A TREASURY OF
Short Stories

Favorites
of the past hundred years
from Turgenev to Thurber
from Balzac
to Hemingway
with biographical sketches
of the authors
Edited by
BERNARDINE KIELTY

SIMON AND SCHUSTER · NEW YORK

PRINTED IN THE UNITED STATES OF AMERICA BY
THE HADDON CRAFTSMEN, INC., SCRANTON, PA.

CONTENTS

OF OUR TIME

EUROPEAN

1

2

3

FOREWORD

ONE OF THE outstanding advantages of an anthology, as I have learned through many months of work on this volume, is the self-inflicted education of the anthologist. One individual at least profits by the orgy of reading and the library prowling. But it must be said that the purpose behind this particular book was primarily neither self-improvement nor teaching. It grew out of an enormous respect for the really good short story, with no other criterion than enjoyment, and from this touchstone it never seriously departed.

The first test in the choice of stories, and the most satisfactory in the end, was savory recollection. Nostalgically I sought out the old not-to-be-forgotten favorites. It was a treat to reread them, but it was disillusioning too. In some cases the discrepancy between young enthusiasm and mature consideration was without doubt a measure of early callowness. But quite as often the story itself proved too closely integrated into the mores of its own day and place, or too much restricted by a technique that had now become shopworn. The strictly regional story thus fell into the discard, most of the dialect stories, and many of the deliberately humorous. Mark Twain's stories, for example—not his novels—no longer seemed funny. Rereading Galsworthy's "The Apple Tree" was like looking at an old picture of an old beau. How could one ever have been so moved! "Marjorie Daw," by Thomas Bailey Aldrich, which once seemed so knowing, had become obvious and artificial.

In the process of the hunt, I called upon friends who in some cases unearthed precious tales almost forgotten. "The Rocking-Horse Winner," by D. H. Lawrence, was one that turned up; Frank Stockton's "The Griffin and the Minor Canon;" and "A Voice in the Night," the thriller by William Hodgson. But the most interesting discovery at this point was the extent to which people's tastes coincided—how many of the stories long remembered turned up again and again.

In the table of contents as finally evolved, I have to confess to frequent lack of logic and to many arbitrary decisions. Concessions were made to literary history, but very few, and possibly not enough for the well-rounded book that some readers may be looking for. There were certain authors, however, who, if slighted, would forever haunt one. What story anthologist would be brave enough, even if he wanted to, to leave out a Kipling, a Chekhov, an O. Henry, or a Sherwood Anderson? Nevertheless, many a well-known name is missing. As a general rule those authors have not been included whose novels—or other media of their art —are outstandingly better than their short stories. This accounts for the conspicuous absence of Willa Cather, one of our greatest novelists, of Sinclair Lewis, of Thomas Hardy, to mention only three. Yet inconsistently there is Balzac, novelist par excellence.

A penchant for the exciting has resulted in what may seem an overweight of mystery and horror, but in my judgment some of the best-written and the most effective stories of the past thirty years have been in this field: the higher the degree of imagination, the more eloquent, apparently, the word and phrase. I have also leaned toward humor. W. W. Jacobs and "Saki" and Bemelmans and Runyon are here for the fun they furnish, though all of them have written serious stories, which, given the chance, they would no doubt themselves have chosen. Passionate and fanatical though the Irish be, I have sidetracked their politics in favor of sentiment, and selected tales for the lilt of their English. I have indulged a woman's predilection for a love story, and have put in a number of tales that revolve about a child.

In some cases celebrated stories are left out because they have already appeared in several anthologies, among them "The Procurator of Judea," by Anatole France, "The Devil and Daniel Webster," by Stephen Vincent Benét, "The Turn of the Screw," by Henry James; less well-known stories by all these masters have been substituted.

The most difficult task was selecting among contemporaries. One feels unsure about the untried: first impressions are so often dependent on immediate circumstance, on local prestige, even on the state of one's digestion. In retrospect we recognize classics among stories unappreciated in their time. But today's popular success may wear as thin as Ravel's *Bolero.*

The physical limitations of what can be put between the boards of a book have also forced decisions. Because of their length it was unfortunately necessary to omit three great stories from twentieth-century Central Europe: Thomas Mann's "Disorder and Early Sorrow," Franz Werfel's "The Man Who Conquered Death," Bruno Frank's "The Moon Watch." I should like also to have had room for Pushkin and Gogol and Bunin, and for James Joyce's "The Dead." In fact, this mechanical difficulty has lopped off centuries. There are tales in the Bible that logically belong here, and in the *Decameron* and in the *Arabian Nights.* But the short story, as we commonly think of it, is pretty much a nineteenth-century product, and as such it is here presented—a modern vehicle of expression starting more or less on its way with Poe, and descending, cut and trimmed and sharpened, down through the years to Faulkner and Hemingway.

Actually the short story is an ideal medium in a swiftly moving modern world. Unlike the novel, it hasn't the time or the space to tell all. By nature it is provocative, it tempts speculation, its last note carries overtones of infinite suggestion. As Bliss Perry said, it may be "the merest sketch of a face, a comic attitude, a tragic incident: it may be a lovely dream, a horrid nightmare, or a page of words that haunt us like music." It is a song, not a symphony.

If there is any formula to be deduced from the considerable exhibition here displayed, it is a very simple one, a formula, as I see it, with two component parts. In the first place, in each story a situation, however subtle or dramatic or ordinary, is resolved: "something happens." In the second place, there is emotional impact. The author has had his moments of vivid experience out of which it has been given him, by his acute sensitivity and his exceptional talents, to carry over to us a miniature cosmos that reflects the full sharp excitement of his original vision. If the author is successful, as in these examples I believe him to have been, the reader himself is also involved. The reader is moved—to laugh, to cry, to exclaim; and the more completely the mood envelops him, the greater the achievement. Aldous Huxley may have seen a bright-eyed boy and sensed in him the infinite tragedy of the misunderstood, and so conceived a Young Archimedes. Stephen Vincent Benét may often have heard the timeworn strains of "I've Been Working on the Railroad," but the time it brought forth an O'Halloran with his Luck was the moment that counted. Sherwood Anderson surely remembered the look a girl gave him—of contempt and superiority—when he wrote "I'm a Fool."

The lives of the writers themselves, summarized here, turned out to be quite as dramatic as their fiction. It was impossible to do them justice in the space allotted, but here again I found the task rewarding out of all proportion: delving into contemporary criticism often irrelevant for my purpose, dipping into diaries and journals and letters, here and there picking up odd but revealing bits, many of which are included in these brief biographical sketches, at the expense, I'm afraid, of more factual detail.

This excursion down through the years has also afforded fleeting glimpses of history. Ephemeral and hazy, but nevertheless there, behind the procession of stories and in the background of the lives of the men and women who wrote them, are the changing culture and modes of thinking, to a certain extent the politics and the immediate education, of each succeeding generation, as these various influences have affected the articulate members.

The best I can hope then is that the reader will have as thoroughly satisfactory a time—picking up this book for recreation—as the compiler had in the process of her so-called work.

BERNARDINE KIELTY

NINETEENTH CENTURY

Ivan Sergeyevich Turgenev
1818-1883

TURGENEV, the Russian who chose to live nearly half his adult life outside his own country, was nonetheless one of Russia's greatest patriots. "No man," said Ernest Renan at Turgenev's funeral, "has been as much as he the incarnation of a whole race: generations of ancestors, lost in the sleep of centuries, speechless, came through him to life and utterance." Although born into the landed gentry, of a family of enormous wealth, Turgenev understood the "little" people, and, by his simple direct stories, awakened Russia to her responsibilities to them.

The incredible ménage in which Turgenev grew up might well have justified a revolution on its own count: five thousand serfs at the command of a single family, and cruelty accepted as a matter of course. (Turgenev's grandmother, it is said, killed a serf with her own hands.) But Turgenev was not a revolutionary, nor was he a propagandist. He was merely a Russian aristocrat who preferred his native tongue to any other, and came to know his serfs not as properties but as persons. Like all young men of his class he was brought up to speak French, and it was only through close companionship with the old serf who used to take him hunting that he learned to love Russian. Together the two strolled the countryside, chatted with villagers and farmers, and became their friends. It was a far-reaching experience for Turgenev, and *A Sportsman's Sketches*, from which "Yermolaï and the Miller's Wife" comes, was his artist's tribute to a people sometimes gay and charming, oftener tired and sad.

After *Fathers and Sons* had been published (1862), and had been completely misunderstood by both critics and the public, Turgenev left Russia in disgust, and for much of the next twenty years lived in France. We read of him at Flaubert's Sunday afternoons at Croisset; in his own green-shuttered house on Montmartre; or at the home of Pauline Garcia (Mme Viardot), the singer, whom he loved long but hopelessly. He continued to write while abroad, but only about Russia. For all his seeming adaptation to Parisian life, the great towering, white-bearded Turgenev remained eternally Russian.

Yermolaï and the Miller's Wife

BY IVAN TURGENEV

ONE evening I went with the huntsman Yermolaï "stand-shooting." . . . But perhaps all my readers may not know what "stand-shooting" is. I will tell you.

A quarter of an hour before sunset in springtime you go out into the woods with your gun, but without your dog. You seek out a spot for yourself on the outskirts of the forest, take a look round, examine your caps, and glance at your companion. A quarter of an hour passes; the sun has set, but it is still light in the forest; the sky is clear and transparent; the birds are chattering and twittering; the young grass shines with the brilliance of emerald. . . . You wait. Gradually the recesses of the forest grow dark; the blood-red glow of the evening sky creeps slowly on to the roots and the trunks of the trees, and keeps rising higher and higher, passes from the lower, still almost leafless branches, to the motionless, slumbering treetops. . . . And now even the topmost branches are darkened; the purple sky fades to dark blue. The forest fragrance grows stronger; there is a scent of warmth and damp earth; the fluttering breeze dies away at your side. The birds go to sleep—not all at once—but after their kinds; first the finches are hushed, a few minutes later the warblers, and after them the yellow buntings. In the forest it grows darker and darker. The trees melt together into great masses of blackness; in the dark-blue sky the first stars come timidly out. All the birds are asleep. Only the redstarts and the nuthatches are still chirping drowsily. . . . And now they too are still. The last echoing call of the peewit rings over our heads; the oriole's melancholy cry sounds somewhere in the distance; then the nightingale's first note. Your heart is weary with suspense, when suddenly—but only sportsmen can understand me—suddenly in the deep hush there is a peculiar croaking and whirring sound, the measured sweep of swift wings is heard, and the snipe, gracefully bending its long beak, sails smoothly down behind a dark bush to meet your shot.

That is the meaning of "stand-shooting." And so I had gone out stand-shooting with Yermolaï; but excuse me, reader: I must first introduce you to Yermolaï.

Picture to yourself a tall, gaunt man of forty-five, with a long, thin nose, a narrow forehead, little gray eyes, a bristling head of hair, and

Translated from the Russian by Constance Garnett. From *A Sportsman's Sketches* by Ivan Turgenev. By permission of The Macmillan Company and A. P. Watt & Son of London.

3

thick sarcastic lips. This man wore, winter and summer alike, a yellow nankeen coat of German cut, but with a sash round the waist; he wore blue pantaloons and a cap of astrakhan, presented to him in a merry hour by a spendthrift landowner. Two bags were fastened on to his sash, one in front, skillfully tied into two halves, for powder and for shot; the other behind for game: wadding Yermolaï used to produce out of his peculiar, seemingly inexhaustible cap. With the money he gained by the game he sold, he might easily have bought himself a cartridge box and powder flask; but he never once even contemplated such a purchase, and continued to load his gun after his old fashion, exciting the admiration of all beholders by the skill with which he avoided the risks of spilling or mixing his powder and shot. His gun was a single-barreled flintlock, endowed, moreover, with a villainous habit of "kicking." It was due to this that Yermolaï's right cheek was permanently swollen to a larger size than the left. How he ever succeeded in hitting anything with this gun, it would take a shrewd man to discover—but he did. He had too a setter dog, by name Valetka, a most extraordinary creature. Yermolaï never fed him. "Me feed a dog!" he reasoned; "why, a dog's a clever beast; he finds a living for himself." And certainly, though Valetka's extreme thinness was a shock even to an indifferent observer, he still lived and had a long life; and in spite of his pitiable position he was not even once lost, and never showed an inclination to desert his master. Once indeed, in his youth, he had absented himself for two days, on courting bent, but this folly was soon over with him. Valetka's most

noticeable peculiarity was his impenetrable indifference to everything in the world. . . . If it were not a dog I was speaking of, I should have called him "disillusioned." He usually sat with his cropped tail curled up under him, scowling and twitching at times, and he never smiled. (It is well known that dogs can smile, and smile very sweetly.) He was exceedingly ugly; and the idle house serfs never lost an opportunity of jeering cruelly at his appearance; but all these jeers, and even blows, Valetka bore with astonishing indifference. He was a source of special delight to the cooks, who would all leave their work at once and give him chase with shouts and abuse, whenever, through a weakness not confined to dogs, he thrust his hungry nose through the half-open door of the kitchen, tempting with its warmth and appetizing smells. He distinguished himself by untiring energy in the chase, and had a good scent; but if he chanced to overtake a slightly wounded hare, he devoured it with relish to the last bone, somewhere in the cool shade under the green bushes, at a respectful distance from Yermolaï, who was abusing him in every known and unknown dialect.

Yermolaï belonged to one of my neighbors, a landowner of the old style. Landowners of the old style don't care for game, and prefer the domestic fowl. Only on extraordinary occasions, such as birthdays, name days, and elections, the cooks of the old-fashioned landowners set to work to prepare some longbeaked birds, and, falling into the state of frenzy peculiar to Russians when they don't quite know what to do, they concoct such marvelous sauces for them that the guests examine the proffered dishes curiously and attentively, but rarely make up their minds to try them. Yermolaï was under orders to provide his master's kitchen with two brace of grouse and partridges once a month. But he might live where and how he pleased. They had given him up, as a man of no use for work of any kind—"bone lazy," as the expression is among us in Orel. Powder and shot, of course, they did not provide him, following precisely the same principle in virtue of which he did not feed his dog. Yermolaï was a very strange kind of man; heedless as a bird, rather fond of talking, awkward and vacant-looking; he was excessively fond of drink, and never could sit still long; in walking he shambled along, and rolled from side to side; and yet he got over fifty miles in the day with his rolling, shambling gait. He exposed himself to the most varied adventures: spent the night in the marshes, in trees, on roofs, or under bridges; more than once he had got shut up in lofts, cellars, or barns; he sometimes lost his gun, his dog, his most indispensable garments; got long and severe thrashings; but he always returned home after a little while, in his clothes, and with his gun and his dog. One could not call him a cheerful man, though one almost always found him in an even frame of mind; he was looked on generally as an eccentric. Yermolaï liked a little chat with a good companion, especially over a glass, but he would not stop long; he would get up and go. "But where the devil are you going? It's dark out-of-doors." "To Tchaplino." "But what's taking you to Tchaplino, ten miles away?" "I am going to stay the night at Sophron's there." "But stay the night here." "No, I can't." And Yermolaï, with his Valetka, would go off into the dark night, through woods and water courses, and the peasant Sophron very likely did not let him into his place, and even, I am afraid, gave him a blow to teach him "not to disturb honest folks." But none could compare with Yermolaï in skill in deep-water fishing in springtime, in catching crayfish with his hands, in tracking game by scent, in snaring quails, in training hawks, in capturing the nightingales who had the greatest variety of notes. . . . One thing he could not do, train a dog; he had not patience enough. He had a wife too. He went to see her once a week. She lived in a wretched, tumbledown little hut, and led a hand-to-mouth existence, never knowing overnight whether she would have food to eat on the morrow; and in every way her lot was a pitiful one. Yermolaï, who seemed such a careless and easygoing fellow, treated his wife with cruel harshness; in his own house he assumed a stern and menacing manner; and his poor wife did everything she could to please him, trembled when he looked at her, and spent her last farthing to buy him vodka; and when he stretched himself majestically on the stove and fell into a heroic sleep, she obsequiously covered him with a sheepskin. I happened myself more than once to catch an involuntary look in him of a kind of savage ferocity; I did not like the expression of his face when he finished off a wounded bird with his teeth. But Yermolaï never remained more than a day at home, and away from home he was once more the same "Yermolka" (i.e., the shooting cap), as he was called for a hundred miles round, and as he sometimes called himself. The lowest house serf was conscious of being superior to this vagabond—and perhaps this was precisely why they treated him with friendliness; the peasants at first amused themselves by chasing him and driving him like a hare over the open country, but afterwards they left him in God's hands, and when once they recognized him as "queer," they no longer tormented him, and even gave him bread and entered into talk with him. . . . This was the man I took as my huntsman, and with him I went stand-shooting to a great birch wood on the banks of the Ista.

Many Russian rivers, like the Volga, have one bank rugged and precipitous, the other bounded by level meadows; and so it is with the Ista. This small river winds extremely capriciously, coils like a snake, and does not keep a straight course for half a mile together; in some places, from the top of a sharp acclivity, one can see the river for ten miles, with its dikes, its pools and mills, and the gardens on its banks, shut in with willows and thick flower gardens. There are fish in the Ista in endless numbers, especially roaches (the peasants take them in hot weather from under the bushes with their hands); little sandpipers flutter whistling along the stony banks, which are streaked with cold clear streams; wild ducks dive in the middle of the pools, and look round warily; in the coves under the overhanging cliffs herons stand out in the shade. . . . We stood in ambush nearly an hour, killed two brace of wood snipe, and, as we wanted to try our luck again at sunrise (stand-shooting can be done as well in the early morning), we resolved to spend the night at the nearest mill. We came out of the wood, and went down the slope. The dark-blue waters of the river

ran below; the air was thick with the mists of night. We knocked at the gate. The dogs began barking in the yard.

"Who is there?" asked a hoarse and sleepy voice.

"We are sportsmen; let us stay the night." There was no reply. "We will pay."

"I will go and tell the master— Sh! curse the dogs! Go to the devil with you!"

We listened as the workman went into the cottage; he soon came back to the gate. "No," he said; "the master tells me not to let you in."

"Why not?"

"He is afraid; you are sportsmen; you might set the mill on fire; you've firearms with you, to be sure."

"But what nonsense!"

"We had our mill on fire like that last year; some fish dealers stayed the night, and they managed to set it on fire somehow."

"But, my good friend, we can't sleep in the open air!"

"That's your business." He went away, his boots clacking as he walked.

Yermolaï promised him various unpleasant things in the future. "Let us go to the village," he brought out at last, with a sigh. But it was two miles to the village.

"Let us stay the night here," I said, "in the open air—the night is warm; the miller will let us have some straw if we pay for it."

Yermolaï agreed without discussion. We began again to knock.

"Well, what do you want?" the workman's voice was heard again; "I've told you you can't."

We explained to him what we wanted. He went to consult the master of the house, and returned with him. The little side gate creaked. The miller appeared, a tall, fat-faced man with a bull neck, round-bellied and corpulent. He agreed to my proposal. A hundred paces from the mill there was a little outhouse open to the air on all sides. They carried straw and hay there for us; the workman set a samovar down on the grass near the river, and, squatting on his heels, began to blow vigorously into the pipe of it. The embers glowed, and threw a bright light on his young face. The miller ran to wake his wife, and suggested at last that I myself should sleep in the cottage; but I preferred to remain in the open air. The miller's wife brought us milk, eggs, potatoes, and bread. Soon the samovar boiled, and we began drinking tea. A mist had risen from the river; there was no wind; from all round came the cry of the corncrake, and faint sounds from the mill wheels of drops that dripped from the paddles and of water gurgling through the bars of the lock. We built a small fire on the ground. While Yermolaï was baking the potatoes in the embers, I had time to fall into a doze. I was waked by a discreetly subdued whispering near me. I lifted my head; before the fire, on a tub turned upside down, the miller's wife sat talking to my huntsman. By her dress, her movements, and her manner of speaking, I had already recognized that she had been in domestic service, and was neither peasant nor city-bred; but now for the first time I got a clear view of her features. She looked about thirty; her thin, pale face still showed the traces of remarkable beauty; what particularly charmed me was her eyes, large and mournful in expression. She was leaning her elbows on her knees, and had her face in her hands. Yermolaï

was sitting with his back to me, and thrusting sticks into the fire.

"They've the cattle plague again at Zheltonhiny," the miller's wife was saying; "Father Ivan's two cows are dead—Lord have mercy on them!"

"And how are your pigs doing?" asked Yermolaï, after a brief pause.

"They're alive."

"You ought to make me a present of a sucking pig."

The miller's wife was silent for a while, then she sighed.

"Who is it you're with?" she asked.

"A gentleman from Kostomarovo."

Yermolaï threw a few pine twigs on the fire; they all caught at once, and a thick white smoke came puffing into his face.

"Why didn't your husband let us into the cottage?"

"He's afraid."

"Afraid! the fat old tub! Arina Timofyevna, my darling, bring me a little glass of spirits."

The miller's wife rose and vanished into the darkness. Yermolaï began to sing in an undertone:

When I went to see my sweetheart,
I wore out all my shoes.

Arina returned with a small flask and a glass. Yermolaï got up, crossed himself, and drank it off at a draught. "Good!" was his comment.

The miller's wife sat down again on the tub.

"Well, Arina Timofyevna, are you still ill?"

"Yes."

"What is it?"

"My cough troubles me at night."

"The gentleman's asleep, it seems," observed Yermolaï after a short silence. "Don't go to a doctor, Arina; it will be worse if you do."

"Well, I am not going."

"But come and pay me a visit."

Arina hung down her head dejectedly.

"I will drive my wife out for the occasion," continued Yermolaï. "Upon my word, I will."

"You had better wake the gentleman, Yermolaï Petrovitch; you see, the potatoes are done."

"Oh, let him snore," observed my faithful servant indifferently; "he's tired with walking, so he sleeps sound."

I turned over in the hay. Yermolaï got up and came to me. "The potatoes are ready; will you come and eat them?"

I came out of the outhouse; the miller's wife got up from the tub and was going away. I addressed her.

"Have you kept this mill long?"

"It's two years since I came on Trinity day."

"And where does your husband come from?"

Arina had not caught my question.

"Where's your husband from?" repeated Yermolaï, raising his voice.

"From Byelev. He's a Byelev townsman."

"And are you too from Byelev?"

"No, I'm a serf; I was a serf."

"Whose?"

"Zvyerkov was my master. Now I am free."

"What Zvyerkov?"

"Alexander Selitch."

"Weren't you his wife's lady's maid?"

"How did you know? Yes."

I looked at Arina with redoubled curiosity and sympathy.

"I know your master," I continued.

"Do you?" she replied in a low voice, and her head drooped.

I must tell the reader why I looked with such sympathy at Arina. During my stay at Petersburg I had become quite by chance acquainted with Mr. Zvyerkov. He had a rather influential position, and was reputed a man of sense and education. He had a wife, fat, sentimental, lachrymose, and spiteful—a vulgar and disagreeable creature; he had too a son, the very type of the young swell of today, pampered and stupid. The exterior of Mr. Zvyerkov himself did not prepossess one in his favor; his little mouselike eyes peeped slyly out of a broad, almost square, face; he had a large, prominent nose, with distended nostrils; his close-cropped gray hair stood up like a brush above his scowling brow; his thin lips were forever twitching and smiling mawkishly. Mr. Zvyerkov's favorite position was standing with his legs wide apart and his fat hands in his trousers pockets. Once I happened somehow to be driving alone with Mr. Zvyerkov in a coach out of town. We fell into conversation. As a man of experience and of judgment, Mr. Zvyerkov began to try to set me in "the path of truth."

"Allow me to observe to you," he drawled at last; "all you young people criticize and form judgments on everything at random; you have little knowledge of your own country; Russia, young gentleman, is an unknown land to you; that's where it is! . . . You are forever reading German. For instance, now you say this and that and the other about anything; for instance, about the house serfs. . . . Very fine; I don't dispute it's all very fine; but you don't know them; you don't know the kind of people they are." (Mr. Zvyerkov blew his nose loudly and took a pinch of snuff.) "Allow me to tell you as an illustration one little anecdote; it may perhaps interest you." (Mr. Zvyerkov cleared his throat.) "You know, doubtless, what my wife is; it would be difficult, I should imagine, to find a more kind-hearted woman, you will agree. For her waiting maids, existence is simply a perfect paradise, and no mistake about it. . . . But my wife has made it a rule never to keep married lady's maids. Certainly it would not do; children come—and one thing and the other—and how is a lady's maid to look after her mistress as she ought, to fit in with her ways; she is no longer able to do it; her mind is on other things. One must look at things through human nature. Well, we were driving once through our village, it must be—let me be correct—yes, fifteen years ago. We saw, at the bailiff's, a young girl, his daughter, very pretty indeed; something even—you know—something attractive in her manners. And my wife said to me: 'Koko'— you understand, of course, that is her pet name for me—'let us take this girl to Petersburg; I like her, Koko . . .' I said, 'Let us take her, by all means.' The bailiff, of course, was at our feet; he could not have expected such good fortune, you can imagine. . . . Well, the girl, of course, cried violently. Of course, it was hard for her at first; the parental home . . . in fact . . . there was nothing surprising in that. However, she soon got used to us: at first we put her in the maidservants' room; they trained her, of course. And what do you think? The girl made wonderful progress; my wife became simply devoted to her, promoted her at last above the rest to wait on herself . . . observe. . . . And one must do her the justice to say, my wife had never such a maid, absolutely never; attentive, modest, and obedient—simply all that could be desired. But my wife, I must confess, spoiled her too much; she dressed her well, fed her from our own table, gave her tea to drink, and so on, as you can imagine! So she waited on my wife like this for ten years. Suddenly, one fine morning, picture to yourself, Arina—her name was Arina—rushes unannounced into my study, and flops down at my feet. That's a thing, I tell you plainly, I can't endure. No human being ought ever to lose sight of their personal dignity. Am I not right? What do you say? 'Your honor, Alexander Selitch, I beseech a favor of you.' 'What favor?' 'Let me be married.' I must confess I was taken aback. 'But you know, you stupid, your mistress has no other lady's maid?' 'I will wait on mistress as before.' 'Nonsense! nonsense! your mistress can't endure married lady's maids.' 'Malanya could take my place.' 'Pray don't argue.' 'I obey your will.' I must confess it was quite a shock. I assure you, I am like that; nothing wounds me so— nothing, I venture to say, wounds me so deeply as ingratitude. I need not tell you—you know what my wife is; an angel upon earth, goodness inexhaustible. One would fancy even the worst of men would be ashamed to hurt her. Well, I got rid of Arina. I thought perhaps she would come to her senses; I was unwilling, do you know, to believe in wicked, black ingratitude in anyone. What do you think? Within six months she thought fit to come to me again with the same request. I felt revolted. But imagine my amazement when, some time later, my wife comes to me in tears, so agitated that I felt positively alarmed. 'What has happened?' 'Arina. . . . You understand . . . I am ashamed to tell it. . . .' 'Impossible! . . . Who is the man?' 'Petrushka, the footman.' My indignation broke out then. I am like that. I don't like half measures! Petrushka was not to blame. We might flog him, but in my opinion he was not to blame. Arina . . . Well, well, well! what more's to be said? I gave orders, of course, that her hair should be cut off, she should be dressed in sackcloth, and sent into the country. My wife was deprived of an excellent lady's maid; but there was no help for it: immorality cannot be tolerated in a household in any case. Better to cut off the infected member at once. There, there! now you can judge the thing for yourself—you know that my wife is . . . yes, yes, yes! indeed! . . . an angel! She had grown attached to Arina, and Arina knew it, and had the face to . . . Eh? no, tell me . . . eh? And what's the use of talking about it? Anyway, there was no help for it. I, indeed— I, in particular, felt hurt, felt wounded for a long time by the ingratitude of this girl. Whatever you say—it's no good to look for feeling, for heart, in these people! You may feed the wolf as you will; he has always a hankering for the woods. Education, by all means! But I only wanted to give you an example . . ."

And Mr. Zvyerkov, without finishing his sentence, turned away his head, and, wrapping himself more closely into his cloak, manfully repressed his involuntary emotion.

The reader now probably understands why I looked with sympathetic interest at Arina.

"Have you long been married to the miller?" I asked her at last.

"Two years."

"How was it? Did your master allow it?"

"They bought my freedom."

"Who?"

"Savely Alexyevich."

"Who is that?"

"My husband." (Yermolaï smiled to himself.) "Has my master perhaps spoken to you of me?" added Arina, after a brief silence.

I did not know what reply to make to her question.

"Arina!" cried the miller from a distance. She got up and walked away.

"Is her husband a good fellow?" I asked Yermolaï.

"So-so."

"Have they any children?"

"There was one, but it died."

"How was it? Did the miller take a liking to her? Did he give much to buy her freedom?"

"I don't know. She can read and write; in their business it's of use. I suppose he liked her."

"And have you known her long?"

"Yes. I used to go to her master's. Their house isn't far from here."

"And do you know the footman Petrushka?"

"Piotr Vassilyevich? Of course, I knew him."

"Where is he now?"

"He was sent for a soldier."

We were silent for a while.

"She doesn't seem well?" I asked Yermolaï at last.

"I should think not! Tomorrow, I say, we shall have a good sport. A little sleep now would do us no harm."

A flock of wild ducks swept whizzing over our heads, and we heard them drop down into the river not far from us. It was now quite dark, and it began to be cold; in the thicket sounded the melodious notes of a nightingale. We buried ourselves in the hay and fell asleep.

Leo Nikolayevich Tolstoi

1828-1910

THOUGH THE pattern of Tolstoi's life matched that of many another Russian noble—for the first half, at any rate—the seething undercurrent of spiritual turmoil set him apart. His university years were a gay social whirl; his army career was traditional. He liked to hunt and drink and gamble. Once he turned over a manuscript, *The Cossacks*, to pay off a gambling debt. His ancestral house was bodily removed from the estate, to pay off another. At the age of thirty-four he made a conventional marriage, took his bride to Yasnaya Polyana, in Tula, and settled down to the role of country gentleman. During these years of comparative serenity he wrote *War and Peace* and most of *Anna Karenina*.

But he had already begun to be restless. Below the surface, even in his gayest days, Tolstoi was troubled, as his books of that time testify. Now he began to question the purpose of existence—to weigh the artificialities of his own living against the simple life of the very poor. And shortly before *Anna Karenina* was finished, when he was almost fifty, the convulsive inner struggle broke forth into the open.

What Tolstoi went through in the three or four years of crisis that followed can be gleaned from *Diary of a Madman*. With the vision of death ever before him, he turned to religion and then abruptly away. He shunned visitors, wept, and sat alone. But out of the long agony emerged Tolstoi the evangelist, who for the next thirty years preached the doctrine of Christian living that made him one of the most revered men of his time: love of one's fellow men and the abnegation of all worldly possessions. Tolstoi's wife never subscribed to his teachings, and their life together was embittered by constant quarreling. Of all his children, only Alexandra, the youngest, was sympathetic, and when her father finally left home, she left with him. They set out secretly at night, destination unknown, and the old man died less than a month later, at a railroad station.

The Death of Ivan Ilyich

BY LEO TOLSTOI

I

INSIDE the great building of the law courts, during the interval in the hearing of the Melvinsky case, the members of the judicial council and the public prosecutor were gathered together in the private room of Ivan Yegorovich Shebek, and the conversation turned upon the celebrated Krasovsky case. Fyodor Vassilievich hotly maintained that the case was not in the jurisdiction of the court. Yegor Ivanovich stood up for his own view; but from the first Piotr Ivanovich, who had not entered into the discussion, took no interest in it, but was looking through the newspapers which had just been brought in.

"Gentlemen!" he said, "Ivan Ilyich is dead!"

"You don't say so!"

"Here, read it," he said to Fyodor Vassilievich, handing him the fresh, still damp-smelling paper.

Within a black margin was printed: "Praskovya Fyodorovna Golovin with heartfelt affliction informs friends and relatives of the decease of her beloved husband, member of the Court of Justice, Ivan Ilyich Golovin, who passed away on the 4th of February. The funeral will take place on Thursday at one o'clock."

Ivan Ilyich was a colleague of the gentlemen present, and all liked him. It was some weeks now since he had been taken ill; his illness had been said to be incurable. His post had been kept open for him, but it had been thought that in case of his death Alexyeev might receive his appointment, and either Vinnikov or Shtabel would succeed to Alexyeev's. So that on hearing of Ivan Ilyich's death, the first thought of each of the gentlemen in the room was of the effect this death might have on the transfer or promotion of themselves or their friends.

"Now I am sure of getting Shtabel's place or Vinnikov's," thought Fyodor Vassilievich. "It was promised me long ago, and the promotion means eight hundred rubles' additional income, besides the grants for office expenses."

"Now I shall have to petition for my brother-in-law to be transferred from Kaluga," thought Piotr Ivanovich. "My wife will be very glad. She won't be able to say now that I've never done anything for her family."

"I thought somehow that he'd never get up from his bed again,"

Translated from the Russian by Constance Garnett. By permission of The Modern Library, Inc.

Piotr Ivanovich said aloud. "I'm sorry!"

"But what was it exactly was wrong with him?"

"The doctors could not decide. That's to say, they did decide, but differently. When I saw him last, I thought he would get over it."

"Well, I positively haven't called there ever since the holidays. I've kept meaning to go."

"Had he any property?"

"I think there's something, very small, of his wife's. But something quite trifling."

"Yes, one will have to go and call. They live such a terribly long way off."

"A long way from you, you mean. Everything's a long way from your place."

"There, he can never forgive me for living the other side of the river," said Piotr Ivanovich, smiling at Shavek. And they began to talk of the great distances between different parts of the town, and went back into the court.

Besides the reflections upon the changes and promotions in the service likely to ensue from this death, the very fact of the death of an intimate acquaintance excited in everyone who heard of it, as such a fact always does, a feeling of relief that "It is he that is dead, and not I."

"Only think! he is dead, but here am I all right," each one thought or felt. The more intimate acquaintances, the so-called friends of Ivan Ilyich, could not help thinking too that now they had the exceedingly tiresome social duties to perform of going to the funeral service and paying the widow a visit of condolence.

The most intimately acquainted with their late colleague were Fyodor Vassilievich and Piotr Ivanovich.

Piotr Ivanovich had been a comrade of his at the school of jurisprudence, and considered himself under obligations to Ivan Ilyich.

Telling his wife at dinner of the news of Ivan Ilyich's death and his reflections as to the possibility of getting her brother transferred into their circuit, Piotr Ivanovich, without lying down for his usual nap, put on his frock coat and drove to Ivan Ilyich's.

At the entrance before Ivan Ilyich's flat stood a carriage and two hired flies. Downstairs in the entry near the hatstand there was leaning against the wall a coffin lid with tassels and braiding freshly rubbed up with pipe clay. Two ladies were taking off their cloaks. One of them he knew, the sister of Ivan Ilyich; the other was a lady he did not know. Piotr Ivanovich's colleague, Shvarts, was coming down; and from the top stair, seeing who it was coming in, he stopped and winked at him, as though to say: "Ivan Ilyich has made a mess of it; it's a very different matter with you and me."

Shvarts' face, with his English whiskers and all his thin figure in his frock coat, had, as it always had, an air of elegant solemnity; and this solemnity, always such a contrast to Shvarts' playful character, had a special piquancy here. So thought Piotr Ivanovich.

Piotr Ivanovich let the ladies pass on in front of him, and walked slowly up the stairs after them. Shvarts had not come down, but was waiting at the top. Piotr Ivanovich knew what for; he wanted obviously to settle with him where their game of "screw" was to be that evening. The ladies went up to the widow's room; while Shvarts, with his lips tightly and gravely shut, and amusement in his eyes, with a twitch of his eyebrows motioned Piotr Ivanovich to the right, to the room where the dead man was.

Piotr Ivanovich went in, as people always do on such occasions, in uncertainty as to what he would have to do there. One thing he felt sure of—that crossing himself never comes amiss on such occasions. As to whether it was necessary to bow down while doing so, he did not feel quite sure and so chose a middle course. On entering the room he began crossing himself, and made a slight sort of bow. So far as the movements of his hands and head permitted him, he glanced while doing so about the room. Two young men, one a high-school boy, nephews probably, were going out of the room, crossing themselves. An old lady was standing motionless; and a lady, with her eyebrows queerly lifted, was saying something to her in a whisper. A deacon in a frock coat, resolute and hearty, was reading something aloud with an expression that precluded all possibility of contradiction. A young peasant who used to wait at table, Gerasim, walking with light footsteps in front of Piotr Ivanovich, was sprinkling something on the floor. Seeing this, Piotr Ivanovich was at once aware of the faint odor of the decomposing corpse. On his last visit to Ivan Ilyich, Piotr Ivanovich had seen this peasant in his room; he was performing the duties of a sicknurse, and Ivan Ilyich liked him particularly. Piotr Ivanovich continued crossing himself and bowing in a direction intermediate between the coffin, the deacon, and the holy pictures on the table in the corner. Then when this action of making the sign of the cross with his hand seemed to him to have been unduly prolonged, he stood still and began to scrutinize the dead man.

The dead man lay, as dead men always do lie, in a peculiarly heavy dead way, his stiffened limbs sunk in the cushions of the coffin, and his head bent back forever on the pillow, and thrust up, as dead men always do, his yellow waxen forehead with bald spots on the sunken temples, and his nose that stood out sharply and, as it were, squeezed on the upper lip. He was much changed, even thinner since Piotr Ivanovich had seen him, but his face—as always with the dead—was more handsome, and, above all, more impressive than it had been when he was alive. On the face was an expression of what had to be done having been done, and rightly done. Besides this, there was too in that expression a reproach or a reminder for the living. This reminder seemed to Piotr Ivanovich uncalled for, or, at least, to have nothing to do with him. He felt something unpleasant; and so Piotr Ivanovich once more crossed himself hurriedly, and, as it struck him, too hurriedly, not quite in accordance with the proprieties, turned and went to the door. Shvarts was waiting for him in the adjoining room, standing with his legs apart and both hands behind his back playing with his top hat. A single glance at the playful, sleek, and elegant figure of Shvarts revived Piotr Ivanovich. He felt that he, Shvarts, was above it, and would not give way to depressing impressions. The mere sight of him said plainly: the incident of the service over the body of Ivan Ilyich cannot possibly constitute a sufficient ground for recognizing the business of the session suspended—in other words, in no way can it hinder us from shuffling and cutting a pack of cards this evening, while the footman sets four unsanctified candles on the table for us; in fact, there is no ground for supposing that this incident could prevent us from spending the evening agreeably. He said as much indeed to Piotr Ivanovich as he came out, proposing that the party should meet at Fyodor Vassilievich's. But apparently it was Piotr Ivanovich's destiny not to play "screw" that evening. Praskovya Fyodorovna, a short, fat woman who, in spite of all efforts in a contrary direction, was steadily broader from her shoulders downwards, all in black, with lace on her head and her eyebrows as queerly arched as those of the lady standing beside the coffin, came out of her own apartments with some other ladies and, conducting them to the dead man's room, said: "The service will take place immediately; come in."

Shvarts, making an indefinite bow, stood still, obviously neither accepting nor declining this invitation. Praskovya Fyodorovna, recognizing Piotr Ivanovich, sighed, went right up to him, took his hand, and said, "I know that you were a true friend of Ivan Ilyich's . . ." and looked at him, expecting from him the suitable action in response to these words. Piotr Ivanovich knew that, just as before he had to cross himself, now what he had to do was to press her hand, to sigh, and to say, "Ah, I was indeed!" And he did so. And as he did so, he felt that the desired result had been attained; that he was touched, and she was touched.

"Come, since it's not begun yet, I have something I want to say to you," said the widow. "Give me your arm."

Piotr Ivanovich gave her his arm,

and they moved toward the inner rooms, passing Shvarts, who winked gloomily at Piotr Ivanovich.

"So much for our 'screw'! Don't complain if we find another partner. You can make a fifth when you do get away," said his humorous glance.

Piotr Ivanovich sighed still more deeply and despondently, and Praskovya Fyodorovna pressed his hand gratefully. Going into her drawing room, which was upholstered with pink cretonne and lighted by a dismal-looking lamp, they sat down at the table, she on a sofa and Piotr Ivanovich on a low ottoman with deranged springs which yielded spasmodically under his weight. Praskovya Fyodorovna was about to warn him to sit on another seat, but felt such a recommendation out of keeping with her position, and changed her mind. Sitting down on the ottoman, Piotr Ivanovich remembered how Ivan Ilyich had arranged this drawing room, and had consulted him about this very pink cretonne with green leaves. Seating herself on the sofa, and pushing by the table (the whole drawing room was crowded with furniture and things), the widow caught the lace of her black fichu in the carving of the table. Piotr Ivanovich got up to disentangle it for her; and the ottoman, freed from his weight, began bobbing up spasmodically under him. The widow began unhooking her lace herself, and Piotr Ivanovich again sat down, suppressing the mutinous ottoman springs under him. But the widow could not quite free herself, and Piotr Ivanovich rose again, and again the ottoman became mutinous and popped up with a positive snap. When this was all over, she took out a clean cambric handkerchief and began weeping.

Piotr Ivanovich had been cooled off by the incident with the lace and the struggle with the ottoman springs, and he sat looking sullen. This awkward position was cut short by the entrance of Sokolov, Ivan Ilyich's butler, who came in to announce that the place in the cemetery fixed on by Praskovya Fyodorovna would cost two hundred rubles. She left off weeping and, with the air of a victim, glancing at Piotr Ivanovich, said in French that it was very terrible for her. Piotr Ivanovich made a silent gesture signifying his unhesitating conviction that it must indeed be so.

"Please smoke," she said in a magnanimous, and at the same time, crushed voice, and she began discussing with Sokolov the question of the price of the site for the grave.

Piotr Ivanovich, lighting a cigarette, listened to her very circumstantial inquiries as to the various prices of sites and her decision as to the one to be selected. Having settled on the site for the grave, she made arrangements also about the choristers. Sokolov went away.

"I see to everything myself," she said to Piotr Ivanovich, moving on one side the albums that lay on the table; and noticing that the table was in danger from the cigarette ash, she promptly passed an ash tray to Piotr Ivanovich, and said: "I consider it affectation to pretend that my grief prevents me from looking after practical matters. On the contrary, if anything could—not console me . . . but distract me, it is seeing after everything for him." She took out her handkerchief again, as though preparing to weep again; and suddenly, as though struggling with herself, she shook herself, and

began speaking calmly: "But I've business to talk about with you."

Piotr Ivanovich bowed, carefully keeping in check the springs of the ottoman, which had at once begun quivering under him.

"The last few days his sufferings were awful."

"Did he suffer very much?" asked Piotr Ivanovich.

"Oh, awfully! For the last moments, hour indeed, he never left off screaming. For three days and nights in succession he screamed incessantly. It was insufferable. I can't understand how I bore it; one could hear it through three closed doors. Ah, what I suffered!"

"And was he really conscious?" asked Piotr Ivanovich.

"Yes," she whispered, "up to the last minute. He said good-by to us a quarter of an hour before his death, and asked Volodya to be taken away too."

The thought of the sufferings of a man he had known so intimately, at first as a lighthearted boy, a schoolboy, then grown up as a partner at whist, in spite of the unpleasant consciousness of his own and this woman's hypocrisy, suddenly horrified Piotr Ivanovich. He saw again that forehead, the nose that seemed squeezing the lip, and he felt frightened for himself. "Three days and nights of awful suffering and death. Why, that may at once, any minute, come upon me too," he thought, and he felt for an instant terrified. But immediately, he could not himself have said how, there came to his support the customary reflection that this had happened to Ivan Ilyich and not to him, and that to him this must not and could not happen; that in thinking thus he was giving way to depression, which was not the right thing to do, as was evident from Shvarts' expression of face. And making these reflections, Piotr Ivanovich felt reassured, and began with interest inquiring details about Ivan Ilyich's end, as though death were a mischance peculiar to Ivan Ilyich, but not at all incidental to himself.

After various observations about the details of the truly awful physical sufferings endured by Ivan Ilyich (these details Piotr Ivanovich learned only through the effect Ivan Ilyich's agonies had had on the nerves of Praskovya Fyodorovna), the widow apparently thought it time to get to business.

"Ah, Piotr Ivanovich, how hard it is, how awfully, awfully hard!" and she began to cry again.

Piotr Ivanovich sighed, and waited for her to blow her nose. When she had done so, he said, "Indeed it is," and again she began to talk, and brought out what was evidently the business she wished to discuss with him; that business consisted in the inquiry as to how on the occasion of her husband's death she was to obtain a grant from the government. She made a show of asking Piotr Ivanovich's advice about a pension. But he perceived that she knew already to the minutest details, what he did not know himself indeed, everything that could be got out of the government on the ground of this death; but that what she wanted to find out was whether there were not any means of obtaining a little more. Piotr Ivanovich tried to imagine such means; but after pondering a little, and out of politeness abusing the government for its stinginess, he said that he believed that it was impossible to obtain more. Then she sighed and began unmistakably looking about for an excuse for getting rid of her

visitor. He perceived this, put out his cigarette, got up, pressed her hand, and went out into the passage.

In the dining room, where was the bric-à-brac clock that Ivan Ilyich had been so delighted at buying, Piotr Ivanovich met the priest and several people he knew who had come to the service for the dead, and saw too Ivan Ilyich's daughter, a handsome young lady. She was all in black. Her very slender figure looked even slenderer than usual. She had a gloomy, determined, almost wrathful expression. She bowed to Piotr Ivanovich as though he were to blame in some way. Behind the daughter, with the same offended air on his face, stood a rich young man, whom Piotr Ivanovich knew, too, an examining magistrate, the young lady's fiancé, as he had heard. He bowed dejectedly to him, and would have gone on into the dead man's room, when from the staircase there appeared the figure of the son, the high-school boy, extraordinarily like Ivan Ilyich. He was the little Ivan Ilyich over again as Piotr Ivanovich remembered him at school. His eyes were red with crying and had that look often seen in unclean boys of thirteen or fourteen. The boy, seeing Piotr Ivanovich, scowled morosely and bashfully. Piotr Ivanovich nodded to him and went into the dead man's room. The service for the dead began—candles, groans, incense, tears, sobs. Piotr Ivanovich stood frowning, staring at his feet in front of him. He did not once glance at the dead man, and right through to the end did not once give way to depressing influences, and was one of the first to walk out. In the hall there was no one. Gerasim, the young peasant, darted out of the dead man's room, tossed over with his strong hand all the fur cloaks to find Piotr Ivanovich's, and gave it him.

"Well, Gerasim, my boy?" said Piotr Ivanovich, so as to say something. "A sad business, isn't it?"

"It's God's will. We shall come to the same," said Gerasim, showing his white, even, peasant teeth in a smile, and like a man in a rush of extra work, he briskly opened the door, called up the coachman, saw Piotr Ivanovich into the carriage, and darted back to the steps as though bethinking himself of what he had to do next.

Piotr Ivanovich had a special pleasure in the fresh air after the smell of incense, of the corpse, and of carbolic acid.

"Where to?" asked the coachman. "It's not too late. I'll still go round to Fyodor Vassilievich's."

And Piotr Ivanovich drove there. And he did, in fact, find them just finishing the first rubber, so that he came just at the right time to take a hand.

II

The previous history of Ivan Ilyich was the simplest, the most ordinary, and the most awful.

Ivan Ilyich died at the age of forty-five, a member of the Judicial Council. He was the son of an official, whose career in Petersburg through various ministries and departments had been such as leads people into that position in which, though it is distinctly obvious that they are unfit to perform any kind of real duty, they yet cannot, owing to their long past service and their official rank, be dismissed; and they therefore receive a specially created fictitious post, and by no means fictitious thousands—from six to ten —on which they go on living till

extreme old age. Such was the privy councilor, the superfluous member of various superfluous institutions, Ilya Efimovich Golovin.

He had three sons. Ivan Ilyich was the second son. The eldest son's career was exactly like his father's, only in a different department, and he was by now close upon that stage in the service in which the same sinecure would be reached. The third son was the unsuccessful one. He had in various positions always made a mess of things, and was now employed in the railway department. And his father and his brothers, and still more their wives, did not merely dislike meeting him, but avoided, except in extreme necessity, recollecting his existence. His sister had married Baron Greff, a Petersburg official of the same stamp as his father-in-law. Ivan Ilyich was *le phénix de la famille*, as people said. He was not so frigid and precise as the eldest son, nor so wild as the youngest. He was the happy mean between them—a shrewd, lively, pleasant, and well-bred man. He had been educated with his younger brother at the school of jurisprudence. The younger brother had not finished the school course, but was expelled when in the fifth class. Ivan Ilyich completed the course successfully. At school he was just the same as he was later on all his life—an intelligent fellow, highly good-humored and sociable, but strict in doing what he considered to be his duty. His duty he considered whatever was so considered by those persons who were set in authority over him. He was not a toady as a boy, nor later on as a grown-up person; but from his earliest years he was attracted, as a fly to the light, to persons of good standing in the world, assimilated their manners and their views of life, and established friendly relations with them. All the enthusiasms of childhood and youth passed, leaving no great traces in him; he gave way to sensuality and to vanity, and latterly when in the higher classes at school to liberalism, but always keeping within certain limits which were unfailingly marked out for him by his instincts.

At school he had committed actions which had struck him beforehand as great vileness, and gave him a feeling of loathing for himself at the very time he was committing them. But later on, perceiving that such actions were committed also by men of good position, and were not regarded by them as base, he was able, not to regard them as good, but to forget about them completely, and was never mortified by recollections of them.

Leaving the school of jurisprudence in the tenth class, and receiving from his father a sum of money for his outfit, Ivan Ilyich ordered his clothes at Sharmer's, hung on his watch chain a medallion inscribed *Respice finem*, said good-by to the prince who was the principal of his school, had a farewell dinner with his comrades at Donon's, and with all his new fashionable belongings— traveling trunk, linen, suits of clothes, shaving and toilet appurtenances, and traveling rug, all ordered and purchased at the very best shops—set off to take the post of secretary on special commissions for the governor of a province, a post which had been obtained for him by his father.

In the province Ivan Ilyich without loss of time made himself a position as easy and agreeable as his position had been in the school of jurisprudence. He did his work, made his career, and at the same time led a life of well-bred social gaiety. Occasionally he visited various districts on official duty, behaved with dignity both with his superiors and his inferiors; and, with exactitude and an incorruptible honesty of which he could not help feeling proud, performed the duties with which he was intrusted, principally having to do with the dissenters. When engaged in official work he was, in spite of his youth and taste for frivolous amusement, exceedingly reserved, official, and even severe. But in social life he was often amusing and witty, and always good-natured, well bred, and *bon enfant*, as was said of him by his chief and his chief's wife, with whom he was like one of the family.

In the province there was, too, a connection with one of the ladies who obtruded their charms on the stylish young lawyer. There was a dressmaker, too, and there were drinking bouts with smart officers visiting the neighborhood, and visits to a certain outlying street after supper; there was a rather cringing obsequiousness in his behavior, too, with his chief, and even his chief's wife. But all this was accompanied with such a tone of the highest breeding that it could not be called by harsh names; it all came under the rubric of the French saying, *Il faut que la jeunesse se passe*. Everything was done with clean hands, in clean shirts, with French phrases, and, what was of most importance, in the highest society, and consequently with the approval of people of rank.

Such was Ivan Ilyich's career for five years, and then came a change in his official life. New methods of judicial procedure were established; new men were wanted to carry them out. And Ivan Ilyich became such a new man. Ivan Ilyich was offered the post of examining magistrate, and he accepted it in spite of the fact that this post was in another province, and he would have to break off all the ties he had formed and form new ones. Ivan Ilyich's friends met together to see him off, had their photographs taken in a group, presented him with a silver cigarette case, and he set off to his new post.

As an examining magistrate, Ivan Ilyich was as *comme il faut*, as well bred, as adroit in keeping official duties apart from private life, and as successful in gaining universal respect, as he had been as secretary of private commissions. The duties of his new office were in themselves of far greater interest and attractiveness for Ivan Ilyich. In his former post it had been pleasant to pass in his smart uniform from Sharmer's through the crowd of petitioners and officials waiting timorously and envying him, and to march with his easy swagger straight into the governor's private room, there to sit down with him to tea and cigarettes. But the persons directly subject to his authority were few. The only such persons were the district police superintendents and the dissenters, when he was serving on special commissions. And he liked treating such persons affably, almost like comrades; liked to make them feel that he, able to annihilate them, was behaving in this simple, friendly way with them. But such people were then few in number. Now as an examining magistrate Ivan Ilyich felt that everyone—everyone without exception—the most dignified, the most self-satisfied people, all were in his hands, and that he had but to write certain words on a sheet of paper with a printed heading, and this dignified, self-satisfied person

would be brought before him in the capacity of a defendant or a witness; and if he did not care to make him sit down, he would have to stand up before him and answer his questions. Ivan Ilyich never abused this authority of his; on the contrary, he tried to soften the expression of it. But the consciousness of this power and the possibility of softening its effect constituted for him the chief interest and attractiveness of his new position. In the work itself, in the preliminary inquiries, that is, Ivan Ilyich very rapidly acquired the art of setting aside every consideration irrelevant to the official aspect of the case, and of reducing every case, however complex, to that form in which it could in a purely external fashion be put on paper, completely excluding his personal view of the matter and, what was of paramount importance, observing all the necessary formalities. All this work was new. And he was one of the first men who put into practical working the reforms in judicial procedure enacted in 1864.

On settling in a new town in his position as examining magistrate, Ivan Ilyich made new acquaintances, formed new ties, took up a new line, and adopted a rather different attitude. He took up an attitude of somewhat dignified aloofness toward the provincial authorities, while he picked out the best circle among the legal gentlemen and wealthy gentry living in the town, and adopted a tone of slight dissatisfaction with the government, moderate liberalism, and lofty civic virtue. With this, while making no change in the elegance of his get-up, Ivan Ilyich in his new office gave up shaving, and left his beard free to grow as it liked. Ivan Ilyich's existence in the new town proved to be very agreeable; the society which took the line of opposition to the governor was friendly and good; his income was larger, and he found a source of increased enjoyment in whist, at which he began to play at this time; and having a faculty for playing cards good-humoredly, and being rapid and exact in his calculations, he was as a rule on the winning side.

After living two years in the new town, Ivan Ilyich met his future wife. Praskovya Fyodorovna Mihel was the most attractive, clever, and brilliant girl in the set in which Ivan Ilyich moved. Among other amusements and recreations after his labors as a magistrate, Ivan Ilyich started a light, playful flirtation with Praskovya Fyodorovna.

Ivan Ilyich when he was an assistant secretary had danced as a rule; as an examining magistrate he danced only as an exception. He danced now as it were under protest, as though to show "that though I am serving on the new reformed legal code, and am of the fifth class in official rank, still if it comes to a question of dancing, in that line, too, I can do better than others." In this spirit he danced now and then toward the end of the evening with Praskovya Fyodorovna, and it was principally during these dances that he won the heart of Praskovya Fyodorovna. She fell in love with him. Ivan Ilyich had no clearly defined intention of marrying; but when the girl fell in love with him, he put the question to himself: "After all, why not get married?"

The young lady, Praskovya Fyodorovna, was of good family, nice-looking. There was a little bit of property. Ivan Ilyich might have reckoned on a more brilliant match, but this was a good match. Ivan

Ilyich had his salary; she, he hoped, would have as much of her own. It was a good family; she was a sweet, pretty, and perfectly *comme il faut* young woman. To say that Ivan Ilyich got married because he fell in love with his wife and found in her sympathy with his views of life would be as untrue as to say that he got married because the people of his world approved of the match. Ivan Ilyich was influenced by both considerations; he was doing what was agreeable to himself in securing such a wife, and at the same time doing what persons of higher standing looked upon as the correct thing.

And Ivan Ilyich got married.

The process itself of getting married and the early period of married life, with the conjugal caresses, the new furniture, the new crockery, the new house linen, all up to the time of his wife's pregnancy, went off very well, so that Ivan Ilyich had already begun to think that so far from marriage breaking up that kind of frivolous, agreeable, lighthearted life, always decorous and always approved by society, which he regarded as the normal life, it would even increase its agreeableness. But at that point, in the early months of his wife's pregnancy, there came in a new element, unexpected, unpleasant, tiresome, and unseemly, which could never have been anticipated, and from which there was no escape.

His wife, without any kind of reason, it seemed to Ivan Ilyich, *de gaieté de cœur*, as he expressed it, began to disturb the agreeableness and decorum of their life. She began without any sort of justification to be jealous, exacting in her demands on his attention, squabbled over everything, and treated him to the coarsest and most unpleasant scenes.

At first Ivan Ilyich hoped to escape from the unpleasantness of this position by taking up the same frivolous and well-bred line that had served him well on other occasions of difficulty. He endeavored to ignore his wife's ill-humor, went on living lightheartedly and agreeably as before, invited friends to play cards, tried to get away himself to the club or to his friends. But his wife began on one occasion with such energy abusing him in such coarse language, and so obstinately persisted in her abuse of him every time he failed in carrying out her demands, obviously having made up her mind firmly to persist till he gave way, that is, stayed at home and was as dull as she was, that Ivan Ilyich took alarm. He perceived that matrimony, at least with his wife, was not invariably conducive to the pleasure and proprieties of life; but, on the contrary, often destructive of them, and that it was therefore essential to erect some barrier to protect himself from these disturbances. And Ivan Ilyich began to look about for such means of protecting himself. His official duties were the only thing that impressed Praskovya Fyodorovna, and Ivan Ilyich began to use his official position and the duties arising from it in his struggle with his wife to fence off his own independent world apart.

With the birth of the baby, the attempts at nursing it, and the various unsuccessful experiments with foods, with the illnesses, real and imaginary, of the infant and its mother, in which Ivan Ilyich was expected to sympathize, though he never had the slightest idea about them, the need for him to fence off a world apart for himself outside his family life became still more imperative. As his wife grew more irritable and exacting, so did Ivan Ilyich more and more transfer the center of gravity of his life to his official work. He became fonder and fonder of official life, and more ambitious than he had been.

Very quickly, not more than a year after his wedding, Ivan Ilyich had become aware that conjugal life, though providing certain comforts, was in reality a very intricate and difficult business toward which one must, if one is to do one's duty, that is, lead the decorous life approved by society, work out for oneself a definite line, just as in the government service.

And such a line Ivan Ilyich did work out for himself in his married life. He expected from his home life only those comforts—of dinner at home, of housekeeper and bed—which it could give him, and, above all, that perfect propriety in external observances required by public opinion. For the rest, he looked for good-humored pleasantness, and if he found it he was very thankful. If he met with antagonism and querulousness, he promptly retreated into the separate world he had shut off for himself in his official life and there he found solace.

Ivan Ilyich was prized as a good official, and three years later he was made assistant public prosecutor. The new duties of this position, their dignity, the possibility of bringing anyone to trial and putting anyone in prison, the publicity of the speeches and the success Ivan Ilyich had in that part of his work—all this made his official work still more attractive to him.

Children were born to him. His wife became steadily more querulous and ill-tempered, but the line Ivan Ilyich had taken up for himself in home life put him almost out of reach of her grumbling.

After seven years of service in the same town, Ivan Ilyich was transferred to another province with the post of public prosecutor. They moved, money was short, and his wife did not like the place they had moved to. The salary was indeed a little higher than before, but their expenses were larger. Besides, a couple of the children died, and home life consequently became even less agreeable for Ivan Ilyich.

For every mischance that occurred in their new place of residence, Praskovya Fyodorovna blamed her husband. The greater number of subjects of conversation between husband and wife, especially the education of the children, led to questions which were associated with previous quarrels, and quarrels were ready to break out at every instant. There remained only those rare periods of being in love which did indeed come upon them, but never lasted long. These were the islands at which they put in for a time, but they soon set off again upon the ocean of concealed hostility that was made manifest in their aloofness from one another. This aloofness might have distressed Ivan Ilyich if he had believed that this ought not to be so, but by now he regarded this position as perfectly normal, and it was indeed the goal toward which he worked in his home life. His aim was to make himself more and more free from the unpleasant aspects of domestic life and to render them harmless and decorous. And he attained this aim by spending less and less time with his family; and when he was forced to be at home, he endeavored to secure his tranquillity by the presence of outsiders. The great thing for Ivan Ilyich was having his office. In the official world all the interest of life was concentrated for him. And this interest absorbed him. The sense of his own power, the consciousness of being able to ruin anyone he wanted to ruin, even the external dignity of his office, when he made his entry into the court or met subordinate officials, his success in the eyes of his superiors and his subordinates, and, above all, his masterly handling of cases, of which he was conscious—all this delighted him and, together with chats with his colleagues, dining out, and whist, filled his life. So that, on the whole, Ivan Ilyich's life still went on in the way he thought it should go—agreeably and decorously.

So he lived for another seven years. His eldest daughter was already sixteen, another child had died, and there was left only one other, a boy at the high school, a subject of dissension. Ivan Ilyich wanted to send him to the school of jurisprudence, while Praskovya Fyodorovna to spite him sent him to the high school. The daughter had been educated at home, and had turned out well; the boy too did fairly well at his lessons.

III

Such was Ivan Ilyich's life for seventeen years after his marriage. He had been by now a long while prosecutor, and had refused several appointments offered him, looking out for a more desirable post, when there occurred an unexpected incident which utterly destroyed his peace of mind. Ivan Ilyich had been expecting to be appointed presiding judge in a university town, but a certain Goppe somehow stole a march on him and secured the appointment. Ivan Ilyich took offense, began upbraiding him, and quarreled with him and with his own superiors. A coolness was felt toward him, and on the next appointment that was made he was again passed over.

This was in the year 1880. That year was the most painful one in Ivan Ilyich's life. During that year it became evident on the one hand that his pay was insufficient for his expenses; on the other hand, that he had been forgotten by everyone, and that what seemed to him the most monstrous, the cruelest injustice appeared to other people as a quite commonplace fact. Even his father felt no obligation to assist him. He felt that everyone had deserted him, and that everyone regarded his position with an income of three thousand five hundred rubles as a quite normal and even fortunate one. He alone, with a sense of the injustice done him, and the everlasting nagging of his wife and the debts he had begun to accumulate, living beyond his means, knew that his position was far from being normal.

The summer of that year, to cut down his expenses, he took a holiday and went with his wife to spend the summer in the country at her brother's.

In the country, with no official duties to occupy him, Ivan Ilyich was for the first time a prey not to simple boredom, but to intolerable depression, and he made up his mind that things could not go on like that, and that it was absolutely necessary to take some decisive steps.

After a sleepless night spent by Ivan Ilyich walking up and down the terrace, he determined to go to Petersburg to take active steps and to get transferred to some other department, so as to revenge himself on them, the people, that is, who had not known how to appreciate him.

Next day, in spite of all the efforts of his wife and his mother-in-law to dissuade him, he set off to Petersburg.

He went with a single object before him—to obtain a post with an income of five thousand. He was ready now to be satisfied with a post in any department, of any tendency, with any kind of work. He must only have a post—a post with five thousand, in the executive department, the banks, the railways, the Empress Marya's institutions, even in the customs duties—what was essential was five thousand, and essential it was, too, to get out of the department in which they had failed to appreciate his value.

And, behold, this quest of Ivan Ilyich's was crowned with wonderful, unexpected success. At Kursk there got into the same first-class carriage F. S. Ilyin, an acquaintance, who told him of a telegram just received by the governor of Kursk announcing a change about to take place in the ministry—Piotr Ivanovich was to be superseded by Ivan Semyonovich.

The proposed change, apart from its significance for Russia, had special significance for Ivan Ilyich from the fact that by bringing to the front a new person, Piotr Petrovich, and obviously, therefore, his friend Zahar Ivanovich, it was in the highest degree propitious to Ivan Ilyich's own plans. Zahar Ivanovich was a friend and schoolfellow of Ivan Ilyich's.

At Moscow the news was confirmed. On arriving at Petersburg, Ivan Ilyich looked up Zahar Ivanovich, and received a positive promise of an appointment in his former department—that of justice.

A week later he telegraphed to his wife: "Zahar Miller's place. At first report I receive appointment."

Thanks to these changes, Ivan Ilyich unexpectedly obtained, in the same department as before, an appointment which placed him two stages higher than his former colleagues, and gave him an income of five thousand, together with the official allowance of three thousand five hundred for traveling expenses. All his ill-humor with his former enemies and the whole department was forgotten, and Ivan Ilyich was completely happy.

Ivan Ilyich went back to the country more lighthearted and good-tempered than he had been for a very long while. Praskovya Fyodorovna was in better spirits, too, and peace was patched up between them. Ivan Ilyich described what respect everyone had shown him in Petersburg; how all those who had been his enemies had been put to shame, and were cringing now before him; how envious they were of his appointment, and still more of the high favor in which he stood in Petersburg.

Praskovya Fyodorovna listened to this, and pretended to believe it, and did not contradict him in anything, but confined herself to making plans for her new arrangements in the town to which they would be moving. And Ivan Ilyich saw with delight that these plans were his plans; that they were agreed; and that his life after this disturbing hitch in its progress was about to regain its true, normal character of lighthearted agreeableness and propriety.

Ivan Ilyich had come back to the country for a short stay only. He had to enter upon the duties of his new office on the 10th of September; and besides, he needed some time to settle in a new place, to move all his belongings from the other province, to purchase and order many things in addition; in short, to arrange things as settled in his own mind and almost exactly as settled in the heart, too, of Praskovya Fyodorovna.

And now when everything was so successfully arranged and when he and his wife were agreed in their aim, and were, besides, so little together, they got on with one another as they had not got on together since the early years of their married life. Ivan Ilyich had thought of taking his family away with him at once; but his sister and his brother-in-law, who had suddenly become extremely cordial and intimate with him and his family, were so pressing in urging them to stay that he set off alone.

Ivan Ilyich started off; and the lighthearted temper produced by his success, and his good understanding with his wife, one thing backing up another, did not desert him all the time. He found a charming set of apartments, the very thing both husband and wife had dreamed of. Spacious, lofty reception rooms in the old style, a comfortable, dignified-looking study for him, rooms for his wife and daughter, a schoolroom for his son, everything as though planned on purpose for them. Ivan Ilyich himself looked after the furnishing of them, chose the wallpapers, bought furniture, by preference antique furniture, which had a peculiar *comme il faut* style to his mind, and it all grew up and grew up, and really attained the ideal he had set before himself. When he had half finished arranging the house, his arrangement surpassed his own expectations. He saw the *comme il faut* character, elegant and free from vulgarity, that the whole would have when it was all ready. As he fell asleep he pictured to himself the reception room as it would be. Looking at the drawing room, not yet finished, he could see the hearth, the screen, the *étagère*, and the little chairs dotted here and there, the plates and dishes on the wall, and the bronzes as they would be when they were all put in their places. He was delighted with the thought of how he would impress Praskovya and Lizanka, who had taste too in this line. They would never expect anything like it. He was particularly successful in coming across and buying cheap old pieces of furniture, which gave a peculiarly aristocratic air to the whole. In his letters he purposely disparaged everything so as to surprise them. All this so absorbed him that the duties of his new office, though he was so fond of his official work, interested him less than he had expected. During sittings of the court he had moments of inattention; he pondered the question which sort of cornices to have on the window blinds, straight or fluted. He was so interested in this business that he often set to work with his own hands, moved a piece of furniture, or hung up curtains himself. One day he went up a ladder to show a workman, who did not understand, how he wanted some hangings draped, made a false step, and slipped; but, like a strong and nimble person, he clung on, and only knocked his side against the corner of a frame. The bruised place ached, but it soon passed off. Ivan Ilyich felt all this time particularly good-

humored and well. He wrote: "I feel fifteen years younger." He thought his house furnishing would be finished in September, but it dragged on to the middle of October. But then the effect was charming; not only he said so, but everyone who saw it told him so, too.

In reality, it was all just what is commonly seen in the houses of people who are not exactly wealthy but want to look like wealthy people, and so succeed only in being like one another—hangings, dark wood, flowers, rugs, and bronzes, everything dark and highly polished, everything that all people of a certain class have so as to be like all people of a certain class. And in his case it was all so like that it made no impression at all; but it all seemed to him somehow special. When he met his family at the railway station and brought them to his newly furnished rooms, all lighted up in readiness, and a footman in a white tie opened the door into an entry decorated with flowers, and then they walked into the drawing room and the study, uttering cries of delight, he was very happy, conducted them everywhere, eagerly drinking in their praises, and beaming with satisfaction. The same evening, while they talked about various things at tea, Praskovya Fyodorovna inquired about his fall, and he laughed and showed them how he had gone flying, and how he had frightened the upholsterer.

"It's all well I'm something of an athlete. Another man might have been killed, and I got nothing worse than a blow here; when it's touched it hurts, but it's going off already; nothing but a bruise."

And they began to live in their new abode, which, as is always the case, when they had got thoroughly settled in they found to be short of just one room, and with their new income, which, as always, was only a little—some five hundred rubles—too little, and everything went very well. Things went particularly well at first, before everything was quite finally arranged, and there was still something to do to the place—something to buy, something to order, something to move, something to make to fit. Though there were indeed several disputes between husband and wife, both were so well satisfied, and there was so much to do, that it all went off without serious quarrels. When there was nothing left to arrange, it became a little dull, and something seemed to be lacking, but by then they were making acquaintances and forming habits, and life was filled up again.

Ivan Ilyich, after spending the morning in the court, returned home to dinner, and at first he was generally in a good humor, although this was apt to be upset a little, and precisely on account of the new abode. Every spot on the tablecloth, on the hangings, the string of a window blind broken, irritated him. He had devoted so much trouble to the arrangement of the rooms that any disturbance of their order distressed him. But, on the whole, the life of Ivan Ilyich ran its course as, according to his conviction, life ought to do—easily, agreeably, and decorously. He got up at nine, drank his coffee, read the newspaper, then put on his official uniform, and went to the court. There the routine of the daily work was already mapped out for him, and he stepped into it at once. People with petitions, inquiries in the office, the office itself, the sittings—public and preliminary. In all this the great thing necessary was to exclude everything with the sap of life in it, which always disturbs the regular course of official business, not to admit any sort of relations with people except the official relations; the motive of all intercourse had to be simply the official motive and the intercourse itself to be only official. A man would come, for instance, anxious for certain information. Ivan Ilyich, not being the functionary on duty, would have nothing whatever to do with such a man. But if this man's relation to him as a member of the court is such as can be formulated on official stamped paper—within the limits of such a relation Ivan Ilyich would do everything, positively everything, he could, and in doing so would observe the semblance of human friendly relations, that is, the courtesies of social life. But where the official relation ended, there everything else stopped, too. This art of keeping the official aspect of things apart from his real life, Ivan Ilyich possessed in the highest degree; and through long practice and natural aptitude, he had brought it to such a pitch of perfection that he even permitted himself at times, like a skilled specialist as it were in jest, to let the human and official relations mingle. He allowed himself this liberty just because he felt he had the power at any moment if he wished it to take up the purely official line again and to drop the human relation. This thing was not simply easy, agreeable, and decorous; in Ivan Ilyich's hands it attained a positively artistic character. In the intervals of business he smoked, drank tea, chatted a little about politics, a little about public affairs, a little about cards, but most of all about appointments in the service. And tired, but feeling like some artist who has skillfully played his part in the performance, one of the first violins in the orchestra, he returned home. At home his daughter and her mother had been paying calls somewhere, or else someone had been calling on them; the son had been at school, had been preparing his lessons with his teachers, and duly learning correctly what was taught at the high school. Everything was as it should be. After dinner, if there were no visitors, Ivan Ilyich sometimes read some book of which people were talking, and in the evening sat down to work, that is, read official papers, compared them with the laws, sorted depositions, and put them under the laws. This he found neither tiresome nor entertaining. It was tiresome when he might have been playing "screw"; but if there were no "screw" going on, it was anyway better than sitting alone or with his wife. Ivan Ilyich's pleasures were little dinners, to which he invited ladies and gentlemen of good social position, and such methods of passing the time with them as were usual with such persons, so that his drawing room might be like all other drawing rooms.

Once they even gave a party—a dance. And Ivan Ilyich enjoyed it, and everything was very successful, except that it led to a violent quarrel with his wife over the tarts and sweetmeats. Praskovya Fyodorovna had her own plan; while Ivan Ilyich insisted on getting everything from an expensive pastry cook, and ordered a great many tarts, and the quarrel was because these tarts were left over and the pastry cook's bill came to forty-five rubles. The quarrel was a violent and unpleasant one, so much so that Praskovya Fyodorovna called him, "Fool, imbecile." And he clutched at his head, and in his anger made some allusion to a divorce. But the party itself was enjoyable. There were all the best people, and Ivan Ilyich danced with Princess Trufonov, the sister of the one so well known in connection with the charitable association called, "Bear My Burden." His official pleasures lay in the gratification of his pride; his social pleasures lay in the gratification of his vanity. But Ivan Ilyich's most real pleasure was the pleasure of playing "screw," the Russian equivalent for bridge. He admitted to himself that, after all, after whatever unpleasant incidents there had been in his life, the pleasure which burned like a candle before all others was sitting with good players, and not noisy partners, at "screw"; and, of course, a four-hand game (playing with five was never a success, though one pretends to like it particularly), and with good cards, to play a shrewd, serious game, then supper and a glass of wine. And after "screw," especially after winning some small stakes (winning large sums was unpleasant), Ivan Ilyich went to bed in a particularly happy frame of mind.

So they lived. They moved in the very best circle, and were visited by people of consequence and young people.

In their views of their circle of acquaintances, the husband, the wife, and the daughter were in complete accord; and without any expressed agreement on the subject, they all acted alike in dropping and shaking off various friends and relations, shabby persons who swooped down upon them in their drawing room with Japanese plates on the walls, and pressed their civilities on them. Soon these shabby persons ceased fluttering about them, and none but the very best society was seen at the Golovins'. Young men began to pay attention to Lizanka; and Petrishtchev, the son of Dmitry Ivanovich Petrishtchev, and the sole heir of his fortune, an examining magistrate, began to be so attentive to Lizanka that Ivan Ilyich had raised the question with his wife whether it would not be as well to arrange a sleigh drive for them, or to get up some theatricals. So they lived. And everything went on in this way without change, and everything was very nice.

IV

All were in good health. One could not use the word ill-health in connection with the symptoms Ivan Ilyich sometimes complained of, namely, a queer taste in his mouth and a sort of uncomfortable feeling on the left side of the stomach.

But it came to pass that this uncomfortable feeling kept increasing, and became not exactly a pain, but a continual sense of weight in his side, and irritable temper. This irritable temper, continually growing and growing, began at last to mar the agreeable easiness and decorum that had reigned in the Golovin household. Quarrels between the husband and wife became more and more frequent, and soon all the easiness and amenity of life had fallen away, and mere propriety was maintained with difficulty. Scenes became again more frequent. Again there were only islands in the sea of contention—and but few of these—at which the husband and wife could meet without an outbreak. And Praskovya Fyodorovna said now, not without grounds, that her husband had a trying temper. With her characteristic exaggeration, she said

he had always had this awful temper, and she had needed all her sweetness to put up with it for twenty years. It was true that it was he now who began the quarrels. His gusts of temper always broke out just before dinner, and often just as he was beginning to eat, at the soup. He would notice that some piece of the crockery had been chipped, or that the food was not nice, or that his son put his elbow on the table, or his daughter's hair was not arranged as he liked it. And whatever it was, he laid the blame of it on Praskovya Fyodorovna. Praskovya Fyodorovna had at first retorted in the same strain, and said all sorts of horrid things to him; but on two occasions, just at the beginning of dinner, he had flown into such a frenzy that she perceived that it was due to physical derangement, and was brought on by taking food, and she controlled herself; she did not reply, but simply made haste to get dinner over. Praskovya Fyodorovna took great credit to herself for this exercise of self-control. Making up her mind that her husband had a fearful temper, and made her life miserable, she began to feel sorry for herself. And the more she felt for herself, the more she hated her husband. She began to wish he were dead; yet could not wish it because then there would be no income. And this exasperated her against him even more. She considered herself dreadfully unfortunate, precisely because even his death could not save her, and she felt irritated and concealed it, and this hidden irritation on her side increased his irritability.

After one violent scene, in which Ivan Ilyich had been particularly unjust, and after which he had said in explanation that he certainly was irritable, but that it was due to illness, she said that if he were ill he ought to take steps, and insisted on his going to see a celebrated doctor.

He went. Everything was as he had expected; everything was as it always is. The waiting and the assumption of dignity, that professional dignity he knew so well, exactly as he assumed it himself in court, and the sounding and listening and questions that called for answers that were foregone conclusions and obviously superfluous, and the significant air that seemed to insinuate—you only leave it all to us, and we will arrange everything, for us it is certain and incontestable how to arrange everything, everything in one way for every man of every sort. It was all exactly as in his court of justice. Exactly the same air as he put on in dealing with a man brought up for judgment, the doctor put on for him.

The doctor said: This and that proves that you have such-and-such a thing wrong inside you; but if that is not confirmed by analysis of this and that, then we must assume this and that, then—and so on. To Ivan Ilyich there was only one question of consequence. Was his condition dangerous or not? But the doctor ignored that irrelevant inquiry. From the doctor's point of view this was a side issue, not the subject under consideration; the only real question was the balance of probabilities between a loose kidney, chronic catarrh, and appendicitis. It was not a question of the life of Ivan Ilyich, but the question between the loose kidney and the intestinal appendix. And this question, as it seemed to Ivan Ilyich, the doctor solved in a brilliant manner in favor of the appendix, with the reservation that analysis of the water might give a fresh clue, and

that then the aspect of the case would be altered. All this was point for point identical with what Ivan Ilyich had himself done in brilliant fashion a thousand times over in dealing with some man on his trial. Just as brilliantly the doctor made his summing up, and triumphantly, gaily even, glanced over his spectacles at the prisoner in the dock. From the doctor's summing up Ivan Ilyich deduced the conclusion—that things looked bad, and that he, the doctor, and most likely everyone else, did not care, but that things looked bad for him. And this conclusion impressed Ivan Ilyich morbidly, arousing in him a great feeling of pity for himself, of great anger against this doctor who could be unconcerned about a matter of such importance.

But he said nothing of that. He got up, and, laying the fee on the table, he said, with a sigh, "We sick people probably often ask inconvenient questions. Tell me, is this generally a dangerous illness or not?"

The doctor glanced severely at him with one eye through his spectacles, as though to say: "Prisoner at the bar, if you will not keep within the limits of the questions allowed you, I shall be compelled to take measures for your removal from the precincts of the court." "I have told you what I thought necessary and suitable already," said the doctor; "the analysis will show anything further." And the doctor bowed him out.

Ivan Ilyich went out slowly and dejectedly, got into his sleigh, and drove home. All the way home he was incessantly going over all the doctor had said, trying to translate all these complicated, obscure, scientific phrases into simple language, and to read in them an answer to the question, It is bad—is it very bad, or nothing much as yet? And it seemed to him that the upshot of all the doctor had said was that it was very bad. Everything seemed dismal to Ivan Ilyich in the streets. The sleigh drivers were dismal, the houses were dismal, the people passing, and the shops were dismal. This ache, this dull gnawing ache, that never ceased for a second, seemed, when connected with the doctor's obscure utterances, to have gained a new, more serious significance. With a new sense of misery· Ivan Ilyich kept watch on it now.

He reached home and began to tell his wife about it. His wife listened; but in the middle of his account his daughter came in with her hat on, ready to go out with her mother. Reluctantly she half sat down to listen to these tedious details, but she could not stand it for long, and her mother did not hear his story to the end.

"Well, I'm very glad," said his wife; "now you must be sure and take the medicine regularly. Give me the prescription; I'll send Gerasim to the chemist's!" And she went to get ready to go out.

He had not taken breath while she was in the room, and he heaved a deep sigh when she was gone.

"Well," he said, "maybe it really is nothing as yet."

He began to take the medicine, to carry out the doctor's directions, which were changed after the analysis of the water. But it was just at this point that some confusion arose, either in the analysis or in what ought to have followed from it. The doctor himself, of course, could not be blamed for it, but it turned out that things had not gone as the doctor had told him. Either

he had forgotten or told a lie, or was hiding something from him.

But Ivan Ilyich still went on just as exactly carrying out the doctor's directions, and in doing so he found comfort at first.

From the time of his visit to the doctor Ivan Ilyich's principal occupation became the exact observance of the doctor's prescriptions as regards hygiene and medicine and the careful observation of his ailment in all the functions of his organism. Ivan Ilyich's principal interest came to be people's ailments and people's health. When anything was said in his presence about sick people, about deaths and recoveries, especially in the case of an illness resembling his own, he listened, trying to conceal his excitement, asked questions, and applied what he heard to his own trouble.

The ache did not grow less; but Ivan Ilyich made great efforts to force himself to believe that he was better. And he succeeded in deceiving himself so long as nothing happened to disturb him. But as soon as he had a mischance, some unpleasant words with his wife, a failure in his official work, an unlucky hand at "screw," he was at once acutely sensible of his illness. In former days he had borne with such mishaps, hoping soon to retrieve the mistake, to make a struggle, to reach success later, to have a lucky hand. But now he was cast down by every mischance and reduced to despair. He would say to himself: "Here I'm only just beginning to get better, and the medicine has begun to take effect, and now this mischance or disappointment." And he was furious against the mischance or the people who were causing him the disappointment and killing him, and he felt that this fury was killing him, but could not check it. One would have thought that it should have been clear to him that this exasperation against circumstances and people was aggravating his disease, and that therefore he ought not to pay attention to the unpleasant incidents. But his reasoning took quite the opposite direction. He said that he needed peace, and was on the watch for everything that disturbed his peace, and at the slightest disturbance of it he flew into a rage. What made his position worse was that he read medical books and consulted doctors. He got worse so gradually that he might have deceived himself, comparing one day with another, the difference was so slight. But when he consulted the doctors, then it seemed to him that he was getting worse, and very rapidly so indeed. And in spite of this, he was continually consulting the doctors.

That month he called on another celebrated doctor. The second celebrity said almost the same as the first, but put his questions differently; and the interview with this celebrity only redoubled the doubts and terrors of Ivan Ilyich. A friend of a friend of his, a very good doctor, diagnosed the disease quite differently; and in spite of the fact that he guaranteed recovery, by his questions and his suppositions he confused Ivan Ilyich even more and strengthened his suspicions. A homeopath gave yet another diagnosis of the complaint, and prescribed medicine, which Ivan Ilyich took secretly for a week; but after a week of the homeopathic medicine he felt no relief, and losing faith both in the other doctor's treatment and in this, he fell into even deeper depression. One day a lady of his acquaintance talked to him

of the healing wrought by the holy pictures. Ivan Ilyich caught himself listening attentively and believing in the reality of the fact alleged. This incident alarmed him. "Can I have degenerated to such a point of intellectual feebleness?" he said to himself. "Nonsense! it's all rubbish. I must not give way to nervous fears, but, fixing on one doctor, adhere strictly to his treatment. That's what I will do. Now it's settled. I won't think about it, but till next summer I will stick to the treatment, and then I shall see. Now I'll put a stop to this wavering!" It was easy to say this, but impossible to carry it out. The pain in his side was always dragging at him, seeming to grow more acute and ever more incessant; it seemed to him that the taste in his mouth was queerer, and there was a loathsome smell even from his breath, and his appetite and strength kept dwindling. There was no deceiving himself; something terrible, new, and so important that nothing more important had ever been in Ivan Ilyich's life, was taking place in him, and he alone knew of it. All about him did not or would not understand, and believed that everything in the world was going on as before. This was what tortured Ivan Ilyich more than anything. Those of his own household, most of all his wife and daughter, who were absorbed in a perfect whirl of visits, did not, he saw, comprehend it at all, and were annoyed that he was so depressed and exacting, as though he were to blame for it. Though they tried indeed to disguise it, he saw he was a nuisance to them; but that his wife had taken up a definite line of her own in regard to his illness, and stuck to it regardless of what he might say or do. This line was expressed thus: "You know," she would say to acquaintances, "Ivan Ilyich cannot, like all other simple-hearted folks, keep to the treatment prescribed him. One day he'll take his drops and eat what he's ordered, and go to bed in good time; the next day, if I don't see to it, he'll suddenly forget to take his medicine, eat sturgeon (which is forbidden by the doctors), yes, and sit up at 'screw' till past midnight."

"Why, when did I do that?" Ivan Ilyich asked in vexation one day at Piotr Ivanovich's.

"Why, yesterday, with Shebek."

"It makes no difference. I couldn't sleep for pain."

"Well, it doesn't matter what you do it for, only you'll never get well like that, and you make us wretched."

Praskovya Fyodorovna's external attitude to her husband's illness, openly expressed to others and to himself, was that Ivan Ilyich was to blame in the matter of his illness, and that the whole illness was another injury he was doing to his wife. Ivan Ilyich felt that the expression of this dropped from her unconsciously, but that made it no easier for him.

In his official life, too, Ivan Ilyich noticed, or fancied he noticed, a strange attitude to him. At one time it seemed to him that people were looking inquisitively at him, as a man who would shortly have to vacate his position; at another time his friends would suddenly begin chaffing him in a friendly way over his nervous fears, as though that awful and horrible, unheard-of thing that was going on within him, incessantly gnawing at him and irresistibly dragging him away somewhere, were the most agreeable subject for joking. Shvarts especially, with his jocoseness, his liveliness, and his *comme il faut* tone, exasper-

ated Ivan Ilyich by reminding him of himself ten years ago.

Friends came sometimes to play cards. They sat down to the card table; they shuffled and dealt the new cards. Diamonds were led and followed by diamonds, the seven. His partner said, "Can't trump," and played the two of diamonds. What then? Why, delightful, capital, it should have been—he had a trump hand. And suddenly Ivan Ilyich feels the gnawing ache, that taste in his mouth, and it strikes him as something grotesque that with that he could be glad of a trump hand.

He looks at Mihail Mihailovich, his partner, how he taps on the table with his red hand, and affably and indulgently abstains from snatching up the trick, and pushes the cards toward Ivan Ilyich so as to give him the pleasure of taking them up, without any trouble, without even stretching out his hand. "What, does he suppose that I'm so weak that I can't stretch out my hand?" thinks Ivan Ilyich, and he forgets the trumps, and trumps his partner's cards, and plays his trump hand without making three tricks; and what's the most awful thing of all is that he sees how upset Mihail Mihailovich is about it, while he doesn't care a bit, and it's awful for him to think why he doesn't care.

They all see that he's in pain, and say to him, "We can stop if you're tired. You go and lie down." Lie down? No, he's not in the least tired; they will play the rubber. All are gloomy and silent. Ivan Ilyich feels that it is he who has brought this gloom upon them, and he cannot disperse it. They have supper, and the party breaks up, and Ivan Ilyich is left alone with the consciousness that his life is poisoned for him and poisons the life of others, and that this poison is not losing its force, but is continually penetrating more and more deeply into his whole existence.

And with the consciousness of this, and with the physical pain in addition, and the terror in addition to that, he must lie in his bed, often not able to sleep for pain the greater part of the night; and in the morning he must get up again, dress, go to the law court, speak, write, or, if he does not go out, stay at home for all the four-and-twenty hours of the day and night, of which each one is a torture. And he had to live thus on the edge of the precipice alone, without one man who would understand and feel for him.

V

In this way one month, then a second, passed by. Just before the New Year his brother-in-law arrived in the town on a visit to them. Ivan Ilyich was at the court when he arrived. Praskovya Fyodorovna had gone out shopping. Coming home and going into his study, he found there his brother-in-law, a healthy, florid man, engaged in unpacking his trunk. He raised his head, hearing Ivan Ilyich's step, and for a second stared at him without a word. That stare told Ivan Ilyich everything. His brother-in-law opened his mouth to utter an "Oh!" of surprise, but checked himself. That confirmed it all.

"What! have I changed?"

"Yes, there is a change."

And all Ivan Ilyich's efforts to draw him into talking of his appearance his brother-in-law met with obstinate silence. Praskovya Fyodorovna came in; the brother-in-law went to see her. Ivan Ilyich locked his door and began gazing at himself in the looking glass, first full face, then in profile. He took up his photograph, taken with his wife, and compared the portrait with what he saw in the looking glass. The change was immense. Then he bared his arm to the elbow, looked at it, pulled the sleeve down again, sat down on an ottoman, and felt blacker than night.

"I mustn't, I mustn't," he said to himself, jumped up, went to the table, opened some official paper, tried to read it, but could not. He opened the door, went into the drawing room. The door into the drawing room was closed. He went up to it on tiptoe and listened.

"No, you're exaggerating," Praskovya Fyodorovna was saying.

"Exaggerating? You can't see it. Why, he's a dead man. Look at his eyes—there's no light in them. But what's wrong with him?"

"No one can tell. Nikolaev" (that was another doctor) "said something, but I don't know. Leshtchetitsky" (this was the celebrated doctor) "said the opposite."

Ivan Ilyich walked away, went to his own room, lay down, and fell to musing. "A kidney—a loose kidney." He remembered all the doctors had told him, how it had detached, and how it was loose; and by an effort of imagination he tried to catch that kidney and to stop it, to strengthen it. So little was needed, he fancied. "No, I'll go again to Piotr Ivanovich" (this was the friend who had for a friend a doctor). He rang, ordered the horse to be put in, and got ready to go out.

"Where are you off to, Jean?" asked his wife with a peculiarly melancholy and exceptionally kind expression.

This exceptionally kind expression exasperated him. He looked darkly at her.

"I want to see Piotr Ivanovich."

He went to the friend who had for a friend a doctor. And with him to the doctor's. He found him in, and had a long conversation with him.

Reviewing the anatomical and physiological details of what, according to the doctor's view, was taking place within him, he understood it all. It was just one thing—a little thing wrong with the intestinal appendix. It might all come right. Only strengthen one sluggish organ, and decrease the undue activity of another, an absorption would take place, and all would be set right. He was a little late for dinner. He ate his dinner, talked cheerfully, but it was a long while before he could go to his own room to work. At last he went to his study, and at once sat down to work. He read his legal documents and did his work, but the consciousness never left him of having a matter of importance very near to his heart which he had put off, but would look into later. When he had finished his work, he remembered that the matter near his heart was thinking about the intestinal appendix. But he did not give himself up to it; he went into the drawing room to tea. There were visitors; and there was talking, playing on the piano, and singing; there was the young examining magistrate, the desirable match for the daughter. Ivan Ilyich spent the evening, as Praskovya Fyodorovna observed, in better spirits than any of them; but he never forgot for an instant that he had an important matter of the intestinal appendix put off for consideration later. At eleven o'clock he said good night and went to his own room. He had slept alone since his illness in a little room adjoining his study. He went in, undressed, and took up a novel of Zola, but did not read it; he fell to thinking. And in his imagination the desired recovery of the intestinal appendix had taken place. There had been absorption, rejection, re-establishment of the regular action.

"Why, it's all simply that," he said to himself. "One only wants to assist nature." He remembered the medicine, got up, took it, lay down on his back, watching for the medicine to act beneficially and overcome the pain. "It's only to take it regularly and avoid injurious influences; why, already I feel rather better, much better." He began to feel his side; it was not painful to the touch. "Yes, I don't feel it—really, much better already." He put out the candle and lay on his side. "The appendix is getting better, absorption." Suddenly he felt the familiar, old, dull, gnawing ache, persistent, quiet, in earnest. In his mouth the same familiar loathsome taste. His heart sank, and his brain felt dim, misty. "My God, my God!" he said, "again, again, and it will never cease." And suddenly the whole thing rose before him in quite a different aspect.

"Intestinal appendix! kidney!" he said to himself. "It's not a question of the appendix, not a question of the kidney, but of life and . . . death. Yes, life has been, and now it's going, going away, and I cannot stop it. Yes. Why deceive myself? Isn't it obvious to everyone, except me, that I'm dying, and it's only a question of weeks, of days—at once, perhaps. There was light, and now there is darkness. I was here, and now I am going! Where?" A cold chill ran over him, his breath stopped. He heard nothing but the throbbing of his heart.

"I shall be no more, then what will there be? There'll be nothing. Where then shall I be when I'm no more? Can this be dying? No; I don't want to!" He jumped up, tried to light the candle; and fumbling with trembling hands, he dropped the candle and the candle-stick on the floor and fell back again on the pillow. "Why trouble? It doesn't matter," he said to himself, staring with open eyes into the darkness. "Death. Yes, death. And they —all of them—don't understand, and don't want to understand, and feel no pity. They are playing." (He caught through the closed doors the faraway cadence of a voice and the accompaniment.) "They don't care, but they will die, too. Fools! Me sooner and them later; but it will be the same for them. And they are merry. The beasts!" Anger stifled him. And he was agonizingly, insufferably miserable. "It cannot be that all men always have been doomed to this awful horror!" He raised himself.

"There is something wrong in it; I must be calm, I must think it all over from the beginning." And then he began to consider. "Yes, the beginning of my illness. I knocked my side, and I was just the same, that day and the days after it; it ached a little, then more, then doctors, then depression, misery, and again doctors; and I've gone on getting closer and closer to the abyss. Strength growing less. Nearer and nearer. And here I am, wasting away, no light in my eyes. I think of how to cure the appendix, but this is death. Can it be death?" Again a horror came over him; gasping for breath, he bent over, began feeling for the matches, and knocked his elbow against the bedside table. It was in his way and hurt him; he felt furious with it, in his anger knocked against it more violently and upset it. And in despair, breathless, he fell back on his spine, waiting for death to come that instant.

The visitors were leaving at that time. Praskovya Fyodorovna was seeing them out. She heard something fall, and came in.

"What is it?"

"Nothing. I dropped something by accident."

She went out, brought a candle. He was lying, breathing hard and fast, like a man who has run a mile, and staring with fixed eyes at her.

"What is it, Jean?"

"Nothing, I say. I dropped something." Why speak? She won't understand, he thought.

She certainly did not understand. She picked up the candle, lighted it for him, and went out hastily. She had to say good-by to a departing guest. When she came back, he was lying in the same position on his back, looking upwards.

"How are you—worse?"

"Yes."

She shook her head, sat down.

"Do you know what, Jean? I wonder if we hadn't better send for Leshtchetitsky to see you here?"

This meant calling in the celebrated doctor, regardless of expense. He smiled malignantly, and said no. She sat a moment longer, went up to him, and kissed him on the forehead.

He hated her with all the force of his soul when she was kissing him, and had to make an effort not to push her away.

"Good night. Please God, you'll sleep."

"Yes."

VI

Ivan Ilyich saw that he was dying, and was in continual despair.

At the bottom of his heart Ivan llyich knew that he was dying; but so far from growing used to this idea, he simply did not grasp it—he was utterly unable to grasp it.

The example of the syllogism that he had learned in Kiseveter's logic— Caius is a man, men are mortal, therefore Caius is mortal—had seemed to him all his life correct only as regards Caius, but not at all as regards himself. In that case it was a question of Caius, a man, an abstract man, and it was per- fectly true, but he was not Caius, and was not an abstract man; he had always been a creature quite, quite different from all others; he had been little Vanya with a mamma and papa, and Mitya and Volodya, with playthings and a coachman and a nurse; afterwards with Katenka, with all the joys and griefs and ecstasies of childhood, boyhood, and youth. What did Caius know of the smell of the leathern ball Vanya had been so fond of? Had Caius kissed his mother's hand like that? Caius had not heard the silk rustle of his mother's skirts. He had not made a riot at school over the pudding. Had Caius been in love like that? Could Caius preside over the sit- tings of the court?

And Caius certainly was mortal, and it was right for him to die; but for me, little Vanya, Ivan Ilyich, with all my feelings and ideas—for me it's a different matter. And it cannot be that I ought to die. That would be too awful.

That was his feeling.

"If I had to die like Caius, I should have known it was so, some inner voice would have told me so. But there was nothing of the sort in me. And I and all my friends, we felt that it was not at all the same as with Caius. And now here

it is!" he said to himself. "It can't be! It can't be, but it is! How is it? How's one to understand it?" And he could not conceive it, and tried to drive away this idea as false, in- correct, and morbid, and to supplant it by other, correct, healthy ideas. But this idea, not as an idea merely, but as it were an actual fact, came back again and stood confronting him.

And to replace this thought he called up other thoughts, one after another, in the hope of finding sup- port in them. He tried to get back into former trains of thought, which in old days had screened off the thought of death. But, strange to say, all that had in old days covered up, obliterated, the sense of death could not now produce the same effect. Latterly, Ivan Ilyich spent the greater part of his time in these efforts to restore his old trains of thought which had shut off death. At one time he would say to him- self, "I'll put myself into my official work; why, I used to live in it." And he would go to the law courts, banishing every doubt. He would enter into conversation with his col- leagues, and would sit carelessly, as his old habit was, scanning the crowd below dreamily, and with both his wasted hands he would lean on the arms of the oak arm- chair just as he always did; and, bending over to a colleague, pass the papers to him and whisper to him, then suddenly dropping his eyes and sitting up straight, he would pronounce the familiar words that opened the proceedings. But suddenly in the middle, the pain in his side, utterly regardless of the stage he had reached in his conduct of the case, began its work. It riveted Ivan Ilyich's attention. He drove away the thought of it, but it still did its work, and then It came and stood confronting him and looked at him, and he felt turned to stone, and the light died away in his eyes, and he began to ask himself again, "Can it be that It is the only truth?" And his colleagues and his subordinates saw with surprise and distress that he, the brilliant, subtle judge, was losing the thread of his speech, was making blunders. He shook himself, tried to regain his self-control, and got somehow to the end of the sitting, and went home with the painful sense that his judicial labors could not as of old hide from him what he wanted to hide; that he could not by means of his official work escape from It. And the worst of it was that It drew him to itself not for him to do anything in particular, but simply for him to look at It straight in the face, to look at It and, doing nothing, suffer unspeakably.

And to save himself from this, Ivan Ilyich sought amusements, other screens, and these screens he found, and for a little while they did seem to save him, but soon again they were not so much broken down as let the light through, as though It pierced through everything, and there was nothing that could shut It off.

Sometimes during those days he would go into the drawing room he had furnished, that drawing room where he had fallen, for which—how bitterly ludicrous it was for him to think of it!—for the decoration of which he had sacrificed his life, for he knew that it was that bruise that had started his illness. He went in and saw that the polished table had been scratched by something. He looked for the cause, and found it in the bronze clasps of the album, which had been twisted on one side.

He took up the album, a costly one, which he had himself arranged with loving care, and was vexed at the carelessness of his daughter and her friends. Here a page was torn, here the photographs had been shifted out of their places. He carefully put it to rights again and bent the clasp back.

Then the idea occurred to him to move all this *établissement* of the albums to another corner where the flowers stood. He called the footman; or his daughter or his wife came to help him. They did not agree with him, contradicted him; he argued, got angry. But all that was very well, since he did not think of It; It was not in sight.

But then his wife would say, as he moved something himself, "Do let the servants do it, you'll hurt yourself again," and all at once It peeped through the screen; he caught a glimpse of It. He caught a glimpse of It, but still he hoped It would hide itself. Involuntarily though, he kept watch on his side; there it is just the same still, aching still, and now he cannot forget it, and It is staring openly at him from behind the flowers. What's the use of it all?

"And it's the fact that here, at that curtain, as if it had been storming a fort, I lost my life. Is it possible? How awful and how silly! It cannot be! It cannot be, and it is."

He went into his own room, lay down, and was again alone with It. Face to face with It, and nothing to be done with it. Nothing but to look at It and shiver.

VII

How it came to pass during the third month of Ivan Ilyich's illness, it would be impossible to say, for it happened little by little, imperceptibly, but it had come to pass that his wife and his daughter and his son and their servants and their acquaintances, and the doctors, and, most of all, he himself—all were aware that all interest in him for other people consisted now in the question how soon he would leave his place empty, free the living from the constraint of his presence, and be set free himself from his sufferings.

He slept less and less; they gave him opium, and began to inject morphine. But this did not relieve him. The dull pain he experienced in the half-asleep condition at first only relieved him as a change, but then it became as bad, or even more agonizing, than the open pain. He had special things to eat prepared for him according to the doctors' prescriptions; but these dishes became more and more distasteful, more and more revolting to him.

Special arrangements, too, had to be made for his other physical needs, and this was a continual misery to him. Misery from the uncleanliness, the unseemliness, and the stench, from the feeling of another person having to assist in it.

But just from this most unpleasant side of his illness there came comfort to Ivan Ilyich. There always came into his room on these occasions to clear up for him the peasant who waited on table, Gerasim.

Gerasim was a clean, fresh, young peasant, who had grown stout and hearty on the good fare in town. Always cheerful and bright. At first the sight of this lad, always cleanly dressed in the Russian style, engaged in this revolting task, embarrassed Ivan Ilyich.

One day, getting up from the night stool, too weak to replace his clothes, he dropped on to a soft low chair and looked with horror at his bare, powerless thighs, with the muscles so sharply standing out on them.

Then there came in with light, strong steps Gerasim, in his thick boots, diffusing a pleasant smell of tar from his boots, and bringing in the freshness of the winter air. Wearing a clean hempen apron, and a clean cotton shirt, with his sleeves tucked up on his strong, bare young arms, without looking at Ivan Ilyich, obviously trying to check the radiant happiness in his face so as not to hurt the sick man, he went up to the night stool.

"Gerasim," said Ivan Ilyich faintly.

Gerasim started, clearly afraid that he had done something amiss, and with a rapid movement turned toward the sick man his fresh, good-natured, simple young face, just beginning to be downy with the first growth of beard.

"Yes, your honor."

"I'm afraid this is very disagreeable for you. You must excuse me. I can't help it."

"Why, upon my word, sir!" And Gerasim's eyes beamed, and he showed his white young teeth in a smile. "What's a little trouble? It's a case of illness with you, sir."

And with his deft, strong arms he performed his habitual task, and went out, stepping lightly. And five minutes later, treading just as lightly, he came back.

Ivan Ilyich was still sitting in the same way in the armchair.

"Gerasim," he said, when the latter had replaced the night stool all sweet and clean, "please help me; come here." Gerasim went up to him. "Lift me up. It's difficult for me alone, and I've sent Dmitry away."

Gerasim went up to him; as

lightly as he stepped he put his strong arms round him, deftly and gently lifted and supported him, with the other hand pulled up his trousers, and would have set him down again. But Ivan Ilyich asked him to carry him to the sofa. Gerasim, without effort, carefully not squeezing him, led him, almost carrying him, to the sofa, and settled him there.

"Thank you; how neatly and well . . . you do everything."

Gerasim smiled again, and would have gone away. But Ivan Ilyich felt his presence such a comfort that he was reluctant to let him go.

"Oh, move that chair near me, please. No, that one, under my legs. I feel easier when my legs are higher."

Gerasim picked up the chair and, without letting it knock, set it gently down on the ground just at the right place, and lifted Ivan Ilyich's legs on to it. It seemed to Ivan Ilyich that he was easier just at the moment when Gerasim lifted his legs higher.

"I'm better when my legs are higher," said Ivan Ilyich. "Put that cushion under me."

Gerasim did so. Again he lifted his legs to put the cushion under them. Again it seemed to Ivan Ilyich that he was easier at that moment when Gerasim held his legs raised. When he laid them down again, he felt worse.

"Gerasim," he said to him, "are you busy just now?"

"Not at all, sir," said Gerasim, who had learned among the town-bred servants how to speak to gentle-folks.

"What have you left to do?"

"Why, what have I to do? I've done everything, there's only the wood to chop for tomorrow."

"Then hold my legs up like that—can you?"

"To be sure, I can." Gerasim lifted the legs up. And it seemed to Ivan Ilyich that in that position he did not feel the pain at all.

"But how about the wood?"

"Don't you trouble about that, sir. We shall have time enough."

Ivan Ilyich made Gerasim sit and hold his legs, and began to talk to him. And, strange to say, he fancied he felt better while Gerasim had hold of his legs.

From that time forward Ivan Ilyich would sometimes call Gerasim, and get him to hold his legs on his shoulders, and he liked talking with him. Gerasim did this easily, readily, simply, and with a good nature that touched Ivan Ilyich. Health, strength, and heartiness in all other people were offensive to Ivan Ilyich; but the strength and heartiness of Gerasim did not mortify him, but soothed him.

Ivan Ilyich's great misery was due to the deception that for some reason or other everyone kept up with him —-that he was simply ill, and not dying, and that he need only keep quiet and follow the doctor's orders, and then some great change for the better would be the result. He knew that whatever they might do, there would be no result except more agonizing sufferings and death. And he was made miserable by this lie, made miserable at their refusing to acknowledge what they all knew and he knew, by their persisting in lying over him about his awful position, and in forcing him too to take part in this lie. Lying, lying, this lying carried on over him on the eve of his death, and destined to bring that terrible, solemn act of his death down to the level of all their visits, curtains, sturgeons for dinner . . . was a horrible agony for Ivan Ilyich. And, strange to say, many times when they had been going through the regular performance over him, he had been within a hair's-breadth of screaming at them: "Cease your lying! You know, and I know, that I'm dying; so do, at least, give over lying!" But he had never had the spirit to do this. The terrible, awful act of his dying was, he saw, by all those about him, brought down to the level of a casual, unpleasant, and to some extent indecorous incident (somewhat as they would behave with a person who should enter a drawing room smelling unpleasant). It was brought down to the level by that very decorum to which he had been enslaved all his life. He saw that no one felt for him, because no one would even grasp his position. Gerasim was the only person who recognized the position, and felt sorry for him. And that was why Ivan Ilyich was at ease only with Gerasim. He felt comforted when Gerasim sometimes supported his legs for whole nights at a stretch, and would not go away to bed, saying, "Don't you worry yourself, Ivan Ilyich, I'll get sleep enough yet," or when suddenly dropping into the familiar peasant forms of speech, he added: "If thou weren't sick, but as 'tis, 'twould be strange if I didn't wait on thee." Gerasim alone did not lie; everything showed clearly that he alone understood what it meant, and saw no necessity to disguise it, and simply felt sorry for his sick, wasting master. He even said this once straight out, when Ivan Ilyich was sending him away.

"We shall all die. So what's a little trouble?" he said, meaning by this to express that he did not complain of the trouble just because he

was taking this trouble for a dying man, and he hoped that for him too someone would be willing to take the same trouble when his time came.

Apart from this deception, or in consequence of it, what made the greatest misery for Ivan Ilyich was that no one felt for him as he would have liked them to feel for him. At certain moments, after prolonged suffering, Ivan Ilyich, ashamed as he would have been to own it, longed more than anything for someone to feel sorry for him, as for a sick child. He longed to be petted, kissed, and wept over, as children are petted and comforted. He knew that he was an important member of the law courts, that he had a beard turning gray, and that therefore it was impossible. But still he longed for it. And in his relations with Gerasim there was something approaching to that. And that was why being with Gerasim was a comfort to him. Ivan Ilyich longs to weep, longs to be petted and wept over, and then there comes in a colleague, Shebek; and instead of weeping and being petted, Ivan Ilyich puts on his serious, severe, earnest face, and from mere inertia gives his views on the effect of the last decision in the Court of Appeal, and obstinately insists upon them. This falsity around him and within him did more than anything to poison Ivan Ilyich's last days.

VIII

It was morning. All that made it morning for Ivan Ilyich was that Gerasim had gone away, and Piotr the footman had come in; he had put out the candles, opened one of the curtains, and began surreptitiously setting the room to rights. Whether it were morning or evening, Friday or Sunday, it all made no difference; it was always just the same thing. Gnawing, agonizing pain never ceasing for an instant; the hopeless sense of life always ebbing away, but still not yet gone; always swooping down on him that fearful, hated death, which was the only reality, and always the same falsity. What were days, or weeks, or hours of the day to him?

"Will you have tea, sir?"

"He wants things done in their regular order. In the morning the family should have tea," he thought, and only said—

"No."

"Would you care to move onto the sofa?"

"He wants to make the room tidy, and I'm in his way. I'm uncleanness, disorder," he thought, and only said—

"No, leave me alone."

The servant still moved busily about his work. Ivan Ilyich stretched out his hand. Piotr went up to offer his services.

"What can I get you?"

"My watch."

Piotr got out the watch, which lay just under his hand, and gave it to him.

"Half-past eight. Are they up?"

"Not yet, sir. Vladimir Ivanovich" (that was his son) "has gone to the high school, and Praskovya Fyodorovna gave orders that she was to be waked if you asked for her. Shall I send word?"

"No, no need. Should I try some tea?" he thought. "Yes, tea . . . bring it."

Piotr was on his way out. Ivan Ilyich felt frightened of being left alone. How keep him? Oh, the medicine. "Piotr, give me my medicine. Oh, well, maybe medicine may

still be some good." He took the spoon, drank it. "No, it does no good. It's all rubbish, deception," he decided, as soon as he tasted the familiar, mawkish, hopeless taste. "No, I can't believe it now. But the pain, why this pain; if it would only cease for a minute." And he groaned. Piotr turned round. "No, go on. Bring the tea."

Piotr went away. Ivan Ilyich, left alone, moaned, not so much from the pain, awful as it was, as from misery. Always the same thing again and again, all these endless days and nights. If it would only be quicker. Quicker to what? Death, darkness. No, no. Anything better than death!

When Piotr came in with the tea on a tray, Ivan Ilyich stared for some time absent-mindedly at him, not grasping who he was and what he wanted. Piotr was disconcerted by this stare. And when he showed he was disconcerted, Ivan Ilyich came to himself.

"Oh, yes," he said, "tea, good, set it down. Only help me to wash and put on a clean shirt."

And Ivan Ilyich began his washing. He washed his hands slowly, and then his face, cleaned his teeth, combed his hair, and looked in the looking glass. He felt frightened at what he saw, especially at the way his hair clung limply to his pale forehead. When his shirt was being changed, he knew he would be still more terrified if he glanced at his body, and he avoided looking at himself. But at last it was all over. He put on his dressing gown, covered himself with a rug, and sat in the armchair to drink his tea. For one moment he felt refreshed; but as soon as he began to drink the tea, again there was the same taste, the same pain. He forced himself to finish it, and lay down, stretched out his legs. He lay down and dismissed Piotr.

Always the same. A gleam of hope flashes for a moment, then again the sea of despair roars about him again, and always pain, always pain, always heartache, and always the same thing. Alone it is awfully dreary; he longs to call someone, but he knows beforehand that with others present it will be worse. "Morphine again—only to forget again. I'll tell him, the doctor, that he must think of something else. It can't go on; it can't go on like this."

One hour, two hours pass like this. Then there is a ring at the front door. The doctor, perhaps. Yes, it is the doctor, fresh, hearty, fat, and cheerful, wearing that expression that seems to say, "You there are in a panic about something, but we'll soon set things right for you." The doctor is aware that this expression is hardly fitting here, but he has put on a frock coat to pay a round of calls.

In a hearty, reassuring manner the doctor rubs his hands.

"I'm cold. It's a sharp frost. Just let me warm myself," he says with an expression as though it's only a matter of waiting a little till he's warm, and as soon as he's warm he'll set everything to rights.

"Well, now, how are you?"

Ivan Ilyich feels that the doctor would like to say, "How's the little trouble?" but that he feels that he can't talk like that, and says, "How did you pass the night?"

Ivan Ilyich looks at the doctor with an expression that asks, "Is it possible you're never ashamed of lying?"

But the doctor does not care to understand this look.

And Ivan Ilyich says, "It's always just as awful. The pain never leaves me, never ceases. If only there were something!"

"Ah, you're all like that, all sick people say that. Come, now I do believe I'm thawed; even Praskovya Fyodorovna, who's so particular, could find no fault with my temperature. Well, now I can say good morning." And the doctor shakes hands.

And dropping his former levity, the doctor, with a serious face, proceeds to examine the patient, feeling his pulse, to take his temperature, and then the tappings and soundings begin.

Ivan Ilyich knows positively and indubitably that it's all nonsense and empty deception; but when the doctor, kneeling down, stretches over him, putting his ear first higher, then lower, and goes through various gymnastic evolutions over him with a serious face, Ivan Ilyich is affected by this, as he used sometimes to be affected by the speeches of the lawyers in court, though he was perfectly well aware that they were telling lies all the while and why they were telling lies.

The doctor, kneeling on the sofa, was still sounding him, when there was the rustle of Praskovya Fyodorovna's silk dress in the doorway, and she was heard scolding Piotr for not having let her know that the doctor had come.

She comes in, kisses her husband, and at once begins to explain that she has been up a long while, and that it was only through a misunderstanding that she was not there when the doctor came.

Ivan Ilyich looks at her, scans her all over, and sets down against her her whiteness and plumpness, and the cleanness of her hands and neck, and the glossiness of her hair.

and the gleam full of life in her eyes. With all the force of his soul he hates her. And when she touches him it makes him suffer from the thrill of hatred he feels for her.

Her attitude to him and his illness is still the same. Just as the doctor had taken up a certain line with the patient which he was not now able to drop, so she too had taken up a line with him—that he was not doing something he ought to do, and was himself to blame, and she was lovingly reproaching him for his neglect, and she could not now get out of this attitude.

"Why, you know, he won't listen to me; he doesn't take his medicine at the right times. And what's worse still, he insists on lying in a position that surely must be bad for him —with his legs in the air."

She described how he made Gerasim hold his legs up.

The doctor smiled with kindly condescension that said, "Oh, well, it can't be helped, these sick people do take up such foolish fancies; but we must forgive them."

When the examination was over, the doctor looked at his watch, and then Praskovya Fyodorovna informed Ivan Ilyich that it must, of course, be as he liked, but she had sent today for a celebrated doctor, and that he would examine him, and have a consultation with Mihail Danilovich (that was the name of their regular doctor).

"Don't oppose it now, please. This I'm doing entirely for my own sake," she said ironically, meaning it to be understood that she was doing it all for his sake, and was only saying this to give him no right to refuse her request. He lay silent, knitting his brows. He felt that he was hemmed in by such a tangle of falsity that it was hard to disentangle anything from it.

Everything she did for him was entirely for her own sake, and she told him she was doing for her own sake what she actually was doing for her own sake as something so incredible that he would take it as meaning the opposite.

At half-past eleven the celebrated doctor came. Again came the sounding, and then grave conversation in his presence and in the other room about the kidney and the appendix, and questions and answers, with such an air of significance that again, instead of the real question of life and death, which was now the only one that confronted him, the question that came uppermost was of the kidney and the appendix, which were doing something not as they ought to do, and were for that reason being attacked by Mihail Danilovich and the celebrated doctor, and forced to mend their ways.

The celebrated doctor took leave of him with a serious, but not a hopeless face. And to the timid question that Ivan Ilyich addressed to him while he lifted his eyes, shining with terror and hope, up toward him, Was there a chance of recovery? he answered that he could not answer for it, but that there was a chance. The look of hope with which Ivan Ilyich watched the doctor out was so piteous that, seeing it, Praskovya Fyodorovna positively burst into tears, as she went out of the door to hand the celebrated doctor his fee in the next room.

The gleam of hope kindled by the doctor's assurance did not last long. Again the same room, the same pictures, the curtains, the wallpaper, the medicine bottles, and ever the same, his aching suffering body. And Ivan Ilyich began to moan; they gave him injections, and he sank into oblivion. When he waked up it was getting dark; they brought him his dinner. He forced himself to eat some broth; and again everything the same, and again the coming night.

After dinner at seven o'clock, Praskovya Fyodorovna came into his room, dressed as though to go to a soiree, with her full bosom laced in tight, and traces of powder on her face. She had in the morning mentioned to him that they were going to the theater. Sarah Bernhardt was visiting the town, and they had a box, which he had insisted on their taking. By now he had forgotten about it, and her smart attire was an offense to him. But he concealed this feeling when he recollected that he had himself insisted on their taking a box and going, because it was an aesthetic pleasure, beneficial and instructive for the children.

Praskovya Fyodorovna came in satisfied with herself, but yet with something of a guilty air. She sat down, asked how he was, as he saw, simply for the sake of asking, and not for the sake of learning anything, knowing indeed that there was nothing to learn, and began telling him how absolutely necessary it was; how she would not have gone for anything, but the box had been taken, and Ellen, their daughter, and Petrishtchev (the examining lawyer, the daughter's suitor) were going, and that it was out of the question to let them go alone. But that she would have liked much better to stay with him. If only he would be sure to follow the doctor's prescription while she was away.

"Oh, and Fyodor Dmitryevich" (the suitor) "would like to come in. May he? And Liza?"

"Yes, let them come in."

The daughter came in, in full dress, her fresh young body bare, while his body made him suffer so. But she made a show of it; she was strong, healthy, obviously in love, and impatient of the illness, suffering, and death that hindered her happiness.

Fyodor Dmitryevich came in too in evening dress, his hair curled à la Capoul, with his long, sinewy neck tightly fenced round by a white collar, with his vast expanse of white chest and strong thighs displayed in narrow black trousers, with one white glove in his hand and a crush opera hat.

Behind him crept in unnoticed the little high-school boy in his new uniform, poor fellow, in gloves, and with that awful blue ring under his eyes that Ivan Ilyich knew the meaning of.

He always felt sorry for his son. And pitiable indeed was his scared face of sympathetic suffering. Except Gerasim, Ivan Ilyich fancied that Volodya was the only one that understood and was sorry.

They all sat down; again they asked how he was. A silence followed. Liza asked her mother about the opera glass. An altercation ensued between the mother and daughter as to who had taken it, and where it had been put. It turned into an unpleasant squabble.

Fyodor Dmitryevich asked Ivan Ilyich whether he had seen Sarah Bernhardt? Ivan Ilyich could not at first catch the question that was asked him, but then he said, "No, have you seen her before?"

"Yes, in *Adrienne Lecouvreur*."

Praskovya Fyodorovna observed that she was particularly good in that part. The daughter made some reply. A conversation sprang up about the art and naturalness of her acting, that conversation that is continually repeated and always the same.

In the middle of the conversation Fyodor Dmitryevich glanced at Ivan Ilyich and relapsed into silence. The others looked at him and became mute, too. Ivan Ilyich was staring with glittering eyes straight before him, obviously furious with them. This had to be set right, but it could not anyhow be set right. This silence had somehow to be broken. No one would venture on breaking it, and all began to feel alarmed that the decorous deception was somehow breaking down, and the facts would be exposed to all. Liza was the first to pluck up courage. She broke the silence. She tried to cover up what they were all feeling, but inadvertently she gave it utterance.

"If we are going, though, it's time to start," she said, glancing at her watch, a gift from her father; and with a scarcely perceptible meaning smile to the young man, referring to something only known to themselves, she got up with a rustle of her skirts.

They all got up, said good-by, and went away. When they were gone, Ivan Ilyich fancied he was easier; there was no falsity—that had gone away with them, but the pain remained. That continual pain, that continual terror, made nothing harder, nothing easier. It was always worse.

Again came minute after minute, hour after hour, still the same and still no end, and ever more terrible the inevitable end.

"Yes, send Gerasim," he said in answer to Piotr's question.

IX

Late at night his wife came back. She came in on tiptoe, but he heard her, opened his eyes, and made haste to close them again. She wanted to send away Gerasim and sit up with him herself instead. He opened his eyes and said, "No, go away."

"Are you in great pain?"

"Always the same."

"Take some opium."

He agreed, and drank it. She went away.

Till three o'clock he slept a miserable sleep. It seemed to him that he and his pain were being thrust somewhere into a narrow, deep, black sack, and they kept pushing him further and further in, and still could not thrust him to the bottom. And this operation was awful to him, and was accompanied with agony. And he was afraid, and yet wanted to fall into it, and struggled and yet tried to get into it. And all of a sudden he slipped, fell, and woke up. Gerasim, still the same, is sitting at the foot of the bed, half dozing peacefully, patient. And he is lying with his wasted legs clad in stockings, raised on Gerasim's shoulders, the same candle burning in the alcove, and the same interminable pain.

"Go away, Gerasim," he whispered.

"It's all right, sir. I'll stay a bit longer."

"No, go away."

He took his legs down, lay sideways on his arm, and he felt very sorry for himself. He only waited till Gerasim had gone away into the next room; he could restrain himself no longer, and cried like a child. He cried at his own helplessness, at his awful loneliness, at the cruelty of people, at the cruelty of God, at the absence of God.

"Why has Thou done all this? What brought me to this? Why, why torture me so horribly?"

He did not expect an answer, and wept indeed that there was and could be no answer. The pain grew more acute again, but he did not stir, did not call.

He said to himself, "Come, more then; come, strike me! But what for? What have I done to Thee? What for?"

Then he was still, ceased weeping, held his breath, and was all attention; he listened, as it were, not to a voice uttering sounds, but to the voice of his soul, to the current of thoughts that rose up within him.

"What is it you want?" was the first clear idea able to be put into words that he grasped.

"What? Not to suffer, to live," he answered.

And again he was utterly plunged into attention so intense that even the pain did not distract him.

"To live? Live how?" the voice of his soul was asking.

"Why, live as I used to live before—happily and pleasantly."

"As you used to live before—happily and pleasantly?" queried the voice. And he began going over in his imagination the best moments of his pleasant life. But strange to say, all these best moments of his pleasant life seemed now not at all what they had seemed then. All—except the first memories of childhood—there, in his childhood there had been something really pleasant in which one could have lived if it had come back. But the creature who had this pleasant experience was no more; it was like a memory of someone else.

As soon as he reached the begin-ning of what had resulted in him as he was now, Ivan Ilyich, all that had seemed joys to him then now melted away before his eyes and were transformed into something trivial, and often disgusting.

And the further he went from childhood, the nearer to the actual present, the more worthless and un-certain were the joys. It began with life at the school of jurisprudence. Then there had still been some-thing genuinely good; then there had been gaiety; then there had been friendship; then there had been hopes. But in the higher classes these good moments were already becoming rarer. Later on, during the first period of his official life, at the governor's, good moments appeared; but it was all mixed, and less and less of it was good. And further on even less was good, and the further he went the less good there was.

His marriage . . . as gratuitous as the disillusion of it and the smell of his wife's breath and the sen-suality, the hypocrisy! And that deadly official life, and anxiety about money, and so for one year, and two, and ten, and twenty, and always the same thing. And the further he went, the more deadly it became. "As though I had been going steadily downhill, imagining that I was going uphill. So it was in fact. In public opinion I was going up-hill, and steadily as I got up it life was ebbing away from me. . . . And now the work's done, there's only to die.

"But what is this? What for? It cannot be! It cannot be that life has been so senseless, so loathsome? And if it really was so loathsome and senseless, then why die, and die in agony? There's something wrong.

"Can it be I have not lived as one

ought?" suddenly came into his
head. "But how not so, when I've
done everything as it should be
done?" he said, and at once dismissed this only solution of all the
enigma of life and death as something utterly out of the question.

"What do you want now? To live?
Live how? Live as you live at the
courts when the usher booms out:
'The judge is coming!' " . . . "The
judge is coming, the judge is coming," he repeated to himself. "Here
he is, the judge! But I'm not to
blame!" he shrieked in fury. "What's
it for?" And he left off crying and,
turning with his face to the wall,
fell to pondering always on the same
question, "What for, why all this
horror?"

But however much he pondered,
he could not find an answer. And
whenever the idea struck him, as it
often did, that it all came of his
never having lived as he ought, he
thought of all the correctness of his
life and dismissed the strange idea.

X

Another fortnight had passed. Ivan
Ilyich could not now get up from
the sofa. He did not like lying in
bed, and lay on the sofa. And lying
almost all the time facing the wall,
in loneliness he suffered all the inexplicable agonies, and in loneliness pondered always that inexplicable question, "What is it?
Can it be true that it's death?" And
an inner voice answered, "Yes, it is
true." "Why these agonies?" and a
voice answered, "For no reason."
Beyond and besides this there was
nothing.

From the very beginning of his
illness, ever since Ivan Ilyich first
went to the doctor's, his life had
been split up into two contradictory

moods, which were continually alternating—one was despair and the
anticipation of an uncomprehended
and awful death; the other was hope
and an absorbed watching over the
actual condition of his body. First
there was nothing confronting him
but a kidney or intestine which had
temporarily declined to perform
their duties, then there was nothing
but unknown awful death, which
there was no escaping.

These two moods had alternated
from the very beginning of the illness; but the further the illness progressed, the more doubtful and fantastic became the conception of the
kidney, and the more real the sense
of approaching death.

He had but to reflect on what he
had been three months before and
what he was now, to reflect how
steadily he had been going downhill,
for every possibility of hope to be
shattered.

Of late, in the loneliness in which
he found himself, lying with his
face to the back of the sofa, a loneliness in the middle of a populous
town and of his numerous acquaintances and his family, a loneliness
than which none more complete
could be found anywhere—not at
the bottom of the sea, not deep
down in the earth—of late in this
fearful loneliness Ivan Ilyich had
lived only in imagination in the
past. One by one the pictures of his
past rose up before him. It always
began from what was nearest in
time and went back to the most
remote, to childhood, and rested
there. If Ivan Ilyich thought of the
stewed prunes that had been offered
him for dinner that day, his mind
went back to the damp, wrinkled
French plum of his childhood, of its
peculiar taste and the flow of saliva
when the stone was sucked; and

along with this memory of a taste there rose up a whole series of memories of that period—his nurse, his brother, his playthings. "I mustn't . . . it's too painful," Ivan Ilyich said to himself, and he brought himself back to the present. The button on the back of the sofa and the creases in the morocco. "Morocco's dear, and doesn't wear well; there was a quarrel over it. But the morocco was different, and different too the quarrel when we tore Father's portfolio and were punished, and Mamma bought us the tarts." And again his mind rested on his childhood, and again it was painful, and he tried to drive it away and think of something else.

And again at that point, together with that chain of associations, quite another chain of memories came into his heart, of how this illness had grown up and become more acute. It was the same there, the further back the more life there had been. There had been both more that was good in life and more of life itself. And the two began to melt into one. "Just as the pain goes on getting worse and worse, so has my whole life gone on getting worse and worse," he thought. One light spot was there at the back, at the beginning of life, and then it kept getting blacker and blacker, and going faster and faster. "In inverse ratio to the square of the distance from death," thought Ivan Ilyich. And the image of a stone falling downwards with increasing velocity sank into his soul. Life, a series of increasing sufferings, falls more and more swiftly to the end, the most fearful sufferings. "I am falling." He shuddered, shifted himself, would have resisted, but he knew beforehand that he could not resist; and again, with eyes weary with gazing at it,

but unable not to gaze at what was before him, he stared at the back of the sofa and waited, waited expecting that fearful fall and shock and dissolution. "Resistance is impossible," he said to himself. "But if one could at least comprehend what it's for? Even that's impossible. It could be explained if one were to say that I hadn't lived as I ought. But that can't be alleged," he said to himself, thinking of all the regularity, correctness, and propriety of his life. "That really can't be admitted," he said to himself, his lips smiling ironically as though someone could see his smile and be deceived by it. "No explanation! Agony, death . . . What for?"

XI

So passed a fortnight. During that fortnight an event occurred that had been desired by Ivan Ilyich and his wife. Petrishtchev made a formal proposal. This took place in the evening. Next day Praskovya Fyodorovna went in to her husband, resolving in her mind how to inform him of Fyodor Dmitryevich's proposal, but that night there had been a change for the worse in Ivan Ilyich. Praskovya Fyodorovna found him on the same sofa, but in a different position. He was lying on his face, groaning, and staring straight before him with a fixed gaze.

She began talking of remedies. He turned his stare on her. She did not finish what she had begun saying; such hatred of her in particular was expressed in that stare.

"For Christ's sake, let me die in peace," he said.

She would have gone away, but at that moment the daughter came in and went up to say good morning to him. He looked at his daughter just as at his wife, and to her inquiries how he was, he told her dryly that they would soon all be rid of him. Both were silent, sat a little while, and went out.

"How are we to blame?" said Liza to her mother. "As though we had done it! I'm sorry for Papa, but why punish us?"

At the usual hour the doctor came. Ivan Ilyich answered, "Yes, no," never taking his exasperated stare from him, and toward the end he said, "Why, you know that you can do nothing, so let me be."

"We can relieve your suffering," said the doctor.

"Even that you can't do; let me be."

The doctor went into the drawing room and told Praskovya Fyodorovna that it was very serious, and that the only resource left them was opium to relieve his sufferings, which must be terrible. The doctor said his physical sufferings were terrible, and that was true; but even more terrible than his physical sufferings were his mental sufferings, and in that lay his chief misery.

His moral sufferings were due to the fact that during that night, as he looked at the sleepy, good-natured, broad-cheeked face of Gerasim, the thought had suddenly come into his head, "What if in reality all my life, my conscious life, has been not the right thing?" The thought struck him that what he had regarded before as an utter impossibility, that he had spent his life not as he ought, might be the truth. It struck him that those scarcely detected impulses of struggle within him against what was considered good by persons of higher position, scarcely detected impulses which he had dismissed, that they might be the real thing, and everything else might be not the right thing. And

his official work, and his ordering of his daily life and of his family, and these social and official interests— all that might be not the right thing. He tried to defend it all to himself. And suddenly he felt all the weakness of what he was defending. And it was useless to defend it.

"But if it's so," he said to himself, "and I am leaving life with the consciousness that I have lost all that was given me, and there's no correcting it, then what?" He lay on his back and began going over his whole life entirely anew. When he saw the footman in the morning, then his wife, then his daughter, then the doctor, every movement they made, every word they uttered, confirmed for him the terrible truth that had been revealed to him in the night. In them he saw himself, saw all in which he had lived, and saw distinctly that it was all not the right thing; it was a horrible, vast deception that concealed both life and death. This consciousness intensified his physical agonies, multiplied them tenfold. He groaned and tossed from side to side and pulled at the covering over him. It seemed to him that it was stifling him and weighing him down. And for that he hated them.

They gave him a big dose of opium; he sank into unconsciousness; but at dinnertime the same thing began again. He drove them all away, and tossed from side to side.

His wife came to him and said, "Jean, darling, do this for my sake" (for my sake?). "It can't do harm, and it often does good. Why, it's nothing. And often in health people——"

He opened his eyes wide.

"What? Take the sacrament? What for? No. Besides . . ."

She began to cry. "Yes, my dear. I'll send for our priest, he's so nice."

"All right, very well," he said.

When the priest came and confessed him he was softened, felt as it were a relief from his doubts, and consequently from his sufferings, and there came a moment of hope. He began once more thinking of the intestinal appendix and the possibility of curing it. He took the sacrament with tears in his eyes.

When they laid him down again after the sacrament for a minute, he felt comfortable, and again the hope of life sprang up. He began to think about the operation, which had been suggested to him. "To live, I want to live," he said to himself. His wife came in to congratulate him; she uttered the customary words and added—

"It's quite true, isn't it, that you're better?"

Without looking at her, he said, "Yes."

Her dress, her figure, the expression of her face, the tone of her voice—all told him the same: "Not the right thing. All that in which you lived and are living is lying, deceit, hiding life and death away from you." And as soon as he had formed that thought, hatred sprang up in him, and with that hatred agonizing physical sufferings, and with these sufferings the sense of inevitable, approaching ruin. Something new was happening; there were screwing and shooting pains, and a tightness in his breathing.

The expression of his face as he uttered that "Yes" was terrible. After uttering that "Yes," looking her straight in the face, he turned on his face, with a rapidity extraordinary in his weakness, and shrieked—

"Go away, go away, let me be!"

XII

From that moment there began the scream that never ceased for three days, and was so awful that through two closed doors one could not hear it without horror. At the moment when he answered his wife he grasped that he had fallen, that there was no return, that the end had come, quite the end, while doubt was still as unsolved, still remained doubt.

"Oo! Oo—o! Oo!" he screamed in varying intonations. He had begun screaming, "I don't want to!" and so had gone on screaming on the same vowel sound—oo!

All those three days, during which time did not exist for him, he was struggling in that black sack into which he was being thrust by an unseen, resistless force. He struggled as the man condemned to death struggles in the hands of the executioner, knowing that he cannot save himself. And every moment he felt that in spite of all his efforts to struggle against it, he was getting nearer and nearer to what terrified him. He felt that his agony was due both to his being thrust into this black hole and still more to his not being able to get right into it. What hindered him from getting into it was the claim that his life had been good. That justification of his life held him fast and would not let him get forward, and it caused him more agony than all.

All at once some force struck him in the chest, in the side, and stifled his breathing more than ever; he rolled forward into the hole, and there at the end there was some sort of light. It had happened with him, as it had sometimes happened to him in a railway carriage, when he had thought he was going forward while he was going back, and all of a sudden recognized his real direction.

"Yes, it has all been not the right thing," he said to himself, "but that's no matter." He could, he could do the right thing. "What is the right thing?" he asked himself, and suddenly he became quiet.

This was at the end of the third day, two hours before his death. At that very moment the schoolboy had stealthily crept into his father's room and gone up to his bedside. The dying man was screaming and waving his arms. His hand fell on the schoolboy's head. The boy snatched it, pressed it to his lips, and burst into tears.

At that very moment Ivan Ilyich had rolled into the hole, and caught sight of the light, and it was revealed to him that his life had not been what it ought to have been, but that that could still be set right. He asked himself, "What is the right thing?"—and became quiet, listening. Then he felt someone was kissing his hand. He opened his eyes and glanced at his son. He felt sorry for him. His wife went up to him. He glanced at her. She was gazing at him with open mouth, the tears unwiped streaming over her nose and cheeks, a look of despair on her face. He felt sorry for her.

"Yes, I'm making them miserable," he thought. "They're sorry, but it will be better for them when I die." He would have said this, but had not the strength to utter it. "Besides, why speak, I must act," he thought. With a glance to his wife he pointed to his son and said—

"Take away . . . sorry for him . . . And you too . . ." He tried to say "forgive," but said "forgo" . . . and too weak to correct himself, shook his hand, knowing that He would understand Whose understanding mattered.

And all at once it became clear to him that what had tortured him and would not leave him was suddenly dropping away all at once on both sides and on ten sides and on all sides. He was sorry for them, must act so that they might not suffer. Set them free and be free himself of those agonies. "How right and how simple!" he thought. "And the pain?" he asked himself. "Where's it gone? Eh, where are you, pain?"

He began to watch for it.

"Yes, here it is. Well, what of it, let the pain be.

"And death. Where is it?"

He looked for his old accustomed terror of death, and did not find it. "Where is it? What death?" There was no terror, because death was not either.

In the place of death there was light.

"So this is it!" he suddenly exclaimed aloud.

"What joy!"

To him all this passed in a single instant, and the meaning of that instant suffered no change after. For those present his agony lasted another two hours. There was a rattle in his throat, a twitching in his wasted body. Then the rattle and the gasping came at longer and longer intervals.

"It is over!" someone said over him.

He caught those words and repeated them in his soul.

"Death is over," he said to himself. "It's no more."

He drew in a breath, stopped midway in the breath, stretched, and died.

Anton Pavlovich Chekhov
1860-1904

CHEKHOV once said that melancholy is to the Russian writer what the potato is to a French chef: it can be dished out in a hundred different ways. Certainly, as he prepared it, melancholy made his reputation in western Europe. In Russia, however, he was best known and loved as a humorist.

Son of an ex-serf who kept a general store in Taganrog, on the Sea of Azov, Chekhov was born into a lively and clever family. The three Chekhov brothers were all artists: two of them began writing comic stories during their university years, and the third drew cartoons. "Schiller Shakespearovich Goethe" was Anton's signature when writing to his brothers. Though he was graduated from the medical school of the University of Moscow, he practiced very little as a doctor. For Chekhov was essentially a writer—as someone said, though medicine was his wife, literature was his mistress. When he had attained enough success to enable him to write as he chose, he abandoned the comic papers and settled down to the serious work by which we know him best. He wrote about lazy, good-humored, kindly peasants living in dirt and ignorance. To Chekhov, those who suffered and succumbed were noble, while those who endured and triumphed over misery were unfeeling and brutal. It was this note of melancholy—Chekhov's "gray mood"—that delighted the aesthetes of the late nineteenth century, tired as they were of the wholesomeness of the Victorians. "A Day in the Country" contributes to this mood.

Chekhov's great love was the theater. Most of his plays— *The Seagull, Uncle Vanya, The Cherry Orchard, The Three Sisters*—were produced by Stanislavsky at the Moscow Art Theater, and in 1901 he married the actress Olga Knipper, who played leading parts in them. Three years later, he died of tuberculosis in Germany. His coffin was sent home in a green freight car marked FOR OYSTERS.

A Day in the Country

BY ANTON CHEKHOV

BETWEEN eight and nine o'clock in the morning.

A dark leaden-colored mass is creeping over the sky toward the sun. Red zigzags of lightning gleam here and there across it. There is a sound of faraway rumbling. A warm wind frolics over the grass, bends the trees, and stirs up the dust. In a minute there will be a spurt of May rain and a real storm will begin.

Fyokla, a little beggar girl of six, is running through the village, looking for Terenty the cobbler. The white-haired, barefoot child is pale. Her eyes are wide-open, her lips are trembling.

"Uncle, where is Terenty?" she asks everyone she meets. No one answers. They are all preoccupied with the approaching storm and take refuge in their huts. At last she meets Silanty Silich, the sacristan, Terenty's bosom friend. He is coming along, staggering from the wind.

"Uncle, where is Terenty?"

"At the kitchen gardens," answers Silanty.

The beggar girl runs behind the huts to the kitchen gardens and there finds Terenty; the tall old man with a thin, pockmarked face, very long legs, and bare feet, dressed in a woman's tattered jacket, is standing near the vegetable plots, looking with drowsy, drunken eyes at the dark storm cloud. On his long crane-like legs he sways in the wind like a starling cote.

"Uncle Terenty!" the white-headed beggar girl addresses him. "Uncle, darling!"

Terenty bends down to Fyokla, and his grim, drunken face is overspread with a smile, such as come into people's faces when they look at something little, foolish, and absurd, but warmly loved.

"Ah! servant of God, Fyokla," he says, lisping tenderly, "where have you come from?"

"Uncle Terenty," says Fyokla, with a sob, tugging at the lapel of the cobbler's coat. "Brother Danilka has had an accident! Come along!"

"What sort of accident? Ough, what thunder! Holy, holy, holy . . . What sort of accident?"

"In the count's copse Danilka stuck his hand into a hole in a tree, and he can't get it out. Come along, Uncle, do be kind and pull his hand out!"

"How was it he put his hand in? What for?"

"He wanted to get a cuckoo's egg out of the hole for me."

54

"The day has hardly begun and already you are in trouble . . ." Terenty shook his head and spat deliberately. "Well, what am I to do with you now? I must come . . . I must, may the wolf gobble you up, you naughty children! Come, little orphan!"

Terenty comes out of the kitchen garden and, lifting high his long legs, begins striding down the village street. He walks quickly without stopping or looking from side to side, as though he were shoved from behind or afraid of pursuit. Fyokla can hardly keep up with him.

They come out of the village and turn along the dusty road toward the count's copse that lies dark blue in the distance. It is about a mile and a half away. The clouds have by now covered the sun, and soon afterwards there is not a speck of blue left in the sky. It grows dark.

"Holy, holy, holy . . ." whispers Fyokla, hurrying after Terenty. The first raindrops, big and heavy, lie, dark dots on the duty road. A big drop falls on Fyokla's cheek and glides like a tear down her chin.

"The rain has begun," mutters the cobbler, kicking up the dust with his bare, bony feet. "That's fine, Fyokla, old girl. The grass and the trees are fed by the rain, as we are by bread. And as for the thunder, don't you be frightened, little orphan. Why should it kill a little thing like you?"

As soon as the rain begins, the wind drops. The only sound is the patter of rain dropping like fine shot on the young rye and the parched road.

"We shall get soaked, Fyokla," mutters Terenty. "There won't be a dry spot left on us. . . . Ho-ho, my girl! It's run down my neck! But

don't be frightened, silly. . . . The grass will be dry again, the earth will be dry again, and we shall be dry again. There is the same sun for us all."

A flash of lightning, some fourteen feet long, gleams above their heads. There is a loud peal of thunder, and it seems to Fyokla that something big, heavy, and round is rolling over the sky and tearing it open, exactly over her head.

"Holy, holy, holy . . ." says Terenty, crossing himself. "Don't be afraid, little orphan! It is not from spite that it thunders."

Terenty's and Fyokla's feet are covered with lumps of heavy, wet clay. It is slippery and difficult to walk, but Terenty strides on more and more rapidly. The weak little beggar girl is breathless and ready to drop.

But at last they go into the count's copse. The washed trees, stirred by a gust of wind, drop a perfect waterfall upon them. Terenty stumbles over stumps and begins to slacken his pace.

"Whereabouts is Danilka?" he asks. "Lead me to him."

Fyokla leads him into a thicket, and, after going a quarter of a mile, points to Danilka. Her brother, a little fellow of eight, with hair as red as ocher and a pale, sickly face, stands leaning against a tree, and, with his head on one side, looking sideways at the sky. In one hand he holds his shabby old cap, the other is hidden in an old lime tree. The boy is gazing at the stormy sky, and apparently not thinking of his trouble. Hearing footsteps and seeing the cobbler he gives a sickly smile and says:

"A terrible lot of thunder, Terenty. . . . I've never heard so much thunder in all my life."

"And where is your hand?"

"In the hole. . . . Pull it out, please, Terenty!"

The wood had broken at the edge of the hole and jammed Danilka's hand; he could push it farther in, but could not pull it out. Terenty snaps off the broken piece, and the boy's hand, red and crushed, is released.

"It's terrible how it's thundering," the boy says again rubbing his hand. "What makes it thunder, Terenty?"

"One cloud runs against the other," answers the cobbler. The party come out of the copse, and walk along the edge of it toward the darkened road. The thunder gradually abates, and its rumbling is heard far away beyond the village.

"The ducks flew by here the other day, Terenty," says Danilka, still rubbing his hand. "They must be nesting in the Gniliya Zaimishtcha marshes. . . . Fyokla, would you like me to show you a nightingale's nest?"

"Don't touch it, you might disturb them," says Terenty, wringing the water out of his cap. "The nightingale is a singing bird, without sin. He has had a voice given him in his throat, to praise God and gladden the heart of man. It's a sin to disturb him."

"What about the sparrow?"

"The sparrow doesn't matter, he's a bad, spiteful bird. He is like a pickpocket in his ways. He doesn't like man to be happy. When Christ was crucified it was the sparrow brought nails to the Jews, and called 'alive! alive!' "

A bright patch of blue appears in the sky.

"Look!" says Terenty. "An ant heap burst open by the rain! They've been flooded, the rogues!"

They bend over the ant heap. The downpour has damaged it; the insects are scurrying to and fro in the mud, agitated, and busily trying to carry away their drowned companions.

"You needn't be in such a taking, you won't die of it!" says Terenty, grinning. "As soon as the sun warms you, you'll come to your senses again. . . . It's a lesson to you, you stupids. You won't settle on low ground another time."

They go on.

"And here are some bees," cries Danilka, pointing to the branch of a young oak tree.

The drenched and chilled bees are huddled together on the branch. There are so many of them that neither bark nor leaf can be seen. Many of them are settled on one another.

"That's a swarm of bees," Terenty informs them. "They were flying looking for a home, and when the rain came down upon them they settled. If a swarm is flying, you need only sprinkle water on them to make them settle. Now if, say, you wanted to take the swarm, you would bend the branch with them into a sack and shake it, and they all fall in."

Little Fyokla suddenly frowns and rubs her neck vigorously. Her brother looks at her neck, and sees a big swelling on it.

"Hey-hey!" laughs the cobbler. "Do you know where you got that from, Fyokla, old girl? There are Spanish flies on some tree in the wood. The rain has trickled off them, and a drop has fallen on your neck—that's what has made the swelling."

The sun appears from behind the clouds and floods the wood, the fields, and the three friends with its warm light. The dark menacing cloud has gone far away and taken the storm with it. The air is warm and fragrant. There is a scent of bird-cherry, meadowsweet, and lilies-of-the-valley.

"That herb is given when your nose bleeds," says Terenty, pointing to a woolly-looking flower. "It does good."

They hear a whistle and a rumble, but not such a rumble as the storm clouds carried away. A goods train races by before the eyes of Terenty, Danilka, and Fyokla. The engine, panting and puffing out black smoke, drags more than twenty vans after it. Its power is tremendous. The children are interested to know how an engine, not alive and without the help of horses, can move and drag such weights, and Terenty undertakes to explain it to them:

"It's all the steam's doing, children. . . . The steam does the work. . . . You see, it shoves under that thing near the wheels, and it . . . you see . . . it works . . ."

They cross the railway line, and, going down from the embankment, walk toward the river. They walk not with any object, but just at random, and talk all the way . . . Danilka asks questions, Terenty answers them.

Terenty answers all his questions, and there is no secret in nature which baffles him. He knows everything. Thus, for example, he knows the names of all the wild flowers, animals, and stones. He knows what herbs cure diseases, he has no difficulty in telling the age of a horse or a cow. Looking at the sunset, at the moon, or the birds, he can tell what sort of weather it will be next day. And indeed, it is not only Terenty who is so wise. Silanty Silich, the innkeeper, the market gardener, the shepherd, and all the villagers, generally speaking, know as much as he does. These people have learned not from books, but in the fields, in the wood, on the riverbank. Their teach- ers have been the birds themselves, when they sang to them, the sun when it left a glow of crimson be- hind it at setting, the very trees, and wild herbs.

Danilka looks at Terenty and greedily drinks in every word. In spring, before one is weary of the warmth and the monotonous green of the fields, when everything is fresh and full of fragrance, who would not want to hear about the golden May beetles, about the cranes, about the gurgling streams, and the corn mounting into ear?

The two of them, the cobbler and the orphan, walk about the fields, talk unceasingly, and are not weary. They could wander about the world endlessly. They walk, and in their talk of the beauty of the earth do not notice the frail little beggar girl tripping after them. She is breath- less and moves with a lagging step. There are tears in her eyes; she would be glad to stop these inex- haustible wanderers, but to whom and where can she go? She has no home or people of her own; whether she likes it or not, she must walk and listen to their talk.

Toward midday, all three sit down on the riverbank. Danilka takes out of his bag a piece of bread, soaked and reduced to a mash, and they begin to eat. Terenty says a prayer when he has eaten the bread, then stretches himself on the sandy bank and falls asleep. While he is asleep, the boy gazes at the water, ponder- ing. He has many different things to think of. He has just seen the storm, the bees, the ants, the train. Now, before his eyes, fishes are whisking about. Some are two inches long and more, others are no bigger than one's nail. A viper, with its head held high, is swimming from one bank to the other.

Only toward the evening our wanderers return to the village. The children go for the night to a deserted barn, where the corn of the commune used to be kept, while Terenty, leaving them, goes to the tavern. The children lie huddled together on the straw, dozing.

The boy does not sleep. He gazes into the darkness, and it seems to him that he is seeing all that he has seen in the day: the storm clouds, the bright sunshine, the birds, the fish, lanky Terenty. The number of his impressions, together with ex-haustion and hunger, are too much for him; he is as hot as though he were on fire, and tosses from side to side. He longs to tell someone all that is haunting him now in the darkness and agitating his soul, but there is no one to tell. Fyokla is too little and could not understand.

"I'll tell Terenty tomorrow," thinks the boy.

The children fall asleep, thinking of the homeless cobbler, and, in the night Terenty comes to them, makes the sign of the cross over them, and puts bread under their heads. And no one sees his love. It is seen only by the moon which floats in the sky and peeps caressingly through the holes in the wall of the deserted barn.

Honoré de Balzac
1799-1850

SOMERSET MAUGHAM says: "I suppose Balzac is the greatest novelist who ever lived." Certainly, he left behind him one of the great literary monuments of all time. At the age of thirty he started writing *La Comédie humaine*, worked almost without stop for twenty years, and died at fifty, worn out from overwork. In those twenty years he had little opportunity for life or family or love, hardly enough for friends.

Balzac wrote sixteen hours daily, sometimes not leaving his room for three days at a time, eating very little, and drinking cup after cup of black coffee. His routine was a dinner of sorts at five in the afternoon, sleep until midnight, then work all night and most of the next day. It is said that the manifold intricacies of the novels and stories that make up the many volumes of *The Human Comedy* were all in his head at the same time. He knew all the details of the lives of every one of his two thousand or more characters, the condition of the country and province from which each came, the nature of the trade or profession each belonged to, and the political changes that were going on in their world. He was in their consciousness, in their clothes, business, palaces, even in their beds. "After Shakespeare, he is our great magazine of documents on human nature," said Taine.

Never satisfied with his finished manuscripts, Balzac went over the proofs time and time again, changing the order of stories, rewriting, spending a fortune on printers' bills for revised proofs.

"A Passion in the Desert" was written in Balzac's first year of work on *La Comédie humaine* and is a part of *Tales from the Military Life*.

A Passion in the Desert

BY HONORÉ DE BALZAC

"THE whole show is dreadful," she cried, coming out of the menagerie of M. Martin. She had just been looking at that daring speculator "working with his hyena"—to speak in the style of the program.

"By what means," she continued, "can he have tamed these animals to such a point as to be certain of their affection for——."

"What seems to you a problem," said I, interrupting, "is really quite natural."

"Oh!" she cried, letting an incredulous smile wander over her lips.

"You think that beasts are wholly without passions?" I asked her. "Quite the reverse; we can communicate to them all the vices arising in our own state of civilization."

She looked at me with an air of astonishment.

"Nevertheless," I continued, "the first time I saw M. Martin, I admit, like you, I did give vent to an exclamation of surprise. I found myself next to an old soldier with the right leg amputated, who had come in with me. His face had struck me. He had one of those intrepid heads, stamped with the seal of warfare, and on which the battles of Napoleon are written. Besides, he had that

frank good-humored expression which always impresses me favorably. He was without doubt one of those troopers who are surprised at nothing, who find matter for laughter in the contortions of a dying comrade, who bury or plunder him quite lightheartedly, who stand intrepidly in the way of bullets; in fact, one of those men who waste no time in deliberation, and would not hesitate to make friends with the devil himself. After looking very attentively at the proprietor of the menagerie getting out of his box, my companion pursed up his lips with an air of mockery and contempt, with that peculiar and expressive twist which superior people assume to show they are not taken in. Then when I was expatiating on the courage of M. Martin, he smiled, shook his head knowingly, and said, 'Well known.'

"How 'well known'? I said. 'If you would only explain to me the mystery I should be vastly obliged.'

"After a few minutes, during which we made acquaintance, we went to dine at the first restaurateur's whose shop caught our eye. At dessert a bottle of champagne completely refreshed and brightened up the memories of this odd old soldier. He told me his story, and I said he had every reason to exclaim, 'Well known.' "

When she got home, she teased me to that extent and made so many promises that I consented to communicate to her the old soldier's confidences. Next day she received the following episode of an epic which one might call "The Frenchman in Egypt."

During the expedition in Upper Egypt under General Desaix, a Provençal soldier fell into the hands of the Mangrabins, and was taken by these Arabs into the deserts beyond the falls of the Nile.

In order to place a sufficient distance between themselves and the French army, the Mangrabins made forced marches, and only rested during the night. They camped round a well overshadowed by palm trees under which they had previously concealed a store of provisions. Not surmising that the notion of flight would occur to their prisoner, they contented themselves with binding his hands, and after eating a few dates, and giving provender to their horses, went to sleep.

When the brave Provençal saw that his enemies were no longer watching him, he made use of his teeth to steal a scimitar, fixed the blade between his knees, and cut the cords which prevented using his hands; in a moment he was free. He at once seized a rifle and dagger, then taking the precaution to provide himself with a sack of dried dates, oats, and powder and shot, and to fasten a scimitar to his waist he leaped onto a horse, and spurred on vigorously in the direction where he thought to find the French army. So impatient was he to see a bivouac again that he pressed on the already tired courser at such speed that its

flanks were lacerated with his spurs, and at last the poor animal died, leaving the Frenchman alone in the desert. After walking some time in the sand with all the courage of an escaped convict, the soldier was obliged to stop, as the day had already ended. In spite of the beauty of an Oriental sky at night, he felt he had not strength enough to go on. Fortunately he had been able to find a small hill, on the summit of which a few palm trees shot up into the air; it was their verdure seen from afar which had brought hope and consolation to his heart. His fatigue was so great that he lay down upon a rock of granite, capriciously cut out like a camp bed; there he fell asleep without taking any precaution to defend himself while he slept. He had made the sacrifice of his life. His last thought was one of regret. He repented having left the Mangrabins, whose nomad life seemed to smile on him now that he was afar from them and without help. He was awakened by the sun, whose pitiless rays fell with all their force on the granite and produced an intolerable heat—for he had had the stupidity to place himself inversely to the shadow thrown by the verdant majestic heads of the palm trees. He looked at the solitary trees and shuddered —they reminded him of the graceful shafts crowned with foliage which characterize the Saracen columns in the cathedral of Arles.

But when, after counting the palm trees, he cast his eye around him, the most horrible despair was infused into his soul. Before him stretched an ocean without limit. The dark sand of the desert spread farther than sight could reach in every direction, and glittered like steel struck with a bright light. It might have been a sea of looking glass, or lakes melted together in a mirror. A fiery vapor carried up in streaks made a perpetual whirlwind over the quivering land. The sky was lit with an Oriental splendor of insupportable purity, leaving naught for the imagination to desire. Heaven and earth were on fire.

The silence was awful in its wild and terrible majesty. Infinity, immensity, closed in upon the soul from every side. Not a cloud in the sky, not a breath in the air, not a flaw on the bosom of the sand, ever moving in diminutive waves; the horizon ended as at sea on a clear day, with one line of light, definite as the cut of a sword.

The Provençal threw his arms around the trunk of one of the palm trees, as though it were the body of a friend, and then in the shelter of the thin straight shadow that the palm cast upon the granite, he wept. Then sitting down he remained as he was, contemplating with profound sadness the implacable scene, which was all he had to look upon. He cried aloud, to measure the solitude. His voice, lost in the hollows of the hill, sounded faintly, and aroused no echo—the echo was in his own heart. The Provençal was twenty-two years old; he loaded his carbine.

"There'll be time enough," he said to himself, laying on the ground the weapon which alone could bring him deliverance.

Looking by turns at the black expanse and the blue expanse, the soldier dreamed of France—he smelled with delight the gutters of Paris—he remembered the towns through which he had passed, the faces of his fellow soldiers, the most minute details of his life. His southern fancy soon showed him the stones of his beloved Provence, in the play of the heat which waved over the spread sheet of the desert. Fearing the danger of this cruel mirage, he went down the opposite side of the hill to that by which he had come up the day before. The remains of a rug showed that this place of refuge had at one time been inhabited; at a short distance he saw some palm trees full of dates. Then the instinct which binds us to life awoke again in his heart. He hoped to live long enough to await the passing of some Arabs, or perhaps he might hear the sound of cannon; for at this time Bonaparte was traversing Egypt.

This thought gave him new life. The palm tree seemed to bend with the weight of the ripe fruit. He shook some of it down. When he tasted this unhoped-for manna, he felt sure that the palms had been cultivated by a former inhabitant— the savory, fresh meat of the dates was proof of the care of his predecessor. He passed suddenly from dark despair to an almost insane joy. He went up again to the top of the hill, and spent the rest of the day in cutting down one of the sterile palm trees, which the night before had served him for shelter. A vague memory made him think of the animals of the desert; and in case they might come to drink at the spring, visible from the base of the rocks but lost farther down, he resolved to guard himself from their visits by placing a barrier at the entrance of his hermitage.

In spite of his diligence, and the strength which the fear of being devoured asleep gave him, he was unable to cut the palm in pieces, though he succeeded in cutting it down. At eventide the king of the desert fell; the sound of its fall resounded far and wide, like a sign in the solitude; the soldier shuddered as though he had heard some voice predicting woe.

But like an heir who does not long bewail a deceased parent, he tore off from this beautiful tree the tall broad green leaves which are its poetic adornment, and used them to mend the mat on which he was to sleep.

Fatigued by the heat and his work, he fell asleep under the red curtains of his wet cave.

In the middle of the night his sleep was troubled by an extraordinary noise; he sat up, and the deep silence around him allowed him to distinguish the alternative accents of a respiration whose savage energy could not belong to a human creature.

A profound terror, increased still further by the darkness, the silence, and his waking images, froze his heart within him. He almost felt his hair stand on end, when by straining his eyes to their utmost he perceived through the shadows two faint yellow lights. At first he attributed these lights to the reflection of his own pupils, but soon the vivid brilliance of the night aided him gradually to distinguish the objects around him in the cave, and he beheld a huge animal lying but two steps from him. Was it a lion, a tiger, or a crocodile?

The Provençal was not educated enough to know under what species his enemy ought to be classed; but his fright was all the greater, as his ignorance led him to imagine all terrors at once; he endured a cruel torture, noting every variation of the breathing close to him without daring to make the slightest movement. An odor, pungent like that of a fox, but more penetrating, profounder— so to speak—filled the cave, and when the Provençal became sensible of this, his terror reached its height, for he could not longer doubt the proximity of a terrible companion, whose royal dwelling served him for shelter.

Presently the reflection of the moon, descending on the horizon, lit up the den, rendering gradually visible and resplendent the spotted skin of a panther.

This lion of Egypt slept, curled up like a big dog, the peaceful possessor of a sumptuous niche at the gate of a hotel; its eyes opened for a moment and closed again; its face was turned toward the man. A thousand confused thoughts passed through the Frenchman's mind; first he thought of killing it with a bullet from his gun, but he saw there was not enough distance between them for him to take proper aim—the shot would miss the mark. And if it were to wake!—the thought made his limbs rigid. He listened to his own heart beating in the midst of the silence, and cursed the too violent pulsations which the flow of blood brought on, fearing to disturb that sleep which allowed him time to think of some means of escape.

Twice he placed his hand on his scimitar, intending to cut off the head of his enemy; but the difficulty of cutting stiff, short hair compelled him to abandon this daring project. To miss would be to die for *certain*, he thought; he preferred the chances of fair fight, and made up his mind to wait till morning; the morning did not leave him long to wait.

He could now examine the panther at ease; its muzzle was smeared with blood.

"She's had a good dinner," he thought, without troubling himself as to whether her feast might have been on human flesh. "She won't be hungry when she gets up."

It was a female. The fur on her belly and flanks was glistening white; many small marks like velvet formed beautiful bracelets round her feet; her sinuous tail was also white, ending with black rings; the over-part of her dress, yellow like un-burnished gold, very lissome and soft, had the characteristic blotches in the form of rosettes which dis-tinguish the panther from every other feline species.

This tranquil and formidable hostess snored in an attitude as graceful as that of a cat lying on a cushion. Her bloodstained paws, nervous and well armed, were stretched out before her face, which rested upon them, and from which radiated her straight, slender whiskers, like threads of silver.

If she had been like that in a cage, the Provençal would doubtless have admired the grace of the ani-mal, and the vigorous contrasts of vivid color which gave her robe an imperial splendor; but just then his sight was troubled by her sinister appearance.

The presence of the panther, even asleep, could not fail to produce the effect which the magnetic eyes of the serpent are said to have on the nightingale.

For a moment the courage of the soldier began to fail before this danger, though no doubt it would have risen at the mouth of a cannon charged with shell. Nevertheless, a bold thought brought daylight in his soul and sealed up the source of the cold sweat which sprang forth on his brow. Like men driven to bay who defy death and offer their body to the smiter, so he, seeing in this merely a tragic episode, resolved to play his part with honor to the last.

"The day before yesterday the Arabs would have killed me per-haps," he said; so considering him-self as good as dead already, he waited bravely, with excited curi-osity, his enemy's awakening.

When the sun appeared, the panther suddenly opened her eyes; then she put out her paws with energy, as if to stretch them and get rid of cramp. At last she yawned, showing the formidable apparatus of her teeth and pointed tongue, rough as a file.

"A regular *petite maîtresse*," thought the Frenchman, seeing her roll herself about so softly and coquettishly. She licked off the blood which stained her paws and muzzle, and scratched her head with re-iterated gestures full of prettiness. "All right, make a little toilet," the Frenchman said to himself, begin-ning to recover his gaiety with his courage; "we'll say good morning to each other presently," and he seized the small, short dagger which he had taken from the Mangrabins. At this moment the panther turned her head toward the man and looked at him fixedly without moving.

The rigidity of her metallic eyes and their insupportable luster made him shudder, especially when the animal walked toward him. But he looked at her caressingly, staring into her eyes in order to magnetize her, and let her come quite close to him; then with a movement both gentle and amorous, as though he were caressing the most beautiful of women, he passed his hand over her whole body, from the head to the tail, scratching the flexible vertebrae which divided the panther's yellow back. The animal waved her tail voluptuously, and her eyes grew gentle; and when for the third time the Frenchman accomplished this interesting flattery, she gave forth one of those purrings by which our cats express their pleasure; but this murmur issued from a throat so powerful and so deep that it resounded through the cave like the last vibrations of an organ in a church. The man, understanding the importance of his caresses, redoubled them in such a way as to surprise and stupefy his imperious courtesan. When he felt sure of having extinguished the ferocity of his capricious companion, whose hunger had so fortunately been satisfied the day before, he got up to go out of the cave; the panther let him go out, but when he had reached the summit of the hill she sprang with the lightness of a sparrow hopping from twig to twig, and rubbed herself against his legs, putting up her back after the manner of all the race of cats. Then regarding her guest with eyes whose glare had softened a little, she gave vent to that wild cry which naturalists compare to the grating of a saw.

"She is exacting," said the Frenchman, smilingly.

He was bold enough to play with her ears; he caressed her belly and scratched her head as hard as he could.

When he saw that he was successful, he tickled her skull with the point of his dagger, watching for the right moment to kill her, but the hardness of her bones made him tremble for his success.

The sultana of the desert showed herself gracious to her slave; she lifted her head, stretched out her neck, and manifested her delight by the tranquillity of her attitude. It suddenly occurred to the soldier that to kill this savage princess with one blow he must poignard her in the throat.

He raised the blade, when the panther, satisfied no doubt, laid herself gracefully at his feet, and cast up at him glances in which, in spite of their natural fierceness, was mingled confusedly a kind of good will. The poor Provençal ate his dates, leaning against one of the palm trees, and casting his eyes alternately on the desert in quest of some liberator and on his terrible companion to watch her uncertain clemency.

The panther looked at the place where the date stones fell, and every time that he threw one down her eyes expressed an incredible mistrust.

She examined the man with an almost commercial prudence. However, this examination was favorable to him, for when he had finished his meager meal she licked his boots with her powerful rough tongue, brushing off with marvellous skill the dust gathered in the creases.

"Ah, but when she's really hungry!" thought the Frenchman. In spite of the shudder this thought caused him, the soldier began to measure curiously the proportions of the panther, certainly one of the most splendid specimens of its race. She was three feet high and four feet long without counting her tail; this powerful weapon, rounded like a cudgel, was nearly three feet long. The head, large as that of a lioness, was distinguished by a rare expression of refinement. The cold cruelty of a tiger was dominant, it was true, but there was also a vague resemblance to the face of a sensual woman. Indeed, the face of this solitary queen had something of the gaiety of a drunken Nero: she had satiated herself with blood, and she wanted to play.

The soldier tried if he might walk up and down, and the panther left him free, contenting herself with following him with her eyes, less like a faithful dog than a big Angora cat, observing everything and every movement of her master.

When he looked around, he saw, by the spring, the remains of his horse; the panther had dragged the carcass all that way; about two thirds of it had been devoured already. The sight reassured him.

It was easy to explain the panther's absence, and the respect she had had for him while he slept. The first piece of good luck emboldened him to tempt the future, and he conceived the wild hope of continuing on good terms with the panther during the entire day, neglecting no means of taming her, and remaining in her good graces.

He returned to her, and had the unspeakable joy of seeing her wag her tail with an almost imperceptible movement at his approach. He sat down then, without fear, by her side, and they began to play together; he took her paws and muzzle, pulled her ears, rolled her over on her back, stroked her warm, delicate flanks. She let him do whatever he liked, and when he began to stroke the hair on her feet she drew her claws in carefully.

The man, keeping the dagger in one hand, thought to plunge it into the belly of the too-confiding panther, but he was afraid that he would be immediately strangled in her last conclusive struggle; besides, he felt in his heart a sort of remorse which bid him respect a creature that had done him no harm. He seemed to have found a friend, in a boundless desert; half unconsciously he thought of his first sweetheart, whom he had nicknamed "Mignonne" by way of contrast, because she was so atrociously jealous that all the time of their love he was in fear of the knife with which she had always threatened him.

This memory of his early days suggested to him the idea of making the young panther answer to this name, now that he began to admire with less terror her swiftness, suppleness, and softness. Toward the end of the day he had familiarized himself with his perilous position; he now almost liked the painfulness of it. At last his companion had got into the habit of looking up at him whenever he cried in a falsetto voice, "Mignonne."

At the setting of the sun Mignonne gave, several times running, a profound melancholy cry. "She's been well brought up," said the lighthearted soldier; "she says her prayers." But this mental joke only occurred to him when he noticed what a pacific attitude his companion remained in. "Come, *ma petite blonde*, I'll let you go to bed first," he said to her, counting on the activity of his own legs to run away as quickly as possible, directly she was asleep, and seek another shelter for the night.

The soldier waited with impatience the hour of his flight, and when it had arrived he walked vigorously in the direction of the Nile; but hardly had he made a quarter of a league in the sand when he heard the panther bounding after him, crying with that sawlike cry more dreadful even than the sound of her leaping.

"Ah!" he said, "then she's taken a fancy to me; she has never met anyone before, and it is really quite flattering to have her first love."

That instant the man fell into one of those movable quicksands so terrible to travelers and from which it is impossible to save oneself. Feeling himself caught, he gave a shriek of alarm; the panther seized him with her teeth by the collar, and, springing vigorously backward, drew him as if by magic out of the whirling sand.

"Ah, Mignonne!" cried the soldier, caressing her enthusiastically; "we're bound together for life and death— but no jokes, mind!" and he retraced his steps.

From that time the desert seemed inhabited. It contained a being to whom the man could talk, and whose ferocity was rendered gentle by him, though he could not explain to himself the reason for their strange friendship. Great as was the soldier's desire to stay upon guard, he slept.

On awakening he could not find Mignonne; he mounted the hill, and in the distance saw her springing toward him after the habit of these animals, who cannot run on account of the extreme flexibility of the vertebral column. Mignonne arrived, her jaws covered with blood; she received the wonted caress of her companion, showing with much purring how happy it made her. Her eyes, full of languor, turned still more gently than the day before toward the Provençal who talked to her as one would to a tame animal.

"Ah! Mademoiselle, you are a nice girl, aren't you? Just look at that! So we like to be made much of, don't we? Aren't you ashamed of yourself? So you have been eating some Arab or other, have you? That doesn't matter. They're animals just the same as you are; but don't you take to eating Frenchmen, or I shan't like you any longer."

She played like a dog with its master, letting herself be rolled over, knocked about, and stroked, alternately; sometimes she herself would provoke the soldier, putting up her paw with a soliciting gesture.

Some days passed in this manner. This companionship permitted the Provençal to appreciate the sublime beauty of the desert; now that he had a living thing to think about, alternations of fear and quiet, and plenty to eat, his mind became filled with contrast and his life began to be diversified.

Solitude revealed to him all her secrets, and enveloped him in her delights. He discovered in the rising and setting of the sun sights unknown to the world. He knew what it was to tremble when he heard over his head the hiss of a bird's wing, so rarely did they pass, or when he saw the clouds, changing and many-colored travelers, melt one into another. He studied in the night time the effect of the moon upon the ocean of sand, where the simoom made waves swift of movement and rapid in their change. He lived the life of the Eastern day, marveling at its wonderful pomp; then, after having reveled in the sight of a hurricane over the plain where the whirling sands made red, dry mists and death-bearing clouds, he would welcome the night with joy, for then fell the healthful freshness of the stars, and he listened to imaginary music in the skies. Then solitude taught him to unroll the treasures of dreams. He passed whole hours in remembering mere nothings, and comparing his present life with his past.

At last he grew passionately fond of the panther; for some sort of affection was a necessity.

Whether it was that his will powerfully projected had modified the character of his companion, or whether, because she found abundant food in her predatory excursions in the desert, she respected the man's life, he began to fear for it no longer, seeing her so well tamed.

He devoted the greater part of his time to sleep, but he was obliged to watch like a spider in its web that the moment of his deliverance might not escape him, if anyone should pass the line marked by the horizon. He had sacrificed his shirt to make a flag with, which he hung at the top of a palm tree, whose foliage he had torn off. Taught by necessity, he found the means of keeping it spread out, by fastening it with little sticks; for the wind might not be blowing at the moment when the passing traveler was looking through the desert.

It was during the long hours, when he had abandoned hope, that he amused himself with the panther. He had come to learn the different inflections of her voice, the expressions of her eyes; he had studied the capricious patterns of all the rosettes which marked the gold of her robe. Mignonne was not even angry when he took hold of the tuft at the end of her tail to count her rings, those graceful ornaments which glittered in the sun like jewelry. It gave him pleasure to contemplate the supple, fine outlines of her form, the whiteness of her belly, the graceful pose of her head. But it was especially when she was playing that he felt most pleasure in looking at her; the agility and youthful lightness of her movements were a continual surprise to him; he wondered at the supple way in which she jumped and climbed, washed herself and arranged her fur, crouched down and prepared to spring. However rapid her spring might be, however slippery the stone she was on, she would always stop short at the word "Mignonne."

One day, in a bright midday sun, an enormous bird coursed through the air. The man left his panther to look at this new guest; but after waiting a moment the deserted sultana growled deeply.

"My goodness! I do believe she's jealous," he cried, seeing her eyes become hard again; "the soul of Virginie has passed into her body; that's certain."

The eagle disappeared into the air, while the soldier admired the curved contour of the panther.

But there was such youth and grace in her form! she was beautiful as a woman! the blond fur of her robe mingled well with the delicate tints of faint white which marked her flanks.

The profuse light cast down by the sun made this living gold, these russet markings, to burn in a way to give them an indefinable attraction.

The man and the panther looked at one another with a look full of meaning; the coquette quivered when she felt her friend stroke her head; her eyes flashed like lightning—then she shut them tightly.

"She has a soul," he said, looking at the stillness of this queen of the sands, golden like them, white like them, solitary and burning like them.

"Well," she said, "I have read your plea in favor of beasts; but how did two so well adapted to understand each other end?"

"Ah, well! you see, they ended as all great passions do end—by a misunderstanding. For some reason *one* suspects the other of treason; they don't come to an explanation through pride, and quarrel and part from sheer obstinacy."

"Yet sometimes at the best moments a single word or a look is enough—but anyhow go on with your story."

"It's horribly difficult, but you will understand, after what the old villain told me over his champagne.

"He said—'I don't know if I hurt her, but she turned round, as if enraged, and with her sharp teeth caught hold of my leg—gently, I daresay; but I, thinking she would devour me, plunged my dagger into her throat. She rolled over, giving a cry that froze my heart; and I saw her dying, still looking at me without anger. I would have given all the world—my cross even, which I had not then—to have brought her to life again. It was as though I had murdered a real person; and the soldiers who had seen my flag, and were come to my assistance, found me in tears.'

"'Well sir,' he said, after a moment of silence, 'since then I have been in war in Germany, in Spain, in Russia, in France; I've certainly carried my carcass about a good deal, but never have I seen anything like the desert. Ah! yes, it is very beautiful!'

"'What did you feel there?' I asked him.

"'Oh! that can't be described, young man. Besides, I am not always regretting my palm trees and my panther. I should have to be very melancholy for that. In the desert, you see, there is everything, and nothing.'

"'Yes, but explain——'

"'Well,' he said, with an impatient gesture, 'it is God without mankind.'"

Gustave Flaubert

1821-1880

LIKE BALZAC, Flaubert dedicated his life to writing. Unlike Balzac, however, in his twenty-seven years of diligent work Flaubert produced only five novels, three short stories, and two plays. "His life," said Henry James, "was that of a pearl diver, breathless in the thick element while he groped for the priceless word. . . . He passed it in reconstructing sentences, exterminating repetitions, calculating and comparing cadences. . . . The horror that haunted all his years was the horror of the cliché, the stereotyped, the things usually said. . . ." His reward was to become the most powerful artistic influence on his own and the following generation of writers. He was "the novelists' novelist."

Flaubert lived with his mother at Croisset, near Rouen, in a fine old house overlooking the Seine. It was a quiet, hard-working, sequestered existence, interrupted only when his friends came out from Paris of a Sunday afternoon to visit him. These were the great writers of a great day—George Sand, seventeen years older than he but his closest friend, Zola, Daudet, the Goncourts, Turgenev, and Maupassant, his disciple. Flaubert never married, though for several years he carried on a somewhat intellectual affair with Louise Colet, the poet, whose salon Barbey d'Aurevilly described as an "academic oyster bed." When Flaubert embarked upon *Madame Bovary*, the liaison ended, with Emma Bovary supplanting Louise.

He was an enormous man, with a head of flaming-red hair and a general appearance of robust strength. But he was never well. In later years he was almost continuously ill, the war of 1870 took further toll of his health, and he aged long before his time. "A Simple Heart," one of the *Trois Contes*, was written in these last desolate years. His mother had died, and he was ill and alone.

A Simple Heart

BY GUSTAVE FLAUBERT

I

MADAME AUBAIN's servant Félicité was the envy of the ladies of Pont-l'Évêque for half a century.

She received four pounds a year. For that she was cook and general servant, and did the sewing, washing, and ironing; she could bridle a horse, fatten poultry, and churn butter—and she remained faithful to her mistress, unamiable as the latter was.

Mme Aubain had married a gay bachelor without money who died at the beginning of 1809, leaving her with two small children and a quantity of debts. She then sold all her property except the farms of Toucques and Geffosses, which brought in two hundred pounds a year at most, and left her house in Saint-Melaine for a less expensive one that had belonged to her family and was situated behind the market.

This house had a slate roof and stood between an alley and a lane that went down to the river. There was an unevenness in the levels of the rooms which made you stumble. A narrow hall divided the kitchen from the "parlor" where Mme Aubain spent her day, sitting in a wicker easy chair by the window.

Against the panels, which were painted white, was a row of eight mahogany chairs. On an old piano under the barometer a heap of wooden and cardboard boxes rose like a pyramid. A stuffed armchair stood on either side of the Louis Quinze chimney piece, which was in yellow marble with a clock in the middle of it modeled like a temple of Vesta. The whole room was a little musty, as the floor was lower than the garden.

The first floor began with "Madame's" room: very large, with a pale-flowered wallpaper and a portrait of "Monsieur" as a dandy of the period. It led to a smaller room, where there were two children's cots without mattresses. Next came the drawing room, which was always shut up and full of furniture covered with sheets. Then there was a corridor leading to a study. The shelves of a large bookcase were respectably lined with books and papers, and its three wings surrounded a broad writing table in dark wood. The two panels at the end of the room were covered with pen drawings, water-color landscapes, and engravings by Audran, all relics of better days and vanished splendor. Félicité's room on the top floor got

From *Three Tales* by Gustave Flaubert. By permission of the publishers. Copyright, 1924, by Alfred A. Knopf, Inc.

its light from a dormer window, which looked over the meadows.

She rose at daybreak to be in time for Mass, and worked till evening without stopping. Then, when dinner was over, the plates and dishes in order, and the door shut fast, she thrust the log under the ashes and went to sleep in front of the hearth with her rosary in her hand. Félicité was the stubbornest of all bargainers; and as for cleanness, the polish on her saucepans was the despair of other servants. Thrifty in all things, she ate slowly, gathering off the table in her fingers the crumbs of her loaf—a twelve-pound loaf expressly baked for her, which lasted for three weeks.

At all times of year she wore a print handkerchief fastened with a pin behind, a bonnet that covered her hair, gray stockings, a red skirt, and a bibbed apron—such as hospital nurses wear—over her jacket.

Her face was thin and her voice sharp. At twenty-five she looked like forty. From fifty onwards she seemed of no particular age; and with her silence, straight figure, and precise movements she was like a woman made of wood, and going by clockwork.

II

She had had her love story like another.

Her father, a mason, had been killed by falling off some scaffolding. Then her mother died, her sisters scattered, and a farmer took her in and employed her, while she was still quite little, to herd the cows at pasture. She shivered in rags and would lie flat on the ground to drink water from the ponds; she was beaten for nothing, and finally turned out for the theft of a shilling which she did not steal. She went to another farm, where she became dairymaid; and as she was liked by her employers her companions were jealous of her.

One evening in August (she was then eighteen) they took her to the assembly at Colleville. She was dazed and stupefied in an instant by the noise of the fiddlers, the lights in the trees, the gay medley of dresses, the lace, the gold crosses, and the throng of people jigging all together. While she kept shyly apart a young man with a well-to-do air, who was leaning on the shaft of a cart and smoking his pipe, came up to ask her to dance. He treated her to cider, coffee, and cake, and bought her a silk handkerchief; and then, imagining she had guessed his meaning, offered to see her home. At the edge of a field of oats he pushed her roughly down. She was frightened and began to cry out; and he went off.

One evening later she was on the Beaumont road. A big hay wagon was moving slowly along; she wanted to get in front of it, and as she brushed past the wheels she recognized Theodore. He greeted her quite calmly, saying she must excuse it all because it was "the fault of the drink." She could not think of any answer and wanted to run away.

He began at once to talk about the harvest and the worthies of the commune, for his father had left Colleville for the farm at Les Écots, so that now he and she were neighbors. "Ah!" she said. He added that they thought of settling him in life. Well, he was in no hurry; he was waiting for a wife to his fancy. She dropped her head; and then he asked her if she thought of marrying. She answered with a smile that it was meant to make fun of her.

"But I am not, I swear!"—and he passed his left hand round her waist.

She walked in the support of his embrace; their steps grew slower. The wind was soft, the stars glittered, the huge wagonload of hay swayed in front of them, and dust rose from the dragging steps of the four horses. Then, without a word of command, they turned to the right. He clasped her once more in his arms, and she disappeared into the shadow.

The week after Theodore secured some assignations with her.

They met at the end of farmyards, behind a wall, or under a solitary tree. She was not innocent as young ladies are—she had learned knowledge from the animals—but her reason and the instinct of her honor would not let her fall. Her resistance exasperated Theodore's passion; so much so that to satisfy it—or perhaps quite artlessly—he made her an offer of marriage. She was in doubt whether to trust him, but he swore great oaths of fidelity.

Soon he confessed to something troublesome; the year before his parents had bought him a substitute for the army, but any day he might be taken again, and the idea of serving was a terror to him. Félicité took this cowardice of his as a sign of affection, and it redoubled hers. She stole away at night to see him, and when she reached their meeting place Theodore racked her with his anxieties and urgings.

At last he declared that he would go himself to the prefecture for information, and would tell her the result on the following Sunday, between eleven and midnight.

When the moment came she sped toward her lover. Instead of him she found one of his friends.

He told her that she would not see Theodore any more. To ensure himself against conscription he had married an old woman, Madame Lehoussais, of Toucques, who was very rich.

There was an uncontrollable burst of grief. She threw herself on the ground, screamed, called to the God of mercy, and moaned by herself in the fields till daylight came. Then she came back to the farm and announced that she was going to leave; and at the end of the month she received her wages, tied all her small belongings with a handkerchief, and went to Pont-l'Évêque.

In front of the inn there she made inquiries of a woman in a widow's cap, who, as it happened, was just looking for a cook. The girl did not know much, but her willingness seemed so great and her demands so small that Mme Aubain ended by saying:

"Very well, then, I will take you."

A quarter of an hour afterwards Félicité was installed in her house.

She lived there at first in a tremble, as it were, at "the style of the house" and the memory of "Monsieur" floating over it all. Paul and Virginie, the first aged seven and the other hardly four, seemed to her beings of a precious substance; she carried them on her back like a horse; it was a sorrow to her that Mme Aubain would not let her kiss them every minute. And yet she was happy there. Her grief had melted in the pleasantness of things all round.

Every Thursday regular visitors came in for a game of boston, and Félicité got the cards and foot-warmers ready beforehand. They arrived punctually at eight and left before the stroke of eleven.

On Monday mornings the dealer who lodged in the covered passage spread out all his old iron on the ground. Then a hum of voices began to fill the town, mingled with the neighing of horses, bleating of lambs, grunting of pigs, and the sharp rattle of carts along the street. About noon, when the market was at its height, you might see a tall, hook-nosed old countryman with his cap pushed back making his appearance at the door. It was Robelin, the farmer of Geffosses. A little later came Liébard, the farmer from Toucques—short, red, and corpulent —in a gray jacket and gaiters shod with spurs.

Both had poultry or cheese to offer their landlord. Félicité was invariably a match for their cunning and they went away filled with respect for her.

At vague intervals Mme Aubain had a visit from the Marquis de Gremanville, one of her uncles, who had ruined himself by debauchery and now lived at Falaise on his last remaining morsel of land. He invariably came at the luncheon hour, with a dreadful poodle whose paws left all the furniture in a mess. In spite of efforts to show his breeding, which he carried to the point of raising his hat every time he mentioned "my late father," habit was too strong for him; he poured himself out glass after glass and fired off improper remarks. Félicité edged him politely out of the house—"You have had enough, Monsieur de Gremanville! Another time!"—and she shut the door on him.

She opened it with pleasure to M. Bourais, who had been a lawyer. His boldness, his white stock, frilled shirt, and roomy brown coat, his way of rounding the arm as he took snuff —his whole person, in fact, created that disturbance of mind which overtakes us at the sight of extraordinary men.

As he looked after the property of

"Madame" he remained shut up with her for hours in "Monsieur's" study, though all the time he was afraid of compromising himself. He respected the magistracy immensely, and had some pretensions to Latin.

To combine instruction and amusement he gave the children a geography book made up of a series of prints. They represented scenes in different parts of the world: cannibals with feathers on their heads, a monkey carrying off a young lady, Bedouins in the desert, the harpooning of a whale, and so on. Paul explained these engravings to Félicité; and that, in fact, was the whole of her literary education. The children's education was undertaken by Guyot, a poor creature employed at the town hall, who was famous for his beautiful hand and sharpened his penknife on his boots.

When the weather was bright the household set off early for a day at Geffosses Farm.

Its courtyard is on a slope, with the farmhouse in the middle, and the sea looks like a gray streak in the distance.

Félicité brought slices of cold meat out of her basket, and they breakfasted in a room adjoining the dairy. It was the only surviving fragment of a country house which was now no more. The wallpaper hung in tatters, and quivered in the drafts. Mme Aubain sat with bowed head, overcome by her memories; the children became afraid to speak. "Why don't you play, then?" she would say, and off they went.

Paul climbed into the barn, caught birds, played at ducks and drakes over the pond, or hammered with his stick on the big casks which boomed like drums. Virginie fed the rabbits or dashed off to pick cornflowers, her quick legs showing their embroidered little drawers.

One autumn evening they went home by the fields. The moon was in its first quarter, lighting part of the sky; and mist floated like a scarf over the windings of the Toucques. Cattle, lying out in the middle of the grass, looked quietly at the four people as they passed. In the third meadow some of them got up and made a half circle in front of the walkers. "There's nothing to be afraid of," said Félicité, as she stroked the nearest on the back with a kind of crooning song; he wheeled round and others did the same. But when they crossed the next pasture there was a formidable bellow. It was a bull, hidden by the mist. Mme Aubain was about to run. "No! no! don't go so fast!" They mended their pace, however, and heard a loud breathing behind them which came nearer. His hoofs thudded on the meadow grass like hammers; why, he was galloping now! Félicité turned round, and tore up clods of earth with both hands and threw them in his eyes. He lowered his muzzle, waved his horns, and quivered with fury, bellowing terribly. Mme Aubain, now at the end of the pasture with her two little ones, was looking wildly for a place to get over the high bank. Félicité was retreating, still with her face to the bull, keeping up a shower of clods which blinded him, and crying all the time, "Be quick! be quick!"

Mme Aubain went down into the ditch, pushed Virginie first and then Paul, fell several times as she tried to climb the bank, and managed it at last by dint of courage.

The bull had driven Félicité to bay against a rail fence; his slaver was streaming into her face; another

second, and he would have gored her. She had just time to slip between two of the rails and the big animal stopped short in amazement.

This adventure was talked of at Pont-l'Évêque for many a year. Félicité did not pride herself on it in the least, not having the barest suspicion that she had done anything heroic.

Virginie was the sole object of her thoughts, for the child developed a nervous complaint as a result of her fright, and M. Poupart, the doctor, advised seabathing at Trouville. It was not a frequented place then. Mme Aubain collected information, consulted Bourais, and made preparations as though for a long journey.

Her luggage started a day in advance, in Liébard's cart. The next day he brought round two horses, one of which had a lady's saddle with a velvet back to it, while a cloak was rolled up to make a kind of seat on the crupper of the other. Mme Aubain rode on that, behind the farmer. Félicité took charge of Virginie, and Paul mounted M. Lechaptois' donkey, lent on condition that great care was taken of it.

The road was so bad that its five miles took two hours. The horses sank in the mud up to their pasterns, and their haunches jerked abruptly in the effort to get out; or else they stumbled in the ruts, and at other moments had to jump. In some places Liébard's mare came suddenly to a halt. He waited patiently until she went on again, talking about the people who had properties along the road, and adding moral reflections to their history. So it was that as they were in the middle of Toucques, and passed under some windows bowered with nasturtiums, he shrugged his shoulders and said:

"There's a Mme Lehoussais lives there; instead of taking a young man she . . ." Félicité did not hear the rest; the horses were trotting and the donkey galloping. They all turned down a bypath; a gate swung open and two boys appeared; and the party dismounted in front of a manure heap at the very threshold of the farmhouse door.

When Mme Liébard saw her mistress she gave lavish signs of joy. She served her a luncheon with a sirloin of beef, tripe, black pudding, a fricassee of chicken, sparkling cider, a fruit tart, and brandied plums; seasoning it all with compliments to Madame, who seemed in better health; Mademoiselle, who was "splendid" now; and Monsieur Paul, who had "filled out" wonderfully. Nor did she forget their deceased grandparents, whom the Liébards had known, as they had been in the service of the family for several generations. The farm, like them, had the stamp of antiquity. The beams on the ceiling were worm-eaten, the walls blackened with smoke, and the windowpanes gray with dust. There was an oak dresser laden with every sort of useful article—jugs, plates, pewter bowls, wolftraps, and sheep shears; and a huge syringe made the children laugh. There was not a tree in the three courtyards without mushrooms growing at the bottom of it or a tuft of mistletoe on its boughs. Several of them had been thrown down by the wind. They had taken root again at the middle; and all were bending under their wealth of apples. The thatched roofs, like brown velvet and of varying thickness, withstood the heaviest squalls. The cart shed, however, was falling into ruin. Mme Aubain said she would see about it, and ordered the animals to be saddled again.

It was another half-hour before they reached Trouville. The little caravan dismounted to pass Écores —it was an overhanging cliff with boats below it—and three minutes later they were at the end of the quay and entered the courtyard of the Golden Lamb, kept by good Mme David.

From the first days of their stay Virginie began to feel less weak, thanks to the change of air and the effect of the sea baths. These, for want of a bathing dress, she took in her chemise; and her nurse dressed her afterwards in a coastguard's cabin which was used by the bathers.

In the afternoons they took the donkey and went off beyond the Black Rocks, in the direction of Hennequeville. The path climbed at first through ground with dells in it like the green sward of a park, and then reached a plateau where grass fields and arable lay side by side. Hollies rose stiffly out of the briary tangle at the edge of the road; and here and there a great withered tree made zigzags in the blue air with its branches.

They nearly always rested in a meadow, with Deauville on their left, Havre on their right, and the open sea in front. It glittered in the sunshine, smooth as a mirror and so quiet that its murmur was scarcely to be heard; sparrows chirped in hiding and the immense sky arched over it all. Mme Aubain sat doing her needlework; Virginie plaited rushes by her side; Félicité pulled up lavender, and Paul was bored and anxious to start home.

Other days they crossed the Toucques in a boat and looked for shells. When the tide went out sea urchins, starfish, and jellyfish were left exposed; and the children ran in pursuit of the foam flakes which scudded in the wind. The sleepy waves broke on the sand and unrolled all along the beach; it stretched away out of sight, bounded on the land side by the dunes which parted it from the Marsh, a wide meadow shaped like an arena. As they came home that way, Trouville, on the hill slope in the background, grew bigger at every step, and its miscellaneous throng of houses seemed to break into a gay disorder.

On days when it was too hot they did not leave their room. From the dazzling brilliance outside light fell in streaks between the laths of the blinds. There were no sounds in the village; and on the pavement below not a soul. This silence round them deepened the quietness of things. In the distance, where men were calking, there was a tap of hammers as they plugged the hulls, and a sluggish breeze wafted up the smell of tar.

The chief amusement was the return of the fishing boats. They began to tack as soon as they had passed the buoys. The sails came down on two of the three masts; and they drew on with the foresail swelling like a balloon, glided through the splash of the waves, and when they had reached the middle of the harbor suddenly dropped anchor. Then the boats drew up against the quay. The sailors threw quivering fish over the side; a row of carts was waiting, and women in cotton bonnets darted out to take the baskets and give their men a kiss.

One of them came up to Félicité one day, and she entered the lodgings a little later in a state of delight. She had found a sister again—and then Nastasie Barette, "wife of Le-roux," appeared, holding an infant at her breast and another child with her right hand, while on her left was a little cabin boy with his hands on his hips and a cap over his ear.

After a quarter of an hour Mme Aubain sent them off; but they were always to be found hanging about the kitchen, or encountered in the course of a walk. The husband never appeared.

Félicité was seized with affection for them. She bought them a blanket, some shirts, and a stove; it was clear that they were making a good thing out of her. Mme Aubain was annoyed by this weakness of hers, and she did not like the liberties taken by the nephew, who said "thee" and "thou" to Paul. So as Virginie was coughing and the fine weather gone, she returned to Pont-l'Évêque.

There M. Bourais enlightened her on the choice of a boys' school. The one at Caen was reputed to be the best, and Paul was sent to it. He said his good-bys bravely, content enough at going to live in a house where he would have companions.

Mme Aubain resigned herself to her son's absence as a thing that had to be. Virginie thought about it less and less. Félicité missed the noise he made. But she found an occupation to distract her; from Christmas onward she took the little girl to catechism every day.

III

After making a genuflexion at the door she walked up between the double row of chairs under the lofty nave, opened Mme Aubain's pew, sat down, and began to look about her. The choir stalls were filled with the boys on the right and the girls on the left, and the curé stood by the lectern. On a painted window in the apse the Holy Ghost looked down upon the Virgin. Another window showed her on her knees before the child Jesus, and a group carved in wood behind the altar shrine represented St. Michael overthrowing the dragon.

The priest began with a sketch of sacred history. The Garden, the Flood, the Tower of Babel, cities in flames, dying nations, and overturned idols passed like a dream before her eyes; and the dizzying vision left her with reverence for the Most High and fear of His wrath. Then she wept at the story of the Passion. Why had they crucified Him, when He loved the children, fed the multitudes, healed the blind, and had willed, in His meekness, to be born among the poor, on the dung heap of a stable? The sowings, harvests, wine presses, all the familiar things the Gospel speaks of, were a part of her life. They had been made holy by God's passing; and she loved the lambs more tenderly for her love of the Lamb, and the doves because of the Holy Ghost.

She found it hard to imagine Him in person, for He was not merely a bird, but a flame as well, and a breath at other times. It may be His light, she thought, which flits at night about the edge of the marshes, His breathing which drives on the clouds, His voice which gives harmony to the bells; and she would sit rapt in adoration, enjoying the cool walls and the quiet of the church.

Of doctrines she understood nothing—did not even try to understand. The curé discoursed, the children repeated their lesson, and finally she went to sleep, waking up with a start when their wooden shoes

clattered on the flagstones as they went away.

It was thus that Félicité, whose religious education had been neglected in her youth, learned the catechism by dint of hearing it; and from that time she copied all Virginie's observances, fasting as she did and confessing with her. On Corpus Christi Day they made a festal altar together.

The first communion loomed distractingly ahead. She fussed over the shoes, the rosary, the book and gloves; and how she trembled as she helped Virginie's mother to dress her!

All through the Mass she was racked with anxiety. She could not see one side of the choir because of M. Bourais; but straight in front of her was the flock of maidens, with white crowns above their hanging veils, making the impression of a field of snow; and she knew her dear child at a distance by her dainty neck and thoughtful air. The bell tinkled. The heads bowed, and there was silence. As the organ pealed, singers and congregation took up the *Agnus Dei*; then the procession of the boys began, and after them the girls rose. Step by step, with their hands joined in prayer, they went toward the lighted altar, knelt on the first step, received the sacrament in turn, and came back in the same order to their places. When Virginie's turn came Félicité leaned forward to see her; and with the imaginativeness of deep and tender feeling it seemed to her that she actually was the child; Virginie's face became hers, she was dressed in her clothes, it was her heart beating in her breast. As the moment came to open her mouth she closed her eyes and nearly fainted.

She appeared early in the sacristy

next morning for monsieur the curé to give her the communion. She took it with devotion, but it did not give her the same exquisite delight.

Mme Aubain wanted to make her daughter into an accomplished person; and as Guyot could not teach her music or English she decided to place her in the Ursuline Convent at Honfleur as a boarder. The child made no objection. Félicité sighed and thought that Madame lacked feeling. Then she reflected that her mistress might be right; matters of this kind were beyond her.

So one day an old spring van drew up at the door, and out of it stepped a nun to fetch the young lady. Félicité hoisted the luggage on to the top, admonished the driver, and put six pots of preserves, a dozen pears, and a bunch of violets under the seat.

At the last moment Virginie broke into a fit of sobbing; she threw her arms round her mother, who kissed her on the forehead, saying over and over, "Come, be brave! be brave!" The step was raised, and the carriage drove off.

Then Mme Aubain's strength gave way; and in the evening all her friends—the Lormeau family, Mme Lechaptois, the Rochefeuille ladies, M. de Houppeville, and Bourais—came in to console her.

To be without her daughter was very painful for her at first. But she heard from Virginie three times a week, wrote to her on the other days, walked in the garden, and so filled up the empty hours.

From sheer habit Félicité went into Virginie's room in the mornings and gazed at the walls. It was boredom to her not to have to comb the child's hair now, lace up her boots, tuck her into bed—and not to see her charming face perpetually and hold her hand when they went out together. In this idle condition she tried making lace. But her fingers were too heavy and broke the threads; she could not attend to anything, she had lost her sleep, and was, in her own words, "destroyed."

To "divert herself" she asked leave to have visits from her nephew Victor.

He arrived on Sundays after Mass, rosy-cheeked, bare-chested, with the scent of the country he had walked through still about him. She laid her table promptly and they had lunch, sitting opposite each other. She ate as little as possible herself to save expense, but stuffed him with food so generously that at last he went to sleep. At the first stroke of vespers she woke him up, brushed his trousers, fastened his tie, and went to church, leaning on his arm with maternal pride.

Victor was always instructed by his parents to get something out of her—a packet of moist sugar, it might be, a cake of soap, spirits, or even money at times. He brought his things for her to mend and she took over the task, only too glad to have a reason for making him come back.

In August his father took him off on a coasting voyage. It was holiday time, and she was consoled by the arrival of the children. Paul, however, was getting selfish, and Virginie was too old to be called "thou" any longer; this put a constraint and barrier between them.

Victor went to Morlaix, Dunkirk, and Brighton in succession and made Félicité a present on his return from each voyage. It was a box made of shells the first time, a coffee cup the next, and on the third occasion a large gingerbread man. Victor was growing handsome. He was well made, had a hint of a mustache, good honest eyes, and a small leather hat pushed backwards like a pilot's. He entertained her by telling stories embroidered with nautical terms.

On a Monday, July 14, 1819 (she never forgot the date), he told her that he had signed on for the big voyage and next night but one he would take the Honfleur boat and join his schooner, which was to weigh anchor from Havre before long. Perhaps he would be gone two years.

The prospect of this long absence threw Félicité into deep distress; one more good-by she must have, and on the Wednesday evening, when Madame's dinner was finished, she put on her clogs and made short work of the twelve miles between Pont-l'Évêque and Honfleur.

When she arrived in front of the Calvary she took the turn to the right instead of the left, got lost in the timber yards, and retraced her steps; some people to whom she spoke advised her to be quick. She went all round the harbor basin, full of ships, and knocked against hawsers; then the ground fell away, lights flashed across each other, and she thought her wits had left her, for she saw horses up in the sky.

Others were neighing by the quayside, frightened at the sea. They were lifted by a tackle and deposited in a boat, where passengers jostled each other among cider casks, cheese baskets, and sacks of grain; fowls could be heard clucking, the captain swore; and a cabin boy stood leaning over the bows, indifferent to it all. Félicité, who had not recognized him, called "Victor!" and he raised his head; all at once, as she was darting forwards, the gangway was drawn back.

The Honfleur packet, women sing-ing as they hauled it, passed out of harbor. Its framework creaked and the heavy waves whipped its bows. The canvas had swung round, no one could be seen on board now; and on the moon-silvered sea the boat made a black speck which paled gradually, dipped, and vanished.

As Félicité passed by the Calvary she had a wish to commend to God what she cherished most, and she stood there praying a long time with her face bathed in tears and her eyes toward the clouds. The town was asleep, coast guards were walking to and fro; and water poured without cessation through the hole in the sluice, with the noise of a torrent. The clocks struck two.

The convent parlor would not be open before day. If Félicité were late Madame would most certainly be annoyed; and in spite of her desire to kiss the other child she turned home. The maids at the inn were waking up as she came in to Pont-l'Évêque.

So the poor slip of a boy was going to toss for months and months at sea! She had not been frightened by his previous voyages. From England or Brittany you came back safe enough; but America, the colonies, the islands—these were lost in a dim region at the other end of the world.

Félicité's thoughts from that moment ran entirely on her nephew. On sunny days she was harassed by the idea of thirst; when there was a storm she was afraid of the lightning on his account. As she listened to the wind growling in the chimney or carrying off the slates she pictured him lashed by that same tempest, at the top of a shattered mast, with his body thrown backwards under a sheet of foam; or else (with a reminiscence of the illustrated geography) he was being eaten by savages, captured in a wood by monkeys, or dying on a desert shore. And never did she mention her anxieties.

Mme Aubain had anxieties of her own, about her daughter. The good sisters found her an affectionate but delicate child. The slightest emotion unnerved her. She had to give up the piano.

Her mother stipulated for regular letters from the convent. She lost patience one morning when the postman did not come, and walked to and fro in the parlor from her armchair to the window. It was really amazing; not a word for four days!

To console Mme Aubain by her own example Félicité remarked:

"As for me, Madame, it's six months since I heard . . ."

"From whom, pray?"

"Why . . . from my nephew," the servant answered gently.

"Oh! your nephew!" And Mme Aubain resumed her walk with a shrug of the shoulders, as much as to say: "I was not thinking of him! And what is more, it's absurd! A scamp of a cabin boy—what does he matter? . . . whereas my daughter . . . why, just think!"

Félicité, though she had been brought up on harshness, felt indignant with Madame—and then forgot. It seemed the simplest thing in the world to her to lose one's head over the little girl. For her the two children were equally important; a bond in her heart made them one, and their destinies must be the same.

She heard from the chemist that Victor's ship had arrived at Havana. He had read this piece of news in a gazette.

Cigars—they made her imagine Havana as a place where no one does anything but smoke, and there was Victor moving among the Negroes in a cloud of tobacco. Could you, she wondered, "in case you needed," return by land? What was the distance from Pont-l'Évêque? She questioned M. Bourais to find out.

He reached for his atlas and began explaining the longitudes; Félicité's consternation provoked a fine pedantic smile. Finally he marked with his pencil a black, imperceptible point in the indentations of an oval spot, and said as he did so, "Here it is." She went over the map; the maze of colored lines wearied her eyes without conveying anything; and on an invitation from Bourais to tell him her difficulty she begged him to show her the house where Victor was living. Bourais threw up his arms, sneezed, and laughed immensely: a simplicity like hers was a positive joy. And Félicité did not understand the reason; how could she when she expected, very likely, to see the actual image of her nephew—so stunted was her mind!

A fortnight afterwards Liébard came into the kitchen at market time as usual and handed her a letter from her brother-in-law. As neither of them could read she took it to her mistress.

Mme Aubain, who was counting the stitches in her knitting, put the work down by her side, broke the seal of the letter, started, and said in a low voice, with a look of meaning:

"It is bad news . . . that they have to tell you. Your nephew . . ."

He was dead. The letter said no more.

Félicité fell onto a chair, leaning her head against the wainscot; and she closed her eyelids, which suddenly flushed pink. Then with bent forehead, hands hanging, and fixed eyes, she said at intervals:

"Poor little lad! poor little lad!"

Liébard watched her and heaved sighs. Mme Aubain trembled a little. She suggested that Félicité should go to see her sister at Trouville. Félicité answered by a gesture that she had no need.

There was a silence. The worthy Liébard thought it was time for them to withdraw.

Then Félicité said:

"They don't care, not they!"

Her head dropped again; and she took up mechanically, from time to time, the long needles on her worktable.

Women passed in the yard with a barrow of dripping linen.

As she saw them through the windowpanes she remembered her washing; she had put it to soak the day before, today she must wring it out; and she left the room.

Her plank and tub were at the edge of the Toucques. She threw a pile of linen on the bank, rolled up her sleeves, and taking her wooden beater dealt lusty blows whose sound carried to the neighboring gardens. The meadows were empty, the river stirred in the wind; and down below long grasses wavered, like the hair of corpses floating in the water. She kept her grief down and was very brave until the evening; but once in her room she surrendered to it utterly, lying stretched on the mattress with her face in the pillow and her hands clenched against her temples.

Much later she heard, from the captain himself, the circumstances of Victor's end. They had bled him too much at the hospital for yellow fever. Four doctors held him at once. He had died instantly, and the chief had said:

"Bah! there goes another!"

His parents had always been brutal to him. She preferred not to see them again; and they made no advances, either because they forgot her or from the callousness of the wretchedly poor.

Virginie began to grow weaker. Tightness in her chest, coughing, continual fever, and veinings on her cheekbones betrayed some deepseated complaint. M. Poupart had advised a stay in Provence. Mme Aubain determined on it, and would have brought her daughter home at once but for the climate of Pont-l'Évêque.

She made an arrangement with a jobmaster, and he drove her to the convent every Tuesday. There is a terrace in the garden, with a view over the Seine. Virginie took walks there over the fallen vine leaves, on her mother's arm. A shaft of sunlight through the clouds made her blink sometimes, as she gazed at the sails in the distance and the whole horizon from the castle of Tancarville to the lighthouses at Havre. Afterwards they rested in the arbor. Her mother had secured a little cask of excellent Malaga; and Virginie laughing at the idea of getting tipsy, drank a thimbleful of it, no more.

Her strength came back visibly. The autumn glided gently away. Félicité reassured Mme Aubain. But one evening, when she had been out on a commission in the neighborhood, she found M. Poupart's gig at the door. He was in the hall, and Mme Aubain was tying her bonnet.

"Give me my foot warmer, purse, gloves! Quicker, come!"

Virginie had inflammation of the lungs; perhaps it was hopeless.

"Not yet!" said the doctor, and they both got into the carriage under whirling flakes of snow. Night was coming on and it was very cold.

Félicité rushed into the church to light a taper. Then she ran after the gig, came up with it in an hour, and jumped lightly in behind. As she hung on by the fringes a thought came into her mind: "The courtyard has not been shut up; supposing burglars got in!" And she jumped down.

At dawn next day she presented herself at the doctor's. He had come in and started for the country again. Then she waited in the inn, thinking that a letter would come by some hand or other. Finally, when it was twilight, she took the Lisieux coach.

The convent was at the end of a steep lane. When she was about halfway up it she heard strange sounds—a death bell tolling. "It is for someone else," thought Félicité, and she pulled the knocker violently.

After some minutes there was a sound of trailing slippers, the door opened ajar, and a nun appeared.

The good sister, with an air of compunction, said that "she had just passed away." On the instant the bell of St. Leonard's tolled twice as fast.

Félicité went up to the second floor.

From the doorway she saw Virginie stretched on her back, with her hands joined, her mouth open, and head thrown back under a black crucifix that leaned toward her, between curtains that hung stiffly, less pale than was her face. Mme Aubain, at the foot of the bed which she clasped with her arms, was choking with sobs of agony. The mother superior stood on the right. Three candlesticks on the chest of drawers made spots of red, and the mist came whitely through the windows. Nuns came and took Mme Aubain away.

For two nights Félicité never left the dead child. She repeated the same prayers, sprinkled holy water over the sheets, came and sat down again, and watched her. At the end of the first vigil she noticed that the face had grown yellow, the lips turned blue, the nose was sharper, and the eyes sunk in. She kissed them several times, and would not have been immensely surprised if Virginie had opened them again; to minds like hers the supernatural is quite simple. She made the girl's toilette, wrapped her in her shroud, lifted her down into her bier, put a garland on her head, and spread out her hair. It was fair, and extraordinarily long for her age. Félicité cut off a big lock and slipped half of it into her bosom, determined that she should never part with it.

The body was brought back to Pont-l'Évêque, as Mme Aubain intended; she followed the hearse in a closed carriage.

It took another three quarters of an hour after the Mass to reach the cemetery. Paul walked in front, sobbing. M. Bourais was behind, and then came the chief residents, the women shrouded in black mantles, and Félicité. She thought of her nephew; and because she had not been able to pay these honors to him her grief was doubled, as though the one were being buried with the other.

Mme Aubain's despair was boundless. It was against God that she first rebelled, thinking it unjust of Him to have taken her daughter from her—she had never done evil and her conscience was so clear! Ah, no! —she ought to have taken Virginie off to the south. Other doctors would have saved her. She accused herself now, wanted to join her child, and broke into cries of distress in the middle of her dreams. One dream haunted her above all. Her husband, dressed as a sailor, was returning from a long voyage, and shedding tears he told her that he had been ordered to take Virginie away. Then they consulted how to hide her somewhere.

She came in once from the garden quite upset. A moment ago—and she pointed out the place—the father and daughter had appeared to her, standing side by side, and they did nothing, but they looked at her.

For several months after this she stayed inertly in her room. Félicité lectured her gently; she must live for her son's sake, and for the other, in remembrance of "her."

"Her," answered Mme Aubain, as though she were just waking up. "Ah, yes! . . . yes! . . . You do not forget her!" This was an allusion to the cemetery, where she was strictly forbidden to go.

Félicité went there every day.

Precisely at four she skirted the houses, climbed the hill, opened the gate, and came to Virginie's grave. It was a little column of pink marble with a stone underneath and a garden plot enclosed by chains. The beds were hidden under a coverlet of flowers. She watered their leaves, freshened the gravel, and knelt down to break up the earth better. When Mme Aubain was able to come there she felt a relief and a sort of consolation.

Then years slipped away, one like another, and their only episodes were the great festivals as they recurred—Easter, the Assumption, All Saints' Day. Household occurrences marked dates that were referred to afterwards. In 1825, for instance,

two glaziers whitewashed the hall; in 1827 a piece of the roof fell into the courtyard and nearly killed a man. In the summer of 1828 it was Madame's turn to offer the consecrated bread; Bourais, about this time, mysteriously absented himself; and one by one the old acquaintances passed away: Guyot, Liébard, Mme Lechaptois, Robelin, and Uncle Gremanville, who had been paralyzed for a long time.

One night the driver of the mail coach announced the Revolution of July in Pont-l'Évêque. A new subprefect was appointed a few days later—Baron de Larsonnière, who had been consul in America, and brought with him, besides his wife, a sister-in-law and three young ladies, already growing up. They were to be seen about on their lawn, in loose blouses, and they had a Negro and a parrot. They paid a call on Mme Aubain which she did not fail to return. The moment they were seen in the distance Félicité ran to let her mistress know. But only one thing could really move her feelings—the letters from her son.

He was swallowed up in a tavern life and could follow no career. She paid his debts, he made new ones; and the sighs that Mme Aubain uttered as she sat knitting by the window reached Félicité at her spinning wheel in the kitchen.

They took walks together along the espaliered wall, always talking of Virginie and wondering if such and such a thing would have pleased her and what, on some occasion, she would have been likely to say.

All her small belongings filled a cupboard in the two-bedded room. Mme Aubain inspected them as seldom as she could. One summer day she made up her mind to it—and some moths flew out of the wardrobe.

Virginie's dresses were in a row underneath a shelf, on which there were three dolls, some hoops, a set of toy pots and pans, and the basin that she used. They took out her petticoats as well, and the stockings and handkerchiefs, and laid them out on the two beds before folding them up again. The sunshine lit up these poor things, bringing out their stains and the creases made by the body's movements. The air was warm and blue, a blackbird warbled, life seemed bathed in a deep sweetness. They found a little plush hat with thick, chestnut-colored pile; but it was eaten all over by moths. Félicité begged it for her own. Their eyes met fixedly and filled with tears; at last the mistress opened her arms, the servant threw herself into them, and they embraced each other, satisfying their grief in a kiss that made them equal.

It was the first time in their lives, Mme Aubain's nature not being expansive. Félicité was as grateful as though she had received a favor, and cherished her mistress from that moment with the devotion of an animal and a religious worship.

The kindness of her heart unfolded.

When she heard the drums of a marching regiment in the street she posted herself at the door with a pitcher of cider and asked the soldiers to drink. She nursed cholera patients and protected the Polish refugees; one of these even declared that he wished to marry her. They quarreled, however; for when she came back from the Angelus one morning she found that he had got into her kitchen and made himself a vinegar salad which he was quietly eating.

After the Poles came Father Colmiche, an old man who was supposed to have committed atrocities in '93. He lived by the side of the river in the ruins of a pigsty. The little boys watched him through the cracks in the wall, and threw pebbles at him which fell on the pallet where he lay constantly shaken by a catarrh; his hair was very long, his eyes inflamed, and there was a tumor on his arm bigger than his head. She got him some linen and tried to clean up his miserable hole; her dream was to establish him in the bakehouse, without letting him annoy Madame. When the tumor burst she dressed it every day; sometimes she brought him cake, and would put him in the sunshine on a truss of straw. The poor old man, slobbering and trembling, thanked her in his worn-out voice, was terrified that he might lose her, and stretched out his hands when he saw her go away. He died; and she had a Mass said for the repose of his soul.

That very day a great happiness befell her; just at dinnertime appeared Mme de Larsonnière's Negro, carrying the parrot in its cage, with perch, chain, and padlock. A note from the baroness informed Mme Aubain that her husband had been raised to a prefecture and they were starting that evening; she begged her to accept the bird as a memento and mark of her regard.

For a long time he had absorbed Félicité's imagination, because he came from America; and that name reminded her of Victor, so much so that she made inquiries of the Negro. She had once gone so far as to say "How Madame would enjoy having him!"

The Negro repeated the remark to his mistress; and as she could not take the bird away with her she chose this way of getting rid of him.

IV

His name was Loulou. His body was green and the tips of his wings rose-pink; his forehead was blue and his throat golden.

But he had the tiresome habits of biting his perch, tearing out his feathers, sprinkling his dirt about, and spattering the water of his tub. He annoyed Mme Aubain, and she gave him to Félicité for good.

She endeavored to train him; soon he could repeat, "Nice boy! Your servant, sir! Good morning, Marie!" He was placed by the side of the door, and astonished several people by not answering to the name Jacquot, for all parrots are called Jacquot. People compared him to a turkey and a log of wood, and stabbed Félicité to the heart each time. Strange obstinacy on Loulou's part!—directly you looked at him he refused to speak.

None the less he was eager for society; for on Sundays, while the Rochefeuille ladies, M. de Houppeville, and new familiars—Onfroy the apothecary, Monsieur Varin, and Captain Mathieu—were playing their game of cards, he beat the windows with his wings and threw himself about so frantically that they could not hear each other speak.

Bourais' face, undoubtedly, struck him as extremely droll. Directly he saw it he began to laugh—and laugh with all his might. His peals rang through the courtyard and were repeated by the echo; the neighbors came to their windows and laughed too; while M. Bourais, gliding along under the wall to escape the parrot's eye, and hiding his profile with his hat, got to the river and then entered

by the garden gate. There was a lack of tenderness in the looks which he darted at the bird.

Loulou had been slapped by the butcher boy for making so free as to plunge his head into his basket; and since then he was always trying to nip him through his shirt. Fabu threatened to wring his neck, although he was not cruel, for all his tattooed arms and large whiskers. Far from it; he really rather liked the parrot, and in a jovial humor even wanted to teach him to swear. Félicité, who was alarmed by such proceedings, put the bird in the kitchen. His little chain was taken off and he roamed about the house.

His way of going downstairs was to lean on each step with the curve of his beak, raise the right foot, and then the left; and Félicité was afraid that these gymnastics brought on fits of giddiness. He fell ill and could not talk or eat any longer. There was a growth under his tongue, such as fowls have sometimes. She cured him by tearing the pellicle off with her fingernails. M. Paul was thoughtless enough one day to blow some cigar smoke into his nostrils, and another time when Mme Lormeau was teasing him with the end of her umbrella he snapped at the ferrule. Finally he got lost.

Félicité had put him on the grass to refresh him, and gone away for a minute, and when she came back— no sign of the parrot! She began by looking for him in the shrubs, by the waterside, and over the roofs, without listening to her mistress's cries of "Take care, do! You are out of your wits!" Then she investigated all the gardens in Pont-l'Évêque, and stopped the passers-by. "You don't ever happen to have seen my parrot, by any chance, do you?" And she gave a description of the parrot to those who did not know him. Suddenly, behind the mills at the foot of the hill she thought she could make out something green that fluttered. But on the top of the hill there was nothing. A hawker assured her that he had come across the parrot just before, at Saint-Melaine, in Mère Simon's shop. She rushed there; they had no idea of what she meant. At last she came home exhausted, with her slippers in shreds and despair in her soul; and as she was sitting in the middle of the garden seat at Madame's side, telling the whole story of her efforts, a light weight dropped on to her shoulder—it was Loulou! What on earth had he been doing? Taking a walk in the neighborhood, perhaps!

She had some trouble in recovering from this, or rather never did recover. As the result of a chill she had an attack of quinsy, and soon afterwards an earache. Three years later she was deaf; and she spoke very loud, even in church. Though Félicité's sins might have been published in every corner of the diocese without dishonor to her or scandal to anybody, his reverence the priest thought it right now to hear her confession in the sacristy only.

Imaginary noises in the head completed her upset. Her mistress often said to her, "Heavens! how stupid you are!" "Yes, Madame," she replied, and looked about for something.

Her little circle of ideas grew still narrower; the peal of church bells and the lowing of cattle ceased to exist for her. All living beings moved as silently as ghosts. One sound only reached her ears now—the parrot's voice.

Loulou, as though to amuse her, reproduced the click-clack of the turnspit, the shrill call of a man selling fish, and the noise of the saw in the joiner's house opposite; when the bell rang he imitated Mme Aubain's "Félicité! the door! the door!"

They carried on conversations, he endlessly reciting the three phrases in his repertory, to which she replied with words that were just as disconnected but uttered what was in her heart. Loulou was almost a son and a lover to her in her isolated state. He climbed up her fingers, nibbled at her lips, and clung to her kerchief; and when she bent her forehead and shook her head gently to and fro, as nurses do, the great wings of her bonnet and the bird's wings quivered together.

When the clouds massed and the thunder rumbled Loulou broke into cries, perhaps remembering the downpour in his native forests. The streaming rain made him absolutely mad; he fluttered wildly about, dashed up to the ceiling, upset everything, and went out through the window to dabble in the garden; but he was back quickly to perch on one of the firedogs and hopped about to dry himself, exhibiting his tail and his beak in turn.

One morning in the terrible winter of 1837 she had put him in front of the fireplace because of the cold. She found him dead, in the middle of his cage: head downwards, with his claws in the wires. He had died from congestion, no doubt. But Félicité thought he had been poisoned with parsley, and though there was no proof of any kind her suspicions inclined to Fabu.

She wept so piteously that her mistress said to her, "Well, then, have him stuffed!"

She asked advice from the chemist, who had always been kind to the parrot. He wrote to Havre, and a person called Fallacher undertook the business. But as parcels sometimes got lost in the coach she decided to take the parrot as far as Honfleur herself.

Along the sides of the road were leafless apple trees, one after the other. Ice covered the ditches. Dogs barked about the farms; and Félicité, with her hands under her cloak, her little black sabots and her basket, walked briskly in the middle of the road.

She crossed the forest, passed High Oak, and reached St. Gatien.

A cloud of dust rose behind her, and in it a mail coach, carried away by the steep hill, rushed down at full gallop like a hurricane. Seeing this woman who would not get out of the way, the driver stood up in front and the postilion shouted too. He could not hold in his four horses, which increased their pace, and the two leaders were grazing her when he threw them to one side with a jerk of the reins. But he was wild with rage, and lifting his arm as he passed at full speed, gave her such a lash from waist to neck with his big whip that she fell on her back.

Her first act, when she recovered consciousness, was to open her basket. Loulou was happily none the worse. She felt a burn in her right cheek, and when she put her hands against it they were red; the blood was flowing.

She sat down on a heap of stones and bound up her face with her handkerchief. Then she ate a crust of bread which she had put in the basket as a precaution, and found a consolation for her wound in gazing at the bird.

When she reached the crest of Ecquemauville she saw the Honfleur lights sparkling in the night sky like a company of stars; beyond, the sea stretched dimly. Then a faintness overtook her and she stopped; her wretched childhood, the disillusion of her first love, her nephew's going away, and Virginie's death all came back to her at once like the waves of an oncoming tide, rose to her throat, and choked her.

Afterwards, at the boat, she made a point of speaking to the captain, begging him to take care of the parcel, though she did not tell him what was in it.

Fellacher kept the parrot a long time. He was always promising it for the following week. After six months he announced that a packing case had started, and then nothing more was heard of it. It really seemed as though Loulou was never coming back. "Ah, they have stolen him!" she thought.

He arrived at last, and looked superb. There he was, erect upon a branch which screwed into a mahogany socket, with a foot in the air and his head on one side, biting a nut which the bird stuffer—with a taste for impressiveness—had gilded.

Félicité shut him up in her room. It was a place to which few people were admitted, and held so many religious objects and miscellaneous things that it looked like a chapel and bazaar in one.

A big cupboard impeded you as you opened the door. Opposite the window commanding the garden a little round one looked into the court; there was a table by the folding bed with a water jug, two combs, and a cube of blue soap in a chipped plate. On the walls hung rosaries, medals, several benign Virgins, and a holy-water vessel made out of coconut; on the chest of drawers, which was covered with a cloth like an altar, was the shell box that Victor had given her, and after that a watering can, a toy balloon, exercise books, the illustrated geography, and a pair of young lady's boots; and, fastened by its ribbons to the nail of the looking glass, hung the little plush hat! Félicité carried observances of this kind so far as to keep one of Monsieur's frock coats. All the old rubbish which Mme Aubain did not want any longer she laid hands on for her room. That was why there were artificial flowers along the edge of the chest of drawers and a portrait of the Comte d'Artois in the little window recess.

With the aid of a bracket Loulou was established over the chimney, which jutted into the room. Every morning when she woke up she saw him there in the dawning light, and recalled old days and the smallest details of insignificant acts in a deep quietness which knew no pain.

Holding, as she did, no communication with anyone, Félicité lived as insensibly as if she were walking in her sleep. The Corpus Christi processions roused her to life again. Then she went round begging mats and candlesticks from the neighbors to decorate the altar they put up in the street.

In church she was always gazing at the Holy Ghost in the window, and observed that there was something of the parrot in him. The likeness was still clearer, she thought, on a crude color print representing the baptism of Our Lord. With his purple wings and emerald body he was the very image of Loulou.

She bought him, and hung him up instead of the Comte d'Artois, so that she could see them both together in one glance. They were linked in her thoughts; and the parrot was consecrated by his association with the Holy Ghost, which became more vivid to her eye and more intelligible. The Father could not have chosen to express Himself through a dove, for such creatures cannot speak; it must have been one of Loulou's ancestors, surely. And though Félicité looked at the picture while she said her prayers she swerved a little from time to time toward the parrot.

She wanted to join the Ladies of the Virgin, but Mme Aubain dissuaded her.

And then a great event loomed up before them—Paul's marriage.

He had been a solicitor's clerk to begin with, and then tried business, the Customs, the Inland Revenue, and made efforts, even, to get into the Rivers and Forests. By an inspiration from heaven he had suddenly, at thirty-six, discovered his real line—the Registrar's Office. And there he showed such marked capacity that an inspector had offered him his daughter's hand and promised him his influence.

So Paul, grown serious, brought the lady to see his mother.

She sniffed at the ways of Pont-l'Évêque, gave herself great airs, and wounded Félicité's feelings. Mme Aubain was relieved at her departure.

The week after came news of M. Bourais' death in an inn in Lower Brittany. The rumor of suicide was confirmed, and doubts arose as to his honesty. Mme Aubain studied his accounts, and soon found out the whole tale of his misdoings—embezzled arrears, secret sales of wood, forged receipts, etc. Besides that he had an illegitimate child, and "relations with a person at Dozulé."

These shameful facts distressed her greatly. In March, 1853, she was seized with a pain in the chest;

her tongue seemed to be covered with film, and leeches did not ease the difficult breathing. On the ninth evening of her illness she died, just at seventy-two.

She passed as being younger, owing to the bands of brown hair which framed her pale, pockmarked face. There were few friends to regret her, for she had a stiffness of manner which kept people at a distance.

But Félicité mourned for her as one seldom mourns for a master. It upset her ideas and seemed contrary to the order of things, impossible and monstrous, that Madame should die before her.

Ten days afterwards, which was the time it took to hurry there from Besançon, the heirs arrived. The daughter-in-law ransacked the drawers, chose some furniture, and sold the rest; and then they went back to their registering.

Madame's armchair, her small round table, her foot warmer, and the eight chairs were gone! Yellow patches in the middle of the panels showed where the engravings had hung. They had carried off the two little beds and the mattresses, and all Virginie's belongings had disappeared from the cupboard. Félicité went from floor to floor dazed with sorrow.

The next day there was a notice on the door, and the apothecary shouted in her ear that the house was for sale.

She tottered, and was obliged to sit down. What distressed her most of all was to give up her room, so suitable as it was for poor Loulou. She enveloped him with a look of anguish when she was imploring the Holy Ghost, and formed the idolatrous habit of kneeling in front of the parrot to say her prayers. Some-

times the sun shone in at the attic window and caught his glass eye, and a great luminous ray shot out of it and put her in an ecstasy.

She had a pension of fifteen pounds a year which her mistress had left her. The garden gave her a supply of vegetables. As for clothes, she had enough to last her to the end of her days, and she economized in candles by going to bed at dusk.

She hardly ever went out, as she did not like passing the dealer's shop, where some of the old furniture was exposed for sale. Since her fit of giddiness she dragged one leg; and as her strength was failing Mère Simon, whose grocery business had collapsed, came every morning to split the wood and pump water for her.

Her eyes grew feeble. The shutters ceased to be thrown open. Years and years passed, and the house was neither let nor sold.

Félicité never asked for repairs because she was afraid of being sent away. The boards on the roof rotted; her bolster was wet for a whole winter. After Easter she spat blood.

Then Mère Simon called in a doctor. Félicité wanted to know what was the matter with her. But she was too deaf to hear, and the only word which reached her was "pneumonia." It was a word she knew, and she answered softly, "Ah! like Madame," thinking it natural that she should follow her mistress.

The time for the festal shrines was coming near. The first one was always at the bottom of the hill, the second in front of the post office, and the third toward the middle of the street. There was some rivalry in the matter of this one, and the women of the parish ended by choosing Mme Aubain's courtyard.

The hard breathing and fever increased. Félicité was vexed at doing nothing for the altar. If only she could at least have put something there! Then she thought of the parrot. The neighbors objected that it would not be decent. But the priest gave her permission, which so intensely delighted her that she begged him to accept Loulou, her sole possession, when she died.

From Tuesday to Saturday, the eve of the festival, she coughed more often. By the evening her face had shriveled, her lips stuck to her gums, and she had vomitings; and at twilight next morning, feeling herself very low, she sent for a priest.

Three kindly women were round her during the extreme unction. Then she announced that she must speak to Fabu. He arrived in his Sunday clothes, by no means at his ease in the funeral atmosphere.

"Forgive me," she said, with an effort to stretch out her arm: "I thought it was you who had killed him."

What did she mean by such stories? She suspected him of murder—a man like him! He waxed indignant, and was on the point of making a row.

"There," said the woman, "she is no longer in her senses, you can see it well enough!"

Félicité spoke to shadows of her own from time to time. The women went away, and Mère Simon had breakfast. A little later she took Loulou and brought him close to Félicité with the words:

"Come, now, say good-by to him!"

Loulou was not a corpse, but the worms devoured him; one of his wings was broken, and the tow was coming out of his stomach. But she was blind now; she kissed him on the forehead and kept him close

against her cheek. Mère Simon took him back from her to put him on the altar.

V

Summer scents came up from the meadows; flies buzzed; the sun made the river glitter and heated the slates. Mère Simon came back into the room and fell softly asleep.

She woke at the noise of bells; the people were coming out from vespers. Félicité's delirium subsided. She thought of the procession and saw it as if she had been there.

All the school children, the church singers, and the firemen walked on the pavement, while in the middle of the road the verger armed with his hallebard and the beadle with a large cross advanced in front. Then came the schoolmaster, with an eye on the boys, and the sister, anxious about her little girls; three of the daintiest, with angelic curls, scattered rose petals in the air; the deacon controlled the band with outstretched arms; and two censer bearers turned back at every step toward the Holy Sacrament, which was borne by monsieur the curé, wearing his beautiful chasuble, under a canopy of dark-red velvet held up by four churchwardens. A crowd of people pressed behind, between the white cloths covering the house walls, and they reached the bottom of the hill.

A cold sweat moistened Félicité's temples. Mère Simon sponged her with a piece of linen, saying to herself that one day she would have to go that way.

The hum of the crowd increased, was very loud for an instant, and then went further away.

A fusillade shook the windowpanes. It was the postilions saluting the monstrance. Félicité rolled her eyes and said as audibly as she could: "Does he look well?" The parrot was weighing on her mind.

Her agony began. A death rattle that grew more and more convulsed made her sides heave. Bubbles of froth came at the corners of her mouth and her whole body trembled.

Soon the booming of the ophicleides, the high voices of the children, and the deep voices of the men were distinguishable. At intervals all was silent, and the tread of feet, deadened by the flowers they walked on, sounded like a flock pattering on grass.

The clergy appeared in the courtyard. Mère Simon clambered on to a chair to reach the attic window, and so looked down straight upon the shrine. Green garlands hung over the altar, which was decked with a flounce of English lace. In the middle was a small frame with relics in it; there were two orange trees at the corners, and all along stood silver candlesticks and china vases, with sunflowers, lilies, peonies, foxgloves, and tufts of hortensia. This heap of blazing color slanted from the level of the altar to the carpet which went on over the pavement; and some rare objects caught the eye. There was a silver-gilt sugar basin with a crown of violets; pendants of Alençon stone glittered on the moss, and two Chinese screens displayed their landscapes. Loulou was hidden under roses, and showed nothing but his blue forehead, like a plaque of lapis lazuli.

The churchwardens, singers, and children took their places round the three sides of the court. The priest went slowly up the steps, and placed his great, radiant golden sun upon the lace. Everyone knelt down. There was a deep silence; and the censers glided to and fro on the full swing of their chains.

An azure vapor rose up into Félicité's room. Her nostrils met it; she inhaled it sensuously, mystically; and then closed her eyes. Her lips smiled. The beats of her heart lessened one by one, vaguer each time and softer, as a fountain sinks, an echo disappears; and when she sighed her last breath she thought she saw an opening in the heavens, and a gigantic parrot hovering above her head.

Guy de Maupassant
1850-1893

WHEN the literary great were gathering at Flaubert's house, a young man, conspicuous for physique rather than culture, used to come in from rowing on the Seine to listen to the conversation. He was Guy de Maupassant, and he too wanted to write, but Flaubert saw no particular promise in him, and the others thought him only an athlete. For seven years, however, just because he happened to be a friend of Maupassant's mother, Flaubert put the young man through a severe apprenticeship, and what was the astonishment of all when Maupassant's first published story came out a masterpiece! The story was the famous "Boule de Suif" ("Ball-of-Fat").

Where Flaubert wrote a single story, Maupassant wrote a dozen. Where the master strained for a single effect, the pupil was a fountain of freedom and variety. Maupassant wrote almost three hundred short stories in ten years, rapid, concise tales, strong, brutal, often obscene. He wrote only of what he perceived through his senses—fields, bodies, clothes, food. No theories or moral prejudices clouded the crystal-clear vision of his best work. He too had a great influence on the generation of writers to come, and to many he still remains the perfect master of the short story.

Maupassant lived and loved too hard, and a few years before he died, he was committed to an insane asylum.

Two Little Soldiers

BY GUY DE MAUPASSANT

EVERY Sunday, the moment they were dismissed, the two little soldiers made off. Once outside the barracks, they struck out to the right through Courbevoie, walking with long rapid strides, as though they were on a march.

When they were beyond the last of the houses, they slackened pace along the bare, dusty roadway which goes toward Bézons.

They were both small and thin, and looked quite lost in their coats, which were too big and too long. Their sleeves hung down over their hands, and they found their enormous red breeches, which compelled them to waddle, very much in the way. Under their stiff, high helmets their faces had little character—two poor, sallow Breton faces, simple with an almost animal simplicity, and with gentle and quiet blue eyes.

They never conversed during these walks, but went straight on, each with the same thought in his head. This thought atoned for the lack of conversation; it was this—that just inside the little wood near Les Champioux they had found a place which reminded them of their own country, where they could feel happy again.

When they arrived under the trees where the roads from Colombes and from Chatou cross, they would take off their heavy helmets and wipe their foreheads. They always halted on the Bézons bridge to look at the Seine, and would remain there two or three minutes, bent double, leaning on the parapet.

Sometimes they would gaze out over the great basin of Argenteuil, where the skiffs might be seen scudding, with their white, careening sails, recalling perhaps the look of the Breton waters, the harbor of Vanne, near which they lived, and the fishing boats standing out across the Morbihan to the open sea.

Just beyond the Seine they bought their provisions from a sausage merchant, a baker, and a wineseller. A piece of blood pudding, four sous' worth of bread, and a liter of *petit bleu* constituted the provisions, which they carried off in their handkerchiefs. After they had left Bézons they traveled slowly and began to talk.

In front of them a barren plain studded with clumps of trees led to the wood, to the little wood which had seemed to them to resemble the one at Kermarivan. Grainfields and hayfields bordered the narrow path, which lost itself in the young green-

ness of the crops, and Jean Kerderen
would always say to Luc le Ganidec:
"It looks like it does near Plouni-
von."

"Yes; exactly."

Side by side they strolled, their
souls filled with vague memories of
their own country, with awakened
images as naïve as the pictures on
the colored broadsheets which you
buy for a penny. They kept on
recognizing, as it were, now a corner
of a field, a hedge, a bit of moorland,
now a crossroad, now a granite cross.
Then, too, they would always stop
beside a certain landmark, a great
stone, because it looked something
like the cromlech at Locneuven.

Every Sunday on arriving at the
first clump of trees Luc le Ganidec
would cut a switch, a hazel switch,
and begin gently to peel off the
bark, thinking meanwhile of the folk
at home. Jean Kerderen carried the
provisions.

From time to time Luc would
mention a name, or recall some deed
of their childhood in a few brief
words, which caused long thoughts.
And their own country, their dear,
distant country, recaptured them
little by little, seizing on their imaginations, and sending to them from
afar her shapes, her sounds, her well-
known prospects, her odors—odors
of the green lands where the salt
sea air was blowing.

No longer conscious of the ex-
halations of the Parisian stables, on
which the earth of the *banlieue* fat-
tens, they scented the perfume of the
flowering broom, which the salt
breeze of the open sea plucks and
bears away. And the sails of the
boats from the riverbanks seemed
like the white wings of the coasting
vessels seen beyond the great plain
which extended from their homes to
the very margin of the sea.

They walked with short steps, Luc
le Ganidec and Jean Kerderen, content and sad, haunted by a sweet
melancholy, by the lingering, ever-
present sorrow of a caged animal
who remembers his liberty.

By the time that Luc had stripped
the slender wand of its bark they
reached the corner of the wood where
every Sunday they took breakfast.
They found the two bricks which
they kept hidden in the thicket, and
kindled a little fire of twigs, over
which to roast the blood pudding at
the end of a bayonet.

When they had had breakfast,
eaten their bread to the last crumb,
and drunk their wine to the last
drop, they remained seated side by
side upon the grass, saying nothing,
their eyes on the distance, their eyelids drooping, their fingers crossed
as at Mass, their red legs stretched
out beside the poppies of the field.
And the leather of their helmets and
the brass of their buttons glittered in
the ardent sun, making the larks,
which sang and hovered above their
heads, cease in mid-song.

Toward noon they began to turn
their eyes from time to time in the
direction of the village of Bézons,
because the girl with the cow was
coming. She passed by them every
Sunday on her way to milk and
change the pasture of her cow—the
only cow in this district which ever
went out of the stable to grass. It
was pastured in a narrow field along
the edge of the wood a little farther
on.

They soon perceived the girl, the
only human being within vision, and
were gladdened by the brilliant reflections thrown off by the tin milk
pail under the rays of the sun. They
never talked about her. They were
simply glad to see her, without understanding why.

She was a big strong wench with red hair, burned by the heat of sunny days, a sturdy product of the environs of Paris.

Once, finding them seated in the place, she said:

"Good morning. You two are always here, aren't you?"

Luc le Ganidec, the bolder, stammered:

"Yes, we come to rest."

That was all. But the next Sunday she laughed on seeing them, laughed with a protecting benevolence and a feminine keenness which knew well enough that they were bashful. And she asked:

"What are you doing there? Are you trying to see the grass grow?"

Luc was cheered up by this, and smiled likewise: "Maybe we are."

"That's pretty slow work," said she.

He answered, still laughing: "Well, yes, it is."

She went on. But coming back with a milk pail full of milk, she stopped again before them, and said:

"Would you like a little? It will taste like home."

With the instinctive feeling that they were of the same peasant race as she, being herself perhaps also far away from home, she had divined and touched the spot.

They were both touched. Then with some difficulty, she managed to make a little milk run into the neck of the glass bottle in which they carried their wine. And Luc drank first, with little swallows, stopping every minute to see whether he had drunk more than his half. Then he handed the bottle to Jean.

She stood upright before them, her hands on her hips, her pail on the ground at her feet, glad at the pleasure which she had given.

Then she departed, shouting:

"*Allons*, adieu! Till next Sunday!"

And as long as they could see her at all, they followed with their eyes her tall silhouette, which faded, growing smaller and smaller, seeming to sink into the verdure of the fields.

When they were leaving the barracks the week after, Jean said to Luc:

"Oughtn't we to buy her something good?"

They were in great embarrassment before the problem of the choice of a delicacy for the girl with the cow. Luc was of the opinion that a little tripe would be the best, but Jean prefered some *berlingots* because he was fond of sweets. His choice fairly made him enthusiastic, and they bought at a grocer's two sous' worth of white and red candies.

They ate their breakfast more rapidly than usual, being nervous with expectation.

Jean saw her first. "There she is!" he cried. Luc added: "Yes, there she is."

While yet some distance off she laughed at seeing them. Then she cried:

"Is everything going as you like it?"

And in unison they asked:

"Are you getting on all right?"

Then she conversed, talked to them of simple things in which they felt an interest—of the weather, of the crops, and of her master.

They were afraid to offer her the candies, which were slowly melting away in Jean's pocket.

At last Luc grew bold, and murmured:

"We have brought you something."

She demanded, "What is it? Tell me."

Then Jean, blushing up to his ears, managed to get at the little paper cornucopia, and held it out.

She began to eat the little bon-
bons, rolling them from one cheek to
the other where they made little
round lumps. The two soldiers,
seated before her, gazed at her with
emotion and delight.

Then she went to milk her cow,
and once more gave them some milk
on coming back.

They thought of her all the week;
several times they even spoke of
her. The next Sunday she sat down
with them for a little longer talk; and
all three, seated side by side, their
eyes lost in the distance, clasping
their knees with their hands, told the
small doings, the minute details of
life in the villages where they had
been born, while over there the cow,
seeing that the milkmaid had stopped
on her way, stretched out toward
her its heavy head with its dripping
nostrils, and gave a long low to call
her.

Soon the girl consented to eat a bit
of bread with them and drink a
mouthful of wine. She often brought
them plums in her pocket, for the
season of plums had come. Her presence sharpened the wits of the two
little Breton soldiers, and they chattered like two birds.

But, one Tuesday, Luc le Ganidec
asked for leave—a thing which had
never happened before—and he did
not return until ten o'clock at night.
Jean racked his brains uneasily for a
reason for his comrade's going out
in this way.

The next Thursday Luc, having
borrowed ten sous from his bed-
fellow, again asked and obtained permission to leave the barracks for
several hours. When he set off with
Jean on their Sunday walk his manner was very queer, quite restless,
and quite changed. Kerderen did not
understand, but he vaguely suspected

something without divining what it
could be.

They did not say a word to one
another until they reached their
usual halting place, where, from
their constant sitting in the same
spot, the grass was quite worn away.
They ate their breakfast slowly.
Neither of them felt hungry.

Before long the girl appeared. As
on every Sunday, they watched her
coming. When she was quite near,
Luc rose and made two steps forward.
She put her milk pail on the ground
and kissed him. She kissed him passionately, throwing her arms about
his neck, without noticing Jean, without remembering that he was there,
without even seeing him.

And he sat there desperate, poor
Jean, so desperate that he did not
understand, his soul quite overwhelmed, his heart bursting, but not
yet understanding himself. Then the
girl seated herself beside Luc, and
they began to chatter.

Jean did not look at them. He now
divined why his comrade had gone
out twice during the week, and he
felt within him a burning grief, a
kind of wound, that sense of rending which is caused by treason.

Luc and the girl went off together
to change the position of the cow.
Jean followed them with his eyes.
He saw them departing side by side.
The red breeches of his comrade
made a bright spot on the road. It
was Luc who picked up the mallet
and hammered down the stake to
which they tied the beast.

The girl stooped to milk her, while
he stroked the cow's sharp spine with
a careless hand. Then they left the
milk pail on the grass, and went
deep into the wood.

Jean saw nothing but the wall of
leaves where they had entered; and
he felt himself so troubled that if he

had tried to rise he would certainly have fallen. He sat motionless, stupefied by astonishment and suffering, with an agony which was simple but deep. He wanted to cry, to run away, to hide himself, never to see anybody any more.

Soon he saw them issuing from the thicket. They returned slowly, holding each other's hands as in the villages do those who are promised. It was Luc who carried the pail.

They kissed one another again before they separated, and the girl went off after having thrown Jean a friendly "Good evening" and a smile which was full of meaning. Today she no longer thought of offering him any milk.

The two little soldiers sat side by side, motionless as usual, silent and calm, their placid faces betraying nothing of all which troubled their hearts. The sun fell on them. Sometimes the cow lowed, looking at them from afar.

At their usual hour they rose to go back. Luc cut a switch. Jean carried the empty bottle to return it to the wineseller at Bézons. Then they sallied out upon the bridge, and, as they did every Sunday, stopped several minutes in the middle to watch the water flowing.

Jean leaned, leaned more and more, over the iron railing, as though he saw in the current something which attracted him. Luc said: "Are you trying to drink?" Just as he uttered the last word Jean's head overbalanced his body, his legs described a circle in the air, and the little blue and red soldier fell in a heap, struck the water, and disappeared.

Luc, his tongue paralyzed with anguish, tried in vain to shout. Farther down he saw something stir; then the head of his comrade rose to the surface of the river and sank immediately. Farther still he again perceived a hand, a single hand, which issued from the stream and then disappeared. That was all.

The bargemen who dragged the river did not find the body that day.

Luc set out alone for the barracks, going at a run, his soul filled with despair. He told of the accident, with tears in his eyes, and a husky voice, blowing his nose again and again: "He leaned over—he—he leaned over—so far—so far that his head turned a somersault; and—and—so he fell—he fell ——"

Choked with emotion, he could say no more. If he had only known!

Alphonse Daudet
1840-1897

DAUDET, "great little novelist," as he was called, had the
light touch. He was strongly influenced, like all his French
contemporaries, by Flaubert, but his own sweetness and
charm showed through in spite of himself. He was also a
follower of Dickens, and was accused of imitating him. In
fact his first novel, about the miseries of an unhappy childhood, is in typical Dickens style. But the special grace of
it remains pure Daudet. His stories are sentimental, comical,
pathetic, a mixture of laughter and tears, and—particularly
Lettres de mon moulin—have probably done more than any
others to make French endurable to beginning students.

Daudet was born in Nîmes, the son of a silk manufacturer,
had his schooling in Lyon, and as a young man went to
Paris. Here he became more Parisian than the Parisians. As
secretary to the Duc de Morny he was very much of the *haut
monde*. He lived an intense artistic life, and his marriage to
Julia Allard, also a writer, was one of complete intellectual
harmony.

On Daudet, as on Maupassant and Flaubert, the Franco-
Prussian War left its mark. "The Last Lesson" concerns those
tragic days of the 1870's, but it might as easily have been the
1940's.

The Last Lesson

BY ALPHONSE DAUDET

I STARTED for school very late that morning and was in great dread of a scolding, especially because M. Hamel had said that he would question us on participles, and I did not know the first word about them. For a moment I thought of running away and spending the day out-of-doors. It was so warm, so bright! The birds were chirping at the edge of the woods; and in the open field back of the sawmill the Prussian soldiers were drilling. It was all much more tempting than the rule for participles, but I had the strength to resist, and hurried off to school.

When I passed the town hall there was a crowd in front of the bulletin board. For the last two years all our bad news had come from there—the lost battles, the draft, the orders of the commanding officer—and I thought to myself, without stopping: "What can be the matter now?"

Then, as I hurried by as fast as I could go, the blacksmith, Wachter, who was there, with his apprentice, reading the bulletin, called after me: "Don't go so fast, bub; you'll get to your school in plenty of time!"

I thought he was making fun of me, and reached M. Hamel's little garden all out of breath.

Usually, when school began, there was a great bustle, which could be heard out in the street, the opening and closing of desks, lessons repeated in unison, very loud, with our hands over our ears to understand better, and the teacher's great ruler rapping on the table. But now it was all so still! I had counted on the commotion to get to my desk without being seen; but, of course, that day everything had to be as quiet as Sunday morning. Through the window I saw my classmates, already in their places, and M. Hamel walking up and down with his terrible iron ruler under his arm. I had to open the door and go in before everybody. You can imagine how I blushed and how frightened I was.

But nothing happened. M. Hamel saw me and said very kindly: "Go to your place quickly, little Franz. We were beginning without you."

I jumped over the bench and sat down at my desk. Not till then, when I had got a little over my fright, did I see that our teacher had on his beautiful green coat, his frilled shirt, and the little black silk cap, all embroidered, that he never wore except on inspection and prize days. Besides, the whole school seemed so strange and solemn. But the thing that surprised me most was to see, on the back benches that were always empty, the village people sitting quietly like ourselves; old Hauser, with his three-cornered hat, the former mayor, the former postmaster, and several others besides. Everybody looked sad; and Hauser had brought an old primer, thumbed at the edges, and he held it open on his knees with his great spectacles lying across the pages.

While I was wondering about it all, M. Hamel mounted his chair, and, in the same grave and gentle one which he had used to me, said:

"My children, this is the last lesson I shall give you. The order has come from Berlin to teach only German in the schools of Alsace and Lorraine. The new master comes tomorrow. This is your last French lesson. I want you to be very attentive."

What a thunderclap these words were to me!

Oh, the wretches; that was what they had put up at the town hall!

My last French lesson! Why, I hardly knew how to write! I should never learn any more! I must stop there, then! Oh, how sorry I was for not learning my lessons, for seeking birds' eggs, or going sliding on the Saar! My books, that had seemed such a nuisance a while ago, so heavy to carry, my grammar, and my history of the saints, were old friends now that I couldn't give up. And M. Hamel, too; the idea that he was going away, that I should never see him again, made me forget all about his ruler and how cranky he was.

Poor man! It was in honor of this last lesson that he had put on his fine Sunday clothes, and now I understood why the old men of the village were sitting there in the back of the room. It was because they were sorry, too, that they had not gone to school more. It was their way of thanking our master for his forty years of faithful service and of showing their respect for the country that was theirs no more.

While I was thinking of all this, I heard my name called. It was my turn to recite. What would I not have given to be able to say that dreadful rule for the participle all through, very loud and clear, and without one mistake? But I got mixed up on the first words and stood there, holding on to my desk, my heart beating, and not daring to look up. I heard M. Hamel say to me:

"I won't scold you, little Franz; you must feel bad enough. See how it is! Every day we have said to ourselves: 'Bah! I've plenty of time. I'll learn it tomorrow.' And now you see where we've come out. Ah, that's the great trouble with Alsace; she puts off learning till tomorrow. Now those fellows out there will have the right to say to you: 'How is it; you pretend to be Frenchmen, and yet you can neither speak nor write your own language?' But you are not the worst, poor little Franz. We've all a great deal to reproach ourselves with.

"Your parents were not anxious enough to have you learn. They preferred to put you to work on a farm or at the mills, so as to have a little more money. And I? I've been to blame also. Have I not often sent you to water my flowers instead of learning your lessons? And when I wanted to go fishing, did I not just give you a holiday?"

Then, from one thing to another, M. Hamel went on to talk of the French language, saying that it was the most beautiful language in the world—the clearest, the most logical; that we must guard it among us and never forget it, because when a people are enslaved, as long as they hold fast to their language it is as if they had the key to their prison. Then he opened a grammar and read us our lesson. I was amazed to see how well I understood it. All he said seemed so easy, so easy! I think, too, that I had never listened so carefully, and that he had never explained everything with so much patience. It seemed almost as if the poor man wanted to give us all he knew before going away, and to put it all into our heads at one stroke.

After the grammar, we had a lesson in writing. That day M. Hamel had new copies for us, written in a beautiful round hand: France, Alsace, France, Alsace. They looked like little flags floating everywhere in the schoolroom, hung from the rod at the top of our desks. You ought to have seen how everyone set to work, and how quiet it was! The only sound was the scratching of the pens over the paper. Once some beetles flew in; but nobody paid any attention to them, not even the littlest ones, who worked right on tracing their fishhooks, as if that was French, too. On the roof the pigeons cooed very low, and I thought to myself:

"Will they make them sing in German, even the pigeons?"

Whenever I looked up from my writing I saw M. Hamel sitting motionless in his chair and gazing first at one thing, then at another, as if he wanted to fix in his mind just how everything looked in that little schoolroom. Fancy! For forty years he had been there in the same place, with his garden outside the window and his class in front of him, just like that. Only the desks and benches had been worn smooth; the walnut trees in the garden were taller, and the hop vine that he had planted himself twined about the windows to the roof. How it must have broken his heart to leave it all, poor man; to hear his sister moving about in the room above, packing their trunks! For they must leave the country next day.

But he had the courage to hear every lesson to the very last. After the writing, we had a lesson in history, and then the babies chanted their ba, be, bi, bo, bu. Down there at the back of the room old Hauser had put on his spectacles and, holding his primer in both hands, spelled the letters with them. You could see that he, too, was crying; his voice trembled with emotion, and it was so funny to hear him that we all wanted to laugh and cry. Ah, how well I remember it, that last lesson!

All at once the church clock struck twelve. Then the Angelus. At the same moment the trumpets of the Prussians, returning from drill, sounded under our windows. M. Hamel stood up, very pale, in his chair. I never saw him look so tall.

"My friends," said he, "I—I——" But something choked him. He could not go on.

Then he turned to the blackboard, took a piece of chalk, and, bearing down with all his might, he wrote as large as he could:

"*Vive la France!*"

Then he stopped and leaned his head against the wall, and, without a word, he made a gesture to us with his hand:

"School is dismissed—you may go."

Anatole France
1844-1924

ANATOLE FRANCE, born Jacques Anatole Thibault, was the son of a bookseller of the Quai Malaquai. His father, a Royalist and a devout Catholic, sent him to an aristocratic Jesuit school where he got an excellent grounding in the classics. But France always claimed it was the Seine booksellers who really educated him, and in spite of his Catholic training, Voltaire and Renan became his ideals. Naturally indolent, he took neither writing nor anything else seriously. During the Franco-Prussian War he served in the army at the siege of Paris, and diverted himself by playing the flute and reading Virgil.

France's early writing was devoted to publishers' blurbs and a weekly magazine article. Although he was later to dominate the French literary scene for a period of thirty years, he might well have died in comparative obscurity had he not come under the influence of a certain strong-minded woman. In 1883 he met Mme Arman de Caillavet, who drove him to work and propelled him into that position of eminence in the social and literary world which he was to hold for so long. For twenty-five years she saw to it that he wrote six days a week. On Sundays she "received," and France "conversed." In fact, he became almost as renowned for his conversation as for his writing. Under her strenuous discipline he wrote the greater part of his best work. "Without her help I should write no books," he said in the dedication of *Crainquebille*.

Though a contemporary of Zola, Turgenev, and Flaubert, France was not so deeply serious. He was the stylist par excellence. "I have passed my life," he said, "twisting dynamite into curlpapers." His world fame receded considerably after 1910, but he still remained a monumental literary figure to the French, and his funeral in 1924 was said to have brought out the biggest crowd in Paris after the Victory Parade of 1919. . . . "Our Lady's Juggler" was the inspiration for Massenet's opera *Le Jongleur de Notre Dame*.

Our Lady's Juggler

BY ANATOLE FRANCE

IN THE days of King Louis there was a poor juggler in France, a native of Compiègne, Barnaby by name, who went about from town to town, performing feats of skill and strength. On fair days he would unfold an old worn-out carpet in the public square, and when by means of a jovial address, which he had learned of a very ancient juggler, and which he never varied in the least, he had drawn together the children and loafers, he assumed extraordinary attitudes, and balanced a tin plate on the tip of his nose. At first the crowd would feign indifference.

But when, supporting himself on his hands face downwards, he threw into the air six copper balls, which glittered in the sunshine, and caught them again with his feet; or when, throwing himself backwards until his heels and the nape of the neck met, giving his body the form of a perfect wheel, he would juggle in this posture with a dozen knives, a murmur of admiration would escape the spectators, and pieces of money rain down upon the carpet.

Nevertheless, like the majority of those who live by their wits, Barnaby of Compiègne had a great struggle to make a living.

Earning his bread in the sweat of his brow, he bore rather more than his share of the penalties consequent upon the misdoings of our father Adam.

Again, he was unable to work as constantly as he would have been willing to do. The warmth of the sun and the broad daylight were as necessary to enable him to display his brilliant parts as to the trees if flower and fruit should be expected of them. In wintertime he was nothing more than a tree stripped of its leaves, and as it were dead. The frozen ground was hard to the juggler, and, like the grasshopper of which Marie de France tells us, the inclement season caused him to suffer both cold and hunger. But as he was simple-natured he bore his ills patiently.

He had never meditated on the origin of wealth, nor upon the inequality of human conditions. He believed firmly that if this life should prove hard, the life to come could not fail to redress the balance, and this hope upheld him. He did not resemble those thievish and miscreant Merry Andrews who sell their souls to the devil. He never blasphemed God's name; he lived uprightly, and although he had no wife

From *Mother of Pearl* by Anatole France. By permission of Dodd, Mead & Company and John Lane, The Bodley Head, Ltd., of London.

of his own, he did not covet his neighbor's, since woman is ever the enemy of the strong man, as it appears by the history of Samson recorded in the Scriptures.

In truth, his was not a nature much disposed to carnal delights, and it was a greater deprivation to him to forsake the tankard than the Hebe who bore it. For whilst not wanting in sobriety, he was fond of a drink when the weather waxed hot. He was a worthy man who feared God, and was very devoted to the Blessed Virgin.

Never did he fail, on entering a church, to fall upon his knees before the image of the Mother of God, and offer up this prayer to her:

"Blessed Lady, keep watch over my life until it shall please God that I die, and when I am dead, ensure to me the possession of the joys of paradise."

Now, on a certain evening after a dreary wet day, as Barnaby pursued his road, sad and bent, carrying under his arm his balls and knives wrapped up in his old carpet, on the watch for some barn where, though he might not sup, he might sleep, he perceived on the road, going in the same direction as himself, a monk, whom he saluted courteously. And as they walked at the same rate they fell into conversation with one another.

"Fellow traveler," said the monk, "how comes it about that you are clothed all in green? Is it perhaps in order to take the part of a jester in some mystery play?"

"Not at all, good father," replied Barnaby. "Such as you see me, I am called Barnaby, and for my calling I am a juggler. There would be no pleasanter calling in the world if it

would always provide one with daily bread."

"Friend Barnaby," returned the monk, "be careful what you say. There is no calling more pleasant than the monastic life. Those who lead it are occupied with the praises of God, the Blessed Virgin, and the saints; and, indeed, the religious life is one ceaseless hymn to the Lord."

Barnaby replied, "Good father, I own that I spoke like an ignorant man. Your calling cannot be in any respect compared to mine, and although there may be some merit in dancing with a penny balanced on a stick on the tip of one's nose, it is not a merit which comes within hail of your own. Gladly would I, like you, good father, sing my office day by day, and especially, the office of the most Holy Virgin, to whom I have vowed a singular devotion. In order to embrace the monastic life I would willingly abandon the art by which from Soissons to Beauvais I am well known in upwards of six hundred towns and villages."

The monk was touched by the juggler's simplicity, and as he was not lacking in discernment, he at once recognized in Barnaby one of those men of whom it is said in the Scriptures: Peace on earth to men of good will. And for this reason he replied, "Friend Barnaby, come with me, and I will have you admitted into the monastery of which I am prior. He who guided Saint Mary of Egypt in the desert set me upon your path to lead you into the way of salvation."

It was in this manner, then, that Barnaby became a monk. In the monastery into which he was received the religious vied with one another in the worship of the Blessed Virgin, and in her honor each employed all the knowledge and all the skill which God had given him.

The prior on his part wrote books dealing according to the rules of scholarship with the virtues of the Mother of God.

Brother Maurice, with a deft hand, copied out these treatises upon sheets of vellum.

Brother Alexander adorned the leaves with delicate miniature paintings. Here were displayed the Queen of Heaven seated upon Solomon's throne, and while four lions were on guard at her feet, around the nimbus which encircled her head hovered seven doves, which are the seven gifts of the Holy Spirit, the gifts, namely, of Fear, Piety, Knowledge, Strength, Counsel, Understanding, and Wisdom. For her companions she had six virgins with hair of gold, namely, Humility, Prudence, Seclusion, Submission, Virginity, and Obedience.

At her feet were two little naked figures, perfectly white, in an attitude of supplication. These were souls imploring her all-powerful intercession for their soul's health, and we may be sure not imploring in vain.

Upon another page facing this, Brother Alexander represented Eve, so that the Fall and the Redemption could be perceived at one and the same time—Eve the Wife abased, and Mary the Virgin exalted.

Furthermore, to the marvel of the beholder, this book contained presentments of the Well of Living Waters, the Fountain, the Lily, the Moon, the Sun, and the Garden enclosed of which the Song of Songs tells us, the Gate of Heaven and the City of God, and all these things were symbols of the Blessed Virgin.

Brother Marbode was likewise one of the most loving children of Mary.

He spent all his days carving images in stone, so that his beard, his eyebrows, and his hair were white with dust, and his eyes continually swollen and weeping; but his strength and cheerfulness were not diminished, although he was now well gone in years, and it was clear that the Queen of Paradise still cherished her servant in his old age. Marbode represented her seated upon a throne, her brow encircled with an orb-shaped nimbus set with pearls. And he took care that the folds of her dress should cover the feet of her, concerning whom the prophet declared: My beloved is as a garden enclosed.

Sometimes, too, he depicted her in the semblance of a child full of grace, and appearing to say, "Thou art my God, even from my mother's womb."

In the priory, moreover, were poets who composed hymns in Latin, both in prose and verse, in honor of the Blessed Virgin Mary, and amongst the company was even a brother from Picardy who sang the miracles of Our Lady in rhymed verse and in the vulgar tongue.

Being a witness of this emulation in praise and the glorious harvest of their labors, Barnaby mourned his own ignorance and simplicity.

"Alas!" he sighed, as he took his solitary walk in the little shelterless garden of the monastery, "wretched wight that I am, to be unable, like my brothers, worthily to praise the Holy Mother of God, to whom I have vowed my whole heart's affection. Alas! alas! I am but a rough man and unskilled in the arts, and I can render you in service, Blessed Lady, neither edifying sermons, nor ingenious paintings, nor statues truthfully sculptured, nor verses whose march is measured to the beat of feet. No gift have I, alas!"

After this fashion he groaned and gave himself up to sorrow. But one evening, when the monks were spending their hour of liberty in conversation, he heard one of them tell the tale of a religious man who could repeat nothing other than the Ave Maria. This poor man was despised for his ignorance; but after his death there issued forth from his mouth five roses in honor of the five letters of the name Mary (Marie), and thus his sanctity was made manifest.

Whilst he listened to this narrative, Barnaby marveled yet once again at the loving-kindness of the Virgin; but the lesson of that blessed death did not avail to console him, for his heart overflowed with zeal, and he longed to advance the glory of his Lady, who is in heaven.

How to compass this he sought, but could find no way, and day by day he became the more cast down, when one morning he awakened filled full with joy, hastened to the chapel, and remained there alone for more than an hour. After dinner he returned to the chapel once more.

And, starting from that moment, he repaired daily to the chapel at such hours as it was deserted, and spent within it a good part of the time which the other monks devoted to the liberal and mechanical arts. His sadness vanished, nor did he any longer groan.

A demeanor so strange awakened the curiosity of the monks.

These began to ask one another for what purpose Brother Barnaby could be indulging so persistently in retreat.

The prior, whose duty it is to let nothing escape him in the behavior of his children in religion, resolved to keep a watch over Barnaby during his withdrawals to the chapel. One day, then, when he was shut up there after his custom, the prior, accompanied by two of the older monks, went to discover through the chinks in the door what was going on within the chapel.

They saw Barnaby before the altar of the Blessed Virgin, head downwards, with his feet in the air, and he was juggling with six balls of copper and a dozen knives. In honor of the Holy Mother of God he was performing those feats, which aforetime had won him most renown. Not recognizing that the simple fellow was thus placing at the service of the Blessed Virgin his knowledge and skill, the two old monks exclaimed against the sacrilege.

The prior was aware how stainless was Barnaby's soul, but he concluded that he had been seized with madness. They were all three preparing to lead him swiftly from the chapel, when they saw the Blessed Virgin descend the steps of the altar and advance to wipe away with a fold of her azure robe the sweat which was dropping from her juggler's forehead.

Then the prior, falling upon his face upon the pavement, uttered these words, "Blessed are the simplehearted, for they shall see God."

"Amen!" responded the old brethren, and kissed the ground.

Hans Christian Andersen

1805-1875

HANS ANDERSEN'S life is like one of his own fairy stories, strange and a little sad. He was born in the small island town of Odense, in Denmark. His father was a poor shoemaker, very young and sickly, and the little family of three lived, ate, and slept in one room. When Hans was eleven his father died, and the little boy, left to his own devices, promptly stopped going to school. He built himself a toy theater, made puppets and clothed them, and read all the plays he could put his hands on, including most of Shakespeare.

His mother wanted Hans to be a tailor, but he preferred to be an opera singer, and at fourteen ran away to Copenhagen, where he hoped to make his fortune. But he was never a success in Copenhagen, neither then nor later. When he found that he had no voice, he turned to dancing, and the director of the Royal Theater, where he tried out as a dancer, took a fancy to the eccentric boy. In time King Ferdinand VI became interested and sent Hans to a fine school. But he was an unwilling student, and his school years were bitter and dark. In his young manhood he wrote plays and poetry, again without much success. He traveled on a stipend from the King and wrote about the countries he visited.

Not until after his first book of *Fairy Tales* was published in 1835 did he become famous, and even then Copenhagen mocked him. "Totally devoid of variety," said the Danish critics. All over the world, however, Hans Christian Andersen's name had by now become celebrated. When he visited England, Charles Dickens was his host. Yet Hans had not made good in the city of his choice and still believed himself a failure. To the end he disdained his fairy stories. . . . Although some of them are old tales retold, most of the fairy tales, including "The Steadfast Tin Soldier," were his own invention.

The Steadfast Tin Soldier

BY HANS CHRISTIAN ANDERSEN

THERE were once five and twenty tin soldiers, all brothers, for they were the offspring of the same old tin spoon. Each man shouldered his gun, kept his eyes well to the front, and wore the smartest red and blue uniform imaginable. The first thing they heard in their new world, when the lid was taken off the box, was a little boy clapping his hands and crying, "Soldiers, soldiers!" It was his birthday and they had just been given to him; so he lost no time in setting them up on the table. All the soldiers were exactly alike, with one exception, and he differed from the rest in having only one leg. For he was made last, and there was not quite enough tin left to finish him. However, he stood just as well on his one leg as the others on two; in fact, he is the very one who is to become famous. On the table where they were being set up were many other toys; but the chief thing which caught the eye was a delightful paper castle. You could see through the tiny windows, right into the rooms. Outside there were some little trees surrounding a small mirror, representing a lake, whose surface reflected the waxen swans which were swimming about on it. It was altogether charming, but the prettiest thing of all was a little maiden standing at the open door of the castle. She, too, was cut out of paper, but she wore a dress of the lightest gauze, with a dainty little blue ribbon over her shoulders, by way of a scarf, set off by a brilliant spangle as big as her whole face. The little maid was stretching out both arms, for she was a dancer, and in the dance one of her legs was raised so high into the air that the tin soldier could see absolutely nothing of it, and supposed that she, like himself, had but one leg.

"That would be the very wife for me!" he thought; "but she is much too grand; she lives in a palace, while I only have a box, and then there are five and twenty of us to share it. No, that would be no place for her! but I must try to make her acquaintance!" Then he lay down full length behind a snuffbox, which stood on the table. From that point he could have a good look at the lady, who continued to stand on one leg without losing her balance.

Late in the evening the other soldiers were put into their box, and the people of the house went to bed. Now was the time for the toys to play; they amused themselves with paying visits, fighting battles, and giving balls. The tin soldiers rustled about in their box, for they wanted to join the games, but they could not get the lid off. The nut-crackers turned somersaults, and the pencil scribbled nonsense on the slate. There was such a noise that the canary woke up and joined in, but his remarks were in verse. The only two who did not move were the tin soldier and the little dancer. She stood as stiff as ever on tiptoe, with her arms spread out; he was equally firm on his one leg, and he did not take his eyes off her for a moment.

Then the clock struck twelve, when pop! up flew the lid of the snuffbox, but there was no snuff in it, no! There was a little black goblin, a sort of Jack-in-the-box.

"Tin soldier!" said the goblin, "have the goodness to keep your eyes to yourself."

But the tin soldier feigned not to hear.

"Ah! you just wait till tomorrow," said the goblin.

In the morning when the children got up they put the tin soldier on the window frame, and, whether it was caused by the goblin or by a puff of wind, I do not know, but all at once the window burst open, and the soldier fell head foremost from the third story.

It was a terrific descent, and he landed at last, with his leg in the air, and rested on his cap, with his bayonet fixed between two paving stones. The maidservant and the little boy ran down at once to look for him; but although they almost trod on him, they could not see him. Had the soldier only called out, "Here I am," they would easily have found him, but he did not think it proper to shout when he was in uniform.

Presently it began to rain, and the drops fell faster and faster, till there was a regular torrent. When it was over two street boys came along.

"Look out!" said one; "there is a tin soldier! He shall go for a sail."

So they made a boat out of a newspaper and put the soldier into the middle of it, and he sailed away down the gutter; both boys ran alongside, clapping their hands. Good heavens! what waves there were in the gutter, and what a current, but then it certainly had rained cats and dogs. The paper boat danced up and down, and now and then whirled round and round. A shudder ran through the tin soldier, but he remained undaunted, and did not move a muscle, only looked straight before him with his gun shouldered. All at once the boat drifted under a long wooden tunnel, and it became as dark as it was in his box.

"Where on earth am I going now!" thought he. "Well, well, it is all the fault of that goblin! Oh, if only the little maiden were with me in the boat it might be twice as dark for all I should care!"

At this moment a big water rat, who lived in the tunnel, came up.

"Have you a pass?" asked the rat. "Hand up your pass!"

The tin soldier did not speak, but clung still tighter to his gun. The boat rushed on, the rat close behind. Phew, how he gnashed his teeth and shouted to the bits of stick and straw, "Stop him, stop him, he hasn't paid his toll; he hasn't shown his pass!" But the current grew stronger and stronger, the tin soldier could already see daylight before him at the end of the tunnel; but he also heard a roaring sound, fit to strike terror to the bravest heart. Just imagine! Where the tunnel ended the stream rushed straight into the big canal. That would be just as dangerous for him as it would be for us to shoot a great rapid.

He was so near the end now that it was impossible to stop. The boat dashed out; the poor tin soldier held himself as stiff as he could; no one should say of him that he even winced.

The boat swirled round three or four times, and filled with water to the edge; it must sink. The tin soldier stood up to his neck in water, and the boat sank deeper and deeper. The paper became limper and limper, and at last the water went over his head—then he thought of the pretty little dancer, whom he was never to see again, and this refrain rang in his ears:

Onward! Onward! Soldier!
For death thou canst not shun.

At last the paper gave way entirely and the soldier fell through —but at the same moment he was swallowed by a big fish.

Oh, how dark it was inside the fish, it was worse than being in the tunnel even; and then it was so narrow! But the tin soldier was as dauntless as ever, and lay full length, shouldering his gun.

The fish rushed about and made the most frantic movements. At last it became quite quiet, and after a time, a flash like lightning pierced it. The soldier was once more in the broad daylight, and someone called out loudly, "A tin soldier!" The fish had been caught, taken to market, sold, and brought into the kitchen, where the cook cut it open with a large knife. She took the soldier up by the waist, with two fingers, and carried him into the parlor, where everyone wanted to see the wonderful man who had traveled about in the stomach of a fish; but the tin soldier was not at all proud. They set him up on the table, and, wonder of wonders! he found himself in the very same room that he had been in before. He saw the very same children, and the toys were still standing on the table, as well as the beautiful castle with the pretty little dancer.

She still stood on one leg, and held the other up in the air. You see she also was unbending. The soldier was so much moved that he was ready to shed tears of tin, but that would not have been fitting. He looked at her, and she looked at him, but they said never a word. At this moment one of the little boys took up the tin soldier, and without rhyme or reason, threw him into the fire. No doubt the little goblin in the snuffbox was to blame for that. The tin soldier stood there, lighted up by the flame, and in the most horrible heat; but whether it was the heat of the real fire, or the warmth of his feelings, he did not know. He had lost all his gay color; it might have been from his perilous journey, or it might have been from grief, who can tell?

He looked at the little maiden, and she looked at him; and he felt that he was melting away, but he still managed to keep himself erect, shouldering his gun bravely.

A door was suddenly opened, the draft caught the little dancer, and she fluttered like a sylph, straight into the fire, to the soldier, blazed up, and was gone!

By this time the soldier was reduced to a mere lump, and when the maid took away the ashes next morning she found him, in the shape of a small tin heart. All that was left of the dancer was her spangle, and that was burned as black as coal.

Friedrich Gerstäcker

1816-1872

ON THE German horizon, dominated by the giant figures of
Goethe and Schiller and Heine, Friedrich Gerstäcker stands
up, a smallish figure beside those others, but an erect one.
Unlike his parochial countrymen of that day, Gerstäcker liked
to travel. Adventure was his métier, Robinson Crusoe his
immediate inspiration. As early as 1837 he was in America,
and wrote about what he saw, opening up vistas to the stay-
at-home Germans. "Germelshausen" is a tale of travel, too,
but of a region farther away than even Gerstäcker ventured.
In this story of the village that appears only every hundred
years, there is the spooky touch of an early Kafka.

Germelshausen

BY FRIEDRICH GERSTÄCKER

In the autumn of the year 184- a
strapping young fellow, knapsack on
back and stick in hand, was walking
with slow and easy stride along the
broad highroad that leads up from
Marisfeld to Wichtelhausen.

He was not one of those journey-
man artisans who travel about from
place to place, seeking work; anyone
could see that at the first glance,
even if the small, neatly made
leather portfolio, which he carried
strapped on his knapsack, had not
betrayed his calling. There was certainly no denying the fact that he
was an artist.

His black, broad-brimmed hat
cocked jauntily on one side, his long,
fair, curly hair, his downy beard, full
but youthful still—everything announced it, even the somewhat
threadbare black velvet jacket, which
seemed likely to be a little too warm
for him on this bright warm morning. He had unbuttoned it, and the
white shirt underneath—for he wore
no waistcoat—was but loosely held
together round his neck by a black
silk scarf.

He might have been about a mile
distant from Marisfeld when the bell
of the village church rang out, and
he halted, leaning upon his stick and
listening intently to the full tones of
the bell, which sounded wondrously
sweet to him across the breezes.

The sounds had long since died
away, and yet he still stood there,
gazing dreamily out over the hill
slopes. His heart was at home with
his loved ones in the dear little village among the Taurus Mountains,
with his mother and his sisters, and
it almost seemed as if a tear was like
to spring to his eye.

But his light and merry heart
would not suffer the intrusion of sad
and melancholy thought. He only
took off his hat, waved a loving,
smiling greeting in the direction in
which he knew his home lay, and
then gripping his stout stick more
firmly he gaily stepped out along the
road, continuing the journey he had
already begun.

Meanwhile the sun was beating
down with considerable warmth
upon the broad, monotonous highway, which was covered with a thick
layer of dust; and our traveler had
already for some time been casting
glances to right and left to see if he
could anywhere discover some
pleasanter footpath.

At one point, indeed, a road did
branch off to the right, but it looked
to him unpromising, and besides, it
would lead him too far out of his

This translation is used by permission of George G. Harrap of London.

way; so he stuck to his original track a little longer, until he at length came to a limpid mountain stream, across which he could discern the ruins of an old stone bridge.

Away on the other side ran a grassy path, leading farther into the valley; so, with no definite purpose in view—for he was only passing through the beautiful Werra Valley to enrich his portfolio—he crossed the brook dry-shod by leaping from one great stone to another, and so reached the close-cropped meadow on the other side, where he advanced rapidly on the springy turf under the shadow of the thick alder bushes, well content with the change.

"Now I have the advantage," he said to himself with a laugh, "of not knowing whither I am bound. There is no tiresome sign post here telling one miles beforehand what is the name of the next village, and invariably giving the wrong distance. How ever do people in these parts measure their miles, I should like to know!

"How wonderfully quiet it is in this valley! To be sure, on Sundays farmers have nothing to do out-of-doors, and since they have to walk behind their plow or by their cart the whole week, they don't care much about going for a walk when Sunday comes; they first of all make up for their arrears of sleep in church during the morning, and after dinner stretch their legs under the table in the tavern. Tavern! hm, a glass of beer wouldn't be such a bad thing in this heat; but until I can get it this clear stream will quench my thirst just as well."

And with that he flung off knapsack and hat, knelt down at the waterside, and drank to his heart's content.

Somewhat cooled by his drink, his glance fell on an old, strangely gnarled willow tree, which he rapidly sketched with practiced hand; and then, completely rested and refreshed, he took up his knapsack again and continued his way, regardless as to where it would lead him.

He had wandered on thus for perhaps an hour or so, jotting down in his sketchbook here a crag, there a peculiar clump of alder bushes, or again a knotty oak branch; the sun had meanwhile mounted higher and higher, and he had just made up his mind to quicken his steps in order at least not to miss his dinner in the next village, when before him in the valley, sitting close to the brook and by an old stone, on which perhaps in times gone by there had stood a sacred shrine, he caught sight of a peasant girl, who was gazing down the road along which he came.

As he was hidden by the alders, he had been able to see her before she saw him; but following the bank of the stream, he had hardly passed beyond the bushes which had hitherto concealed him from her sight, when she leaped to her feet and flew toward him with a cry of pleasure.

Arnold, as the young painter was called, stood amazed, and was soon aware that a beautiful girl of hardly seventeen years, dressed in a peculiar but extremely pretty peasant's costume, was running up to him with outstretched arms.

Arnold of course saw at once that she had mistaken him for someone else, and that this joyful greeting was not meant for him; and the girl no sooner recognized him than she stood stock-still with horror, turned pale at first and then red all over, and finally said with shy embarrassment: "Do not be offended, stranger! I—I thought——"

"That it was your sweetheart, my dear child, didn't you?" laughed the young man. "And now you are vexed that a different person, an uninteresting stranger, has met you! Don't be angry because I am not he."

"Ah, how can you say such things?" said the girl in a distressed whisper. "Why should I be angry?—oh! but if you only knew how delighted I was!"

"Then he certainly does not deserve that you should wait any longer for him," said Arnold, who now for the first time noticed the truly wonderful charm of the graceful peasant girl. "Were I in his place, you would not have had to wait for me in vain for a single moment."

"You do say such strange things," said the girl, abashed. "If he could have come he would certainly be here by now. Perhaps he is ill, or—even dead," she added slowly and with a sigh that came from the depths of her heart.

"And has he let you have no news of himself all this time?"

"No, all this long, long time."

"Then his home is perhaps a long way from here?"

"A long way? Why, yes; quite a great distance from here," said the girl. "In Bischofsroda."

"Bischofsroda?" cried Arnold. "I spent four weeks there only recently, and I know every child in the whole village. What is his name?"

"Heinrich — Heinrich Vollgut," said the girl shyly; "the mayor's son in Bischofsroda."

"Hm," mused Arnold, "I was in and out of the mayor's house, but *his* name was Bauerling, as far as I know, and I never heard the name of Vollgut in the whole village."

"Probably you didn't know all the people there," argued the girl, and over the sorrowful expression which clouded her sweet face there stole a soft, roguish smile, which became her as well and much better than her previous melancholy.

"Well, but from Bischofsroda," said the young man, "you can get here over the mountains easily in two hours, at most in three."

"And yet he is not here," said the girl, sighing deeply again, "though he promised so faithfully."

"Then he'll come, sure enough," Arnold assured her with hearty conviction; "for once anyone has given you a promise, he must surely have a heart of stone if he went back on his word—and that I am sure your Heinrich has not got."

"No," she answered resolutely; "but now I cannot wait any longer for him, as I have to be home for dinner, or else Father will scold me."

"And where is your home?"

"Straight down there in the valley. Hark! there's the bell; they are just coming out of church."

Arnold listened, and at no great distance off he could hear the slow pealing of a bell, but the sound came to him not deep and full, but sharp and discordant, and when he turned his eyes toward the spot it seemed to him almost as if a thick mountain mist lay over that part of the valley.

"Your bell is cracked," he laughed; "it doesn't ring true."

"Yes, I know that," answered the girl calmly; "it has not a pleasant sound, and we should have had it recast long ago, but we are always short of money and time, for hereabouts there are no bellcasters. Yet, what does it matter? We know it all right, and we know what it means when it rings—so even though it is cracked it serves its purpose."

"And what is the name of your village?"

"Germelshausen."

"And can I get to Wichtelhausen from there?"

"Quite easily; by the footpath it takes hardly half an hour—perhaps, indeed, not so much, if you put your best foot forward."

"Then I'll go with you through the village, sweetheart, and if you have a good inn in the place I'll have my dinner there too."

"The inn is only too good," said the maiden with a sigh, as she cast a glance backward to see if her expected lover might not yet be coming.

"Can any inn be too good?"

"For the farmer, yes," said the girl gravely, as she walked slowly by his side along the valley. "Of an evening after his work he still has much to do in the house, and this he neglects if he sits in the public house till late at night."

"But I at any rate have nothing more to neglect today."

"Yes, with townfolk it is rather different; they don't do anything, and consequently haven't got much to neglect either. Yet the farmer has to earn bread for them."

"Well, not exactly so," said Arnold with a laugh. "He has to grow it, I grant you, but we have to earn it for ourselves; and a hard job it is too, many a time, for what the farmer does he sees that he is well paid for it."

"But you don't work, anyhow?"

"Why not, pray?"

"Your hands don't look like it."

"Then I will show you at once how I work and what I work at," laughed Arnold. "Just you sit down on that flat stone under the old lilac tree——"

"And what am I to do there?"

"Just sit down," cried the young painter, who threw off his knapsack and took out his sketchbook and pencil.

"But I must go home."

"I shall be done in five minutes. I should very much like to take a reminder of you away into the world with me; even your Heinrich will have no objection to that!"

"A reminder of me? What a funny man you are!"

"I will take your portrait away with me."

"You are a painter, then?"

"Yes."

"What a lucky thing! Then you might set to work and touch up the pictures in Germelshausen Church; they look so very poor and shabby."

"What is your name?" was Arnold's next question. He had meanwhile opened his portfolio and was rapidly sketching in the girl's charming features.

"Gertrud."

"And what is your father?"

"The mayor of the village. If you are a painter, you must not go to the inn either; I will take you straight home with me, and after dinner you can talk over the whole matter with Father."

"Oh, the pictures in the church?" said Arnold, laughing.

"Of course," said the girl gravely; "and then you must stay with us a long, long time until—our day comes again and the pictures are finished."

"Well, we'll talk about that later, Gertrud," said the young painter, busily plying his pencil the while; "but won't your Heinrich be angry if I am often—very often with you, and if I talk with you a good deal?"

"Heinrich?" said she. "Oh, he won't come now."

"Not today, no; but perhaps tomorrow."

"No," said Gertrud, quite calmly; "as he wasn't there by eleven o'clock, he will stay away until our day comes again."

"Your day? What do you mean by that?"

The girl looked at him with wide-open, earnest eyes, but gave no answer to his question, and her gaze, turning to the clouds floating away high over their heads, fastened upon them with a peculiar expression of pain and melancholy.

Gertrud's beauty at this moment was truly the beauty of an angel, and Arnold forgot all else in the interest which he was taking in the completion of her picture. Nor had he much more time left. The girl suddenly stood up, and tossing a kerchief over her head to shield her from the sun's rays, she said:

"Go I must; the day is so short, and they are expecting me at home."

But Arnold had finished his little picture, and indicating with a few bold strokes the folds of her dress, he held out the sketch to her and said:

"Have I caught your likeness?"

"It is myself!" gasped Gertrud, almost in fright.

"Well, who else could it be?" laughed Arnold.

"And do you wish to keep the picture and take it away with you?" asked the girl shyly, almost wistfully.

"Why, certainly I do," cried the young man, "and then when I am far, far away from here I shall think of you hard, and often."

"But will my father allow that?"

"Allow me to think of you? Is he capable of forbidding me to do so?"

"No—but—to take the picture away with you—out into the world?"

"He can't hinder me, sweetheart," said Arnold tenderly; "but would you

yourself hate to know that it was in my possession?"

"I? No!" was the girl's answer after short reflection; "if only—but I must ask Father about it."

"What a silly child you are!" said the young painter with a laugh; "even a princess would have no objection to an artist securing a sketch of her features for himself. No harm can come to you from it. But please don't run off like that, you wild creature; I am coming with you, you know—or do you want to leave me behind without my dinner? Have you forgotten about the church pictures?"

"Oh! yes, the pictures," said the girl, standing still and waiting for him; but Arnold, who had quickly tied up his portfolio again, was by her side in a moment, and they both continued their way toward the village far quicker than before.

The village, however, was much nearer than Arnold had supposed from the sound of the cracked bell, for what the young man from afar had taken for an alder grove proved to be, on their nearer approach, a row of fruit trees enclosed by a hedge. Closely hidden behind these, yet surrounded on the north and northeast by broad fields, lay the old village with its low church tower and its smoke-blackened cottages.

Here, too, it was that the pair first struck a firm, well-laid street, planted on either side with fruit trees. But over the village lowered a thick mist which Arnold had already perceived from afar, and it dimmed the bright sunshine, which fell upon the gray, old, weather-beaten roofs with a weird and yellowish light.

But Arnold scarcely had eyes for this. Gertrud, stepping out by his side, had meekly slipped her hand in his as they came to the first houses, and clasping it in her own she turned with him into the next street.

A strange feeling thrilled the lusty youth at the touch of her warm hand and almost involuntarily his eyes sought to meet those of the young maiden. But Gertrud did not look in his direction; with eyes fixed modestly on the ground, she conducted her guest to her father's house, and Arnold's attention, too, was at length taken up with the villagers he met, who all passed him by in silence and without a word of greeting.

He could not help noticing this at first, for in all the neighboring villages it would have been deemed a crime not to offer a stranger at least a "Good day" or "God bless you." Here no one thought of such a thing, and, just as in any large town, the people either passed by in silence and without showing any interest, or else stood here and there and looked after them; but no one spoke a word to them—not one of all the passers-by gave a greeting even to the girl.

And how strange the old houses looked, with their pointed gables ornamented with carved work, and their hard thatched roofs weatherworn and gray; and though it was Sunday, no window was polished bright, and the round panes set in leaden frames looked tarnished and dim, and showed on their dull surface shimmering rainbow colors.

Here and there a window would open as they walked by, and pleasant-faced girls or elderly worthy matrons would peep out. The curious dress of the people struck him also, differing essentially as it did from that of the village in the vicinity. And besides all this an almost soundless stillness reigned everywhere so

that Arnold, to whom this silence at last became oppressive, said to his companion:

"Do you observe Sunday in your village so strictly that people when they meet one another haven't even a word of greeting to utter? If one didn't hear a dog barking now and then or a cock crowing, one might really think the whole place dumb and dead."

"It is dinnertime," said Gertrud quietly, "and people are not inclined to talk then; this evening you will find them all the noisier."

"Thank heaven!" exclaimed Arnold, "there are at least some children yonder playing in the street. I had begun to feel quite uncanny; I can tell you they spend Sunday quite differently in Bischofsroda."

"There's my father's house," said Gertrud in a low voice.

"But I can't thrust myself in upon him thus unexpectedly at dinnertime. I might be an unwelcome intruder, and I like to have friendly faces round me at meals.

"So show me rather where the inn is, my child, or let me find it myself, for probably Germelshausen is no exception to the rule of other villages. Generally the public house is quite close to the church, and if you take the church tower to guide you, you can't go far wrong."

"There you are right; that is exactly the case with us," said Gertrud quietly; "but they expect us already at home, and you need have no fear of getting an unfriendly reception."

"Expect us? Ah, you mean yourself and your Heinrich? Yes, Gertrud, if you would take me today in his place, then I would stay with you—until—until you yourself should tell me to go away again."

He had spoken these last words in

such feeling tones, almost against his will, the while gently pressing the hand which still held his, that Gertrud suddenly stopped, looked at him out of her big, grave eyes, and said:

"Would you really wish that?"

"A thousand times yes," cried the young painter, utterly carried away by the girl's wonderful beauty. But Gertrud made no further answer, and pursuing her way as if she was pondering over the words of her companion, she at length came to a halt in front of a tall house, which was approached by a flight of broad, stone steps, protected by iron railings. Speaking in her former shy and timid manner she resumed:

"This is where I live, kind sir, and if it would please you, come in with me to my father, who will no doubt be proud to see you at his table."

II

Before Arnold could return any answer to this invitation the mayor himself appeared in the doorway at the top of the steps, and a window was thrown open, revealing the kindly face of an old lady, who looked out and nodded to them.

"Why, Gertrud," exclaimed the farmer, "what a long time you have stayed out today, and look what a smart young fellow she has brought back with her!"

"My dear sir!"

"Please, no ceremony on the steps! The dumplings are ready; come in, or they'll get hard and cold."

"But that's not Heinrich," cried the old lady from the window. "Now, didn't I always say that he would never come back again?"

"All right, mother, all right," said the mayor, "this one will do very well instead"; and holding out his hand to the stranger, he went on: "A hearty welcome to Germelshausen, young gentleman, wherever the lass may have picked you up. And now come in to dinner and fall to to your heart's content; anything else we can talk of later."

He left the young painter no possible further chance to make any excuses, but vigorously shaking his hand, which Gertrud had released as soon as he had set foot on the stone steps, he took his arm with familiar kindness and conducted him into the spacious living room.

Although he was well acquainted with the habits of the German farmer, who shuts himself off from every breath of fresh air in his room, and not unfrequently even in summer keeps up a fire so as to produce the broiling heat he so delights in, yet what was most noticeable to Arnold at once was the musty, earthy atmosphere which pervaded the house.

The narrow entrance hall was likewise far from inviting. The plaster had fallen from the walls and appeared to have just been hastily swept to one side. The single dim window at the back of the hall hardly admitted the meager light, and the stairs which led to the upper story looked old and out of repair.

Little time, however, was given him to observe all this, for in the very next moment his hospitable host threw open the door of the parlor, and Arnold saw himself in a low but broad and spacious room, which was airy and fresh, with white sand sprinkled over the floor, and which with its large table in the center spread with a snow-white cloth contrasted pleasantly with the rest of the rather dilapidated arrangements of the house.

Besides the old lady, who now

had shut the window and moved her chair up to the table, there were also sitting in the corner a few red-cheeked children; and a buxom peasant woman, who also was wearing a costume utterly different from that of the neighboring villages, was just opening the door to admit the maid, who came in with a large dish.

And now the dumplings were smoking on the board and everyone made for the chairs, to partake of the welcome meal; but no one sat down, and the children, as it seemed to Arnold, cast almost anxious eyes on their father.

The latter advanced to his chair, and leaning his arms upon it, stared dumbly, silently, even gloomily upon the ground. Was he praying? Arnold saw that he kept his lips firmly pressed while his right hand hung down clenched by his side. In his features was no sign of prayer, only an obstinate yet irresolute defiance.

Gertrud then turned quietly to him and laid her hand on his shoulder, while the old lady stood speechless opposite to him, and looked at him with earnestly pleading eyes.

"Let us eat," growled the man, "it's no use, I fear"; and pushing his chair aside, nodded to his guest, dropped into his seat, and, seizing the huge ladle, served out helpings all round.

To Arnold the man's whole behavior was almost uncanny, nor could he feel comfortable amid the depression shown by the others. But the mayor was not the man to eat his dinner to the accompaniment of melancholy thoughts. In answer to his rap on the table the maid came in again, bearing bottles and glasses, and with the rich old wine which he now poured out, a very different and more cheerful state of mind soon pre-vailed among the company round the table.

The glorious beverage ran through Arnold's veins like liquid fire; never in his life had he tasted anything like it. Gertrud drank some too, and so did the old lady, who later seated herself at her spinning wheel in the corner and in a low voice sang a little song of the merry life in Germelshausen. The mayor himself seemed a different being.

He now became as cheerful and jovial as earlier he had been morose and silent, and Arnold himself could not escape the influence of the rich wine.

He could not precisely tell how it came about, but the mayor had taken a violin in his hand and was playing a merry dance, and Arnold with his arm about fair Gertrud's waist whirled with her round the room so madly that he upset the spinning wheel and the chair, bumped into the maid, who was trying to carry away the dinner things, and cut all sorts of merry capers, so that the others almost died of laughter to see him.

Suddenly there was complete silence in the room, and as Arnold looked round at the magistrate in astonishment, the latter pointed with his violin bow out of the window, and then laid the instrument back again in the wooden case from which he had taken it. And Arnold perceived that outside in the street a coffin was being carried by.

Six men dressed in white shirts were bearing it upon their shoulders, and behind them, quite alone, walked an old man, leading a little, fair-haired girl by the hand.

The old man walked along the street as one crushed with grief, but the little girl, who could hardly have been four years old, and probably had no idea who was lying in that black coffin, kept gaily nodding her head wherever she saw a face she knew, and laughed shrilly when two or three dogs scampered by and one of them ran up against the steps of the mayor's house and rolled over and over.

But the silence endured only as long as the coffin was in sight, and Gertrud drew up to the young man and said:

"Now rest a little while; you have been romping quite enough; otherwise, the heavy wine will get into your head more and more. Come, take your hat and let us go for a little walk together. By the time we get back it will be time to go to the inn, for there is a dance this evening."

"A dance? That's splendid," exclaimed Arnold, delighted; "I've come just at the right time. You'll give me the first dance, I hope, Gertrud?"

"Certainly, if you wish."

Arnold had already seized his hat and sketchbook.

"What do you want with the book?" asked the mayor.

"He sketches, Father," said Gertrud, "and he has already drawn me. Just have a look at the pictures."

Arnold opened the sketchbook and held out the picture to her father.

The farmer looked at it quietly for a while, without speaking.

"And do you want to take that home with you," he asked at length, "and perhaps frame it and hang it up in your room?"

"Why not, pray?"

"May he, Father?" asked Gertrud.

"If he does not stay with us," laughed the mayor, "I have no objection—but there's something wanting in the background."

"What?"

"Why, the funeral procession that passed a moment ago. Draw that on the paper, and you may take the picture with you."

"What! the funeral procession with Gertrud!"

"There's room enough," said the mayor obstinately; "you must put it in the sketch, or else I will not permit you to take away with you my lassie's portrait all by itself. In such solemn company no one can possibly think evil of it."

At this strange proposal to give the pretty maiden a funeral party as a guard of honor, Arnold laughingly shook his head. But the old man seemed to have made up his mind, and so, to humor him, he did as he wished. Later on he could quite easily rub out the dismal additional feature.

With practiced hand he drew on the paper the figures that had just passed by, though only from memory, and the whole family crowded round him as he worked, and watched with evident astonishment the rapid completion of the drawing.

"There, have I been successful?" cried Arnold at length, jumping up from his chair and holding out the picture at arm's length.

"Splendidly!" nodded the mayor; "I should never have thought you could finish it so quickly. Now, that will do; out you go with the lassie and have a look at the village; it may be a long while before you have a chance of seeing it again. Be back here by five o'clock sharp—we are having high jinks tonight and you must be there."

The musty room and the wine which had mounted to his head had begun to make Arnold feel heavy and oppressed. He longed to be out-of-doors, and a few minutes later he was striding along the street which led through the village, with fair Gertrud by his side.

As they made their way along there was not the same absence of noise as there had been before; children were playing in the road here and there, old people were sitting at their doors, looking at them, and the whole place with its quaint, ancient houses might have presented quite a pleasant appearance if only the sun had been able to pierce the thick brown smoke which hung like a cloud over the roofs.

"Is the moor or forest on fire hereabouts?" he asked the girl. "This sort of smoke does not hang over any other village and cannot come from the chimneys."

"It is earth vapor," said Gertrud quietly; "but have you never heard of Germelshausen?"

"Never."

"That is strange, and yet the village is old, oh! so old."

"The houses look like it, at any rate, and the people too have such a curious way with them, and their speech sounds quite differently from that of places near at hand. You go very little outside your own village, I expect?"

"Very little," said Gertrud curtly.

"And not a single swallow is left. They can't surely have flown away yet?"

"Oh, a long time ago," answered the girl apathetically; "in Germelshausen they never come now to build their nests. Perhaps they can't stand the earth vapor."

"But surely you don't have that always?"

"Yes, always."

"Then that is the reason why your fruit trees bear no fruit, and yet in Marisfeld this year they had to prop up the branches, so fruitful has the season been."

Gertrud said not a word in answer, and walked on in silence by his side straight through the village until they came to the extreme limit. On the way she gave a kindly nod to a child here and there or spoke a low word or two with one of the young girls—maybe about the evening's dance and the dresses they were to wear.

And as they talked, the girls cast sympathetic glances at the young painter, so that his heart warmed and saddened—he did not quite know why—and for all that he did not dare to ask Gertrud why it should be so.

They had now at length reached the last houses, and if it had been lively in the village itself, here at any rate everything was still and lonely and deathlike. The gardens looked as if they had not been walked in for years and years; grass was growing in the pathways, and it seemed especially noticeable to the young stranger that not a single fruit tree bore a single bit of fruit.

At this point some men met them, going back home from outside the village, and at once Arnold recognized them as the funeral party returning. They moved noiselessly past them into the village again, and almost involuntarily the pair turned their steps to the graveyard.

Arnold tried now to cheer up his companion, who seemed to him so very serious, by telling her about other places where he had been and what the great outer world was like. She had never seen a railway, never even heard of one, and listened with attention and astonishment to his explanations.

Nor had she any knowledge of the electric telegraph, and she knew just as little about all the other more modern inventions; so that the young artist could not understand how it was possible that there should be still living in Germany human beings so secluded, so absolutely cut off from the rest of the world and without the slightest connection with it.

Conversing thus, they reached the cemetery, and here the young stranger was immediately struck by the old-world appearance of the stones and monuments, simple and plain though they were as a general rule.

"Here is an old, old stone," he said, bending down to the nearest one and with difficulty deciphering the scrollwork upon it. "Anna Maria Berthold, maiden name Stieglitz, born 16th December, 1188, died 2nd December, 1224."

"That is my mother," said Gertrud solemnly, and the big, crystal tears filled her eyes and slowly trickled down on to her bodice.

"Your mother, dear child?" said Arnold in astonishment; "your great-great-grandmother perhaps it might have been."

"No," said Gertrud, "my own mother. Father married again, and the one at home is my stepmother."

"But surely it says died 1224?"

"What does the year matter?" said Gertrud mournfully. "It is sad enough to be thus parted from one's mother, and yet," she added sorrowfully under her breath, "perhaps it was well, very well that she was suffered to go to God beforehand."

Arnold bent down over the stone, shaking his head, and made a closer examination of the inscription, in case the first "2" in the date might be an "8," for in the old-time writing such a thing was not impossible, but the second "2" was exactly the same as the first, and it was as yet too soon to write 1884. Perhaps it was the stonemason who had made the mistake, and the girl was so deep in her memories of the departed that he did not like to trouble her any further with questions that were perhaps displeasing to her.

He therefore left her by the gravestone before which she had sunk to her knees and was silently praying, and proceeded to examine some other monuments, but all of them without exception bore dates of many hundred years back, even as far back as A.D. 930 and 900. No more recent gravestone could be discovered, and yet the dead were even now laid to rest in this place, as the latest fresh grave betokened.

From the low churchyard wall there was a splendid view of the old village, and Arnold quickly availed himself of the opportunity of making a sketch of it. But over this place also lay the strange fog, though toward the wood he could see the sunlight falling bright and clear on the mountain slopes.

Then from the village came the sound of the old cracked bell again, and Gertrud, quickly rising from her knees and dashing the tears from her eyes, gently beckoned to the young man to follow her.

Arnold was quickly by her side.

"Now we must sorrow no more," she said with a smile; "the church bell is ringing the end of the service, and now for the dance. Up to the present you have no doubt imagined that the people of Germelshausen are nothing but kill-joys, but tonight you will think the contrary."

"But yonder is the church door," said Arnold, "and I can see nobody coming out."

"That is perfectly natural," laughed the girl, "for no one ever goes in, not even the priest. Only the old verger allows himself no rest, and still rings the service in and out."

"And do none of your people ever go to church?"

"No, neither to Mass nor to confession," said the girl quietly. "We have quarreled with the Pope, who lives among foreigners, and has forbidden it until we return to obedience."

"Why, I've never heard of such a thing in all my life."

"Yes, it is a long time ago," said the girl carelessly.

"Look, there's the verger all alone coming out of church and shutting the door; he never goes to the inn of an evening either, but sits all by himself at home."

"And does the priest go?"

"I should think so, and he is the jolliest of them all. He does not take things to heart."

"And how has all this come about?" asked Arnold, who was amazed not so much at the facts he had heard as at the girl's simplicity.

"It's a long story," Gertrud said, "and the priest has written it all down in a big, thick book. If you are interested, and if you understand Latin, you may read all about it there.

"But," she added by way of warning, "don't speak of it when Father is by, for he doesn't like it. Look, here come the boys and girls out-of-doors already; I must hurry off home now and dress, for I should not like to be the last."

"And the first dance, Gertrud?"

"I dance it with you; you have my promise."

The two walked quickly back to the village, which was now all astir with life, very different from what it was in the morning. Laughing groups of young people were standing about on all sides; the girls were all dressed up for the festival, and the young fellows too were in their best clothes,

while on the face of the inn, as they sped past, festoons of leaves were hanging from window to window, and formed a broad triumphal arch over the door.

Seeing that everyone was tricked out most resplendently, Arnold was unwilling to mingle with the merrymakers dressed in his traveling garb; so he unbuckled his knapsack in the mayor's house, took out of it his smart suit, and had just completed his toilet when Gertrud knocked at the door and called him.

And what a picture of loveliness the girl looked now in her simple yet rich gown, and how cordially she asked him to escort her, saying that her father and mother would not follow on till later!

"Yearning after her Heinrich cannot be depressing her spirits to any particular extent," was the youth's uppermost thought as he drew her arm through his and passed with her to the ballroom through the gathering dusk. But he refrained from giving utterance to such thoughts, for a strange, a wonderful feeling thrilled his breast, and his own heart throbbed violently as he felt the girl's heart beating against his arm.

"To think that tomorrow I must depart," he sighed softly to himself. Although he had not intended it, his words reached the ears of his companion, and she said with a smile:

"Don't trouble about that; we shall be together longer—longer perhaps than you like."

"And would you be glad, Gertrud, if I stayed with you?" asked Arnold, and as he spoke he felt the blood surging in tumultuous waves over forehead and temples.

"Of course I should," said the young girl simply: "you are nice and kind, and Father likes you too, of that I'm sure, and—Heinrich hasn't come, you know," she added in an undertone and somewhat angrily.

"Suppose he came tomorrow?"

"Tomorrow?" said Gertrud, looking at him gravely out of her great dark eyes; "between now and tomorrow lies a long, long night. Tomorrow! You will understand tomorrow what that word means. But today, let us not speak of it," she said abruptly, yet pleasantly; "today is a holiday, to which we have looked forward so long, oh! so long, and do not let us spoil it by gloomy thoughts.

"Here we are at the place; the boys will stare a good deal when they see me bringing a new partner."

Arnold was about to make some reply to her, but his words were drowned by the noisy music which rolled out from within the ballroom. Strange tunes, too, were the musicians playing, not one of which he recognized, and at first he was almost blinded by the flash of the many lights that sparkled before his eyes.

Gertrud led him into the center of the hall, where a bevy of young peasant girls stood chatting together, and not till then did she leave him to himself so that, until the real business of the dance began, he might look about him a little and make the acquaintance of the other young men.

III

At the first moment Arnold felt ill at ease among these many strangers; moreover, their strange costume and their strange speech repelled him, and though the harsh, unwonted accents came sweetly from Gertrud's lips, yet they grated on his ear when pronounced by others. The young fellows were all friendly disposed toward him, however, and one of them approached him, took him by the hand, and said:

"You have done wisely, sir, in choosing to bide with us. We lead a merry life, and the interval passes quickly enough."

"What do you mean by the interval?" asked Arnold, astonished not so much at the expression as because the youth pronounced so firmly his conviction that he had chosen to make the village his home. "Do you mean that I shall come back here?"

"But do you wish to go away?" asked the young peasant sharply.

"Tomorrow, yes, or the day after tomorrow; but I'll come back."

"Tomorrow; oh!" laughed the youth; "then that's all right. Well, we'll talk more about it tomorrow. But now come and I'll show you how we enjoy ourselves, for if you really want to go away tomorrow, you might not after all get a chance of seeing the fun."

The others looked at each other and laughed knowingly, while the young peasant took Arnold by the hand and conducted him all over the house, which was now packed full of a crowd of merrymakers. First they passed through rooms wherein sat cardplayers with great heaps of money lying before them. Next they came to a bowling alley, inlaid with shining flagstones.

In a third room, ring-throwing and other games were being played, and the young girls tripped in and out, laughing and singing and teasing the young men, till all of a sudden a flourish from the band, which up to now had been playing away merrily, gave the signal for the dance to commence, and Gertrud stood at Arnold's side and took his arm.

"Come, we must not be the last," said the lovely girl, "for as the mayor's daughter it is for me to open the ball."

"But what strange tune is that?" said Arnold; "I can't catch the time at all."

"Oh, you soon will," smiled Gertrud; "you'll catch the time in the first five minutes, and I'll tell you how."

With jubilant shouts the whole company, with the exception of the cardplayers, crowded into the ballroom, and Arnold was soon oblivious of everything else in the first blissful feeling of holding the wondrously beautiful maiden in his arms.

Again and again he danced with Gertrud, and no one else seemed to want to claim his partner from him, although the other girls often threw teasing remarks at him as they flew by.

One thing only struck him and alarmed him. Close by the inn stood the ancient church, and the shrill, discordant clang of the cracked bell could be distinctly heard in the ballroom. At the first stroke of the bell it was as if a magician's wand had smitten the dancers.

The music stopped playing in the middle of a beat, the merry surging crowd stood still and motionless, as if spellbound, and everyone silently counted the slow strokes one by one.

But as soon as the last sound died away, the animation and merriment broke out afresh. This was repeated at eight, at nine, at ten o'clock, and when Arnold would fain inquire what was the reason for such a strange proceeding, Gertrud laid her finger on her lips and at the same time looked so solemn and sad that he would not have troubled her further for all the world.

At ten o'clock there was a pause in the dancing, and the musicians, who must have had lungs of iron, headed the procession of young people down to the supper room.

There were merry doings there. The wine simply ran in streams, and Arnold, who could not be behindhand among all the others, reckoned up in his own mind what sort of hole this expensive evening would make in his modest pocket.

But Gertrud was sitting by his side, drinking with him out of the same glass, and how could he give way to any such misgivings? Even though her Heinrich should come tomorrow.

The first stroke of eleven o'clock rang out. Again the loud merriment of the revelers was silenced, again the same breathless listening to the long-drawn strokes.

A peculiar horror overcame him; he could not tell why; and the thought of his mother at home smote through his heart. He slowly raised his glass and drained it in a toast to his absent dear ones.

At the eleventh stroke the company sprang up from the table; the dancing was to begin again and they all scuttled back to the ballroom.

"Who was it you drank your last toast to?" asked Gertrud, as she laid her arm again in his.

Arnold hesitated before replying. Maybe Gertrud would only laugh at him if he told her. But no; she herself had prayed so fervently on that very afternoon by her own mother's grave—and so he said in a low voice:

"My mother."

Gertrud answered never a word, but walked in silence by his side up the stairs. Her laughter had ceased also, and before they took their places for the dance again she asked him:

"Do you love your mother so much?"

"More than life itself."

"And does she love you?"

"Does not a mother love her child?"

"And what if you never went back home to her?"

"Poor Mother!" said Arnold, "her heart would break."

"The dance is just starting again," cried Gertrud quickly; "come along, we mustn't miss a moment more."

So wilder than ever the dance began. The young men, fired by the strong wine, shouted and hurrahed, and shrieked, and such a din arose as threatened to drown the music.

Arnold did not now feel so happy in all this uproar, and Gertrud too had become serious and silent. But with all the others the merriment seemed only to increase, and during a pause the mayor came up to them, gave the young man a hearty slap on the shoulder, and said, laughing:

"That's right, Mr. Painter, shake a merry leg tonight; we shall have plenty of time to have a good long rest. Nay, then, Gertie, why pull such a solemn face? Does that fit in with the dance this day? Merry's the word—there, they're off again!

"Now I must look up my old woman and trip the last dance with her. Take your places; the bandsmen are fairly bursting their cheeks again." And with a huzzah he plunged through the crowd of revelers.

Arnold was embracing Gertrud once more for a fresh dance when the latter suddenly broke away from him, gripped his arm, and whispered softly: "Come!"

Arnold had no time to ask her whither, for she slipped from his grasp and sped away toward the door.

"Whither away, Gertie?" some of her playmates called out to them.

"Coming back in a moment," came the sound of her curt answer, and a few seconds later she was standing with Arnold outside before the house in the sharp night air.

"Where do you propose to go, Gertrud?"

"Come!"

Again she caught his arm and led him through the village, past her father's house, into which she dashed and presently emerged with a small bundle.

"What is the meaning of this?" asked Arnold in alarm.

"Come!" was the only word she said in answer, and past the houses she strode with him until they left the outermost wall of the village behind them. So far they had followed the broad, firm, hard-trodden highway; now Gertrud turned off the road to the left and mounted a little, low hill from the top of which could be seen the brilliantly lighted windows and doors of the inn.

Here she came to a halt, held out her hand to Arnold, and said tenderly:

"My greetings to your mother; farewell!"

"Gertrud," cried Arnold, astonished, aghast, "do you wish to send me away from you thus, now, in the middle of the night? Has any word of mine offended you?"

"No, Arnold," said the girl, calling him by his Christian name for the first time. "Just . . . just because I love you, you must go away."

"But I cannot let you go away from me back to the village like this, all alone and in the dark," pleaded Arnold. "Girl, you don't know how much I love you, how utterly and entirely you have won my heart in these few hours. You know not . . ."

"Say no more," she interrupted him quickly, "we will not say good-by. When the clock has struck twelve —it can hardly want ten minutes yet—return to the inn door; there I shall be expecting you."

"And until then . . . !"

"Stay just where you are. Promise me not to take one step to right or left till the clock has struck the last stroke of twelve."

"I promise, Gertrud; but then . . ."

"Then come," she said, holding out her hand in farewell, and would have left him.

"Gertrud!" cried Arnold, in a pleading, anguished voice.

Gertrud stood a moment as if in hesitation, then suddenly she turned toward him, threw her arms around his neck; and Arnold felt the icy lips of the lovely maiden pressed on his. It was but for a moment; in the next instant she had torn herself away and was flying toward the village. And Arnold in amazement at her strange behavior, yet mindful of his promise, remained standing just where she had left him.

Now for the first time he saw how the weather had changed in these few hours. The wind was howling through the trees, the sky was overcast with heavy racing clouds, and one or two large drops of rain proclaimed the approach of a storm.

Through the darkness of the night the lights glowed bright from the inn, and when the wind came roaring across he could hear in broken waves of sound the riotous blare of the instruments—but not for long. Only for a few moments had he been standing in his place when the clock in the old church tower began to strike. In that same instant the music ceased or was drowned in the howling storm, which raged so violently over the hill slope that Arnold was obliged to stoop down to the ground in order not to lose his balance.

Before him on the ground he felt the bundle which Gertrud had fetched out of the house—his own knapsack and sketchbook—and affrighted, he stood upright again. The clock had finished striking, the hurricane roared past over his head, but nowhere in the village was there any longer a light to be seen. The dogs which but a short while ago had been barking and howling were silent, and a thick, damp mist was rising up from the hollow.

"The time is up," muttered Arnold to himself, hoisting his knapsack on his back, "and I must see Gertrud once again; I cannot part from her like this. The dance is over; the dancers will now be going home, and if the mayor will not put me up for the night I can stay at the inn. Besides, in the darkness I shouldn't find my way through the forest."

He cautiously went down the gentle slope which he and Gertrud had ascended together, in order to strike the broad white road which would bring him to the village, but in vain did he grope about for it among the bushes below.

The ground was soft and swampy, and in his thin boots he sank in up to the ankles; there was everywhere a tangle of alder bushes growing just where he had imagined the road to be. He could not possibly have crossed it in the dark; he could not have failed to feel it the moment he stepped on it; and besides, he knew that the village wall ran right across it—this at any rate he could not miss.

But it was in vain that with anguished haste he sought for it; the ground became more soft, more swampy the farther he advanced, the undergrowth became thicker and everywhere beset with thorns, which tore his clothes and scratched his hands till they bled.

Had he wandered off to the right or to the left and beyond the village? He feared lest he should lose his bearings still more completely, and came to a halt on a fairly dry spot, determined to wait there until the old clock should strike one.

But it did not strike, not a dog barked, no sound of human voice reached him, and with great difficulty, wet to the skin and shivering with cold, he toiled back again to the higher ground of the hill slope where Gertrud had left him.

From this spot he tried, indeed, a few more times to penetrate the thicket and find the village, but in vain. Tired to death, and a prey to a peculiar horror, he at last avoided the low, dark, weird hollow and sought the shelter of a tree, there to spend the night.

And how slowly for him did the hours pass by! For shivering as he was with cold, he was not able to steal from that long night even one moment's sleep. And he was forever straining his ears into the darkness, as again and again he thought he heard the rasping sound of the bell, only to find again and again that he had been mistaken.

At last the first glow of light began to dawn out of the far east. The clouds had dispersed, the sky was once more clear and bright with stars, and the awakening birds twittered softly in the gloomy trees.

Brighter and lighter grew the golden horizon; already he could clearly discern the treetops round about him; but it was in vain that his eye sought the view of the old

brown church tower and the weather-worn roofs. Nothing but a wilderness of alderbushes, dotted here and there with a few stunted willows, stretched out before him. No road was to be seen leading to the right or to the left, no sign of human habitation in the vicinity.

The day broke clearer and clearer. The earliest sunbeams fell upon the broad green expanse that spread out before his gaze; and Arnold, who was at a loss to solve the riddle, wandered some considerable distance back into the valley. He must, he thought, have lost his way in the dark, without knowing it, while he was seeking for the place, and had got too far away. He was now firmly determined to find it again.

At length he came to the stone near which he had drawn Gertrud's picture. This spot he would have recognized again out of thousands, for the old lilac tree with its stiff branches indicated it only too clearly.

He now knew exactly from what direction he had come and where Germelshausen must lie; so he paced rapidly back along the valley, keeping closely to the same track which he and Gertrud had followed yesterday. Over there also he recognized the bend in the slope over which had hung the murky fog, and only the alder bushes still separated him from the nearest houses.

Now he had reached it; he pressed on and—found himself once more in the very same swampy morass in which he had waded about the night before.

Completely at a loss and not trusting his own senses, he was for forcing a way through at this point, but the filthy swamp ooze at length compelled him to make for dry ground again, and there he wandered helplessly backward and forward.

The village had disappeared, and that was the end of it.

Several hours had perhaps been consumed in this fruitless search, and his weary limbs at last refused to serve him any longer. He could go no further; before anything else he must rest. What had been the use of his vain quest? At the first village he came across he could easily find a guide to conduct him to Germelshausen, and then he could not miss the road again.

Dead tired, he flung himself down under a tree—and how utterly ruined was his best suit! This, however, did not trouble him now; he produced his sketchbook and out of it he took Gertrud's portrait. With bitter pain his eyes fastened on the dear, sweet features of the maiden, who, as he realized to his great alarm, had already taken too firm a hold upon his heart.

Then he heard behind him a rustling among the leaves—a dog began to bark; and quickly springing to his feet, he was aware of an old woodsman standing not far away from him and curiously observing the strange figure who was so decently dressed and yet presented such a wild appearance.

"Greeting!" exlaimed Arnold, heartily pleased to meet a human being, and quickly thrusting the picture back into the portfolio. "You could not have been more welcome if I had invited you here, Herr Forester, for I think I have lost my way."

"Hm," said the old man, "if you have been lying here in the bush all night, I should think so too, and hardly half an hour's walk over yonder to Dillstedt and a good inn. Heavens! what a sight you are, for all the world as if you had been dragged neck and crop out of thorns and mud!"

"Are you quite familiar with the forest here?" asked Arnold, who before all things wanted to know where he really was.

"I should think I was," laughed the woodsman as he struck a light and lighted his pipe again.

"What is the name of the nearest village?"

"Dillstedt—straight over there. When you get on to that little hill yonder, you can easily see it lying below you."

"And how far is it from here to Germelshausen?"

"To where?" cried the woodsman, removing his pipe in horror from his lips.

"To Germelshausen."

"God help me!" said the old man, casting a scared look about him; "the forest I know well enough, but how many fathoms deep down below the earth the 'cursed village' lies, God alone knows—nor is it any business of ours."

"The 'cursed village'?" cried Arnold in astonishment.

"Germelshausen—yes," said the woodsman. "Just there in the swamp, where now grow the old willows and alders, it is said to have stood hundreds and hundreds of years ago. Later on it sank away, no man knows why or whither; and the story goes that every hundred years on a certain day it is raised up again to the light of heaven, but I should not wish any Christian man to chance to be there then.

"But, man alive! camping out in the bush last night does not seem to have agreed with you. You look as white as a ghost. There now, just you have a sip out of this flask;

it will do you good—now have a good pull!"

"Thank you."

"Tut, tut, that wasn't half enough —take a proper, first-class pull at it. That's right; that's the real stuff to take. And now make haste and get across to the inn, and into a warm bed."

"In Dillstedt?"

"Why, of course: there's none nearer."

"What about Germelshausen?"

"Be good enough not to mention the place again, especially here on the spot where we are standing. Let the dead rest, and above all those who do not even enjoy rest, but keep on rising again unexpectedly amongst us."

"But only yesterday the village was still standing here," cried Arnold, who had almost lost his trust in his own senses. "I was inside it—eating and drinking and dancing there!"

The woodsman calmly looked the young man up and down, and then said with a smile:

"But it went by some other name, didn't it? Probably you have come straight over from Dillstedt. There was a dance there yesterday evening, and it's not everybody can stand the strong beer that the landlord brews at present."

By the way of answer Arnold opened his portfolio and drew out the drawing that he had made from the churchyard.

"Do you know that village?"

"No," said the woodsman shaking his head; "there's not such a flat tower as that in the whole countryside."

"That is Germelshausen," cried Arnold; "and do the peasant girls in this neighborhood dress as this girl does here?"

"Um—no! and what's that queer-looking funeral procession you have put in the picture?"

Arnold returned no answer. He thrust the sheets back again into the portfolio, and a strange feeling of pain thrilled through him.

"You can't miss the road to Dillstedt," said the woodsman good-naturedly, for a dark suspicion now occurred to him that the stranger might perhaps not be quite right in the head. "But if you would like, I will accompany you till we come to where we can see the place; that won't take me much out of my way."

Arnold declined with many thanks. "I'll find my way over there all right. And so it is only once in every hundred years that they say the village comes up again?"

"So people say," answered the woodsman, "but who can say if it is true?"

Arnold had taken up his knapsack again.

"God be wi' you!" he said, holding out his hand to the woodsman.

"Many thanks," answered he; "where are you going now?"

"To Dillstedt."

"That's right—when you get over the slope you'll come to the broad highroad again."

Arnold turned away, and slowly proceeded on his way. Only when he had reached the top of the slope which commanded a view over the whole of the valley did he pause once again and look back.

"Farewell, Gertrud!" he murmured softly, and as he walked over the hill, the big crystal tears were streaming from his eyes.

Giovanni Verga

1840-1922

ALTHOUGH he lived more than fourscore years, Giovanni
Verga's period of creative writing was very short. In his prime
he was Italy's foremost novelist and short-story writer, but
the works which gave him that position were all written
between 1880 and 1889. Like so many young men with a
literary bent, Verga left home at an early age and went to
the city to seek his fame. Florence was then the cultural
center of Italy. There Verga came under the influence of the
literary circle that frequented the famous *salotti* of the
Countess Maffei. He wrote, but not well and not successfully.
It was not until he left Florence and returned to his home in
the countryside of Sicily that he found real inspiration. He
now wrote of the peasants with whom he had grown up,
stories of local habits and of old customs. *Vita dei campi*
(published in English as *Under the Shadow of Etna*), from
which "The Saint Joseph's Ass" is taken, and *Cavalleria
Rusticana*, more charming as a story than as an opera, are
the books on which his reputation was made.

With the new generation, which turned to d'Annunzio,
Verga fell out of fashion. For thirty years he was all but
forgotten. There was a belated revival of interest when on his
eightieth birthday the government made him a senator, and
when he died two years later, his funeral cortege extended
for miles. D. H. Lawrence's translation of his stories as *Little
Novels of Sicily*, published in 1923, reintroduced Verga to
the English-reading world.

The Saint Joseph's Ass

BY GIOVANNI VERGA

THEY had bought him at the fair at Buccheri when he was quite a foal, when as soon as he saw a she-ass he went up to her to find her teats, for which he got a good many bangs on the head and showers of blows upon the buttocks, and caused a great shouting of "Gee back!" Neighbor Neli, seeing him lively and stubborn as he was, a young creature that licked his nose after it had been hit, giving his ears a shake, said, "This is the chap for me!" And he went straight to the owner, holding in his pocket his hand which clasped the thirty-five shillings.

"It's a fine foal," said the owner, "and it's worth more than five-and-thirty shillings. Never mind if he's got that black-and-white skin, like a magpie. I'll just show you his mother, whom we keep there in the bough shelter because the foal has always got his nose at the teats. You'll see a fine black beast there; she works for me better than a mule, and has brought me more young ones than she has hairs on her back. Upon my soul, I don't know where that magpie jacket has come from, on the foal. But he's sound in the bone, I tell you! And you don't value men according to their faces. Look what a chest and

legs like pillars! Look how he holds his ears! An ass that keeps his ears straight up like that, you can put him in a cart or in the plow as you like, and make him carry ten quarters of buckwheat better than a mule, as true as this is holy day today! Feel his tail, if you and all your family couldn't hang on to it!"

Neighbor Neli knew it better than he; but he wasn't such a fool as to agree, and stood on his own, with his hand in his pocket, shrugging his shoulders and curling his nose, while the owner led the colt round in front of him.

"Hm!" muttered neighbor Neli, "with that hide on him, he's like Saint Joseph's ass. Those colored animals are all Jonahs, and when you ride through the village on their backs everybody laughs at you. What do you want me to make you a present of, for Saint Joseph's ass?"

Then the owner turned his back on him in a rage, shouting that if he didn't know anything about animals, or if he hadn't got the money to pay with, he'd better not come to the fair and make Christians waste their time, on the blessed day that it was.

Neighbor Neli let him swear, and

From *Little Novels of Sicily* by Giovanni Verga, translated by D. H. Lawrence. By permission of The Viking Press, Inc. Copyright, 1925, by Thomas Seltzer, Inc.

went off with his brother, who was pulling him by his jacket sleeve, and saying that if he was going to throw away his money on that ugly beast he deserved to be kicked.

However, on the sly they kept their eye on the Saint Joseph's ass, and on its owner who was pretending to shell some broad beans, with the halter rope between his legs, while neighbor Neli went wandering round among the groups of mules and horses, and stopping to look, and bargaining for first one and then the other of the best beasts, without ever opening the fist which he kept in his pocket with the thirty-five shillings, as if he'd got the money to buy half the fair. But his brother said in his ear, motioning toward the ass of Saint Joseph, "That's the chap for us!"

The wife of the owner of the ass from time to time ran to look what had happened, and finding her husband with the halter in his hand, she said to him, "Isn't the Madonna going to send us anybody today to buy the foal?"

And her husband answered every time: "Not so far! There came one man to try for him, and he liked him. But he drew back when he had to pay for him, and has gone off with his money. See him, that one there, in the white stocking cap, behind the flock of sheep. But he's not bought anything up to now, which means he'll come back."

The woman would have liked to sit down on a couple of stones, just close to her ass, to see if he would be sold. But her husband said to her: "You clear out! If they see we're waiting, they'll never come to bargain."

Meanwhile the foal kept nuzzling with his nose between the legs of the she-asses that passed by, chiefly because he was hungry, and his master, the moment the young thing opened his mouth to bray, fetched him a bang and made him be quiet, because the buyers wouldn't want him if they heard him.

"It's still there," said neighbor Neli in his brother's ear, pretending to come past again to look for the man who was selling broiled chick-peas. "If we wait till Ave Maria we can get him for five shillings less than the price we offered."

The sun of May was hot, so that from time to time, in the midst of the shouting and swarming of the fair, there fell a great silence over all the fairground, as if there was nobody there, and then the mistress of the ass came back to say to her husband: "Don't you hold out for five shillings more or less, because there's no money to buy anything in with, this evening; and then you know the foal will eat five shillings' worth in a month, if he's left on our hands."

"If you're not going," replied her husband, "I'll fetch you a kick you won't forget!"

So the hours of the fair rolled by, but none of those who passed before the ass of Saint Joseph stopped to look at him; for, sure enough, his master had chosen the most humble position, next the low-price cattle, so as not to make him show up too badly beside the beautiful bay mules and the glossy horses! It took a fellow like neighbor Neli to go and bargain for the Saint Joseph's ass, which set everybody in the fair laughing the moment they saw it. With having waited so long in the sun the foal let his head and his ears drop, and his owner had seated himself gloomily on the stones, with his hands also dangling between his knees, and the halter in his hands, watching here and there the long shadows, which began to form in the plain as the sun went down, from the legs of all the beasts which had not found a buyer. Then Neli and his brother, and another friend whom they had picked up for the occasion, came walking that way, looking into the air, so that the owner of the ass also twisted his head away to show he wasn't sitting there waiting for them; and the friend of neighbor Neli said like this, looking vacant, as if the idea had just come to him:

"Oh, look at the ass of Saint Joseph! Why don't you buy him, neighbor Neli?"

"I asked the price of him this morning; he's too dear. Then I should have everybody laughing at me with that black-and-white donkey. You can see that nobody would have him, so far."

"That's a fact, but the color doesn't matter, if a thing is any use to you."

And he asked of the owner: "How much do you expect us to make you a present of, for that Saint Joseph's donkey?"

The wife of the owner of the ass of Saint Joseph, seeing that the bargaining had started again, came edging softly up to them, with her hands clasped under her short cloak.

"Don't mention such a thing!" neighbor Neli began to shout, running away across the plain. "Don't mention such a thing to me, I won't hear a word of it."

"If he doesn't want it, let him go without it," answered the owner. "If he doesn't take it, somebody else will. It's a sad man who had nothing left to sell, after the fair!"

"But I mean him to listen to me, by the blessed devil I do!" squealed the friend. "Can't I say my own fool's say like anybody else?"

And he ran to seize neighbor Neli by the jacket, and he came back to speak a word in the ear of the ass's owner, who now wanted at any cost to go home with his little donkey; so the friend threw his arms round his neck, whispering: "Listen! five shillings more or less, if you don't sell it today; you won't find another softy like my pal here to buy your beast, which isn't worth a cigar."

And he embraced the ass's mistress also, talking in her ear, to get her on his side. But she shrugged her shoulders and replied with a sullen face: "It's my man's business. It's nothing to do with me. But if he lets you have it for less than forty shillings he's a simpleton, in all conscience! It cost us more!"

"I was a lunatic to offer thirty-five shillings this morning," put in neighbor Neli. "You see now whether you've found anybody else to buy it at that price. There's nothing left in all the fair but three or four scabby sheep and the ass of Saint Joseph. Thirty shillings now, if you like."

"Take it," suggested the ass's mistress to her husband, with tears in her eyes. "We haven't a penny to buy anything tonight, and Turiddu has got the fever on him again; he needs some sulphate."

"All the devils!" bawled her husband. "If you don't get out, I'll give you a taste of the halter!"

"Thirty-two-and-six, there!" cried the friend at last, shaking him hard by the jacket collar. "Neither you nor me! This time you've got to take my word, by all the saints in paradise! And I don't ask as much as a glass of wine. You can see the sun's gone down. Then what are you waiting for, the pair of you?"

And he snatched the halter from the owner's hand, while neighbor Neli, swearing, drew out of his pocket the fist with the thirty-five shillings, and gave them him without looking at them, as if he was tearing out his own liver. The friend drew aside with the mistress of the ass, to count the money on a stone, while the owner of the ass rushed through the fair like a young colt, swearing and punching himself on the head.

But then he permitted himself to go back to his wife, who was very slowly and carefully counting over again the money in the handkerchief, and he asked, "Is it right?"

"Yes, it's quite right; Saint Gaetano be praised! Now I'll go to the chemist."

"I've fooled them! I'd have given it him for twenty shillings, if I'd had to; those colored donkeys are all Jonahs."

And neighbor Neli, leading the little donkey behind him down the slope, said: "As true as God's above I've stolen his foal from him! The color doesn't matter. Look what legs, like pillars, neighbor. He's worth forty shillings with your eyes shut."

"If it hadn't been for me," replied the friend, "you wouldn't have done a thing. Here, I've still got two-and-six of yours. And if you like, we'll go and drink your donkey's health with it."

And now the colt stood in need of all his health to earn back the thirty-two-and-six he had cost, and the straw he ate. Meanwhile he took upon himself to keep gamboling behind neighbor Neli, trying to bite his jacket in fun, as if he knew it was the jacket of his new master,

and he didn't care a rap about leaving forever the stable where he had lived in the warmth, near his mother, rubbing his muzzle on the edge of the manger, or butting and capering with the ram, or going to rouse up the pig in its corner. And his mistress, who was once more counting the money in the handkerchief in front of the druggist's counter, she didn't either once think of how she had seen the foal born, all black and white with his skin as glossy as silk, and he couldn't stand on his legs yet, but lay nestling in the sun in the yard, and all the grass which he had eaten to get so big and stout had passed through her hands. The only one who remembered her foal was the she-ass, who stretched out her neck, braying toward the stable door, but when she no longer had her teats swollen with milk, she too forgot about the foal.

"Now this creature," said neighbor Neli, "you'll see he'll carry me ten quarters of buckwheat better than a mule. And at harvest I'll set him threshing."

At the threshing the colt, tied in a string with the other beasts, old mules and broken-down horses, trotted round over the sheaves from morning till night, till he was so tired he didn't even want to open his mouth to bite at the heap of straw when they had put him to rest in the shade, now that a little wind had sprung up, so that the peasants could toss up the grain into the air with broad wooden forks to winnow it, crying, *Viva Maria!*

Then he let his muzzle and his ears hang down, like a grown-up ass, his eye spent, as if he was tired of looking out over the vast white campagna which fumed here and there with the dust from the threshing floors, and it seemed as if he was made for nothing else but to be let die of thirst and made to trot round on the sheaves. At evening he went back to the village with full saddle-bags, and the master's lad went behind him, pricking him between the legs, along the hedges of the byway that seemed alive with the twittering of the tits and the scent of catmint and of rosemary, and the donkey would have liked to snatch a mouthful, if they hadn't made him trot all the time, till the blood ran down his legs, and they had to take him to the vet; but his master didn't care, because the harvest had been a good one, and the colt had earned his thirty-two-and-six. His master said: "Now he's done his work, and if I sell him for twenty shillings I've still made money by him."

The only one who was fond of the foal was the lad who made him trot along the little road, when they were coming home from the threshing floor, and he cried while the farrier was burning the creature's legs with a red-hot iron, so that the colt twisted himself up, with his tail in the air and his ears as erect as when he had roved round the fair-ground, and he tried to get free from the twisted rope which pressed his lips, and he rolled his eyes with pain almost as if he had human understanding when the farrier's lad came to change the red-hot irons, and his skin smoked and frizzled like fish in a frying pan. But neighbor Neli shouted at his son: "Silly fool! what are you crying for? He's done his work now, and seeing that the harvest has gone well, we'll sell him and buy a mule, which will be better for us."

Some things children don't understand; and after they had sold the colt to Farmer Cirino from Licodia,

neighbor Neli's son used to go to visit it in the stable, to stroke its nose and its neck, and the ass would turn to snuff at him as if its heart were still bound to him, whereas donkeys are made to be tied up where their master wishes, and they change their fate as they change their stable. Farmer Cirino from Licodia had bought the Saint Joseph's ass cheap, because it still had the wound in the pastern; and the wife of neighbor Neli, when she saw the ass going by with its new master, said: "There goes our luck; that black-and-white hide brings a jolly threshing floor; and now times go from bad to worse, so that we've even sold the mule again."

Farmer Cirino had yoked the ass to the plow, with the old horse that went like a jewel, drawing out his own brave furrow all day long, for miles and miles, from the time when the larks began to trill in the dawn-white sky till when the robins ran to huddle behind the bare twigs that quivered in the cold, with their short flight and their melancholy chirping, in the mist which rose like a sea. Only, seeing that the ass was smaller than the horse, they had put him a pad of straw on the saddle, under the yoke, and he went at it harder than ever, breaking the frozen sod, pulling with all his might from the shoulder. "This creature saves my horse for me, because he's getting old," said Farmer Cirino. "He's got a heart as big as the plain of Catania, has that ass of Saint Joseph! And you'd never think it."

And he said to his wife, who was following behind him clutched in her scanty cloak, parsimoniously scattering the seed: "If anything should happen to him, think what a loss it would be! We should be ruined, with all the season's work in hand."

And the woman looked at the work in hand, at the little stony, desolate field, where the earth was white and cracked, because there had been no rain for so long, the water coming all in mist, the mist that rots the seed; so that when the time came to hoe the young corn it was like the devil's beard, so sparse and yellow, as if you'd burned it with matches. "In spite of the way we worked that land!" whined Farmer Cirino, tearing off his jacket. "That donkey puts his guts into it like a mule! He's the ass of misfortune, he is."

His wife had a lump in her throat when she looked at that burned-up cornfield, and only answered with the big tears that came to her eyes.

"It isn't the donkey's fault. He brought a good year to neighbor Neli. It's us who are unlucky."

So the ass of Saint Joseph changed masters once more, for Farmer Cirino went back again with his sickle from the cornfield; there was no need to reap it that year, in spite of the fact that they'd hung images of the saints on to the cane hedge, and had spent ninepence having it blessed by the priest. "The devil is after us!" Farmer Cirino went swearing through those ears of corn that stood up straight like feathers, which even the ass wouldn't eat; and he spat into the air at the blue sky that had not a drop of water in it. Then neighbor Luciano the carter, meeting Farmer Cirino leading home the ass with empty saddlebags, asked him: "What do you want me to give you for Saint Joseph's ass?"

"Give me what you like. Curse him and whoever made him," replied Farmer Cirino. "Now we haven't got bread to eat, nor barley to give to the beast."

"I'll give you fifteen shillings because you're ruined; but the ass isn't worth it, he won't last above six months. See what a poor sight he is!"

"You ought to have asked more," Farmer Cirino's wife began to grumble after the bargain was concluded. "Neighbor Luciano's mule has died, and he hasn't the money to buy another. If he hadn't bought the Saint Joseph's ass he wouldn't know what to do with his cart and harness; and you'll see that donkey will bring him riches."

The ass then learned to pull the cart, which was too high on the shafts for him, and weighed so heavily on his shoulders that he wouldn't have lasted even six months, scrambling his way up the steep, rough roads, when it took all neighbor Luciano's cudgeling to put a bit of breath into his body; and when he went downhill it was worse, because all the load came down on top of him, and pressed on him so much that he had to hold on with his back curved up in an arch, with those poor legs that had been burned by fire, so that people seeing him began to laugh, and when he fell down it took all the angels of paradise to get him up again. But neighbor Luciano knew that he pulled his ton and a half of stuff better than a mule, and he got paid two shillings a half ton. "Every day the Saint Joseph's ass lives it means six shillings I earned," he said, "and he costs me less to feed than a mule." Sometimes people toiling up on foot at a snail's pace behind the cart, seeing that poor beast digging his hoofs in with no strength left, and arching his spine, breathing quick, his eye hopeless, suggested: "Put a stone under the wheel, and let that poor beast get his wind." But neighbor Luciano replied: "If I let him go his own pace he'll never earn me any six shillings a day. I've got to mend my own skin with his. When he can't do another stroke I'll sell him to the lime man, for the creature is a good one and will do for him; and it's not true a bit that Saint Joseph's asses are Jonahs. I got him for a crust of bread from Farmer Cirino, now he's come down and is poor."

Then the Saint Joseph's ass fell into the hands of the lime man, who had about twenty donkeys, all thin skeletons just ready to drop, but which managed nevertheless to carry him his little sacks of lime, and lived on mouthfuls of weeds which they could snatch from the roadside as they went. The lime man didn't want him because he was all covered with scars worse than the other beasts, and his legs seared with fire, and his shoulders worn out with the collar, and his withers gnawed by the plow saddle, and his knees broken by his falls, and then that black-and-white skin which in his opinion didn't go at all with his other black animals. "That doesn't matter," replied Luciano. "It'll help you to know your own asses at a distance." And he took off another ninepence from the seven shillings which he had asked, to close the bargain. But even the mistress who had seen him born would no longer have recognized the Saint Joseph's ass, he was so changed, as he went with his nose to the ground and his ears like an umbrella, under the little sacks of lime, twisting his behind at the blows from the boy who was driving the herd. But the mistress herself had also changed by then, with the bad times there had

been, and the hunger she had felt, and the fevers that they'd all caught down on the plain, she, her husband, and her Turiddu, without any money to buy sulphate, for one hasn't got a Saint Joseph's ass to sell every day, not even for thirty-five shillings.

In winter, when work was scarce, and the wood for burning the lime was rarer and farther to fetch, and the frozen little roads hadn't a leaf on their hedges, or a mouthful of stubble along the frozen ditchside, life was harder for those poor beasts; and the owner knew that the winter would carry off half of them for him; so that he usually had to buy a good stock of them in the spring. At night the herd lay in the open, near the kiln, and the beasts did the best for themselves, pressing close up to one another. But those stars that shone like swords pierced them in their vulnerable parts, in spite of their thick hides, and all their sores and galls burned again and trembled in the cold as if they could speak.

However, there are plenty of Christians who are no better off, and even haven't got that rag of a cloak in which the herd boy curled himself up to sleep in front of the furnace. A poor widow lived close by—in a hovel even more dilapidated than the lime kiln, so that the stars pierced through the roof like swords, as if you were in the open, and the wind made the few rags of coverlets flutter. She used to do washing, but it was a lean business, because folk washed their own rags, when they were washed at all, and now that her boy was grown she lived by going down to the village to sell wood. But nobody had known her husband, and nobody knew where she got the wood she sold;

though her boy knew, because he went to glean it here and there, at the risk of being shot at by the estate keepers. "If you had a donkey," said the lime man, who wanted to sell the Saint Joseph's ass because it was no longer any good to him, "you could carry bigger bundles to the village, now that your boy is grown."

The poor woman had a shilling or two tied in a corner of a handkerchief, and she let the lime man get them out of her, because they said that "old stuff goes to die in the house of the crazy."

At least the poor Saint Joseph's ass lived his last days a little better; because the widow cherished him like a treasure, thanks to the pennies he had cost her, and she went out at nights to get him straw and hay, and kept him in the hut beside the bed, so that he helped to keep them all warm, like a little fire, he did, and in this world one hand washes the other. The woman, driving before her the ass laden with wood like a mountain, so that you couldn't see his ears, went building castles in the air; and the boy foraged round the hedges and ventured into the margins of the wood to get the load together, till both mother and son imagined themselves growing rich at the trade; till at last the baron's estate keeper caught the boy in the act of stealing boughs and tanned his hide for him thoroughly with a stick. To cure the boy the doctor swallowed up all the pence in his handkerchief, the stock of wood, and all there was to sell, which wasn't much; so that one

night when the boy was raving with fever, his inflamed face turned toward the wall, and there wasn't a mouthful of bread in the house, the mother went out raving and talking to herself as if she had got the fever as well; and she went and broke down an almond tree close by, though it didn't seem possible that she could have managed to do it, and at dawn she loaded it on the ass to go and sell it. But under the weight, as he tried to get up the steep path, the donkey kneeled down really like Saint Joseph's ass before the Infant Jesus, and couldn't get up again.

"Holy spirits," murmured the woman, "oh, carry that load of wood for me, you yourselves."

And some passers-by pulled the ass by the rope and hit his ears to make him get up.

"Don't you see he's dying," said a carter at last, and so the others left him in peace, since the ass had eyes like a dead fish, and a cold nose, and shivers running over his skin.

The woman thought of her son in his delirium, with his face red with fever, and she stammered: "Now what shall we do? Now what shall we do?"

"If you want to sell him with all the wood I'll give you two shillings for him," said the carter, who had his wagon empty. And as the woman looked at him with vacant eyes, he added, "I'm only buying the wood, because that's all the ass is worth!" And he gave a kick at the carcass, which sounded like a burst drum.

Robert Louis Stevenson
1850-1894

DURING his lifetime and for many years following his death Robert Louis Stevenson was the most beloved of writers, and far and away the most attractive figure in the literary world of his generation. "The most inspiriting, the most fascinating human being that I have ever known," Edmund Gosse said.

Stevenson contracted tuberculosis at an early age and spent a good part of his life traveling in search of health. Born in Edinburgh, he was graduated there as a civil engineer and later admitted to the bar. But Scotland, which he so dearly loved, was the one country that his fragile health could not stand up against. Every year he stayed there he became worse. He tried France and Germany and eventually America. (While in California he married the woman with whom he had long been in love—an American woman of forceful personality, eleven years older than he, and married when he met her. After her divorce they lived in the mining camp described in *The Silverado Squatters*.) In the course of the years he went to Saranac, the New Jersey coast, Davos, and the French Riviera. Finally he bought a schooner, and with his wife and stepson cruised in warm waters on a long last journey that ended in Samoa, where he later died.

At no time could Stevenson work more than a few hours of a few consecutive days, and most of his writing had to be done in bed. But he was indefatigable, and his output—essays, stories, novels, poetry, travel books—is both considerable and brilliant. The full charm of his personality, so inseparable from his writing, comes through most vividly in his letters, collected and published after his death.

In Samoa the natives called Stevenson Tusitala (Teller of Tales). They loved him dearly, and buried him, at his own request, high on a mountain peak.

"A Lodging for the Night" was his first published story, and one of his most successful.

A Lodging for the Night

BY ROBERT LOUIS STEVENSON

IT WAS late in November, 1456. The snow fell over Paris with rigorous, relentless persistence; sometimes the wind made a sally and scattered it in flying vortices; sometimes there was a lull, and flake after flake descended out of the black night air, silent, circuitous, interminable. To poor people, looking up under moist eyebrows, it seemed a wonder where it all came from. Master Francis Villon had propounded an alternative that afternoon at a tavern window: was it only Pagan Jupiter plucking geese upon Olympus? or were the holy angels moulting? He was only a poor Master of Arts, he went on; and as the question somewhat touched upon divinity, he durst not venture to conclude. A silly old priest from Montargis, who was among the company, treated the young rascal to a bottle of wine in honor of the jest and grimaces with which it was accompanied, and swore on his own white beard that he had been just such another irreverent dog when he was Villon's age.

The air was raw and pointed, but not far below freezing; and the flakes were large, damp, and adhesive. The whole city was sheeted up. An army might have marched from end to end and not a footfall given the alarm. If there were any belated birds in heaven, they saw the island like a large white patch, and the bridges like slim white spars, on the black ground of the river. High up overhead the snow settled among the tracery of the cathedral towers. Many a niche was drifted full; many a statue wore a long white bonnet on its grotesque or sainted head. The gargoyles had been transformed into great false noses, drooping towards the point. The crockets were like upright pillows swollen on one side. In the intervals of the wind, there was a dull sound of dripping about the precincts of the church.

The cemetery of St. John had taken its own share of the snow. All the graves were decently covered; tall white housetops stood around in grave array; worthy burghers were long ago in bed, benightcapped like their domiciles; there was no light in all the neighborhood but a little peep from a lamp that hung swinging in the church choir, and tossed the shadows to and fro in time to its oscillations. The clock was hard on ten when the patrol went by with halberds and a lantern, beating their hands; and they saw nothing suspicious about the cemetery of St. John.

Yet there was a small house, backed up against the cemetery wall, which was still awake, and awake to evil purpose, in that snoring district. There was not much to betray it from without; only a stream of warm vapor from the chimney top, a patch where the snow melted on the roof, and a few half-obliterated footprints at the door. But within, behind the shuttered windows, Master Francis Villon the poet, and some of the thievish crew with whom he consorted, were keeping the night alive and passing round the bottle.

A great pile of living embers diffused a strong and ruddy glow from the arched chimney. Before this straddled Dom Nicolas, the Picardy monk, with his skirts picked up and his fat legs bared to the comfortable warmth. His dilated shadow cut the room in half; and the firelight only escaped on either side of his broad person, and in a little pool between his outspread feet. His face had the beery, bruised appearance of the continual drinker's; it was covered with a network of congested veins, purple in ordinary circumstances, but now pale violet, for even with his back to the fire the cold pinched him on the other side. His cowl had half fallen back, and made a strange excrescence on either side of his bull neck. So he straddled, grumbling, and cut the room in half with the shadow of his portly frame.

On the right, Villon and Guy Tabary were huddled together over a scrap of parchment; Villon making a ballade which he was to call the "Ballade of Roast Fish," and Tabary spluttering admiration at his shoulder. The poet was a rag of a man, dark, little, and lean, with hollow cheeks and thin black locks. He carried his four-and-twenty years with feverish animation. Greed had made folds about his eyes, evil smiles had puckered his mouth. The wolf and pig struggled together in his face. It was an eloquent, sharp, ugly, earthly countenance. His hands were small and prehensile, with fingers knotted like a cord; and they were continually flickering in front of him in violent and expressive pantomime. As for Tabary, a broad, complacent, admiring imbecility breathed from his squash nose and slobbering lips: he had become a thief, just as he might have become the most decent of burgesses, by the imperious chance that rules the lives of human geese and human donkeys.

At the monk's other hand, Montigny and Thevenin Pensete played a game of chance. About the first there clung some flavor of good birth and training, as about a fallen angel; something long, lithe, and courtly in the person; something aquiline and darkling in the face. Thevenin, poor soul, was in great feather: he had done a good stroke of knavery that afternoon in the Faubourg St. Jacques, and all night he had been gaining from Montigny. A flat smile illuminated his face; his bald head shone rosily in a garland of red curls; his little protuberant stomach shook with silent chucklings as he swept in his gains.

"Doubles or quits?" said Thevenin.

Montigny nodded grimly.

"Some may prefer to dine in state," wrote Villon, *"on bread and cheese on silver plate. Or, or—*help me out, Guido!"

Tabary giggled.

"Or parsley on a golden dish," scribbled the poet.

The wind was freshening without; it drove the snow before it, and sometimes raised its voice in a victorious whoop, and made sepulchral grumblings in the chimney. The cold was growing sharper as the night went on. Villon, protruding his lips, imitated the gust with something between a whistle and a groan. It was an eerie, uncomfortable talent of the poet's, much detested by the Picardy monk.

"Can't you hear it rattle in the gibbet?" said Villon. "They are all dancing the devil's jig on nothing, up there. You may dance, my gallants, you'll be none the warmer! Whew! what a gust! Down went somebody just now! A medlar the fewer on the three-legged medlar tree!—I say, Dom Nicolas, it'll be cold tonight on the St. Denis Road?" he asked.

Dom Nicolas winked both his big eyes, and seemed to choke upon his Adam's apple. Montfaucon, the great grisly Paris gibbet, stood hard by the St. Denis Road, and the pleasantry touched him on the raw. As for Tabary, he laughed immoderately over the medlars; he had never heard anything more lighthearted; and he held his sides and crowed. Villon fetched him a fillip on the nose, which turned his mirth into an attack of coughing.

"Oh, stop that row," said Villon, "and think of rhymes to 'fish.'"

"Doubles or quits," said Montigny doggedly.

"With all my heart," quoth Thevenin.

"Is there any more in that bottle?" asked the monk.

"Open another," said Villon. "How do you ever hope to fill that big hogshead, your body, with little things like bottles? And how do you expect to get to heaven? How many angels, do you fancy, can be spared to carry up a single monk from Picardy? Or do you think yourself another Elias—and they'll send the coach for you?"

"Hominibus impossible," replied the monk as he filled his glass.

Tabary was in ecstasies.

Villon filliped his nose again.

"Laugh at my jokes, if you like," he said.

"It was very good," objected Tabary.

Villon made a face at him. "Think of rhymes to 'fish,'" he said. "What have you to do with Latin? You'll wish you knew none of it at the great assizes, when the devil calls for Guido Tabary, clericus—the devil with the humpback and redhot fingernails. Talking of the devil," he added in a whisper, "look at Montigny!"

All three peered covertly at the gamester. He did not seem to be enjoying his luck. His mouth was a little to a side; one nostril nearly shut, and the other much inflated. The black dog was on his back, as people say, in terrifying nursery metaphor; and he breathed hard under the gruesome burden.

"He looks as if he could knife him," whispered Tabary, with round eyes.

The monk shuddered, and turned his face and spread his open hands to the red embers. It was the cold that thus affected Dom Nicolas, and not any excess of moral sensibility.

"Come now," said Villon—"about this ballade. How does it run so far?" And beating time with his hand, he read it aloud to Tabary.

They were interrupted at the fourth rhyme by a brief and fatal movement among the gamesters.

The round was completed, and Thevenin was just opening his mouth to claim another victory, when Montigny leaped up, swift as an adder, and stabbed him to the heart. The blow took effect before he had time to utter a cry, before he had time to move. A tremor or two convulsed his frame; his hands opened and shut, his heels rattled on the floor; then his head rolled backward over one shoulder with the eyes wide open, and Thevenin Pensete's spirit had returned to Him who made it.

Everyone sprang to his feet; but the business was over in two two's. The four living fellows looked at each other in rather a ghastly fashion; the dead man contemplating a corner of the roof with a singular and ugly leer.

"My God!" said Tabary; and he began to pray in Latin.

Villon broke out into hysterical laughter. He came a step forward and ducked a ridiculous bow at Thevenin, and laughed still louder. Then he sat down suddenly, all of a heap, upon a stool, and continued laughing bitterly as though he would shake himself to pieces.

Montigny recovered his composure first.

"Let's see what he has about him," he remarked, and he picked the dead man's pockets with a practiced hand, and divided the money into four equal portions on the table. "There's for you," he said.

The monk received his share with a deep sigh, and a single stealthy glance at the dead Thevenin, who was beginning to sink into himself and topple sideways off the chair.

"We're all in for it," cried Villon, swallowing his mirth. "It's a hanging job for every man jack of us that's here—not to speak of those who

aren't." He made a shocking gesture in the air with his raised right hand, and put out his tongue and threw his head on one side, so as to counterfeit the appearance of one who has been hanged. Then he pocketed his share of the spoil, and executed a shuffle with his feet as if to restore the circulation.

Tabary was the last to help himself; he made a dash at the money, and retired to the other end of the apartment.

Montigny stuck Thevenin upright in the chair, and drew out the dagger, which was followed by a jet of blood.

"You fellows had better be moving," he said, as he wiped the blade on his victim's doublet.

"I think we had," returned Villon, with a gulp. "Damn his fat head!" he broke out. "It sticks in my throat like phlegm. What right has a man to have red hair when he is dead?" And he fell all of a heap again upon the stool, and fairly covered his face with his hands.

Montigny and Dom Nicolas laughed aloud, even Tabary feebly chiming in.

"Crybaby," said the monk.

"I always said he was a woman," added Montigny, with a sneer. "Sit up, can't you?" he went on, giving another shake to the murdered body. "Tread out that fire, Nick!"

But Nick was better employed; he was quietly taking Villon's purse, as the poet sat limp and trembling on the stool where he had been making a ballade not three minutes before. Montigny and Tabary dumbly demanded a share of the booty, which the monk silently promised as he passed the little bag into the bosom of his gown. In many ways an artistic nature unfits a man for practical existence.

No sooner had the theft been accomplished than Villon shook himself, jumped to his feet, and began helping to scatter and extinguish the embers. Meanwhile Montigny opened the door and cautiously peered into the street. The coast was clear; there was no meddlesome patrol in sight. Still it was judged wiser to slip out severally; and as Villon was himself in a hurry to escape from the neighborhood of the dead Thevenin, and the rest were in a still greater hurry to get rid of him before he should discover the loss of his money, he was the first by general consent to issue forth into the street.

The wind had triumphed and swept all the clouds from heaven. Only a few vapors, as thin as moonlight, fleeted rapidly across the stars. It was bitter cold; and by a common optical effect, things seemed almost more definite than in the broadest daylight. The sleeping city was absolutely still; a company of white hoods, a field full of little alps, below the twinkling stars. Villon cursed his fortune. Would it were still snowing! Now, wherever he went, he left an indelible trail behind him on the glittering streets; wherever he went he was still tethered to the house by the cemetery of St. John; wherever he went he must weave, with his own plodding feet, the rope that bound him to the crime and would bind him to the gallows. The leer of the dead man came back to him with a new significance. He snapped his fingers as if to pluck up his own spirits, and choosing a street at random, stepped boldly forward in the snow.

Two things preoccupied him as he went: the aspect of the gallows at Montfaucon in this bright, windy phase of the night's existence, for one; and for another, the look of the dead man with his bald head and garland of red curls. Both struck cold upon his heart, and he kept quickening his pace as if he could escape from unpleasant thoughts by mere fleetness of foot. Sometimes he looked back over his shoulder with a sudden nervous jerk; but he was the only moving thing in the white streets, except when the wind swooped round a corner and threw up the snow, which was beginning to freeze, in spouts of glittering dust.

Suddenly he saw, a long way before him, a black clump and a couple of lanterns. The clump was in motion, and the lanterns swung as though carried by men walking. It was a patrol. And though it was merely crossing his line of march he judged it wiser to get out of eyeshot as speedily as he could. He was not in the humor to be challenged, and he was conscious of making a very conspicuous mark upon the snow. Just on his left hand there stood a great hotel, with some turrets and a large porch before the door; it was half ruinous, he remembered, and had long stood empty; and so he made three steps of it, and jumped into the shelter of the porch. It was pretty dark inside, after the glimmer of the snowy streets, and he was groping forward with outspread hands, when he stumbled over some substance which offered an indescribable mixture of resistances, hard and soft, firm and loose. His heart gave a leap, and he sprang two steps back and stared dreadfully at the obstacle. Then he gave a little laugh of relief. It was only a woman, and she dead. He knelt beside her to make sure upon this latter point. She was freezing cold, and rigid like a stick. A little ragged finery fluttered in the wind about her hair and her cheeks had been heavily rouged that same afternoon. Her pockets were quite empty; but in her stocking, underneath the garter, Villon found two of the small coins that went by the name of whites. It was little enough; but it was always something; and the poet was moved with a deep sense of pathos that she should have died before she had spent her money. That seemed to him a dark and pitiable mystery; and he looked from the coins in his hand to the dead woman, and back again to the coins, shaking his head over the riddle of man's life. Henry V of England, dying at Vincennes just after he had conquered France, and this poor jade cut off by a cold draught in a great man's doorway, before she had time to spend her couple of whites—it seemed a cruel way to carry on the world. Two whites would have taken such a little while to squander; and yet it would have been one more good taste in the mouth, one more smack of the lips, before the devil got the soul, and the body was left to birds and vermin. He would like to use all his tallow before the light was blown out and the lantern broken.

While these thoughts were passing through his mind, he was feeling, half mechanically, for his purse. Suddenly his heart stopped beating; a feeling of cold scales passed up the back of his legs, and a cold blow seemed to fall upon his scalp. He stood petrified for a moment; then he felt again with one feverish movement; and then his loss burst upon him, and he was covered at once with perspiration. To spendthrifts money is so living and actual —it is such a thin veil between them and their pleasures! There is only one limit to their fortune—that of

time; and a spendthrift with only a few crowns is the Emperor of Rome until they are spent. For such a person to lose his money is to suffer the most shocking reverse, and fall from heaven to hell, from all to nothing, in a breath. And all the more if he has put his head in the halter for it; if he may be hanged tomorrow for that same purse, so dearly earned, so foolishly departed! Villon stood and cursed; he threw the two whites into the street; he shook his fist at heaven; he stamped, and was not horrified to find himself trampling the poor corpse. Then he began rapidly to retrace his steps towards the house beside the cemetery. He had forgotten all fear of the patrol, which was long gone by at any rate, and had no idea but that of his lost purse. It was in vain that he looked right and left upon the snow; nothing was to be seen. He had not dropped it in the streets. Had it fallen in the house? He would have liked dearly to go in and see; but the idea of the grisly occupant unmanned him. And he saw besides, as he drew near, that their efforts to put out the fire had been unsuccessful; on the contrary, it had broken into a blaze, and a changeful light played in the chinks of door and window, and revived his terror for the authorities and Paris gibbet.

He returned to the hotel with the porch, and groped about upon the snow for the money he had thrown away in his childish passion. But he could only find one white; the other had probably struck sideways and sunk deeply in. With a single white in his pocket, all his projects for a rousing night in some wild tavern vanished utterly away. And it was not only pleasure that fled laughing from his grasp; positive discomfort, positive pain, attacked him as he stood ruefully before the porch. His perspiration had dried upon him; and although the wind had now fallen, a binding frost was setting in stronger with every hour, and he felt benumbed and sick at heart. What was to be done? Late as was the hour, improbable as was success, he would try the house of his adopted father, the chaplain of St. Benoît.

He ran there all the way, and knocked timidly. There was no answer. He knocked again and again, taking heart with every stroke; and at last steps were heard approaching from within. A barred wicket fell open in the iron-studded door, and emitted a gush of yellow light.

"Hold up your face to the wicket," said the chaplain from within.

"It's only me," whimpered Villon.

"Oh, it's only you, is it?" returned the chaplain; and he cursed him with foul unpriestly oaths for disturbing him at such an hour, and bade him be off to hell, where he came from.

"My hands are blue to the wrist," pleaded Villon; "my feet are dead and full of twinges; my nose aches with the sharp air; the cold lies at my heart. I may be dead before morning. Only this once, Father, and before God, I will never ask again!"

"You should have come earlier," said the ecclesiastic coolly. "Young men require a lesson now and then." He shut the wicket and retired deliberately into the interior of the house.

Villon was beside himself; he beat upon the door with his hands and feet, and shouted hoarsely after the chaplain.

"Wormy old fox!" he cried. "If I had my hand under your twist, I would send you flying headlong into the bottomless pit."

A door shut in the interior, faintly audible to the poet down long passages. He passed his hand over his mouth with an oath. And then the humor of the situation struck him, and he laughed and looked lightly up to heaven, where the stars seemed to be winking over his discomfiture.

What was to be done? It looked very like a night in the frosty streets. The idea of the dead woman popped into his imagination, and gave him a hearty fright; what had happened to her in the early night might very well happen to him before morning. And he so young! and with such immense possibilities of disorderly amusement before him! He felt quite pathetic over the notion of his own fate, as if it had been someone else's, and made a little imaginative vignette of the scene in the morning when they should find his body.

He passed all his chances under review, turning the white between his thumb and forefinger. Unfortunately he was on bad terms with some old friends who would once have taken pity on him in such a plight. He had lampooned them in verses; he had beaten and cheated them; and yet now, when he was in so close a pinch, he thought there was at least one who might perhaps relent. It was a chance. It was worth trying at least, and he would go and see.

On the way, two little accidents happened to him which colored his musings in a very different manner. For, first, he fell in with the track of a patrol, and walked in it for some hundred yards, although it lay out of his direction. And this spirited him up; at least he had confused his trail; for he was still possessed with the idea of people tracking him all about Paris over the snow, and collaring him next morning before he was awake. The other matter affected him quite differently. He passed a street corner, where, not so long before, a woman and her child had been devoured by wolves. This was just the kind of weather, he reflected, when wolves might take it into their heads to enter Paris again; and a lone man in these deserted streets would run the chance of something worse than a mere scare. He stopped and looked upon the place with an unpleasant interest—it was the center where several lanes intersected each other; and he looked down them all, one after another, and held his breath to listen, lest he should detect some galloping black things on the snow or hear the sound of howling between him and the river. He remembered his mother telling him the story and pointing out the spot, while he was yet a child. His mother! If he only knew where she lived, he might make sure at least of shelter. He determined he would inquire upon the morrow; nay, he would go and see her, too, poor old girl! So thinking, he arrived at his destination—his last hope for the night.

The house was quite dark, like its neighbors; and yet after a few taps, he heard a movement overhead, a door opening, and a cautious voice asking who was there. The poet named himself in a loud whisper, and waited, not without some trepidation, the result. Nor had he to wait long. A window was suddenly opened, and a pailful of slops splashed down upon the doorstep. Villon had not been unprepared for something of the sort, and had put himself as much in shelter as the nature of the porch admitted; but for all that, he was deplorably drenched below the waist. His hose began to freeze almost at once.

Death from cold and exposure stared him in the face; he remembered he was of phthisical tendency, and began coughing tentatively. But the gravity of the danger steadied his nerves. He stopped a few hundred yards from the door where he had been so rudely used, and reflected with his finger to his nose. He could only see one way of getting a lodging and that was to take it. He had noticed a house not far away, which looked as if it might be easily broken into, and thither he betook himself promptly, entertaining himself on the way with the idea of a room still hot, with a table still loaded with the remains of supper, where he might pass the rest of the black hours and whence he should issue, on the morrow, with an armful of valuable plate. He even considered on what viands and what wines he should prefer; and as he was calling the roll of his favorite dainties, roast fish presented itself to his mind with an odd mixture of amusement and horror.

"I shall never finish that ballade," he thought to himself; and then, with another shudder at the recollection, "Oh, damn his fat head!" he repeated fervently, and spat upon the snow.

The house in question looked dark at first sight; but as Villon made a preliminary inspection in search of the handiest point of attack, a little twinkle of light caught his eye from behind a curtained window.

"The devil!" he thought. "People awake! Some student or some saint, confound the crew. Can't they get drunk and lie in bed snoring like their neighbors! What's the good of curfew, and poor devils of bell ringers jumping at a rope's end in bell towers? What's the use of day, if people sit up all night? The gripes to them!" He grinned as he saw where his logic was leading him. "Every man to his business, after all," added he, "and if they're awake, by the Lord, I may come by a supper honestly for once, and cheat the devil."

He went boldly to the door and knocked with an assured hand. On both previous occasions, he had knocked timidly and with some dread of attracting notice; but now when he had just discarded the thought of a burglarious entry, knocking at a door seemed a mighty simple and innocent proceeding. The sound of his blows echoed through the house with thin, phantasmal reverberations, as though it were quite empty; but these had scarcely died away before a measured tread drew near, a couple of bolts were withdrawn, and one wing was opened broadly, as though no guile or fear of guile were known to those within. A tall figure of a man, muscular and spare, but a little bent, confronted Villon. The head was massive in bulk, but finely sculptured; the nose blunt at the bottom, but refining upward to where it joined a pair of strong and honest eyebrows; the mouth and eyes surrounded with delicate markings, and the whole face based upon a thick white beard, boldly and squarely trimmed. Seen as it was by the light of a flickering hand lamp, it looked perhaps nobler than it had a right to do; but it was a fine face, honorable, rather than intelligent, strong, simple, and righteous.

"You knock late, sir," said the old man in resonant, courteous tones.

Villon cringed, and brought up many servile words of apology; at a crisis of this sort, the beggar was uppermost in him, and the man of genius hid his head with confusion.

"You are cold," repeated the old man, "and hungry? Well, step in." And he ordered him into the house with a noble enough gesture.

"Some great seigneur," thought Villon, as his host, setting down the lamp on the flagged pavement of the entry, shot the bolts once more into their places.

"You will pardon me if I go in front," he said, when this was done; and he preceded the poet upstairs into a large apartment, warmed with a pan of charcoal and lit by a great lamp hanging from the roof. It was very bare of furniture: only some gold plate on a sideboard; some folios; and a stand of armor between the windows. Some smart tapestry hung upon the walls, representing the crucifixion of our Lord in one piece, and in another a scene of shepherds and shepherdesses by a running stream. Over the chimney was a shield of arms.

"Will you seat yourself," said the old man, "and forgive me if I leave you? I am alone in my house tonight, and if you are to eat I must forage for you myself."

No sooner was his host gone than Villon leaped from the chair on which he had just seated himself, and began examining the room, with the stealth and passion of a cat. He weighed the gold flagons in his hand, opened all the folios, and investigated the arms upon the shield, and the stuff with which the seats were lined. He raised the window curtains, and saw that the windows were set with rich stained glass in figures, so far as he could see, of martial import. Then he stood in the middle of the room, drew a long breath and retaining it with puffed cheeks, looked round and round him, turning on his heels, as if to impress every feature of the apartment on his memory.

"Seven pieces of plate," he said. "If there had been ten, I would have risked it. A fine house, and a fine old master, so help me all the saints!"

And just then, hearing the old man's tread returning along the corridor, he stole back to his chair, and began humbly toasting his wet legs before the charcoal pan.

His entertainer had a plate of meat in one hand and a jug of wine in the other. He sat down the plate upon the table, motioning Villon to draw in his chair, and going to the sideboard, brought back two goblets, which he filled.

"I drink to your better fortune," he said gravely, touching Villon's cup with his own.

"To our better acquaintance," said the poet, growing bold. A mere man of the people would have been awed by the courtesy of the old seigneur, but Villon was hardened in that matter; he had made mirth for great lords before now, and found them as black rascals as himself. And so he devoted himself to the viands with a ravenous gusto, while the old man, leaning backward, watched him with steady, curious eyes.

"You have blood on your shoulder, my man," he said.

Montigny must have laid his wet hand upon him as he left the house. He cursed Montigny in his heart.

"It was none of my shedding," he stammered.

"I had not supposed so," returned his host quietly. "A brawl?"

"Well, something of that sort," Villon admitted with a quaver.

"Perhaps a fellow murdered?"

"Oh, no, not murdered," said the poet, more and more confused. "It was all fair play—murdered by acci-

dent. I had no hand in it, God strike me dead!" he added fervently.

"One rogue the fewer, I dare say," observed the master of the house.

"You may dare to say that," agreed Villon, infinitely relieved. "As big a rogue as there is between here and Jerusalem. He turned up his toes like a lamb. But it was a nasty thing to look at. I dare say you've seen dead men in your time, my lord?" he added, glancing at the armor.

"Many," said the old man. "I have followed the wars, as you imagine."

Villon laid down his knife and fork, which he had just taken up again.

"Were any of them bald?" he asked.

"Oh, yes; and with hair as white as mine."

"I don't think I should mind the white so much," said Villon. "His was red." And he had a return of his shuddering and tendency to laughter, which he drowned with a great draught of wine. "I'm a little put out when I think of it," he went on. "I knew him—damn him! And then the cold gives a man fancies—or the fancies give a man cold, I don't know which."

"Have you any money?" asked the old man.

"I have one white," returned the poet, laughing. "I got it out of a dead jade's stocking in a porch. She was as dead as Caesar, poor wench, and as cold as a church, with bits of ribbon sticking in her hair. This is a hard world in winter for wolves and wenches and poor rogues like me."

"I," said the old man, "am Enguerrand de la Feuillée, seigneur de Brisetout, bailly du Patatrac. Who and what may you be?"

Villon rose and made a suitable reverence. "I am called Francis Villon," he said, "a poor Master of Arts of this university. I know some Latin, and a deal of vice. I can make chansons, ballades, lais, virelais, and roundels, and I am very fond of wine. I was born in a garret, and I shall not improbably die upon the gallows. I may add, my lord, that from this night forward I am your lordship's very obsequious servant to command."

"No servant of mine," said the knight; "my guest for this evening, and no more."

"A very grateful guest," said Villon politely, and he drank in dumb show to his entertainer.

"You are shrewd," began the old man, tapping his forehead, "very shrewd; you have learning; you are a clerk; and yet you take a small piece of money off a dead woman in the street. Is it not a kind of theft?"

"It is a kind of theft much practiced in the wars, my lord."

"The wars are the field of honor," returned the old man proudly. "There a man plays his life upon the cast; he fights in the name of his lord the king, his Lord God, and all their lordships the holy saints and angels."

"Put it," said Villon, "that I were really a thief, should I not play my life also, and against heavier odds?"

"For gain but not for honor."

"Gain?" repeated Villon with a shrug. "Gain! The poor fellow wants supper, and takes it. So does the soldier in a campaign. Why, what are all these requisitions we hear so much about? If they are not gain to those who take them, they are loss enough to the others. The men-at-arms drink by a good fire, while the burgher bites his nails to buy them wine and wood. I have seen a good many plowmen swinging on trees about the country; ay, I have seen thirty to one elm, and a very poor figure they made; and when I asked someone how all these came to be hanged, I was told it was because they could not scrape together enough crowns to satisfy the men-at-arms."

"These things are a necessity of war, which the low-born must endure with constancy. It is true that some captains drive overhard; there are spirits in every rank not easily moved by pity; and, indeed, many follow arms who are no better than brigands."

"You see," said the poet, "you cannot separate the soldier from the brigand; and what is a thief but an isolated brigand with circumspect manners? I steal a couple of mutton chops, without so much as disturbing people's sleep; the farmer grumbles a bit, but sups none the less wholesomely on what remains. You come up blowing gloriously on a trumpet, take away the whole sheep, and beat the farmer pitifully into the bargain. I have no trumpet; I am only Tom, Dick, or Harry; I am a rogue and a dog, and hanging's too good for me—with all my heart; but just ask the farmer which of us he prefers, just find out which of us he lies awake to curse on cold nights."

"Look at us two," said his lordship. "I am old, strong, and honored. If I were turned from my house tomorrow, hundreds would be proud to shelter me. Poor people would go out and pass the night in the streets with their children, if I merely hinted that I wished to be alone. And I find you up, wandering homeless, and picking farthings off dead women by the wayside! I fear no man and nothing; I have seen you tremble and lose countenance at a word. I wait God's summons contentedly in my own house, or, if it please the king to call me out again, upon the field of battle. You look for the gallows; a rough, swift death, without hope or honor. Is there no difference between these two?"

"As far as to the moon," Villon acquiesced. "But if I had been born lord of Brisetout, and you had been the poor scholar Francis, would the difference have been any the less? Should not I have been warming my knees at this charcoal pan, and would not you have been groping for farthings in the snow? Should not I have been the soldier, and you the thief?"

"A thief?" cried the old man. "I a thief! If you understood your words, you would repent them."

Villon turned out his hands with a gesture of inimitable impudence. "If your lordship had done me the honor to follow my argument!" he said.

"I do you too much honor in submitting to your presence," said the knight. "Learn to curb your tongue when you speak with old and honorable men, or someone hastier than I may reprove you in a sharper fashion." And he rose and paced the lower end of the apartment, struggling with anger and antipathy. Villon surreptitiously refilled his cup, and settled himself more comfortably in the chair, crossing his knees and leaning his head upon one hand and the elbow against the back of the chair. He was now replete and warm, and he was in nowise frightened for his host, having gauged him as justly as was possible between two such different characters. The night was far spent, and in a very comfortable fashion after

all; and he felt morally certain of a safe departure on the morrow.

"Tell me one thing," said the old man, pausing in his walk. "Are you really a thief?"

"I claim the sacred right of hospitality," returned the poet. "My lord, I am."

"You are very young," the knight continued.

"I should never have been so old," replied Villon, showing his fingers, "if I had not helped myself with these ten talents. They have been my nursing mothers and my nursing fathers."

"You may still repent and change."

"I repent daily," said the poet. "There are few people more given to repentance than poor Francis. As for change, let somebody change my circumstances. A man must continue to eat, if it were only that he may continue to repent."

"The change must begin in the heart," returned the old man solemnly.

"My dear lord," answered Villon, "do you really fancy that I steal for pleasure? I hate stealing, like any other piece of work or of danger. My teeth chatter when I see a gallows. But I must eat, I must drink, I must mix in society of some sort. What the devil! Man is not a solitary animal—*Cui Deus fæminam tradit*. Make me king's pantler—make me abbot of St. Denis; make me bailly of the Patatrac; and then I shall be changed indeed. But as long as you leave me the poor scholar Francis Villon, without a farthing, why, of course, I remain the same."

"The Grace of God is all-powerful."

"I should be a heretic to question it," said Francis. "It has made you lord of Brisetout and bailly of the Patatrac; it has given me nothing but the quick wits under my hat and these ten toes upon my hands. May I help myself to wine? I thank you respectfully. By God's grace, you have a very superior vintage."

The lord of Brisetout walked to and fro with his hands behind his back. Perhaps he was not yet quite settled in his mind about the parallel between thieves and soldiers; perhaps Villon had interested him by some cross-thread of sympathy; perhaps his wits were simply muddled by so much unfamiliar reasoning; but whatever the cause, he somehow yearned to convert the young man to a better way of thinking, and could not make up his mind to drive him forth again into the street.

"There is something more than I can understand in this," he said at length. "Your mouth is full of subtleties, and the devil has led you very far astray; but the devil is only a very weak spirit before God's truth, and all his subtleties vanish at a word of true honor, like darkness at morning. Listen to me once more. I learned long ago that a gentleman should live chivalrously and lovingly to God, and the king, and his lady; and though I have seen many strange things done, I have still striven to command my ways upon that rule. It is not only written in all noble histories, but in every man's heart if he will take care to read. You speak of food and wine, and I know very well that hunger is a difficult trial to endure; but you do not speak of other wants; you say nothing of honor, of faith to God and other men, of courtesy, of love without reproach. It may be that I am not very wise—and yet I think I am—but you seem to me like one who has lost his way and made a great error in life. You are attend-ing to the little wants, and you have totally forgotten the great and only real ones, like a man who should be doctoring toothache on the Judgment Day. For such things as honor and love and faith are not only nobler than food and drink, but indeed I think we desire them more, and suffer more sharply for their absence. I speak to you as I think you will most easily understand me. Are you not, while careful to fill your belly, disregarding another appetite in your heart, which spoils the pleasure of your life and keeps you continually wretched?"

Villon was sensibly nettled under all this sermonizing.

"You think I have no sense of honor!" he cried. "I'm poor enough, God knows! It's hard to see rich people with their gloves, and you blowing in your hands. An empty belly is a bitter thing, although you speak so lightly of it. If you had had as many as I, perhaps you would change your tune. Anyway I'm a thief—make the most of that—but I'm not a devil from hell, God strike me dead. I would have you to know I've an honor of my own, as good as yours, though I don't prate about it all day long, as if it was a God's miracle to have any. It seems quite natural to me; I keep it in its box till it's wanted. Why now, look you here, how long have I been in this room with you? Did you not tell me you were alone in the house? Look at your gold plate! You're strong, if you like, but you're old and unarmed, and I have my knife. What did I want but a jerk of the elbow and here would have been you with the cold steel in your bowels, and there would have been me, clinking in the streets, with an armful of golden cups! Did you suppose I hadn't wit enough to see that? And

I scorned the action. There are your damned goblets, as safe as in a church; there are you, with your heart ticking as good as new; and here am I, ready to go out again as poor as I came in, with my one white that you threw in my teeth! And you think I have no sense of honor—God strike me dead!"

The old man stretched out his right arm. "I will tell you what you are," he said. "You are a rogue, my man, an impudent and blackhearted rogue and vagabond. I have passed an hour with you. Oh! believe me, I feel myself disgraced! And you have eaten and drunk at my table. But now I am sick of your presence; the day has come, and the night-bird should be off to his roost. Will you go before, or after?"

"Which you please," returned the poet, rising. "I believe you to be strictly honorable." He thoughtfully emptied his cup. "I wish I could add you were intelligent," he went on, knocking on his head with his knuckles. "Age! age! the brains stiff and rheumatic."

The old man preceded him from a point of self-respect; Villon followed, whistling, with his thumbs in his girdle.

"God pity you," said the lord of Brisetout at the door.

"Good-by, Papa," returned Villon with a yawn. "Many thanks for the cold mutton."

The door closed behind him. The dawn was breaking over the white roofs. A chill, uncomfortable morning ushered in the day. Villon stood and heartily stretched himself in the middle of the road.

"A very dull old gentleman," he thought. "I wonder what his goblets may be worth."

Maurice Hewlett
1861-1923

MAURICE HEWLETT is in a class by himself, part of no trend
and creating no trend. He was a medievalist, a lecturer on
medieval art, living in a house that dated back to 1350, and
visiting the ancient cities of Italy for a part of every year.
He "used other men's art and wisdom as a springboard," he
said of himself. His best stories are those excursions into the
rich, dark shadows of the Middle Ages with all their romance
and pageantry, the richer and the more romantic for his
scholarly and original mind. His prose has the texture of
tapestry.

But Maurice Hewlett was no escapist: he lived very much
in the present. He considered himself a worker of the English
countryside, and in his later years moved into a workman's
cottage. During World War I he built planes for the British,
made a fortune, and gave it all away, while his wife, a vicar's
daughter whom he married in 1888, became, surprisingly
enough, an aviatrix. . . . *Little Novels of Italy* (published
in 1899), from which "Quattrocentisteria" comes, is probably his most popular book.

Quattrocentisteria

(HOW SANDRO BOTTICELLI SAW SIMONETTA IN THE SPRING)

BY MAURICE HEWLETT

I

Up at Fiesole, among the olives and chestnuts which cloud the steeps, the magnificent Lorenzo was entertaining his guests on a morning in April. The olives were just whitening to silver; they stretched in a trembling sea down the slope. Beyond lay Forence, misty and golden; and round about were the mossy hills, cut sharp and definite against a grape-blue sky, printed with starry buildings and sober ranks of cypress. The sun, catching the mosaics of San Miniato and the brazen cross on the façade, made them shine like sword blades in the quiver of the heat between. For the valley was just a lake of hot air, hot and murky—"fever weather," said the people in the streets—with a glaring summer sun let in between two long spells of fog. 'Twas unnatural at that season, via; but the blessed saints sent the weather and one could only be careful what one was about at sundown.

Up at the Villa, with brisk morning airs rustling overhead, in the cool shades of trees and lawns, it was pleasant to lie still, watching these things, while a silky young exquisite sang to his lute a not-too-audacious ballad about Selvaggia, or Becchina and the saucy Prior of Sant' Onofrio. He sang well too, that dark-eyed boy; the girl at whose feet he was crouched was laughing and blushing at once; and, being very fair, she blushed hotly. She dared not raise her eyes to look into his, and he knew it and was quietly measuring his strength—it was quite a comedy! At each wanton refrain he lowered his voice to a whisper and bent a little forward. And the girl's laughter became hysterical; she was shaking with the effort to control herself. At last she looked up with a sort of sob in her breath and saw his mocking smile and the gleam of the wild beast in his eyes. She grew white, rose hastily, and turned away to join a group of ladies sitting apart. A man with a heavy, rather sullen face and a bush of yellow hair falling over his forehead in a wave was standing aside, watching all this. He folded his arms and scowled under his big brows; and when the girl moved away his eyes followed her.

The lad ended his song in a broad

sarcasm amid bursts of laughter and applause. The Magnificent, sitting in his carved chair, nursed his sallow face and smiled approval. "My brother boasts his invulnerability," he said, turning to his neighbor, "let him look to it, Messer Cupido will have him yet. Already, we can see, he has been let into some of the secrets of the bower." The man bowed and smiled deferentially. "Signor Giuliano has all the qualities to win the love of ladies, and to retain it. Doubtless he awaits his destiny. The Wise Man has said that 'Beauty . . .'" The young poet enlarged on his text with some fire in his thin cheeks, while the company kept very silent. It was much to their liking; even Giuliano was absorbed; he sat on the ground, clasping one knee between his hands, smiling upwards into vacancy, as a man does whose imagination is touched. Lorenzo nursed his sallow face and beat time to the orator's cadences with his foot; he, too, was abstracted and smiling. At the end he spoke; "Our Marsilio himself has never said nobler words, my Agnolo. The mantle of the Attic prophet has descended indeed upon this Florence. And Beauty, as thou sayest, is from heaven. But where shall it be found here below, and how discerned?" The man of the heavy jowl was standing with folded arms, looking from under his brows at the group of girls. Lorenzo saw everything; he noticed him. "Our Sandro will tell us it is yonder. The Star of Genoa shines over Florence and our poor little constellations are gone out. Ecco, my Sandro, gravest and hardiest of painters, go summon Madonna Simonetta and her handmaidens to our symposium. Agnolo will speak further to us of this sovereignty of Beauty."

The painter bowed his head and moved away.

A green alley vaulted with thick ilex and myrtle formed a tapering vista where the shadows lay misty blue and pale shafts of light pierced through fitfully. At the far end it ran out into an open space and a splash of sunshine. A marble Ganymede with lifted arms rose in the middle like a white flame. The girls were there, intent upon some commerce of their own, flashing hither and thither over the grass in a flutter of saffron and green and crimson. Simonetta—Sandro could see—was a little apart, a very tall, isolated figure, clear and cold in a recess of shade, standing easily, resting on one hip with her hands behind her. A soft, straight robe of white clipped her close from shoulder to heel; the lines of her figure were thrust forward by her poise. His eye followed the swell of her bosom, very gentle and girlish, and the long folds of her dress falling thence to her knee. While she stood there, proud and remote, a chance beam of the sun shone on her head so that it seemed to burn. "Heaven salutes the Queen of Heaven—Venus Urania!" With an odd impulse he stopped, crossed himself, and then hurried on.

He told his errand to her; having no eyes for the others.

"Signorina—I am to acquaint her serenity that the divine poet Messer Agnolo is to speak of the sovereign power of beauty; of the Heavenly Beauty whereof Plato taught, as it is believed."

Simonetta arched a slim neck and looked down at the obsequious speaker, or at least he thought so. And he saw how fair she was, a creature how delicate and gracious, with gray eyes frank and wide, and full red lips where a smile (nervous and a little wistful, he judged, rather than defiant) seemed always to hover Such clear-cut, high beauty made him ashamed; but her coloring (for he was a painter) made his heart beat. She was no ice-bound shadow of deity then! but flesh and blood; a girl—a child, of timid, soft contours, of warm roses and blue veins laced in a pearly skin. And she was crowned with a heavy wealth of red-gold hair, twisted in great coils, bound about with pearls, and smoldering like molten metal where it fell rippling along her neck. She dazzled him, so that he could not face her or look further. His eyes dropped. He stood before her moody, disconcerted.

The girls, who had dissolved their company at his approach, listened to what he had to say, linked in knots of twos and threes. They needed no excuses to return; some were philosophers and poetesses; some had left their lovers in the ring round Lorenzo. So they went down the green alley still locked by the arms, by the waist or shoulders. They did not wait for Simonetta. She was a Genoese, and proud as the snow. Why did Giuliano love her? Did he love her, indeed? He was bewitched then, for she was cold, and a brazen creature in spite of it. How dare she bare her neck so! Oh! 'twas Genoese. *"Uomini senza fede e donne senza vergogna,"* they quoted as they ran.

And Simonetta walked alone down the way with her head high; but Sandro stepped behind, at the edge of her trailing white robe. . . .

. . . The poet was leaning against an ancient alabaster vase, soil-stained, yellow with age and its long sojourn in the loam, but with traces of its carved garlands clinging to it still. He fingered it lovingly as he talked. His oration was concluding, and his voice rose high and tremulous; there were sparks in his hollow eyes. . . . "And as this sovereign Beauty is queen of herself, so she is subject to none other, owns to no constraining custom, fears no reproach of man. What she wills, that has the force of a law. Being Beauty, her deeds are lovely and worshipful. Therefore Phryne, whom men, groping in darkness and the dull ways of earth, dubbed courtesan, shone in a court of law before the assembled nobles of Athens, naked and undismayed in the blaze of her fairness. And Athens discerned the goddess and trembled. Yes, and more; even as Aphrodite, whose darling she was, arose pure from the foam, so she too came up out of the sea in the presence of a host, and the Athenians, seeing no shame, thought none, but, rather, reverenced her the more. For what shame is it that the body of one so radiant in clear perfections should be revealed? Is then the garment of the soul, her very mold and image, so shameful? Shall we seek to know her essence by the garment of a garment, or hope to behold that which really is in the shadows we cast upon shadows? Shame is of the brute dullard who thinks shame. The evil ever sees Evil glaring at him. Plato, the golden-mouthed, with the soul of pure fire, has said the truth of this matter in his *De Republica*, the fifth book, where he speaks of young maids sharing the exercise of the palaestra, yea, and the Olympic contests even! For he says, 'Let the wives of our wardens bare themselves, for their virtue will be a robe; and let them share the toils of war and defend their country. And for the man who laughs at naked women exercising their bodies for high reasons, his laughter is a fruit of unripe wisdom, and he himself knows not what he is about; for that is ever the best of sayings that the useful is the noble and the hurtful the base.' " . . .

There was a pause. The name of Plato had had a strange effect upon the company. You will have said they had suddenly entered a church and had felt all lighter interests sink under the weight of the dim, echoing nave. After a few moments the poet spoke again in a quieter tone, but his voice had lost none of the unction which had enriched it. . . . "Beauty is queen; by the virtue of Deity, whose image she is, she reigns, lifts up, fires. Let us beware how we tempt Deity lest we perish ourselves. Actaeon died when he gazed unbidden upon the pure body of Artemis; but Artemis herself rayed her splendor upon Endymion, and Endymion is among the immortals. We fall when we rashly confront Beauty, but that Beauty who comes unawares may nerve our souls to wing to heaven." He ended on a resonant note and then, still looking out over the valley, sank into his seat. Lorenzo, with a fine humility, got up and kissed his thin hand. Giuliano looked at Simonetta, trying to recall her gaze, but she remained standing in her place, seeing nothing of her companions. She was thinking of something, frowning a little and biting her lip, her hands were before her; her slim fingers twisted and locked themselves nervously, like a tangle of snakes. Then she tossed her head, as a young horse might, and looked at Giuliano suddenly, full in the eyes. He rose to meet her with a deprecating smile, cap in hand—but she walked past him, almost brushing him with her gown, but never flinching her full gaze, threaded her way through the group to the back, behind the poet, where Sandro was. He had seen her coming, indeed he had watched her furtively throughout the oration, but her near presence disconcerted him again—and he looked down. She was strongly excited with her quick resolution; her color had risen and her voice faltered when she began to speak. She spoke eagerly, running her words together.

"*Ecco*, Messer Sandro," she whispered, blushing. "You have heard these sayings . . . Who is there in Florence like me?"

"There is no one," said Sandro simply.

"I will be your Lady Venus," she went on breathlessly. "You shall paint me, rising from the sea foam. . . . The Genoese love the sea." She was still eager and defiant; her bosom rose and fell unchecked.

"The Signorina is mocking me; it is impossible; the Signorina knows it."

"Eh, Madonna! is it so shameful to be fair—Star of the Sea as your poets sing at evening? Do you mean that I dare not do it? Listen then, Signor Pittore; tomorrow morning at Mass time you will come to the Villa Vespucci with your brushes and pans and you will ask for Monna Simonetta. Then you will see. Leave it now; it is settled." And she walked away with her head high and the same superb smile on her red lips. Mockery! She was in dead earnest; all her child's feelings were in hot revolt. These women who had whispered to each other, sniggered at her dress, her white neck and her free carriage; Giuliano who had presumed so upon her candor—these prying, censorious Florentines—she would strike them dumb with her amazing loveliness. They sang her a goddess that she might be flattered

and suffer their company: she would
show herself a goddess indeed—the
star of her shining Genoa, where
men were brave and silent and
maidens frank like the sea. Yes, and
then she would withdraw herself
suddenly and leave them forlorn and
dismayed.

As for Sandro, he stood where she
had left him, peering after her with
a mist in his eyes. He seemed to be
looking over the hillside, over the
city glowing afar off gold and purple
in the hot air, to Mont' Oliveto and
the heights, where a line of black
cypresses stood about a low white
building. At one angle of the building was a little turret with a bel-
vedere of round arches. The tallest
cypress just topped the windows.
There his eyes seemed to rest.

II

At Mass time Sandro, folded in
his shabby green cloak, stepped into
the sun on the Ponte Vecchio. The
morning mists were rolling back
under the heat; you began to see the
yellow line of houses stretching
along the turbid river on the far
side, and frowning down upon it
with blank, mud-stained faces.
Above, through steaming air, the sky
showed faintly blue and a campanile to the right loomed pale and
uncertain like a ghost. The sound of
innumerable bells floated over the
still city. Hardly a soul was abroad;
here and there a couple of dusty
peasants were trudging in with
baskets of eggs and jars of milk and
oil; a boat passed down to the fishing, and the oar knocked sleepily in
the rowlock as she cleared the
bridge. And above, on the heights
of Mont' Oliveto, the tapering forms
of cypresses were faintly outlined—
straight bars of shadow—and the

level ridge of a roof ran lightly back
into the soft shroud.

Sandro could mark these things
as he stepped resolutely on to the
bridge, crossed it, and went up a
narrow street among the sleeping
houses. The day held golden promise; it was the day of his life! Meantime the mist clung to him and
nipped him; what had fate in store?
What was to be the issue? In the
Piazza Santo Spirito, gray and
hollow-sounding in the chilly silences, his own footsteps echoed
solemnly as he passed by the door
of the great ragged church. Through
the heavy darkness within light
flickered faintly and went; service
was not begun. A drab crew of
cripples lounged on the steps, yawning and shivering, and two country
girls were strolling to the Mass with
brown arms round each other's
waists. When Sandro's footfall clattered on the stones they stopped by
the door, looking after him, and
laughed to see his dull face and
muffled figure. In the street beyond
he heard a bell jingling, hasty, incessant; and soon a white-robed procession swept by him, fluttering vestments, tapers, and the Host under a
canopy, silk and gold. Sandro
snatched at his cap and dropped on
his knees in the road, crouching low
and muttering under his breath as
the vision went past. He remained
kneeling for a moment after it had
gone, then crossed himself—forehead, breast, lip—and hurried forward. . . . He stepped under the
archway into the Court. There was
a youth with a cropped head and
swarthy neck lounging there, teasing
a spaniel. As the steps sounded on
the flags he looked up; the old green
cloak and clumsy shoes of the visitor
did not interest him; he turned his
back and went on with his game.

Sandro accosted him—Was the Signorina at the house? The boy went on with his game. "Eh, Diavolo! I know nothing at all," he said.

Sandro raised his voice till it rang round the courtyard. "You will go at once and inquire. You will say to the Signorina that Sandro di Mariano Filipepi the Florentine painter is here by her orders; that he waits her pleasure below."

The boy had got up; he and Sandro eyed each other for a little space. Sandro was the taller and had the glance of a hawk. So the porter went. . . .

. . . Presently with throbbing brows he stood on the threshold of Simonetta's chamber. It was the turret room of the villa and its four arched windows looked through a leafy tracery over towards Florence. Sandro could see down below him in the haze the glitter of the Arno and the dusky dome of Brunelleschi cleave the sward of the hills like a great burnished bowl. In the room itself there was tapestry, the Clemency of Scipio, with courtiers in golden cuirasses and tall plumes, and peacocks and huge Flemish horses—a rich profusion of crimson and blue drapery and stout-limbed soldiery. On a bracket, above a green silk curtain was a silver statuette of Madonna and the Bambino Gesu, with a red lamp flickering feebly before. By the windows a low divan heaped with velvet cushions and skins. But for a coffer and a prayer desk and a curtained recess which enshrined Simonetta's bed, the room looked wind-swept and bare.

When he entered Simonetta was standing by the window, leaning her hand against the ledge for support. She was draped from top to toe in a rose-colored mantle which shrouded her head like a nun's wimple and then fell in heavy folds to the ground. She flushed as he came, but saluted him with a grave inclination. Neither spoke. The silent greeting, the full consciousness in each of their parts, gave a curious religious solemnity to the scene—like some familiar but stately Church mystery. Sandro busied himself mechanically with his preparations—he was a lover and his pulse chaotic, but he had come to paint—and when these were done, on tiptoe, as it were, he looked timidly about him round the room, seeking where to pose her. Then he motioned her with the same reverential, preoccupied air, silent still, to a place under the silver Madonna. . . .

. . . There was a momentary quiver of withdrawal. Simonetta blushed vividly and drooped her eyes down to her little bare foot peeping out below the lines of the rosy cloak. The cloak's warmth shone on her smooth skin and rayed over her cheeks. In her flowery loveliness she looked diaphanous, ethereal; and yet you could see what a child she was, with her bright audacity, her ardor and her willfulness flushing and paling about her like the dawn. There she stood trembling on the brink. . . .

Suddenly all her waywardness shot into her eyes; she lifted her arms and the cloak fell back like the shard of a young flower; then, delicate and palpitating as a silver reed, she stood up in the soft light of the morning, and the sun, slanting in between the golden leaves and tendrils, kissed her neck and shrinking shoulder.

Sandro stood facing her, moody and troubled, fingering his brushes and bits of charcoal; his shaggy brows were knit, he seemed to be breathing hard. He collected himself with an effort and looked up at her as she stood before him shrinking, awe-struck, panting at the thing she had done. Their eyes met, and the girl's distress increased; she raised her hand to cover her bosom; her breath came in short gasps from parted lips, but her wide eyes still looked fixedly into his, with such blank panic that a sudden movement might really have killed her. He saw it all; she! there at his mercy. Tears swam and he trembled. Ah! the gracious lady! what divine condescension! what ineffable courtesy! But the artist in him was awakened almost at the same moment; his looks wandered in spite of her piteous candor and his own nothingness. Sandro the poet would have fallen on his face with an *"Exi a me, nam peccator sum."* Sandro the painter was different—no mercy there. He made a snatch at a carbon and raised his other hand with a kind of command—"Holy Virgin! what a line! Stay as you are, I implore you: swerve not one hair's breadth and I have you forever!" There was conquest in his voice.

So Simonetta stood very still, hiding her bosom with her hand, but never took her watch off the enemy. As he ran blindly about doing a hundred urgent indispensable things— noting the light, the line she made, how her arm cut across the folds of the curtain—she dogged him with staring, fascinated eyes, just as a hare, crouching in her form, watches a terrier hunting round her and waits for the end.

But the enemy was disarmed. Sandro the passionate, the lover, the brooding devotee, was gone; so was *la bella* Simonetta the beloved, the behymned. Instead, here was a fretful painter, dashing lines and broad smudges of shade on his paper, while before him rose an exquisite, slender, swaying form, glistening carnation and silver, and, over all, the maddening glow of red-gold hair. Could he but catch those velvet shadows, those delicate, glossy, reflected lights! Body of Bacchus! How could he put them in! What a picture she was! Look at the sun on her shoulder! and her hair— Christ! how it burned! It was a curious moment. The girl who had never understood or cared to understand this humble lover guessed now that he was lost in the artist. She felt that she was simply an effect and she resented it as a crowning insult. Her color rose again, her red lips gathered into a pout. If Sandro had but known, she was his at that instant. He had but to drop the painter, throw down his brushes, set his heart and hot eyes bare—to open his arms and she would have fled into them and nestled there; so fierce was her instinct just then to be loved, she, who had always been loved! But Sandro knew nothing and cared nothing. He was absorbed in the gracious lines of her body, the lithe long neck, the drooping shoulder, the tenderness of her youth; and then the grand open curve of the hip and thigh on which she was poised. He drew them in with a free hand in great sweeping lines, eagerly, almost angrily; once or twice he broke his carbon and— body of a dog!—he snatched at another.

This lasted a few minutes only: even Simonetta, with all her maiden tremors still feverishly acute, hardly noticed the flight of time; she was so hot with the feeling of her wrongs, the slight upon her victorious fairness. Did she not know how fair she was? She was getting very angry;

she had been made a fool of. All Florence would come and gape at the picture and mock her in the streets with bad names and coarse gestures as she rode by. She looked at Sandro. Santa Maria! how hot he was! His hair was drooping over his eyes! He tossed it back every second! And his mouth was open, one could see his tongue working! Why had she not noticed that great mouth before? 'Twas the biggest in all Florence. O! why had he come? She was frightened, remorseful, a child again, with a trembling pathetic mouth and shrinking limbs. And then her heart began to beat under her slim fingers. She pressed them down into her flesh to stay those great masterful throbs. A tear gathered in her eye; larger and larger it grew, and then fell. A shining drop rested on the round of her cheek and rolled slowly down her chin to her protecting hand, and lay there half hidden, shining like a raindrop between two curving petals of a rose.

It was just at that moment the painter looked up from his work and shook his bush of hair back. Something in his sketch had displeased him; he looked up frowning, with a brush between his teeth. When he saw the tearstained, distressful, beautiful face it had a strange effect upon him. He dropped nerveless, like a wounded man, to his knees, and covered his eyes with his hands. "Ah Madonna! for the pity of heaven forgive me! forgive me! I have sinned, I have done thee fearful wrong; I, who still dare to love thee." He uncovered his face and looked up radiant: his own words had inspired him. "Yes," he went on, with a steadfast smile, "I, Sandro, the painter, the poor devil of a painter, have seen thee and I dare to love!" His triumph was short-

lived. Simonetta had grown deadly white, her eyes burned, she had forgotten herself. She was tall and slender as a lily, and she rose, shaking, to her height.

"Thou presumest strangely," she said, in a slow still voice. "Go! Go in peace!"

She was conqueror. In her calm scorn, she was like a young immortal, some cold victorious Cynthia whose chastity had been flouted. Sandro was pale too: he said nothing and did not look at her again. She stood quivering with excitement, watching him with the same intent alertness as he rolled up his paper and crammed his brushes and pencils into the breast of his jacket. She watched him still as he backed out of the room and disappeared through the curtains of the archway. She listened to his footsteps along the corridor, down the stair. She was alone in the silence of the sunny room. Her first thought was for her cloak; she snatched it up and veiled herself, shivering as she looked fearfully round the walls. And then she flung herself on the piled cushions before the window and sobbed piteously, like an abandoned child. The sun slanted in between the golden leaves and tendrils and played in the tangle of her hair. . . .

III

At ten o'clock on the morning of April the twenty-sixth, a great bell began to toll: two beats heavy and slow, and then silence, while the air echoed the reverberation, moaning. Sandro, in shirt and breeches, with bare feet spread broad, was at work in his garret on the old bridge. He stayed his hand as the strong tone struck, bent his head and said a prayer: *"Miserere ei, Domine; requiem eternam dona, Domine"*; the words came out of due order as if he was very conscious of their import. Then he went on. And the great bell went on; two beats together, and then silence. It seemed to gather solemnity and a heavier message as he painted. Through the open window a keen draft of air blew in with dust and a scrap of shaving from the Lung' Arno down below; it circled round his workshop, fluttering the sketches and rags pinned to the walls. He looked out on a bleak landscape. San Miniato in heavy shade, and the white houses by the river staring like dead faces. A strong breeze was abroad; it whipped the brown water and raised little curling billows, ragged and white at the edges, and tossed about snaps of surf. It was cold. Sandro shivered as he shut to his casement; and the stiffening gale rattled at it fitfully. Once again it thrust it open, bringing wild work among the litter in the room. He made fast with the rain driving in his face. And above the howling of the squall he heard the sound of the great bell, steady and unmoved as if too full of its message to be put aside. Yet it was coming to him athwart the wind.

Sandro stood at his casement and looked at the weather—beating rain and yeasty water. He counted, rather nervously, the pulses between each pair of the bell's deep tones. He was impressionable to circumstances, and the coincidence of storm and passing bell awed him. . . . "Either the God of Nature suffers or the fabric of the world is breaking" —he remembered a scrap of talk wafted towards him (as he stood in attendance) from some humanist at Lorenzo's table only yesterday,

above the light laughter and snatches of song. That breakfast party at the Camaldoli yesterday! What a contrast—the even spring weather with the sun in a cloudless sky, and now this icy dead morning with its battle of wind and bell, fighting, he thought—over the failing breath of some strong man. Man! God, more like. "The God of Nature suffers," he murmured as he turned to his work. . . .

Simonetta had not been there yesterday. He had not seen her, indeed, since that nameless day when she had first transported him with the radiance of her bare beauty and then struck him down with a level gaze from steel-cold eyes. And he had deserved it, he had—she had said— "presumed strangely." Three more words only had she uttered and he had slunk out from her presence like a dog. What a goddess! Venus Urania! So she, too, might have ravished a worshiper as he prayed, and, after, slain him for a careless word. Cruel? No, but a goddess. Beauty had no laws; she was above them. Agnolo himself had said it, from Plato. . . . Holy Michael! What a blast! Black and desperate weather. . . . "Either the God of Nature suffers." God shield all Christian souls on such a day! . . .

One came and told him Simonetta Vespucci was dead. Some fever had torn at her and raced through all her limbs, licking up her life as it passed. No one had known of it— it was so swift! But there had just been time to fetch a priest; Fra Matteo, they said, from the Carmine, had shrived her ('twas a bootless task, God knew, for the child had babbled so, her wits wandered, look you), and then he had performed the last office. One had fled to tell the Medici. Giuliano was wild with grief; 'twas as if he had killed her instead of the spring ague—but then, people said he loved her well! And our Lorenzo had bid them swing the great bell of the Duomo—Sandro had heard it perhaps?—and there was to be a public procession and a Requiem sung at Santa Croce before they took her back to Genoa to lie with her fathers. Eh! Bacchus! She was fair and Giuliano had loved her well. 'Twas natural enough then. So the gossip ran out to tell his news to more attentive ears, and Sandro stood in his place, intoning softly, *"Te Deum Laudamus."*

He understood it all. There had been a dark and awful strife—earth shuddering as the black shadow of death swept by. Through tears now the sun beamed broad over the gentle city where she lay lapped in her mossy hills. *"Lux eterna lucet ei,"* he said with a steady smile; *"atque lucebit,"* he added after a pause. He had been painting that day an agonizing Christ, red and languid, crowned with thorns. Some of his own torment seems to have entered it, for, looking at it now, we see, first of all, wild eyeballs staring with the mad earnestness, the purposeless intensity of one seized or "possessed." He put the panel away and looked about for something else, the sketch he had made of Simonetta on that last day. When he had found it, he rolled it straight and set it on his easel. It was not the first charcoal study he had made from life, but a brush drawing on dark paper, done in sepia wash and the lights in white lead. He stood looking into it with his hands clasped. About half a braccia high, faint and shadowy in the pale tint he had used, he saw her there victim rather than goddess.

Standing timidly and wistfully, shrinking rather, veiling herself, maidenlike, with her hands and hair, with lips trembling and dewy eyes, she seemed to him now an immortal who must needs suffer for some great end; live and suffer and die; live again, and suffer and die. It was a doom perpetual like Demeter's, to bear, to nurture, to lose and to find her Persephone. She had stood there immaculate and apprehensive, a wistful victim. Three days before he had seen her thus; and now she was dead. He would see her no more.

Ah! Yes, once more he would see her. . . .

They carried dead Simonetta through the streets of Florence with her pale face uncovered and a crown of myrtle in her hair. People thronging there held their breath, or wept to see such still loveliness; and her poor parted lips wore a patient little smile, and her eyelids were pale violet and lay heavy to her cheek. White, like a bride, with a nosegay of orange-blossom and syringa at her throat, she lay there on her bed with lightly folded hands and the strange aloofness and pre-occupation all the dead have. Only her hair burned about her like a molten copper; and the wreath of myrtle leaves ran forward to her brows and leaped beyond them into a tongue.

The great procession swept forward; black brothers of Misericordia, shrouded and awful, bore the bed or stalked before it with torches that guttered and flared sootily in the dancing light of day. They held the pick of Florence, those scowling shrouds—Giuliano and Lorenzo, Pazzi, Tornabuoni, Soderini or Pulci; and behind, old Cattaneo, battered with storms, walked heavily, swinging his long arms and looking into the day's face as if he would try another fall with Death yet. Priests and acolytes, tapers, banners, vestments and a great silver crucifix, they drifted by, chanting the dirge for Simonetta; and she, as if for a sacrifice, lifted up on her silken bed, lay couched like a white flower edged with the color of flame. . . .

. . . Santa Croce, the great church, stretched forward beyond her into distances of gray mist and cold spaces of light. Its bare vastness was damp like a vault. And she lay in the midst listless, heavy-lidded, apart, with the half smile, as it seemed, of some secret mirth. Round her the great candles smoked and flickered, and Mass was sung at the High Altar for her soul's repose. Sandro stood alone, facing the shining altar but looking fixedly at Simonetta on her couch. He was white and dry—parched lips and eyes that ached and smarted. Was this the end? Was it possible, my God! that the transparent, unearthly thing lying there so prone and pale was dead? Had such loveliness aught to do with life or death? Ah! sweet lady, dear heart, how tired she was, how deadly tired! From where he stood he could see with intolerable anguish the somber rings round her eyes and the violet shadows on the lids, her folded hands and the straight, meek line to her feet. And her poor wan face with its wistful pitiful little smile was turned half aside on the delicate throat, as if in a last appeal —"Leave me now, O Florentines, to my rest. I have given you all I had: ask no more. I was a young girl, a child; too young for your eager strivings. You have killed me with your play; let me be now, let me sleep!" Poor child! Poor child!

Sandro was on his knees with his face pressed against the pulpit and tears running through his fingers as he prayed. . . .

As he had seen her, so he painted. As at the beginning of life in a cold world, passively meeting the long trouble of it, he painted her a rapt Presence floating evenly to our earth. A gray, translucent sea laps silently upon a little creek and, in the hush of a still dawn, the myrtles and sedges on the water's brim are quiet. It is a dream in half tones that he gives us, gray and green and steely blue; and just that, and some homely magic of his own, hint the commerce of another world with man's discarded domain. Men and women are asleep, and as in an early walk you may startle the hares at their play, or see the creatures of the darkness—owls and night hawks and heavy moths—flit with fantastic purpose over the familiar scene, so here it comes upon you suddenly that you have surprised Nature's self at her mysteries; you are let into the secret; you have caught the spirit of the April woodland as she glides over the pasture to the copse. And that, indeed, was Sandro's fortune. He caught her in just such a propitious hour. He saw the sweet wild thing, pure and undefiled by touch of earth; caught her in that pregnant pause of time ere she had lighted. Another moment and a buxom nymph of the grove would fold her in a rosy mantle, colored as the earliest wood anemones are. She would vanish, we know, into the daffodils or a bank of violets. And you might tell her presence there, or in the rustle of the myrtles, or coo of doves mating in the pines; you might feel her genius in the scent of the earth or the kiss of the West wind; but you could only see her in mid-April, and you should look for her over the sea. She always comes with the first warmth of the year.

But daily, before he painted, Sandro knelt in a dark chapel in Santa Croce, while a blue-chinned priest said Mass for the repose of Simonetta's soul.

Sir Arthur Conan Doyle

1859-1930

SHERLOCK HOLMES was born in 1887, in *A Study in Scarlet.* He is said to have been named Sherlock because Arthur Doyle once scored thirty runs in cricket from a bowler named Sherlock; and Holmes, from Oliver Wendell Holmes, Doyle's favorite author. His long face and lean physique were those of one Joseph Bell, a teacher of Doyle's. The detective came to fame in 1891, when *The Adventures of Sherlock Holmes* was published, but fell off a cliff and was killed in *The Memoirs of Sherlock Holmes* in 1893. This, however, was highhandedness the public would not stand for, and because of popular indignation he was resurrected in 1905 in *The Return of Sherlock Holmes.* "When Holmes fell over that cliff he may not have killed himself," was the popular criticism at the time, "but he was never quite the same man afterwards." Holmesians like to say that it was because of the Return that Queen Victoria knighted Doyle. Actually, the knighthood was his reward for a pamphlet explaining satisfactorily England's part in the Boer War.

Conan Doyle was Anglo-Irish. He was brought up a Catholic, was educated in Jesuit schools in England and on the continent, and received his medical degree from Edinburgh University. It was between the long waits for patients that Dr. Doyle began writing. In spite of the enormous popularity of Sherlock Holmes, Doyle always preferred his historical novels —like *The White Company*—and as a matter of fact killed off his hero to free himself for other writing. Sir Arthur Conan Doyle's interest in spiritualism, always considerable, was deepened by the death of his son, who died of pneumonia after being severely wounded in the battle of the Somme.

The Red-Headed League

BY SIR ARTHUR CONAN DOYLE

I HAD called upon my friend, Mr. Sherlock Holmes, one day in the autumn of last year, and found him in deep conversation with a very stout, florid-faced elderly gentleman, with fiery red hair. With an apology for my intrusion, I was about to withdraw, when Holmes pulled me abruptly into the room and closed the door behind me.

"You could not possibly have come at a better time, my dear Watson," he said, cordially.

"I was afraid that you were engaged."

"So I am. Very much so."

"Then I can wait in the next room."

"Not at all. This gentleman, Mr. Wilson, has been my partner and helper in many of my most successful cases, and I have no doubt that he will be of the utmost use to me in yours also."

The stout gentleman half rose from his chair and gave a bob of greeting, with a quick little questioning glance from his small, fat-encircled eyes.

"Try the settee," said Holmes, relapsing into his armchair, and putting his finger tips together, as was his custom when in judicial moods. "I know, my dear Watson, that you share my love of all that is bizarre and outside the conventions and humdrum routine of everyday life. You have shown your relish for it by the enthusiasm which has prompted you to chronicle, and, if you will excuse my saying so, somewhat to embellish so many of my own little adventures."

"Your cases have indeed been of the greatest interest to me," I observed.

"You will remember that I remarked the other day, just before we went into the very simple problem presented by Miss Mary Sutherland, that for strange effects and extraordinary combinations we must go to life itself, which is always far more daring than any effort of the imagination."

"A proposition which I took the liberty of doubting."

"You did, doctor, but none the less you must come round to my view, for otherwise I shall keep on piling fact upon fact on you, until your reason breaks down under them and acknowledges me to be right. Now, Mr. Jabez Wilson here has been good enough to call upon me this morning, and to begin a narrative which promises to be one of the most singular which I have

From *The Adventures of Sherlock Holmes* by Sir Arthur Conan Doyle. By permission of Harper & Brothers, Adrian M. Conan Doyle, and A. P. Watt & Son of London.

listened to for some time. You have heard me remark that the strangest and most unique things are very often connected not with the larger but with the smaller crimes, and occasionally, indeed, where there is room for doubt whether any positive crime has been committed. As far as I have heard, it is impossible for me to say whether the present case is an instance of crime or not, but the course of events is certainly among the most singular that I have ever listened to. Perhaps, Mr. Wilson, you would have the great kindness to recommence your narrative. I ask you, not merely because my friend, Dr. Watson, has not heard the opening part, but also because the peculiar nature of the story makes me anxious to have every possible detail from your lips. As a rule, when I have heard some slight indication of the course of events I am able to guide myself by the thousands of other similar cases which occur to my memory. In the present instance I am forced to admit that the facts are, to the best of my belief, unique."

The portly client puffed out his chest with an appearance of some little pride, and pulled a dirty and wrinkled newspaper from the inside pocket of his greatcoat. As he glanced down the advertisement column, with his head thrust forward, and the paper flattened out upon his knee, I took a good look at the man, and endeavored, after the fashion of my companion, to read the indications which might be presented by his dress or appearance.

I did not gain very much, however, by my inspection. Our visitor bore every mark of being an average commonplace British tradesman, obese, pompous, and slow. He wore rather baggy gray shepherd's check trousers, a not overclean black frock-coat, unbuttoned in the front, and a drab waistcoat with a heavy brassy Albert chain, and a square pierced bit of metal dangling down as an ornament. A frayed top hat and a faded brown overcoat with a wrinkled velvet collar lay upon a chair beside him. Altogether, look as I would, there was nothing remarkable about the man save his blazing red head and the expression of extreme chagrin and discontent upon his features.

Sherlock Holmes' quick eye took in my occupation, and he shook his head with a smile as he noticed my questioning glances. "Beyond the obvious facts that he has at some time done manual labor, that he takes snuff, that he is a Freemason, that he had been in China, and that he has done a considerable amount of writing lately, I can deduce nothing else."

Mr. Jabez Wilson started up in his chair, with his forefinger upon the paper, but his eyes upon my companion.

"How in the name of good fortune, did you know all that, Mr. Holmes?" he asked. "How did you know, for example, that I did manual labor? It's as true as gospel, for I began as a ship's carpenter."

"Your hands, my dear sir. Your right hand is quite a size larger than your left. You have worked with it and the muscles are more developed."

"Well, the snuff, then, and the Freemasonry?"

"I won't insult your intelligence by telling you how I read that, especially as, rather against the strict rules of your order, you use an arc and compass breastpin."

"Ah, of course, I forgot that. But the writing?"

"What else can be indicated by that right cuff so very shiny for five inches, and the left one with the smooth patch near the elbow where you rest it upon the desk."

"Well, but China?"

"The fish which you have tatooed immediately above your wrist could only have been done in China. I have made a small study of tatoo marks, and have even contributed to the literature of the subject. That trick of staining the fishes' scales of a delicate pink is quite peculiar to China. When, in addition, I see a Chinese coin hanging from your watch chain, the matter becomes even more simple."

Mr. Jabez Wilson laughed heartily. "Well, I never!" said he. "I thought at first that you had done something clever, but I see that there was nothing in it after all."

"I begin to think, Watson," said Holmes, "that I make a mistake in explaining. '*Omne ignotum pro magnifico*,' you know, and my poor little reputation, such as it is, will suffer shipwreck if I am so candid. Can you not find the advertisement, Mr. Wilson?"

"Yes, I have got it now," he answered, with his thick, red finger planted halfway down the column. "Here it is. This is what began it all. You just read it for yourself, sir."

I took the paper from him and read as follows:

"To the Red-headed League: On account of the bequest of the late Ezekiah Hopkins, of Lebanon, Pa., U. S. A., there is now another vacancy open which entitles a member of the League to a salary of four pounds a week for purely nominal services. All red-headed men who are sound in body and mind and above the age of twenty-one years are eligible. Apply in person on Monday, at eleven o'clock, to Duncan Ross, at the offices of the League, 7 Pope's Court, Fleet Street."

"What on earth does this mean?" I ejaculated, after I had twice read over the extraordinary announcement.

Holmes chuckled and wiggled in his chair, as was his habit when in high spirits. "It is a little off the beaten track, isn't it?" said he. "And now, Mr. Wilson, off you go at scratch, and tell us all about yourself, your household, and the effect which this advertisement had upon your fortunes. You will first make a note, doctor, of the paper and the date."

"It is *The Morning Chronicle* of April 27, 1890. Just two months ago."

"Very good. Now, Mr. Wilson."

"Well, it is just as I have been telling you, Mr. Sherlock Holmes," said Jabez Wilson, mopping his forehead, "I have a small pawnbroker's business at Coburg Square, near the City. It's not a very large affair, and of late years it has not done more than just give me a living. I used to be able to keep two assistants, but now I only keep one; and I would have a job to pay him but that he is willing to come for half wages, so as to learn the business."

"What is the name of this obliging youth?" asked Sherlock Holmes.

"His name is Vincent Spaulding, and he's not such a youth either. It's hard to say his age. I should not wish a smarter assistant, Mr. Holmes; and I know very well that he could better himself, and earn twice what

I am able to give him. But, after all, if he is satisfied, why should I put ideas in his head?"

"Why, indeed? You seem most fortunate in having an employee who comes under the full market price. It is not a common experience among employers in this age. I don't know that your assistant is not as remarkable as your advertisement."

"Oh, he has his faults, too," said Mr. Wilson. "Never was such a fellow for photography. Snapping away with a camera when he ought to be improving his mind, and then diving down into the cellar like a rabbit into its hole to develop his pictures. That is his main fault; but, on the whole, he's a good worker. There's no vice in him."

"He is still with you, I presume?"

"Yes, sir. He and a girl of fourteen, who does a bit of simple cooking, and keeps the place clean— that's all I have in the house, for I am a widower, and never had any family. We live very quietly, sir, the three of us; and we keep a roof over our heads, and pay our debts, if we do nothing more.

"The first thing that put us out was that advertisement. Spaulding, he came down into the office just this day eight weeks, with this very paper in his hand, and he says:

" 'I wish to the Lord, Mr. Wilson, that I was a red-headed man.'

" 'Why that?' I asks.

" 'Why,' says he, 'here's another vacancy on the League of the Red-headed Men. It's worth quite a little fortune to any man who gets it, and I understand that there are more vacancies than there are men, so that the trustees are at their wits' end what to do with the money. If my hair would only change color

here's a nice little crib all ready for me to step into.'

" 'Why, what is it, then?' I asked. You see, Mr. Holmes, I am a very stay-at-home man, and, as my business came to me instead of my having to go to it, I was often weeks on end without putting my foot over the door mat. In that way I didn't know much of what was going on outside, and I was always glad of a bit of news.

" 'Have you never heard of the League of the Red-headed Men?' he asked with his eyes open.

" 'Never.'

" 'Why, I wonder at that, for you are eligible yourself—for one of the vacancies.'

" 'And what are they worth?' I asked.

" 'Oh, merely a couple of hundred a year, but the work is slight, and it need not interfere very much with one's other occupations.'

"Well, you can easily think that that made me prick up my ears, for the business has not been over good for some years, and an extra couple of hundred would have been very handy.

" 'Tell me all about it,' said I.

" 'Well,' said he, showing me the advertisement, 'you can see for yourself that the League has a vacancy, and there is the address where you should apply for particulars. As far as I can make out, the League was founded by an American millionaire, Ezekiah Hopkins, who was very peculiar in his ways. He was himself red-headed, and he had a great sympathy for all red-headed men; so, when he died, it was found that he had left his enormous fortune in the hands of trustees, with instructions to apply the interests to the providing of easy berths to men whose hair is of that color. From all

I hear it is splendid pay, and very little to do.'

"'But,' said I, 'there would be millions of red-headed men who would apply.'

"'Not so many as you might think,' he answered. 'You see it is really confined to Londoners, and to grown men. This American had started from London when he was young, and he wanted to do the old town a good turn. Then, again, I have heard it is no use your applying if your hair is light red, or dark red, or anything but real, bright, blazing, fiery red. Now, if you cared to apply, Mr. Wilson, you would just walk in; but perhaps it would hardly be worth your while to put yourself out of the way for the sake of a few hundred pounds.'

"Now it is a fact, gentlemen, as you may see for yourselves, that my hair is of a very full and rich tint, so that it seemed to me that, if there was to be any competition in the matter, I stood as good a chance as any man that I had ever met. Vincent Spaulding seemed to know so much about it that I thought he might prove useful, so I just ordered him to put up the shutters for the day, and to come right away with me. He was very willing to have a holiday, so we shut the business up, and started off for the address that was given us in the advertisement.

"I never hope to see such a sight as that again, Mr. Holmes. From north, south, east, and west every man who had a shade of red in his hair had tramped into the City to answer the advertisement. Fleet Street was choked with red-headed folk, and Pope's Court looked like a coster's orange barrow. I should not have thought there were so many in the whole country as were brought together by that single ad-

vertisement. Every shade of color they were—straw, lemon, orange, brick, Irish setter, liver, clay; but, as Spaulding said, there were not many who had the real vivid flame-colored tint. When I saw how many were waiting, I would have given it up in despair; but Spaulding would not hear of it. How he did it I could not imagine, but he pushed and pulled and butted until he got me through the crowd, and right up to the steps which led to the office. There was a double stream upon the stair, some going up in hope, and some coming back dejected; but we wedged in as well as we could, and soon found ourselves in the office."

"Your experience has been a most entertaining one," remarked Holmes, as his client paused and refreshed his memory with a huge pinch of snuff. "Pray continue your very interesting statement."

"There was nothing in the office but a couple of wooden chairs and a deal table, behind which sat a small man, with a head that was even redder than mine. He said a few words to each candidate as he came up, and then he always managed to find some fault in them which would disqualify them. Getting a vacancy did not seem to be such a very easy matter after all. However, when our turn came, the little man was much more favorable to me than to any of the others, and he closed the door as we entered, so that he might have a private word with us.

"'This is Mr. Jabez Wilson,' said my assistant, 'and he is willing to fill a vacancy in the League.'

"'And he is admirably suited for it,' the other answered. 'He has every requirement. I cannot recall when I have seen anything so fine.' He took a step backward, cocked his head on one side, and gazed at my hair until I felt quite bashful. Then suddenly he plunged forward, wrung my hand, and congratulated me warmly on my success.

" 'It would be injustice to hesitate,' said he. 'You will, however, I am sure, excuse me for taking an obvious precaution.' With that he seized my hair in both his hands, and tugged until I yelled with the pain. 'There is water in your eyes,' said he, as he released me. 'I perceive that all is as it should be. But we have to be careful, for we have twice been deceived by wigs and once by paint. I could tell you tales of cobbler's wax which would disgust you with human nature.' He stepped over to the window and shouted through it at the top of his voice that the vacancy was filled. A groan of disappointment came up from below, and the folk all trooped away in different directions, until there was not a red head to be seen except my own and that of the manager.

" 'My name,' said he, 'is Mr. Duncan Ross, and I am myself one of the pensioners upon the fund left by our noble benefactor. Are you a married man, Mr. Wilson? Have you a family?'

"I answered that I had not.

"His face fell immediately.

" 'Dear me!' he said, gravely, 'that is very serious indeed! I am sorry to hear you say that. The fund was, of course, for the propagation and spread of the redheads as well as for their maintenance. It is exceedingly unfortunate that you should be a bachelor.'

"My face lengthened at this, Mr. Holmes, for I thought that I was not to have the vacancy after all; but, after thinking it over for a few minutes, he said that it would be all right.

" 'In the case of another,' said he, 'the objection might be fatal, but we must stretch a point in favor of a man with such a head of hair as yours. When shall you be able to enter upon your new duties?'

" 'Well, it is a little awkward, for I have a business already,' said I.

" 'Oh, never mind about that, Mr. Wilson!' said Vincent Spaulding. 'I shall be able to look after that for you.'

" 'What would be the hours?' I asked.

" 'Ten to two.'

"Now a pawnbroker's business is mostly done of an evening, Mr. Holmes, especially Thursday and Friday evenings, which is just before payday; so it would suit me very well to earn a little in the mornings. Besides, I knew that my assistant was a good man, and that he would see to anything that turned up.

" 'That would suit me very well,' said I. 'And the pay?'

" 'Is four pounds a week.'

" 'And the work?'

" 'Is purely nominal.'

" 'What do you call purely nominal?'

" 'Well, you have to be in the office, or at least in the building, the whole time. If you leave, you forfeit your whole position forever. The will is very clear upon that point. You don't comply with the conditions if you budge from the office during that time.'

" 'It's only four hours a day, and I should not think of leaving,' said I.

" 'No excuse will avail,' said Mr. Duncan Ross, 'neither sickness, nor business, nor anything else. There you must stay, or you lose your billet.'

" 'And the work?'

" 'Is to copy out the *Encyclopædia Britannica*. There is the first volume of it in that press. You must find your own ink, pens, and blotting paper, but we provide this table and chair. Will you be ready tomorrow?"

" 'Certainly,' I answered.

" 'Then, good-by, Mr. Jabez Wilson, and let me congratulate you once more on the important position which you have been fortunate enough to gain.' He bowed me out of the room, and I went home with my assistant hardly knowing what to say or do, I was so pleased at my own good fortune.

"Well, I thought over the matter all day, and by evening I was in low spirits again; for I had quite persuaded myself that the whole affair must be some great hoax or fraud, though what its object might be I could not imagine. It seemed altogether past belief that anyone could make such a will, or that they would pay such a sum for doing anything so simple as copying out the *Encyclopædia Britannica*. Vincent Spaulding did what he could to cheer me up, but by bedtime I had reasoned myself out of the whole thing. However, in the morning I determined to have a look at it anyhow, so I bought a penny bottle of ink, and with a quill pen and seven sheets of foolscap paper I started off for Pope's Court.

"Well, to my surprise and delight everything was as right as possible. The table was set out ready for me, and Mr. Duncan Ross was there to see that I got fairly to work. He started me off upon the letter A, and then he left me; but he would drop in from time to time to see that all was right with me. At two o'clock he bade me good day, complimented me upon the amount that I had written, and locked the door of the office after me.

"This went on day after day, Mr. Holmes, and on Saturday the manager came in and planked down four golden sovereigns for my week's work. It was the same next week, and the same the week after. Every morning I was there at ten, and every afternoon I left at two. By degrees Mr. Duncan Ross took to coming in only once of a morning, and then, after a time, he did not come in at all. Still, of course, I never dared to leave the room for an instant, for I was not sure when he might come, and the billet was such a good one, and suited me so well, that I would not risk the loss of it.

"Eight weeks passed away like this, and I had written about Abbots, and Archery, and Armor, and Architecture, and Attica, and hoped with diligence that I might get on to the B's before very long. It cost me something in foolscap, and I had pretty nearly filled a shelf with my writings. And then suddenly the whole business came to an end."

"To an end?"

"Yes, sir. And no later than this morning. I went to my work as usual at ten o'clock, but the door was shut and locked, with a little square of cardboard hammered onto the middle of the panel with a tack. Here it is, and you can read for yourself."

He held up a piece of white cardboard, about the size of a sheet of notepaper. It read in this fashion:

"THE RED-HEADED LEAGUE IS DISSOLVED.
Oct. 9, 1890."

Sherlock Holmes and I surveyed this curt announcement and the rueful face behind it, until the comical side of the affair so completely overtopped every consideration that we both burst out into a roar of laughter.

"I cannot see that there is anything very funny," cried our client, flushing up to the roots of his flaming hair. "If you can do nothing better than laugh at me, I can go elsewhere."

"No, no," cried Holmes, shoving him back into the chair from which he had half risen. "I really wouldn't miss your case for the world. It is most refreshingly unusual. But there is, if you will excuse my saying so, something just a little funny about it. Pray what steps did you take when you found the card upon the door?"

"I was staggered, sir. I did not know what to do. Then I called at the offices round, but none of them seemed to know anything about it. Finally, I went to the landlord, who is an accountant living on the ground floor, and I asked him if he could tell me what had become of the Red-headed League. He said that he had never heard of any such body. Then I asked him who Mr. Duncan Ross was. He answered that the name was new to him.

" 'Well,' said I, 'the gentleman at No. 4.'

" 'What, the red-headed man?'

" 'Yes.'

" 'Oh,' said he, 'his name was William Morris. He was a solicitor, and was using my room as a temporary convenience until his new premises were ready. He moved out yesterday.'

" 'Where could I find him?'

" 'Oh, at his new offices. He did tell me the address. Yes, 17 King Edward Street, near St. Paul's.'

"I started off, Mr. Holmes, but when I got to that address it was a manufactory of artificial kneecaps, and no one in it had ever heard of either Mr. William Morris, or Mr. Duncan Ross."

"And what did you do then?" asked Holmes.

"I went home to Saxe-Coburg Square, and I took the advice of my assistant. But he could not help me in any way. He could only say that if I waited I should hear by post. But that was not quite good enough, Mr. Holmes. I did not wish to lose such a place without a struggle, so, as I had heard that you were good enough to give advice to poor folk who were in need of it, I came right away to you."

"And you did very wisely," said Holmes. "Your case is an exceedingly remarkable one, and I shall be happy to look into it. From what you have told me I think that it is possible that graver issues hang from it than might at first sight appear."

"Grave enough!" said Mr. Jabez Wilson. "Why, I have lost four pounds a week."

"As far as you are personally concerned," remarked Holmes, "I do not see that you have any grievance against this extraordinary league. On the contrary, you are, as I understand, richer by some thirty pounds, to say nothing of the minute knowledge which you have gained on every subject which comes under the letter A. You have lost nothing by them."

"No, sir. But I want to find out about them, and who they are, and what their object was in playing this prank—if it was a prank—upon me. It was a pretty expensive joke for them, for it cost them two-and-thirty pounds."

"We shall endeavor to clear up these points for you. And, first, one or two questions, Mr. Wilson. This assistant of yours who first called your attention to the advertisement —how long had he been with you?"

"About a month then."

"How did he come?"

"In answer to an advertisement."

"Was he the only applicant?"

"No, I had a dozen."

"Why did you pick him?"

"Because he was handy and would come cheap."

"At half wages, in fact."

"Yes."

"What is he like, this Vincent Spaulding?"

"Small, stout-built, very quick in his ways, no hair on his face, though he's not short of thirty. Has a white splash of acid upon his forehead."

Holmes sat up in his chair in considerable excitement. "I thought as much," said he. "Have you ever observed that his ears are pierced for earrings?"

"Yes, sir. He told me that a gypsy had done it for him when he was a lad."

"Hum!" said Holmes, sinking back in deep thought. "He is still with you?"

"Oh, yes, sir; I have only just left him."

"And has your business been attended to in your absence?"

"Nothing to complain of, sir. There's never very much to do of a morning."

"That will do, Mr. Wilson. I shall be happy to give you an opinion upon the subject in the course of a day or two. Today is Saturday, and I hope that by Monday we may come to a conclusion.

"Well, Watson," said Holmes, when our visitor had left us, "what do you make of it all?"

"I make nothing of it," I answered, frankly. "It is a most mysterious business."

"As a rule," said Holmes, "the more bizarre a thing is the less mysterious it proves to be. It is your commonplace, featureless crimes which are really puzzling, just as a commonplace face is the most difficult to identify. But I must be prompt over this matter."

"What are you going to do, then?" I asked.

"To smoke," he answered. "It is quite a three-pipe problem, and I beg that you won't speak to me for fifty minutes." He curled himself up in his chair, with his thin knees drawn up to his hawklike nose, and there he sat with his eyes closed and his black clay pipe thrusting out like the bill of some strange bird. I had come to the conclusion that he had dropped asleep, and indeed was nodding myself, when he suddenly sprang out of his chair with the gesture of a man who has made up his mind, and put his pipe down upon the mantelpiece.

"Sarasate plays at St. James's Hall this afternoon," he remarked. "What do you think, Watson? Could your patients spare you for a few hours?"

"I have nothing to do today. My practice is never very absorbing."

"Then put on your hat and come. I am going through the City first, and we can have some lunch on the way. I observe that there is a good deal of German music on the program which is rather more to my taste than Italian or French. It is introspective, and I want to introspect. Come along!"

We traveled by the Underground as far as Aldersgate; and a short walk took us to Saxe-Coburg Square, the scene of the singular story which we had listened to in the morning. It was a poky, little, shabby-genteel place, where four lines of dingy, two-storied brick houses looked out into a small railed-in inclosure, where a lawn of weedy grass, and a few clumps of faded laurel bushes made a hard fight against a smoke-laden and uncongenial atmosphere. Three gilt balls and a brown board with JABEZ WILSON in white letters upon a corner house announced the place where our red-headed client carried on his business. Sherlock Holmes stopped in front of it with his head on one side, and looked it all over, with his eyes shining brightly between puckered lids. Then he walked slowly up the street, and then down again to the corner, still looking keenly at the houses. Finally he returned to the pawnbroker's and, having thumped vigorously upon the pavement with his stick two or three times, he went up to the door and knocked. It was instantly opened by a bright-looking, clean-shaven young fellow, who asked him to step in.

"Thank you," said Holmes, "I only wished to ask you how you would go from here to the Strand."

"Third right, fourth left," answered the assistant, promptly, closing the door.

"Smart fellow, that," observed Holmes as we walked away. "He is, in my judgment, the fourth smartest man in London, and for daring I am not sure that he has not a claim to be third. I have known something of him before."

"Evidently," said I, "Mr. Wilson's assistant counts for a good deal in this mystery of the Red-headed League. I am sure that you inquired your way merely in order that you might see him."

"Not him."

"What then?"

"The knees of his trousers."

"And what did you see?"

"What I expected to see."

"Why did you beat the pavement?"

"My dear doctor, this is a time for observation, not for talk. We are spies in an enemy's country. We know something of Saxe-Coburg Square. Let us now explore the parts which lie behind it."

The road in which we found ourselves as we turned round the corner from the retired Saxe-Coburg Square presented as great a contrast to it as the front of a picture does to the back. It was one of the main arteries which convey the traffic of the City to the north and west. The roadway was blocked with the immense stream of commerce flowing in a double tide inward and outward, while the footpaths were black with the hurrying swarm of pedestrians. It was difficult to realize, as we looked at the line of fine shops and stately business premises, that they really abutted on the other side upon the faded and stagnant square which we had just quitted.

"Let me see," said Holmes, standing at the corner, and glancing along the line. "I should like just to remember the order of the houses here. It is a hobby of mine to have an exact knowledge of London. There is Mortimer's, the tobacconist; the little newspaper shop, the Coburg branch of the City and Suburban Bank, the Vegetarian Restaurant, and McFarlane's carriage-building depot. That carries us right on to the other block. And now, doctor, we've done our work, so it's time we had some play. A sandwich and a cup of coffee, and then off to violinland, where all is sweetness, and delicacy, and harmony, and there are no red-headed clients to vex us with their conundrums."

My friend was an enthusiastic musician, being himself not only a very capable performer, but a composer of no ordinary merit. All the afternoon he sat in the stalls wrapped in the most perfect happiness, gently waving his long thin fingers in time to the music, while his gently smiling face and his languid, dreamy eyes were as unlike those of Holmes the sleuth hound, Holmes the relentless, keen-witted, ready-handed criminal agent, as it was possible to conceive. In his singular character the dual nature alternately asserted itself, and his extreme exactness and astuteness represented, as I have often thought, the reaction against the poetic and contemplative mood which occasionally predominated in him. The swing of his nature took him from extreme languor to devouring energy; and, as I knew well, he was never so truly formidable as when, for days on end, he had been lounging in his armchair amid his improvisations and his black-letter editions. Then it was that the lust of the chase would suddenly come upon him, and that his brilliant reasoning power would rise to the level of intuition, until those who were unacquainted with his methods would look askance at him as on a man whose knowledge was not that of other mortals. When I saw him that afternoon so enwrapped in the music at St. James's Hall, I felt that an evil time might be coming upon those whom he had set himself to hunt down.

"You want to go home, no doubt, doctor," he remarked, as we emerged.

"Yes, it would be as well."

"And I have some business to do which will take some hours. This business at Coburg Square is serious.

"A considerable crime is in contemplation. I have every reason to believe that we shall be in time to stop it. But today being Saturday rather complicates matters. I shall want your help tonight."

"At what time?"

"Ten will be early enough."

"I shall be at Baker Street at ten."

"Very well. And, I say, doctor! there may be some little danger, so kindly put your army revolver in your pocket." He waved his hand, turned on his heel, and disappeared in an instant among the crowd.

I trust that I am not more dense than my neighbors, but I was always oppressed with a sense of my own stupidity in my dealing with Sherlock Holmes. Here I had heard what he had heard, I had seen what he had seen, and yet from his words it was evident that he saw clearly not only what had happened, but what was about to happen, while to me the whole business was still confused and grotesque. As I drove home to my house in Kensington I thought over it all, from the extraordinary story of the redheaded copier of the *Encyclopædia* down to the visit to Saxe-Coburg Square, and the ominous words with which he had parted from me. What was this nocturnal expedition, and why should I go armed? Where were we going, and what were we to do? I had the hint from Holmes that this smooth-faced pawnbroker's assistant was a formidable man—a man who might play a deep game. I tried to puzzle it out, but gave it up in despair, and set the matter aside until night should bring an explanation.

It was a quarter-past nine when I started from home and made my way across the Park, and so through Oxford Street to Baker Street. Two hansoms were standing at the door, and, as I entered the passage, I heard the sound of voices from above. On entering his room, I found Holmes in animated conversation with two men, one of whom I recognized as Peter Jones, the official police agent; while the other was a long, thin, sad-faced man, with a very shiny hat and oppressively respectable frock-coat.

"Ha! our party is complete," said Holmes, buttoning up his pea jacket, and taking his heavy hunting crop from the rack. "Watson, I think you know Mr. Jones, of Scotland Yard? Let me introduce you to Mr. Merryweather, who is to be our companion in tonight's adventure."

"We're hunting in couples again, doctor, you see," said Jones, in his consequential way. "Our friend here is a wonderful man for starting a chase. All he wants is an old dog to help him do the running down."

"I hope a wild goose may not prove to be the end of our chase," observed Mr. Merryweather, gloomily.

"You may place considerable confidence in Mr. Holmes, sir," said the police agent, loftily. "He has his own little methods, which are, if he won't mind my saying so, just a little too theoretical and fantastic, but he has the makings of a detective in him. It is not too much to say that once or twice, as in that business of the Sholto murder and the Agra treasure, he has been more nearly correct than the official force."

"Oh, if you say so, Mr. Jones, it is all right!" said the stranger, with deference. "Still, I confess that I miss my rubber. It is the first Saturday night for seven-and-twenty years that I have not had my rubber."

"I think you will find," said Sherlock Holmes, "that you will play for a higher stake tonight than you have ever done yet, and that the play will be more exciting. For you, Mr. Merryweather, the stake will be some thirty thousand pounds; and for you, Jones, it will be the man

upon whom you wish to lay your hands."

"John Clay, the murderer, thief, smasher, and forger. He's a young man, Mr. Merryweather, but he is at the head of his profession, and I would rather have my bracelets on him than on any criminal in London. He's a remarkable man, is young John Clay. His grandfather was a Royal Duke, and he himself has been to Eton and Oxford. His brain is as cunning as his fingers, and though we meet signs of him at every turn, we never know where to find the man himself. He'll crack a crib in Scotland one week, and be raising money to build an orphanage in Cornwall the next. I've been on his track for years, and have never set eyes on him yet."

"I hope that I may have the pleasure of introducing you tonight. I've had one or two little turns also with Mr. John Clay, and I agree with you that he is at the head of his profession. It is past ten, however, and quite time that we started. If you two will take the first hansom, Watson and I will follow in the second."

Sherlock Holmes was not very communicative during the long drive, and lay back in the cab, humming the tunes which he had heard in the afternoon. We rattled through an endless labyrinth of gas-lit streets until we emerged into Farringdon Street.

"We are close there now," my friend remarked. "This fellow Merryweather is a bank director and personally interested in the matter. I thought it as well to have Jones with us also. He is not a bad fellow, though an absolute imbecile in his profession. He has one positive virtue. He is as brave as a bulldog, and as tenacious as a lobster if he gets his claws upon anyone. Here we are, and they are waiting for us."

We had reached the same crowded thoroughfare in which we had found ourselves in the morning. Our cabs were dismissed, and following the guidance of Mr. Merryweather, we passed down a narrow passage, and through a side door which he opened for us. Within there was a small corridor, which ended in a very massive iron gate. This also was opened, and led down a flight of winding stone steps, which terminated at another formidable gate. Mr. Merryweather stopped to light a lantern, and then conducted us down a dark, earth-smelling passage, and so, after opening a third door, into a huge vault or cellar, which was piled all round with crates and massive boxes.

"You are not very vulnerable from above," Holmes remarked, as he held up the lantern and gazed about him.

"Nor from below," said Mr. Merryweather, striking his stick upon the flags which lined the floor. "Why, dear me, it sounds quite hollow!" he remarked, looking up in surprise.

"I must really ask you to be a little more quiet," said Holmes, severely. "You have already imperiled the whole success of our expedition. Might I beg that you would have the goodness to sit down upon one of those boxes, and not to interfere?"

The solemn Mr. Merryweather perched himself upon a crate, with a very injured expression upon his face, while Holmes fell upon his knees upon the floor, and, with the lantern and a magnifying lens, began to examine minutely the cracks between the stones. A few seconds sufficed to satisfy him, for he sprang to his feet again, and put his glass in his pocket.

"We have at least an hour before us," he remarked, "for they can hardly take any steps until the good pawnbroker is safely in bed. Then they will not lose a minute, for the sooner they do their work the longer time they will have for their escape. We are at present, doctor—as no doubt you have divined—in the cellar of the City branch of one of the principal London banks. Mr. Merryweather is the chairman of directors, and he will explain to you that there are reasons why the more daring criminals of London should take a considerable interest in this cellar at present."

"It is our French gold," whispered the director. "We have had several warnings that an attempt might be made upon it."

"Your French gold?"

"Yes. We had occasion some months ago to strengthen our resources, and borrowed, for that purpose, thirty thousand napoleons from the Bank of France. It has become known that we have never had occasion to unpack the money, and that it is still lying in our cellar. The crate upon which I sit contains two thousand napoleons packed between layers of lead foil. Our reserve of bullion is much larger at present than is usually kept in a single branch office, and the directors have had misgivings upon the subject."

"Which were very well justified," observed Holmes. "And now it is time that we arranged our little plans. I expect that within an hour matters will come to a head. In the meantime, Mr. Merryweather, we must put the screen over that dark lantern."

"And sit in the dark?"

"I am afraid so. I had brought a pack of cards in my pocket, and I thought that, as we were a *partie carrée*, you might have your rubber after all. But I see that the enemy's preparations have gone so far that we cannot risk the presence of a light. And, first of all, we must choose our positions. These are daring men, and, though we shall take them at a disadvantage, they may do us some harm, unless we are careful. I shall stand behind this crate, and do you conceal yourself behind those. Then, when I flash a light upon them, close in swiftly. If they fire, Watson, have no compunction about shooting them down."

I placed my revolver, cocked, upon the top of the wooden case behind which I crouched. Holmes shot the slide across the front of his lantern, and left us in pitch darkness —such an absolute darkness as I have never before experienced. The smell of hot metal remained to assure us that the light was still there ready to flash out at a moment's notice. To me, with my nerves worked up to a pitch of expectancy, there was something depressing and subduing in the sudden gloom, and in the cold, dank air of the vault.

"They have but one retreat," whispered Holmes. "That is back through the house into Saxe-Coburg Square. I hope that you have done what I asked you, Jones?"

"I have an inspector and two officers waiting at the front door."

"Then we have stopped all the holes. And now we must be silent and wait."

What a time it seemed! From comparing notes afterwards, it was but an hour and a quarter, yet it appeared to me that the night must have almost gone, and the dawn be breaking above us. My limbs were weary and stiff, for I feared to change my position, yet my nerves were worked up to the highest pitch of tension, and my hearing was so acute that I could not only hear the gentle breathing of my companions, but I could distinguish the deeper, heavier inbreath of the bulky Jones from the thin, sighing note of the bank director. From my position I could look over the case in the direction of the floor. Suddenly my eyes caught the glint of a light.

At first it was but a lurid spark upon the stone pavement. Then it lengthened out until it became a yellow line, and then, without any warning or sound, a gash seemed to open and a hand appeared, a white, almost womanly hand, which felt about in the center of the little area of light. For a minute or more the hand, with its writhing fingers, protruded out of the floor. Then it was withdrawn as suddenly as it appeared, and all was dark again save the single lurid spark, which marked a chink between the stones.

Its disappearance, however, was but momentary. With a rending, tearing sound, one of the broad white stones turned over upon its side, and left a square, gaping hole, through which streamed the light of a lantern. Over the edge there peeped a clean-cut, boyish face, which looked keenly about it, and then, with a hand on either side of the aperture, drew itself shoulder-high and waist-high, until one knee rested upon the edge. In another instant he stood at the side of the hole, and was hauling after him a companion, lithe and small like himself, with a pale face and a shock of very red hair.

"It's all clear," he whispered.

"Have you the chisel and the bags? Great Scot! Jump, Archie, jump, and I'll swing for it!"

Sherlock Holmes had sprung out and seized the intruder by the collar. The other dived down the hole, and I heard the sound of rending cloth as Jones clutched at his skirts. The light flashed upon the barrel of a revolver, but Holmes's hunting crop came down on the man's wrist, and the pistol clinked upon the stone floor.

"It's no use, John Clay," said Holmes, blandly, "you have no chance at all."

"So I see," the other answered, with the utmost coolness. "I fancy that my pal is all right, though I see you have got his coattails."

"There are three men waiting for him at the door," said Holmes.

"Oh, indeed. You seem to have done the thing very completely. I must compliment you."

"And I you," Holmes answered. "Your red-headed idea was very new and effective."

"You'll see your pal again presently," said Jones. "He's quicker at climbing down holes than I am. Just hold out while I fix the derbies."

"I beg that you will not touch me with your filthy hands," remarked our prisoner, as the handcuffs clattered upon his wrists. "You may not be aware that I have royal blood in my veins. Have the goodness also, when you address me, always to say 'sir' and 'please.'"

"All right," said Jones, with a stare and a snigger. "Well, would you please, sir, march upstairs where we can get a cab to carry your highness to the police station."

"That is better," said John Clay, serenely. He made a sweeping bow to the three of us, and walked quietly off in the custody of the detective.

"Really, Mr. Holmes," said Mr. Merryweather, as we followed them from the cellar, "I do not know how the bank can thank you or repay you. There is no doubt that you have detected and defeated in the most complete manner one of the most determined attempts at bank robbery that have ever come within my experience."

"I have had one or two little scores of my own to settle with Mr. John Clay," said Holmes. "I have been at some small expense over this matter, which I shall expect the bank to refund, but beyond that I am amply repaid by having had an experience which is in many ways unique, and by hearing the very remarkable narrative of the Red-headed League."

"You see, Watson," he explained, in the early hours of the morning, as we sat over a glass of whisky and soda in Baker Street, "it was perfectly obvious from the first that the only possible object of this rather fantastic business of the advertisement of the League, and the copying of the *Encyclopædia*, must be to get this not overbright pawn-broker out of the way for a number of hours every day. It was a curious way of managing it, but really it would be difficult to suggest a better. The method was no doubt suggested to Clay's ingenious mind by the color of his accomplice's hair. The four pounds a week was a lure which must draw him, and what was it to them, who were playing for thousands? They put in the advertisement, one rogue has the temporary office, the other rogue incites the man to apply for it, and together they manage to secure his absence every morning in the week.

From the time that I heard of the assistant having come for half wages, it was obvious to me that he had some strong motive for securing the situation."

"But how could you guess what the motive was?"

"Had there been women in the house, I should have suspected a mere vulgar intrigue. That, however, was out of the question. The man's business was a small one, and there was nothing in the house which could account for such elaborate preparations, and such an expenditure as they were at. It must then be something out of the house. What could it be? I thought of the assistant's fondness for photography, and his trick of vanishing into the cellar. The cellar! There was the end of this tangled clew. Then I made inquiries as to this mysterious assistant, and found that I had to deal with one of the coolest and most daring criminals in London. He was doing something in the cellar—something which took many hours a day for months on end. What could it be, once more? I could think of nothing save that he was running a tunnel to some other building.

"So far I had got when we went to visit the scene of action. I surprised you by beating upon the pavement with my stick. I was ascertaining whether the cellar stretched out in front or behind. It was not in front. Then I rang the bell, and, as I hoped, the assistant answered it. We have had some skirmishes, but we had never set eyes upon each other before. I hardly looked at his face. His knees were what I wished to see. You must yourself have remarked how worn,

wrinkled and stained they were. They spoke of those hours of burrowing. The only remaining point was what they were burrowing for. I walked round the corner, saw that the City and Suburban Bank abutted on our friend's premises, and felt that I had solved my problem. When you drove home after the concert I called upon Scotland Yard, and upon the chairman of the bank directors, with the result that you have seen."

"And how could you tell that they would make their attempt tonight?" I asked.

"Well, when they closed their League offices that was a sign that they cared no longer about Mr. Jabez Wilson's presence; in other words, that they had completed their tunnel. But it was essential that they should use it soon, as it might be discovered, or the bullion might be removed. Saturday would suit them better than any other day, as it would give them two days for their escape. For all these reasons I expected them to come tonight."

"You reasoned it out beautifully," I exclaimed, in unfeigned admiration. "It is so long a chain, and yet every link rings true."

"It saved me from ennui," he answered, yawning. "Alas! I already feel it closing in upon me. My life is spent in one long effort to escape from the commonplaces of existence. These little problems help me to do so."

"And you are a benefactor of the race," said I. He shrugged his shoulders. "Well, perhaps, after all, it is of some little use," he remarked. "'*L'homme c'est rien—l'œuvre c'est tout*,' as Gustave Flaubert wrote to George Sand."

Rudyard Kipling

1865-1936

KIPLING was born in Bombay, India. He spoke Hindustani as early as he did English, and by his nurse's side saw at first hand and took for granted the daily drama of life and death in the teeming bazaar. But at the age of six he was sent to England—uprooted from the highly seasoned familiar jungle land and transplanted into a family of strict Victorian relatives who disciplined him according to their lights. It was a miserable period for the young boy. While still in England he went to Westward Ho, North Devon, to school, about which he was to write much later in *Stalky and Co.* But he was not really alive again until, at seventeen, refusing his parents' offer to go to the university, he returned to India.

Then at last Kipling came into his own, and from that point on he was a dynamo of energy. His first work was on a Lahore newspaper, to which he contributed verse and short stories. By the time he was twenty-four he had written *Departmental Ditties, Soldiers Three, Plain Tales from the Hills, The Story of the Gadsbys, In Black and White, Under the Deodars, The Phantom Rickshaw,* and *Wee Willie Winkie* —a good enough life record for any short-story writer. Another newspaper sent him to England, by way of China, Japan, and America, but his reputation had preceded him: by 1889 he was famous in England and, by 1892, the world over. For four years he lived in Brattleboro, Vermont, having married an American, and during this period wrote *Many Inventions,* the *Jungle Books, The Seven Seas,* and *Captains Courageous.*

In later years Kipling's critics dubbed him "the literary aspect of the British Empire," because of his stubbornness in politics. But few contested his eminence as a writer. *Kim* is perhaps the most complete picture of Indian life that any novel has to offer; *Barrack Room Ballads* is the perfect expression of the British colonial soldier's slang and point of view; and his short stories—for variety and vigor, raciness of dialogue and magical color—rank with the best.

Without Benefit of Clergy

BY RUDYARD KIPLING

Before my Spring I garnered
    Autumn's gain,
Out of her time my field was white
    with grain,
    The year gave up her secrets to
      my woe.
Forced and deflowered each sick
    season lay,
In mystery of increase and decay;
I saw the sunset ere men saw the
    day,
    Who am too wise in that I should
    not know.

        —BITTER WATERS

I

"BUT if it be a girl?"

"Lord of my life, it cannot be. I have prayed for so many nights, and sent gifts to Sheikh Badl's shrine so often, that I know God will give us a son—a man-child that shall grow into a man. Think of this and be glad. My mother shall be his mother till I can take him again, and the mullah of the Pattan mosque shall cast his nativity—God send he be born in an auspicious hour!—and then, and then thou wilt never weary of me, thy slave."

"Since when hast thou been a slave, my queen?"

"Since the beginning—till this mercy came to me. How could I be sure of thy love when I knew that I had been bought with silver?"

"Nay, that was the dowry. I paid it to thy mother."

"And she has buried it, and sits upon it all day long like a hen. What talk is yours of dower! I was bought as though I had been a Lucknow dancing girl instead of a child."

"Art thou sorry for the sale?"

"I have sorrowed; but today I am glad. Thou wilt never cease to love me now?—answer, my king."

"Never—never. No."

"Not even though the *mem-log*—the white women of thy own blood—love thee? And remember, I have watched them driving in the evening; they are very fair."

"I have seen fire-balloons by the hundred. I have seen the moon, and—then I saw no more fire-balloons."

Ameera clapped her hands and laughed. "Very good talk," she said. Then with an assumption of great stateliness, "It is enough. Thou hast my permission to depart—if thou wilt."

The man did not move. He was sitting on a low red-lacquered couch in a room furnished only with a blue and white floor cloth, some rugs, and a very complete collection of native cushions. At his feet sat a woman of sixteen, and she was all but all the world in his eyes. By every rule and law she should have been otherwise, for he was an Englishman, and she a Mussulman's daughter bought two years before from her mother, who, being left without money, would have sold Ameera shrieking to the Prince of Darkness if the price had been sufficient.

It was a contract entered into with a light heart; but even before the girl had reached her bloom she came to fill the greater portion of John Holden's life. For her, and the withered hag her mother, he had taken a little house overlooking the great red-walled city, and found— when the marigolds had sprung up by the well in the courtyard and Ameera had established herself according to her own ideas of comfort, and her mother had ceased grumbling at the inadequacy of the cooking places, the distance from the daily market, and at matters of housekeeping in general—that the house was to him his home. Anyone could enter his bachelor's bungalow by day or night, and the life that he led there was an unlovely one. In the house in the city his feet only could pass beyond the outer courtyard to the women's rooms; and when the big wooden gate was bolted behind him he was king in his own territory, with Ameera for queen. And there was going to be added to this kingdom a third person whose arrival Holden felt inclined to resent. It interfered with his perfect happiness. It disarranged the orderly peace of the house that was his own. But Ameera was wild with delight at the thought

of it, and her mother not less so. The love of a man, and particularly a white man, was at the best an inconstant affair, but it might, both women argued, be held fast by a baby's hands. "And then," Ameera would always say, "then he will never care for the white *mem-log*. I hate them all—I hate them all."

"He will go back to his own people in time," said the mother; "but by the blessing of God that time is yet afar off."

Holden sat silent on the couch, thinking of the future, and his thoughts were not pleasant. The drawbacks of a double life are manifold. The Government, with singular care, had ordered him out of the station for a fortnight on special duty in the place of a man who was watching by the bedside of a sick wife. The verbal notification of the transfer had been edged by a cheerful remark that Holden ought to think himself lucky in being a bachelor and a free man. He came to break the news to Ameera.

"It is not good," she said slowly, "but it is not all bad. There is my mother here, and no harm will come to me—unless indeed I die of pure joy. Go thou to thy work and think no troublesome thoughts. When the days are done I believe . . . nay, I am sure. And—and then I shall lay *him* in thy arms, and thou wilt love me forever. The train goes tonight, at midnight is it not? Go now, and do not let thy heart be heavy by cause of me. But thou wilt not delay in returning? Thou wilt not stay on the road to talk to the bold white *mem-log*. Come back to me swiftly, my life."

As he left the courtyard to reach his horse that was tethered to the gatepost, Holden spoke to the white-haired old watchman who guarded the house, and bade him under certain contingencies dispatch the filled-up telegraph form that Holden gave him. It was all that could be done, and with the sensations of a man who has attended his own funeral Holden went away by the night mail to his exile. Every hour of the day he dreaded the arrival of the telegram, and every hour of the night he pictured to himself the death of Ameera. In consequence his work for the State was not of first-rate quality, nor was his temper towards his colleagues of the most amiable. The fortnight ended without a sign from his home, and, torn to pieces by his anxieties, Holden returned to be swallowed up for two precious hours by a dinner at the club, wherein he heard, as a man hears in a swoon, voices telling him how execrably he had performed the other man's duties, and how he had endeared himself to all his associates. Then he fled on horseback through the night with his heart in his mouth. There was no answer at first to his blows on the gate, and he had just wheeled his horse round to kick it in when Pir Khan appeared with a lantern and held his stirrup.

"Has aught occurred?" said Holden.

"The news does not come from my mouth, Protector of the Poor, but——" He held out his shaking hand as befitted the bearer of good news who is entitled to a reward.

Holden hurried through the courtyard. A light burned in the upper room. His horse neighed in the gateway, and he heard a shrill little wail that sent all the blood into the apple of his throat. It was a new voice, but it did not prove that Ameera was alive.

"Who is there?" he called up the narrow brick staircase.

There was a cry of delight from Ameera, and then the voice of the mother, tremulous with old age and pride—"We be two women and—the—man—thy—son."

On the threshold of the room Holden stepped on a naked dagger, that was laid there to avert ill-luck, and it broke at the hilt under his impatient heel.

"God is great!" cooed Ameera in the half-light. "Thou hast taken his misfortunes on thy head."

"Ay, but how is it with thee, life of my life? Old woman, how is it with her?"

"She has forgotten her sufferings for joy that the child is born. There is no harm; but speak softly," said the mother.

"It only needed thy presence to make me all well," said Ameera. "My king, thou hast been very long away. What gifts hast thou for me? Ah, ah! It is I that bring gifts this time. Look, my life, look. Was there ever such a babe? Nay, I am too weak even to clear my arm from him."

"Rest then, and do not talk. I am here, *bachari* [little woman]."

"Well said, for there is a bond and a heel-rope [*peecharee*] between us now that nothing can break. Look—canst thou see in this light? He is without spot or blemish. Never was such a man-child. *Ya illah!* he shall be a pundit—no, a trooper of the Queen. And, my life, dost thou love me as well as ever, though I am faint and sick and worn? Answer truly."

"Yea. I love as I have loved, with all my soul. Lie still, pearl, and rest."

"Then do not go. Sit by my side here—so. Mother, the lord of this house needs a cushion. Bring it."

There was an almost imperceptible movement on the part of the new life that lay in the hollow of Ameera's arm. "Aho!" she said, her voice breaking with love. "The babe is a champion from his birth. He is kicking me in the side with mighty kicks. Was there ever such a babe! And he is ours to us—thine and mine. Put thy hand on his head, but carefully, for he is very young, and men are unskilled in such matters."

Very cautiously Holden touched with the tips of his fingers the downy head.

"He is of the faith," said Ameera; "for lying here in the night watches I whispered the call to prayer and the profession of faith into his ears. And it is most marvelous that he was born upon a Friday, as I was born. Be careful of him, my life; but he can almost grip with his hands."

Holden found one helpless little hand that closed feebly on his finger. And the clutch ran through his body till it settled about his heart. Till then his sole thought had been for Ameera. He began to realize that there was someone else in the world, but he could not feel that it was a veritable son with a soul. He sat down to think, and Ameera dozed lightly.

"Get hence, sahib," said her mother under her breath. "It is not good that she should find you here on waking. She must be still."

"I go," said Holden submissively. "Here be rupees. See that my baba gets fat and finds all that he needs."

The clink of the silver roused Ameera. "I am his mother, and no hireling," she said weakly. "Shall I look to him more or less for the sake of money? Mother, give it back. I have borne my lord a son."

The deep sleep of weakness came upon her almost before the sentence was completed. Holden went down to the courtyard very softly with his heart at ease. Pir Khan, the old watchman, was chuckling with delight. "This house is now complete," he said, and without further comment thrust into Holden's hands the hilt of a saber worn many years ago when he, Pir Khan, served the Queen in the police. The bleat of a tethered goat came from the well curb.

"There be two," said Pir Khan, "two goats of the best. I bought them, and they cost much money; and since there is no birth party assembled their flesh will be all mine. Strike craftily, sahib! 'Tis an ill-balanced saber at the best. Wait till they raise their heads from cropping the marigolds."

"And why?" said Holden, bewildered.

"For the birth sacrifice. What else? Otherwise the child being unguarded from fate may die. The Protector of the Poor knows the fitting words to be said."

Holden had learned them once with little thought that he would ever speak them in earnest. The touch of the cold saber hilt in his palm turned suddenly to the clinging grip of the child upstairs—the child that was his own son—and a dread of loss filled him.

"Strike!" said Pir Khan. "Never life came into the world but life was paid for it. See, the goats have raised their heads. Now! With a drawing cut!"

Hardly knowing what he did Holden cut twice as he muttered the Mahomedan prayer that runs: "Almighty! In place of this my son I offer life for life, blood for blood, head for head, bone for bone, hair for hair, skin for skin." The waiting horse snorted and bounded in his pickets at the smell of the raw blood that spurted over Holden's riding boots.

"Well smitten!" said Pir Khan, wiping the saber. "A swordsman was lost in thee. Go with a light heart, Heaven-born. I am thy servant, and the servant of thy son. May the Presence live a thousand years and . . . the flesh of the goats is all mine?" Pir Khan drew back richer by a month's pay. Holden slung himself into the saddle and rode off through the low-hanging wood smoke of the evening. He was full of riotous exultation, alternating with a vast vague tenderness directed towards no particular object, that made him choke as he bent over the neck of his uneasy horse. "I never felt like this in my life," he thought. "I'll go to the club and pull myself together."

A game of pool was beginning, and the room was full of men. Holden entered, eager to get to the light and the company of his fellows, singing at the top of his voice—

In Baltimore a-walking, a lady I
    did meet!

"Did you?" said the club secretary from his corner. "Did she happen to tell you that your boots were wringing wet? Great goodness, man, it's blood!"

"Bosh!" said Holden, picking his cue from the rack. "May I cut in? It's dew. I've been riding through high crops. My faith! my boots are in a mess though!

And if it be a girl she shall wear
    a wedding ring,
And if it be a boy he shall fight
    for his king,
With his dirk, and his cap, and his
    little jacket blue,
He shall walk the quarter-deck—

"Yellow on blue—green next player," said the marker monotonously.

"*He shall walk the quarter-deck*—Am I green, marker? *He shall walk the quarter-deck*—eh! that's a bad shot—*As his daddy used to do!*"

"I don't see that you have anything to crow about," said a zealous junior civilian acidly. "The Government is not exactly pleased with your work when you relieved Sanders."

"Does that mean a wigging from headquarters?" said Holden with an abstracted smile. "I think I can stand it."

The talk beat up round the everfresh subject of each man's work, and steadied Holden till it was time to go to his dark empty bungalow, where his butler received him as one who knew all his affairs. Holden remained awake for the greater part of the night, and his dreams were pleasant ones.

II

"How old is he now?"

"*Ya illah!* What a man's question! He is all but six weeks old; and on this night I go up to the housetop with thee, my life, to count the stars. For that is auspicious. And he was born on a Friday under the sign of the sun, and it has been told to me that he will outlive us both and get wealth. Can we wish for aught better, beloved?"

"There is nothing better. Let us go up to the roof, and thou shalt count the stars—but a few only for the sky is heavy with cloud."

"The winter rains are late, and maybe they come out of season. Come, before all the stars are hid. I have put on my richest jewels."

"Thou hast forgotten the best of all."

"*Ai!* Ours. He comes also. He has never yet seen the skies."

Ameera climbed the narrow staircase that led to the flat roof. The child, placid and unwinking, lay in the hollow of her right arm, gorgeous in silver-fringed muslin with a small skullcap on his head. Ameera wore all that she valued most. The diamond nose stud that takes the place of the Western patch in drawing attention to the curve of the nostril, the gold ornament in the center of the forehead studded with tallow-drop emeralds and flawed rubies, the heavy circlet of beaten gold that was fastened round her neck by the softness of the pure metal, and the chinking curb-patterned silver anklets hanging low over the rosy anklebone. She was dressed in jade-green muslin as befitted a daughter of the Faith, and from shoulder to elbow and elbow to wrist ran bracelets of silver tied with floss silk, frail glass bangles slipped over the wrist in proof of the slenderness of the hand, and certain heavy gold bracelets that had no part in her country's ornaments but, since they were Holden's gift and fastened with a cunning European snap, delighted her immensely.

They sat down by the low white parapet of the roof, overlooking the city and its lights.

"They are happy down there," said Ameera. "But I do not think that they are as happy as we. Nor do I think the white *mem-log* are as happy. And thou?"

"I know they are not."

"How dost thou know?"

"They give their children over to the nurses."

"I have never seen that," said Ameera with a sigh, "nor do I wish to see. *Ahi!*"—she dropped her head on Holden's shoulder—"I have counted forty stars, and I am tired. Look at the child, love of my life, he is counting too."

The baby was staring with round eyes at the dark of the heavens. Ameera placed him in Holden's arms, and he lay there without a cry.

"What shall we call him among ourselves?" she said. "Look! Art thou ever tired of looking? He carries thy very eyes. But the mouth——"

"Is thine, most dear. Who should know better than I?"

"'Tis such a feeble mouth. Oh, so small! And yet it holds my heart between its lips. Give him to me now. He has been too long away."

"Nay, let him lie; he has not yet begun to cry."

"When he cries thou wilt give him back—eh? What a man of mankind thou art! If he cried he were only the dearer to me. But, my life, what little name shall we give him?"

The small body lay close to Holden's heart. It was utterly helpless and very soft. He scarcely dared to breathe for fear of crushing it. The caged green parrot that is regarded as a sort of guardian-spirit in most native households moved on its perch and fluttered a drowsy wing.

"There is the answer," said Holden. "Mian Mittu has spoken. He shall be the parrot. When he is ready he will talk mightily and run about. Mian Mittu is the parrot in thy—in the Mussulman tongue, is it not?"

"Why put me so far off?" said Ameera fretfully. "Let it be like unto some English name—but not wholly. For he is mine."

"Then call him Tota, for that is likest English."

"Ay, Tota, and that is still the parrot. Forgive me, my lord, for a minute ago, but in truth he is too little to wear all the weight of Mian Mittu for name. He shall be Tota— our Tota to us. Hearest thou, O small one? Littlest, thou art Tota." She touched the child's cheek, and he waking wailed, and it was necessary to return him to his mother, who soothed him with the wonderful rhyme of *Aré koko, Jaré koko!* which says:

> *Oh crow! Go crow! Baby's sleeping sound,*
> *And the wild plums grow in the jungle, only a penny a pound.*
> *Only a penny a pound, baba, only a penny a pound.*

Reassured many times as to the price of those plums, Tota cuddled himself down to sleep. The two sleek, white well-bullocks in the courtyard were steadily chewing the cud of their evening meal; old Pir Khan squatted at the head of Holden's horse, his police saber across his knees, pulling drowsily at a big water pipe that croaked like a bullfrog in a pond. Ameera's mother sat spitting in the lower veranda, and the wooden gate was shut and barred. The music of a marriage procession came to the roof above the gentle hum of the city, and a string of flying foxes crossed the face of the low moon.

"I have prayed," said Ameera after a long pause, "I have prayed for two things. First, that I may die in thy stead if thy death is demanded, and in the second that I may die in the place of the child. I have prayed to the Prophet and to Beebee Miriam [the Virgin Mary]. Thinkest thou either will hear?"

"From thy lips who would not hear the lightest word?"

"I asked for straight talk, and thou hast given me sweet talk. Will my prayers be heard?"

"How can I say? God is very good."

"Of that I am not sure. Listen now. When I die, or the child dies, what is thy fate? Living, thou wilt return to the bold white *mem-log*, for kind calls to kind."

"Not always."

"With a woman, no; with a man it is otherwise. Thou wilt in this life, later on, go back to thine own folk. That I could almost endure, for I should be dead. But in thy very death thou wilt be taken away to a strange place and a paradise that I do not know."

"Will it be paradise?"

"Surely, for who would harm thee? But we two—I and the child—shall be elsewhere, and we cannot come to thee, nor canst thou come to us. In the old days, before the child was born, I did not think of these things; but now I think of them always. It is very hard talk."

"It will fall as it will fall. Tomorrow we do not know, but today and love we know well. Surely we are happy now."

"So happy that it were well to make our happiness assured. And thy Beebee Miriam should listen to me; for she is also a woman. But then she would envy me! It is not seemly for men to worship a woman."

Holden laughed aloud at Ameera's little spasm of jealousy.

"Is it not seemly? Why didst thou not turn me from worship of thee, then?"

"Thou a worshiper! And of me? My king, for all thy sweet words, well I know that I am thy servant and thy slave, and the dust under thy feet. And I would not have it otherwise. See!"

Before Holden could prevent her she stooped forward and touched his feet; recovering herself with a little laugh she hugged Tota closer to her bosom. Then almost savagely—

"Is it true that the bold white *mem-log* live for three times the length of my life? Is it true that they make their marriages not before they are old women?"

"They marry as do others—when they are women."

"That I know, but they wed when they are twenty-five. Is that true?"

"That is true."

"*Ya illah!* At twenty-five! Who would of his own will take a wife even of eighteen? She is a woman—aging every hour. Twenty-five! I shall be an old woman at that age, and—— Those *mem-log* remain young forever. How I hate them!"

"What have they to do with us?"

"I cannot tell. I know only that there may now be alive on this earth a woman ten years older than I who may come to thee and take thy love ten years after I am an old woman, gray-headed, and the nurse of Tota's son. That is unjust and evil. They should die too."

"Now, for all thy years thou art a child, and shalt be picked up and carried down the staircase."

"Tota! Have a care for Tota, my lord! Thou at least art as foolish as any babe!" Ameera tucked Tota out of harm's way in the hollow of her neck, and was carried downstairs laughing in Holden's arms, while Tota opened his eyes and smiled after the manner of the lesser angels.

He was a silent infant, and, almost before Holden could realize that he was in the world, developed into a small gold-colored little god and un-questioned despot of the house over-looking the city. Those were months of absolute happiness to Holden and Ameera—happiness withdrawn from the world, shut in behind the wooden gate that Pir Khan guarded. By day Holden did his work with an immense pity for such as were not so fortunate as himself, and a sympathy for small children that amazed and amused many mothers at the little station gatherings. At nightfall he returned to Ameera—Ameera, full of the wondrous doings of Tota; how he had been seen to clap his hands together and move his fingers with intention and pur-pose—which was manifestly a miracle—how later, he had of his own initiative crawled out of his low bedstead onto the floor and swayed on both feet for the space of three breaths.

"And they were long breaths, for my heart stood still with delight," said Ameera.

Then Tota took the beasts into his counsels—the well-bullocks, the little gray squirrels, the mongoose that lived in a hole near the well, and especially Mian Mittu, the parrot, whose tail he grievously pulled, and Mian Mittu screamed till Ameera and Holden arrived.

"O villain! Child of strength! This to thy brother on the housetop! *Tobah, tobah!* Fie! Fie! But I know a charm to make him wise as Sulei-man and Aflotoun [Solomon and Plato]. Now look," said Ameera. She drew from an embroidered bag a handful of almonds. "See! We count seven. In the name of God!"

She placed Mian Mittu, very angry and rumpled, on the top of his cage, and seating herself between the babe and the bird she cracked and peeled an almond less white than her teeth. "This is a true charm, my life, and do not laugh.

See! I give the parrot one half and Tota the other." Mian Mittu with careful beak took his share from between Ameera's lips, and she kissed the other half into the mouth of the child, who ate it slowly with wondering eyes. "This I will do each day of seven, and without doubt he who is ours will be a bold speaker and wise. Eh, Tota, what wilt thou be when thou art a man and I am gray-headed?" Tota tucked his fat legs into adorable creases. He could crawl, but he was not going to waste the spring of his youth in idle speech. He wanted Mian Mittu's tail to tweak.

When he was advanced to the dignity of a silver belt—which, with a magic square engraved on silver and hung round his neck, made up the greater part of his clothing—he staggered on a perilous journey down the garden to Pir Khan and proffered him all his jewels in exchange for one little ride on Holden's horse, having seen his mother's mother chaffering with peddlers in the veranda. Pir Khan wept and set the untried feet on his own gray head in sign of fealty, and brought the bold adventurer to his mother's arms, vowing that Tota would be a leader of men ere his beard was grown.

One hot evening, while he sat on the roof between his father and mother watching the never-ending warfare of the kites that the city boys flew, he demanded a kite of his own with Pir Khan to fly it, because he had a fear of dealing with anything larger than himself, and when Holden called him a "spark," he rose to his feet and answered slowly in defense of his new-found individuality, *"Hum'park nahin hai. Hum admi hai* [I am no spark, but a man]."

The protest made Holden choke and devote himself very seriously to a consideration of Tota's future. He need hardly have taken the trouble. The delight of that life was too perfect to endure. Therefore it was taken away as many things are taken away in India—suddenly and without warning. The little lord of the house, as Pir Khan called him, grew sorrowful and complained of pains who had never known the meaning of pain. Ameera, wild with terror, watched him through the night, and in the dawning of the second day the life was shaken out of him by fever—the seasonal autumn fever. It seemed altogether impossible that he could die, and neither Ameera nor Holden at first believed the evidence of the little body on the bedstead. Then Ameera beat her head against the wall and would have flung herself down the well in the garden had Holden not restrained her of main force.

One mercy only was granted to Holden. He rode to his office in broad daylight and found waiting him an unusually heavy mail that demanded concentrated attention and hard work. He was not, however, alive to this kindness of the gods.

III

The first shock of a bullet is no more than a brisk pinch. The wrecked body does not send in its protest to the soul till ten or fifteen seconds later. Holden realized his pain slowly, exactly as he had realized his happiness, and with the same imperious necessity for hiding all trace of it. In the beginning he only felt that there had been a loss, and that Ameera needed comforting, where she sat with her head on her knees shivering as Mian Mittu from the housetop called, *Tota! Tota! Tota!* Later all his world and the daily life of it rose up to hurt him. It was an outrage that any one of the children at the bandstand in the evening should be alive and clamorous, when his own child lay dead. It was more than mere pain when one of them touched him, and stories told by overfond fathers of their children's latest performances cut him to the quick. He could not declare his pain. He had neither help, comfort, nor sympathy; and Ameera at the end of each weary day would lead him through the hell of self-questioning reproach which is reserved for those who have lost a child and believe that with a little—just a little—more care it might have been saved.

"Perhaps," Ameera would say, "I did not take sufficient heed. Did I, or did I not? The sun on the roof that day when he played so long alone and I was—*ahi!* braiding my hair—it may be that the sun then bred the fever. If I had warned him from the sun he might have lived. But, oh my life, say that I am guiltless! Thou knowest that I loved him as I love thee. Say that there is no blame on me, or I shall die—I shall die!"

"There is no blame—before God, none. It was written and how could we do aught to save? What has been has been. Let it go, beloved."

"He was all my heart to me. How can I let the thought go when my arm tells me every night that he is not here? *Ahi! Ahi!* O Tota, come back to me—come back again, and let us be all together as it was before!"

"Peace, peace! For thine own sake, and for mine also, if thou lovest me—rest."

"By this I know thou dost not

care; and how shouldst thou? The white men have hearts of stone and souls of iron. Oh, that I had married a man of mine own people—though he beat me—and had never eaten the bread of an alien!"

"Am I an alien—mother of my son?"

"What else—*Sahib?* . . . Oh, forgive me—forgive! The death has driven me mad. Thou art the life of my heart, and the light of my eyes, and the breath of my life, and—and I have put thee from me, though it was but for a moment. If thou goest away, to whom shall I look for help? Do not be angry. Indeed, it was the pain that spoke and not thy slave."

"I know, I know. We be two who were three. The greater need therefore that we should be one."

They were sitting on the roof as of custom. The night was a warm one in early spring, and sheet lightning was dancing on the horizon to a broken tune played by far-off thunder. Ameera settled herself in Holden's arms.

"The dry earth is lowing like a cow for the rain, and I—I am afraid. It was not like this when we counted the stars. But thou lovest me as much as before, though a bond is taken away? Answer!"

"I love more because a new bond has come out of the sorrow that we have eaten together, and that thou knowest."

"Yea, I knew," said Ameera in a very small whisper. "But it is good to hear thee say so, my life, who art so strong to help. I will be a child no more, but a woman and an aid to thee. Listen! Give me my *sitar* and I will sing bravely."

She took the light silver-studded *sitar* and began a song of the great hero Rajah Rasalu. The hand failed on the strings, the tune halted, checked, and at a low note turned off to the poor little nursery rhyme about the wicked crow—

And the wild plums grow in the jungle, only a penny a pound. Only a penny a pound, baba— only . . .

Then came the tears, and the piteous rebellion against fate till she slept, moaning a little in her sleep, with the right arm thrown clear of the body as though it protected something that was not there. It was after this night that life became a little easier for Holden. The ever-present pain of loss drove him into his work, and the work repaid him by filling up his mind for nine or ten hours a day. Ameera sat alone in the house and brooded, but grew happier when she understood that Holden was more at ease, according to the custom of women. They touched happiness again, but this time with caution.

"It was because we loved Tota that he died. The jealousy of God was upon us," said Ameera. "I have hung up a large black jar before our window to turn the evil eye from us, and we must make no protestations of delight, but go softly underneath the stars, lest God find us out. Is that not good talk, worthless one?"

She had shifted the accent on the word that means "beloved," in proof of the sincerity of her purpose. But the kiss that followed the new christening was a thing that any deity might have envied. They went about hence-forward saying, "It is naught, it is naught;" and hoping that all the Powers heard.

The Powers were busy on other things. They had allowed thirty million people four years of plenty wherein men fed well and the crops were certain, and the birth rate rose year by year; the districts reported a purely agricultural population varying from nine hundred to two thousand to the square mile of the overburdened earth; and the Member for Lower Tooting, wandering about India in pot hat and frock coat, talked largely of the benefits of British rule and suggested as the one thing needful the establishment of a duly qualified electoral system and a general bestowal of the franchise. His long-suffering hosts smiled and made him welcome, and when he paused to admire, with pretty picked words, the blossom of the blood-red *dhak* tree that had flowered untimely for a sign of what was coming, they smiled more than ever.

It was the Deputy Commissioner of Kot-Kumharsen, staying at the club for a day, who lightly told a tale that made Holden's blood run cold as he overheard the end.

"He won't bother anyone any more. Never saw a man so astonished in my life. By Jove, I thought he meant to ask a question in the House about it. Fellow passenger in his ship—dined next him—bowled over by cholera and died in eighteen hours. You needn't laugh, you fellows. The Member for Lower Toot-, ing is awfully angry about it; but he's more scared. I think he's going to take his enlightened self out of India."

"I'd give a good deal if he were knocked over. It might keep a few vestrymen of his kidney to their own parish. But what's this about cholera? It's full early for anything of that kind," said the warden of an unprofitable salt lick.

"Don't know," said the Deputy Commissioner reflectively. "We've got locusts with us. There's sporadic cholera all along the north—at least we're calling it sporadic for decency's sake. The spring crops are short in five districts, and nobody seems to know where the rains are. It's nearly March now. I don't want to scare anybody, but it seems to me that Nature's going to audit her accounts with a big red pencil this summer."

"Just when I wanted to take leave, too!" said a voice across the room.

"There won't be much leave this year, but there ought to be a great deal of promotion. I've come in to persuade the Government to put my pet canal on the list of famine-relief works. It's an ill-wind that blows no good. I shall get that canal finished at last."

"Is it the old program then," said Holden; "famine, fever, and cholera?"

"Oh, no. Only local scarcity and an unusual prevalence of seasonal sickness. You'll find it all in the reports if you live till next year. You're a lucky chap. *You* haven't got a wife to send out of harm's way. The hill stations ought to be full of women this year."

"I think you're inclined to exaggerate the talk in the *bazars*," said a young civilian in the Secretariat. "Now I have observed——"

"I daresay you have," said the Deputy Commissioner, "but you've a great deal more to observe, my son. In the meantime, I wish to observe to you——" and he drew him aside to discuss the construction of the canal that was so dear to his heart. Holden went to his bungalow and began to understand that he was not alone in the world, and also that he was afraid for the sake of another—which is the most soul-satisfying fear known to man.

Two months later, as the Deputy had foretold, Nature began to audit her accounts with a red pencil. On the heels of the spring reaping came a cry for bread, and the Government, which had decreed that no man should die of want, sent wheat. Then came the cholera from all four quarters of the compass. It struck a pilgrim gathering of half a million at a sacred shrine. Many died at the feet of their god; the others broke and ran over the face of the land carrying the pestilence with them. It smote a walled city and killed two hundred a day. The people crowded the trains, hanging on to the foot-boards and squatting on the roofs of the carriages, and the cholera followed them, for at each station they dragged out the dead and the dying. They died by the roadside, and the horses of the Englishmen shied at the corpses in the grass. The rains did not come, and the earth turned to iron lest man should escape death by hiding in her. The English sent their wives away to the hills and went about their work, coming forward as they were bidden to fill the gaps in the fighting line. Holden, sick with fear of losing his chiefest treasure on earth, had done his best to persuade Ameera to go away with her mother to the Himalayas.

"Why should I go?" said she one evening on the roof.

"There is sickness, and people are dying, and all the white *mem-log* have gone."

"All of them?"

"All—unless perhaps there remain some old scald-head who vexes her husband's heart by running risk of death."

"Nay; who stays is my sister, and thou must not abuse her, for I will be a scald-head too. I am glad all the bold *mem-log* are gone."

"Do I speak to a woman or a babe? Go to the hills and I will see to it that thou goest like a queen's daughter. Think, child. In a red-lacquered bullock cart, veiled and curtained, with brass peacocks upon the pole and red cloth hangings. I will send two orderlies for guard, and——"

"Peace! Thou art the babe in speaking thus. What use are those toys to me? *He* would have patted the bullocks and played with the housings. For his sake, perhaps— thou hast made me very English—I might have gone. Now, I will not. Let the *mem-log* run."

"Their husbands are sending them, beloved."

"Very good talk. Since when hast thou been my husband to tell me what to do? I have but borne thee a son. Thou art only all the desire of my soul to me. How shall I depart when I know that if evil befall thee by the breadth of so much as my littlest fingernail—is that not small? —I should be aware of it though I were in paradise. And here, this summer thou mayest die—*ai, janee,* die! and in dying they might call to tend thee a white woman, and she would rob me in the last of thy love!"

"But love is not born in a moment or on a deathbed!"

"What dost thou know of love, stoneheart? She would take thy thanks at least and, by God and the Prophet and Beebee Miriam the mother of the Prophet, that I will never endure. My lord and my love, let there be no more foolish talk of going away. Where thou art, I am. It is enough." She put an arm round his neck and a hand on his mouth.

There are not many happinesses so complete as those that are snatched under the shadow of the sword. They sat together and laughed, calling each other openly by every pet name that could move the wrath of the gods. The city below them was

locked up in its own torments. Sulphur fires blazed in the streets; the conches in the Hindu temples screamed and bellowed, for the gods were inattentive in those days. There was a service in the great Mahomedan shrine, and the call to prayer from the minarets was almost unceasing. They heard the wailing in the houses of the dead, and once the shriek of a mother who had lost a child and was calling for its return. In the gray dawn they saw the dead borne out through the city gates, each litter with its own little knot of mourners. Wherefore they kissed each other and shivered.

It was a red and heavy audit, for the land was very sick and needed a little breathing space ere the torrent of cheap life should flood it anew. The children of immature fathers and undeveloped mothers made no resistance. They were cowed and sat still, waiting till the sword should be sheathed in November if it were so willed. There were gaps among the English, but the gaps were filled. The work of superintending famine relief, cholera sheds, medicine distribution, and what little sanitation was possible, went forward because it was so ordered.

Holden had been told to keep himself in readiness to move to replace the next man who should fall. There were twelve hours in each day when he could not see Ameera, and she might die in three. He was considering what his pain would be if he could not see her for three months, or if she died out of his sight. He was absolutely certain that her death would be demanded—so certain that when he looked up from the telegram and saw Pir Khan breathless in the doorway, he laughed aloud. "And?" said he——

"When there is a cry in the night and the spirit flutters into the throat, who has a charm that will restore? Come swiftly, Heaven-born! It is the black cholera."

Holden galloped to his home. The sky was heavy with clouds, for the long-deferred rains were near and the heat was stifling. Ameera's mother met him in the courtyard, whimpering, "She is dying. She is nursing herself into death. She is all but dead. What shall I do, sahib?"

Ameera was lying in the room in which Tota had been born. She made no sign when Holden entered, because the human soul is a very lonely thing and, when it is getting ready to go away, hides itself in a misty borderland where the living may not follow. The black cholera does its work quietly and without explanation. Ameera was being thrust out of life as though the Angel of Death had himself put his hand upon her. The quick breathing seemed to show that she was either afraid or in pain, but neither eyes nor mouth gave any answer to Holden's kisses. There was nothing to be said or done, Holden could only wait and suffer. The first drops of the rain began to fall on the roof, and he could hear shouts of joy in the parched city.

The soul came back a little and the lips moved. Holden bent down to listen. "Keep nothing of mine," said Ameera. "Take no hair from my head. *She* would make thee burn it later on. That flame I should feel. Lower! Stoop lower! Remember only that I was thine and bore thee a son. Though thou wed a white woman tomorrow, the pleasure of receiving in thy arms thy first son is taken from thee forever. Remember me when thy son is born—the one that shall carry thy name before all men.

His misfortunes be on my head. I bear witness—I bear witness"—the lips were forming the words on his ear—"that there is no God but—thee, beloved!"

Then she died. Holden sat still, and all thought was taken from him —till he heard Ameera's mother lift the curtain.

"Is she dead, *sahib?*"

"She is dead."

"Then I will mourn, and afterwards take an inventory of the furniture in this house. For that will be mine. The *sahib* does not mean to resume it? It is so little, so very little, *sahib*, and I am an old woman. I would like to lie softly."

"For the mercy of God be silent a while. Go out and mourn where I cannot hear."

"*Sahib*, she will be buried in four hours."

"I know the custom. I shall go ere she is taken away. The matter is in thy hands. Look to it, that the bed on which—on which she lies ——"

"Aha! That beautiful red-lacquered bed. I have long desired ——"

"That the bed is left here untouched for my disposal. All else in the house is thine. Hire a cart, take everything, go hence, and before sunrise let there be nothing in this house but that which I have ordered thee to respect."

"I am an old woman. I would stay at least for the days of mourning, and the rains have just broken. Whither shall I go?"

"What is that to me? My order is that there is a going. The house gear is worth a thousand rupees and my orderly shall bring thee a hundred rupees tonight."

"That is very little. Think of the cart hire."

"It shall be nothing unless thou goest, and with speed. O woman, get hence and leave me with my dead!"

The mother shuffled down the staircase, and in her anxiety to take stock of the house fittings forgot to mourn. Holden stayed by Ameera's side and the rain roared on the roof. He could not think connectedly by reason of the noise, though he made many attempts to do so. Then four sheeted ghosts glided dripping into the room and stared at him through their veils. They were the washers of the dead. Holden left the room and went out to his horse. He had come in a dead, stifling calm through ankle-deep dust. He found the courtyard a rain-lashed pond alive with frogs; a torrent of yellow water ran under the gate, and a roaring wind drove the bolts of the rain like buckshot against the mud walls. Pir Khan was shivering in his little hut by the gate, and the horse was stamping uneasily in the water.

"I have been told the *sahib's* order," said Pir Khan. "It is well. This house is now desolate. I go also, for my monkey-face would be a reminder of that which has been. Concerning the bed, I will bring that to thy house yonder in the morning; but remember, *sahib*, it will be to thee a knife turning in a green wound. I go upon a pilgrimage, and I will take no money. I have grown fat in the protection of the Presence whose sorrow is my sorrow. For the last time I hold his stirrup."

He touched Holden's foot with both hands and the horse sprang out into the road, where the creaking bamboos were whipping the sky and all the frogs were chuckling. Holden could not see for the rain in his face.

He put his hands before his eyes and muttered—

"Oh you brute! You utter brute!"

The news of his trouble was already in his bungalow. He read the knowledge in his butler's eyes when Ahmed Khan brought in food, and for the first and last time in his life laid a hand upon his master's shoulder, saying, "Eat, *sahib*, eat. Meat is good against sorrow. I also have known. Moreover the shadows come and go, *sahib*; the shadows come and go. These be curried eggs."

Holden could neither eat nor sleep. The heavens sent down eight inches of rain in that night and washed the earth clean. The waters tore down walls, broke roads, and scoured open the shallow graves on the Mahomedan burying ground. All next day it rained, and Holden sat still in his house, considering his sorrow. On the morning of the third day he received a telegram which said only, "Ricketts, Myndonie. Dying. Holden relieve. Immediate." Then he thought that before he departed he would look at the house wherein he had been master and lord. There was a break in the weather, and the rank earth steamed with vapor.

He found that the rains had torn down the mud pillars of the gateway, and the heavy wooden gate that had guarded his life hung lazily from one hinge. There was grass three inches high in the courtyard; Pir Khan's lodge was empty, and the sodden thatch sagged between the beams. A gray squirrel was in possession of the veranda, as if the house had been untenanted for thirty years instead of three days. Ameera's mother had removed everything except some mildewed matting. The *tick-tick* of the little scorpions as they hurried across the floor was the only sound in the house. Ameera's room and the other one where Tota had lived were heavy with mildew; and the narrow staircase leading to the roof was streaked and stained with rain-borne mud. Holden saw all these things, and came out again to meet in the road Durga Dass, his landlord—portly, affable, clothed in white muslin, and driving a Cee-spring buggy. He was overlooking his property to see how the roofs stood the stress of the first rains.

"I have heard," said he, "you will not take this place any more, *sahib*?"

"What are you going to do with it?"

"Perhaps I shall let it again."

"Then I will keep it on while I am away."

Durga Dass was silent for some time. "You shall not take it on, *sahib*," he said. "When I was a young man I also—— but today I am a member of the Municipality. Ho! Ho! No. When the birds have gone what need to keep the nest? I will have it pulled down—the timber will sell for something always. It shall be pulled down, and the Municipality shall make a road across, as they desire, from the burning ghat to the city wall, so that no man may say where this house stood."

Leonard Merrick

1864-1939

LEONARD MILLER was born near London of well-to-do Jewish parents who unfortunately lost their money before the boy had finished his education. Practically penniless at eighteen, he shipped to South Africa. There he worked in the diamond fields, superintending Kaffir laborers, and later in a lawyer's office in Kimberley. When he was able eventually to return to London, he got a small part in a theatrical company on tour. It was at that time that he took Merrick as his stage name, later legalizing it. The theater was always his love, as testified by many of the stories he then wrote. However, he lasted only two years on the stage, and his stories were not a success. There was a precious elegance about them that the public did not take to. But rumor spread among the literati that an important talent was being neglected, and just in time to keep Merrick from starving, a group of the most prominent writers of the day got together a complete set of his work and had it published in 1918, each contributing a preface. Among the writers were Barrie, Wells, W. J. Locke, Sir Arthur Wing Pinero, William Dean Howells, Maurice Hewlett, Sir William Robertson Nicholl, twelve in all, and it is an illuminating commentary that of the twelve, Merrick was acquainted with only three.

There is an alluring nostalgia in Merrick's stories—for the theater, for the lighthearted Bohemian world, for Paris before World War I—a gaiety close to tears. *A Chair on the Boulevard* contains "The Tragedy of a Comic Song," one of several stories about Tricotrin and Pitou, in that faraway, never-to-be-revived Paris.

The Tragedy of a Comic Song

BY LEONARD MERRICK

I LIKE to monopolize a table in a restaurant, unless a friend is with me, so I resented the young man's presence. Besides, he had a melancholy face. If it hadn't been for the piano-organ, I don't suppose I should have spoken to him. As the organ that was afflicting Lisle Street began to volley a comic song of a day that was dead, he started.

"That tune!" he murmured in French. If I did not deceive myself, tears sprang to his eyes.

I was curious. Certainly, on both sides of the Channel, we had long ago had more than enough of the tune—no self-respecting organ-grinder rattled it now. That the young Frenchman should wince at the tune I understood. But that he should weep!

I smiled sympathetically. "We suffered from it over here as well," I remarked.

"I did not know," he said, in English that reproved my French, "it was sung in London also—*Partant pour le moulin?*"

"Under another name," I told him, "it was an epidemic."

Clearly, the organ had stirred distressing memories in him, for though we fell to chatting, I could see that he neither talked nor dined with any relish. As luck would have it, too, the instrument of torture resumed its repertoire well within hearing, and when *Partant pour le moulin* was reached again, he clasped his head.

"You find it so painful?" I inquired.

"Painful?" he exclaimed. "Monsieur, it is my 'istory, that comic tune! It is to me romance, tragedy, ruin. Will you hear? Wait! I shall range my ideas. Listen."

It is Paris, at Montmartre—we are before the door of a laundress. A girl approaches. Her gaze is troubled, she frowns a little. What ails her? I shall tell you: the laundress has refused to deliver her washing until her bill is paid. And the girl cannot pay it—not till Saturday—and she has need of things to put on. It is a moment of anxiety. She opens the door. Some minutes pass. The girl reappears, holding under her arm a little parcel. Good! she has triumphed. In coming out she sees a young man, pale, abstracted, who stands before the shop. He does not attempt to enter. He stands motionless, regarding the window with an air forlorn.

"Ah," she says to herself, "here is another customer who cannot pay his bill!"

But wait a little. After 'alf an hour what happens? She sees the young man again! This time he stands before a modest restaurant. Does he go in? No, again no! He regards the window sorrowfully. He sighs. The dejection of his attitude would melt a stone.

"Poor boy," she thought; "he cannot pay for a dinner either!"

The affair is not finished. How the summer day is beautiful—she will do some footing! Figure yourself that once more she perceives the young man. Now it is before the *mont-de-piété*, the pawnbroker's. She watches him attentively. Here, at least, he will enter, she does not doubt. She is wrong. It is the same thing—he regards, he laments, he turns away!

"Oh, *mon Dieu*," she said. "Nothing remains to him to pawn even!"

It is too strong! She addressed him:

"Monsieur!"

But, when she has said "Monsieur," there is the question how she shall continue. Now the young man regards the girl instead of the pawnbroker's. Her features are pretty—or "pretty well"; her costume has been made by herself, but it is not bad; and she has chic—above all she has chic. He asks:

"What can I have the pleasure to do for you?"

Remark that she is bohemian, and he also. The conversation was like this:

"Monsieur, three times this morning I have seen you. It was impossible that I resist speaking. You have grief?"

"Frightful!" he said.

"Perhaps," she added timidly, "you have hunger also?"

"A hunger insupportable, mademoiselle!"

"I myself am extremely hard up, monsieur, but will you permit that I offer you what I can?"

"Angel!" the young man exclaimed. "There must be wings under your coat. But I beg of you not to fly yet. I shall tell you the reason of my grief. If you will do me the honor to seat yourself at the café opposite, we shall be able to talk more pleasantly."

This appeared strange enough, this invitation from a young man who she had supposed was starving; but wait a little! Her amazement increased when, to pay for the wine he had ordered, her companion threw on to the table a bank note with a gesture absolutely careless.

She was in danger of distrusting her eyes.

"Is it a dream?" she cried. "Is it a vision from the *Thousand and One Nights*, or is it really a bank note?"

"Mademoiselle, it is the mess of pottage," the young man answered gloomily. "It is the cause of my sadness: for that miserable money, and more that is to come, I have sold my birthright."

She was on a ship—no, what is it, your expression?—"at sea"!

"I am a poet," he explained; "but perhaps you may not know my work; I am not celebrated. I am Tricotrin, mademoiselle — Gustave Tricotrin, at your feet! For years I have written, aided by ambition, and an uncle who manufactures silk in Lyon. Well, the time is arrived when he is monstrous, this uncle. He says to me, 'Gustave, this cannot last—you make no living, you make nothing but debts.' (My tragedies he ignores.) 'Either you must be a poet who makes money, or you must be a partner who makes silk. How could I defy him?—he holds the purse. It was unavoidable that I stopped. He has given me a sum to satisfy my creditors, and Monday I depart for Lyon. In the meantime, I take tender farewells of the familiar scenes I shall perhaps never behold again."

"How I have been mistaken!" she exclaimed. And then: "But the hunger you confessed?"

"Of the soul, mademoiselle," said the poet—"the most bitter!"

"And you have no difficulties with the laundress?"

"None," he groaned. "But in the bright days of poverty that have fled forever, I have had many difficulties with her. This morning I reconstituted the situation—I imagined myself without a sou, and without a collar."

"The little restaurant," she questioned, "where I saw you dining on the odor?"

"I figured fondly to myself that I was ravenous and that I dared not enter. It was sublime."

"The *mont-de-piété*?"

"There imagination restored to me the vanished moments when I have mounted with suspense, and my least deplorable suit of clothes." His emotion was profound. "It is my youth to which I am bidding adieu!" he cried. "It is more than that—it is my aspirations and my renown!"

"But you have said that you have no renown," she reminded him.

"So much the more painful," said the young man; "the hussy we could not win is always the fairest—I part from renown even more despairingly than from youth."

She felt an amusement, and interest. But soon it was the turn of him to feel an interest—the interest that had consequences so important, so 'eartbreaking, so *fatales!* He had demanded of her, most naturally, her history, and this she related to

him in a style dramatic. Myself, I have not the style dramatic, though I avow to you I admire that.

"We are in a provincial town," she said to the young man, "we are in Rouen—the workroom of a modiste. Have no embarrassment, Monsieur Tricotrin, you, at least, are invisible to the girls who sew! They sew all day and talk little—already they are *tristes*, resigned. Among them sits one who is different—one passionate, ambitious—a girl who burns to be *divette*, singer, who is devoured by longings for applause, fashion, wealth. She has made the acquaintance of a little pastry cook. He has become fascinated, they are affianced. In a month she will be married."

The young man, Tricotrin, well understood that the girl she described was herself.

"What does she consider while she sits sewing?" she continued. "That the pastry cook loves her, that he is generous, that she will do her most to be to him a good wife? Not at all. Far from that! She considers, on the contrary, that she was a fool to promise him; she considers how she shall escape—from him, from Rouen, from her ennui—she seeks to fly to Paris. Alas! she has no money, not a franc. And she sews—always she sews in the dull room—and her spirit rebels."

"Good!" said the poet. "It is a capital first installment."

"The time goes on. There remains only a week to the marriage morning. The little home is prepared, the little pastry cook is full of joy. *Alors*, one evening they go out; for her the sole attraction in the town is the hall of varieties. Yes, it is third class, it is not great things; however, it is the only one in Rouen. He purchases two tickets.

What a misfortune—it is the last temptation to her! They stroll back; she takes his arm—under the moon, under the stars; but she sees only the lamps of Paris!—she sees only that he can say nothing she cares to hear!"

"Ah, unhappy man!" murmured the poet.

"They sit at a café table, and he talks, the fiancé, of the bliss that is to come to them. She attends to not a word, not a syllable. While she smiles, she questions herself, frenzied, how she can escape. She has commanded a *sirop*. As she lifts her glass to the siphon, her gaze falls on the ring she wears—the ring of their betrothal. 'To the future, *cher ange!*' says the fiancé. 'To the future, *vieux chéri!*' she says. And she laughs in her heart—for she resolves to sell the ring!"

Tricotrin had become absolutely enthralled.

"She obtained for the ring forty-five francs the next day—and for the little pastry cook all is finished. She wrote him a letter—'Good-by.' He has lost his reason. Mad with despair, he has flung himself before an electric car, and is killed. . . . It is strange," she added to the poet, who regarded her with consternation, "that I did not think sooner of the ring that was always on my finger, *n'est-ce pas?* It may be that never before had I felt so furious an impulse to desert him. It may be also—that there was no ring and no pastry cook!" And she broke into peals of laughter.

"Ah, *mon Dieu*," exclaimed the young man, "but you are enchanting! Let us go to breakfast—you are the kindred soul I have looked for all my life. By-the-bye, I may as well know your name?"

Then, Monsieur, this poor girl who had trembled before her laundress, she told him a name which was going, in a while, to crowd the Ambassadeurs and be famous through all Paris—a name which was to mean caprices, folly, extravagance the most willful and reckless. She answered—and it said nothing yet—"My name is Paulette Fleury."

The piano-organ stopped short, as if it knew the Frenchman had reached a crisis in his narrative. He folded his arms and nodded impressively.

"*Voilà!* Monsieur. I 'ave introduced you to Paulette Fleury! It was her beginning."

He offered me a cigarette, and frowned, lost in thought, at the lady who was chopping bread behind the counter.

"Listen," he resumed.

They have breakfasted; they have fed the sparrows around their chairs, and they have strolled under the green trees in the sunshine. She was singing then at a little café-concert the most obscure. It is arranged, before they part, that in the evening he shall go to applaud her.

He had a friend, young also, a composer, named Nicolas Pitou. I cannot express to you the devotion that existed between them. Pitou was employed at a publisher's, but the publisher paid him not much better than his art. The comrades have shared everything: the loans from the *mont-de-piété*, the attic, and the dreams. In Montmartre it was said "Tricotrin and Pitou" as one says "Orestes and Pylades." It is beautiful such affection, *hein?* Listen!

Tricotrin has recounted to his friend his meeting with Paulette, and when the hour for the concert is arrived, Pitou accompanied him. The musician, however, was, perhaps, the more sedate. He has gone with little expectation; his interest was not high.

What a surprise he has had! He has found her an actress—an artist to the ends of the fingers. Tricotrin was astonished also. The two friends, the poet and the composer, said, *"Mon Dieu!"* They regarded the one the other. They said, *"Mon Dieu!"* again. Soon Pitou has requested of Tricotrin an introduction. It is agreed. Tricotrin has presented his friend, and invited the *chanteuse* to drink a bock—a glass of beer. . . . Apropos, you take a liqueur, Monsieur, yes? What liqueur you take? Sst, *garçon!* . . . Well, you conjecture, no doubt, what I shall say? Before the bock was finished, they were in love with her—both!

At the door of her lodging, Paulette has given to each a pressure of the hand, and said gently, "Till tomorrow."

"I worship her!" Tricotrin told Pitou.

"I have found my ideal!" Pitou answered Tricotrin.

It is superb, such friendship, *hein?*

In the mind of the poet who had accomplished tragedies majestic— in the mind of the composer, the most classical in Montmartre—there had been born a new ambition; it was to write a comic song for Paulette Fleury!

It appears to you droll, perhaps? Monsieur, to her lover, the humblest *divette* is more than Patti. In all the world there can be no joy so thrilling as to hear the music of one's brain sung by the woman one adores— unless it be to hear the woman one adores give forth one's verse. I believe it has been accepted as a fact, this; nevertheless it is true.

Yes, already the idea had come to them, and Paulette was well pleased when they told her of it. Oh, she knew they loved her, both, and with both she coquetted. But with their intention she did not coquet; as to that she was in earnest. Every day they discussed it with enthusiasm— they were to write a song that should make for her a furore.

What happened? I shall tell you. Monday, when Tricotrin was to depart for Lyon, he informed his uncle that he will not go. No less than that! His uncle was furious—I do not blame him—but naturally Tricotrin has argued, "If I am to create for Paulette her great chance, I must remain in Paris to study Paulette! I cannot create in an atmosphere of commerce. I require the Montmartrois, the boulevards, the inspiration of her presence." Isn't it?

And Pitou—whose very soul had been enraptured in his leisure by a fugue he was composing—Pitou would have no more of it. He allowed the fugue to grow dusty, while day and night he thought always of refrains that ran "Zim-la-zim-la zim-boum-boum!" Constantly they conferred, the comrades. They told the one the other how they loved her; and then they beat their heads, and besought of Providence a fine idea for the comic song.

It was the thought supreme. The silk manufacturer has washed his 'ands of Tricotrin, but he has not cared—there remained to him still one of the bank notes. As for Pitou, who neglected everything except to find his melody for Paulette, the publisher has given him the sack. Their acquaintances ridiculed the sacrifices made for her. But, Monsieur, when a man loves truly, to make a sacrifice for the woman is to make a present to himself.

Nevertheless I avow to you that they fretted because of her co-quetry. One hour it seemed that Pitou had gained her heart; the next her encouragement has been all to Tricotrin. Sometimes they have said to her:

"Paulette, it is true we are as Orestes and Pylades, but there can be only one King of Eden at the time. Is it Orestes or Pylades that you mean to crown?"

Then she would laugh and reply: "How can I say? I like you both so much I can never make up my mind which to like best."

It was not satisfactory.

And always she added, "In the meantime where is the song?"

Ah, the song, that song, how they have sought it!—on the Butte, and in the Bois, and round the Halles. Often they have tramped Paris till daybreak, meditating the great chance for Paulette. And at last the poet has discovered it: for each verse a different phase of life, but through it all the pursuit of gaiety, the fever of the dance—the gaiety of youth, the gaiety of dotage, the gaiety of despair! It should be the song of the pleasure-seekers—the voices of Paris when the lamps are lit.

Monsieur, if we sat 'ere in the restaurant until it closed, I could not describe to you how passionately Tricotrin, the devoted Tricotrin worked for her. He has studied her without cease; he has studied her attitudes, her expressions. He has taken his lyric as if it were material and cut it to her figure; he has taken it as if it were plaster, and molded it upon her mannerisms. There was not a *moue* that she made, not a

pretty trick that she had, not a word what she like to sing for which he did not provide an opportunity. At the last line, when the pen fell from his fingers, he shouted to Pitou, "Comrade, be brave—I have won her!"

And Pitou? Monsieur, if we sat 'ere till they prepared the tables for *déjeuner* tomorrow, I could not describe to you how passionately Pitou, and the devoted Pitou, worked that she might have a grand popularity by his music. At dawn, when he has found that *strepitoso* passage, which is the hurrying of the feet, he wakened the poet and cried, *"Mon ami,* I pity you—she is mine!" It was the souls of two men when it was finished, that comic song they made for her! It was the song the organ has ground out—*Partant pour le moulin.*

And then they rehearsed it, the three of them, over and over, inventing always new effects. And then the night for the song is arrived. It has rained all day, and they have walked together in the rain—the singer, and the men who loved her, both—to the little café-concert where she would appear.

They tremble in the room, among the crowd, Pitou and Tricotrin; they are agitated. There are others who sing—it says nothing to them. In the room, in the Future, there is only Paulette!

It is very hot in the café-concert, and there is too much noise. At last they ask her: "Is she nervous?" She shakes her head: *"Mais non!"* She smiles to them.

Attend! It is her turn. Ouf; but it is hot in the café-concert, and there is too much noise! She mounts the platform. The audience are careless; it continues, the jingle of the glasses, the hum of talk. She begins. Beneath the table Tricotrin has gripped the hand of Pitou.

Wait! Regard the crowd that look at her! The glasses are silent, now, *hein?* The talk has stopped. To a great actress is come her chance. There is *not* too much noise in the café-concert!

But, when she finished! What an uproar! Never will she forget it. A thousand times she has told the story, how it was written—the song —and how it made her famous. Before two weeks she was the attraction of the Ambassadeurs, and all Paris has raved of Paulette Fleury.

Tricotrin and Pitou were mad with joy. Certainly Paris did not rave of Pitou nor Tricotrin—there have not been many that remembered who wrote the song; and it earned no money for them, either, because it was hers—and gift of their love. Still, they were enraptured. To both of them she owed equally, and more than ever it was a question which would be the happy man.

Listen! When they are gone to call on her one afternoon she was not at 'ome. What had happened? I shall tell you. There was a noodle, rich—what you call a "Johnnie in the Stalls"—who became infatuated with her at the Ambassadeurs. He

whistled *Partant pour le moulin* all the days, and went to hear it all the nights. Well, she was not at 'ome because she had married him. Absolutely they were married! Her lovers have been told it at the door.

What a moment! Figure yourself what they have suffered, both! They had worshiped her, they had made sacrifices for her, they had created for her her grand success; and, as a consequence of that song, she was the wife of the "Johnnie in the Stalls"!

Far down the street, but yet distinct, the organ revived the tune again. My Frenchman shuddered, and got up.

"I cannot support it," he murmured. "You understand? The associations are too pathetic."

"They must be harrowing," I said. "Before you go, there is one thing I should like to ask you, if I may. Have I had the honor of meeting Monsieur Tricotrin, or Monsieur Pitou?"

He stroked his hat, and gazed at me in sad surprise. "Ah, but neither, Monsieur," he groaned. "The associations are much more 'arrowing than that—I was the 'Johnnie in the Stalls'!"

W. W. Jacobs
1863-1943

EVEN if his stories are not world-shaking, it would be unforgivable to overlook William Wymark Jacobs. A shy, modest little man, Jacobs was for thirty years one of the most successful and dearly loved short-story writers in the English-speaking world. Like so many good writers, he was a civil-service employee. He worked in the savings-bank department of the post office, and wrote only on the side until he became popular enough to support himself by his writing. He toiled over every page, often taking an entire morning to write a single sentence. If he finished a four-thousand-word story in a month he considered himself lucky and took a holiday. His best stories are about Wapping, the dock area of London, where his father was a dock manager: "A world of sleepy little ports," writes J. B. Priestley, "tiny coasting vessels, trim cottages, happy little taverns, pretty saucy girls with a string of admirers, comic policemen, lovelorn third-mates, henpecked sea-captains, philosophical night-watchmen."

Jacobs had a low voice and gentle manners, a lovely sense of humor, and eyes with a twinkle. His only strong aversion was woman suffrage, whereas his wife, the mother of his five children, was a militant suffragist who once smashed a window with a brick to attract a London bobby's notice. It did, and she went to jail for a month. . . . "The Money Box" came out in *Odd Craft*, in 1903.

The Money Box

BY W. W. JACOBS

SAILORMEN are not good 'ands at saving money as a rule, said the night watchman, as he wistfully toyed with a bad shilling on his watch chain, though to 'ear 'em talk of saving when they're at sea and there isn't a pub within a thousand miles of 'em, you might think different.

It ain't for the want of trying either with some of 'em, and I've known men do all sorts o' things as soon as they was paid off, with a view to saving. I knew one man as used to keep all but a shilling or two in a belt next to 'is skin so that he couldn't get at it easy, but it was all no good. He was always running short in the most inconvenient places. I've seen 'im wriggle for five minutes right off, with a tramcar conductor standing over 'im and the other people in the tram reading their papers with one eye and watching him with the other.

Ginger Dick and Peter Russet—two men I've spoke of to you afore—tried to save their money once. They'd got so sick and tired of spending it all in p'r'aps a week or ten days arter coming ashore, and 'aving to go to sea agin sooner than they 'ad intended, that they determined some way or other to 'ave things different.

They was homeward bound on a steamer from Melbourne when they made their minds up; and Isaac Lunn, the oldest fireman aboard—a very steady old teetotaler—gave them a lot of good advice about it. They all wanted to rejoin the ship when she sailed agin, and 'e offered to take a room ashore with them and mind their money, giving 'em what 'e called a moderate amount each day.

They would ha' laughed at any other man, but they knew that old Isaac was as honest as could be and that their money would be safe with 'im, and at last, after a lot of palaver, they wrote out a paper saying as they were willing for 'im to 'ave their money and give it to 'em bit by bit, till they went to sea agin.

Anybody but Ginger Dick and Peter Russet or a fool would ha' known better than to do such a thing, but old Isaac 'ad got such a oily tongue and seemed so fair-minded about wot 'e called moderate drinking that they never thought wot they was letting themselves in for, and when they took their pay—close on sixteen pounds each—they put the odd change in their pockets

From *Odd Craft* by W. W. Jacobs. By permission of the publishers, Charles Scribner's Sons. Copyright, 1903, 1931, by W. W. Jacobs.

and 'anded the rest over to him.

The first day they was as pleased as Punch. Old Isaac got a nice, respectable bedroom for them all, and arter they'd 'ad a few drinks they humored 'im by 'aving a nice 'ot cup o' tea, and then goin' off with 'im to see a magic-lantern performance.

It was called *The Drunkard's Downfall,* and it begun with a young man going into a nice-looking pub and being served by a nice-looking barmaid with a glass of ale. Then it got on to 'arf pints and pints in the next picture, and arter Ginger 'ad seen the lost young man put away six pints in about 'arf a minute, 'e got such a raging thirst on 'im that 'e couldn't sit still, and 'e whispered to Peter Russet to go out with 'im.

"You'll lose the best of it if you go now," ses old Isaac, in a whisper; "in the next picture there's little frogs and devils sitting on the edge of the pot as 'e goes to drink."

Ginger Dick got up and nodded to Peter.

"Arter that 'e kills 'is mother with a razor," ses old Isaac, pleading with 'im and 'olding on to 'is coat.

Ginger Dick sat down agin, and when the murder was over 'e said it made 'im feel faint, and 'im and Peter Russet went out for a breath of fresh air. They 'ad three at the first place, and then they moved on to another and forgot all about Isaac and the dissolving views until ten o'clock, when Ginger, who 'ad been very liberal to some friends 'e'd made in a pub, found 'e'd spent 'is last penny.

"This comes o' listening to a parcel o' teetotalers," 'e ses, very cross, when 'e found that Peter 'ad spent all 'is money too. "Here we are just beginning the evening and not a farthing in our pockets."

They went off 'ome in a very bad temper. Old Isaac was asleep in 'is bed, and when they woke 'im up and said that they was going to take charge of their money themselves 'e kept dropping off to sleep agin and snoring that 'ard they could scarcely hear themselves speak. Then Peter tipped Ginger a wink and pointed to Isaac's trousers, which were 'anging over the foot of the bed.

Ginger Dick smiled and took 'em up softly, and Peter Russet smiled too; but 'e wasn't best pleased to see old Isaac a smiling in 'is sleep, as though 'e was 'aving amusing dreams. All Ginger found was a ha'penny, a bunch o' keys, and a cough lozenge. In the coat and waistcoat 'e found a few tracks folded up, a broken penknife, a ball of string, and some other rubbish. Then 'e set down on the foot o' their bed and made eyes over at Peter.

"Wake 'im up agin," ses Peter, in a temper.

Ginger Dick got up and, leaning over the bed, took old Isaac by the shoulders and shook 'im as if 'e'd been a bottle o' medicine. "Time to get up, lads?" ses old Isaac, putting one leg out o' bed.

"No, it ain't," ses Ginger, very rough; "we ain't been to bed yet. We want our money back."

Isaac drew 'is leg back into bed agin. "Goo' night," he ses, and fell fast asleep.

"He's shamming, that's wot 'e is," ses Peter Russet. "Let's look for it. It must be in the room somewhere."

They turned the room upside down pretty near, and then Ginger Dick struck a match and looked up the chimney, but all e' found was that it 'adn't been swept for about twenty years, and wot with temper and soot 'e looked so frightful that Peter was arf afraid of 'im.

"I've 'ad enough of this," ses Ginger, running up to the bed and 'olding his sooty fist under old Isaac's nose. "Now, then, where's that money? If you don't give us our money, our 'ard-earned money, inside o' two minutes, I'll break every bone in your body."

"This is wot comes o' trying to do you a favor, Ginger," ses the old man, reproachfully.

"Don't talk to me," ses Ginger, "cos I won't have it. Come on; where is it?"

Old Isaac looked at 'im, and then he gave a sigh and got up and put on 'is boots and 'is trousers.

"I thought I should 'ave a little trouble with you," he ses, slowly, "but I was prepared for that."

"You'll 'ave more if you don't hurry up," ses Ginger, glaring at 'im.

"We don't want to 'urt you, Isaac," ses Peter Russet, "we on'y want our money."

"I know that," ses Isaac; "you keep still, Peter, and see fair play, and I'll knock you silly arterwards."

He pushed some o' the things into a corner and then 'e spat on 'is 'ands, and began to prance up and down, and duck 'is 'ead about and hit the air in a way that surprised 'em.

"I ain't hit a man for five years," 'e ses, still dancing up and down— "fighting's sinful except in a good cause—but afore I got a new 'art, Ginger, I'd lick three men like you afore breakfast, just to git up a appetite."

"Look 'ere," ses Ginger; "you're an old man and I don't want to 'urt you; tell us where our money is, our 'ard-earned money, and I won't lay a finger on you."

"I'm taking care of it for you," ses the old man.

Ginger Dick gave a howl and rushed at him, and the next moment Isaac's fist shot out and give 'im a drive that sent 'im spinning across the room until 'e fell in a heap in the fireplace. It was like a kick from a 'orse, and Peter looked very serious as 'e picked 'im up and dusted 'im down.

"You should keep your eye on 'is fist," he ses, sharply.

It was a silly thing to say, seeing that that was just wot 'ad 'appened, and Ginger told 'im wot 'e'd do for 'im when 'e'd finished with Isaac. He went at the old man agin, but 'e never 'ad a chance, and in about three minutes 'e was very glad to let Peter 'elp 'im into bed.

"It's your turn to fight him now, Peter," he ses. "Just move this piller so as I can see."

"Come on lad," ses the old man.

Peter shook 'is 'ead. "I have no wish to 'urt you, Isaac," he ses, kindly; "excitement like fighting is dangerous for an old man. Give us our money and we'll say no more about it."

"No, my lads," ses Isaac. "I've undertook to take charge o' this money and I'm going to do it; and I 'ope that when we all sign on aboard the *Planet* there'll be a matter o' twelve pounds each left. Now, I don't want to be 'arsh with you, but I'm going back to bed, and if I 'ave to get up and dress agin you'll wish yourselves dead."

He went back to bed agin, and Peter, taking no notice of Ginger Dick, who kept calling 'im a coward, got into bed alongside of Ginger and fell fast asleep.

They all 'ad breakfast in a coffee shop next morning, and arter it was over Ginger, who 'adn't spoke a word till then, said that 'e and Peter Russet wanted a little money to go on with. He said they preferred to get their meals alone, as Isaac's face took their appetite away.

"Very good," ses the old man. "I don't want to force my company on nobody," and after thinking 'ard for a minute or two he put 'is 'and in 'is trouser pocket and gave them eighteen-pence each.

"Wot's this for?" ses Ginger, staring at the money. "Matches?"

"That's your day's allowance," ses Isaac, "and it's plenty. There's ninepence for your dinner, fourpence for your tea, and twopence for a crust o' bread and cheese for supper. And if you must go and drown yourselves in beer, that leaves threepence each to go and do it with."

Ginger tried to speak to 'im, but 'is feelings was too much for 'im, and 'e couldn't. Then Peter Russet swallered something 'e was going to say and asked old Isaac very perlite to make it a quid for 'im because he was going down to Colchester to see 'is mother, and 'e didn't want to go empty-'anded.

"You're a good son, Peter," ses old Isaac, "and I wish there was more like you. I'll come down with you, if you like; I've got nothing to do."

Peter said it was very kind of 'im, but 'e'd sooner go alone, owing to his mother being very shy afore strangers.

"Well, I'll come down to the station and take a ticket for you," ses Isaac.

Then Peter lost 'is temper altogether, and banged 'is fist on the table and smashed arf the crockery. He asked Isaac whether 'e thought 'im and Ginger Dick was a couple o' children, and 'e said if 'e didn't give 'em all their money right away 'e'd give 'im in charge to the first policeman they met.

"I'm afraid you didn't intend for

to go and see your mother, Peter," ses the old man.

"Look 'ere," ses Peter, "are you going to give us that money?"

"Not if you went down on your bended knees," ses the old man.

"Very good," says Peter, getting up and walking outside; "then come along o' me to find a policeman."

"I'm agreeable," ses Isaac, "but I've got the paper you signed."

Peter said 'e didn't care twopence if 'e'd got fifty papers, and they walked along looking for a policeman, which was a very unusual thing for them to do.

"I 'ope for your sakes it won't be the same policeman that you and Ginger Dick set on in Gun Alley the night afore you shipped on the *Planet*," ses Isaac, pursing up 'is lips.

" 'Tain't likely to be," ses Peter, beginning to wish 'e 'adn't been so free with 'is tongue.

"Still, if I tell 'im, I dessay he'll soon find 'im," ses Isaac; "there's one coming along now, Peter; shall I stop 'im?"

Peter Russet looked at 'im and then he looked at Ginger, and they walked by, grinding their teeth. They stuck to Isaac all day, trying to get their money out of 'im, and the names they called 'im was a surprise even to themselves. And at night they turned the room topsy-turvy agin looking for their money and 'ad more unpleasantness when they wanted Isaac to get up and let 'em search the bed.

They 'ad breakfast together agin next morning and Ginger tried another tack. He spoke quite nice to Isaac, and 'ad three large cups o' tea to show 'im 'ow 'e was beginning to like it, and when the old man gave 'em their eighteen-pences 'e smiled and said 'e'd like a few shillings extra that day.

"It'll be all right, Isaac," he ses. "I wouldn't 'ave a drink if you asked me to. Don't seem to care for it now. I was saying so to you on'y last night, wasn't I, Peter?"

"You was," ses Peter; "so was I."

"Then I've done you good, Ginger," ses Isaac, clapping 'im on the back.

"You 'ave," ses Ginger, speaking between his teeth, "and I thank you for it. I don't want drink; but I thought o' going to a music 'all this evening."

"Going to wot?" ses old Isaac, drawing 'imself up and looking very shocked.

"A music 'all," ses Ginger, trying to keep 'is temper.

"A music 'all," ses Isaac; "why, it's worse than a pub, Ginger. I should be a very poor friend o' yours if I let you go there—I couldn't think of it."

"Wot's it got to do with you, you gray-whiskered serpent?" screams Ginger, arf mad with rage. "Why don't you leave us alone? Why don't you mind your own business? It's our money."

Isaac tried to talk to 'im, but 'e wouldn't listen, and he made such a fuss that at last the coffee-shop keeper told 'im to go outside. Peter follered 'im out, and being very upset they went and spent their day's allowance in the first hour, and then they walked about the streets quarreling as to the death they'd like old Isaac to 'ave when 'is time came.

They went back to their lodgings at dinnertime; but there was no sign of the old man, and, being 'ungry and thirsty, they took all their spare clothes to a pawnbroker and got enough money to go on with. Just to show their independence they went to two music 'alls, and with a sort of idea that they was doing Isaac a bad turn they spent every farthing afore they got 'ome, and sat up in bed telling 'im about the spree they'd 'ad.

At five o'clock in the morning Peter woke up and saw, to 'is surprise, that Ginger Dick was dressed and carefully folding up old Isaac's clothes. At first 'e thought that Ginger 'ad gone mad, taking care of the old man's things like that, but afore 'e could speak Ginger noticed that 'e was awake, and stepped over to 'im and whispered to 'im to dress without making a noise. Peter did as 'e was told, and, more puzzled than ever, saw Ginger make up all the old man's clothes in a bundle and creep out of the room on tiptoe.

"Going to 'ide 'is clothes?" 'e ses.

"Yes," ses Ginger, leading the way downstairs; "in a pawnshop. We'll make the old man pay for to-day's amusements."

Then Peter see the joke and 'e begun to laugh so 'ard that Ginger 'ad to threaten to knock 'is head off to quiet 'im. Ginger laughed 'imself when they got outside, and at last, after walking about till the shops opened, they got into a pawnbroker's and put old Isaac's clothes up for fifteen shillings.

First thing they did was to 'ave a good breakfast, and after that they came out smiling all over and began to spend a 'appy day. Ginger was in tiptop spirits and so was Peter, and the idea that old Isaac was in bed while they was drinking 'is clothes pleased them more than anything. Twice that evening policemen spoke to Ginger for dancing on the pavement, and by the time the money was spent it took Peter all 'is time to get 'im 'ome.

Old Isaac was in bed when they got there, and the temper 'e was in was shocking; but Ginger sat on 'is bed and smiled at 'im as if 'e was saying compliments to 'im.

"Where's my clothes?" ses the old man, shaking 'is fist at the two of 'em.

Ginger smiled at 'im; then 'e shut 'is eyes and dropped off to sleep.

"Where's my clothes?" ses Isaac, turning to Peter.

"Clothes?" ses Peter, staring at 'im.

"Where are they?" ses Isaac.

It was a long time afore Peter could understand wot 'e meant, but as soon as 'e did 'e started to look for 'em. Drink takes people in different ways, and the way it always took Peter was to make 'im one o' the most obliging men that ever lived. He spent arf the night crawling about on all fours looking for the clothes, and four or five times old Isaac woke up from dreams of earthquakes to find Peter 'ad got jammed under 'is bed, and was wondering what 'ad 'appened to 'im.

None of 'em was in the best o' tempers when they woke up next morning, and Ginger 'ad 'ardly got 'is eyes open before Isaac was asking 'im about 'is clothes agin.

"Don't bother me about your clothes," ses Ginger; "talk about something else for a change."

"Where are they?" ses Isaac, sitting on the edge of 'is bed.

Ginger yawned and felt in 'is waistcoat pocket—for neither of 'em 'ad undressed—and then 'e took the pawn ticket out and threw it on the floor. Isaac picked it up, and then 'e began to dance about the room as if 'e'd gone mad.

"Do you mean to tell me you've pawned my clothes?" he shouts.

"Me and Peter did," ses Ginger, sitting up in bed and getting ready for a row.

Isaac dropped on the bed agin all of a 'eap. "And wot am I to do?" he ses.

"If you be'ave yourself," ses Ginger, "and give us our money, me and Peter'll go and get 'em out agin. When we've 'ad breakfast, that is. There's no hurry."

"But I 'aven't got the money," ses Isaac; "it was all sewn up in the lining of the coat. I've on'y got about five shillings. You've made a nice mess of it, Ginger, you 'ave."

"You're a silly fool, Ginger, that's wot you are," ses Peter.

"Sewn up in the lining of the coat?" ses Ginger, staring.

"The bank notes was," ses Isaac, "and three pounds in gold 'idden in the cap. Did you pawn that too?"

Ginger got up in 'is excitement and walked up and down the room. "We must go and get 'em out at once," he ses.

"And where's the money to do it with?" ses Peter.

Ginger 'adn't thought of that, and it struck 'im all of a heap. None of 'em seemed to be able to think of a way of getting the other ten shillings wot was wanted, and Ginger was so upset that 'e took no notice of the things Peter kept saying to 'im.

"Let's go and ask to see 'em, and say we left a railway ticket in the pocket," ses Peter.

Isaac shook 'is 'ead. "There's on'y one way to do it," he ses. "We shall 'ave to pawn your clothes, Ginger, to get mine out with."

"That's the on'y way, Ginger," ses Peter, brightening up. "Now, wot's the good o' carrying on like that? It's no worse for you to be without your clothes for a little while than it was for pore old Isaac."

It took 'em quite arf an hour afore they could get Ginger to see it. First of all 'e wanted Peter's clothes to be took instead of 'is, and when Peter pointed out that they was too shabby to fetch ten shillings 'e 'ad a lot o' nasty things to say about wearing such old rags, and at last, in a terrible temper, 'e took 'is clothes off and pitched 'em in a 'eap on the floor.

"If you ain't back in arf an hour, Peter," 'e ses, scowling at 'im, "you'll 'ear from me, I can tell you."

"Don't you worry about that," ses Isaac, with a smile. "I'm going to take 'em." "You?" ses Ginger; "but you can't. You ain't got no clothes."

"I'm going to wear Peter's," ses Isaac, with a smile.

Peter asked 'im to listen to reason, but it was all no good. He'd got the pawn ticket, and at last Peter, forgetting all he'd said to Ginger Dick about using bad langwidge, took 'is clothes off, one by one, and dashed 'em on the floor, and told Isaac some of the things 'e thought of 'im.

The old man didn't take any notice of 'im. He dressed 'imself up very slow and careful in Peter's clothes, and then 'e drove 'em nearly crazy by wasting time making 'is bed.

"Be as quick as you can, Isaac," ses Ginger, at last; "think of us two a-sitting 'ere waiting for you."

"I sha'n't forget it," ses Isaac, and 'e came back to the door after 'e'd gone arfway down the stairs to ask 'em not to go out on the drink while 'e was away.

It was nine o'clock when he went, and at 'ha'-past nine Ginger began to get impatient and wondered wot 'ad 'appened to 'im, and when ten o'clock came and no Isaac they was both leaning out of the winder with blankets over their shoulders, looking up the road. By eleven o'clock Peter was in very low spirits and

Ginger was so mad 'e was afraid to speak to 'im.

They spent the rest o' that day 'anging out of the winder, but it was not till ha'-past four in the afternoon that Isaac, still wearing Peter's clothes and carrying a couple of large green plants under 'is arm, turned into the road, and from the way 'e was smiling they thought it must be all right.

"Wot 'ave you been such a long time for?" ses Ginger, in a low, fierce voice, as Isaac stopped underneath the winder and nodded up to 'em.

"I met a old friend," ses Isaac.

"Met a old friend?" ses Ginger, in a passion. "Wot d'ye mean, wasting time like while we was sitting up 'ere waiting and starving?"

"I 'adn't seen 'im for years," ses Isaac, "and time slipped away afore I noticed it."

"I dessay," ses Ginger, in a bitter voice. "Well, is the money all right?"

"I don't know," ses Isaac; "I ain't got the clothes."

"Wot?" ses Ginger, nearly falling out of the winder. "Well, wot 'ave you done with mine, then? Where are they? Come upstairs."

"I won't come upstairs, Ginger," ses Isaac, "because I'm not quite sure whether I've done right. But I'm not used to going into pawnshops, and I walked about trying to make up my mind to go in and couldn't."

"Well, wot did you do then?" ses Ginger, 'ardly able to contain hisself.

"While I was trying to make up my mind," ses old Isaac, "I see a man with a barrer of lovely plants. 'E wasn't asking money for 'em, only old clothes."

"Old clothes?" ses Ginger, in a voice as if 'e was being suffocated.

"I thought they'd be a bit o' green for you to look at," ses the old man, 'olding the plants up; "there's no knowing 'ow long you'll be up there. The big one is yours, Ginger, and the other is for Peter."

"'Ave you gone mad, Isaac?" ses Peter, in a trembling voice, arter Ginger 'ad tried to speak and couldn't.

Isaac shook 'is 'ead and smiled up at 'em, and then, arter telling Peter to put Ginger's blanket a little more round 'is shoulders, for fear 'e should catch cold, 'e said 'e'd ask the landlady to send 'em up some bread and butter and a cup o' tea.

They 'eard 'im talking to the landlady at the door, and then 'e went off in a hurry without looking behind 'im, and the landlady walked up and down on the other side of the road with 'er apron stuffed in 'er mouth, pretending to be looking at 'er chimney pots.

Isaac didn't turn up at all that night, and by next morning those two unfortunate men see 'ow they'd been done. It was quite plain to them that Isaac 'ad been deceiving them, and Peter was pretty certain that 'e took the money out of the bed while 'e was fussing about making it. Old Isaac kept 'em there for three days, sending 'em in their clothes bit by bit and two shillings a day to live on; but they didn't set eyes on 'im agin until they all signed on aboard the *Planet*, and they didn't set eyes on their money until they was two miles below Gravesend.

Joseph Conrad

1857-1924

JOSEPH CONRAD, one of the geniuses of English literature, was born into a revolutionary Polish family named Korzeniowsky, and knew no English until he was twenty years old. Brought up in a country without a seacoast, he yearned for the ocean, and later made his reputation on novels and stories of the sea. Although his achievements were of the highest and his output was large, he started to write only after he was thirty and then in a language foreign to him.

Conrad learned English from a newspaper and from hearing it spoken by men of the sea. After four years on French vessels, he entered the British Merchant Marine as a seaman, worked up to master, and for many years served as first or second in command on ships plying between England and the Orient. It was not until 1889 that he started his first novel, *Almayer's Folly*, which, with the interruptions of sea voyages and a serious illness contracted in the Congo, took him five years to write. After retiring from the sea, Conrad began to write in earnest, driven not only by his unrelenting genius, but also by debt, for he had a wife and two children to support. Writing never came easy to him, and he kept at it to the point of exhaustion.

Conrad's novels and stories have the grandeur of space and distance, the mystery that lies behind a lost shore in the tropics and the dark tangle of riverbanks. They are stories of men far from home who carry some burden of guilt in their hearts. It has been suggested that Conrad's soul was tortured for deserting his own country, spiritually as well as physically, and that every story he tells is his own story.

The Secret Sharer

BY JOSEPH CONRAD

CHAPTER ONE

On my right hand there were lines of fishing stakes resembling a mysterious system of half-submerged bamboo fences, incomprehensible in its division of the domain of tropical fishes, and crazy of aspect as if abandoned forever by some nomad tribe of fishermen now gone to the other end of the ocean; for there was no sign of human habitation as far as the eye could reach. To the left a group of barren islets, suggesting ruins of stone walls, towers, and blockhouses, had its foundations set in a blue sea that itself looked solid, so still and stable did it lie below my feet; even the track of light from the westering sun shone smoothly, without that animated glitter which tells of an imperceptible ripple. And when I turned my head to take a parting glance at the tug which had just left us anchored outside the bar, I saw the straight line of the flat shore joined to the stable sea, edge to edge, with a perfect and unmarked closeness, in one leveled floor half brown, half blue under the enormous dome of the sky. Corresponding in their insignificance to the islets of the sea, two small clumps of trees, one on each side of the only fault in the impeccable joint, marked the mouth of the river Meinam we had just left on the first preparatory stage of our homeward journey; and, far back on the inland level, a larger and loftier mass, the grove surrounding the great Paknam pagoda, was the only thing on which the eye could rest from the vain task of exploring the monotonous sweep of the horizon. Here and there gleams as of a few scattered pieces of silver marked the windings of the great river; and on the nearest of them, just within the bar, the tug steaming right into the land became lost to my sight, hull and funnel and masts, as though the impassive earth had swallowed her up without an effort, without a tremor. My eye followed the light cloud of her smoke, now here, now there, above the plain, according to the devious curves of the stream, but always fainter and farther away, till I lost it at last behind the miter-shaped hill of the great pagoda. And then I was left alone with my ship, anchored at the head of the Gulf of Siam.

She floated at the starting point of a long journey, very still in an immense stillness, the shadows of

From 'Twixt Land and Sea by Joseph Conrad. By permission of Doubleday & Company, Inc., and J. M. Dent & Sons, Ltd. of London. Copyright, 1912, by Doubleday & Company, Inc.

her spars flung far to the eastward by the setting sun. At that moment I was alone on her decks. There was not a sound in her—and around us nothing moved, nothing lived, not a canoe on the water, not a bird in the air, not a cloud in the sky. In this breathless pause at the threshold of a long passage we seemed to be measuring our fitness for a long and arduous enterprise, the appointed task of both our existences to be carried out, far from all human eyes, with only sky and sea for spectators and for judges.

There must have been some glare in the air to interfere with one's sight, because it was only just before the sun left us that my roaming eyes made out beyond the highest ridges of the principal islet of the group something which did away with the solemnity of perfect solitude. The tide of darkness flowed on swiftly; and with tropical suddenness a swarm of stars came out above the shadowy earth, while I lingered yet, my hand resting lightly on my ship's rail as if on the shoulder of a trusted friend. But, with all that multitude of celestial bodies staring down at one, the comfort of quiet communion with her was gone for good. And there were also disturbing sounds by this time—voices, footsteps forward; the steward flitted along the main-deck, a busily ministering spirit; a hand bell tinkled urgently under the poop deck. . . .

I found my two officers waiting for me near the supper table, in the lighted cuddy. We sat down at once, and as I helped the chief mate, I said:

"Are you aware that there is a ship anchored inside the islands? I saw her mastheads above the ridge as the sun went down."

He raised sharply his simple face, overcharged by a terrible growth of whisker, and emitted his usual ejaculations: "Bless my soul, sir! You don't say so!"

My second mate was a round-cheeked, silent young man, grave beyond his years, I thought; but as our eyes happened to meet I detected a slight quiver on his lips. I looked down at once. It was not my part to encourage sneering on board my ship. It must be said, too, that I knew very little of my officers. In consequence of certain events of no particular significance, except to myself, I had been appointed to the command only a fortnight before. Neither did I know much of the hands forward. All these people had been together for eighteen months or so, and my position was that of the only stranger on board. I mention this because it has some bearing on what is to follow. But what I felt most was my being a stranger to the ship; and if all the truth must be told, I was somewhat of a stranger to myself. The youngest man on board (barring the second mate), and untried as yet by a position of the fullest responsibility, I was willing to take the adequacy of the others for granted. They had simply to be equal to their tasks; but I wondered how far I should turn out faithful to that ideal conception of one's own personality every man sets up for himself secretly.

Meantime the chief mate, with an almost visible effect of collaboration on the part of his round eyes and frightful whiskers, was trying to evolve a theory of the anchored ship. His dominant trait was to

take all things into earnest consideration. He was of a painstaking turn
of mind. As he used to say, he
"liked to account to himself" for
practically everything that came in
his way, down to a miserable scorpion he had found in his cabin a
week before. The why and the
wherefore of that scorpion—how it
got on board and came to select his
room rather than the pantry (which
was a dark place and more what a
scorpion would be partial to), and
how on earth it managed to drown
itself in the inkwell of his writing
desk—had exercised him infinitely.
The ship within the islands was
much more easily accounted for; and
just as we were about to rise from
table he made his pronouncement.
She was, he doubted not, a ship
from home lately arrived. Probably
she drew too much water to cross
the bar except at the top of spring
tides. Therefore she went into that
natural harbor to wait for a few days
in preference to remaining in an
open roadstead.

"That's so," confirmed the second
mate, suddenly, in his slightly
hoarse voice. "She draws over
twenty feet. She's the Liverpool
ship *Sephora* with a cargo of coal.
Hundred and twenty-three days from
Cardiff."

We looked at him in surprise.

"The tugboat skipper told me
when he came on board for your
letters, sir," explained the young
man. "He expects to take her up the
river the day after tomorrow."

After thus overwhelming us with
the extent of his information he
slipped out of the cabin. The mate
observed regretfully that he "could
not account for that young fellow's
whims." What prevented him telling us all about it at once, he
wanted to know.

I detained him as he was making
a move. For the last two days the
crew had had plenty of hard work,
and the night before they had very
little sleep. I felt painfully that I—
a stranger—was doing something
unusual when I directed him to let
all hands turn in without setting an
anchor watch. I proposed to keep
on deck myself till one o'clock or
thereabouts. I would get the second
mate to relieve me at that hour.

"He will turn out the cook and the
steward at four," I concluded, "and
then give you a call. Of course at
the slightest sign of any sort of
wind we'll have the hands up and
make a start at once."

He concealed his astonishment.
"Very well, sir." Outside the cuddy
he put his head in the second mate's
door to inform him of my unheard-of
caprice to take a five hours' anchor
watch on myself. I heard the other
raise his voice incredulously—
"What? The Captain himself?" Then
a few more murmurs, a door closed,
then another. A few moments later
I went on deck.

My strangeness, which had made
me sleepless, had prompted that unconventional arrangement, as if I
had expected in those solitary hours
of the night to get on terms with
the ship of which I knew nothing,
manned by men of whom I knew
very little more. Fast alongside a
wharf, littered like any ship in port
with a tangle of unrelated things, invaded by unrelated shore people, I
had hardly seen her yet properly.
Now, as she lay cleared for sea, the
stretch of her main deck seemed to
me very fine under the stars. Very
fine, very roomy for her size, and
very inviting. I descended the poop
and paced the waist, my mind pic-
turing to myself the coming passage
through the Malay Archipelago,

down the Indian Ocean, and up the Atlantic. All its phases were familiar enough to me, every characteristic, all the alternatives which were likely to face me on the high seas— everything! . . . except the novel responsibility of command. But I took heart from the reasonable thought that the ship was like other ships, the men like other men, and that the sea was not likely to keep any special surprises expressly for my discomfiture.

Arrived at that comforting conclusion, I bethought myself of a cigar and went below to get it. All was still down there. Everybody at the after end of the ship was sleeping profoundly. I came out again on the quarter deck, agreeably at ease in my sleeping suit on that warm breathless night, barefooted, a glowing cigar in my teeth, and, going forward, I was met by the profound silence of the fore end of the ship. Only as I passed the door of the forecastle I heard a deep, quiet, trustful sigh of some sleeper inside. And suddenly I rejoiced in the great security of the sea as compared with the unrest of the land, in my choice of that untempted life presenting no disquieting problems, invested with an elementary moral beauty by the absolute straightforwardness of its appeal and by the singleness of its purpose.

The riding light in the forerigging burned with a clear, untroubled, as if symbolic, flame, confident and bright in the mysterious shades of the night. Passing on my way aft along the other side of the ship, I observed that the rope side ladder, put over, no doubt, for the master of the tug when he came to fetch away our letters, had not been hauled in as it should have been. I became annoyed at this, for ex-

actitude in some small matters is the very soul of discipline. Then I reflected that I had myself peremptorily dismissed my officers from duty, and by my own act had prevented the anchor watch being formally set and things properly attended to. I asked myself whether it was wise ever to interfere with the established routine of duties even from the kindest of motives. My action might have made me appear eccentric. Goodness only knew how that absurdly whiskered mate would "account" for my conduct, and what the whole ship thought of that informality of their new captain. I was vexed with myself.

Not from compunction certainly, but, as it were mechanically, I proceeded to get the ladder in myself. Now a side ladder of that sort is a light affair and comes in easily, yet my vigorous tug, which should have brought it flying on board, merely recoiled upon my body in a totally unexpected jerk. What the devil! . . . I was so astounded by the immovableness of that ladder that I remained stock-still, trying to account for it to myself like that imbecile mate of mine. In the end, of course, I put my head over the rail.

The side of the ship made an opaque belt of shadow on the darkling glassy shimmer of the sea. But I saw at once something elongated and pale floating very close to the ladder. Before I could form a guess a faint flash of phosphorescent light, which seemed to issue suddenly from the naked body of a man, flickered in the sleeping water with the elusive, silent play of summer lightning in a night sky. With a gasp I saw revealed to my stare a pair of feet, the long legs, a broad livid back immersed right up to the neck in a greenish cadaverous glow. One hand, awash, clutched the bottom rung of the ladder. He was complete but for the head. A headless corpse! The cigar dropped out of my gaping mouth with a tiny plop and a short hiss quite audible in the absolute stillness of all things under heaven. At that I suppose he raised up his face, a dimly pale oval in the shadow of the ship's side. But even then I could only barely make out down there the shape of his black-haired head. However, it was enough for the horrid, frostbound sensation which had gripped me about the chest to pass off. The moment of vain exclamations was past, too. I only climbed on the spare spar and leaned over the rail as far as I could, to bring my eyes nearer to that mystery floating alongside.

As he hung by the ladder, like a resting swimmer, the sea lightning played about his limbs at every stir; and he appeared in it ghastly, silvery, fishlike. He remained as mute as a fish, too. He made no motion to get out of the water, either. It was inconceivable that he should not attempt to come on board, and strangely troubling to suspect that perhaps he did not want to. And my first words were prompted by just that troubled incertitude.

"What's the matter?" I asked in my ordinary tone, speaking down to the face upturned exactly under mine.

"Cramp," it answered, no louder. Then slightly anxious, "I say, no need to call anyone."

"I was not going to," I said.

"Are you alone on deck?"

"Yes."

I had somehow the impression that he was on the point of letting go the ladder to swim away beyond my ken—mysterious as he came. But, for the moment, this being appearing as if he had risen from the bottom of the sea (it was certainly the nearest land to the ship) wanted only to know the time. I told him. And he, down there, tentatively:

"I suppose your captain's turned in?"

"I am sure he isn't," I said.

He seemed to struggle with himself, for I heard something like the low, bitter murmur of doubt. "What's the good?" His next words came out with a hesitating effort.

"Look here, my man. Could you call him out quietly?"

I thought the time had come to declare myself.

"I am the captain."

I heard a "By Jove!" whispered at the level of the water. The phosphorescence flashed in the swirl of the water all about his limbs, his other hand seized the ladder.

"My name's Leggatt."

The voice was calm and resolute. A good voice. The self-possession of that man had somehow induced a corresponding state in myself. It was very quietly that I remarked:

"You must be a good swimmer."

"Yes. I've been in the water practically since nine o'clock. The question for me now is whether I am to let go this ladder and go on swimming till I sink from exhaustion, or—to come on board here."

I felt this was no mere formula of desperate speech, but a real alternative in the view of a strong soul. I should have gathered from this that he was young; indeed, it is only the young who are ever confronted by such clear issues. But at the time it was pure intuition on my part. A mysterious communication was established already between us two—in the face of that silent, darkened tropical sea. I was young, too; young enough to make no comment. The man in the water began suddenly to climb up the ladder, and I hastened away from the rail to fetch some clothes.

Before entering the cabin I stood still, listening in the lobby at the foot of the stairs. A faint snore came through the closed door of the chief mate's room. The second mate's door was on the hook, but the darkness in there was absolutely soundless. He, too, was young and could sleep like a stone. Remained the steward, but he was not likely to wake up before he was called. I got a sleeping suit out of my room and, coming back on deck, saw the naked man from the sea sitting on the main hatch, glimmering white in the darkness, his elbows on his knees and his head in his hands. In a moment he had concealed his damp body in a sleeping suit of the same gray-stripe pattern as the one I was wearing and followed me like my double on the poop. Together we moved right aft, barefooted, silent.

"What is it?" I asked in a deadened voice, taking the lighted lamp out of the binnacle, and raising it to his face.

"An ugly business."

He had rather regular features; a good mouth; light eyes under somewhat heavy, dark eyebrows; a smooth, square forehead; no growth on his cheeks; a small, brown mustache, and a well-shaped, round chin. His expression was concentrated, meditative, under the inspecting light of the lamp I held up to his face; such as a man thinking hard in solitude might wear. My sleeping suit was just right for his size. A well-knit young fellow of twenty-five at most. He caught his lower lip with the edge of white, even teeth.

"Yes," I said, replacing the lamp in the binnacle. The warm, heavy tropical night closed upon his head again.

"There's a ship over there," he murmured.

"Yes, I know. The *Sephora*. Did you know of us?"

"Hadn't the slightest idea. I am the mate of her——" He paused and corrected himself. "I should say I *was*."

"Aha! Something wrong?"

"Yes. Very wrong indeed. I've killed a man."

"What do you mean? Just now?"

"No, on the passage. Weeks ago. Thirty-nine south. When I say a man——"

"Fit of temper," I suggested, confidently.

The shadowy, dark head, like mine, seemed to nod imperceptibly above the ghostly gray of my sleeping suit. It was, in the night, as though I had been faced by my own reflection in the depths of a somber and immense mirror.

"A pretty thing to have to own up to for a Conway boy," murmured my double, distinctly.

"You're a Conway boy?"

"I am," he said, as if startled. Then, slowly . . . "Perhaps you too——"

It was so; but being a couple of years older I had left before he joined. After a quick interchange of dates a silence fell; and I thought suddenly of my absurd mate with his terrific whiskers and the "Bless my soul—you don't say so" type of intellect. My double gave me an inkling of his thoughts by saying: "My father's a parson in Norfolk. Do you see me before a judge and jury on that charge? For myself I can't see the necessity. There are fellows that an angel from heaven —— And I am not that. He was one of those creatures that are just simmering all the time with a silly sort of wickedness. Miserable devils that have no business to live at all. He wouldn't do his duty and wouldn't let anybody else do theirs. But what's the good of talking! You know well enough the sort of ill-conditioned snarling cur——"

He appealed to me as if our experiences had been as identical as our clothes. And I knew well enough the pestiferous danger of such a character where there are no means of legal repression. And I knew well enough also that my double there was no homicidal ruffian. I did not think of asking him for details, and he told me the story roughly in brusque, disconnected sentences. I needed no more. I saw it all going on as though I were myself inside that other sleeping suit.

"It happened while we were setting a reefed foresail, at dusk. Reefed foresail! You understand the sort of weather. The only sail we had left to keep the ship running; so you may guess what it had been like for days. Anxious sort of job, that. He gave me some of his cursed insolence at the sheet. I tell you I was overdone with this terrific weather that seemed to have no end to it. Terrific, I tell you—and a deep ship. I believe the fellow himself was half crazed with funk. It was no time for gentlemanly reproof, so I turned round and felled him like an ox. He up and at me. We closed just as an awful sea made for the ship. All hands saw it coming and took to the rigging, but I had him by the throat, and went on shaking him like a rat, the men above us yelling, 'Look out! look out!' Then a crash as if the sky had fallen on my head. They say that for over ten minutes hardly anything was to be seen of the ship—just the three masts and a bit of the forecastle head and of the poop all awash driving along in a smother of foam. It was a miracle that they found us, jammed together behind the forebits. It's clear that I meant business, because I was holding him by the throat still when they picked us up. He was black in the face. It was too much for them. It seems they rushed us aft together, gripped as we were, screaming 'Murder!' like a lot of lunatics, and broke into the cuddy. And the ship running for her life, touch and go all the time, any minute her last in a sea fit to turn your hair gray only a-looking at it. I understand that the skipper, too, started raving like the rest of them. The man had been deprived of sleep for more than a week, and to have this sprung on him at the height of a furious gale nearly drove him out of his mind. I wonder they didn't fling me overboard after getting the carcass of their precious shipmate out of my fingers. They had rather a job to separate us, I've been told. A sufficiently fierce story to make an old judge and a respectable jury sit up a bit. The first thing I heard when I came to myself was the maddening howling of that endless gale, and on that the voice of the old man. He was hanging on to my bunk, staring into my face out of his sou'wester.

"'Mr. Leggatt, you have killed a man. You can act no longer as chief mate of this ship.'"

His care to subdue his voice made it sound monotonous. He rested a hand on the end of the skylight to steady himself with, and all that time did not stir a limb, so far as I could see. "Nice little tale for a quiet tea party," he concluded in the same tone.

One of my hands, too, rested on the end of the skylight; neither did I stir a limb, so far as I knew. We stood less than a foot from each other. It occurred to me that if old "Bless my soul—you don't say so" were to put his head up the companion and catch sight of us, he would think he was seeing double, or imagine himself come upon a scene of weird witchcraft; the strange captain having a quiet confabulation by the wheel with his own gray ghost. I became very much concerned to prevent anything of the sort. I heard the other's soothing undertone.

"My father's a parson in Norfolk," it said. Evidently he had forgotten he had told me this important fact before. Truly a nice little tale.

"You had better slip down into my stateroom now," I said, moving off stealthily. My double followed my movements; our bare feet made no sound; I let him in, closed the door with care, and, after giving a call to the second mate, returned on deck for my relief.

"Not much sign of any wind yet," I remarked when he approached.

"No, sir. Not much," he assented, sleepily, in his hoarse voice, with just enough deference, no more, and barely suppressing a yawn.

"Well, that's all you have to look out for. You have got your orders."

"Yes, sir."

I paced a turn or two on the poop and saw him take up his position face forward with his elbow in the ratlines of the mizzen rigging before I went below. The mate's faint snoring was still going on peacefully. The cuddy lamp was burning over the table on which stood a vase with flowers, a polite attention from the ship's provision merchant—the last flowers we should see for the next three months at the very least. Two bunches of bananas hung from the beam symmetrically, one on each side of the rudder casing. Everything was as before in the ship—except that two of her captain's sleeping suits were simultaneously in use, one motionless in the cuddy, the other keeping very still in the captain's stateroom.

It must be explained here that my cabin had the form of the capital letter L, the door being within the angle and opening into the short part of the letter. A couch was to the left, the bed place to the right; my writing desk and the chronometers' table faced the door. But anyone opening it, unless he stepped right inside, had no view of what I call the long (or vertical) part of the letter. It contained some lockers surmounted by a bookcase; and a few clothes, a thick jacket or two, caps, oilskin coat, and such like, hung on hooks. There was at the bottom of that part a door opening into my bathroom, which could be entered also directly from the saloon. But that way was never used.

The mysterious arrival had discovered the advantage of this particular shape. Entering my room, lighted strongly by a big bulkhead lamp swung on gimbals above my writing desk, I did not see him anywhere till he stepped out quietly from behind the coats hung in the recessed part.

"I heard somebody moving about, and went in there at once," he whispered.

I, too, spoke under my breath.

"Nobody is likely to come in

here without knocking and getting permission."

He nodded. His face was thin and the sunburn faded, as though he had been ill. And no wonder. He had been, I heard presently, kept under arrest in his cabin for nearly seven weeks. But there was nothing sickly in his eyes or in his expression. He was not a bit like me, really; yet, as we stood leaning over my bed place, whispering side by side, with our dark heads together and our backs to the door, anybody bold enough to open it stealthily would have been treated to the uncanny sight of a double captain busy talking in whispers with his other self.

"But all this doesn't tell me how you came to hang on to our side ladder," I inquired, in the hardly audible murmurs we used, after he had told me something more of the proceedings on board the *Sephora* once the bad weather was over.

"When we sighted Java Head I had had time to think all those matters out several times over. I had six weeks of doing nothing else, and with only an hour or so every evening for a tramp on the quarterdeck."

He whispered, his arms folded on the side of my bed place, staring through the open port. And I could imagine perfectly the manner of this thinking out—a stubborn if not a steadfast operation; something of which I should have been perfectly incapable.

"I reckoned it would be dark before we closed with the land," he continued, so low that I had to strain my hearing near as we were to each other, shoulder touching shoulder almost. "So I asked to speak to the old man. He always seemed very sick when he came to see me—as if he could not look me in the face. You know, that foresail saved the ship. She was too deep to have run long under bare poles. And it was I that managed to set it for him. Anyway, he came. When I had him in my cabin—he stood by the door looking at me as if I had the halter round my neck already—I asked him right away to leave my cabin door unlocked at night while the ship was going through Sunda Straits. There would be the Java coast within two or three miles, off Angier Point. I wanted nothing more. I've had a prize for swimming my second year in the Conway."

"I can believe it," I breathed out.

"God only knows why they locked me in every night. To see some of their faces you'd have thought they were afraid I'd go about at night strangling people. Am I a murdering brute? Do I look it? By jove! if I had been he wouldn't have trusted himself like that into my room. You'll say I might have chucked him aside and bolted out, there and then—it was dark already. Well, no. And for the same reason I wouldn't think of trying to smash the door. There would have been a rush to stop me at the noise, and I did not mean to get into a confounded scrimmage. Somebody else might have got killed—for I would not have broken out only to get chucked back, and I did not want any more of that work. He refused, looking more sick than ever. He was afraid of the men, and also of that old second mate of his who had been sailing with him for years —a gray-headed old humbug; and his steward, too, had been with him devil knows how long—seventeen years or more—a dogmatic sort of loafer who hated me like poison, just because I was the chief mate. No chief mate ever made more than one voyage in the *Sephora*, you know. Those two old chaps ran the ship. Devil only knows what the skipper wasn't afraid of (all his nerve went to pieces altogether in that hellish spell of bad weather we had)—of what the law would do to him—of his wife, perhaps. Oh, yes! she's on board. Though I don't think she would have meddled. She would have been only too glad to have me out of the ship in any way. The 'brand of Cain' business, don't you see. That's all right. I was ready enough to go off wandering on the face of the earth—and that was price enough to pay for an Abel of that sort. Anyhow, he wouldn't listen to me. 'This thing must take its course. I represent the law here." He was shaking like a leaf. 'So you won't?' 'No!' 'Then I hope you will be able to sleep on that,' I said, and turned my back on him. 'I wonder that *you* can,' cries he, and locks the door.

"Well after that, I couldn't. Not very well. That was three weeks ago. We have had a slow passage through the Java Sea; drifted about Carimata for ten days. When we anchored here they thought, I suppose, it was all right. The nearest land (and that's five miles) is the ship's destination; the consul would soon set about catching me; and there would have been no object in bolting to these islets there. I don't suppose there's a drop of water on them. I don't know how it was, but tonight that steward, after bringing me my supper, went out to let me eat it, and left the door unlocked. And I ate it—all there was, too. After I had finished I strolled out on the quarter-deck. I don't know that I meant to do anything. A

breath of fresh air was all I wanted, I believe. Then a sudden temptation came over me. I kicked off my slippers and was in the water before I had made up my mind fairly. Somebody heard the splash and they raised an awful hullabaloo. 'He's gone! Lower the boats! He's committed suicide! No, he's swimming.' Certainly I was swimming. It's not so easy for a swimmer like me to commit suicide by drowning. I landed on the nearest islet before the boat left the ship's side. I heard them pulling about in the dark, hailing, and so on, but after a bit they gave up. Everything quieted down and the anchorage became as still as death. I sat down on a stone and began to think. I felt certain they would start searching for me at daylight. There was no place to hide on those stony things—and if there had been, what would have been the good? But now I was clear of that ship, I was not going back. So after a while I took off all my clothes, tied them up in a bundle with a stone inside, and dropped them in the deep water on the outer side of that islet. That was suicide enough for me. Let them think what they liked, but I didn't mean to drown myself. I meant to swim till I sank—but that's not the same thing. I struck out for another of these little islands, and it was from that one that I first saw your riding light. Something to swim for. I went on easily, and on the way I came upon a flat rock a foot or two above water. In the daytime, I dare say, you might make it out with a glass from your poop. I scrambled up on it and rested myself for a bit. Then I made another start. That last spell must have been over a mile."

His whisper was getting fainter and fainter, and all the time he stared straight out through the port-hole, in which there was not even a star to be seen. I had not interrupted him. There was something that made comment impossible in his narrative, or perhaps in himself; a sort of feeling, a quality, which I can't find a name for. And when he ceased, all I found was a futile whisper: "So you swam for our light?"

"Yes—straight for it. It was something to swim for. I couldn't see any stars low down because the coast was in the way, and I couldn't see the land, either. The water was like glass. One might have been swimming in a confounded thousand-feet deep cistern with no place for scrambling out anywhere; but what I didn't like was the notion of swimming round and round like a crazed bullock before I gave out; and as I didn't mean to go back . . . No. Do you see me being hauled back, stark naked, off one of these little islands by the scruff of the neck and fighting like a wild beast? Somebody would have got killed for certain, and I did not want any of that. So I went on. Then your ladder——"

"Why didn't you hail the ship?" I asked, a little louder.

He touched my shoulder lightly. Lazy footsteps came right over our heads and stopped. The second mate had crossed from the other side of the poop and might have been hanging over the rail for all we knew.

"He couldn't hear us talking—could he?" My double breathed into my very ear, anxiously.

His anxiety was in answer, a sufficient answer, to the question I had put to him. An answer containing all the difficulty of that situation. I closed the porthole quietly, to make sure. A louder word might have been overheard.

"Who's that?" he whispered then.

"My second mate. But I don't know much more of the fellow than you do."

And I told him a little about myself. I had been appointed to take charge while I least expected anything of the sort, not quite a fortnight ago. I didn't know either the ship or the people. Hadn't had the time in port to look about me or size anybody up. And as to the crew, all they knew was that I was appointed to take the ship home. For the rest, I was almost as much of a stranger on board as himself, I said. And at the moment I felt it most acutely. I felt that it would take very little to make me a suspect person in the eyes of the ship's company.

He had turned about meantime; and we, the two strangers in the ship, faced each other in identical attitudes.

"Your ladder——" he murmured, after a silence. "Who'd have thought of finding a ladder handing over at night in a ship anchored out here! I felt just then a very unpleasant faintness. After the life I've been leading for nine weeks, anybody would have got out of condition. I wasn't capable of swimming round as far as your rudder chains. And, lo and behold! there was a ladder to get hold of. After I gripped it I said to myself, 'What's the good?' When I saw a man's head looking over I thought I would swim away presently and leave him shouting—in whatever language it was. I didn't mind being looked at. I—I liked it. And then you speaking to me so quietly—as if you had expected me —made me hold on a little longer. It had been a confounded lonely time—I don't mean while swimming. I was glad to talk a little to somebody that didn't belong to the

Sephora. As to asking for the captain, that was a mere impulse. It could have been no use, with all the ship knowing about me and the other people pretty certain to be round here in the morning. I don't know—I wanted to be seen, to talk with somebody, before I went on. I don't know what I would have said. . . . 'Fine night, isn't it?' or something of the sort."

"Do you think they will be round here presently?" I asked with some incredulity.

"Quite likely," he said, faintly.

He looked extremely haggard all of a sudden. His head rolled on his shoulders.

"H'm. We shall see then. Meantime get into that bed," I whispered. "Want help? There."

It was a rather high bed place with a set of drawers underneath. This amazing swimmer really needed the lift I gave him by seizing his leg. He tumbled in, rolled over on his back, and flung one arm across his eyes. And then, with his face nearly hidden, he must have looked exactly as I used to look in that bed. I gazed upon my other self for a while before drawing across carefully the two green serge curtains which ran on a brass rod. I thought for a moment of pinning them together for greater safety, but I sat down on the couch, and once there I felt unwilling to rise and hunt for a pin. I would do it in a moment. I was extremely tired, in a peculiarly intimate way, by the strain of stealthiness, by the effort of whispering and the general secrecy of this excitement. It was three o'clock by now and I had been on my feet since nine, but I was not sleepy; I could not have gone to sleep. I sat there, fagged out, looking at the curtains, trying to clear my mind of the con-

fused sensation of being in two places at once, and greatly bothered by an exasperating knocking in my head. It was a relief to discover suddenly that it was not in my head at all, but on the outside of the door. Before I could collect myself the words "Come in" were out of my mouth, and the steward entered with a tray, bringing in my morning coffee. I had slept, after all, and I was so frightened that I shouted, "This way! I am here, steward," as though he had been miles away. He put down the tray on the table next the couch and only then said, very quietly, "I can see you are here, sir." I felt him give me a keen look, but I dared not meet his eyes just then. He must have wondered why I had drawn the curtains of my bed before going to sleep on the couch. He went out, hooking the door open as usual.

I heard the crew washing decks above me. I knew I would have been told at once if there had been any wind. Calm, I thought, and I was doubly vexed. Indeed, I felt dual more than ever. The steward reappeared suddenly in the doorway. I jumped up from the couch so quickly that he gave a start.

"What do you want here?"

"Close your port, sir—they are washing decks."

"It is closed," I said, reddening.

"Very well, sir." But he did not move from the doorway and returned my stare in an extraordinary, equivocal manner for a time. Then his eyes wavered, all his expression changed, and in a voice unusually gentle, almost coaxingly:

"May I come in to take the empty cup away, sir?"

"Of course!" I turned my back on him while he popped in and out. Then I unhooked and closed the door and even pushed the bolt. This sort of thing could not go on very long. The cabin was as hot as an oven, too. I took a peep at my double, and discovered that he had not moved, his arm was still over his eyes; but his chest heaved; his hair was wet; his chin glistened with perspiration. I reached over him and opened the port.

"I must show myself on deck," I reflected.

Of course, theoretically, I could do what I liked, with no one to say nay to me within the whole circle of the horizon; but to lock my cabin door and take the key away I did not dare. Directly I put my head out of the companion I saw the group of my two officers, the second mate barefooted, the chief mate in long India-rubber boots, near the break of the poop, and the steward half-way down the poop ladder talking to them eagerly. He happened to catch sight of me and dived, the second ran down on the main deck shouting some order or other, and the chief mate came to meet me, touching his cap.

There was a sort of curiosity in his eye that I did not like. I don't know whether the steward had told them that I was "queer" only, or downright drunk, but I know the man meant to have a good look at me. I watched him coming with a smile which, as he got into point-blank range, took effect and froze his very whiskers. I did not give him time to open his lips.

"Square the yards by lifts and braces before the hands go to breakfast."

It was the first particular order I had given on board that ship; and I stayed on deck to see it executed, too. I had felt the need of asserting myself without loss of time. That

sneering young cub got taken down a peg or two on that occasion, and I also seized the opportunity of having a good look at the face of every fore-mast man as they filed past me to go to the after braces. At breakfast time, eating nothing myself, I pre-sided with such frigid dignity that the two mates were only too glad to escape from the cabin as soon as decency permitted; and all the time the dual working of my mind dis-tracted me almost to the point of in-sanity. I was constantly watching myself, my secret self, as dependent on my actions as my own person-ality, sleeping in that bed, behind that door which faced me as I sat at the head of the table. It was very much like being mad, only it was worse because one was aware of it.

I had to shake him for a solid minute, but when at last he opened his eyes it was in the full possession of his senses, with an inquiring look.

"All's well so far," I whispered. "Now you must vanish into the bath-room."

He did so, as noiseless as a ghost, and then I rang for the steward, and facing him boldly, directed him to tidy up my stateroom while I was having my bath—"and be quick about it." As my tone admitted of no excuses, he said, "Yes, sir," and ran off to fetch his dustpan and brushes. I took a bath and did most of my dressing, splashing, and whistling softly for the steward's edification, while the secret sharer of my life stood drawn up bolt up-right in that little space, his face looking very sunken in daylight, his eyelids lowered under the stern, dark line of his eyebrows drawn to-gether by a slight frown.

When I left him there to go back to my room the steward was finish-ing dusting. I sent for the mate and engaged him in some insignificant conversation. It was, as it were, trifling with the terrific character of his whiskers; but my object was to give him an opportunity for a good look at my cabin. And then I could at last shut, with a clear conscience, the door of my stateroom and get my double back into the recessed part. There was nothing else for it. He had to sit still on a small folding stool, half smothered by the heavy coats hanging there. We listened to the steward going into the bathroom out of the saloon, filling the water bottles there, scrubbing the bath, setting things to rights, whisk, bang, clatter—out again into the saloon—turn the key—click. Such was my scheme for keeping my second self invisible. Nothing better could be contrived under the circumstances. And there we sat; I at my writing desk ready to appear busy with some papers, he behind me out of sight of the door. It would not have been prudent to talk in daytime; and I could not have stood the excitement of that queer sense of whispering to myself. Now and then, glancing over my shoulder, I saw him far back there, sitting rigidly on the low stool, his bare feet close together, his arms folded, his head hanging on his breast—and perfectly still. Anybody would have taken him for me.

I was fascinated by it myself. Every moment I had to glance over my shoulder. I was looking at him when a voice outside the door said: "Beg pardon, sir."

"Well!" . . . I kept my eyes on him, and so when the voice outside the door announced, "There's a ship's boat coming our way, sir," I saw him give a start—the first movement he had made for hours. But he did not raise his bowed head.

"All right. Get the ladder over."

I hesitated. Should I whisper something to him? But what? His immobility seemed to have been never disturbed. What could I tell him he did not know already? . . . Finally I went on deck.

CHAPTER TWO

The skipper of the *Sephora* had a thin red whisker all round his face, and the sort of complexion that goes with hair of that color; also the particular, rather smeary shade of blue in the eyes. He was not exactly a showy figure; his shoulders were high, his stature but middling—one leg slightly more bandy than the other. He shook hands, looking vaguely around. A spiritless tenacity was his main characteristic, I judged. I behaved with a politeness which seemed to disconcert him. Perhaps he was shy. He mumbled to me as if he were ashamed of what he was saying; gave his name (it was something like Archbold—but at this distance of years I hardly am sure), his ship's name, and a few other particulars of that sort, in the manner of a criminal making a reluctant and doleful confession. He had had terrible weather on the passage out—terrible—terrible—wife aboard, too.

By this time we were seated in the cabin and the steward brought in a tray with a bottle and glasses. "Thanks! No." Never took liquor. Would have some water, though. He drank two tumblerfuls. Terrible thirsty work. Every since daylight had been exploring the islands round his ship.

"What was that for—fun?" I asked, with an appearance of polite interest.

"No!" He sighed. "Painful duty."

As he persisted in his mumbling

and I wanted my double to hear every word, I hit upon the notion of informing him that I regretted to say I was hard of hearing.

"Such a young man, too!" he nodded, keeping his smeary blue, unintelligent eyes fastened upon me. "What was the cause of it—some disease?" he inquired, without the least sympathy and as if he thought that, if so, I'd got no more than I deserved.

"Yes; disease," I admitted in a cheerful tone which seemed to shock him. But my point was gained, because he had to raise his voice to give me his tale. It is not worth while to record that version. It was just over two months since all this had happened, and he had thought so much about it that he seemed completely muddled as to its bearings, but still immensely impressed.

"What would you think of such a thing happening on board your own ship? I've had the *Sephora* for these fifteen years. I am a well-known shipmaster."

He was densely distressed—and perhaps I should have sympathized with him if I had been able to detach my mental vision from the unsuspected sharer of my cabin as though he were my second self. There he was on the other side of the bulkhead, four or five feet from us, no more, as we sat in the saloon. I looked politely at Captain Archbold (if that was his name), but it was the other I saw, in a gray sleeping suit, seated on a low stool, his bare feet close together, his arms folded, and every word said between us falling into the ears of his dark head bowed on his chest.

"I have been at sea now, man and boy, for seven-and-thirty years, and I've never heard of such a thing happening in an English ship. And

that it should be my ship. Wife on board, too."

I was hardly listening to him.

"Don't you think," I said, "that the heavy sea which, you told me, came aboard just then might have killed the man? I have seen the sheer weight of a sea kill a man very neatly, by simply breaking his neck."

"Good God!" he uttered, impressively, fixing his smeary blue eyes on me. "The sea! No man killed by the sea ever looked like that." He seemed positively scandalized at my suggestion. And as I gazed at him certainly not prepared for anything original on his part, he advanced his head close to mine and thrust his tongue out at me so suddenly that I couldn't help starting back.

After scoring over my calmness in this graphic way he nodded wisely. If I had seen the sight, he assured me, I would never forget it as long as I lived. The weather was too bad to give the corpse a proper sea burial. So next day at dawn they took it up on the poop, covering its face with a bit of bunting; he read a short prayer, and then, just as it was, in its oilskins and long boots, they launched it amongst those mountainous seas that seemed ready every moment to swallow up the ship herself and the terrified lives on board of her.

"That reefed foresail saved you," I threw in.

"Under God—it did," he exclaimed fervently. "It was by a special mercy, I firmly believe, that it stood some of those hurricane squalls."

"It was the setting of that sail which——" I began.

"God's own hand in it," he interrupted me. "Nothing less could have done it. I don't mind telling you that I hardly dared give the order. It seemed impossible that we could touch anything without losing it, and then our last hope would have been gone."

The terror of that gale was on him yet. I let him go on for a bit, then said, casually—as if returning to a minor subject:

"You were very anxious to give up your mate to the shore people, I believe?"

He was. To the law. His obscure tenacity on that point had in it something incomprehensible and a little awful; something, as it were, mystical, quite apart from his anxiety that he should not be suspected of "countenancing any doings of that sort." Seven-and-thirty virtuous years at sea, of which over twenty of immaculate command, and the last fifteen in the *Sephora*, seemed to have laid him under some pitiless obligation.

"And you know," he went on, groping shame-facedly amongst his feelings, "I did not engage that young fellow. His people had some interest with my owners. I was in a way forced to take him on. He looked very smart, very gentlemanly, and all that. But do you know—I never liked him, somehow. I am a plain man. You see, he wasn't exactly the sort for the chief mate of a ship like the *Sephora*."

I had become so connected in thoughts and impressions with the secret sharer of my cabin that I felt as if I, personally, were being given to understand that I, too, was not the sort that would have done for the chief mate of a ship like the *Sephora*. I had no doubt of it in my mind.

"Not at all the style of man. You understand," he insisted, superfluously, looking hard at me.

I smiled urbanely. He seemed at a loss for a while.

"I suppose I must report a suicide."

"Beg pardon?"

"Sui-cide! That's what I'll have to write to my owners directly I get in."

"Unless you manage to recover him before tomorrow," I assented, dispassionately. . . . "I mean, alive."

He mumbled something which I really did not catch, and I turned my ear to him in a puzzled manner. He fairly bawled:

"The land—I say, the mainland is at least seven miles off my anchorage."

"About that."

My lack of excitement, of curiosity, of surprise, of any sort of pronounced interest, began to arouse his distrust. But except for the felicitous pretense of deafness I had not tried to pretend anything. I had felt utterly incapable of playing the part of ignorance properly, and therefore was afraid to try. It is also certain that he had brought some ready-made suspicions with him, and that he viewed my politeness as a strange and unnatural phenomenon. And yet how else could I have received him? Not heartily! That was impossible for psychological reasons, which I need not state here. My only object was to keep off his inquiries. Surlily? Yes, but surliness might have provoked a point-blank question. From its novelty to him and from its nature, punctilious courtesy was the manner best calculated to restrain the man. But there was the danger of his breaking through my defense bluntly. I could not, I think, have met him by a direct lie, also for psychological (not moral) reasons. If he had only known how afraid I was of his putting my feeling of identity with the other to the test! But, strangely enough—(I thought of it only afterwards)—I believe that he was not a little disconcerted by the reverse side of that weird situation, by something in me that reminded him of the man he was seeking—suggested a mysterious similitude to the young fellow he had distrusted and disliked from the first.

However that might have been, the silence was not very prolonged. He took another oblique step.

"I reckon I had no more than a two-mile pull to your ship. Not a bit more."

"And quite enough, too, in this awful heat," I said.

Another pause full of mistrust followed. Necessity, they say, is mother of invention, but fear, too, is not barren of ingenious suggestions. And I was afraid he would ask me point-blank for news of my other self.

"Nice little saloon, isn't it?" I remarked, as if noticing for the first time the way his eyes roamed from one closed door to the other. "And very well fitted out, too. Here, for instance," I continued, reaching over the back of my seat negligently and flinging the door open, "is my bathroom."

He made an eager movement, but hardly gave it a glance. I got up, shut the door of the bathroom, and invited him to have a look round, as if I were very proud of my accommodation. He had to rise and be shown round, but he went through the business without any raptures whatever.

"And now we'll have a look at my stateroom," I declared, in a voice as loud as I dared to make it, crossing the cabin to the starboard side with purposely heavy steps.

He followed me in and gazed around. My intelligent double had vanished. I played my part.

"Very convenient—isn't it?"

"Very nice. Very comf . . ." He didn't finish and went out brusquely as if to escape from some unrighteous wiles of mine. But it was not to be. I had been too frightened not to feel vengeful; I felt I had him on the run, and I meant to keep him on the run. My polite insistence must have had something menacing in it, because he gave in suddenly. And I did not let him off a single item; mate's room, pantry, storerooms, the very sail locker which was also under the poop—he had to look into them all. When at last I showed him out on the quarter-deck he drew a long, spiritless sigh, and mumbled dismally that he must really be going back to his ship now. I desired my mate, who had joined us, to see to the captain's boat.

The man of whiskers gave a blast on the whistle which he used to wear hanging round his neck, and yelled, "*Sephora's* away!" My double down there in my cabin must have heard, and certainly could not feel more relieved than I. Four fellows came running out from somewhere forward and went over the side, while my own men, appearing on deck too, lined the rail. I escorted my visitor to the gangway ceremoniously, and nearly overdid it. He was a tenacious beast. On the very ladder he lingered, and in that unique, guiltily conscientious manner of sticking to the point:

"I say . . . you . . . you don't think that——"

I covered his voice loudly:

"Certainly not. . . . I am delighted. Good-by."

I had an idea of what he meant to say, and just saved myself by the

privilege of defective hearing. He
was too shaken generally to insist,
but my mate, close witness of that
parting, looked mystified and his
face took on a thoughtful cast. As I
did not want to appear as if I wished
to avoid all communication with my
officers, he had the opportunity to
address me.

"Seems a very nice man. His
boat's crew told our chaps a very
extraordinary story, if what I am
told by the steward is true. I suppose you had it from the captain,
sir?"

"Yes. I had a story from the captain."

"A very horrible affair—isn't it,
sir?"

"It is."

"Beats all these tales we hear
about murders in Yankee ships."

"I don't think it beats them. I
don't think it resembles them in the
least."

"Bless my soul—you don't say so!
But of course I've no acquaintance
whatever with American ships, not
I, so I couldn't go against your
knowledge. It's horrible enough for
me. . . . But the queerest part is that
those fellows seemed to have some
idea the man was hidden aboard
here. They had really. Did you ever
hear of such a thing?"

"Preposterous—isn't it?"

We were walking to and fro
athwart the quarter-deck. No one of
the crew forward could be seen (the
day was Sunday), and the mate
pursued:

"There was some little dispute
about it. Our chaps took offense. 'As
if we would harbor a thing like
that,' they said. 'Wouldn't you like
to look for him in our coalhole?'
Quite a tiff. But they made it up in
the end. I suppose he did drown
himself. Don't you, sir?"

"I don't suppose anything."

"You have no doubt in the matter, sir?"

"None whatever."

I left him suddenly. I felt I was
producing a bad impression, but
with my double down there it was
most trying to be on deck. And it
was almost as trying to be below.
Altogether a nerve-trying situation.
But on the whole I felt less torn in
two when I was with him. There
was no one in the whole ship whom
I dared take into my confidence.
Since the hands had got to know his
story, it would have been impossible
to pass him off for anyone else, and
an accidental discovery was to be
dreaded now more than ever. . . .

The steward being engaged in
laying the table for dinner, we could
talk only with our eyes when I first
went down. Later in the afternoon
we had a cautious try at whispering.
The Sunday quietness of the ship
was against us; the stillness of air
and water around her was against
us; the elements, the men were
against us—everything was against
us in our secret partnership; time itself—for this could not go on forever. The very trust in Providence
was, I suppose, denied to his guilt.
Shall I confess that this thought cast
me down very much? And as to the
chapter of accidents which counts
for so much in the book of success,
I could only hope that it was closed.
For what favorable accident could
be expected?

"Did you hear everything?" were
my first words as soon as we took up
our position side by side, leaning
over my bed place.

He had. And the proof of it was
his earnest whisper, "The man told
you he hardly dared to give the
order."

I understood the reference to be to that saving foresail.

"Yes. He was afraid of it being lost in the setting."

"I assure you he never gave the order. He may think he did, but he never gave it. He stood there with me on the break of the poop after the main topsail blew away, and whimpered about our last hope— positively whimpered about it and nothing else—and the night coming on! To hear one's skipper go on like that in such weather was enough to drive any fellow out of his mind. It worked me up into a sort of desperation. I just took it into my own hands and went away from him, boiling, and—— But what's the use telling you? You know! . . . Do you think that if I had not been pretty fierce with them I should have got the men to do anything? Not It! The bo's'n perhaps? Perhaps! It wasn't a heavy sea—it was a sea gone mad! I suppose the end of the world will be something like that; and a man may have the heart to see it coming once and be done with it—but to have to face it day after day—— I don't blame anybody. I was precious little better than the rest. Only—I was an officer of that old coal wagon, any-how——"

"I quite understand," I conveyed that sincere assurance into his ear. He was out of breath with whisper-ing; I could hear him pant slightly. It was all very simple. The same strung-up force which had given twenty-four men a chance, at least, for their lives, had, in a sort of re-coil, crushed an unworthy mutinous existence.

But I had no leisure to weigh the merits of the matter—footsteps in the saloon, a heavy knock. "There's enough wind to get under way with, sir." Here was the call of a new claim upon my thoughts and even upon my feelings.

"Turn the hands up," I cried through the door. "I'll be on deck directly."

I was going out to make the acquaintance of my ship. Before I left the cabin our eyes met—the eyes of the only two strangers on board. I pointed to the recessed part where the little campstool awaited him and laid my finger on my lips. He made a gesture—somewhat vague—a little mysterious, accom-panied by a faint smile, as if of regret.

This is not the place to enlarge upon the sensations of a man who feels for the first time a ship move under his feet to his own independ-ent word. In my case they were not unalloyed. I was not wholly alone with my command; for there was that stranger in my cabin. Or rather, I was not completely and wholly with her. Part of me was absent. That mental feeling of being in two places at once affected me physically as if the mood of secrecy had pene-trated my very soul. Before an hour had elapsed since the ship had begun to move, having occasion to ask the mate (he stood by my side) to take a compass bearing of the Pagoda, I caught myself reaching up to his ear in whispers. I say I caught myself, but enough had escaped to startle the man. I can't describe it otherwise than by saying that he shied. A grave, preoccupied manner, as though he were in pos-session of some perplexing intelli-gence, did not leave him henceforth. A little later I moved away from the rail to look at the compass with such a stealthy gait that the helmsman noticed it—and I could not help noticing the unusual roundness of his eyes. These are trifling instances, though it's to no commander's advantage to be suspected of ludicrous eccentricities. But I was also more seriously affected. There are to a seaman certain words, gestures, that should in given conditions come as naturally, as instinctively as the winking of a menaced eye. A certain order should spring on to his lips without thinking; a certain sign should get itself made, so to speak, without reflection. But all unconscious alertness had abandoned me. I had to make an effort of will to recall myself back (from the cabin) to the conditions of the moment. I felt that I was appearing an irresolute commander to those people who were watching me more or less critically.

And, besides, there were the scares. On the second day out, for instance, coming off the deck in the afternoon (I had straw slippers on my bare feet) I stopped at the open pantry door and spoke to the steward. He was doing something there with his back to me. At the sound of my voice he nearly jumped out of his skin, as the saying is, and incidentally broke a cup.

"What on earth's the matter with you?" I asked, astonished.

He was extremely confused. "Beg your pardon, sir. I made sure you were in your cabin."

"You see I wasn't."

"No, sir. I could have sworn I had heard you moving in there not a moment ago. It's most extraordinary . . . very sorry, sir."

I passed on with an inward shudder. I was so identified with my secret double that I did not even mention the fact in those scanty, fearful whispers we exchanged. I suppose he had made some slight noise of some kind or other. It would have been miraculous if he

hadn't at one time or another. And yet, haggard as he appeared, he looked always perfectly self-controlled, more than calm—almost invulnerable. On my suggestion he remained almost entirely in the bathroom, which, upon the whole, was the safest place. There could be really no shadow of an excuse for anyone ever wanting to go in there, once the steward had done with it. It was a very tiny place. Sometimes he reclined on the floor, his legs bent, his head sustained on one elbow. At others I would find him on the campstool, sitting in his gray sleeping suit and with his cropped dark hair like a patient, unmoved convict. At night I would smuggle him into my bed place, and we would whisper together, with the regular footfalls of the officer of the watch passing and repassing over our heads. It was an infinitely miserable time. It was lucky that some tins of fine preserves were stowed in a locker in my stateroom; hard bread I could always get hold of; and so he lived on stewed chicken, *pâté de foie gras*, asparagus, cooked oysters, sardines—on all sorts of abominable sham delicacies out of tins. My early-morning coffee he always drank; and it was all I dared do for him in that respect.

Every day there was the horrible maneuvering to go through so that my room and then the bathroom should be done in the usual way. I came to hate the sight of the steward, to abhor the voice of that harmless man. I felt that it was he who would bring on the disaster of discovery. It hung like a sword over our heads.

The fourth day out, I think (we were then working down the east side of the Gulf of Siam, tack for tack, in light winds and smooth water)—the fourth day, I say, of this miserable juggling with the unavoidable, as we sat at our evening meal, that man, whose slightest movement I dreaded, after putting down the dishes ran up on deck busily. This could not be dangerous. Presently he came down again; and then it appeared that he had remembered a coat of mine which I had thrown over a rail to dry after having been wetted in a shower which had passed over the ship in the afternoon. Sitting stolidly at the head of the table I became terrified at the sight of the garment on his arm. Of course he made for my door. There was no time to lose.

"Steward," I thundered. My nerves were so shaken that I could not govern my voice and conceal my agitation. This was the sort of thing that made my terrifically whiskered mate tap his forehead with his forefinger. I had detected him using that gesture while talking on deck with a confidential air to the carpenter. It was too far to hear a word, but I had no doubt that this pantomime could only refer to the strange new captain.

"Yes, sir," the pale-faced steward turned resignedly to me. It was this maddening course of being shouted at, checked without rhyme or reason, arbitrarily chased out of my cabin, suddenly called into it, sent flying out of his pantry on incomprehensible errands, that accounted for the growing wretchedness of his expression.

"Where are you going with that coat?"

"To your room, sir."

"Is there another shower coming?"

"I'm sure I don't know, sir. Shall I go up again and see, sir?"

"No! never mind."

My object was attained, as of course my other self in there would have heard everything that passed. During this interlude my two officers never raised their eyes off their respective plates; but the lip of that confounded cub, the second mate, quivered visibly.

I expected the steward to hook my coat on and come out at once. He was very slow about it; but I dominated my nervousness sufficiently not to shout after him. Suddenly I became aware (it could be heard plainly enough) that the fellow for some reason or other was opening the door of the bathroom. It was the end. The place was literally not big enough to swing a cat in. My voice died in my throat and I went stony all over. I expected to hear a yell of surprise and terror, and made a movement, but had not the strength to get on my legs. Everything remained still. Had my second self taken the poor wretch by the throat? I don't know what I could have done next moment if I had not seen the steward come out of my room, close the door, and then stand quietly by the sideboard.

"Saved," I thought. "But, no! Lost! Gone! He was gone!"

I laid my knife and fork down and leaned back in my chair. My head swam. After a while, when sufficiently recovered to speak in a steady voice, I instructed my mate to put the ship round at eight o'clock himself.

"I won't come on deck," I went on. "I think I'll turn in, and unless the wind shifts I don't want to be disturbed before midnight. I feel a bit seedy."

"You did look middling bad a little while ago," the chief mate remarked without showing any great concern.

They both went out, and I stared at the steward clearing the table. There was nothing to be read on that wretched man's face. But why did he avoid my eyes, I asked myself. Then I thought I should like to hear the sound of his voice.

"Steward!"

"Sir!" Startled as usual.

"Where did you hang up that coat?"

"In the bathroom, sir." The usual anxious tone. "It's not quite dry yet, sir."

For some time longer I sat in the cuddy. Had my double vanished as he had come? But of his coming there was an explanation, whereas his disappearance would be inexplicable. . . . I went slowly into my dark room, shut the door, lighted the lamp, and for a time dared not turn round. When at last I did I saw him standing bolt-upright in the narrow recessed part. It would not be true to say I had a shock, but an irresistible doubt of his bodily existence flitted through my mind. Can it be, I asked myself, that he is not visible to other eyes than mine? It was like being haunted. Motionless, with a grave face, he raised his hands slightly at me in a gesture which meant clearly, "Heavens! what a narrow escape!" Narrow indeed. I think I had come creeping quietly as near insanity as any man who has not actually gone over the border. That gesture restrained me, so to speak.

The mate with the terrific whiskers was now putting the ship on the other tack. In the moment of profound silence which follows upon the hands going to their stations I heard on the poop his raised voice: "Hard alee!" and the distant shout of the order repeated on the main-deck. The sails, in that light breeze, made but a faint fluttering noise. It ceased. The ship was coming round slowly; I held my breath in the renewed stillness of expectation; one wouldn't have thought that there was a single living soul on her decks. A sudden brisk shout, "Mainsail haul!" broke the spell, and in the noisy cries and rush overhead of the men running away with the main brace we two, down in my cabin, came together in our usual position by the bed place.

He did not wait for my question. "I heard him fumbling here and just managed to squat myself down in the bath," he whispered to me. "The fellow only opened the door and put his arm in to hang the coat up. All the same——"

"I never thought of that," I whispered back, even more appalled than before at the closeness of the shave, and marveling at that something unyielding in his character which was carrying him through so finely. There was no agitation in his whisper. Whoever was being driven distracted, it was not he. He was sane. And the proof of his sanity was continued when he took up the whispering again.

"It would never do for me to come to life again."

It was something that a ghost might have said. But what he was alluding to was his old captain's reluctant admission of the theory of suicide. It would obviously serve his turn—if I had understood at all the view which seemed to govern the unalterable purpose of his action.

"You must maroon me as soon as ever you can get amongst these islands off the Cambodge shore," he went on.

"Maroon you! We are not living in a boy's adventure tale," I protested. His scornful whispering took me up.

"We aren't indeed! There's nothing of a boy's tale in this. But there's nothing else for it. I want no more. You don't suppose I am afraid of what can be done to me? Prison or gallows or whatever they may please. But you don't see me coming back to explain such things to an old fellow in a wig and twelve respectable tradesmen, do you? What can they know whether I am guilty or not—or of *what* I am guilty, either? That's my affair. What does the Bible say? 'Driven off the face of the earth.' Very well, I am off the face of the earth now. As I came at night so I shall go."

"Impossible!" I murmured. "You can't."

"Can't? . . . Not naked like a soul on the Day of Judgment. I shall freeze on to this sleeping-suit. The Last Day is not yet—and . . . you have understood thoroughly. Didn't you?"

I felt suddenly ashamed of myself. I may say truly that I understood—and my hesitation in letting that man swim away from my ship's side had been a mere sham sentiment, a sort of cowardice.

"It can't be done now till next night," I breathed out. "The ship is on the off-shore tack and the wind may fail us."

"As long as I know that you understand," he whispered. "But of course you do. It's a great satisfaction to have got somebody to understand. You seem to have been there on purpose." And in the same whisper, as if we two whenever we talked had to say things to each other which were not fit for the world to hear, he added, "It's very wonderful."

We remained side by side talking in our secret way—but sometimes silent or just exchanging a whispered word or two at long intervals. And as usual he stared through the port. A breath of wind came now and again into our faces. The ship might have been moored in dock, so gently and on an even keel she slipped through the water, that did not murmur even at our passage, shadowy and silent like a phantom sea.

At midnight I went on deck, and to my mate's great surprise put the ship round on the other tack. His terrible whiskers flitted round me in silent criticism. I certainly should not have done it if it had been only a question of getting out of that sleepy gulf as quickly as possible. I believe he told the second mate, who relieved him, that it was a great want of judgment. The other only yawned. That intolerable cub shuffled about so sleepily and lolled against the rails in such a slack, improper fashion that I came down on him sharply.

"Aren't you properly awake yet?"

"Yes, sir! I am awake."

"Well, then, be good enough to hold yourself as if you were. And keep a lookout. If there's any current we'll be closing with some islands before daylight."

The east side of the gulf is fringed with islands, some solitary, others in groups. On the blue background of the high coast they seem to float on silvery patches of calm water, arid and gray, or dark green and rounded like clumps of evergreen bushes, with the larger ones, a mile or two long, showing the outlines of ridges, ribs of gray rock under the dank mantle of matted leafage. Unknown to trade, to travel, almost to geography, the manner of life they harbor is an unsolved secret. There must be villages—settlements of fishermen at least—on the largest of them, and some communication with the world is probably kept up by native craft. But all that forenoon, as we headed for them, fanned along by the faintest of breezes, I saw no sign of man or canoe in the field of the telescope I kept on pointing at the scattered group.

At noon I gave no orders for a change of course, and the mate's whiskers became much concerned and seemed to be offering themselves unduly to my notice. At last I said:

"I am going to stand right in. Quite in—as far as I can take her."

The stare of extreme surprise imparted an air of ferocity also to his eyes, and he looked truly terrific for a moment.

"We're not doing well in the middle of the gulf," I continued, casually. "I am going to look for the land breezes tonight."

"Bless my soul! Do you mean, sir, in the dark amongst the lot of all them islands and reefs and shoals?"

"Well—if there are any regular land breezes at all on this coast one must get close inshore to find them, mustn't one?"

"Bless my soul!" he exclaimed again under his breath. All that afternoon he wore a dreamy, contemplative appearance which in him was a mark of perplexity. After dinner I went into my stateroom as if I meant to take some rest. There we two bent our dark heads over a half-unrolled chart lying on my bed.

"There," I said. "It's got to be Koh-ring. I've been looking at it ever since sunrise. It has got two hills and a low point. It must be inhabited. And on the coast opposite there is what looks like the mouth of a biggish river—with some towns,

no doubt, not far up. It's the best chance for you that I can see."

"Anything. Koh-ring let it be."

He looked thoughtfully at the chart as if surveying chances and distances from a lofty height—and following with his eyes his own figure wandering on the blank land of Cochin-China, and then passing off that piece of paper clean out of sight into uncharted regions. And it was as if the ship had two captains to plan her course for her. I had been so worried and restless running up and down that I had not had the patience to dress that day. I had remained in my sleeping suit, with straw slippers and a soft floppy hat. The closeness of the heat in the gulf had been most oppressive, and the crew were used to see me wandering in that airy attire.

"She will clear the south point as she heads now," I whispered into his ear. "Goodness only knows when, though, but certainly after dark. I'll edge her in to half a mile, as far as I may be able to judge in the dark——"

"Be careful," he murmured, warningly—and I realized suddenly that all my future, the only future for which I was fit, would perhaps go irretrievably to pieces in any mishap to my first command.

I could not stop a moment longer in the room. I motioned him to get out of sight and made my way on the poop. That unplayful cub had the watch. I walked up and down for a while thinking things out, then beckoned him over.

"Send a couple of hands to open the two quarter-deck ports," I said, mildly.

He actually had the impudence, or else so forgot himself in his wonder at such an incomprehensible order, as to repeat:

"Open the quarter-deck ports! What for, sir?"

"The only reason you need concern yourself about is because I tell you to do so. Have them open wide and fastened properly."

He reddened and went off, but I believe made some jeering remark to the carpenter as to the sensible practice of ventilating a ship's quarter-deck. I know he popped into the mate's cabin to impart the fact to him because the whiskers came on deck, as it were by chance, and stole glances at me from below—for signs of lunacy or drunkenness, I suppose.

A little before supper, feeling more restless than ever, I rejoined, for a moment, my second self. And to find him sitting so quietly was surprising, like something against nature, inhuman.

I developed my plan in a hurried whisper.

"I shall stand in as close as I dare and then put her round. I will presently find means to smuggle you out of here into the sail-locker, which communicates with the lobby. But there is an opening, a sort of square for hauling the sails out, which gives straight on the quarter-deck and which is never closed in fine weather, so as to give air to the sails. When the ship's way is deadened in stays and all the hands are aft at the main-braces you will have a clear road to slip out and get overboard through the open quarter-deck port. I've had them both fastened up. Use a rope's end to lower yourself into the water so as to avoid a splash—you know. It could be heard and cause some beastly complication."

He kept silent for a while, then whispered, "I understand."

"I won't be there to see you go,"

I began with an effort. "The rest . . . I only hope I have understood, too."

"You have. From first to last"— and for the first time there seemed to be a faltering, something strained in his whisper. He caught hold of my arm, but the ringing of the supper bell made me start. He didn't though; he only released his grip.

After supper I didn't come below again till well past eight o'clock. The faint, steady breeze was loaded with dew; and the wet, darkened sails held all there was of propelling power in it. The night, clear and starry, sparkled darkly, and the opaque, lightless patches shifting slowly against the low stars were the drifting islets. On the port bow there was a big one more distant and shadowily imposing by the great space of sky it eclipsed.

On opening the door I had a back view of my very own self looking at a chart. He had come out of the recess and was standing near the table.

"Quite dark enough," I whispered.

He stepped back and leaned against my bed with a level, quiet glance. I sat on the couch. We had nothing to say to each other. Over our heads the officer of the watch moved here and there. Then I heard him move quickly. I knew what that meant. He was making for the companion; and presently his voice was outside my door.

"We are drawing in pretty fast, sir. Land looks rather close."

"Very well," I answered. "I am coming on deck directly."

I waited till he was gone out of the cuddy, then rose. My double moved too. The time had come to exchange our last whispers, for neither of us was ever to hear each other's natural voice.

"Look here!" I opened a drawer

and took out three sovereigns. "Take this anyhow. I've got six and I'd give you the lot, only I must keep a little money to buy some fruit and vegetables for the crew from native boats as we go through Sunda Straits."

He shook his head.

"Take it," I urged him, whispering desperately. "No one can tell what——"

He smiled and slapped meaningly the only pocket of the sleeping jacket. It was not safe, certainly. But I produced a large old silk handkerchief of mine, and tying the three pieces of gold in a corner, pressed it on him. He was touched, I suppose, because he took it at last and tied it quickly round his waist under the jacket, on his bare skin.

Our eyes met; several seconds elapsed, till, our glances still mingled, I extended my hand and turned the lamp out. Then I passed through the cuddy, leaving the door of my room wide open. . . . "Steward!"

He was still lingering in the pantry in the greatness of his zeal, giving a rub-up to a plated cruet stand the last thing before going to bed. Being careful not to wake up the mate, whose room was opposite, I spoke in an undertone.

He looked round anxiously. "Sir!"

"Can you get me a little hot water from the galley?"

"I am afraid, sir, the galley fire's been out for some time now."

"Go and see."

He flew up the stairs.

"Now," I whispered, loudly, into the saloon—too loudly, perhaps, but I was afraid I couldn't make a sound. He was by my side in an instant—the double captain slipped past the stairs—through a tiny dark passage . . . a sliding door. We were in the sail locker, scrambling on our knees over the sails. A sudden thought struck me. I saw myself wandering barefooted, bareheaded, the sun beating on my dark poll. I snatched off my floppy hat and tried hurriedly in the dark to ram it on my other self. He dodged and fended off silently. I wonder what he thought had come to me before he understood and suddenly desisted. Our hands met gropingly, lingered united in a steady, motionless clasp for a second. . . . No word was breathed by either of us when they separated.

I was standing quietly by the pantry door when the steward returned.

"Sorry, sir. Kettle barely warm. Shall I light the spirit lamp?"

"Never mind."

I came out on deck slowly. It was now a matter of conscience to shave the land as close as possible—for now he must go overboard whenever the ship was put in stays. Must! There could be no going back for him. After a moment I walked over to leeward and my heart flew into my mouth at the nearness of the land on the bow. Under any other circumstances I would not have held on a minute longer. The second mate had followed me anxiously.

I looked on till I felt I could command my voice.

"She will weather," I said then in a quiet tone.

"Are you going to try that, sir?" he stammered out incredulously.

I took no notice of him and raised my tone just enough to be heard by the helmsman.

"Keep her good full."

"Good full, sir."

The wind fanned my cheek, the sails slept, the world was silent. The strain of watching the dark loom of the land grow bigger and denser was too much for me. I had shut my eyes—because the ship must go closer. She must! The stillness was intolerable. Were we standing still?

When I opened my eyes the second view started my heart with a thump. The black southern hill of Koh-ring seemed to hang right over the ship like a towering fragment of the ever-lasting night. On that enormous mass of blackness there was not a gleam to be seen, not a sound to be heard. It was gliding irresistibly towards us and yet seemed already within reach of the hand. I saw the vague figures of the watch grouped in the waist, gazing in awed silence.

"Are you going on, sir?" inquired an unsteady voice at my elbow.

I ignored it. I had to go on.

"Keep her full. Don't check her way. That won't do now," I said, warningly.

"I can't see the sails very well," the helmsman answered me, in strange, quavering tones.

Was she close enough? Already she was, I won't say in the shadow of the land, but in the very blackness of it, already swallowed up as it were, gone too close to be recalled, gone from me altogether.

"Give the mate a call," I said to the young man who stood at my elbow as still as death. "And turn all hands up."

My tone had a borrowed loudness reverberated from the height of the land. Several voices cried out together: "We are all on deck, sir."

Then stillness again, with the great shadow gliding closer, towering higher, without a light, without a sound. Such a hush had fallen on the ship that she might have been a bark of the dead floating in slowly under the very gate of Erebus.

"My God! Where are we?"

It was the mate moaning at my elbow. He was thunderstruck, and as it were deprived of the moral support of his whiskers. He clapped his hands and absolutely cried out, "Lost!"

"Be quiet," I said, sternly.

He lowered his tone, but I saw the shadowy gesture of his despair. "What are we doing here?"

"Looking for the land wind."

He made as if to tear his hair, and addressed me recklessly.

"She will never get out. You have done it, sir. I knew it'd end in something like this. She will never weather, and you are too close now to stay. She'll drift ashore before she's round. O my God!"

I caught his arm as he was raising it to batter his poor devoted head, and shook it violently.

"She's ashore already," he wailed, trying to tear himself away.

"Is she? . . . Keep good full there!"

"Good full, sir," cried the helmsman in a frightened, thin, childlike voice.

I hadn't let go the mate's arm and went on shaking it. "Ready about, do you hear? You go forward"—shake—"and stop there"—shake—"and hold your noise"—shake—"and see these head-sheets properly overhauled"—shake, shake—shake.

And all the time I dared not look towards the land lest my heart should fail me. I released my grip at last and he ran forward as if fleeing for dear life.

I wondered what my double there in the sail locker thought of this commotion. He was able to hear everything—and perhaps he was able to understand why, on my conscience, it had to be thus close—nc less. My first order "Hard alee!" re-echoed ominously under the towering shadow of Koh-ring as if I had shouted in a mountain gorge. And then I watched the land intently. In that smooth water and light wind it was impossible to feel the ship coming-to. No! I could not feel her. And my second self was making now ready to ship out and lower himself overboard. Perhaps he was gone already . . . ?

The great black mass brooding over our very mastheads began to pivot away from the ship's side silently. And now I forgot the secret stranger ready to depart, and remembered only that I was a total stranger to the ship. I did not know her. Would she do it? How was she to be handled?

I swung the mainyard and waited helplessly. She was perhaps stopped, and her very fate hung in the balance, with the black mass of Koh-ring like the gate of the everlasting night towering over her taffrail. What would she do now? Had she way on her yet? I stepped to the side swiftly, and on the shadowy water I could see nothing except a faint phosphorescent flash revealing the glassy smoothness of the sleeping surface. It was impossible to tell—and I had not learned yet the feel of my ship. Was she moving? What I needed was something easily seen, a piece of paper, which I could throw overboard and watch. I had nothing on me. To run down for it I didn't dare. There was no time. All at once my strained, yearning stare distinguished a white object floating within a yard of the ship's side. White on the black water. A phosphorescent flash passed under it. What was that thing? . . . I recognized my own floppy hat. It must have fallen off

his head . . . and he didn't bother. Now I had what I wanted—the saving mark for my eyes. But I hardly thought of my other self, now gone from the ship, to be hidden forever from all friendly faces, to be a fugitive and a vagabond on the earth, with no brand of the curse on his sane forehead to stay a slaying hand . . . too proud to explain.

And I watched the hat—the expression of my sudden pity for his mere flesh. It had been meant to save his homeless head from the dangers of the sun. And now—behold—it was saving the ship, by serving me for a mark to help out the ignorance of my strangeness. Ha! It was drifting forward, warning me just in time that the ship had gathered sternway.

"Shift the helm," I said in a low voice to the seaman standing still like a statue.

The man's eyes glistened wildly in the binnacle light as he jumped round to the other side and spun round the wheel.

I walked to the break of the poop. On the overshadowed deck all hands stood by the forebraces waiting for my order. The stars ahead seemed to be gliding from right to left. And all was so still in the world that I heard the quiet remark, "She's round," passed in a tone of intense relief between two seamen.

"Let go and haul."

The foreyards ran round with a great noise, amidst cheery cries. And now the frightful whiskers made themselves heard giving various orders. Already the ship was drawing ahead. And I was alone with her. Nothing! no one in the world should stand now between us, throwing a shadow on the way of silent knowledge and mute affection, the perfect communion of a seaman with his first command.

Walking to the taffrail, I was in time to make out, on the very edge of a darkness thrown by a towering black mass like the very gateway of Erebus—yes, I was in time to catch an evanescent glimpse of my white hat left behind to mark the spot where the secret sharer of my cabin and of my thoughts, as though he were my second self, had lowered himself into the water to take his punishment: a free man, a proud swimmer striking out for a new destiny.

Edgar Allan Poe

1809-1849

POE's life was as lurid as his stories. Born of a pair of strolling actors who died when he was very young, he was brought up by respectable foster parents who did what they could to make a Virginia gentleman of him. But, in turn, he was forced out of the University of Virginia because of gambling debts, expelled from West Point for absence from roll call, and lost the editorship of the *Southern Literary Messenger* because of drinking. His foster father disinherited him, and he was left at the age of twenty-two, penniless, ill, and untrained for work. Five years later he married a child of fourteen, who soon became ill and died slowly for six years, while her husband lost job after job. After her death he had many platonic love affairs, all of which went wrong. He was a congenital alcoholic, one glass putting him into a state of frenzy. He was constantly borrowing money. He told so many varied stories about himself that his biographers have all disagreed on facts, and the personality that has emerged is blurred but consistently purple.

When it came to his writing, however, Poe had both feet on the ground. He wrote strictly for money. A hard worker, he studied the market, both English and American magazines, and gave the public what it wanted. He hunted through newspapers for plots, amalgamated stories of other writers, and on occasion reused his own material. "The Cask of Amontillado" is reminiscent of *"La Grande Bretèche"* of Balzac. His stories give the effect of high emotional tension. Actually, he wrote them coldly and quite without passion. His poetry, on the other hand, reveals the inner man, and both his poetry and his criticism are oftentimes considered finer than his stories. Yet more than a hundred years after his death it is for his stories that he is remembered. He still remains one of the most popular American short-story writers.

The Cask of Amontillado

BY EDGAR ALLAN POE

THE thousand injuries of Fortunato I had borne as I best could, but when he ventured upon insult, I vowed revenge. You, who so well know the nature of my soul will not suppose, however, that I gave utterance to a threat. *At length* I would be avenged; this was a point definitely settled— but the very definitiveness with which it was resolved precluded the idea of risk. I must not only punish, but punish with impunity. A wrong is unredressed when retribution over- takes its redresser. It is equally unre- dressed when the avenger fails to make himself felt as such to him who has done the wrong.

It must be understood that neither by word nor deed had I given For- tunato cause to doubt my good will. I continued, as was my wont, to smile in his face, and he did not perceive that my smile *now* was at the thought of his immolation.

He had a weak point—this Fortu- nato—although in other regards he was a man to be respected and even feared. He prided himself on his connoisseurship in wine. Few Italians have the true virtuoso spirit. For the most part their enthusiasm is adopted to suit the time and opportunity to practice imposture upon the British and Austrian millionaires. In painting and gemmary Fortunato, like his countrymen, was a quack, but in the matter of old wines he was sincere. In this respect I did not differ from him materially—I was skillful in the Italian vintages myself, and bought largely whenever I could.

It was about dusk, one evening during the supreme madness of the carnival season, that I encountered my friend. He accosted me with ex- cessive warmth, for he had been drinking much. The man wore motley. He had on a tight-fitting partistriped dress, and his head was surmounted by the conical cap and bells. I was so pleased to see him that I thought I should never have done wringing his hand.

I said to him—"My dear For- tunato, you are luckily met. How re- markably well you are looking to- day! But I have received a pipe of what passes for Amontillado, and I have my doubts."

"How?" said he, "Amontillado? A pipe? Impossible! And in the middle of the carnival?"

"I have my doubts," I replied; "and I was silly enough to pay the full Amontillado price without con- sulting you in the matter. You were not to be found, and I was fearful of losing a bargain."

"Amontillado!"

"I have my doubts."

"Amontillado!"

"And I must satisfy them."

"Amontillado!"

"As you are engaged, I am on my way to Luchesi. If anyone has a critical turn, it is he. He will tell me——"

"Luchesi cannot tell Amontillado from sherry."

"And yet some fools will have it that his taste is a match for your own."

"Come, let us go."

"Whither?"

"To your vaults."

"My friend, no; I will not impose upon your good nature. I perceive you have an engagement. Luchesi ——"

"I have no engagement; come."

"My friend, no. It is not the engagement, but the severe cold with which I perceive you are afflicted. The vaults are insufferably damp. They are encrusted with niter."

"Let us go, nevertheless. The cold is merely nothing. Amontillado! You have been imposed upon; and as for Luchesi, he cannot distinguish sherry from Amontillado."

Thus speaking, Fortunato possessed himself of my arm. Putting on a mask of black silk, and drawing a roquelaure closely about my person, I suffered him to hurry me to my palazzo.

There were no attendants at home; they had absconded to make merry in honor of the time. I had told them that I should not return until the morning, and had given them explicit orders not to stir from the house. These orders were sufficient, I well knew, to insure their immediate disappearance, one and all, as soon as my back was turned.

I took from their sconces two flambeaux, and giving one to Fortunato, bowed him through several suites of rooms to the archway that led into the vaults. I passed down a long and winding staircase, requesting him to be cautious as he followed. We came at length to the foot of the descent, and stood together on the damp ground of the catacombs of the Montresors.

The gait of my friend was unsteady, and the bells upon his cap jingled as he strode.

"The pipe," said he.

"It is farther on," said I; "but observe the white webwork which gleams from these cavern walls."

He turned towards me, and looked into my eyes with two filmy orbs that distilled the rheum of intoxication.

"Niter?" he asked, at length.

"Niter," I replied. "How long have you had that cough?"

"Ugh! ugh! ugh!—ugh! ugh! ugh! —ugh! ugh! ugh!—ugh! ugh! ugh! —ugh! ugh! ugh!"

My poor friend found it impossible to reply for many minutes.

"It is nothing," he said, at last.

"Come," I said, with decision, "we will go back; your health is precious. You are rich, respected, admired, beloved; you are happy, as once I was. You are a man to be missed. For me it is no matter. We will go back; you will be ill, and I cannot be responsible. Besides, there is Luchesi——"

"Enough," he said; "the cough is a mere nothing: it will not kill me. I shall not die of a cough."

"True—true," I replied; "and, indeed, I had no intention of alarming you unnecessarily—but you should use all proper caution. A draught of this Médoc will defend us from the damps."

Here I knocked off the neck of a

bottle which I drew from a long row of its fellows that lay upon the mold.

"Drink," I said, presenting him the wine.

He raised it to his lips with a leer. He paused and nodded to me familiarly, while his bells jingled.

"I drink," he said, "to the buried that repose around us."

"And I to your long life."

He again took my arm, and we proceeded.

"These vaults," he said, "are extensive."

"The Montresors," I replied, "were a great and numerous family."

"I forget your arms."

"A huge human foot d'or, in a field azure; the foot crushes a serpent rampant whose fangs are imbedded in the heel."

"And the motto?"

"*Nemo me impune lacessit.*"*

"Good!" he said.

The wine sparkled in his eyes and the bells jingled. My own fancy grew warm with the Médoc. We had passed through walls of piled bones, with casks and puncheons intermingling, into the inmost recesses of the catacombs. I paused again, and this time I made bold to seize Fortunato by an arm above the elbow.

"The niter!" I said; "see, it increases. It hangs like moss upon the vaults. We are below the river's bed. The drops of moisture trickle among the bones. Come, we will go back ere it is too late. Your cough——"

"It is nothing," he said; "let us go on. But first, another draught of the Médoc."

I broke and reached him a flagon of De Grâve. He emptied it at a breath. His eyes flashed with a fierce

* No one dare attack me with impunity (the motto of Scotland).

light. He laughed and threw the bottle upwards with a gesticulation I did not understand.

I looked at him in surprise. He repeated the movement—a grotesque one.

"You do not comprehend?" he said.

"Not I," I replied.

"Then you are not of the brotherhood."

"How?"

"You are not of the masons."

"Yes, yes," I said, "yes, yes."

"You? Impossible! A mason?"

"A mason," I replied.

"A sign," he said.

"It is this," I answered, producing a trowel from beneath the folds of my roquelaure.

"You jest," he exclaimed, recoiling a few paces. "But let us proceed to the Amontillado."

"Be it so," I said, replacing the tool beneath the cloak, and again offering him my arm. He leaned upon it heavily. We continued our route in search of the Amontillado. We passed through a range of low arches, descended, passed on, and descending again, arrived at a deep crypt, in which the foulness of the air caused our flambeaux rather to glow than flame.

At the most remote end of the crypt there appeared another less spacious. Its walls had been lined with human remains piled to the vault overhead, in the fashion of the great catacombs of Paris. Three sides of this interior crypt were still ornamented in this manner. From the fourth the bones had been thrown down, and lay promiscuously upon the earth, forming at one point a mound of some size. Within the wall thus exposed by the displacing of the bones, we perceived a still interior recess, in depth about **four** feet, in width three, in height six or seven. It seemed to have been constructed for no especial use within itself, but formed merely the interval between two of the colossal supports of the roof of the catacombs, and was backed by one of their circumscribing walls of solid granite.

It was in vain that Fortunato, uplifting his dull torch, endeavored to pry into the depths of the recess. Its termination the feeble light did not enable us to see.

"Proceed," I said; "herein is the Amontillado. As for Luchesi——"

"He is an ignoramus," interrupted my friend, as he stepped unsteadily forward, while I followed immediately at his heels. In an instant he had reached the extremity of the niche, and finding his progress arrested by the rock, stood stupidly bewildered. A moment more and I had fettered him to the granite. In its surface were two iron staples, distant from each other about two feet, horizontally. From one of these depended a short chain, from the other a padlock. Throwing the links about his waist, it was but the work of a few seconds to secure it. He was too much astounded to resist. Withdrawing the key I stepped back from the recess.

"Pass your hand," I said, "over the wall; you cannot help feeling the niter. Indeed it is *very* damp. Once more let me *implore* you to return. No? Then I must positively leave you. But I must first render you all the little attentions in my power."

"The Amontillado!" ejaculated my friend, not yet recovered from his astonishment.

"True," I replied; "the Amontillado."

As I said these words I busied myself among the pile of bones of which I have before spoken. Throwing them aside, I soon uncovered a quantity of building stone and mortar. With these materials and with the aid of my trowel, I began vigorously to wall up the entrance of the niche.

I had scarcely laid the first tier of the masonry when I discovered that the intoxication of Fortunato had in a great measure worn off. The earliest indication I had of this was a low moaning cry from the depth of the recess. It was *not* the cry of a drunken man. There was then a long and obstinate silence. I laid the second tier, and the third, and the fourth; and then I heard the furious vibrations of the chain. The noise lasted for several minutes, during which, that I might hearken to it with the more satisfaction, I ceased my labors and sat down upon the bones. When at last the clanking subsided, I resumed the trowel, and finished without interruption the fifth, the sixth, and the seventh tier. The wall was now nearly upon a level with my breast. I again paused, and holding the flambeaux over the masonwork, threw a few feeble rays upon the figure within.

A succession of loud and shrill screams, bursting suddenly from the throat of the chained form, seemed to thrust me violently back. For a brief moment I hesitated—I trembled. Unsheathing my rapier, I began to grope with it about the recess; but the thought of an instant reassured me. I placed my hand upon the solid fabric of the catacombs, and felt satisfied. I reapproached the wall. I replied to the yells of him who clamored. I re-echoed—I aided—I surpassed them in volume and in strength. I did this, and the clamorer grew still.

It was now midnight, and my task was drawing to a close. I had completed the eighth, the ninth, and the tenth tier. I had finished a portion of the last and the eleventh; there remained but a single stone to be fitted and plastered in. I struggled with its weight; I placed it partially in its destined position. But now there came from out the niche a low laugh that erected the hairs upon my head. It was succeeded by a sad voice, which I had difficulty in recognizing as that of the noble Fortunato. The voice said—

"Ha! ha! ha!—he! he! he!—a very good joke indeed—an excellent jest. We will have many a rich laugh about it at the palazzo—he! he! he! —over our wine—he! he! he!"

"The Amontillado!" I said.

"He! he! he!—he! he! he!—yes, the Amontillado. But is it not getting late? Will not they be awaiting us at the palazzo, the Lady Fortunato and the rest? Let us be gone."

"Yes," I said, "let us be gone."

"*For the love of God, Montresor!*"

"Yes," I said, "for the love of God!"

But to these words I hearkened in vain for a reply. I grew impatient. I called aloud:

"Fortunato!"

No answer, I called again:

"Fortunato!"

No answer still. I thrust a torch through the remaining aperture and let it fall within. There came forth in return only a jingling of the bells. My heart grew sick—on account of the dampness of the catacombs. I hastened to make an end of my labor. I forced the last stone into its position; I plastered it up. Against the new masonry I re-erected the old rampart of bones. For the half of a century no mortal has disturbed them. *In pace requiescat!*

Ambrose Bierce
1842-1916 (?)

"BITTER BIERCE" was a wit and a storyteller. The wit was vitriolic, and the stories—tales of death and cruelty and horror—sprang from a morbid fancy. Born in Ohio, Bierce fought with distinction throughout the Civil War, worked for a time in England, but spent most of his life in San Francisco. There he was journalist, editor, columnist—virtually literary dictator of the West Coast. It was a normal, wholesome life. Yet his obsession with the gruesome and the supernatural was strangely justified in his end: no one knows where, how, or when he died. In 1913, at the age of seventy-one, he went to Mexico. He wrote several letters on the way, and in one to his daughter said he had attached himself to Villa's army—the army of Pancho Villa, the rebel. After that there was nothing. Like the "Horseman in the Sky" he charged, warrior that he was, into the unknown.

A Horseman in the Sky

BY AMBROSE BIERCE

I

ONE sunny afternoon in the autumn of the year 1861 a soldier lay in a clump of laurel by the side of a road in western Virginia. He lay at full length upon his stomach, his feet resting upon the toes, his head upon the left forearm. His extended right hand loosely grasped his rifle. But for the somewhat methodical disposition of his limbs and a slight rhythmic movement of the cartridge box at the back of his belt he might have been thought to be dead. He was asleep at his post of duty. But if detected he would be dead shortly afterward, death being the just and legal penalty of his crime.

The clump of laurel in which the criminal lay was in the angle of a road which after ascending southward a steep acclivity to that point turned sharply to the west, running along the summit for perhaps one hundred yards. There it turned southward again and went zigzagging downward through the forest. At the salient of that second angle was a large flat rock, jutting out northward, overlooking the deep valley from which the road ascended. The rock capped a high cliff; a stone dropped from its outer edge would have fallen sheer downward one thousand feet to the tops of the pines. The angle where the soldier lay was on another spur of the same cliff. Had he been awake he would have commanded a view, not only of the short arm of the road and the jutting rock, but of the entire profile of the cliff below it. It might well have made him giddy to look.

The country was wooded everywhere except at the bottom of the valley to the northward, where there was a small natural meadow, through which flowed a stream scarcely visible from the valley's rim. This open ground looked hardly larger than an ordinary dooryard, but was really several acres in extent. Its green was more vivid than that of the inclosing forest. Away beyond it rose a line of giant cliffs similar to those upon which we are supposed to stand in our survey of the savage scene, and through which the road had somehow made its climb to the summit. The configuration of the valley, indeed, was such that from this point of observation it seemed entirely shut in, and one could but have wondered how the road which found a way out of it had found a way into it, and whence came and

From *In the Midst of Life* by Ambrose Bierce. By permission of Albert and Charles Boni, Inc.

257

whither went the waters of the stream that parted the meadow more than a thousand feet below.

No country is so wild and difficult but men will make it a theater of war; concealed in the forest at the bottom of that military rattrap, in which half a hundred men in possession of the exits might have starved an army to submission, lay five regiments of Federal infantry. They had marched all the previous day and night and were resting. At nightfall they would take to the road again, climb to the place where their unfaithful sentinel now slept, and descending the other slope of the ridge fall upon a camp of the enemy at about midnight. Their hope was to surprise it, for the road led to the rear of it. In case of failure, their position would be perilous in the extreme; and fail they surely would should accident or vigilance apprise the enemy of the movement.

II

The sleeping sentinel in the clump of laurel was a young Virginian named Carter Druse. He was the son of wealthy parents, an only child, and had known such ease and cultivation and high living as wealth and taste were able to command in the mountain country of western Virginia. His home was but a few miles from where he now lay. One morning he had risen from the breakfast table and said, quietly but gravely: "Father, a Union regiment has arrived at Grafton. I am going to join it."

The father lifted his leonine head, looked at the son a moment in silence, and replied: "Well, go, sir, and whatever may occur do what you conceive to be your duty. Vir-

ginia, to which you are a traitor, must get on without you. Should we both live to the end of the war, we will speak further of the matter. Your mother, as the physician has informed you, is in a most critical condition; at the best she cannot be with us longer than a few weeks, but that time is precious. It would be better not to disturb her."

So Carter Druse, bowing reverently to his father, who returned the salute with a stately courtesy that masked a breaking heart, left the home of his childhood to go soldiering. By conscience and courage, by deeds of devotion and daring, he soon commended himself to his fellows and his officers; and it was to these qualities and to some knowledge of the country that he owed his selection for his present perilous duty at the extreme outpost. Nevertheless, fatigue had been stronger than resolution and he had fallen asleep. What good or bad angel came in a dream to rouse him from his state of crime, who shall say? Without a movement, without a sound, in the profound silence and the languor of the late afternoon, some invisible messenger of fate touched with unsealing finger the eyes of his consciousness—whispered into the ear of his spirit the mysterious awakening word which no human lips ever have spoken, no human memory ever has recalled. He quietly raised his forehead from his arm and looked between the masking stems of the laurels, instinctively closing his right hand about the stock of his rifle.

His first feeling was a keen artistic delight. On a colossal pedestal, the cliff—motionless at the extreme edge of the capping rock, and sharply outlined against the sky— was an equestrian statue of impressive dignity. The figure of the man sat the figure of the horse, straight and soldierly, but with the repose of a Grecian god carved in the marble which limits the suggestion of activity. The gray costume harmonized with its aerial background; the metal of accouterment and caparison was softened and subdued by the shadow; the animal's skin had no points of high light. A carbine strikingly foreshortened lay across the pommel of the saddle, kept in place by the right hand grasping it at the "grip"; the left hand, holding the bridle rein, was invisible. In silhouette against the sky the profile of the horse was cut with the sharpness of a cameo; it looked across the heights of air to the confronting cliffs beyond. The face of the rider, turned slightly away, showed only an outline of temple and beard; he was looking downward to the bottom of the valley. Magnified by its lift against the sky and by the soldier's testifying sense of the formidableness of a near enemy the group appeared of heroic, almost colossal, size.

For an instant Druse had a strange, half-defined feeling that he had slept to the end of the war and was looking upon a noble work of art reared upon that eminence to commemorate the deeds of an heroic past of which he had been an inglorious part. The feeling was dispelled by a slight movement of the group: the horse, without moving its feet, had drawn its body slightly backward from the verge; the man remained immobile as before. Broad awake and keenly alive to the significance of the situation, Druse now brought the butt of his rifle against his cheek by cautiously pushing the barrel forward through the bushes, cocked the piece, and glanc-

ing through the sights covered a vital spot of the horseman's breast. A touch upon the trigger and all would have been well with Carter Druse. At that instant the horseman turned his head and looked in the direction of his concealed foeman— seemed to look into his very face, into his eyes, into his brave, compassionate heart.

Is it then so terrible to kill an enemy in war—an enemy who has surprised a secret vital to the safety of one's self and comrades—an enemy more formidable for his knowledge than all his army for its numbers? Carter Druse grew pale; he shook in every limb, turned faint, and saw the statuesque group before him as black figures, rising, falling, moving unsteadily in arcs of circles in a fiery sky. His hand fell away from his weapon, his head slowly dropped until his face rested on the leaves in which he lay. This courageous gentleman and hardy soldier was near swooning from intensity of emotion.

It was not for long; in another moment his face was raised from earth, his hands resumed their places on the rifle, his forefinger sought the trigger; mind, heart, and eyes were clear, conscience and reason sound. He could not hope to capture that enemy; to alarm him would but send him dashing to his camp with his fatal news. The duty of the soldier was plain: the man must be shot dead from ambush—without warning, without a moment's spiritual preparation, with never so much as an unspoken prayer, he must be sent to his account. But no—there is a hope; he may have discovered nothing—perhaps he is but admiring the sublimity of the landscape. If permitted, he may turn and ride carelessly away in the direction whence he came. Surely it will be possible to judge at the instant of his withdrawing whether he knows. It may well be that his fixity of attention—Druse turned his head and looked through the deeps of air downward, as from the surface to the bottom of a translucent sea. He saw creeping across the green meadow a sinuous line of figures of men and horses—some foolish commander was permitting the soldiers of his escort to water their beasts in the open, in plain view from a dozen summits!

Druse withdrew his eyes from the valley and fixed them again upon the group of man and horse in the sky, and again it was through the sights of his rifle. But this time his aim was at the horse. In his memory, as if they were a divine mandate, rang the words of his father at their parting: "Whatever may occur, do what you conceive to be your duty." He was calm now. His teeth were firmly but not rigidly closed; his nerves were as tranquil as a sleeping babe's —not a tremor affected any muscle of his body; his breathing, until suspended in the act of taking aim, was regular and slow. Duty had conquered; the spirit had said to the body: "Peace, be still." He fired.

III

An officer of the Federal force, who in a spirit of adventure or in quest of knowledge had left the hidden bivouac in the valley, and with aimless feet had made his way to the lower edge of a small open space near the foot of the cliff, was considering what he had to gain by pushing his exploration further. At a distance of a quarter mile before him, but apparently at a stone's throw, rose from its fringe of pines the gigantic face of rock, towering to so great a height above him that it made him giddy to look up to where its edge cut a sharp, rugged line against the sky. It presented a clean, vertical profile against a background of blue sky to a point half the way down, and of distant hills, hardly less blue, thence to the tops of the trees at its base. Lifting his eyes to the dizzy altitude of its summit the officer saw an astonishing sight—a man on horseback riding down into the valley through the air!

Straight upright sat the rider, in military fashion, with a firm seat in the saddle, a strong clutch upon the rein to hold his charger from too impetuous a plunge. From his bare head his long hair streamed upward, waving like a plume. His hands were concealed in the cloud of the horse's lifted mane. The animal's body was as level as if every hoof stroke encountered the resistant earth. Its motions were those of a wild gallop, but even as the officer looked they ceased, with all the legs thrown sharply forward as in the act of alighting from a leap.

But this was a flight!

Filled with amazement and terror by this apparition of a horseman in the sky—half believing himself the chosen scribe of some new Apocalypse, the officer was overcome by the intensity of his emotions; his legs failed him and he fell. Almost at the same instant he heard a crashing sound in the trees —a sound that died without an echo —and all was still.

The officer rose to his feet, trembling. The familiar sensation of an abraded shin recalled his dazed faculties. Pulling himself together he ran rapidly obliquely away from the cliff to a point distant from its foot; thereabout he expected to find his man; and thereabout he naturally failed. In the fleeting instant of his vision his imagination had been so wrought upon by the apparent grace and ease and intention of the marvelous performance that it did not occur to him that the line of march of aerial cavalry is directly downward, and that he could find the objects of his search at the very foot of the cliff. A half-hour later he returned to camp.

This officer was a wise man; he knew better than to tell an incredible truth. He said nothing of what he had seen. But when the commander asked him if in his scout he had learned anything of advantage to the expedition he answered:

"Yes, sir; there is no road leading down into this valley from the southward."

The commander, knowing better, smiled.

IV

After firing his shot, Private Carter Druse reloaded his rifle and re-sumed his watch. Ten minutes had hardly passed when a Federal sergeant crept cautiously to him on hands and knees. Druse neither turned his head nor looked at him, but lay without motion or sign of recognition.

"Did you fire?" the sergeant whispered.

"Yes."

"At what?"

"A horse. It was standing on yonder rock—pretty far out. You see it is no longer there. It went over the cliff."

The man's face was white, but he showed no other sign of emotion. Having answered, he turned away his eyes and said no more. The sergeant did not understand.

"See here, Druse," he said, after a moment's silence, "it's no use making a mystery. I order you to report. Was there anybody on the horse?"

"Yes."

"Well?"

"My father."

The sergeant rose to his feet and walked away. "Good God!" he said.

Sarah Orne Jewett
1849-1909

SARAH ORNE JEWETT was the first—and the best—of the many Maine writers. She came of seafaring stock. Her grandfather was a shipowner, and her home was one of the fine old colonial mansions that sea captains built in the great days of the clippers. By her time the China trade had fallen off, and the children of former governors and judges and ladies of that past splendid day were just plain folk. But they still retained their dignity and self-respect, which Miss Jewett understood. As a little girl she used to ride with her doctor-father on his rounds, visiting remote farmhouses and fishing shacks, listening to strong Maine talk which she never forgot. Like Jane Austen she knew her own corner of the world and never tried to write beyond it.

Sarah Jewett has been called the New England nun. A Yankee she certainly was, but not provincial. Her great friend was Annie Fields of Boston, in whose famous salon she met Dr. Holmes, Henry James, Phillips Brooks, William Dean Howells, Longfellow, Whittier, Thomas Bailey Aldrich. She read Zola, Turgenev, and Tolstoi; and Flaubert's maxim: *"Ecrire la vie ordinaire comme on écrit l'histoire,"* was pinned up over her desk. Her stories have charm and delicacy and humor. A hundred writers since have tried to catch that same fragrance, on that same farmer-fisherman coast, but there is not one to match her. "The Hiltons' Holiday" was her favorite story, according to Willa Cather, who once said, incidentally, that she considered the three great American novels to be *Huckleberry Finn*, *The Scarlet Letter*, and Sarah Orne Jewett's *The Country of the Pointed Firs*.

The Hiltons' Holiday

BY SARAH ORNE JEWETT

I

THERE was a bright, full moon in the clear sky, and the sunset was still shining faintly in the west. Dark woods stood all about the old Hilton farmhouse, save down the hill, westward, where lay the shadowy fields which John Hilton, and his father before him, had cleared and tilled with much toil— the small fields to which they had given the industry and even affection of their honest lives.

John Hilton was sitting on the doorstep of his house. As he moved his head in and out of the shadows, turning now and then to speak to his wife, who sat just within the doorway, one could see his good face, rough and somewhat unkempt, as if he were indeed a creature of the shady woods and brown earth, instead of the noisy town. It was late in the long spring evening, and he had just come from the lower field as cheerful as a boy, proud of having finished the planting of his potatoes.

"I had to do my last row mostly by feelin'," he said to his wife. "I'm proper glad I pushed through, an' went back an' ended off after supper. 'Twould have taken me a good part o' tomorrow mornin', an' broke my day."

"'Tain't no use for ye to work yourself all to pieces, John," answered the woman quickly. "I declare it does seem harder than ever that we couldn't have kep' our boy; he'd been comin' fourteen years old this fall, most a grown man, and he'd work right 'longside of ye now the whole time."

"'Twas hard to lose him; I do seem to miss little John," said the father sadly. "I expect there was reasons why 'twas best. I feel able an' smart to work; my father was a girt strong man, an' a monstrous worker afore me. 'Tain't that; but I was thinkin' by myself today what a sight o' company the boy would ha' been. You know, small's he was, how I could trust to leave him anywheres with the team, and how he'd beseech to go with me wherever I was goin'; always right in my tracks I used to tell 'em. Poor little John, for all he was so young he had a great deal o' judgment; he'd ha' made a likely man."

The mother sighed heavily as she sat within the shadow.

"But then there's the little girls, a sight o' help an' company," urged the father eagerly, as if it were wrong to dwell upon sorrow and loss. "Katy, she's most as good as a boy, except that she ain't very rugged. She's a real little farmer, she's helped me a sight this spring; an' you've got Susan Ellen, that makes a complete little housekeeper for ye as far as she's learnt. I don't see but we're better off than most folks, each on us having a workmate."

"That's so, John," acknowledged Mrs. Hilton wistfully, beginning to rock steadily in her straight, splint-bottomed chair. It was always a good sign when she rocked.

"Where be the little girls so late?" asked their father. " 'Tis gettin' long past eight o'clock. I don't know when we've all set up so late, but it's so kind o' summerlike an' pleasant. Why, where be they gone?"

"I've told ye; only over to Becker's folks," answered the mother. "I don't see myself what keeps 'em so late; they beseeched me after supper till I let 'em go. They're all in a dazzle with the new teacher; she asked 'em to come over. They say she's unusual smart with 'reth-metic, but she has a kind of a gorpen look to me. She's goin' to give Katy some pieces for her doll, but I told Katy she ought to be ashamed wantin' dolls' pieces, big as she's gettin' to be. I don't know's she ought, though; she ain't but nine this summer."

"Let her take her comfort," said the kindhearted man. "Them things draws her to the teacher, an' makes them acquainted. Katy's shy with new folks, more so'n Susan Ellen, who's of the business kind. Katy's shy-feelin' and wishful."

"I don't know but she is," agreed the mother slowly. "Ain't it sing'lar how well acquainted you be with that one, an' I with Susan Ellen? 'Twas always so from the first. I'm doubtful sometimes our Katy ain't one that'll be like to get married— anyways not about here. She lives right with herself, but Susan Ellen ain't nothin' when she's alone, she's always after company; all the boys is waitin' on her a'ready. I ain't afraid but she'll take her pick when the time comes. I expect to see Susan Ellen well settled—she feels grown up now—but Katy don't care one mite 'bout none o' them things. She wants to be rovin' out-o'-doors. I do believe she'd stand an' hark to a bird the whole forenoon."

"Perhaps she'll grow up to be a teacher," suggested John Hilton. "She takes to her book more 'n the other one. I should like one on 'em to be a teacher same's my mother was. They're good girls as anybody's got."

"So they be," said the mother, with unusual gentleness, and the creak of her rocking chair was heard, regular as the ticking of a clock. The night breeze stirred in the great woods, and the sound of a brook that went falling down the hillside grew louder and louder. Now and then one could hear the plaintive chirp of a bird. The moon glittered with whiteness like a winter moon, and shone upon the low-roofed house until its small window-panes gleamed like silver, and one could almost see the colors of a blooming bush of lilac that grew in a sheltered angle by the kitchen door. There was an incessant sound of frogs in the lowlands.

"Be you sound asleep, John?" asked the wife presently.

"I don't know but what I was a'most," said the tired man, starting a little. "I should laugh if I was to fall sound asleep right here on the step; 'tis the bright night, I expect, makes my eyes feel heavy, an' 'tis so peaceful. I was up an' dressed a little past four an' out to work. Well, well!" and he laughed sleepily and rubbed his eyes. "Where's the little girls? I'd better step along an' meet 'em."

"I wouldn't just yet; they'll get home all right, but 'tis late for 'em certain. I don't want 'em keepin' Mis' Becker's folks up neither. There, le's wait a few minutes," urged Mrs. Hilton.

"I've be'n a-thinkin' all day I'd like to give the child'n some kind of a treat," said the father, wide awake now. "I hurried up my work 'cause I had it so in mind. They don't have the opportunities some do, an' I want 'em to know the world, an' not stay right here on the farm like a couple o' bushes."

"They're a sight better off not to be so full o' notions as some is," protested the mother suspiciously.

"Certain," answered the farmer; "but they're good, bright child'n, an' commencin' to take a sight o' notice. I want 'em to have all we can give 'em. I want 'em to see how other folks does things."

"Why, so do I"—here the rocking chair stopped ominously—"but so long's they're contented——"

"Contented ain't all in this world; hopper-toads may have that quality an' spend all their time a-blinkin'. I don't know's bein' contented is all there is to look for in a child. Ambition's somethin' to me."

"Now you've got your mind on to some plot or other." (The rocking chair began to move again.) "Why can't you talk right out?"

"'Tain't nothin' special," answered the good man, a little ruffled; he was never prepared for his wife's mysterious powers of divination. "Well there, you do find things out

the master! I only thought perhaps I'd take 'em tomorrow, an' go off somewhere if 'twas a good day. I've been promisin' for a good while I'd take 'em to Topham Corners; they've never been there since they was very small."

"I believe you want a good time yourself. You ain't never got over bein' a boy." Mrs. Hilton seemed much amused. "There, go if you want to an' take 'em; they've got their summer hats an' new dresses. I don't know o' nothin' that stands in the way. I should sense it better if there was a circus or anythin' to go to. Why don't you wait an' let the girls pick 'em some strawberries or nice ros'berries, and then they could take an' sell 'em to the stores?"

John Hilton reflected deeply. "I should like to get me some good yellow-turnip seed to plant late. I ain't more'n satisfied with what I've been gettin' o' late years o' Ira Speed. An' I'm goin' to provide me with a good hoe; mine's gettin' wore out an' all shackly. I can't seem to fix it good."

"Them's excuses," observed Mrs. Hilton, with friendly tolerance. "You just cover up the hoe with somethin', if you get it—I would. Ira Speed's so jealous he'll remember it of you this twenty year, your goin' an' buyin' a new hoe o' anybody but him."

"I've always thought 'twas a free country," said John Hilton soberly. "I don't want to vex Ira neither; he favors us all he can in trade. 'Tis difficult for him to spare a cent, but he's as honest as daylight."

At this moment there was a sudden sound of young voices, and a pair of young figures came out from the shadow of the woods into the moonlighted open space. An old cock crowed loudly from his perch in the shed, as if he were a herald of royalty. The little girls were hand in hand, and a brisk young dog capered about them as they came.

"Wa'n't it dark gittin' home through the woods this time o' night?" asked the mother hastily, and not without reproach.

"I don't love to have you gone so late; Mother an' me was timid about ye, and you've kep' Mis' Becker's folks up, I expect," said their father regretfully. "I don't want to have it said that my little girls ain't got good manners."

"The teacher had a party," chirped Susan Ellen, the elder of the two children. "Goin' home from school she asked the Grover boys, an' Mary an' Sarah Speed. An' Mis' Becker was real pleasant to us: she passed round some cake, an' handed us sap sugar on one of her best plates, an' we played games an' sung some pieces too. Mis' Becker thought we did real well. I can pick out most of a tune on the cabinet organ; teacher says she'll give me lessons."

"I want to know, dear!" exclaimed John Hilton.

"Yes, an' we played Copenhagen, an' took sides spellin', an' Katy beat everybody spellin' there was there."

Katy had not spoken; she was not so strong as her sister, and while Susan Ellen stood a step or two away addressing her eager little audience, Katy had seated herself close to her father on the doorstep. He put his arm around her shoulders, and drew her close to his side, where she stayed.

"Ain't you got nothin' to tell, daughter?" he asked, looking down fondly; and Katy gave a pleased little sigh for answer.

"Tell 'em what's goin' to be the last day o' school, and about our trimmin' the schoolhouse," she said;

and Susan Ellen gave the program in most spirited fashion.

"'Twill be a great time," said the mother, when she had finished. "I don't see why folks wants to go traipsin' off to strange places when such things is happenin' right about 'em." But the children did not observe her mysterious air. "Come, you must step yourselves right to bed!"

They all went into the dark, warm house; the bright moon shone steadily all night, and the lilac flowers were shaken by no breath of wind until the early dawn.

II

The Hiltons always waked early. So did their neighbors, the crows and song sparrows and robins, the light-footed foxes and squirrels in the woods. When John Hilton waked, before five o'clock, an hour later than usual because he had sat up so late, he opened the house door and came out into the yard, crossing the short green turf hurriedly as if the day were too far spent for any loitering. The magnitude of the plan for taking a whole day of pleasure confronted him seriously, but the weather was fair, and his wife, whose disapproval could not have been set aside, had accepted and even smiled upon the great project. It was inevitable now that he and the children should go to Topham Corners. Mrs. Hilton had the pleasure of waking them, and telling the news.

In a few minutes they came frisking out to talk over the great plans. The cattle were already fed, and their father was milking. The only sign of high festivity was the wagon pulled out into the yard, with both seats put in as if it were Sunday;

but Mr. Hilton still wore his every-day clothes, and Susan Ellen suffered instantly from disappointment.

"Ain't we goin', Father?" she asked complainingly; but he nodded and smiled at her, even though the cow, impatient to get to pasture, kept whisking her rough tail across his face. He held his head down and spoke cheerfully, in spite of this vexation.

"Yes, sister, we're goin' certain', an' goin' to have a great time too." Susan Ellen thought that he seemed like a boy at that delightful moment, and felt new sympathy and pleasure at once. "You go an' help Mother about breakfast an' them things; we want to get off quick's we can. You coax Mother now, both on ye, an' see if she won't go with us."

"She said she wouldn't be hired to," responded Susan Ellen. "She says it's goin' to be hot, an' she's laid out to go over an 'see how her aunt Tamsen Brooks is this afternoon.

The father gave a little sigh; then he took heart again. The truth was that his wife made light of the contemplated pleasure, and, much as he usually valued her companionship and approval, he was sure that they should have a better time without her. It was impossible, however, not to feel guilty of dis-loyalty at the thought. Even though she might be completely unconscious of his best ideals, he only loved her and the ideals the more, and bent his energies to satisfying her indefinite expectations. His wife still kept much of that youthful beauty which Susan Ellen seemed likely to reproduce.

An hour later the best wagon was ready, and the great expedition set forth. The little dog sat apart, and barked as if it fell entirely upon him to voice the general excitement.

Both seats were in the wagon, but the empty place testified to Mrs. Hilton's unyielding disposition. She had wondered why one broad seat would not do, but John Hilton meekly suggested that the wagon looked better with both. The little girls sat on the back seat dressed alike in their Sunday hats of straw with blue ribbons, and their little plaid shawls pinned neatly about their small shoulders. They wore gray thread gloves, and sat very straight. Susan Ellen was half a head the taller, but otherwise, from behind, they looked much alike. As for their father, he was in his Sunday best—a plain black coat, and a winter hat of felt, which was heavy and rusty-looking for that warm early summer day. He had it in mind to buy a new straw hat at Topham, so that this with the turnip seed and the hoe made three important reasons for going.

"Remember an' lay off your shawls when you get there an' carry them over your arms," said the mother, clucking like an excited hen to her chickens. "They'll do to keep the dust off your new dresses goin' an' comin'. An' when you eat your dinners don't get spots on you, an' don't point at folks as you ride by, an' stare, or they'll know you come from the country. An', John, you call into Cousin Ad'line Marlow's an' see how they all be, an' tell her I expect her over certain to stop awhile be-fore hayin'. It always eases her phthisic to git up here on the high land, an' I've got a new notion about doin' over her best-room carpet sence I see her that'll save rippin' one breadth. An' don't come home all wore out; an', John, don't you go an 'buy me no kickshaws to fetch home. I ain't a child, an' you ain't got no money to waste. I expect you'll go, like's not, an' buy you some kind of a foolish boy's hat; do look an' see if it's reasonable good straw, an' won't splinter all off round the edge. An' you mind, John——"

"Yes, yes, hold on!" cried John impatiently; then he cast a last affectionate, reassuring look at her face, flushed with the hurry and responsibility of starting them off in proper shape. "I wish you was goin' too," he said, smiling. "I do so!" Then the old horse started, and they went out at the bars, and began the careful long descent of the hill. The young dog, tethered to the lilac bush, was frantic with piteous appeals; the little girls piped their eager good-bys again and again, and their father turned many times to look back and wave his hand. As for their mother, she stood alone and watched them out of sight.

There was one place far out on the highroad where she could catch a last glimpse of the wagon, and she waited what seemed a very long time until it appeared and then was lost to sight again behind a low hill. "They're nothin' but a pack o' child'n together," she said aloud; and then felt lonelier than she expected. She even stooped and patted the unresigned little dog as she passed him, going into the house.

The occasion was so much more important than anyone had foreseen that both the little girls were speechless. It seemed at first like going to church in new clothes; or to a funeral; they hardly knew how to behave at the beginning of a whole day of pleasure. They made grave bows at such persons of their acquaintance as happened to be straying in the road. Once or twice they stopped before a farmhouse, while their father talked an inconsiderately long time with someone about

the crops and the weather, and even dwelt upon town business and the doings of the selectmen, which might be talked of at any time. The explanations that he gave of their excursion seemed quite unnecessary. It was made entirely clear that he had a little business to do at Topham Corners, and thought he had better give the little girls a ride; they had been very steady at school, and he had finished planting, and could take the day as well as not. Soon, however, they all felt as if such an excursion were an everyday affair, and Susan Ellen began to ask eager questions, while Katy silently sat apart, enjoying herself as she never had done before. She liked to see the strange houses, and the children who belonged to them; it was delightful to find flowers that she knew growing all along the road, no matter how far she went from home. Each small homestead looked its best and pleasantest, and shared the exquisite beauty that early summer made— shared the luxury of greenness and floweriness that decked the rural world. There was an early peony or a late lilac in almost every dooryard.

It was seventeen miles to Topham. After a while they seemed very far from home, having left the hills far behind, and descended to a great level country with fewer tracts of woodland, and wider fields where the crops were much more forward. The houses were all painted, and the roads were smoother and wider. It had been so pleasant driving along that Katy dreaded going into the strange town when she first caught sight of it, though Susan Ellen kept asking with bold fretfulness if they were not almost there. They counted the steeples of four churches, and their father presently showed them the Topham Academy, where their grandmother once went to school, and told them that perhaps someday they would go there too. Katy's heart gave a strange leap; it was such a tremendous thing to think of, but instantly the suggestion was transformed for her into one of the certainties of life. She looked with solemn awe at the tall belfry, and the long rows of windows in the front of the academy, there where it stood high and white among the clustering trees. She hoped that they were going to drive by, but something forbade her taking the responsibility of saying so.

Soon the children found themselves among the crowded village houses. Their father turned to look at them with affectionate solicitude.

"Now sit up straight and appear pretty," he whispered to them. "We're among the best people now, an' I want folks to think well of you."

"I guess we're as good as they be," remarked Susan Ellen, looking at some innocent passers-by with dark suspicion, but Katy tried indeed to sit straight, and folded her hands prettily in her lap, and wished with all her heart to be pleasing for her father's sake. Just then an elderly woman saw the wagon and the sedate party it carried, and smiled so kindly that it seemed to Katy as if Topham Corners had welcomed and received them. She smiled back again as if this hospitable person were an old friend, and entirely forgot that the eyes of all Topham had been upon her.

"There, now we're coming to an elegant house that I want you to see; you'll never forget it," said John Hilton. "It's where Judge Masterson lives, the great lawyer; the handsomest house in the county, everybody says."

"Do you know him, Father?" asked Susan Ellen.

"I do," answered John Hilton proudly. "Him and my mother went to school together in their young days, and were always called the two best scholars of their time. The Judge called to see her once; he stopped to our house to see her when I was a boy. An' then, some years ago—you've heard me tell how I was on the jury, an' when he heard my name spoken he looked at me sharp, and asked if I wa'n't the son of Catharine Winn, an' spoke most beautiful of your grandmother, an' how well he remembered their young days together."

"I like to hear about that," said Katy.

"She had it pretty hard, I'm afraid, up on the old farm. She keepin' school in our district when Father married her—that's the main reason I backed 'em down when they wanted to tear the old schoolhouse all to pieces," confided John Hilton, turning eagerly. "They all say she lived longer up here on the hill than she could anywhere, but she never had her health. I wa'n't but a boy when she died. Father an' me lived alone afterward till the time your mother come; 'twas a good while, too; I wa'n't married so young as some. 'Twas lonesome, I tell you; Father was plumb discouraged losin' of his wife, an' her long sickness an' all set him back, an' we'd work all day on the land an' never say a word. I s'pose 'tis bein' so lonesome early in life that makes me so pleased to have some nice girls growin' up round me now."

There was a tone in her father's voice that drew Katy's heart toward him with new affection. She dimly understood, but Susan Ellen was less interested. They had often heard this story before, but to one child it was always new and to the other old. Susan Ellen was apt to think it tiresome to hear about her grandmother, who, being dead, was hardly worth talking about.

"There's Judge Masterson's place," said their father in an everyday manner, as they turned a corner, and came into full view of the beautiful old white house standing behind its green trees and terraces and lawns. The children had never imagined anything so stately and fine, and even Susan Ellen exclaimed with pleasure. At that moment they saw an old gentleman, who carried himself with great dignity, coming slowly down the wide box-bordered path toward the gate.

"There he is now, there's the judge!" whispered John Hilton excitedly, reining his horse quickly to the green roadside. "He's goin' downtown to his office; we can wait right here an' see him. I can't expect him to remember me; it's been a good many years. Now you are goin' to see the great Judge Masterson!"

There was a quiver of expectation in their hearts. The judge stopped at his gate, hesitating a moment before he lifted the latch, and glanced up the street at the country wagon with its two prim little girls on the back seat, and the eager man who drove. They seemed to be waiting for something; the old horse was nibbling at the fresh roadside grass. The judge was used to being looked at with interest, and responded now with a smile as he came out to the sidewalk, and unexpectedly turned their way. Then he suddenly lifted his hat with grave politeness, and came directly toward them.

"Good morning, Mr. Hilton," he said. "I am very glad to see you, sir"; and Mr. Hilton, the little girls' own father, took off his hat with equal courtesy, and bent forward to shake hands.

Susan Ellen cowered and wished herself away, but little Katy sat straighter than ever, with joy in her father's pride and pleasure shining in her pale, flowerlike little face.

"These are your daughters, I am sure," said the old gentleman kindly, taking Susan Ellen's limp and reluctant hand; but when he looked at Katy, his face brightened. "How she recalls your mother!" he said with great feeling. "I am glad to see this dear child. You must come to see me with your father, my dear," he added, still looking at her. "Bring both the little girls, and let them run about the old garden; the cherries are just getting ripe," said Judge Masterson hospitably. "Perhaps you will have time to stop this afternoon as you go home?"

"I should call it a great pleasure if you would come and see us again some time. You may be driving our way, sir," said John Hilton.

"Not very often in these days," answered the old judge. "I thank you for the kind invitation. I should like to see the fine view again from your hill westward. Can I serve you in any way while you are in town? Good-by, my little friends!"

Then they parted, but not before Katy, the shy Katy, whose hand the judge still held unconsciously while he spoke, had reached forward as he said good-by, and lifted her face to kiss him. She could not have told why, except that she felt drawn to something in the serious, worn face. For the first time in her life the child had felt the charm of manners; perhaps she owned a kinship between that which made him what he was, and the spark of nobleness and purity in her own simple soul. She turned again and again to look back at him as they drove away.

"Now you have seen one of the first gentlemen in the county," said their father. "It was worth comin' twice as far"—but he did not say any more, nor turn as usual to look in the children's faces.

In the chief business street of Topham a great many country wagons like the Hiltons' were fastened to the posts, and there seemed to our holiday-makers to be a great deal of noise and excitement.

"Now I've got to do my errands, and we can let the horse rest and feed," said John Hilton. "I'll slip his headstall right off, an' put on his halter. I'm goin' to buy him a real good treat o' oats. First we'll go an' buy me my straw hat; I feel as if this one looked a little past to wear in Topham. We'll buy the things we want, an' then we'll walk all along the street, so you can look in the windows an' see the han'some things, same's your mother likes to. What was it Mother told you about your shawls?"

"To take 'em off an' carry 'em over our arms," piped Susan Ellen, without comment but in the interest of alighting and finding themselves afoot upon the pavement the shawls were forgotten. The children stood at the doorway of a shop while their father went inside, and they tried to see what the Topham shapes of bonnets were like, as their mother had advised them; but everything was exciting and confusing, and they could arrive at no decision. When Mr. Hilton came out with a hat in his hand to be seen in a better light, Katy whispered that she wished he would buy a shiny one like Judge Masterson's; but her father only smiled and shook his head, and said that they were plain folks, he and Katy. There were dry-goods for sale in the same shop, and a young clerk who was measuring linen kindly pulled off some pretty labels with gilded edges and gay pictures, and gave them to the little girls, to their exceeding joy. He may have had small sisters at home, this friendly lad, for he took pains to find two pretty blue boxes besides, and was rewarded by their beaming gratitude.

It was a famous day; they even became used to seeing so many people pass. The village was full of its morning activity, and Susan Ellen gained a new respect for her father, and an increased sense of her own consequence, because even in Topham several persons knew him and called him familiarly by name. The meeting with an old man who had once been a neighbor seemed to give Mr. Hilton the greatest pleasure. The old man called to them from a house doorway as they were passing, and they all went in. The children seated themselves wearily on the wooden step, but their father shook his old friend eagerly by the hand, and declared that he was delighted to see him so well and enjoying the fine weather.

"Oh, yes," said the old man, in a feeble, quavering voice, "I'm astonishin' well for my age. I don't complain, John, I don't complain."

They talked long together of people whom they had known in the past, and Katy, being a little tired, was glad to rest, and sat still with her hands folded, looking about the front yard. There were some kinds of flowers that she never had seen before.

"This is the one that looks like my mother," her father said, and touched Katy's shoulder to remind her to stand up and let herself be seen. "Judge Masterson saw the resemblance; we met him at his gate this morning."

"Yes, she certain does look like your mother, John," said the old man, looking pleasantly at Katy, who found that she liked him better than at first. "She does, certain; the best of young folks is, they remind us of the old ones. 'Tis nateral to cling to life, folks say, but for me, I git impatient at times. Most everybody's gone now, an' I want to be goin'. 'Tis somethin' before me, an' I want to have it over with. I want to be there 'long o' the rest o' the folks. I expect to last quite a while, though; I may see ye couple o' times more, John."

John Hilton responded cheerfully, and the children were urged to pick some flowers. The old man awed them with his impatience to be gone. There was such a townful of people about him, and he seemed as lonely as if he were the last survivor of a former world. Until that moment they had felt as if everything were just beginning.

"Now I want to buy somethin' pretty for your mother," said Mr. Hilton, as they went soberly away down the street, the children keeping fast hold of his hands. "By now the old horse will have eat his dinner and had a good rest, so pretty soon we can jog along home. I'm goin' to take you round by the academy, and the old North Meetinghouse where Dr. Barstow used to preach. Can't you think o' somethin' that your mother'd want?" he asked suddenly, confronted by a man's difficulty of choice.

"She was talkin' about wantin' a new pepper box, one day; the top o' the old one won't stay on," suggested Susan Ellen, with delightful readiness. "Can't we have some candy, Father?"

"Yes, ma'am," said John Hilton, smiling and swinging her hand to and fro as they walked. "I feel as if some would be good myself. What's all this?" They were passing a photographer's doorway with its enticing array of portraits. "I do declare!" he exclaimed excitedly, "I'm goin' to have our pictures taken; 'twill please your mother more 'n a little."

This was, perhaps, the greatest triumph of the day, except the delightful meeting with the judge; they sat in a row, with the father in the middle, and there was no doubt as to the excellence of the likeness. The best hats had to be taken off because they cast a shadow, but they were not missed, as their owners had feared. Both Susan Ellen and Katy looked their brightest and best; their eager young faces would forever shine there; the joy of the holiday was mirrored in the little picture. They did not know why their father was so pleased with it; they would not know until age had dowered them with the riches of association and remembrance.

Just at nightfall the Hiltons reached home again, tired out and happy. Katy had climbed over into the front seat beside her father, because that was always her place when they went to church on Sundays. It was a cool evening, there was a fresh sea wind that brought a light mist with it, and the sky was fast growing cloudy. Somehow the children looked different; it seemed to their mother as if they had grown older and taller since they went away in the morning, and as if they belonged to the town now as much as to the country. The greatness of their day's experience had left her far behind; the day had been silent and lonely without them, and she had their supper ready, and been watching anxiously, ever since five o'clock. As for the children themselves they had little to say at first— they had eaten their luncheon early on the way to Topham. Susan Ellen was childishly cross, but Katy was pathetic and wan. They could hardly wait to show the picture, and their mother was as much pleased as everybody had expected.

"There, what did make you wear your shawls?" she exclaimed a moment afterward, reproachfully. "You ain't been an' wore 'em all day long? I wanted folks to see how pretty your new dresses was, if I did make 'em. Well, well! I wish more 'n ever now I'd gone an' seen to ye!"

"An' here's the pepper box!" said Katy, in a pleased, unconscious tone.

"That really is what I call beautiful," said Mrs. Hilton, after a long and doubtful look. "Our other one was only tin. I never did look so high as a chiny one with flowers, but I can get us another any time for every day. That's a proper hat, as good as you could have got, John. Where's your new hoe?" she asked as he came toward her from the barn, smiling with satisfaction.

"I declare to Moses if I didn't forget all about it," meekly acknowledged the leader of the great ex-cursion. "That an' my yellow-turnip seed, too; they went clean out o' my head, there was so many other things to think of. But 'tain't no sort o' matter; I can get a hoe just as well to Ira Speed's."

His wife could not help laughing. "You an' the little girls have had a great time. They was full o' wonder to me about everything, and I expect they'll talk about it for a week. I guess we was right about havin' 'em see somethin' more o' the world."

"Yes," answered John Hilton, with humility, "yes, we did have a beautiful day. I didn't expect so much. They looked as nice as anybody, and appeared so modest an' pretty. The little girls will remember it perhaps by an' by. I guess they won't never forget this day they had 'long o' Father."

It was evening again, the frogs were piping in the lower meadows, and in the woods, higher up the great hill, a little owl began to hoot. The sea air, salt and heavy, was blowing in our country at the end of the hot bright day. A lamp was lighted in the house, the happy children were talking together, and supper was waiting. The father and mother lingered for a moment outside and looked down over the shadowy fields; then they went in, without speaking. The great day was over, and they shut the door.

Frank Stockton
1834-1902

FRANCIS RICHARD STOCKTON, dean of American humorists
of the Brownstone Age, was descended from an old family
that settled in America in the middle seventeenth century,
and one of his ancestors was a signer of the Declaration of Independence. As a young man in Philadelphia he worked as
wood engraver and invented an engraving tool. Later in
New York he was an editor on *The Century Magazine* and
for eight years edited *St. Nicholas*. But most of his writing
life was passed quietly in Nutley, New Jersey, where he
dictated from a hammock.

Stockton was lame and never in good health, but always
equable of temper. A very witty man, with a fund of good
stories, he was excellent company and had many friends. He
wrote several children's books, but the novels that made
him famous were *Rudder Grange*, about a servant girl on a
houseboat, and *The Casting Away of Mrs. Lecks and Mrs.
Aleshine*, about two widows shipwrecked on an island in
the Pacific. Like so many funny men, Stockton wrote slowly
and painfully, often laboring as long as an hour for the right
word. His humor stemmed from personal individuality and
did not depend on dialect or colloquialism. A story of his,
"The Lady or the Tiger?" caused a sensation when it came
out in 1882, and was later made into a musical comedy. But
"The Griffin and the Minor Canon" is much more typical
of his best work.

The Griffin and the Minor Canon

BY FRANK STOCKTON

Over the great door of an old, old church which stood in a quiet town of a faraway land there was carved in stone the figure of a large griffin. The old-time sculptor had done his work with great care, but the image he had made was not a pleasant one to look at. It had a large head, with enormous open mouth and savage teeth; from its back arose great wings, armed with sharp hooks and prongs; it had stout legs in front, with projecting claws; but there were no legs behind—the body running out into a long and powerful tail, finished off at the end with a barbed point. This tail was coiled up under him, the end sticking up just back of his wings.

The sculptor, or the people who had ordered this stone figure, had evidently been very much pleased with it, for little copies of it, also on stone, had been placed here and there along the sides of the church, not very far from the ground, so that people could easily look at them, and ponder on their curious forms. There were a great many other sculptures on the outside of this church—saints, martyrs, grotesque heads of men, beasts, and birds, as well as those of other creatures which cannot be named, because nobody knows exactly what they were; but none were so curious and interesting as the great griffin over the door, and the little griffins on the sides of the church.

A long, long distance from the town, in the midst of dreadful wilds scarcely known to man, there dwelt the Griffin whose image had been put up over the church door. In some way or other, the old-time sculptor had seen him and afterward, to the best of his memory, had copied his figure in stone.

The Griffin had never known this, until, hundreds of years afterward, he heard from a bird, from a wild animal, or in some manner which it is not now easy to find out, that there was a likeness of him on the old church in the distant town.

Now, this Griffin had no idea how he looked. He had never seen a mirror, and the streams where he lived were so turbulent and violent that a quiet piece of water, which would reflect the image of anything looking into it, could not be found. Being, as far as could be ascertained, the very last of his race, he had never seen another griffin. Therefore it was that, when he heard of this stone image of himself, he became very anxious to know what he looked like, and at last he determined to go to the old church, and see for himself what manner of being he was.

So he started off from the dreadful wilds, and flew on and on until he came to the countries inhabited by men, where his appearance in the air created great consternation; but he alighted nowhere, keeping up a steady flight until he reached the suburbs of the town which had his image on its church. Here, late in the afternoon, he lighted in a green meadow by the side of a brook, and stretched himself on the grass to rest. His great wings were tired, for he had not made such a long flight in a century, or more.

The news of his coming spread quickly over the town, and the people, frightened nearly out of their wits by the arrival of so strange a visitor, fled into their houses, and shut themselves up. The Griffin called loudly for someone to come to him but the more he called, the more afraid the people were to show themselves. At length he saw two laborers hurrying to their homes through the fields, and in a terrible voice he commanded them to stop. Not daring to disobey, the men stood, trembling.

"What is the matter with you all?" cried the Griffin. "Is there not a man in your town who is brave enough to speak to me?"

"I think," said one of the laborers, his voice shaking so that his words could hardly be understood, "that—perhaps—the Minor Canon—would come."

"Go, call him, then!" said the Griffin; "I want to see him."

The Minor Canon, who was an assistant in the old church, had just finished the afternoon services, and was coming out of a side door, with three aged women who had formed the weekday congregation. He was a young man of a kind disposition, and very anxious to do good to the people of the town. Apart from his duties in the church, where he conducted services every weekday, he visited the sick and the poor, counseled and assisted persons who were in trouble, and taught a school composed entirely of the bad children in the town with whom nobody else would have anything to do. Whenever the people wanted something difficult done for them, they always went to the Minor Canon. Thus it was that the laborer thought of the young priest when he found that someone must come and speak to the Griffin.

The Minor Canon had not heard of the strange event, which was known to the whole town except himself and the three old women, and when he was informed of it, and was told that the Griffin had asked to see him, he was greatly amazed and frightened.

"Me!" he exclaimed. "He has never heard of me! What should he want with me?"

"Oh! you must go instantly!" cried the two men. "He is very angry now because he has been kept waiting so long; and nobody knows what may happen if you don't hurry to him."

The poor Minor Canon would rather have had his hand cut off than go out to meet an angry Griffin; but he felt that it was his duty to go, for it would be a woeful thing if injury should come to the people of the town because he was not brave enough to obey the summons of the Griffin. So, pale and frightened, he started off.

"Well," said the Griffin, as soon as the young man came near, "I am glad to see that there is someone who has the courage to come to me."

The Minor Canon did not feel very brave, but he bowed his head.

"Is this the town," said the Griffin, "where there is a church with a likeness of myself over one of the doors?"

The Minor Canon looked at the frightful creature before him and saw that it was, without doubt, exactly like the stone image on the church. "Yes," he said, "you are right."

"Well, then," said the Griffin, "will you take me to it? I wish very much to see it."

The Minor Canon instantly thought that if the Griffin entered the town without the people's knowing what he came for, some of them would probably be frightened to death, and so he sought to gain time to prepare their minds.

"It is growing dark, now," he said, very much afraid, as he spoke, that his words might enrage the Griffin, "and objects on the front of the church cannot be seen clearly. It will be better to wait until morning, if you wish to get a good view of the stone image of yourself."

"That will suit me very well," said the Griffin. "I see you are a man of good sense. I am tired, and I will take a nap here on this soft grass, while I cool my tail in the little stream that runs near me. The end of my tail gets red-hot when I am angry or excited, and it is quite warm now. So you may go; but be sure and come early tomorrow morning, and show me the way to the church."

The Minor Canon was glad enough to take his leave, and hurried into the town. In front of the church he found a great many people assembled to hear his report of his interview with the Griffin. When

they found that he had not come to spread ruin, but simply to see his stony likeness on the church, they showed neither relief nor gratification, but began to upbraid the Minor Canon for consenting to conduct the creature into the town.

"What could I do?" cried the young man. "If I should not bring him he would come himself, and, perhaps, end by setting fire to the town with his red-hot tail."

Still the people were not satisfied, and a great many plans were proposed to prevent the Griffin from coming into the town. Some elderly persons urged that the young men should go out and kill him; but the young men scoffed at such a ridiculous idea.

Then someone said that it would be a good thing to destroy the stone image, so that the Griffin would have no excuse for entering the town; and this plan was received with such favor that many of the people ran for hammers, chisels, and crowbars, with which to tear down and break up the stone griffin. But the Minor Canon resisted this plan with all the strength of his mind and body. He assured the people that this action would enrage the Griffin beyond measure, for it would be impossible to conceal from him that his image had been destroyed during the night. But the people were so determined to break up the stone griffin that the Minor Canon saw that there was nothing for him to do but to stay there and protect it. All night he walked up and down in front of the church door, keeping away the men who brought ladders, by which they might mount to the great stone griffin, and knock it to pieces with their hammers and crowbars. After many hours the people were obliged to give up their attempts, and went home to sleep; but the Minor Canon remained at his post till early morning, and then he hurried away to the field where he had left the Griffin.

The monster had just awakened, and rising to his forelegs and shaking himself he said that he was ready to go into the town. The Minor Canon, therefore, walked back, the Griffin flying slowly through the air, at a short distance above the head of his guide. Not a person was to be seen in the streets, and they went directly to the front of the church, where the Minor Canon pointed out the stone griffin.

The real Griffin settled down in the little square before the church and gazed earnestly at his sculptured likeness. For a long time he looked at it. First he put his head on one side, and then he put it on the other; then he shut his right eye and gazed with his left, after which he shut his left eye and gazed with his right. Then he moved a little to one side and looked at the image, then he moved the other way. After a while he said to the Minor Canon, who had been standing by all this time:

"It is, it must be, an excellent likeness! That breadth between the eyes, that expansive forehead, those massive jaws! I feel that it must resemble me. If there is any fault to find with it, it is that the neck seems a little stiff. But that is nothing. It is an admirable likeness—admirable!"

The Griffin sat looking at his image all the morning and all the afternoon. The Minor Canon had been afraid to go away and leave him, and had hoped all through the day that he would soon be satisfied with his inspection and fly away home. But by evening the poor

young man was very tired, and felt that he must eat and sleep. He frankly said this to the Griffin, and asked him if he would not like something to eat. He said this because he felt obliged in politeness to do so; but as soon as he had spoken the words, he was seized with dread lest the monster should demand half a dozen babies, or some tempting repast of that kind.

"Oh, no," said the Griffin; "I never eat between the equinoxes. At the vernal and at the autumnal equinox I take a good meal, and that lasts me for half a year. I am extremely regular in my habits, and do not think it healthful to eat at odd times. But if you need food, go and get it, and I will return to the soft grass where I slept last night and take another nap."

The next day the Griffin came again to the little square before the church, and remained there until evening, steadfastly regarding the stone griffin over the door. The Minor Canon came out once or twice to look at him, and the Griffin seemed very glad to see him; but the young clergyman could not stay as he had done before, for he had many duties to perform. Nobody went to the church, but the people came to the Minor Canon's house, and anxiously asked him how long the Griffin was going to stay.

"I do not know," he answered, "but I think he will soon be satisfied with regarding his stone likeness, and then he will go away."

But the Griffin did not go away. Morning after morning he came to the church; but after a time he did not stay there all day. He seemed to have taken a great fancy to the Minor Canon, and followed him about as he worked. He would wait for him at the side door of the church, for the Minor Canon held services every day, morning and evening, though nobody came now. "If anyone should come," he said to himself, "I must be found at my post." When the young man came out, the Griffin would accompany him in his visits to the sick and the poor, and would often look into the windows of the schoolhouse where the Minor Canon was teaching his unruly scholars. All the other schools were closed, but the parents of the Minor Canon's scholars forced them to go to school, because they were so bad they could not endure them all day at home—Griffin or no Griffin. But it must be said they generally behaved very well when that great monster sat up on his tail and looked in at the schoolroom window.

When it was found that the Griffin showed no sign of going away, all the people who were able to do so left the town. The canons and the higher officers of the church had fled away during the first day of the Griffin's visit, leaving behind only the Minor Canon and some of the men who opened the doors and swept the church. All the citizens who could afford it shut up their houses and traveled to distant parts, and only the working people and the poor were left behind. After some days these ventured to go about and attend to their business, for if they did not work they would starve. They were getting a little used to seeing the Griffin; and having been told that he did not eat between equinoxes, they did not feel so much afraid of him as before.

Day by day the Griffin became more and more attached to the Minor Canon. He kept near him a great part of the time, and often spent the night in front of the little house where the young clergyman

lived alone. This strange companionship was often burdensome to the Minor Canon; but, on the other hand, he could not deny that he derived a great deal of benefit and instruction from it. The Griffin had lived for hundreds of years, and had seen much, and he told the Minor Canon many wonderful things.

"It is like reading an old book," said the young clergyman to himself; "but how many books I would have had to read before I would have found out what the Griffin has told me about the earth, the air, the water, about minerals, and metals, and growing things, and all the wonders of the world!"

Thus the summer went on, and drew toward its close. And now the people of the town began to be very much troubled again.

"It will not be long," they said, "before the autumnal equinox is here, and then that monster will want to eat. He will be dreadfully hungry, for he has taken so much exercise since his last meal. He will devour our children. Without doubt, he will eat them all. What is to be done?"

To this question no one could give an answer, but all agreed that the Griffin must not be allowed to remain until the approaching equinox. After talking over the matter a great deal, a crowd of the people went to the Minor Canon at a time when the Griffin was not with him.

"It is all your fault," they said, "that that monster is among us. You brought him here, and you ought to see that he goes away. It is only on your account that he stays here at all; for, although he visits his image every day, he is with you the greater part of the time. If you were not here, he would not stay. It is your duty to go away, and then he will follow you, and we shall be free from the dreadful danger which hangs over us."

"Go away!" cried the Minor Canon, greatly grieved at being spoken to in such a way. "Where shall I go? If I go to some other town, shall I not take this trouble there? Have I a right to do that?"

"No," said the people, "you must not go to any other town. There is no town far enough away. You must go to the dreadful wilds where the Griffin lives; and then he will follow you and stay there."

They did not say whether or not they expected the Minor Canon to stay there also, and he did not ask them anything about it. He bowed his head, and went into his house to think. The more he thought, the more clear it became to his mind that it was his duty to go away, and thus free the town from the presence of the Griffin.

That evening he packed a leathern bag full of bread and meat, and early the next morning he set out on his journey to the dreadful wilds. It was a long, weary, and doleful journey, especially after he had gone beyond the habitations of men; but the Minor Canon kept on bravely, and never faltered.

The way was longer than he had expected, and his provisions soon grew so scanty that he was obliged to eat but a little every day; but he kept up his courage, and pressed on, and, after many days of toilsome travel, he reached the dreadful wilds.

When the Griffin found that the Minor Canon had left the town he seemed sorry, but showed no desire to go and look for him. After a few days had passed he became much annoyed, and asked some of the people where the Minor Canon had gone. But, although the citizens had been so anxious that the young clergyman should go to the dreadful wilds, thinking that the Griffin would immediately follow him, they were now afraid to mention the Minor Canon's destination, for the monster seemed angry already, and if he should suspect their trick he would, doubtless, become very much enraged. So everyone said he did not know, and the Griffin wandered about disconsolate. One morning he looked into the Minor Canon's schoolhouse, which was always empty now, and thought that it was a shame that everything should suffer on account of the young man's absence.

"It does not matter so much about the church," he said, "for nobody went there; but it is a pity about the school. I think I will teach it myself until he returns."

It was the hour for opening the school, and the Griffin went inside and pulled the rope which rang the school bell. Some of the children who heard the bell ran in to see what was the matter, supposing it to be a joke of one of their companions; but when they saw the Griffin they stood astonished and scared.

"Go tell the other scholars," said the monster, "that school is about to open, and that if they are not all here in ten minutes I shall come after them."

In seven minutes every scholar was in place.

Never was seen such an orderly school. Not a boy or girl moved or uttered a whisper. The Griffin climbed into the master's seat, his wide wings spread on each side of him, because he could not lean back in his chair while they stuck out behind, and his great tail coiled around, in front of the desk, the barbed end sticking up, ready to tap any boy or girl who might misbehave.

The Griffin now addressed the scholars, telling them that he intended to teach them while their master was away. In speaking he tried to imitate, as far as possible, the mild and gentle tones of the Minor Canon; but it must be admitted that in this he was not very successful. He had paid a good deal of attention to the studies of the school, and he determined not to try to teach them anything new, but to review them in what they had been studying; so he called up the various classes, and questioned them upon their previous lessons. The children racked their brains to remember what they had learned. They were so afraid of the Griffin's displeasure that they recited as they had never recited before. One of the boys, far down in his class, answered so well that the Griffin was astonished.

"I should think you would be at the head," said he. "I am sure you have never been in the habit of reciting so well. Why is this?"

"Because I did not choose to take the trouble," said the boy, trembling in his boots. He felt obliged to speak the truth, for all the children thought that the great eyes of the Griffin could see right through them, and that he would know when they told a falsehood.

"You ought to be ashamed of yourself," said the Griffin. "Go down to the very tail of the class; and if you are not at the head in two days, I shall know the reason why."

The next afternoon this boy was Number One.

It was astonishing how much these children now learned of what they had been studying. It was as if they had been educated over again. The Griffin used no severity toward them, but there was a look about him which made them unwilling to go to bed until they were sure they knew their lessons for the next day.

The Griffin now thought that he ought to visit the sick and the poor; and he began to go about the town for this purpose. The effect upon the sick was miraculous. All, except those who were very ill indeed, jumped from their beds when they heard he was coming, and declared themselves quite well. To those who could not get up he gave herbs and roots, which none of them had ever before thought of as medicines, but which the Griffin had seen used in various parts of the world; and most of them recovered. But, for all that, they afterward said that, no matter what happened to them, they hoped that they should never again have such a doctor coming to their bedsides, feeling their pulses and looking at their tongues.

As for the poor, they seemed to have utterly disappeared. All those who had depended upon charity for their daily bread were now at work in some way or other; many of them offering to do odd jobs for their neighbors just for the sake of their meals—a thing which before had been seldom heard of in the town. The Griffin could find no one who needed his assistance.

The summer had now passed, and the autumnal equinox was rapidly approaching. The citizens were in a state of great alarm and anxiety. The Griffin showed no signs of going away, but seemed to have settled himself permanently among them. In a short time the day for his semiannual meal would arrive, and then what would happen? The monster would certainly be very hungry, and would devour all their children.

Now they greatly regretted and lamented that they had sent away the Minor Canon; he was the only one on whom they could have depended in this trouble, for he could talk freely with the Griffin, and so find out what could be done. But it would not do to be inactive. Some step must be taken immediately. A meeting of the citizens was called, and two old men were appointed to go and talk to the Griffin. They were instructed to offer to prepare a splendid dinner for him on equinox day— one which would entirely satisfy his hunger. They would offer him the fattest mutton, the most tender beef, fish, and game of various sorts, and anything of the kind that he might fancy. If none of these suited, they were to mention that there was an orphan asylum in the next town.

"Anything would be better," said the citizens, "than to have our dear children devoured."

The old men went to the Griffin; but their propositions were not received with favor.

"From what I have seen of the people of this town," said the monster, "I do not think I could relish anything which was prepared by them. They appear to be all cowards and, therefore, mean and selfish. As for eating one of them, old or young, I could not think of it for a moment. In fact, there was only one creature in the whole place for whom I could have had any appetite, and that is the Minor Canon, who has gone away. He was brave, and good, and honest, and I think I should have relished him."

"Ah!" said one of the old men very politely, "in that case I wish we had not sent him to the dreadful wilds!"

"What!" cried the Griffin. "What do you mean? Explain instantly what you are talking about!"

The old man, terribly frightened at what he had said, was obliged to tell how the Minor Canon had been sent away by the people, in the hope that the Griffin might be induced to follow him.

When the monster heard this he became furiously angry. He dashed away from the old men, and, spreading his wings, flew backward and forward over the town. He was so much excited that his tail became red-hot, and glowed like a meteor against the evening sky. When at last he settled down in the little field where he usually rested, and thrust his tail into the brook, the steam arose like a cloud, and the water of the stream ran hot through the town. The citizens were greatly frightened, and bitterly blamed the old man for telling about the Minor Canon.

"It is plain," they said, "that the Griffin intended at last to go and look for him, and we should have been saved. Now who can tell what misery you have brought upon us."

The Griffin did not remain long in the little field. As soon as his tail was cool he flew to the town hall and rang the bell. The citizens knew that they were expected to come there; and although they were afraid to go, they were still more afraid to stay away; and they crowded into the hall. The Griffin was on the platform at one end, flapping his wings and walking up and down, and the end of his tail was still so warm that it slightly scorched the boards as he dragged it after him.

When everybody who was able to come was there, the Griffin stood still and addressed the meeting.

"I have had a very low opinion

of you," he said, "ever since I discovered what cowards you are, but I had no idea that you were so ungrateful, selfish, and cruel as I now find you to be. Here was your Minor Canon, who labored day and night for your good, and thought of nothing else but how he might benefit you and make you happy; and as soon as you imagine yourselves threatened with a danger—for well I know you are dreadfully afraid of me—you send him off, caring not whether he returns or perishes, hoping thereby to save yourselves. Now, I had conceived a great liking for that young man, and had intended, in a day or two, to go and look him up. But I have changed my mind about him. I shall go and find him, but I shall send him back here to live among you, and I intend that he shall enjoy the reward of his labor and his sacrifices.

"Go, some of you, to the officers of the church, who so cowardly ran away when I first came here, and tell them never to return to this town under penalty of death. And if, when your Minor Canon comes back to you, you do not bow yourselves before him, put him in the highest place among you, and serve and honor him all his life, beware of my terrible vengeance! There were only two good things in this town: the Minor Canon and the stone image of myself over your church door. One of these you have sent away, and the other I shall carry away myself."

With these words he dismissed the meeting, and it was time, for the end of his tail had become so hot that there was danger of it setting fire to the building.

The next morning the Griffin came to the church, and tearing the stone image of himself from its fastenings over the great door he grasped it with his powerful forelegs and flew up into the air. Then, after hovering over the town for a moment, he gave his tail an angry shake and took up his flight to the dreadful wilds. When he reached this desolate region, he set the stone griffin upon a ledge of a rock which rose in front of the dismal cave he called his home. There the image occupied a position somewhat similar to that it had had over the church door; and the Griffin, panting with the exertion of carrying such an enormous load to so great a distance, lay down upon the ground and regarded it with much satisfaction. When he felt somewhat rested he went to look for the Minor Canon. He found the young man, weak and half starved, lying under the shadow of a rock. After picking him up and carrying him to his cave, the Griffin flew away to a distant marsh, where he procured some roots and herbs which he well knew were strengthening and beneficial to man, though he had never tasted them himself. After eating these the Minor Canon was greatly revived, and sat up and listened while the Griffin told him what had happened in the town.

"Do you know," said the monster, when he had finished, "that I have had, and still have, a great liking for you?"

"I am very glad to hear it," said the Minor Canon, with his usual politeness.

"I am not at all sure that you would be," said the Griffin, "if you thoroughly understood the state of the case; but we will not consider that now. If some things were different, other things would be otherwise. I have been so enraged by discovering the manner in which you have been treated that I have determined that you shall at last enjoy the rewards and honors to which you are entitled. Lie down and have a good sleep, and then I will take you back to the town."

As he heard these words, a look of trouble came over the young man's face.

"You need not give yourself any anxiety," said the Griffin, "about my return to the town. I shall not remain there. Now that I have that admirable likeness of myself in front of my cave, where I can sit at my leisure, and gaze upon its noble features and magnificent proportions, I have no wish to see that abode of cowardly and selfish people."

The Minor Canon, relieved from his fears, lay back, and dropped into a doze; and when he was sound asleep the Griffin took him up, and carried him back to the town. He arrived just before daybreak, and putting the young man gently on the grass in the little field where he himself used to rest, the monster, without having been seen by any of the people, flew back to his home.

When the Minor Canon made his appearance in the morning among the citizens, the enthusiasm and cordiality with which he was received were truly wonderful. He was taken to a house which had been occupied by one of the banished high officers of the place, and everyone was anxious to do all that could be done for his health and comfort. The people crowded into the church when he held services, so

that the three old women who used to be his weekday congregation could not get to the best seats, which they had always been in the habit of taking; and the parents of the bad children determined to reform them at home, in order that he might be spared the trouble of keeping up his former school. The Minor Canon was appointed to the highest office of the old church, and before he died, he became a bishop.

During the first years after his return from the dreadful wilds, the people of the town looked up to him as a man to whom they were bound to do honor and reverence; but they often, also, looked up to the sky to see if there were any signs of the Griffin coming back. However, in the course of time, they learned to honor and reverence their former Minor Canon without the fear of being punished if they did not do so.

But they need never have been afraid of the Griffin. The autumnal equinox day came round, and the monster ate nothing. If he could not have the Minor Canon, he did not care for anything. So, lying down, with his eyes fixed upon the great stone griffin, he gradually declined, and died. It was a good thing for some of the people of the town that they did not know this.

If you should ever visit the old town, you would still see the little griffins on the sides of the church; but the great stone griffin that was over the door is gone.

Stephen Crane
1871-1900

STEPHEN CRANE's short life was restless and uneven and intensely American. Born in Newark, New Jersey, the fourteenth child of a Methodist pastor, he was the typical American boy, playing baseball, boxing, and hunting. In college he became the youngest captain and the best shortstop the Syracuse University baseball team ever had. But he was unable to finish his education. His mother, who had supported the family after her husband's death, died when Stephen was eighteen, and for the next five years he lived in New York and nearly starved. The Bowery was his stamping ground, and his first novel, *Maggie: A Girl of the Streets*, was about the people he saw there. Publishers would have none of it: it was "too honest." So young Crane borrowed money to have it printed himself, sold it on newsstands at fifty cents a copy, and at the end of a year had disposed of fewer than a hundred copies. "The Pace of Youth," written only a little later, received no greater notice.

Not until *The Red Badge of Courage* was published in 1895 did Stephen Crane reach success. Though he was born six years after the Civil War ended, this might have been actual reporting. The editors who had formerly turned him down now hounded him for stories. Overnight the boy who often hadn't a roof over his head knew comparative security, but he spent what he earned as fast as he got it.

After reporting the Greco-Turkish and the Spanish-American wars, Crane rented an old English castle and for a short time settled down with his wife to the role of American-turned-English-squire, with dogs and horses and a constant houseful of guests. His hospitality was so lavish as to bring ridicule upon him from the many English and Americans who took advantage of it. He had had tuberculosis for several years, and before going to England had married the woman who had nursed him through two serious attacks—a woman older than he and of no great refinement, who nonetheless made him the best of wives. Again he grew ill, once more was in debt and unable to work. He died before he was twenty-nine.

Crane was the first of the modern generation of American writers, more of today than of yesterday.

The Pace of Youth

BY STEPHEN CRANE

STIMSON stood in a corner and glowered. He was a fierce man and had indomitable whiskers, albeit he was very small.

"That young tarrier," he whispered to himself. "He wants to quit makin' eyes at Lizzie. This is too much of a good thing. First thing you know, he'll get fired."

His brow creased in a frown, he strode over to the huge open doors and looked at a sign. "Stimson's Mammoth Merry-Go-Round," it read, and the glory of it was great. Stimson stood and contemplated the sign. It was an enormous affair; the letters were as large as men. The glow of it, the grandeur of it was very apparent to Stimson. At the end of his contemplation, he shook his head thoughtfully, determinedly. "No, no," he muttered. "This is too much of a good thing. First thing you know, he'll get fired."

A soft booming sound of surf, mingled with the cries of bathers, came from the beach. There was a vista of sand and sky and sea that drew to a mystic point far away in the northward. In the mighty angle, a girl in a red dress was crawling slowly like some kind of a spider on the fabric of nature. A few flags hung lazily above where the bath-houses were marshaled in compact squares. Upon the edge of the sea stood a ship with its shadowy sails painted dimly upon the sky, and high overhead in the still, sun-shot air a great hawk swung and drifted slowly.

Within the Merry-Go-Round there was a whirling circle of ornamental lions, giraffes, camels, ponies, goats, glittering with varnish and metal that caught swift reflections from windows high above them. With stiff wooden legs, they swept on in a never-ending race, while a great orchestrion clamored in wild speed. The summer sunlight sprinkled its gold upon the garnet canopies carried by the tireless racers and upon all the devices of decoration that made Stimson's machine magnificent and famous. A host of laughing children bestrode the animals, bending forward like charging cavalrymen, and shaking reins and whooping in glee. At intervals they leaned out perilously to clutch at iron rings that were tendered to them by a long wooden arm. At the intense moment before the swift grab for the rings one could see their little nervous bodies quiver with eagerness; the

From *Midnight Sketches* by Stephen Crane. By permission of the publishers. Copyright, 1898, 1902 and 1926, by Alfred A. Knopf, Inc.

laughter rang shrill and excited. Down in the long rows of benches, crowds of people sat watching the game, while occasionally a father might arise and go near to shout encouragement, cautionary commands, or applause at his flying offspring. Frequently mothers called out: "Be careful, Georgie!" The orchestrion bellowed and thundered on its platform, filling the ears with its long monotonous song. Over in a corner, a man in a white apron and behind a counter roared above the tumult: "Popcorn! Popcorn!"

A young man stood upon a small, raised platform erected in a manner of a pulpit, and just without the line of the circling figures. It was his duty to manipulate the wooden arm and affix the rings. When all were gone into the hands of the triumphant children, he held forth a basket, into which they returned all save the coveted brass one, which meant another ride free and made the holder very illustrious. The young man stood all day upon his narrow platform affixing rings or holding forth the basket. He was a sort of general squire in these lists of childhood. He was very busy.

And yet Stimson, the astute, had noticed that the young man frequently found time to twist about on his platform and smile at a girl who shyly sold tickets behind a silvered netting. This, indeed, was the great reason of Stimson's glowering. The young man upon the raised platform had no manner of license to smile at the girl behind the silvered netting. It was a most gigantic insolence. Stimson was amazed at it. "By Jiminy," he said to himself again, "that fellow is smiling at my daughter." Even in this tone of great wrath it could be discerned that Stimson was filled with wonder that any youth should dare smile at the daughter in the presence of the august father.

Often the dark-eyed girl peered between the shining wires, and, upon being detected by the young man, she usually turned her head quickly to prove to him that she was not interested. At other times, however, her eyes seemed filled with a tender fear lest he should fall from that exceedingly dangerous platform. As for the young man, it was plain that these glances filled him with valor, and he stood carelessly upon his perch, as if he deemed it of no consequence that he might fall from it. In all the complexities of his daily life and duties he found opportunity to gaze ardently at the vision behind the netting.

This silent courtship was conducted over the heads of the crowd who thronged about the bright machine. The swift eloquent glances of the young man went noiselessly and unseen with their message. There had finally become established between the two in this manner a subtle understanding and companionship. They communicated accurately all that they felt. The boy told his love, his reverence, his hope in the changes of the future. The girl told him that she loved him, and she did not love him, and she did not know if she loved him. Sometimes a little sign saying "Cashier" in gold letters, and hanging upon the silvered netting, got directly in range and interfered with the tender message.

The love affair had not continued without anger, unhappiness, despair. The girl had once smiled brightly upon a youth who came to buy some tickets for his little sister, and the young man upon the platform, observing this smile, had been filled with gloomy rage. He stood like a dark statue of vengeance upon his pedestal and thrust out the basket to the children with a gesture that was full of scorn for their hollow happiness, for their insecure and temporary joy. For five hours he did not once look at the girl when she was looking at him. He was going to crush her with his indifference; he was going to demonstrate that he had never been serious. However, when he narrowly observed her in secret he discovered that she seemed more blithe than was usual with her. When he found that his apparent indifference had not crushed her he suffered greatly. She did not love him, he concluded. If she had loved him she would have been crushed. For two days he lived a miserable existence upon his high perch. He consoled himself by thinking of how unhappy he was, and by swift, furtive glances at the loved face. At any rate he was in her presence, and he could get a good view from his perch when there was no interference by the little sign: "Cashier."

But suddenly, swiftly, these clouds vanished, and under the imperial blue sky of the restored confidence they dwelt in peace, a peace that was satisfaction, a peace that, like a babe, put its trust in the treachery of the future. This confidence endured until the next day, when she, for unknown cause, suddenly refused to look at him. Mechanically he continued his task, his brain dazed, a tortured victim of doubt, fear, suspicion. With his eyes he supplicated her to telegraph an explanation. She replied with a stony glance that froze his blood. There was a great difference in their respective reasons for becoming angry. His were always foolish, but apparent, plain as the moon. Hers were subtle, feminine, as incomprehensible as the stars, as mysterious as the shadows at night.

They fell and soared and soared and fell in this manner until they knew that to live without each other would be a wandering in deserts. They had grown so intent upon the uncertainties, the variations, the guessings of their affair that the world had become but a huge immaterial background. In time of peace their smiles were soft and prayerful, caresses confided to the air. In time of war, their youthful hearts, capable of profound agony, were wrung by the intricate emotions of doubt. They were the victims of the dread angel of affectionate speculation that forces the brain endlessly on roads that lead nowhere.

At night, the problem of whether she loved him confronted the young man like a specter, looming as high as a hill and telling him not to delude himself. Upon the following day, this battle of the night displayed itself in the renewed fervor of his glances and in their increased number. Whenever he thought he could detect that she too was suffering, he felt a thrill of joy.

But there came a time when the young man looked back upon these contortions with contempt. He believed then that he had imagined his pain. This came about when the redoubtable Stimson marched forward to participate.

"This has got to stop," Stimson had said to himself, as he stood and watched them. They had grown careless of the light world that clattered about them; they were become so engrossed in their personal drama that the language of their eyes was almost as obvious as gestures. And Stimson, through his keenness, his wonderful, infallible penetration, suddenly came into possession of these obvious facts. "Well, of all the nerves," he said, regarding with a new interest the young man upon the perch.

He was a resolute man. He never hesitated to grapple with a crisis. He decided to overturn everything at once, for, although small, he was very fierce and impetuous. He resolved to crush this dreaming.

He strode over to the silvered netting. "Say, you want to quit your everlasting grinning at that idiot," he said, grimly.

The girl cast down her eyes and made a little heap of quarters into a stack. She was unable to withstand the terrible scrutiny of her small and fierce father.

Stimson turned from his daughter and went to a spot beneath the platform. He fixed his eyes upon the young man and said—

"I've been speakin' to Lizzie. You better attend strictly to your own business or there'll be a new man here next week." It was as if he had blazed away with a shotgun. The young man reeled upon his perch. At last he in a measure regained his composure and managed to stammer:

"A—all right, sir." He knew that denials would be futile with the terrible Stimson. He agitatedly began to rattle the rings in the basket, and pretend that he was obliged to count them or inspect them in some way. He, too, was unable to face the great Stimson.

For a moment, Stimson stood in fine satisfaction and gloated over the effects of his threat.

"I've fixed them," he said complacently, and went out to smoke a cigar and revel in himself. Through his mind went the proud reflection that people who came in contact with his granite will usually ended in quick and abject submission.

One evening, a week after Stimson had indulged in the proud reflection that people who came in contact with his granite will usually ended in quick and abject submission, a young feminine friend of the girl behind the silvered netting came to her there and asked her to walk on the beach after "Stimson's Mammoth Merry-Go-Round" was closed for the night. The girl assented with a nod.

The young man upon the perch holding the rings saw this nod and judged its meaning. Into his mind came an idea of defeating the watchfulness of the redoubtable Stimson.

When the Merry-Go-Round was closed and the two girls started for the beach, he wandered off aimlessly in another direction, but he kept them in view, and as soon as he was assured that he had escaped the vigilance of Stimson, he followed them.

The electric lights on the beach made a broad band of tremoring light, extending parallel to the sea, and upon the wide walk there slowly paraded a great crowd, intermingling, intertwining, sometimes colliding. In the darkness stretched the vast purple expanse of the ocean, and the deep indigo sky above was peopled with yellow stars. Occasionally out upon the water a whirling mass of froth suddenly flashed into view, like a great ghostly robe appearing, and then vanished, leaving the sea in its darkness, whence came those bass tones of the water's unknown emotion. A wind, cool, reminiscent of the wave wastes, made the women hold their wraps about their throats, and caused the men to grip the rims of their straw hats. It carried the noise of the band in the pavilion in gusts. Sometimes people unable to hear the music glanced up at the pavilion and were reassured upon beholding the distant leader still gesticulating and bobbing, and the other members of the band with their lips glued to their instruments. High in the sky soared an unassuming moon, faintly silver.

For a time the young man was afraid to approach the two girls; he followed them at a distance and called himself a coward. At last, however, he saw them stop on the outer edge of the crowd and stand silently listening to the voices of the sea. When he came to where they stood, he was trembling in his agitation. They had not seen him.

"Lizzie," he began. "I——"

The girl wheeled instantly and put her hand to her throat.

"Oh, Frank, how you frightened me," she said—inevitably.

"Well, you know, I—I——" he stuttered.

But the other girl was one of those beings who are born to attend at tragedies. She had for love a reverence, an admiration that was greater the more that she contemplated the fact that she knew nothing of it. This couple, with their emotions, awed her and made her humbly wish that she might be destined to be of some service to them. She was very homely.

When the young man faltered before them, she, in her sympathy, actually overestimated the crisis, and felt that he might fall dying at their feet. Shyly, but with courage, she marched to the rescue.

"Won't you come and walk on the beach with us?" she said.

The young man gave her a glance

of deep gratitude which was not without the patronage which a man in his condition naturally feels for one who pities it. The three walked on.

Finally, the being who was born to attend at this tragedy said that she wished to sit down and gaze at the sea, alone.

They politely urged her to walk on with them, but she was obstinate. She wished to gaze at the sea, alone. The young man swore to himself that he would be her friend until he died.

And so the two young lovers went on without her. They turned once to look at her.

"Jennie's awful nice," said the girl.

"You bet she is," replied the young man, ardently.

They were silent for a little time.

"You were angry at me yesterday."

"No, I wasn't."

"Yes, you were, too. You wouldn't look at me once all day."

"No, I wasn't angry. I was only putting on."

Though she had, of course, known it, this confession seemed to make her very indignant. She flashed a resentful glance at him.

"Oh, you were, indeed?" she said with a great air.

For a few minutes she was so haughty with him that he loved her to madness. And directly this poem, which stuck at his lips, came forth lamely in fragments.

When they walked back toward the other girl and saw the patience of her attitude, their hearts swelled in a patronizing and secondary tenderness for her.

They were very happy. If they had been miserable they would have charged this fairy scene of the night with a criminal heartlessness; but as they were joyous, they vaguely wondered how the purple sea, the yellow stars, the changing crowds under the electric lights could be so phlegmatic and stolid.

They walked home by the lakeside way, and out upon the water those gay paper lanterns, flashing, fleeting, and careening, sang to them, sang a chorus of red and violet, and green and gold; a song of mystic bands of the future.

One day, when business paused during a dull sultry afternoon, Stimson went uptown. Upon his return, he found that the popcorn man, from his stand over in a corner, was keeping an eye upon the cashier's cage, and that nobody at all was attending to the wooden arm and the iron rings. He strode forward like a sergeant of grenadiers.

"Where in thunder is Lizzie?" he demanded, a cloud of rage in his eyes.

The popcorn man, although associated long with Stimson, had never got over being dazed.

"They've—they've—gone round to th'—th'—house," he said with difficulty, as if he had just been stunned.

"Whose house?" snapped Stimson.

"Your—your house, I s'pose," said the popcorn man.

Stimson marched round to his home. Kingly denunciations surged, already formulated, to the tip of his tongue, and he bided the moment when his anger could fall upon the heads of that pair of children. He found his wife convulsive and in tears.

"Where's Lizzie?"

And then she burst forth—"Oh—John—John—they've run away, I know they have. They drove by here not three minutes ago. They must have done it on purpose to bid me good-by, for Lizzie waved her hand sadlike, and then, before I could get out to ask where they were going or what, Frank whipped up the horse."

Stimson gave vent to a dreadful roar.

"Get my revolver—get a hack— get my revolver, do you hear— what the devil——" His voice became incoherent.

He had always ordered his wife about as if she were a battalion of infantry, and despite her misery, the training of years forced her to spring mechanically to obey; but suddenly she turned to him with a shrill appeal.

"Oh, John—not—the—revolver."

"Confound it, let go of me!" he roared again, and shook her from him.

He ran hatless upon the street. There were a multitude of hacks at the summer resort, but it was ages to him before he could find one. Then he charged it like a bull.

"Uptown!" he yelled, as he tumbled into the rear seat.

The hackman thought of severed arteries. His galloping horse distanced a large number of citizens who had been running to find what caused such contortions by the little hatless man.

It chanced as the bouncing hack went along near the lake, Stimson gazed across the calm gray expanse and recognized a color in a bonnet and a pose of a head. A buggy was traveling along a highway that led to Sorington. Stimson bellowed— "There—there—there they are—in that buggy."

The hackman became inspired with the full knowledge of the situation. He struck a delirious blow with the whip. His mouth expanded in a grin of excitement and joy. It came to pass that this old vehicle, with its drowsy horse and its dusty-eyed and tranquil driver, seemed suddenly to awaken, to become animated and fleet. The horse ceased to ruminate on his state, his air of reflection vanished. He became intent upon his aged legs and spread them in quaint and ridiculous devices for speed. The driver, his eyes shining, sat critically in his seat. He watched each motion of this rattling machine down before him. He resembled an engineer. He used the whip with judgment and deliberation as the engineer would have used coal or oil. The horse clacked swiftly upon the macadam, the wheels hummed, the body of the vehicle wheezed and groaned.

Stimson, in the rear seat, was erect in that impassive attitude that comes sometimes to the furious man when he is obliged to leave the battle to others. Frequently, however, the tempest in his breast came to his face and he howled—

"Go it—go it—you're gaining; pound 'im! Thump the life out of 'im; hit 'im hard, you fool!" His hand grasped the rod that supported the carriage top, and it was clenched so that the nails were faintly blue.

Ahead, that other carriage had been flying with speed, as from realization of the menace in the rear. It bowled away rapidly, drawn by the eager spirit of a young and modern horse. Stimson could see the buggy top bobbing, bobbing. That little pane, like an eye, was a derision to him. Once he leaned forward and bawled angry sentences. He began to feel impotent; his whole expedition was a tottering of an old man upon a trail of birds. A sense of age made him shake again with wrath. That other vehicle, that was youth, with youth's pace; it was swift-flying with the hope of dreams. He began to comprehend those two children ahead of him, and he knew a sudden and strange awe, because he understood the power of their young blood, the power to fly strongly into the future and feel and hope again, even at that time when his bones must be laid in the earth. The dust rose easily from the hot road and stifled the nostrils of Stimson.

The highway vanished far away in a point with a suggestion of intolerable length. The other vehicle was becoming so small that Stimson could no longer see the derisive eye.

At last the hackman drew rein to his horse and turned to look at Stimson.

"No use, I guess," he said.

Stimson made a gesture of acquiescence, rage, despair. As the hackman turned his dripping horse about, Stimson sank with the astonishment and grief of a man who had been defied by the universe. He had been in a great perspiration, and now his bald head felt cool and uncomfortable. He put up his hand with a sudden recollection that he had forgotten his hat.

At last he made a gesture. It meant that at any rate he was not responsible.

Jack London
1876-1916

In 1913 Jack London was the best-known and highest-paid writer in the world. He made over a million dollars on fifty books, and spent it all. He built himself a mansion, bought a ranch, sailed a yacht, and died a suicide because of debt, overwork, and liquor. Born in San Francisco, the illegitimate son of a strolling Irish astrologer and a hard-working, unlucky mother, London lived a precarious childhood, working on ice wagons, paper routes, and in bowling alleys, and grew up with a strong yearning for luxury and respectability. But at fifteen he was a tramp, at sixteen an oyster pirate, owner of the *Razzle-Dazzle*, at eighteen in Coxey's Army, and at twenty in Alaska, carrying under his arm *The Origin of Species, Das Kapital,* and *Paradise Lost*. He returned from the Klondike without any gold nuggets, but with the germ of *The Call of the Wild* in his imagination. Always reaching out for something beyond him, he finally found escape in his own stories. The day of the wide-open spaces had already passed, but he re-created it—a primitive world with a superman to fight against it. He himself was strong, handsome, blue-eyed—the romantic and tragic figure of his own tales.

London's reputation in Russia, Germany, and France has long outlasted his vogue at home. Certainly, up to the day of Hollywood, he did more than anyone else to color the European idea of America.

To Build a Fire

BY JACK LONDON

DAY had broken cold and gray, exceedingly cold and gray, when the man turned aside from the main Yukon trail and climbed the high earthbank where a dim and little traveled trail led eastward through the fat spruce timberland. It was a steep bank, and he paused for breath at the top, excusing the act to himself by looking at his watch. It was nine o'clock. There was no sun nor hint of sun, though there was not a cloud in the sky. It was a clear day, and yet there seemed an intangible pall over the face of things, a subtle gloom that made the day dark, and that was due to the absence of sun. This fact did not worry the man. He was used to the lack of sun. It had been days since he had seen the sun, and he knew that a few more days must pass before that cheerful orb, due south, would just peep above the skyline and dip immediately from view.

The man flung a look back along the way he had come. The Yukon lay a mile wide and hidden under three feet of ice. On top of this ice were as many feet of snow. It was all pure white, rolling in gentle undulations where the ice jams of the freeze-up had formed.

North and south, as far as his eye could see, it was unbroken white, save for a dark hairline that curved and twisted from around the spruce-covered island to the south, and that curved and twisted away into the north, where it disappeared behind another spruce-covered island. This dark hairline was the trail—the main trail—that led south five hundred miles to the Chilcoot Pass, Dyea, and salt water; and that led north seventy miles to Dawson, and still on to the north a thousand miles to Nulato, and finally to St. Michael on Bering Sea, a thousand miles and half a thousand more.

But all this—that mysterious, far-reaching hairline trail, the absence of sun from the sky, the tremendous cold, and the strangeness and weirdness of it all—made no impression on the man. It was not because he was long used to it. He was a newcomer in the land, a *chechaquo*, and this was his first winter. The trouble with him was that he was without imagination. He was quick and alert in the things of life, but only in the things, and not in the significances. Fifty degrees below zero meant eighty-odd degrees of frost. Such fact impressed him as being cold and uncomfortable, and that

was all. It did not lead him to
meditate upon his frailty as a creature of temperature, and upon man's
frailty in general, able only to live
within certain narrow limits of heat
and cold; and from there on it did
not lead him to the conjectural field
of immortality and man's place in
the universe. Fifty degrees below
zero stood for a bite of frost that
hurt and that must be guarded
against by the use of mittens, ear
flaps, warm moccasins, and thick
socks. Fifty degrees below zero was
to him just precisely fifty degrees
below zero. That there should be
anything more to it than that was a
thought that never entered his
head.

As he turned to go on, he spat
speculatively. There was a sharp,
explosive crackle that startled him.
He spat again. And again, in the
air, before it could fall to the
snow, the spittle crackled. He knew
that at fifty below spittle crackled
on the snow, but this spittle had
crackled in the air. Undoubtedly it
was colder than fifty below—how
much colder he did not know. But
the temperature did not matter. He
was bound for the old claim on the
left fork of Henderson Creek, where
the boys were already. They had
come over across the divide from
the Indian Creek country, while he
had come the roundabout way to
take a look at the possibilities of
getting out logs in the spring from
the islands in the Yukon. He would
be in to camp by six o'clock; a bit
after dark, it was true, but the
boys would be there, a fire would
be going, and a hot supper would
be ready. As for lunch, he pressed
his hand against the protruding
bundle under his jacket. It was also
under his shirt, wrapped up in a
handkerchief and lying against the
naked skin. It was the only way to
keep the biscuits from freezing. He
smiled agreeably to himself as he
thought of those biscuits, each cut
open and sopped in bacon grease,
and each enclosing a generous slice
of fried bacon.

He plunged in among the big
spruce trees. The trail was faint.
A foot of snow had fallen since
the last sled had passed over, and
he was glad he was without a sled,
traveling light. In fact, he carried
nothing but the lunch wrapped in
the handkerchief. He was surprised,
however, at the cold. It certainly
was cold, he concluded, as he
rubbed his numb nose and cheekbones with his mittened hand. He
was a warm-whiskered man, but the
hair on his face did not protect the
high cheekbones and the eager nose
that thrust itself aggressively into
the frosty air.

At the man's heels trotted a dog,
a big native husky, the proper wolf
dog, gray-coated and without any
visible or temperamental difference
from its brother, the wild wolf. The
animal was depressed by the tremendous cold. It knew that it was
no time for traveling. Its instinct
told it a truer tale than was told
to the man by the man's judgment.
In reality, it was not merely colder
than fifty below zero; it was colder
than sixty below, than seventy
below. It was seventy-five below
zero. Since the freezing point is
thirty-two above zero, it meant that
one hundred and seven degrees of
frost obtained. The dog did not
know anything about thermometers.
Possibly in its brain there was no
sharp consciousness of a condition
of very cold such as was in the
man's brain. But the brute had its
instinct. It experienced a vague but
menacing apprehension that sub-

dued it and made it slink along at the man's heels, and that made it question eagerly every unwonted movement of the man as if expecting him to go into camp or to seek shelter somewhere and build a fire. The dog had learned fire, and it wanted fire, or else to burrow under the snow and cuddle its warmth away from the air.

The frozen moisture of its breathing had settled on its fur in a fine powder of frost, and especially were its jowls, muzzle, and eyelashes whitened by its crystaled breath. The man's red beard and mustache were likewise frosted, but more solidly, the deposit taking the form of ice and increasing with every warm, moist breath he exhaled. Also, the man was chewing tobacco, and the muzzle of ice held his lips so rigidly that he was unable to clear his chin when he expelled the juice. The result was that a crystal beard of the color and solidity of amber was increasing its length on his chin. If he fell down it would shatter itself, like glass, into brittle fragments. But he did not mind the appendage. It was the penalty all tobacco chewers paid in that country, and he had been out before in two cold snaps. They had not been so cold as this, he knew, but by the spirit thermometer at Sixty Mile he knew they had been registered at fifty below and at fifty-five.

He held on through the level stretch of woods for several miles, crossed a wide flat of niggerheads, and dropped down a bank to the frozen bed of a small stream. This was Henderson Creek, and he knew he was ten miles from the forks. He looked at his watch. It was ten o'clock. He was making four miles an hour, and he calculated that he would arrive at the forks at half-past

twelve. He decided to celebrate that event by eating his lunch there.

The dog dropped in again at his heels, with a tail drooping discouragement, as the man swung along the creek bed. The furrow of the old sled trail was plainly visible, but a dozen inches of snow covered the marks of the last runners. In a month no man had come up or down that silent creek. The man held steadily on. He was not much given to thinking, and just then particularly he had nothing to think about save that he would eat lunch at the forks and that at six o'clock he would be in camp with the boys. There was nobody to talk to; and, had there been, speech would have been impossible because of the ice muzzle on his mouth. So he continued monotonously to chew tobacco and to increase the length of his amber beard.

Once in a while the thought reiterated itself that it was very cold and that he had never experienced such cold. As he walked along he rubbed his cheekbones and nose with the back of his mittened hand. He did this automatically, now and again changing hands. But rub as he would, the instant he stopped his cheekbones went numb, and the following instant the end of his nose went numb. He was sure to frost his cheeks; he knew that, and experienced a pang of regret that he had not devised a nose strap of the sort Bud wore in cold snaps. Such a strap passed across the cheeks, as well, and saved them. But it didn't matter much, after all. What were frosted cheeks? A bit painful, that was all; they were never serious.

Empty as a man's mind was of thoughts, he was keenly observant, and he noticed the changes in the creek, the curves and bends and timber jams, and always he sharply noted where he placed his feet. Once, coming around a bend, he shied abruptly, like a startled horse, curved away from the place where he had been walking, and retreated several paces back along the trail. The creek he knew was frozen clear to the bottom—no creek could contain water in that arctic winter—but he knew also that there were springs that bubbled out from the hillsides and ran along under the snow and on top the ice of the creek. He knew that the coldest snaps never froze these springs, and he knew likewise their danger. They were traps. They hid pools of water under the snow that might be three inches deep, or three feet. Sometimes a skin of ice half an inch thick covered them, and in turn was covered by the snow. Sometimes there were alternate layers of water and ice skin, so that when one broke through he kept on breaking through for a while, sometimes wetting himself to the waist.

That was why he had shied in such panic. He had felt the give under his feet and heard the crackle of a snow-hidden ice skin. And to get his feet wet in such a temperature meant trouble and danger. At the very least it meant delay, for he would be forced to stop and build a fire, and under its protection to bare his feet while he dried his socks and moccasins. He stood and studied the creek bed and its banks, and decided that the flow of water came from the right. He reflected awhile, rubbing his nose and cheeks, then skirted to the left, stepping gingerly and testing the footing for each step. Once clear of the danger, he took a fresh chew of

tobacco and swung along at his four-mile gait.

In the course of the next two hours he came upon several similar traps. Usually the snow above the hidden pools had a sunken, candied appearance that advertised the danger. Once again, however, he had a close call; and once, suspecting danger, he compelled the dog to go on in front. The dog did not want to go. It hung back until the man shoved it forward, and then it went quickly across the white, unbroken surface. Suddenly it broke through, floundered to one side, and got away to firmer footing. It had wet its forefeet and legs, and almost immediately the water that clung to it turned to ice. It made quick efforts to lick the ice off its legs, then dropped down in the snow and began to bite out the ice that had formed between the toes. This was a matter of instinct. To permit the ice to remain would mean sore feet. It did not know this. It merely obeyed the mysterious prompting that arose from the deep crypts of its being. But the man knew, having achieved a judgment on the subject, and he removed the mitten from his right hand and helped tear out the ice-particles. He did not expose his fingers more than a minute, and was astonished at the swift numbness that smote them. It certainly was cold. He pulled on the mitten hastily, and beat the hand savagely across his chest.

At twelve o'clock the day was at its brightest. Yet the sun was too far south on its winter journey to clear the horizon. The bulge of the earth intervened between it and Henderson Creek, where the man walked under a clear sky at noon and cast no shadow. At half-past twelve, to the minute, he arrived at the forks of the creek. He was pleased at the speed he had made. If he kept it up, he would certainly be with the boys by six. He unbuttoned his jacket and shirt and drew forth his lunch. The action consumed no more than a quarter of a minute, yet in that brief moment the numbness laid hold of the exposed fingers. He did not put the mitten on, but, instead, struck the fingers a dozen sharp smashes against his leg. Then he sat down on a snow-covered log to eat. The sting that followed upon the striking of his fingers against his leg ceased so quickly that he was startled. He had had no chance to take a bite of biscuit. He struck the fingers repeatedly and returned them to the mitten, baring the other hand for the purpose of eating. He tried to take a mouthful, but the ice muzzle prevented. He had forgotten to build a fire and thaw out. He chuckled at his foolishness, and as he chuckled he noted the numbness creeping into the exposed fingers. Also, he noted that the stinging which had first come to his toes when he sat down was already passing away. He wondered whether the toes were warm or numb. He moved them inside the moccasins and decided that they were numb.

He pulled the mitten on hurriedly and stood up. He was a bit frightened. He stamped up and down until the stinging returned into the feet. It certainly was cold, was his thought. That man from Sulphur Creek had spoken the truth when telling how cold it sometimes got in the country. And he had laughed at him at the time! That showed one must not be too sure of things. There was no mistake about it, it *was* cold. He strode up and down, stamping his feet and threshing his arms, until reassured by the returning warmth. Then he got out matches and proceeded to make a fire. From the undergrowth, where high water of the previous spring had lodged a supply of seasoned twigs, he got his firewood. Working carefully from a small beginning, he soon had a roaring fire, over which he thawed the ice from his face and in the protection of which he ate his biscuits. For the moment the cold of space was outwitted. The dog took satisfaction in the fire, stretching out close enough for warmth and far enough away to escape being singed.

When the man had finished, he filled his pipe and took his comfortable time over a smoke. Then he pulled on his mittens, settled the earflaps of his cap firmly about his ears, and took the creek trail up the left fork. The dog was disappointed and yearned back toward the fire. This man did not know cold. Possibly all the generations of his ancestry had been ignorant of cold, of real cold, of cold one hundred and seven degrees below freezing point. But the dog knew; all its ancestry knew, and it had inherited the knowledge. And it knew that it was not good to walk abroad in such fearful cold. It was the time to lie snug in a hole in the snow and wait for a curtain of cloud to be drawn across the face of outer space whence this cold came. On the other hand, there was no keen intimacy between the dog and the man. The one was the toil slave of the other, and the only caresses it had ever received were the caresses of the whiplash and of harsh and menac- effort to communicate its apprehen- ing throat sounds that threatened the whiplash. So the dog made no

sion to the man. It was not concerned in the welfare of the man;
it was for its own sake that it
yearned back toward the fire. But
the man whistled, and spoke to it
with the sound of whiplashes, and
the dog swung in at the man's heels
and followed after.

The man took a chew of tobacco
and proceeded to start a new amber
beard. Also, his moist breath quickly
powdered with white his mustache,
eyebrows, and lashes. There did
not seem to be so many springs on
the left fork of the Henderson, and
for half an hour the man saw no
signs of any. And then it happened.
At a place where there were no
signs, where the soft, unbroken
snow seemed to advertise solidity
beneath, the man broke through. It
was not deep. He wet himself halfway to the knees before he
floundered out to the firm crust.

He was angry, and cursed his
luck aloud. He had hoped to get
into camp with the boys at six
o'clock, and this would delay him an
hour, for he would have to build
a fire and dry out his footgear. This
was imperative at that low temperature—he knew that much; and he
turned aside to the bank, which he
climbed. On top, tangled in the un-
derbrush about the trunks of several
small spruce trees, was a high-
water deposit of dry firewood—
sticks and twigs, principally, but
also larger portions of seasoned
branches and fine, dry, last year's
grasses. He threw down several
large pieces on top of the snow.
This served for a foundation and
prevented the young flame from
drowning itself in the snow it otherwise would melt. The flame he got
by touching a match to a small
shred of birch bark that he took
from his pocket. This burned even

more readily than paper. Placing it
on the foundation, he fed the young
flame, with wisps of dry grass
and with the tiniest dry twigs.

He worked slowly and carefully,
keenly aware of his danger. Gradually, as the flame grew stronger,
he increased the size of the twigs
with which he fed it. He squatted in
the snow, pulling the twigs out from
their entanglement in the brush and
feeding directly to the flame. He
know there must be no failure.
When it is seventy-five below zero,
a man must not fail in his first attempt to build a fire—that is, if
his feet are wet. If his feet are dry,
and he fails, he can run along the
trail for a half a mile and restore
his circulation. But the circulation of
wet and freezing feet cannot be restored by running when it is seventy-
five below. No matter how fast he
runs, the wet feet will freeze the
harder.

All this the man knew. The old-
timer on Sulphur Creek had told
him about it the previous fall, and
now he was appreciating the advice.
Already all sensation had gone out
of his feet. To build the fire he had
been forced to remove his mittens, and the fingers had quickly
gone numb. His pace of four miles
an hour had kept his heart pump-
ing blood to the surface of his body
and to all the extremities. But the
instant he stopped, the action of
the pump eased down. The cold
of space smote the unprotected tip
of the planet, and he, being on that
unprotected tip, received the full
force of the blow. The blood of his
body recoiled before it. The blood
was alive, like the dog, and like the
dog it wanted to hide away and
cover itself up from the fearful
cold. So long as he walked four
miles an hour, he pumped that

blood, willy-nilly, to the surface; but now it ebbed away and sank down into the recesses of his body. The extremities were the first to feel its absence. His wet feet froze the faster, and his exposed fingers numbed the faster, though they had not yet begun to freeze. Nose and cheeks were already freezing, while the skin of all his body chilled as it lost its blood.

But he was safe. Toes and nose and cheeks would be only touched by the frost, for the fire was beginning to burn with strength. He was feeding it with twigs the size of his finger. In another minute he would be able to feed it with branches the size of his wrist, and then he could remove his wet footgear, and, while it dried, he could keep his naked feet warm by the fire, rubbing them at first, of course, with snow. The fire was a success. He was safe. He remembered the advice of the old-timer on Sulphur Creek, and smiled. The old-timer had been very serious in laying down the law that no man must travel alone in the Klondike after fifty below. Well, there he was; he had had the accident; he was alone; and he had saved himself. Those old-timers were rather womanish, some of them, he thought. All a man had to do was to keep his head, and he was all right. Any man who was a man could travel alone. But it was surprising, the rapidity with which his cheeks and nose were freezing. And he had not thought his fingers could go lifeless in so short a time. Lifeless they were, for he could scarcely make them move together to grip a twig, and they seemed remote from his body and from him. When he touched a twig, he had to look and see whether or not he had hold of it. The wires were pretty well down between him and his finger ends.

All of which counted for little. There was the fire, snapping and crackling and promising life with every dancing flame. He started to untie his moccasins. They were coated with ice; the thick German socks were like sheaths of iron halfway to the knees; and the moccasin strings were like rods of steel all twisted and knotted as by some conflagration. For moment he tugged with his numb fingers, then, realizing the folly of it, he drew his sheath knife.

But before he could cut the strings, it happened. It was his own fault or, rather, his mistake. He should not have built the fire under the spruce tree. He should have built it in the open. But it had been easier to pull the twigs from the brush and drop them directly on the fire. Now the tree under which he had done this carried a weight of snow on its boughs. No wind had blown for weeks, and each bough was fully freighted. Each time he had pulled a twig he had communicated a slight agitation to the tree—an imperceptible agitation, so far as he was concerned, but an agitation sufficient to bring about the disaster. High up in the tree one bough capsized its load of snow. This fell on the boughs beneath, capsizing them. This process continued, spreading out and involving the whole tree. It grew like an avalanche, and it descended without warning upon the man and the fire, and the fire was blotted out! Where it had burned was a mantle of fresh and disordered snow.

The man was shocked. It was as though he had just heard his own sentence of death. For a moment he sat and stared at the spot where the fire had been. Then he grew very calm. Perhaps the old-timer on Sulphur Creek was right. If he had only had a trail mate he would have been in no danger now. The trail mate could have built the fire. Well, it was up to him to build the fire over again, and this second time there must be no failure. Even if he succeeded, he would most likely lose some toes. His feet must be badly frozen by now, and there would be some time before the second fire was ready.

Such were his thoughts, but he did not sit and think them. He was busy all the time they were passing through his mind. He made a new foundation for a fire, this time in the open, where no treacherous tree could blot it out. Next, he gathered dry grasses and tiny twigs from the high-water flotsam. He could not bring his fingers together to pull them out, but he was able to gather them by the handful. In this way he got many rotten twigs and bits of green moss that were undesirable, but it was the best he could do. He worked methodically, even collecting an armful of the larger branches to be used later when the fire gathered strength. And all the while the dog sat and watched him, a certain yearning wistfulness in its eyes, for it looked upon him as the fire provider, and the fire was slow in coming.

When all was ready, the man reached in his pocket for a second piece of birch bark. He knew the bark was there, and, though he could not feel it with his fingers, he could hear its crisp rustling as he fumbled for it. Try as he would, he could not clutch hold of it. And all the time, in his consciousness, was the knowledge that each instant his feet were freezing. This thought tended to put him in a panic, but he fought against it and kept calm. He pulled on his mittens with his teeth, and threshed his arms back and forth, beating his hands with all his might against his sides. He did this sitting down, and he stood up to do it; and all the while the dog sat in the snow, its wolf brush of a tail curled around warmly over its forefeet, its sharp wolf ears pricked forward intently as it watched the man. And the man, as he beat and threshed with his arms and hands, felt a great surge of envy as he regarded the creature that was warm and secure in its natural covering.

After a time he was aware of the first faraway signals of sensation in his beaten fingers. The faint tingling grew stronger till it evolved into a stinging ache that was excruciating, but which the man hailed with satisfaction. He stripped the mitten from his right hand and fetched forth the birch bark. The exposed fingers were quickly going numb again. Next he brought out his bunch of sulphur matches. But the tremendous cold had already driven the life out of his fingers. In his effort to separate one match from the others, the whole bunch fell in the snow. He tried to pick it out of the snow, but failed. The dead fingers could neither touch nor clutch. He was very careful. He drove the thought of his freezing feet, and nose, and cheeks, out of his mind, devoting his whole soul to the matches. He watched, using the sense of vision in place of that of touch, and when he saw his fingers on each side the bunch, he closed them—that is, he willed to close them, for the wires were down, and the fingers did not obey. He pulled the mitten on the right hand, and beat it fiercely against his knee. Then, with both mittened hands, he scooped the bunch of matches, along with much snow, into his lap. Yet he was no better off.

After some manipulation he managed to get the bunch between the heels of his mittened hands. In this fashion he carried it to his mouth. The ice crackled and snapped when by a violent effort he opened his mouth. He drew the lower jaw in, curled the upper lip out of the way, and scraped the bunch with his upper teeth in order to separate a match. He succeeded in getting one, which he dropped on his lap. He was no better off. He could not pick it up. Then he devised a way. He picked it up in his teeth and scratched it on his leg. Twenty times he scratched before he succeeded in lighting it. As it flamed he held it with his teeth to the birch bark. But the burning brimstone went up his nostrils and into his lungs, causing him to cough spasmodically. The match fell into the snow and went out.

The old-timer on Sulphur Creek was right, he thought in the moment of controlled despair that ensued: after fifty below, a man should travel with a partner. He beat his hands, but failed in exciting any sensation. Suddenly he bared both hands, removing the mittens with his teeth. He caught the whole bunch between the heels of his hands. His arm muscles not being frozen enabled him to press the hand heels tightly against the matches. Then he scratched the bunch along his leg. It flared into flame, seventy sulphur matches at once! There was no wind to blow them out. He kept his head to one side to escape the strangling fumes, and held the blazing bunch to the

birch bark. As he so held it, he became aware of sensation in his hand. His flesh was burning. He could smell it. Deep down below the surface he could feel it. The sensation developed into pain that grew acute. And still he endured it, holding the flame of the matches clumsily to the bark that would not light readily because his own burning hands were in the way, absorbing most of the flame.

At last, when he could endure no more, he jerked his hands apart. The blazing matches fell sizzling into the snow, but the birch bark was alight. He began laying dry grasses and the tiniest twigs on the flame. He could not pick and choose, for he had to lift the fuel between the heels of his hands. Small pieces of rotten wood and green moss clung to the twigs, and he bit them off as well as he could with his teeth. He cherished the flame carefully and awkwardly. It meant life, and it must not perish. The withdrawal of blood from the surface of his body now made him begin to shiver, and he grew more awkward. A large piece of green moss fell squarely on the little fire. He tried to poke it out with his fingers, but his shivering frame make him poke too far, and he disrupted the nucleus of the little fire, the burning grasses and tiny twigs separating and scattering. He tried to poke them together again, but in spite of the tenseness of the effort, his shivering got away with him, and the twigs were hopelessly scattered. Each twig gushed a puff of smoke and went out. The fire provider had failed. As he looked apathetically about him, his eyes chanced on the dog, sitting across the ruins of the fire from him, in the snow, making restless, hunching movements, slightly lifting one forefoot and then the other, shifting its weight back and forth on them with wistful eagerness.

The sight of the dog put a wild idea into his head. He remembered the tale of the man, caught in a blizzard, who killed a steer and crawled inside the carcass, and so was saved. He would kill the dog and bury his hands in the warm body until the numbness went out of them. Then he could build another fire. He spoke to the dog, calling it to him; but in his voice was a strange note of fear that frightened the animal, who had never known the man to speak in such way before. Something was the matter, and its suspicious nature sensed danger—it knew not what danger, but somewhere, somehow, in its brain arose an apprehension of the man. It flattened its ears down at the sound of the man's voice, and its restless, hunching movements and the liftings and shiftings of its forefeet became more pronounced; but it would not come to the man. He got on his hands and knees and crawled toward the dog. This unusual posture again excited suspicion, and the animal sidled mincingly away.

The man sat up in the snow for a moment and struggled for calmness. Then he pulled on his mittens, by means of his teeth, and got upon his feet. He glanced down at first in order to assure himself that he was really standing up, for the absence of sensation in his feet left him unrelated to the earth. His erect position in itself started to drive the webs of suspicion from the dog's mind; and when he spoke peremptorily, with the sound of whiplashes in his voice, the dog rendered its customary allegiance and came to him. As it came within reaching distance, the man lost his control. His arms flashed out to the dog, and he experienced genuine surprise when he discovered that his hands could not clutch, that there was neither bend nor feeling in the fingers. He had forgotten for the moment that they were frozen and that they were freezing more and more. All this happened quickly, and before the animal could get away, he encircled its body with his arms. He sat down in the snow, and in this fashion held the dog, while it snarled and whined and struggled.

But it was all he could do, hold its body encircled in his arms and sit there. He realized that he could not kill the dog. There was no way to do it. With his helpless hands he could neither draw nor hold his sheath knife nor throttle the animal. He released it, and it plunged wildly away, with tail between its legs, and still snarling. It halted forty feet away and surveyed him curiously, with ears sharply pricked forward. The man looked down at his hands in order to locate them, and found them hanging on the ends of his arms. It struck him as curious that one should have to use his eyes in order to find out where his hands were. He began threshing his arms back and forth, beating the mittened hands against his sides. He did this for five minutes, violently, and his heart pumped enough blood up to the surface to put a stop to his shivering. But no sensation was aroused in the hands. He had an impression that they hung like weights on the ends of his arms, but when he tried to run the impression down, he could not find it.

A certain fear of death, dull and oppressive, came to him. This fear quickly became poignant as he realized that it was no longer a mere matter of freezing his fingers and toes, or of losing his hands and feet, but that it was a matter of life and death with the chances against him. This threw him into a panic, and he turned and ran up the creek bed along the old, dim trail. The dog joined in behind and kept up with him. He ran blindly, without intention, in fear such as he had never known in his life. Slowly, as he plowed and floundered through the snow, he began to see things again—the banks of the creek, the old timber jams, the leafless aspens, and the sky. The running made him feel better. He did not shiver. Maybe, if he ran on, his feet would thaw out; and, anyway, if he ran far enough, he would reach camp and the boys. Without doubt he would lose some fingers and toes and some of his face; but the boys would take care of him, and save the rest of him when he got there. And at the same time there was another thought in his mind that said he would never get to the camp and the boys; that it was too many miles away, that the freezing had too great a start on him, and that he would soon be stiff and dead. This thought he kept in the background and refused to consider. Sometimes it pushed itself forward and demanded to be heard, but he thrust it back and strove to think of other things.

It struck him as curious that he could run at all on feet so frozen that he could not feel them when they struck the earth and took the weight of his body. He seemed to himself to skim along above the surface, and to have no connection with the earth. Somewhere he had once seen a winged Mercury, and he wondered if Mercury felt as he felt when skimming over the earth.

His theory of running until he reached camp and the boys had one flaw in it: he lacked the endurance. Several times he stumbled, and finally he tottered, crumpled up, and fell. When he tried to rise, he failed. He must sit and rest, he decided, and next time he would merely walk and keep on going. As he sat and regained his breath, he noted that he was feeling quite warm and comfortable. He was not shivering, and it even seemed that a warm glow had come to his chest and trunk. And yet, when he touched his nose or cheeks, there was no sensation. Running would not thaw them out. Nor would it thaw out his hands and feet. Then the thought came to him that the frozen portions of his body must be extending. He tried to keep this thought down, to forget it, to think of something else; he was aware of the panicky feeling that it caused, and he was afraid of the panic. But the thought asserted itself, and persisted, until it produced a vision of his body totally frozen. This was too much, and he made another wild run along the trail. Once he slowed down to a walk, but the thought of the freezing extending itself made him run again.

And all the time the dog ran with him, at his heels. When he fell down a second time, it curled its tail over its forefeet and sat in front of him, facing him, curiously eager and intent. The warmth and security of the animal angered him, and he cursed it till it flattened down its ears appeasingly. This time the shivering came more quickly upon the man. He was losing in his battle with the frost. It was creeping into his body from all sides. The thought of it drove him on, but he ran no more than a hundred feet, when he staggered and pitched headlong. It was his last panic. When he had recovered his breath and control, he sat up and entertained in his mind the conception of meeting death with dignity. However, the conception did not come to him in such terms. His idea of it was that he had been making a fool of himself, running around like a chicken with its head cut off—such was the simile that occurred to him. Well, he was bound to freeze anyway, and he might as well take it decently. With this new-found peace of mind came the first glimmerings of drowsiness. A good idea, he thought, to sleep off to death. It was like taking an anesthetic. Freezing was not so bad as people thought. There were lots worse ways to die.

He pictured the boys finding his body next day. Suddenly he found himself with them, coming along the trail and looking for himself. And, still with them, he came around a turn in the trail and found himself lying in the snow. He did not belong with himself any more, for even then he was out of himself, standing with the boys and looking at himself in the snow. It certainly was cold, was his thought. When he got back to the States he could tell the folks what real cold was. He drifted on from this to a vision of the old-timer on Sulphur Creek. He could see him quite clearly, warm and comfortable, and smoking a pipe.

"You were right, old hoss; you were right," the man mumbled to the old-timer of Sulphur Creek.

Then the man drowsed off into what seemed to him the most comfortable and satisfying sleep he had ever known. The dog sat facing him and waiting. The brief day drew to a close in a long, slow twilight. There were no signs of a fire to be made, and, besides, never in the dog's experience had it known a man to sit like that in the snow and make no fire. As the twilight drew on, its eager yearning for the fire mastered it, and with a great lifting and shifting of forefeet, it whined softly, then flattened its ears down in anticipation of being chidden by the man. But the man remained silent. Later, the dog whined loudly. And still later it crept close to the man and caught the scent of death. This made the animal bristle and back away. A little longer it delayed, howling under the stars that leaped and danced and shone brightly in the cold sky. Then it turned and trotted up the trail in the direction of the camp it knew, where were the other food providers and fire providers.

O. Henry
1862-1910

THE short-short story with the twist at the end—anathema
to present-day serious writers and a disastrous influence on a
whole generation of story writers, but immensely popular in its
day—is the O. Henry formula. The first stories under the
name of O. Henry were written in the Ohio penitentiary,
where for three years William Sydney Porter was an inmate.
Whether or not he was guilty of the crime of embezzlement
of bank funds for which he was sentenced has never been
entirely clear. He had, however, taken the law into his own
hands: he evaded his trial by running away, and spent a year
traveling about Mexico and Central America with a notorious
outlaw, Al Jennings, living on the proceeds of Jennings'
$30,000 robbery. After his prison term he became staff short-
story writer on the New York *World*, where in thirty
months he wrote one hundred and thirteen stories. He
was allowed only one page to a story, hence the functional
origin of the "short-short" of 2500 words. There was always
a deadline to meet, always an editor on his back who had
given him an advance, and through it all he is said to have
consumed two quarts of whisky a day. He died of tuberculosis at forty-eight, with an output of six hundred pieces of
fiction to his credit. His funeral service was held at the
Little Church Around the Corner, in New York, at the same
time a wedding was being performed.

Though born in North Carolina, O. Henry loved the byways, back alleys, and humor of the New York streets. His
figures still sit on the benches of Madison Square and weave
their way down the Bowery.

The Coming-Out of Maggie

BY O. HENRY

Every Saturday night the Clover Leaf Social Club gave a hop in the hall of the Give and Take Athletic Association on the East Side. In order to attend one of these dances you must be a member of the Give and Take—or, if you belong to the division that starts off with the right foot in waltzing, you must work in Rhinegold's paper-box factory. Still, any Clover Leaf was privileged to escort or be escorted by an outsider to a single dance. But mostly each Give and Take brought the paper-box girl that he affected; and few strangers could boast of having shaken a foot at the regular hops.

Maggie Toole, on account of her dull eyes, broad mouth, and left-handed style of footwork in the two-step, went to the dances with Anna McCarty and her "fellow." Anna and Maggie worked side by side in the factory, and were the greatest chums ever. So Anna always made Jimmy Burns take her by Maggie's house every Saturday night so that her friend could go to the dance with them.

The Give and Take Athletic Association lived up to its name. The hall of the Association in Orchard Street was fitted out with muscle-making inventions. With the fibers thus builded up the members were wont to engage the police and rival social and athletic organizations in joyous combat. Between these more serious occupations the Saturday night hops with the paper-box factory girls came as a refining influence and as an efficient screen. For sometimes the tip went round, and if you were among the elect that tiptoed up the dark back stairway you might see as neat and satisfying a little welter-weight affair to a finish as ever happened inside the ropes.

On Saturdays Rhinegold's paper-box factory closed at 3 P. M. On one such afternoon Anna and Maggie walked homeward together. At Maggie's door Anna said, as usual: "Be ready at seven, sharp, Mag; and Jimmy and me'll come by for you."

But what was this? Instead of the customary humble and grateful thanks from the nonescorted one there was to be perceived a high-poised head, a prideful dimpling at the corners of a broad mouth, and almost a sparkle in a dull brown eye.

"Thanks, Anna," said Maggie; "but you and Jimmy needn't bother tonight. I've a gentleman friend that's coming round to escort me to the hop."

The comely Anna pounced upon her friend, shook her, chided and beseeched her. Maggie Toole catch a fellow! Plain, dear, loyal, unattractive Maggie, so sweet as a chum, so unsought for a two-step or a moonlit bench in the little park. How was it? When did it happen? Who was it?

"You'll see tonight," said Maggie, flushed with the wine of the first grapes she had gathered in Cupid's vineyard. "He's swell all right. He's two inches taller than Jimmy, and an up-to-date dresser. I'll introduce him, Anna, just as soon as we get to the hall."

Anna and Jimmy were among the first Clover Leafs to arrive that evening. Anna's eyes were brightly fixed upon the door of the hall to catch the first glimpse of her friend's "catch."

At 8:30 Miss Toole swept into the hall with her escort. Quickly her triumphant eye discovered her chum under the wing of her faithful Jimmy.

"Oh, gee!" cried Anna, "Mag ain't made a hit—oh, no! Swell fellow? well, I guess! Style? Look at 'um."

"Go as far as you like," said Jimmy, with sandpaper in his voice. "Cop him out if you want him. These new guys always win out with the push. Don't mind me. He don't squeeze all the limes, I guess. Huh!"

"Shut up, Jimmy. You know what I mean. I'm glad for Mag. First fellow she ever had. Oh, here they come."

Across the floor Maggie sailed like a coquettish yacht convoyed by a stately cruiser. And truly, her companion justified the encomiums of the faithful chum. He stood two inches taller than the average Give and Take athlete; his dark hair curled; his eyes and his teeth flashed whenever he bestowed his frequent smiles. The young men of the Clover Leaf Club pinned not their faith to the graces of person as much as they did to its prowess, its achievements in hand-to-hand conflicts, and its preservation from the legal duress that constantly menaced it. The member of the association who would bind a paper-box maiden to his conquering chariot scorned to employ Beau Brummell airs. They were not considered honorable methods of warfare. The swelling biceps, the coat straining at its buttons over the chest, the air of conscious conviction of the supereminence of the male in the cosmogony of creation, even a calm display of bow legs as subduing and enchanting agents in the gentle tourneys of Cupid—these were the approved arms and ammunition of the Clover Leaf gallants. They viewed, then, the genuflexions and alluring poses of this visitor with their chins at a new angle.

"A friend of mine, Mr. Terry O'Sullivan," was Maggie's formula of introduction. She led him around the room, presenting him to each new-arriving Clover Leaf. Almost was she pretty now, with the unique luminosity in her eyes that comes to a girl with her first suitor and a kitten with its first mouse.

"Maggie Toole's got a fellow at last," was the word that went round among the paper-box girls. "Pipe Mag's floorwalker"—thus the Give and Take expressed their indifferent contempt.

Usually at the weekly hops Maggie kept a spot on the wall warm with her back. She felt and showed so much gratitude whenever a self-sacrificing partner invited her to dance that his pleasure was cheapened and diminished. She had even grown used to noticing Anna joggle the reluctant Jimmy with her elbow as a signal for him to invite her chum to walk over his feet through a two-step.

But tonight the pumpkin had turned to a coach and six. Terry O'Sullivan was a victorious Prince Charming, and Maggie Toole winged her first butterfly flight. And though our tropes of fairyland be mixed with those of entomology they shall not spill one drop of ambrosia from the rose-crowned melody of Maggie's one perfect night.

The girls besieged her for introductions to her "fellow." The Clover Leaf young men, after two years of blindness, suddenly perceived charms in Miss Toole. They flexed their compelling muscles before her and bespoke her for the dance.

Thus she scored; but to Terry O'Sullivan the honors of the evening fell thick and fast. He shook his curls; he smiled and went easily through the seven motions for acquiring grace in your own room before an open window ten minutes each day. He danced like a faun; he introduced manner and style and atmosphere; his words came trippingly upon his tongue, and—he waltzed twice in succession with the paper-box girl that Dempsey Donovan brought.

Dempsey was the leader of the association. He wore a dress suit, and could chin the bar twice with one hand. He was one of "Big Mike" O'Sullivan's lieutenants, and was never troubled by trouble. No cop dared to arrest him. Whenever he broke a pushcart man's head or shot a member of the Heinrick B. Sweeney Outing and Literary Asso-

ciation in the kneecap, an officer would drop around and say:

"The Cap'n'd like to see ye a few minutes round to the office whin ye have time, Dempsey, me boy."

But there would be sundry gentlemen there with large gold fob chains and black cigars; and somebody would tell a funny story, and then Dempsey would go back and work half an hour with the six-pound dumbbells. So, doing a tight-rope act on a wire stretched across Niagara was a safe terpsichorean performance compared with waltzing twice with Dempsey Donovan's paper-box girl. At 10 o'clock the jolly round face of "Big Mike" O'Sullivan shone at the door for five minutes upon the scene. He always looked in for five minutes, smiled at the girls, and handed out real perfectos to the delighted boys.

Dempsey Donovan was at his elbow instantly, talking rapidly. "Big Mike" looked carefully at the dancers, smiled, shook his head and departed.

The music stopped. The dancers scattered to the chairs along the walls. Terry O'Sullivan, with his entrancing bow, relinquished a pretty girl in blue to her partner, and started back to find Maggie. Dempsey intercepted him in the middle of the floor.

Some fine instinct that Rome must have bequeathed to us caused nearly everyone to turn and look at them —there was a subtle feeling that two gladiators had met in the arena. Two or three Give and Takes with tight coat sleeves drew nearer.

"One moment, Mr. O'Sullivan," said Dempsey. "I hope you're enjoying yourself. Where did you say you lived?"

The two gladiators were well matched. Dempsey had, perhaps,

ten pounds of weight to give away. The O'Sullivan had breadth with quickness. Dempsey had a glacial eye, a dominating slit of a mouth, an indestructible jaw, a complexion like a belle's, and the coolness of a champion. The visitor showed more fire in his contempt and less control over his conspicuous sneer. They were enemies by the law written when the rocks were molten. They were each too splendid, too nighty, too incomparable to divide pre-eminence. One only must survive.

"I live on Grand," said O'Sullivan, insolently; "and no trouble to find me at home. Where do you live?"

Dempsey ignored the question.

"You say your name's O'Sullivan," he went on. "Well, 'Big Mike' says he never saw you before."

"Lots of things he never saw," said the favorite of the hop.

"As a rule," went on Dempsey, huskily sweet, "O'Sullivans in this district know one another. You escorted one of our lady members here, and we want a chance to make good. If you've got a family tree let's see a few historical O'Sullivan buds come out on it. Or do you want us to dig it out of you by the roots?"

"Suppose you mind your own business," suggested O'Sullivan, blandly.

Dempsey's eye brightened. He held up an inspired forefinger as though a brilliant idea had struck him.

"I've got it now," he said cordially. "It was just a little mistake. You ain't no O'Sullivan. You are a ringtailed monkey. Excuse us for not recognizing you at first."

O'Sullivan's eye flashed. He made a quick movement, but Andy Geoghan was ready and caught his arm.

Dempsey nodded at Andy and William McMahan, the secretary of the club, and walked rapidly toward a door at the rear of the hall. Two other members of the Give and Take Association swiftly joined the little group. Terry O'Sullivan was now in the hands of the Board of Rules and Social Referees. They spoke to him briefly and softly, and conducted him out through the same door at the rear.

This movement on the part of the Clover Leaf members requires a word of elucidation. Back of the association hall was a smaller room rented by the club. In this room personal difficulties that arose on the ballroom floor were settled, man to man, with the weapons of nature, under the supervision of the board. No lady could say that she had witnessed a fight at a Clover Leaf hop in several years. Its gentlemen members guaranteed that.

So easily and smoothly had Dempsey and the board done their preliminary work that many in the hall had not noticed the checking of the fascinating O'Sullivan's social triumph. Among these was Maggie. She looked about for her escort.

"Smoke up!" said Rose Cassidy. "Wasn't you on? Demps Donovan picked a scrap with your Lizzie-boy, and they've waltzed out to the slaughter room with him. How's my hair look done up this way, Mag?"

Maggie laid a hand on the bosom of her cheesecloth waist.

"Gone to fight with Dempsey!" she said, breathlessly. "They've got to be stopped. Dempsey Donovan can't fight him. Why, he'll—he'll kill him!"

"Ah, what do you care?" said Rose. "Don't some of 'em fight every hop?"

But Maggie was off, darting her

zigzag way through the maze of dancers. She burst through the rear door into the dark hall and then threw her solid shoulder against the door of the room of single combat. It gave way, and in the instant that she entered her eye caught the scene —the board standing about with open watches; Dempsey Donovan in his shirt sleeves dancing, light-footed, with the wary grace of the modern pugilist, within easy reach of his adversary; Terry O'Sullivan standing with arms folded and a murderous look in his dark eyes. And without slacking the speed of her entrance she leaped forward with a scream—leaped in time to catch and hang upon the arm of O'Sullivan that was suddenly up-lifted, and to whisk from it the long, bright stiletto that he had drawn from his bosom.

The knife fell and rang upon the floor. Cold steel drawn in the rooms of the Give and Take Association! Such a thing had never happened before. Everyone stood motionless for a minute. Andy Geoghan kicked the stiletto with the toe of his shoe curiously, like an antiquarian who has come upon some ancient weapon unknown to his learning.

And then O'Sullivan hissed something unintelligible between his teeth. Dempsey and the board exchanged looks. And then Dempsey looked at O'Sullivan without anger, as one looks at a stray dog, and nodded his head in the direction of the door.

"The back stairs, Giuseppi," he said, briefly. "Somebody'll pitch your hat down after you."

Maggie walked up to Dempsey Donovan. There was a brilliant spot of red in her cheeks, down which slow tears were running. But she looked him bravely in the eye.

"I knew it, Dempsey," she said, and her eyes grew dull even in their tears. "I knew he was a Guinea. His name's Tony Spinelli. I hurried in when they told me you and him was scrappin'. Them Guineas always carries knives. But you don't understand, Dempsey. I never had a fellow in my life. I got tired of comin' with Anna and Jimmy every night, so I fixed it with him to call himself O'Sullivan, and brought him along. I knew there'd be nothin' doin' for him if he came as a Dago. I guess I'll resign from the club now."

Dempsey turned to Andy Geoghan.

"Chuck that cheese slicer out of the window," he said, "and tell 'em inside that Mr. O'Sullivan has had a telephone message to go down to Tammany Hall."

And then he turned back to Maggie.

"Say, Mag," he said, "I'll see you home. And how about next Saturday night? Will you come to the hop with me if I call around for you?"

It was remarkable how quickly Maggie's eyes could change from dull to a shining brown.

"With you, Dempsey?" she stammered. "Say—will a duck swim?"

Henry James
1843-1916

WHEN Henry James left Turgenev's house one rainy afternoon, he jumped over gutters in his excitement. He had met
Flaubert, Zola, and Daudet. In the course of that year he was
to meet them often in large friendly gatherings, and the
impression on the young American writer was deep and
lasting. It was after this period in Paris that James moved
to Europe for good, making his home in England and, like
his French masters, consecrating his life to art. He did not
marry. He seems to have had no romance in his life and no
drama—except a consuming passion for his work, which was
for so many years unrewarded by the general reading public.

Although one of his early novels, *Daisy Miller*, gave him
a certain amount of popularity, James never for a writing
moment let public taste and inclination affect him. In fact,
the continued mild approval of that early book, after he had
reached the magnificent period of *The Wings of the Dove*
and *The Golden Bowl*, made him despair of intelligent comprehension. At forty he wrote in his notebook: "I must make
some great efforts during the next few years, if I wish not
to have been a failure. I shall have been a failure unless I do
something *great*." For thirty years he persisted in his gigantic
task, publishing from one to three volumes every year, with
diminishing success. Yet today critics acclaim him as perhaps
our foremost American novelist.

Intimately familiar with three nationalities, James liked to
write about the interplay of race and class, particularly of
Americans in relation to European society. His is a leisurely
world where there is no need for concern with practical matters, whose people have fine consciences and are preoccupied
with problems of ethical conduct. His intricate analysis of
their psychological processes makes James' novels move
slowly, while, by the same virtue, the gradual revelation of
motive makes them intensely dramatic.

As to his short stories, Ludwig Lewisohn says, "The real
lover of fiction will return to his tales again and again, and,
no matter how many years or what experiences have intervened, will find them full and flawless. The intention of each
is carried out. . . . Each has the high tranquillity of tone that
belongs to the completely achieved work of art."

The Altar of the Dead

BY HENRY JAMES

I

HE HAD a mortal dislike, poor Stransom, to lean anniversaries, and loved them still less when they made a pretense of a figure. Celebrations and suppressions were equally painful to him, and but one of the former found a place in his life. He had kept each year in his own fashion the date of Mary Antrim's death. It would be more to the point perhaps to say that this occasion kept *him*: it kept him at least effectually from doing anything else. It took hold of him again and again with a hand of which time had softened but never loosened the touch. He waked to his feast of memory as consciously as he would have waked to his marriage morn. Marriage had had of old but too little to say to the matter: for the girl who was to have been his bride there had been no bridal embrace. She had died of a malignant fever after the wedding day had been fixed, and he had lost before fairly tasting it an affection that promised to fill his life to the brim.

Of that benediction, however, it would have been false to say this life could really be emptied: it was still ruled by a pale ghost, still ordered by a sovereign presence. He had not been a man of numerous passions, and even in all these years no sense had grown stronger with him than the sense of being bereft. He had needed no priest and no altar to make him forever widowed. He had done many things in the world—he had done almost all but one: he had never, never forgotten. He had tried to put into his existence whatever else might take up room in it, but had failed to make it more than a house of which the mistress was eternally absent. She was most absent of all on the recurrent December day that his tenacity set apart. He had no arranged observance of it, but his nerves made it all their own. They drove him forth without mercy, and the goal of his pilgrimage was far. She had been buried in a London suburb, a part then of Nature's breast, but which he had seen lose one after another every feature of freshness. It was in truth during the moments he stood there that his eyes beheld the place least. They looked at another image, they opened to another light. Was it a credible future? Was it an incredible past? Whatever the answer it was an immense escape from the actual.

It's true that if there weren't other dates than this there were other memories; and by the time George Stransom was fifty-five such memories had greatly multiplied. There were other ghosts in his life than the ghost of Mary Antrim. He had perhaps not had more losses than most men, but he had counted his losses more; he hadn't seen death more closely, but had in a manner felt it more deeply. He had formed little by little the habit of numbering his Dead: it had come to him early in life that there was something one had to do for them. They were there in their simplified intensified essence, their conscious absence and expressive patience, as personally there as if they had only been stricken dumb. When all sense of them failed, all sound of them ceased, it was as if their purgatory were really still on earth; they asked so little that they got, poor things, even less, and died again, died every day, of the hard usage of life. They had no organized service, no reserved place, no honor, no shelter, no safety. Even ungenerous people provided for the living, but even those who were called most generous did nothing for the others. So on George Stransom's part had grown up with the years a resolve that he at least would do something, do it, that is, for his own—would perform the great charity without reproach. Every man *had* his own, and every man had, to meet this charity, the ample resources of the soul.

It was doubtless the voice of Mary Antrim that spoke for them best; as the years at any rate went by he found himself in regular communion with these postponed pensioners, those whom indeed he always called in his thoughts the Others. He spared them the mo-

ments, he organized the charity. Quite how it had risen he probably never could have told you, but what came to pass was that an altar, such as was after all within everybody's compass, lighted with perpetual candles and dedicated to these secret rites, reared itself in his spiritual spaces. He had wondered of old, in some embarrassment, whether he had a religion; being very sure, and not a little content, that he hadn't at all events the religion some of the people he had known wanted him to have. Gradually this question was straightened out for him: it became clear to him that the religion instilled by his earliest consciousness had been simply the religion of the Dead. It suited his inclination, it satisfied his spirit, it gave employment to his piety. It answered his love of great offices, of a solemn and splendid ritual; for no shrine could be more bedecked and no ceremonial more stately than those to which his worship was attached. He had no imagination about these things but that they were accessible to any who should feel the need of them. The poorest could build such temples of the spirit—could make them blaze with candles and smoke with incense, make them flush with pictures and flowers. The cost, in the common phrase, of keeping them up fell wholly on the generous heart.

II

He had this year, on the eve of his anniversary, as happened, an emotion not unconnected with that range of feeling. Walking home at the close of a busy day he was arrested in the London street by the particular effect of a shop front that lighted the dull brown air with its mercenary grin and before which several persons were gathered. It was the window of a jeweler whose diamonds and sapphires seemed to laugh, in flashes like high notes of sound, with the mere joy of knowing how much more they were "worth" than most of the dingy pedestrians staring at them from the other side of the pane. Stransom lingered long enough to suspend, in a vision, a string of pearls about the white neck of Mary Antrim, and then was kept an instant longer by the sound of a voice he knew. Next him was a mumbling old woman, and beyond the old woman a gentleman with a lady on his arm. It was from him, from Paul Creston, the voice had proceeded: he was talking with the lady of some precious object in the window. Stransom had no sooner recognized him than the old woman turned away; but just with this growth of opportunity came a felt strangeness that stayed him in the very act of laying his hand on his friend's arm. It lasted but the instant, only that space sufficed for the flash of a wild question. Was *not* Mrs. Creston dead?—the ambiguity met him there in the short drop of her husband's voice, the drop conjugal, if it ever was, and in the way the two figures leaned to each other. Creston, making a step to look at something else, came nearer, glanced at him, started and exclaimed—behavior the effect of which was at first only to leave Stransom staring, staring back across the months at the different face, the wholly other face, the poor man had shown him last, the blurred ravaged mask bent over the open grave by which they had stood together. That son of affliction wasn't in mourning now; he detached his arm from his companion's to grasp the hand of the older friend. He colored as well as smiled in the

strong light of the shop when Stransom raised a tentative hat to the lady. Stransom had just time to see she was pretty before he found himself gaping at a fact more portentous. "My dear fellow, let me make you acquainted with my wife."

Creston had blushed and stammered over it, but in half a minute, at the rate we live in polite society, it had practically become, for our friend, the mere memory of a shock. They stood there and laughed and talked; Stransom had instantly whisked the shock out of the way, to keep it for private consumption. He felt himself grimace, he heard himself exaggerate the proper, but was conscious of turning not a little faint. That new woman, that hired performer Mrs. Creston? Mrs. Creston had been more living for him than any woman but one. This lady had a face that shone as publicly as the jeweler's window, and in the happy candor with which she wore her monstrous character was an effect of gross immodesty. The character of Paul Creston's wife thus attributed to her was monstrous for reasons Stransom could judge his friend to know perfectly that he knew. The happy pair had just arrived from America, and Stransom hadn't needed to be told this to guess the nationality of the lady. Somehow it deepened the foolish air that her husband's confused cordiality was unable to conceal. Stransom recalled that he had heard of poor Creston's having, while his bereavement was still fresh, crossed the sea for what people in such predicaments call a little change. He had found little change indeed, he had brought the little change back; it was the little change that stood there and that, do what he would, he couldn't, while he showed those high front teeth of his, look other than a conscious ass about. They were going into the shop, Mrs. Creston said, and she begged Mr. Stransom to come with them and help to decide. He thanked her, opening his watch and pleading an engagement for which he was already late, and they parted while she shrieked into the fog, "Mind now you come to see me right away!" Creston had had the delicacy not to suggest that, and Stransom hoped it hurt him somewhere to hear her scream it to all the echoes.

He felt quite determined, as he walked away, never in his life to go near her. She was perhaps a human being, but Creston oughtn't to have shown her without precautions, oughtn't indeed to have shown her at all. His precautions should have been those of a forger or a murderer, and the people at home would never have mentioned extradition. This was a wife for foreign service or purely external use; a decent consideration would have spared her the injury of comparisons. Such was the first flush of George Stransom's reaction; but as he sat alone that night—there were particular hours he always passed alone—the harshness dropped from it and left only the pity. *He* could spend an evening with Kate Creston, if the man to whom she had given everything couldn't. He had known her twenty years, and she was the only woman for whom he might perhaps have been unfaithful. She was all cleverness and sympathy and charm; her house had been the very easiest in all the world and her friendship the very firmest. Without accidents he had loved her, without accidents everyone had loved her: she had made the passions about her as regular as the moon makes the tides. She had been also of course far too good

for her husband, but he never suspected it, and in nothing had she been more admirable than in the exquisite art with which she tried to keep everyone else (keeping Creston was no trouble) from finding it out. Here was a man to whom she had devoted her life and for whom she had given it up—dying to bring into the world a child of his bed; and she had had only to submit to her fate to have, ere the grass was green on her grave, no more existence for him than a domestic servant he had replaced. The frivolity, the indecency of it made Stransom's eyes fill; and he had that evening a sturdy sense that he alone, in a world without delicacy, had a right to hold up his head. While he smoked, after dinner, he had a book in his lap, but he had no eyes for his page: his eyes, in the swarming void of things, seemed to have caught Kate Creston's, and it was into their sad silences he looked. It was to him her sentient spirit had turned, knowing it to be of her he would think. He thought for a long time of how the closed eyes of dead women could still live—how they could open again, in a quiet lamplit room, long after they had looked their last. They had looks that survived—had them as great poets had quoted lines.

The newspaper lay by his chair—the thing that came in the afternoon and the servants thought one wanted; without sense for what was in it he had mechanically unfolded and then dropped it. Before he went to bed he took it up, and this time, at the top of a paragraph, he was caught by five words that made him start. He stood staring, before the fire, at the "Death of Sir Acton Hague, K.C.B.," the man who ten years earlier had been the nearest of his friends and whose deposition from this eminence had practically left it without an occupant. He had seen him after their rupture, but hadn't now seen him for years. Standing there before the fire he turned cold as he read what had befallen him. Promoted a short time previous to the governorship of the Westward Islands, Acton Hague had died, in the bleak honor of this exile, of an illness consequent on the bite of a poisonous snake. His career was compressed by the newspaper into a dozen lines, the perusal of which excited on George Stransom's part no warmer feeling than one of relief at the absence of any mention of their quarrel, an incident accidentally tainted at the time, thanks to their joint immersion in large affairs, with a horrible publicity. Public indeed was the wrong Stransom had, to his own sense, suffered, the insult he had blankly taken from the only man with whom he had ever been intimate; the friend, almost adored, of his University years, the subject, later, of his passionate loyalty: so public that he had never spoken of it to a human creature, so public that he had completely overlooked it. It had made the difference for him that friendship too was all over, but it had only made just that one. The shock of interests had been private, intensely so; but the action taken by Hague had been in the face of men. Today it all seemed to have occurred merely to the end that George Stransom should think of him as "Hague" and measure exactly how much he himself could resemble a stone. He went cold, suddenly and horribly cold, to bed.

III

The next day, in the afternoon, in the great gray suburb, he knew his long walk had tired him. In the dreadful cemetery alone he had been on his feet an hour. Instinctively, coming back, they had taken him a devious course, and it was a desert in which no circling cabman hovered over possible prey. He paused on a corner and measured the dreariness; then he made out through the gathered dusk that he was in one of those tracts of London which are less gloomy by night than by day, because, in the former case, of the civil gift of light. By day there was nothing, but by night there were lamps, and George Stransom was in a mood that made lamps good in themselves. It wasn't that they could show him anything, it was only that they could burn clear. To his surprise, however, after a while, they did show him something: the arch of a high doorway approached by a low terrace of steps, in the depth of which—it formed a dim vestibule —the raising of a curtain at the moment he passed gave him a glimpse of an avenue of .gloom with a glow of tapers at the end. He stopped and looked up, recognizing the place as a church. The thought quickly came to him that since he was tired he might rest there; so that after a moment he had in turn pushed up the leathern curtain and gone in. It was a temple of the old persuasion, and there had evidently been a function—perhaps a service for the dead; the high altar was still a blaze of candles. This was an exhibition he always liked, and he dropped into a seat with relief. More than it had ever yet come home to him it struck him as good there should be churches.

This one was almost empty and the other altars were dim; a verger shuffled about, an old woman coughed, but it seemed to Stransom there was hospitality in the thick sweet air. Was it only the savor of the incense or was it something of larger intention? He had at any rate quitted the great gray suburb and come nearer to the warm center. He presently ceased to feel intrusive, gaining at last even a sense of community with the only worshiper in his neighborhood, the somber presence of a woman, in mourning unrelieved, whose back was all he could see of her and who had sunk deep into prayer at no great distance from him. He wished he could sink, like her, to the very bottom, be as motionless, as rapt in prostration. After a few moments he shifted his seat; it was almost indelicate to be so aware of her. But Stransom subsequently quite lost himself, floating away on the sea of light. If occasions like this had been more frequent in his life he would have had more present the great original type, set up in a myriad temples, of the unapproachable shrine he had erected in his mind. That shrine had begun in vague likeness to church pomps, but the echo had ended by growing more distinct than the sound. The sound now rang out, the type blazed at him with all its fires and with a mystery of radiance in which endless meanings could glow. The thing became as he sat there his appropriate altar and each starry candle an appropriate vow. He numbered them, named them, grouped them— it was the silent roll call of his Dead. They made together a brightness vast and intense, a brightness in which the mere chapel of his thoughts grew so dim that as it faded away he asked himself if he shouldn't find his real comfort in some material act, some outward worship.

This idea took possession of him while, at a distance, the black-robed lady continued prostrate; he was quietly thrilled with his conception, which at last brought him to his feet in the sudden excitement of a plan. He wandered softly through the aisles, pausing in the different chapels, all save one applied to a special devotion. It was in this clear recess, lampless and unapplied, that he stood longest—the length of time it took him fully to grasp the conception of gilding it with his bounty. He should snatch it from no other rites and associate it with nothing profane; he would simply take it as it should be given up to him and make it a masterpiece of splendor and a mountain of fire. Tended sacredly all the year, with the sanctifying church round it, it would always be ready for his offices. There would be difficulties, but from the first they presented themselves only as difficulties surmounted. Even for a person so little affiliated the thing would be a matter of arrangement. He saw it all in advance, and how bright in especial the place would become to him in the intermissions of toil and the dusk of afternoons; how rich in assurance at all times, but especially in the indifferent world. Before withdrawing he drew nearer again to the spot where he had first sat down, and in the movement he met the lady whom he had seen praying and who was now on her way to the door. She passed him quickly, and he had only a glimpse of her pale face and her unconscious, almost sightless eyes. For that instant she looked faded and handsome.

This was the origin of the rites more public, yet certainly esoteric, that he at last found himself able to establish. It took a long time, it took a year, and both the process and the result would have been—for any who knew—a vivid picture of his good faith. No one did know, in fact—no one but the bland ecclesiastics whose acquaintance he had promptly sought, whose objections he had softly overridden, whose curiosity and sympathy he had artfully charmed, whose assent to his eccentric munificence he had eventually won, and who had asked for concessions in exchange for indulgences. Stransom had of course at an early stage of his enquiry been referred to the Bishop, and the Bishop had been delightfully human, the Bishop had been almost amused. Success was within sight, at any rate, from the moment the attitude of those whom it concerned became liberal in response to liberality. The altar and the sacred shell that half encircled it, consecrated to an ostensible and customary worship, were to be splendidly maintained; all that Stransom reserved to himself was the number of his lights and the free enjoyment of his intention. When the intention had taken complete effect the enjoyment became even greater than he had ventured to hope. He liked to think of this effect when far from it, liked to convince himself of it yet again when near. He was not often indeed so near as that a visit to it hadn't perforce something of the patience of a pilgrimage; but the time he gave to his devotion came to seem to him more a contribution to his other interests than a betrayal of them. Even a loaded life might be easier when one had added a new necessity to it.

How much easier was probably never guessed by those who simply knew there were hours when he

disappeared and for many of whom there was a vulgar reading of what they used to call his plunges. These plunges were into depths quieter than the deep sea caves, and the habit had at the end of a year or two become the one it would have cost him most to relinquish. Now they had really, his Dead, something that was indefeasibly theirs; and he liked to think that they might in cases be the Dead of others, as well as that the Dead of others might be invoked there under the protection of what he had done. Whoever bent a knee on the carpet he had laid down appeared to him to act in the spirit of his intention. Each of his lights had a name for him, and from time to time a new light was kindled. This was what he had fundamentally agreed for, that there should always be room for them all. What those who passed or lingered saw was simply the most resplendent of the altars called suddenly into vivid usefulness, with a quiet elderly man, for whom it evidently had a fascination, often seated there in a maze or a doze; but half the satisfaction of the spot for this mysterious and fitful worshiper was that he found the years of his life there, and the ties, the affections, the struggles, the submissions, the conquests, if there had been such, a record of that adventurous journey in which the beginnings and the endings of human relations are the lettered milestones. He had in general little taste for the past as a part of his own history; at other times and in other places it mostly seemed to him pitiful to consider and impossible to repair; but on these occasions he accepted it with something of that positive gladness with which one adjusts one's self to an ache that begins to succumb to treatment. To the treatment of time the malady of life begins at a given moment to succumb; and these were doubtless the hours at which that truth most came home to him. The day was written for him there on which he had first become acquainted with death, and the successive phases of the acquaintance were marked each with a flame.

The flames were gathering thick at present, for Stransom had entered that dark defile of our earthly descent in which someone dies every day. It was only yesterday that Kate Creston had flashed out her white fire; yet already there were younger stars ablaze on the tips of the tapers. Various persons in whom his interest had not been intense drew closer to him by entering this company. He went over it, head by head, till he felt like the shepherd of a huddled flock, with a shepherd's vision of differences imperceptible. He knew his candles apart, up to the color of the flame, and would still have known them had their positions all been changed. To other imaginations they might stand for other things—that they should stand for something to be hushed before was all he desired; but he was intensely conscious of the personal note of each and of the distinguishable way it contributed to the concert. There were hours at which he almost caught himself wishing that certain of his friends would now die, that he might establish with them in this manner a connection more charming than, as it happened, it was possible to enjoy with them in life. In regard to those from whom one was separated by the long curves of the globe such a connection could only be an improvement: it brought them in-

stantly within reach. Of course there were gaps in the constellation, for Stransom knew he could only pretend to act for his own, and it wasn't every figure passing before his eyes into the great obscure that was entitled to a memorial. There was a strange sanctification in death, but some characters were more sanctified by being forgotten than by being remembered. The greatest blank in the shining page was the memory of Acton Hague, of which he inveterately tried to rid himself. For Acton Hague no flame could ever rise on any altar of his.

IV

Every year, the day he walked back from the great graveyard, he went to church as he had done the day his idea was born. It was on this occasion, as it happened, after a year had passed, that he began to observe his altar to be haunted by a worshiper at least as frequent as himself. Others of the faithful, and in the rest of the church, came and went, appealing sometimes, when they disappeared, to a vague or to a particular recognition; but this unfailing presence was always to be observed when he arrived and still in possession when he departed. He was surprised, the first time, at the promptitude with which it assumed an identity for him—the identity of the lady whom two years before, on his anniversary, he had seen so intensely bowed, and of whose tragic face he had had so flitting a vision. Given the time that had passed, his recollection of her was fresh enough to make him wonder. Of himself she had of course no impression, or rather had had none at first: the time came when her manner of transacting her business suggested her having gradually guessed his call to be of the same order. She used his altar for her own purpose —he could only hope that, sad and solitary as she always struck him, she used it for her own Dead. There were interruptions, infidelities, all on his part, calls to other associations and duties; but as the months went on he found her whenever he returned, and he ended by taking pleasure in the thought that he had given her almost the contentment he had given himself. They worshiped side by side so often that there were moments when he wished he might be sure, so straight did their prospect stretch away of growing old together in their rites. She was younger than he, but she looked as if her Dead were at least as numerous as his candles. She had no color, no sound, no fault, and another of the things about which he had made up his mind was that she had no fortune. Always blackrobed, she must have had a succession of sorrows. People weren't poor, after all, whom so many losses could overtake; they were positively rich when they had had so much to give up. But the air of this devoted and indifferent woman, who always made, in any attitude, a beautiful accidental line, conveyed somehow to Stransom that she had known more kinds of trouble than one.

He had a great love of music and little time for the joy of it; but occasionally, when workaday noises were muffled by Saturday afternoons, it used to come back to him that there were glories. There were moreover friends who reminded him of this and side by side with whom he found himself sitting out concerts. On one of these winter evenings, in Saint James's Hall, he be-

came aware after he had seated himself that the lady he had so often seen at church was in the place next him and was evidently alone, as he also this time happened to be. She was at first too absorbed in the consideration of the program to heed him, but when she at last glanced at him he took advantage of the movement to speak to her, greeting her with the remark that he felt as if he already knew her. She smiled as she said, "Oh yes, I recognize you"; yet in spite of this admission of long acquaintance it was the first he had seen of her smile. The effect of it was suddenly to contribute more to that acquaintance than all the previous meetings had done. He hadn't "taken in," he said to himself, that she was so pretty. Later, that evening—it was while he rolled along in a hansom on his way to dine out—he added that he hadn't taken in that she was so interesting. The next morning in the midst of his work he quite suddenly and irrelevantly reflected that his impression of her, beginning so far back, was like a winding river that had at last reached the sea.

His work in fact was blurred a little all that day by the sense of what had now passed between them. It wasn't much, but it had just made the difference. They had listened together to Beethoven and Schumann; they had talked in the pauses, and at the end, when at the door, to which they moved together, he had asked her if he could help her in the matter of getting away. She had thanked him and put up her umbrella, slipping into the crowd without an allusion to their meeting yet again and leaving him to remember at leisure that not a word had been exchanged about the usual scene of that coincidence.

This omission struck him now as natural and then again as perverse. She mightn't in the least have allowed his warrant for speaking to her, and yet if she hadn't he would have judged her an underbred woman. It was odd that when nothing had really ever brought them together he should have been able successfully to assume they were in a manner old friends—that this negative quantity was somehow more than they could express. His success, it was true, had been qualified by her quick escape, so that there grew up in him an absurd desire to put it to some better test. Save in so far as some other poor chance might help him, such a test could be only to meet her afresh at church. Left to himself he would have gone to church the very next afternoon, just for the curiosity of seeing if he should find her there. But he wasn't left to himself, a fact he discovered quite at the last, after he had virtually made up his mind to go. The influence that kept him away really revealed to him how little to himself his Dead *ever* left him. He went only for *them*—for nothing else in the world.

The force of this revulsion kept him away ten days: he hated to connect the place with anything but his offices or to give a glimpse of the curiosity that had been on the point of moving him. It was absurd to weave a tangle about a matter so simple as a custom of devotion that might with ease have been daily or hourly; yet the tangle got itself woven. He was sorry, he was disappointed: it was as if a long happy spell had been broken and he had lost a familiar security. At the last, however, he asked himself if he was to stay away forever from the fear of this muddle about

motives. After an interval neither longer nor shorter than usual he re-entered the church with a clear conviction that he should scarcely heed the presence or the absence of the lady of the concert. This indifference didn't prevent his at once noting that for the only time since he had first seen her she wasn't on the spot. He had now no scruple about giving her time to arrive, but she didn't arrive, and when he went away still missing her he was profanely and consentingly sorry. If her absence made the tangle more intricate, that was all her own doing. By the end of another year it was very intricate indeed; but by that time he didn't in the least care, and it was only his cultivated consciousness that had given him scruples. Three times in three months he had gone to church without finding her, and he felt he hadn't needed these occasions to show him his suspense had dropped. Yet it was, incongruously, not indifference, but a refinement of delicacy that had kept him from asking the sacristan, who would of course immediately have recognized his description of her, whether she had been seen at other hours. His delicacy had kept him from asking any question about her at any time, and it was exactly the same virtue that had left him so free to be decently civil to her at the concert.

This happy advantage now served him anew, enabling him when she finally met his eyes—it was after a fourth trial—to predetermine quite fixedly his awaiting her retreat. He joined her in the street as soon as she had moved, asking her if he might accompany her a certain distance. With her placid permission he went as far as a house in the neighborhood at which she had business: she let him know it was not where she lived. She lived, as she said, in a mere slum, with an old aunt, a person in connection with whom she spoke of the engrossment of humdrum duties and regular occupations. She wasn't, the mourning niece, in her first youth, and her vanished freshness had left something behind that, for Stransom, represented the proof it had been tragically sacrificed. Whatever she gave him the assurance of she gave without references. She might have been a divorced duchess—she might have been an old maid who taught the harp.

V

They fell at last into the way of walking together almost every time they met, though for a long time still they never met but at church. He couldn't ask her to come and see him, and as if she hadn't a proper place to receive him she never invited her friend. As much as himself she knew the world of London, but from an undiscussed instinct of privacy they haunted the region not mapped on the social chart. On the return she always made him leave her at the same corner. She looked with him, as a pretext for a pause, at the depressed things in suburban shop fronts; and there was never a word he had said to her that she hadn't beautifully understood. For long ages he never knew her name, any more than she had ever pronounced his own; but it was not their names that mattered, it was only their perfect practice and their common need.

These things made their whole relation so impersonal that they hadn't the rules or reasons people found in ordinary friendships. They

didn't care for the things it was supposed necessary to care for in the intercourse of the world. They ended one day—they never knew which of them expressed it first—by throwing out the idea that they didn't care for each other. Over this idea they grew quite intimate; they rallied to it in a way that marked a fresh start in their confidence. If to feel deeply together about certain things wholly distinct from themselves didn't constitute a safety, where was safety to be looked for? Not lightly nor often, not without occasion nor without emotion, any more than in any other reference by serious people to a mystery of their faith; but when something had happened to warm, as it were, the air for it, they came as near as they could come to calling their Dead by name. They felt it was coming very near to utter their thought at all. The word "they" expressed enough; it limited the mention, it had a dignity of its own, and if, in their talk, you had heard our friends use it, you might have taken them for a pair of pagans of old alluding decently to the domesticated gods. They never knew—at least Stransom never knew—how they had learned to be sure about each other. If it had been with each a question of what the other was there for, the certitude had come in some fine way of its own. Any faith, after all, has the instinct of propagation, and it was as natural as it was beautiful that they should have taken pleasure on the spot in the imagination of a following. If the following was for each but a following of one it had proved in the event sufficient. Her debt, however, of course, was much greater than his, because while she had only given him a worshiper he had given her a splendid temple. Once she said she pitied him for the length of his list —she had counted his candles almost as often as himself—and this made him wonder what could have been the length of hers. He had wondered before at the coincidence of their losses, especially as from time to time a new candle was set up. On some occasion some accident led him to express this curiosity, and she answered as if in surprise that he hadn't already understood. "Oh for me, you know, the more there are the better—there could never be too many. I should like hundreds and hundreds—I should like thousands; I should like a great mountain of light."

Then of course in a flash he understood. "Your Dead are only One?" She hung back at this as never yet. "Only One," she answered, coloring as if now he knew her guarded secret. It really made him feel he knew less than before, so difficult was it for him to reconstitute a life in which a single experience had so belittled all others. His own life, round its central hollow, had been packed close enough. After this she appeared to have regretted her confession, though at the moment she spoke there had been pride in her very embarrassment. She declared to him that his own was the larger, the dearer possession—the portion one would have chosen if one had been able to choose; she assured him she could perfectly imagine some of the echoes with which his silences were peopled. He knew she couldn't: one's relation to what one had loved and hated had been a relation too distinct from the relations of others. But this didn't affect the fact that they were growing old together in their piety. She was a feature of

that piety, but even at the ripe stage of acquaintance in which they occasionally arranged to meet at a concert or to go together to an exhibition she was not a feature of anything else. The most that happened was that his worship became paramount. Friend by friend dropped away till at last there were more emblems on his altar than houses left him to enter. She was more than any other the friend who remained, but she was unknown to all the rest. Once when she had discovered, as they called it, a new star, she used the expression that the chapel at last was full.

"Oh no," Stransom replied, "there's a great thing wanting for that! The chapel will never be full till a candle is set up before which all the others will pale. It will be the tallest candle of all."

Her mild wonder rested on him. "What candle do you mean?"

"I mean, dear lady, my own."

He had learned after a long time that she earned money by her pen, writing under a pseudonym she never disclosed in magazines he never saw. She knew too well what he couldn't read and what she couldn't write, and she taught him to cultivate indifference with a success that did much for their good relations. Her invisible industry was a convenience to him; it helped his contented thought of her, the thought that rested in the dignity of her proud obscure life, her little remunerated art and her little impenetrable home. Lost, with her decayed relative, in her dim suburban world, she came to the surface for him in distant places. She was really the priestess of his altar, and whenever he quitted England he committed it to her keeping. She proved to him afresh that women have more

of the spirit of religion than men;
he felt his fidelity pale and faint in
comparison with hers. He often said
to her that since he had so little
time to live he rejoiced in her having so much; so glad was he to
think she would guard the temple
when he should have been called.
He had a great plan for that, which
of course he told her too, a bequest
of money to keep it up in undimin-
ished state. Of the administration
of this fund he would appoint her
superintendent, and if the spirit
should move her she might kindle a
taper even for him.

"And who will kindle one even
for me?" she then seriously asked.

VI

She was always in mourning, yet
the day he came back from the longest absence he had yet made her appearance immediately told him she
had lately had a bereavement. They
met on this occasion as she was
leaving the church, so that postponing his own entrance he instantly
offered to turn round and walk
away with her. She considered, then
she said: "Go in now, but come and
see me in an hour." He knew the
small vista of her street, closed at
the end and as dreary as an empty
pocket, where the pairs of shabby
little houses, semidetached but in-
dissolubly united, were like married
couples on bad terms. Often, however, as he had gone to the beginning he had never gone beyond.
Her aunt was dead—that he immediately guessed, as well as that it
made a difference; but when she
had for the first time mentioned
her number he found himself, on her
leaving him, not a little agitated
by this sudden liberality. She wasn't
a person with whom, after all, one

got on so very fast: it had taken
him months and months to learn her
name, years and years to learn her
address. If she had looked, on this
reunion, so much older to him, how
in the world did he look to her? She
had reached the period of life he
had long since reached, when, after
separations, the marked clock-face
of the friend we meet announces
the hour we have tried to forget.
He couldn't have said what he expected as, at the end of his waiting,
he turned the corner where for years
he had always paused; simply not
to pause was a sufficient cause for
emotion. It was an event, somehow;
and in all their long acquaintance
there had never been an event. This
one grew larger when, five minutes
later, in the faint elegance of her
little drawing room, she quavered
out a greeting that showed the
measure she took of it. He had a
strange sense of having come for
something in particular; strange because literally there was nothing particular between them, nothing save
that they were at one on their great
point, which had long ago become
a magnificent matter of course. It
was true that after she had said,
"You can always come now, you
know," the thing he was there for
seemed already to have happened.
He asked her if it was the death of
her aunt that made the difference;
to which she replied: "She never
knew I knew you. I wished her not
to." The beautiful clearness of her
candor—her faded beauty was like
a summer twilight—disconnected
the words from any image of deceit.
They might have struck him as the
record of a deep dissimulation, but
she had always given him a sense
of noble reasons. The vanished aunt
was present, as he looked about him,
in the small complacencies of the

room, the beaded velvet and the fluted moreen; and though, as we know, he had the worship of the Dead, he found himself not definitely regretting this lady. If she wasn't in his long list, however, she was in her niece's short one, and Stransom presently observed to the latter that now at least, in the place they haunted together, she would have another object of devotion.

"Yes, I shall have another. She was very kind to me. It's that that's the difference."

He judged, wondering a good deal before he made any motion to leave her, that the difference would somehow be very great and would consist of still other things than her having let him come in. It rather chilled him, for they had been happy together as they were. He extracted from her at any rate an intimation that she should now have means less limited, that her aunt's tiny fortune had come to her, so that there was henceforth only one to consume what had formerly been made to suffice for two. This was a joy to Stransom, because it had hitherto been equally impossible for him either to offer her presents or contentedly to stay his hand. It was too ugly to be at her side that way, abounding himself and yet not able to overflow—a demonstration that would have been signally a false note. Even her better situation too seemed only to draw out in a sense the loneliness of her future. It would merely help her to live more and more for their small ceremonial, and this at a time when he himself had begun wearily to feel that, having set it in motion, he might depart. When they had sat a while in the pale parlor she got up—"This isn't *my* room: let us go into mine." They had only to cross the narrow

hall, as he found, to pass quite into another air. When she had closed the door of the second room, as she called it, he felt at last in real possession of her. The place had the flush of life—it was expressive; its dark red walls were articulate with memories and relics. These were simple things—photographs and water colors, scraps of writing framed and ghosts of flowers embalmed; but a moment sufficed to show him they had a common meaning. It was here she had lived and worked, and she had already told him she would make no change of scene. He read the reference in the objects about her—the general one to places and times; but after a minute he distinguished among them a small portrait of a gentleman. At a distance and without their glasses his eyes were only so caught by it as to feel a vague curiosity. Presently this impulse carried him nearer, and in another moment he was staring at the picture in stupefaction and with the sense that some sound had broken from him. He was further conscious that he showed his companion a white face when he turned round on her gasping: "Acton Hague!"

She matched his great wonder. "Did you know him?"

"He was the friend of all my youth—of my early manhood. And *you* knew him?"

She colored at this and for a moment her answer failed; her eyes embraced everything in the place, and a strange irony reached her lips as she echoed: "Knew him?"

Then Stransom understood, while the room heaved like the cabin of a ship, that its whole contents cried out with him, that it was a museum in his honor, that all her later years had been addressed to him and that the shrine he himself had reared had been passionately converted to this use. It was all for Acton Hague that she had kneeled every day at his altar. What need had there been for a consecrated candle when he was present in the whole array? The revelation so smote our friend in the face that he dropped into a seat and sat silent. He had quickly felt her shaken by the force of his shock, but as she sank on the sofa beside him and laid her hand on his arm he knew almost as soon that she mightn't resent it as much as she'd have liked.

VII

He learned in that instant two things: one being that even in so long a time she had gathered no knowledge of his great intimacy and his great quarrel; the other that in spite of this ignorance, strangely enough, she supplied on the spot a reason for his stupor. "How extraordinary," he presently exclaimed, "that we should never have known!"

She gave a wan smile which seemed to Stransom stranger even than the fact itself. "I never, never spoke of him."

He looked again about the room. "Why then, if your life had been so full of him?"

"Mayn't I put you that question as well? Hadn't your life also been full of him?"

"Anyone's, everyone's life who had the wonderful experience of knowing him. *I* never spoke of him," Stransom added in a moment, "because he did me—years ago—an unforgettable wrong." She was silent, and with the full effect of his presence all about them it almost startled

her guest to hear no protest escape her. She accepted his words; he turned his eyes to her again to see in what manner she accepted them. It was with rising tears and a rare sweetness in the movement of putting out her hand to take his own. Nothing more wonderful had ever appeared to him than, in that little chamber of remembrance and homage, to see her convey with such exquisite mildness that as from Acton Hague any injury was credible. The clock ticked in the stillness—Hague had probably given it to her—and while he let her hold his hand with a tenderness that was almost an assumption of responsibility for his old pain as well as his new, Stransom after a minute broke out: "Good God, how he must have used *you!*"

She dropped his hand at this, got up and, moving across the room, made straight a small picture to which, on examining it, he had given a slight push. Then turning round on him with her pale gaiety recovered, "I've forgiven him!" she declared.

"I know what you've done," said Stransom; "I know what you've done for years." For a moment they looked at each other through it all with their long community of service in their eyes. This short passage made, to his sense, for the woman before him, an immense, an absolutely naked confession; which was presently, suddenly blushing red and changing her place again, what she appeared to learn he perceived in it. He got up and "How you must have loved him!" he cried.

"Women aren't like men. They can love even where they've suffered."

"Women are wonderful," said

Stransom. "But I assure you I've forgiven him too."

"If I had known of anything so strange I wouldn't have brought you here."

"So that we might have gone on in our ignorance to the last?"

"What do you call the last?" she asked, smiling still.

At this he could smile back at her. "You'll see—when it comes."

She thought of that. "This is better perhaps; but as we were—it was good."

He put her the question. "Did it never happen that he spoke of me?"

Considering more intently she made no answer, and he then knew he should have been adequately answered by her asking how often he himself had spoken of their terrible friend. Suddenly a brighter light broke in her face and an excited idea sprang to her lips in the appeal: "You *have* forgiven him?"

"How, if I hadn't, could I linger here?"

She visibly winced at the deep but unintended irony of this; but even while she did so she panted quickly: "Then in the lights on your altar——?"

"There's never a light for Acton Hague!"

She stared with a dreadful fall. "But if he's one of your Dead?"

"He's one of the world's, if you like—he's one of yours. But he's not one of mine. Mine are only the Dead who died possessed of me. They're mine in death because they were mine in life."

"*He* was yours in life then, even if for a while he ceased to be. If you forgave him you went back to him. Those whom we've once loved——"

"Are those who can hurt us most," Stransom broke in.

"Ah it's not true—you've *not* forgiven him!" she wailed with a passion that startled him.

He looked at her as never yet. "What was it he did to you?"

"Everything!" Then abruptly she put out her hand in farewell. "Goodby."

He turned as cold as he had turned that night he read the man's death. "You mean that we meet no more?"

"Not as we've met—not *there!*"

He stood aghast at this snap of their great bond, at the renouncement that rang out in the word she so expressively sounded. "But what's changed—for you?"

She waited in all the sharpness of a trouble that for the first time since he had known her made her splendidly stern. "How can you understand now when you didn't understand before?"

"I didn't understand before only because I didn't know. Now that I know, I see what I've been living with for years," Stransom went on very gently.

She looked at him with a larger allowance, doing this gentleness justice. "How can I then, on this new knowledge of my own, ask you to continue to live with it?"

"I set up my altar, with its multiplied meanings," Stransom began; but she quickly interrupted him.

"You set up your altar, and when I wanted one most I found it magnificently ready. I used it with the gratitude I've always shown you, for I knew it from of old to be dedicated to Death. I told you long ago that my Dead weren't many. Yours were, but all you had done for them was none too much for *my* worship! You had placed a great life for Each—I gathered them together for One!"

"We had simply different intentions," he returned. "That, as you say, I perfectly knew, and I don't see why your intention shouldn't still sustain you."

"That's because you're generous—you can imagine and think. But the spell's broken."

It seemed to poor Stransom, in spite of his resistance, that it really was, and the prospect stretched gray and void before him. All he could say, however, was: "I hope you'll try before you give up."

"If I had known you had ever known him I should have taken for granted he had his candle," she presently answered. "What's changed, as you say, is that on making the discovery I find he never has had it. That makes *my* attitude" —she paused as thinking how to express it, then said simply—"all wrong."

"Come once again," he pleaded.

"Will you give him his candle?" she asked.

He waited, but only because it would sound ungracious; not because of a doubt of his feeling. "I can't do that!" he declared at last.

"Then good-by." And she gave him her hand again.

He had got his dismissal; besides which, in the agitation of everything that had opened out to him, he felt the need to recover himself as he could only do in solitude. Yet he lingered—lingered to see if she had no compromise to express, no attenuation to propose. But he only met her great lamenting eyes, in which indeed he read that she was as sorry for him as for anyone else. This made him say: "At least, in any case, I may see you here."

"Oh yes, come if you like. But I don't think it will do."

He looked round the room once more, knowing how little he was

sure it would do. He felt also stricken and more and more cold, and his chill was like an ague in which he had to make an effort not to shake. Then he made doleful reply: "I must try on my side—if you can't try on yours." She came out with him to the hall and into the doorway, and here he put her the question he held he could least answer from his own wit. "Why have you never let me come before?"

"Because my aunt would have seen you, and I should have had to tell her how I came to know you."

"And what would have been the objection to that?"

"It would have entailed other explanations; there would at any rate have been that danger."

"Surely she knew you went every day to church," Stransom objected.

"She didn't know what I went for."

"Of me then she never even heard?"

"You'll think I was deceitful. But I didn't need to be!"

He was now on the lower doorstep, and his hostess held the door half closed behind him. Through what remained of the opening he saw her framed face. He made a supreme appeal. "What *did* he do to you?"

"It would have come out—*she* would have told you. That fear at my heart—that was my reason!" And she closed the door, shutting him out.

VIII

He had ruthlessly abandoned her —that of course was what he had done. Stransom made it all out in solitude, at leisure, fitting the unmatched pieces gradually together and dealing one by one with a hundred obscure points. She had known Hague only after her present friend's relations with him had wholly terminated; obviously indeed a good while after; and it was natural enough that of his previous life she should have ascertained only what he had judged good to communicate. There were passages it was quite conceivable that even in moments of the tenderest expansion he should have withheld. Of many facts in the career of a man so in the eye of the world there was of course a common knowledge; but this lady lived apart from public affairs, and the only time perfectly clear to her would have been the time following the dawn of her own drama. A man in her place would have "looked up" the past—would even have consulted old newspapers. It remained remarkable indeed that in her long contact with the partner of her retrospect no accident had lighted a train; but there was no arguing about that; the accident had in fact come: it had simply been that security had prevailed. She had taken what Hague had given her, and her blankness in respect of his other connections was only a touch in the picture of that plasticity Stransom had supreme reason to know so great a master could have been trusted to produce.

This picture was for a while all our friend saw; he caught his breath again and again as it came over him that the woman with whom he had had for years so fine a point of contact was a woman whom Acton Hague, of all men in the world, had more or less fashioned. Such as she sat there today she was ineffaceably stamped with him. Beneficent, blameless as Stransom held her,

he couldn't rid himself of the sense that he had been, as who should say, swindled. She had imposed upon him hugely, though she had known it as little as he. All this later past came back to him as a time grotesquely misspent. Such at least were his first reflections; after a while he found himself more divided and only, at the end of it, more troubled. He imagined, recalled, reconstituted, figured out for himself the truth she had refused to give him; the effect of which was to make her seem to him only more saturated with her fate. He felt her spirit, through the whole strangeness, finer than his own to the very degree in which she might have been, in which she certainly had been, more wronged. A woman, when wronged, was always more wronged than a man, and there were conditions when the least she could have got off with was more than the most he could have to bear. He was sure this rare creature wouldn't have got off with the least. He was awestruck at the thought of such a surrender—such a prostration. Molded indeed she had been by powerful hands, to have converted her injury into an exaltation so sublime. The fellow had only had to die for everything that was ugly in him to be washed out in a torrent. It was vain to try to guess what had taken place, but nothing could be clearer than that she had ended by accusing herself. She absolved him at every point, she adored her very wounds. The passion by which he had profited had rushed back after its ebb, and now the tide of tenderness, arrested forever at flood, was too deep even to fathom. Stransom sincerely considered that he had forgiven him; but how little he had achieved the miracle that she had achieved! His forgiveness was silence, but hers was mere unuttered sound. The light she had demanded for his altar would have broken his silence with a blare; whereas all the lights in the church were for her too great a hush.

She had been right about the difference—she had spoken the truth about the change: Stransom was soon to know himself as perversely but sharply jealous. *His* tide had ebbed, not flowed; if he had "forgiven" Acton Hague, that forgiveness was a motive with a broken spring. The very fact of her appeal for a material sign, a sign that should make her dead lover equal there with the others, presented the concession to her friend as too handsome for the case. He had never thought of himself as hard, but an exorbitant article might easily render him so. He moved round and round this one, but only in widening circles —the more he looked at it the less acceptable it seemed. At the same time he had no illusion about the effect of his refusal; he perfectly saw how it would make for a rupture. He left her alone a week, but when at last he again called this conviction was cruelly confirmed. In the interval he had kept away from the church, and he needed no fresh assurance from her to know she hadn't entered it. The change was complete enough: it had broken up her life. Indeed it had broken up his, for all the fires of his shrine seemed to him suddenly to have been quenched. A great indifference fell upon him, the weight of which was in itself a pain; and he never knew what his devotion had been for him till in that shock it ceased like a dropped watch. Neither did he know with how large a confidence he had counted on the final service

that had now failed: the mortal deception was that in this abandonment the whole future gave way.

These days of her absence proved to him of what she was capable; all the more that he never dreamed she was vindictive or even resentful. It was not in anger she had forsaken him; it was in simple submission to hard reality, to the stern logic of life. This came home to him when he sat with her again in the room in which her late aunt's conversation lingered like the tone of a cracked piano. She tried to make him forget how much they were estranged, but in the very presence of what they had given up it was impossible not to be sorry for her. He had taken from her so much more than she had taken from him. He argued with her again, told her she could now have the altar to herself; but she only shook her head with pleading sadness, begging him not to waste his breath on the impossible, the extinct. Couldn't he see that in relation to her private need the rites he had established were practically an elaborate exclusion? She regretted nothing that had happened; it had all been right so long as she didn't know, and it was only that now she knew too much and that from the moment their eyes were open they would simply have to conform. It had doubtless been happiness enough for them to go on together so long. She was gentle, grateful, resigned; but this was only the form of a deep immovability. He saw he should never more cross the threshold of the second room, and he felt how much this alone would make a stranger of him and give a conscious stiffness to his visits. He would have hated to plunge again into that well of reminders, but he enjoyed quite as little the vacant alternative.

After he had been with her three or four times it struck him that to have come at last into her house had had the horrid effect of diminishing their intimacy. He had known her better, had liked her in greater freedom, when they merely walked together or kneeled together. Now they only pretended; before they had been nobly sincere. They began to try their walks again, but it proved a lame imitation, for these things, from the first, beginning or ending, had been connected with their visits to the church. They had either strolled away as they came out or gone in to rest on the return. Stransom, besides, now faltered; he couldn't walk as of old. The omission made everything false; it was a dire mutilation of their lives. Our friend was frank and monotonous, making no mystery of his remonstrance and no secret of his predicament. Her response, whatever it was, always came to the same thing—an implied invitation to him to judge, if he spoke of predicaments, of how much comfort she had in hers. For him indeed was no comfort even in complaint, since every allusion to what had befallen them but made the author of their trouble more present. Acton Hague was between them—that was the essence of the matter, and never so much between them as when they were face to face. Then Stransom, while still wanting to banish him, had the strangest sense of striving for an ease that would involve having accepted him. Deeply disconcerted by what he knew, he was still worse tormented by really not knowing. Perfectly aware that it would have been horribly vulgar to abuse his old friend or to tell his companion the story of their quarrel, it yet vexed him that her depth of reserve

should give him no opening and should have the effect of a magnanimity greater even than his own.

He challenged himself, denounced himself, asked himself if he were in love with her that he should care so much what adventures she had had. He had never for a moment allowed he was in love with her; therefore nothing could have surprised him more than to discover he was jealous. What but jealousy could give a man that sore contentious wish for the detail of what would make him suffer? Well enough he knew indeed that he should never have it from the only person who today could give it to him. She let him press her with his somber eyes, only smiling at him with an exquisite mercy and breathing equally little the word that would expose her secret and the world that would appear to deny his literal right to bitterness. She told nothing, she judged nothing; she accepted everything but the possibility of her return to the old symbols. Stransom divined that for her too they had been vividly individual, had stood for particular hours or particular attributes—particular links in her chain. He made it clear to himself, as he believed, that his difficulty lay in the fact that the very nature of the plea for his faithless friend constituted a prohibition; that it happened to have come from *her* was precisely the vice that attached to it. To the voice of impersonal generosity he felt sure he would have listened; he would have deferred to an advocate who, speaking from abstract justice, knowing of his denial without having known Hague, should have had the imagination to say: "Ah, remember only the best of him; pity him; provide for him." To provide for him on the very ground of having discovered another of his turpitudes was not to pity but to glorify him. The more Stransom thought the more he made out that whatever this relation of Hague's it could only have been a deception more or less finely practiced. Where had it come into the life that all men saw? Why had one never heard of it if it had had the frankness of honorable things? Stransom knew enough of his other ties, of his obligations and appearances, not to say enough of his general character, to be sure there had been some infamy. In one way or another this creature had been coldly sacrificed. That was why at the last as well as the first he must still leave him out and out.

IX

And yet this was no solution, especially after he had talked again to his friend of all it had been his plan she should finally do for him. He had talked in the other days, and she had responded with a frankness qualified only by a courteous reluctance, a reluctance that touched him, to linger on the question of his death. She had then practically accepted the charge, suffered him to feel he could depend upon her to be the eventual guardian of his shrine; and it was in the name of what had so passed between them that he appealed to her not to forsake him in his age. She listened at present with shining coldness and all her habitual forbearance to insist on her terms; her deprecation was even still tenderer, for it expressed the compassion of her own sense that he was abandoned. Her terms, however, remained the same, and scarcely the less audible for not being uttered; though he was sure that secretly even more than he she

felt bereft of the satisfaction his solemn trust was to have provided her. They both missed the rich future, but she missed it most, because after all it was to have been entirely hers; and it was her acceptance of the loss that gave him the full measure of her preference for the thought of Acton Hague over any other thought whatever. He had humor enough to laugh rather grimly when he said to himself: "Why the deuce does she like him so much more than she likes me?"— the reasons being really so conceivable. But even his faculty of analysis left the irritation standing, and this irritation proved perhaps the greatest misfortune that had ever overtaken him. There had been nothing yet that made him so much want to give up. He had of course by this time well reached the age of renouncement; but it had not hitherto been vivid to him that it was time to give up everything.

Practically, at the end of six months, he had renounced the friendship once so charming and comforting. His privation had two faces, and the face it had turned to him on the occasion of his last attempt to cultivate that friendship was the one he could look at least. This was the privation he inflicted; the other was the privation he bore. The conditions she never phrased he used to murmur to himself in solitude: "One more, one more—only just one." Certainly he was going down; he often felt it when he caught himself, over his work, staring at vacancy and giving voice to that inanity. There was proof enough besides in his being so weak and so ill. His irritation took the form of melancholy, and his melancholy that of the conviction that his health had quite failed. His altar moreover had ceased to exist; his chapel, in his dreams, was a great dark cavern. All the lights had gone out—all his Dead had died again. He couldn't exactly see at first how it had been in the power of his late companion to extinguish them, since it was neither for her nor by her that they had been called into being. Then he understood that it was essentially in his own soul the revival had taken place, and that in the air of this soul they were now unable to breathe. The candles might mechanically burn, but each of them had lost its luster. The church had become a void; it was his presence, her presence, their common presence, that had made the indispensable medium. If anything was wrong everything was—her silence spoiled the tune.

Then when three months were gone he felt so lonely that he went back; reflecting that as they had been his best society for years his Dead perhaps wouldn't let him forsake them without doing something more for him. They stood there, as he had left them, in their tall radiance, the bright cluster that had already made him, on occasions when he was willing to compare small things with great, liken them to a group of sea lights on the edge of the ocean of life. It was a relief to him, after a while, as he sat there, to feel they had still a virtue. He was more and more easily tired, and he always drove now; the action of his heart was weak and gave him none of the reassurance conferred by the action of his fancy. None the less he returned yet again, returned several times, and finally, during six months, haunted the place with a renewal of frequency and a strain of impatience. In winter the church was unwarmed and exposure to cold forbidden him, but the glow of his shrine was an influence in which he could almost bask. He sat and wondered to what he had reduced his absent associate and what she now did with the hours of her absence. There were other churches, there were other altars, there were other candles; in one way or another her piety would still operate; he couldn't absolutely have deprived her of her rites. So he argued, but without contentment; for he well enough knew there was no other such rare semblance of the mountain of light she had once mentioned to him as the satisfaction of her need. As this semblance again gradually grew great to him and his pious practice more regular, he found a sharper and sharper pang in the imagination of her darkness; for never so much as in these weeks had his rites been real, never had his gathered company seemed so to respond and even to invite. He lost himself in the large luster, which was more and more what he had from the first wished it to be—as dazzling as the vision of heaven in the mind of a child. He wandered in the fields of light; he passed, among the tall tapers, from tier to tier, from fire to fire, from name to name, from the white intensity of one clear emblem, of one saved soul, to another. It was in the quiet sense of having saved his souls that his deep strange instinct rejoiced. This was no dim theological rescue, no boon of a contingent world; they were saved better than faith or works could save them, saved for the warm world they had shrunk from dying to, for actuality, for continuity, for the certainty of human remembrance.

By this time he had survived all his friends; the last straight flame was three years old, there was no one to add to the list. Over and over he called his roll, and it appeared to him compact and complete. Where should he put in another, where, if there were no other objection, would it stand in its place in the rank? He reflected, with a want of sincerity of which he was quite conscious, that it would be difficult to determine that place. More and more, besides, face to face with his little legion, reading over endless histories, handling the empty shells and playing with the silence—more and more he could see that he had never introduced an alien. He had had his great compassions, his indulgences—there were cases in which they had been immense; but what had his devotion after all been if it hadn't been at bottom a respect? He was, however, himself surprised at his stiffness; by the end of the winter the responsibility of it was what was uppermost in his thoughts. The refrain had grown old to them, that plea for just one more. There came a day when, for simple exhaustion, if symmetry should demand just one he was ready so far to meet symmetry. Symmetry was harmony, and the idea of harmony began to haunt him; he said to himself that harmony was of course everything. He took, in fancy, his composition to pieces, redistributing it into other lines, making other juxtapositions and contrasts. He shifted this and that candle, he made the spaces different, he effaced the disfigurement of a possible gap. There were subtle and complex relations, a scheme of cross reference, and moments in which he seemed to catch a glimpse of the void so sensible to the woman who wandered in exile or sat where he had seen her with the portrait of Acton

Hague. Finally, in this way, he arrived at a conception of the total, the ideal, which left a clear opportunity for just another figure. "Just one more—to round it off; just one more, just one," continued to hum in his head. There was a strange confusion in the thought, for he felt the day to be near when he too should be one of the Others. What in this event would the Others matter to him, since they only mattered to the living? Even as one of the Dead what would his altar matter to him, since his particular dream of keeping it up had melted away? What had harmony to do with the case if his lights were all to be quenched? What he had hoped for was an instituted thing. He might perpetuate it on some other pretext, but his special meaning would have dropped. This meaning was to have lasted with the life of the one other person who understood it.

In March he had an illness during which he spent a fortnight in bed, and when he revived a little he was told of two things that had happened. One was that a lady whose name was not known to the servants (she left none) had been three times to ask about him; the other was that in his sleep and on an occasion when his mind evidently wandered he was heard to murmur again and again: "Just one more— just one." As soon as he found himself able to go out, and before the doctor in attendance had pronounced him so, he drove to see the lady who had come to ask about him. She was not at home; but this gave him the opportunity, before his strength should fail again, to take his way to the church. He entered it alone; he had declined, in a happy manner he possessed of being able to decline effectively, the company of his servant or of a nurse. He knew now perfectly what these good people thought; they had discovered his clandestine connection, the magnet that had drawn him for so many years, and doubtless attached a significance of their own to the odd words they had repeated to him. The nameless lady was the clandestine connection—a fact nothing could have made clearer than his indecent haste to rejoin her. He sank on his knees before his altar while his head fell over on his hands. His weakness, his life's weariness overtook him. It seemed to him he had come for the great surrender. At first he asked himself how he should get away; then, with the failing belief in the power, the very desire to move gradually left him. He had come, as he always came, to lose himself; the fields of light were still there to stray in; only this time, in straying, he would never come back. He had given himself to his Dead, and it was good: this time his Dead would keep him. He couldn't rise from his knees; he believed he should never rise again; all he could do was to lift his face and fix his eyes on his lights. They looked unusually, strangely splendid, but the one that always drew him most had an unprecedented luster. It was the central voice of the choir, the glowing heart of the brightness, and on this occasion it semed to expand, to spread great wings of flame. The whole altar flared—dazzling and blinding; but the source of the vast radiance burned clearer than the rest, gathering itself into form, and the form was human beauty and human charity, was the far-off face of Mary Antrim. She smiled at him from the glory of heaven—she brought the glory down with her to take him. He bowed his head in

submission and at the same moment another wave rolled over him. Was it the quickening of joy to pain? In the midst of his joy at any rate he felt his buried face grow hot as with some communicated knowledge that had the force of a reproach. It suddenly made him contrast that very rapture with the bliss he had refused to another. This breath of the passion immortal was all that other had asked; the descent of Mary Antrim opened his spirit with a great compunctious throb for the descent of Acton Hague. It was as if Stransom had read what her eyes said to him.

After a moment he looked round in a despair that made him feel as if the source of life were ebbing. The church had been empty—he was alone; but he wanted to have something done, to make a last appeal. This idea gave him strength for an effort; he rose to his feet with a movement that made him turn, supporting himself by the back of a bench. Behind him was a prostrate figure, a figure he had seen before; a woman in deep mourning, bowed in grief or in prayer. He had seen her in other days—the first time of his entrance there, and he now slightly wavered, looking at her again till she seemed aware he had noticed her. She raised her head and met his eyes: the partner of his long worship had come back. She looked across at him an instant with a face wondering and scared; he saw he had made her afraid. Then quickly rising she came straight to him with both hands out.

"Then you *could* come? God sent you!" he murmured with a happy smile.

"You're very ill—you shouldn't be here," she urged in anxious reply.

"God sent me too, I think. I was

ill when I came, but the sight of you does wonders." He held her hands, which steadied and quickened him. "I've something to tell you."

"Don't tell me!" she tenderly pleaded; "let me tell you. This afternoon, by a miracle, the sweetest of miracles, the sense of our difference left me. I was out—I was near, thinking, wandering alone, when, on the spot, something changed in my heart. It's my confession—there it is. To come back, to come back on the instant—the idea gave me wings. It was as if I suddenly saw something—as if it all became possible. I could come for what you yourself came for: that was enough. So here I am. It's not for my own—that's over. But I'm here for *them*." And breathless, infinitely relieved by her low precipitate explanation, she looked with eyes that reflected all its splendor at the magnificence of their altar.

"They're here for you," Stransom said, "They're present tonight as they've never been. They speak for you—don't you see?—in a passion of light; they sing out like a choir of angels. Don't you hear what they

say?—they offer the very thing you asked of me."

"Don't talk of it—don't think of it; forget it!" She spoke in hushed supplication, and while the alarm deepened in her eyes she disengaged one of her hands and passed an arm round him to support him better, to help him to sink into a seat.

He let himself go, resting on her; he dropped upon the bench and she fell on her knees beside him, his own arm round her shoulder. So he remained an instant, staring up at his shrine. "They say there's a gap in the array—they say it's not full, complete. Just one more," he went on, softly—"isn't that what you wanted? Yes, one more, one more."

"Ah no more—no more!" she wailed, as with a quick new horror of it, under her breath.

"Yes, one more," he repeated, simply; "just one!" And with this his head dropped on her shoulder; she felt that in his weakness he had fainted. But alone with him in the dusky church a great dread was on her of what might still happen, for his face had the whiteness of death.

Edith Wharton
1862-1937

BORN in New York of Rhinelander and Schermerhorn stock, Edith Newbold Jones began writing at the age of eleven, when she produced a novel. "Oh, how do you do, Mrs. Brown?" the novel opened. "If I only had known you were going to call, I should have tidied up the drawing room." To which her mother said, "Drawing rooms are always tidy." Mrs. Jones, fearing from this precocious attempt at novel writing that her little girl might be getting too intellectual, put her shoulder behind the task of fitting young Edith into the lunching, afternoon-calling, park-driving pattern to which she belonged by birth. "Never talk about money," her mother once admonished her as a part of this pattern, "and think about it as little as possible."

When, later, Edith Wharton took matters into her own hands and became a professional novelist, her friends refrained politely, as her books grew in popularity, from even mentioning the fact that she wrote. In two early novels, *The House of Mirth* and *The Custom of the Country*, she tried to show up the would-be aristocracy of her own New York and Boston. "Have you ever known a respectable woman?" someone asked her indignantly, after the experiences of Lily Bart and Undine Sprague had been whispered over teacups.

At the age of twenty-three Edith married Edward Wharton, a Boston banker, who shortly after their marriage became ill. Because of his health, the Whartons went to France to live, and it was there that Edith Wharton came into her literary own. The two strong personality influences in her life were Henry James and S. Weir Mitchell, her doctor. Dr. Mitchell is said to have urged her to write to relieve her nervous tension. And Henry James, a close friend, became her spiritual mentor. Like James, she had the greatest conscientiousness in her creative work: even when most successful, she was aware of artistic shortcomings. She had a photographic memory and wrote her three most distinctively American novels—*Ethan Frome, Summer,* and *The Age of Innocence*—while in France.

Afterward

BY EDITH WHARTON

I

"Oh, there is one, of course, but you'll never know it." The assertion, laughingly flung out six months earlier in a bright June garden, came back to Mary Boyne with a new perception of its significance as she stood, in the December dusk, waiting for the lamps to be brought into the library.

The words had been spoken by their friend Alida Stair, as they sat at tea on her lawn at Pangbourne, in reference to the very house of which the library in question was the central, the pivotal "feature." Mary Boyne and her husband, in quest of a country place in one of the southern or southwestern counties, had, on their arrival in England, carried their problem straight to Alida Stair, who had successfully solved it in her own case; but it was not until they had rejected, almost capriciously, several practical and judicious suggestions that she threw out: "Well, there's Lyng, in Dorsetshire. It belongs to Hugo's cousins, and you can get it for a song."

The reason she gave for its being obtainable on these terms—its remoteness from a station, its lack of electric light, hot-water pipes, and other vulgar necessities—were exactly those pleasing in favor with two romantic Americans perversely in search of the economic drawbacks which were associated, in their tradition, with unusual architectural felicities.

"I should never believe I was living in an old house unless I was thoroughly uncomfortable," Ned Boyne, the more extravagant of the two, had jocosely insisted; "the least hint of 'convenience' would make me think it had been bought out of an exhibition, with the pieces numbered, and set up again." And they had proceeded to enumerate, with humorous precision, their various doubts and demands, refusing to believe that the house their cousin recommended was *really* Tudor till they learned it had no heating system, or that the village church was literally in the grounds till she assured them of the deplorable uncertainty of the water supply.

"It's too uncomfortable to be true!" Edward Boyne had continued to exult as the avowal of each disadvantage was successively wrung from her; but he had cut short his rhapsody to ask, with a relapse to distrust: "And the ghost? You've been concealing from us the fact that there is no ghost!"

Mary, at the moment, had laughed with him, yet almost with her laugh, being possessed of several sets of independent perceptions, had been struck by a note of flatness in Alida's answering hilarity.

"Oh, Dorsetshire's full of ghosts, you know."

"Yes, yes; but that won't do. I don't want to have to drive ten miles to see somebody else's ghost. I want one of my own on the premises. *Is there a ghost at Lyng?*"

His rejoinder had made Alida laugh again, and it was then that she had flung back tantalizingly: "Oh, there *is* one, of course, but you'll never know it."

"Never know it?" Boyne pulled her up. "But what in the world constitutes a ghost except the fact of its being known for one?"

"I can't say. But that's the story."

"That there's a ghost, but that nobody knows it's a ghost?"

"Well—not till afterward, at any rate."

"Till afterward?"

"Not till long long afterward."

"But if it's once been identified as an unearthly visitant, why hasn't its *signalement* been handed down in the family? How has it managed to preserve its incognito?"

Alida could only shake her head. "Don't ask me. But it has."

"And then suddenly"—Mary spoke up as if from cavernous depths of divination—"suddenly, long afterward, one says to one's self, '*That was it?*'"

She was startled at the sepulchral sound with which her question fell on the banter of the other two, and she saw the shadow of the same surprise flit across Alida's pupils. "I suppose so. One just has to wait."

"Oh, hang waiting!" Ned broke in. "Life's too short for a ghost who can only be enjoyed in retrospect. Can't we do better than that, Mary?"

But it turned out that in the event they were not destined to, for within three months of their conversation with Mrs. Stair they were settled at Lyng, and the life they had yearned for, to the point of planning it in advance in all its daily details, had actually begun for them.

It was to sit, in the thick December dusk, by just such a wide-hooded fireplace, under just such black oak rafters, with the sense that beyond the mullioned panes the downs were darkened to a deeper solitude: it was for the ultimate indulgence of such sensations that Mary Boyne, abruptly exiled from New York by her husband's business, had endured for nearly fourteen years the soul-deadening ugliness of a Middle Western town, and that Boyne had ground on doggedly at his engineering till, with a suddenness that still made her blink, the prodigious windfall of the Blue Star Mine had put them at a stroke in possession of life and the leisure to taste it. They had never for a moment meant their new state to be one of idleness; but they meant to give themselves only to harmonious activities. She had her vision of painting and gardening (against a background of gray walls), he dreamed of the production of his long-planned book on the "Economic Basis of Culture"; and with such absorbing work ahead no existence could be too sequestered: they could not get far enough from the world, or plunge deep enough into the past.

Dorsetshire had attracted them from the first by an air of remoteness out of all proportion to its geographical position. But to the Boynes it was one of the ever-recurring wonders of the whole incredibly compressed island—a nest of counties, as they put it—that for the production of its effects so little of a given quality went so far: that so few miles made a distance, and so short a distance a difference.

"It's that," Ned had once enthusiastically explained, "that gives such depth to their effects, such relief to their contrasts. They've been able to lay the butter so thick on every delicious mouthful."

The butter had certainly been laid on thick at Lyng: the old house hidden under a shoulder of the downs had almost all the finer marks of commerce with a protracted past. The mere fact that it was neither large nor exceptional made it, to the Boynes, abound the more completely in its special charm—the charm of having been for centuries a deep dim reservoir of life. The life had probably not been of the most vivid order: for long periods, no doubt, it had fallen as noiselessly into the past as the quiet drizzle of autumn fell, hour after hour, into the fish pond between the yews; but these backwaters of existence sometimes breed, in their sluggish depths, strange acuities of emotion, and Mary Boyne had felt from the first the mysterious stir of intenser memories.

The feeling had never been stronger than on this particular afternoon when, waiting in the library for the lamps to come, she rose from her seat and stood among the shadows of the hearth. Her husband had gone off, after luncheon, for one of his long tramps on the downs. She had noticed of late that he preferred to go alone; and, in the tried security of their personal relations, had been driven to conclude that his book was bothering him, and that he needed the afternoons to turn over in solitude the problems left from the morning's work. Certainly the book was not going as smoothly as she had thought it would, and there were lines of perplexity between his eyes such as had never been there in his engineering days. He had often, then, looked fagged to the verge of illness, but the native demon of "worry" had never branded his brow. Yet the few pages he had so far read to her—the introduction, and a summary of the opening chapter—showed a firm hold on his subject, and an increasing confidence in his powers.

The fact threw her into deeper perplexity, since, now that he had done with "business" and its disturbing contingencies, the one other possible source of anxiety was eliminated. Unless it were his health, then? But physically he had gained since they had come to Dorsetshire, grown robuster, ruddier and fresher-eyed. It was only within the last week that she had felt in him the undefinable change which made her restless in his absence, and as tongue-tied in his presence as though it were *she* who had a secret to keep from him!

The thought that there *was* a secret somewhere between them struck her with a sudden rap of wonder, and she looked about her down the long room.

"Can it be the house?" she mused.

The room itself might have been full of secrets. They seemed to be piling themselves up, as evening fell, like the layers and layers of velvet shadow dropping from the low ceiling, the rows of books, the smoke-blurred sculpture of the hearth.

"Why, of course—the house is haunted!" she reflected.

The ghost—Alida's imperceptible ghost—after figuring largely in the banter of their first month or two at Lyng, had been gradually left aside as too ineffectual for imaginative use. Mary had, indeed, as became the tenant of a haunted house, made the customary inquiries among her rural neighbours, but, beyond a vague "They du say so, Ma'am," the villagers had nothing to impart. The elusive specter had apparently never had sufficient identity for a legend to crystallize about it, and after a time the Boynes had set the matter down to their profit-and-loss account, agreeing that Lyng was one of the few houses good enough in itself to dispense with supernatural enhancements.

"And I suppose, poor ineffectual demon, that's why it beats its beautiful wings in vain in the void," Mary had laughingly concluded.

"Or, rather," Ned answered in the same strain, "why, amid so much that's ghostly, it can never affirm its separate existence as *the* ghost." And thereupon their invisible housemate had finally dropped out of their references, which were numerous enough to make them soon unaware of the loss.

Now, as she stood on the hearth, the subject of their earlier curiosity revived in her with a new sense of its meaning—a sense gradually acquired through daily contact with the scene of the lurking mystery. It was the house itself, of course, that was possessed the ghost-seeing faculty, that communed visually but secretly with its own past; if one could only get into close enough communion with the house, one might surprise its secret, and acquire the ghost-sight on one's own account. Perhaps, in his long hours in this very room, where she never trespassed till the afternoon, her husband *had* acquired it already, and was silently carrying about the weight of whatever it had revealed to him. Mary was too well versed in the code of the spectral world not to know that one could not talk about the ghosts one saw: to do so was almost as great a breach of taste as to name a lady in a club. But this explanation did not really satisfy her. "What, after all, except for the fun of the shudder," she reflected, "would he really care for any of their old ghosts?" And thence she was thrown back once more on the fundamental dilemma; the fact that one's greater or less susceptibility to spectral influences had no particular bearing on the case, since, when one *did* see a ghost at Lyng, one did not know it.

"Not till long afterward," Alida Stair had said. Well, supposing Ned *had* seen one when they first came, and had known only within the last week what had happened to him? More and more under the spell of the hour, she threw back her thoughts to the early days of their tenancy, but at first only to recall a lively confusion of unpacking, settling, arranging of books, and calling to each other from remote corners of the house as, treasure after treasure, it revealed itself to them. It was in this particular connection that she presently recalled a certain soft afternoon of the previous October, when, passing from the first rapturous flurry of exploration to a detailed inspection of the old house, she had pressed (like a novel heroine) a panel that opened on a flight of corkscrew stairs leading to a flat ledge of the roof—

the roof which, from below, seemed to slope away on all sides too abruptly for any but practiced feet to scale.

The view from this hidden coign was enchanting, and she had flown down to snatch Ned from his papers and give him the freedom of her discovery. She remembered still how, standing at her side, he had passed his arm about her while their gaze flew to the long tossed horizon line of the downs, and then dropped contentedly back to trace the arabesque of yew hedges about the fish pond, and the shadow of the cedar on the lawn.

"And now the other way," he had said, turning her about within his arm; and closely pressed to him, she had absorbed, like some long satisfying draught, the picture of the gray-walled court, the squat lions on the gates, and the lime avenue reaching up to the highroad under the downs.

It was just then, while they gazed and held each other, that she had felt his arm relax, and heard a sharp "Hullo!" that made her turn to glance at him.

Distinctly, yes, she now recalled that she had seen, as she glanced, a shadow of anxiety, of perplexity, rather, fall across his face; and, following his eyes, had beheld the figure of a man—a man in loose grayish clothes, as it appeared to her —who was sauntering down the lime avenue to the court with the doubtful gait of a stranger who seeks his way. Her shortsighted eyes had given her but a blurred impression of slightness and grayishness, with something foreign, or at least un-local, in the cut of the figure or its dress; but her husband had apparently seen more—seen enough to make him push past her with a

hasty "Wait!" and dash down the stairs without pausing to give her a hand.

A slight tendency to dizziness obliged her, after a provisional clutch at the chimney against which they had been leaning, to follow him first more cautiously; and when she had reached the landing she paused again, for a less definite reason, leaning over the banister to strain her eyes through the silence of the brown sun-flecked depths. She lingered there till, somewhere in those depths, she heard the closing of a door; then, mechanically impelled, she went down the shallow flight of steps till she reached the lower hall.

The front door stood open on the sunlight of the court, and hall and court were empty. The library door was open, too, and after listening in vain for any sound of voices within, she crossed the threshold, and found her husband alone, vaguely fingering the papers on his desk.

He looked up, as if surprised at her entrance, but the shadow of anxiety had passed from his face, leaving it even, as she fancied, a little brighter and clearer than usual.

"What was it? Who was it?" she asked.

"Who?" he repeated, with the surprise still all on his side.

"The man we saw coming toward the house."

He seemed to reflect. "The man? Why, I thought I saw Peters; I dashed after him to say a word about the stable drains, but he had disappeared before I could get down."

"Disappeared? But he seemed to be walking so slowly when we saw him."

Boyne shrugged his shoulders. "So I thought; but he must have got up steam in the interval. What do you say to our trying a scramble up Meldon Steep before sunset?"

That was all. At the time the occurrence had been less than nothing, had, indeed, been immediately obliterated by the magic of their first vision from Meldon Steep, a height which they had dreamed of climbing ever since they had first seen its bare spine rising above the roof of Lyng. Doubtless it was the mere fact of the other incident's having occurred on the very day of their ascent to Meldon that had kept it stored away in the fold of memory from which it now emerged; for in itself it had no mark of the portentous. At the moment there could have been nothing more natural than that Ned should dash himself from the roof in pursuit of dilatory tradesmen. It was the period when they were always on the watch for one or the other of the specialists employed about the place; always lying in wait for them, and rushing out at them with questions, reproaches or reminders. And certainly in the distance the gray figure had looked like Peters.

Yet now, as she reviewed the scene, she felt her husband's explanation of it to have been invalidated by the look of anxiety on his face. Why had the familiar appearance of Peters made him anxious? Why, above all, if it was of such prime necessity to confer with him on the subject of the stable drains, had the failure to find him produced such a look of relief? Mary could not say that any one of these questions had occurred to her at the time, yet, from the promptness with which they now marshaled themselves at her summons, she had a sense that they must all along have been there, waiting their hour.

II

Weary with her thoughts, she moved to the window. The library was now quite dark, and she was surprised to see how much faint light the outer world still held.

As she peered out into it across the court, a figure shaped itself far down the perspective of bare limes; it looked a mere blot of deeper gray in the grayness, and for an instant, as it moved toward her, her heart thumped to the thought "It's the ghost!"

She had time, in that long instant, to feel suddenly that the man of whom, two months earlier, she had had a distant vision from the roof, was now, at his predestined hour, about to reveal himself as *not* having been Peters; and her spirit sank under the impending fear of the disclosure. But almost with the next tick of the clock the figure, gaining substance and character, showed itself even to her weak sight as her husband's; and she turned to meet him, as he entered, with the confession of her folly.

"It's really too absurd," she laughed out, "but I never *can* remember!"

"Remember what?" Boyne questioned as they drew together.

"That when one sees the Lyng ghost one never knows it."

Her hand was on his sleeve, and he kept it there, but with no response in his gesture or in the lines of his preoccupied face.

"Did you think you'd seen it?" he asked, after an appreciable interval.

"Why, I actually took *you* for it, my dear, in my mad determination to spot it!"

"Me—just now?" His arm dropped away, and he turned from her with a faint echo of her laugh. "Really, dearest, you'd better give it up, if that's the best you can do."

"Oh, yes, I give it up. Have *you*?" she asked, turning round on him abruptly.

The parlormaid had entered with letters and a lamp, and the light struck up into Boyne's face as he bent above the tray she presented.

"Have *you*?" Mary perversely insisted, when the servant had disappeared on her errand of illumination.

"Have I what?" he rejoined absently, the light bringing out the sharp stamp of worry between his brows as he turned over the letters.

"Given up trying to see the ghost." Her heart beat a little faster at the experiment she was making.

Her husband, laying his letters aside, moved away into the shadow of the hearth.

"I never tried," he said, tearing open the wrapper of a newspaper.

"Well, of course," Mary persisted, "the exasperating thing is that there's no use trying, since one can't be sure till so long afterward."

He was unfolding the paper as if he had hardly heard her; but after a pause, during which the sheets rustled spasmodically between his hands, he looked up to ask, "Have you any idea *how long*?"

Mary had sunk into a low chair beside the fireplace. From her seat she glanced over, startled, at her husband's profile, which was projected against the circle of lamplight.

"No; none. Have *you*?" she retorted, repeating her former phrase with an added stress of intention.

Boyne crumpled the paper into a bunch, and then, inconsequently, turned back with it toward the lamp.

"Lord, no! I only meant," he explained, with a faint tinge of impatience, "is there any legend, any tradition, as to that?"

"Not that I know of," she answered; but the impulse to add "What makes you ask?" was checked by the reappearance of the parlormaid, with tea and a second lamp.

With the dispersal of shadows, and the repetition of the daily domestic office, Mary Boyne felt herself less oppressed by that sense of something mutely imminent which had darkened her afternoon. For a few moments she gave herself to the details of her task, and when she looked up from it she was struck to the point of bewilderment by the change in her husband's face. He had seated himself near the farther lamp, and was absorbed in the perusal of his letters; but was it something he had found in them, or merely the shifting of her own point of view, that had restored his features to their normal aspect? The longer she looked the more definitely the change affirmed itself. The lines of tension had vanished, and such traces of fatigue as lingered were of the kind easily attributable to steady mental effort. He glanced up, as if drawn by her gaze, and met her eyes with a smile.

"I'm dying for my tea, you know; and here's a letter for you," he said.

She took the letter he held out in exchange for the cup she proffered him, and, returning to her seat, broke the seal with the languid gesture of the reader whose interests are all enclosed in the circle of one cherished presence.

Her next conscious motion was that of starting to her feet, the letter falling to them as she rose, while she held out to her husband a newspaper clipping.

"Ned! What's this? What does it mean?"

He had risen at the same instant, almost as if hearing her cry before she uttered it; and for a perceptible space of time he and she studied each other, like adversaries watching for an advantage, across the space between her chair and his desk.

"What's what? You fairly made me jump!" Boyne said at length, moving toward her with a sudden half-exasperated laugh. The shadow of apprehension was on his face again, not now a look of fixed foreboding, but a shifting vigilance of lips and eyes that gave her the sense of his feeling himself invisibly surrounded.

Her hand shook so that she could hardly give him the clipping.

"This article—from the *Waukesha Sentinel*—that a man named Elwell has brought suit against you—that there was something wrong about the Blue Star Mine. I can't understand more than half."

They continued to face each other as she spoke, and to her astonishment she saw that her words had the almost immediate effect of dissipating the strained watchfulness of his look.

"Oh, *that!*" He glanced down the printed slip, and then folded it with the gesture of one who handles something harmless and familiar. "What's the matter with you this afternoon, Mary? I thought you'd got bad news."

She stood before him with her undefinable terror subsiding slowly under the reassurance of his tone.

"You knew about this, then—it's all right?"

"Certainly I knew about it; and it's all right."

"But what *is* it? I don't under-stand. What does this man accuse you of?"

"Pretty nearly every crime in the calendar." Boyne had tossed the clipping down, and thrown himself into an armchair near the fire. "Do you want to hear the story? It's not particularly interesting—just a squabble over interests in the Blue Star."

"But who is this Elwell? I don't know the name."

"Oh, he's a fellow I put into it—gave him a hand up. I told you all about him at the time."

"I dare say. I must have forgotten." Vainly she strained back among her memories. "But if you helped him, why does he make this return?"

"Probably some shyster lawyer got hold of him and talked him over. It's all rather technical and complicated. I thought that kind of thing bored you."

His wife felt a sting of compunction. Theoretically, she deprecated the American wife's detachment from her husband's professional interests, but in practice she had always found it difficult to fix her attention on Boyne's report of the transactions in which his varied interests involved him. Besides, she had felt during their years of exile, that, in a community where the amenities of living could be obtained only at the cost of efforts as arduous as her husband's professional labors, such brief leisure as he and she could command should be used as an escape from immediate preoccupations, a flight to the life they always dreamed of living. Once or twice, now that this new life had actually drawn its magic circle about them, she had asked herself if she had done right; but hitherto such conjectures had been no more than the retrospective excursions of an active fancy. Now for the first time, it startled her a little to find how little she knew of the material foundation on which her happiness was built.

She glanced at her husband, and was again reassured by the composure of his face; yet she felt the need of more definite grounds for her reassurance.

"But doesn't this suit worry you? Why have you never spoken to me about it?"

He answered both questions at once. "I didn't speak of it at first because it *did* worry me—annoyed me, rather. But it's all ancient history now. Your correspondent must have got hold of a back number of the *Sentinel*."

She felt a quick thrill of relief. "You mean it's over? He's lost his case?"

There was a just perceptible delay in Boyne's reply. "The suit's been withdrawn—that's all."

But she persisted, as if to exonerate herself from the inward charge of being too easily put off. "Withdrawn it because he saw he had no chance?"

"Oh, he had no chance," Boyne answered.

She was still struggling with a dimly felt perplexity at the back of her thoughts.

"How long ago was it withdrawn?"

He paused, as if with a slight return of his former uncertainty. "I've just had the news now; but I've been expecting it."

"Just now—in one of your letters?"

"Yes; in one of my letters."

She made no answer, and was aware only, after a short interval of waiting, that he had risen, and strolling across the room, had placed himself on the sofa at her side. She felt him, as he did so, pass an arm about her, she felt his hand seek hers and clasp it, and turning slowly, drawn by the warmth of his cheek, she met his smiling eyes.

"It's all right—it's all right?" she questioned, through the flood of her dissolving doubts; and "I give you my word it was never righter!" he laughed back at her, holding her close.

III

One of the strangest things she was afterward to recall out of all the next day's strangeness was the sudden and complete recovery of her sense of security.

It was in the air when she woke in her low-ceiled, dusky room; it went with her downstairs to the breakfast table, flashed out at her from the fire, and reduplicated itself from the flanks of the urn and the sturdy flutings of the Georgian teapot. It was as if, in some round-about way, all her diffused fears of the previous day, with their moment of sharp concentration about the newspaper article—as if this dim questioning of the future, and startled return upon the past, had between them liquidated the arrears of some haunting moral obligation. If she had indeed been careless of her husband's affairs, it was, her new state seemed to prove, because her faith in him instinctively justified such carelessness; and his right to her faith had now affirmed itself in the very face of menace and suspicion. She had never seen him more untroubled, more naturally and unconsciously himself, than after the cross-examination to which she had subjected him: it was almost as if he had been aware of her doubts, and had wanted the air cleared as much as she did.

It was as clear, thank heaven! as the bright outer light that surprised her almost with a touch of summer when she issued from the house for her daily round of the gardens. She had left Boyne at his desk, indulging herself, as she passed the library door, by a last peep at his quiet face, where he bent, pipe in mouth, above his papers; and now she had her own morning's task to perform. The task involved, on such charmed winter days, almost as much happy loitering about the different quarters of her demesne as if spring were already at work there. There were such endless possibilities still before her, such opportunities to bring out the latent graces of the old place, without a single irreverent touch of alteration, that the winter was all too short to plan what spring and autumn executed. And her recovered sense of safety gave, on this particular morning, a peculiar zest to her progress through the sweet still place. She went first to the kitchen garden, where the espaliered pear trees drew complicated patterns on the walls, and pigeons were fluttering and preening about the silvery-slated roof of their cot. There was something wrong about the piping of the hothouse and she was expecting an authority from Dorchester, who was to drive out between trains and make a diagnosis of the boiler. But when she dipped into the damp heat of the greenhouses, among the spiced scents and waxy pinks and reds of old-fashioned exotics—even the flora of Lyng was in the note!—she learned that the great man had not arrived, and, the day being too rare to waste in an artificial atmosphere, she came out again and paced along the springy turf of the bowling green to the gardens behind the house. At their farther end rose a grass terrace, looking across the fish pond and yew hedges to the long house front with its twisted chimneystacks and blue roof angles all drenched in the pale gold moisture of the air.

Seen thus, across the level tracery of the gardens, it sent her, from open windows and hospitably smoking chimneys, the look of some warm human presence, of a mind slowly ripened on a sunny wall of experience. She had never before had such a sense of her intimacy with it, such a conviction that its secrets were all beneficent, kept, as they said to children, "for one's good," such a trust in its power to gather up her life and Ned's into the harmonious pattern of the long long story it sat there weaving in the sun.

She heard steps behind her, and turned, expecting to see the gardener accompanied by the engineer from Dorchester. But only one figure was in sight, that of a youngish slightly built man, who, for reasons she could not on the spot have given, did not remotely resemble her notion of an authority on hothouse boilers. The newcomer, on seeing her, lifted his hat, and paused with the air of a gentleman—perhaps a traveler— who wishes to make it known that his intrusion is involuntary. Lyng occasionally attracted the more cultivated traveler, and Mary half expected to see the stranger dissemble a camera, or justify his presence by producing it. But he made no gesture of any sort, and after a moment she asked, in a tone responding to the courteous hesitation of his attitude: "Is there anyone you wish to see?"

"I came to see Mr. Boyne," he answered. His intonation, rather than his accent, was faintly American, and Mary, at the note, looked at him more closely. The brim of his soft felt hat cast a shade on his face, which, thus obscured, wore to her shortsighted gaze a look of seriousness, as of a person arriving "on business," and civilly but firmly aware of his rights.

Past experience had made her equally sensible to such claims; but she was jealous of her husband's morning hours, and doubtful of his having given anyone the right to intrude on them.

"Have you an appointment with my husband?" she asked.

The visitor hesitated, as if unprepared for the question.

"I think he expects me," he replied.

It was Mary's turn to hesitate. "You see this is his time for work: he never sees anyone in the morning."

He looked at her a moment without answering; then, as if accepting her decision, he began to move away. As he turned, Mary saw him pause and glance up at the peaceful house front. Something in his air suggested weariness and disappointment, the dejection of the traveler who has come from far off and whose hours are limited by the timetable. It occurred to her that if this were the case her refusal might have made his errand vain, and a sense of compunction caused her to hasten after him.

"May I ask if you have come a long way?"

He gave her the same grave look. "Yes—I have come a long way."

"Then, if you'll go to the house, no doubt my husband will see you now. You'll find him in the library."

She did not know why she had added the last phrase, except from a vague impulse to atone for her previous inhospitality. The visitor seemed about to express his thanks, but her attention was distracted by the approach of the gardener with a companion who bore all the marks of being the expert from Dorchester.

"This way," she said, waving the stranger to the house; and an instant later she had forgotten him in the absorption of her meeting with the boilermaker.

The encounter led to such far-reaching results that the engineer ended by finding it expedient to ignore his train, and Mary was beguiled into spending the remainder of the morning in absorbed confabulation among the flowerpots. When the colloquy ended, she was surprised to find that it was nearly luncheon time, and she half expected, as she hurried back to the house, to see her husband coming out to meet her. But she found no one in the court but an undergardener raking the gravel, and the hall, when she entered it, was so silent that she guessed Boyne to be still at work.

Not wishing to disturb him, she turned into the drawing room, and there, at her writing table, lost herself in renewed calculations of the outlay to which the morning's conference had pledged her. The fact that she could permit herself such follies had not yet lost its novelty; and somehow, in contrast to the vague fears of the previous days, it now seemed an element of her recovered security, of the sense that, as Ned had said, things in general had never been "righter."

She was still luxuriating in a lavish play of figures when the parlormaid, from the threshold, roused her with an enquiry as to the expediency of serving luncheon. It was one of their jokes that Trimmle announced luncheon as if she were divulging a state secret, and Mary, intent upon her papers, merely murmured an absent-minded assent.

She felt Trimmle wavering doubtfully on the threshold, as if in rebuke of such unconsidered assent; then her retreating steps sounded down the passage, and Mary, pushing away her papers, crossed the hall and went to the library door. It was still closed, and she wavered in her turn, disliking to disturb her husband, yet anxious that he should not exceed his usual measure of work. As she stood there, balancing her impulses, Trimmle returned with the announcement of luncheon, and Mary, thus impelled, opened the library door.

Boyne was not at his desk, and she peered about her, expecting to discover him before the bookshelves, somewhere down the length of the room; but her call brought no response, and gradually it became clear to her that he was not there.

She turned back to the parlor-maid.

"Mr. Boyne must be upstairs. Please tell him that luncheon is ready."

Trimmle appeared to hesitate between the obvious duty of obedience and an equally obvious conviction of the foolishness of the injunction laid on her. The struggle resulted in her saying: "If you please, Madam, Mr. Boyne's not upstairs."

"Not in his room? Are you sure?"

"I'm sure, Madam."

Mary consulted the clock. "Where is he, then?"

"He's gone out," Trimmle announced, with the superior air of one who has respectfully waited for the question that a well-ordered mind would have put first.

Mary's conjecture had been right, then. Boyne must have gone to the gardens to meet her, and since she had missed him, it was clear that he had taken the shorter way by the south door, instead of going round to the court. She crossed the hall to the French window opening directly on the yew garden, but the parlor-maid, after another moment of inner conflict, decided to bring out: "Please, Madam, Mr. Boyne didn't go that way."

Mary turned back. "Where *did* he go? And when?"

"He went out of the front door, up the drive, Madam." It was a matter of principle with Trimmle never to answer more than one question at a time.

"Up the drive? At this hour?" Mary went to the door herself, and glanced across the court through the tunnel of bare limes. But its perspective was as empty as when she had scanned it on entering.

"Did Mr. Boyne leave no message?"

Trimmle seemed to surrender herself to a last struggle with the forces of chaos.

"No, Madam. He just went out with the gentleman."

"The gentleman? What gentleman?" Mary wheeled about, as if to front this new factor.

"The gentleman who called, Madam," said Trimmle resignedly.

"When did a gentleman call? Do explain yourself, Trimmle!"

Only the fact that Mary was very hungry, and that she wanted to consult her husband about the greenhouses, would have caused her to lay so unusual an injunction on her attendant; and even now she was detached enough to note in Trimmle's eye the dawning defiance of the respectful subordinate who has been pressed too hard.

"I couldn't exactly say the hour, Madam, because I didn't let the gentleman in," she replied, with an air of discreetly ignoring the irregularity of her mistress's course.

"You didn't let him in?"

"No, Madam. When the bell rang I was dressing, and Agnes——"

"Go and ask Agnes, then," said Mary.

Trimmle still wore her look of patient magnanimity. "Agnes would not know, Madam, for she had unfortunately burnt her hand in trimming the wick of the new lamp from town"—Trimmle, as Mary was aware, had always been opposed to the new lamp—"and so Mrs. Dockett sent the kitchenmaid instead."

Mary looked again at the clock. "It's after two! Go and ask the kitchenmaid if Mr. Boyne left any word."

She went in to luncheon without waiting, and Trimmle presently brought her there the kitchenmaid's statement that the gentleman had called about eleven o'clock, and that Mr. Boyne had gone out with him without leaving any message. The kitchenmaid did not even know the caller's name, for he had written it on a slip of paper, which he had folded and handed to her, with the injunction to deliver it at once to Mr. Boyne.

Mary finished her luncheon, still wondering, and when it was over, and Trimmle had brought the coffee to the drawing room, her wonder had deepened to a first faint tinge of disquietude. It was unlike Boyne to absent himself without explanation at so unwonted an hour, and the difficulty of identifying the visitor whose summons he had

apparently obeyed made his disappearance the more unaccountable. Mary Boyne's experience as the wife of a busy engineer, subject to sudden calls and compelled to keep irregular hours, had trained her to the philosophic acceptance of surprises; but since Boyne's withdrawal from business he had adopted a Benedictine regularity of life. As if to make up for the dispersed and agitated years, with their "stand-up" lunches, and dinners rattled down to the joltings of the dining cars, he cultivated the last refinements of punctuality and monotony, discouraging his wife's fancy for the unexpected, and declaring that to a delicate taste there were infinite gradations of pleasure in the recurrences of habit.

Still, since no life can completely defend itself from the unforeseen, it was evident that all Boyne's precautions would sooner or later prove unavailable, and Mary concluded that he had cut short a tiresome visit by walking with his caller to the station, or at least accompanying him for part of the way.

This conclusion relieved her from farther preoccupation, and she went out herself to take up her conference with the gardener. Thence she walked to the village post office, a mile or so away; and when she turned toward home the early twilight was setting in.

She had taken a footpath across the downs, and as Boyne, meanwhile, had probably returned from the station by the highroad, there was little likelihood of their meeting. She felt sure, however, of his having reached the house before her; so sure that, when she entered it herself, without even pausing to inquire of Trimmle, she made directly for the library. But the library was still empty, and with an unwonted exactness of visual memory she observed that the papers on her husband's desk lay precisely as they had lain when she had gone in to call him to luncheon.

Then of a sudden she was seized by a vague dread of the unknown. She had closed the door behind her on entering, and as she stood alone in the long silent room, her dread seemed to take shape and sound, to be there breathing and lurking among the shadows. Her short-sighted eyes strained through them, half discerning an actual presence, something aloof, that watched and knew; and in the recoil from that intangible presence she threw herself on the bellrope and gave it a sharp pull.

This sharp summons brought Trimmle in precipitately with a lamp, and Mary breathed again at this sobering reappearance of the usual.

"You may bring tea if Mr. Boyne is in," she said, to justify her ring.

"Very well, Madam. But Mr. Boyne is not in," said Trimmle, putting down the lamp.

"Not in? You mean he's come back and gone out again?"

"No, Madam. He's never been back."

The dread stirred again, and Mary knew that now it had her fast.

"Not since he went out with—the gentleman?"

"Not since he went out with the gentleman."

"But who was the gentleman?" Mary insisted, with the shrill note of someone trying to be heard through a confusion of noises.

"That I couldn't say, Madam." Trimmle, standing there by the lamp, seemed suddenly to grow less round and rosy, as though eclipsed by the same creeping shade of apprehension.

"But the kitchenmaid knows—wasn't it the kitchenmaid who let him in?"

"She doesn't know either, Madam, for he wrote his name on a folded paper."

Mary, through her agitation, was aware that they were both designating the unknown visitor by a vague pronoun, instead of the conventional formula which, till then, had kept their allusions within the bounds of conformity. And at the same moment her mind caught at the suggestion of the folded paper.

"But he must have a name! Where's the paper?"

She moved to the desk, and began to turn over the documents that littered it. The first that caught her eye was an unfinished letter in her husband's hand, with his pen lying across it, as though dropped there at a sudden summons.

"My dear Parvis"—who was Parvis?—"I have just received your letter announcing Elwell's death, and while I suppose there is now no farther risk of trouble, it might be safer——"

She tossed the sheet aside, and continued her search; but no folded paper was discoverable among the letters and pages of manuscript which had been swept together in a heap, as if by a hurried or a startled gesture.

"But the kitchenmaid saw him. Send her here," she commanded, wondering at her dullness in not thinking sooner of so simple a solution.

Trimmle vanished in a flash, as if thankful to be out of the room, and when she reappeared, conducting the agitated underling, Mary had regained her self-possession, and had her questions ready.

The gentleman was a stranger, yes—that she understood. But what had he said? And, above all, what had he looked like? The first question was easily enough answered, for the disconcerting reason that he had said so little—had merely asked for Mr. Boyne, and, scribbling something on a bit of paper, had requested that it should at once be carried in to him.

"Then you don't know what he wrote? You're not sure it *was* his name?"

The kitchenmaid was not sure, but supposed it was, since he had written it in answer to her inquiry as to whom she should announce.

"And when you carried the paper in to Mr. Boyne, what did he say?"

The kitchenmaid did not think that Mr. Boyne had said anything, but she could not be sure, for just as she had handed him the paper and he was opening it, she had become aware that the visitor had followed her into the library, and she had slipped out, leaving the two gentlemen together.

"But then, if you left them in the library, how do you know that they went out of the house?"

This question plunged the witness into a momentary inarticulateness, from which she was rescued by Trimmle, who, by means of ingenious circumlocutions, elicited the statement that before she could cross the hall to the back passage she had heard the two gentlemen behind her, and had seen them go out of the front door together.

"Then, if you saw the strange gentleman twice, you must be able to tell me what he looked like."

But with this final challenge to her powers of expression it became clear that the limit of the kitchenmaid's endurance had been reached. The obligation of going to the front door to "show in" a visitor was in itself so subversive of the fundamental order of things that it had thrown her faculties into hopeless disarray, and she could only stammer out, after various panting efforts: "His hat, mum, was different-like, as you might say——"

"Different? How different?" Mary flashed out, her own mind, in the same instant, leaping back to an image left on it that morning, and then lost under layers of subsequent impressions.

"His hat had a wide brim, you mean? and his face was pale—a youngish face?" Mary pressed her, with a white-lipped intensity of interrogation. But if the kitchenmaid found any adequate answer to this challenge, it was swept away for her listener down the rushing current of her own convictions. The stranger—the stranger in the garden! Why had Mary not thought of him before? She needed no one now to tell her that it was he who had called for her husband and gone away with him. But who was he, and why had Boyne obeyed him?

IV

It leaped out at her suddenly, like a grin out of the dark, that they had often called England so little— "such a confoundedly hard place to get lost in."

A confoundedly hard place to get lost in! That had been her husband's phrase. And now, with the whole machinery of official investigation sweeping its flashlights from shore to shore, and across the dividing straits; now, with Boyne's name blazing from the walls of every town and village, his portrait (how that wrung her!) hawked up and down the country like the image of a hunted criminal; now the little compact populous island, so policed, surveyed and administered, revealed itself as a Sphinx-like guardian of abysmal mysteries, staring back into his wife's anguished eyes as if with the wicked joy of knowing something they would never know!

In the fortnight since Boyne's disappearance there had been no word of him, no trace of his movements. Even the usual misleading reports that raise expectancy in tortured bosoms had been few and fleeting. No one but the kitchenmaid had seen Boyne leave the house, and no one else had seen "the gentleman" who accompanied him. All inquiries in the neighborhood failed to elicit the memory of a stranger's presence that day in the neighborhood of Lyng. And no one had met Edward Boyne, either alone or in company, in any of the neighboring villages, or on the road across the downs, or at either of the local railway stations. The sunny English noon had swallowed him as completely as if he had gone out into Cimmerian night.

Mary, while every official means of investigation was working at its highest pressure, had ransacked her husband's papers for any trace of antecedent complications, of entanglements or obligations unknown to her, that might throw a ray into the darkness. But if any such had existed in the background of Boyne's life, they had vanished like the slip of paper on which the visitor had written his name. There remained no possible thread of guidance except—if it were indeed an exception —the letter which Boyne had apparently been in the act of writing when he received his mysterious summons. That letter, read and reread by his wife, and submitted by her to the police, yielded little enough to feed conjecture.

"I have just heard of Elwell's death, and while I suppose there is now no farther risk of trouble, it might be safer——" That was all. The "risk of trouble" was easily explained by the newspaper clipping which had apprised Mary of the suit brought against her husband by one of his associates in the Blue Star enterprise. The only new information conveyed by the letter was the fact of its showing Boyne, when he wrote it, to be still apprehensive of the results of the suit, though he had told his wife that it had been withdrawn, and though the letter itself proved that the plaintiff was dead. It took several days of cabling to fix the identity of the "Parvis" to whom the fragment was addressed, but even after these inquiries had shown him to be a Waukesha lawyer, no new facts concerning the Elwell suit were elicited. He appeared to have had no direct concern in it, but to have been conversant with the facts merely as an acquaintance, and possibly intermediary; and he declared himself unable to guess with what object Boyne intended to seek his assistance.

This negative information, sole fruit of the first fortnight's search, was not increased by a jot during the slow weeks that followed. Mary knew that the investigations were still being carried on, but she had a vague sense of their gradually slackening, as the actual march of time seemed to slacken. It was as though the days, flying horror-struck from the shrouded image of the one inscrutable day, gained assurance as the distance lengthened, till at last they fell back into their normal gait. And so with the human imaginations at work on the dark event. No doubt it occupied them still, but week by week and hour by hour it grew less absorbing, took up less space, was slowly but inevitably crowded out of the foreground of consciousness by the new problems perpetually bubbling up from the cloudy caldron of human experience.

Even Mary Boyne's consciousness gradually felt the same lowering of velocity. It still swayed with the incessant oscillations of conjecture; but they were slower, more rhythmical in their beat. There were even moments of weariness when, like the victim of some poison which leaves the brain clear, but holds the body motionless, she saw herself domesticated with the Horror, accepting its perpetual presence as one of the fixed conditions of life.

These moments lengthened into hours and days, till she passed into a phase of stolid acquiescence. She watched the routine of daily life with the incurious eye of a savage on whom the meaningless processes of civilization make but the faintest impression. She had come to regard herself as part of the routine, a spoke of the wheel, revolving with its motion; she felt almost like the furniture of the room in which she sat, an insensate object to be dusted and pushed about with the chairs and tables. And this deepening apathy held her fast at Lyng, in spite of the entreaties of friends and the usual medical recommendation of "change." Her friends supposed that her refusal to move was inspired by the belief that her husband would one day return to the spot from which he had vanished, and a beautiful legend grew up about this imaginary state of waiting. But in reality she had no such belief: the depths of anguish enclosing her were no longer lighted by flashes of hope. She was sure that Boyne would never come back, that he had gone out of her sight as completely as if Death itself had waited that day on the threshold. She had even renounced one by one, the various theories as to his disappearance which had been advanced by the press, the police, and her own agonized imagination. In sheer lassitude her mind turned from these alternatives of horror, and sank back into the blank fact that he was gone.

No, she would never know what had become of him—no one would ever know. But the house *knew*; the library in which she spent her long lonely evenings knew. For it was here that the last scene had been enacted, here that the stranger had come, and spoken the word which had caused Boyne to rise and follow him. The floor she trod had left his tread; the books on the shelves had seen his face; and there were moments when the intense consciousness of the old dusky walls seemed about to break out into some audible revelation of their secret. But the revelation never came, and she knew it would never come. Lyng was not one of the garrulous old houses that betray the secrets entrusted to them. Its very legend proved that it had always been the mute accomplice, the incorruptible custodian, of the mysteries it had surprised. And Mary Boyne, sitting face to face with its silence, felt the futility of seeking to break it by any human means.

V

"I don't say it *wasn't* straight, and yet I don't say it *was* straight. It was business."

Mary, at the words, lifted her head with a start, and looked intently at the speaker.

When, half an hour before, a card with "Mr. Parvis" on it had been brought up to her, she had been immediately aware that the name had been a part of her consciousness ever since she had read it at the head of Boyne's unfinished letter. In the library she had found awaiting her a small sallow man with a bald head and gold eyeglasses, and it sent a tremor through her to know that this was the person to whom her husband's last known thought had been directed.

Parvis, civilly, but without vain preamble—in the manner of a man who has his watch in his hand—had set forth the object of his visit. He had "run over" to England on business, and finding himself in the neighborhood of Dorchester, had not wished to leave it without paying his respects to Mrs. Boyne; and without asking her, if the occasion offered, what she meant to do about Bob Elwell's family.

The words touched the spring of some obscure dread in Mary's bosom. Did her visitor, after all, know what Boyne had meant by his unfinished phrase? She asked for an elucidation of his question, and noticed at once that he seemed surprised at her continued ignorance of the subject. Was it possible that she really knew as little as she said?

"I know nothing—you must tell me," she faltered out; and her visitor thereupon proceeded to unfold his story. It threw, even to her confused perceptions, and imperfectly initiated vision, a lurid glare on the whole hazy episode of the Blue Star Mine. Her husband had made his money in that brilliant speculation at the cost of "getting ahead" of someone less alert to seize the chance; and the victim of his ingenuity was young Robert Elwell, who had "put him on" to the Blue Star scheme.

Parvis, at Mary's first cry, had thrown her a sobering glance through his impartial glasses.

"Bob Elwell wasn't smart enough, that's all; if he had been he might have turned round and served Boyne the same way. It's the kind of thing that happens every day in business. I guess it's what the scientists call the survival of the fittest—see?" said Mr. Parvis, evidently pleased with the aptness of his analogy.

Mary felt a physical shrinking from the next question she tried to frame: it was as though the words on her lips had a taste that nauseated her.

"But then—you accuse my husband of doing something dishonorable?"

Mr. Parvis surveyed the question dispassionately. "Oh, no, I don't. I don't even say it wasn't straight." He glanced up and down the long lines of books, as if one of them might have supplied him with the definition he sought. "I don't say it *wasn't* straight, and yet I don't say it *was* straight. It was business." After all, no definition in his category could be more comprehensive than that.

Mary sat staring at him with a look of terror. He seemed to her like the indifferent emissary of some evil power.

"But Mr. Elwell's lawyers apparently did not take your view, since I suppose the suit was withdrawn by their advice."

"Oh, yes; they knew he hadn't a leg to stand on, technically. It was when they advised him to withdraw the suit that he got desperate. You see, he'd borrowed most of the money he lost in the Blue Star, and he was up a tree. That's why he shot himself when they told him he had no show."

The horror was sweeping over Mary in great deafening waves.

"He shot himself? He killed himself because of *that*?"

"Well, he didn't kill himself, exactly. He dragged on two months before he died." Parvis emitted the statement as unemotionally as a gramophone grinding out its "record."

"You mean that he tried to kill himself, and failed? And tried again?"

"Oh, he didn't have to *try* again," said Parvis grimly.

They sat opposite each other in silence, he swinging his eyeglasses thoughtfully about his finger, she, motionless, her arms stretched along her knees in an attitude of rigid tension.

"But if you knew all this," she began at length, hardly able to force her voice above a whisper, "how is it that when I wrote you at the time of my husband's disappearance you said you didn't understand his letter?"

Parvis received this without perceptible embarrassment: "Why, I didn't understand it—strictly speaking. And it wasn't the time to talk about it, if I had. The Elwell business was settled when the suit was withdrawn. Nothing I could have told you would have helped you to find your husband."

Mary continued to scrutinize him. "Then why are you telling me now?"

Still Parvis did not hesitate. "Well, to begin with, I supposed you knew more than you appear to—I mean about the circumstances of Elwell's death. And then people are talking of it now; the whole matter's been

raked up again. And I thought if you didn't know you ought to."

She remained silent, and he continued: "You see, it's only come out lately what a bad state Elwell's affairs were in. His wife's a proud woman, and she fought on as long as she could, going out to work, and taking sewing at home when she got too sick—something with the heart, I believe. But she had his mother to look after, and the children, and she broke down under it, and finally had to ask for help. That called attention to the case, and the papers took it up, and a subscription was started. Everybody out there liked Bob Elwell, and most of the prominent names in the place are down on the list, and people began to wonder why——"

Parvis broke off to fumble in an inner pocket. "Here," he continued, "here's an account of the whole thing from the *Sentinel*—a little sensational, of course. But I guess you'd better look it over."

He held out a newspaper to Mary, who unfolded it slowly, remembering, as she did so, the evening when, in that same room, the perusal of a clipping from the *Sentinel* had first shaken the depths of her security.

As she opened the paper, her eyes, shrinking from the glaring headlines, "Widow of Boyne's Victim Forced to Appeal for Aid," ran down the column of text to two portraits inserted in it. The first was her husband's, taken from a photograph made the year they came to England. It was the picture of him that she liked best, the one that stood on the writing table upstairs in her bedroom. As the eyes in the photograph met hers, she felt it would be impossible to read what was said of him, and closed her lids with the sharpness of the pain.

"I thought if you felt disposed to put your name down——" she heard Parvis continue.

She opened her eyes with an effort, and they fell on the other portrait. It was that of a youngish man, slightly built, with features somewhat blurred by the shadow of a projecting hat brim. Where had she seen that outline before? She stared at it confusedly, her heart hammering in her ears. Then she gave a cry.

"This is the man—the man who came for my husband!"

She heard Parvis start to his feet, and was dimly aware that she had slipped backward into the corner of the sofa, and that he was bending above her in alarm. She straightened herself, and reached out for the paper, which she had dropped. "It's the man! I should know him anywhere!" she persisted in a voice that sounded to her own ears like a scream.

Parvis's answer seemed to come to her from far off, down endless fog-muffled windings.

"Mrs. Boyne, you're not very well. Shall I call somebody? Shall I get a glass of water?"

"No, no, no!" She threw herself toward him, her hand frantically clutching the newspaper. "I tell you, it's the man! I know him! He spoke to me in the garden!"

Parvis took the journal from her, directing his glasses to the portrait. "It can't be, Mrs. Boyne. It's Robert Elwell."

"Robert Elwell?" Her white stare seemed to travel into space. "Then it was Robert Elwell who came for him."

"Came for Boyne? The day he went away from here?" Parvis's voice dropped as hers rose. He bent over, laying a fraternal hand on her, as if to coax her gently back into her seat. "Why, Elwell was dead! Don't you remember?"

Mary sat with her eyes fixed on the picture, unconscious of what he was saying.

"Don't you remember Boyne's unfinished letter to me—the one you found on his desk that day? It was written just after he'd heard of Elwell's death." She noticed an odd shake in Parvis's unemotional voice. "Surely you remember," he urged her.

Yes, she remembered: that was the profoundest horror of it. Elwell had died the day before her husband's disappearance; and this was Elwell's portrait; and it was the portrait of the man who had spoken to her in the garden. She lifted her head and looked slowly about the library. The library could have borne witness that it was also the portrait of the man who had come in that day to call Boyne from his unfinished letter. Through the misty surgings of her brain she heard the faint boom of half-forgotten words—words spoken by Alida Stair on the lawn at Pangbourne before Boyne and his wife had ever seen the house at Lyng, or had imagined that they might one day live there.

"This was the man who spoke to me," she repeated.

She looked again at Parvis. He was trying to conceal his disturbance under what he probably imagined to be an expression of indulgent commiseration; but the edges of his lips were blue. "He thinks me mad; but I'm not mad," she reflected; and suddenly there flashed upon her a way of justifying her strange affirmation.

She sat quiet, controlling the quiver of her lips, and waiting till she could trust her voice; then she said, looking straight at Parvis: "Will you answer me one question, please? When was it that Robert Elwell tried to kill himself?"

"When—when?" Parvis stammered.

"Yes; the date. Please try to remember."

She saw that he was growing still more afraid of her. "I have a reason," she insisted.

"Yes, yes. Only I can't remember. About two months before, I should say."

"I want the date," she repeated.

Parvis picked up the newspaper. "We might see here," he said, still humoring her. He ran his eyes down the page. "Here it is. Last October—the——"

She caught the words from him. "The twentieth, wasn't it?" With a sharp look at her, he verified. "Yes, the twentieth. Then you *did* know?"

"I know now." Her gaze continued to travel past him. "Sunday, the twentieth—that was the day he came first."

Parvis's voice was almost inaudible. "Came *here* first?"

"Yes."

"You saw him twice, then?"

"Yes, twice." She just breathed it at him. "He came first on the twentieth of October. I remember the date because it was the day we went up Meldon Steep for the first time." She felt a faint gasp of inward laughter at the thought that but for that she might have forgotten.

Parvis continued to scrutinize her, as if trying to intercept her gaze.

"We saw him from the roof," she went on. "He came down the lime avenue toward the house. He was dressed just as he is in that picture. My husband saw him first. He was frightened, and ran down ahead of me; but there was no one there. He had vanished."

"Elwell had vanished?" Parvis faltered.

"Yes." Their two whispers seemed to grope for each other. "I couldn't think what had happened. I see now. He *tried* to come then; but he wasn't dead enough—he couldn't reach us. He had to wait for two months to die; and then he came back again—and Ned went with him."

She nodded at Parvis with the look of triumph of a child who has worked out a difficult puzzle. But suddenly she lifted her hands with a desperate gesture, pressing them to her temples.

"Oh, my God! I sent him to Ned—I told him where to go! I sent him to this room!" she screamed.

She felt the walls of books rush toward her, like inward falling ruins; and she heard Parvis, a long way off, through the ruins, crying to her, and struggling to get at her. But she was numb to his touch, she did not know what he was saying. Through the tumult she heard but one clear note, the voice of Alida Stair, speaking on the lawn at Pangbourne.

"You won't know till afterward," it said. "You won't know till long, long afterward."

OF OUR TIME

Isak Dinesen

1885-1962

Isak Dinesen, the Baroness Blixen, was a strong and original personality, a Danish woman who lived in an ancient ancestral home near Elsinore, whose father came to America in the '70's and trapped for three years with the Minnesota Indians. True daughter of her father, she lived seventeen years of her life in Kenya Colony and ran a coffee plantation single-handed for much of that time. *Out of Africa* is her tribute to this African adventure and to her Kikuyu native servants—a fascinating account of a strange but enormously satisfying experience. *Seven Gothic Tales* and *Winter's Tales*, two volumes of long short stories, were written in English, which no doubt accounts for the freshness and originality of word and phrase. They are strange tales—as Dorothy Canfield describes them: "tense, fierce, hard, controlled, overcivilized, savage." "Sorrow-Acre" comes from *Winter's Tales*.

Sorrow-Acre

BY ISAK DINESEN

THE low, undulating Danish landscape was silent and serene, mysteriously wide awake in the hour before sunrise. There was not a cloud in the pale sky, not a shadow along the dim, pearly fields, hills and woods. The mist was lifting from the valleys and hollows, the air was cool, the grass and the foliage dripping wet with morning dew. Unwatched by the eyes of man, and undisturbed by his activity, the country breathed a timeless life, to which language was inadequate.

All the same, a human race had lived on this land for a thousand years, had been formed by its soil and weather, and had marked it with its thoughts, so that now no one could tell where the existence of the one ceased and the other began. The thin gray line of a road, winding across the plain and up and down hills, was the fixed materialization of human longing, and of the human notion that it is better to be in one place than another.

A child of the country would read this open landscape like a book. The irregular mosaic of meadows and cornlands was a picture, in timid green and yellow, of the people's struggle for its daily bread; the centuries had taught it to plow and sow much within these elegant, geo-

in this way. On a distant hill the immovable wings of a windmill, in a small blue cross against the sky, delineated a later stage in the career of bread. The blurred outline of thatched roofs—a low, brown growth of the earth—where the huts of the village thronged together, told the history, from his cradle to his grave, of the peasant, the creature nearest to the soil and dependent on it, prospering in a fertile year and dying in years of drought and pests.

A little higher up, with the faint horizontal line of the white cemetery wall round it, and the vertical contour of tall poplars by its side, the red-tiled church bore witness, as far as the eye reached, that this was a Christian country. The child of the land knew it as a strange house, inhabited only for a few hours every seventh day, but with a strong, clear voice in it to give out the joys and sorrows of the land: a plain, square embodiment of the nation's trust in the justice and mercy of heaven. But where, amongst cupular woods and groves, the lordly, pyramidal silhouette of the cut lime avenues rose in the air, there a big country house lay.

The child of the land would read much within these elegant, geometrical ciphers on the hazy blue. They spoke of power, the lime trees paraded round a stronghold. Up here was decided the destiny of the surrounding land and of the men and beasts upon it, and the peasant lifted his eyes to the green pyramids with awe. They spoke of dignity, decorum, and taste. Danish soil grew no finer flower than the mansion to which the long avenue led. In its lofty rooms life and death bore themselves with stately grace. The country house did not gaze upward, like the church, nor down to the ground like the huts; it had a wider earthly horizon than they, and was related to much noble architecture all over Europe. Foreign artisans had been called in to panel and stucco it, and its own inhabitants traveled and brought back ideas, fashions, and things of beauty. Paintings, tapestries, silver, and glass from distant countries had been made to feel at home here, and now formed part of Danish country life.

The big house stood as firmly rooted in the soil of Denmark as the peasants' huts, and was as faithfully allied to her four winds and her changing seasons, to her animal life, trees, and flowers. Only its interests lay in a higher plane. Within the domain of the lime trees it was no longer cows, goats, and pigs on which the minds and the talk ran, but horses and dogs. The wild fauna, the game of the land, that the peasant shook his fist at, when he saw it on his young green rye or in his ripening wheat field, to the residents of the country houses were the main pursuit and the joy of existence.

The writing in the sky solemnly proclaimed continuance, a worldly immortality. The great country houses had held their ground through many generations. The families who lived in them revered the past as they honored themselves, for the history of Denmark was their own history.

A Rosenkrantz had sat at Rosenholm, a Juel at Hverringe, a Skeel at Gammel-Estrup as long as people remembered. They had seen kings and schools of style succeed one another and, proudly and humbly, had made over their personal existence to that of their land, so that amongst their equals and with the peasants they passed by its name: Rosenholm, Hverringe, Gammel-Estrup. To the King and the country, to his family and to the individual lord of the manor himself it was a matter of minor consequence which particular Rosenkrantz, Juel, or Skeel, out of a long row of fathers and sons, at the moment in his person incarnated the fields and woods, the peasants, cattle and game of the estate. Many duties rested on the shoulders of the big landowners—towards God in heaven, towards the King, his neighbor, and himself—and they were all harmoniously consolidated into the idea of his duties towards his land. Highest amongst these ranked his obligation to uphold the sacred continuance, and to produce a new Rosenkrantz, Juel, or Skeel for the service of Rosenholm, Hverringe, and Gammel-Estrup.

Female grace was prized in the manors. Together with good hunting and fine wine it was the flower and emblem of the higher existence led there, and in many ways the families prided themselves more on their daughters than on their sons.

The ladies who promenaded in the lime avenues, or drove through them in heavy coaches with four horses, carried the future of the name in their laps and were, like dignified and debonair caryatides, holding up the houses. They were themselves conscious of their value, kept up their price, and moved in a sphere of pretty worship and self-worship. They might even be thought to add to it, on their own, a graceful, arch, paradoxical haughtiness. For how free were they, how powerful! Their lords might rule the country, and allow themselves many liberties, but when it came to that supreme matter of legitimacy which was the vital principle of their world, the center of gravity lay with them.

The lime trees were in bloom. But in the early morning only a faint fragrance drifted through the garden, an airy message, an aromatic echo of the dreams during the short summer night.

In a long avenue that led from the house all the way to the end of the garden, where, from a small white pavilion in the classic style, there was a great view over the fields, a young man walked. He was plainly dressed in brown, with pretty linen and lace, bare-headed, with his hair tied by a ribbon. He was dark, a strong and sturdy figure with fine eyes and hands; he limped a little on one leg.

The big house at the top of the avenue, the garden and the fields had been his childhood's paradise. But he had traveled and lived out of Denmark, in Rome and Paris, and he was at present appointed to the Danish Legation to the Court of King George, the brother of the late, unfortunate young Danish Queen. He had not seen his ancestral home for nine years. It made him laugh to find, now, everything so much smaller than he remembered it, and at the same time he

was strangely moved by meeting it again. Dead people came towards him and smiled at him; a small boy in a ruff ran past him with his hoop and kite, in passing gave him a clear glance and laughingly asked: "Do you mean to tell me that you are I?" He tried to catch him in the flight, and to answer him: "Yes, I assure you that I am you," but the light figure did not wait for a reply.

The young man, whose name was Adam, stood in a particular relation to the house and the land. For six months he had been heir to it all; nominally he was so even at this moment. It was this circumstance which had brought him from England, and on which his mind was dwelling, as he walked along slowly.

The old lord up at the manor, his father's brother, had had much misfortune in his domestic life. His wife had died young, and two of his children in infancy. The one son then left to him, his cousin's playmate, was a sickly and morose boy. For ten years the father traveled with him from one watering place to another, in Germany and Italy, hardly ever in other company than that of his silent, dying child, sheltering the faint flame of life with both hands, until such time as it could be passed over to a new bearer of the name. At the same time another misfortune had struck him: he fell into disfavor at Court, where till now he had held a fine position. He was about to rehabilitate his family's prestige through the marriage which he had arranged for his son, when before it could take place the bridegroom died, not yet twenty years old.

Adam learned of his cousin's death, and his own changed fortune, in England, through his ambitious and triumphant mother. He sat with her letter in his hand and did not know what to think about it.

If this, he reflected, had happened to him while he was still a boy, in Denmark, it would have meant all the world to him. It would be so now with his friends and school-fellows, if they were in his place, and they would, at this moment, be congratulating or envying him. But he was neither covetous nor vain by nature; he had faith in his own talents and had been content to know that his success in life depended on his personal ability. His slight infirmity had always set him a little apart from other boys; it had, perhaps, given him a keener sensibility of many things in life, and he did not, now, deem it quite right that the head of the family should limp on one leg. He did not even see his prospects in the same light as his people at home. In England he had met with greater wealth and magnificence than they dreamed of; he had been in love with, and made happy by, an English lady of such rank and fortune that to her, he felt, the finest estate of Denmark would look but like a child's toy farm.

And in England, too, he had come in touch with the great new ideas of the age: of nature, of the right and freedom of man, of justice and beauty. The universe, through them, had become infinitely wider to him; he wanted to find out still more about it and was planning to travel to America, to the new world. For a moment he felt trapped and imprisoned, as if the dead people of his name, from the family vault at home, were stretching out their parched arms for him.

But at the same time he began to dream at night of the old house and garden. He had walked in these avenues in dream, and had smelled the scent of the flowering limes. When at Ranelagh an old gypsy woman looked at his hand and told him that a son of his was to sit in the seat of his fathers, he felt a sudden, deep satisfaction, queer in a young man who till now had never given his sons a thought.

Then, six months later, his mother again wrote to tell him that his uncle had himself married the girl intended for his dead son. The head of the family was still in his best age, not over sixty, and although Adam remembered him as a small, slight man, he was a vigorous person; it was likely that his young wife would bear him sons.

Adam's mother in her disappointment lay the blame on him. If he had returned to Denmark, she told him, his uncle might have come to look upon him as a son, and would not have married; nay, he might have handed the bride over to him. Adam knew better. The family estate, differing from the neighboring properties, had gone down from father to son ever since a man of their name first sat there. The tradition of direct succession was the pride of the clan and a sacred dogma to his uncle; he would surely call for a son of his own flesh and bone.

But at the news the young man was seized by a strange, deep, aching remorse towards his old home in Denmark. It was as if he had been making light of a friendly and generous gesture, and disloyal to someone unfailingly loyal to him. It would be but just, he thought, if from now the place should disown and forget him. Nostalgia, which before he had never known, caught hold of him; for the first time he walked in the streets and parks of London as a stranger.

He wrote to his uncle and asked if he might come and stay with him, begged leave from the Legation and took ship for Denmark. He had come to the house to make his peace with it; he had slept little in the night, and was up so early and walking in the garden, to explain himself, and to be forgiven.

While he walked, the still garden slowly took up its day's work. A big snail, of the kind that his grandfather had brought back from France, and which he remembered eating in the house as a child, was already, with dignity, dragging a silver train down the avenue. The birds began to sing; in an old tree under which he stopped a number of them were worrying an owl; the rule of the night was over.

He stood at the end of the avenue and saw the sky lightening. An ecstatic clarity filled the world; in half an hour the sun would rise. A rye field here ran along the garden; two roe-deer were moving in it and looked roseate in the dawn. He gazed out over the fields, where as a small boy he had ridden his pony, and towards the wood where he had killed his first stag. He remembered the old servants who had taught him; some of them were now in their graves.

The ties which bound him to this place, he reflected, were of a mystic nature. He might never again come back to it, and it would make no difference. As long as a man of his own blood and name should sit in the house, hunt in the fields and be obeyed by the people in the huts, wherever he traveled on earth, in England or amongst the red Indians of America, he himself would still be safe, would still have

a home, and would carry weight in the world.

His eyes rested on the church. In old days, before the time of Martin Luther, younger sons of great families, he knew, had entered the Church of Rome, and had given up individual wealth and happiness to serve the greater ideals. They, too, had bestowed honor upon their homes and were remembered in its registers. In the solitude of the morning half in jest he let his mind run as it listed; it seemed to him that he might speak to the land as to a person, as to the mother of his race. "Is it only my body that you want," he asked her, "while you reject my imagination, energy, and emotions? If the world might be brought to acknowledge that the virtue of our name does not belong to the past only, will it give you no satisfaction?" The landscape was so still that he could not tell whether it answered him yes or no.

After a while he walked on, and came to the new French rose garden laid out for the young mistress of the house. In England he had acquired a freer taste in gardening, and he wondered if he could liberate these blushing captives, and make them thrive outside their cut hedges. Perhaps, he meditated, the elegantly conventional garden would be a floral portrait of his young aunt from Court, whom he had not yet seen.

As once more he came to the pavilion at the end of the avenue his eyes were caught by a bouquet of delicate colors which could not possibly belong to the Danish summer morning. It was in fact his uncle himself, powdered and silk-stockinged, but still in a brocade dressing gown, and obviously sunk in deep thought. "And what business, or what meditations," Adam asked himself, "drags a connoisseur of the beautiful, but three months married to a wife of seventeen, from his bed into his garden before sunrise?" He walked up to the small, slim, straight figure.

His uncle on his side showed no surprise at seeing him, but then he rarely seemed surprised at anything. He greeted him, with a compliment on his matuntiality, as kindly as he had done on his arrival last evening. After a moment he looked to the sky, and solemnly proclaimed: "It will be a hot day." Adam, as a child, had often been impressed by the grand, ceremonial manner in which the old lord would state the common happenings of existence; it looked as if nothing had changed here, but all was what it used to be.

The uncle offered the nephew a pinch of snuff. "No, thank you, Uncle," said Adam, "it would ruin my nose to the scent of your garden, which is as fresh as the Garden of Eden, newly created." "From every tree of which," said his uncle, smiling, "thou, my Adam, mayest freely eat." They slowly walked up the avenue together.

The hidden sun was now already gilding the top of the tallest trees. Adam talked of the beauties of nature, and of the greatness of Nordic scenery, less marked by the hand of man than that of Italy. His uncle took the praise of the landscape as a personal compliment, and congratulated him because he had not, in likeness to many young travelers in foreign countries, learned to despise his native land. No, said Adam, he had lately in England longed for the fields and woods of his Danish home. And he had there become acquainted with a new piece of Danish poetry which had enchanted him more than any English or French work. He named the author, Johannes Ewald, and quoted a few of the mighty, turbulent verses.

"And I have wondered, while I read," he went on after a pause, still moved by the lines he himself had declaimed, "that we have not till now understood how much our Nordic mythology in moral greatness surpasses that of Greece and Rome. If it had not been for the physical beauty of the ancient gods, which has come down to us in marble, no modern mind could hold them worthy of worship. They were mean, capricious, and treacherous. The gods of our Danish forefathers are as much more divine than they as the Druid is nobler than the Augur. For the fair gods of Asgaard did possess the sublime human virtues; they were righteous, trustworthy, benevolent and even, within a barbaric age, chivalrous." His uncle here for the first time appeared to take any real interest in the conversation. He stopped, his majestic nose a little in the air. "Ah, it was easier to them," he said.

"What do you mean, Uncle?" Adam asked. "It was a great deal easier," said his uncle, "to the northern gods than to those of Greece to be, as you will have it, righteous and benevolent. To my mind it even reveals a weakness in the souls of our ancient Danes that they should consent to adore such divinities." "My dear uncle," said Adam, smiling, "I have always felt that you would be familiar with the modes of Olympus. Now please let me share your insight, and tell me why virtue should come easier to our Danish gods than to those of milder climates." "They were not as powerful," said his uncle.

"And does power," Adam again

asked, "stand in the way of virtue?"
"Nay," said his uncle gravely. "Nay,
power is in itself the supreme virtue.
But the gods of which you speak
were never all-powerful. They had,
at all times, by their side those
darker powers which they named
the Jotuns, and who worked the
suffering, the disasters, the ruin of
our world. They might safely give
themselves up to temperance and
kindness. The omnipotent gods," he
went on, "have no such facilitation.
With their omnipotence they take
over the woe of the universe."

They had walked up the avenue
till they were in view of the house.
The old lord stopped and ran his
eyes over it. The stately building
was the same as ever; behind the
two tall front windows, Adam knew,
was now his young aunt's room. His
uncle turned and walked back.

"Chivalry," he said, "chivalry, of
which you were speaking, is not a
virtue of the omnipotent. It must
needs imply mighty rival powers
for the knight to defy. With a
dragon inferior to him in strength,
what figure will St. George cut? The
knight who finds no superior forces
ready to hand must invent them,
and combat windmills; his knighthood itself stipulates dangers, vileness, darkness on all sides of him.
Nay, believe me, my nephew, in
spite of his moral worth, your
chivalrous Odin of Asgaard as a
Regent must take rank below that
of Jove who avowed his sovereignty,
and accepted the world which he
ruled. But you are young," he
added, "and the experience of the
aged to you will sound pedantic."

He stood immovable for a moment and then with deep gravity
proclaimed: "The sun is up."

The sun did indeed rise above the
horizon. The wide landscape was
suddenly animated by its splendor,
and the dewy grass shone in a
thousand gleams.

"I have listened to you, Uncle,"
said Adam, "with great interest. But
while we have talked you yourself
have seemed to me preoccupied; your
eyes have rested on the field outside
the garden, as if something of great
moment, a matter of life and death,
was going on there. Now that the
sun is up, I see the mowers in the
rye and hear them whetting their
sickles. It is, I remember you telling me, the first day of the harvest.
That is a great day to a landowner
and enough to take his mind away
from the gods. It is very fine
weather, and I wish you a full
barn."

The elder man stood still, his
hands on his walking stick. "There
is indeed," he said at last, "something going on in that field, a matter of life and death. Come, let us
sit down here, and I will tell you
the whole story." They sat down
on the seat that ran all along the
pavilion, and while he spoke the old
lord of the land did not take his
eyes off the rye field.

"A week ago, on Thursday night,"
he said, "someone set fire to my barn
at Rødmosegaard—you know the
place, close to the moor—and
burned it all down. For two or three
days we could not lay hands on the
offender. Then on Monday morning
the keeper at Rødmose, with the
wheelwright over there, came up to
the house; they dragged with them
a boy, Goske Piil, a widow's son,
and they made their Bible oath
that he had done it; they had themselves seen him sneaking round the
barn by nightfall on Thursday.
Goske had no good name on the
farm; the keeper bore him a grudge
upon an old matter of poaching,

and the wheelwright did not like him either, for he did, I believe, suspect him with his young wife. The boy, when I talked to him, swore to his innocence, but he could not hold his own against the two old men. So I had him locked up, and meant to send him in to our judge and the district, with a letter.

"The judge is a fool, and would naturally do nothing but what he thought I wished him to do. He might have the boy sent to the convict prison for arson, or put amongst the soldiers as a bad character and a poacher. Or again, if he thought that that was what I wanted, he could let him off.

"I was out riding in the fields, looking at the corn that was soon ripe to be mowed, when a woman, the widow, Goske's mother, was brought up before me, and begged to speak to me. Anne-Marie is her name. You will remember her; she lives in the small house east of the village. She has not got a good name in the place either. They tell as a girl she had a child and did away with it.

"From five days' weeping her voice was so cracked that it was difficult for me to understand what she said. Her son, she told me at last, had indeed been over at Rødmose on Thursday, but for no ill purpose; he had gone to see someone. He was her only son, she called the Lord God to witness on his innocence, and she wrung her hands to me that I should save the boy for her.

"We were in the rye field that you and I are looking at now. That gave me an idea. I said to the widow: 'If in one day, between sunrise and sunset, with your own hands you can mow this field, and it be well done,

I will let the case drop and you shall keep your son. But if you cannot do it, he must go, and it is not likely that you will then ever see him again.'

"She stood up then and gazed over the field. She kissed my riding boot in gratitude for the favor shown to her."

The old lord here made a pause, and Adam said: "Her son meant much to her?" "He is her only child," said his uncle. "He means to her her daily bread and support in old age. It may be said that she holds him as dear as her own life. As," he added, "within a higher order of life, a son to his father means the name and the race, and he holds him as dear as life everlasting. Yes, her son means much to her. For the mowing of that field is a day's work to three men, or three days' work to one man. Today, as the sun rose, she set to her task. And down there, by the end of the field, you will see her now, in a blue headcloth, with the man I have set to follow her and to ascertain that she does the work unassisted, and with two or three friends by her, who are comforting her."

Adam looked down, and did indeed see a woman in a blue headcloth, and a few other figures in the corn.

They sat for a while in silence. "Do you yourself," Adam then said, "believe the boy to be innocent?" "I cannot tell," said his uncle. "There is no proof. The word of the keeper and the wheelwright stand against the boy's word. If indeed I did the one thing or the other, it would be merely a matter of chance, or maybe of sympathy. The boy," he said after a moment, "was my son's playmate, the only other child that I ever

knew him to like or to get on with."
"Do you," Adam again asked, "hold
it possible to her to fulfill your condition?" "Nay, I cannot tell," said
the old lord. "To an ordinary person
it would not be possible. No ordinary person would ever have taken
it on at all. I chose it so. We are
quibbling with the law, Anne-Marie
and I."

Adam for a few minutes followed
the movement of the small group in
the rye. "Will you walk back?" he
asked. "No," said his uncle, "I think
that I shall stay here till I have
seen the end of the thing." "Until
sunset?" Adam asked with surprise.
"Yes," said the old lord. Adam said:
"It will be a long day." "Yes," said
his uncle, "a long day. But," he
added, as Adam rose to walk away,
"if, as you said, you have got that
tragedy of which you spoke in your
pocket, be as kind as to leave it
here, to keep me company." Adam
handed him the book.

In the avenue he met two footmen who carried the old lord's morning chocolate down to the pavilion
on large silver trays.

As now the sun rose in the sky,
and the day grew hot, the lime trees
gave forth their exuberance of
scent, and the garden was filled with
unsurpassed, unbelievable sweetness.
Towards the still hour of midday the
long avenue reverberated like a
soundboard with a low, incessant
murmur: the humming of a million
bees that clung to the pendulous,
thronging clusters of blossoms and
were drunk with bliss.

In all the short lifetime of Danish
summer there is no richer or more
luscious moment than that week
wherein the lime trees flower. The
heavenly scent goes to the head and
to the heart; it seems to unite the
fields of Denmark with those of

Elysium; it contains both hay,
honey, and holy incense, and is
half fairyland and half apothecary's
locker. The avenue was changed
into a mystic edifice, a dryad's cathedral, outward from summit to base
lavishly adorned, set with multi-
tudinous ornaments, and golden in
the sun. But behind the walls the
vaults were benignly cool and somber, like ambrosial sanctuaries in a
dazzling and burning world, and in
here the ground was still moist.

Up in the house, behind the silk
curtains of the two front windows,
the young mistress of the estate
from the wide bed stuck her feet
into two little high-heeled slippers.
Her lace-trimmed nightgown had
slid up above her knee and down
from the shoulder; her hair, done
up in curling pins for the night, was
still frosty with the powder of yesterday, her round face flushed with
sleep. She stepped out to the middle
of the floor and stood there, looking extremely grave and thoughtful,
yet she did not think at all. But
through her head a long procession
of pictures marched, and she was
unconsciously endeavoring to put
them in order, as the pictures of her
existence had used to be.

She had grown up at Court; it
was her world, and there was
probably not in the whole country
a small creature more exquisitely
and innocently drilled to the stately
measure of a palace. By favor of
the old Dowager Queen she bore
her name and that of the King's
sister, the Queen of Sweden: Sophie
Magdalena. It was with a view to
these things that her husband,
when he wished to restore his status in high places, had chosen her
as a bride, first for his son and then
for himself. But her own father, who
held an office in the Royal House-

hold and belonged to the new Court aristocracy, in his day had done the same thing the other way round, and had married a country lady, to get a foothold within the old nobility of Denmark. The little girl had her mother's blood in her veins. The country to her had been an immense surprise and delight.

To get into her castle-court she must drive through the farm yard, through the heavy stone gateway in the barn itself, wherein the rolling of her coach for a few seconds re-echoed like thunder. She must drive past the stables and the timber mare, from which sometimes a miscreant would follow her with sad eyes, and might here startle a long string of squalling geese, or pass the heavy, scowling bull, led on by a ring in his nose and kneading the earth in dumb fury. At first this had been to her, every time, a slight shock and a jest. But after a while all these creatures and things, which belonged to her, seemed to become part of herself. Her mothers, the old Danish country ladies, were robust persons, undismayed by any kind of weather; now she herself had walked in the rain and had laughed and glowed in it like a green tree.

She had taken her great new home in possession at a time when all the world was unfolding, mating, and propagating. Flowers, which she had known only in bouquets and festoons, sprung from the earth round her; birds sang in all the trees. The newborn lambs seemed to her daintier than her dolls had been. From her husband's Hanoverian stud, foals were brought to her to give names; she stood and watched as they poked their soft noses into their mothers' bellies to drink. Of this strange process she had till now only vaguely heard. She had hap-

pened to witness, from a path in the park, the rearing and screeching stallion on the mare. All this luxuriance, lust, and fecundity was displayed before her eyes, as for her pleasure.

And for her own part, in the midst of it, she was given an old husband who treated her with punctilious respect because she was to bear him a son. Such was the compact; she had known of it from the beginning. Her husband, she found, was doing his best to fulfill his part of it, and she herself was loyal by nature and strictly brought up. She would not shirk her obligation. Only she was vaguely aware of a discord of an incompatibility within her majestic existence, which prevented her from being as happy as she had expected to be.

After a time her chagrin took a strange form: as the consciousness of an absence. Someone ought to have been with her who was not. She had no experience in analyzing her feelings; there had not been time for that at Court. Now, as she was more often left to herself, she vaguely probed her own mind. She tried to set her father in that void place, her sisters, her music master, an Italian singer whom she had admired; but none of them would fill it for her. At times she felt lighter at heart, and believed the misfortune to have left her. And then again it would happen, if she were alone, or in her husband's company, and even within his embrace, that everything round her would cry out: Where? Where? so that she let her wild eyes run about the room in search for the being who should have been there, and who had not come.

When, six months ago, she was informed that her first young bridegroom had died and that she was to marry his father in his place, she had not been sorry. Her youthful suitor, the one time she had seen him, had appeared to her infantile and insipid; the father would make a statelier consort. Now she had sometimes thought of the dead boy, and wondered whether with him life would have been more joyful. But she soon again dismissed the picture, and that was the sad youth's last recall to the stage of this world.

Upon one wall of her room there hung a long mirror. As she gazed into it new images came along. The day before, driving with her husband, she had seen, at a distance, a party of village girls bathe in the river, and the sun shining on them. All her life she had moved amongst naked marble deities, but it had till now never occurred to her that the people she knew should themselves be naked under their bodices and trains, waistcoats and satin breeches, that indeed she herself felt naked within her clothes. Now, in front of the looking glass, she tardily untied the ribbons of her nightgown, and let it drop to the floor.

The room was dim behind the drawn curtains. In the mirror her body was silvery like a white rose; only her cheeks and mouth, and the tips of her fingers and breasts had a faint carmine. Her slender torso was formed by the whalebones that had clasped it tightly from her childhood; above the slim, dimpled knee a gentle narrowness marked the place of the garter. Her limbs were rounded as if, at whatever place they might be cut through with a sharp knife, a perfectly circular transverse incision would be obtained. The side and belly were so smooth that her own gaze slipped and glided, and grasped for a hold. She was not altogether like a statue,

she found, and lifted her arms above her head. She turned to get a view of her back, the curves below the waistline were still blushing from the pressure of the bed. She called to mind a few tales about nymphs and goddesses, but they all seemed a long way off, so her mind returned to the peasant girls in the river. They were, for a few minutes, idealized into playmates, or sisters even, since they belonged to her as did the meadow and the blue river itself. And within the next moment the sense of forlornness once more came upon her, a *horror vaccui* like a physical pain. Surely, surely someone should have been with her now, her other self, like the image in the glass, but nearer, stronger, alive. There was no one, the universe was empty round her.

A sudden, keen itching under her knee took her out of her reveries, and awoke in her the hunting instincts of her breed. She wetted a finger on her tongue, slowly brought it down and quickly slapped it to the spot. She felt the diminutive, sharp body of the insect against the silky skin, pressed the thumb to it, and triumphantly lifted up the small prisoner between her finger tips. She stood quite still, as if meditating upon the fact that a flea was the only creature risking its life for her smoothness and sweet blood.

Her maid opened the door and came in, loaded with the attire of the day—shift, stays, hoop, and petticoats. She remembered that she had a guest in the house, the new nephew arrived from England. Her husband had instructed her to be kind to their young kinsman, disinherited, so to say, by her presence in the house. They would ride out on the land together.

In the afternoon the sky was no

longer blue as in the morning. Large clouds slowly towered upon it, and the great vault itself was colorless, as if diffused into vapors round the white-hot sun in zenith. A low thunder ran along the western horizon; once or twice the dust of the roads rose in tall spirals. But the fields, the hills, and the woods were as still as a painted landscape.

Adam walked down the avenue to the pavilion, and found his uncle there, fully dressed, his hands upon his walking stick and his eyes on the rye field. The book that Adam had given him lay by his side. The field now seemed alive with people. Small groups stood here and there in it, and a long row of men and women were slowly advancing towards the garden in the line of the swath.

The old lord nodded to his nephew, but did not speak or change his position. Adam stood by him as still as himself.

The day to him had been strangely disquieting. At the meeting again with old places the sweet melodies of the past had filled his senses and his mind, and had mingled with new, bewitching tunes of the present. He was back in Denmark, no longer a child but a youth, with a keener sense of the beautiful, with tales of other countries to tell, and still a true son of his own land and enchanted by its loveliness as she had never been before.

But through all these harmonies the tragic and cruel tale which the old lord had told him in the morning, and the sad contest which he knew to be going on so near by, in the cornfield, had re-echoed, like the recurrent, hollow throbbing of a muffled drum, a redoubtable sound. It came back time after time, so that he had felt himself to change color and to answer absently. It

brought with it a deeper sense of pity with all that lived than he had ever known. When he had been riding with his young aunt, and their road ran along the scene of the drama, he had taken care to ride between her and the field, so that she should not see what was going on there, or question him about it. He had chosen the way home through the deep, green wood for the same reason.

More dominantly even than the figure of the woman struggling with her sickle for her son's life, the old man's figure, as he had seen it at sunrise, kept him company through the day. He came to ponder on the part which that lonely, determinate form had played in his own life. From the time when his father died, it had impersonated to the boy law and order, wisdom of life and kind guardianship. What was he to do, he thought, if after eighteen years these filial feelings must change, and his second father's figure take on to him a horrible aspect, as a symbol of the tyranny and oppression of the world? What was he to do if ever the two should come to stand in opposition to each other as adversaries?

At the same time an unaccountable, a sinister alarm and dread on behalf of the old man himself took hold of him. For surely here the Goddess Nemesis could not be far away. This man had ruled the world round him for a longer period than Adam's own lifetime and had never been gainsaid by anyone. During the years when he had wandered through Europe with a sick boy of his own blood as his sole companion he had learned to set himself apart from his surroundings, and to close himself up to all outer life, and he had become insusceptible to the ideas and feelings of other human beings. Strange fancies might there have run in his mind, so that in the end he had seen himself as the only person really existing, and the world as a poor and vain shadow play, which had no substance to it.

Now, in senile willfulness, he would take in his hand the life of those simpler and weaker than himself, of a woman, using it to his own ends, and he feared of no retributive justice. Did he not know, the young man thought, that there were powers in the world, different from and more formidable than the short-lived might of a despot?

With the sultry heat of the day this foreboding of impending disaster grew upon him, until he felt ruin threatening not the old lord only, but the house, the name and himself with him. It seemed to him that he must cry out a warning to the man he had loved, before it was too late.

But as now he was once more in his uncle's company, the green calm of the garden was so deep that he did not find his voice to cry out. Instead a little French air which his aunt had sung to him up in the house kept running in his mind.— "C'est un trop doux effort . . ." He had good knowledge of music; he had heard the air before, in Paris, but not so sweetly sung.

After a time he asked: "Will the woman fulfill her bargain?" His uncle unfolded his hands. "It is an extraordinary thing," he said animatedly, "that it looks as if she might fulfill it. If you count the hours from sunrise till now, and from now till sunset, you will find the time left her to be half of that already gone. And see! She has now mowed two thirds of the field. But then we will naturally have to reckon with her strength declining as she works on. All in all, it is an idle pursuit in you or me to bet on the issue of the matter; we must wait and see. Sit down, and keep me company in my watch." In two minds Adam sat down.

"And here," said his uncle, and took up the book from the seat, "is your book, which has passed the time finely. It is great poetry, ambrosia to the ear and the heart. And it has, with our discourse on divinity this morning, given me stuff for thought. I have been reflecting upon the law of retributive justice." He took a pinch of snuff, and went on. "A new age," he said, "has made to itself a god in its own image, an emotional god. And now you are already writing a tragedy on your god."

Adam had no wish to begin a debate on poetry with his uncle, but he also somehow dreaded a silence, and said: "It may be, then, that we hold tragedy to be, in the scheme of life, a noble, a divine phenomenon."

"Aye," said his uncle solemnly," "a noble phenomenon, the noblest on earth. But of the earth only and never divine. Tragedy is the privilege of man, his highest privilege. The God of the Christian Church Himself, when He wished to experience tragedy, had to assume human form. And even at that," he added thoughtfully, "the tragedy was not wholly valid, as it would have become had the hero of it been, in very truth, a man. The divinity of Christ conveyed to it a divine note, the moment of comedy. The real tragic part, by the nature of things, fell to the executors, not to the victim. Nay, my nephew, we should not adulterate the pure elements of the cosmos. Tragedy should remain the right of human beings, subject, in their conditions or in their own nature, to the dire law of necessity. To them it is salvation and beatification. But the gods, whom we must believe to be unacquainted with and incomprehensive of necessity, can have no knowledge of the tragic. When they are brought face to face with it they will, according to my experience, have the good taste and decorum to keep still, and not interfere.

"No," he said after a pause, "the true art of the gods is the comic. The comic is a condescension of the divine to the world of man; it is the sublime vision, which cannot be studied, but must ever be celestially granted. In the comic the gods see their own being reflected as in a mirror, and while the tragic poet is bound by strict laws, they will allow the comic artist a freedom as unlimited as their own. They do not even withhold their own existence from his sports. Jove may favor Lucianos of Samosata. As long as your mockery is in true godly taste you may mock at the gods and still remain a sound devotee. But in pitying, or condoling with your god, you deny and annihilate him, and such is the most horrible of atheisms.

"And here on earth, too," he went on, "we, who stand in lieu of the gods and have emancipated ourselves from the tyranny of necessity, should leave to our vassals their monopoly of tragedy, and for ourselves accept the comic with grace. Only a boorish and cruel master— a parvenu, in fact—will make a jest of his servants' necessity, or force the comic upon them. Only a timid and pedantic ruler, a petit-maître, will fear the ludicrous on his own behalf. Indeed," he finished his long speech, "the very same fatality, which, in striking the burgher or peasant, will become tragedy, with the aristocrat is exalted to the comic. By the grace and wit of our acceptance hereof our aristocracy is known."

Adam could not help smiling a little as he heard the apotheosis of the comic on the lips of the erect, ceremonious prophet. In this ironic smile he was, for the first time, estranging himself from the head of his house.

A shadow fell across the landscape. A cloud had crept over the sun; the country changed color beneath it, faded and bleached, and even all sounds for a minute seemed to die out of it.

"Ah, now," said the old lord, "if it is going to rain, and the rye gets wet, Anne-Marie will not be able to finish in time. And who comes there?" he added, and turned his head a little.

Preceded by a lackey a man in riding boots and a striped waistcoat with silver buttons, and with his hat in his hand, came down the avenue. He bowed deeply, first to the old lord and then to Adam. "My bailiff," said the old lord. "Good afternoon, Bailiff. What news have you to bring?" The bailiff made a sad gesture. "Poor news only, my lord," he said. "And how poor news?" asked his master. "There is," said the bailiff with weight, "not a soul at work on the land, and not a sickle going except that of Anne-Marie in this rye field. The mowing has stopped; they are all at her heels. It is a poor day for a first day of the harvest." "Yes, I see," said the old lord. The bailiff went on. "I have spoken kindly to them," he said, "and I have sworn at them; it is all one. They might as well all be deaf."

"Good bailiff," said the old lord, "leave them in peace; let them do as they like. This day may, all the same, do them more good than many others. Where is Goske, the boy, Anne-Marie's son?" "We have set him in the small room by the barn," said the bailiff. "Nay, let him be brought down," said the old lord; "let him see his mother at work. But what do you say—will she get the field mowed in time?" "If you ask me, my lord," said the bailiff, "I believe that she will. Who would have thought so? She is only a small woman. It is as hot a day today as, well, as I do ever remember. I myself, you yourself, my lord, could not have done what Anne-Marie has done today." "Nay, nay, we could not, Bailiff," said the old lord.

The bailiff pulled out a red handkerchief and wiped his brow, somewhat calmed by venting his wrath. "If," he remarked with bitterness, "they would all work as the widow works now, we would make a profit on the land." "Yes," said the old lord, and fell into thought, as if calculating the profit it might make. "Still," he said, "as to the question of profit and loss, that is more intricate than it looks. I will tell you something that you may not know: The most famous tissue ever woven was raveled out again every night. But come," he added, "she is close by now. We will go and have a look at her work ourselves." With these words he rose and set his hat on.

The cloud had drawn away again; the rays of the sun once more burned the wide landscape, and as the small party walked out from under the shade of the trees the dead-still heat was heavy as lead; the sweat sprang out on their faces and their eyelids smarted. On the narrow path they had to go one by one, the old lord stepping along first, all black, and the footman, in

his bright livery, bringing up the rear.

The field was indeed filled with people like a market place; there were probably a hundred or more men and women in it. To Adam the scene recalled pictures from his Bible: the meeting between Esau and Jacob in Edom, or Boas' reapers in his barley field near Bethlehem. Some were standing by the side of the field, others pressed in small groups close to the mowing woman, and a few followed in her wake, binding up sheaves where she had cut the corn, as if thereby they thought to help her, or as if by all means they meant to have part in her work. A younger woman with a pail on her head kept close to her side, and with her a number of half-grown children. One of these first caught sight of the lord of the estate and his suite, and pointed to him. The binders let their sheaves drop, and as the old man stood still many of the onlookers drew close round him.

The woman on whom till now the eyes of the whole field had rested— a small figure on the large stage— was advancing slowly and unevenly, bent double as if she were walking on her knees, and stumbling as she walked. Her blue headcloth had slipped back from her head; the gray hair was plastered to the skull with sweat, dusty and stuck with straw. She was obviously totally unaware of the multitude round her; neither did she now once turn her head or her gaze towards the new arrivals.

Absorbed in her work she again and again stretched out her left hand to grasp a handful of corn, and her right hand with the sickle in it to cut it off close to the soil, in waverings, groping pulls, like a tired swimmer's strokes. Her course took her so close to the feet of the old lord that his shadow fell on her. Just then she staggered and swayed sideways, and the woman who followed her lifted the pail from her head and held it to her lips. Anne-Marie drank without leaving her hold on her sickle, and the water ran from the corners of her mouth. A boy, close to her, quickly bent one knee, seized her hands in his own and, steadying and guiding them, cut off a gripe of rye. "No, no," said the old lord, "you must not do that, boy. Leave Anne-Marie in peace to her work." At the sound of his voice the woman, falteringly, lifted her face in his direction.

The bony and tanned face was streaked with sweat and dust; the eyes were dimmed. But there was not in its expression the slightest trace of fear or pain. Indeed amongst all the grave and concerned faces of the field hers was the only one perfectly calm, peaceful, and mild. The mouth was drawn together in a thin line, a prim, keen, patient little smile, such as will be seen in the face of an old woman at her spinning wheel or her knitting, eager on her work, and happy in it. And as the younger women lifted back the pail, she immediately again fell to her mowing, with an ardent, tender craving, like that of a mother who lays a baby to the nipple. Like an insect that bustles along in high grass, or like a small vessel in a heavy sea, she butted her way on, her quiet face once more bent upon her task.

The whole throng of onlookers, and with them the small group from the pavilion, advanced as she advanced, slowly and as if drawn by a string. The bailiff, who felt the intense silence of the field heavy on

him, said to the old lord: "The rye will yield better this year than last," and got no reply. He repeated his remark to Adam, and at last to the footman, who felt himself above a discussion on agriculture, and only cleared his throat in answer. In a while the bailiff again broke the silence. "There is the boy," he said and pointed with his thumb. "They have brought him down." At that moment the woman fell forward on her face and was lifted up by those nearest to her.

Adam suddenly stopped on the path, and covered his eyes with his hand. The old lord without turning asked him if he felt incommoded by the heat. "No," said Adam, "but stay. Let me speak to you." His uncle stopped, with his hand on the stick and looking ahead, as if regretful of being held back.

"In the name of God," cried the young man in French, "force not this woman to continue." There was a short pause. "But I force her not, my friend," said his uncle in the same language. "She is free to finish at any moment." "At the cost of her child only," again cried Adam. "Do you not see that she is dying? You know not what you are doing, or what it may bring upon you."

The old lord, perplexed by this unexpected animadversion, after a second turned all round, and his pale, clear eyes sought his nephew's face with stately surprise. His long, waxen face, with two symmetrical curls at the sides, had something of the mien of an idealized and ennobled old sheep or ram. He made sign to the bailiff to go on. The footman also withdrew a little, and the uncle and nephew were, so to say, alone on the path. For a minute neither of them spoke.

"In this very place where we now

stand," said the old lord, then, with hauteur, "I gave Anne-Marie my word."

"My uncle!" said Adam. "A life is a greater thing even than a word. Recall that word, I beseech you, which was given in caprice, as a whim. I am praying you more for your sake than for my own, yet I shall be grateful to you all my life if you will grant me my prayer."

"You will have learned in school," said his uncle, "that in the beginning was the word. It may have been pronounced in caprice, as a whim, the Scripture tells us nothing about it. It is still the principle of our world, its law of gravitation. My own humble word has been the principle of the land on which we stand, for an age of man. My father's word was the same, before my day."

"You are mistaken," cried Adam. "The word is creative—it is imagination, daring, and passion. By it the world was made. How much greater are these powers which bring into being than any restricting or controlling law! You wish the land on which we look to produce and propagate; you should not banish from it the forces which cause, and which keep up life, nor turn it into a desert by dominance of law. And when you look at the people, simpler than we and nearer to the heart of nature, who do not analyze their feelings, whose life is one with the life of the earth, do they not inspire in you tenderness, respect, reverence even? This woman is ready to die for her son; will it ever happen to you or me that a woman willingly gives up her life for us? And if it did indeed come to pass, should we make so light of it as not to give up a dogma in return?"

"You are young," said the old lord. "A new age will undoubtedly applaud you. I am old-fashioned, I have been quoting to you texts a thousand years old. We do not, perhaps, quite understand one another. But with my own people I am, I believe, in good understanding. Anne-Marie might well feel that I am making light of her exploit, if now, at the eleventh hour, I did nullify it by a second word. I myself should feel so in her place. Yes, my nephew, it is possible, did I grant you your prayer and pronounce such an amnesty, that I should find it void against her faithfulness, and that we would still see her at her work, unable to give it up, as a shuttle in the rye field, until she had it all mowed. But she would then be a shocking, a horrible sight, a figure of unseemly fun, like a small planet running wild in the sky, when the law of gravitation had been done away with."

"And if she dies at her task," Adam exclaimed, "her death and its consequences will come upon your head."

The old lord took off his hat and gently ran his hand over his powdered head. "Upon my head?" he said. "I have kept up my head in many weathers. Even," he added proudly, "against the cold wind from high places. In what shape will it come upon my head, my nephew?" "I cannot tell," cried Adam in despair. "I have spoken to warn you. God only knows." "Amen," said the old lord with a little delicate smile. "Come, we will walk on." Adam drew in his breath deeply.

"No," he said in Danish. "I cannot come with you. This field is yours; things will happen here as you decide. But I myself must go away. I beg you to let me have, this evening, a coach as far as town. For I could not sleep another night under your roof, which I have honored beyond any on earth." So many conflicting feelings at his own speech thronged in his breast that it would have been impossible for him to give them words.

The old lord, who had already begun to walk on, stood still, and with him the lackey. He did not speak for a minute, as if to give Adam time to collect his mind. But the young man's mind was in uproar and would not be collected.

"Must we," the old man asked, in Danish, "take leave here, in the rye field? I have held you dear, next to my own son. I have followed your career in life from year to year, and have been proud of you. I was happy when you wrote to say that you were coming back. If now you will go away, I wish you well." He shifted his walking stick from the right hand to the left and gravely looked his nephew in the face.

Adam did not meet his eyes. He was gazing out over the landscape. In the late mellow afternoon it was resuming its colors, like a painting brought into proper light; in the meadows the little black stacks of peat stood gravely distinct upon the green sward. On this same morning he had greeted it all, like a child running laughingly to its mother's bosom; now already he must tear himself from it, in discordance, and forever. And at the moment of parting it seemed infinitely dearer than any time before, so much beautified and solemnized by the coming separation that it looked like the place in a dream, a landscape out of paradise, and he wondered if it was really the same. But, yes—there before him was, once more, the hunting ground of long ago. And there was the road on which he had ridden today.

"But tell me where you mean to go from here," said the old lord slowly. "I myself have traveled a good deal in my days. I know the word of leaving, the wish to go away. But I have learned by experience that, in reality, the word has a meaning only to the place and the people which one leaves. When you have left my house—although it will see you go with sadness—as far as it is concerned the matter is finished and done with. But to the person who goes away it is a different thing, and not so simple. At the moment that he leaves one place he will be already, by the laws of life, on his way to another, upon this earth. Let me know, then, for the sake of our old acquaintance, to which place you are going when you leave here. To England?"

"No," said Adam. He felt in his heart that he could never again go back to England or to his easy and carefree life there. It was not far enough away; deeper waters than the North Sea must now be laid between him and Denmark. "No, not to England," he said. "I shall go to America, to the new world." For a moment he shut his eyes, trying to form to himself a picture of existence in America, with the gray Atlantic Ocean between him and these fields and woods.

"To America?" said his uncle and drew up his eyebrows. "Yes, I have heard of America. They have got freedom there, a big waterfall, savage red men. They shoot turkeys, I have read, as we shoot partridges. Well, if it be your wish, go to America, Adam, and be happy in the new world."

He stood for some time, sunk in thought, as if he had already sent off the young man to America, and had done with him. When at last he spoke, his words had the character of a monologue, enunciated by the person who watches things come and go, and himself stays on.

"Take service, there," he said, "with the power which will give you an easier bargain than this: That with your own life you may buy the life of your son."

Adam had not listened to his uncle's remarks about America, but the conclusive, solemn words caught his ear. He looked up. As if for the first time in his life, he saw the old man's figure as a whole, and conceived how small it was, so much smaller than himself, pale, a thin black anchorite upon his own land. A thought ran through his head: "How terrible to be old!" The abhorrence of the tyrant, and the sinister dread on his behalf, which had followed him all day, seemed to die out of him, and his pity with all creation to extend even to the somber form before him.

His whole being had cried out for harmony. Now, with the possibility of forgiving, of a reconciliation, a sense of relief went through him; confusedly he bethought himself of Anne-Marie drinking the water held to her lips. He took off his hat, as his uncle had done a moment ago, so that to a beholder at a distance it would seem that the two dark-clad gentlemen on the path were repeatedly and respectfully saluting one another, and brushed the hair from his forehead. Once more the tune of the garden room rang in his mind:

"*Mourir pour ce qu'on aime*
C'est un trop doux effort . . ."

He stood for a long time immobile and dumb. He broke off a few ears of rye, kept them in his hand, and looked at them.

He saw the ways of life, he thought, as a twined and tangled design, complicated and mazy; it was not given him or any mortal to command or control it. Life and death, happiness and woe, the past and the present, were interlaced within the pattern. Yet to the initiated it might be read as easily as our ciphers—which to the savage must seem confused and incomprehensible—will be read by the schoolboy. And out of the contrasting elements concord rose. All that lived must suffer; the old man, whom he had judged hardly, had suffered, as he had watched his son die, and had dreaded the obliteration of his being. He himself would come to know ache, tears, and remorse, and, even through these, the fullness of life. So might now, to the woman in the rye field, her ordeal be a triumphant procession. For to die for the one you loved was an effort too sweet for words.

As now he thought of it, he knew that all his life he had sought the unity of things, the secret which connects the phenomena of existence. It was this strife, this dim presage, which had sometimes made him stand still and inert in the midst of the games of his playfellows, or which had, at other moments—on moonlight nights, or in his little boat on the sea—lifted the boy to ecstatic happiness. Where other young people, in their pleasures or their amours, had searched for contrast and variety, he himself had yearned only to comprehend in full the oneness of the world. If things had come differently to him, if his young cousin had not died, and the events that followed his death had not brought him to Denmark, his search for understanding and harmony might have taken him to America, and he might have found them there, in the virgin forests of a new world. Now they have been disclosed to him today, in the place where he had played as a child. As the song is one with the voice that sings it, as the road is one with the goal, as lovers are made one in their embrace, so is man one with his destiny, and he shall love it as himself.

He looked up again, towards the horizon. If he wished to, he felt, he might find out what it was that had brought to him, here, the sudden conception of the unity of the universe. When this same morning he had philosophized, lightly and for his own sake, on his feeling of belonging to this land and soil, it had been the beginning of it. But since then it had grown; it had become a mightier thing, a revelation to his soul. Some time he would look into it, for the law of cause and effect was a wonderful and fascinating study. But not now. This hour was consecrated to greater emotions, to a surrender to fate and to the will of life.

"No," he said at last. "If you wish it I shall not go. I shall stay here."

At that moment a long, loud roll of thunder broke the stillness of the afternoon. It re-echoed for a while amongst the low hills, and it reverberated within the young man's breast as powerfully as if he had been seized and shaken by hands. The landscape had spoken. He remembered that twelve hours ago he had put a question to it, half in jest, and not knowing what he did. Here it gave him its answer.

What it contained he did not know; neither did he inquire. In his promise to his uncle he had given himself over to the mightier powers of the world. Now what must come must come.

"I thank you," said the old lord, and made a little stiff gesture with his hand. "I am happy to hear you say so. We should not let the difference in our ages, or of our views, separate us. In our family we have been wont to keep peace and faith with one another. You have made my heart lighter."

Something within his uncle's speech faintly recalled to Adam the misgivings of the afternoon. He rejected them; he would not let them trouble the new, sweet felicity which his resolution to stay had brought him.

"I shall go on now," said the old lord. "But there is no need for you to follow me. I will tell you tomorrow how the matter has ended."

"No," said Adam, "I shall come back by sunset, to see the end of it myself."

All the same he did not come back. He kept the hour in his mind, and all through the evening the consciousness of the drama, and the profound concern and compassion with which, in his thoughts, he followed it, gave to his speech, glance, and movements a grave and pathetic substance. But he felt that he was, in the rooms of the manor, and even by the harpsichord on which he accompanied his aunt to her air from *Alceste*, as much in the center of things as if he had stood in the rye field itself, and as near to those human beings whose fate was now decided there. Anne-Marie and he were both in the hands of destiny, and destiny would, by different ways, bring each to the designated end.

Later on he remembered what he had thought that evening.

But the old lord stayed on. Late in the afternoon he even had an idea; he called down his valet to the pavilion and made him shift his clothes on him and dress him up in a brocaded suit that he had worn at Court. He let a lace-trimmed shirt be drawn over his head and stuck out his slim legs to have them put into thin silk stockings and buckled shoes. In this majestic attire he dined alone, of a frugal meal, but took a bottle of Rhenish wine with it, to keep up his strength. He sat on for a while, a little sunk in his seat; then, as the sun neared the earth, he straightened himself, and took the way down to the field.

The shadows were now lengthening, azure blue along all the eastern slopes. The lonely trees in the corn marked their site by narrow blue pools running out from their feet, and as the old man walked a thin, immensely elongated reflection stirred behind him on the path. Once he stood still; he thought he heard a lark singing over his head, a springlike sound; his tired head held no clear perception of the season; he seemed to be walking, and standing, in a kind of eternity.

The people in the field were no longer silent, as they had been in the afternoon. Many of them talked loudly among themselves, and a little farther away a woman was weeping.

When the bailiff saw his master, he came up to him. He told him, in great agitation, that the widow would, in all likelihood, finish the mowing of the field within a quarter of an hour.

"Are the keeper and the wheelwright here?" the old lord asked him. "They have been here," said the bailiff, "and have gone away, five times. Each time they have said that they would not come back. But they have come back again, all the same, and they are here now." "And where is the boy?" the old lord asked again. "He is with her," said the bailiff. "I have given him leave to follow her. He has walked close to his mother all the afternoon, and you will see him now by her side, down there."

Anne-Marie was now working her way up towards them more evenly than before, but with extreme slowness, as if at any moment she might come to a standstill. This excessive tardiness, the old lord reflected, if it had been purposely performed, would have been an inimitable, dignified exhibition of skilled art; one might fancy the Emperor of China advancing in like manner on a divine procession or rite. He shaded his eyes with his hand, for the sun was now just beyond the horizon, and its last rays made light, wild, many-colored specks dance before his sight. With such splendor did the sunset emblazon the earth and the air that the landscape was turned into a melting pot of glorious metals. The meadows and the grasslands became pure gold; the barley field near by, with its long ears, was a live lake of shining silver.

There was only a small patch of straw standing in the rye field, when the woman, alarmed by the change in the light, turned her head a little to get a look at the sun. The while she did not stop her work, but grasped one handful of corn and cut it off, then another, and another. A great stir, and a sound like a manifold, deep sigh, ran through the crowd. The field was now mowed from one end to the other. Only the mower herself did not realize the fact; she stretched out her hand anew, and when she found nothing in it, she seemed puzzled or disappointed. Then she let her arms drop, and slowly sank to her knees.

Many of the women burst out weeping, and the swarm drew close round her, leaving only a small open space at the side where the old lord stood. Their sudden nearness frightened Anne-Marie; she made a slight, uneasy movement, as if terrified that they should put their hands on her.

The boy, who had kept by her all day, now fell on his knees beside her. Even he dared not touch her, but held one arm low behind her back and the other before her, level with her collarbone, to catch hold of her if she should fall, and all the time he cried aloud. At that moment the sun went down.

The old lord stepped forward and solemnly took off his hat. The crowd became silent, waiting for him to speak. But for a minute or two he said nothing. Then he addressed her, very slowly.

"Your son is free, Anne-Marie," he said. He again waited a little, and added: "You have done a good day's work, which will long be remembered."

Anne-Marie raised her gaze only as high as his knees, and he understood that she had not heard what he said. He turned to the boy. "You tell your mother, Goske," he said, gently, "what I have told her."

The boy had been sobbing wildly, in raucous, broken moans. It took him some time to collect and control himself. But when at last he spoke, straight into his mother's face, his voice was low, a little impatient, as if he were conveying an everyday message to her. "I am free, Mother," he said. "You have done a good day's work that will long be remembered."

At the sound of his voice she lifted her face to him. A faint, bland shadow of surprise ran over it, but still she gave no sign of having heard what he said, so that the people round them began to wonder if the exhaustion had turned her deaf. But after a moment she slowly and waveringly raised her hand, fumbling in the air as she aimed at his face, and with her fingers touched his cheek. The cheek was wet with tears, so that at the contact her finger tips lightly stuck to it, and she seemed unable to overcome the infinitely slight resistance, or to withdraw her hand. For a minute the two looked each other in the face. Then, softly and lingeringly, like a sheaf of corn that falls to the ground, she sank forward onto the boy's shoulder, and he closed his arms round her.

He held her thus, pressed against him, his own face buried in her hair and headcloth, for such a long time that those nearest to them, frightened because her body looked so small in his embrace, drew closer, bent down, and loosened his grip. The boy let them do so without a word or a movement. But the woman who held Anne-Marie, in her arms to lift her up, turned her face to the old lord. "She is dead," she said.

The people who had followed Anne-Marie all through the day kept standing and stirring in the field for many hours, as long as the evening light lasted, and longer. Long after some of them had made a stretcher from branches of the trees and had carried away the dead woman, others wandered on, up and down the stubble, imitating and measuring her course from one end of the rye field to the other, and binding up the last sheaves, where she had finished her mowing.

The old lord stayed with them for a long time, stepping along a little, and again standing still.

In the place where the woman had died the old lord later on had a stone set up, with a sickle engraved in it. The peasants on the land then named the rye field "Sorrow-Acre." By this name it was known a long time after the story of the woman and her son had itself been forgotten.

Frank O'Connor
1903-

FRANK O'CONNOR, an Irishman of the Aran Isles, was a notable figure in the Black and Tan war, hiding from the authorities, secretly carrying arms, calling upon the country-side to rebel. But once the Free State was in existence, it saw fit to intern him, and during his confinement he reverted to his real work—writing and studying languages. From childhood on he had spoken Gaelic and read all the poetry available in that tongue. After his release from prison he proved his erudition by a study of Turgenev, written in Gaelic, which won him a prize.

O'Connor's stories seem to tell themselves. He "is doing for Ireland what Chekhov did for Russia," W. B. Yeats once said of him. If for nothing else than the lilt of the Irish-English in them, these stories should not be missed.

The Storyteller

BY FRANK O'CONNOR

AFRIC and Nance went up the mountain, two little girls in shapeless, colorless smocks of coarse frieze. With them went the lamb. Afric had found it on the mountain, and it insisted on accompanying her everywhere. It was an idiotic, astonished animal which stopped dead and bucked and scampered entirely without reason. It was drawing on to dusk.

Shadow was creeping up the mountain. First light faded from the sea, then from the rocks, then from the roadway and the fields. Soon it would dwindle from the bog; everything there would fill with rich color and the long channels of dark bog water would burn like mirrors between the purple walls of turf.

Behind each of the channels was ranged a file of turf stacks, black sods heaped to dry and looking like great pine cones.

"And the priest came," continued Nance, pursuing a litany.

"And what did he say?"

"He said—he said Grandfather would die tonight."

"You said 'twas the doctor said that."

"The priest said it, too."

"Hike, you divil!" yelled Afric. The lamb had walked straight up to the edge of a bog pool, bent down in innocent rapture and then tossed itself high into the air and off sideways like a crow.

"And Mom said you were to stop talking about the boat."

"What boat?"

"The boat you said would come for Grandfather. Mom said there was no boat."

"There is a boat. Grandfather said it. And lights."

"Mom said there's no lights either."

"Mom doesn't know. Grandfather knows better."

"Mom said Grandfather didn't mean it."

"Ha!" said Afric scornfully.

"'Tis true."

"And I suppose he didn't mean about Shaun O'Mullarkey and the Sprid either. Or about Con of the fairies and the Demon Hurler. Or about the Gillygooley. Or the Gawley Cullawney and his mother."

"Mom said," continued Nance in the tone of one reciting a lesson, "that 'twould be better for Grandfather now if he hadn't so much old stories and paid heed to his prayers when he had the chance."

"Grandfather always said his

prayers. Grandfather knew more prayers than Mom."

"Mom said he told barbarous stories."

"But if they were true?"

"Mom says they weren't true, that they were all lies and that God punishes people for telling lies and that's why Grandfather is afraid to die. He's afraid of what God will do to him for telling lies."

"Ha!" sniffed Afric again, but with less confidence.

The mountain did not inspire confidence. The shadow, quickening its mighty motion, rose before them among the naked rocks. Two tiny stars came out, vibrating in the green sky. A pair of horses, head down before them, suddenly took fright and rushed away with a great snorting, their manes tossing and loose stones flying from their hoofs. To the right, a cliff, a pale veil dropped sheer to the edge of a dark lake, and from its foot the land went down in terraces of gray stone to the sea's edge, a ghost-pale city without lights or sound.

It was queer, Afric thought, the way Grandfather had stopped telling them stories all at once, the way he seemed to fix his eyes on the wall. Even when she had asked him about the boat he had only muttered, "Whisht, child, whisht!" But all the same Afric knew that Mom must be wrong. Grandfather had meant it all. There must be some other reason for his silence.

"Maybe death will come like a traveling man, like it came to some," she said thoughtfully. "A man with long, long legs and a bandage over his eyes. Maybe that's why Grandfather would be afraid—a big man the size of a mountain. I'd be afraid of him myself, I'm thinking."

It was almost dark when they reached the mountaintop. There was a cold wind there, the grasses swayed and whistled, and their bare feet squelched calf-deep in the quaggy ground with its almost invisible hollows. Plunging on, they lost sight of the sea, the other side of the mountain came into view. A chain of lakes with edges like the edges of countries on the maps in school shone out of all the savage darkness, and beyond them, very far away, another inlet of the sea.

They almost failed to see the fire. It was in a deep natural hollow. It burned under a curiously shaped metal drum. On top of the drum was another metal container, narrow below and broad above like a bucket, and a jointed pipe led from this into a barrel with a tap on it. Under the tap was a mug covered by a strip of muslin. Four children were solemnly seated on the edge of the pit, looking down on this queer contraption, their bare legs dangling in the firelight, their faces and heads in shadow. They were not speaking, but looking with fascinated, solemn eyes at the still. Afric's father was standing before it, his hands in his trousers' pockets. He was a tall, handsome man, big-shouldered, broad-chested, with a wide gray kindly face and gray eyes, but now he seemed melancholy and withdrawn.

"What way is your grandfather?" he asked.

"Mom said to tell you there was no change," said Nance.

Nance and Afric sat within the hollow out of the wind so that the heads and shoulders of the other children rose up on every side against the starlit sky like idols grouped in a circle. The lamb seemed to take the greatest interest in the whole proceedings, sniffed at the turf, the tub, the barrel, backed away from them, staggered to the mouth of the hollow and scampered back as though horribly shocked by something, licked the legs of the little girls and gazed with blank eyes into the fire. Its antics caused a sudden diversion among the four other children; they laughed without restraint. Then, as though they had grown self-conscious, they fell silent. Two wiped their noses in the sleeves of their little frieze jackets. Then they rose and went off silently down the mountain. After a few moments the other two did exactly the same thing. It was growing very dark.

Then their Uncle Padraic came, and, standing against the sky, leaned on a turf-cutting spade. You nearly always saw Padraic leaning on something; a wall, a turf rick, the pillar of a gate—there always seemed to be something for Padraic to lean on. Whatever it was, his whole body fell lifelessly about it. He stood like that now against the sky, his hands resting in a crossed position on the handle, his chin resting on his hands. He was a tall, gaunt, gentle man, wearing a frieze vest without sleeves over a knitted gansey and very much patched frieze trousers. He didn't say anything, but seemed to breathe out an atmosphere of tranquillity. It looked as if he could go on leaning forever without opening his mouth.

"Himself is the same way," said their father.

Padraic spat sideways and rested his chin again upon his crossed hands.

"He is."

They fell silent again. Their father dipped a mug in the barrel of ale and passed it up to his brother-in-law. Padraic drank and carefully emptied the mug onto the ground before returning it.

"One of ye better go for more turf," said their father.

"I will," said Afric. "Keep a hold on the lamb, Nance."

She took the bag and began to run down the mountain. It was a high hollow starry night full of strange shadows. From behind her she heard Nance's cry of distress, and a few moments later something warm and white and woolly came between her flying feet and nearly threw her. She flung herself head foremost on the soft turf, rolling round and round downhill, while the lamb rolled idiotically on top of her, its warm nose seeking her face. There was a smell of earth and grass which made her drunk. She boxed the lamb's ears, caught it by the budding horns, pushed, shoved, wrestled and rolled with it.

"Ah, lambeen, lambeen, lambeen! You foolish lambeen! I'm going for turf and the fairies will catch you, the fairies will catch you! Look, lambeen, they're searching for you with little lanterns!"

She filled her bag with turf. The bog was now wild and dark. The channels of bog water were shining with inky brightness; as though the bog were all a-tremble they shook, but with a suave oily motion that barely broke the reflected starlight. Below, very far below, were a few lights along the shore.

She recognized her own house on the little spit of land that pushed out into the bay. There was light only in the west window in the room where her grandfather was lying. She could imagine all the others in the kitchen in the firelight: her mother and the baby, her mother's two sisters, old Brigid, their mother, sucking her pipe, and Padraic's children. They would be talking in low voices, and then her mother or old

Brigid would go into the west room to the old man who would tell no more stories, and they would talk to him of the will of God, but still his face, pale as the little beard about his chin, would be bitter because he did not wish to die. Not wish to die and he eighty and more! And up on the mountain were she and her father, making poteen which would be drunk at the old man's wake, because he was a famous and popular man and people would come from twenty miles around on ponies and in traps to pray for his soul.

Maybe he was dying now! But Afric felt sure if he was dying there would be some sign, as there always was in the stories he told: along the road a huge man, dressed in rags, a bandage about his eyes and his hands outstretched, feeling his way to their house; all the air filled with strange lights while the spirits waited; a shining boat making its way across the dark water without a sail. Surely there would be signs like that! She looked about her furtively, suddenly trembling and all attune for the wonder. But there was nothing. Not a sound. In sudden panic she repulsed the lamb and began to run, her bag of dry sods knocking her shoulders.

It was all placid and homely up there. Padraic was sitting on an upturned tub, smoking. It was so silent you could hear the noise of the stream near by, loud in the darkness. Her father came up from it, carrying a bucket.

"He had a long day," he said, as though continuing a conversation.

"He had a long day," agreed Padraic, not looking up. He spat and sucked his pipe again.

"He was a good man," said Afric's father.

"He was. He was a good father to you."

"He was so. 'Tis a pity he couldn't be more resigned."

" 'Twas what they were saying."

"He said a queer thing last night."

"Did he now?"

"He says a man sees the world when he comes into it and goes out of it; the rest is only foolishness— that's what he said."

" 'Tis a deep saying."

" 'Tis deep."

"But there's meaning in it," Padraic went on.

"I dare say."

"There is. He was always a deep man, a patient, long-thinking man."

Afric was astonished. She never remembered her uncle to have spoken as much.

"Do you remember," he continued, "on the boat? He never liked one of us to do a thing in a hurry. 'Mother was drowned a year ago,' he'd say, 'and she'd have been round the lake since then.' That's what he'd always say."

"He would so."

" 'Tis a pity he didn't do more with himself—a clever man."

" 'Tis. But he wouldn't stop in America."

"He wouldn't sure."

"There was nothing he cared about only the stories."

"No, then. And he was a wonder with them."

"He was. You wouldn't miss a day in a bog or a night in the boat with him. Often he'd keep you that way you wouldn't know you were hungry." Afric's father spat. It was not often he made such admissions. "And there were times we were hungry."

"You never took after him, Con."

"No, then. 'Twasn't in me, I suppose. But 'twasn't in our generation. I'd get great pleasure listening to him, but I could never tell a story myself."

"The place won't be the same without him," said Padraic, rising.

"Ye'd better go home with yeer uncle," said her father.

"I'll stop with you, Father," said Afric.

He thought for a moment.

"Do so," he said.

She knew then he was lonely.

When Padraic and Nance had gone, everything seemed lonelier than before, but she didn't mind because her father was with her. He wrapped his coat about her. The lamb snuggled up beside her. And now she let the mountain come alive with all its stories and its magic. Because she knew it was up here the spirits lived and planned their descents on the little cottages; at night you could often see them from the bay, moving across the mountain with their little lanterns. Sometimes, the lights would be close together and you would know it was a fairy funeral. A man from the place, making poteen in the mountains at night, had come across just such a funeral, and the spirits had laid the coffin at his feet. He had opened it, and inside was a beautiful girl with long yellow hair. As he looked at her she had opened her eyes and he had brought her home with him. She had told him she was a girl from Tuam, and when inquiries were made it was found that a girl from Tuam had been buried that same day; but she wouldn't go back to her own people and remained always with the man who had saved her and married him.

Afric could see her father moving about in the smoky light, his legs seeming immense. Sometimes she saw his face when he bent to the fire. Then he sat on the upturned tub

with his head between his hands. She went to sleep at last.

When she woke again the helmet of shadow had tilted. It was cold. The high hollow drum of the sky had half filled with low drifting vapors. Someone—she did not know who—was speaking to her father. Then he caught her in his arms, and the jolting and slithering of his feet in the long slopes wakened her completely. He stumbled on blindly as though he did not know she was in his arms. Even when she looked at him he did not seem to be aware of her.

There was a little crowd kneeling even at the door of the west room. The kitchen was in darkness only for the firelight, and this and the flickering of candles made the west room unusually bright and gay. The people kneeling there rose and made way for her father. He put her gently down on a stool by the fire and went in, taking off his hat. The low murmur of prayer went on again. Afric tiptoed to the room door. Yes, the west room was very bright. Her grandfather's great bearded head was lying, very pale and wasted, over the bowed heads under the light of two candles. Her father was kneeling awkwardly by the bedside, covering his face with his hands. Her grandmother, old Brigid, suddenly began to keen and sway from side to side.

Afric went out. She looked up and down the lane. She was looking with a sort of fascinated terror for the big man with the bandage over his eyes. There was no sign of him. The lane was quiet only for the whispering of the bushes and a blackbird's first bewildered, drowsy fluting. There were no lights, no voices. Frightened as she was, she ran down the lane to the little cove where her father's boat was drawn up among the slimy rocks and seaweed. Over it was a grassy knoll. She ran there and threw herself on her face and hands lest anyone should spy her and take fright. The light was breaking over the water. But no boat came shining to her out of the brightness. The blackbird having tried his voice threw it out in a sudden burst of song, and the lesser birds joined in with twitters and chuckles. In the little cove there was a ducking of water among the dried weeds, a vague pushing to and fro. She rose, her smock wet, and looked down into the cove. There was no farewell, no clatter of silver oars in rowlocks as magic took her child away. Nothing, nothing at all. With a strange choking in her throat she went slowly back to the house. She thought that maybe she knew now why her grandfather had been so sad.

Liam O'Flaherty
1897-

LIAM O'FLAHERTY is the typical wild fighting Irishman. At
eighteen he joined the Irish Guards and fought in Belgium;
in the Irish Civil War, with a small "army" he held the
Rotunda in Dublin for a week; then for three years he followed
the sea, going round the world as a stoker, trimmer, or
seaman. He talks loud and plays hard, and his first stories
were of the same timbre—until Edward Garnett, seeing
promise in them, told him to go home and "write a story
about a cow." This he did—went back to the Aran Isles, off
Galway, where he was born, and where he still has a home,
and wrote stories as idyllic as his nature is strenuous and
rebellious.

The Old Hunter

BY LIAM O'FLAHERTY

Mr. Stephen Mullen, the horse dealer of Ballyhaggard, went to an auction one day. He was a tall, slim man with a red face and white eyebrows. Being a very popular man, on account of his dry wit and his good temper, he met many friends in the town where the auction was being held, and the result was that he spent the morning in the hotels drinking. Slightly intoxicated, he arrived at the auction when everything was sold except an old hunter called Morrissey.

Mr. Mullen went up to the auctioneer, a friend of his, and asked him had he anything left. The auctioneer pointed to the old hunter.

"That's the lot," he said.

"What's that?" said Mr. Mullen, shutting one eye and cocking his head sideways.

"Pooh!" said the auctioneer, "there's enough iron in that old rascal to keep a factory going for a month. Tell you what, these bank clerks and shopkeepers that are buying horses now with their ill-gotten gains don't know a . . ."

"Hech, hech," said Mr. Mullen, "let's have a look at him. I might give ye the price of a drink for him."

They walked over to the hunter. He was a finely built animal, but he looked like a man that had just left a nursing home after a serious nervous breakdown. His bones were sticking through his hide, and though he held his head proudly in the air, it was obvious that he did so out of respect for his ancestry and not because of any consciousness of his strength. He was of a bay color and somebody had fired his left hind leg, so clumsily and in such a cruel manner that it appeared to have been done with a red-hot crowbar. The pelt was quite naked of hair and the flesh was singed in streaks.

"Look at that," said Mr. Mullen, pointing to the leg. "Did ye get him from a tinker, or what?"

"Lord have mercy on yer soul," said the auctioneer, "that fellah has a pedigree as long as yer arm. Come here, I'll show ye."

"Ye needn't bother," said Mr. Mullen. "What good is a pedigree to a dying man? The Master o' the Hounds might give a few bob for him for the pack."

Mr. Mullen wrinkled up his face in a smile and he looked at the auctioneer with his mouth open. He really wanted the horse because he liked the old fellow's head, but he wanted to get him for next to nothing. The auctioneer also wanted

From *Short Stories of Liam O'Flaherty*. By permission of Jacques Chambrun, Inc. Published by Jonathan Cape of London, 1937.

to get rid of him very badly, but still, he wanted to strike a good bargain.

"Now drop the coddin', Mr. Mullen," he said, "and buy the horse if ye want him. Sure I needn't tell you what a horse is, whether he is a horse or a mule. Man alive, sure a few square meals 'ud change that fellah so much ye wouldn't know him. Look at him . . ."

"Aye," said Mullen coldly, "let's have a look at them. I mean at his insides. I bet he's got a smoker's heart and a liver stitched together with the best silk thread. If I buy him, would ye get him carted home for me?"

"I can see it's out for coddin' me ye are," said the auctioneer, turning to go away.

"Very well," said Mr. Mullen, clearing his throat, "I'll make ye an offer for him."

"What's that?" said the auctioneer, halting abruptly and turning around to Mr. Mullen.

"I've got thirty bob on me," said Mullen, contracting his white eyebrows. "I'll give ye the lot, though it's good money wasted."

The auctioneer pursed up his lips and stared at Mr. Mullen for a few moments as if he were dumfounded.

"D'ye really mean it?" he said.

Mr. Mullen nodded.

"Take him home, for God's sake," said the auctioneer, waving his hands.

Mr. Mullen paid for the horse and took him home. He led him along beside his own horse, and it was the devil of a job to keep him in hand. My boy, he had his head in the wind and champed along, rearing and trying to break loose.

"Good Lord," thought Mr. Mullen, "that fellah is a corker only for his age."

Mr. Mullen went to a party that night and there was heavy drinking. In his cups he began to boast about the old hunter he had bought for thirty shillings. Everybody made fun of him about it, so Mr. Mullen boasted that he would ride the old horse to the meet of the Ballyhaggard hounds next day.

"Wait till you see," he cried. "I'll leave you all so far behind that I'll have the fox's skin dressed before you arrive."

Next day Mr. Mullen's head was as big as a pot, and when he remembered his boast he was disgusted with himself. But he was a man of his word and he ordered the old hunter to be saddled for him. He drank a considerable amount of raw whisky and mounted him. Off he went to the meet.

Everybody in the district turns out with the hounds, from Lord Clonmore to Mr. Mulligan the butcher of Murren. All sorts of ungainly beasts appear. In fact, Mr. Murchison the new Protestant curate once joined, mounted on a cart horse, which a scoundrel called The Tiger Donnelly sold him as an Irish hunter. Since the war and the revolution all sorts of people have been thrown together in the district, so that, as Mr. Mullen says, "There's no class about anything nowadays." But when Mr. Mullen himself appeared that day on Morrissey, everybody agreed that such an extraordinary animal had never been seen before. It was like a mortally sick man appearing at a wedding, half drunk and insisting on being the most hilarious person present.

"Bravo, Mr. Mullen," said Lord Clonmore. "The dead have arisen. Eh?"

Everybody laughed and Mr. Mullen was mortally insulted, but when the Cavalcade set off, by Jove, Morrissey behaved himself marvelously. Like a good thoroughbred of the old school, he showed every ounce that was in him. He cleared the ditches and fences as lightly as those wonderful horses for which the Galway Blazers were famous, fellows that could live a week on a raw turnip and cross a bog without wetting their fetlocks. Mr. Mullen kept refreshing himself now and again with stimulants, and as a consequence rode even more daringly than was his custom; but the old hunter carried him all day without a single stumble, until at last, just before the finish, he arrived at the drain that flows from the workhouse, about a mile outside the town. There is no more filthy or evil-smelling drain in the world. There is no necessity to describe it.

But when Morrissey arrived at this drain at full speed, he stopped dead. Undoubtedly the animal was too well bred to face it. Mr. Mullen was pitched over the horse's head and he fell headlong into the stinking place. Several people pulled up, but Mr. Mullen crawled out, uninjured. Seeing him, everybody went into hysterics with laughter. He was indescribable, and in fact unrecognizable. Morrissey lowered his head, sniffed at Mr. Mullen and set off back at a mad canter.

"It must have turned his stomach," laughed a red-haired farmer.

"Yer a lot of scoundrels," shouted Mr. Mullen, struggling to his feet and holding out his dripping hands that were as black and sticky as if he had dipped them in tar.

Morrissey was found again and brought back to the stables. Mr. Mullen went home and had a bath, and by that time his anger had worn off and he himself was able to laugh at the joke. Next morning he went to look at Morrissey. The poor animal was quite stiff with his efforts of the previous day. But he still had his head in the air and he whinnied joyfully when he saw Mr. Mullen. That softened Mr. Mullen's heart towards him.

"Damn it," he said to the stable boy, "he's a great old horse. I'll take him down to the shore and give him a dip in the salt water to soften his legs."

He rode Morrissey down to the strand. It was a fine day, but there was a rather heavy ground swell and the waves broke on the sand with a thundering noise. This thundering noise and the menacing aspect of the dark green waves, rising suddenly within a few feet of the shore and falling with a thud, terrified the horse. It was impossible to get him to walk in the tide. At last Mr. Mullen managed to get him near the surf, when the tide had receded for a particularly long distance, as it does now and again, after a certain number of short waves have broken. Then as the horse was stamping about and snorting, trying to get away from the water, an enormous wave rose suddenly and almost enveloped him. Instead of trying to rush backward, he was so confused by the rush of water under his stomach that he plunged out to sea. Mr. Mullen tried to head him off, but it was no use. Presently another equally large wave arose, passed right over the horse and the rider, so that they both turned a somersault. Mr. Mullen was thrown from the saddle and he became entangled somehow in the horse's legs. When he came to the surface, after having saved himself, the horse was five yards away and Mr. Mullen was in deep water. He swam a few strokes, struck ground and then looked behind him. There was the horse, swimming mightily out towards the open sea.

"God Almighty!" cried Mr. Mullen. "With ten pounds worth of a saddle on him."

Mr. Mullen dashed up on to the strand and began to call some boatmen that were there. They ran over to him.

"Hey," he cried, "if he drowns, will he sink or float?"

"God save us," they cried, "who are ye talking about?"

"My horse, damn it," cried Mr. Mullen; "he's gone out to sea. Don't ye see him? Look."

"Aw, snakes alive," they said, when they saw the dark object, heaving along sideways, like an unwieldy porpoise.

"He'll float sure enough," said one man, "with the water he'll swallow."

"All right then," said Mr. Mullen, "get me a boat. I want to save the saddle. The horse isn't worth his keep, but the saddle is worth money. Get a boat for me."

They rushed down a boat and put to sea after the horse. When they had gone out almost half a mile, they met the horse swimming back towards them.

"There he is," cried one boatman.

"He's floating, sure enough," said Mr. Mullen. "Get alongside him and get the saddle."

"It's not floatin' he is but swimmin' like a warrior," said the boatman.

"God!" said Mr. Mullen.

They were all amazed and they lay on their oars, as Morrissey swept past them towards the beach, going at a terrific pace. They followed him, and when they reached the strand, Morrissey was standing there, shivering and exhausted. Mr. Mullen took off his hat and struck his forehead.

"Well, that horse beats all I ever saw," he said. "Here, I'll buy a bottle of whisky over this. Come on, men."

After that Mr. Mullen and the horse that went to sea became quite famous in the district. So that Mr. Mullen grew fond of the horse and he kept him all that winter in his stables with plenty of food. But he made no attempt to ride him, and although the fame of the horse spread afar, still nobody made an offer for him. Because even though he was famous for having swam a mile out to sea and then swam back again, he was also famous for having thrown Mr. Mullen into the workhouse drain.

Then in the following April another extraordinary thing happened to the horse. I must say that he had improved considerably during the winter. He had fattened a great deal and his hide was becoming almost glossy. The mark on his hind leg was not so outrageous, and to an ordinary person he seemed a perfectly sound horse. But to a horseman he was still an old crock. One of those game old things, whether they are old colonels who insist on wearing tight waists in their seventieth year, or old horses or old battered fighting cocks that take a step ferociously and then glare, wagging their chaps aggressively as if they were in the prime of their lives—I say, he was one of those game old things that make a virtue of looking fit even when they might be excused drooping their heads and lying down to die. But all the buyers admired him and left him alone. Then Mr. Stanley Edwards came to the town.

Mr. Edwards might be called a crock as well as the old hunter. He spent a greater part of each year in a nursing home. The remainder of the year he spent in the pursuit of extravagant pleasures, not always very well considered. His money was tied up in this country, otherwise it is very probable that he would never spend a week in it. But when he had done a great bout in London, he always had to return to Ireland to get some more money. After one of those bouts and a month in the hospital, he engaged a villa in Ballyhaggard to take the sea air. A few days after his arrival in the town he came to Mr. Mullen. Mr. Mullen looked him up and down, rather surprised that such a weakling should come to him for anything.

"Well," he said, "what could I do for you?"

"Look here," said Mr. Edwards, "I have to live for a few months in this ghastly place. I'm sick and I have very little money. I have been here three days and I'm quite fed up with walking up and down the shore and talking to lunatics around here. I want a horse. Can you get me one?"

"Let me see," said Mr. Mullen, looking at him shrewdly, "you'd want a quiet horse, I suppose?"

"I want a horse," said Mr. Edwards pettishly. "It doesn't matter what he is. If he breaks my neck it might be a jolly good idea."

"I see," said Mr. Mullen. "I think I've got the very thing that'll suit you."

"Oh! Look here," said Mr. Edwards rather nervously. "I don't mean I want some . . . eh . . . crazy thing. You know . . . a . . . oh, well . . ."

"You leave it to me," said Mr. Mullen. "You can try him out before you buy him."

Morrissey was brought out and Mr. Edwards immediately mounted him and trotted off. Mr. Edwards looked a very poor figure on horseback. Some wit said that he was born to be a ragpicker, because his gaunt frame bent like a willow rod and his nose was so long that he could use it in the same way that an elephant uses the top of his trunk. But such a slight weight suited the old horse and he went off very gallantly indeed, with that twirl in his right hind leg, which is a sign of old age in a horse and which warns off the cunning buyer but which is very attractive; like the smart twirl of the spurred boot which tells the swagger cavalry officer.

Mr. Mullen looked after the horse, scratching his chin and thinking that he would be very glad to accept a five-pound note for him.

After an hour, Mr. Edwards returned, perspiring but looking very happy. A good hour's trotting on a well-bred horse on a fine spring morning would make a corpse almost come to life again.

"Go all right?" said Mr. Mullen, smiling his most engaging smile.

"Splendid," said Mr. Edwards, sitting the horse and wiping his forehead, as if he were loath to dismount. "How much do you want for him?"

"I'll take thirty pounds at a pinch," said Mr. Mullen, after a moment's apparent thought and looking at Mr. Edwards as if he were going to do him a favor, which, however, gave him a great deal of pain.

"Oh!" said Mr. Edwards, a little surprised.

Then he dismounted and looked curiously at Mr. Mullen.

"It's a lot," he said.

"Oh! Well," said Mr. Mullen, making a gesture with his hands, "a horse isn't a bicycle."

"Quite," said Mr. Edwards. "Now, let me see."

He walked around the horse and

passed his hand over the horse's body in various places. Mr. Mullen was very glad to see that he touched the wrong places. Then Mr. Edwards stood at a distance from the horse and looked at him. He seemed very loath to leave him. Mr. Mullen began to feel very comfortable.

"Look here," said Mr. Edwards at length, "I'll come back tomorrow and have another ride. May I?"

"Why, certainly," said Mr. Mullen affably. "You can have a look at his pedigree now if you like."

"Oh, has he got a pedigree?" said Mr. Edwards.

"Lord, yes," said Mr. Mullen, "yards of it."

Here it must be stated that although Mr. Edwards was a wealthy country gentleman, he kept motorcars instead of horses and knew nothing about the animals except on race courses. So that a pedigree seemed to him as good a guarantee of perfection as the maker's name on a Rolls-Royce.

"Let's have a look at it," he said. Mr. Mullen produced the pedigree and Mr. Edwards inspected it.

"In that case," he said, "I'll buy the horse right away."

"It's like taking milk from a child," thought Mr. Mullen, as Mr. Edwards wrote out the check.

Everybody expected Mr. Edwards to break his neck, and some people said that Mr. Mullen played rather a scurvy trick on the poor fellow, but during the whole of that summer the horse was seen on the roads almost every day, trotting along in the pink of condition. And what was more,

Mr. Edwards became quite a new man. Whether it was the sea air or the riding that did it, he regained his health to an extraordinary extent. He did not become robust, but he was no longer an invalid and he led a decent healthy life. In fact, just before he went away, he came to Mr. Mullen and said: "Look here, Mr. Mullen, you've saved my life."

"Glad to hear it," said Mr. Mullen, without winking an eye.

In September Mr. Edwards left the district, but instead of going to England, as was his custom, he returned to his property in County Kilkenny. Nothing more was heard of him or of the horse for two years. And then two months ago I met Mr. Mullen in Dublin. We were having a drink together and talking about various things, when he suddenly gripped my arm and said:

"D'ye remember that horse, Morrissey, I had, the fellah that threw me into the drain?"

I nodded.

"Ye remember I sold him to a chap called Edwards from Kilkenny. Well, I've just been down there to a show. Met him there. He's still got the horse, going as strong as a three-year-old and . . . d'ye know what I'm going to tell ye? That horse saved his life, as he said himself. When I asked him about the horse, he said: 'I wouldn't part with that horse for a thousand. I haven't left this district since I saw you last, and I can drink two bottles of port now after dinner without turning a hair.'"

So that, indeed, it seems that there is something in a pedigree.

Sean O'Faoláin
1900-

LESS fiery and passionate by temperament than his two
northern compatriots, O'Connor and O'Flaherty, this Irish
revolutionist is a Master of Arts from the National University
of Ireland and from Harvard, a member of the Irish Royal
Academy of Letters, a schoolteacher, and a university lecturer.
But it is not for his learning that the world knows him. It is
for the poetry of his prose. The revolution that colored the
thinking of his student days is reflected with quite as much
passion in his stories as in the stories of those others, but the
texture is on the whole softer. Through the O'Faoláin stories
trail Irish mist and beautiful girls, the blue of the southern
mountains and the atmosphere of the town streets of his
native Cork. *A Nest of Simple Folk* is probably his best-
known novel. "Sinners" comes from the book of short stories,
A Purse of Coppers.

Sinners

BY SEAN O'FAOLÁIN

THE canon, barely glancing at his two waiting penitents, entered the confessional. From inside he looked wearily across at the rows of penitents on each side of Father Deeley's box, all still as statues where they sat against the wall, or leaned forward to let the light of the single electric bulb, high up in the windy roof, fall on their prayer books. Deeley would give each about ten minutes, and that meant he would not absolve the last until near midnight. "More trouble with the sacristan," sighed the canon, and closed the curtains and lifted his hand towards the slide of the grille.

He paused. To banish a sudden restiveness he said a prayer. He often said that prayer—an Aspiration against Anger. He had remembered that on the other side of the grille was a little serving girl he had sent out of the box last Saturday night because she had been five years away from confession and did not seem to be a bit sorry for it. He lifted his hand, but paused again. To add to his difficulty—for it was no help to know what, under the *sigillum*, he must pretend not to know—he had just been told in the sacristy by her employer that a pair of her best boots was missing. Why

on earth, he sighed, did people reveal such things to him? Did he *want* to know the sins of his penitents? Was the confession being made to him, or to God? Was it . . . ? He lowered his hand, ashamed of his irritation, and repeated the prayer. Then he drew the slide, cupped his ear in his palm to listen, and saw her hands clasping and unclasping, as if her courage was a little bird between her palms trying to escape.

"My poor child," he said, ever so gently, dutifully pretending to know nothing about her, "tell me how long it is since your last confession."

"It's a long time, Father," she whispered.

"How long?" To encourage her he added: "Over a year?"

"Yes, Father."

"How much? Tell me, my poor child, tell me. Two years?"

"More, Father."

"Three years?"

"More, Father."

"Well, well, you must tell me, you know."

In spite of himself his voice was a little pettish. The title "Father" instead of "Canon" was annoying him too. She noted the change of voice, for she said, hurriedly:

" 'Tis that, Father."

"'Tis what?" asked the canon a shade too loudly.

"Over three years, Father," she prevaricated.

He wondered if he could dare let the prevarication go; but his conscience would not let him.

"My dear child, how much over three years is it?"

"'Tis, 'tis, Father, 'tis . . ."

The canon forestalled the lie.

"My dear child, how much over three years is it? Is it four years? And would you mind calling me *Canon?*"

The breathing became faster.

"'Tis, Father. I mean, 'tis more, *Canon*, Father."

"Well, how much? I can't make your confession for you, you know."

"'Tis a bit more, Father."

"But how much?" broke from the canon.

"Two months," lied the maid, and her hands made a flutter of whiteness in the dark.

The canon almost wished he could break the seal of the confessional and reveal to her that he knew exactly who she was, and how long she had been away; all he dared say was:

"I suspect you're telling me a lie."

"Oh, God, Father, it's gospel truth."

"But"—the canon tapped the cushion—"there's no use in telling me if it's not the truth. For God's sake, my poor child," he controlled himself, "maybe it's five years?"

"'Tis five years," admitted the maid in so low a voice that he barely heard it.

He sighed with satisfaction. He straightened his hair on his forehead. Then he leaned nearer to hear her sins, nearer and nearer until his ear was pressed against the lattice.

"Now," he warned, "that is a long time, my child. But, thank God, you have come back at last. You must try hard to remember all—all—your sins. Let me help you. My poor little child! Take the first commandment."

But when he heard the shudder of her breath he knew he had made a bad mistake; she would be seeing a long list of broken commandments before her and she would slur over many of her sins in order to shorten the ordeal.

"I mean to say," went on the canon, annoyed with his own stupidity, "that is one way of doing it. Do you wish to make your confession that way?"

"Yes, Father."

"Very well."

"The first commandment . . ." She stopped in confusion and he realized that she did not even know what the commandment was.

"Did you ever miss Mass on Sundays?" he helped her out, although his knees were beginning to dance with impatience.

"Oh, never, never in my whole life."

"Good. Did you ever swear? Take the Lord's name in vain?"

"Tututut!" said the girl in horror at the very idea.

"Did you ever disobey your parents, cause them pain in any way, give back-answers?"

"I have no parents, Father. Mrs. Higg—my mistress got me from the Orphanage."

"Ah! Well . . . er . . . lies? Anger? Have you told lies, or given way to anger?"

"Wisha, I suppose I did, Father. I suppose I told a little lie now and again."

"How often in those five years? On an average? I mean, is it a weakness you have? A habit?"

"God help us, Father, I don't tell

many. I only tell 'em when I do be afraid."

"Well, we will say you told lies occasionally. Now the sixth commandment. Have you ever sinned in thought, word, or deed against Holy Purity? The opposite sex, for example. Have you ever misbehaved in any way with men?"

"Oh!" gasped the maid, and her voice thickened.

"Stealing?" prompted the canon, and he waited for her to say that she had stolen Mrs. Higgins's boots.

"I never in my life, Father, stole as much as the head off of a pin. Except when I was small I once stole an apple in the nuns' orchard. And then they caught me and gave me a flaking. And they took the last bite out of my mouth."

"You never stole articles of dress?" threatened the canon, and he suddenly realized that there were only three very unlikely commandments left. "Clothes? Hats? Gloves? Shoes?"

"Never, Father."

There was a long pause.

"Boots?" he whispered.

Suddenly the girl was sobbing violently.

"Father," she wept, "Mrs. Higgins is telling you lies about me. I hate that wan. I . . . I . . . I hate her. I do. She's always prying and poking and prodding at me. She took me from the nuns five years ago and she never gave me a minute's rest. She calls me low names. She tells me I can't be good or wholesome to come out of an orphanage. She is picking at me from dawn to dusk. She's an old bitch. . . ."

"My child! My child!"

"I did take the boots. I took them. But I didn't steal them. Sure I haven't a boot on my foot and she has lashings and leavings of 'em. I was going to put them back."

"My child, to take them is the same as to steal them."

"What does she want them for? But she's that mean. Her own daughter ran away from her two years ago and married an Englishman who's half a Freemason. The poor girl told me with her own mouth, only last week, how she's half starved by that husband of hers and they have no money to have a family. But do you think her mother would give her a penny?"

The girl sobbed on. The canon groaned and drew himself up to ease his chest. He could hear the wind whistling up in the roof and he could see the long queue on each side of Father Deeley's box, all still as statues in the dusk of the aisle. Seeing them he groaned again as much as to say: "What's the use? They all deceive themselves. They all think everyone is sinful but themselves only. Or if they say they are sinners, and feel it—it only lasts while they are in the church. Then they go out and are filled with envy and pride and they have no charity." He leaned back.

"My child, my child, my child! For five years you have stayed away from God. If you had died you would have died with that mortal sin on your soul and gone to hell for all eternity. It's the law of the Church, and the law of God, that you *must*, you *must* go to confession at least once a year. Why did you stay away? Look at the way your mind is deformed so that you can't even recognize a sin when you commit it. Is there some sin you haven't told me that you were ashamed to tell?"

"No, Father."

"Didn't your good mistress send you to confession at least every month during those five years?"

"She sent me every week. But it

was always of a Saturday night. And one Saturday night I didn't go because I wanted to buy a blouse before the shops shut. Then it was six months before I knew it and I was afraid to go. And, anyway, sure what had I to tell?"

The canon waved his hands weakly and with great sarcasm he said:

"Did you *never* commit a sin?"

"I suppose I told a lie, Father. And there was the apple in the nuns' orchard."

Furiously the priest turned to her, determined to wring the truth from her. In her compartment he heard Lady Nolan-White, his second penitent, coughing impatiently.

"My dear child, you simply must have committed sins during those five years. Be honest with yourself. Come now! Look! Take the most common sin of all. Have you, ever, had what we, vulgarly, call a . . . er . . . call a boy?"

"I had—once—Father."

"Well, now!" He rubbed his forehead like a man in a great heat and he strained towards her as if he were struggling with her demon. "You were, what do we say . . . er . . . walking out with him?"

"Yes," panted the girl. "In the back lane."

"Well, what shall we say? Did, what do you say, did, er, did any intimacy take place with him?"

"I don't know, Father."

"You know what it is to be immodest, don't you?" cried the canon.

Her breath was panting in and out. She said nothing. She stared at him.

"My poor, poor child, you seem to have small experience of the world. But we must get at the truth. Did he—did you—did either of you ever

go beyond the bounds of propriety?"

"I dunno, Father."

Loudly the canon expelled his breath. He was becoming exhausted, but he would not give in. He rubbed his hair all the wrong way, which gave him a wild look. He took off his pince-nez and wiped them.

"You understand plain English, don't you? Now, tell me, tell Almighty God the truth of the thing. Did you ever allow him to take liberties with you?"

"Yes, Father. I mean no, Father. We were in the lane. No, Father. We didn't do nothing. Nothing much, I mean."

"Five years," moaned the canon, and he hammered his thigh with his fist. "And nothing to tell. What kind of Christians . . . ?" He determined to make one last effort, just one more effort. "Did he ever touch your body?" he asked bluntly.

"No, Father. Well, I mean—no, Father."

Seeing that she was beginning to whimper again he threw up his hands.

"All right, child," he said gently. "Say your Act of Contrition and I'll give you Absolution."

"Father," she whispered, her eyes black through the grille, "I was in bed with him once."

The canon looked at her. She drew back. He leaned away and looked from a distance at the crisscrossed face behind the grille. Then he began to smile, slowly expanding his mouth into a wide beam of relief.

"My child," he whispered, "did anyone ever tell you that you were a little deficient in the head? I mean, you weren't very smart at school, were you?"

"I was always at the top of the school, Father. Mother Mary Gonzaga wanted to make a teacher of me."

"And," growled the canon, now utterly exasperated, and dancing his knees up and down on the balls of his feet like a man in the agony of toothache, "do you kneel there and tell me that you think it no sin to go to bed with a man? Who," he added, casually, "isn't your husband?"

"I meant no harm, Father," she palpitated, "and it's not what is in your mind at all, for we didn't do nothing, and if it wasn't for the thunder and lightning that terrified me, I wouldn't do it at all. Mrs. Higgins was down in Crosshaven with Mrs. Kinwall, that's her daughter, and I was all alone in the house, and I was afraid of the dark and the thunder, so Mikey said he'd stay with me, so he stayed, and then it was late and I was 'fraid to be by myself in the bed, so he said: 'I'll mind you,' so I said: 'All right, Mikey, but none of that,' and he said: 'All right, Madgie, none of that,' and there wasn't any of that, Father."

She stared at the canon, who was blowing and puffing and shaking his head as if the whole world were suddenly gone mad.

"It was no harm, Father," she wailed, seeing he did not believe her.

"Once?" asked the canon shortly. "You did this once?"

"Yes, Father."

"Are you sorry for it?" he demanded briefly.

"If it was a sin. Was it, Father?"

"It was!" he roared. "People can't be allowed to do this kind of thing. It was a serious occasion of sin. Anything might have happened. Are you sorry?"—and he wondered if he should throw her out of the box again.

"I'm sorry, Father."

"Tell me a sin of your past life."

"The apple in the orchard, Father."

"Say an Act of Contrition."

She ran through it swiftly, staring at him all the while. There were beads of perspiration on her upper lip.

"Say three Rosaries for your penance."

He shot the slide to and sank back, worn out. From force of habit he drew the opposite slide and at once he got the sweet scent of jasmine, but when Lady Nolan-White was in the middle of her Confiteor he waved his two hands madly in the air and said, hastily:

"Excuse me, one moment . . . I can't . . . it's all absurd . . . its impossible. . . ."

And he drew the slide on her astonished, beautiful, rouged face. He put on his biretta, low down on his nose, and stalked out into the aisle. He parted the curtains on Lady Nolan-White and said:

"It's quite impossible . . . You don't understand it . . . Good night!"

He stalked up the dim aisle, and when he met two urchins gossiping in a corner he banged their little skulls together, and at once he became disgusted with himself to see them cowering from him in fright. He passed on, his hand under the tail of his surplice, dancing it up and down. When he saw two old women by the great Calvary, rubbing spittle into the Magdalen's foot and then rubbing the spittle to their eyes or throat, he groaned out: "Oh, dear, oh, dear," and strode on towards Father Deeley's box. There he counted heads—fourteen penitents on one side and twelve on the other —looked at his gold watch and saw it was a quarter-past eight.

He strode back to the center compartment and flung aside the curtains. Out of the dimness the warm cherubic face of the young curate looked at him—a pink Italian saint. Slowly the glow of spiritual elevation died from his face as the canon's insistent whisper hissed down at him:

"Father Deeley, it won't do. I assure you it's absolutely impossible. Half-past eight and twenty-six people yet to hear confession. They're just deceiving you. They want to gabble. I am an old man and I understand them. Think of the sacristan. Electric light, too! And gas going until midnight. The organization of the Church . . ."

And so on. All the time he kept stretching and relaxing the mechanical bow of his genteel smile, and he spoke in the most polite voice. But Deeley's face grew troubled, and pained, and seeing it the canon groaned inwardly. He remembered a curate he had once who played the organ every day for hours on end, until the parishioners complained that they couldn't pray with the noise he made; the canon recalled how he had gone up into the loft to ask him to stop, and the curate had lifted to him a face like an angel's, and how within one half minute it had become the face of a cruel, bitter old man.

"All right, Father Deeley," he said hastily, forestalling protests. "You are young. I know. Still, you are young. . . ."

"I am not young," said Deeley furiously. "I know my duty. It's a matter of conscience. I can sit in the dark if you are so mean that you . . ."

"All right, all right, all right," waved the canon, smiling furiously. "We are all old nowadays. Experience counts for nothing. . . ."

"Canon," said Deeley, intensely, putting his two fists on his chest, "when I was in the seminary, I used to say to myself: 'Deeley,' I used to say, 'when you are a priest . . .'"

"Oh," begged the canon, cracking his face in a smile, "don't, I beg you, please don't tell me your life story!"

Whereupon he whirled away, his head in the air, switching on and off the electric light of his smile to penitents he did not know and had never seen in his life before. He found himself before the high altar. He saw the sacristan standing on a stepladder before it, arranging the flowers for the morning, and he thought it would be well to apologize to him for Deeley's late hours. But the sacristan kept turning a vase round and round, and at last he realized that the little man was cross with him already, was deliberately delaying up there, and would not come down until he was gone.

Sighing, he went away, and after writing some letters he realized that his stomach had ceased to belong to him and would be out on its own devices until morning, like a hound that escapes from its kennel. Wearily he took his hat and cane and decided to take a long walk to calm his nerves.

It was a tender night of floating moonlight, cosily damp, and it soothed him to look down on the city and see the roofs as white as if there was frost on them. More calm, he returned home. The river was like milk. The streets were asleep. He hummed quietly to himself and felt at peace with all men. The clocks of the city chimed at one another in a good-humored mood, slow and with silvery, singing echoes. Then he heard a woman's voice talking from the high window of a cement-faced house, and he saw that it was Mrs. Higgins's house. She was in a white nightdress.

"That's a fine story!" she cried down to the pavement. "Ha! A cockalorum of a story! Wait until I see the canon. At confession, indeed! Wait until I see the nuns! Oh, you jade! You unfortunate, poor sinner!"

He saw the little girlish figure cowering down in the doorway.

"Mrs. Higgins," she wailed, "it's gospel truth. The canon threw me out again. I told him all sorts of lies. I had to go to Father Deeley. He kept me half an hour. Oh, Mrs. Higgins," wailed the child. "It's gospel truth."

"Aha!" prated the nightdress. "But you're a nice thing. Wait until I tell . . ."

The canon felt the hound of his stomach jump from the kennel again. His entrails came bodily up to his neck. He marched by, blowing and puffing.

"Oh, my God!" he whined. "Have pity on me. Oh, my God! Have pity on me!"

He turned towards the dark presbytery deep among the darkest lanes.

D. H. Lawrence
1885-1930

"To BE with Lawrence," Aldous Huxley said, "was a kind of adventure, a voyage of discovery into newness and otherness. . . . He seemed to know, by personal experience, what it was like to be a tree or a daisy or a breaking wave or even the mysterious moon itself. . . . One of his great charms as a companion was that he could never be bored and so could never be boring. . . . He could cook, he could sew . . . fires always burned when he laid them, and a floor, after Lawrence had scrubbed it, was thoroughly clean."

David Herbert Lawrence, the son of a coal miner, was born in poverty. At the age of sixteen he became a clerk and, a few years later, a teacher. Like Katherine Mansfield and Robert Louis Stevenson, he was tubercular and forever seeking health in far-off lands—in Italy, France, New Mexico, and Mexico. His wife was Baroness Frieda von Richthofen, the sister of the German ace of World War I; his friends were Katherine Mansfield and Middleton Murry and other young writers of the rebellious postwar generation.

Close to nature as he was Lawrence found the primitive life sound and sane; and squeamishness about sex seemed to him a hangover of Victorian prudery, an unnatural, superimposed code. He himself was described as a puritan by those who knew him well; but in his fight against hypocrisy, particularly in regard to sex, he brought the censor down upon him and paid by having some of his best books banned: *Women in Love* was rejected by London publishers, *The Rainbow* was condemned by the courts and the entire edition destroyed, *Lady Chatterley's Lover* was suppressed until recently, and his book of poems, *Pansies*, was suppressed the year before he died.

Because women, in his philosophy, were nearer than men to the center of the primitive life, they were the core of the universe to him. *Sons and Lovers* is about his mother; most of his other novels are about Frieda. In their turn, three women have written intimate books about him—his wife, Dorothy Brett, and Mabel Dodge Luhan. . . . Lawrence wrote novels, poetry, plays, travel books, and essays, yet his short stories may well outlive them all. "The Rocking-Horse Winner" is one of his less known but most charming stories.

The Rocking-Horse Winner

BY D. H. LAWRENCE

THERE was a woman who was beautiful, who started with all the advantages, yet she had no luck. She married for love, and the love turned to dust. She had bonny children, yet she felt they had been thrust upon her, and she could not love them. They looked at her coldly, as if they were finding fault with her. And hurriedly she felt she must cover up some fault in herself. Yet wh.t it was that she must cover up she never knew. Nevertheless, when her children were present, she always felt the center of her heart go hard. This troubled her, and in her manner she was all the more gentle and anxious for her children, as if she loved them very much. Only she herself knew that at the center of her heart was a hard little place that could not feel love, no, not for anybody. Everybody else said of her: "She is such a good mother. She adores her children." Only she herself, and her children themselves, knew it was not so. They read it in each other's eyes.

There were a boy and two little girls. They lived in a pleasant house, with a garden, and they had discreet servants, and felt themselves superior to anyone in the neighborhood.

Although they lived in style, they felt always an anxiety in the house. There was never enough money. The mother had a small income, and the father had a small income, but not nearly enough for the social position which they had to keep up. The father went in to town to some office. But though he had good prospects, these prospects never materialized. There was always the grinding sense of the shortage of money, though the style was always kept up.

At last the mother said, "I will see if I can't make something." But she did not know where to begin. She racked her brains, and tried this thing and the other, but could not find anything successful. The failure made deep lines come into her face. Her children were growing up, they would have to go to school. There must be more money, there must be more money. The father, who was always very handsome and expensive in his tastes, seemed as if he never would be able to do anything worth doing. And the mother, who had a great belief in herself, did not succeed any better, and her tastes were just as expensive.

And so the house came to be haunted by the unspoken phrase:

There must be more money! There must be more money! The children could hear it all the time, though nobody said it aloud. They heard it at Christmas, when the expensive and splendid toys filled the nursery. Behind the shining modern rocking horse, behind the smart doll's house, a voice would start whispering: "There must be more money! There must be more money!" And the children would stop playing, to listen for a moment. They would look into each other's eyes, to see if they had all heard. And each one saw in the eyes of the other two that they too had heard. "There must be more money! There must be more money!"

It came whispering from the springs of the still-swaying rocking horse, and even the horse, bending his wooden, champion head, heard it. The big doll, sitting so pink and smirking in her new pram, could hear it quite plainly, and seemed to be smirking all the more self-consciously because of it. The foolish puppy, too, that took the place of the Teddy bear, he was looking so extraordinarily foolish for no other reason but that he heard the secret whisper all over the house: "There must be more money!"

Yet nobody ever said it aloud. The whisper was everywhere, and therefore no one spoke it. Just as no one ever says: "We are breathing!" in spite of the fact that breath is coming and going all the time.

"Mother," said the boy Paul one day, "why don't we keep a car of our own? Why do we always use Uncle's, or else a taxi?"

"Because we're the poor members of the family," said the mother.

"But why are we, Mother?"

"Well—I suppose," she said slowly and bitterly, "it's because your father has no luck."

The boy was silent for some time.

"Is luck money, Mother?" he asked, rather timidly.

"No, Paul. Not quite. It's what causes you to have money."

"Oh!" said Paul vaguely. "I thought when Uncle Oscar said filthy lucker, it meant money."

"Filthy lucre does mean money," said the mother. "But it's lucre, not luck."

"Oh!" said the boy. "Then what is luck, Mother?"

"It's what causes you to have money. If you're lucky you have money. That's why it's better to be born lucky than rich. If you're rich, you may lose your money. But if you're lucky, you will always get more money."

"Oh! Will you? And is Father not lucky?"

"Very unlucky, I should say," she said bitterly.

The boy watched her with unsure eyes.

"Why?" he asked.

"I don't know. Nobody ever knows why one person is lucky and another unlucky."

"Don't they? Nobody at all? Does nobody know?"

"Perhaps God. But He never tells."

"He ought to, then. And aren't you lucky either, Mother?"

"I can't be, if I married an unlucky husband."

"But by yourself, aren't you?"

"I used to think I was, before I married. Now I think I am very unlucky indeed."

"Why?"

"Well—never mind! Perhaps I'm not really," she said.

The child looked at her, to see if she meant it. But he saw, by the lines of her mouth, that she was only trying to hide something from him.

"Well, anyhow," he said stoutly, "I'm a lucky person."

"Why?" said his mother, with a sudden laugh.

He stared at her. He didn't even know why he had said it.

"God told me," he asserted, brazening it out.

"I hope He did, dear!" she said, again with a laugh, but rather bitter.

"He did, Mother!"

"Excellent!" said the mother, using one of her husband's exclamations.

The boy saw she did not believe him; or rather, that she paid no attention to his assertions. This angered him somewhere, and made him want to compel her attention.

He went off by himself, vaguely, in a childish way, seeking for the clue to "luck." Absorbed, taking no heed of other people, he went about with a sort of stealth, seeking inwardly for luck. He wanted luck, he wanted it, he wanted it. When the two girls were playing dolls in the nursery, he would sit on his big rocking horse, charging madly into space, with a frenzy that made the little girls peer at him uneasily. Wildly the horse careered, the waving dark hair of the boy tossed, his eyes had a strange glare in them. The little girls dared not speak to him.

When he had ridden to the end of his mad little journey, he climbed down and stood in front of his rocking horse, staring fixedly into its lowered face. Its red mouth was slightly open, its big eye was wide and glassy-bright.

"Now!" he would silently command the snorting steed. "Now, take me to where there is luck! Now take me!"

And he would slash the horse on the neck with the little whip he had asked Uncle Oscar for. He knew the horse could take him to where there was luck, if only he forced it. So he would mount again, and start on his furious ride, hoping at last to get there. He knew he could get there.

"You'll break your horse, Paul!" said the nurse.

"He's always riding like that! I wish he'd leave off!" said his sister Joan.

But he only glared down on them in silence. Nurse gave him up. She could make nothing of him. Anyhow, he was growing beyond her.

One day his mother and his Uncle Oscar came in when he was on one of his furious rides. He did not speak to them.

"Hallo, you young jockey! Riding a winner?" said his uncle.

"Aren't you growing too big for a rocking horse? You're not a very little boy any longer, you know," said his mother.

But Paul only gave a blue glare from his big, rather close-set eyes. He would speak to nobody when he was in full tilt. His mother watched him with an anxious expression on her face.

At last he suddenly stopped forcing his horse into the mechanical gallop, and slid down.

"Well, I got there," he announced fiercely, his blue eyes still flaring, and his sturdy long legs straddling apart.

"Where did you get to?" asked his mother.

"Where I wanted to go," he flared back at her.

"That's right, son!" said Uncle Oscar. "Don't you stop till you get there. What's the horse's name?"

"He doesn't have a name," said the boy.

"Gets on without all right?" asked the uncle.

"Well, he has different names. He was called Sansovino last week."

"Sansovino, eh? Won the Ascot. How did you know his name?"

"He always talks about horse races with Bassett," said Joan.

The uncle was delighted to find that his small nephew was posted with all the racing news. Bassett, the young gardener, who had been wounded in the left foot in the war and had got his present job through Oscar Cresswell, whose batman he had been, was a perfect blade of the "turf." He lived in the racing events, and the small boy lived with him.

Oscar Cresswell got it all from Bassett.

"Master Paul comes and asks me, so I can't do more than tell him, sir," said Bassett, his face terribly serious, as if he were speaking of religious matters.

"And does he ever put anything on a horse he fancies?"

"Well—I don't want to give him away—he's a young sport, a fine sport, sir. Would you mind asking him himself? He sort of takes a pleasure in it, and perhaps he'd feel I was giving him away, sir, if you don't mind."

Bassett was serious as a church.

The uncle went back to his nephew, and took him off for a ride in the car.

"Say, Paul, old man, do you ever put anything on a horse?" the uncle asked.

The boy watched the handsome man closely.

"Why, do you think I oughtn't to?" he parried.

"Not a bit of it! I thought perhaps you might give me a tip for the Lincoln."

The car sped on into the country, going down to Uncle Oscar's place in Hampshire.

"Honor bright?" said the nephew.

"Honor bright, son!" said the uncle.

"Well, then, Daffodil."

"Daffodil! I doubt it, sonny. What about Mirza?"

"I only know the winner," said the boy. "That's Daffodil."

"Daffodil, eh?"

There was a pause. Daffodil was an obscure horse comparatively.

"Uncle!"

"Yes, son?"

"You won't let it go any further, will you? I promised Bassett."

"Bassett be damned, old man! What's he got to do with it?"

"We're partners. We've been partners from the first. Uncle, he lent me my first five shillings, which I lost. I promised him, honor bright, it was only between me and him; only you gave me that ten-shilling note I started winning with, so I thought you were lucky. You won't let it go any further, will you?"

The boy gazed at his uncle from those big, hot, blue eyes, set rather close together. The uncle stirred and laughed uneasily.

"Right you are, son! I'll keep your tip private. Daffodil, eh? How much are you putting on him?"

"All except twenty pounds," said the boy. "I keep that in reserve."

The uncle thought it a good joke.

"You keep twenty pounds in reserve, do you, you young romancer? What are you betting, then?"

"I'm betting three hundred," said the boy gravely.

"But it's between you and me, Uncle Oscar! Honor bright?"

The uncle burst into a roar of laughter.

"It's between you and me all right, you young Nat Gould," he said, laughing. "But where's your three hundred?"

"Bassett keeps it for me. We're partners."

"You are, are you! And what is Bassett putting on Daffodil?"

"He won't go quite as high as I do, I expect. Perhaps he'll go a hundred and fifty."

"What, pennies?" laughed the uncle.

"Pounds," said the child, with a surprised look at his uncle. "Bassett keeps a bigger reserve than I do."

Between wonder and amusement Uncle Oscar was silent. He pursued the matter no further, but he determined to take his nephew with him to the Lincoln races.

"Now, son," he said, "I'm putting twenty on Mirza, and I'll put five for you on any horse you fancy. What's your pick?"

"Daffodil, Uncle."

"No, not the fiver on Daffodil!"

"I should if it was my own fiver," said the child.

"Good! Good! Right you are! A fiver for me and a fiver for you on Daffodil."

The child had never been to a race meeting before, and his eyes were blue fire. He pursed his mouth tight, and watched. A Frenchman just in front had put his money on Lancelot. Wild with excitement, he flayed his arms up and down, yelling "Lancelot! Lancelot!" in his French accent.

Daffodil came in first, Lancelot second, Mirza third. The child, flushed with eyes blazing, was curiously serene. His uncle brought him four five-pound notes, four to one.

"What am I to do with these?" he cried, waving them before the boy's eyes.

"I suppose we'll talk to Bassett," said the boy. "I expect I have fifteen hundred now; and twenty in reserve; and this twenty."

His uncle studied him for some moments.

"Look here, son!" he said. "You're not serious about Bassett and that fifteen hundred, are you?"

"Yes, I am. But it's between you and me, Uncle. Honor bright!"

"Honor bright all right, son! But I must talk to Bassett."

"If you'd like to be a partner, uncle, with Bassett and me, we could all be partners. Only, you'd have to promise, honor bright, Uncle, not to let it go beyond us three. Bassett and I are lucky, and you must be lucky, because it was your ten shillings I started winning with. . . ."

Uncle Oscar took both Bassett and Paul into Richmond Park for an afternoon, and there they talked.

"It's like this, you see, sir," Bassett said. "Master Paul would get me talking about racing events, spinning yarns, you know, sir. And he was always keen on knowing if I'd made or if I'd lost. It's about a year since, now, that I put five shillings on Blush of Dawn for him: and we lost. Then the luck turned, with that ten shillings he had from you: that we put on Singhalese. And since that time, it's been pretty steady, all things considering. What do you say, Master Paul?"

"We're all right when we're sure," said Paul. "It's when we're not quite sure that we go down."

"Oh, but we're careful then," said Bassett.

"But when are you sure?" smiled Uncle Oscar.

"It's Master Paul, sir," smiled Bassett, in a secret, religious voice. "It's as if he had it from heaven. Like Daffodil, now, for the Lincoln. That was as sure as eggs."

"Did you put anything on Daffodil?" asked Oscar Cresswell.

"Yes, sir. I made my bit."

"And my nephew?"

Bassett was obstinately silent, looking at Paul.

"I made twelve hundred, didn't I, Bassett? I told uncle I was putting three hundred on Daffodil."

"That's right," said Bassett, nodding.

"But where's the money?" asked the uncle.

"I keep it safe locked up, sir. Master Paul he can have it any minute he likes to ask for it."

"What, fifteen hundred pounds?"

"And twenty! And forty, that is, with the twenty he made on the course."

"It's amazing!" said the uncle.

"If Master Paul offers you to be partners, sir, I would, if I were you: if you'll excuse me," said Bassett.

Oscar Cresswell thought about it. "I'll see the money," he said.

They drove home again, and, sure enough, Bassett came round to the gardenhouse with fifteen hundred pounds in notes. The twenty pounds' reserve was left with Joe Glee, in the Turf Commission deposit.

"You see, it's all right, Uncle, when I'm sure! Then we go strong, for all we're worth. Don't we, Bassett?"

"We do that, Master Paul."

"And when are you sure?" said the uncle, laughing.

"Oh, well, sometimes I'm absolutely sure, like about Daffodil," said the boy; "and sometimes I have an idea; and sometimes I haven't even an idea, have I, Bassett? Then we're careful, because we mostly go down."

"You do, do you! And when you're sure, like about Daffodil, what makes you sure, sonny?"

"Oh, well, I don't know," said the boy uneasily. "I'm sure, you know, Uncle, that's all."

"It's as if he had it from heaven, sir," Bassett reiterated.

"I should say so!" said the uncle.

But he became a partner. And when the Leger was coming on, Paul was "sure" about Lively Spark, which was a quite inconsiderable horse. The boy insisted on putting a thousand on the horse, Bassett went for five hundred, and Oscar Cresswell two hundred. Lively Spark came in first, and the betting had been ten to one against him. Paul had made ten thousand.

"You see," he said, "I was absolutely sure of him."

Even Oscar Cresswell had cleared two thousand.

"Look here, son," he said, "this sort of thing makes me nervous."

"It needn't, Uncle! Perhaps I shan't be sure again for a long time."

"But what are you going to do with your money?" asked the uncle.

"Of course," said the boy, "I started it for Mother. She said she had no luck, because Father is unlucky, so I thought if I was lucky, it might stop whispering."

"What might stop whispering?"

"Our house. I hate our house for whispering."

"What does it whisper?"

"Why—why"—the boy fidgeted—"why, I don't know. But it's always short of money, you know, Uncle."

"I know it, son, I know it."

"You know people send Mother writs, don't you, Uncle?"

"I'm afraid I do," said the uncle.

"And then the house whispers, like people laughing at you behind your back. It's awful, that is! I thought if I was lucky——"

"You might stop it," added the uncle.

The boy watched him with big blue eyes, that had an uncanny cold fire in them, and he said never a word.

"Well, then!" said the uncle. "What are we doing?"

"I shouldn't like Mother to know I was lucky," said the boy.

"Why not, son?"

"She'd stop me."

"I don't think she would."

"Oh!"—and the boy writhed in an odd way—"I don't want her to know, Uncle."

"All right, son! We'll manage it without her knowing."

They managed it very easily. Paul, at the other's suggestion, handed over five thousand pounds to his uncle, who deposited it with the family lawyer, who was then to inform Paul's mother that a relative had put five thousand pounds into his hands, which sum was to be paid out a thousand pounds at a time, on the mother's birthday, for the next five years.

"So she'll have a birthday present of a thousand pounds for five successive years," said Uncle Oscar. "I hope it won't make it all the harder for her later."

Paul's mother had her birthday in November. The house had been "whispering" worse than ever lately, and, even in spite of his luck, Paul could not bear up against it. He was very anxious to see the effect of the birthday letter, telling his mother about the thousand pounds.

When there were no visitors, Paul now took his meals with his parents, as he was beyond the nursery control. His mother went into town nearly every day. She had discovered that she had an odd knack of sketching furs and dress materials, so she worked secretly in the studio of a friend who was the chief "artist" for the leading drapers. She drew the figures of ladies in furs and ladies in silk and sequins for the newspaper advertisements. This young woman artist earned several thousand pounds a year, but Paul's mother only made several hundreds, and she was again dissatisfied. She so wanted to be first in something, and she did not succeed, even in making sketches for drapery advertisements.

She was down to breakfast on the morning of her birthday. Paul watched her face as she read her letters. He knew the lawyer's letter. As his mother read it, her face hardened and became more expressionless. Then a cold, determined look came on her mouth. She hid the letter under the pile of others, and said not a word about it.

"Didn't you have anything nice in the post for your birthday, Mother?" asked Paul.

"Quite moderately nice," she said, her voice cold and absent.

She went away to town without saying more.

But in the afternoon Uncle Oscar appeared. He said Paul's mother had had a long interview with the lawyer, asking if the whole five thousand could not be advanced at once, as she was in debt.

"What do you think, Uncle?" said the boy.

"I leave it to you, son."

"Oh, let her have it, then! We can get some more with the other," said the boy.

"A bird in the hand is worth two in the bush, laddie!" said Uncle Oscar.

"But I'm sure to know for the Grand National; or the Lincolnshire; or else the Derby. I'm sure to know for one of them," said Paul.

So Uncle Oscar signed the agreement, and Paul's mother touched the whole five thousand. Then something very curious happened. The voices in the house suddenly went mad, like a chorus of frogs on a spring evening. There were certain new furnishings, and Paul had a tutor. He was really going to Eton, his father's school, in the following autumn. There were flowers in the winter, and blossoming of the luxury Paul's mother had been used to. And yet the voices in the house, behind the sprays of mimosa and almond blossom, and from under the piles of iridescent cushions, simply trilled and screamed in a sort of ecstasy: "There must be more money; Oh-h-h; there must be more money. Oh, now, now-w! Now-w-w —there must be more money!—more than ever! More than ever!"

It frightened Paul terribly. He studied away at his Latin and Greek with his tutors, but his intense hours were spent with Bassett. The Grand National had gone by: he had not "known," and had lost a hundred pounds. Summer was at hand. He was in agony for the Lincoln. But even for the Lincoln he didn't "know," and he lost fifty pounds. He became wild-eyed and strange, as if something were going to explode in him.

"Let it alone, son! Don't you bother about it!" urged Uncle Oscar. But it was as if the boy couldn't really hear what his uncle was saying.

"I've got to know for the Derby! I've got to know for the Derby," the child reiterated, his big blue eyes blazing with a sort of madness.

His mother noticed how over wrought he was.

"You'd better go to the seaside. Wouldn't you like to go now to the seaside, instead of waiting? I think you'd better," she said, looking down at him anxiously, her heart curiously heavy because of him.

But the child lifted his uncanny blue eyes.

"I couldn't possibly go before the Derby, Mother!" he said. "I couldn't possibly go before the Derby, Mother!" he said. "I couldn't possibly!"

"Why not?" she said, her voice becoming heavy when she was opposed. "Why not? You can still go from the seaside to see the Derby with your Uncle Oscar, if that's what you wish. No need for you to wait here. Besides, I think you care too much about these races. It's a bad sign. My family has been a gambling family, and you won't know till you grow up how much damage it has done. But it has done damage. I shall have to send Bassett away, and ask Uncle Oscar not to talk racing to you, unless you promise to be reasonable about it: go away to the seaside and forget it. You're all nerves!"

"I'll do what you like, Mother, so long as you don't send me away till after the Derby," the boy said.

"Send you away from where? Just from this house?"

"Yes," he said, gazing at her.

"Why, you curious child, what makes you care about this house so much, suddenly? I never knew you loved it."

He gazed at her without speaking. He had a secret within a secret, something he had not divulged, even to Bassett or to his Uncle Oscar.

But his mother, after standing undecided and a little bit sullen for some moments, said:

"Very well, then! Don't go to the seaside till after the Derby, if you don't wish it. But promise me you won't let your nerves go to pieces. Promise you won't think so much about horse racing and events, as you call them!"

"Oh, no," said the boy casually. "I won't think much about them, Mother. You needn't worry. I wouldn't worry, Mother, if I were you."

"If you were me and I were you," said his mother, "I wonder what we should do!"

"But you know you needn't worry, Mother, don't you?" the boy repeated.

"I should be awfully glad to know it," she said wearily.

"Oh, well, you can, you know. I mean, you ought to know you needn't worry," he insisted.

"Ought I? Then I'll see about it," she said.

Paul's secret of secrets was his wooden horse, that which had no name. Since he was emancipated from a nurse and a nursery governess, he had had his rocking horse removed to his own bedroom at the top of the house.

"Surely, you're too big for a rocking horse!" his mother had remonstrated.

"Well, you see, Mother, till I can have a real horse, I like to have some sort of animal about," had been his quaint answer.

"Do you feel he keeps you company?" she laughed.

"Oh, yes! He's very good, he always keeps me company, when I'm there," said Paul.

So the horse, rather shabby, stood in an arrested prance in the boy's bedroom.

The Derby was drawing near, and the boy grew more and more tense. He hardly heard what was spoken to him, he was very frail, and his eyes were really uncanny. His mother had sudden strange seizures of uneasiness about him. Sometimes, for half-an-hour, she would feel a sudden anxiety about him that was almost anguish. She wanted to rush to him at once, and know he was safe.

Two nights before the Derby, she was at a big party in town, when one of her rushes of anxiety about her boy, her firstborn, gripped her heart till she could hardly speak. She fought with the feeling, might and main, for she believed in common sense. But it was too strong. She had to leave the dance and go downstairs to telephone to the country. The children's nursery governess was terribly surprised and startled at being rung up in the night.

"Are the children all right, Miss Wilmot?"

"Oh, yes, they are quite all right."

"Master Paul? Is he all right?"

"He went to bed as right as a trivet. Shall I run up and look at him?"

"No," said Paul's mother reluctantly. "No! Don't trouble. It's all right. Don't sit up. We shall be home fairly soon." She did not want her son's privacy intruded upon.

"Very good," said the governess.

It was about one o'clock when Paul's mother and father drove up to their house. All was still. Paul's mother went to her room and slipped off her white fur cloak. She had told her maid not to wait up for her.

She heard her husband downstairs, mixing a whisky and soda.

And then, because of the strange anxiety at her heart, she stole upstairs to her son's room. Noiselessly she went along the upper corridor. Was there a faint noise? What was it?

She stood, with arrested muscles, outside his door, listening. There was a strange, heavy, and yet not loud noise. Her heart stood still. It was a soundless noise, yet rushing and powerful. Something huge, in violent, hushed motion. What was it? What in God's name was it? She ought to know. She felt that she knew the noise. She knew what it was.

Yet she could not place it. She couldn't say what it was. And on and on it went, like a madness.

Softly, frozen with anxiety and fear, she turned the door handle.

The room was dark. Yet in the space near the window, she heard and saw something plunging to and fro. She gazed in fear and amazement.

Then suddenly she switched on the light, and saw her son, in his green pajamas, madly surging on the rocking horse. The blaze of light suddenly lit him up, as he urged the wooden horse, and lit her up, as she stood, blonde, in her dress of pale green and crystal, in the doorway.

"Paul!" she cried. "Whatever are you doing?"

"It's Malabar!" he screamed, in a powerful, strange voice. "It's Malabar!"

His eyes blazed at her for one strange and senseless second, as he ceased urging his wooden horse. Then he fell with a crash to the ground, and she, all her tormented motherhood flooding upon her, rushed to gather him up.

But he was unconscious, and unconscious he remained, with some brain fever. He talked and tossed, and his mother sat stonily by his side.

"Malabar! It's Malabar! Bassett, Bassett, I know! It's Malabar!"

So the child cried, trying to get up and urge the rocking horse that gave him his inspiration.

"What does he mean by Malabar?" asked the heart-frozen mother.

"I don't know," said the father stonily.

"What does he mean by Malabar?" she asked her brother Oscar.

"It's one of the horses running for the Derby," was the answer.

And, in spite of himself, Oscar Cresswell spoke to Bassett, and himself put a thousand on Malabar; at fourteen to one.

The third day of the illness was critical; they were waiting for a change. The boy, with his rather long, curly hair, was tossing ceaselessly on the pillow. He neither slept nor regained consciousness, and his eyes were like blue stones. His mother sat, feeling her heart had gone, turned actually into a stone.

In the evening, Oscar Cresswell did not come, but Bassett sent a message saying could he come up for one moment, just one moment? Paul's mother was very angry at the intrusion, but on second thoughts she agreed. The boy was the same. Perhaps Bassett might bring him to consciousness.

The gardener, a shortish fellow with a little brown mustache, and sharp little brown eyes, tiptoed into the room, touched his imaginary cap to Paul's mother, and stole to the bedside, staring with glittering, smallish eyes at the tossing, dying child.

"Master Paul!" he whispered. "Master Paul! Malabar came in first all right, a clean win. I did as you told me. You've made over seventy thousand pounds, you have; you've got over eighty thousand. Malabar came in all right, Master Paul."

"Malabar! Malabar! Did I say Malabar, Mother? Did I say Malabar? Do you think I'm lucky, Mother? I knew Malabar, didn't I? Over eighty thousand pounds! I call that lucky, don't you Mother? Over eighty thousand pounds! I knew, didn't I know I knew? Malabar came in all right. If I ride my horse till I'm sure, then I tell you, Bassett, you can go as high as you

like. Did you go for all you were worth, Bassett?"

"I went a thousand on it, Master Paul."

"I never told you, Mother, that if I can ride my horse, and get there, then I'm absolutely sure—oh, absolutely! Mother, did I ever tell you? I am lucky!"

"No, you never did," said the mother.

But the boy died in the night.

And even as he lay dead, his mother heard her brother's voice saying to her: "My God, Hester, you're eighty-odd thousand to the good, and a poor devil of a son to the bad. But, poor devil, poor devil, he's best gone out of a life where he rides his rocking horse to find a winner."

Katherine Mansfield

1888-1923

KATHERINE MANSFIELD did not live long and did not write much. During most of her adulthood she suffered from tuberculosis and moved from country to country, from mountain to shore, seeking a cure. Only six small volumes of stories, a book of poems, some literary reviews, letters, and a journal remain. Yet her influence has spread into all corners of the writing world. She was an exciting person, quick, gay to exuberance, eager, amusing, slightly ironical—and deeply emotional. All her feelings and experience, all her special flavor, are in her stories.

No one could have devised a more precarious existence than Katherine Mansfield lived by her own direction. Born in a well-to-do family in New Zealand, Kathleen Beauchamp had a happy, normal childhood. At thirteen she was sent to school in London for five years, and after returning home for a short time, left it for good. Still under twenty-one and determined to make her way in London on an allowance of a hundred pounds a year, she first tried music. Coming of a musical family—the kind that played trios in the evening at home—she was a good cellist, and had a lovely voice. But she married her music teacher, lived with him only a few days, and after that changed her career to writing. While staying in a small Bavarian town, where she gave birth to a stillborn child, she wrote her first stories, *In a German Pension*. She lived and worked with John Middleton Murry for six years before they were able to marry, and during those years came the war, and her own ill-health. Not until *Bliss and Other Stories* was published in 1920 did she become known to the general reading public. But it was too late: her hold on life was too fragile. The war had been a tremendous spiritual shock to her and a deep personal tragedy when her dearly loved brother was killed almost immediately after going into action. "Though he is lying in the middle of a little wood in France, and I am still walking upright and feeling the sun and the wind from the sea, I am just as dead as he is," she wrote in her diary. She too died in France, and is buried there.

The Doll's House

BY KATHERINE MANSFIELD

WHEN dear old Mrs. Hay went back to town after staying with the Burnells she sent the children a doll's house. It was so big that the carter and Pat carried it into the courtyard, and there it stayed, propped up on two wooden boxes beside the feed-room door. No harm could come to it; it was summer. And perhaps the smell of paint would have gone off by the time it had to be taken in. For, really, the smell of paint coming from that doll's house ("Sweet of old Mrs. Hay, of course; most sweet and generous!")—but the smell of paint was quite enough to make anyone seriously ill, in Aunt Beryl's opinion. Even before the sacking was taken off. And when it was. . . .

There stood the doll's house, a dark, oily, spinach green, picked out with bright yellow. Its two solid little chimneys, glued onto the roof, were painted red and white, and the door, gleaming with yellow varnish, was like a little slab of toffee. Four windows, real windows, were divided into panes by a broad streak of green. There was actually a tiny porch too, painted yellow, with big lumps of congealed paint hanging along the edge.

But perfect, perfect little house! Who could possibly mind the smell? It was part of the joy, part of the newness.

"Open it quickly, someone!"

The hook at the side was stuck fast. Pat pried it open with his penknife, and the whole house front swung back, and—there you were, gazing at one and the same moment into the drawing room and dining room, the kitchen and two bedrooms. That is the way for a house to open! Why don't all houses open like that? How much more exciting than peering through the slit of a door into a mean little hall with a hatstand and two umbrellas! That is—isn't it? —what you long to know about a house when you put your hand on the knocker. Perhaps it is the way God opens houses at dead of night when He is taking a quiet turn with an angel. . . .

"O-oh!" The Burnell children sounded as though they were in despair. It was too marvelous; it was too much for them. They had never seen anything like it in their lives. All the rooms were papered. There were pictures on the walls, painted on the paper, with gold frames complete. Red carpet covered all the floors except the kitchen; red plush chairs in the drawing room, green in the dining room; tables, beds with real bedclothes, a cradle, a stove, a dresser with tiny plates and one big jug. But what Kezia liked more than anything, what she liked frightfully, was the lamp. It stood in the middle of the dining-room table, an exquisite little amber lamp with a white globe. It was even filled all ready for lighting, though, of course, you couldn't light it. But there was something inside that looked like oil, and that moved when you shook it.

The father and mother dolls, who sprawled very stiff as though they had fainted in the drawing room, and their two little children asleep upstairs, were really too big for the doll's house. They didn't look as though they belonged. But the lamp was perfect. It seemed to smile at Kezia, to say: "I live here." The lamp was real.

The Burnell children could hardly walk to school fast enough the next morning. They burned to tell everybody, to describe, to—well—to boast about their doll's house before the school bell rang.

"I'm to tell," said Isabel, "because I'm the eldest. And you two can join in after. But I'm to tell first."

There was nothing to answer. Isabel was bossy, but she was always right, and Lottie and Kezia knew too well the powers that went with being eldest. They brushed through the thick buttercups at the road edge and said nothing.

"And I'm to choose who's to come and see it first. Mother said I might."

For it had been arranged that while the doll's house stood in the courtyard they might ask the girls at school, two at a time, to come and look. Not to stay to tea, of course, or to come traipsing through the house. But just to stand quietly in the courtyard while Isabel pointed out the beauties, and Lottie and Kezia looked pleased. . . .

But hurry as they might, by the time they had reached the tarred palings of the boys' playground the bell had begun to jangle. They only just had time to whip off their hats and fall into line before the roll was called. Never mind. Isabel tried to make up for it by looking very important and mysterious and by whispering behind her hand to the girls near her: "Got something to tell you at playtime."

Playtime came and Isabel was surrounded. The girls of her class nearly fought to put their arms round her, to walk away with her, to beam flatteringly, to be her special friend. She held quite a court under the huge pine trees at the side of the playground. Nudging, giggling together, the little girls pressed up close. And the only two who stayed outside the ring were the two who were always outside, the little Kelveys. They knew better than to come anywhere near the Burnells.

For the fact was the school the Burnell children went to was not at all the kind of place their parents would have chosen if there had been any choice. But there was none. It was the only school for miles. And the consequence was all the children in the neighborhood, the Judge's little girls, the doctor's daughters, the storekeeper's children, the milkman's, were forced to mix together. Not to speak of there being an equal number of rude, rough little boys as well. But the line had to be drawn somewhere. It was drawn at the Kelveys. Many of the children, including the Burnells, were not allowed even to speak to them. They walked past the Kelveys with their heads in the air, and as they set the fashion in all matters of behavior, the Kelveys were shunned by everybody. Even the teacher had a special voice for them, and a special smile for the other children when Lil Kelvey came up to her desk with a bunch of dreadfully common-looking flowers.

They were the daughters of a spry, hardworking little washerwoman, who went about from house to house by the day. This was awful enough. But where was Mr. Kelvey? Nobody knew for certain. But everybody said he was in prison. So they were the daughters of a washerwoman and a jailbird. Very nice company for other people's children! And they looked it. Why Mrs. Kelvey made them so conspicuous was hard to understand. The truth was they were dressed in "bits" given to her by the people for whom she worked. Lil, for instance, who was a stout, plain child, with big freckles, came to school in a dress made from a green art-serge tablecloth of the Burnells', with red plush sleeves from the Logans' curtains. Her hat, perched on top of her high forehead, was a grown-up woman's hat, once the property of Miss Lecky, the postmistress. It was turned up at the back and trimmed with a large scarlet quill. What a little guy she looked! It was impossible not to laugh. And her little sister, our Else, wore a long white dress, rather like a nightgown, and a pair of little boy's boots. But whatever our Else wore, she would have looked strange. She was a tiny wishbone of a child, with cropped hair and enormous solemn eyes—a little white owl. Nobody had ever seen her smile; she scarcely ever spoke. She went through life holding on to Lil, with a piece of Lil's skirt screwed up in her hand. Where Lil went our Else followed. In the playground, on the road going to and from school, there was Lil marching in front and our Else holding on behind. Only when she wanted anything, or when she was out of breath, our Else gave Lil a tug, a twitch, and Lil stopped

and turned round. The Kelveys never failed to understand each other.

Now they hovered at the edge; you couldn't stop them listening. When the little girls turned round and sneered, Lil, as usual, gave her silly, shamefaced smile, but our Else only looked.

And Isabel's voice, so very proud, went on telling. The carpet made a great sensation, but so did the beds with real bedclothes, and the stove with an oven door.

When she finished, Kezia broke in. "You've forgotten the lamp, Isabel."

"Oh, yes," said Isabel, "and there's a teeny little lamp, all made of yellow glass, with a white globe, that stands on the dining-room table. You couldn't tell it from a real one."

"The lamp's best of all," cried Kezia. She thought Isabel wasn't making half enough of the little lamp. But nobody paid any attention. Isabel was choosing the two who were to come back with them that afternoon and see it. She chose Emmie Cole and Lena Logan. But when the others knew they were all to have a chance, they couldn't be nice enough to Isabel. One by one they put their arms round Isabel's waist and walked her off. They had something to whisper to her, a secret. "Isabel's my friend."

Only the little Kelveys moved away forgotten; there was nothing more for them to hear.

Days passed, and as more children saw the doll's house, the fame of it spread. It became the one subject, the rage. The one question was: "Have you seen Burnells' doll's house? Oh, ain't it lovely!" "Haven't you seen it? Oh, I say!"

Even the dinner hour was given up to talking about it. The little girls sat under the pines eating their thick mutton sandwiches and big slabs of johnnycake spread with butter. While always, as near as they could get, sat the Kelveys, our Else holding on to Lil, listening too, while they chewed their jam sandwiches out of a newspaper soaked with large red blobs. . . .

"Mother," said Kezia, "can't I ask the Kelveys just once?"

"Certainly not, Kezia."

"But why not?"

"Run away, Kezia; you know quite well why not."

At last everybody had seen it except them. On that day the subject rather flagged. It was the dinner hour. The children stood together under the pine trees, and suddenly, as they looked at the Kelveys eating out of their paper, always by themselves, always listening, they wanted to be horrid to them. Emmie Cole started the whisper.

"Lil Kelvey's going to be a servant when she grows up."

"O-oh, how awful!" said Isabel Burnell, and she made eyes at Emmie.

Emmie swallowed in a very meaning way and nodded to Isabel as she'd seen her mother do on those occasions.

"It's true—it's true—it's true," she said.

Then Lena Logan's little eyes snapped. "Shall I ask her?" she whispered.

"Bet you don't," said Jessie May.

"Pooh, I'm not frightened," said Lena. Suddenly she gave a little squeal and danced in front of the other girls. "Watch! Watch me! Watch me now!" said Lena. And sliding, gliding, dragging one foot, giggling behind her hand, Lena went over to the Kelveys.

Lil looked up from her dinner. She wrapped the rest quickly away.

Our Else stopped chewing. What was coming now?

"Is it true you're going to be a servant when you grow up, Lil Kelvey?" shrilled Lena.

Dead silence. But instead of answering, Lil only gave her silly, shamefaced smile. She didn't seem to mind the question at all. What a sell for Lena! The girls began to titter.

Lena couldn't stand that. She put her hands on her hips; she shot forward. "Yah, yer father's in prison!" she hissed, spitefully.

This was such a marvelous thing to have said that the little girls rushed away in a body, deeply, deeply excited, wild with joy. Someone found a long rope, and they began skipping. And never did they skip so high, run in and out so fast, or do such daring things as on that morning.

In the afternoon Pat called for the Burnell children with the buggy and they drove home. There were visitors. Isabel and Lottie, who liked visitors, went upstairs to change their pinafores. But Kezia thieved out at the back. Nobody was about; she began to swing on the big white gates of the courtyard. Presently, looking along the road, she saw two little dots. They grew bigger, they were coming towards her. Now she could see that one was in front and one close behind. Now she could see that they were the Kelveys. Kezia stopped swinging. She slipped off the gate as if she was going to run away. Then she hesitated. The Kelveys came nearer, and beside them walked their shadows, very long, stretching right across the road with their heads in the buttercups. Kezia clambered back on the gate; she had made up her mind; she swung out.

"Hullo," she said to the passing Kelveys.

They were so astounded that they

stopped. Lil gave her silly smile. Our Else stared.

"You can come and see our doll's house if you want to," said Kezia, and she dragged one toe on the ground. But at that Lil turned red and shook her head quickly.

"Why not?" asked Kezia.

Lil gasped, then she said: "Your ma told our ma you wasn't to speak to us."

"Oh, well," said Kezia. She didn't know what to reply. "It doesn't matter. You can come and see our doll's house all the same. Come on. Nobody's looking."

But Lil shook her head still harder.

"Don't you want to?" asked Kezia.

Suddenly there was a twitch, a tug at Lil's skirt. She turned round. Our Else was looking at her with big, imploring eyes; she was frowning; she wanted to go. For a moment Lil looked at our Else very doubtfully. But then our Else twitched her skirt again. She started forward. Kezia led the way. Like two little stray cats they followed across the courtyard to where the doll's house stood.

"There it is," said Kezia.

There was a pause. Lil breathed loudly, almost snorted; our Else was still as a stone.

"I'll open it for you," said Kezia kindly. She undid the hook and they looked inside.

"There's the drawing room and the dining room, and that's the ——"

"Kezia!"

Oh, what a start they gave!

"Kezia!"

It was Aunt Beryl's voice. They turned round. At the back door stood Aunt Beryl, staring as if she couldn't believe what she saw.

"How dare you ask the little Kelveys into the courtyard?" said her cold, furious voice. "You know as well as I do you're not allowed to talk to them. Run away, children, run away at once. And don't come back again," said Aunt Beryl. And she stepped into the yard and shooed them out as if they were chickens.

"Off you go immediately!" she called, cold and proud.

They did not need telling twice. Burning with shame, shrinking together, Lil huddling along like her mother, our Else dazed, somehow they crossed the big courtyard and squeezed through the white gate.

"Wicked, disobedient little girl!" said Aunt Beryl bitterly to Kezia, and she slammed the doll's house to.

The afternoon had been awful. A letter had come from Willie Brent, a terrifying, threatening letter, saying if she did not meet him that evening in Pulman's Bush, he'd come to the front door and ask the reason why! But now that she had frightened those little rats of Kelveys and given Kezia a good scolding, her heart felt lighter. That ghastly pressure was gone. She went back to the house humming.

When the Kelveys were well out of sight of Burnells', they sat down to rest on a big red drainpipe by the side of the road. Lil's cheeks were still burning; she took off the hat with the quill and held it on her knee. Dreamily they looked over the hay paddocks, past the creek, to the group of wattles where Logan's cows stood waiting to be milked. What were their thoughts?

Presently our Else nudged up close to her sister. But now she had forgotten the cross lady. She put out a finger and stroked her sister's quill; she smiled her rare smile.

"I seen the little lamp," she said, softly.

Then both were silent once more.

W. Somerset Maugham

1874-

ALTHOUGH English by descent, Somerset Maugham was born in France, brought up there, and spoke French before he did English. Both his parents having died by the time he was ten years old, the small boy was taken away from the environment he knew and put into the hands of an English clergyman uncle. Many years later, in his semiautobiographical novel, *Of Human Bondage*, he was to describe the years of young sorrow and heartbreak that followed. In preference to the ministry he chose to study medicine and qualified as a physician. But his only practice was a year's internship in the Lambeth slums. He had always cherished a deep desire to write, and once he had satisfied his uncle in the way of education, and had recovered sufficiently from an attack of tuberculosis to be able to work, he returned to the Continent —to Spain, Italy, and France—and wrote steadily for ten years. In 1907 his first successful play was produced, and from that time on his pen was gold.

Maugham's aim in fiction writing, often expressed, and achieved with consummate success through the years, is to entertain. "Let no one think that entertainment is a cheap and shoddy thing; let him leave such a belief to the most snobbish and vulgar of the highbrows; entertainment is a form of pleasure and pleasure is in itself good." On this principle he has written about thirty volumes of short stories and novels, nearly as many plays, and innumerable pieces of excellent sharp criticism. Seldom has a creative writer been able to present himself so objectively as has Maugham in *The Summing Up*, which is not so much an autobiography as a mature estimate of his own work, his personality, and his philosophy.

During World War I Maugham served with British Intelligence, and in World War II with the British Ministry of Information.

Mackintosh

BY W. SOMERSET MAUGHAM

He splashed about for a few minutes in the sea; it was too shallow to swim in and for fear of sharks he could not go out of his depth; then he got out and went into the bathhouse for a shower. The coldness of the fresh water was grateful after the heavy stickiness of the salt Pacific, so warm, though it was only just after seven, that to bathe in it did not brace you but rather increased your languor; and when he had dried himself, slipping into a bath gown, he called out to the Chinese cook that he would be ready for breakfast in five minutes. He walked barefoot across the patch of coarse grass which Walker, the administrator, proudly thought was a lawn, to his own quarters and dressed. This did not take long, for he put on nothing but a shirt and a pair of duck trousers and then went over to his chief's house on the other side of the compound. The two men had their meals together, but the Chinese cook told him that Walker had set out on horseback at five and would not be back for another hour.

Mackintosh had slept badly and he looked with distaste at the pawpaw and the eggs and bacon which were set before him. The mosquitoes had been maddening that night; they flew about the net under which he slept in such numbers that their humming, pitiless and menacing, had the effect of a note, infinitely drawn out, played on a distant organ, and whenever he dozed off he awoke with a start in the belief that one had found its way inside his curtains. It was so hot that he lay naked. He turned from side to side. And gradually the dull roar of the breakers on the reef, so unceasing and so regular that generally you did not hear it, grew distinct on his consciousness, its rhythm hammered on his tired nerves and he held himself with clenched hands in the effort to bear it. The thought that nothing could stop that sound, for it would continue to all eternity, was almost impossible to bear, and, as though his strength were a match for the ruthless forces of nature, he had an insane impulse to do some violent thing. He felt he must cling to his self-control or he would go mad. And now, looking out of the window at the lagoon and the strip of foam which marked the reef, he shuddered with hatred of the brilliant scene. The cloudless sky was like an inverted bowl that hemmed it in. He lit his pipe and turned over the pile

From *The Trembling of a Leaf* by W. Somerset Maugham. By permission of the author, Doubleday & Company, Inc., and William Heinemann, Ltd., of London.

of Auckland papers that had come over from Apia a few days before. The newest of them was three weeks old. They gave an impression of incredible dullness.

Then he went into the office. It was a large, bare room with two desks in it and a bench along one side. A number of natives were seated on this, and a couple of women. They gossiped while they waited for the administrator, and when Mackintosh came in they greeted him.

"*Talofa li.*"

He returned their greeting and sat down at his desk. He began to write, working on a report which the governor of Samoa had been clamoring for and which Walker, with his usual dilatoriness, had neglected to prepare. Mackintosh as he made his notes reflected vindictively that Walker was late with his report because he was so illiterate that he had an invincible distaste for anything to do with pens and paper; and now when it was at last ready, concise and neatly official, he would accept his subordinate's work without a word of appreciation, with a sneer rather or a gibe, and send it on to his own superior as though it were his own composition. He could not have written a word of it. Mackintosh thought with rage that if his chief penciled in some insertion it would be childish in expression and faulty in language. If he remonstrated or sought to put his meaning into an intelligible phrase, Walker would fly into a passion and cry:

"What the hell do I care about grammar? That's what I want to say and that's how I want to say it."

At last Walker came in. The natives surrounded him as he entered, trying to get his immediate attention, but he turned on them

roughly and told them to sit down and hold their tongues. He threatened that if they were not quiet he would have them all turned out and see none of them that day. He nodded to Mackintosh.

"Hulloa, Mac; up at last? I don't know how you can waste the best part of the day in bed. You ought to have been up before dawn like me. Lazy beggar."

He threw himself heavily into his chair and wiped his face with a large bandanna.

"By heaven, I've got a thirst."

He turned to the policeman who stood at the door, a picturesque figure in his white jacket and *lava-lava*, the loincloth of the Samoan, and told him to bring *kava*. The *kava* bowl stood on the floor in the corner of the room, and the policeman filled a half coconut shell and brought it to Walker. He poured a few drops on the ground, murmured the customary words to the company, and drank with relish. Then he told the policeman to serve the waiting natives, and the shell was handed to each one in order of birth or importance and emptied with the same ceremonies.

Then he set about the day's work. He was a little man, considerably less than of middle height, and enormously stout; he had a large, fleshy face, clean-shaven, with the cheeks hanging on each side in great dewlaps, and three vast chins; his small features were all dissolved in fat; and, but for a crescent of white hair at the back of his head, he was completely bald. He reminded you of Mr. Pickwick. He was grotesque, a figure of fun, and yet, strangely enough, not without dignity. His blue eyes, behind large gold-rimmed spectacles, were shrewd and vivacious, and there was a great deal of determination in his face. He was sixty, but his native vitality triumphed over advancing years. Notwithstanding his corpulence his movements were quick, and he walked with a heavy, resolute tread as though he sought to impress his weight upon the earth. He spoke in a loud, gruff voice.

It was two years now since Mackintosh had been appointed Walker's assistant. Walker, who had been for a quarter of a century administrator of Talua, one of the larger islands in the Samoan group, was a man known in person or by report through the length and breadth of the South Seas; and it was with lively curiosity that Mackintosh looked forward to his first meeting with him. For one reason or another he stayed a couple of weeks at Apia before he took up his post and both at Chaplin's hotel and at the English club he heard innumerable stories about the administrator. He thought now with irony of his interest in them. Since then he had heard them a hundred times from Walker himself. Walker knew that he was a character, and, proud of his reputation, deliberately acted up to it. He was jealous of his "legend" and anxious that you should know the exact details of any of the celebrated stories that were told of him. He was ludicrously angry with anyone who had told them to the stranger incorrectly.

There was a rough cordiality about Walker which Mackintosh at first found not unattractive, and Walker, glad to have a listener to whom all he said was fresh, gave of his best. He was good-humored, hearty, and considerate. To Mackintosh, who had lived the sheltered life of a government official in London till at the age of thirty-four an attack of pneumonia, leaving him

with the threat of tuberculosis, had forced him to seek a post in the Pacific, Walker's existence seemed extraordinarily romantic. The adventure with which he started on his conquest of circumstance was typical of the man. He ran away to sea when he was fifteen and for over a year was employed in shoveling coal on a collier. He was an undersized boy and both men and mates were kind to him, but the captain for some reason conceived a savage dislike of him. He used the lad cruelly so that, beaten and kicked, he often could not sleep for the pain that racked his limbs. He loathed the captain with all his soul. Then he was given a tip for some race and managed to borrow twenty-five pounds from a friend he had picked up in Belfast. He put it on the horse, an outsider, at long odds. He had no means of repaying the money if he lost, but it never occurred to him that he could lose. He felt himself in luck. The horse won and he found himself with something over a thousand pounds in hard cash. Now his chance had come. He found out who was the best solicitor in the town—the collier lay then somewhere on the Irish coast—went to him, and, telling him that he heard the ship was for sale, asked him to arrange the purchase for him. The solicitor was amused at his small client, he was only sixteen and did not look so old, and, moved perhaps by sympathy, promised not only to arrange the matter for him but to see that he made a good bargain. After a little while Walker found himself the owner of the ship. He went back to her and had what he described as the most glorious moment of his life when he gave the skipper notice and told him that he must get off *his* ship in half an hour. He made the mate captain and sailed on the collier for another nine months, at the end of which he sold her at a profit.

He came out to the islands at the age of twenty-six as a planter. He was one of the few white men settled in Talua at the time of the German occupation and had then already some influence with the natives. The Germans made him administrator, a position which he occupied for twenty years, and when the island was seized by the British he was confirmed in his post. He ruled the island despotically, but with complete success. The prestige of this success was another reason for the interest that Mackintosh took in him.

But the two men were not made to get on. Mackintosh was an ugly man, with ungainly gestures, a tall thin fellow, with a narrow chest and bowed shoulders. He had sallow, sunken cheeks, and his eyes were large and sombre. He was a great reader, and when his books arrived and were unpacked Walker came over to his quarters and looked at them. Then he turned to Mackintosh with a coarse laugh.

"What in hell have you brought all this muck for?" he asked.

Mackintosh flushed darkly.

"I'm sorry you think it muck. I brought my books because I want to read them."

"When you said you'd got a lot of books coming I thought there'd be something for me to read. Haven't you got any detective stories?"

"Detective stories don't interest me."

"You're a damned fool then."

"I'm content that you should think so."

Every mail brought Walker a mass of periodical literature, papers from New Zealand and magazines from America, and it exasperated him that Mackintosh showed his contempt for these ephemeral publications. He had no patience with the books that absorbed Mackintosh's leisure and thought it only a pose that he read Gibbon's *Decline and Fall* or Burton's *Anatomy of Melancholy*. And since he had never learned to put any restraint on his tongue, he expressed his opinion of his assistant freely. Mackintosh began to see the real man, and under the boisterous good humor he discerned a vulgar cunning which was hateful; he was vain and domineering, and it was strange that he had notwithstanding a shyness which made him dislike people who were not quite of his kidney. He judged others, naïvely, by their language, and if it was free from the oaths and the obscenity which made up the greater part of his own conversation, he looked upon them with suspicion. In the evening the two men played piquet. He played badly but vaingloriously, crowing over his opponent when he won and losing his temper when he lost. On rare occasions a couple of planters or traders would drive over to play bridge, and then Walker showed himself in what Mackintosh considered a characteristic light. He played regardless of his partner, calling up in his desire to play the hand, and argued interminably, beating down opposition by the loudness of his voice. He constantly revoked, and when he did so said with an ingratiating whine: "Oh, you wouldn't count it against an old man who can hardly see." Did he know that his opponents thought it as well to keep on the right side of him and hesitated to insist on the rigor of the game? Mackintosh watched him with an icy contempt. When the game was over, while they smoked their pipes and drank whisky, they would begin telling stories. Walker told with gusto the story of his marriage. He had got so drunk at the wedding feast that the bride had fled and he had never seen her since. He had had numberless adventures, commonplace and sordid, with the women of the island and he described them with a pride in his own prowess which was an offense to Mackintosh's fastidious ears. He was a gross, sensual old man. He thought Mackintosh a poor fellow because he would not share his promiscuous amours and remained sober when the company was drunk.

He despised him also for the orderliness with which he did his official work. Mackintosh liked to do everything just so. His desk was always tidy, his papers were always neatly docketed, he could put his hand on any document that was needed, and he had at his fingers' ends all the regulations that were required for the business of their administration.

"Fudge, fudge," said Walker. "I've run this island for twenty years without red tape, and I don't want it now."

"Does it make it any easier for you that when you want a letter you have to hunt half an hour for it?" answered Mackintosh.

"You're nothing but a damned official. But you're not a bad fellow; when you've been out here a year or two you'll be all right. What's wrong about you is that you won't drink. You wouldn't be a bad sort if you got soused once a week."

The curious thing was that Walker remained perfectly unconscious of the dislike for him which every month increased in the breast of his subordinate. Although he laughed at him, as he grew accustomed to him, he began almost to like him. He had

a certain tolerance for the peculiarities of others, and he accepted Mackintosh as a queer fish. Perhaps he liked him, unconsciously, because he could chaff him. His humor consisted of coarse banter and he wanted a butt. Mackintosh's exactness, his morality, his sobriety, were all fruitful subjects; his Scot's name gave an opportunity for the usual jokes about Scotland; he enjoyed himself thoroughly when two or three men were there and he could make them all laugh at the expense of Mackintosh. He would say ridiculous things about him to the natives, and Mackintosh, his knowledge of Samoan still imperfect, would see their unrestrained mirth when Walker had made an obscene reference to him. He smiled good-humoredly.

"I'll say this for you, Mac," Walker would say in his gruff loud voice, "you can take a joke."

"Was it a joke?" smiled Mackintosh. "I didn't know."

"Scots wha hae!" shouted Walker, with a bellow of laughter. "There's only one way to make a Scotchman see a joke and that's by a surgical operation."

Walker little knew that there was nothing Mackintosh could stand less than chaff. He would wake in the night, the breathless night of the rainy season, and brood sullenly over the gibe that Walker had uttered carelessly days before. It rankled. His heart swelled with rage, and he pictured to himself ways in which he might get even with the bully. He had tried answering him, but Walker had a gift of repartee, coarse and obvious, which gave him an ad vantage. The dullness of his intellect made him impervious to a delicate shaft. His self-satisfaction made it impossible to wound him. His loud voice, his bellow of laughter, were weapons against which Mackintosh had nothing to counter, and he learned that the wisest thing was never to betray his irritation. He learned to control himself. But his hatred grew till it was a monomania. He watched Walker with an insane vigilance. He fed his own self-esteem by every instance of meanness on Walker's part, by every exhibition of childish vanity, of cunning and of vulgarity. Walker ate greedily, noisily, filthily, and Mackintosh watched him with satisfaction. He took note of the foolish things he said and of his mistakes in grammar. He knew that Walker held him in small esteem, and he found a bitter satisfaction in his chief's opinion of him; it increased his own contempt for the narrow, complacent old man. And it gave him a singular pleasure to know that Walker was entirely unconscious of the hatred he felt for him. He was a fool who liked popularity, and he blandly fancied that everyone admired him. Once Mackintosh had overheard Walker speaking of him.

"He'll be all right when I've licked him into shape," he said. "He's a good dog and he loves his master."

Mackintosh silently, without a movement of his long, sallow face, laughed long and heartily.

But his hatred was not blind; on the contrary, it was peculiarly clear-sighted, and he judged Walker's capabilities with precision. He ruled his small kingdom with efficiency. He was just and honest. With opportunities to make money he was a poorer man than when he was first appointed to his post, and his only support for his old age was the pension which he expected when at last he retired from official life. His pride was that with an assistant and a half-caste clerk he was able to administer the island more competently than Upolu, the island of which Apia is the chief town, was administered with its army of functionaries. He had a few native policemen to sustain his authority, but he made no use of them. He governed by bluff and his Irish humor.

"They insisted on building a jail for me," he said. "What the devil do I want a jail for? I'm not going to put the natives in prison. If they do wrong I know how to deal with them."

One of his quarrels with the higher authorities at Apia was that he claimed entire jurisdiction over the natives of his island. Whatever their crimes he would not give them up to courts competent to deal with them, and several times an angry correspondence had passed between him and the Governor at Upolu. For he looked upon the natives as his children. And that was the amazing thing about this coarse, vulgar, selfish man; he loved the island on which he had lived so long with passion, and he had for the natives a strange rough tenderness which was quite wonderful.

He loved to ride about the island on his old gray mare and he was never tired of its beauty. Sauntering along the grassy roads among the coconut trees he would stop every now and then to admire the loveliness of the scene. Now and then he would come upon a native village and stop while the head man brought him a bowl of *kava*. He would look at the little group of bell-shaped huts with their high thatched roofs, like beehives, and a smile would spread over his fat face. His eyes rested happily on the spreading green of the breadfruit trees.

"By George, it's like the garden of Eden."

Sometimes his rides took him along the coast and through the trees he had a glimpse of the wide sea, empty, with never a sail to disturb the loneliness; sometimes he climbed a hill so that a great stretch of country, with little villages nestling among the tall trees, was spread out before him like the kingdom of the world, and he would sit there for an hour in an ecstasy of delight. But he had no words to express his feelings and to relieve them would utter an obscene jest; it was as though his emotion was so violent that he needed vulgarity to break the tension.

Mackintosh observed this sentiment with an icy disdain. Walker had always been a heavy drinker, he was proud of his capacity to see men half his age under the table when he spent a night in Apia, and he had the sentimentality of the toper. He could cry over the stories he read in his magazines and yet would refuse a loan to some trader in difficulties whom he had known for twenty years. He was close with his money. Once Mackintosh said to him:

"No one could accuse you of giving money away."

He took it as a compliment. His enthusiasm for nature was but the driveling sensibility of the drunkard. Nor had Mackintosh any sympathy for his chief's feeling towards the natives. He loved them because they were in his power, as a selfish man loves his dog, and his mentality was on a level with theirs. Their humor was obscene and he was never at a loss for the lewd remark. He understood them and they understood him. He was proud of his influence over them. He looked upon them as his children and he mixed himself in all their affairs. But he was very jealous of his authority: if he ruled them with a rod of iron, brooking no contradiction, he would not suffer any of the white men on the island to take advantage of them. He watched the missionaries suspiciously and, if they did anything of which he disapproved, was able to make life so unendurable to them that if he could not get them removed they were glad to go of their own accord. His power over the natives was so great that on his word they would refuse labor and food to their pastor. On the other hand he showed the traders no favor. He took care that they should not cheat the natives; he saw that they got a fair reward for their work and their copra and that the traders made no extravagant profit on the wares they sold them. He was merciless to a bargain that he thought unfair. Sometimes the traders would complain at Apia that they did not get fair opportunities. They suffered for it. Walker then hesitated at no calumny, at no outrageous lie, to get even with them, and they found that if they wanted not only to live at peace, but to exist at all, they had to accept the situation on his own terms. More than once the store of a trader obnoxious to him had been burned down, and there was only the appositeness of the event to show that the administrator had instigated it. Once a Swedish half-caste, ruined by the burning, had gone to him and roundly accused him of arson. Walker laughed in his face.

"You dirty dog. Your mother was a native and you try to cheat the natives. If your rotten old store is burned down it's a judgment of Providence; that's what it is, a judgment of Providence. Get out."

And as the man was hustled out by two native policemen the administrator laughed fatly.

"A judgment of Providence."

And now Mackintosh watched him enter upon the day's work. He began with the sick, for Walker added doctoring to his other activities, and he had a small room behind the office full of drugs. An elderly man came forward, a man with a crop of curly gray hair, in a blue *lava-lava*, elaborately tatooed, with the skin of his body wrinkled like a wineskin.

"What have you come for?" Walker asked him abruptly.

In a whining voice the man said that he could not eat without vomiting and that he had pains here and pains there.

"Go to the missionaries," said Walker. "You know that I only cure children."

"I have been to the missionaries and they do me no good."

"Then go home and prepare yourself to die. Have you lived so long and still want to go on living? You're a fool."

The man broke into querulous expostulation, but Walker, pointing to a woman with a sick child in her arms, told her to bring it to his desk. He asked her questions and looked at the child.

"I will give you medicine," he said. He turned to the half-caste clerk. "Go into the dispensary and bring me some calomel pills."

He made the child swallow one there and then and gave another to the mother.

"Take the child away and keep it warm. Tomorrow it will be dead or better."

He leaned back in his chair and lit his pipe.

"Wonderful stuff, calomel. I've saved more lives with it than all the hospital doctors at Apia put together."

Walker was very proud of his skill, and with the dogmatism of ignorance had no patience with the members of the medical profession.

"The sort of case I like," he said, "is the one that all the doctors have given up as hopeless. When the doctors have said they can't cure you, I say to them, 'come to me.' Did I ever tell you about the fellow who had a cancer?"

"Frequently," said Mackintosh.

"I got him right in three months."

"You've never told me about the people you haven't cured."

He finished this part of the work and went on to the rest. It was a queer medley. There was a woman who could not get on with her husband and a man who complained that his wife had run away from him.

"Lucky dog," said Walker. "Most men wish their wives would too."

There was a long complicated quarrel about the ownership of a few yards of land. There was a dispute about the sharing out of a catch of fish. There was a complaint against a white trader because he had given short measure. Walker listened attentively to every case, made up his mind quickly, and gave his decision. Then he would listen to nothing more; if the complainant went on he was hustled out of the office by a policeman. Mackintosh listened to it all with sullen irritation. On the whole, perhaps, it might be admitted that rough justice was done, but it exasperated the assistant that his chief trusted his instinct rather than the evidence. He would not listen to reason. He browbeat the witnesses and when they did not see what he wished them to called them thieves and liars.

He left to the last a group of men who were sitting in the corner of the room. He had deliberately ignored them. The party consisted of an old chief, a tall, dignified man with short, white hair, in a new *lava-lava*, bearing a huge fly wisp as a badge of office, his son, and half a dozen of the important men of the village. Walker had had a feud with them and had beaten them. As was characteristic of him he meant now to rub in his victory, and because he had them down to profit by their helplessness. The facts were peculiar. Walker had a passion for building roads. When he had come to Talua there were but a few tracks here and there, but in course of time he had cut roads through the country, joining the villages together, and it was to this that a great part of the island's prosperity was due. Whereas in the old days it had been impossible to get the produce of the land, copra chiefly, down to the coast where it could be put on schooners or motor launches and so taken to Apia, now transport was easy and simple. His ambition was to make a road right round the island and a great part of it was already built.

"In two years I shall have done it, and then I can die or they can fire me, I don't care."

His roads were the joy of his heart and he made excursions constantly to see that they were kept in order. They were simple enough, wide tracks, grass covered, cut through the scrub or through the plantations; but trees had to be rooted out, rocks dug up or blasted, and here and there leveling had been necessary. He was proud that he had surmounted by his own skill such difficulties as they presented. He rejoiced in his disposition of them so that they were not only convenient, but showed off the beauties of the island which his soul loved. When he spoke of his roads he was almost a poet. They meandered through those lovely scenes, and Walker had taken care that here and there they should run in a straight line, giving you a green vista through the tall trees, and here and there should turn and curve so that the heart was rested by the diversity. It was amazing that this coarse and sensual man should exercise so subtle an ingenuity to get the effects which his fancy suggested to him. He had used in making his roads all the fantastic skill of a Japanese gardener. He received a grant from headquarters for the work but took a curious pride in using but a small part of it, and the year before had spent only a hundred pounds of the thousand assigned to him.

"What do they want money for?" he boomed. "They'll only spend it on all kinds of muck they don't want; what the missionaries leave them, that is to say."

For no particular reason, except perhaps pride in the economy of his administration and the desire to contrast his efficiency with the wasteful methods of the authorities at Apia, he got the natives to do the work he wanted for wages that were almost nominal. It was owing to this that he had lately had difficulty with the village whose chief men now were come to see him. The chief's son had been in Upolu for a year and on coming back had told his people of the large sums that were paid at Apia for the public works. In long, idle talks he had inflamed their hearts with the desire for gain. He held out to them visions of vast wealth and they thought of the whisky they could buy—it was dear, since there was a law that it must not be sold to natives, and so it cost them double what the white man had to pay for it—they thought of the great sandalwood boxes in which they kept their treasures, and the scented soap and potted salmon, the luxuries for which the Kanaka will sell his soul; so that when the administrator sent for them and told them he wanted a road made from their village to a certain point along the coast and offered them twenty pounds, they asked him a hundred. The chief's son was called Manuma. He was a tall, handsome fellow, copper-colored, with his fuzzy hair dyed red with lime, a wreath of red berries round his neck, and behind his ear a flower like a scarlet flame against his brown face. The upper part of his body was naked, but to show that he was no longer a savage, since he had lived in Apia, he wore a pair of dungarees instead of a *lava-lava*. He told them that if they held together the administrator would be obliged to accept their terms. His heart was set on building the road and when he found they would not work for less he would give them what they asked. But they must not move; whatever he said they must not abate their claim; they had asked a hundred and that they must keep to. When they mentioned the figure, Walker burst into a shout of his long, deep-voiced laughter. He told them not to make fools of themselves, but to set about the work at once. Because he was in a good humor that day he promised to give them a feast when the road was finished. But when he found that no attempt was made to start work, he went to the village and asked the men what silly game they were playing. Manuma had coached them well. They were quite calm, they did not attempt to argue—and argument is a passion with the Kanaka—they merely shrugged their shoulders: they would do it for a hundred pounds, and if he would not give them that they would do no

work. He could please himself. They did not care. Then Walker flew into a passion. He was ugly then. His short fat neck swelled ominously, his red face grew purple, he foamed at the mouth. He set upon the natives with invective. He knew well how to wound and how to humiliate. He was terrifying. The older men grew pale and uneasy. They hesitated. If it had not been for Manuma, with his knowledge of the great world, and their dread of his ridicule, they would have yielded. It was Manuma who answered Walker.

"Pay us a hundred pounds and we will work."

Walker, shaking his fist at him, called him every name he could think of. He riddled him with scorn. Manuma sat still and smiled. There may have been more bravado than confidence in his smile, but he had to make a good show before the others. He repeated his words.

"Pay us a hundred pounds and we will work."

They thought that Walker would spring on him. It would not have been the first time that he had thrashed a native with his own hands; they knew his strength, and though Walker was three times the age of the young man and six inches shorter they did not doubt that he was more than a match for Manuma. No one had ever thought of resisting the savage onslaught of the administrator. But Walker said nothing. He chuckled.

"I am not going to waste my time with a pack of fools," he said. "Talk it over again. You know what I have offered. If you do not start in a week, take care."

He turned round and walked out of the chief's hut. He untied his old mare and it was typical of the relations between him and the natives that one of the elder men hung on to the off stirrup while Walker from a convenient boulder hoisted himself heavily into the saddle.

That same night when Walker according to his habit was strolling along the road that ran past his house, he heard something whizz past him and with a thud strike a tree. Something had been thrown at him. He ducked instinctively. With a shout, "Who's that?" he ran towards the place from which the missile had come and he heard the sound of a man escaping through the bush. He knew it was hopeless to pursue in the darkness, and besides he was soon out of breath, so he stopped and made his way back to the road. He looked about for what had been thrown, but could find nothing. It was quite dark. He went quickly back to the house and called Mackintosh and the Chinese boy.

"One of those devils has thrown something at me. Come along and let's find out what it was."

He told the boy to bring a lantern and the three of them made their way back to the place. They hunted about the ground, but could not find what they sought. Suddenly the boy gave a guttural cry. They turned to look. He held up the lantern, and there, sinister in the light that cut the surrounding darkness, was a long knife sticking into the trunk of a coconut tree. It had been thrown with such force that it required quite an effort to pull it out.

"By George, if he hadn't missed me I'd have been in a nice state."

Walker handled the knife. It was one of those knives, made in imitation of the sailor knives brought to the islands a hundred years before by the first white men, used to divide the coconuts in two so that the copra might be dried. It was a mur-

derous weapon, and the blade, twelve inches long, was very sharp. Walker chuckled softly.

"The devil, the impudent devil."

He had no doubt it was Manuma who had flung the knife. He had escaped death by three inches. He was not angry. On the contrary, he was in high spirits; the adventure exhilarated him, and when they got back to the house, calling for drinks, he rubbed his hands gleefully.

"I'll make them pay for this!"

His little eyes twinkled. He blew himself out like a turkeycock, and for the second time within half an hour insisted on telling Mackintosh every detail of the affair. Then he asked him to play piquet, and while they played he boasted of his intentions. Mackintosh listened with tightened lips.

"But why should you grind them down like this?" he asked. "Twenty pounds is precious little for the work you want them to do."

"They ought to be precious thankful I give them anything."

"Hang it all, it's not your own money. The government allots you a reasonable sum. They won't complain if you spend it."

"They're a bunch of fools at Apia."

Mackintosh saw that Walker's motive was merely vanity. He shrugged his shoulders.

"It won't do you much good to score off the fellows at Apia at the cost of your life."

"Bless you, they wouldn't hurt me, these people. They couldn't do without me. They worship me. Manuma is a fool. He only threw that knife to frighten me."

The next day Walker rode over again to the village. It was called Matautu. He did not get off his horse. When he reached the chief's house he saw that the men were sitting round the floor in a circle, talking, and he guessed they were discussing again the question of the road. The Samoan huts are formed in this way: trunks of slender trees are placed in a circle at intervals of perhaps five or six feet; a tall tree is set in the middle and from this downwards slopes the thatched roof. Venetian blinds of coconut leaves can be pulled down at night or when it is raining. Ordinarily the hut is open all round so that the breeze can blow through freely. Walker rode to the edge of the hut and called out to the chief.

"Oh, there, Tangatu, your son left his knife in a tree last night. I have brought it back to you."

He flung it down on the ground in the midst of the circle, and with a low burst of laughter ambled off.

On Monday he went out to see if they had started work. There was no sign of it. He rode through the village. The inhabitants were about their ordinary avocations. Some were weaving mats of the pandanus leaf, one old man was busy with a *kava* bowl, the children were playing, the women went about their household chores. Walker, a smile on his lips, came to the chief's house.

"*Talofa-li*," said the chief.

"*Talofa*," answered Walker.

Manuma was making a net. He sat with a cigarette between his lips and looked up at Walker with a smile of triumph.

"You have decided that you will not make the road?"

The chief answered.

"Not unless you pay us one hundred pounds."

"You will regret it." He turned to Manuma. "And you, my lad, I shouldn't wonder if your back was very sore before you're much older."

He rode away chuckling. He left the natives vaguely uneasy. They feared the fat sinful old man, and neither the missionaries' abuse of him nor the scorn which Manuma had learned in Apia made them forget that he had a devilish cunning and that no man had ever braved him without in the long run suffering for it. They found out within twenty-four hours what scheme he had devised. It was characteristic. For next morning a great band of men, women, and children came into the village and the chief men said that they had made a bargain with Walker to build the road. He had offered them twenty pounds and they had accepted. Now the cunning lay in this, that the Polynesians have rules of hospitality which have all the force of laws; an etiquette of absolute rigidity made it necessary for the people of the village not only to give lodging to the strangers, but to provide them with food and drink as long as they wished to stay. The inhabitants of Matautu were outwitted. Every morning the workers went out in a joyous band, cut down trees, blasted rocks, leveled here and there and then in the evening tramped back again, and ate and drank, ate heartily, danced, sang hymns, and enjoyed life. For them it was a picnic. But soon their hosts began to wear long faces; the strangers had enormous appetites, and the plantains and the breadfruit vanished before their rapacity; the alligator-pear trees, whose fruit sent to Apia might sell for good money, were stripped bare. Ruin stared them in the face. And then they found that the strangers were working very slowly. Had they received a hint from Walker that they might take their time? At this rate by the time the road was finished there would not be a scrap of food in the village. And worse than this, they were a laughingstock; when one or other of them went to some distant hamlet on an errand he found that the story had got there before him, and he was met with derisive laughter. There is nothing the Kanaka can endure less than ridicule. It was not long before much angry talk passed among the sufferers. Manuma was no longer a hero; he had to put up with a good deal of plain speaking, and one day what Walker had suggested came to pass: a heated argument turned into a quarrel and half a dozen of the young men set upon the chief's son and gave him such a beating that for a week he lay bruised and sore on the pandanus mats. He turned from side to side and could find no ease. Every day or two the administrator rode over on his old mare and watched the progress of the road. He was not a man to resist the temptation of taunting the fallen foe, and he missed no opportunity to rub into the shamed inhabitants of Matautu the bitterness of their humiliation. He broke their spirit. And one morning, putting their pride in their pockets, a figure of speech, since pockets they had not, they all set out with the strangers and started working on the road. It was urgent to get it done quickly if they wanted to save any food at all, and the whole village joined in. But they worked silently, with rage and mortification in their hearts, and even the children toiled in silence. The women wept as they carried away bundles of brushwood. When Walker saw them he laughed so much that he almost rolled out of his saddle. The news spread quickly and tickled the people of

the island to death. This was the greatest joke of all, the crowning triumph of that cunning old white man whom no Kanaka had ever been able to circumvent; and they came from distant villages, with their wives and children, to look at the foolish folk who had refused twenty pounds to make the road and now were forced to work for nothing. But the harder they worked the more easily went the guests. Why should they hurry, when they were getting good food for nothing and the longer they took about the job the better the joke became? At last the wretched villagers could stand it no longer, and they were come this morning to beg the administrator to send the strangers back to their own homes. If he would do this they promised to finish the road themselves for nothing. For him it was a victory complete and unqualified. They were humbled. A look of arrogant complacence spread over his large, naked face, and he seemed to swell in his chair like a great bullfrog. There was something sinister in his appearance, so that Mackintosh shivered with disgust. Then in his booming tones he began to speak.

"Is it for my good that I make the road? What benefit do you think I get out of it? It is for you, so that you can walk in comfort and carry your copra in comfort. I offered to pay you for your work, though it was for your own sake the work was done. I offered to pay you generously. Now *you* must pay. I will send the people of Manua back to their homes if you will finish the road and pay the twenty pounds that I have to pay them."

There was an outcry. They sought to reason with him. They told him they had not the money. But to everything they said he replied with brutal gibes. Then the clock struck. "Dinnertime," he said. "Turn them all out."

He raised himself heavily from his chair and walked out of the room. When Mackintosh followed him he found him already seated at table, a napkin tied round his neck, holding his knife and fork in readiness for the meal the Chinese cook was about to bring. He was in high spirits.

"I did 'em down fine," he said, as Mackintosh sat down. "I shan't have much trouble with the roads after this."

"I suppose you were joking," said Mackintosh icily.

"What do you mean by that?"

"You're not really going to make them pay twenty pounds?"

"You bet your life I am."

"I'm not sure you've got any right to."

"Ain't you? I guess I've got the right to do any damned thing I like on this island."

"I think you've bullied them quite enough."

Walker laughed fatly. He did not care what Mackintosh thought.

"When I want your opinion I'll ask for it."

Mackintosh grew very white. He knew by bitter experience that he could do nothing but keep silence, and the violent effort at self-control made him sick and faint. He could not eat the food that was before him and with disgust he watched Walker shovel meat into his vast mouth. He was a dirty feeder, and to sit at table with him needed a strong stomach. Mackintosh shuddered. A tremendous desire seized him to humiliate that gross and cruel man; he would give anything in the world to see him in the dust,

suffering as much as he had made others suffer. He had never loathed the bully with such loathing as now.

The day wore on. Mackintosh tried to sleep after dinner, but the passion in his heart prevented him; he tried to read, but the letters swam before his eyes. The sun beat down pitilessly, and he longed for rain; but he knew that rain would bring no coolness; it would only make it hotter and more steamy. He was a native of Aberdeen and his heart yearned suddenly for the icy winds that whistled through the granite streets of that city. Here he was a prisoner, imprisoned not only by that placid sea, but by his hatred for that horrible old man. He pressed his hands to his aching head. He would like to kill him. But he pulled himself together. He must do something to distract his mind, and since he could not read he thought he would set his private papers in order. It was a job which he had long meant to do and which he had constantly put off. He unlocked the drawer of his desk and took out a handful of letters. He caught sight of his revolver. An impulse, no sooner realized than set aside, to put a bullet through his head and so escape from the intolerable bondage of life flashed through his mind. He noticed that in the damp air the revolver was slightly rusted, and he got an oil rag and began to clean it. It was while he was thus occupied that he grew aware of someone slinking round the door. He looked up and called:

"Who is there?"

There was a moment's pause, then Manuma showed himself.

"What do you want?"

The chief's son stood for a moment, sullen and silent, and when he spoke it was with a strangled voice.

"We can't pay twenty pounds. We haven't the money."

"What am I to do?" said Mackintosh. "You heard what Mr. Walker said."

Manuma began to plead, half in Samoan and half in English. It was a singsong whine, with the quavering intonations of a beggar, and it filled Mackintosh with disgust. It outraged him that the man should let himself be so crushed. He was a pitiful object.

"I can do nothing," said Mackintosh irritably. "You know that Mr. Walker is master here."

Manuma was silent again. He still stood in the doorway.

"I am sick," he said at last. "Give me some medicine."

"What is the matter with you?"

"I do not know. I am sick. I have pains in my body."

"Don't stand there," said Mackintosh sharply. "Come in and let me look at you."

Manuma entered the little room and stood before the desk.

"I have pains here and here."

He put his hands to his loins and his face assumed an expression of pain. Suddenly Mackintosh grew conscious that the boy's eyes were resting on the revolver which he had laid on the desk when Manuma appeared in the doorway. There was a silence between the two which to Mackintosh was endless. He seemed to read the thoughts which were in the Kanaka's mind. His heart beat violently. And then he felt as though something possessed him so that he acted under the compulsion of a foreign will. He himself did not make the movements of his body, but a power that was strange to him. His throat was suddenly dry, and he put his hand to it mechanically in order

to help his speech. He was impelled to avoid Manuma's eyes.

"Just wait here," he said, his voice sounding as though someone had seized him by the windpipe, "and I'll fetch you something from the dispensary."

He got up. Was it his fancy that he staggered a little? Manuma stood silently, and though he kept his eyes averted, Mackintosh knew that he was looking dully out of the door. It was this other person that possessed him, that drove him out of the room, but it was himself that took a handful of muddled papers and threw them on the revolver in order to hide it from view. He went to the dispensary. He got a pill and poured out some blue draught into a small bottle, and then came out into the compound. He did not want to go back into his own bungalow, so he called to Manuma.

"Come here."

He gave him the drugs and instructions how to take them. He did not know what it was that made it impossible for him to look at the Kanaka. While he was speaking to him he kept his eyes on his shoulder. Manuma took the medicine and slunk out of the gate.

Mackintosh went into the dining room and turned over once more the old newspapers. But he could not read them. The house was very still. Walker was upstairs in his room asleep, the Chinese cook was busy in the kitchen, the two policemen were out fishing. The silence that seemed to brood over the house was unearthly, and there hammered in Mackintosh's head the question whether the revolver still lay where he had placed it. He could not bring himself to look. The uncertainty was horrible, but the certainty would be more horrible still. He sweated. At last he could stand the silence no longer, and he made up his mind to go down the road to the trader's, a man named Jervis, who had a store about a mile away. He was a half-caste, but even that amount of white blood made him possible to talk to. He wanted to get away from his bungalow, with the desk littered with untidy papers, and underneath them something, or nothing. He walked along the road. As he passed the fine hut of a chief a greeting was called out to him. Then he came to the store. Behind the counter sat the trader's daughter, a swarthy broad-featured girl in a pink blouse and a white drill skirt. Jervis hoped he would marry her. He had money, and he had told Mackintosh that his daughter's husband would be well to do. She flushed a little when she saw Mackintosh.

"Father's just unpacking some cases that have come in this morning. I'll tell him you're here."

He sat down and the girl went out behind the shop. In a moment her mother waddled in, a huge old woman, a chiefess, who owned much land in her own right; and gave him her hand. Her monstrous obesity was an offense, but she managed to convey an impression of dignity. She was cordial without obsequiousness; affable, but conscious of her station.

"You're quite a stranger, Mr. Mackintosh. Teresa was saying only this morning: 'Why, we never see Mr. Mackintosh now.' "

He shuddered a little as he thought of himself as that old native's son-in-law. It was notorious that she ruled her husband, notwithstanding his white blood, with a firm hand. Hers was the authority and hers the business head. She might be no more than Mrs. Jervis to the white people, but her father

had been a chief of the blood royal, and his father and his father's father had ruled as kings. The trader came in, small beside his imposing wife, a dark man with a black beard going gray, in ducks, with handsome eyes and flashing teeth. He was very British, and his conversation was slangy, but you felt he spoke English as a foreign tongue; with his family he used the language of his native mother. He was a servile man, cringing and obsequious.

"Ah, Mr. Mackintosh, this is a joyful surprise. Get the whisky, Teresa; Mr. Mackintosh will have a gargle with us."

He gave all the latest news of Apia, watching his guest's eyes the while, so that he might know the welcome thing to say.

"And how is Walker? We've not seen him just lately. Mrs. Jervis is going to send him a sucking pig one day this week."

"I saw him riding home this morning," said Teresa.

"Here's how," said Jervis, holding up his whisky.

Mackintosh drank. The two women sat and looked at him, Mrs. Jervis in her black Mother Hubbard, placid and haughty, and Teresa, anxious to smile whenever she caught his eye, while the trader gossiped insufferably.

"They were saying in Apia it was about time Walker retired. He ain't so young as he was. Things have changed since he first come to the islands and he ain't changed with them."

"He'll go too far," said the old chiefess. "The natives aren't satisfied."

"That was a good joke about the road," laughed the trader. "When I told them about it in Apia they fair split their sides with laughing. Good old Walker."

Mackintosh looked at him savagely. What did he mean by talking of him in that fashion? To a half-caste trader he was Mr. Walker. It was on his tongue to utter a harsh rebuke for the impertinence. He did not know what held him back.

"When he goes I hope you'll take his place, Mr. Mackintosh," said Jervis. "We all like you on the island. You understand the natives. They're educated now, they must be treated differently to the old days. It wants an educated man to be administrator now. Walker was only a trader same as I am."

Teresa's eyes glistened.

"When the time comes if there's anything anyone can do here, you bet your bottom dollar we'll do it. I'd get all the chiefs to go over to Apia and make a petition."

Mackintosh felt horribly sick. It had not struck him that if anything happened to Walker it might be he who would succeed him. It was true that no one in his official position knew the island so well. He got up suddenly and scarcely taking his leave walked back to the compound. And now he went straight to his room. He took a quick look at his desk. He rummaged among the papers.

The revolver was not there.

His heart thumped violently against his ribs. He looked for the revolver everywhere. He hunted in the chairs and in the drawers. He looked desperately, and all the time he knew he would not find it. Suddenly he heard Walker's gruff, hearty voice.

"What the devil are you up to, Mac?"

He started. Walker was standing in the doorway and instinctively he turned round to hide what lay upon his desk.

"Tidying up?" quizzed Walker. "I've told 'em to put the gray in the trap. I'm going down to Tafoni to bathe. You'd better come along."

"All right," said Mackintosh.

So long as he was with Walker nothing could happen. The place they were bound for was about three miles away, and there was a fresh-water pool, separated by a thin barrier of rock from the sea, which the administrator had blasted out for the natives to bathe in. He had done this at spots round the island, wherever there was a spring; and the fresh water, compared with the sticky warmth of the sea, was cool and invigorating. They drove along the silent grassy road, splashing now and then through fords, where the sea had forced its way in, past a couple of native villages, the bell-shaped huts spaced out roomily and the white chapel in the middle, and at the third village they got out of the trap, tied up the horse, and walked down to the pool. They were accompanied by four or five girls and a dozen children. Soon they were all splashing about, shouting and laughing, while Walker, in a *lava-lava*, swam to and fro like an unwieldy porpoise. He made lewd jokes with the girls, and they amused themselves by diving under him and wriggling away when he tried to catch them. When he was tired he lay down on a rock, while the girls and children surrounded him; it was a happy family; and the old man, huge, with his crescent of white hair and his shining bald crown, looked like some old sea god. Once Mackintosh caught a queer soft look in his eyes.

"They're dear children," he said. "They look upon me as their father."

And then without a pause he turned to one of the girls and made an obscene remark which sent them all into fits of laughter. Mackintosh started to dress. With his thin legs and thin arms he made a grotesque figure, a sinister Don Quixote, and Walker began to make coarse jokes about him. They were acknowledged with little smothered laughs. Mackintosh struggled with his shirt. He knew he looked absurd, but he hated being laughed at. He stood silent and glowering.

"If you want to get back in time for dinner you ought to come soon."

"You're not a bad fellow, Mac. Only you're a fool. When you're doing one thing you always want to do another. That's not the way to live."

But all the same he raised himself slowly to his feet and began to put on his clothes. They sauntered back to the village, drank a bowl of *kava* with the chief, and then, after a joyful farewell from all the lazy villagers, drove home.

After dinner, according to his habit, Walker, lighting his cigar, prepared to go for a stroll. Mackintosh was suddenly seized with fear.

"Don't you think it's rather unwise to go out at night by yourself just now?"

Walker stared at him with his round blue eyes.

"What the devil do you mean?"

"Remember the knife the other night. You've got those fellows' backs up."

"Pooh! They wouldn't dare."

"Someone dared before."

"That was only a bluff. They wouldn't hurt me. They look upon me as a father. They know that whatever I do is for their own good."

Mackintosh watched him with contempt in his heart. The man's self-complacency outraged him, and yet something, he knew not what, made him insist.

"Remember what happened this morning. It wouldn't hurt you to stay at home just tonight. I'll play piquet with you."

"I'll play piquet with you when I come back. The Kanaka isn't born yet who can make me alter my plans."

"You'd better let me come with you."

"You stay where you are."

Mackintosh shrugged his shoulders. He had given the man full warning. If he did not heed it that was his own lookout. Walker put on his hat and went out. Mackintosh began to read; but then he thought of something; perhaps it would be as well to have his own whereabouts quite clear. He crossed over to the kitchen and, inventing some pretext, talked for a few minutes with the cook. Then he got out the gramophone and put a record on it, but while it ground out its melancholy tune, some comic song of a London music hall, his ear was strained for a sound away there in the night. At his elbow the record reeled out its loudness, the words were raucous, but notwithstanding he seemed to be surrounded by an unearthly silence. He heard the dull roar of the breakers against the reef. He heard the breeze sigh, far up, in the leaves of the coconut trees. How long would it be? It was awful.

He heard a hoarse laugh.

"Wonders will never cease. It's not often you play yourself a tune, Mac."

Walker stood at the window, red-faced, bluff and jovial.

"Well, you see I'm alive and kicking. What were you playing for?"

Walker came in.

"Nerves a bit dicky, eh? Playing a tune to keep your pecker up?"

"I was playing your requiem."

"What the devil's that?"

"'Alf o' bitter an' a pint of stout."

"A rattling good song too. I don't mind how often I hear it. Now I'm ready to take your money off you at piquet."

They played and Walker bullied his way to victory, bluffing his opponent, chaffing him, jeering at his mistakes, up to every dodge, browbeating him, exulting. Presently Mackintosh recovered his coolness, and standing outside himself, as it were, he was able to take a detached pleasure in watching the overbearing old man and in his own cold reserve. Somewhere Manuma sat quietly and awaited his opportunity.

Walker won game after game and pocketed his winnings at the end of the evening in high good humor.

"You'll have to grow a little bit older before you stand much chance against me, Mac. The fact is I have a natural gift for cards."

"I don't know that there's much gift about it when I happen to deal you fourteen aces."

"Good cards come to good players," retorted Walker. "I'd have won if I'd had your hands."

He went on to tell long stories of the various occasions on which he had played cards with notorious sharpers and to their consternation had taken all their money from them. He boasted. He praised himself. And Mackintosh listened with absorption. He wanted now to feed his hatred; and everything Walker said, every gesture, made him more detestable. At last Walker got up.

"Well, I'm going to turn in," he said with a loud yawn. "I've got a long day tomorrow."

"What are you going to do?"

"I'm driving over to the other side of the island. I'll start at five, but I don't expect I shall get back to dinner till late."

They generally dined at seven.

"We'd better make it half-past seven then."

"I guess it would be as well."

Mackintosh watched him knock the ashes out of his pipe. His vitality was rude and exuberant. It was strange to think that death hung over him. A faint smile flickered in Mackintosh's cold, gloomy eyes.

"Would you like me to come with you?"

"What in God's name should I want that for? I'm using the mare and she'll have enough to do to carry me; she don't want to drag you over thirty miles of road."

"Perhaps you don't quite realize what the feeling is at Matautu. I think it would be safer if I came with you."

Walker burst into contemptuous laughter.

"You'd be a fine lot of use in a scrap. I'm not a great hand at getting the wind up."

Now the smile passed from Mackintosh's eyes to his lips. It distorted them painfully.

"*Quem deus vult perdere prius dementat.*"

"What the hell is that?" said Walker.

"Latin," answered Mackintosh as he went out.

And now he chuckled. His mood had changed. He had done all he could and the matter was in the hands of fate. He slept more soundly than he had done for weeks. When he awoke next morning he went out. After a good night he found a pleasant exhilaration in the freshness of the early air. The sea was a more vivid blue, the sky more brilliant, than on most days, the trade wind was fresh, and there was a ripple on the lagoon as the breeze brushed over it like velvet brushed the wrong way. He felt himself stronger and younger. He entered upon the day's work with zest. After luncheon he slept again, and as evening drew on he had the bay saddled and sauntered through the bush. He seemed to see it all with new eyes. He felt more normal. The extraordinary thing was that he was able to put Walker out of his mind altogether. So far as he was concerned he might never have existed.

He returned late, hot after his ride, and bathed again. Then he sat on the veranda, smoking his pipe, and looked at the day declining over the lagoon. In the sunset the lagoon, rosy and purple and green, was very beautiful. He felt at peace with the world and with himself. When the cook came out to say that dinner was ready and to ask whether he should wait, Mackintosh smiled at him with friendly eyes. He looked at his watch.

"It's half-past seven. Better not wait. One can't tell when the boss'll be back."

The boy nodded, and in a moment Mackintosh saw him carry across the yard a bowl of steaming soup. He got up lazily, went into the dining room, and ate his dinner. Had it happened? The uncertainty was amusing and Mackintosh chuckled in the silence. The food did not seem so monotonous as usual, and even though there was hamburger steak, the cook's invariable dish when his poor invention failed him, it tasted by some miracle succulent and spiced. After dinner he strolled over lazily to his bungalow to get a book. He liked the intense stillness, and now that the

night had fallen the stars were blazing in the sky. He shouted for a lamp and in a moment the Chink pattered over on his bare feet, piercing the darkness with a ray of light. He put the lamp on the desk and noiselessly slipped out of the room. Mackintosh stood rooted to the floor, for there, half hidden by untidy papers, was his revolver. His heart throbbed painfully, and he broke into a sweat. It was done then.

He took up the revolver with a shaking hand. Four of the chambers were empty. He paused a moment and looked suspiciously out into the night, but there was no one there. He quickly slipped four cartridges into the empty chambers and locked the revolver in his drawer.

He sat down to wait.

An hour passed, a second hour passed. There was nothing. He sat at his desk as though he were writing, but he neither wrote nor read. He merely listened. He strained his ears for a sound traveling from a far distance. At last he heard hesitating footsteps and knew it was the Chinese cook.

"Ah-Sung," he called.

The boy came to the door.

"Boss velly late," he said. "Dinner no good."

Mackintosh stared at him, wondering whether he knew what had happened, and whether, when he knew, he would realize on what terms he and Walker had been. He went about his work, sleek, silent, and smiling, and who could tell his thoughts?

"I expect he's had dinner on the way, but you must keep the soup hot at all events."

The words were hardly out of his mouth when the silence was suddenly broken into by a confusion, cries, and a rapid patter of naked feet. A number of natives ran into the compound, men and women and children; they crowded round Mackintosh and they all talked at once. They were unintelligible. They were excited and frightened and some of them were crying. Mackintosh pushed his way through them and went to the gateway. Though he had scarcely understood what they said he knew quite well what had happened. And as he reached the gate the dogcart arrived. The old mare was being led by a tall Kanaka, and in the dogcart crouched two men, trying to hold Walker up. A little crowd of natives surrounded it.

The mare was led into the yard and the natives surged in after it. Mackintosh shouted to them to stand back and the two policemen, sprang suddenly from God knows where, pushed them violently aside. By now he had managed to understand that some lads who had been fishing, on their way back to their village had come across the cart on the home side of the ford. The mare was nuzzling about the herbage and in the darkness they could just see the great white bulk of the old man sunk between the seat and the dashboard. At first they thought he was drunk and they peered in, grinning, but then they heard him groan, and guessed that something was amiss. They ran to the village and called for help. It was when they returned, accompanied by half a hundred people, that they discovered Walker had been shot.

With a sudden thrill of horror Mackintosh asked himself whether he was already dead. The first thing at all events was to get him out of the cart, and that, owing to Walker's corpulence, was a difficult job. It took four strong men to lift him. They jolted him and he uttered a dull groan. He was still alive. At last they carried him into the house, up the stairs, and placed him on his bed. Then Mackintosh was able to see him, for in the yard, lit only by half a dozen hurricane lamps, everything had been obscured. Walker's white ducks were stained with blood, and the men who had carried him wiped their hands, red and sticky, on their *lava-lavas*. Mackintosh held up the lamp. He had not expected the old man to be so pale. His eyes were closed. He was breathing still, his pulse could be just felt, but it was obvious that he was dying. Mackintosh had not bargained for the shock of horror that convulsed him. He saw that the native clerk was there, and in a voice hoarse with fear told him to go into the dispensary and get what was necessary for a hypodermic injection. One of the policemen had brought up the whisky, and Mackintosh forced a little into the old man's mouth. The room was crowded with natives. They sat about the floor, speechless now and terrified, and every now and then one wailed aloud. It was very hot, but Mackintosh felt cold, his hands and his feet were like ice, and he had to make a violent effort not to tremble in all his limbs. He did not know what to do. He did not know if Walker was bleeding still, and if he was, how he could stop the bleeding.

The clerk brought the hypodermic needle.

"You give it to him," said Mackintosh. "You're more used to that sort of thing than I am."

His head ached horribly. It felt as though all sorts of little savage things were beating inside it, trying to get out. They watched for the effect of the injection. Presently Walker opened his eyes slowly. He did not seem to know where he was.

"Keep quiet," said Mackintosh. "You're at home. You're quite safe."

Walker's lips outlined a shadowy smile.

"They've got me," he whispered.

"I'll get Jervis to send his motor-boat to Apia at once. We'll get a doctor out by tomorrow afternoon."

There was a long pause before the old man answered,

"I shall be dead by then."

A ghastly expression passed over Mackintosh's pale face. He forced himself to laugh.

"What rot! You keep quiet and you'll be as right as rain."

"Give me a drink," said Walker. "A stiff one."

With shaking hand Mackintosh poured out whisky and water, half and half, and held the glass while Walker drank greedily. It seemed to restore him. He gave a long sigh and a little color came into his great fleshy face. Mackintosh felt extraordinarily helpless. He stood and stared at the old man.

"If you'll tell me what to do I'll do it," he said.

"There's nothing to do. Just leave me alone. I'm done for."

He looked dreadfully pitiful as he lay on the great bed, a huge, bloated, old man; but so wan, so weak, it was heart-rending. As he rested, his mind seemed to grow clearer.

"You were right, Mac," he said presently. "You warned me."

"I wish to God I'd come with you."

"You're a good chap, Mac, only you don't drink."

There was another long silence, and it was clear that Walker was sinking. There was an internal hemorrhage and even Mackintosh in his ignorance could not fail to see that his chief had but an hour or two to live. He stood by the side of the bed stock-still. For half an hour perhaps Walker lay with his eyes closed, then he opened them.

"They'll give you my job," he said, slowly. "Last time I was in Apia I told them you were all right. Finish my road. I want to think that'll be done. All round the island."

"I don't want your job. You'll get all right."

Walker shook his head wearily.

"I've had my day. Treat them fairly, that's the great thing. They're children. You must always remember that. You must be firm with them, but you must be kind. And you must be just. I've never made a bob out of them. I haven't saved a hundred pounds in twenty years. The road's the great thing. Get the road finished."

Something very like a sob was wrung from Mackintosh.

"You're a good fellow, Mac. I always liked you."

He closed his eyes, and Mackintosh thought that he would never open them again. His mouth was so dry that he had to get himself something to drink. The Chinese cook silently put a chair for him. He sat down by the side of the bed and waited. He did not know how long a time passed. The night was endless. Suddenly one of the men sitting there broke into uncontrollable sobbing, loudly, like a child, and Mackintosh grew aware that the room was crowded by this time with natives. They sat all over the floor on their haunches, men and women, staring at the bed.

"What are all these people doing here?" said Mackintosh. "They've got no right. Turn them out, turn them out, all of them."

His words seemed to rouse Walker, for he opened his eyes once more, and now they were all misty. He wanted to speak, but he was so weak that Mackintosh had to strain his ears to catch what he said.

"Let them stay. They're my children. They ought to be here."

Mackintosh turned to the natives.

"Stay where you are. He wants you. But be silent."

A faint smile came over the old man's white face.

"Come nearer," he said.

Mackintosh bent over him. His eyes were closed and the words he said were like a wind sighing through the fronds of the coconut trees.

"Give me another drink. I've got something to say."

This time Mackintosh gave him his whisky neat. Walker collected his strength in a final effort of will.

"Don't make a fuss about this. In 'ninety-five when there were troubles white men were killed, and the fleet came and shelled the villages. A lot of people were killed who'd had nothing to do with it. They're damned fools at Apia. If they make a fuss they'll only punish the wrong people. I don't want anyone punished."

He paused for a while to rest.

"You must say it was an accident. No one's to blame. Promise me that."

"I'll do anything you like," whispered Mackintosh.

"Good chap. One of the best. They're children. I'm their father. A father don't let his children get into trouble if he can help it."

A ghost of a chuckle came out of his throat. It was astonishingly weird and ghastly.

"You're a religious chap, Mac. What's that about forgiving them? You know."

For a while Mackintosh did not answer. His lips trembled.

"Forgive them, for they know not what they do?"

"That's right. Forgive them. I've loved them, you know, always loved them."

He sighed. His lips faintly moved, and now Mackintosh had to put his ears quite close to them in order to hear.

"Hold my hand," he said.

Mackintosh gave a gasp. His heart seemed wrenched. He took the old man's hand, so cold and weak, a coarse, rough hand, and held it in his own. And thus he sat until he nearly started out of his seat, for the silence was suddenly broken by a long rattle. It was terrible and unearthly. Walker was dead. Then the natives broke out with loud cries. The tears ran down their faces, and they beat their breasts.

Mackintosh disengaged his hand from the dead man's, and staggering like one drunk with sleep he went out of the room. He went to the locked drawer in his writing desk and took out the revolver. He walked down to the sea and walked into the lagoon; he waded out cautiously, so that he should not trip against a coral rock, till the water came to his armpits. Then he put a bullet through his head.

An hour later half a dozen slim brown sharks were splashing and struggling at the spot where he fell.

Aldous Huxley

1894-1963

SON of Leonard Huxley, writer, Greek scholar, and editor of *The Cornhill Magazine;* grandson of Thomas Huxley; grand-nephew of Matthew Arnold; nephew of Mrs. Humphry Ward; brother of Julian Huxley, scientist—Aldous Huxley lived up to his illustrious family. His knowledge was tremendous, *The Encyclopædia Britannica* his favorite reading. As someone once said, a fraction of his writing, with its theories on everything, expounded as it is in clear and beautiful prose, would have been enough to make the reputation of an eighteenth-century celebrity. Specifically, his novel *Point Counter Point,* along with *Crome Yellow* and *Antic Hay,* is probably the final word on his generation in the decade of its prime: the English intelligentsia of the middle twenties— that cynical, brilliant, anarchic little group, now mature and scattered, which had its vitriolic say-so and undoubtedly left its mark.

Between the ages of seventeen and twenty, Aldous Huxley lost his eyesight and wrote a novel which he was never able to read. By the time he had recovered partial eyesight, the manuscript was lost. He got through Oxford with the aid of a magnifying glass, and continued to suffer from extreme nearsightedness until, many years later, in California, he improved his sight by a technique of direct, conscious effort. This made such a deep impression on him that he translated it into his philosophy: "becoming the master of one's circumstances instead of their slave."

Like Henry James, Huxley wrote, in both his short stories and his novels, of one class of people only—of those who, though they made nothing of it, have had the advantage of birth, means, position, and culture. But whereas James respected his creatures, Huxley, on the whole, despised them. . . . "Young Archimedes" is the title story of a volume of short stories.

Young Archimedes

BY ALDOUS HUXLEY

IT WAS the view which finally made us take the place. True, the house had its disadvantages. It was a long way out of town and had no telephone. The rent was unduly high, the drainage system poor. On windy nights, when the ill-fitting panes were rattling so furiously in the window frames that you could fancy yourself in an hotel omnibus, the electric light, for some mysterious reason, used invariably to go out and leave you in the noisy dark. There was a splendid bathroom; but the electric pump, which was supposed to send up water from the rainwater tanks in the terrace, did not work. Punctually every autumn the drinking well ran dry. And our landlady was a liar and a cheat.

But these are the little disadvantages of every hired house, all over the world. For Italy they were not really at all serious. I have seen plenty of houses which had them all and a hundred others, without possessing the compensating advantages of ours—the southward-facing garden and terrace for the winter and spring, the large cool rooms against the midsummer heat, the hilltop air and freedom from mosquitoes, and finally the view.

And what a view it was! Or rather, what a succession of views. For it was different every day; and without stirring from the house one had the impression of an incessant change of scene: all the delights of travel without its fatigues. There were autumn days when all the valleys were filled with mist and the crest of the Apennines rose darkly out of a flat white lake. There were days when the mist invaded even our hilltop and we were enveloped in a soft vapor in which the mist-colored olive trees, that sloped away below our windows towards the valley, disappeared as though into their own spiritual essence; and the only firm and definite things in the small, dim world within which we found ourselves confined were the two tall black cypresses growing on a little projecting terrace a hundred feet down the hill. Black, sharp, and solid, they stood there, twin pillars of Hercules at the extremity of the known universe; and beyond them there was only pale cloud and round them only the cloudy olive trees.

These were the wintry days; but there were days of spring and autumn, days unchallengingly cloudless, or—more lovely still—made various by the huge floating shapes of vapor that, snowy above the

From *Young Archimedes and Other Stories* by Aldous Huxley. By permission of Harper & Brothers. Copyright, 1924, by Aldous Huxley. In Canada, from *The Little Mexican*, by permission of Messrs. Chatto & Windus, London, and the Oxford University Press, Canadian Branch.

faraway, snow-capped mountains, gradually unfolded, against the pale bright blue, enormous heroic gestures. And in the height of the sky the bellying draperies, the swans, the aerial marbles, hewed and left unfinished by gods grown tired of creation almost before they had begun, drifted sleeping along the wind, changing form as they moved. And the sun would come and go behind them; and now the town in the valley would fade and almost vanish in the shadow, and now, like an immense fretted jewel between the hills, it would glow as though by its own light. And looking across the nearer tributary valley that wound from below our crest down towards the Arno, looking over the low dark shoulder of hill on whose extreme promonotory stood the towered church of San Miniato, one saw the huge dome airily hanging on its ribs of masonry, the square campanile, the sharp spire of Santa Croce, and the canopied tower of the Signoria, rising above the intricate maze of houses, distinct and brilliant, like small treasures carved out of precious stones. For a moment only, and then their light would fade away once more, and the traveling beam would pick out, among the indigo hill beyond, a single golden crest.

There were days when the air was wet with passed or with approaching rain, and all the distances seemed miraculously near and clear. The olive trees detached themselves one from another on the distant slopes; the faraway villages were lovely and pathetic like the most exquisite small toys. There were days in summertime, days of impending thunder when, bright and sunlit against huge bellying masses of black and purple, the hills and the white houses shone as it were precariously, in a dying

splendor, on the brink of some fearful calamity.

How the hills changed and varied! Every day and every hour of the day, almost, they were different. There would be moments when, looking across the plains of Florence, one would see only a dark blue silhouette against the sky. The scene had no depth; there was only a hanging curtain painted flatly with the symbols of the mountains. And then, suddenly almost, with the passing of a cloud, or when the sun had declined to a certain level in the sky, the flat scene transformed itself; and where there had been only a painted curtain, now there were ranges behind ranges of hills, graduated tone after tone from brown, or gray, or a green gold to faraway blue. Shapes that a moment before had been fused together indiscriminately into a single mass now came apart into their constituents. Fiesole, which had seemed only a spur of Monte Morello, now revealed itself as the jutting headland of another system of hills, divided from the nearest bastions of its greater neighbor by a deep and shadowy valley.

At noon, during the heats of summer, the landscape became dim, powdery, vague and almost colorless under the midday sun; the hills disappeared into the trembling fringes of the sky. But as the afternoon wore on the landscape emerged again, it dropped its anonymity, it climbed back out of nothingness into form and life. And its life, as the sun sank and slowly sank through the long afternoon, grew richer, grew more intense with every moment. The level light, with its attendant long, dark shadows, laid bare, so to speak, the anatomy of the land; the hills —each western escarpment shining, and each slope averted from the sunlight profoundly shadowed—became massive, jutty, and solid. Little folds of dimples in the seemingly even ground revealed themselves. Eastward from our hilltop, across the plain of the Ema, a great bluff casts its ever-increasing shadow; in the surrounding brightness of the valley a whole town lay eclipsed within it. And as the sun expired on the horizon, the further hills flushed in its warm light, till their illumined flanks were the color of tawny roses; but the valleys were already filled with the blue mist of the evening. And it mounted, mounted; the fire went out of the western windows of the populous slopes; only the crests were still alight, and at last they too were all extinct. The mountains faded and fused together again into a flat painting of mountains against the pale evening sky. In a little while it was night; and if the moon were full, a ghost of the dead scene still haunted the horizons.

Changed in its beauty, this wide landscape always preserved a quality of humanness and domestication which made it, to my mind at any rate, the best of all landscapes to live with. Day by day one traveled through its different beauties; but the journey, like our ancestors' Grand Tour, was always a journey through civilization. For all its mountains, its deep slopes and deep valleys, the Tuscan scene is dominated by its inhabitants. They have cultivated every rood of ground that can be cultivated; their houses are thickly scattered even over the hills, and the valleys are populous. Solitary on the hilltop, one is not alone in a wilderness. Man's traces are across the country, and already—one feels it with satisfaction as one looks out across it—for centuries, for thousands of years; it has been his, sub-missive, tamed, and humanized. The wide, blank moorlands, the sands, the forests of innumerable trees—these are places for occasional visitation, healthful to the spirit which submits itself to them for not too long. But fiendish influences as well as divine haunt these total solitudes. The vegetative life of plants and things is alien and hostile to the human. Men cannot live at ease except where they have mastered their surroundings and where their accumulated lives outnumber and outweigh the vegetative lives about them. Stripped of its dark wood, planted, terraced and tilled almost to the mountains' tops, the Tuscan landscape is humanized and safe. Sometimes upon those who live in the midst of it there comes a longing for some place that is solitary, inhuman, lifeless, or peopled only with alien life. But the longing is soon satisfied, and one is glad to return to the civilized and submissive scene.

I found that house on the hilltop the ideal dwelling place. For there, safe in the midst of a humanized landscape, one was yet alone; one could be as solitary as one liked. Neighbors whom one never sees at close quarters are the ideal and perfect neighbors.

Our nearest neighbors, in terms of physical proximity, lived very near. We had two sets of them, as a matter of fact, almost in the same house with us. One was the peasant family, who lived in a long, low building, part dwelling house, part stables, storerooms and cow sheds, adjoining the villa. Our other neighbors—intermittent neighbors, however, for they only ventured out of town every now and then, during the most flawless weather—were the owners of the villa, who had reserved for themselves the smaller wing of the huge L-shaped house—a mere dozen rooms or so—leaving the remaining eighteen or twenty to us.

They were a curious couple, our proprietors. An old husband, gray, listless, tottering, seventy at least; and a signora of about forty, short, very plump, with tiny fat hands and feet and a pair of very large, very dark black eyes, which she used with all the skill of a born comedian. Her vitality, if you could have harnessed it and made it do some useful work, would have supplied a whole town with electric light. The physicists talk of deriving energy from the atom; they would be more profitably employed nearer home—in discovering some way of tapping those enormous stores of vital energy which accumulate in unemployed women of sanguine temperament and which, in the present imperfect state of social and scientific organization, vent themselves in ways that are generally so deplorable in interfering with other people's affairs, in working up emotional scenes, in thinking about love and making it, and in bothering men till they cannot get on with their work.

Signora Bondi got rid of her superfluous energy, among other ways, by "doing in" her tenants. The old gentleman, who was a retired merchant with a reputation for the most perfect rectitude, was allowed to have no dealings with us. When we came to see the house, it was the wife who showed us round. It was she who, with a lavish display of charm, with irresistible rollings of the eyes, expatiated on the merits of the place, sang the praises of the electric pump, glorified the bathroom (considering which, she insisted, the rent was remarkably moderate), and when we suggested calling in a sur-

veyor to look over the house, earnestly begged us, as though our well-being were her only consideration, not to waste our money unnecessarily in doing anything so superfluous. "After all," she said, "we are honest people. I wouldn't dream of letting you the house except in perfect condition. Have confidence." And she looked at me with an appealing, pained expression in her magnificent eyes, as though begging me not to insult her by my coarse suspiciousness. And leaving us no time to pursue the subject of surveyors any further, she began assuring us that our little boy was the most beautiful angel she had ever seen. By the time our interview with Signora Bondi was at an end, we had definitely decided to take the house.

"Charming woman," I said, as we left the house. But I think that Elizabeth was not quite so certain of it as I.

Then the pump episode began.

On the evening of our arrival in the house we switched on the electricity. The pump made a very professional whirring noise; but no water came out of the taps in the bathroom. We looked at one another doubtfully.

"Charming woman?" Elizabeth raised her eyebrows.

We asked for interviews; but somehow the old gentleman could never see us, and the Signora was invariably out or indisposed. We left notes; they were never answered. In the end, we found that the only method of communicating with our landlords, who were living in the same house with us, was to go down into Florence and send a registered express letter to them. For this they had to sign two separate receipts and even, if we chose to pay forty centimes more, a third incriminating document, which was then returned to us. There could be no pretending, as there always was with ordinary letters or notes, that the communication had never been received. We began at last to get answers to our complaints. The Signora, who wrote all the letters, started by telling us that, naturally, the pump didn't work, as the cisterns were empty, owing to the long drought. I had to walk three miles to the post office in order to register my letter reminding her that there had been a violent thunderstorm only last Wednesday, and that the tanks were consequently more than half full. The answer came back: bath water had not been guaranteed in the contract; and if I wanted it, why hadn't I had the pump looked at before I took the house? Another walk into town to ask the Signora next door whether she remembered her adjurations to us to have confidence in her, and to inform her, that the existence in a house of a bathroom was in itself an implicit guarantee of bath water. The reply to that was that the Signora couldn't continue to have communications with people who wrote so rudely to her. After that I put the matter into the hands of a lawyer. Two months later the pump was actually replaced. But we had to serve a writ on the lady before she gave in. And the costs were considerable.

One day, towards the end of the episode, I met the old gentleman in the road, taking his big Maremman dog for a walk—or being taken, rather, for a walk by the dog. For where the dog pulled the old gentleman had perforce to follow. And when it stopped to smell, or scratch the ground, or leave against a gatepost its visiting card or an offensive challenge, patiently, at his end of the

leash, the old man had to wait. I passed him standing at the side of the road, a few hundred yards below our house. The dog was sniffing at the roots of one of the twin cypresses which grew one on either side of the entry to a farm; I heard the beast growling indignantly to itself, as though it scented an intolerable insult. Old Signor Bondi, leashed to his dog, was waiting. The knees inside the tubular gray trousers were slightly bent. Leaning on his cane, he stood gazing mournfully and vacantly at the view. The whites of his old eyes were discolored, like ancient billiard balls. In the gray, deeply wrinkled face, his nose was dyspeptically red. His white mustache, ragged and yellowing at the fringes, drooped in a melancholy curve. In his black tie he wore a very large diamond; perhaps that was what Signora Bondi had found so attractive about him.

I took off my hat as I approached. The old man stared at me absently, and it was only when I was already almost past him that he recollected who I was.

"Wait," he called after me, "wait!" And he hastened down the road in pursuit. Taken utterly by surprise and at a disadvantage—for it was engaged in retorting to the affront imprinted on the cypress roots—the dog permitted itself to be jerked after him. Too much astonished to be anything but obedient, it followed its master. "Wait!"

I waited.

"My dear sir," said the old gentleman, catching me by the lapel of my coat and blowing most disagreeably in my face, "I want to apologize." He looked around him, as though afraid that even here he might be overheard. "I want to apologize," he went on, "about the wretched pump business. I assure you that, if it had been only my affair, I'd have put the thing right as soon as you asked. You were quite right: a bathroom is an implicit guarantee of bath water. I saw from the first that we should have no chance if it came to court. And besides, I think one ought to treat one's tenants as handsomely as one can afford to. But my wife"—he lowered his voice—"the fact is that she likes this sort of thing, even when she knows that she's in the wrong and must lose. And besides, she hoped, I dare say, that you'd get tired of asking and have the job done yourself. I told her from the first that we ought to give in; but she wouldn't listen. You see, she enjoys it. Still, now she sees that it must be done. In the course of the next two or three days you'll be having your bath water. But I thought I'd just like to tell you how . . ." But the Maremmano, which had recovered by this time from its surprise of a moment since, suddenly bounded, growling, up the road. The old gentleman tried to hold the beast, strained at the leash, tottered unsteadily, then gave way and allowed himself to be dragged off. ". . . how sorry I am," he went on, as he receded from me, "that this little misunderstanding . . ." But it was no use. "Good-by." He smiled politely, made a little deprecating gesture, as though he had suddenly remembered a pressing engagement, and had no time to explain what it was. "Good-by." He took off his hat and abandoned himself completely to the dog.

A week later the water really did begin to flow, and the day after our first bath Signora Bondi, dressed in dove-gray satin and wearing all her pearls, came to call.

"Is it peace now?" she asked, with a charming frankness, as she shook hands.

We assured her that, so far as we were concerned, it certainly was.

"But why did you write me such dreadfully rude letters?" she said, turning on me a reproachful glance that ought to have moved the most ruthless malefactor to contrition. "And then that writ. How could you? To a lady . . ."

I mumbled something about the pump and our wanting baths.

"But how could you expect me to listen to you while you were in that mood? Why didn't you set about it differently—politely, charmingly?" She smiled at me and dropped her fluttering eyelids.

I thought it best to change the conversation. It is disagreeable, when one is in the right, to be made to appear in the wrong.

A few weeks later we had a letter —duly registered and by express messenger—in which the Signora asked us whether we proposed to renew our lease (which was only for six months), and notifying us that, if we did, the rent would be raised twenty-five per cent, in consideration of the improvements which had been carried out. We thought ourselves lucky, at the end of much bargaining, to get the lease renewed for a whole year with an increase in the rent of only fifteen per cent.

It was chiefly for the sake of the view that we put up with these intolerable extortions. But we had found other reasons, after a few days' residence, for liking the house. Of these the most cogent was that, in the peasant's youngest child, we had discovered what seemed the perfect playfellow for our own small boy. Between little Guido—for that was his name—and the youngest of his brothers and sisters there was a gap of six or seven years. His two older brothers worked with their father in the fields; since the time of the mother's death, two or three years before we knew them, the eldest sister had ruled the house, and the younger, who had just left school, helped her and in betweenwhiles kept an eye on Guido, who by this time, however, needed very looking after; for he was between six and seven years old and as precocious, self-assured, and responsible as the children of the poor, left as they are to themselves almost from the time they can walk, generally are.

Though fully two and a half years older than little Robin—and at that age thirty months are crammed with half a lifetime's experience—Guido took no undue advantage of his superior intelligence and strength. I have never seen a child more patient, tolerant, and untyrannical. He never laughed at Robin for his clumsy efforts to imitate his own prodigious feats; he did not tease or bully, but helped his small companion when he was in difficulties and explained when he could not understand. In return, Robin adored him, regarded him as the model and perfect Big Boy, and slavishly imitated him in every way he could.

These attempts of Robin's to imitate his companion were often exceedingly ludicrous. For by an obscure psychological law, words and actions in themselves quite serious become comic as soon as they are copied; and the more accurately, if the imitation is a deliberate parody, the funnier—for an overloaded imitation of someone we know does not make us laugh so much as one that is almost indistinguishably like the original. The bad imitation is only ludicrous when it is a piece of sincere and earnest flattery which

does not quite come off. Robin's imitations were mostly of this kind. His heroic and unsuccessful attempts to perform the feats of strength and skill, which Guido could do with ease, were exquisitely comic. And his careful, long-drawn imitations of Guido's habits and mannerisms were no less amusing. Most ludicrous of all, because most earnestly undertaken and most incongruous in the imitator, were Robin's impersonations of Guido in a pensive mood. Guido was a thoughtful child given to brooding and sudden abstractions. One would find him sitting in a corner by himself, chin in hand, elbow on knee, plunged, to all appearances, in the profoundest meditation. And sometimes, even in the midst of his play, he would suddenly break off, to stand, his hands behind his back, frowning and staring at the ground. When this happened, Robin became overawed and a little disquieted. In a puzzled silence he looked at his companion. "Guido," he would say softly, "Guido." But Guido was generally too much preoccupied to answer; and Robin, not venturing to insist, would creep near him, and throwing himself as nearly as possible into Guido's attitude—standing Napoleonically, his hands clasped behind him, or sitting in the posture of Michelangelo's Lorenzo the Magnificent—would try to meditate too. Every few seconds he would turn his bright blue eyes towards the elder child to see whether he was doing it quite right. But at the end of a minute he began to grow impatient; meditation wasn't his strong point. "Guido," he called again and, louder, "Guido!" And he would take him by the hand and try to pull him away. Sometimes Guido roused himself from his reverie and went back to the interrupted game. Sometimes he paid no attention. Melancholy, perplexed, Robin had to take himself off to play by himself. And Guido would go on sitting or standing there, quite still; and his eyes, if one looked into them, were beautiful in their grave and pensive calm.

They were large eyes, set far apart and, what was strange in a dark-haired Italian child, of a luminous pale blue-gray color. They were not always grave and calm, as in these pensive moments. When he was playing, when he talked or laughed, they lit up; and the surface of those clear, pale lakes of thought seemed, as it were, to be shaken into brilliant sun-flashing ripples. Above those eyes was a beautiful forehead, high and steep and domed in a curve that was like a subtle curve of a rose petal. The nose was straight, the chin small and rather pointed, the mouth drooped a little sadly at the corners.

I have a snapshot of the two children sitting together on the parapet of the terrace. Guido sits almost facing the camera, but looking a little to one side and downwards; his hands are crossed in his lap and his expression, his attitude are thoughtful, grave, and meditative. It is Guido in one of those moods of abstraction into which he would pass even at the height of laughter and play—quite suddenly and completely, as though he had all at once taken it into his head to go away and left the silent and beautiful body behind, like an empty house, to wait for his return. And by its side sits little Robin, turning to look up at him, his face half averted from the camera, but the curve of his cheek showing that he is laughing; one little raised hand is caught at the top of a gesture, the other clutches

at Guido's sleeves, as though he were urging him to come away and play. And the legs dangling from the parapet have been seen by the blinking instrument in the midst of an impatient wriggle; he is on the point of slipping down and running off to play hide-and-seek in the garden. All the essential characteristics of both the children are in that little snapshot.

"If Robin were not Robin," Elizabeth used to say, "I could almost wish he were Guido."

And even at that time, when I took no particular interest in the child, I agreed with her. Guido seemed to me one of the most charming little boys I had ever seen.

We were not alone in admiring him. Signora Bondi when, in those cordial intervals between our quarrels, she came to call, was constantly speaking of him. "Such a beautiful, beautiful child!" she would exclaim with enthusiasm. "It's really a waste that he should belong to peasants who can't afford to dress him properly. If he were mine, I should put him into black velvet; or little white knickers and a white knitted silk jersey with a red line at the collar and cuffs; or perhaps a white sailor suit would be pretty. And in winter a little fur coat, with a squirrelskin cap, and possibly Russian boots . . ." Her imagination was running away with her. "And I'd let his hair grow, like a page's, and have it just curled up a little at the tips. And a straight fringe across his forehead. Everyone would turn round and stare after us if I took him out with me in Via Tornabuoni."

What you want, I should have liked to tell her, is not a child; it's a clockwork doll or a performing monkey. But I did not say so—partly because I could not think of the

Italian for a clockwork doll and partly because I did not want to risk having the rent raised another fifteen per cent.

"Ah, if I only had a little boy like that!" She sighed and modestly dropped her eyelids. "I adore children. I sometimes think of adopting one—that is, if my husband would allow it."

I thought of the poor old gentleman being dragged along at the heels of his big white dog and inwardly smiled.

"But I don't know if he would," the signora was continuing, "I don't know if he would." She was silent for a moment, as though considering a new idea.

A few days later, when we were sitting in the garden after luncheon, drinking our coffee, Guido's father instead of passing with a nod and the usual cheerful good day, halted in front of us and began to talk. He was a fine handsome man, not very tall, but well proportioned, quick and elastic in his movements, and full of life. He had a thin brown face, featured like a Roman's and lit by a pair of the most intelligent-looking gray eyes I ever saw. They exhibited almost too much intelligence when, as not infrequently happened, he was trying, with an assumption of perfect frankness and a childlike innocence, to take one in or get something out of one. Delighting in itself, the intelligence shone there mischievously. The face might be ingenuous, impassive, almost imbecile in its expression; but the eyes on these occasions gave him completely away. One knew, when they glittered like that, that one would have to be careful.

Today, however, there was no dangerous light in them. He wanted nothing out of us, nothing of any value—only advice, which is a commodity, he knew, that most people are only too happy to part with. But he wanted advice on what was, for us, rather a delicate subject: on Signora Bondi. Carlo had often complained to us about her. The old man is good, he told us, very good and kind indeed. Which meant, I dare say, among other things, that he could easily be swindled. But his wife. . . . Well, the woman was a beast. And he would tell us stories of her insatiable rapacity: she was always claiming more than the half of the produce which, by the laws of the *métayage* systems, was the proprietor's due. He complained of her suspiciousness: she was forever accusing him of sharp practices, of downright stealing—him, he struck his breast, the soul of honesty. He complained of her shortsighted avarice: she wouldn't spend enough on manure, wouldn't buy him another cow, wouldn't have electric light installed in the stables. And we had sympathized, but cautiously, without expressing too strong an opinion on the subject. The Italians are wonderfully noncommittal in their speech; they will give nothing away to an interested person until they are quite certain that it is right and necessary and, above all, safe to do so. We had lived long enough among them to imitate their caution. What we said to Carlo would be sure, sooner or later, to get back to Signora Bondi. There was nothing to be gained by unnecessarily embittering our relations with the lady—only another fifteen per cent, very likely, to be lost.

Today he wasn't so much complaining as feeling perplexed. The Signora had sent for him, it seemed, and asked him how he would like it if she were to make an offer—it was all very hypothetical in the cautious Italian style—to adopt little Guido. Carlo's first instinct had been to say that he wouldn't like it at all. But an answer like that would have been too coarsely committal. He had preferred to say that he would think about it. And now he was asking for our advice.

Do what you think best, was what in effect we replied. But we gave it distantly but distinctly to be understood that we didn't think that Signora Bondi would make a very good foster mother for the child. And Carlo was inclined to agree. Besides he was very fond of the boy.

"But the thing is," he concluded rather gloomily, "that if she has really set her heart on getting hold of the child, there's nothing she won't do to get him—nothing."

He too, I could see, would have liked the physicists to start on unemployed childless women of sanguine temperament before they tried to tackle the atom. Still, I reflected, as I watched him striding away along the terrace, singing powerfully from a brazen gullet as he went, there was force there, there was life enough in those elastic limbs, behind those bright gray eyes, to put up a good fight even against the accumulated vital energies of Signora Bondi.

It was a few days after this that my gramophone and two or three boxes of records arrived from England. They were a great comfort to us on the hilltop, providing as they did the only thing in which that spiritually fertile solitude—otherwise a perfect Swiss Family Robinson's island—was lacking: music. There is not much music to be heard nowadays in Florence. The times when Dr. Burney could tour through Italy, listening to an unending succession of new operas, symphonies, quartets, cantatas, are gone. Gone are the days when a learned musician, inferior only to the Reverend Father Martini of Bologna, could admire what the peasants sang and the strolling players thrummed and scraped on their instruments. I have traveled for weeks through the peninsula and hardly heard a note that was not *Salome* or the Fascists' song. Rich in nothing else that makes life agreeable or even supportable, the northern metropolises are rich in music. That is perhaps the only inducement that a reasonable man can find for living there. The other attractions—organized gaiety, people, miscellaneous conversation, the social pleasures—what are those, after all, but an expense of spirit that buys nothing in return? And then the cold, the darkness, the moldering dirt, the damp and squalor. . . . No, where there is no necessity that retains, music can be the only inducement. And that, thanks to the ingenious Edison, can now be taken about in a box and unpacked in whatever solitude one chooses to visit. One can live at Benin, or Nuneaton, or Tozeur in the Sahara, and still hear Mozart quartets, and selections from *The Well-Tempered Clavichord*, and the Fifth Symphony, and the Brahms clarinet quintet, and motets by Palestrina.

Carlo, who had gone down to the station with his mule and cart to fetch the packing case, was vastly interested in the machine.

"One will hear some music again," he said, as he watched me unpacking the gramophone and the disks. "It is difficult to do much oneself."

Still, I reflected, he managed to do a good deal. On warm nights we used to hear him, where he sat at the door of his house, playing his guitar and softly singing; the eldest boy shrilled out the melody on the mandolin and sometimes the whole family would join in, and the darkness would be filled with their passionate, throaty singing. Piedigrotta songs they mostly sang; and the voices drooped slurringly from note to note, lazily climbed or jerked themselves with sudden sobbing emphases from one tone to another. At a distance and under the stars the effect was not unpleasing.

"Before the war," he went on, "in normal times" (and Carlo had a hope, even a belief, that the normal times were coming back and that life would soon be as cheap and easy as it had been in the days before the flood), "I used to go and listen to the operas at the Politeama. Ah, they were magnificent. But it costs five lire now to get in."

"Too much," I agreed.

"Have you got *Trovatore?*" he asked.

I shook my head.

"*Rigoletto?*"

"I'm afraid not."

"*Bohème? Fanciulla del West? Pagliacci?*"

I had to go on disappointing him.

"Not even *Norma?* Or the *Barbiere?*"

I put on Battistini in "*Là ci darem*" out of *Don Giovanni*. He agreed that the singing was good; but I could see that he didn't much like the music, Why not? He found it difficult to explain.

"It's not like *Pagliacci,*" he said at last.

"Not palpitating?" I suggested, using a word with which I was sure he would be familiar; for it occurs in every Italian political speech and patriotic leading article.

"Not palpitating," he agreed.

And I reflected that it is precisely by the difference between *Pagliacci* and *Don Giovanni*, between the palpitating and the nonpalpitating, that modern music taste is separated from the old. The corruption of the best, I thought, is the worst. Beethoven taught music to palpitate with his intellectual and spiritual passion. It has gone on palpitating ever since, but with the passion of inferior men. Indirectly, I thought, Beethoven is responsible for *Parsifal, Pagliacci,* and the *Poem of Fire*; still more indirectly for *Samson and Delilah* and "Ivy, cling to me." Mozart's melodies may be brilliant, memorable, infectious; but they don't palpitate, don't catch you between wind and water, don't send the listener off into erotic ecstasies.

Carlo and his elder children found my gramophone, I am afraid, rather a disappointment. They were too polite, however, to say so openly; they merely ceased, after the first day or two, to take any interest in the machine and the music it played. They preferred the guitar and their own singing.

Guido, on the other hand, was immensely interested. And he liked, not the cheerful dance tunes, to whose sharp rhythms our little Robin loved to go stamping round and round the room, pretending that he was a whole regiment of soldiers, but the genuine stuff. The first record he heard, I remember, was that of the slow movement of Bach's Concerto in D Minor for two violins. That was the disk I put on the turntable as soon as Carlo had left me. It seemed to me, so to speak, the most musical piece of music with which I would refresh my long-parched mind—the coolest and clearest of all draughts. The movement had just got under way and was beginning to unfold its pure and melancholy beauties in accordance with the laws of the most exacting intellectual logic, when the two children, Guido in front and little Robin breathlessly following, came clattering into the room from the loggia.

Guido came to a halt in front of the gramophone and stood there, motionless, listening. His pale blue-gray eyes opened themselves wide; making a little nervous gesture that I had often noticed in him before, he plucked at his lower lip with his thumb and forefinger. He must have taken a deep breath; for I noticed that, after listening for a few seconds, he sharply expired and drew in a fresh gulp of air. For an instant he looked at me—a questioning, astonished, rapturous look—gave a little laugh that ended in a kind of nervous shudder, and turned back towards the source of the incredible sounds. Slavishly imitating his elder comrade, Robin had also taken up his stand in front of the gramophone, and in exactly the same position, glancing at Guido from time to time to make sure that he was doing everything, down to plucking at his lip, in the correct way. But after a minute or so he became bored.

"Soldiers," he said, turning to me; "I want soldiers. Like in London." He remembered the ragtime and the jolly marches round and round the room.

I put my fingers to my lips. "Afterwards," I whispered.

Robin managed to remain silent and still for perhaps another twenty seconds. Then he seized Guido by the arm, shouting, *"Vieni,* Guido! Soldiers. *Soldati. Vieni giuocare soldati."*

It was then, for the first time, that I saw Guido impatient. *"Vai!"* he whispered angrily, slapped at Robin's clutching hand and pushed him

roughly away. And he leaned a little closer to the instrument, as though to make up by yet intenser listening for what the interruption had caused him to miss.

Robin looked at him, astonished. Such a thing had never happened before. Then he burst out crying and came to me for consolation.

When the quarrel was made up—and Guido was sincerely repentant, was as nice as he knew how to be when the music had stopped and his mind was free to think of Robin once more—I asked him how he liked the music. He said he thought it was beautiful. But *bello* in Italian is too vague a word, too easily and frequently uttered, to mean very much.

"What did you like best?" I insisted. For he had seemed to enjoy it so much that I was curious to find out what had really impressed him.

He was silent for a moment, pensively frowning. "Well," he said at last, "I liked the bit that went like this." And he hummed a long phrase. "And then there's the other thing singing at the same time—but what are those things," he interrupted himself, "that sing like that?"

"They're called violins," I said.

"Violins." He nodded. "Well, the other violin goes like this." He hummed again. "Why can't one sing both at once? And what is in that box? What makes it make that noise?" The child poured out his questions.

I answered him as best I could, showing him the little spirals on the disk, the needle, the diaphragm. I told him to remember how the string of the guitar trembled when one plucked it; sound is a shaking in the air, I told him, and I tried to explain how those shakings get printed on the black disk. Guido listened to me very gravely, nodding from time to time. I had the impression that he understood perfectly well everything I was saying.

By this time, however, poor Robin was so dreadfully bored that in pity for him I had to send the two children out into the garden to play. Guido went obediently; but I could see that he would have preferred to stay indoors and listen to more music. A little while later, when I looked out, he was hiding in the dark recesses of the big bay tree, roaring like a lion, and Robin laughing, but a little nervously, as though he were afraid that the horrible noise might possibly turn out, after all, to be the roaring of a real lion, was beating the bush with a stick, and shouting, "Come out, come out! I want to shoot you."

After lunch, when Robin had gone upstairs for his afternoon sleep, he reappeared. "May I listen to music now?" he asked. And for an hour he sat there in front of the instrument, his head cocked slightly on one side, listening while I put on one disk after another.

Thenceforward he came every afternoon. Very soon he knew all my library of records, had his preferences and dislikes, and could ask for what he wanted by humming the principal theme.

"I don't like that one," he said of Strauss's *Till Eulenspiegel.* "It's like what we sing in our house. Not really like, you know. But somehow rather like, all the same. You understand?" He looked at us perplexedly and appealingly, as though begging us to understand what he meant and so save him from going on explaining. We nodded. Guido went on. "And then," he said, "the end doesn't seem to come properly out of the beginning. It's not like the one you

played the first time." He hummed a bar or two from the slow movement of Bach's D Minor Concerto.

"It isn't," I suggested, "like saying: All little boys like playing. Guido is a little boy. Therefore Guido likes playing."

He frowned. "Yes, perhaps that's it," he said at last. "The one you played first is more like that. But, you know," he added, with an excessive regard for truth, "I don't like playing as much as Robin does."

Wagner was among his dislikes; so was Debussy. When I played the record of one of Debussy's arabesques, he said, "Why does he say the same thing over and over again? He ought to say something new, or go on, or make the thing grow. Can't he think of anything different?" But he was less censorious about the *Après-midi d'un faune.* "The things have beautiful voices," he said.

Mozart overwhelmed him with delight. The duet from *Don Giovanni,* which his father had found insufficiently palpitating, enchanted Guido. But he preferred the quartets and the orchestral pieces.

"I like music," he said, "better than singing."

Most people, I reflected, like singing better than music; are more interested in the executant than in what he executes, and find the impersonal orchestra less moving than the soloist. The touch of the pianist is the human touch, and the soprano's high C is the personal note. It is for the sake of this touch, that note, that audiences fill the concert halls.

Guido, however, preferred music. True, he liked *"Là ci darem";* he liked *"Deh vieni alla finestra";* he thought *"Che soave zefiretto"* so lovely that almost all our concerts had to begin with it. But he preferred the other things. The *Figaro* overture was one of his favorites. There is a passage not far from the beginning of the piece, when the first violins suddenly go rocketing up into the heights of loveliness; as the music approached that point, I used always to see a smile developing and gradually brightening on Guido's face, and when, punctually, the thing happened, he clapped his hands and laughed aloud with pleasure.

On the other side of the same disk, it happened, was recorded Beethoven's *Egmont* overture. He liked that almost better than *Figaro*. "It has more voices," he explained. And I was delighted by the acuteness of the criticism; for it is precisely in the richness of its orchestration that *Egmont* goes beyond *Figaro*.

But what stirred him almost more than anything was the *Coriolan* overture. The third movement of the Fifth Symphony, the second movement of the Seventh, the slow movement of the Emperor Concerto—all these things ran it pretty close. But none excited him so much as *Coriolan*. One day he made me play it three or four times in succession; then he put it away.

"I don't think I want to hear that any more," he said.

"Why not?"

"It's too . . . too . . ." he hesitated, "too big," he said at last. "I don't really understand it. Play me the one that goes like this." He hummed the phrase from the D Minor Concerto.

"Do you like that one better?" I asked.

He shook his head. "No, it's not that exactly. But it's easier."

"Easier?" It seemed to me rather a queer word to apply to Bach.

"I understand it better."

One afternoon, while we were in the middle of our concert, Signora Bondi was ushered in. She began at once to be overwhelmingly affectionate towards the child; kissed him, patted his head, paid him the most outrageous compliments on his appearance. Guido edged away from her.

"And do you like music?" she asked.

The child nodded.

"I think he has a gift," I said. "At any rate, he has a wonderful ear and a power of listening and criticizing such as I've never met with in a child of that age. We're thinking of hiring a piano for him to learn on."

A moment later I was cursing myself for my undue frankness in praising the boy. For Signora Bondi began immediately to protest that, if she could have the upbringing of the child, she would give him the best masters, bring out his talent, make an accomplished maestro of him—and, on the way, an infant prodigy. And at that moment, I am sure, she saw herself sitting maternally, in pearls and black satin, in the lea of the huge Steinway, while an angelic Guido, dressed like little Lord Fauntleroy, rattled out Liszt and Chopin to the loud delight of a thronged auditorium. She saw the bouquets and all the elaborate floral tributes, heard the clapping and the few well-chosen words with which the veteran maestri, touched almost to tears, would hail the coming of the little genius. It became more than ever important for her to acquire the child.

"You've sent her away fairly ravening," said Elizabeth, when Signora Bondi had gone. "Better tell her next time that you made a mistake, and that the boy's got no musical talent whatever."

In due course a piano arrived. After giving him the minimum of preliminary instruction, I let Guido loose on it. He began by picking out for himself, the melodies he had heard, reconstructing the harmonies in which they were embedded. After a few lessons, he understood the rudiments of musical notation and could read a simple passage at sight, albeit very slowly. The whole process of reading was still strange to him; he had picked up his letters somehow, but nobody had yet taught him to read whole words and sentences.

I took occasion, next time I saw Signora Bondi, to assure her that Guido had disappointed me. There was nothing in his musical talent, really. She professed to be very sorry to hear it; but I could see that she didn't for a moment believe me. Probably she thought that we were after the child too, and wanted to bag the infant prodigy for ourselves, before she could get in her claim, thus depriving her of what she regarded almost as her feudal right. For, after all, weren't they her peasants? If anyone was to profit by adopting the child it ought to be herself.

Tactfully, diplomatically, she renewed her negotiations with Carlo. The boy, she put it to him, had genius. It was the foreign gentleman who had told her so, and he was the sort of man, clearly, who knew about such things. If Carlo would let her adopt the child, she'd have him trained. He'd become a great maestro and get engagements in the Argentine and the United States, in Paris and London. He'd earn millions and millions. Think of Caruso, for example. Part of the millions, she

explained, would of course come to Carlo. But before they began to roll in, those millions, the boy would have to be trained. But training was very expensive. In his own interest, as well as that of his son, he ought to let her take charge of the child. Carlo said he would think it over, and again applied to us for advice. We suggested that it would be best in any case to wait a little and see what progress the boy made.

He made, in spite of my assertions to Signora Bondi, excellent progress. Every afternoon, while Robin was asleep, he came for his concert and his lesson. He was getting along famously with his reading; his small fingers were acquiring strength and agility. But what to me was more interesting was that he had begun to make up little pieces on his own account. A few of them I took down as he played them and I have them still. Most of them, strangely enough, as I thought then, are canons. He had a passion for canons. When I explained to him the principles of the form he was enchanted.

"It is beautiful," he said, with admiration. "Beautiful, beautiful. And so easy!"

Again the word surprised me. The canon is not, after all, so conspicuously simple. Thenceforward he spent most of his time at the piano in working out little canons for his own amusement. They were often remarkably ingenious. But in the invention of other kinds of music he did not show himself so fertile as I had hoped. He composed and harmonized one or two solemn little airs like hymn tunes, with a few sprightlier pieces in the spirit of the military march. They were extraordinary, of course, as being the inventions of a child. But a great many children can do extraordinary things;

we are all geniuses up to the age of ten. But I had hoped that Guido was a child who was going to be a genius at forty; in which case what was extraordinary for an ordinary child was not extraordinary enough for him. "He's hardly a Mozart," we agreed, as we played his little pieces over. I felt, it must be confessed, almost aggrieved. Anything less than a Mozart, it seemed to me, was hardly worth thinking about.

He was not a Mozart. No. But he was somebody, as I was to find out, quite as extraordinary. It was one morning in the early summer that I made the discovery. I was sitting in the warm shade of our westward-facing balcony, working. Guido and Robin were playing in the little enclosed garden below. Absorbed in my work, it was only, I suppose, after the silence had prolonged itself a considerable time that I became aware that the children were making remarkably little noise. There was no shouting, no running about; only a quiet talking. Knowing by experience that when children are quiet it generally means that they are absorbed in some delicious mischief, I got up from my chair and looked over the balustrade to see what they were doing. I expected to catch them dabbling in water, making a bonfire, covering themselves with tar. But what I actually saw was Guido, with a burnt stick in his hand, demonstrating on the smooth paving stones of the path, that the square on the hypotenuse of a right-angled triangle is equal to the sum of the squares on the other two sides.

Kneeling on the floor, he was drawing with the point of his blackened stick on the flagstones. And Robin, kneeling imitatively beside him, was growing, I could

see, rather impatient with this very slow game.

"Guido," he said. But Guido paid no attention. Pensively frowning, he went on with his diagram. "Guido!" The younger child bent down and then craned round his neck so as to look up into Guido's face. "Why don't you draw a train?"

"Afterwards," said Guido. "But I just want to show you this first. It's *so* beautiful," he added cajolingly.

"But I want a train," Robin persisted.

"In a moment. Do just wait a moment." The tone was almost imploring. Robin armed himself with renewed patience. A minute later Guido had finished both his diagrams.

"There!" he said triumphantly, and straightened himself up to look at them. "Now I'll explain."

And he proceded to prove the theorem of Pythagoras—not in Euclid's way, but by the simpler and more satisfying method which was, in all probability, employed by Pythagoras himself. He had drawn a square and dissected it, by a pair of crossed perpendiculars, into two squares and two equal rectangles. The equal rectangles he divided up by their diagonals into four equal right-angled triangles. The two squares are then seen to be the squares on the two sides of any of these triangles other than the hypotenuse. So much for the first diagram. In the next he took the four right-angled triangles into which the rectangles had been divided and rearranged them round the original square so that their right angles filled the corners of the square, the hypotenuses looked inwards, and the greater and less sides of the triangles were in continuation along the sides of the squares (which are each equal to the sum of these sides). In this way the original square is redissected into four right-angled triangles and the square on the hypotenuse. The four triangles are equal to the two rectangles of the original dissection. Therefore the square on the hypotenuse is equal to the sum of the two squares—the squares on the two other sides—into which, with the rectangles, the original square was first dissected.

In very untechnical language, but clearly and with a relentless logic, Guido expounded his proof. Robin listened, with an expression on his bright, freckled face of perfect incomprehension.

"*Treno*," he repeated from time to time. "*Treno*. Make a train."

"In a moment," Guido implored. "Wait a moment. But do just look at this. Do." He coaxed and cajoled. "It's so beautiful. It's so easy."

So easy . . . The theorem of Pythagoras seemed to explain for me Guido's musical predilections. It was not an infant Mozart we had been cherishing; it was a little Archimedes with, like most of his kind, an incidental musical twist.

"*Treno, treno!*" shouted Robin, growing more and more restless as the exposition went on. And when Guido insisted on going on with his proof, he lost his temper. "*Cattivo* Guido," he shouted, and began to hit out at him with his fists.

"All right," said Guido resignedly. "I'll make a train." And with his stick of charcoal he began to scribble on the stones.

I looked on for a moment in silence. It was not a very good train. Guido might be able to invent for himself and prove the theorem of Pythagoras: but he was not much of a draftsman.

"Guido!" I called. The two children turned and looked up. "Who taught you to draw those squares?" It was inconceivable, of course, that somebody might have taught him.

"Nobody." He shook his head. Then, rather anxiously, as though he were afraid there might be something wrong about drawing squares, he went on to apologize and explain. "You see," he said, "it seemed to me so beautiful. Because those squares"—he pointed at the two small squares in the first figure—"are just as big as this one." And, indicating the square on the hypotenuse in the second diagram, he looked up at me with a deprecating smile.

I nodded. "Yes, it's very beautiful," I said—"it's very beautiful indeed."

An expression of delighted relief appeared on his face; he laughed with pleasure. "You see it's like this," he went on, eager to initiate me into the glorious secret he had discovered. "You cut these two long squares"—he meant the rectangles—"into two slices. And then there are four slices, all just the same, because, because—— Oh, I ought to have said that before—because these long squares are the same because those lines, you see . . ."

"But I want a train," protested Robin.

Leaning on the rail of the balcony, I watched the children below. I thought of the extraordinary thing I had just seen and of what it meant.

I thought of the vast differences between human beings. We classify men by the color of their eyes and hair, the shape of their skulls. Would it not be more sensible to divide them up into intellectual species? There would be even wider gulfs between the extreme mental types than between a Bushman and a Scandinavian. This child, I thought, when he grows up, will be to me, intellectually, what a man is to his dog. And there are other men and women who are, perhaps, almost as dogs to me.

Perhaps the men of genius are the only true men. In all the history of the race there have been only a few thousand real men. And the rest of us—what are we? Teachable animals. Without the help of the real man, we should have found out almost nothing at all. Almost all the ideas with which we are familiar could never have occurred to minds like ours. Plant the seeds there and they will grow; but our minds could never spontaneously have generated them.

There have been whole nations of dogs, I thought; whole epochs in which no Man was born. From the dull Egyptians the Greeks took crude experience and rules of thumb and made sciences. More than a thousand years passed before Archimedes had a comparable successor. There has been only one Buddha, one Jesus, only one Bach that we know of, one Michelangelo.

Is it by a mere chance, I wondered, that a Man is born from time to time? What causes a whole constellation of them to come contemporaneously into being and from out of a single people? Taine thought that Leonardo, Michelangelo, and Raphael were born when they were because the time was ripe for great painters and the Italian scene congenial. In the mouth of a rationalizing nineteenth-century Frenchman the doctrine is strangely mystical; it may be none the less true for that. But what of those born out of time? Blake, for example. What of those?

This child, I thought, has had the fortune to be born at a time when he will be able to make good use of his capacities. He will find the most elaborate analytical methods lying ready to his hand; he will have a prodigious experience behind him. Suppose him born while Stonehenge was building; he might have spent a lifetime discovering the rudiments, guessing darkly where now he might have had a chance of proving. Born at the time of the Norman Conquest, he would have had to wrestle with all the preliminary difficulties created by an inadequate symbolism; it would have taken him long years, for example, to learn the art of dividing MMMCCCCLXXXVIII by MCMXIX. In five years, nowadays, he will learn what it took generations of Men to discover.

And I thought of the fate of all the Men born so hopelessly out of time that they could achieve little or nothing of value. Beethoven born in Greece, I thought, would have had to be content to play thin melodies on the flute or lyre; in those intellectual surroundings it would hardly have been possible for him to imagine the nature of harmony.

From drawing trains, the children in the garden below had gone onto playing trains. They were trotting round and round; with blown round cheeks and pouting mouth like the cherubic symbol of a wind, Robin puff-puffed and Guido, holding the skirt of his smoke, shuffled behind him, tooting. They ran forward, backed, stopped at imaginary stations, shunted, roared over bridges, crashed through tunnels, met with occasional collisions and derailments. The young Archimedes seemed to be just as happy as the little towheaded barbarian. A few minutes ago he had been busy with the theorem of Pythagoras. Now, tooting indefatigably along imaginary rails, he was perfectly content to shuffle backwards and forwards among the flower beds, between the pillars of the loggia, in and out of the dark tunnels of the laurel tree. The fact that one is going to be Archimedes does not prevent one from being an ordinary cheerful child meanwhile. I thought of this strange talent distinct and separate from the rest of the mind, independent, almost, of experience. The typical child prodigies are musical and mathematical; the other talents ripen slowly under the influence of emotional experience and growth. Till he was thirty Balzac gave proof of nothing but ineptitude; but at four the young Mozart was already a musician, and some of Pascal's most brilliant work was done before he was out of his teens.

In the weeks that followed, I alternated the daily piano lessons with lessons in mathematics. Hints rather than lessons they were; for I only made suggestions, indicated methods, and left the child himself to work out the ideas in detail. Thus I introduced him to algebra by showing him another proof of the theorem of Pythagoras. In this proof one drops a perpendicular from the right angle on to the hypotenuse, and arguing from the fact that the two triangles thus created are similar to one another and to the original triangle, and that the proportions which their corresponding sides bear to one another are therefore equal, one can show in algebraical form that C^2+D^2 (the squares on the other two sides) are equal to A^2+B^2 (the squares on the two segments of The hypotenuses) $+2AB$; which last, it is easy to show geometrically, is equal to $(A+B)^2$, or the square on the hypotenuse. Guido was as much enchanted by the rudiments of algebra as he would have been if I had given him an engine worked by steam, with a methylated spirit lamp to heat the boiler; more enchanted, perhaps—for the engine would have got broken, and, remaining always itself, would in any case have lost its charm, while the rudiments of algebra continued to grow and blossom in his mind with an unfailing luxuriance. Every day he made the discovery of something which seemed to him exquisitely beautiful; the new toy was inexhaustible in its potentialities.

In the intervals of applying algebra to the second book of Euclid, we experimented with circles; we stuck bamboos into the parched earth, measured their shadows at different hours of the day, and drew exciting conclusions from our observations. Sometimes, for fun, we cut and folded sheets of paper so as to make cubes and pyramids. One afternoon Guido arrived carrying carefully between his small and rather grubby hands a flimsy dodecahedron.

"*E tanto bello!*" he said, as he showed us his paper crystal; and when I asked him how he had managed to make it, he merely smiled and said it had been so easy. I looked at Elizabeth and laughed. But it would have been more symbolically to the point, I felt, if I had gone down on all fours, wagged the spiritual outgrowth of my os coccyx, and barked my astonished admiration.

It was an uncommonly hot summer. By the beginning of July our little Robin, unaccustomed to these high temperatures, began to look pale and tired; he was listless, had lost his appetite and energy. The doctor advised mountain air. We decided to spend the next ten or twelve weeks in Switzerland. My parting gift to Guido was the first six books of Euclid in Italian. He turned over the pages, looking ecstatically at the figures.

"If only I knew how to read properly," he said. "I'm so stupid. But now I shall really try to learn."

From our hotel near Grindelwald we sent the child, in Robin's name, various postcards of cows, alphorns, Swiss chalets, edelweiss, and the like. We received no answers to these cards; but then we did not expect answers. Guido could not write, and there was no reason why his father or his sisters should take the trouble to write for him. No news, we took it, was good news. And then one day, early in September, there arrived at the hotel a strange letter. The manager had it stuck up on the glass-fronted notice board in the hall, so that all the guests might see it, and whoever conscientiously thought that it belonged to him might claim it. Passing the board on the way in to lunch, Elizabeth stopped to look at it.

"But it must be from Guido," she said.

I came and looked at the envelope over her shoulder. It was unstamped and black with postmarks. Traced out in pencil, the big uncertain capital letters sprawled across its face. In the first line was written: AL BABBO DI ROBIN, and there followed a travestied version of the name of the hotel and the place. Round the address bewildered postal officials had scrawled suggested emendations. The letter had wandered for a fortnight at least, back and forth across the face of Europe.

"Al Babbo di Robin. To Robin's father." I laughed. "Pretty smart of the postmen to have got it here at all." I went to the manager's office, set forth the justice of my claim to the letter and, having paid the fifty-centime surcharge for the missing stamp, had the case unlocked and the letter given me. We went in to lunch.

"The writing's magnificent," we agreed, laughing, as we examined the address at close quarters. "Thanks to Euclid," I added. "That's what comes of pandering to the ruling passion."

But when I opened the envelope and looked at its contents I no longer laughed. The letter was brief and almost telegraphic in style. SONO DALLA PADRONA, it ran, NON MI PIACE HA RUBATO IL MIO LIBRO NON VOGLIO SUONARE PIU VOGLIO TORNARE A CASA VENGA SUBITO GUIDO.

"What is it?"

I handed Elizabeth the letter. "That blasted woman's got hold of him," I said.

Busts of men in Homburg hats, angels bathed in marble tears extinguishing torches, statues of little girls, cherubs, veiled figures, allegories and ruthless realisms—the strangest and most diverse idols beckoned and gesticulated as we passed. Printed indelibly on tin and embedded in the living rock, the brown photographs looked out, under glass, from the humbler crosses, headstones, and broken pillars. Dead ladies in cubistic geometrical fashions of thirty years ago —two cones of black satin meeting point to point at the waist, and the arms: a sphere to the elbow, a polished cylinder below—smiled mournfully out of their marble frames; the smiling frames; the smiling faces, the white hands, were the only recognizably human things that emerged from the solid geometry of their clothes. Men with black mustaches, men with white beards, young clean-shaven men, stared or averted their gaze to show a Roman profile. Children in their stiff best opened wide their eyes, smiled hopefully in anticipation of the little bird that was to issue from the camera's muzzle, smiled skeptically in the knowledge that it wouldn't, smiled laboriously and obediently because they had been told to. In spiky Gothic cottages of marble the richer dead reposed; through grilled doors one caught a glimpse of pale Inconsolables weeping, of distraught Geniuses guarding the secret of the tomb. The less prosperous sections of the majority slept in communities, close-crowded but elegantly housed under smooth continuous marble floors, whose every flagstone was the mouth of a separate grave.

These Continental cemeteries, I thought, as Carlo and I made our way among the dead, are more frightful than ours, because these people pay more attention to their dead than we do. That primordial cult of corpses, that tender solicitude for their material well-being, which led the ancients to house their dead in stone, while they themselves lived between wattles and under thatch, still lingers here; persists, I thought, more vigorously than with us. There are a hundred gesticulating statues here for every one in an English graveyard. There are more family vaults, more "luxuriously appointed" (as they say of liners and hotels) than one would find at home. And embedded in every tombstone there are photographs to remind the powdered bones within what form they will have to resume on the Day of Judgment; beside each are little hanging lamps to burn optimistically on All Souls' Day. To the Man who built the Pyramids they are nearer, I thought, than we.

"If I had known," Carlo kept re-peating, "if only I had known." His voice came to me through my reflections as though from a distance. "At the time he didn't mind at all. How should I have known that he would take it so much to heart afterwards? And she deceived me, she lied to me."

I assured him yet once more that it wasn't his fault. Though, of course, it was, in part. It was mine too, in part; I ought to have thought of the possibility and somehow guarded against it. And he shouldn't have let the child go, even temporarily and on trial, even though the woman was bringing pressure to bear on him. And the pressure had been considerable. They had worked on the same holding for more than a hundred years, the men of Carlo's family; and now she had made the old man threaten to turn him out. It would be a dreadful thing to leave the place; and besides, another place wasn't so easy to find. It was made quite plain, however, that he could stay if he let her have the child. Only for a little to begin with; just to see how he got on. There would be no compulsion whatever on him to stay if he didn't like it. And it would be all to Guido's advantage; and to his father's, too, in the end. All that the Englishman had said about his not being such a good musician as he had thought at first was obviously untrue—mere jealousy and little-mindedness: the man wanted to take credit for Guido himself, that was all. And the boy, it was obvious, would learn nothing from him. What he needed was a real good profes-sional master.

All the energy that, if the physicists had known their business, would have been driving dynamos, went into this campaign. It began the moment we were out of the house, intensively. She would have more chance of success, the Signora doubtless thought, if we weren't there. And besides, it was essential to take the opportunity when it offered itself and get hold of the child before we could make our bid—for it was obvious to her that we wanted Guido just as much as she did.

Day after day she renewed the assault. At the end of a week she sent her husband to complain about the state of the vines: they were in a shocking condition; he had decided, or very nearly decided, to give Carlo notice. Meekly, shamefacedly, in obedience to higher orders, the old gentleman uttered his threats. Next day Signora Bondi returned to the attack. The padrone, she declared, had been in a towering passion; but she'd do her best, her very best, to mollify him. And after a significant pause she went on to talk about Guido.

In the end Carlo gave in. The woman was too persistent and she held too many trump cards. The child could go and stay with her for a month or two on trial. After that, if he really expressed a desire to remain with her, she would formally adopt him.

At the idea of going for a holiday to the seaside—and it was to the seaside, Signora Bondi told him, that they were going—Guido was pleased and excited. He had heard a lot about the sea from Robin. *"Tanta acqua!"* It had sounded almost too good to be true. And now he was actually to go and see this marvel. It was very cheerfully that he parted from his family.

But after the holiday by the sea was over, and Signora Bondi had brought him back to her town house in Florence, he began to be homesick. The Signora, it was true, treated him exceedingly kindly, bought him new clothes, took him out to tea in the Via Tornabuoni and filled him up with cakes, iced strawberry-ade, whipped cream, and chocolates. But she made him practice the piano more than he liked, and what was worse, she took away his Euclid, on the score that he wasted too much time with it. And when he said that he wanted to go home, she put him off with promises and excuses and downright lies. She told him that she couldn't take him at once, but that next week, if he were good and worked hard at his piano meanwhile, next week . . . And when the time came she told him that his father didn't want him back. And she redoubled her petting, gave him expensive presents, and stuffed him with yet unhealthier foods. To no purpose. Guido didn't like his new life, didn't want to practice scales, pined for his book, and longed to be back with his brothers and sisters. Signora Bondi, meanwhile, continued to hope that time and chocolates would eventually make the child hers; and to keep his family at a distance, she wrote to Carlo every few days letters which still purported to come from the seaside (she took the trouble to send them to a friend, who posted them back again to Florence), and in which she painted the most charming picture of Guido's happiness.

It was then that Guido wrote his letter to me. Abandoned, as he supposed, by his family—for that they should not take the trouble to come to see him when they were so near was only to be explained on the hypothesis that they really had given him up—he must have looked to me as his last and only hope. And the letter, with its fantastic address, had been nearly a fortnight on its way. A fortnight—it must have seemed hundreds of years; and as the centuries succeeded one another, gradually, no doubt, the poor child became convinced that I too had abandoned him. There was no hope left.

"Here we are," said Carlo.

I looked up and found myself confronted by an enormous monument. In a kind of grotto hollowed in the flanks of a monolith of gray sandstone, Sacred Love, in bronze, was embracing a funeral urn. And in bronze letters riveted into the stone was a long legend to the effect that the inconsolable Ernesto Bondi had raised this monument to the memory of his beloved wife, Anunziata, as a token of his undying love for one whom, snatched from him by a premature death, he hoped very soon to join beneath this stone. The first Signora Bondi had died in 1912. I thought of the old man leashed to his white dog; he must always, I reflected, have been a most uxorious husband.

"They buried him here."

We stood there for a long time in silence. I felt the tears coming into my eyes as I thought of the poor child lying there underground. I thought of those luminous grave eyes, and the curve of that beautiful forehead, the droop of the melancholy mouth, of the expression of delight which illumined his face when he learned of some new idea that pleased him, when he heard a piece of music that he liked. And this beautiful small being was dead; and the spirit that inhabited this form, the amazing spirit, that too had been destroyed almost before it had begun to exist.

And the unhappiness that must have preceded the final act, the child's despair, the conviction of his utter abandonment—those were terrible to think of, terrible.

"I think we had better come away now," I said at least, and touched Carlo on the arm. He was standing there like a blind man, his eyes shut, his face slightly lifted towards the light; from between his closed eyelids the tears welled out, hung for a moment, and trickled down his cheeks. His lips trembled and I could see that he was making an effort to keep them still. "Come away," I repeated.

The face which had been still in its sorrow was suddenly convulsed; he opened his eyes, and through the tears they were bright with a violent anger. "I shall kill her," he said, "I shall kill her. When I think of him throwing himself out, falling through the air . . ." With his two hands he made a violent gesture, bringing them down from over his head and arresting them with a sudden jerk when they were on the level with his breast. "And then crash." He shuddered. "She's as much responsible as though she had pushed him down herself. I shall kill her." He clenched his teeth.

To be angry is easier than to be sad, less painful. It is comforting to think of revenge. "Don't talk like that," I said. "It's no good. It's stupid. And what would be the point?" He had had those fists before, when grief became too painful and he had tried to escape from it. Anger had been the easiest way of escape. I had had, before this, to persuade him back into the harder path of grief. "It's stupid to talk like that," I repeated, and I led him away through the ghastly labyrinth of tombs, where death seemed more terrible even than it is.

By the time we had left the cemetery, and were walking down from San Miniato towards the Piazzale Michelangelo below, he had become calmer. His anger had subsided again into the sorrow from which it had derived all its strength and its bitterness. In the Piazzale we halted for a moment to look down at the city in the valley below us. It was a day of floating clouds—great shapes, white, golden, and gray; and between them patches of a thin, transparent blue. Its lantern level, almost, with our eyes, the dome of the cathedral revealed itself in all its grandiose lightness, its vastness and aerial strength. On the innumerable brown and rosy roofs of the city the afternoon sunlight lay softly, sumptuously, and the towers were as though varnished and enameled with an old gold. I thought of all the Men who had lived here and left the visible traces of their spirit and conceived extraordinary things. I thought of the dead child.

Evelyn Waugh

1903-

EVELYN WAUGH began his writing career as one of the "bright young men" of the postwar world, the son of Arthur Waugh, critic and publisher, and brother of Alec Waugh, novelist. He scattered his talents early, teaching school and working on a newspaper, then studying, as he says, "carpentry and fashionable society." In the latter he succeeded brilliantly. It was the day of the Riviera and the Lido, treasure hunts and yachts, escapades and casual infidelities—the English counterpart of America's Jazz Age, with all the glitter and sophistication intensified. Waugh's novels, *Vile Bodies, Black Mischief, A Handful of Dust, Decline and Fall,* are the bitter, disillusioned, cynical but highly amusing results of observation and experience. During this time he himself married, was divorced, and became a Catholic. In a serious vein, he has written travel books on Abyssinia, Mexico, and India, and his novel *Brideshead Revisited* is a magnificent re-creation of that same between-wars England, now become a romantic memory and misted over with the opal glow of Waugh's special Catholicism.

Bella Fleace Gave a Party

BY EVELYN WAUGH

BALLINGAR is four and a half hours from Dublin if you catch the early train from Broadstone Station and five and a quarter if you wait until the afternoon. It is the market town of a large and comparatively well-populated district. There is a pretty Protestant Church in 1820 Gothic on one side of the square and a vast, unfinished Catholic cathedral opposite it, conceived in that irresponsible medley of architectural orders that is so dear to the hearts of transmontane pietists. Celtic lettering of a sort is beginning to take the place of the Latin alphabet on the shop fronts that complete the square. These all deal in identical goods in varying degrees of dilapidation; Mulligan's Store, Flannigan's Store, Riley's Store, each sells thick black boots, hanging in bundles, soapy colonial cheese, hardware and haberdashery, oil and saddlery, and each is licensed to sell ale and porter for consumption on or off the premises. The shell of the barracks stands with empty window frames and blackened interior as a monument to emancipation. A typical Irish town.

Fleacetown is fifteen miles from Ballingar, on a direct uneven road through typical Irish country; vague purple hills in the far distance and towards them, on one side of the road, fitfully visible among drifting patches of white mist, unbroken miles of bog, dotted with occasional stacks of cut peat. On the other side the ground slopes up to the north, divided irregularly into spare fields by banks and stone walls over which the Ballingar hounds have some of their most eventful hunting. Moss lies on everything; in a rough green rug on the walls and banks, soft green velvet on the timber—blurring the transitions so that there is no knowing where the ground ends and trunk and masonry begin. All the way from Ballingar there is a succession of whitewashed cabins and a dozen or so fair-size farmhouses; but there is no gentleman's house, for all this was Fleace property in the days before the Land Commission. The demesne land is all that belongs to Fleacetown now, and this is let for pasture to neighboring farmers. Only a few beds are cultivated in the walled kitchen garden; the rest has run to rot, thorned bushes barren of edible fruit spreading everywhere among weedy flowers reverting rankly to type. The hothouses have been drafty skeletons for ten years. The great gates set in their Georgian arch are permanently padlocked, the

From *Mr. Lovejoy's Little Outing* by Evelyn Waugh. By permission of Harold Matson. Published by Little, Brown & Co. Copyright, 1936, by Evelyn Waugh.

lodges are derelict, and the line of the main drive is only just discernible through the meadows. Access to the house is half a mile further up through a farm gate, along a track befouled by cattle.

But the house itself, at the date with which we are dealing, was in a condition of comparatively good repair; compared, that is to say, with Ballingar House or Castle Boycott or Knode Hall. It did not, of course, set up to rival Gordontown, where the American Lady Gordon had installed electric light, central heating and a lift, or Mock House or Newhill, which were leased to sporting Englishmen, or Castle Mockstock, since Lord Mockstock married beneath him. These four houses with their neatly raked gravel, bathrooms and dynamos, were the wonder and ridicule of the country. But Fleacetown, in fair competition with the essentially Irish houses of the Free State, was unusually habitable.

Its roof was intact; and it is the roof which makes the difference between the second and third grades of Irish country houses. Once that goes you have moss in the bedrooms, ferns on the stairs and cows in the library, and in a very few years you have to move into the dairy or one of the lodges. But so long as he has, literally, a roof over his head, an Irishman's house is still his castle. There were weak bits in Fleacetown, but general opinion held that the leads were good for another twenty years and would certainly survive the present owner.

Miss Annabel Rochfort-Doyle-Fleace, to give her the full name under which she appeared in books of reference, though she was known to the entire countryside as Bella Fleace, was the last of her family. There had been Fleaces and Fleysers

living about Ballingar since the days of Strongbow, and farm buildings marked the spot where they had inhabited a stockaded fort two centuries before the immigration of the Boycotts or Gordons or Mockstocks. A family tree emblazed by a nineteenth-century genealogist, showing how the original stock had merged with the equally ancient Rochforts and the respectable though more recent Doyles, hung in the billiard room. The present home had been built on extravagant lines in the middle of the eighteenth century, when the family, though enervated, was still wealthy and influential. It would be tedious to trace its gradual decline from fortune; enough to say that it was due to no heroic debauchery. The Fleaces just got unobtrusively poorer in the way that families do who make no effort to help themselves. In the last generations, too, there had been marked traces of eccentricity. Bella Fleace's mother— an O'Hara of Newhill—had from the day of her marriage until her death suffered from the delusion that she was a Negress. Her brother, from whom she had inherited, devoted himself to oil painting; his mind ran on the simple subject of assassination and before his death he had executed pictures of practically every such incident in history from Julius Caesar to General Wilson. He was at work on a painting, his own murder, at the time of the troubles, when he was, in fact, ambushed and done to death with a shotgun on his own drive.

It was under one of her brother's paintings—Abraham Lincoln in his box at the theater—that Miss Fleace was sitting one colorless morning in November when the idea came to her to give a Christmas party. It would be unnecessary to describe her appearance closely, and somewhat confusing, because it seemed in contradiction to much of her character. She was over eighty, very untidy and very red; streaky gray hair was twisted behind her head into a horsy bun, wisps hung round her cheeks; her nose was prominent and blue-veined; her eyes pale blue, blank and mad; she had a lively smile and spoke with a marked Irish intonation. She walked with the aid of a stick, having been lamed many years back when her horse rolled her among loose stones late in a long day with the Ballingar Hounds; a tipsy sporting doctor had completed the mischief, and she had not been able to ride again. She would appear on foot when hounds drew the Fleacetown coverts and loudly criticize the conduct of the huntsman, but every year fewer of her old friends turned out; strange faces appeared.

They knew Bella, though she did not know them. She had become a byword in the neighborhood, a much-valued joke.

"A rotten day," they would report. "We found our fox, but lost again almost at once. But we saw Bella. Wonder how long the old girl will last. She must be nearly ninety. My father remembers when she used to hunt—went like smoke, too."

Indeed, Bella herself was becoming increasingly occupied with the prospect of death. In the winter before the one we are talking of, she had been extremely ill. She emerged in April, rosy-cheeked as ever, but slower in her movements and mind. She gave instructions that better attention must be paid to her father's and brother's graves, and in June took the unprecedented step of inviting her heir to visit her. She always refused to see this young man up till now. He was an Englishman,

a very distant cousin, named Banks. He lived in South Kensington and occupied himself in the Museum. He arrived in August and wrote long and very amusing letters to all his friends describing his visit, and later translated his experiences into a short story for the *Spectator*. Bella disliked him from the moment he arrived. He had horn-rimmed spectacles and a BBC voice. He spent most of his time photographing the Fleacetown chimney pieces and the molding of the doors. One day he came to Bella bearing a pile of calf-bound volumes from the library.

"I say, did you know you had these?" he asked.

"I did," Bella lied.

"All first editions. They must be extremely valuable."

"You put them back where you found them."

Later, when he wrote to thank her for his visit—enclosing prints of some of his photographs—he mentioned the books again. This set Bella thinking. Why should that young puppy go poking round the house putting a price on everything? She wasn't dead yet, Bella thought. And the more she thought of it, the more repugnant it became to think of Archie Banks carrying off her books to South Kensington and removing the chimney pieces and, as he threatened, writing an essay about the house for the *Architectural Review*. She had often heard that the books were valuable. Well, there were plenty of books in the library and she did not see why Archie Banks should profit by them. So she wrote a letter to a Dublin bookseller. He came to look through the library, and after a while he offered her twelve hundred pounds for the lot, or a thousand for the six books which had attracted Archie Bank's attention. Bella was not sure that she had the right to sell things out of the house; a wholesale clearance would be noticed. So she kept the sermons and military history which made up most of the collection, the Dublin bookseller went off with the first editions, which eventually fetched rather less than he had given, and Bella was left with winter coming on and a thousand pounds in hand.

It was then that it occurred to her to give a party. There were always several parties given round Ballingar at Christmastime, but of late years Bella had not been invited to any, partly because many of her neighbors had never spoken to her, partly because they did not think she would want to come, and partly because they would not have known what to do with her if she had. As a matter of fact she loved parties. She liked sitting down to supper in a noisy room, she liked dance music and gossip about which of the girls was pretty and who was in love with them, and she liked drink and having things brought to her by men in pink evening coats. And though she tried to console herself with contemptuous reflections about the ancestry of the hostesses, it annoyed her very much whenever she heard of a party being given in the neighborhood to which she was not asked.

And so it came about that, sitting with the *Irish Times* under the picture of Abraham Lincoln and gazing across the bare trees of the park to the hills beyond, Bella took it into her head to give a party. She rose immediately and hobbled across the room to the bell rope. Presently her butler came into the morning room; he wore the green baize apron in which he cleaned the silver and in his hand he carried the plate brush

to emphasize the irregularity of the summons.

"Was it yourself ringing?" he asked.

"It was, who else?"

"And I at the silver!"

"Riley," said Bella with some solemnity, "I propose to give a ball at Christmas."

"Indeed!" said her butler. "And for what would you want to be dancing at your age?" But as Bella adumbrated her idea, a sympathetic light began to glitter in Riley's eye. "There's not been such a ball in the country for twenty-five years. It will cost a fortune."

"It will cost a thousand pounds," said Bella proudly.

The preparations were necessarily stupendous. Seven new servants were recruited in the village and set to work dusting and cleaning and polishing, clearing out furniture and pulling up carpets. Their industry served only to reveal fresh requirements; plaster moldings, long rotten, crumbled under the feather brooms, worm-eaten mahogany floorboards came up with the tin tacks; bare brick was disclosed behind the cabinets in the great drawing room. A second wave of the invasion brought painters, paperhangers and plumbers, and in a moment of enthusiasm Bella had the cornice and the capitals of the pillars in the hall regilded; windows were reglazed, banisters fitted into gaping sockets, and the stair carpet shifted so that the worn strips were less noticeable.

In all these works Bella was indefatigable. She trotted from drawing room to hall, down the long gallery, up the staircase, admonishing the hireling servants, lending a hand with the lighter objects of furniture, sliding, when the time came, up and down the mahogany floor of the drawing room to work in the French chalk. She unloaded chests of silver in the attics, found long-forgotten services of china, went down with Riley into the cellars to count the few remaining and now flat and acid bottles of champagne. And in the evenings when the manual laborers had retired exhausted to their gross recreations, Bella sat up far into the night turning the pages of cookery books, comparing the estimates of rival caterers, inditing long and detailed letters to the agents for dance bands and, most important of all, drawing up her list of guests and addressing the high double piles of engraved cards that stood in her escritoire.

Distance counts for little in Ireland. People will readily drive three hours to pay an afternoon call, and for a dance of such importance no journey was too great. Bella had her list painfully compiled from works of reference, Riley's more up-to-date social knowledge and her own suddenly animated memory. Cheerfully, in a steady childish handwriting, she transferred the names to the cards and addressed the envelopes. It was the work of several late sittings. Many of those whose names were transcribed were dead or bedridden; some whom she just remembered seeing as small children were reaching retiring age in remote corners of the globe; many of the houses she wrote down were blackened shells, burned during the troubles and never rebuilt; some had "no one living in them, only farmers." But at last, none too early, the last envelope was addressed. A final lap with the stamps and then later than usual she rose from the desk. Her limbs were stiff, her eyes dazzled, her tongue cloyed with the gum of the Free State post office; she felt a little

dizzy, but she locked her desk that evening with the knowledge that the most serious part of the work of the party was over. There had been several notable and deliberate omissions from that list.

"What's all this I hear about Bella giving a party?" said Lady Gordon to Lady Mockstock. "I haven't had a card."

"Neither have I yet. I hope the old thing hasn't forgotten me. I certainly intend to go. I've never been inside the house. I believe she's got some lovely things."

With true English reserve the lady whose husband had leased Mock Hall never betrayed the knowledge that any party was in the air at all at Fleacetown.

As the last days approached Bella concentrated more upon her own appearance. She had bought few clothes of recent years, and the Dublin dressmaker with whom she used to deal had shut up shop. For a delirious instant she played with the idea of a journey to London and even Paris, and considerations of time alone obliged her to abandon it. In the end she discovered a shop to suit her, and purchased a very magnificent gown of crimson satin; to this she added long white gloves and satin shoes. There was no tiara, alas! among her jewels, but she unearthed large numbers of bright, nondescript Victorian rings, some chains and lockets, pearl brooches, turquoise earrings, and a collar of garnets. She ordered a coiffeur down from Dublin to dress her hair.

On the day of the ball she woke early, slightly feverish with nervous excitement, and wriggled in bed till she was called, restlessly rehearsing in her mind every detail of the arrangements. Before noon she had been to supervise the setting of hundreds of candles in the sconces round the ballroom and supper room, and in the three great chandeliers of cut Waterford glass; she had seen the supper tables laid out with silver and glass and stood the massive wine coolers by the buffet; she had helped bank the staircase and hall with chrysanthemums. She had no luncheon that day, though Riley urged her with samples of the delicacies already arrived from the caterer's. She felt a little faint; lay down for a short time, but soon rallied to sew with her own hands the crested buttons on to the liveries of the hired servants.

The invitations were timed for eight o'clock. She wondered whether that would be too early—she had heard tales of parties that began very late—but as the afternoon dragged on unendurably, and rich twilight enveloped the house, Bella became glad that she had set a short term on this exhausting wait.

At six she went up to dress. The hairdresser was there with a bag full of tongs and combs. He brushed and coiled her hair and whiffed it up and generally manipulated it until it became orderly and formal and apparently far more copious. She put on all her jewelry and, standing before the cheval glass in her room, could not forbear a gasp of surprise. Then she limped downstairs.

The house looked magnificent in the candlelight. The band was there, the twelve hired footmen, Riley in knee breeches and black silk stockings.

It struck eight. Bella waited. Nobody came.

She sat down on a gilt chair at the head of the stairs, looked steadily before her with her blank, blue eyes. In the hall, in the cloakroom, in the supper room, the hired footmen looked at one another with knowing winks. "What does the old girl expect? No one'll have finished dinner before ten."

The linkmen on the steps stamped and chafed their hands.

At half-past twelve Bella rose from her chair. Her face gave no indication of what she was thinking. "Riley, I think I will have some supper. I am not feeling altogether well."

She hobbled slowly to the dining room.

"Give me a stuffed quail and a glass of wine. Tell the band to start playing."

The *Blue Danube* waltz flooded the house. Bella smiled approval and swayed her head a little to the rhythm.

"Riley, I am really quite hungry. I've had nothing all day. Give me another quail and some more champagne."

Alone among the candles and the hired footmen, Riley served his mistress with an immense supper. She enjoyed every mouthful.

Presently she rose. "I am afraid there must be some mistake. No one seems to be coming to the ball. It is very disappointing after all our trouble. You may tell the band to go home."

But just as she was leaving the dining room there was a stir in the hall. Guests were arriving. With wild resolution Bella swung herself up the stairs. She must get to the top before the guests were announced. One hand on the banister, one on her stick, pounding heart, two steps at a time. At last she reached the landing and turned to face the company. There was a mist before her eyes and a singing in her ears. She breathed with effort, but dimly she saw four figures advancing and saw Riley meet them and heard him announce

"Lord and Lady Mockstock, Sir Samuel and Lady Gordon."

Suddenly the daze in which she had been moving cleared. Here on the stairs were the two women she had not invited—Lady Mockstock the draper's daughter, Lady Gordon the American.

She drew herself up and fixed them with her blank, blue eyes.

"I had not expected this honor," she said. "Please forgive me if I am unable to entertain you."

The Mockstocks and the Gordons stood aghast; saw the mad blue eyes of their hostess, her crimson dress; the ballroom beyond, looking immense in its emptiness; heard the dance music echoing through the empty house. The air was charged with the scent of chrysanthemums. And then the drama and unreality of the scene were dispelled. Miss Fleace suddenly sat down, and holding out her hands to her butler, said, "I don't quite know what's happening."

He and two of the hired footmen carried the old lady to a sofa. She spoke only once more. Her mind was still on the same subject. "They came uninvited, those two . . . and nobody else."

A day later she died.

Mr. Banks arrived for the funeral and spent a week sorting out her effects. Among them he found in her escritoire, stamped, addressed, but unposted, the invitations to the ball.

Elizabeth Bowen

1899-

THE *jeune fille*, so likely to be a comic figure in American fiction, is more often than not a tender, sad little girl in British stories. Margaret Kennedy (*The Constant Nymph*), Rosamond Lehmann (*Invitation to the Waltz*), Kate O'Brien, and Maggie Owen have all written about her with compassion, but Elizabeth Bowen, especially in her beautiful novel *The Death of the Heart*, uncovers the touching tragedy of innocence with an intensity and a poignancy that surpass them all. She is Irish, married to an Oxford professor, and lives, when she can, at Bowen's Court in County Cork, the estate given one of her ancestors by Cromwell. But life has not always been so smooth: for four years, from the age of nineteen to twenty-three, she lived alone in London, like Katherine Mansfield, on a small income her father gave her, and tried to write. She had to pawn and sell her belongings, but she did succeed. Her first short story was published when she was twenty, and from then on she has thought of little else but writing.

Elizabeth Bowen is classed with Virginia Woolf and Katherine Mansfield, but her stories—like her life—are more ordered and more objective. The tragedy she senses stems not from her own tortured soul, but from deep sympathy for and understanding of others.

Joining Charles

BY ELIZABETH BOWEN

EVERYBODY in the White House was awake early that morning, even the cat. At an unprecedented hour in the thick gray dusk Polyphemus slipped upstairs and began to yowl at young Mrs. Charles's door, under which came out a pale yellow line of candlelight. On an ordinary morning he could not have escaped from the kitchen so easily, but last night the basement door had been left unbolted; all the doors were open downstairs, for the household had gone to bed at a crisis of preparation for the morrow. Sleep was to be no more than an interim, and came to most of them thinly and interruptedly. The rooms were littered with objects that had an air of having been put down momentarily, corded boxes were packed up in the hall, and a spectral breakfast table waiting all night in the parlor reappeared slowly as dawn came in through the curtains.

Young Mrs. Charles came across to the door on her bare feet and, shivering, let in Polyphemus. She was still in pajamas, but her two suitcases were packed to the brim, with tissue paper smoothed on the tops of them: she must have been moving about for hours. She was always, superstitiously, a little afraid of Polyphemus and made efforts to propitiate him on all occasions; his expression of omniscience had imposed upon her thoroughly. His coming in now made her a little conscious; she stood still, one hand on the knob of the dressing-table drawer, and put the other hand to her forehead—what must she do? Between the curtains, drawn a little apart, light kept coming in slowly, solidifying the objects round her, which till now had been uncertain, wavering silhouettes in candlelight. So night fears gave place to the realities of daytime.

Polyphemus continued to melt round the room, staring malignly at nothing. Presently Agatha tapped and came in in her dressing gown; her plaits hung down each side of her long, kind face, and she carried a cup of tea.

"Better drink this," said Agatha. "What can I do?" She drew back the curtains a little more in her comfortable, common-sense way to encourage the daylight. Leaning for a moment out of the window she breathed in critically the morning air; the bare upland country was sheathed but not hidden by mist. "You're going to have a beautiful day," said Agatha.

Mrs. Charles shivered, then began

tugging a comb through her short hair. She had been awake a long time and felt differently from Agatha about the day; she looked at her sister-in-law haggardly. "I dreamed and dreamed," said Mrs. Charles. "I kept missing my boat, saw it sliding away from the quay; and when I turned to come back to you all England was sliding away too, in the other direction, and I don't know where I was left—and I dreamed, too, of course, about losing my passport."

"One would think you had never traveled before," said Agatha tranquilly. She sat down on the end of the narrow bed where Mrs. Charles had slept for the last time, and shaking out Mrs. Charles's garments, passed them to her one by one, watching her dress as though she had been a child. Mrs. Charles felt herself being marveled at; her own smallness and youth had become objective to her at the White House; a thing, all she had, to offer them over again every day to be softened and pleased by.

As she pulled on the clothes she was to wear for so long she began to feel formal and wary, the wife of a competent banker going to join him at Lyon. The expression of her feet in those new brogues was quite unfamiliar; the feet of a "nice little woman." Her hair, infected by this feeling of strangeness that flowed to her very extremities, lay in a different line against her head. For a moment the face of a ghost from the future stared at her out of the looking glass. She turned quickly to Agatha, but her sister-in-law had left her while she was buttoning her jumper at the neck and had gone downstairs to print some more labels. It had occurred to Agatha that there would be less chance of losing the luggage

(a contingency by which this untraveled family seemed to be haunted) if Louise were to tie on new labels, with more explicit directions, at Paris, where she would have to reregister. Agatha was gone, and the cup of tea, untasted, grew cold on the dressing table.

The room looked bare without her possessions and withdrawn, as though it had already forgotten her. At this naked hour of parting she had forgotten it also; she supposed it would come back in retrospect so distinctly as to be a kind of torment. It was a smallish room with sloping ceilings, and a faded paper rambled over by roses. It had white curtains and was never entirely dark; it had so palpably a life of its own that she had been able to love it with intimacy and a sense of return, as one could never have loved an inanimate thing. Lying in bed one could see from the one window nothing but sky or sometimes a veil of rain; when one got up and looked out there were fields, wild and bare, and an unbroken skyline to emphasize the security of the house.

The room was up on the top floor, in one of the gables; a big household cannot afford a spare bedroom of any pretensions. To go downstairs one had to unlatch the nursery gate at the head of the top flight. Last time Charles was home it had been very unfortunate; he had barked his shins on the gate and shouted angrily to his mother to know what the thing was still there for. Louise fully realized that it was being kept for Charles's children.

During that first visit with Charles she had hardly been up to the second floor, where the younger girls slept in the old nursery. There had been no confidences; she and Charles occupied very connubially a room Mrs.

Ray gave up to them that had been hers since her marriage. It was not till Louise came back here alone that the White House opened its arms to her and she began to be carried away by this fullness, this intimacy and queer seclusion of family life. She and the girls were in and out of each other's room; Doris told sagas of high school, Maisie was always just on the verge of a love affair, and large grave Agatha began to drop the formality with which she had greeted a married woman and sister-in-law. She thought Agatha would soon have forgotten she was anything but her own child if it had ever been possible for Agatha to forget Charles.

It would have been terrible if Louise had forgotten, as she so nearly had, to pack Charles's photograph. There it had stood these three months, propped up on the mantelpiece, a handsome convention in sepia, becomingly framed, from which the young wife, falling asleep or waking, had turned away her face instinctively. She folded back a layer of tissue paper before shutting her suitcase and poked down a finger to feel the edge of the frame and reassure herself. There it was, lying face down, wrapped up in her dressing gown, and she would have seen Charles before she looked again at his photograph. The son and brother dominating the White House would be waiting on the Lyon platform to enfold her materially.

Mrs. Charles glanced round the room once more, then went downstairs slowly. Through the house she could hear doors opening and shutting and people running about because of her. She felt ashamed that her packing was finished and there was nothing for her to do. Whenever she had pictured herself leaving the White House it had been in the evening, with curtains drawn, and they had all just come out to the door for a minute to say good-by to her, then gone back to the fire. It had been more painful but somehow easier. Now she felt lonely; they had all gone away from her, there was nobody there.

She went shyly into the morning room as though for the first time and knelt down on the rug in front of a young fire. There was a sharp smell of wood smoke; thin little flames twisted and spat through the kindling. A big looking glass, down to the ground, reflected her kneeling there; small and childish among the solemn mahogany furniture; more like somebody sent back to school than someone rejoining a virile and generous husband who loved her. Her cropped fair hair turned under against her cheek and was cut in a straight line over the eyebrows. She had never had a home before, and had been able to boast till quite lately that she had never been homesick. After she married there had been houses in which she lived with Charles, but still she had not known what it meant to be homesick.

She hoped that, after all, nobody would come in for a moment or two; she had turned her head and was looking out at the lawn with its fringe of trees not yet free from the mist, and at the three blackbirds hopping about on it. The blackbirds made her know all at once what it meant to be going away; she felt as though someone had stabbed her a long time ago but she were only just feeling the knife. She could not take her eyes from the blackbirds, till one with a wild fluty note skimmed off into the trees and the other two followed it. Polyphemus had come in after her and was looking out at them, pressing himself against the windowpane.

"Polyphemus," said Mrs. Charles in her oddly unchildish voice, "have you any illusions?" Polyphemus lashed his tail.

By midday (when she would be nearly at Dover) the fire would be streaming up briskly, but by that time the sun would be pouring in at the windows and no one would need a fire at all. The mornings were not cold yet, the girls were active, and it was only because of her going away that the fire had been lighted. Perhaps Agatha, who never hurt anything's feelings, would come in and sit not too far away from it with her basket of mending, making believe to be glad of the heat. "I don't suppose there'll be fires at Lyon," thought Mrs. Charles. Somewhere, in some foreign room, tomorrow evening when the endearments were over or there was a pause in them, Charles would lean back in his chair with a gusty sigh, arch his chest up, stretch out his legs and say: "Well, come on. Tell me about the family."

Then she would have to tell him about the White House. Her cheeks burned as she thought how it would all come out. There seemed no chance yet of Agatha or Maisie getting married. That was what Charles would want to know chiefly about his sisters. He had a wholesome contempt for virginity. He would want to know how Doris, whom he rather admired, was "coming along." Those sisters of Charles's always sounded rather dreadful young women, not the sort that Agatha, Maisie, or Doris would care to know. It seemed to Charles funny—he often referred to it—that Agatha wanted babies so badly and went all tender and conscious when babies were mentioned.

"She'll make no end of a fuss over our kids," Charles would say. The White House seemed to Charles, all the same, very proper as an institution; it was equally proper that he should have a contempt for it. He helped to support the girls and his mother, for one thing, and that did place them all at a disadvantage. But they were dear, good souls.—Mrs. Charles knelt with her hands on her knees and the hands clenched slowly from anger and helplessness.

Mrs. Ray, the mother of Charles, suddenly knelt down by his wife and put an arm round her shoulders without saying a word. She did these impulsive things gracefully. Mrs. Charles relaxed and leaned sideways a little against the kind shoulder. She had nothing to say, so they watched the fire struggle and heard the hall clock counting away the seconds.

"Have you got enough clothes on?" said Mother after a minute. "It's cold in trains. I never do think you wear enough clothes."

Mrs. Charles, nodding, unbuttoned her coat and showed a ribbed sweater pulled on over her jumper. "Sensible of me!" she proudly remarked.

"You're learning to be quite a sensible little thing," Mother said lightly. "I expect Charles will notice a difference. Tell Charles not to let you go out in the damp in your evening shoes. But I expect he knows how to take care of you."

"Indeed, yes," said Mrs. Charles, nodding.

"You're precious, you see." Mother smoothed back the hair from against Mrs. Charles's cheek to look at her thoughtfully, like a gentle skeptic at some kind of miracle. "Remember to write me about the flat: I want to know everything: wallpapers, views from the windows, sizes of rooms—— We'll be thinking about you both tomorrow."

"I'll be thinking of you."

"Oh, no, you won't," said Mother, with perfect finality.

"Perhaps not," Mrs. Charles quickly amended.

Mother's son Charles was generous, sensitive, gallant, and shrewd. The things he said, the things he had made, his imprint, were all over the White House. Sometimes he looked out at Louise with bright eyes from the family talk, so striking, so unfamiliar that she fell in love with the stranger for moments together as a married woman should not. He was quiet and never said very much, but he noticed; he had an infallible understanding and entered deeply, it seemed, into the sisters' lives. He was so good; he was so keen for them all to be happy. He had the strangest way of anticipating one's wishes. He was master of an inimitable drollery—to hear him chaff Agatha! Altogether he was a knightly person, transcending modern convention. His little wife had come to them all in a glow from her wonderful lover. No wonder she was so quiet; they used to try and read him from her secret, sensitive face.

A thought of their Charles without his Louise troubled them all with a pang when Louise was her dearest. Charles in Lyon, uncomplaining, lonely, tramping the town after business to look for a flat. The return of Louise to him, to the home he had found for her, her room upstairs already aghast and vacant, the emptiness that hung over them, gave them the sense of pouring out an oblation. The girls were heavy, with the faces of Flemish Madonnas; Doris achieved

some resemblance to Charles, but without being handsome. They had cheerful dispositions, but were humble when they considered themselves; they thought Louise must have a great deal of love in her to give them so much when there was a Charles in her life.

Mrs. Ray, with a groan at her "old stiff bones," got up from the hearthrug and sat on a chair. She thought of something to say, but was not quite ready to say it till she had taken up her knitting. She had hoped to have finished this pair of socks in time to send out by Louise with his others; she hadn't been able to—Mrs. Ray sighed. "You're making my boy very happy," she said, with signs in her manner of the difficulty one has in expressing these things.

Louise thought: "Oh, I love you!" There was something about the hands, the hair, the expression, the general being of Mother that possessed her entirely, that she did not think she could live without. She knelt staring at Mother, all in a tumult. Why be so lonely, why never escape? She was too lonely, it couldn't be borne; not even for the sake of the White House. Not this morning, so early, with the buffeting strangeness of travel before her, with her wrists so chilly and the anticipation of seasickness making her stomach ache. The incommunicableness of even these things, these little ills of the body, bore Mrs. Charles down. She was tired of being brave alone, she was going to give it up.

It is with mothers that understanding and comfort are found. She wanted to put down her head on a bosom, this bosom, and say: "I'm unhappy. Oh, help me! I can't go on. I don't love my husband. It's death to be with him. He's grand, but he's rotten all through——" She needed to be fortified.

"Mother——" said Louise.

"Mm-mm?"

"If things were not a success out there—— If one weren't a good wife always——" Mother smoothed her knitting out and began to laugh; an impassable resolute chuckle.

"What a thing——" she said. "What an idea!"

Louise heard steps in the hall and began kneading her hands together, pulling the fingers helplessly. "Mother," she said, "I feel——"

Mother looked at her; out of the eyes looked Charles. The steady, gentle look, their interchange, lasted moments. Steps came hurrying over the flags of the hall.

"I can't go——"

Doris came in with the teapot. She wasn't grown up, her movements were clumsy and powerful, more like a boy's. She should have been Charles. Her heavy plait came tumbling over her shoulders as she bent to put down the teapot—round and brown with a bluish glaze on it. Sleep and tears in the dark had puffed up her eyelids, which seemed to open with difficulty: her small eyes dwindled into her face. "Breakfast," she said plaintively.

Rose, the servant, brought in a plate of boiled eggs—nice and light for the journey—and put them down compassionately.

"Even Rose," thought Mrs. Charles, getting up and coming to the table obediently because they all expected her to, "even Rose——" She looked at the breakfast cups with poppies scattered across them as though she had not seen them before or were learning an inventory. Doris had begun to eat as though nothing else mattered. She took no notice of Louise, pretending, perhaps, to make things easier for herself, that Louise were already gone.

"Oh Doris, not the tussore tie with the red shirt." Whatever White House might teach Mrs. Charles about common sense, it was her mission to teach them about clothes. "Not," said Mrs. Charles, with bravado rising to an exaggeration of pathos, "not on my last day!"

"I dressed in the dark; I couldn't see properly," said Doris.

"You won't get eggs for breakfast in France," said Maisie with a certain amount of triumph as she came in and sat down.

"I wonder what the flat'll be like?" said Maisie. "Do write and tell us about the flat—describe the wallpapers and everything."

"Just think," said Doris, "of Charles buying the furniture! 'Donnez-moi une chaise!' 'Bien, Monsieur.' 'Non. Ce n'est pas assez confortable pour ma femme.'"

"Fancy!" said Maisie, laughing very much. "And fancy if the flat's high up."

"There'll be central heating and stoves. Beautiful fug. She actually won't be chilly." Mrs. Charles was always chilly: this was a household joke.

"Central heating is stuffy——"

Doris broke away suddenly from the conversation. "Oh!" said she violently. "Oh, Louise, you are lucky!"

A glow on the streets and on the pale, tall houses: Louise walking with Charles. Frenchmen runnning in blousy overalls (Doris saw), French poodles, French girls in plaid skirts putting the shutters back, French ladies on iron balconies, leaning over, watching Charles go up the street with Louise and help Louise over the crossings; Charles and

Louise together. A door, a lift, a flat, a room, a kiss! "Charles, Charles, you are so splendid! Mother loves you and the girls love you and I love you——" "Little woman!" A French curtain fluttering in the high, fresh wind, the city under the roofs—forgotten. All this Doris watched: Louise watched Doris.

"Yes," smiled Louise. "I am lucky."

"Even to be going to France," said Doris, and stared with her dog's eyes.

Louise wanted to take France in her two hands and make her a present of it. "You'll be coming out soon, Doris, someday." (It was not likely that Charles would have her—and did one, anyhow, dare let the White House into the flat?)

"Do you really think so?"

"Why not, if Mother can spare you?"

"Louise!" cried Maisie reproachfully—she had been sitting watching—"you aren't eating."

Agatha, sitting next her, covered up her confusion with gentle comforting noises, cut the top off an egg and advanced it coaxingly. That was the way one made a child eat; she was waiting to do the same for Charles's and Louise's baby when it was old enough. Louise now almost saw the baby sitting up between them, but it was nothing to do with her.

"You'll be home in less than the two years, I shouldn't be surprised," said Mother startlingly. It was strange, now one came to think of it, that any question of coming back to the White House had not been brought up before. They might know Mrs. Charles would be coming back, but they did not (she felt) believe it. So she smiled at Mother as though they were playing a game.

"Well, two years at the very least," Mother said with energy.

They all cast their minds forward. Louise saw herself in the strong pale light of the future walking up to the White House and (for some reason) ringing the bell like a stranger. She stood ringing and ringing and nobody answered or even looked out of a window. She began to feel that she had failed them somehow, that something was missing. Of course it was. When Louise came back next time she must bring them a baby. Directly she saw herself coming up the steps with a child in her arms she knew at once what was wanted. Wouldn't Agatha be delighted? Wouldn't Maisie "run on"? Wouldn't Doris hang awkwardly round and make jokes, poking her big finger now and then between the baby's curling pink ones? As for Mother—at the supreme moment of handing the baby to Mother, Louise had a spasm of horror and nearly dropped it. For the first time she looked at the baby's face and saw it was Charles's.

"It would do no good," thought Mrs. Charles, cold all of a sudden and hardened against them all, "to have a baby of Charles's."

They all sat looking not quite at each other, not quite at her. Maisie said (thinking perhaps of the love affair that never completely materialized): "A great deal can happen in two years," and began to laugh confusedly in an emotional kind of way. Mother and Agatha looked across at each other. "Louise, don't forget to send us a wire," said Mother, as though she had been wondering all this time she had sat so quiet behind the teapot whether Louise would remember to do this.

"Or Charles might send the wire."

"Yes," said Louise, "that would be better."

Polyphemus, knowing his moment, sprang up on to Mrs. Charles's knee. His black tail, stretched out over the tablecloth, lashed sideways, knocking the knives and forks crooked. His one green eye sardonically penetrated her. He knew. He had been given to Charles as a dear little kitten. He pressed against her, treading her lap methodically and mewing soundlessly, showing the purple roof of his mouth. "Ask Charles," suggested Polyphemus, "what became of my other eye." "I know," returned Mrs. Charles silently. "They don't, they haven't been told; you've a voice, I haven't —what about it?" "Satan!" breathed Mrs. Charles, and caressed fascinatedly the fur just over his nose.

"Funny," mused Agatha, watching, "you never have cared for Polyphemus, and yet he likes you. He's a very transparent cat; he is wonderfully honest."

"He connects her with Charles," said Maisie, also enjoying this interchange between the wife and the cat. "He's sending some kind of a message—he's awfully clever."

"Too clever for me," said Mrs. Charles, and swept Polyphemus off her knee with finality. Agatha was going as far as the station; she went upstairs for her hat and coat. Mrs. Charles rose also, picked up her soft felt hat from a chair and pulled it on numbly, in front of the long glass, arranging two little bits of hair at the sides against her cheeks. "Either I am dreaming," she thought, "or someone is dreaming me."

Doris roamed round the room and came up to her. "A book left behind, Louise; *Framley Parsonage*, one of your books."

"Keep it for me."

"For two years—all that time?"

"Yes, I'd like you to."

Doris sat down on the floor and began to read *Framley Parsonage*. She went into it deeply—she had to go somewhere; there was nothing to say; she was suddenly shy of Louise again as she had been at first, as though they had never known each other—perhaps they never had.

"Haven't you read it before?"

"No, never, I'll write and tell you, shall I, what I think of it?"

"I've quite forgotten what I think of it," said Louise, standing above her, laughing and pulling on her gloves. She laughed as though she were at a party, moving easily now under the smooth compulsion of Somebody's dreaming mind. Agatha had come in quietly. "Hush!" she said in a strained way to both of them, standing beside the window in hat and coat as though she were the traveler. "Hush!" She was listening for the taxi. Mother and Maisie had gone.

Wouldn't the taxi come, perhaps? What if it never came? An intolerable jar for Louise, to be deprived of going; a tear in the mesh of the dream that she could not endure. "Make the taxi come soon!" she thought, praying now for departure. "Make it come soon!"

Being listened for with such concentration must have frightened the taxi, for it didn't declare itself; there was not a sound to be heard on the road. If it were not for the hospitality of *Framley Parsonage* where, at this moment, would Doris have been? She bent to the pages absorbedly and did not look up; the leaves of the book were thin and turned over noisily. Louise fled from the morning room into the hall.

Out in the dark hall Mother was bending over the pile of boxes, reading and rereading the labels upside down and from all aspects. She often said that labels could not be printed clearly enough. As Louise hurried past she stood up, reached out an arm and caught hold of her. Only a little light came down from the staircase window; they could hardly see each other. They stood like two figures in a picture, without understanding, created to face one another.

"Louise," whispered Mother, "if things should be difficult—— Marriage isn't easy. If you should be disappointed—I know, I feel—you do understand? If Charles——"

"Charles?"

"I do love **you, I** do. You would tell me?"

But Louise, kissing her coldly and gently, said: "Yes, I know. But there isn't really, Mother, anything to tell."

Roald Dahl
1916-

SIX-FOOT-SIX Roald Dahl, the son of Norwegian parents, was born in England and educated there. At the age of twenty-one he was already as far away as Tanganyika, working for an oil company, and when war broke out he joined the RAF and fought over the Western Desert and in the Greek and Syrian campaigns, spending fifteen weeks with a fractured skull in an Alexandria hospital. His first story, written in 1942, was sold at once to an American magazine and was followed in quick succession by others, brilliant, exhilarating and unpredictable. He is one of the few writers whose collections of short stories are popular successes. *Someone Like You* and *Kiss Kiss* were both best sellers.

Beware of the Dog

BY ROALD DAHL

Down below there was only a vast white undulating sea of cloud. Above there was the sun, and the sun was white like the clouds, because it is never yellow when one looks at it from high in the air.

He was still flying the Spitfire. His right hand was on the stick, and he was working the rudder bar with his left leg alone. It was quite easy. The machine was flying well, and he knew what he was doing.

Everything is fine, he thought. I'm doing all right. I'm doing nicely. I know my way home. I'll be there in half an hour. When I land I shall taxi in and switch off my engine and I shall say, help me to get out, will you. I shall make my voice sound ordinary and natural and none of them will take any notice. Then I shall say, someone help me to get out. I can't do it alone because I've lost one of my legs. They'll all laugh and think that I'm joking, and I shall say, all right, come and have a look, you unbelieving bastards. Then Yorky will climb up onto the wing and look inside. He'll probably be sick because of all the blood and the mess. I shall laugh and say, for God's sake, help me out.

He glanced down again at his right leg. There was not much of it

left. The cannon shell had taken him on the thigh, just above the knee, and now there was nothing but a great mess and a lot of blood. But there was no pain. When he looked down, he felt as though he were seeing something that did not belong to him. It had nothing to do with him. It was just a mess which happened to be there in the cockpit; something strange and unusual and rather interesting. It was like finding a dead cat on the sofa.

He really felt fine, and because he still felt fine, he felt excited and unafraid.

I won't even bother to call up on the radio for the blood wagon, he thought. It isn't necessary. And when I land I'll sit there quite normally and say, some of you fellows come and help me out, will you, because I've lost one of my legs. That will be funny. I'll laugh a little while I'm saying it; I'll say it calmly and slowly, and they'll think I'm joking. When Yorky comes up onto the wing and gets sick, I'll say, Yorky, you old son of a bitch, have you fixed my car yet? Then when I get out I'll make my report and later I'll go up to London. I'll take that half bottle of whisky with me and I'll give it to Bluey. We'll sit in her room and drink it. I'll get the water out of the bathroom tap. I won't say much until it's time to go to bed, then I'll say, Bluey, I've got a surprise for you. I lost a leg today. But I don't mind so long as you don't. It doesn't even hurt. We'll go everywhere in cars. I always hated walking, except when I walked down the street of the coppersmiths in Bagdad, but I could go in a rickshaw. I could go home and chop wood, but the head always flies off the ax. Hot water, that's what it needs; put it in the bath and make the handle swell. I chopped lots of wood last time I went home, and I put the ax in the bath. . . .

Then he saw the sun shining on the engine cowling of his machine. He saw the rivets in the metal, and he remembered where he was. He realized that he was no longer feeling good; that he was sick and giddy. His head kept falling forward onto his chest because his neck seemed no longer to have any strength. But he knew that he was flying the Spitfire, and he could feel the handle of the stick between the fingers of his right hand.

I'm going to pass out, he thought. Any moment now I'm going to pass out.

He looked at his altimeter. Twenty-one thousand. To test himself he tried to read the hundreds as well as the thousands. Twenty-one thousand and what? As he looked the dial became blurred, and he could not even see the needle. He knew then that he must bail out; that there was not a second to lose, otherwise he would become unconscious. Quickly, frantically, he tried to slide back the hood with his left hand, but he had not the strength. For a second he took his right hand off the stick, and with both hands he

managed to push the hood back. The rush of cold air on his face seemed to help. He had a moment of great clearness, and his actions became orderly and precise. That is what happens with a good pilot. He took some quick deep breaths from his oxygen mask, and as he did so, he looked out over the side of the cockpit. Down below there was only a vast white sea of cloud, and he realized that he did not know where he was.

It'll be the Channel, he thought. I'm sure to fall in the drink.

He throttled back, pulled off his helmet, undid his straps, and pushed the stick hard over to the left. The Spitfire dripped its port wing, and turned smoothly over onto its back. The pilot fell out.

As he fell he opened his eyes, because he knew that he must not pass out before he had pulled the cord. On one side he saw the sun; on the other he saw the whiteness of the clouds, and as he fell, as he somersaulted in the air, the white clouds chased the sun and the sun chased the clouds. They chased each other in a small circle; they ran faster and faster, and there was the sun and the clouds and the clouds and the sun, and the clouds came nearer until suddenly there was no longer any sun, but only a great whiteness. The whole world was white, and there was nothing in it. It was so white that sometimes it looked black, and after a time it was either white or black, but mostly it was white. He watched it as it turned from white to black, and then back to white again, and the white stayed for a long time, but the black lasted only for a few seconds. He got into the habit of going to sleep during the white periods, and of waking up just in time to see the world when it was black. But the black was very quick. Sometimes it was only a flash, like someone switching off the light, and switching it on again at once, and so whenever it was white, he dozed off.

One day, when it was white, he put out a hand and he touched something. He took it between his fingers and crumpled it. For a time he lay there, idly letting the tips of his fingers play with the thing which they had touched. Then slowly he opened his eyes, looked down at his hand, and saw that he was holding something which was white. It was the edge of a sheet. He knew it was a sheet because he could see the texture of the material and the stitchings on the hem. He screwed up his eyes, and opened them again quickly. This time he saw the room. He saw the bed in which he was lying; he saw the gray walls and the door and the green curtains over the window. There were some roses on the table by his bed.

Then he saw the basin on the table near the roses. It was a white enamel basin, and beside it there was a small medicine glass.

This is a hospital, he thought. I am in a hospital. But he could remember nothing. He lay back on his pillow, looking at the ceiling and wondering what had happened. He was gazing at the smooth grayness of the ceiling which was so clean and gray, and then suddenly he saw a fly walking upon it. The sight of this fly, the suddenness of seeing this small black speck on a sea of gray, brushed the surface of his brain, and quickly, in that second, he remembered everything. He remembered the Spitfire and he remembered the altimeter showing twenty-one thousand feet. He remembered the pushing back of the

hood with both hands, and he remembered the bailing out. He remembered his leg.

It seemed all right now. He looked down at the end of the bed, but he could not tell. He put one hand underneath the bedclothes and felt for his knees. He found one of them, but when he felt for the other, his hand touched something which was soft and covered in bandages.

Just then the door opened and a nurse came in.

"Hello," she said. "So you've waked up at last."

She was not good-looking, but she was large and clean. She was between thirty and forty and she had fair hair. More than that he did not notice.

"Where am I?"

"You're a lucky fellow. You landed in a wood near the beach. You're in Brighton. They brought you in two days ago, and now you're all fixed up. You look fine."

"I've lost a leg," he said.

"That's nothing. We'll get you another one. Now you must go to sleep. The doctor will be coming to see you in about an hour." She picked up the basin and the medicine glass and went out.

But he did not sleep. He wanted to keep his eyes open because he was frightened that if he shut them again everything would go away. He lay looking at the ceiling. The fly was still there. It was very energetic. It would run forward very fast for a few inches, then it would stop. Then it would run forward again, stop, run forward, stop, and every now and then it would take off and buzz around viciously in small circles. It always landed back in the same place on the ceiling and started running and stopping all over again. He watched it for so long that after a while it was no longer a fly, but only a black speck upon a sea of gray, and he was still watching it when the nurse opened the door, and stood aside while the doctor came in. He was an Army doctor, a major, and he had some last war ribbons on his chest. He was bald and small, but he had a cheerful face and kind eyes.

"Well, well," he said. "So you've decided to wake up at last. How are you feeling?"

"I feel all right."

"That's the stuff. You'll be up and about in no time."

The doctor took his wrist to feel his pulse.

"By the way," he said, "some of the lads from your squadron were ringing up and asking about you. They wanted to come along and see you, but I said that they'd better wait a day or two. Told them you were all right, and that they could come and see you a little later on. Just lie quiet and take it easy for a bit. Got something to read?" He glanced at the table with the roses. "No. Well, nurse will look after you. She'll get you anything you want." With that he waved his hand and went out, followed by the large clean nurse.

When they had gone, he lay back and looked at the ceiling again. The fly was still there and as he lay watching it he heard the noise of an airplane in the distance. He lay listening to the sound of its engines. It was a long way away. I wonder what it is, he thought. Let me see if I can place it. Suddenly he jerked his head sharply to one side. Anyone who has been bombed can tell the noise of a Junkers 88. They can tell most other German bombers for that matter, but especially a Junkers 88. The engines seem to sing a duet. There is a deep vibrating bass voice and with it there is a high pitched

tenor. It is the singing of the tenor which makes the sound of a JU-88 something which one cannot mistake.

He lay listening to the noise, and he felt quite certain about what it was. But where were the sirens, and where the guns? That German pilot certainly had a nerve coming near Brighton alone in daylight.

The aircraft was always far away, and soon the noise faded away into the distance. Later on there was another. This one, too, was far away, but there was the same deep undulating bass and the high singing tenor, and there was no mistaking it. He had heard that noise every day during the battle.

He was puzzled. There was a bell on the table by the bed. He reached out his hand and rang it. He heard the noise of footsteps down the corridor, and the nurse came in.

"Nurse, what were those airplanes?"

"I'm sure I don't know. I didn't hear them. Probably fighters or bombers. I expect they were returning from France. Why, what's the matter?"

"They were JU-88's. I'm sure they were JU-88's. I know the sound of the engines. There were two of them. What were they doing over here?"

The nurse came up to the side of his bed and began to straighten out the sheets and tuck them in under the mattress.

"Gracious me, what things you imagine. You mustn't worry about a thing like that. Would you like me to get you something to read?"

"No, thank you."

She patted his pillow and brushed back the hair from his forehead with her hand.

"They never come over in daylight any longer. You know that. They were probably Lancasters or Flying Fortresses."

"Nurse."

"Yes."

"Could I have a cigarette?"

"Why certainly you can."

She went out and came back almost at once with a packet of Players and some matches. She handed one to him and when he had put it in his mouth, she struck a match and lit it.

"If you want me again," she said, "just ring the bell," and she went out.

Once toward evening he heard the noise of another aircraft. It was far away, but even so he knew that it was a single-engined machine. But he could not place it. It was going fast; he could tell that. But it wasn't a Spit, and it wasn't a Hurricane. It did not sound like an American engine either. They make more noise. He did not know what it was, and it worried him greatly. Perhaps I am very ill, he thought. Perhaps I am imagining things. Perhaps I am a little delirious. I simply do not know what to think.

That evening the nurse came in with a basin of hot water and began to wash him.

"Well," she said, "I hope you don't still think that we're being bombed."

She had taken off his pajama top and was soaping his right arm with a flannel. He did not answer.

She rinsed the flannel in the water, rubbed more soap on it, and began to wash his chest.

"You're looking fine this evening," she said. "They operated on you as soon as you came in. They did a marvelous job. You'll be all right. I've got a brother in the RAF," she added. "Flying bombers."

He said, "I went to school in Brighton."

She looked up quickly. "Well, that's fine," she said. "I expect you'll know some people in the town."

"Yes," he said, "I know quite a few."

She had finished washing his chest and arms, and now she turned back the bedclothes, so that his left leg was uncovered. She did it in such a way that his bandaged stump remained under the sheets. She undid the cord of his pajama trousers and took them off. There was no trouble because they had cut off the right trouser leg, so that it could not interfere with the bandages. She began to wash his left leg and the rest of his body. This was the first time he had had a bed bath, and he was embarrassed. She laid a towel under his leg, and she was washing his foot with the flannel. She said, "This wretched soap won't lather at all. It's the water. It's as hard as nails."

He said, "None of the soap is very good now and, of course, with hard water it's hopeless." As he said it he remembered something. He remembered the baths which he used to take at school in Brighton, in the long stone-floored bathroom which had four baths in a room. He remembered how the water was so soft that you had to take a shower afterwards to get all the soap off your body, and he remembered how the foam used to float on the surface of the water, so that you could not see your legs underneath. He remembered that sometimes they were given calcium tablets because the school doctor used to say that soft water was bad for the teeth.

"In Brighton," he said, "the water isn't . . ."

He did not finish the sentence. Something had occurred to him; something so fantastic and absurd that for a moment he felt like telling the nurse about it and having a good laugh.

She looked up. "The water isn't what?" she said.

"Nothing," he answered. "I was dreaming."

She rinsed the flannel in the basin, wiped the soap off his leg, and dried him with a towel.

"It's nice to be washed," he said. "I feel better." He was feeling his face with his hands. "I need a shave."

"We'll do that tomorrow," she said. "Perhaps you can do it yourself then."

That night he could not sleep. He lay awake thinking of the Junkers 88's and of the hardness of the water. He could think of nothing else. They were JU-88's, he said to himself. I know they were. And yet it is not possible, because they would not be flying around so low over here in broad daylight. I know that it is true, and yet I know that it is impossible. Perhaps I am ill. Perhaps I am behaving like a fool and do not know what I am doing or saying. Perhaps I am delirious. For a long time he lay awake thinking these things, and once he sat up in bed and said aloud, "I will prove that I am not crazy. I will make a little speech about something complicated and intellectual. I will talk about what to do with Germany after the war." But before he had time to begin, he was asleep.

He woke just as the first light of day was showing through the slit in the curtains over the window. The room was still dark, but he could tell that it was already beginning to get light outside. He lay looking at the gray light which was showing through the slit in the curtain, and as he lay there he remembered the day before. He remembered the Junkers 88's and the hardness of the water; he remembered the large pleasant nurse and the kind doctor, and now the small grain of doubt took root in his mind and it began to grow.

He looked around the room. The nurse had taken the roses out the night before, and there was nothing except the table with a packet of cigarettes, a box of matches and an ash tray. Otherwise, it was bare. It was no longer warm or friendly. It was not even comfortable. It was cold and empty and very quiet.

Slowly the grain of doubt grew, and with it came fear, a light, dancing fear that warned but did not frighten; the kind of fear that one gets not because one is afraid, but because one feels that there is something wrong. Quickly the doubt and the fear grew so that he became restless and angry, and when he touched his forehead with his hand, he found that it was damp with sweat. He knew then that he must do something; that he must find some way of proving to himself that he was either right or wrong, and he looked up and saw again the window and the green curtains. From where he lay, that window was right in front of him, but it was fully ten yards away. Somehow he must reach it and look out. The idea became an obsession with him, and soon he could think of nothing except the window. But what about his leg? He put his hand underneath the bedclothes and felt the thick bandaged stump which was all that was left on the right-hand side. It seemed all right. It didn't hurt. But it would not be easy.

He sat up. Then he pushed the bedclothes aside and put his left leg on the floor. Slowly, carefully, he swung his body over until he had both hands on the floor as well; and then he was out of bed, kneeling on the carpet. He looked at the stump. It was very short and thick, covered with bandages. It was beginning to hurt and he could feel it throbbing. He wanted to collapse, lie down on the carpet and do nothing, but he knew that he must go on.

With two arms and one leg, he crawled over towards the window. He would reach forward as far as he could with his arms, then he would give a little jump and slide his left leg along after them. Each time he did, it jarred his wound so that he gave a soft grunt of pain, but he continued to crawl across the floor on two hands and one knee. When he got to the window he reached up, and one at a time he placed both hands on the sill. Slowly he raised himself up until he was standing on his left leg. Then quickly he pushed aside the curtains and looked out.

He saw a small house with a gray tiled roof standing alone beside a narrow lane, and immediately behind it there was a plowed field. In front of the house there was an untidy garden, and there was a green hedge separating the garden from the lane. He was looking at the hedge when he saw the sign. It was just a piece of board nailed to the top of a short pole, and because the hedge had not been trimmed for a long time, the branches had grown out around the sign so that it seemed almost as though it had been placed in the middle of the hedge. There was something written on the board with white paint, and he pressed his head against the glass of the window, trying to read what it said. The first letter was a G, he could see that. The second was an A, and the third was an R. One after another he managed to see what the letters were. There were three words, and slowly he spelled the letters out aloud to himself as he managed to read them. G-A-R-D-E A-U C-H-I-E-N. *Garde au chien*. That is what it said.

He stood there balancing on one leg and holding tightly to the edges of the window sill with his hands, staring at the sign and at the white-washed lettering of the words. For a moment he could think of nothing at all. He stood there looking at the sign, repeating the words over and over to himself, and then slowly he began to realize the full meaning of the thing. He looked up at the cottage and at the plowed field. He looked at the small orchard on the left of the cottage and he looked at the green countryside beyond. "So this is France," he said. "I am in France."

Now the throbbing in his right thigh was very great. It felt as though someone was pounding the end of his stump with a hammer, and suddenly the pain became so intense that it affected his head and for a moment he thought he was going to fall. Quickly he knelt down again, crawled back to the bed and hoisted himself in. He pulled the bedclothes over himself and lay back on the pillow, exhausted. He could still think of nothing at all except the small sign by the hedge, and the plowed field and the orchard. It was the words on the sign that he could not forget.

It was some time before the nurse came in. She came carrying a basin of hot water and she said, "Good morning, how are you today?"

He said, "Good morning, nurse."

The pain was still great under the bandages, but he did not wish to tell this woman anything. He looked at her as she busied herself with getting the washing things ready. He looked at her more carefully now. Her hair was very fair. She was tall and big-boned, and her face seemed pleasant. But there was something a little uneasy about her eyes. They were never still. They never looked at anything for more than a moment and they moved too quickly from one place to another in the room. There was something about her movements also. They were too sharp and nervous to go well with the casual manner in which she spoke.

She set down the basin, took off his pajama top and began to wash him.

"Did you sleep well?"

"Yes."

"Good," she said. She was washing his arms and his chest.

"I believe there's someone coming down to see you from the Air Ministry after breakfast," she went on. "They want a report or something. I expect you know all about it. How you got shot down and all that. I won't let him stay long, so don't worry."

He did not answer. She finished washing him, and gave him a toothbrush and some tooth powder. He brushed his teeth, rinsed his mouth and spat the water out into the basin.

Later she brought him his breakfast on a tray, but he did not want to eat. He was still feeling weak and sick, and he wished only to lie still and think about what had happened. And there was a sentence running through his head. It was a sentence which Johnny, the Intelligence Officer of his squadron, always repeated to the pilots every day before they went out. He could see Johnny now, leaning against the wall of the dispersal hut with his pipe in his hand, saying, "And if they get you, don't forget, just your name, rank and number. Nothing else. For God's sake, say nothing else."

"There you are," she said as she put the tray on his lap. "I've got you an egg. Can you manage all right?"

"Yes."

She stood beside the bed. "Are you feeling all right?"

"Yes."

"Good. If you want another egg I might be able to get you one."

"This is all right."

"Well, just ring the bell if you want any more." And she went out.

He had just finished eating, when the nurse came in again.

She said, "Wing Commander Roberts is here. I've told him that he can only stay for a few minutes."

She beckoned with her hand and the Wing Commander came in.

"Sorry to bother you like this," he said.

He was an ordinary RAF officer, dressed in a uniform which was a little shabby, and he wore wings and a DFC. He was fairly tall and thin with plenty of black hair. His teeth, which were irregular and widely spaced, stuck out a little even when he closed his mouth. As he spoke he took a printed form and a pencil from his pocket, and he pulled up a chair and sat down.

"How are you feeling?"

There was no answer.

"Tough luck about your leg. I know how you feel. I hear you put up a fine show before they got you."

The man in the bed was lying quite still, watching the man in the chair.

The man in the chair said, "Well, let's get this stuff over. I'm afraid you'll have to answer a few questions so that I can fill in this combat report. Let me see now, first of all, what was your squadron?"

The man in the bed did not move. He looked straight at the Wing Commander and he said, "My name is Peter Williamson. My rank is Squadron Leader and my number is nine seven two four five seven."

M. R. James
1862-1936

MONTAGUE RHODES JAMES, choice of connoisseurs, has written a greater number of consistently first-rate ghost stories than anyone else. His ghosts are malignant and sinister. They have seen everything and been everywhere: into the unknowable, the unseeable, the evil corners, and the dank, dark distances.

Though they may have been the consummate achievement, ghost stories have not been the directive in James's long career. After a precocious childhood, during which, before he was ten, he had written the lives of nineteen saints, he was, in turn, scholar at Eton, prizewinner many times at Cambridge, excavator at Cyprus, cataloguer of medieval manuscripts at Cambridge, provost at King's College, and provost of Eton from 1918 until his death. "The Mezzotint" is included here as less familiar than the widely reprinted "Casting of the Runes."

The Mezzotint

BY M. R. JAMES

SOME time ago I believe I had the pleasure of telling you the story of an adventure which happened to a friend of mine by the name of Dennistoun, during his pursuit of objects of art for the museum of Cambridge.

He did not publish his experiences very widely upon his return to England; but they could not fail to become known to a good many of his friends, and among others to the gentleman who at that time presided over an art museum at another university. It was to be expected that the story should make a considerable impression on the mind of a man whose vocation lay in lines similar to Dennistoun's, and that he should be eager to catch at any explanation of the matter which tended to make it seem improbable that he should ever be called upon to deal with so agitating an emergency. It was, indeed, somewhat consoling to him to reflect that he was not expected to acquire ancient MSS. for his institution; that was the business of the Shelburnian Library. The authorities of that institution might, if they pleased, ransack obscure corners of the Continent for such matters. He was glad to be obliged at the moment to confine his attention to enlarging the already unsurpassed collection of English topographical drawings and engravings possessed by his museum. Yet, as it turned out, even a department so homely and familiar as this may have its dark corners, and to one of these Mr. Williams was unexpectedly introduced.

Those who have taken even the most limited interest in the acquisition of topographical pictures are aware that there is one London dealer whose aid is indispensable to their researches. Mr. J. W. Britnell publishes at short intervals very admirable catalogues of a large and constantly changing stock of engravings, plans, and old sketches of mansions, churches, and towns in England and Wales. These catalogues were, of course, the ABC of his subject to Mr. Williams: but as his museum already contained an enormous accumulation of topographical pictures, he was a regular, rather than a copious, buyer; and he rather looked to Mr. Britnell to fill up gaps in the rank and file of his collection than to supply him with rarities.

Now, in February of last year there appeared upon Mr. Williams's desk at the museum a catalogue from Mr. Britnell's emporium, and accom-

From *The Collected Ghost Stories of M. R. James*. By arrangement with Longmans, Green & Co., Inc.

panying it was a typewritten communication from the dealer himself. This letter ran as follows:

Dear Sir,
We beg to call your attention to No. 978 in our accompanying catalogue, which we shall be glad to send on approval.
Yours faithfully,
J. W. Britnell.

To turn to No. 978 in the accompanying catalogue was with Mr. Williams (as he observed to himself) the work of a moment, and in the place indicated he found the following entry:

978.—*Unknown. Interesting mezzotint: View of a manor house, early part of the century. 15 by 10 inches; black frame. £2 2s.*

It was not specially exciting, and the price seemed high. However, as Mr. Britnell, who knew his business and his customer, seemed to set store by it, Mr. Williams wrote a postcard asking for the article to be sent on approval, along with some other engravings and sketches which appeared in the same catalogue. And so he passed without much excitement of anticipation to the ordinary labors of the day.

A parcel of any kind always arrives a day later than you expect it, and that of Mr. Britnell proved, as I believe the right phrase goes, no exception to the rule. It was delivered at the museum by the afternoon post of Saturday, after Mr. Williams had left his work, and it was accordingly brought round to his rooms in college by the attendant, in order that he might not have to wait over Sunday before looking through it and returning such of the contents as he did not propose to keep. And here

he found it when he came in to tea, with a friend.

The only item with which I am concerned was the rather large, black-framed mezzotint of which I have already quoted the short description given in Mr. Britnell's catalogue. Some more details of it will have to be given, though I cannot hope to put before you the look of the picture as clearly as it is present to my own eye. Very nearly the exact duplicate of it may be seen in a good many old inn parlors, or in the passages of undisturbed country mansions at the present moment. It was a rather indifferent mezzotint, and an indifferent mezzotint is, perhaps, the worst form of engraving known. It presented a full-face view of a not very large manor house of the last century, with three rows of plain sashed windows with rusticated masonry about them, a parapet with balls or vases at the angles, and a small portico in the center. On either side were trees, and in front a considerable expanse of lawn. The legend "A. W. F. sculpsit" was engraved on the narrow margin; and there was no further inscription. The whole thing gave the impression that it was the work of an amateur. What in the world Mr. Britnell could mean by affixing the price of £2 2s. to such an object was more than Mr. Williams could imagine. He turned it over with a good deal of contempt; upon the back was a paper label, the left-hand half of which had been torn off. All that remained were the ends of two lines of writing: the first had the letters—*ngley Hall*; the second—*ssex.*

It would, perhaps, be just worth while to identify the place represented, which he could easily do with the help of a gazetteer, and then he would send it back to Mr.

Britnell, with some remarks reflecting upon the judgment of that gentleman.

He lighted the candles, for it was now dark, made the tea, and supplied the friend with whom he had been playing golf (for I believe the authorities of the university I write of indulge in that pursuit by way of relaxation); and tea was taken to the accompaniment of a discussion which golfing persons can imagine for themselves, but which the conscientious writer has no right to inflict upon any nongolfing persons.

The conclusion arrived at was that certain strokes might have been better, and that in certain emergencies neither player had experienced that amount of luck which a human being has a right to expect. It was now that the friend—let us call him Professor Binks—took up the framed engraving, and said:

"What's this place, Williams?"

"Just what I am going to try to find out," said Williams, going to the shelf for a gazetteer. "Look at the back. Somethingley Hall, either in Sussex or Essex. Half the name's gone, you see. You don't happen to know it, I suppose?"

"It's from that man Britnell, I suppose, isn't it?" said Binks. "Is it for the museum?"

"Well, I think I should buy it if the price was five shillings," said Williams; "but for some unearthly reason he wants two guineas for it. I can't conceive why. It's a wretched engraving, and there aren't even any figures to give it life."

"It's not worth two guineas, I should think," said Binks; "but I don't think it's so badly done. The moonlight seems rather good to me; and I should have thought there *were* figures, or at least a figure, just on the edge in front."

"Let's look," said Williams. "Well, it's true the light is rather cleverly given. Where's your figure? Oh, yes! Just the head, in the very front of the picture."

And indeed there was—hardly more than a black blot on the extreme edge of the engraving—the head of a man or woman, a good deal muffled up, the back turned to the spectator, and looking towards the house.

Williams had not noticed it before.

"Still," he said, "though it's a cleverer thing than I thought, I can't spend two guineas of museum money on a picture of a place I don't know."

Professor Binks had his work to do, and soon went; and very nearly up to Hall time Williams was engaged in a vain attempt to identify the subject of his picture. "If the vowel before the *ng* had only been left, it would have been easy enough," he thought; "but as it is, the name may be anything from Guestingley to Langley, and there are many more names ending like this than I thought; and this rotten book has no index of terminations."

Hall in Mr. Williams's college was at seven. It need not be dwelt upon; the less so as he met there colleagues who had been playing golf during the afternoon, and words with which we have no concern were freely bandied across the table—merely golfing words, I would hasten to explain.

I suppose an hour or more to have been spent in what is called common room after dinner. Later in the evening some few retired to Williams's rooms, and I have little doubt that whist was played and tobacco smoked. During a lull in these operations Williams picked up the mezzotint from the table without looking at it, and handed it to a person mildly interested in art, telling him where it had come from, and the other particulars which we already know.

The gentleman took it carelessly, looked at it, then said, in a tone of some interest:

"It's really a very good piece of work, Williams; it has quite a feeling of the romantic period. The light is admirably managed, it seems to me, and the figure, though it's rather too grotesque, is somehow very impressive."

"Yes, isn't it?" said Williams, who was just then busy giving whisky and soda to others of the company, and was unable to come across the room to look at the view again.

It was by this time rather late in the evening, and the visitors were on the move. After they went Williams was obliged to write a letter or two and clear up some odd bits of work. At last, some time past midnight, he was disposed to turn in, and he put out his lamp after lighting his bedroom candle. The picture lay face upwards on the table where the last man who looked at it had put it, and it caught his eye as he turned the lamp down. What he saw made him very nearly drop the candle on the floor, and he declares now that if he had been left in the dark at that moment he would have had a fit. But, as that did not happen, he was able to put down the light on the table and take a good look at the picture. It was indubitable—rankly impossible, no doubt, but absolutely certain. In the middle of the lawn in front of the unknown house there was a figure where no figure had been at five o'clock that afternoon. It was crawling on all-fours towards the house, and it was muffled in a strange black garment with a white cross on the back.

I do not know what is the ideal course to pursue in a situation of this kind. I can only tell you what Mr. Williams did. He took the picture by one corner and carried it across the passage to a second set of rooms which he possessed. There he locked it up in a drawer, sported the doors of both sets of rooms, and retired to bed; but first he wrote out and signed an account of the extraordinary change which the picture had undergone since it had come into his possession.

Sleep visited him rather late; but it was consoling to reflect that the behavior of the picture did not depend upon his own unsupported testimony. Evidently the man who had looked at it the night before had seen something of the same kind as he had, otherwise he might have been tempted to think that something gravely wrong was happening either to his eyes or his mind. This possibility being fortunately precluded, two matters awaited him on the morrow. He must take stock of the picture very carefully, and call in a witness for the purpose, and he must make a determined effort to ascertain what house it was that was represented. He would therefore ask his neighbor Nisbet to breakfast with him, and he would subsequently spend a morning over the gazetteer.

Nisbet was disengaged, and arrived about 9:30. His host was not quite dressed, I am sorry to say, even at this late hour. During breakfast nothing was said about the mezzotint by Williams, save that he had a picture on which he wished for Nisbet's opinion. But those who are familiar with university life can picture for themselves the wide and delightful range of subjects over which the conversation of two Fellows of Canterbury College is likely to extend during a Sunday morning breakfast. Hardly a topic was left unchallenged, from golf to lawn tennis. Yet I am bound to say that Williams was rather distraught; for his interest naturally centered in that very strange picture which was now reposing, face downwards, in the drawer in the room opposite.

The morning pipe was at last lighted, and the moment had arrived for which he looked. With very considerable—almost tremulous—excitement, he ran across, unlocked the drawer, and, extracting the picture— still face downwards—ran back, and put it into Nisbet's hands.

"Now," he said, "Nisbet, I want you to tell me exactly what you see in that picture. Describe it, if you don't mind, rather minutely. I'll tell you why afterwards."

"Well," said Nisbet, "I have here a view of a country house—English, I presume—by moonlight."

"Moonlight? You're sure of that?"

"Certainly. The moon appears to be on the wane, if you wish for details, and there are clouds in the sky."

"All right. Go on. I'll swear," added Williams in an aside, "there was no moon when I saw it first."

"Well, there's not much more to be said," Nisbet continued. "The house has one—two—three rows of windows, five in each row, except at the bottom, where there's a porch instead of the middle one, and——"

"But what about figures?" said Williams with marked interest.

"There aren't any," said Nisbet; "but——"

"What! No figure on the grass in front?"

"Not a thing."

"You'll swear to that?"

"Certainly I will. But there's just one other thing."

"What?"

"Why, one of the windows on the ground floor—left of the door—is open."

"Is it really so? My goodness! he must have got in," said Williams, with great excitement; and he hurried to the back of the sofa on which Nisbet was sitting, and, catching the picture from him, verified the matter for himself.

It was quite true. There was no figure, and there was the open window. Williams, after a moment of speechless surprise, went to the writing table and scribbled for a short time. Then he brought two papers to Nisbet, and asked him first to sign one—it was his own description of the picture, which you have just heard—and then to read the other which was Williams's statement written the night before.

"What can it all mean?" said Nisbet.

"Exactly," said Williams. "Well, one thing I must do—or three things, now I think of it. I must find out from Garwood"—this was his last night's visitor—"what he saw, and then I must get the thing photographed before it goes further, and then I must find out what the place is."

"I can do the photographing myself," said Nisbet, "and I will. But, you know, it looks very much as if we were assisting at the working out of a tragedy somewhere. The question is, Has it happened already, or is it going to come off? You must find out what the place is. Yes," he said, looking at the picture again, "I expect you're right: he has got in. And if I don't mistake there'll be the devil to pay in one of the rooms upstairs."

"I'll tell you what," said Williams: "I'll take the picture across to old Green" (this was the senior Fellow of the College, who had been Bursar for many years). "It's quite likely he'll know it. We have property in Essex and Sussex, and he must have been over the two counties a lot in his time."

"Quite likely he will," said Nisbet; "but just let me take my photograph first. But look here, I rather think Green isn't up today. He wasn't in Hall last night, and I think I heard him say he was going down for the Sunday."

"That's true, too," said Williams; "I know he's gone to Brighton. Well, if you'll photograph it now, I'll go across to Garwood and get his statement, and you keep an eye on it while I'm gone. I'm beginning to think two guineas is not a very exorbitant price for it now."

In a short time he had returned, and brought Mr. Garwood with him. Garwood's statement was to the effect that the figure, when he had seen it, was clear of the edge of the picture, but had not got far across the lawn. He remembered a white mark on the back of its drapery, but could not have been sure it was a cross. A document to this effect was then drawn up and signed, and Nisbet proceeded to photograph the picture.

"Now what do you mean to do?" he said. "Are you going to sit and watch it all day?"

"Well, no, I think not," said Williams. "I rather imagine we're meant to see the whole thing. You see, between the time I saw it last night and this morning there was time for lots of things to happen, but the creature only got into the house. It could easily have got through its business in the time and gone to its own place again; but the fact of the window being open, I think, must mean that it's in there now. So I feel quite easy about leaving it. And besides, I have a kind of idea that it wouldn't change much, if at all, in the daytime. We might go out for a walk this afternoon, and come in to tea, or whenever it gets dark. I shall leave it out on the table here, and sport the door. My skip can get in, but no one else."

The three agreed that this would be a good plan; and, further, that if they spent the afternoon together they would be less likely to talk about the business to other people; for any rumor of such a transaction as was going on would bring the whole of the Phasmatological Society about their ears.

We may give them a respite until five o'clock.

At or near that hour the three were entering Williams's staircase. They were at first slightly annoyed to see that the door of his rooms was unsported; but in a moment it was remembered that on Sunday the skips came for orders an hour or so earlier than on weekdays. However, a surprise was awaiting them. The first thing they saw was the picture leaning up against a pile of books on the table, as it had been left, and the next thing was Williams's skip, seated on a chair opposite, gazing at it with undisguised horror. How was this? Mr. Filcher (the name is not my own invention) was a servant of considerable standing, and set the standard of etiquette to all his own college and to several neighboring ones, and nothing could be more alien to his practice than to be found sitting on his master's chair, or appearing to take any particular notice of his master's furniture or pictures. Indeed, he seemed to feel this himself. He started violently when the three men were in the room, and got up with a marked effort. Then he said:

"I ask your pardon, sir, for taking such a freedom as to set down."

"Not at all, Robert," interposed Mr. Williams. "I was meaning to ask you some time what you thought of that picture."

"Well, sir, of course I don't set up my opinion again yours, but it ain't the pictur I should 'ang where my little girl could see it, sir."

"Wouldn't you, Robert? Why not?"

"No, sir. Why, the pore child, I recollect once she see a Door Bible, with picturs not 'alf what that is, and we 'ad to set up with her three or four nights afterwards, if you'll believe me; and if she was to ketch a sight of this skelinton here, or whatever it is, carrying off the pore baby, she would be in a taking. You know 'ow it is with children; 'ow nervish they git with a little thing and all. But what I should say, it don't seem a right pictur to be laying about, sir, not where anyone that's liable to be startled could come on it. Should you be wanting anything this evening, sir? Thank you, sir."

With these words the excellent man went to continue the round of his masters, and you may be sure the gentlemen whom he left lost no time in gathering round the engraving. There was the house, as before, under the waning moon and the drifting clouds. The window that had been open was shut, and the figure was once more on the lawn: but not this time crawling cautiously on hands and knees. Now it was erect and stepping swiftly, with long strides, towards the front of the picture. The moon was behind it, and the black drapery hung down over its face so that only hints of that

could be seen, and what was visible made the spectators profoundly thankful that they could see no more than a white domelike forehead and a few straggling hairs. The head was bent down, and the arms were tightly clasped over an object which could be dimly seen and identified as a child, whether dead or living it was not possible to say. The legs of the appearance alone could be plainly discerned, and they were horribly thin.

From five to seven the three companions sat and watched the picture by turns. But it never changed. They agreed at last that it would be safe to leave it, and that they would return after Hall and await further developments.

When they assembled again, at the earliest possible moment, the engraving was there, but the figure was gone, and the house was quiet under the moonbeams. There was nothing for it but to spend the evening over gazetteers and guidebooks. Williams was the lucky one at last, and perhaps he deserved it. At 11:30 P.M. he read from Murray's *Guide to Essex* the following lines:

16½ miles, Anningley. *The church has been an interesting building of Norman date, but was extensively classicized in the last century. It contains the tomb of the family of Francis, whose mansion, Anningley Hall, a solid Queen Anne house, stands immediately beyond the churchyard in a park of about 80 acres. The family is now extinct, the last heir having disappeared mysteriously in infancy in the year 1802. The father, Mr. Arthur Francis, was locally known as a talented amateur engraver in mezzotint. After his son's disappearance he lived in complete retirement at the Hall, and was found dead in his studio on the third anniversary of the disaster, having just completed an engraving of the house, impressions of which are of considerable rarity.*

This looked like business, and, indeed, Mr. Green on his return at once identified the house as Anningley Hall.

"Is there any kind of explanation of the figure, Green?" was the question which Williams naturally asked.

"I don't know, I'm sure, Williams. What used to be said in the place when I first knew it, which was before I came up here, was just this: old Francis was always very much down on these poaching fellows, and whenever he got a chance he used to get a man whom he suspected of it turned off the estate, and by degrees he got rid of them all but one. Squires could do a lot of things then that they daren't think of now. Well, this man that was left was what you find pretty often in that country—the last remains of a very old family. I believe they were Lords of the Manor at one time. I recollect just the same thing in my own parish."

"What, like the man in *Tess o' the Durbervilles*," Williams put in.

"Yes, I dare say; it's not a book I could ever read myself. But this fellow could show a row of tombs in the church there that belonged to his ancestors, and all that went to sour him a bit; but Francis, they said, could never get at him—he always kept just on the right side of the law—until one night the keepers found him at it in a wood right at the end of the estate. I could show you the place now; it marches with some land that used to belong to an uncle of mine. And you can imagine there was a row; and this

man Gawdy (that was the name, to be sure—Gawdy; I thought I should get it—Gawdy), he was unlucky enough, poor chap! to shoot a keeper. Well, that was what Francis wanted, and grand juries—you know what they would have been then—and poor Gawdy was strung up in double-quick time; and I've been shown the place he was buried in, on the north side of the church— you know the way in that part of the world: anyone that's been hanged or made away with themselves, they bury them that side. And the idea was that some friend of Gawdy's—not a relation, because he had none, poor devil! he was the last of his line: kind of *spes ultima gentis*—mu.. have planned to get hold of Francis's boy and put an end to *his* line, too. I don't know— it's rather an out-of-the-way thing for an Essex poacher to think of— but, you know, I should say now it looks more as if old Gawdy had managed the job himself. Booh! I hate to think of it! Have some whisky, Williams!"

The facts were communicated by Williams to Dennistoun, and by him to a mixed company, of which I was one, and the Sadducean Professor of Ophiology another. I am sorry to say that the latter, when asked what he thought of it, only remarked: "Oh, those Bridgeford people will say anything"—a sentiment which met with the reception it deserved.

I have only to add that the picture is now in the Ashleian Museum; that it has been treated with a view to discovering whether sympathetic ink has been used in it, but without effect; that Mr. Britnell knew nothing of it save that he was sure it was uncommon; and that, though carefully watched, it has never been known to change again.

E. M. Forster

1879-

EDWARD MORGAN FORSTER is another scholar whose fancy and erudition have combined in rare storytelling. He has written only spasmodically. Although four novels were published before 1911, it was fourteen years before his next and greatest novel came out: *A Passage to India,* that brilliant study of contrasting ideals and ways of life of a cultivated Indian and a Britisher, generally considered the best novel about India. *Aspects of the Novel,* a series of Cambridge lectures brought out in book form, and *Abinger Harvest,* reviews and articles, represent the main body of his critical work, and *The Eternal Moment* and *The Celestial Omnibus* are his short-story excursions into fantasy. "The Story of a Panic" was the first story he ever wrote. "After I came down in my boyhood from Cambridge," he tells in his introduction to *The Collected Tales,* an anthology of his short stories, "I traveled in Italy for a year. I think it was in the May of 1902 that I took a walk near Ravello. I sat down in a valley, a few miles above the town, and suddenly the first chapter of 'The Story of a Panic' rushed into my mind as if it had waited for me up there. I wrote it out as soon as I returned to the hotel."

For many years Forster has concerned himself with the affairs of men, in particular with the rights of authors, and such relevant matters as censorship, book burning, and book banning. He is once more at Cambridge.

The Story of a Panic

BY E. M. FORSTER

EUSTACE'S career—if career it can be called—certainly dates from that afternoon in the chestnut woods above Ravello. I confess at once that I am a plain, simple man, with no pretensions to literary style. Still, I do flatter myself that I can tell a story without exaggerating, and I have therefore decided to give an unbiased account of the extraordinary events of eight years ago.

Ravello is a delightful place with a delightful little hotel in which we met some charming people. There were the two Miss Robinsons, who had been there for six weeks with Eustace, their nephew, then a boy of about fourteen. Mr. Sandbach had also been there some time. He had held a curacy in the north of England, which he had been compelled to resign on account of ill health, and while he was recruiting at Ravello he had taken in hand Eustace's education—which was then sadly deficient—and was endeavoring to fit him for one of our great public schools. Then there was Mr. Leyland, a would-be artist, and, finally, there was the nice landlady, Signora Scafetti, and the nice English-speaking waiter, Emmanuele—though at the time of which I am speaking Emmanuele was away, visiting a sick father.

To this little circle I, my wife, and my two daughters made, I venture to think, a not unwelcome addition. But though I liked most of the company well enough, there were two of them to whom I did not take at all. They were the artist, Leyland, and the Miss Robinsons' nephew, Eustace.

Leyland was simply conceited and odious, and as those qualities will be amply illustrated in my narrative, I need not enlarge upon them here. But Eustace was something besides: he was indescribably repellent.

I am fond of boys as a rule, and was quite disposed to be friendly. I and my daughters offered to take him out—"No, walking was such a fag." Then I asked him to come and bathe— "No, he could not swim."

"Every English boy should be able to swim," I said; "I will teach you myself."

"There, Eustace dear," said Miss Robinson; "here is a chance for you."

But he said he was afraid of the water!—a boy afraid!—and of course I said no more.

I would not have minded so much if he had been a really studious boy,

From *The Celestial Omnibus* by E. M. Forster. By permission of Alfred A. Knopf, Inc.

but he neither played hard nor worked hard. His favorite occupations were lounging on the terrace in an easy chair and loafing along the highroad, with his feet shuffling up the dust and his shoulders stooping forward. Naturally enough, his features were pale, his chest contracted, and his muscles undeveloped. His aunts thought him delicate; what he really needed was discipline.

That memorable day we all arranged to go for a picnic up in the chestnut woods—all, that is, except Janet, who stopped behind to finish her water color of the Cathedral—not a very successful attempt, I am afraid.

I wander off into these irrelevant details because in my mind I cannot separate them from an account of the day; and it is the same with the conversation during the picnic: all is imprinted on my brain together. After a couple of hours' ascent we left the donkeys that had carried the Miss Robinsons and my wife, and all proceeded on foot to the head of the valley—Vallone Fontana Caroso is its proper name, I find.

I have visited a good deal of fine scenery before and since, but have found little that has pleased me more. The valley ended in a vast hollow, shaped like a cup, into which radiated ravines from the precipitous hills around. Both the valley and the ravines and the ribs of hill that divided the ravines were covered with leafy chestnut, so that the general appearance was that of a many-fingered green hand, palm upwards, which was clutching convulsively to keep us in its grasp. Far down the valley we could see Ravello and the sea, but that was the only sign of another world.

"Oh, what a perfectly lovely place!" said my daughter Rose. "What a picture it would make!"

"Yes," said Mr. Sandbach. "Many a famous European gallery would be proud to have a landscape a tithe as beautiful as this upon its walls."

"On the contrary," said Leyland, "it would make a very poor picture. Indeed, it is not paintable at all."

"And why is that?" said Rose, with far more deference than he deserved.

"Look, in the first place," he replied, "how intolerably straight against the sky is the line of the hill. It would need breaking up and diversifying. And where we are standing the whole thing is out of perspective. Besides, all the coloring is monotonous and crude."

"I do not know anything about pictures," I put in, "and I do not pretend to know; but I know what is beautiful when I see it, and I am thoroughly content with this."

"Indeed, who could help being contented!" said the elder Miss Robinson; and Mr. Sandbach said the same.

"Ah!" said Leyland, "you all confuse the artistic view of nature with the photographic."

Poor Rose had brought her camera with her, so I thought this positively rude. I did not wish any unpleasantness; so I merely turned away and assisted my wife and Miss Mary Robinson to put out the lunch —not a very nice lunch.

"Eustace, dear," said his aunt, "come and help us here."

He was in a particularly bad temper that morning. He had, as usual, not wanted to come, and his aunts had nearly allowed him to stop at the hotel to vex Janet. But I, with their permission, spoke to him rather sharply on the subject of exercise; and the result was that he had come, but was even more taciturn and moody than usual.

Obedience was not his strong point. He invariably questioned every command, and only executed it grumbling. I should always insist on prompt and cheerful obedience, if I had a son.

"I'm—coming—Aunt—Mary," he at last replied, and dawdled to cut a piece of wood to make a whistle, taking care not to arrive till we had finished.

"Well, well, sir!" said I, "you stroll in at the end and profit by our labors." He sighed, for he could not endure being chaffed. Miss Mary, very unwisely, insisted on giving him the wing of the chicken, in spite of all my attempts to prevent her. I remember that I had a moment's vexation when I thought that, instead of enjoying the sun and the air and the woods, we were all engaged in wrangling over the diet of a spoiled boy.

But after lunch he was a little less in evidence. He withdrew to a tree trunk and began to loosen the bark from his whistle. I was thankful to see him employed, for once in a way. We reclined and took a *dolce far niente*.

Those sweet chestnuts of the South are puny striplings compared with our robust Northerners. But they clothed the contours of the hills and valleys in a most pleasing way, their veil being only broken by two clearings, in one of which we were sitting.

And because these few trees were cut down, Leyland burst into a petty indictment of the proprietor.

"All the poetry is going from nature," he cried; "her lakes and marshes are drained, her seas banked up, her forests cut down. Every-where we see the vulgarity of desolation spreading."

I have had some experience of estates, and answered that cutting was very necessary for the health of the larger trees. Besides, it was unreasonable to expect the proprietor to derive no income from his lands.

"If you take the commercial side of landscape, you may feel pleasure in the owner's activity. But to me the mere thought that a tree is convertible into cash is disgusting."

"I see no reason," I observed politely, "to despise the gifts of nature because they are of value."

It did not stop him. "It is no matter," he went on, "we are all hopelessly steeped in vulgarity. I do not except myself. It is through us, and to our shame, that the Nereids have left the waters and the Oreads the mountains, that the woods no longer give shelter to Pan."

"Pan!" cried Mr. Sandbach, his mellow voice filling the valley as if it had been a great green church, "Pan is dead. That is why the woods do not shelter him." And he began to tell the striking story of the mariners who were sailing near the coast at the time of the birth of Christ, and three times heard a loud voice saying: "The great god Pan is dead."

"Yes. The great god Pan is dead," said Leyland. And he abandoned himself to that mock misery in which artistic people are so fond of indulging. His cigar went out, and he had to ask me for a match.

"How very interesting," said Rose. "I do wish I knew some ancient history."

"It is not worth your notice," said Mr. Sandbach. "Eh, Eustace?"

Eustace was finishing his whistle. He looked up, with the irritable frown in which his aunts allowed him to indulge, and made no reply.

The conversation turned to various topics and then died out. It was a cloudless afternoon in May, and the pale green of the young chestnut leaves made a pretty contrast with the dark blue of the sky. We were all sitting at the edge of the small clearing for the sake of the view, and the shade of the chestnut saplings behind us was manifestly insufficient. All sounds died away—at least, that is my account; Miss Robinson says that the clamor of the birds was the first sign of uneasiness that she discerned. All sounds died away, except that, far in the distance, I could hear two boughs of a great chestnut grinding together as the tree swayed. The grinds grew shorter and shorter, and finally that sound stopped also. As I looked over the green fingers of the valley, everything was absolutely motionless and still; and that feeling of suspense which one so often experiences when nature is in repose began to steal over me.

Suddenly we were all electrified by the excruciating noise of Eustace's whistle. I never heard any instrument give forth so ear-splitting and discordant a sound.

"Eustace, dear," said Miss Mary Robinson, "you might have thought of your poor Aunt Julia's head."

Leyland, who had apparently been asleep, sat up.

"It is astonishing how blind a boy is to anything that is elevating or beautiful," he observed. "I should not have thought he could have found the wherewithal out here to spoil our pleasure like this."

Then the terrible silence fell upon us again. I was now standing up and watching a cat's-paw of wind that was running down one of the ridges opposite, turning the light green to dark as it traveled. A fanci-

ful feeling of foreboding came over me; so I turned away, to find, to my amazement, that all the others were also on their feet, watching it too.

It is not possible to describe coherently what happened next; but I, for one, am not ashamed to confess that, though the fair blue sky was above me, and the green spring woods beneath me, and the kindest of friends around me, yet I became terribly frightened, more frightened than I ever wish to become again, frightened in a way I never have known either before or after. And in the eyes of the others, too, I saw blank, expressionless fear, while their mouths strove in vain to speak and their hands to gesticulate. Yet all around us were prosperity, beauty, and peace, and all was motionless, save the cat's-paw of wind, now traveling up the ridge on which we stood.

Who moved first has never been settled. It is enough to say that in one second we were tearing away along the hillside. Leyland was in front, then Mr. Sandbach, then my wife. But I only saw for a brief moment; for I ran across the little clearing and through the woods and over the undergrowth and the rocks and down the dry torrent beds into the valley below. The sky might have been black as I ran, and the trees short grass, and the hillside a level road; for I saw nothing and heard nothing and felt nothing, since all the channels of sense and reason were blocked. It was not the spiritual fear that one has known at other times; but brutal overmastering physical fear, stopping up the ears, and dropping clouds before the eyes, and filling the mouth with foul tastes. And it was no ordinary humiliation that survived; for I had been afraid, not as a man, but as a beast.

II

I cannot describe our finish any better than our start; for our fear passed away as it had come, without cause. Suddenly I was able to see, and hear, and cough, and clear my mouth. Looking back, I saw that the others were stopping too; and in a short time we were all together, though it was long before we could speak, and longer before we dared to.

No one was seriously injured. My poor wife had sprained her ankle, Leyland had torn one of his nails on a tree trunk, and I myself had scraped and damaged my ear. I never noticed it till I had stopped.

We were all silent, searching one another's faces. Suddenly Miss Mary Robinson gave a terrible shriek. "Oh, merciful heavens! Where is Eustace?" And then she would have fallen if Mr. Sandbach had not caught her.

"We must go back, we must go back at once," said my Rose, who was quite the most collected of the party. "But I hope—I feel he is safe."

Such was the cowardice of Leyland that he objected. But, finding himself in a minority, and being afraid of being left alone, he gave in. Rose and I supported my poor wife. Mr. Sandbach and Miss Robinson helped Miss Mary, and we returned slowly and silently, taking forty minutes to ascend the path that we had descended in ten.

Our conversation was naturally disjointed, as no one wished to offer an opinion on what had happened. Rose was the most talkative; she startled us all by saying that she had very nearly stopped where she was.

"Do you mean to say that you weren't—that you didn't feel compelled to go?" said Mr. Sandbach.

"Oh, of course, I did feel frightened"—she was the first to use the word—"but I somehow felt that if I could stop on, it would be quite different, that I shouldn't be frightened at all, so to speak." Rose never did express herself clearly; still, it is greatly to her credit that she, the youngest of us, should have held on so long at that terrible time.

"I should have stopped, I do believe," she continued, "if I had not seen Mamma go."

Rose's experience comforted us a little about Eustace. But a feeling of terrible foreboding was on us all as we painfully climbed the chestnut-covered slopes and neared the little clearing. When we reached it our tongues broke loose. There, at the further side, were the remains of our lunch, and close to them, lying motionless on his back, was Eustace.

With some presence of mind I at once cried out: "Hey, you young monkey! Jump up!" But he made no reply, nor did he answer when his poor aunts spoke to him. And, to my unspeakable horror, I saw one of those green lizards dart out from under his shirt cuff as we approached.

We stood watching him as he lay there so silently, and my ears began to tingle in expectation of the outbursts of lamentations and tears.

Miss Mary fell on her knees beside him and touched his hand, which was convulsively entwined in the long grass.

As she did so, he opened his eyes and smiled.

I have often seen that peculiar smile since, both on the possessor's face and on the photographs of him that are beginning to get into the illustrated papers. But, till then, Eustace had always worn a peevish, discontented frown; and we were all unused to this disquieting smile, which always seemed to be without adequate reason.

His aunts showered kisses on him, which he did not reciprocate, and then there was an awkward pause. Eustace seemed so natural and undisturbed; yet, if he had not had astonishing experiences himself, he ought to have been all the more astonished at our extraordinary behavior. My wife, with ready tact, endeavored to behave as if nothing had happened.

"Well, Mr. Eustace," she said, sitting down as she spoke, to ease her foot, "how have you been amusing yourself since we have been away?"

"Thank you, Mrs. Tytler, I have been very happy."

"And where have you been?"

"Here."

"And lying down all the time, you idle boy?"

"No, not all the time."

"What were you doing before?"

"Oh, standing or sitting."

"Stood and sat doing nothing! Don't you know the poem 'Satan finds some mischief still for——' "

"Oh, my dear madam, hush! hush!" Mr. Sandbach's voice broke in; and my wife, naturally mortified by the interruption, said no more and moved away. I was surprised to see Rose immediately take her place and, with more freedom than she generally displayed, run her fingers through the boy's tousled hair.

"Eustace! Eustace!" she said hurriedly, "tell me everything—every single thing."

Slowly he sat up—till then he had lain on his back.

"Oh, Rose——" he whispered, and, my curiosity being aroused, I moved nearer to hear what he was going to say. As I did so, I caught sight of some goats' footmarks in the moist earth beneath the trees.

"Apparently you have had a visit from some goats," I observed. "I had no idea they fed up here."

Eustace laboriously got onto his feet and came to see; and when he saw the footmarks he lay down and rolled on them, as a dog rolls in dirt.

After that there was a grave silence, broken at length by the solemn speech of Mr. Sandbach.

"My dear friends," he said, "it is best to confess the truth bravely. I know that what I am going to say now is what you are all now feeling. The Evil One has been very near us in bodily form. Time may yet discover some injury that he has wrought among us. But at present, for myself at all events, I wish to offer up thanks for a merciful deliverance."

With that he knelt down, and, as the others knelt, I knelt too, though I do not believe in the Devil being allowed to assail us in visible form, as I told Mr. Sandbach afterwards. Eustace came too, and knelt quietly enough between his aunts after they had beckoned to him. But when it was over he at once got up and began hunting for something.

"Why! Someone has cut my whistle in two," he said. (I had seen Leyland with an open knife in his hand—a superstitious act which I could hardly approve.)

"Well, it doesn't matter," he continued.

"And why doesn't it matter?" said Mr. Sandbach, who has ever since tried to entrap Eustace into an account of that mysterious hour.

"Because I don't want it any more."

"Why?"

At that he smiled; and, as no one

seemed to have anything more to say, I set off as fast as I could through the wood and hauled up a donkey to carry my poor wife home. Nothing occurred in my absence, except that Rose had again asked Eustace to tell her what had happened; and he, this time, had turned away his head and had not answered her a single word.

As soon as I returned, we all set off. Eustace walked with difficulty, almost with pain, so that when we reached the other donkeys, his aunts wished him to mount one of them and ride all the way home. I make it a rule never to interfere between relatives, but I put my foot down at this. As it turned out, I was perfectly right, for the healthy exercise, I suppose, began to thaw Eustace's sluggish blood and loosen his stiffened muscles. He stepped out manfully, for the first time in his life, holding his head up and taking deep drafts of air into his chest. I observed with satisfaction to Miss Mary Robinson that Eustace was at last taking some pride in his personal appearance.

Mr. Sandbach sighed, and said that Eustace must be carefully watched, for we none of us understood him yet. Miss Mary Robinson being very much—over much, I think—guided by him, sighed too.

"Come, come, Miss Robinson," I said, "there's nothing wrong with Eustace. Our experiences are mysterious, not his. He was astonished at our sudden departure, that's why he was so strange when we returned. He's right enough—improved, if anything."

"And is the worship of athletics, the cult of insensate activity, to be counted as an improvement?" put in Leyland, fixing a large, sorrowful eye on Eustace, who had stopped to scramble onto a rock to pick some cyclamen. "The passionate desire to rend from nature the few beauties that have been still left her—that is to be counted as an improvement too?"

It is mere waste of time to reply to such remarks, especially when they come from an unsuccessful artist, suffering from a damaged finger. I changed the conversation by asking what we should say at the hotel. After some discussion it was agreed that we should say nothing, either there or in our letters home. Importunate truth telling, which brings only bewilderment and discomfort to the hearers, is, in my opinion, a mistake; and, after a long discussion, I managed to make Mr. Sandbach acquiesce in my view.

Eustace did not share in our conversation. He was racing about, like a real boy, in the wood to the right. A strange feeling of shame prevented us from openly mentioning our fright to him. Indeed, it seemed almost reasonable to conclude that it had made but little impression on him. So it disconcerted us when he bounded back with an armful of flowering acanthus, calling out:

"Do you suppose Gennaro'll be there when we get back?"

Gennaro was the stopgap waiter, a clumsy, impertinent fisher lad, who had been had up from Minori in the absence of the nice English-speaking Emmanuele. It was to him that we owed our scrappy lunch; and I could not conceive why Eustace desired to see him, unless it was to make mock with him of our behavior.

"Yes, of course he will be there," said Miss Robinson. "Why do you ask, dear?"

"Oh, I thought I'd like to see him."

"And why?" snapped Mr. Sandbach.

"Because, because I do, I do; because, because I do." He danced away into the darkening wood to the rhythm of his words.

"This is very extraordinary," said Mr. Sandbach. "Did he like Gennaro before?"

"Gennaro has only been here two days," said Rose, "and I know that they haven't spoken to each other a dozen times."

Each time Eustace returned from the wood his spirits were higher. Once he came whooping down on us as a wild Indian, and another time he made believe to be a dog. The last time he came back with a poor dazed hare, too frightened to move, sitting on his arm. He was getting too uproarious, I thought; and we were all glad to leave the wood and start upon the steep staircase path that leads down into Ravello. It was late and turning dark; and we made all the speed we could, Eustace scurrying in front of us like a goat.

Just where the staircase path debouches on the white highroad, the next extraordinary incident of this extraordinary day occurred. Three old women were standing by the wayside. They, like ourselves, had come down from the woods, and they were resting their heavy bundles of fuel on the low parapet of the road. Eustace stopped in front of them and, after a moment's deliberation, stepped forward and— kissed the left-hand one on the cheek!

"My good fellow!" exclaimed Mr. Sandbach, "are you quite crazy?"

Eustace said nothing, but offered the old woman some of his flowers and then hurried on. I looked back; and the old woman's companions seemed as much astonished at the proceeding as we were. But she herself had put the flowers in her bosom and was murmuring blessings.

This salutation of the old lady was the first example of Eustace's strange behavior, and we were both surprised and alarmed. It was useless talking to him, for he either made silly replies or else bounded away without replying at all.

He made no reference to Gennaro on the way home, and I hoped that that was forgotten. But when we came to the Piazza, in front of the Cathedral, he screamed out: "Gennaro! Gennaro!" at the top of his voice, and began running up the little alley that led to the hotel. Sure enough, there was Gennaro at the end of it, with his arms and legs sticking out of the nice little English-speaking waiter's dress suit, and a dirty fisherman's cap on his head— for, as the poor landlady truly said, however much she superintended his toilet, he always managed to introduce something incongruous into it before he had done.

Eustace sprang to meet him, and leaped right up into his arms and put his own arms round his neck. And this in the presence, not only of us, but also of the landlady, the chambermaid, the facchino, and of two American ladies who were coming for a few days' visit to the little hotel.

I always make a point of behaving pleasantly to Italians, however little they may deserve it; but this habit of promiscuous intimacy was perfectly intolerable and could only lead to familiarity and mortification for all. Taking Miss Robinson aside, I asked her permission to speak seriously to Eustace on the subject of intercourse with social inferiors. She granted it; but I determined to wait till the absurd boy had calmed down a little from the excitement of the day. Meanwhile Gennaro, instead of attending to the wants of the two new ladies, carried Eustace into the house, as if it was the most natural thing in the world.

"*Ho capito*," I heard him say as he passed me. "*Ho capito*" is the Italian for "I have understood"; but, as Eustace had not spoken to him, I could not see the force of the remark. It served to increase our bewilderment, and by the time we sat down at the dinner table, our imaginations and our tongues were alike exhausted.

I omit from this account the various comments that were made, as few of them seem worthy of being recorded. But for three or four hours seven of us were pouring forth our bewilderment in a stream of appropriate and inappropriate exclamations. Some traced a connection between our behavior in the afternoon and the behavior of Eustace now. Others saw no connection at all. Mr. Sandbach still held to the possibility of infernal influences, and also said that he ought to have a doctor. Leyland only saw the development of "that unspeakable Philistine, the boy." Rose maintained, to my surprise, that everything was excusable; while I began to see that the young gentleman wanted a sound thrashing. The poor Miss Robinsons swayed helplessly about between these diverse opinions; inclining now to careful supervision, now to acquiescence, now to corporal chastisement, now to Eno's Fruit Salt.

Dinner passed off fairly well, though Eustace was terribly fidgety, Gennaro as usual dropping the knives and spoons, and hawking and clearing his throat. He only knew a few words of English, and we were all reduced to Italian for making known our wants. Eustace, who had picked up a little somehow, asked for some oranges. To my annoyance, Gennaro in his answer made use of the second person singular—a form only used when addressing those who are both intimates and equals. Eustace had brought it on himself; but an impertinence of this kind was an affront to us all, and I was determined to speak, and to speak at once.

When I heard him clearing the table I went in, and, summoning up my Italian, or rather Neapolitan— the Southern dialects are execrable— I said: "Gennaro! I heard you address Signor Eustace with '*Tu*.'"

"It is true."

"You are not right. You must use '*Lei*' or '*Voi*'—more polite forms. And remember that, though Signor Eustace is sometimes silly and foolish —this afternoon for example—yet you must always behave respectfully to him; for he is a young English gentleman, and you are a poor Italian fisher boy."

I know that speech sounds terribly snobbish, but in Italian one can say things that one would never dream of saying in English. Besides, it is no good speaking delicately to persons of that class. Unless you put things plainly, they take a vicious pleasure in misunderstanding you.

An honest English fisherman would have landed me one in the eye in a minute for such a remark, but the wretched downtrodden Italians have no pride. Gennaro only sighed and said: "It is true."

"Quite so," I said, and turned to go. To my indignation I heard him add: "But sometimes it is not important."

"What do you mean?" I shouted.

He came close up to me with horrid gesticulating fingers.

"Signor Tytler, I wish to say this:

If Eustazio asks me to call him 'Voi,' I will call him 'Voi.' Otherwise, no."

With that he seized up a tray of dinner things and fled from the room with them; and I heard two more wineglasses go on the courtyard floor.

I was now fairly angry, and strode out to interview Eustace. But he had gone to bed, and the landlady, to whom I also wished to speak, was engaged. After more vague wonderings, obscurely expressed owing to the presence of Janet and the two American ladies, we all went to bed, too, after a harassing and most extraordinary day.

III

But the day was nothing to the night.

I suppose I had slept for about four hours, when I woke suddenly thinking I heard a noise in the garden. And immediately, before my eyes were open, cold terrible fear seized me—not fear of something that was happening, like the fear in the wood, but fear of something that might happen.

Our room was on the first floor, looking out onto the garden—or terrace, it was rather: a wedge-shaped block of ground covered with roses and vines, and intersected with little asphalt paths. It was bounded on the small side by the house; round the two long sides ran a wall, only three feet above the terrace level, but with a good twenty-feet drop over it into the olive yards, for the ground fell very precipitously away.

Trembling all over, I stole to the window. There, pattering up and down the asphalt paths, was something white. I was too much alarmed to see clearly; and in the uncertain light of the stars the thing took all

manner of curious shapes. Now it was a great dog, now an enormous white bat, now a mass of quickly traveling cloud. It would bounce like a ball, or take short flights like a bird, or glide slowly like a wraith. It gave no sound—save the pattering sound of what, after all, must be human feet. And at last the obvious explanation forced itself upon my disordered mind; and I realized that Eustace had got out of bed, and that we were in for something more.

I hastily dressed myself and went down into the dining room, which opened upon the terrace. The door was already unfastened. My terror had almost entirely passed away, but for quite five minutes I struggled with a curious cowardly feeling, which bade me not interfere with the poor strange boy, but leave him to his ghostly patterings and merely watch him from the window, to see he took no harm.

But better impulses prevailed and, opening the door, I called out:

"Eustace! What on earth are you doing? Come in at once."

He stopped his antics and said: "I hate my bedroom. I could not stop in it, it is too small."

"Come! Come! I'm tired of affectation. You've never complained of it before."

"Besides I can't see anything—no flowers, no leaves, no sky; only a stone wall." The outlook of Eustace's room certainly was limited; but, as I told him, he had never complained of it before.

"Eustace, you talk like a child. Come in! Prompt obedience, if you please."

He did not move.

"Very well; I shall carry you in by force," I added, and made a few steps towards him. But I was soon convinced of the futility of pursuing a boy through a tangle of asphalt paths, and went in instead, to call Mr. Sandbach and Leyland to my aid.

When I returned with them he was worse than ever. He would not even answer us when we spoke, but began singing and chattering to himself in a most alarming way.

"It's a case for the doctor now," said Mr. Sandbach, gravely tapping his forehead.

He had stopped his running and was singing, first low, then loud— singing five-finger exercises, scales, hymn tunes, scraps of Wagner—anything that came into his head. His voice—a very untuneful voice—grew stronger and stronger, and he ended with a tremendous shout which boomed like a gun among the mountains and awoke everyone who was still sleeping in the hotel. My poor wife and the two girls appeared at their respective windows, and the American ladies were heard violently ringing their bell.

"Eustace," we all cried, "stop! Stop, dear boy, and come into the house."

He shook his head and started off again—talking this time. Never have I listened to such an extraordinary speech. At any other time it would have been ludicrous, for here was a boy, with no sense of beauty and a puerile command of words, attempting to tackle themes which the greatest poets have found almost beyond their power. Eustace Robinson, aged fourteen, was standing in his nightshirt saluting, praising, and blessing, the great forces and manifestations of nature.

He spoke first of night and the stars and planets above his head, of the swarms of fireflies below him, of the invisible sea below the fireflies, of the great rocks covered with anemones and shells that were slumbering in the invisible sea. He spoke of the rivers and waterfalls, of the ripening bunches of grapes, of the smoking cone of Vesuvius and the hidden fire channels that made the smoke, of the myriads of lizards who were lying curled up in the crannies of the sultry earth, of the showers of white rose leaves that were tangled in his hair. And then he spoke of the rain and the wind by which all things are changed, of the air through which all things live, and of the woods in which all things can be hidden.

Of course, it was all absurdly highfaluting: yet I could have kicked Leyland for audibly observing that it was "a diabolical caricature of all that was most holy and beautiful in life."

"And then"—Eustace was going on in the pitiable conversational doggerel which was his only mode of expression—"and then there are men, but I can't make them out so well." He knelt down by the parapet and rested his head on his arms.

"Now's the time," whispered Leyland. I hate stealth, but we darted forward and endeavored to catch hold of him from behind. He was away in a twinkling, but turned round at once to look at us. As far as I could see in the starlight, he was crying. Leyland rushed at him again, and we tried to corner him along the asphalt paths, but without the slightest approach to success.

We returned, breathless and discomfited, leaving him to his madness in the further corner of the terrace. But my Rose had an inspiration.

"Papa," she called from the window, "if you get Gennaro, he might be able to catch him for you."

I had no wish to ask a favor of Gennaro, but, as the landlady had by now appeared on the scene, I begged her to summon him from the charcoal bin in which he slept, and make him try what he could do.

She soon returned, and was shortly followed by Gennaro, attired in a dress coat, without either waistcoat, shirt, or vest, and a ragged pair of what had been trousers, cut short above the knees for purposes of wading. The landlady, who had quite picked up English ways, rebuked him for the incongruous and even indecent appearance which he presented.

"I have a coat and I have trousers. What more do you desire?"

"Never mind, Signora Scafetti," I put in. "As there are no ladies here, it is not of the slightest consequence." Then, turning to Gennaro, I said: "The aunts of Signor Eustace wish you to fetch him into the house."

He did not answer.

"Do you hear me? He is not well. I order you to fetch him into the house."

"Fetch! Fetch!" said Signora Scafetti, and shook him roughly by the arm.

"Eustazio is well where he is."

"Fetch! Fetch!" Signora Scafetti screamed, and let loose a flood of Italian, most of which, I am glad to say, I could not follow. I glanced up nervously at the girls' window, but they hardly know as much as I do, and I am thankful to say that none of us caught one word of Gennaro's answer.

The two yelled and shouted at each other for quite ten minutes, at the end of which Gennaro rushed back to his charcoal bin and Signora Scafetti burst into tears, as well she might, for she greatly valued her English guests.

"He says," she sobbed, "that Signor Eustace is well where he is,

and that he will not fetch him. I can do no more."

But I could, for, in my stupid British way, I have got some insight into the Italian character. I followed Mr. Gennaro to his place of repose and found him wriggling down onto a dirty sack.

"I wish you to fetch Signor Eustace to me," I began.

He hurled at me an unintelligible reply.

"If you fetch him, I will give you this." And out of my pocket I took a new ten-lira note.

This time he did not answer.

"This note is equal to ten lire in silver," I continued, for I knew that the poor-class Italian is unable to conceive of a single large sum.

"I know it."

"That is, two hundred soldi."

"I do not desire them. Eustazio is my friend."

I put the note into my pocket.

"Besides, you would not give it me."

"I am an Englishman. The English always do what they promise."

"That is true." It is astonishing how the most dishonest of nations trust us. Indeed, they often trust us more than we trust one another. Gennaro knelt up on his sack. It was too dark to see his face, but I could feel his warm garlicky breath coming out in gasps, and I knew that the eternal avarice of the South had laid hold upon him.

"I could not fetch Eustazio to the house. He might die there."

"You need not do that," I replied patiently. "You need only bring him to me; and I will stand outside in the garden." And to this, as if it were something quite different, the pitiable youth consented.

"But give me first the ten lire."

"No"—for I knew the kind of person with whom I had to deal. Once faithless, always faithless.

We returned to the terrace, and Gennaro, without a single word, pattered off towards the pattering that could be heard at the remoter end. Mr. Sandbach, Leyland, and myself moved away a little from the house and stood in the shadow of the white climbing roses, practically invisible.

We heard "Eustazio" called, followed by absurd cries of pleasure from the poor boy. The pattering ceased, and we heard them talking. Their voices got nearer, and presently I could discern them through the creepers, the grotesque figure of the young man, and the slim little white-robed boy. Gennaro had his arm round Eustace's neck, and Eustace was talking away in his fluent, slipshod Italian.

"I understand almost everything," I heard him say. "The trees, hills, stars, water, I can see all. But isn't it odd! I can't make out men a bit. Do you know what I mean?"

"*Ho capito*," said Gennaro gravely, and took his arm off Eustace's shoulder. But I made the new note crackle in my pocket; and he heard it. He stuck his hand out with a jerk; and the unsuspecting Eustace gripped it in his own.

"It is odd!" Eustace went on—they were quite close now—"It almost seems as if—as if——"

I darted out and caught hold of his arm, and Leyland got hold of the other arm, and Mr. Sandbach hung onto his feet. He gave shrill, heart-piercing screams; and the white roses, which were falling early that year, descended in showers on him as we dragged him into the house.

As soon as we entered the house he stopped shrieking; but floods of tears silently burst forth and spread over his upturned face.

"Not to my room," he pleaded. "It is so small."

His infinitely dolorous look filled me with strange pity, but what could I do? Besides, his window was the only one that had bars to it.

"Never mind, dear boy," said kind Mr. Sandbach. "I will bear you company till the morning."

At this his convulsive struggles began again. "Oh, please, not that. Anything but that. I will promise to lie still and not to cry more than I can help, if I am left alone."

So we laid him on the bed and drew the sheets over him and left him sobbing bitterly, and saying: "I nearly saw everything, and now I can see nothing at all."

We informed the Miss Robinsons of all that had happened, and returned to the dining room, where we found Signora Scafetti and Gennaro whispering together. Mr. Sandbach got pen and paper and began writing to the English doctor at Naples. I at once drew out the note and flung it down on the table to Gennaro.

"Here is your pay," I said sternly, for I was thinking of the Thirty Pieces of Silver.

"Thank you very much, sir," said Gennaro, and grabbed it.

He was going off, when Leyland, whose interest and indifference were always equally misplaced, asked him what Eustace had meant by saying he could "not make out men a bit."

"I cannot say. Signor Eustazio" (I was glad to observe a little deference at last) "has a subtle brain. He understands many things."

"But I heard you say you understood," Leyland persisted.

"I understand, but I cannot explain. I am a poor Italian fisher lad. Yet, listen: I will try." I saw to my alarm that his manner was changing, and tried to stop him. But he sat down on the edge of the table and started off, with some absolutely incoherent remarks.

"It is sad," he observed at last. "What has happened is very sad. But what can I do? I am poor. It is not I."

I turned away in contempt. Leyland went on asking questions. He wanted to know who it was that Eustace had in his mind when he spoke.

"That is easy to say," Gennaro gravely answered. "It is you, it is I. It is all in this house, and many outside it. If he wishes for mirth, we discomfort him. If he asks to be alone, we disturb him. He longed for a friend, and found none for fifteen years. Then he found me, and the first night I—I who have been in the woods and understood things too—betray him to you, and send him in to die. But what could I do?"

"Gently, gently," said I.

"Oh, assuredly he will die. He will lie in the small room all night, and in the morning he will be dead. That I know for certain."

"There, that will do," said Mr. Sandbach. "I shall be sitting with him."

"Filomena Giusti sat all night with Caterina, but Caterina was dead in the morning. They would not let her out, though I begged, and prayed, and cursed, and beat the door, and climbed the wall. They were ignorant fools, and thought I wished to carry her away. And in the morning she was dead."

"What is all this?" I asked Signora Scafetti.

"All kinds of stories will get about," she replied, "and he, least of anyone, has reason to repeat them."

"And I am alive now," he went on, "because I had neither parents nor relatives nor friends, so that, when the first night came, I could run through the woods and climb the rocks and plunge into the water, until I had accomplished my desire!"

We heard a cry from Eustace's room—a faint but steady sound, like the sound of wind in a distant wood heard by one standing in tranquillity.

"That," said Gennaro, "was the last noise of Caterina. I was hanging onto her window then, and it blew out past me."

And, lifting up his hand, in which my ten-lira note was safely packed, he solemnly cursed Mr. Sandbach, and Leyland, and myself, and Fate, because Eustace was dying in the upstairs room. Such is the working of the Southern mind; and I verily believe that he would not have moved even then, had not Leyland, that unspeakable idiot, upset the lamp with his elbow. It was a patent self-extinguishing lamp, bought by Signora Scafetti, at my special request, to replace the dangerous thing that she was using. The result was that it went out; and the mere physical change from light to darkness had more power over the ignorant animal nature of Gennaro than the most obvious dictates of logic and reason.

I felt, rather than saw, that he had left the room and shouted out to Mr. Sandbach: "Have you got the key of Eustace's room in your pocket?" But Mr. Sandbach and Leyland were both on the floor, having mistaken each other for Gennaro, and some more precious time was wasted in finding a match. Mr. Sandbach had only just time to say that he had left the key in the door, in case the Miss Robinsons wished to pay Eustace a visit, when we heard a noise on the stairs, and there was Gennaro, carrying Eustace down.

We rushed out and blocked up the passage, and they lost heart and retreated to the upper landing.

"Now they are caught," cried Signora Scafetti. "There is no other way out."

We were cautiously ascending the staircase, when there was a terrific scream from my wife's room, followed by a heavy thud on the asphalt path. They had leapt out of her window.

I reached the terrace just in time to see Eustace jumping over the parapet of the garden wall. This time I knew for certain he would be killed. But he alighted in an olive tree, looking like a great white moth, and from the tree he slid onto the earth. And as soon as his bare feet touched the clods of earth he uttered a strange loud cry, such as I should not have thought the human voice could have produced, and disappeared among the trees below.

"He has understood and he is saved," cried Gennaro, who was still sitting on the asphalt path. "Now instead of dying he will live!"

"And you, instead of keeping the ten lire, will give them up," I retorted, for at this theatrical remark I could contain myself no longer.

"The ten lire are mine," he hissed back, in a scarcely audible voice. He clasped his hand over his breast to protect his ill-gotten gains, and, as he did so, he swayed forward and fell upon his face on the path. He had not broken any limbs, and a leap like that would never have killed an Englishman, for the drop was not great. But those miserable Italians have no stamina. Something had gone wrong inside him, and he was dead.

The morning was still far off, but the morning breeze had begun, and more rose leaves fell on us as we carried him in. Signora Scafetti burst into screams at the sight of the dead body, and, far down the valley towards the sea, there still resounded the shouts and the laughter of the escaping boy.

"Saki" (H. H. Munro)

1870-1916

HECTOR HUGH MUNRO was a Scot, born in Burma, and, like Kipling, was sent back to England at an early age to be brought up by two strict aunts. In his early twenties he returned to India and worked there with the Burma Military Police. He had always been delicate, and thirteen months in Burma weakened him so dangerously that he was obliged to return once more to England. His health recovered, he wrote "Alice in Westminster"—political sketches in the Lewis Carroll style, published in the *Westminster Gazette*; and later, during six years as foreign correspondent in Russia and the Balkans, he wrote and sent back to England many of the humorous short stories by which he is best remembered. His pseudonym was Saki, cupbearer in the *Rubáiyát*.

In World War I Munro enlisted as a private, in spite of several offers of a commission, and went to France as corporal at the age of forty-six. In November, 1916, he was killed in the battle of Beaumont-Hamel.

Saki had a rare sense of humor, and his stories, like himself, are full of high spirits, wit, and urbanity. "The empty glass we turn down for him," said Christopher Morley, "is the fragile hollow-stemmed goblet meant for dryest champagne: it is of the finest."

The Open Window

BY "SAKI" (H. H. MUNRO)

"My AUNT will be down presently, Mr. Nuttel," said a very self-possessed young lady of fifteen; "in the meantime you must try and put up with me."

Framton Nuttel endeavored to say the correct something which should duly flatter the niece of the moment without unduly discounting the aunt that was to come. Privately he doubted more than ever whether these formal visits on a succession of total strangers would do much towards helping the nerve cure which he was supposed to be undergoing.

"I know how it will be," his sister had said when he was preparing to migrate to this rural retreat; "you will bury yourself down there and not speak to a living soul, and your nerves will be worse than ever from moping. I shall just give you letters of introduction to all the people I know there. Some of them, as far as I can remember, were quite nice."

Framton wondered whether Mrs. Sappleton, the lady to whom he was presenting one of the letters of introduction, came into the nice division.

"Do you know many of the people round here?" asked the niece, when she judged that they had had sufficient silent communion.

"Hardly a soul," said Framton. "My sister was staying here, at the rectory, you know, some four years ago, and she gave me letters of introduction to some of the people here."

He made the last statement in a tone of distinct regret.

"Then you know practically nothing about my aunt?" pursued the self-possessed young lady.

"Only her name and address," admitted the caller. He was wondering whether Mrs. Sappleton was in the married or widowed state. An undefinable something about the room seemed to suggest masculine habitation.

"Her great tragedy happened just three years ago," said the child; "that would be since your sister's time."

"Her tragedy?" asked Framton; somehow in this restful country spot tragedies seemed out of place.

"You may wonder why we keep that window wide open on an October afternoon," said the niece, indicating a large French window that opened on to a lawn.

"It is quite warm for the time of the year," said Framton; "but has that window got anything to do with the tragedy?"

"Out through that window, three

years ago to a day, her husband and her two young brothers went off for their day's shooting. They never came back. In crossing the moor to their favorite snipe-shooting ground they were all three engulfed in a treacherous piece of bog. It had been that dreadful wet summer, you know, and places that were safe in other years gave way suddenly without warning. Their bodies were never recovered. That was the dreadful part of it." Here the child's voice lost its self-possessed note and became falteringly human. "Poor aunt always thinks that they will come back someday, they and the little brown spaniel that was lost with them, and walk in at that window just as they used to do. That is why the window is kept open every evening till it is quite dusk. Poor dear aunt, she has often told me how they went out, her husband with his white waterproof coat over his arm, and Ronnie, her youngest brother, singing 'Bertie, why do you bound?' as he always did to tease her, because she said it got on her nerves. Do you know, sometimes on still, quiet evenings like this, I almost get a creepy feeling that they will all walk in through that window——"

She broke off with a little shudder. It was a relief to Framton when the aunt bustled into the room with a whirl of apologies for being late in making her appearance.

"I hope Vera has been amusing you?" she said.

"She has been very interesting," said Framton.

"I hope you don't mind the open window," said Mrs. Sappleton briskly; "my husband and brothers will be home directly from shooting, and they always come in this way. They've been out for snipe in the marshes today, so they'll make a fine

mess over my poor carpets. So like you menfolk, isn't it?"

She rattled on cheerfully about the shooting and the scarcity of birds, and the prospects for duck in the winter. To Framton it was all purely horrible. He made a desperate but only partially successful effort to turn the talk on to a less ghastly topic; he was conscious that his hostess was giving him only a fragment of her attention, and her eyes were constantly straying past him to the open window and the lawn beyond. It was certainly an unfortunate coincidence that he should have paid his visit on this tragic anniversary.

"The doctors agree in ordering me complete rest, an absence of mental excitement, and avoidance of anything in the nature of violent physical exercise," announced Framton, who labored under the tolerably widespread delusion that total strangers and chance acquaintances are hungry for the least detail of one's ailments and infirmities, their cause and cure. "On the matter of diet they are not so much in agreement," he continued.

"No?" said Mrs. Sappleton, in a voice which only replaced a yawn at the last moment. Then she suddenly brightened into alert attention—but not to what Framton was saying.

"Here they are at last!" she cried. "Just in time for tea, and don't they look as if they were muddy up to the eyes!"

Framton shivered slightly and turned towards the niece with a look intended to convey sympathetic comprehension. The child was staring out through the open window with a dazed horror in her eyes. In a chill shock of nameless fear Framton swung round in his seat and looked in the same direction.

In the deepening twilight three figures were walking across the lawn towards the window; they all carried guns under their arms, and one of them was additionally burdened with a white coat hung over his shoulders. A tired brown spaniel kept close at their heels. Noiselessly they neared the house, and then a hoarse young voice chanted out of the dusk: "I said, Bertie, why do you bound?"

Framton grabbed wildly at his stick and hat; the hall door, the gravel drive, and the front gate were dimly noted stages in his headlong retreat. A cyclist coming along the road had to run into the hedge to avoid imminent collision.

"Here we are, my dear," said the bearer of the white mackintosh, coming in through the window; "fairly muddy, but most of it's dry. Who was that who bolted out as we came up?"

"A most extraordinary man, a Mr. Nuttel," said Mrs. Sappleton; "could only talk about his illnesses, and dashed off without a word of good-by or apology when you arrived. One would think he had seen a ghost."

"I expect it was the spaniel," said the niece calmly; "he told me he had a horror of dogs. He was once hunted into a cemetery somewhere on the banks of the Ganges by a pack of pariah dogs, and had to spend the night in a newly dug grave with the creatures snarling and grinning and foaming just above him. Enough to make anyone lose their nerve."

Romance at short notice was her speciality.

Oliver Onions
1873-1961

THE matter of George Oliver Onions' name always aroused controversy. According to the best information, he used the first two thirds (George Oliver) in private life, the second two thirds as a writer, and Onions *is* pronounced like the vegetable. He studied art in Paris, lived in the Latin Quarter for many years, and made his living from posters, advertising, illustrating. As a writer he was an original, living in a world quite his own—"a world in which the sudden blowing of a curtain or a light shining behind a window may suggest a terror, a drama, a solution." Although he wrote and rewrote many times for his own satisfaction, it is said that he was completely indifferent to the effect of his work on the public. "The Beckoning Fair One" comes from that especially choice volume, *Widdershins*.

The Beckoning Fair One

BY OLIVER ONIONS

THE three or four "To Let" boards had stood within the low paling as long as the inhabitants of the little triangular "Square" could remember, and if they had ever been vertical it was a very long time ago. They now overhung the palings each at its own angle, and resembled nothing so much as a row of wooden choppers, ever in the act of falling upon some passer-by, yet never cutting off a tenant for the old house from the stream of his fellows. Not that there was ever any great "stream" through the square; the stream passed a furlong and more away, beyond the intricacy of tenements and alleys and byways that had sprung up since the old house had been built, hemming it in completely; and probably the house itself was only suffered to stand pending the falling in of a lease or two, when doubtless a clearance would be made of the whole neighborhood.

It was of bloomy old red brick, and built into its walls were the crowns and clasped hands and other insignia of insurance companies long since defunct. The children of the secluded square had swung upon the low gate at the end of the entrance alley until little more than the solid top bar of it remained, and the alley itself ran past boarded basement windows on which tramps had chalked their cryptic marks. The path was washed and worn uneven by the spilling of water from the eaves of the encroaching next house, and cats and dogs had made the approach their own. The chances of a tenant did not seem such as to warrant the keeping of the "To Let" boards in a state of legibility and repair, and as a matter of fact they were not so kept.

For six months Oleron had passed the old place twice a day or oftener, on his way from his lodgings to the room, ten minutes' walk away, he had taken to work in; and for six months no hatchetlike notice board had fallen across his path. This might have been due to the fact that he usually took the other side of the square. But he chanced one morning to take the side that ran past the broken gate and the rain-worn entrance alley, and to pause before one of the inclined boards. The board bore, besides the agent's name, the announcement, written apparently about the time of Oleron's own early youth, that the key was to be had at Number Six.

Now Oleron was already paying, for his separate bedroom and work-

From *Widdershins* by Oliver Onions. By permission of the author and A. P. Watt & Son of London. Published by Secker & Warburg, London.

room, more than an author who, without private means, habitually disregards his public, can afford; and he was paying in addition a small rent for the storage of the greater part of his grandmother's furniture. Moreover, it invariably happened that the book he wished to read in bed was at his working quarters half a mile and more away, while the note or letter he had sudden need of during the day was as likely as not to be in the pocket of another coat hanging behind his bedroom door. And there were other inconveniences in having a divided domicile. Therefore Oleron, brought suddenly up by the hatchetlike notice board, looked first down through some scanty privet bushes at the boarded basement windows, then up at the blank and grimy windows of the first floor, and so up to the second floor and the flat stone coping of the leads. He stood for a minute thumbing his lean and shaven jaw; then, with another glance at the board, he walked slowly across the square to Number Six.

He knocked, and waited for two or three minutes, but, although the door stood open, received no answer. He was knocking again when a long-nosed man in shirt sleeves appeared.

"I was asking a blessing on our food," he said in severe explanation.

Oleron asked if he might have the key of the old house; and the long-nosed man withdrew again.

Oleron waited for another five minutes on the step; then the man, appearing again and masticating some of the food of which he had spoken, announced that the key was lost.

"But you won't want it," he said. "The entrance door isn't closed, and a push'll open any of the others. I'm

an agent for it, if you're thinking of taking it——"

Oleron recrossed the square, descended the two steps at the broken gate, passed along the alley, and turned in at the old wide doorway. To the right, immediately within the door, steps descended to the roomy cellars, and the staircase before him had a carved rail, and was broad and handsome and filthy. Oleron ascended it, avoiding contact with the rail and wall, and stopped at the first landing. A door facing him had been boarded up, but he pushed at that on his right hand, and an insecure bolt or staple yielded. He entered the empty first floor.

He spent a quarter of an hour in the place, and then came out again. Without mounting higher, he descended and recrossed the square to the house of the man who had lost the key.

"Can you tell me how much the rent is?" he asked.

The man mentioned a figure, the comparative lowness of which seemed accounted for by the character of the neighborhood and the abominable state of unrepair of the place.

"Would it be possible to rent a single floor?"

The long-nosed man did not know; they might. . . .

"Who are they?"

The man gave Oleron the name of a firm of lawyers in Lincoln's Inn.

"You might mention my name— Barrett," he added.

Pressure of work prevented Oleron from going down to Lincoln's Inn that afternoon, but he went on the morrow, and was instantly offered the whole house as a purchase for fifty pounds down, the remainder of the purchase money to remain on mortgage. It took him half an hour to disabuse the lawyer's mind of the idea that he wished anything more of the place than to rent a single floor of it. This made certain hums and haws of a difference, and the lawyer was by no means certain that it lay within his power to do as Oleron suggested; but it was finally extracted from him that, provided the notice boards were allowed to remain up, and that, provided it was agreed that in the event of the whole house letting, the arrangement should terminate automatically without further notice, something might be done. That the old place should suddenly be let over his head seemed to Oleron the slightest of risks to take, and he promised a decision within a week. On the morrow he visited the house again, went through it from top to bottom, and then went home to his lodgings to take a bath.

He was immensely taken with that portion of the house he had already determined should be his own. Scraped clean and repainted, and with that old furniture of Oleron's grandmother's, it ought to be entirely charming. He went to the storage warehouse to refresh his memory of his half-forgotten belongings, and to take measurements; and thence he went to a decorator's. He was very busy with his regular work, and could have wished that the notice board had caught his attention either a few months earlier or else later in the year; but the quickest way would be to suspend work entirely until after his removal. . . .

A fortnight later his first floor was painted throughout in a tender, elderflower white, the paint was dry, and Oleron was in the middle of his installation. He was animated, delighted; and he rubbed his hands as he polished and made disposals of his grandmother's effects—the tall lattice-paned china cupboard with its Derby and Mason and Spode, the large folding Sheraton table, the long, low bookshelves (he had had two of them "copied"), the chairs, the Sheffield candlesticks, the riveted rose bowls. These things he set against his newly painted elderwhite walls—walls of wood paneled in the happiest proportions, and molded and coffered to the low-seated window recesses in a mood of gaiety and rest that the builders of rooms no longer know. The ceilings were lofty, and faintly painted with an old pattern of stars, even the tapering moldings of his iron fireplace were as delicately designed as jewelry; and Oleron walked about rubbing his hands, frequently stopping for the mere pleasure of the glimpses from white room to white room. . . .

"Charming, charming!" he said to himself. "I wonder what Elsie Bengough will think of this!"

He bought a bolt and a Yale lock for his door, and shut off his quarters from the rest of the house. If he now wanted to read in bed, his book could be had for stepping into the next room. All the time, he thought how exceedingly lucky he was to get the place. He put up a hatrack in the little square hall, and hung up his hats and caps and coats; and passers through the small triangular square late at night, looking up over the little serried row of wooden "To Let" hatchets, could see the light within Oleron's red blinds, or else the sudden darkening of one blind and the illumination of another, as Oleron, candlestick in hand, passed from room to room, making final settlings of his furniture, or preparing to resume the work that his removal had interrupted.

II

As far as the chief business of his life—his writing—was concerned, Paul Oleron treated the world a good deal better than he was treated by it; but he seldom took the trouble to strike a balance, or to compute how far, at forty-four years of age, he was behind his points on the handicap. To have done so wouldn't have altered matters, and it might have depressed Oleron. He had chosen his path, and was committed to it beyond possibility of withdrawal. Perhaps he had chosen it in the days when he had been easily swayed by something a little disinterested, a little generous, a little noble; and had he ever thought of questioning himself he would still have held to it that a life without nobility and generosity and disinterestedness was no life for him. Only quite recently, and rarely, had he even vaguely suspected that there was more in it than this; but it was no good anticipating the day when, he supposed, he would reach that maximum point of his powers beyond which he must inevitably decline, and be left face to face with the question whether it would not have profited him better to have ruled his life by less exigent ideals.

In the meantime, his removal into the old house with the insurance marks built into its brick merely interrupted *Romilly Bishop* at the fifteenth chapter.

As this tall man with the lean, ascetic face moved about his new abode, arranging, changing, altering, hardly yet into his working stride again, he gave the impression of almost spinsterlike precision and nicety. For twenty years past, in a score of lodgings, garrets, flats, and rooms furnished and unfurnished, he had been accustomed to do many things for himself, and he had discovered that it saves time and temper to be methodical. He had arranged with the wife of the long-nosed Barrett, a stout Welsh woman with a falsetto voice, the Merionethshire accent of which long residence in London had not perceptibly modified, to come across the square each morning to prepare his breakfast, and also to "turn the place out" on Saturday mornings; and for the rest, he even welcomed a little housework as a relaxation from the strain of writing.

His kitchen, together with the adjoining strip of an apartment into which a modern bath had been fitted, overlooked the alley at the side of the house; and at one end of it was a large closet with a door, and a square sliding hatch in the upper part of the door. This had been a powder closet, and through the hatch the elaborately dressed head had been thrust to receive the click and puff of the powder pistol. Oleron puzzled a little over this closet; then, as its use occurred to him, he smiled faintly, a little moved, he knew not by what. . . . He would have to put it to a very different purpose from its original one; it would probably have to serve as his larder. . . . It was in this closet that he made a discovery. The back of it was shelved, and, rummaging on an upper shelf that ran deeply into the wall, Oleron found a couple of mushroom-shaped old wooden wig stands. He did not know how they had come to be there. Doubtless the painters had turned them up somewhere or other, and had put them there. But his five rooms, as a whole, were short of cupboard and closet room; and it was only by the exercise of some ingenuity that he was able to find places for the bestowal of his household linen, his boxes, and his seldom-used but not-to-be-destroyed accumulations of papers.

It was in the early spring that Oleron entered on his tenancy, and he was anxious to have *Romilly* ready for publication in the coming autumn. Nevertheless, he did not intend to force its production. Should it demand longer in the doing, so much the worse; he realized its importance, its crucial importance, in his artistic development, and it must have its own length and time. In the workroom he had recently left he had been making excellent progress; *Romilly* had begun, as the saying is, to speak and act of herself; and he did not doubt she would continue to do so the moment the distraction of his removal was over. This distraction was almost over; he told himself it was time he pulled himself together again; and on a March morning he went out, returned again with two great bunches of yellow daffodils, placed one bunch on his mantelpiece between the Sheffield sticks and the other on the table before him, and took out the half-completed manuscript of *Romilly Bishop*.

But before beginning work he went to a small rosewood cabinet and took from a drawer his checkbook and passbook. He toted them up, and his monklike face grew thoughtful. His installation had cost him more than he had intended it should, and his balance was rather less than fifty pounds, with no immediate prospect of more.

"Hm! I'd forgotten rugs and chintz curtains and so forth mounted up so," said Oleron. "But it would have been a pity to spoil the place for the want of ten pounds or so. . . . Well, *Romilly* simply *must* be out

for the autumn, that's all. So here goes——"

He drew his papers towards him.

But he worked badly; or, rather, he did not work at all. The square outside had its own noises, frequent and new, and Oleron could only hope that he would speedily become accustomed to these. First came hawkers, with their carts and cries; at midday the children, returning from school, trooped into the square and swung on Oleron's gate; and when the children had departed again for afternoon school, an itinerant musician with a mandolin posted himself beneath Oleron's window and began to strum. This was a not unpleasant distraction, and Oleron, pushing up his window, threw the man a penny. Then he returned to his table again. . . .

But it was no good. He came to himself, at long intervals, to find that he had been looking about his room and wondering how it had formerly been furnished—whether a settee in buttercup or petunia satin had stood under the farther window, whether from the center molding of the light lofty ceiling had depended a glimmering crystal chandelier, or where the tambour frame or the piquet table had stood. . . . No, it was no good; he had far better be frankly doing nothing than getting fruitlessly tired; and he decided that he would take a walk, but, chancing to sit down for a moment, dozed in his chair instead.

"This won't do," he yawned when he awoke at half-past four in the afternoon; "I must do better than this tomorrow——"

And he felt so deliciously lazy that for some minutes he even contemplated the breach of an appointment he had for the evening.

The next morning he sat down to

work without even permitting himself to answer one of his three letters —two of them tradesmen's accounts, the third a note from Miss Bengough, forwarded from his old address. It was a jolly day of white and blue, with a gay noisy wind and a subtle turn in the color of growing things; and over and over again, once or twice a minute, his room became suddenly light and then subdued again, as the shining white clouds rolled northeastwards over the square. The soft fitful illumination was reflected in the polished surface of the table and even in the footworn old floor; and the morning noises had begun again.

Oleron made a pattern of dots on the paper before him, and then broke off to move the jar of daffodils exactly opposite the center of a creamy panel. Then he wrote a sentence that ran continuously for a couple of lines, after which it broke off into notes and jottings. For a time he succeeded in persuading himself that in making these memoranda he was really working; and then he rose and began to pace his room. As he did so, he was struck by an idea. It was that the place might possibly be a little better for more positive color. It was, perhaps, a thought *too* pale—mild and sweet as a kind old face, but a little devitalized, even wan. . . . Yes, decidedly it would be a robuster note —more and richer flowers, and possibly some warm and gay stuff for cushions for the window seats. . . .

"Of course, I really can't afford it," he muttered, as he went for a two-foot and began to measure the width of the window recesses. . . .

In stooping to measure a recess, his attitude suddenly changed to one of interest and attention. Presently he rose again, rubbing his hands with gentle glee.

"Oho, oho!" he said. "These look to me very much like window boxes, nailed up. We must look into this! Yes, those are boxes, or I'm . . . oho, this is an adventure!"

On that wall of his sitting room there were two windows (the third was in another corner), and, beyond the open bedroom door, on the same wall, was another. The seats of all had been painted, repainted, and painted again; and Oleron's investigating finger had barely detected the old nailheads beneath the paint. Under the ledge over which he stooped an old keyhole also had been puttied up. Oleron took out his penknife.

He worked carefully for five minutes, and then went into the kitchen for a hammer and chisel. Driving the chisel cautiously under the seat, he started the whole lid slightly. Again using the penknife, he cut along the hinged edge and outward along the ends; and then he fetched a wedge and a wooden mallet.

"Now for our little mystery——" he said.

The sound of the mallet on the wedge seemed, in that sweet and pale apartment, somehow a little brutal—nay, even shocking. The paneling rang and rattled and vibrated to the blows like a sounding board. The whole house seemed to echo; from the roomy cellarage to the garrets above a flock of echoes seemed to awake; and the sound got a little on Oleron's nerves. All at once he paused, fetched a duster, and muffled the mallet. . . . When the edge was sufficiently raised he put his fingers under it and lifted. The paint flaked and starred a little; the rusty old nails squeaked and grunted; and the lid came up, laying open the box beneath. Oleron looked into it. Save for a couple of inches of scurf and mold and old cobwebs it was empty.

"No treasure there," said Oleron, a little amused that he should have fancied there might have been. "*Romilly* will still have to be out by the autumn. Let's have a look at the others."

He turned to the second window. The raising of the two remaining seats occupied him until well into the afternoon. That of the bedroom, like the first, was empty; but from the second seat of his sitting room he drew out something yielding and folded and furred over an inch thick with dust. He carried the object into the kitchen, and having swept it over a bucket, took a duster to it.

It was some sort of a large bag, of an ancient friezelike material, and when unfolded it occupied the greater part of the small kitchen floor. In shape it was an irregular, a very irregular, triangle, and it had a couple of wide flaps, with the remains of straps and buckles. The patch that had been uppermost in the folding was of a faded yellowish brown; but the rest of it was of shades of crimson that varied according to the exposure of the parts of it.

"Now whatever can that have been?" Oleron mused as he stood surveying it. . . . "I give it up. Whatever it is, it's settled my work for today, I'm afraid——"

He folded the object up carelessly and thrust it into a corner of the kitchen; then, taking pans and brushes and an old knife, he returned to the sitting room and began to scrape and to wash and to line with paper his newly discovered receptacles. When he had finished, he put his spare boots and books and papers into them; and he closed the lids again, amused with his little adventure, but also a little anxious for the hour to come when he should settle fairly down to his work again.

III

It piqued Oleron a little that his friend, Miss Bengough, should dismiss with a glance the place he himself had found so singularly winning. Indeed she scarcely lifted her eyes to it. But then she had always been more or less like that—a little indifferent to the graces of life, careless of appearances, and perhaps a shade more herself when she ate biscuits from a paper bag than when she dined with greater observance of the convenances. She was an unattached journalist of thirty-four, large, showy, fair as butter, pink as a dog rose, reminding one of a florist's picked specimen bloom, and given to sudden and ample movements and moist and explosive utterances. She "pulled a better living out of the pool" (as she expressed it) than Oleron did; and by cunningly disguised puffs of drapers and haberdashers she "pulled" also the greater part of her very varied wardrobe. She left small whirlwinds of air behind her when she moved, in which her veils and scarves fluttered and spun.

Oleron heard a flurry of her skirts on his staircase and her single loud knock at his door when he had been a month in his new abode. Her garments brought in the outer air, and she flung a bundle of ladies' journals down on a chair.

"Don't knock off for me," she said across a mouthful of large-headed hatpins as she removed her hat and veil. "I didn't know whether you were straight yet, so I've brought some sandwiches for lunch. You've got coffee, I suppose?—No, don't get up—I'll find the kitchen——"

"Oh, that's all right, I'll clear these things away. To tell the truth, I'm rather glad to be interrupted," said Oleron.

He gathered his work together and put it away. She was already in the kitchen; he heard the running of water into the kettle. He joined her, and ten minutes later followed her back to the sitting room with the coffee and sandwiches on a tray. They sat down, with the tray on a small table between them.

"Well, what do you think of the new place?" Oleron asked as she poured out coffee.

"Hm! . . . Anybody'd think you were going to get married, Paul."

He laughed.

"Oh no. But it's an improvement on some of them, isn't it?"

"Is it? I suppose it is; I don't know, I liked the last place, in spite of the black ceiling and no water tap. How's *Romilly*?"

Oleron thumbed his chin.

"Hm! I'm rather ashamed to tell you. The fact is, I've not got on very well with it. But it will be all right on the night, as you used to say."

"Stuck?"

"Rather stuck."

"Got any of it you care to read to me? . . ."

Oleron had long been in the habit of reading portions of his work to Miss Bengough occasionally. Her comments were always quick and practical, sometimes directly useful, sometimes indirectly suggestive. She, in return for his confidence, always kept all mention of her own work sedulously from him. His, she said, was "real work"; hers merely filled

space, not always even grammatically.

"I'm afraid there isn't," Oleron replied, still meditatively dry-shaving his chin. Then he added, with a little burst of candor, "The fact is, Elsie, I've not written—not actually written—very much more of it— *any* more of it, in fact. But, of course, that doesn't mean I haven't progressed. I've progressed, in one sense, rather alarmingly. I'm now thinking of reconstructing the whole thing."

Miss Bengough gave a gasp. "Reconstructing!"

"Making Romilly herself a different type of woman. Somehow, I've begun to feel that I'm not getting the most out of her. As she stands, I've certainly lost interest in her to some extent."

"But—but——" Miss Bengough protested, "you had her so real, so *living*, Paul!"

Oleron smiled faintly. He had been quite prepared for Miss Bengough's disapproval. He wasn't surprised that she liked Romilly as she at present existed; she would. Whether she realized it or not, there was much of herself in his fictitious creation. Naturally Romilly would seem "real," "living," to her. . . .

"But are you really serious, Paul?" Miss Bengough asked presently, with a round-eyed stare.

"Quite serious."

"You're really going to scrap those fifteen chapters?"

"I didn't exactly say that."

"That fine, rich love scene?"

"I should only do it reluctantly, and for the sake of something I thought better."

"And that beautiful, *beaut*iful description of Romilly on the shore?"

"It wouldn't necessarily be wasted," he said a little uneasily.

But Miss Bengough made a large and windy gesture, and then let him have it.

"Really, you are *too* trying!" she broke out. "I do wish sometimes you'd remember you're human, and live in a world! You know I'd be the *last* to wish you to lower your standard one inch, but it wouldn't be lowering it to bring it within human comprehension. Oh, you're sometimes altogether too godlike! . . . Why, it would be a wicked, criminal waste of your powers to destroy those fifteen chapters! Look at it reasonably, now. You've been working for nearly twenty years; you've now got what you've been working for almost within your grasp; your affairs are at a most critical stage (oh, don't tell me; I know you're about at the end of your money); and here you are, deliberately proposing to withdraw a thing that will probably make your name, and to substitute for it something that ten to one nobody on earth will ever want to read—and small blame to them! Really, you try my patience!"

Oleron had shaken his head slowly as she had talked. It was an old story between them. The noisy, able, practical journalist was an admirable friend—up to a certain point; beyond that . . . well, each of us knows that point beyond which we stand alone. Elsie Bengough sometimes said that had she had one-tenth part of Oleron's genius there were few things she could not have done—thus making that genius a quantitatively divisible thing, a sort of ingredient, to be added to or subtracted from in the admixture of his work. That it was a qualitative thing, essential, indivisible, informing, passed her comprehension. Their spirits parted company at that point. Oleron knew it. She did not appear to know it.

"Yes, yes, yes," he said a little wearily, by and by, "practically you're quite right, entirely right, and I haven't a word to say. If I could only turn *Romilly* over to you you'd make an enormous success of her. But that can't be, and I, for my part, am seriously doubting whether she's worth my while. You know what that means."

"What does it mean?" she demanded bluntly.

"Well," he said, smiling wanly, "what *does* it mean when you're convinced a thing isn't worth doing? You simply don't do it."

Miss Bengough's eyes swept the ceiling for assistance against this impossible man.

"What utter rubbish!" she broke out at last. "Why, when I saw you last you were simply oozing *Romilly*; you were turning her off at the rate of four chapters a week; if you hadn't moved you'd have had her three-parts done by now. What on earth possessed you to move right in the middle of your most important work?"

Oleron tried to put her off with a recital of inconveniences, but she wouldn't have it. Perhaps in her heart she partly suspected the reason. He was simply mortally weary of the narrow circumstances of his life. He had had twenty years of it—twenty years of garrets and roof chambers and dingy flats and shabby lodgings, and he was tired of dinginess and shabbiness. The reward was as far off as ever—or if it was not, he no longer cared as once he would have cared to put out his hand and take it. It is all very well to tell a man who is at the point of exhaustion that only another effort is required of him; if he cannot make it he is as far off as ever. . . .

"Anyway," Oleron summed up, "I'm happier here than I've been for a long time. That's some sort of a justification."

"And doing no work," said Miss Bengough pointedly.

At that a trifling petulance that had been gathering in Oleron came to a head.

"And why should I do nothing but work?" he demanded. "How much happier am I for it? I don't say I don't love my work—when it's done; but I hate doing it. Sometimes it's an intolerable burden that I simply long to be rid of. Once in many weeks it has a moment, one moment, of glow and thrill for me; I remember the days when it was all glow and thrill; and now I'm forty-four, and it's becoming drudgery. Nobody wants it; I'm ceasing to want it myself; and if any ordinary sensible man were to ask me whether I didn't think I was a fool to go on, I think I should agree that I was."

Miss Bengough's comely pink face was serious.

"But you knew all that, many, many years ago, Paul—and still you chose it," she said in a low voice.

"Well, and how should I have known?" he demanded. "I didn't know. I was told so. My heart, if you like, told me so, and I thought I knew. Youth always thinks it knows; then one day it discovers that it is nearly fifty——"

"Forty-four, Paul——"

—"forty-four, then—and it finds that the glamour isn't in front, but behind. Yes, I knew and chose, if *that's* knowing and choosing . . . but it's a costly choice we're called on to make when we're young!"

Miss Bengough's eyes were on the floor. Without moving them she

said, "You're not regretting it, Paul?"

"Am I not?" he took her up. "Upon my word, I've lately thought I am! What *do* I get in return for it all?"

"You know what you get," she replied.

He might have known from her tone what else he could have had for the holding up of a finger—herself. She knew, but could not tell him, that he could have done no better thing for himself. Had he, any time these ten years, asked her to marry him, she would have replied quietly, "Very well; when?" He had never thought of it. . . .

"Yours is the real work," she continued quietly. "Without you we jackals couldn't exist. You and a few like you hold everything upon your shoulders."

For a minute there was a silence. Then it occurred to Oleron that this was common vulgar grumbling. It was not his habit. Suddenly he rose and began to stack cups and plates on the tray.

"Sorry you catch me like this, Elsie," he said, with a little laugh. ". . . No, I'll take them out; then we'll go for a walk if you like. . . ."

He carried out the tray, and then began to show Miss Bengough round his flat. She made few comments. In the kitchen she asked what an old faded square of reddish frieze was, that Mrs. Barrett used as a cushion for her wooden chair.

"That? I should be glad if you could tell *me* what it is," Oleron replied as he unfolded the bag and related the story of its finding in the window seat.

"I think I know what it is," said Miss Bengough. "It's been used to wrap up a harp before putting it into its case."

"By Jove, that's probably just what it was," said Oleron. "I could make neither head nor tail of it. . . ."

They finished the tour of the flat, and returned to the sitting room.

"And who lives in the rest of the house?" Miss Bengough asked.

"I dare say a tramp sleeps in the cellar occasionally. Nobody else."

"Hm! . . . Well, I'll tell you what I think about it, if you like."

"I should like."

"You'll never work here."

"Oh?" said Oleron quickly. "Why not?"

"You'll never finish *Romilly* here. Why, I don't know, but you won't. I know it. You'll have to leave before you get on with that book."

He mused for a moment, and then said:

"Isn't that a little—prejudiced, Elsie?"

"Perfectly ridiculous. As an argument it hasn't a leg to stand on. But there it is," she replied, her mouth once more full of the large-headed hatpins.

Oleron was reaching down his hat and coat. He laughed.

"I can only hope you're entirely wrong," he said, "for I shall be in a serious mess if *Romilly* isn't out in the autumn."

IV

As Oleron sat by his fire that evening, pondering Miss Bengough's prognostication that difficulties awaited him in his work, he came to the conclusion that it would have been far better had she kept her beliefs to herself. No man does a thing better for having his confidence damped at the outset, and to speak of difficulties is in a sense to make them. Speech itself becomes a deterrent act, to which other discouragements accrete until the very event of which warning is given is as likely as not to come to pass. He heartily confounded her. An influence hostile to the completion of *Romilly* had been born.

And in some illogical, dogmatic way women seem to have, she had attached this antagonistic influence to his new abode. Was ever anything so absurd! "You'll never finish *Romilly* here." . . . Why not? Was this her idea of the luxury that saps the springs of action and brings a man down to indolence and dropping out of the race? The place was well enough—it was entirely charming, for that matter—but it was not so demoralizing as all that! No; Elsie had missed her mark that time. . . .

He moved his chair to look round the room that smiled, positively smiled, in the firelight. He too smiled, as if pity was to be entertained for a maligned apartment. Even that slight lack of robust color he had remarked was not noticeable in the soft glow. The drawn chintz curtains— they had a flowered and trellised pattern, with baskets and oaten pipes—fell in long quiet folds to the window seats; the rows of bindings in old bookcases took the light richly; the last trace of sallowness had gone with the daylight; and, if the truth must be told, it had been Elsie herself who had seemed a little out of the picture.

That reflection struck him a little, and presently he returned to it. Yes, the room had, quite accidentally, done Miss Bengough a disservice that afternoon. It had, in some subtle but unmistakable way, placed her, marked a contrast of qualities. Assuming for the sake of argument the slightly ridiculous proposition that the room in which Oleron sat *was* characterized by a certain sparsity and lack of vigor; so much the worse

for Miss Bengough; she certainly
erred on the side of redundancy and
general muchness. And if one must
contrast abstract qualities, Oleron
inclined to the austere in taste. . . .

Yes, here Oleron had made a distinct discovery; he wondered he had
not made it before. He pictured
Miss Bengough again as she had
appeared that afternoon—large,
showy, moistly pink, with that quality of the prize bloom exuding, as it
were from her; and instantly she
suffered in his thought. He even
recognized now that he had noticed
something odd at the time, and that
unconsciously his attitude, even
while she had been there, had been
one of criticism. The mechanism of
her was a little obvious; her melting
humidity was the result of analyz-
able processes; and behind her there
had seemed to lurk some dim shape
emblematic of mortality. He had
never, during the ten years of their
intimacy, dreamed for a moment of
asking her to marry him; none the
less, he now felt for the first time a
thankfulness that he had not done
so. . . .

Then, suddenly and swiftly, his
face flamed that he should be thinking thus of his friend. What! Elsie
Bengough, with whom he had spent
weeks and weeks of afternoons—she,
the good chum, on whose help he
would have counted had all the
rest of the world failed him—she,
whose loyalty to him would not, he
knew, swerve as long as there was
breath in her—Elsie to be even in
thought dissected thus! He was an
ingrate and a cad. . . .

Had she been there in that moment he would have abased himself
before her.

For ten minutes and more he sat,
still gazing into the fire, with that
humiliating red fading slowly from

his cheeks. All was still within and
without, save for a tiny musical
tinkling that came from his kitchen
—the dripping of water from an imperfectly turned-off tap into the
vessel beneath it. Mechanically he
began to beat with his fingers to the
faintly heard falling of the drops;
the tiny regular movement seemed
to hasten that shameful withdrawal
from his face. He grew cool once
more; and when he resumed his
meditation he was all unconscious
that he took it up again at the same
point. . . .

It was not only her florid super-
fluity of build that he had approached in the attitude of criticism;
he was conscious also of the wide
differences between her mind and his
own. He felt no thankfulness that
up to a certain point their natures
had ever run companionably side by
side; he was now full of questions
beyond that point. Their intellects
diverged; there was no denying it;
and, looking back, he was inclined
to doubt whether there had been
any real coincidence. True, he had
read his writings to her and she had
appeared to speak comprehendingly
and to the point; but what can a
man do who, having assumed that
another sees as he does, is suddenly
brought up sharp by something that
falsifies and discredits all that has
gone before? He doubted all now.
. . . It did for a moment occur to
him that the man who demands of
a friend more than can be given to
him is in danger of losing that
friend, but he put the thought aside.

Again he ceased to think, and
again moved his finger to the distant
dripping of the tap. . . .

And now (he resumed by and
by), if these things were true of
Elsie Bengough, they were also true
of the creation of which she was the

prototype—Romilly Bishop. And since he could say of Romilly what for very shame he could not say of Elsie, he gave his thoughts rein. He did so in that smiling, firelighted room, to the accompaniment of the faintly heard tap.

There was no longer any doubt about it; he hated the central character of his novel. Even as he had described her physically she overpowered the senses; she was coarse-fibered, overcolored, rank. It became true the moment he formulated his thought; Gulliver had described the Brobdingnagian maids of honor thus: and mentally and spiritually she corresponded—was unsensitive, limited, common. The model (he closed his eyes for a moment)—the model stuck out through fifteen vulgar and blatant chapters to such a pitch that, without seeing the reason, he had been unable to begin the sixteenth. He marveled that it had only just dawned upon him.

And *this* was to have been his Beatrice, his vision! As Elsie she was to have gone into the furnace of his art, and she was to have come out the woman all men desire! Her thoughts were to have been culled from his own finest, her form from his dearest dreams, and her setting wherever he could find one fit for her worth. He had brooded long before making the attempt; then one day he had felt her stir within him as a mother feels a quickening, and he had added chapter to chapter. . . .

And those fifteen sodden chapters were what he had produced!

Again he sat, softly moving his finger. . . .

Then he bestirred himself.

She must go, all fifteen chapters of her. That was settled. For what was to take her place his mind was a blank; but one thing at a time; a man is not excused from taking the wrong course because the right one is not immediately revealed to him. Better would come if it was to come; in the meantime——

He rose, fetched the fifteen chapters, and read them over before he should drop them into the fire.

But instead of putting them into the fire he let them fall from his hand. He became conscious of the dripping of the tap again. It had a tinkling gamut of four or five notes, on which it rang irregular changes, and it was foolishly sweet and dulcimerlike. In his mind Oleron could see the gathering of each drop, its little tremble on the lip of the tap, and the tiny percussion of its fall "Plink—plunk," minimized almost to inaudibility. Following the lowest note there seemed to be a brief phrase, irregularly repeated; and presently Oleron found himself waiting for the recurrence of this phrase. It was quite pretty. . . .

But it did not conduce to wakefulness, and Oleron dozed over his fire.

When he awoke again the fire had burned low and the flames of the candles were licking the rims of the Sheffield sticks. Sluggishly he rose, yawned, went his nightly round of door locks and window fastenings, and passed into his bedroom. Soon, he slept soundly.

But a curious little sequel followed on the morrow. Mrs. Barrett usually tapped, not at his door, but at the wooden wall beyond which lay Oleron's bed; and then Oleron rose, put on his dressing gown, and admitted her. He was not conscious that as he did so that morning he hummed an air; but Mrs. Barrett lingered with her hand on the doorknob and her face a little averted and smiling.

"De-ar me!" her soft falsetto rose. "But that will be a very o-ald tune, Mr. Oleron! I will not have heard it this for-ty years!"

"What tune?" Oleron asked.

"The tune, indeed, that you was humming, sir."

Oleron had his thumb in the flap of a letter. It remained there.

"*I* was humming? . . . Sing it, Mrs. Barrett."

Mrs. Barrett prut-prutted.

"I have no voice for singing, Mr. Oleron; it was Ann Pugh was the singer of our family; but the tune will be very o-ald, and it is called 'The Beckoning Fair One.'"

"Try to sing it," said Oleron, his thumb still in the envelope; and Mrs. Barrett, with much dimpling and confusion, hummed the air.

"They do say it was sung to a harp, Mr. Oleron, and it will be very o-ald," she concluded.

"And *I* was singing that?"

"Indeed you was. I would not be likely to tell you lies."

With a "Very well—let me have breakfast," Oleron opened his letter; but the trifling circumstance struck him as more odd than he would have admitted to himself. The phrase he had hummed had been that which he had associated with the falling from the tap on the evening before.

V

Even more curious than that the commonplace dripping of an ordinary water tap should have tallied so closely with an actually existing air was another result it had, namely, that it awakened, or seemed to awaken, in Oleron an abnormal sensitiveness to other noises of the old house. It has been remarked that silence obtains its fullest and most impressive quality when it is broken by some minute sound; and, truth to tell, the place was never still. Perhaps the mildness of the spring air operated on its torpid old timbers; perhaps Oleron's fires caused it to stretch its old anatomy; and certainly a whole world of insect life bored and burrowed in its balks and joists. At any rate Oleron had only to sit quiet in his chair and to wait for a minute or two in order to become aware of such a change in the auditory scale as comes upon a man who, conceiving the midsummer woods to be motionless and still, all at once finds his ear sharpened to the crepitation of a myriad insects.

And he smiled to think of man's arbitrary distinction between that which has life and that which has not. Here, quite apart from such recognizable sounds as the scampering of mice, the falling of plaster behind his paneling, and the popping of purses or coffins from his fire, was a whole house talking to him had he but known its language. Beams settled with a tired sigh into their old mortices; creatures ticked in the walls; joints cracked, boards complained; with no palpable stirring of the air, window sashes changed their positions with a soft knock in their frames. And whether the place had life in this sense or not, it had at all events a winsome personality. It needed but an hour of musing for Oleron to conceive the idea that, as his own body stood in friendly relation to his soul, so, by an extension and an attenuation, his habitation might fantastically be supposed to stand in some relation to himself. He even amused himself with the farfetched fancy that he might so identify himself with the place that some future tenant, taking possession, might regard it as in a sense haunted. It would be rather a joke if he, a perfectly harmless author, with nothing on his mind worse than a novel he had discovered he must begin again, should turn out to be laying the foundation of a future ghost! . . .

In proportion, however, as he felt this growing attachment to the fabric of his abode, Elsie Bengough, from being merely unattracted, began to show a dislike of the place that was more and more marked. And she did not scruple to speak of her aversion.

"It doesn't belong to today at all, and for you especially it's bad," she said with decision. "You're only too ready to let go your hold on actual things and slip into apathy; *you* ought to be in a place with concrete floors and a patent gas meter and a tradesmen's lift. And it would do you all the good in the world if you had a job that made you scramble and rub elbows with your fellow men. Now, if I could get you a job, for, say, two or three days a week, one that would allow you heaps of time for your proper work—would you take it?"

Somehow, Oleron resented a little being diagnosed like this. He thanked Miss Bengough, but without a smile.

"Thank you, but I don't think so. After all, each of us has his own life to live," he could not refrain from adding.

"His own life to live! . . . How long is it since you were out, Paul?"

"About two hours."

"I don't mean to buy stamps or to post a letter. How long is it since you had anything like a stretch?"

"Oh, some little time perhaps. I don't know."

"Since I was here last?"

"I haven't been out much."

"And has *Romilly* progressed much better for your being cooped up?"

"I think she has. I'm laying the foundations of her. I shall begin the actual writing presently."

It seemed as if Miss Bengough had forgotten their tussle about the first *Romilly*. She frowned, turned half away, and then quickly turned again.

"Ah! . . . So you've still got that ridiculous idea in your head?"

"If you mean," said Oleron slowly, "that I've discarded the old *Romilly*, and am at work on a new one, you're right. I have still got that idea in my head."

Something uncordial in his tone struck her; but she was a fighter. His own absurd sensitiveness hardened her. She gave a "Pshaw!" of impatience.

"Where is the old one?" she demanded abruptly.

"Why?" asked Oleron.

"I want to see it. I want to show some of it to you. I want, if you're not woolgathering entirely, to bring you back to your senses."

This time it was he who turned his back. But when he turned round again he spoke more gently.

"It's no good, Elsie. I'm responsible for the way I go, and you must allow me to go it—even if it should seem wrong to you. Believe me, I am giving thought to it. . . . The manuscript? I was on the point of burning it, but I didn't. It's in that window seat, if you must see it."

Miss Bengough crossed quickly to the window seat, and lifted the lid. Suddenly she gave a little exclamation, and put the back of her hand to her mouth. She spoke over her shoulder:

"You ought to knock those nails in, Paul," she said.

He strode to her side.

"What? What is it? What's the matter?" he asked. "I did knock them in—or, rather, pulled them out."

"You left enough to scratch with," she replied, showing her hand. From the upper wrist to the knuckle of the little finger a welling red wound showed.

"Good—gracious!" Oleron ejaculated. . . . "Here, come to the bathroom and bathe it quickly——"

He hurried her to the bathroom, turned on warm water, and bathed and cleansed the bad gash. Then still holding the hand, he turned cold water on it, uttering broken phrases of astonishment and concern.

"Good Lord, how did that happen! As far as I knew I'd . . . is this water too cold? Does that hurt? I can't imagine how on earth . . . there; that'll do—"

"No—one moment longer—I can bear it," she murmured, her eyes closed. . . .

Presently he led her back to the sitting room and bound the hand in one of his handkerchiefs; but his face did not lose its expression of perplexity. He had spent half a day in opening and making serviceable the three window boxes, and he could not conceive how he had come to leave an inch and a half of rusty nail standing in the wood. He himself had opened the lids of each of them a dozen times and had not noticed any nail; but there it was. . . .

"It shall come out now, at all events," he muttered, as he went for a pair of pincers. And he made no mistake about it that time.

Elsie Bengough had sunk into a chair, and her face was rather white; but in her hand was the manuscript of *Romilly*. She had not finished with *Romilly* yet. Presently she returned to the charge.

"Oh, Paul, it will be the greatest mistake you ever, *ever* made if you do not publish this!" she said.

He hung his head, genuinely distressed. He couldn't get that incident of the nail out of his head, and *Romilly* occupied a second place in his thoughts for the moment. But still she insisted; and when presently he spoke it was almost as if he asked her pardon for something.

"What can I say, Elsie? I can only hope that when you see the new version, you'll see how right I am. And if in spite of all you *don't* like her, well . . ." he made a hopeless gesture. "Don't you see that I *must* be guided by my own lights?"

She was silent.

"Come, Elsie," he said gently. "We've got along well so far; don't let us split on this."

The last words had hardly passed his lips before he regretted them. She had been nursing her injured hand, with her eyes once more closed; but her lips and lids quivered simultaneously. Her voice shook as she spoke.

"I can't help saying it, Paul, but you are so greatly changed."

"Hush, Elsie," he murmured soothingly; "you've had a shock; rest for a while. How could I change?"

"I don't know, but you are. You've not been yourself ever since you came here. I wish you'd never seen the place. It's stopped your work, it's making you into a person I hardly know, and it's made me horribly anxious about you. . . . Oh, how my hand is beginning to throb!"

"Poor child!" he murmured. "Will you let me take you to a doctor and have it properly dressed?"

"No—I shall be all right presently —I'll keep it raised——"

She put her elbow on the back of her chair, and the bandaged hand rested lightly on his shoulder.

At that touch an entirely new anxiety stirred suddenly within him. Hundreds of times previously, on their jaunts and excursions, she had slipped her hand within his arm as she might have slipped it into the arm of a brother, and he had accepted the little affectionate gesture as a brother might have accepted it. But now, for the first time, there rushed into his mind a hundred startling questions. Her eyes were still closed, and her head had fallen pathetically back; and there was a lost and ineffable smile on her parted lips. The truth broke in upon him. Good God! . . . And he had never divined it!

And stranger than all was that, now that he did see that she was lost in love of him, there came to him, not sorrow and humility and abasement, but something else that he struggled in vain against—something entirely strange and new, that, had he analyzed it, he would have found to be petulance and irritation and resentment and ungentleness. The sudden selfish prompting mastered him before he was aware. He all but gave it words. What was she doing there at all? Why was she not getting on with her own work? Why was she here interfering with his? Who had given her this guardianship over him that lately she had put forward so assertively?— "Changed?" It was she, not himself, who had changed. . . .

But by the time she had opened her eyes again he had overcome his resentment sufficiently to speak gently, albeit with reserve.

"I wish you would let me take you to a doctor."

She rose.

"No, thank you, Paul," she said. "I'll go now. If I need a dressing I'll get one; take the other hand, please. Good-by——"

He did not attempt to detain her. He walked with her to the foot of the stairs. Halfway along the narrow alley she turned.

"It would be a long way to come if you happened not to be in," she said; "I'll send you a postcard the next time."

At the gate she turned again.

"Leave here, Paul," she said, with a mournful look. "Everything's wrong with this house."

Then she was gone.

Oleron returned to his room. He crossed straight to the window box. He opened the lid and stood long looking at it. Then he closed it again and turned away.

"That's rather frightening," he muttered. "It's simply not possible that I should not have removed that nail. . . ."

VI

Oleron knew very well what Elsie had meant when she had said that her next visit would be preceded by a postcard. She, too, had realized that at last, at last he knew—knew, and didn't want her. It gave him a miserable, pitiful pang, therefore, when she came again within a week, knocking at the door unannounced. She spoke from the landing; she did not intend to stay, she said; and he had to press her before she would so much as enter.

Her excuse for calling was that she had heard of an inquiry for short stories that he might be wise to follow up. He thanked her. Then, her business over, she seemed anxious to get away again. Oleron did not seek to detain her; even he saw through the pretext of the stories; and he accompanied her down the stairs.

But Elsie Bengough had no luck whatever in that house. A second accident befell her. Halfway down the staircase there was the sharp sound of splintering wood, and she checked a loud cry. Oleron knew the woodwork to be old, but he himself had ascended and descended frequently enough without mishap. . . .

Elsie had put her foot through one of the stairs.

He sprang to her side in alarm. "Oh, I say! My poor girl!"

She laughed hysterically.

"It's my weight—I know I'm getting fat——"

"Keep still—let me clear these splinters away," he muttered between his teeth.

She continued to laugh and sob that it was her weight—she was getting fat——

He thrust downwards at the broken boards. The extrication was no easy matter, and her torn boot showed him how badly the foot and ankle within it must be abraded.

"Good God—good God!" he muttered over and over again.

"I shall be too heavy for anything soon," she sobbed and laughed.

But she refused to reascend and to examine her hurt.

"No, let me go quickly—let me go quickly," she repeated.

"But it's a frightful gash!"

"No—not so bad—let me get away quickly—I'm—I'm not wanted."

At her word, that she was not wanted, his head dropped as if she had given him a buffet.

"Elsie!" he choked, brokenly and shocked.

But she too made a quick gesture, as if she put something violently aside.

"Oh, Paul, not *that*—not *you*—of course I do mean that too in a sense —oh, you know what I mean! . . .

But if the other can't be, spare me this now! I—I wouldn't have come, but—but oh, I did, I *did* try to keep away!"

It was intolerable, heartbreaking; but what could he do—what could he say? He did not love her. . . .

"Let me go—I'm not wanted—let me take away what's left of me——"

"Dear Elsie—you are very dear to me——"

But again she made the gesture, as of putting something violently aside.

"No, not that—not anything less —don't offer me anything less— leave me a little pride——"

"Let me get my hat and coat— let me take you to a doctor," he muttered.

But she refused. She refused even the support of his arm. She gave another unsteady laugh.

"I'm sorry I broke your stairs, Paul. . . . You will go and see about the short stories, won't you?"

He groaned.

"Then if you won't see a doctor, will you go across the square and let Mrs. Barrett look at you? Look, there's Barrett passing now——"

The long-nosed Barrett was looking curiously down the alley, but as Oleron was about to call him he made off without a word. Elsie seemed anxious for nothing so much as to be clear of the place, and finally promised to go straight to a doctor, but insisted on going alone.

"Good-by," she said.

And Oleron watched her until she was past the hatchetlike "To Let" boards, as if he feared that even they might fall upon her and maim her.

That night Oleron did not dine. He had far too much on his mind. He walked from room to room of his flat, as if he could have walked away

from Elsie Bengough's haunting cry
that still rang in his ears. "I'm not
wanted—don't offer me anything
less—let me take away what's left
of me——"

Oh, if he could only have persuaded himself that he loved her!

He walked until twilight fell, then
without lighting candles, he stirred
up the fire and flung himself into a
chair.

Poor, poor Elsie! . . .

But even while his heart ached
for her, it was out of the question.
If only he had known! If only he had
used common observation! But those
walks, those sisterly takings of the
arm—what a fool he had been! . . .
Well, it was too late now. It
was she, not he, who must now
act—act by keeping away. He would
help her all he could. He himself
would not sit in her presence. If
she came, he would hurry her out
again as fast as he could. . . . Poor,
poor Elsie!

His room grew dark; the fire
burned dead; and he continued to
sit, wincing from time to time as a
fresh tortured phrase rang again in
his ears.

Then suddenly, he knew not why,
he found himself anxious for her in
a new sense—uneasy about her personal safety. A horrible fancy that
even then she might be looking over
an embankment down into dark
water, that she might even now be
glancing up at the hook on the door,
took him. Women had been known
to do those things. . . . Then there
would be an inquest, and he himself would be called upon to identify
her, and would be asked how she
had come by an ill-healed wound on
the hand and a bad abrasion of the
ankle. Barrett would say that he
had seen her leaving his house. . . .
Then he recognized that his

thoughts were morbid. By an effort
of will he put them aside, and sat
for a while listening to the faint
creakings and tickings and rappings
within his paneling. . . .

If only he could have married
her! . . . But he couldn't. Her face
had risen before him again as he
had seen it on the stairs, drawn with
pain and ugly and swollen with
tears. Ugly—yes, positively blub-
bered; if tears were women's
weapons, as they were said to be,
such tears were weapons turned
against themselves . . . suicide
again. . . .

Then all at once he found himself
attentively considering her two accidents.

Extraordinary they had been, both
of them. He *could not* have left that
old nail standing in the wood; why,
he had fetched tools specially from
the kitchen; and he was convinced
that that step that had broken beneath her weight had been as sound
as the others: It was inexplicable.
If these things could happen, anything could happen. There was not
a beam nor a jamb in the place that
might not fall without warning, not
a plank that might not crash inwards, not a nail that might not
become a dagger. The whole place
was full of life even now; as he sat
there in the dark he heard its crowds
of noises as if the house had been
one great microphone. . . .

Only half conscious that he did
so, he had been sitting for some time
identifying these noises, attributing
to each crack or creak or knock its
material cause; but there was one
noise which, again not fully conscious of the omission, he had not
sought to account for. It had last
come some minutes ago; it came
again now—a sort of soft sweeping
rustle that seemed to hold an almost

inaudibly minute cracking. For half a minute or so it had Oleron's attention; then his heavy thoughts were of Elsie Bengough again.

He was nearer to loving her in that moment than he had ever been. He thought how to some men their loved ones were but the dearer for those poor mortal blemishes that tell us we are but sojourners on earth, with a common fate not far distant that makes it hardly worth while to do anything but love for the time remaining. Strangling sobs, blearing tears, bodies buffeted by sickness, hearts and minds callous and hard with the rubs of the world—how little love there would be were these things a barrier to love! In that sense he did love Elsie Bengough. What her happiness had never moved in him her sorrow almost awoke. . . .

Suddenly his meditation went. His ear had once more become conscious of that soft and repeated noise—the long sweep with the almost inaudible crackle in it. Again and again it came, with a curious insistence and urgency. It quickened a little as he became increasingly attentive . . . It seemed to Oleron that it grew louder. . . .

All at once he started bolt upright in his chair, tense and listening. The silky rustle came again; he was trying to attach it to something. . . .

The next moment he had leaped to his feet, unnerved and terrified. His chair hung poised for a moment, and then went over, setting the fire irons clattering as it fell. There was only one noise in the world like that which had caused him to spring thus to his feet. . . .

The next time it came Oleron felt behind him at the empty air with his hand, and backed slowly until he found himself against the wall.

"God in heaven!" The ejaculation broke from Oleron's lips. The sound had ceased.

The next moment he had given a high cry.

"What is it? What's there? *Who's* there?"

A sound of scuttling caused his knees to bend under him for a moment; but that, he knew, was a mouse. That was not something that his stomach turned sick and his mind reeled to entertain. That other sound, the like of which was not in the world, had now entirely ceased; and again he called. . . .

He called and continued to call; and then another terror, a terror of the sound of his own voice, seized him. He did not dare to call again. His shaking hand went to his pocket for a match, but found none. He thought there might be matches on the mantelpiece——

He worked his way to the mantelpiece round a little recess, without for a moment leaving the wall. Then his hand encountered the mantelpiece, and groped along it. A box of matches fell to the hearth. He could just see them in the firelight, but his hand could not pick them up until he had cornered them inside the fender.

Then he rose and struck a light. The room was as usual. He struck a second match. A candle stood on the table. He lighted it, and the flame sank for a moment and then burned up clear. Again he looked round.

There was nothing.

There was nothing; but there had been something, and might still be something. Formerly, Oleron had smiled at the fantastic thought that, by a merging and interplay of identities between himself and his beautiful room, he might be preparing a ghost for the future; it had not occurred to him *that there might have been a similar merging and coalescence in the past.* Yet with this staggering impossibility he was now face to face. Something did persist in the house; it had a tenant other than himself; and that tenant, whatsoever or whosoever, had appalled Oleron's soul by producing the sound of a woman brushing her hair.

VII

Without quite knowing how he came to be there Oleron found himself striding over the loose board he had temporarily placed on the step broken by Miss Bengough. He was hatless, and descending the stairs. Not until later did there return to him a hazy memory that he had left the candle burning on the table, had opened the door no wider than was necessary to allow the passage of his body, and had sidled out, closing the door softly behind him. At the foot of the stairs another shock awaited him. Something dashed with a flurry up from the disused cellars and disappeared out of the door. It was only a cat, but Oleron gave a childish sob.

He passed out of the gate, and stood for a moment under the "To Let" boards, plucking foolishly at his lip and looking up at the glimmer of light behind one of his red blinds. Then, still looking over his shoulder, he moved stumblingly up the square. There was a small public house round the corner; Oleron had never entered it; but he entered it now, and put down a shilling that missed the counter by inches.

"B-b-bran-brandy," he said, and then stooped to look for the shilling.

He had the little sawdusted bar to himself; what company there was —carters and laborers and the small

tradesmen of the neighborhood—was gathered in the farther compartment, beyond the space where the white-haired landlady moved among her taps and bottles. Oleron sat down on a hardwood settee with a perforated seat, drank half his brandy and then, thinking he might as well drink it as spill it, finished it.

Then he fell to wondering which of the men whose voices he heard across the public house would undertake the removal of his effects on the morrow.

In the meantime he ordered more brandy.

For he did not intend to go back to that room where he had left the candle burning. Oh no! He couldn't have faced even the entry and the staircase with the broken step—certainly not that pith-white, fascinating room. He would go back for the present to his old arrangement, of workroom and separate sleeping quarters; he would go to his old landlady at once—presently—when he had finished his brandy—and see if she could put him up for the night. His glass was empty now. . . .

He rose, had it refilled, and sat down again.

And if anybody asked his reason for removing again? Oh, he had reason enough—reason enough! Nails that put themselves back into wood again and gashed people's hands, steps that broke when you trod on them, and women who came into a man's place and brushed their hair in the dark, were reasons enough! He was querulous and injured about it all. He had taken the place for himself, not for invisible women to brush their hair in; that lawyer fellow in Lincoln's Inn should be told so, too, before many hours were out; it was outrageous, letting people in for agreements like that!

A cut-glass partition divided the compartment where Oleron sat from the space where the white-haired landlady moved; but it stopped seven or eight inches above the level of the counter. There was no partition at the farther bar. Presently Oleron, raising his eyes, saw that faces were watching him through the aperture. The faces disappeared when he looked at them.

He moved to a corner where he could not be seen from the other bar; but this brought him into line with the white-haired landlady.

She knew him by sight—had doubtless seen him passing and repassing; and presently she made a remark on the weather. Oleron did not know what he replied, but it sufficed to call forth the further remark that the winter had been a bad one for influenza, but that the spring weather seemed to be coming at last. . . . Even this slight contact with the commonplace steadied Oleron a little; an idle, nascent wonder whether the landlady brushed her hair every night, and, if so, whether it gave out those little electric cracklings, was shut down with a snap; and Oleron was better.

With his next glass of brandy he was all for going back to his flat. Not go back? Indeed, he would go back! They should very soon see whether he was to be turned out of his place like that! He began to wonder why he was doing the rather unusual thing he was doing at that moment, unusual for him—sitting hatless, drinking brandy, in a public house. Suppose he were to tell the white-haired landlady all about it— to tell her that a caller had scratched her hand on a nail, had later had the bad luck to put her foot through a rotten stair, and that he himself, in an old house full of squeaks and creaks and whispers, had heard a minute noise and had bolted from it in fright—what would she think of him? That he was mad, of course. . . . Pshaw! The real truth of the matter was that he hadn't been doing enough work to occupy him. He had been dreaming his days away, filling his head with a lot of moonshine about a new *Romilly* (as if the old one was not good enough), and now he was surprised that the devil should enter an empty head!

Yes, he would go back. He would take a walk in the air first—he hadn't walked enough lately—and then he would take himself in hand, settle the hash of that sixteenth chapter of *Romilly* (fancy, he had actually been fool enough to think of destroying fifteen chapters!) and thenceforward he would remember that he had obligations to his fellow men and work to do in the world. There was the matter in a nutshell.

He finished his brandy and went out.

He had walked for some time before any other bearing of the matter than that on himself occurred to him. At first, the fresh air had increased the heady effect of the brandy he had drunk; but afterwards his mind grew clearer than it had been since morning. And the clearer it grew, the less final did his boastful self-assurances become, and the firmer his conviction that, when all explanations had been made, there remained something that could not be explained. His hysteria of an hour before had passed; he grew steadily calmer; but the disquieting conviction remained. A deep fear took possession of him. It was a fear for Elsie.

For something in his place was inimical to her safety. Of themselves, her two accidents might not have persuaded him of this; but she herself had said it. *"I'm not wanted here. . . ."* And she had declared that there was something wrong with the place. She had seen it before he had. Well and good. One thing stood out clearly: namely, that if this was so, she must be kept away for quite another reason than that which had so confounded and humiliated Oleron. Luckily she had expressed her intention of staying away; she must be held to that intention. He must see to it.

And he must see to it all the more that he now saw his first impulse, never to set foot in the place again, was absurd. People did not do that kind of thing. With Elsie made secure, he could not with any respect to himself suffer himself to be turned out by a shadow, nor even by a danger merely because it was a danger. He had to live somewhere, and he would live there. He must return.

He mastered the faint chill of fear that came with the decision, and turned in his walk abruptly. Should fear grow on him again he would, perhaps, take one more glass of brandy. . . .

But by the time he reached the short street that led to the square he was too late for more brandy. The little public house was still lighted, but closed, and one or two men were standing talking on the curb. Oleron noticed that a sudden silence fell on them as he passed, and he noticed further that the long-nosed Barrett, whom he passed a little lower down, did not return his good night. He turned in at the broken gates, hesitated merely an instant in the alley, and then mounted his stairs again.

Only an inch of candle remained in the Sheffield stick, and Oleron did not light another one. Deliberately he forced himself to take it up and to make the tour of his five rooms before retiring. It was as he returned from the kitchen across his little hall that he noticed that a letter lay on the floor. He carried it into his sitting room, and glanced at the envelope before opening it.

It was unstamped, and had been put into the door by hand. Its handwriting was clumsy, and it ran from beginning to end without comma or period. Oleron read the first line, turned to the signature, and then finished the letter.

It was from the man Barrett, and it informed Oleron that he, Barrett, would be obliged if Mr. Oleron would make other arrangements for the preparing of his breakfasts and the cleaning out of his place. The sting lay in the tail, that is to say, the postscript. This consisted of a text of Scripture. It embodied an allusion that could only be to Elsie Bengough. . . .

A seldom-seen frown had cut deeply into Oleron's brow. So! That was it! Very well; they would see about that on the morrow. . . . For the rest, this seemed merely another reason why Elsie should keep away. . . .

Then his suppressed rage broke out. . . .

The foul-minded lot! The devil himself could not have given a leer at anything that had ever passed between Paul Oleron and Elsie Bengough, yet this nosing rascal must be prying and talking! . . .

Oleron crumpled the paper up, held it in the candle flame, and then ground the ashes under his heel.

One useful purpose, however, the letter had served: it had created in Oleron a wrathful blaze that effectually banished pale shadows. Nevertheless, one other puzzling circumstance was to close the day. As he undressed, he chanced to glance at his bed. The coverlets bore an impress as if somebody had lain on them. Oleron could not remember that he himself had lain down during the day—offhand, he would have said that certainly he had not; but after all he could not be positive. His indignation for Elsie, acting possibly with the residue of the brandy in him, excluded all other consider- ations; and he put out his candle, lay down, and passed immediately into a deep and dreamless sleep, which, in the absence of Mrs. Bar- rett's morning call, lasted almost once round the clock.

VIII

To the man who pays heed to that voice within him which warns him that twilight and danger are settling over his soul, terror is apt to appear an absolute thing, against which his heart must be safeguarded in a twink unless there is to take place an alteration in the whole range and scale of his nature. Mercifully, he has never far to look for safeguards. Of the immediate and small and com- mon and momentary things of life, of usages and observances and modes and conventions, he builds up forti- fications against the powers of dark- ness. He is even content that, not terror only, but joy also, should for working purposes be placed in the category of the absolute things; and the last treason he will commit will be that breaking down of terms and limits that strikes, not at one man, but at the welfare of the souls of all.

In his own person, Oleron began to commit this treason. He began to commit it by admitting the inexpli- cable and horrible to an increasing familiarity. He did it insensibly, un-

consciously, by a neglect of the things that he now regarded it as an impertinence in Elsie Bengough to have prescribed. Two months before, the words "a haunted house," ap- plied to his lovely bemusing dwelling, would have chilled his marrow; now, his scale of sensation becoming de- pressed, he could ask "Haunted by what?" and remain unconscious that horror, when it can be proved to be relative, by so much loses its proper quality. He was setting aside the landmarks. Mists and confusion had begun to enwrap him.

And he was conscious of nothing so much as of a voracious inquisitive- ness. He wanted *to know*. He was resolved to know. Nothing but the knowledge would satisfy him; and craftily he cast about for means whereby he might attain it.

He might have spared his craft. The matter was the easiest imagi- nable. As in time past he had known, in his writing, moments when his thoughts had seemed to rise of them- selves and to embody themselves in words not to be altered afterwards, so now the questions he put himself seemed to be answered even in the moment of their asking. There was exhilaration in the swift, easy proc- esses. He had known no such joy in his own power since the days when his writing had been a daily fresh- ness and a delight to him. It was almost as if the course he must pur- sue was being dictated to him.

And the first thing he must do, of course, was to define the problem. He defined it in terms of mathe- matics. Granted that he had not the place to himself; granted that the old house had inexpressibly caught and engaged his spirit; granted that, by virtue of the common denomi- nator of the place, this unknown co- tenant stood in some relation to himself: what next? Clearly, the nature of the other numerator must be ascertained.

And how? Ordinarily this would not have seemed simple, but to Oleron it was now pellucidly clear. The key, *of course*, lay in his half-written novel—or rather, in both *Romillys*, the old and the proposed new one.

A little while before Oleron would have thought himself mad to have embraced such an opinion; now he accepted the dizzying hypothesis without a quiver.

He began to examine the first and second *Romillys*.

From the moment of his doing so the thing advanced by leaps and bounds. Swiftly he reviewed the history of the *Romilly* of the fifteen chapters. He remembered clearly now that he had found her insufficient on the very first morning on which he had sat down to work in his new place. Other instances of his aversion leaped up to confirm his obscure investigation. There had come the night when he had hardly forborne to throw the whole thing into the fire; and the next morning he had begun the planning of the new *Romilly*. It had been on that morning that Mrs. Barrett, overhearing him humming a brief phrase that the dripping of a tap the night before had suggested, had informed him that he was singing some air he had never in his life heard before, called "The Beckoning Fair One." . . .

The Beckoning Fair One! . . .

With scarcely a pause in thought he continued:

The first *Romilly* having been definitely thrown over, the second had instantly fastened herself upon him, clamoring for birth in his brain. He even fancied now, looking back, that there had been something like

passion, hate almost, in the supplanting, and that more than once a stray thought given to his discarded creation had—(it was astonishing how credible Oleron found the almost unthinkable idea)—had offended the supplanter.

Yet that a malignancy almost homicidal should be extended to his fiction's poor mortal prototype. . . .

In spite of his inuring to a scale in which the horrible was now a thing to be fingered and turned this way and that, a "Good God!" broke from Oleron.

This intrusion of the first *Romilly's* prototype into his thought again was a factor that for the moment brought his inquiry into the nature of his problem to a termination; the mere thought of Elsie was fatal to anything abstract. For another thing, he could not yet think of that letter of Barrett's, nor of a little scene that had followed it, without a mounting of color and a quick contraction of the brow. For, wisely or not, he had had that argument out at once. Striding across the square on the following morning, he had bearded Barrett on his own doorstep. Coming back again a few minutes later, he had been strongly of opinion that he had only made matters worse. The man had been vagueness itself. He had not been able to be either challenged or browbeaten into anything more definite than a muttered farrago in which the words "Certain things . . . Mrs. Barrett . . . respectable house . . . if the cap fits . . . proceedings that shall be nameless," had been constantly repeated.

"Not that I make any charge——" he had concluded.

"Charge!" Oleron had cried.

"I 'ave my idears of things, as I don't doubt you 'ave yours——"

"Ideas—mine!" Oleron had cried

wrathfully, immediately dropping his voice as heads had appeared at windows of the square. "Look you here, my man; you've an unwholesome mind, which probably you can't help, but a tongue which you can help, and shall! If there is a breath of this repeated . . ."

"I'll not be talked to on my own doorstep like this by anybody . . ." Barrett had blustered. . . .

"You shall, and I'm doing it . . ."

"Don't you forget there's a Gawd above all, Who 'as said . . ."

"You're a low scandalmonger! . . ."

And so forth, continuing badly what was already badly begun. Oleron had returned wrathfully to his own house, and thenceforward, had seen Barrett's face at odd times, lifting blinds or peering round curtains, as if he sought to put himself in possession of heaven knew what evidence, in case it should be required of him.

The unfortunate occurrence made certain minor differences in Oleron's domestic arrangements. Barrett's tongue, he gathered, had already been busy; he was looked at askance by the dwellers of the square; and he judged it better, until he should be able to obtain other help, to make his purchases of provisions a little farther afield rather than at the small shops of the immediate neighborhood. For the rest, housekeeping was no new thing to him, and he would resume his old bachelor habits. . . .

Besides, he was deep in certain rather abstruse investigations, in which it was better that he should not be disturbed.

He was looking out of his window one midday rather tired, not very well, and glad that it was not very likely he would have to stir out-of-doors, when he saw Elsie Bengough crossing the square towards his house. The weather had broken; it was a raw and gusty day; and she had to force her way against the wind that set her ample skirts bellying about her opulent figure and her veil spinning and streaming behind her.

Oleron acted swiftly and instinctively. Seizing his hat, he sprang to the door and descended the stairs at a run. A sort of panic had seized him. She must be prevented from setting foot in the place. As he ran along the alley he was conscious that his eyes went up to the eaves as if something drew them. He did not know that a slate might not accidentally fall. . . .

He met her at the gate, and spoke with curious volubleness.

"This is really too bad, Elsie! Just as I'm urgently called away! I'm afraid it can't be helped though, and that you'll have to think me an inhospitable beast." He poured it out just as it came into his head.

She asked if he was going to town.

"Yes, yes—to town," he replied. "I've got to call on—on Chambers. You know Chambers, don't you? No, I remember you don't; a big man you once saw me with. . . . I ought to have gone yesterday, and"—this he felt to be a brilliant effort—"and he's going out of town this afternoon. To Brighton. I had a letter from him this morning."

He took her arm and led her up the square. She had to remind him that his way to town lay in the other direction.

"Of course—how stupid of me!" he said, with a little loud laugh. "I'm so used to going the other way with you—of course; it's the other way to the bus. Will you come along with me? I am so awfully sorry it's happened like this. . . ."

They took the street to the bus terminus.

This time Elsie bore no signs of having gone through interior struggles. If she detected anything unusual in his manner she made no comment, and he, seeing her calm, began to talk less recklessly through silences. By the time they reached the bus terminus, nobody, seeing the pallid-faced man without an overcoat and the large ample-skirted girl at his side, would have supposed that one of them was ready to sink on his knees for thankfulness that he had, as he believed, saved the other from a wildly unthinkable danger.

They mounted to the top of the bus, Oleron protesting that he should not miss his overcoat, and that he found the day, if anything, rather oppressively hot. They sat down on a front seat.

Now that this meeting was forced upon him, he had something else to say that would make demands upon his tact. It had been on his mind for some time, and was, indeed, peculiarly difficult to put. He revolved it for some minutes, and then, remembering the success of his story of a sudden call to town, cut the knot of his difficulty with another lie.

"I'm thinking of going away for a little while, Elsie," he said.

She merely said, "Oh?"

"Somewhere for a change. I need a change. I think I shall go tomorrow, or the day after. Yes, tomorrow, I think."

"Yes," she replied.

"I don't quite know how long I shall be," he continued. "I shall have to let you know when I am back."

"Yes, let me know," she replied in an even tone.

The tone was, for her, suspiciously even. He was a little uneasy.

"You don't ask me where I'm going," he said, with a little cumbrous effort to rally her.

She was looking straight before her, past the bus driver.

"I know," she said.

He was startled. "How, you know?"

"You're not going anywhere," she replied.

He found not a word to say. It was a minute or so before she continued, in the same controlled voice she had employed from the start.

"You're not going anywhere. You weren't going out this morning. You only came out because I appeared; don't behave as if we were strangers, Paul."

A flush of pink had mounted to his cheeks. He noticed that the wind had given her the pink of early rhubarb. Still he found nothing to say.

"Of course, you ought to go away," she continued. "I don't know whether you look at yourself often in the glass, but you're rather noticeable. Several people have turned to look at you this morning. So, of course, you ought to go away. But you won't, and I know why."

He shivered, coughed a little, and then broke silence.

"Then if you know, there's no use in continuing this discussion," he said curtly.

"Not for me, perhaps, but there is for you," she replied. "Shall I tell you what I know?"

"No," he said in a voice slightly raised.

"No?" she asked, her round eyes earnestly on him.

"No."

Again he was getting out of patience with her; again he was conscious of the strain. Her devotion and fidelity and love plagued him; she was only humiliating both herself and him. It would have been bad enough had he ever, by word or deed, given her cause for thus fastening herself on him . . . but there; that was the worst of that kind of life for a woman. Women such as she, businesswomen, in and out of offices all the time, always, whether they realized it or not, made comradeship a cover for something else. They accepted the unconventional status, came and went freely, as men did, were honestly taken by men at their own valuation—and then it turned out to be the other thing after all, and they went and fell in love. No wonder there was gossip in shops and squares and public houses! In a sense the gossipers were in the right of it. Independent, yet not efficient; with some of womanhood's graces foregone, and yet with all the woman's hunger and need; half sophisticated, yet not wise; Oleron was tired of it all. . . .

And it was time he told her so.

"I suppose," he said tremblingly, looking down between his knees, "I suppose the real trouble is in the life women who earn their own living are obliged to lead."

He could not tell in what sense she took the lame generality; she merely replied, "I suppose so."

"It can't be helped," he continued, "but you do sacrifice a good deal."

She agreed: a good deal; and then she added after a moment, "What, for instance?"

"You may or may not be gradually attaining a new status, but you're in a false position today."

"It was very likely," she said; she "hadn't thought of it much in that light ———"

"And," he continued desperately, "you're bound to suffer. Your most innocent acts are misunderstood; motives you never dreamed of are

attributed to you; and in the end it comes to"—he hesitated a moment and then took the plunge—"to the sidelong look and the leer."

She took his meaning with perfect ease. She merely shivered a little as she pronounced the name.

"Barrett?"

His silence told her the rest.

Anything further that was to be said must come from her. It came as the bus stopped at a stage and fresh passengers mounted the stairs.

"You'd better get down here and go back, Paul," she said. "I understand perfectly—perfectly. It isn't Barrett. You'd be able to deal with Barrett. It's merely convenient for you to say it's Barrett. I know what it is . . . but you said I wasn't to tell you that. Very well. But before you go let me tell you why I came up this morning."

In a dull tone he asked her why. Again she looked straight before her as she replied:

"I came to force your hand. Things couldn't go on as they have been going, you know; and now that's all over."

"All over," he repeated stupidly.

"All over. I want you now to consider yourself, as far as I'm concerned, perfectly free. I make only one reservation."

He hardly had the spirit to ask her what that was.

"If *I* merely need *you*," she said, "please don't give that a thought; that's nothing; I shan't come near for that. But," she dropped her voice, "if *you're* in need of *me*, Paul—I shall know if you are, *and you will be*—then I shall come at no matter what cost. You understand that?"

He could only groan.

"So that's understood," she concluded. "And I think that's all. Now go back. I should advise you to walk back, for you're shivering—good-by ——"

She gave him a cold hand, and he descended. He turned on the edge of the curb as the bus started again. For the first time in all the years he had known her she parted from him with no smile and no wave of her long arm.

IX

He stood on the curb plunged in misery, looking after her as long as she remained in sight; but almost instantly with her disappearance he felt the heaviness lift a little from his spirit. She had given him his liberty; true, there was a sense in which he had never parted with it, but now was no time for splitting hairs; he was free to act, and all was clear ahead. Swiftly the sense of lightness grew on him: it became a positive rejoicing in his liberty; and before he was halfway home he had decided what must be done next.

The vicar of the parish in which his dwelling was situated lived within ten minutes of the square. To his house Oleron turned his steps. It was necessary that he should have all the information he could get about this old house with the insurance marks and the sloping "To Let" boards, and the vicar was the person most likely to be able to furnish it. This last preliminary out of the way, and—aha! Oleron chuckled—things might be expected to happen!

But he gained less information than he had hoped for. The house, the vicar said, was old—but there needed no vicar to tell Oleron that; it was reputed (Oleron pricked up his ears) to be haunted—but there were few old houses about which some rumor did not circulate among the ignorant; and the deplorable lack of faith of the modern world,

the vicar thought, did not tend to dissipate these superstitions. For the rest, his manner was the soothing manner of one who prefers not to make statements without knowing how they will be taken by his hearer. Oleron smiled as he perceived this.

"You may leave my nerves out of the question," he said. "How long has the place been empty?"

"A dozen years, I should say," the vicar replied.

"And the last tenant—did you know him—or her?" Oleron was conscious of a tingling of his nerves as he offered the vicar the alternative of sex.

"Him," said the vicar. "A man. If I remember rightly, his name was Madley; an artist. He was a great recluse; seldom went out of the place, and—" the vicar hesitated and then broke into a little gush of candor "—and since you appear to have come for this information, and since it is better that the truth should be told than that garbled versions should get about, I don't mind saying that this man Madley died there, under somewhat unusual circumstances. It was ascertained at the post-mortem that there was not a particle of food in his stomach, although he was found to be not without money. And his frame was simply worn out. Suicide was spoken of, but you'll agree with me that deliberate starvation is, to say the least, an uncommon form of suicide. An open verdict was returned."

"Ah!" said Oleron. . . . "Does there happen to be any comprehensive history of this parish?"

"No; partial ones only. I myself am not guiltless of having made a number of notes on its purely ecclesiastical history, its registers and so forth, which I shall be happy to show you if you would care to see them:

but it is a large parish, I have only one curate, and my leisure, as you will readily understand . . ."

The extent of the parish and the scantiness of the vicar's leisure occupied the remainder of the interview, and Oleron thanked the vicar, took his leave, and walked slowly home.

He walked slowly for a reason, twice turning away from the house within a stone's-throw of the gate and taking another turn of twenty minutes or so. He had a very ticklish piece of work now before him; it required the greatest mental concentration; it was nothing less than to bring his mind, if he might, into such a state of unpreoccupation and receptivity that he should see the place as he had seen it on that morning when, his removal accomplished, he had sat down to begin the sixteenth chapter of the first *Romilly*.

For, could he recapture that first impression, he now hoped for far more from it. Formerly he had carried no end of mental lumber. Before the influence of the place had been able to find him out at all, it had had the inertia of those dreary chapters to overcome. No results had shown. The process had been one of slow saturation, charging, filling up to a brim. But now he was light, unburdened, rid at last both of that *Romilly* and of her prototype. Now for the new unknown, coy, jealous, bewitching, Beckoning Fair! . . .

At half-past two of the afternoon he put his key into the Yale lock, entered, and closed the door behind him. . . .

His fantastic attempt was instantly and astonishingly successful. He could have shouted with triumph as he entered the room; it was as if he had *escaped* into it. Once more,

as in the days when his writing had had a daily freshness and wonder and promise for him, he was conscious of that new ease and mastery and exhilaration and release. The air of the place seemed to hold more oxygen; as if his own specific gravity had changed, his very tread seemed less ponderable. The flowers in the bowls, the fair proportions of the meadowsweet-colored panels and moldings, the polished floor, and the lofty and faintly starred ceiling, fairly laughed their welcome. Oleron actually laughed back, and spoke aloud.

"Oh, you're pretty, pretty!" he flattered it.

Then he lay down on his couch.

He spent that afternoon as a convalescent who expected a dear visitor might have spent it—in a delicious vacancy, smiling now and then as if in his sleep, and ever lifting drowsy and contented eyes to his alluring surroundings. He lay thus until darkness came, and, with darkness, the nocturnal noises of the old house. . . .

But if he waited for any specific happening, he waited in vain.

He waited similarly in vain on the morrow, maintaining, though with less ease, that sensitized-platelike condition of his mind. Nothing occurred to give it an impression. Whatever it was which he so patiently wooed, it seemed to be both shy and exacting.

Then on the third day he thought he understood. A look of gentle drollery and cunning came into his eyes, and he chuckled.

"Oho, oho! . . . Well, if the wind sits in *that* quarter we must see what else there is to be done. What is there, now? . . . No, I won't send for Elsie; we don't need a wheel to break the butterfly on; we won't go to those lengths, my butterfly. . . ."

He was standing musing, thumbing his lean jaw, looking aslant; suddenly he crossed to his hall, took down his hat, and went out.

"My lady is coquettish, is she? Well, we'll see what a little neglect will do," he chuckled as he went down the stairs.

He sought a railway station, got into a train, and spent the rest of the day in the country. Oh, yes: Oleron thought *he* was the man to deal with Fair Ones who beckoned, and invited, and then took refuge in shyness and hanging back!

He did not return until after eleven that night.

"*Now*, my Fair Beckoner!" he murmured as he walked along the alley and felt in his pocket for his keys. . . .

Inside his flat, he was perfectly composed, perfectly deliberate, exceedingly careful not to give himself away. As if to intimate that he intended to retire immediately, he lighted only a single candle; and as he set out with it on his nightly round he affected to yawn. He went first into his kitchen. There was a full moon, and a lozenge of moonlight, almost peacock blue by contrast with his candle flame, lay on the floor. The window was uncurtained, and he could see the reflection of the candle, and, faintly, that of his own face, as he moved about. The door of the powder closet stood a little ajar, and he closed it before sitting down to remove his boots on the chair with the cushion made of the folded harp bag. From the kitchen he passed to the bathroom. There, another slant of blue moonlight cut the window sill and lay across the pipes on the wall. He visited his seldom-used study, and stood for a moment gazing at the silvered roofs across the square. Then, walking straight through his sitting room, his stockinged feet making no noise, he entered his bedroom and put the candle on the chest of drawers. His face all this time wore no expression save that of tiredness. He had never been wilier nor more alert.

His small bedroom fireplace was opposite the chest of drawers on which the mirror stood, and his bed and the window occupied the remaining sides of the room. Oleron drew down his blind, took off his coat, and then stooped to get his slippers from under the bed.

He could have given no reason for the conviction, but that the manifestation that for two days had been withheld was close at hand he never for an instant doubted. Nor, though he could not for the faintest guess of the shape it might take, did he experience fear. Startling or surprising it might be; he was prepared for that; but that was all; his scale of sensation had become depressed. His hand moved this way and that under the bed in search of his slippers. . . .

But for all his caution and method and preparedness, his heart all at once gave a leap and a pause that was almost horrid. His hand had found the slippers, but he was still on his knees; save for this circumstance he would have fallen. The bed was a low one; the groping for the slippers accounted for the turn of his head to one side; and he was careful to keep the attitude until he had partly recovered his self-possession. When presently he rose there was a drop of blood on his lower lip where he had caught at it with his teeth, and his watch had jerked out of the pocket of his waistcoat and was dangling at the end of its short leather guard. . . .

Then, before the watch had

ceased its little oscillation, he was himself again.

In the middle of his mantelpiece there stood a picture, a portrait of his grandmother; he placed himself before this picture, so that he could see in the glass of it the steady flame of the candle that burned behind him on the chest of drawers. He could see also in the picture glass the little glancings of light from the bevels and facets of the objects about the mirror and candle. But he could see more. These twinklings and reflections and rereflections did not change their position; but there was one gleam that had motion. It was fainter than the rest, and it moved up and down through the air. It was the reflection of the candle on Oleron's black vulcanite comb, and each of its downward movements was accompanied by a silky and crackling rustle.

Oleron, watching what went on in the glass of his grandmother's portrait, continued to play his part. He felt for his dangling watch and began slowly to wind it up. Then, for a moment ceasing to watch, he began to empty his trousers pockets and to place methodically in a little row on the mantelpiece the pennies and halfpennies he took from them. The sweeping, minutely electric noise filled the whole bedroom, and had Oleron altered his point of observation he could have brought the dim gleam of the moving comb so into position that it would almost have outlined his grandmother's head.

Any other head of which it might have been following the outline was invisible.

Oleron finished the emptying of his pockets; then, under cover of another simulated yawn, not so much summoning his resolution as overmastered by an exorbitant curiosity, he swung suddenly round. That which was being combed was still not to be seen, but the comb did not stop. It had altered its angle a little, and had moved a little to the left. It was passing, in fairly regular sweeps, from a point rather more than five feet from the ground, in a direction roughly vertical, to another point a few inches below the level of the chest of drawers.

Oleron continued to act to admiration. He walked to his little washstand in the corner, poured out water, and began to wash his hands. He removed his waistcoat, and continued his preparation for bed. The combing did not cease, and he stood for a moment in thought. Again his eyes twinkled. The next was very cunning ——

"Hm! . . . *I think I'll read for a quarter of an hour,*" he said aloud. . . .

He passed out of the room.

He was away a couple of minutes; when he returned again the room was suddenly quiet. He glanced at the chest of drawers; the comb lay still, between the collar he had removed and a pair of gloves. Without hesitation Oleron put out his hand and picked it up. It was an ordinary eighteen-penny comb, taken from a card in a chemist's shop, of a substance of a definite specific gravity, and no more capable of rebellion against the laws by which it existed than are the worlds that keep their orbits through the void. Oleron put it down again; then he glanced at the bundle of papers he held in his hand. What he had gone to fetch had been the fifteen chapters of the original *Romilly.*

"Hm!" he muttered as he threw the manuscript into a chair. . . . "As

I thought. . . . She's just blindly, ragingly, murderously jealous."

On the night after that, and on the following night, and for many nights and days, so many that he began to be uncertain about the count of them, Oleron, courting, cajoling, neglecting, threatening, beseeching, eaten out with unappeased curiosity and regardless that his life was becoming one consuming passion and desire, continued his search for the unknown conumerator of his abode.

X

As time went on, it came to pass that few except the postman mounted Oleron's stairs; and since men who do not write letters receive few, even the postman's tread became so infrequent that it was not heard more than once or twice a week. There came a letter from Oleron's publishers, asking when they might expect to receive the manuscript of his new book; he delayed for some days to answer it, and finally forgot it. A second letter came, which also he failed to answer. He received no third.

The weather grew bright and warm. The privet bushes among the chopperlike notice boards flowered, and in the streets where Oleron did his shopping the baskets of flower women lined the kerbs. Oleron purchased flowers daily; his room clamored for flowers, fresh and continually renewed; and Oleron did not stint its demands. Nevertheless, the necessity for going out to buy them began to irk him more and more, and it was with a greater and ever greater sense of relief that he returned home again. He began to be conscious that again his scale of sensation had suffered a subtle change—a change that was not res-

toration to its former capacity, but an extension and enlarging that once more included terror. It admitted it in an entirely new form. *Lux orco, tenebræ Joci.* The name of this terror was agoraphobia. Oleron had begun to dread air and space and the horror that might pounce upon the unguarded back.

Presently he so contrived it that his food and flowers were delivered daily at his door. He rubbed his hands when he had hit upon this expedient. That was better! Now he could please himself whether he went out or not. . . .

Quickly he was confirmed in his choice. It became his pleasure to remain immured.

But he was not happy—or, if he was, his happiness took an extraordinary turn. He fretted discontentedly, could sometimes have wept for mere weakness and misery; and yet he was dimly conscious that he would not have exchanged his sadness for all the noisy mirth of the world outside. And speaking of noise: noise, much noise, now caused him the acutest discomfort. It was hardly more to be endured than that newborn fear that kept him, on the increasingly rare occasions when he did go out, sidling close to walls and feeling friendly railings with his hand. He moved from room to room softly and in slippers, and sometimes stood for many seconds closing a door so gently that not a sound broke the stillness that was in itself a delight. Sunday now became an intolerable day to him, for, since the coming of the fine weather, there had begun to assemble in the square under his windows each Sunday morning certain members of the sect to which the long-nosed Barrett adhered. These came with a great drum and large brass-bellied

instruments; men and women up-
lifted anguished voices, struggling
with their God; and Barrett himself,
with upraised face and closed eyes
and working brows, prayed that the
sound of his voice might penetrate
the ears of all unbelievers—as it
certainly did Oleron's. One day, in
the middle of one of these rhapso-
dies, Oleron sprang to his blind and
pulled it down, and heard as he
did so his own name made the
object of a fresh torrent of outpouring.

And sometimes, but not as expecting a reply, Oleron stood still and
called softly. Once or twice he called
"Romilly" and then waited; but
more often his whispering did not
take the shape of a name.

There was one spot in particular
of his abode that he began to haunt
with increasing persistency. This
was just within the opening of his
bedroom door. He had discovered
one day that by opening every door
in his place (always excepting the
outer one, which he only opened un-
willingly) and by placing himself
on this particular spot, he could
actually see to a greater or less extent into each of his five rooms without changing his position. He could
see the whole of his sitting room, all
of his bedroom except the part hidden by the open door, and glimpses
of his kitchen, bathroom, and of his
rarely used study. He was often in
this place, breathless and with his
finger on his lip. One day, as he
stood there, he suddenly found himself wondering whether this Madley,
of whom the vicar had spoken, had
ever discovered the strategic importance of the bedroom entry.

Light, moreover, now caused him
greater disquietude than did darkness. Direct sunlight, of which, as
the sun passed daily round the

house, each of his rooms had now its
share, was like a flame in his brain;
and even diffused light was a dull
and numbing ache. He began, at
successive hours of the day, one
after another, to lower his crimson
blinds. He made short and daring
excursions in order to do this; but he
was ever careful to leave his retreat open, in case he should have
sudden need of it. Presently this
lowering of the blinds had become
a daily methodical exercise, and his
rooms, when he had been his round,
had the blood-red half light of a
photographer's darkroom.

One day, as he drew down the
blind of his little study and backed
in good order out of the room again,
he broke into a soft laugh.

"*That* bilks Mr. Barrett!" he said;
and the baffling of Barrett continued
to afford him mirth for an hour.

But on another day, soon after,
he had a fright that left him
trembling also for an hour. He had
seized the cord to darken the window
over the seat in which he had found
the harp bag, and was standing with
his back well protected in the em-
brasure, when he thought he saw the
tail of a black-and-white check skirt
disappear round the corner of the
house. He could not be sure—had
he run to the window of the other
wall, which was blinded, the skirt
must have been already past—but
he was *almost* sure that it was Elsie.
He listened in an agony of suspense
for her tread on the stairs. . . .

But no tread came, and after three
or four minutes he drew a long
breath of relief.

"By Jove, but that would have
compromised me horribly!" he
muttered. . . .

And he continued to mutter from
time to time, "Horribly compromising . . . *no* woman would stand that

. . . not *any* kind of woman . . . oh, compromising in the extreme!"

Yet he was not happy. He could not have assigned the cause of the fits of quiet weeping which took him sometimes; they came and went, like the fitful illumination of the clouds that traveled over the square; and perhaps, after all, if he was not happy, he was not unhappy. Before he could be unhappy something must have been withdrawn, and nothing had yet been withdrawn from him, for nothing had been granted. He was waiting for that granting, in that flower-laden, frightfully enticing apartment of his, with the pith-white walls tinged and subdued by the crimson blinds to a bloodlike gloom.

He paid no heed to it that his stock of money was running perilously low, nor that he had ceased to work. Ceased to work? He had not ceased to work. They knew very little about it who supposed that Oleron had ceased to work! He was in truth only now beginning to work. He was preparing such a work . . . such a work . . . such a Mistress was a-making in the gestation of his Art . . . let him but get this period of probation and poignant waiting over and men should see. . . . How *should* men know her, this Fair One of Oleron's, until Oleron himself knew her? Lovely radiant creations are not thrown off like How d'ye-do's. The men to whom it is committed to father them must weep wretched tears, as Oleron did, swell with vain presumptuous hopes, as Oleron did, must pursue, as Oleron pursued, the capricious, fair, mocking, slippery, eager Spirit that, ever eluding, ever sees to it that the chase does not slacken. Let Oleron but hunt this Huntress a little longer . . . he would have her sparkling and panting in his arms yet. . . . Oh no: they were very far from the truth who supposed that Oleron had ceased to work!

And if all else was falling away from Oleron, gladly he was letting it go. So do we all when our Fair Ones beckon. Quite at the beginning we wink, and promise ourselves that we will put Her Ladyship through her paces, neglect her for a day, turn her own jealous wiles against her, flout and ignore her when she comes wheedling; perhaps there lurks within us all the time a heartless sprite who is never fooled; but in the end all falls away. She beckons, beckons, and all goes. . . .

And so Oleron kept his strategic post within the frame of his bedroom door, and watched, and waited, and smiled, with his finger on his lips. . . . It was his duteous service, his worship, his troth plighting, all that he had ever known of Love. And when he found himself, as he now and then did, hating the dead man Madley, and wishing that he had never lived, he felt that that, too, was an acceptable service. . . .

But, as he thus prepared himself, as it were, for a Marriage, and moped and chafed more and more that the Bride made no sign, he made a discovery that he ought to have made weeks before.

It was through a thought of the dead Madley that he made it. Since that night when he had thought in his greenness that a little studied neglect would bring the lovely Beckoner to her knees, and had made use of her own jealousy to banish her, he had not set eyes on those fifteen discarded chapters of *Romilly*. He had thrown them back into the window seat, forgotten their very existence. But his own jealousy of Madley had put him in mind of hers of her jilted rival of flesh and blood, and he remembered them. . . . Fool that he had been! Had he, then, expected his Desire to manifest herself while there still existed the evidence of his divided allegiance? What, and she with a passion so fierce and centered that it had not hesitated at the destruction, twice attempted, of her rival? Fool that he had been! . . .

But if *that* was all the pledge and sacrifice she required she should have it—ah, yes, and quickly!

He took the manuscript from the window seat, and brought it to the fire.

He kept his fire always burning now; the warmth brought out the last vestige of odor of the flowers with which his room was banked. He did not know what time it was; long since he had allowed his clock to run down—it had seemed a foolish measurer of time in regard to the stupendous things that were happening to Oleron; but he knew it was late. He took the *Romilly* manuscript and knelt before the fire.

But he had not finished removing the fastening that held the sheets together before he suddenly gave a start, turned his head over his shoulder, and listened intently. The sound he had heard had not been loud—it had been, indeed, no more than a tap, twice or thrice repeated—but it had filled Oleron with alarm. His face grew dark as it came again.

He heard a voice outside on his landing.

"Paul! . . . Paul! . . ."

It was Elsie's voice.

"Paul! . . . I know you're in . . . I want to see you. . . ."

He cursed her under his breath, but kept perfectly still. He did not intend to admit her.

"Paul! . . . You're in trouble. . . .

I believe you're in danger . . . at least come to the door! . . ."

Oleron smothered a low laugh. It somehow amused him that she, in such danger herself, should talk to him of *his* danger! . . . Well, if she was, serve her right; she knew, or said she knew, all about it.

"Paul! . . . Paul! . . ."

"*Paul! . . . Paul! . . .*" He mimicked her under his breath.

"Oh, Paul, it's *horrible!* . . ."

Horrible, was it? thought Oleron. Then let her get away. . . .

"I only want to help you, Paul. . . . I didn't promise not to come if you needed me. . . ."

He was impervious to the pitiful sob that interrupted the low cry. The devil take the woman! Should he shout to her to go away and not come back? No: let her call and knock and sob. She had a gift for sobbing; she mustn't think her sobs would move him. They irritated him, so that he set his teeth and shook his fist at her, but that was all. Let her sob.

"*Paul! . . . Paul! . . .*"

With his teeth hard set, he dropped the first page of *Romilly* into the fire. Then he began to drop the rest in, sheet by sheet.

For many minutes the calling behind his door continued; then suddenly it ceased. He heard the sound of her feet slowly descending the stairs. He listened for the noise of a fall or a cry or a crash of a piece of the handrail of the upper landing; but none of these things came. She was spared. Apparently her rival suffered her to crawl abject and beaten away. Oleron heard the passing of her steps under his window; then she was gone.

He dropped the last page into the fire, and then, with a low laugh rose. He looked fondly round his room.

"Lucky to get away like that," he remarked. "She wouldn't have got away if I'd given her as much as a word or a look! What devils these women are! . . . But no; I oughtn't to say that; one of 'em showed forbearance. . . ."

Who showed forbearance? And what was forborne? Ah, Oleron knew! . . . Contempt, no doubt, had been at the bottom of it, but that didn't matter: the pestering creature had been allowed to go unharmed. Yes, she was lucky; Oleron hoped she knew it. . . .

And now, now, now for his reward!

Oleron crossed the room. All his doors were open; his eyes shone as he placed himself within that of his bedroom.

Fool that he had been, not to think of destroying the manuscript sooner! . . .

How, in a houseful of shadows, should he know his own Shadow? How, in a houseful of noises, distinguish the summons he felt to be at hand? Ah, trust him! He would know! The place was full of a jugglery of dim lights. The blind at his elbow that allowed the light of a street lamp to struggle vaguely through—the glimpse of greeny-blue moonlight seen through the distant kitchen door—the sulky glow of the fire under the black ashes of the burned manuscript—the glimmering of the tulips and the moon daisies and narcissi in the bowls and jugs and jars—these did not so trick and bewilder his eyes that he would not know his Own! It was he, not she, who had been delaying the shadowy Bridal; he hung his head for a moment in mute acknowledgment; then he bent his eyes on the deceiving, puzzling gloom again. He would have called her name had he known

it—but now he would not ask her to share even a name with the other. . . .

His own face, within the frame of the door, glimmered white as the narcissi in the darkness. . . .

A shadow, light as fleece, seemed to take shape in the kitchen (the time had been when Oleron would have said that a cloud had passed over the unseen moon). The low illumination on the blind at his elbow grew dimmer (the time had been when Oleron would have concluded that the lamplighter going his rounds had turned low the flame of the lamp). The fire settled, letting down the black and charred papers; a flower fell from a bowl, and lay indistinct upon the floor; all was still; and then a stray draft moved through the old house, passing before Oleron's face. . . .

Suddenly, inclining his head, he withdrew a little from the door jamb. The wandering draft caused the door to move a little on its hinges. Oleron trembled violently, stood for a moment longer, and then, putting his hand out to the knob, softly drew the door to, sat down on the nearest chair, and waited, as a man might await the calling of his name that should summon him to some weighty, high and privy Audience. . . .

XI

One knows not whether there can be human compassion for anemia of the soul. When the pitch of Life is dropped, and the spirit is so put over and reversed that that only is horrible which before was sweet and worldly and of the day, the human relation disappears. The sane soul turns appalled away, lest not merely itself, but sanity should suffer. We are not gods. We cannot drive out devils. We must see selfishly to it that devils do not enter into ourselves.

And this we must do even though Love so transfuse us that we may well deem our nature to be half divine. We shall but speak of honor and duty in vain. The letter dropped within the dark door will lie unregarded, or, if regarded for a brief instant between two unspeakable lapses, left and forgotten again. The telegram will be undelivered, nor will the whistling messenger (wiselier guided than he knows to whistle) be conscious as he walks away of the drawn blind that is pushed aside an inch by a finger and then fearfully replaced again. No: let the miserable wrestle with his own shadows; let him, if indeed he be so mad, clip and strain and enfold and couch the succubus; but let him do so in a house into which not an air of heaven penetrates, nor a bright finger of the sun pierces the filthy twilight. The lost must remain lost. Humanity has other business to attend to.

For the handwriting of the two letters that Oleron, stealing noiselessly one June day into his kitchen to rid his sitting room of an armful of fetid and decaying flowers, had seen on the floor within his door, had had no more meaning for him than if it had belonged to some dim and faraway dream. And at the beating of the telegraph boy upon the door, within a few feet of the bed where he lay, he had gnashed his teeth and stopped his ears. He had pictured the lad standing there, just beyond his partition, among packets of provisions and bundles of dead and dying flowers. For his outer landing was littered with these. Oleron had feared to open his door to take them

in. After a week, the errand lads had reported that there must be some mistake about the order, and had left no more. Inside, in the red twilight, the old flowers turned brown and fell and decayed where they lay.

Gradually his power was draining away. The Abomination fastened on Oleron's power. The steady sapping sometimes left him for many hours of prostration gazing vacantly up at his red-tinged ceiling, idly suffering such fancies as came of themselves to have their way with him. Even the strongest of his memories had no more than a precarious hold upon his attention. Sometimes a flitting half memory, of a novel to be written, a novel it was important that he should write, tantalized him for a space before vanishing again; and sometimes whole novels, perfect, splendid, established to endure, rose magically before him. And sometimes the memories were absurdly remote and trivial, of garrets he had inhabited and lodgings that had sheltered him, and so forth. Oleron had known a good deal about such things in his time, but all that was now past. He had at last found a place which he did not intend to leave until they fetched him out—a place that some might have thought a little on the greensick side, that others might have considered to be a little too redolent of long-dead and morbid things for a living man to be mewed up in, but ah, so irresistible, with such an authority of its own, with such an associate of its own, and a place of such delights when once a man had ceased to struggle against its inexorable will! A novel? Somebody ought to write a novel about a place like that! There must be lots to write about in a place like that if one could but get to the bottom of it! It had probably already been painted, by a man called Madley who had lived there . . . but Oleron had not known this Madley—had a strong feeling that he wouldn't have liked him—would rather he had lived somewhere else —really couldn't stand the fellow— hated him, Madley, in fact. (Aha! That was a joke!) He seriously doubted whether the man had led the life he ought; Oleron was in two minds sometimes whether he wouldn't tell that long-nosed guardian of the public morals across the way about him; but probably he knew, and had made his praying hullabaloos for him also. That was his line. Why, Oleron himself had had a dust-up with him about something or other . . . some girl or other . . . Elsie Bengough her name was, he remembered. . . .

Oleron had moments of deep uneasiness about this Elsie Bengough. Or rather, he was not so much uneasy about her as restless about the things she did. Chief of these was the way in which she persisted in thrusting herself into his thoughts; and, whenever he was quick enough, he sent her packing the moment she made her appearance there. The truth was that she was not merely a bore; she had always been that; it had now come to the pitch when her very presence in his fancy was inimical to the full enjoyment of certain experiences. . . . She had no tact; really ought to have known that people are not at home to the thoughts of everybody all the time; ought in mere politeness to have allowed him certain seasons quite to himself; and was monstrously ignorant of things if she did not know, as she appeared not to know, that there were certain special hours when a man's veins ran with fire and daring

and power, in which . . . well, in which he had a reasonable right to treat folk as he had treated that prying Barrett—to shut them out completely. . . . But no: up she popped, the thought of her, and ruined all. Bright towering fabrics, by the side of which even those perfect, magical novels of which he dreamed were dun and gray, vanished utterly at her intrusion. It was as if a fog should suddenly quench some fair-beaming star, as if at the threshold of some golden portal prepared for Oleron a pit should suddenly gape, as if a batlike shadow should turn the growing dawn to mirk and darkness again. . . . Therefore, Oleron strove to stifle even the nascent thought of her.

Nevertheless, there came an occasion on which this woman Bengough absolutely refused to be suppressed. Oleron could not have told exactly when this happened; he only knew by the glimmer of the street lamp on his blind that it was some time during the night, and that for some time she had not presented herself.

He had no warning, none, of her coming; she just came—was there. Strive as he would, he could not shake off the thought of her nor the image of her face. She haunted him.

But for her to come at *that* moment of all moments! . . . Really, it was past belief! How *she* could endure it, Oleron could not conceive! Actually, to look on, as it were, at the triumph of a Rival. . . . Good God! It was monstrous! Tact—reticence—he had never credited her with an overwhelming amount of either: but he had never attributed mere—oh, there was no word for it! Monstrous—monstrous! Did she intend thenceforward. . . . Good God! To look on! . . .

Oleron felt the blood rush up to the roots of his hair with anger against her.

"Damnation take her!" he choked. . . .

But the next moment his heat and resentment had changed to a cold sweat of cowering fear. Panic-stricken, he strove to comprehend what he had done. For though he knew not what, he knew he had done something, something fatal, irreparable, blasting. Anger he had felt, but not *this* blaze of ire that suddenly flooded the twilight of his consciousness with a white infernal light. *That* appalling flash was not his—not his *that* open rift of bright and searing hell—not his, not his! His had been the hand of a child, preparing a puny blow; but what was *this other* horrific hand that was drawn back to strike in the same place? Had *he* set that in motion? Had *he* provided the spark that had touched off the whole accumulated power of that formidable and relentless place? He did not know. He only knew that that poor igniting particle in himself was blown out, that—Oh, impossible!—a clinging kiss (how else to express it?) had changed on his very lips to a gnashing and a removal, and that for very pity of the awful odds he must cry out to her against whom he had lately raged to guard herself . . . guard herself. . . .

"*Look out!*" he shrieked aloud. . . .

The revulsion was instant. As if a cold slow billow had broken over him, he came to to find that he was lying in his bed, that the mist and horror that had for so long enwrapped him had departed, that he was Paul Oleron, and that he was sick, naked, helpless, and unutterably abandoned and alone. His faculties, though weak, answered at last to his calls upon them; and he knew that it must have been a hideous nightmare that had left him sweating and shaking thus.

Yes, he was himself, Paul Oleron, a tired novelist, already past the summit of his best work, and slipping downhill again empty-handed from it all. He had struck short in his life's aim. He had tried too much, had overestimated his strength, and was a failure, a failure. . . .

It all came to him in the single word, enwrapped and complete; it needed no sequential thought; he was a failure. He had missed. . . .

And he had missed not one happiness, but two. He had missed the ease of this world, which men love, and he had missed also that other shining prize for which men forego ease, the snatching and holding and triumphant bearing up aloft of which is the only justification of the mad adventurer who hazards the enterprise. And there was no second attempt. Fate has no morrow. Oleron's morrow must be to sit down to profitless, ill-done, unrequired work again, and so on the morrow after that, and the morrow after that, and as many morrows as there might be. . . .

He lay there, weakly yet sanely considering it. . . .

And since the whole attempt had failed, it was hardly worth while to consider whether a little might not be saved from the general wreck. No good would ever come of that half-finished novel. He had intended that it should appear in the autumn; was under contract that it should appear; no matter; it was better to pay forfeit to his publishers than to waste what days were left. He was spent; age was not far off; and paths of wisdom and sadness were the properest for the remainder of the journey. . . .

If only he had chosen the wife, the child, the faithful friend at the fireside, and let them follow an *ignis fatuus* that list! . . .

In the meantime it began to puzzle him exceedingly why he should be so weak, that his room should smell so overpoweringly of decaying vegetable matter, and that his hand, chancing to stray to his face in the darkness, should encounter a beard.

"Most extraordinary!" he began to mutter to himself. "Have I been ill? Am I ill now? And if so, why have they left me alone? . . ." Extraordinary! . . .

He thought he heard a sound from the kitchen or bathroom. He rose a little on his pillow, and listened. . . . Ah! He was not alone, then! It certainly would have been extraordinary if they had left him ill and alone—Alone? Oh no. He would be looked after. He wouldn't be left, ill, to shift for himself. If everybody else had forsaken him, he could trust Elsie Bengough, the dearest chum he had, for that . . . bless her faithful heart!

But suddenly a short, stifled, spluttering cry rang sharply out:

"Paul!"

It came from the kitchen.

And in the same moment it flashed upon Oleron, he knew not how, that two, three, five, he knew not how many minutes before, another sound, unmarked at the time but suddenly transfixing his attention now, had striven to reach his intelligence. This sound had been the slight touch of metal on metal—just such a sound as Oleron made when he put his key into the lock.

"Hallo! . . . Who's that?" he called sharply from his bed.

He had no answer.

He called again. "Hallo! . . . Who's there? . . . Who is it?"

This time he was sure he heard noises, soft and heavy, in the kitchen.

"This is a queer thing altogether," he muttered. "By Jove, I'm as weak as a kitten too. . . . Hallo, there! Somebody called, didn't they? . . . Elsie! Is that you? . . ."

Then he began to knock with his hand on the wall at the side of his bed.

"Elsie! . . . Elsie! . . . You called, didn't you? . . . Please come here, whoever it is! . . ."

There was a sound as of a closing door, and then silence. Oleron began to get rather alarmed.

"It may be a nurse," he muttered; "Elsie'd have to get me a nurse, of course. She'd sit with me as long as she could spare the time, brave lass, and she'd get a nurse for the rest. . . . But it was awfully like her voice. . . . Elsie, or whoever it is! . . . I can't make this out at all. I must go and see what's the matter. . . ."

He put one leg out of bed. Feeling its feebleness, he reached with his hand for the additional support of the wall. . . .

But before putting out the other leg he stopped and considered, picking at his new-found beard. He was suddenly wondering whether he *dared* go into the kitchen. It was such a frightfully long way; no man knew what horror might not leap and huddle on his shoulders if he went so far; when a man has an overmastering impulse to get back into bed he ought to take heed of the warning and obey it. Besides, why should he go? What was there to go for? If it was that Bengough creature again, let her look after herself; Oleron was not going to have things cramp themselves on his defenseless back for the sake of such a spoilsport as *she*! ... If she was in, let her let herself out again, and the sooner the better for her! Oleron simply couldn't be bothered. He had his work to do. On the morrow, he must set about the writing of a novel with a heroine so winsome, capricious, adorable, jealous, wicked, beautiful, inflaming, and altogether evil, that men should stand amazed. She was coming over him now; he knew by the alteration of the very air of the room when she was near him; and that soft thrill of bliss that had begun to stir in him never came unless she was beckoning, beckoning. . . .

He let go the wall and fell back into bed again as—oh, unthinkable! —the other half of the kiss that a gnash had interrupted was placed (how else convey it?) on his lips, robbing him of very breath. . . .

XII

In the bright June sunlight a crowd filled the square, and looked up at the windows of the old house with the antique insurance marks in its walls of red brick and the agents' notice boards hanging like wooden choppers over the paling. Two constables stood at the broken gate of the narrow entrance alley, keeping folk back. The women kept to the outskirts of the throng, moving now and then as if to see the drawn red blinds of the old house from a new angle, and talking in whispers. The children were in the houses, behind closed doors.

A long-nosed man had a little group about him, and he was telling some story over and over again; and another man, little and fat and wide-eyed, sought to capture the long-nosed man's audience with some relation in which a key figured.

". . . and it was revealed to me that there'd been something that very afternoon," the long-nosed man was saying. "I was standing there, where Constable Saunders is—or rather, I was passing about my business, when they came out. There was no deceiving me, oh, no deceiving *me*! *I* saw her face. . . ."

"What was it like, Mr. Barrett?" a man asked.

"It was like hers whom our Lord said to, 'Woman, doth any man accuse thee?'—white as paper, and no mistake! Don't tell *me*! . . . And so I walks straight across to Mrs. Barrett, and 'Jane,' I says, 'this must stop, and stop at once; we are commanded to avoid evil,' I says, 'and it must come to an end now; let him get help elsewhere.' And she says to me, 'John,' she says, 'it's four-an'-six-pence a week'—them was her words. 'Jane,' I says, 'if it was forty-six thousand pounds it should stop' . . . and from that day to this she hasn't set foot inside that gate."

There was a short silence: then,

"Did Mrs. Barrett ever . . . *see* anything, like?" somebody vaguely inquired.

Barrett turned austerely on the speaker.

"What Mrs. Barrett saw and Mrs. Barrett didn't see shall not pass these lips; even as it is written, keep thy tongue from speaking evil," he said.

Another man spoke.

"He was pretty near canned up in the Wagon and Horses that night, weren't he, Jim?"

"Yes, 'e 'adn't 'alf copped it. . . ."

"Not standing treat much, neither; he was in the bar, all on his own. . . ."

"So 'e was; we talked about it. . . ."

The fat, scared-eyed man made another attempt.

"She got the key off of me—she 'ad the number of it—she come into my shop of a Tuesday evening. . . ."

Nobody heeded him.

"Shut your heads," a heavy laborer commented gruffly, "she hasn't been found yet. 'Ere's the inspectors; we shall know more in a bit."

Two inspectors had come up and were talking to the constables who guarded the gate. The little fat man ran eagerly forward, saying that she had bought the key of him. "I remember the number, because of its being three one's and three three's—111333!" he exclaimed excitedly.

An inspector put him aside.

"Nobody's been in?" he asked of one of the constables.

"No, sir."

"Then you, Brackley, come with us; you, Smith, keep the gate. There's a squad on its way."

The two inspectors and the constable passed down the alley and entered the house. They mounted the wide carved staircase.

"This don't look as if he'd been out much lately," one of the inspectors muttered as he kicked aside a litter of dead leaves and paper that lay outside Oleron's door. "I don't think we need knock—break a pane, Brackley."

The door had two glazed panels; there was a sound of shattered glass; and Brackley put his hand through the hole his elbow had made and drew back the latch.

"Faugh!" . . . choked one of the inspectors as they entered. "Let some light and air in, quick. It stinks like a hearse——"

The assembly out in the square saw the red blinds go up and the windows of the old house flung open.

"That's better," said one of the inspectors, putting his head out of a window and drawing a deep breath. . . . "That seems to be the bedroom in there; will you go in, Simms, while I go over the rest? . . ."

They had drawn up the bedroom blind also, and the waxy-white, emaciated man on the bed had made a blinker of his hand against the torturing flood of brightness. Nor could he believe that his hearing was not playing tricks with him, for there were two policemen in his room, bending over him and asking where "she" was. He shook his head.

"This woman Bengough . . . goes by the name of Miss Elsie Bengough . . . d'ye hear? Where is she? . . . No good, Brackley; get him up; be careful with him; I'll just shove *my* head out of the window, I I think. . . ."

The other inspector had been through Oleron's study and had found nothing, and was now in the kitchen, kicking aside an ankle-deep mass of vegetable refuse that cumbered the floor. The kitchen window had no blind, and was overshadowed by the blank end of the house across the alley. The kitchen appeared to be empty.

But the inspector, kicking aside the dead flowers, noticed that a shuffling track that was not of his making had been swept to a cupboard in the corner. In the upper part of the door of the cupboard was a square panel that looked as if it slid on runners. The door itself was closed.

The inspector advanced, put out his hand to the little knob, and slid the hatch along its groove.

Then he took an involuntary step back again.

Framed in the aperture, and falling forward a little before it jammed again in its frame, was something that resembled a large lumpy pudding, done up in a pudding bag of faded browny red frieze.

"Ah!" said the inspector.

To close the hatch again he would have had to thrust that pudding back with his hand; and somehow he did not quite like the idea of touching it. Instead, he turned the handle of the cupboard itself. There was weight behind it, so much weight that, after opening the door three or four inches and peering inside, he had to put his shoulder to it in order to close it again. In closing it he left sticking out, a few inches from the floor, a triangle of black and white check skirt.

He went into the small hall.

"All right!" he called.

They had got Oleron into his clothes. He still used his hands as blinkers, and his brain was very confused. A number of things were happening that he couldn't understand. He couldn't understand the extraordinary mess of dead flowers there seemed to be everywhere; he couldn't understand why there should be police officers in his room; he couldn't understand why one of these should be sent for a four-wheeler and a stretcher; and he couldn't understand what heavy article they seemed to be moving about in the kitchen—his kitchen. . . .

"What's the matter?" he muttered sleepily. . . .

Then he heard a murmur in the square, and the stopping of a four-wheeler outside. A police officer was at his elbow again, and Oleron wondered why, when he whispered something to him, he should run off a string of words—something about "used in evidence against you." They had lifted him to his feet, and were assisting him towards the door. . . .

No, Oleron couldn't understand it at all.

They got him down the stairs and along the alley. Oleron was aware of confused angry shoutings; he gathered that a number of people wanted to lynch somebody or other. Then his attention became fixed on a little fat frightened-eyed man who appeared to be making a statement that an officer was taking down in a notebook.

"I'd seen her with him . . . they was often together . . . she came into my shop and said it was for him . . . I thought it was all right . . . 111333 the number was," the man was saying.

The people seemed to be very angry; many police were keeping them back; but one of the inspectors had a voice that Oleron thought quite kind and friendly. He was telling somebody to get somebody else into the cab before something or other was brought out; and Oleron noticed that a four-wheeler was drawn up at the gate. It appeared that it was himself who was to be put into it; and as they lifted him up he saw that the inspector tried to stand between him and something that stood behind the cab, but was not quick enough to prevent Oleron seeing that this something was a hooded stretcher. The angry voices sounded like a sea; something hard, like a stone, hit the back of the cab; and the inspector followed Oleron in and stood with his back to the window nearer the side where the people were. The door they had put Oleron in at remained open, apparently till the other inspector should come; and through the opening Oleron had a glimpse of the hatchetlike "To Let" boards among the privet trees. One of them said that the key was at Number Six. . . .

Suddenly the raging of voices was hushed. Along the entrance alley shuffling steps were heard, and the other inspector appeared at the cab door.

"Right away," he said to the driver.

He entered, fastened the door after him, and blocked up the second window with his back. Between the two inspectors Oleron slept peacefully. The cab moved down the square, the other vehicle went up the hill. The mortuary lay that way.

Virginia Woolf
1882-1941

VIRGINIA STEPHEN's father was a scholar and an essayist—Sir Leslie Stephen; his first wife was a daughter of Thackeray, and his friends were the illustrious of the day: Hardy, Meredith, Stevenson, Ruskin, Bryce. In this household, the Stephen girls, Virginia and her sisters, grew up shy and lovely, "in plain black dresses," as William Rothenstein describes them, "with white lace collars and wrist bands, looking as though they had walked straight out of a canvas by Watts or Burne-Jones."

After Virginia's marriage to Leonard Woolf in 1912, the new Woolf house in Bloomsbury became quite as intellectual a gathering place as her father's had been, with the emphasis now on Freud and psychoanalysis, and Virginia the center, rather than a sideline observer. The Woolfs had a small hand press at this time on which they got out limited editions under the imprint of the Hogarth Press; this, after the war, developed into a successful publishing house. In 1918 they published T. S. Eliot's *Poems,* and *Prelude,* by an obscure young author named Katherine Mansfield. Like Katherine Mansfield, Virginia Woolf wrote with freshness of a gracious and lovely world, but hers is a world pervaded with loneliness. In March, 1941, she disappeared from her home and was later found drowned. The note she left behind read: "I have the feeling that I shall go mad and cannot go on any longer in these terrible times." "A Haunted House" comes from the posthumous volume of stories by that title.

A Haunted House

BY VIRGINIA WOOLF

WHATEVER hour you woke there was a door shutting. From room to room they went, hand in hand, lifting here, opening there, making sure—a ghostly couple.

"Here we left it," she said. And he added, "Oh, but here too!" "It's upstairs," she murmured. "And in the garden," he whispered. "Quietly," they said, "or we shall wake them."

But it wasn't that you woke us. Oh, no. "They're looking for it; they're drawing the curtain," one might say, and so read on a page or two. "Now they've found it," one would be certain, stopping the pencil on the margin. And then, tired of reading, one might rise and see for oneself, the house all empty, the doors standing open, only the wood pigeons bubbling with content and the hum of the threshing machine sounding from the farm. "What did I come in here for? What did I want to find?" My hands were empty. "Perhaps its upstairs then?" The apples were in the loft. And so down again, the garden still as ever, only the book had slipped into the grass.

But they had found it in the drawing room. Not that one could ever see them. The windowpanes reflected apples, reflected roses; all the leaves were green in the glass. If they moved in the drawing room, the apple only turned its yellow side. Yet, the moment after, if the door was opened, spread about the floor, hung upon the walls, pendant from the ceiling—what? My hands were empty. The shadow of a thrush crossed the carpet; from the deepest wells of silence the wood pigeon drew its bubble of sound. "Safe, safe, safe," the pulse of the house beat softly. "The treasure buried; the room . . ." the pulse stopped short. Oh, was that the buried treasure?

A moment later the light had faded. Out in the garden then? But the trees spun darkness for a wandering beam of sun. So fine, so rare, coolly sunk beneath the surface the beam I sought always burned behind the glass. Death was the glass; death was between us; coming to the woman first, hundreds of years ago, leaving the house, sealing all the windows; the rooms were darkened. He left it, left her, went North, went East, saw the stars turned in the Southern sky; sought the house, found it dropped beneath the Downs. "Safe, safe, safe," the pulse of the house beat gladly. "The Treasure yours."

The wind roars up the avenue.

Trees stoop and bend this way and that. Moonbeams splash and spill wildly in the rain. But the beam of the lamp falls straight from the window. The candle burns stiff and still. Wandering through the house, opening the windows, whispering not to wake us, the ghostly couple seek their joy.

"Here we slept," she says. And he adds, "Kisses without number." "Waking in the morning——" "Silver between the trees——" "Upstairs——" "In the garden——" "When summer came——" "In winter snowtime——" "The doors go shutting far in the distance, gently knocking like the pulse of a heart.

Nearer they come; cease at the doorway. The wind falls, the rain slides silver down the glass. Our eyes darken; we hear no steps beside us; we see no lady spread her ghostly cloak. His hands shield the lantern.

"Look," he breathes. "Sound asleep. Love upon their lips."

Stooping, holding their silver lamp above us, long they look and deeply. Long they pause. The wind drives straightly; the flame stoops slightly. Wild beams of moonlight cross both floor and wall, and, meeting, stain the faces bent; the faces pondering; the faces that search the sleepers and seek their hidden joy.

"Safe, safe, safe," the heart of the house beats proudly. "Long years——" he sighs. "Again you found me." "Here," she murmurs, "sleeping; in the garden reading; laughing, rolling apples in the loft. Here we left our treasure——" Stooping, their light lifts the lids upon my eyes. "Safe! safe! safe!" the pulse of the house beats wildly. Waking, I cry "Oh, is this *your* buried treasure? The light in the heart."

A. E. Coppard
1878-1957

THIS most poetic and fastidious of English short-story writers was born of a tailor and a housemaid. He left school at the age of nine and was apprenticed to a London tailor in Whitechapel. But his mind was not on his work. Later, as an office boy, he began reading poetry. Still later, as clerk and accountant in Oxford, he made the acquaintance and became the friend of a group of writing students, among them Aldous Huxley, L. A. G. Strong, and Richard Hughes. This intercourse with eager writers was the release he needed: he tossed his job out the window, got himself a hut in the Chiltern Hills, and settled down, though in poverty, to write. He completely justified his action by *Adam and Eve and Pinch Me*, a volume of stories that became the first publication of the Golden Cockerel Press and is now a collector's item. (In fact, all of Coppard's books have brought high prices. Yet, more than once, he had to return to clerical work to support his family.) Although he is usually classed with the postwar "younger" writers, he was really not one of them, by age or mood. He had no sociological ax to grind; only a tale to tell.

Adam and Eve and Pinch Me

BY A. E. COPPARD

AND in the whole of his days, vividly at the end of the afternoon—he repeated it again and again to himself—the kind country spaces had *never* absorbed *quite* so rich a glamour of light, so miraculous a bloom of clarity. He could feel streaming in his own mind, in his bones, the same crystalline brightness that lay upon the land. Thoughts and images went flowing through him as easily and amiably as fish swim in their pools; and as idly, too, for one of his speculations took up the theme of his family name. There was such an agreeable oddness about it, just as there was about all the luminous sky today, that it touched him as just a little remarkable. What *did* such a name connote, signify, or symbolize? It was a rann of a name, but it had euphony! Then again, like the fish, his ambulating fancy flashed into other shallows, and he giggled as he paused, peering at the buds in the brake. Turning back towards his house again he could see, beyond its roofs, the spire of the Church tinctured richly as the vane: all round him was a new grandeur upon the grass of the fields, and the spare trees had shadows below that seemed to support them in the man-

ner of a plinth, more real than themselves, and the dikes and any chance heave of the level fields were underlined, as if for special emphasis, with long shades of mysterious blackness.

With a little drift of emotion that had at other times assailed him in the wonder and ecstasy of pure light, Jaffa Codling pushed through the slit in the black hedge and stood within his own garden. The gardener was at work. He could hear the voices of the children about the lawn at the other side of the house. He was very happy, and the place was beautiful, a fine white many-windowed house rising from a lawn bowered with plots of mold, turreted with shrubs, and overset with a vast walnut tree. This house had deep clean eaves, a roof of faint-colored slates that, after rain, glowed dully, like onyx or jade, under the red chimneys, and halfway up at one end was a balcony set with black balusters. He went to a French window that stood open and stepped into the dining room. There was no one within, and, on that lonely instant, a strange feeling of emptiness dropped upon him. The clock ticked almost as if it had been caught in some indecent act; the air was dim and troubled after that glory outside. Well, now, he would go up at once to the study and write down for his new book the ideas and images he had accumulated—beautiful rich thoughts they were—during that wonderful afternoon. He went to mount the stairs and he was passed by one of the maids; humming a silly song she brushed past him rudely, but he was an easygoing man—maids were unteachably tiresome—and reaching the landing he sauntered towards his room. The door stood slightly open and he could hear voices within. He put his hand upon the door . . . it would not open any further. What the devil . . . he pushed—like the bear in the tale—and he pushed, and he pushed—was there something against it on the other side? He put his shoulder to it . . . some wedge must be there, and *that* was extraordinary. Then his whole apprehension was swept up and whirled as by an avalanche—Mildred, his wife, was in there; he could hear her speaking to a man in fair soft tones and the rich phrases that could be used only by a woman yielding a deep affection for him. Codling kept still. Her words burned on his mind and thrilled him as if spoken to himself. There was a movement in the room, then utter silence. He again thrust savagely at the partly open door, but he could not stir it. The silence within continued. He beat upon the door with his fists, crying: "Mildred, Mildred!" There was no response, but he could hear the rocking armchair commence to swing to and fro. Pushing his hand round the edge of the door he tried to thrust his head between the opening. There was not space for this, but he could just peer into the corner of a mirror hung near, and this is what he saw: the chair at one end of its swing, a man sitting in it, and upon one arm of it Mildred, the beloved woman, with her lips upon the man's face, caressing him with her hands. Codling made another effort to get into the room—as vain as it was violent. "Do you hear me, Mildred?" he shouted. Apparently neither of them heard him; they rocked to and fro while he gazed stupefied. What, in the name of God . . . What was this . . . was she bewitched . . . were there such things after all as magic, devilry!

He drew back and held himself quite steadily. The chair stopped swaying, and the room grew awfully still. The sharp ticking of the clock in the hall rose upon the house like the tongue of some perfunctory mocker. Couldn't they hear the clock? . . . Couldn't they hear his heart? He had to put his hand upon his heart, for, surely, in that great silence inside there, they would hear its beat, growing so loud now that it seemed almost to stun him! Then in a queer way he found himself reflecting, observing, analyzing his own actions and intentions. He found some of them to be just a little spurious, counterfeit. He felt it would be easy, so perfectly easy to flash in one blast of anger and annihilate the two. He would do nothing of the kind. There was no occasion for it. People didn't really do that sort of thing, or, at least, not with a genuine passion. There was no need for anger. His curiosity was satisfied, quite satisfied, he was certain, he had not the remotest interest in the man. A welter of unexpected thoughts swept upon his mind as he stood there. As a writer of books he was often stimulated by the emotions and impulses of other people, and now his own surprise was beginning to intrigue him, leaving him, O, quite unstirred emotionally, but interesting him profoundly.

He heard the maid come stepping up the stairway again, humming her silly song. He did not want a scene, or to be caught eavesdropping, and so turned quickly to another door. It was locked. He sprang to one beyond it; the handle would not turn. "Bah! what's *up* with 'em?" But the girl was now upon him, carrying a tray of coffee things. "O, Mary!" he exclaimed casually, "I . . ." To his astonishment the girl stepped past him as if she did not hear or see him, tapped open the door of his study, entered, and closed the door behind her. Jaffa Codling then got really angry. "Hell! were the blasted servants in it!" He dashed to the door again and tore at the handle. It would not even turn, and, though he wrenched with fury at it, the room was utterly sealed against him. He went away for a chair with which to smash the effrontery of that door. No, he wasn't angry, either with his wife or this fellow—Gilbert, she had called him—who had a strangely familiar aspect as far as he had been able to take it in; but when one's servants . . . faugh!

The door opened and Mary came forth smiling demurely. He was a few yards further along the corridor at that moment. "Mary!" he shouted, "leave the door open!" Mary carefully closed it and turned her back on him. He sprang after her with bad words bursting from him as she went towards the stairs and flitted lightly down, humming all the way as if in derision. He leaped downwards after her three steps at a time, but she trotted with amazing swiftness into the kitchen and slammed the door in his face.

Codling stood, but kept his hands carefully away from the door, kept them behind him. "No, no," he whispered cunningly, "there's something fiendish about door handles today, I'll go and get a bar, or a butt of timber," and, jumping out into the garden for some such thing, the miracle happened to him. For it was nothing else than a miracle, the unbelievable, the impossible, simple and laughable if you will, but having as much validity as any miracle can ever invoke. It was simple and laughable because by all the known physical laws he should have collided with his gardener, who happened to pass the window with his wheelbarrow as Codling jumped out on to the path. And it was unbelievable that they should not, and impossible that they *did* not collide; and it was miraculous, because Codling stood for a brief moment in the garden path and the wheelbarrow of Bond, its contents, and Bond himself passed apparently through the figure of Codling as if he were so much air, as if he were not a living breathing man but just a common ghost. There was no impact, just a momentary breathlessness. Codling stood and looked at the retreating figure going on utterly unaware of him. It is interesting to record that Codling's first feelings were mirthful. He giggled. He was jocular. He ran along in front of the gardener, and let him pass through him once more; then after him again; he scrambled into the man's barrow, and was wheeled about by this incomprehensible thickheaded gardener who was dead to all his master's efforts to engage his attention. Presently he dropped the wheelbarrow and went away, leaving Codling to cogitate upon the occurrence. There was no room for doubt, some essential part of him had become detached from the obviously not less vital part. He felt he was essential because he was responding to the experience, he was reacting in the normal way to normal stimuli, although he happened for the time being to be invisible to his fellows and unable to communicate with them. How had it come about—this queer thing? How could he discover what part of him had cut loose, as it were? There was no question of this being death; death wasn't funny, it wasn't a joke; he had still all his human instincts. You didn't get angry with a faithless wife or joke with a fool of a gardener if you were dead, certainly not! He had realized enough of himself to know he was the usual man of instincts, desires, and prohibitions, complex and contradictory; his family history for a million or two years would have denoted that, not explicitly—obviously impossible—but suggestively. He had found himself doing things he had no desire to do, doing things he had a desire *not* to do, thinking thoughts that had no contiguous meaning, no meanings that could be related to his general experience. At odd times he had been chilled—aye, and even agreeably surprised—at the immense potential evil in himself. But still, this was no mere Jekyll and Hyde affair, that a man and his own ghost should separately inhabit the same world was a horse of quite another color. The other part of him was alive and active somewhere . . . as alive . . . as alive . . . yes, as *he* was, but dashed if he knew where! What a lark when they got back to each other and compared notes! In his tales he had brooded over so many imagined personalities, followed in the track of so many psychological enigmas that he *had* felt at times a stranger to himself. What if, after all, that brooding had given him the faculty of projecting this figment of himself into the world of men. Or was he some unrealized latent element of being without its natural integument, doomed now to drift over the ridge of the world forever. Was it his personality, his spirit? Then how was the dashed thing working? Here was he with the most wonderful happening in human experience, and he couldn't differentiate or disinter things. He was like a new Adam flung into some old Eden.

There was Bond tinkering about with some plants a dozen yards in front of him. Suddenly his three children came round from the other side of the house, the youngest boy leading them, carrying in his hand a small sword which was made, not of steel, but of some more brightly shining material; indeed it seemed at one moment to be of gold, and then again of flame, transmuting everything in its neighborhood into the likeness of flame, the hair of the little girl Eve, a part of Adam's tunic; and the fingers of the boy Gabriel as he held the sword were like pale tongues of fire. Gabriel, the youngest boy, went up to the gardener and gave the sword into his hands, saying: "Bond, is this sword any good?" Codling saw the gardener take the weapon and examine it with a careful sort of smile; his great gnarled hands became immediately transparent, the blood could be seen moving diligently about the veins. Codling was so interested in the sight that he did not gather in the gardener's reply. The little boy was dissatisfied and repeated his question, "No, but Bond, *is* this sword any good?" Codling rose, and stood by invisible.

The three beautiful children were grouped about the great angular figure of the gardener in his soiled clothes, looking up now into his face, and now at the sword, with anxiety in all their puckered eyes. "Well, Marse Gabriel," Codling could hear him reply, "as far as a sword goes, it may be a good un, or it may be a bad un, but, good as it is, it can never be anything but a bad thing." He then gave it back to them; the boy Adam held the haft of it, and the girl Eve rubbed the blade with curious fingers. The younger boy stood looking up at the gardener with unsatisfied gaze. "But, Bond, *can't* you say if this sword's any *good?*" Bond turned to his spade and trowels. "Mebbe the shape of it's wrong, Marse Gabriel, though it seems a pretty handy size." Saying this he moved off across the lawn. Gabriel turned to his brother and sister and took the sword from them: they all followed after the gardener and once more Gabriel made enquiry: "Bond, is this sword any *good?*" The gardener again took it and made a few passes in the air like a valiant soldier at exercise. Turning then, he lifted a bright curl from the head of Eve and cut it off with a sweep of the weapon. He held it up to look at it critically and then let it fall to the ground. Codling sneaked behind him and, picking it up, stood stupidly looking at it. "Mebbe, Marse Gabriel," the gardener was saying, "it ud be better made of steel, but it has a smartish edge on it." He went to pick up the barrow, but Gabriel seized it with a spasm of anger, and cried out: "No, no, Bond, will you say, just yes or no, Bond, is this sword any *good?*" The gardener stood still, and looked down at the little boy, who repeated his question— "just yes or no, Bond!" "No, Marse

Gabriel!" "Thank you, Bond!" replied the child with dignity, "that's all we wanted to know," and calling to his mates to follow him, he ran away to the other side of the house.

Codling stared again at the beautiful lock of hair in his hand, and felt himself grow so angry that he picked up a strange-looking flowerpot at his feet and hurled it at the retreating gardener. It struck Bond in the middle of the back and, passing clean through him, broke on the wheel of his barrow, but Bond seemed to be quite unaware of this catastrophe. Codling rushed after, and, taking the gardener by the throat, he yelled, "Damn you, will you tell me what all this means?" But Bond proceeded calmly about his work unnoticing, carrying his master about as if he were a clinging vapor, or a scarf hung upon his neck. In a few moments, Codling dropped exhausted to the ground. "What . . . O hell . . . what, what am I to do?" he groaned. "What has happened to me? What shall I *do?* What *can* I do?" He looked at the broken flowerpot. "Did I invent that?" He pulled out his watch. "That's a real watch, I hear it ticking, and it's six o'clock." Was he dead or disembodied or mad? What was this infernal lapse of identity? And who the devil, yes, who was it upstairs with Mildred? He jumped to his feet and hurried to the window; it was shut; to the door, it was fastened; he was powerless to open either. Well! well! this was experimental psychology with a vengeance, and he began to chuckle again. He'd have to write to McDougall about it. Then he turned and saw Bond wheeling across the lawn towards him again. "*Why* is that fellow always shoving that infernal green barrow around?" he asked, and, the fit of fury seizing him again, he rushed towards Bond, but, before he reached him, the three children danced into the garden again, crying, with great excitement, "Bond, O Bond!" The gardener stopped and set down the terrifying barrow; the children crowded about him, and Gabriel held out another shining thing, asking: "Bond, is this box any good?" The gardener took the box and at once his eyes lit up with interest and delight. "O, Marse Gabriel, where'd ye get it? Where'd ye get it?" "Bond," said the boy impatiently, "is the box any *good?*" "Any good?" echoed the man. "Why, Marse Gabriel, Marse Adam, Miss Eve, look yere!" Holding it down in front of them, he lifted the lid from the box and a bright-colored bird flashed out and flew round and round above their heads. "O," screamed Gabriel with delight, "it's a kingfisher!" "That's what it is," said Bond, "a kingfisher!" "Where?" asked Adam. "Where?" asked Eve. "There it flies—round the fountain—see it? see it!" "No," said Adam. "No," said Eve.

"O, do, do, see it," cried Gabriel, "here it comes, it's coming!" and, holding his hands on high, and standing on his toes, the child cried out as happy as the bird which Codling saw flying above them.

"I can't see it," said Adam.

"Where is it, Gaby?" asked Eve.

"Oh, you stupids," cried the boy. "*There* it goes. There it goes . . . there . . . it's gone!"

He stood looking brightly at Bond, who replaced the lid.

"What shall we do now?" he exclaimed eagerly. For reply, the gardener gave the box into his hand, and walked off with the barrow. Gabriel took the box over to the fountain. Codling, unseen, went after him, almost as excited as the boy;

Eve and her brother followed. They sat upon the stone tank that held the falling water. It was difficult for the child to unfasten the lid; Codling attempted to help him, but he was powerless. Gabriel looked up into his father's face and smiled. Then he stood up and said to the others: "Now, *do* watch it this time."

They all knelt carefully beside the water. He lifted the lid and, behold, a fish like a gold carp, but made wholly of fire, leaped from the box into the fountain. The man saw it dart down into the water, he saw the water bubble up behind it, he heard the hiss that the junction of fire and water produced, and saw a little track of steam follow the bubbles about the tank until the figure of the fish was consumed and disappeared. Gabriel, in ecstasies, turned to his sister with blazing happy eyes, exclaiming:

"There! Evey!"

"What was it?" asked Eve, nonchalantly, "I didn't see anything."

"More didn't I," said Adam.

"Didn't you see that lovely fish?"

"No," said Adam.

"No," said Eve.

"Oh, stupids," cried Gabriel, "it went right past the bottom of the water."

"Let's get a fishin' hook," said Adam.

"No, no, no," said Gabriel, replacing the lid of the box. "O no."

Jaffa Codling had remained on his knees staring at the water so long that, when he looked around him again, the children had gone away. He got up and went to the door, and that was closed; the windows, fastened. He went moodily to a garden bench and sat on it with folded arms. Dusk had begun to fall into the shrubs and trees, the grass to grow dull, the air chill, the sky to muster its gloom. Bond had overturned his barrow, stalled his tools in the lodge, and gone to his home in the village. A curious cat came round the house and surveyed the man who sat chained to his seven-horned dilemma. It grew dark and fearfully silent. Was the world empty now? Some small thing, a snail, perhaps, crept among the dead leaves in the hedge, with a sharp, irritating noise. A strange flood of mixed thoughts poured through his mind until at last one idea disentangled itself, and he began thinking with tremendous fixity of little Gabriel. He wondered if he could brood or meditate, or "will" with sufficient power to bring him into the garden again. The child had just vaguely recognized him for a moment at the waterside. He'd try that dodge, telepathy was a mild kind of a trick after so much of the miraculous. If he'd lost his blessed body, at least the part that ate and smoked and talked to Mildred . . . He stopped as his mind stumbled on a strange recognition. . . . What a joke, of course . . . idiot . . . not to have seen *that*. He stood up in the garden with joy . . . of course, *he* was upstairs with Mildred, it was himself, the other bit of him, that Mildred had been talking to. What a howling fool he'd been.

He found himself concentrating his mind on the purpose of getting the child Gabriel into the garden once more, but it was with a curious mood that he endeavored to establish this relationship. He could not fix his will into any calm intensity of power, or fixity of purpose, or pleasurable mental ecstasy. The utmost force seemed to come with a malicious threatening splenetic "entreaty." That damned snail in the hedge broke the thread of his meditation; a dog began to bark sturdily from a

distant farm; the faculties of his mind became joggled up like a child's picture puzzle, and he brooded unintelligibly upon such things as skating and steam engines, and Elizabethan drama so lapped about with themes like jealousy and chastity. Really now, Shakespeare's Isabella was the most consummate snob in . . . He looked up quickly to his wife's room and saw Gabriel step from the window to the balcony as if he were fearful of being seen. The boy lifted up his hands and placed the bright box on the rail of the balcony. He looked up at the faint stars for a moment or two, and then carefully released the lid of the box. What came out of it and rose into the air appeared to Codling to be just a piece of floating light, but as it soared above the roof he saw it grow to be a little ancient ship, with its hull and fully set sails and its three masts all of faint primrose flame color. It cleaved through the air, rolling slightly as a ship through the wave, in widening circles above the house, making a curving ascent until it lost the shape of a vessel and became only a moving light hurrying to some sidereal shrine. Codling glanced at the boy on the balcony, but in that brief instant something had happened, the ship had burst like a rocket and released three colored drops of fire which came falling slowly, leaving beautiful gray furrows of smoke in their track. Gabriel leaned over the rail with outstretched palms, and, catching the green star and the blue one as they drifted down to him, he ran with a rill of laughter back into the house. Codling sprang forward just in time to catch the red star; it lay vividly blasting his own palm for a monstrous second, and then, slipping through, was gone. He stared at the ground, at the balcony, the sky, and then heard an exclamation . . . his wife stood at his side.

"Gilbert! How you frightened me!" she cried. "I thought you were in your room; come along in to dinner." She took his arm and they walked up the steps into the dining room together. "Just a moment," said her husband, turning to the door of the room. His hand was upon the handle, which turned easily in his grasp, and he ran upstairs to his own room. He opened the door. The light was on, the fire was burning brightly, a smell of cigarette smoke about, pen and paper upon his desk, the Japanese book knife, the gilt matchbox, everything all right, no one there. He picked up a book from his desk. . . . *Monna Vanna*. His bookplate was in it—*Ex Libris*—*Gilbert Cannister*. He put it down beside the green dish; two yellow oranges were in the green dish, and two most deliberately green Canadian apples rested by their side. He went to the door and swung it backwards and forwards quite easily. He sat on his desk trying to piece the thing together, glaring at the print and the bookknife and the smart matchbox, until his wife came up behind him exclaiming: "Come along, Gilbert!"

"Where are the kids, old man?" he asked her, and, before she replied, he had gone along to the nursery. He saw the two cots, his boy in one, his girl in the other. He turned whimsically to Mildred, saying, "There *are* only two, *are* there?" Such a question did not call for reply, but he confronted her as if expecting some assuring answer. She was staring at him with her bright beautiful eyes.

"Are there?" he repeated.

"How strange you should ask me that now!" she said. . . . "If you're a very good man . . . perhaps . . ."

"Mildred!"

She nodded brightly.

He sat down in the rocking chair, but got up again saying to her gently—"We'll call him Gabriel."

"But, suppose——"

"No, no," he said, stopping her lovely lips, "I know all about him." And he told her a pleasant little tale.

William Hope Hodgson
1901-

"THE Voice in the Night" is probably the weirdest of short thrillers. After reading it, one is not surprised to find that almost nothing can be discovered about the author: no publisher or agent can tell whence he came and where he went. No *Who's Who*, encyclopedia, or almanac knows anything about him. Perhaps the destruction of records in wartime London is responsible. But his unforgettable story speaks for itself.

The Voice in the Night

BY WILLIAM HOPE HODGSON

It was a dark, starless night. We were becalmed in the Northern Pacific. Our exact position I do not know; for the sun had been hidden during the course of a weary, breathless week, by a thin haze which had seemed to float above us, about the height of our mastheads, at whiles descending and shrouding the surrounding sea.

With there being no wind, we had steadied the tiller, and I was the only man on deck. The crew, consisting of two men and a boy, were sleeping forward in their den; while Will—my friend, and the master of our little craft—was aft in his bunk on the port side of the little cabin.

Suddenly, from out of the surrounding darkness, there came a nail:

"Schooner, ahoy!"

The cry was so unexpected that I gave no immediate answer, because of my surprise.

It came again—a voice curiously throaty and inhuman, calling from somewhere upon the dark sea away on our port broadside:

"Schooner, ahoy!"

"Hullo!" I sung out, having gathered my wits somewhat. "What are you? What do you want?"

"You need not be afraid," answered the queer voice, having probably noticed some trace of confusion in my tone. "I am only an old—man."

The pause sounded oddly; but it was only afterwards that it came back to me with any significance.

"Why don't you come alongside, then?" I queried somewhat snappishly; for I liked not his hinting at my having been a trifle shaken.

"I—I—can't. It wouldn't be safe. I——" The voice broke off, and there was silence.

"What do you mean?" I asked, growing more and more astonished. "What not safe? Where are you?"

I listened for a moment; but there came no answer. And then, a sudden indefinite suspicion, of I knew not what, coming to me, I stepped swiftly to the binnacle, and took out the lighted lamp. At the same time, I knocked on the deck with my heel to waken Will. Then I was back at the side, throwing the yellow funnel of light out into the silent immensity beyond our rail. As I did so, I heard a slight, muffled cry, and then the sound of a splash as though someone had dipped oars abruptly. Yet I cannot say that I saw anything with certainty; save, it seemed to me, that with the first flash of the

By permission of Mrs. William Hope Hodgson.

589

light, there had been something upon the waters, where now there was nothing.

"Hullo, there!" I called. "What foolery is this!"

But there came only the indistinct sounds of a boat being pulled away into the night.

Then I heard Will's voice, from the direction of the after scuttle:

"What's up, George?"

"Come here, Will!" I said.

"What is it?" he asked, coming across the deck.

I told him the queer thing which had happened. He put several questions; then, after a moment's silence, he raised his hands to his lips, and hailed:

"Boat, ahoy!"

From a long distance away there came back to us a faint reply, and my companion repeated his call. Presently, after a short period of silence, there grew on our hearing the muffled sound of oars; at which Will hailed again.

This time there was a reply:

"Put away the light."

"I'm damned if I will," I muttered; but Will told me to do as the voice bade, and I shoved it down under the bulwarks.

"Come nearer," he said, and the oar strokes continued. Then, when apparently some half-dozen fathoms distant, they again ceased.

"Come alongside," exclaimed Will. "There's nothing to be frightened of aboard here!"

"Promise that you will not show the light?"

"What's to do with you?" I burst out, "that you're so infernally afraid of the light?"

"Because——" began the voice, and stopped short.

"Because what?" I asked quickly.

Will put his hand on my shoulder.

"Shut up a minute, old man," he said in a low voice. "Let me tackle him."

He leaned more over the rail.

"See here, Mister," he said, "this is a pretty queer business, you coming upon us like this, right out in the middle of the blessed Pacific. How are we to know what sort of a hanky-panky trick you're up to? You say there's only one of you. How are we to know, unless we get a squint at you—eh? What's your objection to the light, anyway?"

As he finished, I heard the noise of the oars again, and then the voice came; but now from a greater distance, and sounding extremely hopeless and pathetic.

"I am sorry—sorry! I would not have troubled you, only I am hungry, and—so is she."

The voice died away, and the sound of the oars, dipping irregularly, was borne to us.

"Stop!" sung out Will. "I don't want to drive you away. Come back! We'll keep the light hidden, if you don't like it."

He turned to me:

"It's a damned queer rig, this; but I think there's nothing to be afraid of?"

There was a question in his tone, and I replied.

"No, I think the poor devil's been wrecked around here, and gone crazy."

The sound of the oars drew nearer.

"Shove that lamp back in the binnacle," said Will; then he leaned over the rail and listened. I replaced the lamp, and came back to his side. The dipping of the oars ceased some dozen yards distant.

"Won't you come alongside now?" asked Will in an even voice. "I have had the lamp put back in the binnacle."

"I—I cannot," replied the voice. "I dare not come nearer. I dare not even pay you for the—the provisions."

"That's all right," said Will, and hesitated. "You're welcome to as much grub as you can take——" Again he hesitated.

"You are very good," exclaimed the voice. "May God, Who understands everything, reward you——" It broke off huskily.

"The—the lady?" said Will abruptly. "Is she——"

"I have left her behind upon the island," came the voice.

"What island?" I cut in.

"I know not its name," returned the voice. "I would to God——!" it began, and checked itself as suddenly.

"Could we not send a boat for her?" asked Will at this point.

"No!" said the voice, with extraordinary emphasis. "My God! No!" There was a moment's pause; then it added, in a tone which seemed a merited reproach:

"It was because of our want I ventured—because her agony tortured me."

"I am a forgetful brute," exclaimed Will. "Just wait a minute, whoever you are, and I will bring you up something at once."

In a couple of minutes he was back again, and his arms were full of various edibles. He paused at the rail.

"Can't you come alongside for them?" he asked.

"No—I *dare not*," replied the voice, and it seemed to me that in its tones I detected a note of stifled craving—as though the owner hushed a mortal desire. It came to me then in a flash that the poor old

creature out there in the darkness was *suffering* for actual need of that which Will held in his arms; and yet, because of some unintelligible dread, refraining from dashing to the side of our schooner, and receiving it. And with the lightninglike conviction, there came the knowledge that the Invisible was not mad; but sanely facing some intolerable horror.

"Damn it, Will!" I said, full of many feelings, over which predominated a vast sympathy. "Get a box. We must float off the stuff to him in it."

This we did—propelling it away from the vessel, out into the darkness, by means of a boathook. In a minute, a slight cry from the Invisible came to us, and we knew that he had secured the box.

A little later, he called out a farewell to us, and so heartful a blessing that I am sure we were the better for it. Then, without more ado, we heard the ply of oars across the darkness.

"Pretty soon off," remarked Will, with perhaps just a little sense of injury.

"Wait," I replied. "I think somehow he'll come back. He must have been badly needing that food."

"And the lady," said Will. For a moment he was silent; then he continued:

"It's the queerest thing ever I've tumbled across, since I've been fishing."

"Yes," I said, and fell to pondering.

And so the time slipped away—an hour, another, and still Will stayed with me; for the queer adventure had knocked all desire for sleep out of him.

The third hour was three parts through, when we heard again the sound of oars across the silent ocean.

"Listen!" said Will, a low note of excitement in his voice.

"He's coming, just as I thought," I muttered.

The dipping of the oars grew nearer, and I noted that the strokes were firmer and longer. The food had been needed.

They came to a stop a little distance off the broadside, and the queer voice came again to us through the darkness:

"Schooner, ahoy!"

"That you?" asked Will.

"Yes," replied the voice. "I left you suddenly; but—but there was great need."

"The lady?" questioned Will.

"The—lady is grateful now on earth. She will be more grateful soon in—in heaven."

Will began to make some reply, in a puzzled voice; but became confused, and broke off short. I said nothing. I was wondering at the curious pauses, and, apart from my wonder, I was full of a great sympathy.

The voice continued:

"We—she and I, have talked, as we shared the result of God's tenderness and yours——"

Will interposed; but without coherence.

"I beg of you not to—to belittle your deed of Christian charity this night," said the voice. "Be sure that it has not escaped His notice."

It stopped, and there was a full minute's silence. Then it came again:

"We have spoken together upon that which—which has befallen us. We had thought to go out, without telling any, of the terror which has come into our—lives. She is with me in believing that tonight's happenings are under a special ruling, and that it is God's wish that we should tell to you all that we have suffered since—since——"

"Yes?" said Will softly.

"Since the sinking of the *Albatross.*"

"Ah!" I exclaimed involuntarily. "She left Newcastle for 'Frisco some six months ago, and hasn't been heard of since."

"Yes," answered the voice. "But some few degrees to the North of the line she was caught in a terrible storm, and dismasted. When the day came, it was found that she was leaking badly, and presently, it falling to a calm, the sailors took to the boats, leaving—leaving a young lady —my fiancée—and myself upon the wreck.

"We were below, gathering together a few of our belongings, when they left. They were entirely callous, through fear, and when we came up upon the decks, we saw them only as small shapes afar off upon the horizon. Yet we did not despair, but set to work and constructed a small raft. Upon this we put such few matters as it would hold, including a quantity of water and some ship's biscuit. Then, the vessel being very deep in the water, we got ourselves on to the raft, and pushed off.

"It was later, when I observed that we seemed to be in the way of some tide or current, which bore us from the ship at an angle; so that in the course of three hours, by my watch, her hull became invisible to our sight, her broken masts remaining in view for a somewhat longer period. Then, towards evening, it grew misty, and so through the night. The next day we were still encompassed by the mist, the weather remaining quiet.

"For four days we drifted through this strange haze, until, on the evening of the fourth day, there grew

upon our ears the murmur of breakers at a distance. Gradually it became
plainer, and, somewhat after midnight, it appeared to sound upon
either hand at no very great space.
The raft was raised upon a swell
several times, and then we were in
smooth water, and the noise of the
breakers was behind.

"When the morning came, we
found that we were in a sort of great
lagoon; but of this we noticed little
at the time; for close before us,
through the enshrouding mist,
loomed the hull of a large sailing
vessel. With one accord, we fell
upon our knees and thanked God;
for we thought that here was an end
to our perils. We had much to learn.

"The raft drew near to the ship,
and we shouted on them to take us
aboard; but none answered. Presently the raft touched against the side
of the vessel, and, seeing a rope
hanging downwards, I seized it and
began to climb. Yet I had much ado
to make my way up, because of a
kind of gray, lichenous fungus which
had seized upon the rope, and which
blotched the side of the ship lividly.

"I reached the rail and clambered
over it, on to the deck. Here I saw
that the decks were covered, in
great patches, with the gray masses,
some of them rising into nodules
several feet in height; but at the
time I thought less of this matter
than of the possibility of there being
people aboard the ship. I shouted;
but none answered. Then I went to
the door below the poop deck. I
opened it, and peered in. There was
a great smell of staleness, so that I
knew in a moment that nothing
living was within, and with the
knowledge, I shut the door quickly;
for I felt suddenly lonely.

"I went back, to the side where I
had scrambled up. My—my sweetheart was still sitting quietly upon
the raft. Seeing me look down she
called up to know whether there
were any aboard of the ship. I replied that the vessel had the appearance of having been long deserted;
but that if she would wait a little I
would see whether there was anything in the shape of a ladder by
which she could ascend to the deck.
Then we would make a search
through the vessel together. A little
later, on the opposite side of the
decks, I found a rope side ladder.
This I carried across, and a minute
afterwards she was beside me.

"Together we explored the cabins
and apartments in the after part of
the ship; but nowhere was there any
sign of life. Here and there, within
the cabins themselves, we came
across odd patches of that queer
fungus; but this, as my sweetheart
said, could be cleansed away.

"In the end, having assured ourselves that the after portion of the
vessel was empty, we picked our
ways to the bows, between the ugly
gray nodules of that strange growth;
and here we made a further search,
which told us that there was indeed
none aboard but ourselves.

"This being now beyond any
doubt, we returned to the stern of
the ship and proceeded to make ourselves as comfortable as possible.
Together we cleared out and cleaned
two of the cabins; and after that I
made examination whether there was
anything eatable in the ship. This I
soon found was so, and thanked God
in my heart for His goodness. In
addition to this I discovered the
whereabouts of the fresh-water
pump, and having fixed it I found
the water drinkable, though somewhat unpleasant to the taste.

"For several days we stayed
aboard the ship, without attempting

to get to the shore. We were busily engaged in making the place habitable. Yet even thus early we became aware that our lot was even less to be desired than might have been imagined; for though, as a first step, we scraped away the odd patches of growth that studded the floors and walls of the cabins and saloon, yet they returned almost to their original size within the space of twenty-four hours, which not only discouraged us, but gave us a feeling of vague unease.

"Still we would not admit ourselves beaten, so set to work afresh, and not only scraped away the fungus, but soaked the places where it had been, with carbolic, a canful of which I had found in the pantry. Yet, by the end of the week the growth had returned in full strength, and, in addition, it had spread to other places, as though our touching it had allowed germs from it to travel elsewhere.

"On the seventh morning, my sweetheart woke to find a small patch of it growing on her pillow, close to her face. At that, she came to me, so soon as she could get her garments upon her. I was in the galley at the time lighting the fire for breakfast.

"'Come here, John,' she said, and led me aft. When I saw the thing upon her pillow I shuddered, and then and there we agreed to go right out of the ship and see whether we could not fare to make ourselves more comfortable ashore.

"Hurriedly we gathered together our few belongings, and even among these I found that the fungus had been at work; for one of her shawls had a little lump of it growing near one edge. I threw the whole thing over the side, without saying anything to her.

"The raft was still alongside, but it was too clumsy to guide, and I lowered down a small boat that hung across the stern, and in this we made our way to the shore. Yet, as we drew near to it, I became gradually aware that here the vile fungus, which had driven us from the ship, was growing riot. In places it rose into horrible, fantastic mounds, which seemed almost to quiver, as with a quiet life, when the wind blew across them. Here and there it took on the forms of vast fingers, and in others it just spread out flat and smooth and treacherous. Odd places, it appeared as grotesque stunted trees, seeming extraordinarily kinked and gnarled—the whole quaking vilely at times.

"At first, it seemed to us that there was no single portion of the surrounding shore which was not hidden beneath the masses of the hideous lichen; yet, in this, I found we were mistaken; for somewhat later, coasting along the shore at a little distance, we descried a smooth white patch of what appeared to be fine sand, and there we landed. It was not sand. What it was I do not know. All that I have observed is that upon it the fungus will not grow; while everywhere else, save where the sandlike earth wanders oddly, pathwise, amid the gray desolation of the lichen, there is nothing but that loathsome grayness.

"It is difficult to make you understand how cheered we were to find one place that was absolutely free from the growth, and here we deposited our belongings. Then we went back to the ship for such things as it seemed to us we should need. Among other matters, I managed to bring ashore with me one of the ship's sails, with which I constructed two small tents, which, though exceedingly rough-shaped, served the purposes for which they were intended. In these we lived and stored our various necessities, and thus for a matter of some four weeks all went smoothly and without particular unhappiness. Indeed, I may say with much of happiness—for—we were together.

"It was on the thumb of her right hand that the growth first showed. It was only a small circular spot, much like a little gray mole. My God! how the fear leaped to my heart when she showed me the place. We cleansed it, between us, washing it with carbolic and water. In the morning of the following day she showed her hand to me again. The gray warty thing had returned. For a little while, we looked at one another in silence. Then, still wordless, we started again to remove it. In the midst of the operation she spoke suddenly.

" 'What's that on the side of your face, dear?' Her voice was sharp with anxiety. I put my hand up to feel.

" 'There! Under the hair by your ear. A little to the front a bit.' My finger rested upon the place, and then I knew.

" 'Let us get your thumb done first,' I said. And she submitted, only because she was afraid to touch me until it was cleansed. I finished washing and disinfecting her thumb, and then she turned to my face. After it was finished we sat together and talked awhile of many things; for there had come into our lives sudden, very terrible thoughts. We were, all at once, afraid of something worse than death. We spoke of loading the boat with provisions and water and making our way out on to the sea; yet we were helpless, for many causes, and—and the growth had attacked us already. We

decided to stay. God would do with us what was His will. We would wait.

"A month, two months, three months passed and the places grew somewhat, and there had come others. Yet we fought so strenuously with the fear that its headway was but slow, comparatively speaking.

"Occasionally we ventured off to the ship for such stores as we needed. There we found that the fungus grew persistently. One of the nodules on the main deck became soon as high as my head.

"We had now given up all thought or hope of leaving the island. We had realized that it would be unallowable to go among healthy humans, with the thing from which we were suffering.

"With this determination and knowledge in our minds we knew that we should have to husband our food and water; for we did not know, at that time, but that we should possibly live for many years.

"This reminds me that I have told you that I am an old man. Judged by years this is not so. But— but——"

He broke off; then continued somewhat abruptly:

"As I was saying, we knew that we should have to use care in the matter of food. But we had no .idea then how little food there was left, of which to take care. It was a week later that I made the discovery that all the other bread tanks—which I had supposed full—were empty, and that (beyond odd tins of vegetables and meat, and some other matters) we had nothing on which to depend, but the bread in the tank which I had already opened.

"After learning this I bestirred myself to do what I could, and set to work at fishing in the lagoon; but with no success. At this I was somewhat inclined to feel desperate until the thought came to me to try outside the lagoon, in the open sea.

"Here, at times, I caught odd fish; but so infrequently that they proved of but little help in keeping us from the hunger which threatened. It seemed to me that our deaths were likely to come by hunger, and not by the growth of the thing which had seized upon our bodies.

"We were in this state of mind when the fourth month wore out. Then I made a very horrible discovery. One morning, a little before midday, I came off from the ship with a portion of the biscuits which were left. In the mouth of her tent I saw my sweetheart sitting, eating something.

"'What is it, my dear?' I called out as I leaped ashore. Yet, on hearing my voice, she seemed confused, and, turning, slyly threw something towards the edge of the little clearing. It fell short, and a vague suspicion having arisen within me, I walked across and picked it up. It was a piece of the gray fungus.

"As I went to her with it in my hand, she turned deadly pale; then a rose red.

"I felt strangely dazed and frightened.

"'My dear! My dear!' I said, and could say no more. Yet at my words she broke down and cried bitterly. Gradually, as she calmed, I got from her the news that she had tried it the preceding day, and—and liked it. I got her to promise on her knees not to touch it again, however great our hunger. After she had promised she told me that the desire for it had come suddenly, and that, until the moment of desire, she had experienced nothing towards it but the most extreme repulsion.

"Later in the day, feeling strangely restless, and much shaken with the thing which I had discovered, I made my way along one of the twisted paths—formed by the white, sandlike substance—which led among the fungoid growth. I had, once before, ventured along there; but not to any great distance. This time, being involved in perplexing thought, I went much further than hitherto.

"Suddenly I was called to myself by a queer hoarse sound on my left. Turning quickly I saw that there was movement among an extraordinarily shaped mass of fungus, close to my elbow. It was swaying uneasily, as though it possessed life of its own. Abruptly, as I stared, the thought came to me that the thing had a grotesque resemblance to the figure of a distorted human creature. Even as the fancy flashed into my brain, there was a slight, sickening noise of tearing, and I saw that one of the branchlike arms was detaching itself from the surrounding gray masses, and coming towards me. The head of the thing—a shapeless gray ball, inclined in my direction. I stood stupidly, and the vile arm brushed across my face. I gave out a frightened cry, and ran back a few paces. There was a sweetish taste upon my lips where the thing had touched me. I licked them, and was immediately filled with an inhuman desire. I turned and seized a mass of the fungus. Then more, and—more. I was insatiable. In the midst of devouring, the remembrance of the morning's discovery swept into my amazed brain. It was sent by God. I dashed the fragment I held to the ground. Then, utterly wretched and feeling a dreadful guiltiness, I made my way back to the little encampment.

"I think she knew, by some marvelous intuition which love must have given, so soon as she set eyes on me. Her quiet sympathy made it easier for me, and I told her of my sudden weakness; yet omitted to mention the extraordinary thing which had gone before. I desired to spare her all unnecessary terror.

"But, for myself, I had added an intolerable knowledge, to breed an incessant terror in my brain; for I doubted not but that I had seen the end of one of these men who had come to the island in the ship in the lagoon; and in that monstrous ending I had seen our own.

"Thereafter we kept from the abominable food, though the desire for it had entered into our blood. Yet our drear punishment was upon us; for, day by day, with monstrous rapidity, the fungoid growth took hold of our poor bodies. Nothing we could do would check it materially, and so—and so—we who had been human, became—— Well, it matters less each day. Only—only we had been man and maid!

"And day by day the fight is more dreadful, to withstand the hunger-lust for the terrible lichen.

"A week ago we ate the last of the biscuit, and since that time I have caught three fish. I was out here fishing tonight when your schooner drifted upon me out of the mist. I hailed you. You know the rest, and may God, out of His great heart, bless you for your goodness to a—a couple of poor outcast souls."

There was the dip of an oar—another. Then the voice came again, and for the last time, sounding through the slight surrounding mist, ghostly and mournful.

"God bless you! Good-by!"

"Good-by," we shouted together, hoarsely, our hearts full of many emotions.

I glanced about me. I became aware that the dawn was upon us.

The sun flung a stray beam across the hidden sea; pierced the mist dully, and lit up the receding boat with a gloomy fire. Indistinctly I saw something nodding between the oars. I thought of a sponge—a great, gray nodding sponge—— The oars continued to ply. They were gray—as was the boat—and my eyes searched a moment vainly for the conjunction of hand and oar. My gaze flashed back to the—head. It nodded forward as the oars went backward for the stroke. Then the oars were dipped, the boat shot out of the patch of light, and the—the thing went nodding into the mist.

John Collier

1901-

AN OCCASIONAL poem, some oddly fantastic stories, a book or two privately printed because of English censorship laws, make up the body of John Collier's work. He was educated privately, and has lived gracefully and lightheartedly, it would seem from all accounts, in Oxfordshire, England, and in Hollywood and Virginia. He once edited the works of John Aubrey, a seventeenth-century writer whose wit sounds much like Collier's own. *His Monkey Wife: Or Married to a Chimp* was Collier's first novel, and *Full Circle* another—a novel of England in 1995, destroyed by war, her people returned to savagery. But it is his stories that are best known in America. An excellent collection of his most impish, *A Touch of Nutmeg*, edited by Clifton Fadiman, contains "Bird of Prey."

"Collier's humor has nothing to do with phrases or even situations," says Fadiman; "it proceeds from a peculiar flipness of tone all his own, acetic, casual, always surprising. . . . He has the genuine *soufflé* touch."

Bird of Prey

BY JOHN COLLIER

THE house they call the engineer's house is now deserted. The new man from Baton Rouge gave it up after living less than a month in it, and built himself a two-room shack with his own money, on the very farthest corner of the company's land.

The roof has caved in, and most of the windows are smashed. Oddly enough, no birds nest in the shelter of the eaves, or take advantage of the forsaken rooms. An empty house is normally fine harborage for rats and mice and bats, but there is no squeak, or rustle, or scamper to disturb the quiet of this one. Only creatures utterly foreign, utterly remote from the most distant cousinhood to man, only the termite, the tarantula, and the scorpion indifferently make it their home.

All in a few years Edna Spalding's garden has been wiped out as if it had never existed. The porch where she and Jack sat so happily in the evenings is rotten under its load of wind-blown twigs and sand. A young tree has already burst up the boards outside the living-room window, so that they fan out like the stiff fingers of someone who is afraid. In this corner there still stands a strongly made parrot's perch, the wood of which has been left untouched even by the termite and the boring beetle.

The Spaldings brought a parrot with them when first they came. It was a sort of extra wedding present, given them at the last moment by Edna's mother. It was something from home for Edna to take into the wilds.

The parrot was already old, and he was called Tom, and, like other parrots, he sat on his perch, and whistled and laughed and uttered his few remarks, which were often very appropriate. Edna and Jack were both very fond of him, and they were overwhelmingly fond of each other. They liked their house, and the country, and Jack's colleagues, and everything in life seemed to be delightful.

One night they had just fallen asleep when they were awakened by a tremendous squawking and fluttering outside on the porch. "Oh, Jack!" cried Edna. "Get up! Hurry! Run! It's one of those cats from the men's camp has got hold of poor Tom!"

Jack sprang out of bed, but caught his foot in the sheet, and landed on his elbow on the floor. Between rubbing his elbow and distentangling his foot, he wasted a good many seconds before he was up again and

From *Presenting Moonshine and Other Stories* by John Collier. By permission of Harold Matson. Copyright, 1941, by John Collier.

598

had dashed through the living room and out upon the porch.

All this time, which seemed an age, the squawking and fluttering increased, but as he flung open the door it ceased as suddenly as it had begun. The whole porch was bathed in the brightest moonlight, and at the farther end the perch was clearly visible, and on the floor beneath it was poor old Tom parrot, gasping amid a litter of his own feathers, and crying, "Oh! Oh! Oh!"

At any rate he was alive. Jack looked right and left for traces of his assailant, and at once noticed the long, heavy trailers of the vine were swinging violently although there was not a breath of wind. He went to the rail and looked out and around, but there was no sign of a cat. Of course, it was not likely there would be. Jack was more interested in the fact that the swaying vines were spread over a length of several feet, which seemed a very great deal of disturbance for a fleeing cat to make. Finally he looked up, and he thought he saw a bird— a big bird, an enormous bird—flying away; he just caught a glimpse of it as it crossed the brightness of the moon.

He turned back, and picked up old Tom. The poor parrot's chain was broken, and his heart was pounding away like mad, and still, like a creature hurt and shocked beyond all endurance, he cried, "Oh! Oh! Oh!"

This was all the more odd, for it was seldom the old fellow came out with a new phrase, and Jack would have laughed heartily, except it sounded too pathetic. So he carefully examined the poor bird, and finding no injury beyond the loss of a handful of feather from his neck, he replaced him on the perch, and turned to reassure Edna, who now appeared in the doorway.

"Is he dead?" cried she.

"No," said Jack. "He's had a bit of shock, though. Something got hold of him."

"I'll bring him a piece of sugar," said Edna. "That's what he loves. That'll make him feel better."

She soon brought the sugar, which Tom took in his claw, but though usually he would nibble it up with the greatest avidity, this time he turned his lackluster eye only once upon it, and gave a short, bitter, despairing sort of laugh, and let it fall to the ground.

"Let him rest," said Jack. "He has had a bad tousling."

"It was a cat," said Edna. "It was one of those beastly blacks that the men have at the camp."

"Maybe," said Jack. "On the other hand—I don't know. I thought I saw an enormous bird flying away."

"It couldn't be an eagle," said Edna. "There are none ever seen here."

"I know," said Jack. "Besides, they don't fly at night. Nor do the buzzards. It might have been an owl, I suppose, but——"

"But what?" said Edna.

"But it looked very much larger than an owl," said Jack.

"It was your fancy," said Edna. "It was one of those beastly cats that did it."

This point was discussed very frequently during the next few days. Everybody was consulted, and everybody had an opinion. Jack might have been a little doubtful at first, for he had caught only the briefest glimpse as the creature crossed the moon, but opposition made him more certain, and the discussions sometimes got rather heated.

"Charlie says it was all your imagination," said Edna. "He says no owl would ever attack a parrot."

"How the devil does he know?" said Jack. "Besides, I said it was bigger than an owl."

"He says that shows you imagine things," said Edna.

"Perhaps he would like me to think I do," said Jack. "Perhaps you both would."

"Oh, Jack!" cried Edna. She was deeply hurt, and not without reason, for it showed that Jack was still thinking of a ridiculous mistake he had made, a real mistake, of the sort that young husbands sometimes do make, when they come suddenly into a room and people are startled without any real reason for it. Charlie was young and free and easy and good-looking, and he would put his hand on your shoulder without even thinking about it, and nobody minded.

"I should not have said that," said Jack.

"No, indeed you shouldn't," said Edna, and she was right.

The parrot said nothing at all. All these days he had been moping and ailing, and seemed to have forgotten even how to ask for sugar. He only groaned and moaned to himself, ruffled up his feathers, and every now and then shook his head in the most rueful, miserable, despairing way you can possibly imagine.

One day, however, when Jack came home from work, Edna put her finger to her lips and beckoned him to the window. "Watch Tom," she whispered.

Jack peered out. There was the old bird, lugubriously climbing down from his perch and picking some dead stalks from the vine, which he carried up till he gained a corner where the balustrade ran into the wall, and added his gatherings to others that were already there. He trod round and round, twisted his stalks in and out, and, always with the same doleful expression, paid great attention to the nice disposal of a feather or two, a piece of wool, a fragment of cellophane. There was no doubt about it.

"There's no doubt about it," said Jack.

"He's making a nest!" cried Edna.

"He!" cried Jack. "He! I like that. The old impostor! the old male impersonator! She's going to lay an egg. Thomasina—that's her name from now on."

Thomasina it was. Two or three days later the matter was settled beyond the shadow of a doubt. There, one morning, in the ramshackle nest, was an egg.

"I thought she was sick because of that shaking she got," said Jack. "She was broody, that's all."

"It's a monstrous egg," said Edna. "Poor birdie!"

"What do you expect, after God knows how many years?" said Jack, laughing. "Some birds lay eggs nearly as big as themselves—the kiwi or something. Still, I must admit it's a whopper."

"She doesn't look well," said Edna.

Indeed, the old parrot looked almost as sick as a parrot can be, which is several times sicker than any other living creature. Her eyes closed up, her head sank, and if a finger was put out to scratch her she turned her beak miserably away. However, she sat conscientiously on the prodigious egg she had laid, though every day she seemed a little feebler than before.

"Perhaps we ought to take the egg away," said Jack. "We could get it blown, and keep it as a memento."

"No," said Edna. "Let her have it. It's all she's had in all these years."

Here Edna made a mistake, and she realized it a few mornings later. "Jack," she called. "Do come. It's Tom—Thomasina, I mean. I'm afraid she's going to die!"

"We ought to have taken the egg away," said Jack, coming out with his mouth full of breakfast food. "She's exhausted herself. It's no good anyway. It's bound to be sterile."

"Look at her!" cried Edna.

"She's done for," said Jack, and at that moment the poor old bird keeled over and gasped her last.

"The egg killed her," said Jack, picking it up. "I said it would. Do you want to keep it? Oh, good Lord!" He put the egg down very quickly. "It's alive," he said.

"What?" said Edna. "What do you mean?"

"It gave me a turn," said Jack. "It's most extraordinary. It's against nature. There's a chick inside that egg, tapping."

"Let it out," said Edna. "Break the shell."

"I was right," said Jack. "It was a bird I saw. It must have been a stray parrot. Only it looked so big."

"I'm going to break the shell with a spoon," said Edna, running to fetch one.

"It'll be a lucky bird," said Jack when she returned. "Born with a silver spoon in its beak, so to speak. Be careful."

"I will," said Edna. "Oh, I do hope it lives."

With that she gingerly cracked the shell, the tapping increased, and soon they saw a well-developed beak tearing its way through. In another moment the chick was born.

"Golly!" cried Jack. "What a monster!"

"It's because it's young," said Edna. "It'll grow lovely. Like its mother."

"Maybe," said Jack. "I must be off. Put it in the nest. Feed it pap. Keep it warm. Don't monkey with it too much. Good-by, my love."

That morning Jack telephoned home two or three times to find out how the chick was, and if it ate. He rushed home at lunchtime. In the evening everyone came around to peep at the nestling and offer advice.

Charlie was there. "It ought to be fed every hour at least," said he. "That's how it is in nature."

"He's right," said Jack. "For the first month at least, that's how it should be."

"It looks as if I'm going to be tied down a bit," said Edna ruefully.

"I'll look in when I pass and relieve your solitude," said Charlie.

"I'll manage to rush home now and then in the afternoons," said Jack a little too thoughtfully.

Certainly the hourly feeding seemed to agree with the chick, which grew at an almost alarming speed. It became covered with down, feathers sprouted; in a few months it was fully grown, and not in the least like its mother. For one thing, it was coal-black.

"It must be a hybrid," said Jack. "There is a black parrot; I've seen them in zoos. They didn't look much like this, though. I've half a mind to send a photograph of him somewhere."

"He looks so wicked," said Edna.

"He looks cunning," said Jack. "That bird knows everything, believe me. I bet he'll talk soon."

"It gave a sort of laugh," said Edna. "I forgot to tell you."

"When?" cried Jack. "A laugh?"

"Sort of," said Edna. "But it was horrible. It made Charlie nearly jump out of his skin."

"Charlie!" cried Jack. "You didn't say he'd been here."

"Well, you know how often he drops in," said Edna.

"Do I?" said Jack. "I hope I do. God! What was that?"

"That's what I meant," said Edna, "a sort of laugh."

"What a horrible sound!" said Jack.

"Listen, Jack," said Edna. "I wish you wouldn't be silly about Charlie. You are, you know."

Jack looked at her. "I know I am," said he. "I know it when I look at you. And then I think I never will be again. But somehow it's got stuck in my mind, and the least little thing brings it on. Maybe I'm just a bit crazy, on that one subject."

"Well, he'll be transferred soon," said Edna. "And that'll be the end of it."

"Where did you hear that?" said Jack.

"He told me this afternoon," said Edna. "He was on his way back from getting the mail when he dropped in. That's why he told me first. Otherwise he'd have told you first. Only he hasn't seen you yet. Do you see?"

"Yes, I see," said Jack. "I wish I could be psychoanalyzed or something."

Soon Charlie made his farewells, and departed for his job on the company's other project. Edna was secretly glad to see him go: she wanted no problems, however groundless, to exist between herself and Jack. A few days later she felt sure that all the problems were solved forever.

"Jack," said she when he came home in the evening.

"Yes," said he.

"Something new," said she. "Don't play with that bird. Listen to me."

"Call him Polly," said Jack. They had named it Polly to be on the safe side. "You don't want to call him 'that bird.' The missus doesn't love you, Poll."

"Do you know, I don't!" said Edna, with quite startling vehemence. "I don't like him at all, Jack. Let's give him away."

"What? For heaven's sake!" cried Jack. "This rare, black, specially hatched Poll? This parrot of romantic origin? The cleverest Poll that ever——"

"That's it," said Edna. "He's too darned clever. Jack, I hate him. He's horrible."

"What? Has he said something you don't like?" said Jack, laughing. "I bet he will, when he talks. But what's the news, anyway?"

"Come inside," said Edna. "I'm not going to tell you with that creature listening." She led the way into the bedroom. "The news is," said she, "that I've got to be humored. And if I don't like anything, it's got to be given away. It's not going to be born with a beak because its mother was frightened by a hateful monstrosity of a parrot."

"What?" said Jack.

"That's what," said Edna, smiling and nodding.

"A brat?" cried Jack in delight. "A boy! Or a girl! It's bound to be one or the other. Listen: I was afraid to tell you how much I wanted one, Edna. Oh, boy! This is going to make everything very, very fine. Lie down. You're delicate. Put your feet up. I'm going to fix dinner. This is practice. Stay still. Oh, boy! Oh, boy! Oh, boy!"

He went out through the living room on his way to the kitchen. As he passed the window he caught sight of the parrot on the dark porch outside, and he put his head through to speak to it.

"Have you heard the news?" said he. "Behold a father! You're going to be cut right out, my bird. You're going to be given away. Yes, sir, it's a baby."

The parrot gave a long low whistle. "You don't say so?" said he in a husky voice, a voice of apprehension, a quite astonishing imitation of Charlie's voice. "What about Jack?"

"What's that?" said Jack startled.

"He'll think it's his," whispered the parrot in Edna's voice. "He's fool enough for anything. Kiss me, darling. Phew-w-! You don't say so? What about Jack? He'll think it's his, he's fool enough for anything. Kiss me, darling. Phew-w-w!"

Jack went out into the kitchen, and sat down with his head in his hands for several minutes.

"Hurry up!" cried Edna from the bedroom, "Hurry up—Father!"

"I'm coming," said Jack.

He went to his desk, and took out the revolver. Then he went into the bedroom.

The parrot laughed. Then, lifting its claw, it took the chain in its beak, and bit through it as if it were paper.

Jack came out, holding the gun, his hand over his eyes. "Fool enough for anything!" and the parrot laughed.

Jack turned the gun on himself. As he did so, in the infinitesimal interval between the beginning and the end of the movement of his finger on the trigger, he saw the bird grow, spread its dark wings, and its eyes flamed, and it changed, and it launched itself towards him.

The gun went off. Jack dropped to the floor. The parrot, or whatever it was, sailing down, seized what came out of his ruined mouth, and wheeled back through the window, and was soon far away, visible for a moment only as it swept on broader wings past the new-risen moon.

Sherwood Anderson

1876-1941

No OTHER writer offers greater contrast with the polished, erudite Englishmen who were his contemporaries than Sherwood Anderson, the lad from the Middle West. Son of a roving, loud-mouthed father, Anderson grew up in half a dozen Ohio towns, had very little schooling after the age of fourteen, and, after serving in the Spanish-American War, settled down as manager of a paint factory in Elyria, Ohio. Not until he was nearly forty did Anderson break the pattern of this typical small-town existence. At this point, like most of the heroes about whom he was later to write, he made his escape. In the middle of dictating a letter in the paint factory, he stood up, walked out of the office, and never returned. The episode has been variously explained as a Gauguin jump for freedom and a nervous breakdown resulting in temporary amnesia.

At any rate, Anderson went to Chicago, where he came under the influence of Dreiser, Floyd Dell, and Carl Sandburg, and where he eventually produced *Winesburg, Ohio*, a book that had a profound effect on American short-story writers. After he had found his literary voice, Anderson wanted to tell all the stories of all the people of America—teachers, stable boys, Negroes, young artists, all of them, like himself, longing for freedom. The best of these stories are about his own boyhood, thinly fictionized—like "I'm a Fool."

After a few years of wandering, from New York to Europe to New Orleans, Anderson finally settled down in Virginia, where he lived for the last seventeen years of his life. Here he continued writing, and edited two newspapers, one Republican and one Democratic.

I'm a Fool

BY SHERWOOD ANDERSON

It was a hard jolt for me, one of the most bitterest I ever had to face. And it all came about through my own foolishness too. Even yet, sometimes, I want to cry or swear or kick myself. Perhaps even now, after all this time, there will be a kind of satisfaction in making myself look cheap by telling of it.

It began at three o'clock one October afternoon as I sat in the grandstand at the fall trotting and pacing meet at Sandusky, Ohio.

To tell the truth, I felt a little foolish that I should be sitting in the grandstand at all. During the summer before I had left my home town with Harry Whitehead and, with a nigger named Burt, had taken a job as swipe with one of the two horses Harry was campaigning through the fall race meets that year. Mother cried and my sister Mildred, who wanted to get a job as school teacher in our town that fall, stormed and scolded about the house all during the week before I left. They both thought it something disgraceful that one of our family should take a place as a swipe with race horses. I've an idea Mildred thought my taking the place would stand in the way of her getting the job she'd been working so long for.

But after all I had to work and there was no other work to be got. A big lumbering fellow of nineteen couldn't just hang around the house and I had got too big to mow people's lawns and sell newspapers. Little chaps who could get next to people's sympathies by their sizes were always getting jobs away from me. There was one fellow who kept saying to everyone who wanted a lawn mowed or a cistern cleaned that he was saving money to work his way through college, and I used to lie awake nights thinking up ways to injure him without being found out. I kept thinking of wagons running over him and bricks falling on his head as he walked along the street. But never mind him.

I got the place with Harry and I liked Burt fine. We got along splendid together. He was a big nigger with a lazy sprawling body and soft kind eyes, and when it came to a fight he could hit like Jack Johnson. He had Bucephalus, a big black pacing stallion that could do 2.09 or 2.10 if he had to, and I had a little gelding named Doctor Fritz that never lost a race all fall when Harry wanted him to win.

We set out from home late in July in a boxcar with the two horses, and after that, until late November, we kept moving along to the race meets and the fairs. It was a peachy time for me, I'll say that. Sometimes, now, I think that boys who are raised regular in houses, and never have a fine nigger like Burt for best friend, and go to high schools and college, and never steal anything or get drunk a little, or learn to swear from fellows who know how, or come walking up in front of a grandstand in their shirt sleeves and with dirty horsey pants on when the races are going on and the grandstand is full of people all dressed up—— What's the use talking about it? Such fellows don't know nothing at all. They've never had no opportunity.

But I did. Burt taught me how to rub down a horse and put the bandages on after a race and steam a horse out and a lot of valuable things for any man to know. He could wrap a bandage on a horse's leg so smooth that if it had been the same color you would think it was his skin, and I guess he'd have been a big driver, too, and got to the top like Murphy and Walter Cox and the others if he hadn't been black.

Gee whizz, it was fun. You got to a county-seat town maybe, say, on a Saturday or Sunday, and the fair began the next Tuesday and lasted until Friday afternoon. Doctor Fritz would be, say, in the 2.25 trot on Tuesday afternoon and on Thursday afternoon Bucephalus would knock 'em cold in the "free-for-all" pace. It left you a lot of time to hang around and listen to horse talk, and see Burt knock some yap cold that got too gay, and you'd find out about horses and men and pick up a lot of stuff you could use all the rest of your life if you had some sense and

salted down what you heard and felt and saw.

And then at the end of the week when the race meet was over, and Harry had run home to tend up to his livery-stable business, you and Burt hitched the two horses to carts and drove slow and steady across country to the place for the next meeting so as not to overheat the horses, etc., etc., you know.

Gee whizz, gosh amighty, the nice hickory nut and beechnut and oaks and other kinds of trees along the roads, all brown and red, and the good smells, and Burt singing a song that was called *Deep River*, and the country girls at the windows of houses and everything. You can stick your colleges up your nose for all me. I guess I know where I got my education.

Why, one of those little burgs of towns you come to on the way, say now, on a Saturday afternoon, and Burt says, "Let's lay up here." And you did.

And you took the horses to a livery stable and fed them and you got your good clothes out of a box and put them on.

And the town was full of farmers gaping, because they could see you were race-horse people, and the kids maybe never see a nigger before and was afraid and run away when the two of us walked down their main street.

And that was before prohibition and all that foolishness, and so you went into a saloon, the two of you, and all the yaps come and stood around, and there was always someone pretended he was horsey and knew things and spoke up and began asking questions, and all you did was to lie and lie all you could about what horses you had, and I said I owned them, and then some fellow said, "Will you have a drink of whisky?" and Burt knocked his eye out the way he could say, offhand like, "Oh, well, all, all right, I'm agreeable to a little nip. I'll split a quart with you." Gee whizz.

But that isn't what I want to tell my story about. We got home late in November and I promised Mother I'd quit the race horses for good. There's a lot of things you've got to promise a mother because she don't know any better.

And so, there not being any work in our town any more than when I left there to go to the races, I went off to Sandusky and got a pretty good place taking care of the horses for a man who owned a teaming and delivery and storage business there. It was a pretty good place with good eats and a day off each week and sleeping on a cot in the big barn, and mostly just shoveling in hay and oats to a lot of big good enough skates of horses that couldn't have trotted a race with a toad. I wasn't dissatisfied and I could send money home.

And then, as I started to tell you, the fall races come to Sandusky and I got the day off and I went. I left the job at noon and had on my good clothes and my new brown derby hat I'd just bought the Saturday before, and a stand-up collar.

First of all I went downtown and walked about with the dudes. I've always thought to myself, "put up a good front," and so I did it. I had forty dollars in my pocket and so I went into the West House, a big hotel, and walked up to the cigar stand. "Give me three twenty-five-cent cigars," I said. There was a lot of horse men and strangers and dressed-up people from other towns standing around in the lobby and in the bar, and I mingled amongst them. In the bar there was a fellow with a cane and a Windsor tie on, that it made me sick to look at him. I like a man to be a man and dress up, but not to go put on that kind of airs. So I pushed him aside, kind of rough, and had me a drink of whisky. And then he looked at me as though he thought he'd get gay, but he changed his mind and didn't say anything. And then I had another drink of whisky, just to show him something, and went out and had a hack out to the races all to myself, and when I got there I bought myself the best seat I could get up in the grandstand, but didn't go in for any of these boxes. That's putting on too many airs.

And so there I was, sitting up in the grandstand as gay as you please and looking down on the swipes coming out with their horses and with their dirty horsey pants on and the horse blankets swung over their shoulders same as I had been doing all the year before. I liked one thing about the same as the other, sitting up there and feeling grand and being down there and looking up at the yaps and feeling grander and more important too. One thing's about as good as another if you take it just right. I've often said that.

Well, right in front of me, in the grandstand that day, there was a fellow with a couple of girls and they was about my age. The young fellow was a nice guy all right. He was the kind maybe that goes to college and then comes to be a lawyer or maybe a newspaper editor or something like that, but he wasn't stuck on himself. There are some of that kind are all right and he was one of the ones.

He had his sister with him and another girl and the sister looked around over his shoulder, accidental at first, not intending to start anything—she wasn't that kind—and her eyes and mine happened to meet.

You know how it is. Gee, she was a peach. She had on a soft dress, kind of a blue stuff, and it looked carelessly made, but was well sewed and made and everything. I knew that much. I blushed when she looked right at me and so did she. She was the nicest girl I've ever seen in my life. She wasn't stuck on herself and she could talk proper grammar without being like a schoolteacher or something like that. What I mean is, she was O.K. I think maybe her father was well to do, but not rich to make her chesty because she was his daughter, as some are. Maybe he owned a drugstore or a drygoods store in their home town, or something like that. She never told me and I never asked.

My own people are all O.K. too, when you come to that. My grandfather was Welsh and over in the old country, in Wales, he was—but never mind that.

The first heat of the first race come off and the young fellow setting there with the two girls left them and went down to make a bet. I knew what he was up to, but he didn't talk big and noisy and let everyone around know he was a sport, as some do. He wasn't that kind. Well, he come back and I heard him tell the two girls what horse he'd bet on, and when the heat was trotted they all half got to their feet and acted in the excited, sweaty way people do when they've got money down on a race, and the horse they bet on is up there pretty close at the end, and they think maybe he'll come on with a rush, but he never does because he hasn't got the old juice in him, come right down to it.

And, then, pretty soon, the horses came out for the 2.18 pace and there was a horse in it I knew. He was a horse Bob French had in his string, but Bob didn't own him. He was a horse owned by a Mr. Mathers down at Marietta, Ohio.

This Mr. Mathers had a lot of money and owned a coal mine or something, and he had a swell place out in the country, and he was stuck on race horses, but was a Presbyterian or something, and I think more than likely his wife was one, too, maybe a stiffer one than himself. So he never raced his horses hisself, and the story round the Ohio race tracks was that when one of his horses got ready to go to the races he turned him over to Bob French and pretended to his wife he was sold.

So Bob had the horses and he did pretty much as he pleased and you can't blame Bob; at least, I never did. Sometimes he was out to win and sometimes he wasn't. I never cared much about that when I was swiping a horse. What I did want to know was that my horse had the speed and could go out in front if you wanted him to.

And, as I'm telling you, there was Bob in this race with one of Mr. Mathers' horses, was named "About Ben Ahem" or something like that, and was fast as a streak. He was a gelding and had a mark of 2.21, but could step in .08 or .09.

Because when Burt and I were out, as I've told you, the year before, there was a nigger Burt knew, worked for Mr. Mathers, and we went out there one day when we didn't have no race on at the Marietta Fair and our boss Harry had gone home.

And so everyone was gone to the fair but just this one nigger, and he took us all through Mr. Mathers' swell house and he and Burt tapped a bottle of wine Mr. Mathers had hid in his bedroom, back in a closet, without his wife knowing, and he showed us this Ahem horse. Burt was always stuck on being a driver, but didn't have much chance to get to the top, being a nigger, and he and the other nigger gulped that whole bottle of wine and Burt got a little lit up.

So the nigger let Burt take this About Ben Ahem and step him a mile in a track Mr. Mathers had all to himself, right there on the farm. And Mr. Mathers had one child, a daughter, kinda sick and not very good-looking, and she came home and we had to hustle and get About Ben Ahem stuck back in the barn.

I'm only telling you to get everything straight. At Sandusky, that afternoon I was at the fair, this young fellow with the two girls was fussed, being with the girls and losing his bet. You know how a fellow is that way. One of them was his girl and the other his sister. I had figured that out.

"Gee whizz," I says to myself, "I'm going to give him the dope."

He was mighty nice when I touched him on the shoulder. He and the girls were nice to me right from the start and clear to the end. I'm not blaming them.

And so he leaned back and I gave him the dope on About Ben Ahem. "Don't bet a cent on this first heat because he'll go like an oxen hitched to a plow, but when the first heat is over go right down and lay on your pile." That's what I told him.

Well, I never saw a fellow treat anyone sweller. There was a fat man sitting beside the little girl that had looked at me twice by this time, and I at her, and both blushing, and what did he do but have the nerve

to turn and ask the fat man to get up and change places with me so I could set with his crowd.

Gee whizz, amighty. There I was. What a chump I was to go and get gay up there in the West House bar, and just because that dude was standing there with a cane and that kind of a necktie on, to go and get all balled up and drink that whisky, just to show off.

Of course, she would know, me setting right beside her and letting her smell of my breath. I could have kicked myself right down out of that grandstand and all around that race track and made a faster record than most of the skates of horses they had there that year.

Because that girl wasn't any mutt of a girl. What wouldn't I have given right then for a stick of chewing gum to chew, or a lozenger, or some licorice, or most anything. I was glad I had those twenty-five-cent cigars in my pocket, and right away I give that fellow one and lit one myself. Then that fat man got up and we changed places and there I was plunked down beside her.

They introduced themselves, and the fellow's best girl he had with him was named Miss Elinor Woodbury, and her father was a manufacturer of barrels from a place called Tiffin, Ohio. And the fellow himself was named Wilbur Wessen and his sister was Miss Lucy Wessen.

I suppose it was their having such swell names got me off my trolley. A fellow, just because he has been a swipe with a race horse, and works taking care of horses for a man in the teaming, delivery and storage business, isn't any better or worse than anyone else. I've often thought that, and said it, too.

But you know how a fellow is. There's something in that kind of nice clothes, and the kind of nice eyes she had, and the way she looked at me, awhile before, over her brother's shoulder, and me looking back at her, and both of us blushing.

I couldn't show her up for a boob, could I?

I made a fool of myself, that's what I did. I said my name was Walter Mathers from Marietta, Ohio, and then I told all three of them the smashingest lie you ever heard. What I said was that my father owned the horse About Ben Ahem, and that he had let him out to this Bob French for racing purposes, because our family was proud and had never gone into racing that way, in our own name, I mean. Then I had got started, and they were all leaning over and listening, and Miss Lucy Wessen's eyes were shining, and I went the whole hog.

I told about our place down at Marietta, and about the big stables and the grand brick house we had on a hill, up above the Ohio River, but I knew enough not to do it in no bragging way. What I did was to start things and then let them drag the rest out of me. I acted just as reluctant to tell as I could. Our family hasn't got any barrel factory, and, since I've known us, we've always been pretty poor, but not asking anything of anyone at that, and my grandfather, over in Wales —but never mind that.

We set there talking like we had known each other for years and years, and I went and told them that my father had been expecting maybe this Bob French wasn't on the square, and had sent me up to Sandusky on the sly to find out what I could.

And I bluffed it through I had found out all about the 2.18 pace in which About Ben Ahem was to start.

I said he would lose the first heat by pacing like a lame cow and then he would come back and skin 'em alive after that. And to back up what I said I took thirty dollars out of my pocket and handed it to Mr. Wilbur Wessen and asked him would he mind, after the first heat, to go down and place it on About Ben Ahem for whatever odds he could get. What I said was that I didn't want Bob French to see me and none of the swipes.

Sure enough the first heat come off and About Ben Ahem went off his stride, up the back stretch, and looked like a wooden horse or a sick one, and come in to be last. Then this Wilbur Wessen went down to the betting place under the grandstand and there I was with the two girls, and when that Miss Woodbury was looking the other way once, Lucy Wessen kinda, with her shoulder you know, kinda touched me. You know how a woman can do. They get close, but not getting gay either. You know what they do. Gee whizz.

And then they give me a jolt. What they had done when I didn't know was to get together, and they had decided Wilbur Wessen would bet fifty dollars, and the two girls had gone and put in ten dollars each of their own money, too. I was sick then, but I was sicker later.

About the gelding, About Ben Ahem, and their winning their money I wasn't worried a lot about that. It come out O.K. Ahem stepped the next three heats like a bushel of spoiled eggs going to market before they could be found out, and Wilbur Wessen had got nine to two for the money. There was something else eating at me.

Because Wilbur come back after he had bet the money, and after that he spent most of his time talking to that Miss Woodbury, and Lucy Wessen and I was left alone together like on a desert island. Gee, if I'd only been on the square or if there had been any way of getting myself on the square. There ain't any Walter Mathers, like I said to her and them, and there hasn't ever been one, but if there was, I bet I'd go to Marietta, Ohio, and shoot him tomorrow.

There I was, big boob that I am. Pretty soon the race was over, and Wilbur had gone down and collected our money, and we had a hack downtown, and he stood us a swell dinner at the West House, and a bottle of champagne beside.

And I was with that girl and she wasn't saying much, and I wasn't saying much either. One thing I know. She wasn't stuck on me because of the lie about my father being rich and all that. There's a way you know. . . . Craps amighty. There's a kind of girl you see just once in your life, and if you don't get busy and make hay then you're gone for good and all and might as well go jump off a bridge. They give you a look from inside of them somewhere, and it ain't no vamping, and what it means is—you want that girl to be your wife, and you want nice things around her like flowers and swell clothes, and you want her to have the kids you're going to have, and you want good music played and no ragtime. Gee whizz.

There's a place over near Sandusky, across a kind of bay, and it's called Cedar Point. And when we had had that dinner we went over to it in a launch, all by ourselves. Wilbur and Miss Lucy and that Miss Woodbury had to catch a ten-o'clock train back to Tiffin. Ohio, because

when you're out with girls like that you can't get careless and miss any trains and stay out all night like you can with some kinds of Janes.

And Wilbur blowed himself to the launch and it cost him fifteen cold plunks, but I wouldn't ever have knew it if I hadn't listened. He wasn't no tin horn kind of a sport.

Over at the Cedar Point place we didn't stay around where there was a gang of common kind of cattle at all.

There was big dance halls and dining places for yaps, and there was a beach you could walk along and get where it was dark, and we went there.

She didn't talk hardly at all and neither did I, and I was thinking how glad I was my mother was all right, and always made us kids learn to eat with a fork at table and not swill soup and not be noisy and rough like a gang you see around a race track that way.

Then Wilbur and his girl went away up the beach and Lucy and I set down in a dark place where there was some roots of old trees the water had washed up, and after that, the time, till we had to go back in the launch and they had to catch their trains, wasn't nothing at all. It went like winking your eye.

Here's how it was. The place we were setting in was dark, like I said, and there was roots from that old stump sticking up like arms, and there was a watery smell, and the night was like—as if you could put your hand out and feel it—so warm and soft and dark and sweet like an orange.

I most cried and I most swore and I most jumped up and danced, I was so mad and happy and sad.

When Wilbur come back from being alone with his girl, and she saw him coming, Lucy she says, "We got to go to the train now," and she was most crying, too, but she never knew nothing I knew, and she couldn't be so all busted up. And then, before Wilbur and Miss Woodbury got up to where she was, she put her face up and kissed me quick and put her head up against me and she was all quivering and—— Gee whizz.

Sometimes I hope I have cancer and die. I guess you know what I mean. We went in the launch across the bay to the train like that, and it was dark too. She whispered and said it was like she and I could get out of the boat and walk on the water, and it sounded foolish, but I knew what she meant.

And then quick, we were right at the depot, and there was a big gang of yaps, the kind that goes to the fairs, and crowded and milling around like cattle, and how could I tell her? "It won't be long because you'll write and I'll write to you." That's all she said.

I got a chance like a hay barn afire. A swell chance I got.

And maybe she would write me, down at Marietta that way, and the letter would come back, and stamped on the front of it by the U.S.A. "there ain't any such guy," or something like that, whatever they stamp on a letter that way.

And me trying to pass myself off

for a bigbug and a swell—to her, as decent a little body as God ever made. Craps amighty. A swell chance I got.

And then the train come in and she got on, and Wilbur Wessen come and shook hands with me, and that Miss Woodbury was nice too, and bowed to me and I at her and the train went and I busted out and cried like a kid.

Gee, I could have run after that train and made Dan Patch look like a freight train after a wreck, but socks amighty, what was the use? Did you ever see such a fool?

I'll bet you what—if I had an arm broke right now or a train had run over my foot—I wouldn't go to no doctor at all. I'd go set down and let her hurt and hurt—that's what I'd do.

I'll bet you what—if I hadn't a drunk that booze I'd a never been such a boob as to go tell such a lie— that couldn't never be made straight to a lady like her.

I wish I had that fellow right here that had on a Windsor tie and carried a cane. I'd smash him for fair. Gosh darn his eyes. He's a big fool—that's what he is.

And if I'm not another you just go find me one and I'll quit working and be a bum and give him my job. I don't care nothing for working and earning money and saving it for no such boob as myself.

Ring Lardner

1885-1933

SPORTS writer for many years, and so-called funnyman of the twenties, Ringgold Wilmer Lardner was above all a satirist. Underneath a hilarious surface humor his stories are deadly serious. His heroes—caddies, doughboys, baseball players, Broadway producers, Long Island socialites— are, almost without exception, morons and heels, and never by word or phrase does their creator excuse or forgive them their banality and cheapness.

Whereas the Jazz Age made F. Scott Fitzgerald soft and sentimental, it left Lardner cold and ruthless. To those who knew him well he was a frustrated, unhappy man who despised his own achievements. When his publishers decided on an anthology of his best stories, they had to look for them in the public libraries and have old issues of magazines photostated, because Lardner had thrown his copies away. It was this anthology, *How to Write Short Stories,* that eventually gave him a reputation as a serious writer. . . . For a Lardner enthusiast his best is a hard choice among "Alibi Ike," "Haircut," "Champion," "I Can't Breathe," and "Some Like Them Cold." "Some Like Them Cold" comes from *Round Up.*

Some Like Them Cold

BY RING LARDNER

N. Y., Aug. 3.

DEAR MISS GILLESPIE: How about our bet now as you bet me I would forget all about you the minute I hit the big town and would never write you a letter. Well girlie it looks like you lose so pay me. Seriously we will call all bets off as I am not the kind that bet on a sure thing and it sure was a sure thing that I would not forget a girlie like you and all that is worrying me is whether it may not be the other way round and you are wondering who this fresh guy is that is writeing you this letter. I bet you are so will try and refreshen your memory.

Well girlie I am the handsome young man that was wondering round the Lasalle st. station Monday and "happened" to sit down beside of a mighty pretty girlie who was waiting to meet her sister from Toledo and the train was late and I am glad of it because if it had not of been that little girlie and I would never of met. So for once I was a lucky guy but still I guess it was time I had some luck as it was certainly tough luck for you and I to both be liveing in Chi all that time and never get together till a half hour before I was leaveing town for good.

Still "better late than never" you know and maybe we can make up for lost time though it looks like we would have to do our makeing up at long distants unless you make good on your threat and come to N. Y. I wish you would do that little thing girlie as it looks like that was the only way we would get a chance to play round together as it looks like they was little or no chance of me comeing back to Chi as my whole future is in the big town. N. Y. is the only spot and specially for a man that expects to make my liveing in the song writeing game as here is the Mecca for that line of work and no matter how good a man may be they don't get no recognition unless they live in N. Y.

Well girlie you asked me to tell you all about my trip. Well I remember you saying that you would give anything to be makeing it yourself but as far as the trip itself was conserned you ought to be thankfull you did not have to make it as you would of sweat your head off. I know I did specially wile going through Ind. Monday P. M. but Monday night was the worst of all trying to sleep and finely I give it up and just layed there with the prespiration rolling off of me though I

From *How to Write Short Stories* by Ring W. Lardner. By permission of the publishers, Charles Scribner's Sons. Copyright, 1924, by Charles Scribner's Sons.

615

was laying on top of the covers and nothing on but my underwear.

Yesterday was not so bad as it rained most of the A. M. comeing through N. Y. state and in the P. M. we road along side of the Hudson all P. M. Some river girlie and just looking at it makes a man forget all about the heat and everything else except a certain girlie who I seen for the first time Monday and then only for a half hour but she is the kind of a girlie that a man don't need to see her only once and they would be no danger of forgetting her. There I guess I better lay off that subject or you will think I am a "fresh guy."

Well that is about all to tell you about the trip only they was one amuseing incidence that come off yesterday which I will tell you. Well they was a dame got on the train at Toledo Monday and had the birth opp. mine but I did not see nothing of her that night as I was out smoking till late and she hit the hay early but yesterday A. M. she come in the dinner and sit at the same table with me and tried to make me and it was so raw that the dinge waiter seen it and give me the wink and of course I paid no tension and I waited till she got through so as they would be no danger of her folling me out but she stopped on the way out to get a tooth pick and when I come out she was out on the platform with it so I tried to brush right by but she spoke up and asked me what time it was and I told her and she said she guessed her watch was slow so I said maybe it just seemed slow on acct. of the company it was in.

I don't know if she got what I was driveing at or not but any way she give up trying to make me and got off at Albany. She was a good looker but I have no time for gals that tries to make strangers on a train.

Well if I don't quit you will think I am writeing a book but will expect a long letter in answer to this letter and we will see if you can keep your promise like I have kept mine. Don't dissapoint me girlie as I am all alone in a large city and hearing from you will keep me from getting home sick for old Chi though I never thought so much of the old town till I found out you lived there. Don't think that is kidding girlie as I mean it.

You can address me at this hotel as it looks like I will be here right along as it is on 47th st. right off of old Broadway and handy to everything and am only paying $21 per wk. for my rm. and could of got one for $16 but without bath but am glad to pay the differents as am lost without my bath in the A. M. and sometimes at night too.

Tomorrow I expect to commence fighting the "battle of Broadway" and will let you know how I come out that is if you answer this letter. In the mean wile girlie au reservoir and don't do nothing I would not do.

Your new friend (?)
Chas. F. Lewis.

Chicago, Ill., Aug. 6.
My Dear Mr. Lewis: Well, that certainly was a "surprise party" getting your letter and you are certainly a "wonder man" to keep your word as I am afraid most men of your sex are gay deceivers but maybe you are "different." Any way it sure was a surprise and will gladly pay the bet if you will just tell me what it was we bet. Hope it was not money as I am a "working girl" but if it was not more than a dollar or two will try to dig it up even if I have to "beg, borrow or steal."

Suppose you will think me a "case" to make a bet and then forget what it was, but you must remember, Mr. Man, that I had just met you and was "dazzled." Joking aside I was rather "fussed" and will tell you why. Well, Mr. Lewis, I suppose you see lots of girls like the one you told me about that you saw on the train who tried to "get acquainted" but I want to assure you that I am not one of those kind and sincerely hope you will believe me when I tell you that you was the first man I ever spoke to meeting them like that and my friends and the people who know me would simply faint if they knew I ever spoke to a man without a "proper introduction."

Believe me, Mr. Lewis, I am not that kind and I don't know now why I did it only that you was so "different" looking if you know what I mean and not at all like the kind of men that usually try to force their attentions on every pretty girl they see. Lots of times I act on impulse and let my feelings run away from me and sometimes I do things on the impulse of the moment which I regret them later on, and that is what I did this time, but hope you won't give me cause to regret it and I know you won't as I know you are not that kind of a man a specially after what you told me about the girl on the train. But any way as I say, I was in a "daze" so can't remember what it was we bet, but will try and pay it if it does not "break" me.

Sis's train got in about ten minutes after yours had gone and when she saw me what do you think was the first thing she said? Well, Mr. Lewis, she said: "Why Mibs (That is a pet name some of my friends have given me) what has happened to you? I never seen you have as much color."

So I passed it off with some remark about the heat and changed the subject as I certainly was not going to tell her that I had just been talking to a man who I had never met or she would of dropped dead from the shock. Either that or she would not of believed me as it would be hard for a person who knows me well to imagine me doing a thing like that as I have quite a reputation for "squelching" men who try to act fresh. I don't mean anything personal by that, Mr. Lewis, as am a good judge of character and could tell without you telling me that you are not that kind.

Well, Sis and I have been on the "go" ever since she arrived as I took yesterday and today off so I could show her the "sights" though she says she would be perfectly satisfied to just sit in the apartment and listen to me "rattle on." Am afraid I am a great talker, Mr. Lewis, but Sis says it is as good as a show to hear me talk as I tell things in such a different way as I cannot help from seeing the humorous side of everything and she says she never gets tired of listening to me, but of course she is my sister and thinks the world of me, but she really does laugh like she enjoyed my craziness.

Maybe I told you that I have a tiny little apartment which a girl friend of mine and I have together and it is hardly big enough to turn round in, but still it is "home" and I am a great home girl and hardly ever care to go out evenings except occasionally to the theatre or dance. But even if our "nest" is small we are proud of it and Sis complimented us on how cozy it is and how "homey" it looks and she said she did not see how we could afford to have everything so nice and Edith (my girl friend) said: "Mibs deserves all the credit for that. I never knew a girl who could make a little money go a long ways like she can." Well, of course she is my best friend and always saying nice things about me, but I do try and I hope I get results. Have always said that good taste and being careful is a whole lot more important than lots of money thought it is nice to have it.

You must write and tell me how you are getting along in the "battle of Broadway" (I laughed when I read that) and whether the publishers like your songs though I know they will. Am crazy to hear them and hear you play the piano as I love good jazz music even better than classical, though I suppose it is terrible to say such a thing. But I usually say just what I think though sometimes I wish afterwards I had not of. But still I believe it is better for a girl to be her own self and natural instead of always acting. But am afraid I will never have a chance to hear you play unless you come back to Chi and pay us a visit as my "threat" to come to New York was just a "threat" and I don't see any hope of ever getting there unless some rich New Yorker should fall in love with me and take me there to live. Fine chance for poor little me, eh Mr. Lewis?

Well, I guess I have "rattled on" long enough and you will think I am writing a book unless I quit and besides, Sis has asked me as a special favor to make her a pie for dinner. Maybe you don't know it, Mr. Man, but I am quite famous for my pie and pastry, but I don't suppose a "genius" is interested in common things like that.

Well, be sure and write soon and tell me what N.Y. is like and all about it and don't forget the little girlie who was "bad" and spoke to a strange man in the station and have been blushing over it ever since.

Your friend (?)
Mabelle Gillespie.

N. Y., Aug. 10

Dear Girlie I bet you will think I am a fresh guy commenceing that way but Miss Gillespie is too cold and a man can not do nothing cold in this kind of weather specially in this man's town which is the hottest place I ever been in and I guess maybe the reason why New Yorkers is so bad is because they think they are all ready in H—— and can not go no worse place no matter how they behave themselves. Honest girlie I certainly envy you being where there is a breeze off the old Lake and Chi may be dirty but I never heard of nobody dying because they was dirty but four people died here yesterday on acct. of the heat and I seen two different women flop right on Broadway and had to be taken away in the ambulance and it could not of been because they was dressed too warm because it would be impossible for the women here to leave off any more cloths.

Well have not had much luck yet in the battle of Broadway as all the heads of the big music publishers is out of town on their vacation and the big boys is the only ones I will do business with as it would be silly for a man with the stuff I have got to waste my time on somebody that is just on the staff and have not got the final say. But I did play a couple of my numbers for the people up to Levy's and Goebel's and they went crazy over them in both places. So it looks like all I have to do is wait for the big boys to get back and then play my numbers for them and I will be all set. What I want is to get taken on the staff of one of the big firms as that gives a man the inside and they will plug your numbers more if you are on the staff. In the mean wile have not got nothing to worry me but am just seeing the sights of the big town as have saved up enough money to play round for a wile and any way a man that can play piano like I can don't never have to worry about starveing. Can certainly make the old music box talk girlie and am always good for a $75 or $100 job.

Well have been here a week now and on the go every minute and I thought I would be lonesome down here but no chance of that as I have been treated fine by the people I have met and have sure met a bunch of them. One of the boys liveing in the hotel is a vaudeville actor and he is a member of the Friars club and took me over there to dinner the other night and some way another the bunch got wise that I could play piano so of course I had to sit down and give them some of my numbers and everybody went crazy over them. One of the boys I met there was Paul Sears the song writer but he just writes the lyrics and has wrote a bunch of hits and when he heard some of my melodies he called me over to one side and said he would like to work with me on some numbers. How is that girlie as he is one of the biggest hit writers in N. Y.

N. Y. has got some mighty pretty girlies and I guess it would not be hard to get acquainted with them and in fact several of them has tried to make me since I been here but I always figure that a girl must be something wrong with her if she tries to make a man that she don't know nothing about so I pass them all up. But I did meet a couple of pips that a man here in the hotel

went up on Riverside Drive to see them and insisted on me going along and they got on some way that I could make a piano talk so they was nothing but I must play for them so I sit down and played some of my own stuff and they went crazy over it.

One of the girls wanted I should come up and see her again, and I said I might but I think I better keep away as she acted like she wanted to vamp me and I am not the kind that likes to play round with a gal just for their company and dance with them etc. but when I see the right gal that will be a different thing and she won't have to beg me to come and see her as I will camp right on her trail till she says yes. And it won't be none of these N. Y. fly by nights neither. They are all right to look at but a man would be a sucker to get serious with them as they might take you up and next thing you know you would have a wife on your hands that don't know a dish rag from a waffle iron.

Well girlie will quit and call it a day as it is too hot to write any more and I guess I will turn on the cold water and lay in the tub a wile and then turn in. Don't forget to write to
Your friend,
Chas. F. Lewis.

Chicago, Ill., Aug. 13.
Dear Mr. Man: Hope you won't think me a "silly Billy" for starting my letter that way but "Mr. Lewis" is so formal and "Charles" is too much the other way and any way I would not dare call a man by their first name after only knowing them only two weeks. Though I may as well confess that Charles is my favorite name for a man and have always been crazy about it as it was my father's name. Poor old dad, he

died of cancer three years ago, but left enough insurance so that mother and we girls were well provided for and do not have to do anything to support ourselves though I have been earning my own living for two years to make things easier for mother and also because I simply can't bear to be doing nothing as I feel like a "drone." So I flew away from the "home nest" though mother felt bad about it as I was her favorite and she always said I was such a comfort to her as when I was in the house she never had to worry about how things would go.

But there I go gossiping about my domestic affairs just like you would be interested in them though I don't see how you could be though personly I always like to know all about my friends, but I know men are different so will try and not bore you any longer. Poor Man, I certainly feel sorry for you if New York is as hot as all that. I guess it has been very hot in Chi, too, at least everybody has been complaining about how terrible it is. Suppose you will wonder why I say "I guess" and you will think I ought to know if it is hot. Well, sir, the reason I say "I guess" is because I don't feel the heat like others do or at least I don't let myself feel it. That sounds crazy I know, but don't you think there is a good deal in mental suggestion and not letting yourself feel things? I believe that if a person simply won't allow themselves to be affected by disagreeable things, why such things won't bother them near as much. I know it works with me and that is the reason why I am never cross when things go wrong and "keep smiling" no matter what happens and as far as the heat is concerned, why I just don't let myself feel it and my friends say I don't even

look hot no matter if the weather is boiling and Edith, my girl friend, often says that I am like a breeze and it cools her off just to have me come in the room. Poor Edie suffers terribly during the hot weather and says it almost makes her mad at me to see how cool and unruffled I look when everybody else is perspiring and have red faces etc.

I laughed when I read what you said about New York being so hot that people thought it was the "other place." I can appreciate a joke, Mr. Man, and that one did not go "over my head." Am still laughing at some of the things you said in the station though they probably struck me funnier than they would most girls as I always see the funny side and sometimes something is said and I laugh and the others wonder what I am laughing at as they cannot see anything in it themselves, but it is just the way I look at things so of course I cannot explain to them why I laughed and they think I am crazy. But I had rather part with almost anything rather than my sense of humour as it helps me over a great many rough spots.

Sis has gone back home though I would of liked to of kept her here much longer, but she had to go though she said she would of liked nothing better than to stay with me and just listen to me "rattle on." She always says it is just like a show to hear me talk as I always put things in such a funny way and for weeks after she has been visiting me she thinks of some of the things I said and laughs over them. Since she left Edith and I have been pretty quiet though poor Edie wants to be on the "go" all the time and tries to make me go out with her every evening to the pictures and scolds me when I say I had rather stay home and read and calls me a "book worm." Well, it is true that I had rather stay home with a good book than go to some crazy old picture and the last two nights I have been reading myself to sleep with Robert W. Service's poems. Don't you love Service or don't you care for "high-brow" writings?

Personly there is nothing I love more than to just sit and read a good book or sit and listen to some-body play the piano, I mean if they can really play and I really believe I like popular music better than the classical though I suppose that is a terrible thing to confess, but I love all kinds of music but a specially the piano when it is played by somebody who can really play.

Am glad you have not "fallen" for the "ladies" who have tried to make your acquaintance in New York. You are right in thinking there must be something wrong with girls who try to "pick up" strange men as no girl with self respect would do such a thing and when I say that, Mr. Man, I know you will think it is a funny thing for me to say on ac-count of the way our friendship started, but I mean it and I assure you that was the first time I ever done such a thing in my life and would never of thought of doing it had I not known you were the right kind of a man as I flatter myself that I am a good judge of character and can tell pretty well what a per-son is like by just looking at them and I assure you I had made up my mind what kind of a man you were before I allowed myself to answer your opening remark. Otherwise I am the last girl in the world that would allow myself to speak to a person without being introduced to them.

When you write again you must

tell me all about the girl on River-side Drive and what she looks like and if you went to see her again and all about her. Suppose you will think I am a little old "curiosity shop" for asking all those questions and will wonder why I want to know. Well, sir, I won't tell you why, so there, but I insist on you answering all questions and will scold you if you don't. Maybe you will think that the reason why I am so curious is be-cause I am "jealous" of the lady in question. Well, sir, I won't tell you whether I am or not, but will keep you "guessing." Now, don't you wish you knew?

Must close or you will think I am going to "rattle on" forever or maybe you have all ready become disgusted and torn my letter up. If so all I can say is poor little me— she was a nice little girl and meant well, but the man did not appreciate her.

There! Will stop or you will think I am crazy if you do not all ready.

Yours (?)

Mabelle.

N. Y., Aug. 20.

Dear Girlie: Well girlie I suppose you thought I was never going to answer your letter but have been busier than a one armed paper hanger the last week as have been working on a number with Paul Sears who is one of the best lyric writers in N. Y. and has turned out as many hits as Berlin or Davis or any of them. And believe me girlie he has turned out another hit this time that is he and I have done it together. It is all done now and we are just waiting for the best chance to place it but will not place it no-wheres unless we get the right kind of a deal but maybe will publish it ourselves.

The song is bound to go over big as Sears has wrote a great lyric and I have give it a great tune or at least every body that has heard it goes crazy over it and it looks like it would go over bigger than any song since Mammy and would not be surprised to see it come out the hit of the year. If it is handled right we will make a bbl. of money and Sears says it is a cinch we will clean up as much as $25000 apiece which is pretty fair for one song but this one is not like the most of them but has got a great lyric and I have wrote a melody that will knock them out of their seats. I only wish you could hear it girlie and hear it the way I play it. I had to play it over and over about 50 times at the Friars last night.

I will copy down the lyric of the chorus so you can see what it is like and get the idea of the song though of course you can't tell much about it unless you hear it played and sang. The title of the song is When They're Like You and here is the chorus:

"*Some like them hot, some like them cold.*
Some like them when they're not too darn old.
Some like them fat, some like them lean.
Some like them only at sweet sixteen.
Some like them dark, some like them light.
Some like them in the park, late at night.
Some like them fickle, some like them true,
But the time I like them is when they're like you."

How is that for a lyric and I only wish I could play my melody for you as you would go nuts over it but will send you a copy as soon as the song is published and you can get some of your friends to play it over for you and I know you will like it though it is a different melody when I play it or when somebody else plays it.

Well girlie you will see how busy I have been and am libel to keep right on being busy as we are not going to let the grass grow under our feet but as soon as we have this number placed we will get busy on another one as a couple like that will put me on Easy st. even if they don't go as big as we expect but even 25 grand is a big bunch of money and if a man could only turn out one hit a year and make that much out of it I would be on Easy st. and no more hammering on the old music box in some cabaret.

Who ever we take the song to we will make them come across with one grand for advance royaltys and that will keep me going till I can turn out another one. So the future looks bright and rosey to yours truly and I am certainly glad I come to the big town though sorry I did not do it a whole lot quicker.

This is a great old town girlie and when you have lived here a wile you wonder how you ever stood for a burg like Chi which is just a hick town along side of this besides being dirty etc. and a man is a sucker to stay there all their life specially a man in my line of work as N. Y. is the Mecca for a man that has got the musical gift. I figure that all the time I spent in Chi I was just wasteing my time and never really started to live till I come down here and I have to laugh when I think of the boys out there that is trying to make a liveing in the song writeing game and most of them starve to death all their life and the first week I am down here I meet a man like Sears and the next thing you know we have turned out a song that will make us a fortune.

Well girlie you asked me to tell you about the girlie up on the Drive that tried to make me and asked me to come and see her again. Well I can assure you you have no reason to be jealous in that quarter as I have not been back to see her as I figure it is wasteing my time to play round with a dame like she that wants to go out somewheres every night and if you married her she would want a house on 5th ave. with a dozen servants so I have passed her up as that is not my idea of home.

What I want when I get married is a real home where a man can stay home and work and maybe have a few of his friends in once in a wile and entertain them or go to a good musical show once in a wile and have a wife that is in sympathy with you and not nag at you all the wile but be a real help mate. The girlie up on the Drive would run me ragged and have me in the poor house inside of a year even if I was makeing 25 grand out of one song. Besides she wears a make up that you would have to blast to find out what her face looks like. So I have not been back there and don't intend to see her again so what is the use of me telling you about her. And the only other girlie I have met is a sister of Paul Sears who I met up to his house wile we was working on the song but she don't hardly count as she has not got no use for the boys but treats them like dirt and Paul says she is the coldest proposition he ever seen.

Well I don't know no more to write and besides have got a date to go out to Paul's place for dinner and play some of my stuff for him so as he can see if he wants to set words to some more of my melodies. Well

don't do nothing I would not do and have as good a time as you can in old Chi and will let you know how we come along with the song.

Chas. F. Lewis.

Chicago, Ill., Aug. 23.
Dear Mr. Man: I am thrilled to death over the song and think the words awfully pretty and am crazy to hear the music which I know must be great. It must be wonderful to have the gift of writing songs and then hear people play and sing them and just think of making $25,000 in such a short time. My, how rich you will be and I certainly congratulate you though am afraid when you are rich and famous you will have no time for insignificant little me or will you be an exception and remember your "old" friends even when you are up in the world? I sincerely hope so.

Will look forward to receiving a copy of the song and will you be sure and put your name on it? I am all ready very conceited just to think that I know a man that writes songs and makes all that money.

Seriously I wish you success with your next song and I laughed when I read your remark about being busier than a one armed paper hanger. I don't see how you think up all those comparisons and crazy things to say. The next time one of the girls asks me to go out with them I am going to tell them I can't go because I am busier than a one armed paper hanger and then they will think I made it up and say: "The girl is clever."

Seriously I am glad you did not go back to see the girl on the Drive and am also glad you don't like girls who makes themselves up so much as I think it is disgusting and would rather go round looking like a ghost than put artificial color on my face. Fortunately I have a complexion that does not need "fixing" but even if my coloring was not what it is I would never think of lowering myself to "fix" it. But I must tell you a joke that happened just the other day when Edith and I were out at lunch and there was another girl in the restaurant whom Edie knew and she introduced her to me and I noticed how this girl kept staring at me and finally she begged my pardon and asked if she could ask me a personal question and I said yes and she asked me if my complexion was really "mine." I assured her it was and she said: "Well, I thought so because I did not think anybody could put it on so artistically. I certainly envy you." Edie and I both laughed.

Well, if that girl envies me my complexion, why I envy you living in New York. Chicago is rather dirty though I don't let that part of it bother me as I bathe and change my clothing so often that the dirt does not have time to "settle." Edie often says she cannot see how I always keep so clean looking and says I always look like I had just stepped out of a band box. She also calls me a fish (jokingly) because I spend so much time in the water. But seriously I do love to bathe and never feel so happy as when I have just "cleaned up" and put on fresh clothing.

Edie has just gone out to see a picture and was cross at me because I would not go with her. I told her I was going to write a letter and she wanted to know to whom and I told her and she said: "You write to him so often that a person would almost think you was in love with him." I just laughed and turned it off, but she does say the most em-barrassing things and I would be angry if it was anybody but she that said them.

Seriously I had much rather sit here and write letters or read or just sit and dream than go out to some crazy old picture show except once in awhile I do like to go to the theater and see a good play and a specially a musical play if the music is catchy. But as a rule I am contented to just stay home and feel cozy and lots of evenings Edie and I sit here without saying hardly a word to each other though she would love to talk but she knows I had rather be quiet and she often says it is just like living with a deaf and dumb mute to live with me because I make so little noise round the apartment. I guess I was born to be a home body as I so seldom care to go "gadding."

Though I do love to have company once in awhile, just a few congenial friends whom I can talk to and feel at home with and play cards or have some music. My friends love to drop in here, too, as they say Edie and I always give them such nice things to eat. Though poor Edie has not much to do with it, I am afraid, as she hates anything connected with cooking which is one of the things I love best of anything and I often say that when I begin keeping house in my own home I will insist on doing most of my own work as I would take so much more interest in it than a servant, though I would want somebody to help me a little if I could afford it as I often think a woman that does all her own work is liable to get so tired that she loses interest in the bigger things of life like books and music. Though after all what bigger thing is there than home making a specially for a woman?

I am sitting in the dearest old chair that I bought yesterday at a little store on the North Side. That is my one extravagance, buying furniture and things for the house, but I always say it is economy in the long run as I will always have them and have use for them and when I can pick them up at a bargain I would be silly not to. Though heaven knows I will never be "poor" in regards to furniture and rugs and things like that as mother's house in Toledo is full of lovely things which she says she is going to give to Sis and myself as soon as we have real homes of our own. She is going to give me the first choice as I am her favorite. She has the loveliest old things that you could not buy now for love or money including lovely old rugs and a piano which Sis wanted to have a player attachment put on it but I said it would be an insult to the piano so we did not get one. I am funny about things like that, a specially old furniture and feel towards them like people whom I love.

Poor mother, I am afraid she won't live much longer to enjoy her lovely old things as she has been suffering for years from stomach trouble and the doctor says it has been worse lately instead of better and her heart is weak besides. I am going home to see her a few days this fall as it may be the last time. She is very cheerful and always says she is ready to go now as she had had enough joy out of life and all she would like would be to see her girls settled down in their own homes before she goes.

There I go, talking about my domestic affairs again and I will bet you are bored to death though personly I am never bored when my friends tell me about themselves.

But I won't "rattle on" any longer, but will say good night and don't forget to write and tell me how you come out with the song and thanks for sending me the words to it. Will you write a song about me some time? I would be thrilled to death! But I am afraid I am not the kind of girl that inspires men to write songs about them, but am just a quiet "mouse" that loves home and am not giddy enough to be the heroine of a song.

Well, Mr. Man, good night and don't wait so long before writing again to

Yours (?)
Mabelle.

N. Y., Sept. 8.

Dear Girlie: Well girlie have not got your last letter with me so cannot answer what was in it as I have forgotten if there was anything I was supposed to answer and besides have only a little time to write as I have a date to go out on a party with the Sears. We are going to the Georgie White show and afterwards somewheres for supper. Sears is the boy who wrote the lyric to my song and it is him and his sister I am going on the party with. The sister is a cold fish that has no use for men but she is show crazy and insists on Paul taking her to 3 or 4 of them a week.

Paul wants me to give up my room here and come and live with them as they have plenty of room and I am running a little low on money but don't know if I will do it or not as am afraid I would freeze to death in the same house with a girl like the sister as she is ice cold but she don't hang round the house much as she is always takeing trips or going to shows or somewheres.

So far we have not had no luck

with the song. All the publishers we
have showed it to has went crazy
over it but they won't make the right
kind of a deal with us and if they
don't loosen up and give us a decent
royalty rate we are liabel to put the
song out ourselves and show them
up. The man up to Goebel's told us
the song was O. K. and he liked it
but it was more of a production
number than anything else and ought
to go in a show like the Follies but
they won't be in N. Y. much longer
and what we ought to do is hold it
till next spring.

Mean wile I am working on some
new numbers and also have taken a
position with the orchestra at the
Wilton and am going to work there
starting next week. They pay good
money $60 and it will keep me going.

Well girlie that is about all the
news. I believe you said your father
was sick and hope he is better and
also hope you are getting along O. K.
and take care of yourself. When you
have nothing else to do write to your
friend,

Chas. F. Lewis.

Chicago, Ill., Sept. 11.
Dear Mr. Lewis: Your short note
reached me yesterday and must say
I was puzzled when I read it. It
sounded like you was mad at me
though I cannot think of any reason
why you should be. If there was
something I said in my last letter
that offended you I wish you would
tell me what it was and I will ask
your pardon though I cannot remember anything I could of said that you
could take offense at. But if there
was something, why I assure you,
Mr. Lewis, that I did not mean
anything by it. I certainly did not
intend to offend you in any way.

Perhaps it is nothing I wrote you,
but you are worried on account of

the publishers not treating you fair in
regards to your song and that is
why your letter sounded so distant.
If that is the case I hope that by this
time matters have rectified themselves and the future looks brighter.
But any way, Mr. Lewis, don't allow
yourself to worry over business cares
as they will all come right in the end
and I always think it is silly for
people to worry themselves sick over
temporary troubles, but the best way
is to "keep smiling" and look for the
"silver lining" in the cloud. That is
the way I always do and no matter
what happens, I manage to smile
and my girl friend, Edie, calls me
Sunny because I always look on the
bright side.

Remember also, Mr. Lewis, that
$60 is a salary that a great many
men would like to be getting and are
living on less than that and supporting a wife and family on it. I
always say that a person can get
along on whatever amount they make
if they manage things in the right
way.

So if it is business troubles, Mr.
Lewis, I say don't worry, but look
on the bright side. But if it is something I wrote in my last letter that
offended you I wish you would tell
me what it was so I can apologize
as I assure you I meant nothing and
would not say anything to hurt you
for the world.

Please let me hear from you soon
as I will not feel comfortable until
I know I am not to blame for the
sudden change.

Sincerely,
Mabelle Gillespie.

N. Y., Sept. 24.
Dear Miss Gillespie: Just a few
lines to tell you the big news or at
least it is big news to me. I am engaged to be married to Paul Sears'

sister and we are going to be married early next month and live in Atlantic City where the orchestra I have been playing with has got an engagement in one of the big cabarets.

I know this will be a surprise to you as it was even a surprise to me as I did not think I would ever have the nerve to ask the girlie the big question as she was always so cold and acted like I was just in the way. But she said she supposed she would have to marry somebody some time and she did not dislike me as much as most of the other men her brother brought round and she would marry me with the understanding that she would not have to be a slave and work round the house and also I would have to take her to a show or somewheres every night and if I could not take her myself she would "run wild" alone. Atlantic City will be O. K. for that as a lot of new shows opens down there and she will be able to see them before they get to the big town. As for her being a slave, I would hate to think of marrying a girl and then have them spend their lives in druggery round the house. We are going to live in a hotel till we find something better but will be in no hurry to start house keeping as we will have to buy all new furniture.

Betsy is some doll when she is all fixed up and believe me she knows how to fix herself up. I don't know what she uses but it is weather proof and I have been out in a rain storm with her and we both got drowned but her face stayed on. I would almost think it was real only she tells me different.

Well girlie I may write to you again once in a wile as Betsy says she don't give a damn if I write to all the girls in the world just so I don't make her read the answers but that is all I can think of to say now except good bye and good luck and may the right man come along soon and he will be a lucky man getting a girl that is such a good cook and got all that furniture etc.

But just let me give you a word of advice before I close and that is don't never speak to strange men who you don't know nothing about as they may get you wrong and think you are trying to make them. It just happened that I knew better so you was lucky in my case but the luck might not last.

> Your friend,
> Chas. F. Lewis.

Chicago, Ill., Sept. 27.
My Dear Mr. Lewis: Thanks for your advice and also thank your fiance for her generosity in allowing you to continue your correspondence with her "rivals," but personly I have no desire to take advantage of that generosity as I have something better to do than read letters from a man like you, a specially as I have a man friend who is not so generous as Miss Sears and would strongly object to my continuing a correspondence with another man. It is at his request that I am writing this note to tell you not to expect to hear from me again.

Allow me to congratulate you on your engagement to Miss Sears and I am sure she is to be congratulated too, though if I met the lady I would be tempted to ask her to tell me her secret, namely how she is going to "run wild" on $60.

> Sincerely,
> Mabelle Gillespie.

Damon Runyon

1884-1946

DAMON RUNYON, like Ring Lardner, was a sports writer, a humorist, and a recorder of the way America talks. His notable contribution to the short story is the eloquent use of slang and wisecracks so unashamedly American that when the English publish his stories—and how the English love them! —they add a glossary. Unlike Lardner's sardonic humor, Runyon's is good-natured. He rather liked the "dopes" about whom he wrote.

Runyon was brought up in Colorado. He fought in the Spanish-American War, enlisting at fourteen, spent two years in the Philippines, worked on several California and Colorado newspapers, reported the war in Mexico when Pershing was pursuing Pancho Villa, and World War I in France. But he was above all a New Yorker. After he died, in 1946, his ashes were scattered at his own request over Manhattan—"the place that I have truly loved and that was so good to me." They were dropped from a plane by Captain Rickenbacker, who was a long-time friend.

Blood Pressure

BY DAMON RUNYON

It is maybe eleven-thirty of a Wednesday night, and I am standing at the corner of Forty-eighth Street and Seventh Avenue, thinking about my blood pressure, which is a proposition I never before think much about.

In fact, I never hear of my blood pressure before this Wednesday afternoon when I go around to see Doc Brennan about my stomach, and he puts a gag on my arm and tells me that my blood pressure is higher than a cat's back, and the idea is for me to be careful about what I eat, and to avoid excitement, or I may pop off all of a sudden when I am least expecting it.

"A nervous man such as you with a blood pressure away up in the paint cards must live quietly," Doc Brennan says. "Ten bucks, please," he says.

Well, I am standing there thinking it is not going to be so tough to avoid excitement the way things are around this town right now, and wishing I have my ten bucks back to bet it on Sun Beau in the fourth race at Pimlico the next day, when all of a sudden I look up, and who is in front of me but Rusty Charley.

Now if I have any idea Rusty Charley is coming my way, you can go and bet all the coffee in Java I will be somewhere else at once, for Rusty Charley is not a guy I wish to have any truck with whatever. In fact, I wish no part of him. Furthermore, nobody else in this town wishes to have any part of Rusty Charley, for he is a hard guy indeed. In fact, there is no harder guy anywhere in the world. He is a big wide guy with two large hard hands and a great deal of very bad disposition, and he thinks nothing of knocking people down and stepping on their kissers if he feels like it.

In fact, this Rusty Charley is what is called a gorill, because he is known to often carry a gun in his pants pocket, and sometimes to shoot people down as dead as door nails with it if he does not like the way they wear their hats—and Rusty Charley is very critical of hats. The chances are Rusty Charley shoots many a guy in this man's town, and those he does not shoot he sticks with his chiv—which is a knife— and the only reason he is not in jail is because he just gets out of it, and the law does not have time to think up something to put him back in again for.

Anyway, the first thing I know about Rusty Charley being in my neighborhood is when I hear him saying: "Well, well, well, here we are!"

Then he grabs me by the collar, so it is no use of me thinking of taking it on the lam away from there, although I greatly wish to do so.

"Hello, Rusty," I say, very pleasant. "What is the score?"

"Everything is about even," Rusty says. "I am glad to see you, because I am looking for company. I am over in Philadelphia for three days on business."

"I hope and trust that you do all right for yourself in Philly, Rusty," I say; but his news makes me very nervous, because I am a great hand for reading the papers and I have a pretty good idea what Rusty's business in Philly is. It is only the day before that I see a little item from Philly in the papers about how Gloomy Gus Smallwood, who is a very large operator in the alcohol business there, is guzzled right at his front door.

Of course I do not know that Rusty Charley is the party who guzzles Gloomy Gus Smallwood, but Rusty Charley is in Philly when Gus is guzzled, and I can put two and two together as well as anybody. It is the same thing as if there is a bank robbery in Cleveland, Ohio, and Rusty Charley is in Cleveland, Ohio, or near there. So I am very nervous, and I figure it is a sure thing my blood pressure is going up every second.

"How much dough do you have on you?" Rusty says. "I am plumb broke."

"I do not have more than a couple of bobs, Rusty," I say. "I pay a doctor ten bucks today to find out my blood pressure is very bad. But of course you are welcome to what I have."

"Well, a couple of bobs is no good to high-class guys like you and me," Rusty says. "Let us go to Nathan Detroit's crap game and win some money."

Now, of course, I do not wish to go to Nathan Detroit's crap game; and if I do wish to go there I do not wish to go with Rusty Charley, because a guy is sometimes judged by the company he keeps, especially around crap games, and Rusty Charley is apt to be considered bad company. Anyway, I do not have any dough to shoot craps with, and if I do have dough to shoot craps with, I will not shoot craps with it at all, but will bet it on Sun Beau, or maybe take it home and pay off some of the overhead around my joint, such as rent.

Furthermore, I remember what Doc Brennan tells me about avoiding excitement, and I know there is apt to be excitement around Nathan Detroit's crap game if Rusty Charley goes there, and maybe run my blood pressure up and cause me to pop off very unexpected. In fact, I already feel my blood jumping more than somewhat inside me, but naturally I am not going to give Rusty Charley any argument, so we go to Nathan Detroit's crap game.

This crap game is over a garage in Fifty-second Street this particular night, though sometimes it is over a restaurant in Forty-seventh Street, or in back of a cigar store in Forty-fourth Street. In fact, Nathan Detroit's crap game is apt to be anywhere, because it moves around every night, as there is no sense in a crap game staying in one spot until the coppers find out where it is.

So Nathan Detroit moves his crap game from spot to spot, and citizens wishing to do business with him have to ask where he is every night; and of course almost everybody on Broadway knows this, as Nathan Detroit has guys walking up and down, and around and about, telling the public his address, and giving out the password for the evening.

Well, Jack the Beefer is sitting in an automobile outside the garage in Fifty-second Street when Rusty Charley and I come along, and he says "Kansas City," very low, as we pass, this being the password for the evening; but we do not have to use any password whatever when we climb the stairs over the garage, because the minute Solid John, the doorman, peeks out through his peephole when we knock, and sees Rusty Charley with me, and he opens up very quick indeed, and gives us a big castor-oil smile, for nobody in this town is keeping doors shut on Rusty Charley very long.

It is a very dirty room over the garage, and full of smoke, and the crap game is on an old pool table; and around the table and packed in so close you cannot get a knitting needle between any two guys with a mawl, are all the high shots in town, for there is plenty of money around at this time, and many citizens are very prosperous. Furthermore, I wish to say there are some very tough guys around the table, too, including guys who will shoot you in the head, or maybe the stomach, and think nothing whatever about the matter.

In fact, when I see such guys as Harry the Horse, from Brooklyn, and Sleepout Sam Levinsky, and Lone Louie, from Harlem, I know this is a bad place for my blood pressure, for these are very tough guys indeed, and are known as such to one and all in this town.

But there they are wedged up against the table with Nick the Greek, Big Nig, Gray John, Okay Okun, and many other high shots, and they all have big coarse G notes in their hands which they are tossing around back and forth as if these G notes are nothing but pieces of waste paper.

On the outside of the mob at the table are a lot of small operators who are trying to cram their fists in between the high shots now and then to get down a bet, and there are also guys present who are called Shylocks, because they will lend you dough when you go broke at the table, on watches, or rings, or maybe cuff links, at very good interest.

Well, as I say, there is no room at the table for as many as one more very thin guy when we walk into the joint, but Rusty Charley lets out a big hello as we enter, and the guys all look around, and the next minute there is space at the table big enough not only for Rusty Charley but for me too. It really is quite magical the way there is suddenly room for us when there is no room whatever for anybody when we come in.

"Who is the gunner?" Rusty Charley asks, looking all around.

"Why, you are, Charley," Big Nig, the stick man in the game, says very quick, handing Charley a pair of dice, although afterward I hear that his pal is right in the middle of a roll trying to make nine when we step up to the table. Everybody is very quiet, just looking at Charley. Nobody pays any attention to me, because I am known to one and all as a guy who is just around, and nobody figures me in on any part of Charley, although Harry the Horse looks at me once in a way that I know is no good for my blood pressure, or for anybody else's blood pressure as far as this goes.

Well, Charley takes the dice and turns to a little guy in a derby hat who is standing next to him scrooching back so Charley will not notice him, and Charley lifts the derby hat off the little guy's head, and rattles the dice in his hand, and chucks them into the hat and goes "Hah!" like crap shooters always do when they are rolling the dice. Then Charley peeks into the hat and says "Ten," although he does not let anybody else look in the hat, not even me, so nobody knows if Charley throws a ten, or what.

But, of course, nobody around is going to up and doubt that Rusty Charley throws a ten, because Charley may figure it is the same thing as calling him a liar, and Charley is such a guy as is apt to hate being called a liar.

Now Nathan Detroit's crap game is what is called a head-and-head game, although some guys call it a fading game, because the guys bet against each other rather than against the bank, or house. It is just the same kind of game as when two guys get together and start shooting craps against each other, and Nathan Detroit does not have to ·bother with a regular crap table and a layout such as they have in gambling houses. In fact, about all Nathan Detroit has to do with the game is to find a spot, furnish the dice and take his percentage which is by no means bad.

In such a game as this there is no real action until a guy is out on a point, and then the guys around commence to bet he makes this point, or that he does not make this point, and the odds in any country in the world that a guy does not make a ten

with a pair of dice before he rolls seven, is two to one.

Well, when Charley says he rolls ten in the derby hat nobody opens their trap, and Charley looks all around the table, and all of a sudden he sees Jew Louie at one end, although Jew Louie seems to be trying to shrink himself up when Charley's eyes light on him.

"I will take the odds for five C's," Charley says, "and Louie, you get it" —meaning he is letting Louie bet him $1000 to $500 that he does not make his ten.

Now Jew Louie is a small operator at all times and more of a Shylock than he is a player, and the only reason he is up there against the table at all at this moment is because he moves up to lend Nick the Greek some dough; and ordinarily there is no more chance of Jew Louie betting a thousand to five hundred on any proposition whatever than there is of him giving his dough to the Salvation Army, which is no chance at all. It is a sure thing he will never think of betting a thousand to five hundred a guy will not make ten with the dice, and when Rusty Charley tells Louie he has such a bet, Louie starts trembling all over.

The others around the table do not say a word, and so Charley rattles the dice again in his duke, blows on them, and chucks them into the derby hat and says "Hah!" But, of course, nobody can see in the derby hat except Charley, and he peeks in at the dice and says "Five." He rattles the dice once more and chucks them into the derby and says "Hah!" and then after peeking into the hat at the dice he says "Eight." I am commencing to sweat for fear he may heave a seven in the hat and blow his bet, and I know Charley has no idea of paying off, no matter what he heaves.

On the next chuck, Charley yells "Money!"—meaning he finally makes his ten, although nobody sees it but him; and he reaches out his hand to Jew Louie, and Jew Louie hands him a big fat G note, very, very slow. In all my life I never see a sadder-looking guy than Louie when he is parting with his dough. If Louie has any idea of asking Charley to let him see the dice in the hat to make sure about the ten, he does not speak about the matter, and as Charley does not seem to wish to show the ten around, nobody else says anything either, probably figuring Rusty Charley is not a guy who is apt to let anybody question his word especially over such a small matter as a ten.

"Well," Charley says, putting Louie's G note in his pocket, "I think this is enough for me tonight," and he hands the derby hat back to the little guy who owns it and motions me to come on, which I am glad to do, as the silence in the joint is making my stomach go up and down inside me, and I know this is bad for my blood pressure. Nobody as much as opens his face from the time we go in until we start out, and you will be surprised how nervous it makes you to be in a big crowd with everybody dead still, especially when you figure it a spot that is liable to get hot any minute. It is only just as we get to the door that anybody speaks, and who is it but Jew Louie, who pipes up and says to Rusty Charley like this:

"Charley," he says, "do you make it the hard way?"

Well, everybody laughs, and we go on out, but I never hear myself whether Charley makes his ten with a six and a four, or with two fives—which is the hard way to make a ten with the dice—although I often wonder about the matter afterward.

I am hoping that I can now get away from Rusty Charley and go on home, because I can see he is the last guy in world to have around a blood pressure, and, furthermore, that people may get the wrong idea of me if I stick around with him, but when I suggest going to Charley, he seems to be hurt.

"Why," Charley says, "you are a fine guy to be talking of quitting a pal just as we are starting out. You will certainly stay with me because I like company, and we will go down to Ikey the Pig's and play stuss. Ikey is an old friend of mine, and I owe him a complimentary play."

Now, of course, I do not wish to go to Ikey the Pig's, because it is a place away downtown, and I do not wish to play stuss, because this is a game which I am never able to figure out myself, and, furthermore, I remember Doc Brennan says I ought to get a little sleep now and then; but I see no use in hurting Charley's feelings, especially as he is apt to do something drastic to me if I do not go.

So he calls a taxi, and we start downtown for Ikey the Pig's, and the jockey who is driving the short goes so fast that it makes my blood pressure go up a foot to a foot and a half from the way I feel inside, although Rusty Charley pays no attention to the speed. Finally I stick my head out the window and ask the jockey to please take it a little easy, as I wish to get where I am going all in one piece, but the guy only keeps busting along.

We are at the corner of Nineteenth and Broadway when all of a sudden Rusty Charley yells at the jockey to pull up a minute, which the guy does. Then Charley steps out of the cab and says to the jockey like this:

"When a customer asks you to take it easy, why do you not be nice and take it easy? Now see what you get."

And Rusty Charley hauls off and clips the jockey a punch on the chin that knocks the poor guy right off the seat into the street, and then Charley climbs into the seat himself and away we go with Charley driving, leaving the guy stretched out as stiff as a board. Now Rusty Charley once drives a short for a living himself, until the coppers get an idea that he is not always delivering his customers to the right address, especially such as may happen to be drunk when he gets them, and he is a pretty fair driver, but he only looks one way, which is straight ahead.

Personally, I never wish to ride with Charley in a taxicab under any circumstances, especially if he is driving, because he certainly drives very fast. He pulls up a block from Ikey the Pig's, and says we will leave the short there until somebody finds it and turns it in, but just as we are walking away from the short up steps a copper in uniform and claims we cannot park the short in this spot without a driver.

Well, Rusty Charley just naturally hates to have coppers give him any advice, so what does he do but peek up and down the street to see if anybody is looking, and then haul off and clout the copper on the chin, knocking him bowlegged. I wish to say I never see a more accurate puncher than Rusty Charley, because he always connects with that old button. As the copper tumbles, Rusty Charley grabs me by the arm and starts me running up a side street,

and after we go about a block we dodge into Ikey the Pig's.

It is what is called a stuss house, and many prominent citizens of the neighborhood are present playing stuss. Nobody seems any too glad to see Rusty Charley, although Ikey the Pig lets on he is tickled half to death. This Ikey the Pig is a short fat-necked guy who will look very natural at New Year's, undressed, and with an apple in his mouth, but it seems he and Rusty Charley are really old-time friends, and think fairly well of each other in spots.

But I can see that Ikey the Pig is not so tickled when he finds Charley is there to gamble, although Charley flashes his G note at once, and says he does not mind losing a little dough to Ikey just for old time's sake. But I judge Ikey the Pig knows he is never going to handle Charley's G note, because Charley puts it back in his pocket and it never comes out again even though Charley gets off loser playing stuss right away.

Well, at five o'clock in the morning, Charley is stuck one hundred and thirty G's, which is plenty of money even when a guy is playing on his muscle, and of course Ikey the Pig knows there is no chance of getting one hundred and thirty cents off of Rusty Charley, let alone that many thousands. Everybody else is gone by this time and Ikey wishes to close up. He is willing to take Charley's marker for a million if necessary to get Charley out, but the trouble is in stuss a guy is entitled to get back a percentage even if he gives a marker, and the percentage will wreck Ikey's joint.

Furthermore, Rusty Charley says he will not quit loser under such circumstances because Ikey is his friend, so what happens Ikey finally sends out and hires a cheater by the name of Dopey Goldberg, who takes to dealing the game and in no time he has Rusty Charley even by cheating in Rusty Charley's favor.

Personally, I do not pay much attention to the play but grab myself a few winks of sleep in a chair in a corner, and the rest seems to help my blood pressure no little. In fact, I am not noticing my blood pressure at all when Rusty Charley and I get out of Ikey the Pig's, because I figure Charley will let me go home and I can go to bed. But although it is six o'clock, and coming on broad daylight when we leave Ikey's, Charley is still full of zing, and nothing will do him but we must go to a joint that is called the Bohemian Club.

Well, this idea starts my blood pressure going again, because the Bohemian Club is nothing but a deadfall where guys and dolls go when there is positively no other place in town open, and it is run by a guy by the name of Knife O'Halloran, who comes from down around Greenwich Village and is considered a very bad character. It is well known to one and all that a guy is apt to lose his life in Knife O'Halloran's any night, even if he does nothing more than drink Knife O'Halloran's liquor.

But Rusty Charley insists on going there, so naturally I go with him; and at first everything is very quiet and peaceful, except that a lot of guys and dolls in evening clothes, who wind up there after being in the night clubs all night, are yelling in one corner of the joint. Rusty Charley and Knife O'Halloran are having a drink together out of a bottle which Knife carries in his pocket, so as not to get it mixed up with the liquor he sells his customers, and are cutting up old touches of the time when they run with the

Hudson Dusters together, when all of a sudden in comes four coppers in plain clothes.

Now these coppers are off duty and are meaning no harm to anybody, and are only wishing to have a dram or two before going home, and the chances are they will pay no attention to Rusty Charley if he minds his own business, although of course they know who he is very well indeed and will take great pleasure in putting the old sleeve on him if they only have a few charges against him, which they do not. So they do not give him a tumble. But if there is one thing Rusty Charley hates it is a copper, and he starts eying them from the minute they sit down at a table, and by and by I hear him say to Knife O'Halloran like this:

"Knife," Charley says, "what is the most beautiful sight in the world?"

"I do not know, Charley," Knife says. "What is the most beautiful sight in the world?"

"Four dead coppers in a row," Charley says.

Well, at this I personally ease myself over toward the door, because I never wish to have any trouble with coppers, and especially with four coppers, so I do not see everything that comes off. All I see is Rusty Charley grabbing at the big foot which one of the coppers kicks at him, and then everybody seems to go into a huddle, and the guys and dolls in evening dress start squawking, and my blood pressure goes up to maybe a million.

I get outside the door, but I do not go away at once as anybody with any sense will do, but stand there listening to what is going on inside, which seems to be nothing more than a loud noise like ker-bump, ker-bump, ker-bump. I am not afraid there will be any shooting, because as far as Rusty Charley is concerned he is too smart to shoot any coppers, which is the worst thing a guy can do in this town, and the coppers are not likely to start any blasting because they will not wish it to come out that they are in a joint such as the Bohemian Club off duty. So I figure they will all just take it out in pulling and hauling.

Finally the noise inside dies down, and by and by the door opens and out comes Rusty Charley, dusting himself off here and there with his hands and looking very much pleased, indeed, and through the door before it flies shut again I catch a glimpse of a lot of guys stretched out on the floor. Furthermore, I can still hear guys and dolls hollering.

"Well, well," Rusty Charley says, "I am commencing to think you take the wind on me, and am just about to get mad at you, but here you are. Let us go away from this joint, because they are making so much noise inside you cannot hear yourself think. Let us go to my joint and make my old woman cook us up some breakfast, and then we can catch some sleep. A little ham and eggs will not be bad to take right now."

Well, naturally ham and eggs are appealing to me no little at this time, but I do not care to go to Rusty Charley's joint. As far as I am personally concerned, I have enough of Rusty Charley to do me a long, long time, and I do not care to enter into his home life to any extent whatever, although to tell the truth I am somewhat surprised to learn he has any such life. I believe I do once hear that Rusty Charley marries one of the neighbor's children, and that he lives somewhere over on Tenth Avenue in the Forties, but nobody really knows much about this, and everybody figures if it is true his wife must lead a terrible dog's life.

But while I do not wish to go to Charley's joint I cannot very well refuse a civil invitation to eat ham and eggs, especially as Charley is looking at me in a very much surprised way because I do not seem so glad and I can see that it is not everyone that he invites to his joint. So I thank him, and say there is nothing I will enjoy more than ham and eggs such as his old woman will cook for us, and by and by we are walking along Tenth Avenue up around Forty-fifth Street.

It is still fairly early in the morning, and business guys are opening up their joints for the day, and little children are skipping along the sidewalks going to school and laughing tee-hee, and old dolls are shaking bed-clothes and one thing and another out of the windows of the tenement houses, but when they spot Rusty Charley and me everybody becomes very quiet, indeed, and I can see that Charley is greatly respected in his own neighborhood. The business guys hurry into their joints, and the little children stop skipping and tee-heeing and go tiptoeing along, and the old dolls yank in their noodles, and a great quiet comes to the street. In fact, about all you can hear is the heels of Rusty Charley and me hitting on the sidewalk.

There is an ice wagon with a couple of horses hitched to it standing in front of a store, and when he sees the horses Rusty Charley seems to get a big idea. He stops and looks the horses over very carefully, although as far as I can see they are nothing but horses, and big and fat, and sleepy-looking horses, at that. Finally Rusty Charley says to me like this:

"When I am a young guy," he says, "I am a very good puncher with my right hand, and often I hit a horse on the skull with my fist and knock it down. I wonder," he says, "if I lose my punch. The last copper I hit back there gets up twice on me."

Then he steps up to one of the ice-wagon horses and hauls off and biffs it right between the eyes with a right-hand smack that does not travel more than four inches, and down goes old Mister Horse to his knees looking very much surprised, indeed. I see many a hard puncher in my day, including Dempsey when he really can punch, but I never see a harder punch than Rusty Charley gives this horse.

Well, the ice-wagon driver comes bursting out of the store all heated up over what happens to his horse, but he cools out the minute he sees Rusty Charley, and goes on back into the store, leaving the horse still taking a count, while Rusty Charley and I keep walking. Finally we come to the entrance of a tenement house that Rusty Charley says is where he lives, and in front of this house is a wop with a pushcart loaded with fruit and vegetables and one thing and another, which Rusty Charley tips over as we go into the house, leaving the wop yelling very loud, and maybe cussing us in wop for all I know. I am very glad, personally, we finally get somewhere, because I can feel that my blood pressure is getting worse every minute I am with Rusty Charley.

We climb two flights of stairs, and then Charley opens a door and we step into a room where there is a pretty little red-headed doll about knee high to a flivver, who looks as if she may just get out of the hay, because her red hair is flying around every which way on her head, and her eyes seem still gummed up with sleep. At first I think she is a very cute sight, indeed, and then I see something in her eyes that tells me this doll, whoever she is, is feeling very hostile to one and all.

"Hello, tootsie," Rusty Charley says. "How about some ham and eggs for me and my pal here? We are all tired out going around and about."

Well, the little red-headed doll just looks at him without saying a word. She is standing in the middle of the floor with one hand behind her, and all of a sudden she brings this hand around, and what does she have in it but a young baseball bat, such as kids play ball with, and which cost maybe two bits; and the next thing I know I hear something go ker-bap, and I can see she smacks Rusty Charley on the side of the noggin with the bat.

Naturally I am greatly horrified at this business, and figure Rusty Charley will kill her at once, and then I will be in a jam for witnessing the murder and will be held in jail several years like all witnesses to anything in this man's town; but Rusty Charley only falls into a big rocking chair in a corner of the room and sits there with one hand to his head, saying, "Now hold on, tootsie," and "Wait a minute there, honey." I recollect hearing him say, "We have company for breakfast," and then the little red-headed doll turns on me and gives me a look such as I will always remember, although I smile at her very pleasant and mention it is a nice morning.

Finally she says to me like this:

"So you are the trambo who keeps my husband out all night, are you, you trambo?" she says, and with this she starts for me, and I start for the door; and by this time my blood pressure is all out of whack, because I can see that Mrs. Rusty Charley is excited more than somewhat. I get my hand on the knob and just then something hits me alongside the noggin, which I afterward figure must be the baseball bat, although I remember having a sneaking idea the roof caves in on me.

How I get the door open I do not know, because I am very dizzy in the head and my legs are wobbling, but when I think back over the situation I remember going down a lot of steps very fast, and by and by the fresh air strikes me, and I figure I am in the clear. But all of a sudden I feel another strange sensation back of my head and something goes plop against my noggin, and I figure at first that maybe my blood pressure runs up so high that it squirts out the top of my bean. Then I peek around over my shoulder just once to see that Mrs. Rusty Charley is stand-ing beside the wop peddler's cart snatching fruit and vegetables of one kind and another off the cart and chucking them at me.

But what she hits me with back of the head is not an apple, or a peach, or a rutabaga, or a cabbage, or even a casaba melon, but a brick-bat that the wop has on his cart to weight down the paper sacks in which he sells his goods. It is this brickbat which makes a lump on the back of my head so big that Doc Brennan thinks it is a tumor when I go to him the next day about my stomach, and I never tell him any different.

"But," Doc Brennan says, when he takes my blood pressure again, "your pressure is down below normal now, and as far as it is concerned you are in no danger whatever. It only goes to show what just a little bit of quiet living will do for a guy," Doc Brennan says. "Ten bucks, please," he says.

F. Scott Fitzgerald
1896-1940

Francis Scott Key Fitzgerald will always be remembered as the spokesman of the Jazz Age, that period of extravagance, excitement, and sadness which mirrored America's postwar disillusionment. It was the day of women's new-found freedom—with suffrage, cigarettes, short hair, and short skirts; of oil scandals and come-easy money; of the "flivver" and the back seat; of schoolboys with hip flasks; of bright young people adrift. Fitzgerald, himself one of the Jazz Age's "sad young men," one of "the beautiful and the damned," had the temperament to do justice to this glittering mirage of life. He was young and gay and handsome like his heroes; his wife was the beautiful, impassioned heroine; Long Island week ends, the swift, low-slung car, the ever-present highball, the extravagance, the flappers, and the waste were the ever-recurring elements in both his life and his stories.

Fitzgerald was a born writer. Stories poured out of him, and in his heyday he was one of America's most prolific and popular writers, making and losing quantities of golden useless dollars. *This Side of Paradise* (1920) established him, and *The Great Gatsby* (1925), written at the height of his fame, is usually considered his best work. The last ten years of his life were years of illness, unhappiness, and semiobscurity, but they produced *Tender Is the Night* and an unfinished novel about the movie world, *The Last Tycoon*, which was published posthumously.

Babylon Revisited

BY F. SCOTT FITZGERALD

"And where's Mr. Campbell?" Charlie asked.

"Gone to Switzerland. Mr. Campbell's a pretty sick man, Mr. Wales."

"I'm sorry to hear that. And George Hardt?" Charlie inquired.

"Back in America, gone to work."

"And where is the Snow Bird?"

"He was in here last week. Anyway, his friend, Mr. Schaeffer, is in Paris."

Two familiar names from the long list of a year and a half ago. Charlie scribbled an address in his notebook and tore out the page.

"If you see Mr. Schaeffer, give him this," he said. "It's my brother-in-law's address. I haven't settled on a hotel yet."

He was not really disappointed to find Paris was so empty. But the stillness in the Ritz bar was strange and portentous. It was not an American bar any more—he felt polite in it, and not as if he owned it. It had gone back into France. He felt the stillness from the moment he got out of the taxi and saw the doorman, usually in a frenzy of activity at this hour, gossiping with a *chasseur* by the servants' entrance.

Passing through the corridor, he heard only a single, bored voice in the once-clamorous women's room.

When he turned into the bar he traveled the twenty feet of green carpet with his eyes fixed straight ahead by old habit; and then, with his foot firmly on the rail, he turned and surveyed the room, encountering only a single pair of eyes that fluttered up from a newspaper in the corner. Charlie asked for the head barman, Paul, who in the latter days of the bull market had come to work in his own custom-built car—disembarking, however, with due nicety at the nearest corner. But Paul was at his country house today and Alix giving him information.

"No, no more," Charlie said, "I'm going slow these days."

Alix congratulated him: "You were going pretty strong a couple of years ago."

"I'll stick to it all right," Charlie assured him. "I've stuck to it for over a year and a half now."

"How do you find conditions in America?"

"I haven't been to America for months. I'm in business in Prague, representing a couple of concerns there. They don't know about me down there."

Alix smiled.

"Remember the night of George Hardt's bachelor dinner here?" said

Charlie. "By the way, what's become of Claude Fessenden?"

Alix lowered his voice confidentially: "He's in Paris, but he doesn't come here any more. Paul doesn't allow it. He ran up a bill of thirty thousand francs, charging all his drinks and his lunches, and usually his dinner, for more than a year. And when Paul finally told him he had to pay, he gave him a bad check."

Alix shook his head sadly.

"I don't understand it, such a dandy fellow. Now he's all bloated up—" He made a plump apple of his hands.

Charlie watched a group of strident queens installing themselves in a corner.

"Nothing affects them," he thought. "Stocks rise and fall, people loaf or work, but they go on forever." The place oppressed him. He called for the dice and shook with Alix for the drink.

"Here for long, Mr. Wales?"

"I'm here for four or five days to see my little girl."

"Oh-h! You have a little girl?"

Outside, the fire-red, gas-blue, ghost-green signs shone smokily through the tranquil rain. It was late afternoon and the streets were in movement; the *bistros* gleamed. At the corner of the Boulevard des Capucines he took a taxi. The Place de la Concorde moved by in pink majesty; they crossed the logical Seine, and Charlie felt the sudden provincial quality of the Left Bank.

Charlie directed his taxi to the Avenue de l'Opera, which was out of his way. But he wanted to see the blue hour spread over the magnificent façade, and imagine that the cab horns, playing endlessly the first few bars of *Le Plus que Lent,* were the trumpets of the Second Empire.

They were closing the iron grill in front of Brentano's Book-store, and people were already at dinner behind the trim little bourgeois hedge of Duval's. He had never eaten at a really cheap restaurant in Paris. Five-course dinner, four francs fifty, eighteen cents, wine included. For some odd reason he wished that he had.

As they rolled on to the Left Bank and he felt its sudden provincialism, he thought, "I spoiled this city for myself. I didn't realize it, but the days came along one after another, and then two years were gone, and everything was gone, and I was gone."

He was thirty-five, and good to look at. The Irish mobility of his face was sobered by a deep wrinkle between his eyes. As he rang his brother-in-law's bell in the Rue Palatine, the wrinkle deepened till it pulled down his brows; he felt a cramping sensation in his belly. From behind the maid who opened the door darted a lovely little girl of nine who shrieked "Daddy!" and flew up, struggling like a fish, into his arms. She pulled his head around by one ear and set her cheek against his.

"My old pie," he said.

"Oh, daddy, daddy, daddy, daddy, dads, dads, dads!"

She drew him into the salon, where the family waited, a boy and girl his daughter's age, his sister-in-law and her husband. He greeted Marion with his voice pitched carefully to avoid either feigned enthusiasm or dislike, but her response was more frankly tepid, though she minimized her expression of unalterable distrust by directing her regard toward his child. The two men clasped hands in a friendly way and Lincoln Peters rested his for a moment on Charlie's shoulder.

The room was warm and comfortably American. The three children moved intimately about, playing through the yellow oblongs that led to other rooms; the cheer of six o'clock spoke in the eager smacks of the fire and the sounds of French activity in the kitchen. But Charlie did not relax; his heart sat up rigidly in his body and he drew confidence from his daughter, who from time to time came close to him, holding in her arms the doll he had brought.

"Really extremely well," he declared in answer to Lincoln's question. "There's a lot of business there that isn't moving at all, but we're doing even better than ever. In fact, damn well. I'm bringing my sister over from America next month to keep house for me. My income last year was bigger than it was when I had money. You see, the Czechs——"

His boasting was for a specific purpose; but after a moment, seeing a faint restiveness in Lincoln's eye, he changed the subject:

"Those are fine children of yours, well brought up, good manners."

"We think Honoria's a great little girl too."

Marion Peters came back from the kitchen. She was a tall woman with worried eyes, who had once possessed a fresh American loveliness. Charlie had never been sensitive to it and was always surprised when people spoke of how pretty she had been. From the first there had been an instinctive antipathy between them.

"Well, how do you find Honoria?" she asked.

"Wonderful. I was astonished how much she's grown in ten months. All the children are looking well."

"We haven't had a doctor for a year. How do you like being back in Paris?"

"It seems very funny to see so few Americans around."

"I'm delighted," Marion said vehemently. "Now at least you can go into a store without their assuming you're a millionaire. We've suffered like everybody, but on the whole it's a good deal pleasanter."

"But it was nice while it lasted," Charlie said. "We were a sort of royalty, almost infallible, with a sort of magic around us. In the bar this afternoon"—he stumbled, seeing his mistake—"there wasn't a man I knew."

She looked at him keenly. "I should think you'd have had enough of bars."

"I only stayed a minute. I take one drink every afternoon, and no more."

"Don't you want a cocktail before dinner?" Lincoln asked.

"I take only one drink every afternoon, and I've had that."

"I hope you keep to it," said Marion.

Her dislike was evident in the coldness with which she spoke, but Charlie only smiled; he had larger plans. Her very aggressiveness gave him an advantage, and he knew enough to wait. He wanted them to initiate the discussion of what they knew had brought him to Paris.

At dinner he couldn't decide whether Honoria was most like him or her mother. Fortunate if she didn't combine the traits of both that had brought them to disaster. A great wave of protectiveness went over him. He thought he knew what to do for her. He believed in character; he wanted to jump back a whole generation and trust in character again as the eternally valuable element. Everything wore out.

He left soon after dinner, but not to go home. He was curious to see

Paris by night with clearer and more judicious eyes than those of other days. He bought a *strapontin* for the Casino and watched Josephine Baker go through her chocolate arabesques.

After an hour he left and strolled toward Montmartre, up the Rue Pigalle into the Place Blanche. The rain had stopped and there were a few people in evening clothes disembarking from taxis in front of cabarets, and *cocottes* prowling singly or in pairs, and many Negroes. He passed a lighted door from which issued music, and stopped with the sense of familiarity; it was Bricktop's, where he had parted with so many hours and so much money. A few doors farther on he found another ancient rendezvous and incautiously put his head inside. Immediately an eager orchestra burst into sound, a pair of professional dancers leaped to their feet and a maître d'hôtel swooped toward him, crying, "Crowd just arriving, sir!" But he withdrew quickly.

"You have to be damn drunk," he thought.

Zelli's was closed, the bleak and sinister cheap hotels surrounding it were dark; up in the Rue Blanche there was more light and a local, colloquial French crowd. The Poet's Cave had disappeared, but the two great mouths of the Café of Heaven and the Café of Hell still yawned—even devoured, as he watched, the meager contents of a tourist bus—a German, a Japanese, and an American couple who glanced at him with frightened eyes.

So much for the effort and ingenuity of Montmartre. All the catering to vice and waste was on an utterly childish scale, and he suddenly realized the meaning of the word "dissipate"—to dissipate into thin air; to make nothing out of

something. In the little hours of the night every move from place to place was an enormous human jump, an increase of paying for the privilege of slower and slower motion.

He remembered thousand-franc notes given to an orchestra for playing a single number, hundred-franc notes tossed to a doorman for calling a cab.

But it hadn't been given for nothing.

It had been given, even the most wildly squandered sum, as an offering to destiny that he might not remember the things most worth remembering, the things that now he would always remember—his child taken from his control, his wife escaped to a grave in Vermont.

In the glare of a *brasserie* a woman spoke to him. He bought her some eggs and coffee, and then, eluding her encouraging stare, gave her a twenty-franc note and took a taxi to his hotel.

II

He woke upon a fine fall day—football weather. The depression of yesterday was gone and he liked the people on the streets. At noon he sat opposite Honoria at Le Grand Vatel, the only restaurant he could think of not reminiscent of champagne dinners and long luncheons that began at two and ended in a blurred and vague twilight.

"Now, how about vegetables? Oughtn't you to have some vegetables?"

"Well, yes."

"Here's *épinards* and *chou-fleur* and carrots and *haricots*."

"I'd like *chou-fleur*."

"Wouldn't you like to have two vegetables?"

"I usually only have one at lunch."

The waiter was pretending to be inordinately fond of children. "*Qu'elle est mignonne la petite? Elle parle exactement comme une française.*"

"How about dessert? Shall we wait and see?"

The waiter disappeared. Honoria looked at her father expectantly.

"What are we going to do?"

"First, we're going to that toy store in the Rue Saint-Honoré and buy you anything you like. And then we're going to the vaudeville at the Empire."

She hesitated. "I like it about the vaudeville, but not the toy store."

"Why not?"

"Well, you brought me this doll." She had it with her. "And I've got lots of things. And we're not rich any more, are we?"

"We never were. But today you are to have anything you want."

"All right," she agreed resignedly.

When there had been her mother and a French nurse he had been inclined to be strict; now he extended himself, reached out for a new tolerance; he must be both parents to her and not shut any of her out of communication.

"I want to get to know you," he said gravely. "First let me introduce myself. My name is Charles J. Wales, of Prague."

"Oh, daddy!" her voice cracked with laughter.

"And who are you, please?" he persisted, and she accepted a rôle immediately: "Honoria Wales, Rue Palatine, Paris."

"Married or single?"

"No, not married. Single."

He indicated the doll. "But I see you have a child, madame."

Unwilling to disinherit it, she took it to her heart and thought quickly: "Yes, I've been married, but I'm not married now. My husband is dead."

He went on quickly, "And the child's name?"

"Simone. That's after my best friend at school."

"I'm very pleased that you're doing so well at school."

"I'm third this month," she boasted. "Elsie"—that was her cousin—"is only about eighteenth, and Richard is about at the bottom."

"You like Richard and Elsie, don't you?"

"Oh, yes. I like Richard quite well and I like her all right."

Cautiously and casually he asked: "And Aunt Marion and Uncle Lincoln—which do you like best?"

"Oh, Uncle Lincoln, I guess."

He was increasingly aware of her presence. As they came in, a murmur of ". . . adorable" followed them, and now the people at the next table bent all their silences upon her, staring as if she were something no more conscious than a flower.

"Why don't I live with you?" she asked suddenly. "Because mamma's dead?"

"You must stay here and learn more French. It would have been hard for daddy to take care of you so well."

"I don't really need much taking care of any more. I do everything for myself."

Going out of the restaurant, a man and a woman unexpectedly hailed him!

"Well, the old Wales!"

"Hello there, Lorraine. . . . Dunc."

Sudden ghosts out of the past: Duncan Schaeffer, a friend from college. Lorraine Quarrles, a lovely, pale blonde of thirty; one of a crowd who had helped them make months into days in the lavish times of three years ago.

"My husband couldn't come this year," she said, in answer to his question. "We're poor as hell. So he gave me two hundred a month and told me I could do my worst on that. . . . This your little girl?"

"What about coming back and sitting down?" Duncan asked.

"Can't do it." He was glad for an excuse. As always, he felt Lorraine's passionate, provocative attraction, but his own rhythm was different now.

"Well, how about dinner?" she asked.

"I'm not free. Give me your address and let me call you."

"Charlie, I believe you're sober," she said judicially. "I honestly believe he's sober, Dunc. Pinch him and see if he's sober."

Charlie indicated Honoria with his head. They both laughed.

"What's your address?" said Duncan skeptically.

He hesitated, unwilling to give the name of his hotel.

"I'm not settled yet. I'd better call you. We're going to see the vaudeville at the Empire."

"There! That's what I want to do," Lorraine said. "I want to see some clowns and acrobats and jugglers. That's just what we'll do, Dunc."

"We've got to do an errand first," said Charlie. "Perhaps we'll see you there."

"All right, you snob. . . . Good-by, beautiful little girl."

"Good-by."

Honoria bobbed politely.

Somehow, an unwelcome encounter. They liked him because he was functioning, because he was serious; they wanted to see him, because he was stronger than they were now, because they wanted to draw a certain sustenance from his strength.

At the Empire, Honoria proudly refused to sit upon her father's folded coat. She was already an individual with a code of her own, and Charlie was more and more absorbed by the desire of putting a little of himself into her before she crystallized utterly. It was hopeless to try to know her in so short a time.

Between the acts they came upon Duncan and Lorraine in the lobby where the band was playing.

"Have a drink?"

"All right, but not up at the bar. We'll take a table."

"The perfect father."

Listening abstractedly to Lorraine, Charlie watched Honoria's eyes leave their table, and he followed them wistfully about the room, wondering what they saw. He met her glance and she smiled.

"I liked that lemonade," she said.

What had she said? What had he expected? Going home in a taxi afterward, he pulled her over until her head rested against his chest.

"Darling, do you ever think about your mother?"

"Yes, sometimes," she answered vaguely.

"I don't want you to forget her. Have you got a picture of her?"

"Yes, I think so. Anyhow, Aunt Marion has. Why don't you want me to forget her?"

"She loved you very much."

"I loved her too."

They were silent for a moment.

"Daddy, I want to come and live with you," she said suddenly.

His heart leaped; he had wanted it to come like this.

"Aren't you perfectly happy?"

"Yes, but I love you better than anybody. And you love me better than anybody, don't you, now that mummy's dead?"

"Of course I do. But you won't always like me best, honey. You'll grow up and meet somebody your

own age and go marry him and forget you ever had a daddy."

"Yes, that's true," she agreed tranquilly.

He didn't go in. He was coming
back at nine o'clock and he wanted
to keep himself fresh and new for
the thing he must say then.

"When you're safe inside, just
show yourself in that window."

"All right. Good-by, dads, dads,
dads, dads."

He waited in the dark street until
she appeared, all warm and glowing,
in the window above and kissed her
fingers out into the night.

III

They were waiting. Marion sat
behind the coffee service in a
dignified black dinner dress that just
faintly suggested mourning. Lincoln
was walking up and down with the
animation of one who had already
been talking. They were as anxious
as he was to get into the question.
He opened it almost immediately:

"I suppose you know what I want
to see you about—why I really came
to Paris."

Marion played with the black stars
on her necklace and frowned.

"I'm awfully anxious to have a
home," he continued. "And I'm
awfully anxious to have Honoria in
it. I appreciate your taking in Honoria for her mother's sake, but things
have changed now"—he hesitated
and then continued more forcibly—
"changed radically with me, and I
want to ask you to reconsider the
matter. It would be silly for me to
deny that about three years ago I
was acting badly ——"

Marion looked up at him with
hard eyes.

"—but all that's over. As I told
you, I haven't had more than a

drink a day for over a year, and I
take that drink deliberately, so that
the idea of alcohol won't get too big
in my imagination. You see the
idea?"

"No," said Marion succinctly.

"It's a sort of stunt I set myself.
It keeps the matter in proportion."

"I get you," said Lincoln. "You
don't want to admit it's got any attraction for you."

"Something like that. Sometimes
I forget and don't take it. But I try
to take it. Anyhow, I couldn't afford
to drink in my position. The people
I represent are more than satisfied
with what I've done, and I'm bringing my sister over from Burlington
to keep house for me, and I want
awfully to have Honoria too. You
know that even when her mother
and I weren't getting along well we
never let anything that happened
touch Honoria. I know she's fond of
me and I know I'm able to take care
of her and—well, there you are.
How do you feel about it?"

He knew that now he would have
to take a beating. It would last an
hour or two hours, and it would be
difficult, but if he modulated his inevitable resentment to the chastened
attitude of the reformed sinner, he
might win his point in the end.

Keep your temper, he told himself. You don't want to be justified.
You want Honoria.

Lincoln spoke first: "We've been
talking it over ever since we got
your letter last month. We're happy
to have Honoria here. She's a dear
little thing, and we're glad to be
able to help her, but of course that
isn't the question ——"

Marion interrupted suddenly.
"How long are you going to stay
sober, Charlie?" she asked.

"Permanently, I hope."

"How can anybody count on that?"

"You know I never did drink heavily until I gave up business and came over here with nothing to do. Then Helen and I began to run around with ——"

"Please leave Helen out of it. I can't bear to hear you talk about her like that."

He stared at her grimly; he had never been certain how fond of each other the sisters were in life.

"My drinking only lasted about a year and a half—from the time we came over until I—collapsed."

"It was time enough."

"It was time enough," he agreed.

"My duty is entirely to Helen," she said. "I try to think what she would have wanted me to do. Frankly, from the night you did that terrible thing you haven't really existed for me. I can't help that. She was my sister."

"Yes."

"When she was dying she asked me to look out for Honoria. If you hadn't been in a sanatorium then, it might have helped matters."

He had no answer.

"I'll never in my life be able to forget the morning when Helen knocked at my door, soaked to the skin and shivering, and said you'd locked her out."

Charlie gripped the sides of the chair. This was more difficult than he expected; he wanted to launch out into a long expostulation and explanation, but he only said: "The night I locked her out—" and she interrupted, "I don't feel up to going over that again."

After a moment's silence Lincoln said: "We're getting off the subject. You want Marion to set aside her legal guardianship and give you Honoria. I think the main point for her is whether she has confidence in you or not."

"I don't blame Marion," Charlie said slowly, "but I think she can have entire confidence in me. I had a good record up to three years ago. Of course, it's within human possibilities I might go wrong any time. But if we wait much longer I'll lose Honoria's childhood and my chance for a home." He shook his head, "I'll simply lose her, don't you see?"

"Yes, I see," said Lincoln.

"Why didn't you think of all this before?" Marion asked.

"I suppose I did, from time to time, but Helen and I were getting along badly. When I consented to the guardianship, I was flat on my back in a sanatorium and the market had cleaned me out. I knew I'd acted badly, and I thought if it would bring any peace to Helen, I'd agree to anything. But now it's different. I'm functioning, I'm behaving damn well, so far as ——"

"Please don't swear at me," Marion said.

He looked at her, startled. With each remark the force of her dislike became more and more apparent. She had built up all her fear of life into one wall and faced it toward him. This trivial reproof was possibly the result of some trouble with the cook several hours before. Charlie became increasingly alarmed at leaving Honoria in this atmosphere of hostility against himself; sooner or later it would come out, in a word here, a shake of the head there, and some of that distrust would be irrevocably implanted in Honoria. But he pulled his temper down out of his face and shut it up inside him; he had won a point, for Lincoln realized the absurdity of Marion's remark and asked her lightly since when she had objected to the word "damn."

"Another thing," Charlie said: "I'm able to give her certain advantages now. I'm going to take a French governess to Prague with me. I've got a lease on a new apartment——"

He stopped, realizing that he was blundering. They couldn't be expected to accept with equanimity the fact that his income was again twice as large as their own.

"I suppose you can give her more luxuries than we can," said Marion. "When you were throwing away money we were living along watching every ten francs. . . . I suppose you'll start doing it again."

"Oh, no," he said. "I've learned. I worked hard for ten years, you know —until I got lucky in the market, like so many people. Terribly lucky. It didn't seem any use working any more, so I quit. It won't happen again."

There was a long silence. All of them felt their nerves straining, and for the first time in a year Charlie wanted a drink. He was sure now that Lincoln Peters wanted him to have his child.

Marion shuddered suddenly; part of her saw that Charlie's feet were planted on the earth now, and her own maternal feeling recognized the naturalness of his desire; but she had lived for a long time with a prejudice—a prejudice founded on a curious disbelief in her sister's happiness, and which, in the shock of one terrible night, had turned to hatred for him. It had all happened at a point in her life where the discouragement of ill health and adverse circumstances made it necessary for her to believe in tangible villainy and a tangible villain.

"I can't help what I think!" she cried out suddenly. "How much you were responsible for Helen's death, I don't know. It's something you'll have to square with your own conscience."

An electric current of agony surged through him; for a moment he was almost on his feet, an unuttered sound echoing in his throat. He hung on to himself for a moment, another moment.

"Hold on there," said Lincoln uncomfortably. "I never thought you were responsible for that."

"Helen died of heart trouble," Charlie said dully.

"Yes, heart trouble." Marion spoke as if the phrase had another meaning for her.

Then, in the flatness that followed her outburst, she saw him plainly and she knew he had somehow arrived at control over the situation. Glancing at her husband, she found no help from him, and as abruptly as if it were a matter of no importance, she threw up the sponge.

"Do what you like!" she cried, springing up from her chair. "She's your child. I'm not the person to stand in your way. I think if it were my child I'd rather see her——" She managed to check herself. "You two decide it. I can't stand this. I'm sick. I'm going to bed."

She hurried from the room; after a moment Lincoln said:

"This has been a hard day for her. You know how strongly she feels——" His voice was almost apologetic: "When a woman gets an idea in her head."

"Of course."

"It's going to be all right. I think she sees now that you—can provide for the child, and so we can't very well stand in your way or Honoria's way."

"Thank you, Lincoln."

"I'd better go along and see how she is."

"I'm going."

He was still trembling when he reached the street, but a walk down the Rue Bonaparte to the *quais* set him up, and as he crossed the Seine, fresh and new by the *quai* lamps, he felt exultant. But back in his room he couldn't sleep. The image of Helen haunted him. Helen whom he had loved so until they had senselessly begun to abuse each other's love, tear it into shreds. On that terrible February night that Marion remembered so vividly, a slow quarrel had gone on for hours. There was a scene at the Florida, and then he attempted to take her home, and then she kissed young Webb at a table; after that there was what she had hysterically said. When he arrived home alone he turned the key in the lock in wild anger. How could he know she would arrive an hour later alone, that there would be a snowstorm in which she wandered about in slippers, too confused to find a taxi? Then the aftermath, her escaping pneumonia by a miracle, and all the attendant horror. They were "reconciled," but that was the beginning of the end, and Marion, who had seen with her own eyes and who imagined it to be one of many scenes from her sister's martyrdom, never forgot.

Going over it again brought Helen nearer, and in the white, soft light that steals upon half sleep near morning he found himself talking to her again. She said that he was perfectly right about Honoria and that she wanted Honoria to be with him. She said she was glad he was being good and doing better. She said a lot of other things—very friendly things—but she was in a swing in a white dress, and swinging faster and faster all the time, so that at the end he could not hear clearly all that she said.

IV

He woke up feeling happy. The door of the world was open again. He made plans, vistas, futures for Honoria and himself, but suddenly he grew sad, remembering all the plans he and Helen had made. She had not planned to die. The present was the thing—work to do and someone to love. But not to love too much, for he knew the injury that a father can do to a daughter or a mother to a son by attaching them too closely: afterward, out in the world, the child would seek in the marriage partner the same blind tenderness and, failing probably to find it, turn against love and life.

It was another bright, crisp day. He called Lincoln Peters at the bank where he worked and asked if he could count on taking Honoria when he left for Prague. Lincoln agreed that there was no reason for delay. One thing—the legal guardianship. Marion wanted to retain that a while longer. She was upset by the whole matter, and it would oil things if she felt that the situation was still in her control for another year. Charlie agreed, wanting only the tangible, visible child.

Then the question of a governess. Charlie sat in a gloomy agency and talked to a cross Béarnaise and to a buxom Breton peasant, neither of whom he could have endured. There were others whom he would see to-morrow.

He lunched with Lincoln Peters at Griffons, trying to keep down his exultation.

"There's nothing quite like your own child," Lincoln said. "But you understand how Marion feels too."

"She's forgotten how hard I worked for seven years there," Charlie said. "She just remembers one night."

"There's another thing." Lincoln hesitated. "While you and Helen were tearing around Europe throwing money away, we were just getting along. I didn't touch any of the prosperity because I never got ahead enough to carry anything but my insurance. I think Marion felt there was some kind of injustice in it— you not even working toward the end, and getting richer and richer."

"It went just as quick as it came," said Charlie.

"Yes, a lot of it stayed in the hands of *chasseurs* and saxophone players and maîtres d'hôtel—well, the big party's over now. I just said that to explain Marion's feeling about those crazy years. If you drop in about six o'clock tonight before Marion's too tired, we'll settle the details on the spot."

Back at his hotel, Charlie found a *pneumatique* that had been re-directed from the Ritz bar where Charlie had left his address for the purpose of finding a certain man.

Dear Charlie: You were so strange when we saw you the other day that I wondered if I did something to offend you. If so, I'm not conscious of it. In fact, I have thought about you too much for the last year, and it's always been in the back of my mind that I might see you if I came over here. We did have such good times that crazy spring, like the night you and I stole the butcher's tricycle, and the time we tried to call on the president and you had the old derby rim and the wire cane. Everybody seems so old lately, but I don't feel old a bit. Couldn't

we get together some time today for old time's sake? I've got a vile hang-over for the moment, but will be feeling better this afternoon and will look for you about five in the sweat-shop at the Ritz.

Always devotedly,
Lorraine

His first feeling was one of awe that he had actually, in his mature years, stolen a tricycle and pedaled Lorraine all over the Étoile between the small hours and dawn. In retrospect it was a nightmare. Locking out Helen didn't fit in with any other act of his life, but the tricycle incident did—it was one of many. How many weeks or months of dissipation to arrive at 'hat condition of utter irresponsibility?

He tried to picture how Lorraine had appeared to him then—very attractive; Helen was unhappy about it, though she said nothing. Yesterday, in the restaurant, Lorraine had seemed trite, blurred, worn away. He emphatically did not want to see her, and he was glad Alix had not given away his hotel address. It was a relief to think, instead, of Honoria, to think of Sundays spent with her and of saying good morning to her and of knowing she was there in his house at night, drawing her breath in the darkness.

At five he took a taxi and bought presents for all the Peters—a piquant cloth doll, a box of Roman soldiers, flowers for Marion, big linen handkerchiefs for Lincoln.

He saw, when he arrived in the apartment, that Marion had accepted the inevitable. She greeted him now as though he were a recalcitrant member of the family, rather than a menacing outsider. Honoria had been told she was going; Charlie was glad to see that her tact made her conceal her excessive happiness. Only on his lap did she whisper her delight and the question "When?" before she slipped away with the other children.

He and Marion were alone for a minute in the room, and on an impulse he spoke out boldly:

"Family quarrels are bitter things. They don't go according to any rules. They're not like aches or wounds; they're more like splits in the skin that won't heal because there's not enough material. I wish you and I could be on better terms."

"Some things are hard to forget," she answered. "It's a question of confidence." There was no answer to this and presently she asked, "When do you propose to take her?"

"As soon as I can get a governess. I hoped the day after tomorrow."

"That's impossible. I've got to get her things in shape. Not before Saturday."

He yielded. Coming back into the room, Lincoln offered him a drink.

"I'll take my daily whisky," he said.

It was warm here, it was a home, people together by a fire. The children felt very safe and important; the mother and father were serious, watchful. They had things to do for the children more important than his visit here. A spoonful of medicine was, after all, more important than the strained relations between Marion and himself. They were not dull people, but they were very much in the grip of life and circumstances. He wondered if he couldn't do something to get Lincoln out of his rut at the bank.

A long peal at the door-bell; the *bonne de toute faire* passed through and went down the corridor. The door opened upon another long ring, and then voices, and the three in the salon looked up expectantly; Richard moved to bring the corridor within his range of vision, and Marion rose. Then the maid came back along the corridor, closely followed by the voices, which developed under the light into Duncan Schaeffer and Lorraine Quarrles.

They were gay, they were hilarious, they were roaring with laughter. For a moment Charlie was astounded; unable to understand how they ferreted out the Peters' address.

"Ah-h-h!" Duncan wagged his finger roguishly at Charlie. "Ah-h-h!"

They both slid down another cascade of laughter. Anxious and at a loss, Charlie shook hands with them quickly and presented them to Lincoln and Marion. Marion nodded, scarcely speaking. She had drawn back a step toward the fire; her little girl stood beside her, and Marion put an arm about her shoulder.

With growing annoyance at the intrusion, Charlie waited for them to explain themselves. After some concentration Duncan said:

"We came to invite you to dinner. Lorraine and I insist that all this shishi, cagy business 'bout your address got to stop."

Charlie came closer to them, as if to force them backward down the corridor.

"Sorry, but I can't. Tell me where you'll be and I'll phone you in half an hour."

This made no impression. Lorraine sat down suddenly on the side of a chair, and focusing her eyes on Richard, cried, "Oh, what a nice little boy! Come here, little boy." Richard glanced at his mother, but did not move. With a perceptible shrug of her shoulders, Lorraine turned back to Charlie:

"Come and dine. Sure your cousins won' mine. See you so sel'om. Or solemn."

"I can't," said Charlie sharply. "You two have dinner and I'll phone you."

Her voice became suddenly unpleasant. "All right, we'll go. But I remember once when you hammered on my door at four A.M. I was enough of a good sport to give you a drink. Come on, Dunc."

Still in slow motion, with blurred, angry faces, with uncertain feet, they retired along the corridor.

"Good night," Charlie said.

"Good night!" responded Lorraine emphatically.

When he went back into the salon Marion had not moved, only now her son was standing in the circle of her other arm. Lincoln was still swinging Honoria back and forth like a pendulum from side to side.

"What an outrage!" Charlie broke out. "What an absolute outrage!"

Neither of them answered. Charlie dropped into an armchair, picked up his drink, set it down again and said:

"People I haven't seen for two years having the colossal nerve ——"

He broke off. Marion had made the sound "Oh!" in one swift, furious breath, turned her body from him with a jerk and left the room.

Lincoln set down Honoria carefully.

"You children go in and start your soup," he said, and when they obeyed, he said to Charlie:

"Marion's not well and she can't stand shocks. That kind of people make her really physically sick."

"I didn't tell them to come here. They wormed your name out of somebody. They deliberately ——"

"Well, it's too bad. It doesn't help matters. Excuse me a minute."

Left alone, Charlie sat tense in his chair. In the next room he could hear the children eating, talking in monosyllables, already oblivious to the scene between their elders. He heard a murmur of conversation from a farther room and then the ticking bell of a telephone receiver picked up, and in a panic he moved to the other side of the room and out of earshot.

In a minute Lincoln came back. "Look here, Charlie. I think we'd better call off dinner for tonight. Marion's in bad shape."

"Is she angry with me?"

"Sort of," he said, almost roughly. "She's not strong and ——"

"You mean she's changed her mind about Honoria?"

"She's pretty bitter right now. I don't know. You phone me at the bank tomorrow."

"I wish you'd explain to her I never dreamed these people would come here. I'm just as sore as you are."

"I couldn't explain anything to her now."

Charlie got up. He took his coat and hat and started down the corridor. Then he opened the door of the dining room and said in a strange voice, "Good night, children."

Honoria rose and ran around the table to hug him.

"Good night, sweetheart," he said vaguely, and then trying to make his voice more tender, trying to conciliate something, "Good night, dear children."

V

Charlie went directly to the Ritz bar with the furious idea of finding Lorraine and Duncan, but they were not there, and he realized that in any case there was nothing he could do. He had not touched his drink at the Peters', and now he ordered a whisky-and-soda. Paul came over to say hello.

"It's a great change," he said sadly. "We do about half the business we did. So many fellows I hear about back in the States lost everything, maybe not in the first crash, but then in the second. Your friend George Hardt lost every cent, I hear. Are you back in the States?"

"No, I'm in business in Prague."

"I heard that you lost a lot in the crash."

"I did," and he added grimly, "but I lost everything I wanted in the boom."

"Selling short?"

"Something like that."

Again the memory of those days swept over him like a nightmare— the people they had met traveling; then people who couldn't add a row of figures or speak a coherent sentence. The little man Helen had consented to dance with at the ship's party, who had insulted her ten feet from the table; the women and girls carried screaming with drink or drugs out of public places ——

—The men who locked their wives out in the snow, because the snow of twenty-nine wasn't real snow. If you didn't want it to be snow, you just paid some money.

He went to the phone and called the Peters' apartment; Lincoln answered.

"I called up because this thing is on my mind. Has Marion said anything definite?"

"Marion's sick," Lincoln answered shortly. "I know this thing isn't altogether your fault, but I can't have her go to pieces about it. I'm afraid we'll have to let it slide for six months; I can't take the chance of working her up to this state again."

"I see."

"I'm sorry, Charlie."

He went back to his table. His whisky glass was empty, but he shook his head when Alix looked at it questioningly. There wasn't much he could do now except send Honoria some things; he would send her a lot of things tomorrow. He thought rather angrily that this was just money—he had given so many people money. . . .

"No, no more," he said to another waiter. "What do I owe you?"

He would come back someday; they couldn't make him pay forever. But he wanted his child, and nothing was much good now, beside that fact. He wasn't young any more, with a lot of nice thoughts and dreams to have by himself. He was absolutely sure Helen wouldn't have wanted him to be so alone.

Katharine Brush
1902-1952

IF SCOTT FITZGERALD is the Jazz Age, Katharine Ingham Brush is Flaming Youth. The stories and novels by which her reputation was made are the most glittering of that tinsel age: *Young Man of Manhattan, Red-Headed Woman,* and the girl in "Night Club" are all children of the boom world, carefree, irresponsible, unhappy. Katharine Brush herself was a Connecticut Yankee from way back, transplanted to the glamour of New York. She began writing practically in childhood: first a diary, then verse, finally stories that came out in *College Humor.* Her best-seller novels and her later magazine stories made her an enormous amount of money, which she invested in fun and travel, in clothes and a famous New York duplex apartment—all of which she described most engagingly in her autobiography, *This Is on Me,* as much a frank disclosure of her foibles as a story of success.

Night Club

BY KATHARINE BRUSH

PROMPTLY at quarter of ten P.M. Mrs. Brady descended the steps of the Elevated. She purchased from the newsdealer in the cubbyhole beneath them a next month's magazine and a tomorrow morning's paper and, with these tucked under one plump arm, she walked. She walked two blocks north on Sixth Avenue; turned and went west. But not far west. Westward half a block only, to the place where the gay green awning marked "Club Français" paints a stripe of shade across the glimmering sidewalk. Under this awning Mrs. Brady halted briefly, to remark to the six-foot doorman that it looked like rain and to await his performance of his professional duty. When the small green door yawned open, she sighed deeply and plodded in.

The foyer was a blackness, an airless velvet blackness like the inside of a jeweler's box. Four drum-shaped lamps of golden silk suspended from the ceiling gave it light (a very little) and formed the jewels: gold signets, those, or cuff links for a giant. At the far end of the foyer there were black stairs, faintly dusty, rippling upward toward an amber radiance. Mrs. Brady approached and ponderously mounted the stairs, clinging with one fist to the mangy velvet rope that railed their edge.

From the top, Miss Lena Levin observed the ascent. Miss Levin was the checkroom girl. She had dark-at-the-roots blonde hair and slender hips upon which, in moments of leisure, she wore her hands, like buckles of ivory loosely attached.

This was a moment of leisure. Miss Levin waited behind her counter. Row upon row of hooks, empty as yet, and seeming to beckon—wee curved fingers of iron—waited behind her.

"Late," said Miss Levin, "again."

"Go wan!" said Mrs. Brady. "It's only ten to ten. *Whew!* Them *stairs!*"

She leaned heavily, sideways, against Miss Levin's counter, and, applying one palm to the region of her heart, appeared at once to listen and to count. "Feel!" she cried then in a pleased voice.

Miss Levin obediently felt.

"Them stairs," continued Mrs. Brady darkly, "with my bad heart, will be the death of me. Whew! Well, dearie? What's the news?"

"You got a paper," Miss Levin languidly reminded her.

"Yeah!" agreed Mrs. Brady with sudden vehemence. "I got a paper!" She slapped it upon the counter.

From *Harper's Bazaar* of September, 1927. By permission of the author. Copyright, 1927, by Katharine Brush.

"An' a lot of time I'll get to *read* my paper, won't I now? On a Saturday night!" She moaned. "Other nights is bad enough, dear knows—but *Saturday* nights! How I dread 'em! Every Saturday night I say to my daughter, I say, 'Geraldine, I can't,' I say, 'I can't go through it again, an' that's all there is to it,' I say. 'I'll *quit!*' I say. An' I *will*, too!" added Mrs. Brady firmly, if indefinitely.

Miss Levin, in defense of Saturday nights, mumbled some vague something about tips.

"Tips!" Mrs. Brady hissed it. She almost spat it. Plainly money was nothing, nothing at all, to this lady. "I just wish," said Mrs. Brady, and glared at Miss Levin, "I just wish *you* had to spend one Saturday night, just one, in that dressing room! Bein' pushed an' stepped on and near knocked down by that gang of hussies, an' them orderin' an' bossin' you round like you was *black*, an' usin' your things an' then sayin' they're sorry, they got no change, they'll be back. Yeah! They *never* come back!"

"There's Mr. Costello," whispered Miss Levin through lips that, like a ventriloquist's, scarcely stirred.

"An' as I was sayin'," Mrs. Brady said at once brightly, "I got to leave you. Ten to ten, time I was on the job."

She smirked at Miss Levin, nodded, and right-about-faced. There, indeed, Mr. Costello was. Mr. Billy Costello, manager, proprietor, monarch of all he surveyed. From the doorway of the big room where the little tables herded in a ring around the waxen floor, he surveyed Mrs. Brady, and in such a way that Mrs. Brady, momentarily forgetting her bad heart, walked fast, scurried faster, almost ran.

The door of her domain was set politely in an alcove, beyond silken curtains looped up at the sides. Mrs. Brady reached it breathless, shouldered it open, and groped for the electric switch. Lights sprang up, a bright white blaze, intolerable for an instant to the eyes, like sun on snow. Blinking, Mrs. Brady shut the door.

The room was a spotless, white-tiled place, half beauty shop, half dressing room. Along one wall stood washstands, sturdy triplets in a row, with pale-green liquid soap in glass balloons afloat above them. Against the opposite wall there was a couch. A third wall backed an elongated glass-topped dressing table; and over the dressing table and over the washstands long rectangular sheets of mirror reflected lights, doors, glossy tiles, lights multiplied. . . .

Mrs. Brady moved across this glitter like a thick dark cloud in a hurry. At the dressing table she came to a halt, and upon it she laid her newspaper, her magazine, and her purse —a black purse worn gray with much clutching. She divested herself of a rusty black coat and a hat of the mushroom persuasion, and hung both up in a corner cupboard which she opened by means of one of a quite preposterous bunch of keys. From a nook in the cupboard she took down a lace-edged handkerchief with long streamers. She untied the streamers and tied them again around her chunky black alpaca waist. The handkerchief became an apron's baby cousin.

Mrs. Brady relocked the cupboard door, fumbled her key ring over, and unlocked a capacious drawer of the dressing table. She spread a fresh towel on the plate-glass top, in the geometrical center, and upon the towel she arranged with care a procession of things fished from the drawer. Things for the hair. Things for the complexion. Things for the eyes, the lashes, the brows, the lips, and the fingernails. Things in boxes and things in jars and things in tubes and tins. Also an ash tray, matches, pins, a tiny sewing kit, a pair of scissors. Last of all, a hand-printed sign, a nudging sort of sign:

NOTICE!

THESE ARTICLES, PLACED HERE FOR YOUR CONVENIENCE, ARE THE PROPERTY OF THE *MAID*.

And directly beneath the sign, propping it up against the looking glass, a china saucer, in which Mrs. Brady now slyly laid decoy money: two quarters and two dimes, in four-leaf-clover formation.

Another drawer of the dressing table yielded a bottle of Bromo-seltzer, a bottle of aromatic spirits of ammonia, a tin of sodium bicarbonate, and a teaspoon. These were lined up on a shelf above the couch.

Mrs. Brady was now ready for anything. And (from the grim, thin pucker of her mouth) expecting it.

Music came to her ears. Rather, the beat of music, muffled, rhythmic, remote. *Umpa-um, umpa-um, umpa-um-umm*—Mr. "Fiddle" Baer and his band, hard at work on the first fox-trot of the night. It was teasing, foot-tapping music; but the large solemn feet of Mrs. Brady were still. She sat on the couch and opened her newspaper; and for some moments she read uninterruptedly, with special attention to the murders, the divorces, the breaches of promise, the funnies.

Then the door swung inward, admitting a blast of Mr. Fiddle Baer's best, a whiff of perfume, and a girl.

Mrs. Brady put her paper away.

The girl was petite and darkly beautiful; wrapped in fur and mounted on tall jeweled heels. She entered humming the ragtime song the orchestra was playing, and while she stood near the dressing table, stripping off her gloves, she continued to hum it softly to herself:

Oh, I know my baby loves me,
I can tell my baby loves me.

Here the dark little girl got the left glove off, and Mrs. Brady glimpsed a platinum wedding ring.

'Cause there ain't no maybe
In my baby's
Eyes.

The right glove came off. The dark little girl sat down in one of the chairs that faced the dressing table. She doffed her wrap, casting it carelessly over the chair back. It had a cloth-of-gold lining, and the name of a Paris house was embroidered in curlicues on the label. Mrs. Brady hovered solicitously near.

The dark little girl, still humming, looked over the articles, "placed here for your convenience," and picked up the scissors. Having cut off a very small hangnail with the air of one performing a perilous major operation, she seized and used the manicure buffer, and after that the eyebrow pencil. Mrs. Brady's mind, hopefully calculating the tip, jumped and jumped again like a taxi meter.

Oh, I know my baby loves me——

The dark little girl applied powder and lipstick belonging to herself. She examined the result searchingly in the mirror and sat back, satisfied. She cast some silver *Klink! Klink!* into Mrs. Brady's saucer, and half rose. Then, remembering something, she settled down again.

The ensuing thirty seconds were spent by her in pulling off her platinum wedding ring, tying it in a corner of a lace handkerchief, and tucking the handkerchief down the bodice of her tight white velvet gown.

"There!" she said.

She swooped up her wrap and trotted toward the door, jeweled heels merrily twinkling.

'Cause there ain't no maybe——

The door fell shut.

Almost instantly it opened again, and another girl came in. A blonde, this. She was pretty in a round-eyed, doll-like way; but Mrs. Brady, regarding her, mentally grabbed the spirits of ammonia bottle. For she looked terribly ill. The round eyes were dull, the pretty silly little face was drawn. The thin hands, picking at the fastenings of a specious beaded bag, trembled and twitched.

Mrs. Brady cleared her throat. "Can I do something for you, miss?"

Evidently the blonde girl had believed herself alone in the dressing room. She started violently and glanced up, panic in her eyes. Panic, and something else. Something very like murderous hate—but for an instant only, so that Mrs. Brady, whose perceptions were never quick, missed it altogether.

"A glass of water?" suggested Mrs. Brady.

"No," said the girl, "no." She had one hand in the beaded bag now. Mrs. Brady could see it moving, causing the bag to squirm like a live thing and the fringe to shiver. "Yes!" she cried abruptly. "A glass of water —please—you get it for me."

She dropped on to the couch. Mrs. Brady scurried to the water cooler in the corner, pressed the spigot with a determined thumb. Water trickled out thinly. Mrs. Brady pressed harder, and scowled, and thought, "Something's wrong with

this thing. I mustn't forget, next time I see Mr. Costello——"

When again she faced her patient, the patient was sitting erect. She was thrusting her clenched hand back into the beaded bag again.

She took only a sip of the water, but it seemed to help her quite miraculously. Almost at once color came to her cheeks, life to her eyes. She grew young again—as young as she was. She smiled up at Mrs. Brady.

"Well!" she exclaimed. "What do you know about that!" She shook her honey-colored head. "I can't imagine what came over me."

"Are you better now?" inquired Mrs. Brady.

"Yes. Oh, yes. I'm better now. You see," said the blonde girl confidentially, "we were at the theater, my boy friend and I, and it was hot and stuffy—I guess that must have been the trouble."

She paused, and the ghost of her recent distress crossed her face. "God! I thought that last act *never* would end!" she said.

While she attended to her hair and complexion, she chattered gaily to Mrs. Brady, chattered on with scarcely a stop for breath, and laughed much. She said, among other things, that she and her "boy friend" had not known one another very long, but that she was "ga-ga" about him. "He is about me, too," she confessed. "He thinks I'm grand."

She fell silent then, and in the looking glass her eyes were shadowed, haunted. But Mrs. Brady, from where she stood, could not see the looking glass; and half a minute later the blonde girl laughed and began again. When she went out she seemed to dance out on little winged feet; and Mrs. Brady, sighing, thought it must be nice to be young . . . and happy like that.

The next arrivals were two. A tall, extremely smart young woman in black chiffon entered first, and held the door open for her companion; and the instant the door was shut, she said, as though it had been on the tip of her tongue for hours, "Amy, what under the sun *happened?*"

Amy, who was brown-eyed, brown-bobbed-haired, and patently annoyed about something, crossed to the dressing table and flopped into a chair before she made reply.

"Nothing," she said wearily then.

"That's nonsense!" snorted the other. "Tell me. Was it something she said? She's a tactless ass, of course. Always was."

"No, not anything she said. It was——" Amy bit her lip. "All right! I'll tell you. Before we left your apartment I just happened to notice that Tom had disappeared. So I went to look for him—I wanted to ask him if he'd remembered to tell the maid where we were going— Skippy's subject to croup, you know, and we always leave word. Well, so I went into the kitchen, thinking Tom might be there mixing cocktails—and there he was—and there *she* was!"

The full red mouth of the other young woman pursed itself slightly. Her arched brows lifted. "Well?"

Her matter-of-factness appeared to infuriate Amy. "He was *kissing* her!" she flung out.

"Well?" said the other again. She chuckled softly and patted Amy's shoulder, as if it were the shoulder of a child. "You're surely not going to let *that* spoil your whole evening? Amy *dear!* Kissing may once have been serious and significant—but it isn't nowadays. Nowadays, it's like

shaking hands. It means nothing."

But Amy was not consoled. "I hate her!" she cried desperately. "Redheaded *thing!* Calling me 'darling' and 'honey,' and s-sending me handkerchiefs for C-Christmas— and then sneaking off behind closed doors and k-kissing my h-h-hus-band——"

At this point Amy broke down, but she recovered herself sufficiently to add with venom, "I'd like to slap her!"

"Oh, oh, oh," smiled the tall young woman, "I wouldn't do that!"

Amy wiped her eyes with what might well have been one of the Christmas handkerchiefs, and con-fronted her friend. "Well, what *would* you do, Vera? If you were I?"

"I'd forget it," said Vera, "and have a good time. I'd kiss somebody myself. You've no idea how much better you'd feel!"

"I don't do——" Amy began in-dignantly; but as the door behind her opened and a third young woman —redheaded, ear-ringed, exquisite— lilted in, she changed her tone. "Oh, hello!" she called sweetly, beaming at the newcomer via the mirror. "We were wondering what had become of you!"

The redheaded girl, smiling easily back, dropped her cigarette on the floor and crushed it out with a silver-shod toe. "Tom and I were talking to Fiddle Baer," she explained. "He's going to play 'Clap Yo' Hands' next, because it's my favorite. Lend me a comb, will you?"

"There's a comb there," said Vera, indicating Mrs. Brady's business comb.

"But imagine using it!" murmured the redheaded girl. "Amy, darling, haven't you one?"

Amy produced a tiny comb from her rhinestone purse. "Don't forget to bring it when you come," she said, and stood up. "I'm going on out, I want to tell Tom something." She went.

The redheaded young woman and the tall black-chiffon one were alone, except for Mrs. Brady. The redheaded one beaded her incredible lashes. The tall one, the one called Vera, sat watching her. Presently she said, "Sylvia, look here." And Sylvia looked. Anybody, addressed in that tone, would have.

"There is one thing," Vera went on quietly, holding the other's eyes, "that I want understood. And that is, 'Hands off!' Do you hear me?"

"I don't know what you mean."

"You do know what I mean!"

The redheaded girl shrugged her shoulders. "Amy told you she saw us, I suppose."

"Precisely. And," went on Vera, gathering up her possessions and rising, "as I said before, you're to keep away." Her eyes blazed sudden white-hot rage. "Because, as you very well know, he belongs to *me*," she said, and departed, slamming the door.

Between eleven o'clock and one Mrs. Brady was very busy indeed. Never for more than a moment during those two hours was the dressing room empty. Often it was jammed, full to overflowing with curled cropped heads, with ivory arms and shoulders, with silk and lace and chiffon, with legs. The door flapped in and back, in and back. The mirrors caught and held—and lost—a hundred different faces. Powder veiled the dressing table with a thin white dust; cigarette stubs, scarlet at the tips, choked the ash receiver. Dimes and quarters clattered into Mrs. Brady's saucer—and were transferred to Mrs. Brady's purse.

The original seventy cents remained. That much, and no more, would Mrs. Brady gamble on the integrity of womankind.

She earned her money. She threaded needles and took stitches. She powdered the backs of necks. She supplied towels for soapy, dripping hands. She removed a speck from a teary blue eye and pounded the heel on a slipper. She curled the straggling ends of a black bob and a gray bob, pinned a velvet flower on a lithe round waist, mixed three doses of bicarbonate of soda, took charge of a shed pink-satin girdle, collected, on hands and knees, several dozen fake pearls that had wept from a broken string.

She served chorus girls and school-girls, gay young matrons and gayer young mistresses, a lady who had divorced four husbands, and a lady who had poisoned one, the secret (more or less) sweetheart of a Most Distinguished Name, and the Brains of a bootleg gang. . . . She saw things. She saw a yellow check, with the ink hardly dry. She saw four tiny bruises, such as fingers might make, on an arm. She saw a girl strike another girl, not playfully. She saw a bundle of letters some man wished he had not written, safe and deep in a brocaded handbag.

About midnight the door flew open and at once was pushed shut, and a gray-eyed, lovely child stood backed against it, her palms flattened on the panels at her sides, the draperies of her white chiffon gown settling lightly to rest around her.

There were already five damsels of varying ages in the dressing room. The latest arrival marked their presence with a flick of her eyes and, standing just where she was, she called peremptorily, "Maid!"

Mrs. Brady, standing just where *she* was, said, "Yes, miss?"

"Please come here," said the girl.

Mrs. Brady, as slowly as she dared, did so.

The girl lowered her voice to a tense half whisper. "Listen! Is there any way I can get out of here except through this door I came in?"

Mrs. Brady stared at her stupidly.

"Any window?" persisted the girl. "Or anything?"

Here they were interrupted by the exodus of two of the damsels-of-varying-ages. Mrs. Brady opened the door for them—and in so doing caught a glimpse of a man who waited in the hall outside, a debonair, old-young man with a girl's furry wrap hung over his arm, and his hat in his hand.

The door clicked. The gray-eyed girl moved out from the wall, against which she had flattened herself—for all the world like one eluding pursuit in a cinema.

"What about that window?" she demanded, pointing.

"That's all the farther it opens," said Mrs. Brady.

"Oh! And it's the only one—isn't it?"

"It is."

"Damn," said the girl. "Then there's *no* way out?"

"No way but the door," said Mrs. Brady testily.

The girl looked at the door. She seemed to look *through* the door, and to despise and to fear what she saw. Then she looked at Mrs. Brady. "Well," she said, "then I s'pose the only thing for me to do is to stay in here."

She stayed. Minutes ticked by. Jazz crooned distantly, stopped, struck up again. Other girls came and went. Still the gray-eyed girl sat on the couch, with her back to the wall and her shapely legs crossed, smoking cigarettes, one from the stub of another.

After a long while she said, "Maid!"

"Yes, miss?"

"Peek out that door, will you, and see if there's anyone standing there."

Mrs. Brady peeked, and reported that there was. There was a gentleman with a little bit of a black mustache standing there. The same gentleman, in fact, who was standing there "just after you came in."

"Oh, Lord," sighed the gray-eyed girl. "Well . . . I can't stay here all *night*, that's one sure thing."

She slid off the couch, and went listlessly to the dressing table. There she occupied herself for a minute or two. Suddenly, without a word, she darted out.

Thirty seconds later Mrs. Brady was elated to find two crumpled one-dollar bills lying in her saucer. Her joy, however, died a premature death. For she made an almost simultaneous second discovery. A saddening one. Above all, a puzzling one.

"Now what for," marveled Mrs. Brady, "did she want to walk off with them *scissors?*"

This at twelve-twenty-five.

At twelve-thirty a quartet of excited young things burst in, babbling madly. All of them had their evening wraps with them; all talked at once. One of them, a Dresden-china girl with a heart-shaped face, was the center of attraction. Around her the rest fluttered like monstrous butterflies; to her they addressed their shrill exclamatory cries.

"Babe," they called her.

Mrs. Brady heard snatches: "Not in this state unless . . ." "Well, you can in Maryland, Jimmy says." "Oh, there must be some place nearer than . . ." "Isn't this marvelous?" "When did it happen, Babe? When did you decide?"

"Just now," the girl with the heart-shaped face sang softly, "when we were dancing."

The babble resumed, "But listen, Babe, what'll your mother and father . . . ?" "Oh, never mind, let's hurry." "Shall we be warm enough with just these thin wraps, do you think? Babe, will you be warm enough? Sure?"

Powder flew and little pocket combs marched through bright marcels. Flushed cheeks were painted pinker still.

"My pearls," said Babe, "are *old*. And my dress and my slippers are *new*. Now, let's see—what can I *borrow*?"

A lace handkerchief, a diamond bar pin, a pair of earrings were proffered. She chose the bar pin, and its owner unpinned it proudly, gladly.

"I've got blue garters!" exclaimed a shrill little girl in a silver dress.

"Give me one, then," directed Babe. "I'll trade with you. . . . There! That fixes that."

More babbling, "Hurry! Hurry up!" . . . "Listen, are you *sure* we'll be warm enough? Because we can stop at my house, there's nobody home." "Give me that puff, Babe, I'll powder your back." "And just to think a week ago you'd never even met each other!" "Oh, hurry *up*, let's get *started*!" "I'm ready." "So'm I." "Ready, Babe? You look adorable." "Come on, everybody."

They were gone again, and the dressing room seemed twice as still and vacant as before.

A minute of grace, during which Mrs. Brady wiped the spilled powder away with a damp gray rag.

Then the door jumped open again. Two evening gowns appeared and made for the dressing table in a bee line. Slim tubular gowns they were, one green, one palest yellow. Yellow hair went with the green gown, brown hair with the yellow. The green-gowned, yellow-haired girl wore gardenias on her left shoulder, four of them, and a flashing bracelet on each fragile wrist. The other girl looked less prosperous; still, you would rather have looked at her.

Both ignored Mrs. Brady's cosmetic display as utterly as they ignored Mrs. Brady, producing full field equipment of their own.

"Well," said the girl with gardenias, rouging energetically, "how do you like him?"

"Oh-h—all right."

"Meaning, 'Not any,' hmm? I suspected as much!" The girl with gardenias turned in her chair and scanned her companion's profile with disapproval. "See here, Marilee," she drawled, "are you going to be a damn fool *all* your life?"

"He's fat," said Marilee dreamily. "Fat, and—greasy, sort of. I mean, greasy in his mind. Don't you know what I mean?"

"I know *one* thing," declared the other. "I know Who He Is! And if I were you, that's all I'd need to know. *Under the circumstances*."

The last three words, stressed meaningly, affected the girl called Marilee curiously. She grew grave. Her lips and lashes drooped. For some seconds she sat frowning a little, breaking a black-sheathed lipstick in two and fitting it together again.

"She's worse," she said finally.

"Worse?"

Marilee nodded.

"Well," said the girl with gardenias, "there you are. It's the climate. She'll never be anything *but* worse, if she doesn't get away. Out West. Arizona or somewhere."

"I know," murmured Marilee.

The other girl opened a tin of eye shadow. "Of course," she said dryly, "suit yourself. She's not *my* sister."

Marilee said nothing. Quiet she sat, breaking the lipstick, mending it, breaking it.

"Oh, well," she breathed finally, wearily, and straightened up. She propped her elbows on the plate-glass dressing-table top and leaned toward the mirror, and with the lipstick she began to make her coral-pink mouth very red and gay and reckless and alluring.

Nightly at one o'clock Vane and Moreno dance for the Club Français. They dance a tango, they dance a waltz; then, by way of encore, they do a Black Bottom, and a trick of their own called the Wheel. They dance for twenty, thirty minutes. And while they dance you do not leave your table—for this is what you came to see. Vane and Moreno. The new New York thrill. The sole justification for the five-dollar couvert extorted by Billy Costello.

From one until half-past, then, was Mrs. Brady's recess. She had been looking forward to it all the evening long. When it began—when the opening chords of the tango music sounded stirringly from the room outside—Mrs. Brady brightened. With a right good will she sped the parting guests.

Alone, she unlocked her cupboard and took out her magazine—the magazine she had bought three hours before. Heaving a great breath of relief and satisfaction, she plumped herself on the couch and fingered the pages.

Immediately she was absorbed, her eyes drinking up printed lines, her lips moving soundlessly.

The magazine was Mrs. Brady's favorite. Its stories were true stories, taken from life (so the editor said); and to Mrs. Brady they were live, vivid threads in the dull, drab pattern of her night.

Dorothy Parker
1893-

THEY say that Dorothy Parker has mellowed, that her sharp wit no longer pricks and tears and destroys. But her name will remain engraved in the gilt of the twenties as the Naughty Girl of the pen during those postwar years. Her verse, sharp and swift as an arrow, carries a neat distillation of poison. Her stories are sardonic, satirical, scathing.

Like most humorists, as we have said before, Dorothy Rothschild Parker toils over her writing, writes all too little, and is very serious: since the days when she worked so intensely for the freedom of Sacco and Vanzetti, she has embraced many liberal causes. She was born in West End, New Jersey, and was educated at the Blessed Sacrament Convent in New York.

A Telephone Call

BY DOROTHY PARKER

PLEASE, God, let him telephone me now. Dear God, let him call me now. I won't ask anything else of You, truly I won't. It isn't very much to ask. It would be so little to You, God, such a little, little thing. Only let him telephone now. Please, God. Please, please, please.

If I didn't think about it, maybe the telephone might ring. Sometimes it does that. If I could think of something else. If I could think of something else. Maybe if I counted five hundred by fives, it might ring by that time. I'll count slowly. I won't cheat. And if it rings when I get to three hundred, I won't stop; J won't answer it until I get to five hundred. Five, ten, fifteen, twenty, twenty-five, thirty, thirty-five, forty, forty-five, fifty. . . . Oh, please ring. Please.

This is the last time I'll look at the clock. I will not look at it again. It's ten minutes past seven. He said he would telephone at five o'clock. "I'll call you at five, darling." I think that's where he said "darling." I'm almost sure he said it there. I know he called me "darling" twice, and the other time was when he said good-by. "Good-by, darling." He was busy, and he can't say much in the office, but he called me "darling" twice. He couldn't have minded my calling him up. I know you shouldn't keep telephoning them—I know they don't like that. When you do that, they know you are thinking about them and wanting them, and that makes them hate you. But I hadn't talked to him in three days— not in three days. And all I did was ask him how he was; it was just the way anybody might have called him up. He couldn't have minded that. He couldn't have thought I was bothering him. "No, of course you're not," he said. And he said he'd telephone me. He didn't have to say that. I didn't ask him to, truly I didn't. I'm sure I didn't. I don't think he would say he'd telephone me, and then just never do it. Please don't let him do that, God. Please don't.

"I'll call you at five, darling." "Good-by, darling." He was busy, and he was in a hurry, and there were people around him, but he called me "darling" twice. That's mine, that's mine. I have that, even if I never see him again. Oh, but that's so little. That isn't enough. Nothing's enough, if I never see him again. Please let me see him again, God. Please, I want him so much. I want him so much. I'll be good, God. I will try to be better, I will, if

665

You will let me see him again. If You will let him telephone me. Oh, let him telephone me now.

Ah, don't let my prayer seem too little to You, God. You sit up there, so white and old, with all the angels about You and the stars slipping by. And I come to You with a prayer about a telephone call. Ah, don't laugh, God. You see, You don't know how it feels. You're so safe, there on Your throne, with the blue swirling under You. Nothing can touch You; no one can twist Your heart in his hands. This is suffering, God, this is bad, bad suffering. Won't You help me? For Your Son's sake, help me. You said You would do whatever was asked of You in His name. Oh, God, in the name of Thine only beloved Son, Jesus Christ, our Lord, let him telephone me now.

I must stop this. I mustn't be this way. Look. Suppose a young man says he'll call a girl up, and then something happens, and he doesn't. That isn't so terrible, is it? Why, it's going on all over the world, right this minute. Oh, what do I care what's going on all over the world? Why can't that telephone ring? Why can't it, why can't it? Couldn't you ring? Ah, please, couldn't you? You damned, ugly, shiny thing. It would hurt you to ring, wouldn't it? Oh, that would hurt you. Damn you, I'll pull your filthy roots out of the wall, I'll smash your smug black face in little bits. Damn you to hell.

No, no, no. I must stop. I must think about something else. This is what I'll do. I'll put the clock in the other room. Then I can't look at it. If I do have to look at it, then I'll have to walk into the bedroom, and that will be something to do. Maybe, before I look at it again, he will call me. I'll be so sweet to him, if he calls me. If he says he can't see

me tonight, I'll say, "Why, that's all right, dear. Why, of course it's all right." I'll be the way I was when I first met him. Then maybe he'll like me again. I was always sweet, at first. Oh, it's so easy to be sweet to people before you love them.

I think he must still like me a little. He couldn't have called me "darling" twice today, if he didn't still like me a little. It isn't all gone, if he still likes me a little; even if it's only a little, little bit. You see, God, if You would just let him telephone me, I wouldn't have to ask You anything more. I would be sweet to him, I would be gay, I would be just the way I used to be, and then he would love me again. And then I would never have to ask You for anything more. Don't You see, God? So won't You please let him telephone me? Won't You please, please, please?

Are You punishing me, God, because I've been bad? Are You angry with me because I did that? Oh, but, God, there are so many bad people —You could not be hard only to me. And it wasn't very bad; it couldn't have been bad. We didn't hurt anybody, God. Things are only bad when they hurt people. We didn't hurt one single soul; You know that. You know it wasn't bad, don't You, God? So won't You let him telephone me now?

If he doesn't telephone me, I'll know God is angry with me. I'll count five hundred by fives, and if he hasn't called me then, I will know God isn't going to help me, ever again. That will be the sign. Five, ten, fifteen, twenty, twenty-five, thirty, thirty-five, forty, forty-five, fifty, fifty-five. . . It was bad. I knew it was bad. All right, God, send me to hell. You think You're frightening me with Your hell, don't You? You think Your hell is worse than mine.

I mustn't. I mustn't do this. Suppose he's a little late calling me up —that's nothing to get hysterical about. Maybe he isn't going to call— maybe he's coming straight up here without telephoning. He'll be cross if he sees I have been crying. They don't like you to cry. He doesn't cry. I wish to God I could make him cry. I wish I could make him cry and tread the floor and feel his heart heavy and big and festering in him. I wish I could hurt him like hell.

He doesn't wish that about me. I don't think he even knows how he makes me feel. I wish he could know, without my telling him. They don't like you to tell them they've made you cry. They don't like you to tell them you're unhappy because of them. If you do, they think you're possessive and exacting. And then they hate you. They hate you whenever you say anything you really think. You always have to keep playing little games. Oh, I thought we didn't have to; I thought this was so big I could say whatever I meant. I guess you can't, ever. I guess there isn't ever anything big enough for that. Oh, if he would just telephone, I wouldn't tell him I had been sad about him. They hate sad people. I would be so sweet and so gay, he couldn't help but like me. If he would only telephone. If he would only telephone.

Maybe that's what he is doing. Maybe he is coming on here without calling me up. Maybe he's on his way now. Something might have happened to him. No, nothing could ever happen to him. I can't picture anything happening to him. I never picture him run over. I never see him lying still and long and dead. I wish he were dead. That's a terrible wish. That's a lovely wish. If he were

dead, he would be mine. If he were dead, I would never think of now and the last few weeks. I would remember only the lovely times. It would be all beautiful. I wish he were dead. I wish he were dead, dead, dead.

This is silly. It's silly to go wishing people were dead just because they don't call you up the very minute they said they would. Maybe the clock's fast; I don't know whether it's right. Maybe he's hardly late at all. Anything could have made him a little late. Maybe he had to stay at his office. Maybe he went home, to call me up from there, and somebody came in. He doesn't like to telephone me in front of people. Maybe he's worried, just a little, little bit, about keeping me waiting. He might even hope that I would call him up. I could do that. I could telephone him.

I mustn't. I mustn't, I mustn't. Oh, God, please don't let me telephone him. Please keep me from doing that. I know, God, just as well as You do, that if he were worried about me, he'd telephone no matter where he was or how many people there were around him. Please make me know that, God. I don't ask You to make it easy for me—You can't do that, for all that You could make a world. Only let me know it, God. Don't let me go on hoping. Don't let me say comforting things to myself. Please don't let me hope, dear God. Please don't.

I won't telephone him. I'll never telephone him again as long as I live. He'll rot in hell, before I'll call him up. You don't have to give me strength, God; I have it myself. If he wanted me, he could get me. He knows where I am. He knows I'm waiting here. He's so sure of me, so sure. I wonder why they hate you, as soon as they are sure of you. I should think it would be so sweet to be sure.

It would be so easy to telephone him. Then I'd know. Maybe it wouldn't be a foolish thing to do. Maybe he wouldn't mind. Maybe he'd like it. Maybe he has been trying to get me. Sometimes people try and try to get you on the telephone, and they say the number doesn't answer. I'm not just saying that to help myself; that really happens. You know that really happens, God. Oh, God, keep me away from that telephone. Keep me away. Let me still have just a little bit of pride. I think I'm going to need it, God. I think it will be all I'll have.

Oh, what does pride matter, when I can't stand it if I don't talk to him? Pride like that is such a silly, shabby little thing. The real pride, the big pride, is in having no pride. I'm not saying that just because I want to call him. I am not. That's true, I know that's true. I will be big. I will be beyond little prides.

Please, God, keep me from telephoning him. Please, God.

I don't see what pride has to do with it. This is such a little thing, for me to be bringing in pride, for me to be making such a fuss about. I may have misunderstood him. Maybe he said for me to call him up, at five. "Call me at five, darling." He could have said that, perfectly well. It's so possible that I didn't hear him right. "Call me at five, darling." I'm almost sure that's what he said. God, don't let me talk this way to myself. Make me know, please make me know.

I'll think about something else. I'll just sit quietly. If I could sit still. If I could sit still. Maybe I could read. Oh, all the books are about people who love each other, truly and sweetly. What do they want to write about that for? Don't they know it isn't true? Don't they know it's a lie, it's a God damned lie? What do they have to tell about that for, when they know how it hurts? Damn them, damn them, damn them.

I won't. I'll be quiet. This is nothing to get excited about. Look. Suppose he were someone I didn't know very well. Suppose he were another girl. Then I'd just telephone and say, "Well, for goodness' sake, what happened to you?" That's what I'd do, and I'd never even think about it. Why can't I be casual and natural, just because I love him? I can be. Honestly, I can be. I'll call him up, and be so easy and pleasant. You see if I won't, God. Oh, don't let me call him. Don't, don't, don't.

God, aren't You really going to let him call me? Are You sure, God? Couldn't You please relent? Couldn't You? I don't even ask You to let him telephone me this minute, God; only let him do it in a little while. I'll count five hundred by fives. I'll do it so slowly and so fairly. If he hasn't telephoned then, I'll call him. I will. Oh, please, dear God, dear kind God, my blessed Father in Heaven, let him call before then. Please, God. Please.

Five, ten, fifteen, twenty, twenty-five, thirty, thirty-five. . . .

Ernest Hemingway
1898-1961

ALTHOUGH the world rarely thinks of him as such, Ernest Hemingway was an American Middle Westerner, born in Oak Park, Illinois, and brought up in Michigan. His father, a doctor, wanted him to take up medicine, and his mother wanted him to be a cellist. But World War I settled the controversy with young Hemingway joining the ambulance service in France, and later transferring to the Italian shock troops, the Arditi, with whom he was seriously wounded. In 1921 he made his way to Paris along with hundreds of other spiritual as well as physical war casualties, and settled into the artistic, romantic Bohemian world of the Left Bank. There, in 1926, he produced the definitive novel of the "lost generation," *The Sun Also Rises,* and followed it three years later with *A Farewell to Arms.* The Great War, in which millions of his generation had died, had failed; promises had been broken, civilization cheapened. Hemingway, more articulate than others, expressed his hatred of sham, his revulsion from the idealism which had let him down, in stories of violence and brutality. No one worked harder than he did to reach his end: the transference of human experience into fiction in as true a form as language will permit. Hemingway was not satirical, never tried for atmosphere. His writing is as objective as Henry James's, as clear cut as a line drawing. Hundreds of writers since have tried to match his diamond-hard brilliance; thousands of Hemingway-shadowed characters have talked their way through the "tough" stories that have filled American magazines. But the father of the "hard-boiled" school, the real Hemingway, has not been equaled.

The background of Hemingway's fiction reflects his own experiences. After months in Spain, for example, he wrote *For Whom the Bell Tolls.* His home in Cuba inspired *The Old Man of the Sea.* And so, from a journey he made to Africa, we have "The Snows of Kilimanjaro," which he once said he considered his best story.

He received the Pulitzer Prize for literature in 1953, and the Nobel Prize for literature in 1954.

The Snows of Kilimanjaro

BY ERNEST HEMINGWAY

Kilimanjaro is a snow-covered mountain 19,710 feet high, and is said to be the highest mountain in Africa. Its western summit is called the Masai "Ngàje Ngài," the House of God. Close to the western summit there is the dried and frozen carcass of a leopard. No one has explained what the leopard was seeking at that altitude.

"THE MARVELOUS thing is that it's painless," he said. "That's how you know when it starts."

"Is it really?"

"Absolutely. I'm awfully sorry about the odor though. That must bother you."

"Don't! Please don't."

"Look at them," he said. "Now is it sight or is it scent that brings them like that?"

The cot the man lay on was in the wide shade of a mimosa tree and as he looked out past the shade onto the glare of the plain there were three of the big birds squatted obscenely, while in the sky, a dozen more sailed, making quick-moving shadows as they passed.

"They've been there since the day the truck broke down," he said. "Today's the first time any have lit on the ground. I watched the way they sailed very carefully at first in case I ever wanted to use them in a story. That's funny now."

"I wish you wouldn't," she said.

"I'm only talking," he said. "It's much easier if I talk. But I don't want to bother you."

"You know it doesn't bother me," she said. "It's that I've gotten so very nervous not being able to do anything. I think we might make it as easy as we can until the plane comes."

"Or until the plane doesn't come."

"Please tell me what I can do. There must be something I can do."

"You can take the leg off and that might stop it, though I doubt it. Or you can shoot me. You're a good shot now. I taught you to shoot, didn't I?"

"Please don't talk that way. Couldn't I read to you?"

"Read what?"

"Anything in the book bag that we haven't read."

"I can't listen to it," he said. "Talking is the easiest. We quarrel and that makes the time pass."

"I don't quarrel. I never want to quarrel. Let's not quarrel any more. No matter how nervous we get. Maybe they will be back with another truck today. Maybe the plane will come."

"I don't want to move," the man said. "There is no sense in moving now except to make it easier for you."

"That's cowardly."

"Can't you let a man die as comfortably as he can without calling him names? What's the use of slanging me?"

"You're not going to die."

"Don't be silly. I'm dying now. Ask those bastards." He looked over to where the huge, filthy birds sat, their naked heads sunk in the hunched feathers. A fourth planed down, to run quick-legged and then waddle slowly toward the others.

"They are around every camp. You never notice them. You can't die if you don't give up."

"Where did you read that? You're such a bloody fool."

"You might think about someone else."

"For Christ's sake," he said "that's been my trade."

He lay then and was quiet for a while and looked across the heat shimmer of the plain to the edge of the bush. There were a few Tommies that showed minute and white against the yellow and, far off, he saw a herd of zebra, white against the green of the bush. This was a pleasant camp under big trees against a hill, with good water, and close by, a nearly dry water hole where sand grouse flighted in the mornings.

"Wouldn't you like me to read?" she asked. She was sitting on a canvas chair beside his cot. "There's a breeze coming up."

"No thanks."

"Maybe the truck will come."

"I don't give a damn about the truck."

"I do."

"You give a damn about so many things that I don't."

"Not so many, Harry."

"What about a drink?"

"It's supposed to be bad for you. It said in Black's to avoid all alcohol. You shouldn't drink."

"Molo!" he shouted.

"Yes Bwana."

"Bring whiskey-soda."

"Yes Bwana."

"You shouldn't," she said. "That's what I mean by giving up. It says it's bad for you. I know it's bad for you."

"No," he said. "It's good for me."

So now it was all over, he thought. So now he would never have a chance to finish it. So this was the way it ended in a bickering over a drink. Since the gangrene started in his right leg he had no pain and with the pain the horror had gone and all he felt now was a great tiredness and anger that this was the end of it. For this, that now was coming, he had very little curiosity. For years it had obsessed him; but now it meant nothing in itself. It was strange how easy being tired enough made it.

Now he would never write the things that he had saved to write until he knew enough to write them well. Well, he would not have to fail at trying to write them either. Maybe you could never write them, and that was why you put them off and delayed the starting. Well, he would never know, now.

"I wish we'd never come," the woman said. She was looking at him holding the glass and biting her lip. "You never would have gotten anything like this in Paris. You always said you loved Paris. We could have stayed in Paris or gone anywhere. I'd have gone anywhere. I said I'd go anywhere you wanted. If you wanted to shoot we could have gone shooting in Hungary and been comfortable."

"Your bloody money," he said.

"That's not fair," she said. "It was always yours as much as mine. I left everything and I went wherever you wanted to go and I've done what you wanted to do. But I wish we'd never come here."

"You said you loved it."

"I did when you were all right. But now I hate it. I don't see why that had to happen to your leg. What have we done to have that happen to us?"

"I suppose what I did was to forget to put iodine on it when I first scratched it. Then I didn't pay any attention to it because I never infect. Then, later, when it got bad, it was probably using that weak carbolic solution when the other antiseptics ran out that paralyzed the minute blood vessels and started the gangrene." He looked at her. "What else?"

"I don't mean that."

"If we would have hired a good mechanic instead of a half-baked Kikuyu driver, he would have checked the oil and never burned out that bearing in the truck."

"I don't mean that."

"If you hadn't left your own people, your God-damned Old Westbury, Saratoga, Palm Beach people to take me on———"

"Why, I loved you. That's not fair. I love you now. I'll always love you. Don't you love me?"

"No," said the man. "I don't think so. I never have."

"Harry, what are you saying? You're out of your head."

"No. I haven't any head to go out of."

"Don't drink that," she said. "Dar-ling, please don't drink that. We have to do everything we can."

"You do it," he said. "I'm tired."

Now in his mind he saw a railway station at Karagatch and he was standing with his pack and that was the headlight of the Simplon-Orient cutting the dark now and he was leaving Thrace then after the retreat. That was one of the things he had saved to write, with, in the morning at breakfast, looking out the window and seeing snow on the mountains in Bulgaria and Nansen's Secretary asking the old man if it were snow and the old man looking at it and saying, No, that's not snow. It's too early for snow. And the Secretary repeating to the other girls, No, you see. It's not snow and then all saying, It's not snow we were mistaken. But it was the snow all right and he sent them on into it when he evolved exchange of populations. And it was snow they tramped along in until they died that winter.

It was snow too that fell all Christmas week that year up in the Gauertal, that year they lived in the woodcutter's house with the big square porcelain stove that filled half the room, and they slept on mattresses filled with beech leaves, the time the deserter came with his feet bloody in the snow. He said the police were right behind him and they gave him woolen socks and held the gendarmes talking until the tracks had drifted over.

In Schrunz, on Christmas day, the snow was so bright it hurt your eyes when you looked out from the weinstube and saw everyone coming home from church. That was where they walked up the sleigh-smoothed urine-yellowed road along the river with the steep pine hills, skis heavy

*on the shoulder, and where they ran
that great run down the glacier
above the Madlener-haus, the snow
as smooth to see as cake frosting and
as light as powder and he remembered the noiseless rush the speed
made as you dropped down like a
bird.*

*They were snowbound a week in
the Madlener-haus that time in the
blizzard playing cards in the smoke
by the lantern light and the stakes
were higher all the time as Herr
Lent lost more. Finally he lost it all.
Everything, the skischule money and
all the season's profit and then his
capital. He could see him with his
long nose, picking up the cards and
then opening, "Sans Voir." There was
always gambling then. When there
was no snow you gambled and when
there was too much you gambled.
He thought of all the time in his life
he had spent gambling.*

*But he had never written a line
of that, nor of that cold, bright
Christmas day with the mountains
showing across the plain that Barker
had flown across the lines to bomb
the Austrian officers' leave train,
machine-gunning them as they
scattered and ran. He remembered
Barker afterwards coming into the
mess and starting to tell about it.
And how quiet it got and then somebody saying, "You bloody murderous
bastard."*

*Those were the same Austrians
they killed then that he skied with
later. No not the same. Hans, that
he skied with all that year, had been
in the Kaiser-Jägers and when they
went hunting hares together up the
little valley above the sawmill they
had talked of the fighting on Pasubio
and of the attack on Pertica and
Asalone and he had never written a
word of that. Nor of Monte Corno,*

*nor the Siete Commum, nor of
Arsiedo.*

*How many winters had he lived in
the Voralberg and the Arlberg? It
was four and then he remembered
the man who had the fox to sell
when they had walked into Bludenz,
that time to buy presents, and the
cherry-pit taste of good kirsch, the
fast-slipping rush of running powder-
snow on crust, singing "Hi! Ho! said
Rolly!" as you ran down the last
stretch to the steep drop, taking it
straight, then running the orchard in
three turns and out across the ditch
and onto the icy road behind the
inn. Knocking your bindings loose,
kicking the skis free and leaning
them up against the wooden wall of
the inn, the lamplight coming from
the window, where inside, in the
smoky, new-wine-smelling warmth,
they were playing the accordion.*

"Where did we stay in Paris?" he
asked the woman who was sitting
by him in a canvas chair, now, in
Africa.

"At the Crillon. You know that."

"Why do I know that?"

"That's where we always stayed."

"No. Not always."

"There and at the Pavillon Henri-
Quatre in St. Germain. You said you
loved it there."

"Love is a dunghill," said Harry.
"And I'm the cock that gets on it to
crow."

"If you have to go away," she
said, "is it absolutely necessary to
kill off everything you leave behind?
I mean do you have to take away
everything? Do you have to kill your
horse and your wife and burn your
saddle and your armor?"

"Yes," he said. "Your damned
money was my armor. My Swift and
my Armour."

"Don't."

"All right. I'll stop that. I don't want to hurt you."

"It's a little bit late now."

"All right then. I'll go on hurting you. It's more amusing. The only thing I ever really liked to do with you I can't do now."

"No, that's not true. You liked to do many things and everything you wanted to do I did."

"Oh, for Christ sake stop bragging, will you?"

He looked at her and saw her crying.

"Listen," he said. "Do you think that it is fun to do this? I don't know why I'm doing it. It's trying to kill to keep yourself alive, I imagine. I was all right when we started talking. I didn't mean to start this, and now I'm crazy as a coot and being as cruel to you as I can be. Don't pay any attention, darling, to what I say. I love you, really. You know I love you. I've never loved anyone else the way I love you."

He slipped into the familiar lie he made his bread and butter by.

"You're sweet to me."

"You bitch," he said. "You rich bitch. That's poetry. I'm full of poetry now. Rot and poetry. Rotten poetry."

"Stop it. Harry, why do you have to turn into a devil now?"

"I don't like to leave anything," the man said. "I don't like to leave things behind."

It was evening now and he had been asleep. The sun was gone behind the hill and there was a shadow all across the plain and the small animals were feeding close to camp; quick dropping heads and switching tails, he watched them keeping well out away from the bush now. The birds no longer waited on the ground. They were all perched heavily in a tree. There were many more of them. His personal boy was sitting by the bed.

"Memsahib's gone to shoot," the boy said. "Does Bwana want?"

"Nothing."

She had gone to kill a piece of meat and, knowing how he liked to watch the game, she had gone well away so she would not disturb this little pocket of the plain that he could see. She was always thoughtful, he thought. On anything she knew about, or had read, or that she had ever heard.

It was not her fault that when he went to her he was already over. How could a woman know that you meant nothing that you said; that you spoke only from habit and to be comfortable? After he no longer meant what he said, his lies were more successful with women than when he had told them the truth.

It was not so much that he lied as that there was no truth to tell. He had had his life and it was over and then he went on living it again with different people and more money, with the best of the same places, and some new ones.

You kept from thinking and it was all marvelous. You were equipped with good insides so that you did not go to pieces that way, the way most of them had, and you made an attitude that you cared nothing for the work you used to do, now that you could no longer do it. But, in yourself, you said that you would write about these people; about the very rich; that you were really not of them but a spy in their country; that you would leave it and write of it and for once it would be written by someone who knew what he was writing of. But he would never do it, because each day of not writing, of comfort, of being that which he despised, dulled his ability and softened his will to work so that, finally, he did no work at all. The people he knew now were all much more comfortable when he did not work. Africa was where he had been happiest in the good time of his life, so he had come out here to start again. They had made this safari with the minimum of comfort. There was no hardship; but there was no luxury and he had thought that he could get back into training that way. That in some way he could work the fat off his soul the way a fighter went into the mountains to work and train in order to burn it out of his body.

She had liked it. She said she loved it. She loved anything that was exciting, that involved a change of scene, where there were new people and where things were pleasant. And he had felt the illusion of returning strength of will to work. Now if this was how it ended, and he knew it was, he must not turn like some snake biting itself because its back was broken. It wasn't this woman's fault. If it had not been she it would have been another. If he lived by a lie he should try to die by it. He heard a shot beyond the hill.

She shot very well this good, this rich bitch, this kindly caretaker and destroyer of his talent. Nonsense. He had destroyed his talent himself. Why should he blame this woman because she kept him well? He had destroyed his talent by not using it, by betrayals of himself and what he believed in, by drinking so much that he blunted the edge of his perceptions, by laziness, by sloth, and by snobbery, by pride and by prejudice, by hook and by crook. What was this? A catalogue of old books? What was his talent anyway? It was a talent all right but instead of using it, he had traded on it. It was never what he had done, but always what he could do. And he had chosen to make his living with something else instead of a pen or a pencil. It was strange, too, wasn't it, that when he fell in love with another woman, that woman should always have more money than the last one? But when he was no longer in love, when he was only lying, as to this woman, now, who had the most money of all, who had all the money there was, who had had a husband and children, who had taken lovers and been dissatisfied with them, and who loved him dearly as a writer, as a man, as a companion and as a proud possession; it was strange that when he did not love her at all and was lying, that he should be able to give her more for her money than when he had really loved.

We must all be cut out for what we do, he thought. However you make your living is where your talent lies. He had sold vitality, in one form or another, all his life and when your affections are not too involved you give much better value for the money. He had found that out but he would never write that, now, either. No, he would not write that, although it was well worth writing.

Now she came in sight, walking across the open toward the camp. She was wearing jodhpurs and carrying her rifle. The two boys had a Tommie slung and they were coming along behind her. She was still a good-looking woman, he thought, and she had a pleasant body. She had a great talent and appreciation for the bed, she was not pretty, but he liked her face, she read enormously, liked to ride and shoot and, certainly, she drank too much. Her husband had died when she was still a comparatively young woman and for a while she had devoted herself to her two just-grown children, who did not need her and were embarrassed at having her about, to her stable of horses, to books, and to bottles. She liked to read in the evening before dinner and she drank Scotch and soda while she read. By dinner she was fairly drunk and after a bottle of wine at dinner she was usually drunk enough to sleep.

That was before the lovers. After she had the lovers she did not drink so much because she did not have to be drunk to sleep. But the lovers bored her. She had been married to a man who had never bored her and these people bored her very much.

Then one of her two children was killed in a plane crash and after that was over she did not want the lovers, and drink being no anesthetic she had to make another life. Suddenly, she had been acutely frightened of being alone. But she wanted someone that she respected with her.

It had begun very simply. She liked what he wrote and she had always envied the life he led. She thought he did exactly what he wanted to. The steps by which she had acquired him and the way in which she had finally fallen in love with him were all part of a regular progression in which she had built herself a new life and he had traded away what remained of his old life.

He had traded it for security, for comfort too, there was no denying that, and for what else? He did not know. She would have bought him anything he wanted. He knew that. She was a damned nice woman too. He would as soon be in bed with her as anyone; rather with her, because she was richer, because she was very pleasant and appreciative and because she never made scenes. And now this life that she had built again was coming to a term because he had not used iodine two weeks ago when a thorn had scratched his knee as they moved forward trying to photograph a herd of waterbuck standing, their heads up, peering while their nostrils searched the air, their ears spread wide to hear the first noise that would send them rushing into the bush. They had bolted, too, before he got the picture.

Here she came now.

He turned his head on the cot to look toward her. "Hello," he said.

"I shot a Tommy ram," she told him. "He'll make you good broth and I'll have them mash some potatoes with the Klim. How do you feel?"

"Much better."

"Isn't that lovely? You know I thought perhaps you would. You were sleeping when I left."

"I had a good sleep. Did you walk far?"

"No. Just around behind the hill. I made quite a good shot on the Tommy."

"You shoot marvelously, you know."

"I love it. I've loved Africa. Really. If *you're* all right it's the most fun that I've ever had. You don't know the fun it's been to shoot with you. I've loved the country."

"I love it too."

"Darling, you don't know how marvelous it is to see you feeling better. I couldn't stand it when you felt that way. You won't talk to me like that again, will you? Promise me?"

"No," he said. "I don't remember what I said."

"You don't have to destroy me. Do you? I'm only a middle-aged woman who loves you and wants to do what you want to do. I've been destroyed two or three times already. You wouldn't want to destroy me again, would you?"

"I'd like to destroy you a few times in bed," he said.

"Yes. That's the good destruction. That's the way we're made to be destroyed. The plane will be here tomorrow."

"How do you know?"

"I'm sure. It's bound to come. The boys have the wood all ready and the grass to make the smudge. I went down and looked at it again today. There's plenty of room to land and we have the smudges ready at both ends."

"What makes you think it will come tomorrow?"

"I'm sure it will. It's overdue now. Then, in town, they will fix up your leg and then we will have some good destruction. Not that dreadful talking kind."

"Should we have a drink? The sun is down."

"Do you think you should?"

"I'm having one."

"We'll have one together. *Molo, letti dui whisky-soda!*" she called.

"You'd better put on your mosquito boots," he told her.

"I'll wait till I bathe . . ."

While it grew dark they drank and just before it was dark and there was no longer enough light to shoot, a hyena crossed the open on his way around the hill.

"That bastard crosses there every night," the man said. "Every night for two weeks."

"He's the one makes the noise at night. I don't mind it. They're a filthy animal though."

Drinking together, with no pain now except the discomfort of lying in one position, the boys lighting a fire, its shadow jumping on the tents, he could feel the return of acquiescence in this life of pleasant surrender. She *was* very good to him. He had been cruel and unjust in the afternoon. She was a fine woman, marvelous really. And just then it occurred to him that he was going to die.

It came with a rush; not as a rush of water nor of wind; but of a sudden evil-smelling emptiness and the odd thing was that the hyena slipped lightly along the edge of it.

"What is it, Harry?" she asked him.

"Nothing," he said. "You had better move over to the other side. To windward."

"Did Molo change the dressing?"

"Yes. I'm just using the boric now."

"How do you feel?"

"A little wobbly."

"I'm going in to bathe," she said. "I'll be right out. I'll eat with you and then we'll put the cot in."

So, he said to himself, we did well to stop the quarreling. He had never quarreled much with this woman, while with the women that he loved he had quarreled so much they had finally, always, with the corrosion of the quarreling, killed what they had together. He had loved too much, demanded too much, and he wore it all out.

He thought about alone in Constantinople that time, having quarreled in Paris before he had gone

out. He had whored the whole time
and then, when that was over, and
he had failed to kill his loneliness,
but only made it worse, he had written her, the first one, the one who
left him, a letter telling her how he
had never been able to kill it. . . .
How when he thought he saw her
outside the Regence one time it
made him go all faint and sick inside, and that he would follow a
woman who looked like her in some
way, along the Boulevard, afraid to
see it was not she, afraid to lose the
feeling it gave him. How everyone
he had slept with had only made
him miss her more. How what she
had done could never matter since
he knew he could not cure himself
of loving her. He wrote this letter
at the Club, cold sober, and mailed it
to New York asking her to write him
at the office in Paris. That seemed
safe. And that night missing her so
much it made him feel hollow sick
inside, he wandered up past Taxim's,
picked a girl up and took her out to
supper. He had gone to a place to
dance with her afterward, she
danced badly, and left her for a hot
Armenian slut, that swung her belly
against him so it almost scalded.
He took her away from a British
gunner subaltern after a row. The
gunner asked him outside and they
fought in the street on the cobbles
in the dark. He'd hit him twice,
hard, on the side of the jaw and
when he didn't go down he knew he
was in for a fight. The gunner hit
him in the body, then beside his eye.
He swung with his left again and
landed and the gunner fell on him
and grabbed his coat and tore the
sleeve off and he clubbed him twice
behind the ear and then smashed
him with his right as he pushed
him away. When the gunner went
down his head hit first and he ran

with the girl because they heard the
M.P.'s coming. They got into a taxi
and drove out to Rimmily Hissa
along the Bosphorus, and around,
and back in the cool night and went
to bed and she felt as overripe as she
looked but smooth, rose-petal, sirupy,
smooth-bellied, big-breasted and
needed no pillow under her buttocks,
and he left her before she was awake
looking blousy enough in the first
daylight and turned up at the Pera
Palace with a black eye, carrying his
coat because one sleeve was missing.

That same night he left for
Anatolia and he remembered, later
on that trip, riding all day through
fields of the poppies that they raised
for opium and how strange it made
you feel, finally, and all the distances seemed wrong, to where they
had made the attack with the newly
arrived Constantine officers, that did
not know a God-damned thing, and
the artillery had fired into the troops
and the British observer had cried
like a child.

That was the day he'd first seen
dead men wearing white ballet skirts
and upturned shoes with pompons
on them. The Turks had come
steadily and lumpily and he had seen
the skirted men running and the
officers shooting into them and running then themselves and he and the
British observer had run too until
his lungs ached and his mouth was
full of the taste of pennies and they
stopped behind some rocks and there
were the Turks coming as lumpily as
ever. Later he had seen the things
that he could never think of and later
still he had seen much worse. So
when he got back to Paris that time
he could not talk about it or stand
to have it mentioned. And there in
the café as he passed was that American poet with a pile of saucers in
front of him and a stupid look on his

*potato face talking about the Dada
movement with a Rumanian who
said his name was Tristan Tzara,
who always wore a monocle and had
a headache, and, back at the apartment with his wife that now he
loved again, the quarrel all over, the
madness all over, glad to be home,
the office sent his mail up to the flat.
So then the letter in answer to the
one he'd written came in on a plat-
ter one morning and when he saw
the handwriting he went cold all
over and tried to slip the letter
underneath another. But his wife
said, "Who is that letter from, dear?"
and that was the end of the beginning of that.*

*He remembered the good times
with them all, and the quarrels.
They always picked the finest places
to have the quarrels. And why had
they always quarreled when he was
feeling best? He had never written
any of that because, at first, he never
wanted to hurt anyone and then it
seemed as though there was enough
to write without it. But he had
always thought that he would write
it finally. There was so much to
write. He had seen the world
change; not just the events; although
he had seen many of them and had
watched the people, but he had seen
the subtler change and he could remember how the people were at different times. He had been in it and
he had watched it and it was his
duty to write of it; but now he never
would.*

"How do you feel?" she said. She
had come out from the tent now
after her bath.

"All right."

"Could you eat now?" He saw
Molo behind her with the folding
table and the other boy with the
dishes.

"I want to write," he said.

"You ought to take some broth to
keep your strength up."

"I'm going to die tonight," he said.
"I don't need my strength up."

"Don't be melodramatic, Harry,
please," she said.

"Why don't you use your nose?
I'm rotted halfway up my thigh
now. What the hell should I fool with
broth for? Molo bring whisky-soda."

"Please take the broth," she said
gently.

"All right."

The broth was too hot. He had to
hold it in the cup until it cooled
enough to take it and then he just
got it down without gagging.

"You're a fine woman," he said.
"Don't pay any attention to me."

She looked at him with her well-
known, well-loved face from *Spur*
and *Town and Country*, only a little
the worse for drink, only a little the
worse for bed, but *Town and Country* never showed those good breasts
and those useful thighs and those
lightly small-of-back-caressing hands,
and as he looked and saw her well-
known pleasant smile, he felt death
come again. This time there was no
rush. It was a puff, as of a wind that
makes a candle flicker and the flame
go tall.

"They can bring my net out later
and hang it from the tree and build
the fire up. I'm not going in the
tent tonight. It's not worth moving.
It's a clear night. There won't be
any rain."

So this was how you died, in
whispers that you did not hear. Well,
there would be no more quarreling.
He could promise that. The one
experience that he had never had he
was not going to spoil now. He
probably would. You spoiled everything. But perhaps he wouldn't.

"You can't take dictation, can you?"

"I never learned," she told him.

"That's all right."

There wasn't time, of course, although it seemed as though it telescoped so that you might put it all into one paragraph if you could get it right.

There was a log house, chinked white with mortar, on a hill above the lake. There was a bell on a pole by the door to call the people in to meals. Behind the house were fields and behind the fields was the timber. A line of Lombardy poplars ran from the house to the dock. Other poplars ran along the point. A road went up to the hills along the edge of the timber and along that road he picked blackberries. Then that log house was burned down and all the guns that had been on deer-foot racks above the open fireplace were burned and afterwards their barrels, with the lead melted in the magazines, and the stocks burned away, lay out on the heap of ashes that were used to make lye for the big iron soap kettles, and you asked Grandfather if you could have them to play with, and he said, no. You see they were his guns still and he never bought any others. Nor did he hunt any more. The house was rebuilt in the same place out of lumber now and painted white and from its porch you saw the poplars and the lake beyond; but there were never any more guns. The barrels of the guns that had hung on the deer feet on the wall of the log house lay out there on the heap of ashes and no one ever touched them.

In the Black Forest, after the war, we rented a trout stream and there were two ways to walk to it. One was down the valley from Triberg and around the valley road in the shade of the trees that bordered the white road, and then up a side road that went up through the hills past many small farms, with the big Schwarzwald houses, until that road crossed the stream. That was where our fishing began.

The other way was to climb steeply up to the edge of the woods and then go across the top of the hills through the pine woods, and then out to the edge of a meadow and down across this meadow to the bridge. There were birches along the stream and it was not big, but narrow, clear and fast, with pools where it had cut under the roots of the birches. At the Hotel in Triberg the proprietor had a fine season. It was very pleasant and we were all great friends. The next year came the inflation and the money he had made the year before was not enough to buy supplies to open the hotel and he hanged himself.

You could dictate that, but you could not dictate the Place Contrescarpe where the flower sellers dyed their flowers in the street and the dye ran over the paving where the autobus started and the old men and the women, always drunk on wine and bad marc; and the children with their noses running in the cold; the smell of dirty sweat and poverty and drunkenness at the Café des Amateurs and the whores at the Bal Musette they lived above. The Concièrge who entertained the trooper of the Garde Républicaine in her loge, his horse-hair-plumed helmet on a chair. The locataire across the hall whose husband was a bicycle racer and her joy that morning at the Crémerie when she had opened L'Auto and seen where he placed third in Paris-Tours, his first big race. She had blushed and laughed and then gone upstairs crying with the yellow sporting paper in her hand. The husband of the woman who ran the Bal Musette drove a taxi and when he, Harry, had to take an early plane the husband knocked upon the door to wake him and they each drank a glass of white wine at the zinc of the bar before they started. He knew his neighbors in that quarter then because they all were poor.

Around that Place there were two kinds: the drunkards and the sportifs. The drunkards killed their poverty that way; the sportifs took it out in exercise. They were the descendants of the Communards and it was no struggle for them to know their politics. They knew who had shot their fathers, their relatives, their brothers, and their friends when the Versailles troops came in and took the town after the Commune and executed anyone they could catch with callused hands, or who wore a cap, or carried any other sign he was a workingman. And in that poverty, and in that quarter across the street from a Boucherie Chevaline and a wine co-operative he had written the start of all he was to do. There never was another part of Paris that he loved like that, the sprawling trees, the old white plastered houses painted brown below, the long green of the autobus in that round square, the purple flower dye upon the paving, the sudden drop down the hill of the rue Cardinal Lemoine to the River, and the other way the narrow crowded world of the rue Mouffetard. The street then ran up toward the Panthéon and the other that he always took with the bicycle, the only asphalted street in all that quarter, smooth under the tires, with the high narrow houses and the cheap tall hotel where Paul Verlaine had died. There were only two rooms in

the apartments where they lived and he had a room on the top floor of that hotel that cost him sixty francs a month where he did his writing, and from it he could see the roofs and chimney pots and all the hills of Paris.

From the apartment you could only see the wood-and-coal man's place. He sold wine too, bad wine. The golden horse's head outside the Boucherie Chevaline where the carcasses hung yellow gold and red in the open window, and the green-painted co-operative where they bought their wine; good wine and cheap. The rest was plaster walls and the windows of the neighbors. The neighbors who, at night, when someone lay drunk in the street, moaning and groaning in that typical French ivresse that you were propaganded to believe did not exist, would open their windows and then the murmur of talk.

"Where is the policeman? When you don't want him the bugger is always there. He's sleeping with some concierge. Get the Agent." Till someone threw a bucket of water from a window and the moaning stopped. "What's that? Water. Ah, that's intelligent." And the windows shutting. Marie, his femme de ménage, protesting against the eight-hour day saying, "If a husband works until six he gets only a little drunk on the way home and does not waste too much. If he works only until five he is drunk every night and one has no money. It is the wife of the workingman who suffers from this shortening of hours."

"Wouldn't you like some more broth?" the woman asked him now.

"No, thank you very much. It is awfully good."

"Try just a little."

"I would like a whisky-soda."

"It's not good for you."

"No. It's bad for me. Cole Porter wrote the words and the music. This knowledge that you're going mad for me."

"You know I like you to drink."

"Oh yes. Only it's bad for me."

When she goes, he thought, I'll have all I want. Not all I want but all there is. Ayee he was tired. Too tired. He was going to sleep a little while. He lay still and death was not there. It must have gone around another street. It went in pairs, on bicycles, and moved absolutely silently on the pavements.

No, he had never written about Paris. Not the Paris that he cared about. But what about the rest that he had never written?

What about the ranch and the silvered gray of the sagebrush, the quick, clear water in the irrigation ditches, and the heavy green of the alfalfa. The trail went up into the hills and the cattle in the summer were shy as deer. The bawling and the steady noise and slow moving mass raising a dust as you brought them down in the fall. And behind the mountains, the clear sharpness of the peak in the evening light and, riding down along the trail in the moonlight, bright across the valley. Now he remembered coming down through the timber in the dark holding the horse's tail when you could not see and all the stories that he meant to write.

About the half-wit chore boy who was left at the ranch that time and told not to let anyone get any hay, and that old bastard from the Forks who had beaten the boy when he had worked for him stopping to get some feed. The boy refusing and the old man saying he would beat him

again. The boy got the rifle from the kitchen and shot him when he tried to come into the barn and when they came back to the ranch he'd been dead a week, frozen in the corral, and the dogs had eaten part of him. But what was left you packed on a sled wrapped in a blanket and roped on and you got the boy to help you haul it, and the two of you took it out over the road on skis, and sixty miles down to town to turn the boy over. He having no idea that he would be arrested. Thinking he had done his duty and that you were his friend and he would be rewarded. He'd helped to haul the old man in so everybody could know how bad the old man had been and how he'd tried to steal some feed that didn't belong to him, and when the sheriff put the handcuffs on the boy he couldn't believe it. Then he'd started to cry. That was one story he had saved to write. He knew at least twenty good stories from out there and he had never written one. Why?

"You tell them why," he said.

"Why what, dear?"

"Why nothing."

She didn't drink so much, now, since she had him. But if he lived he would never write about her, he knew that now. Nor about any of them. The rich were dull and they drank too much, or they played too much backgammon. They were dull and they were repetitious. He remembered poor Julian and his romantic awe of them and how he had started a story once that began, "The very rich are different from you and me." And how someone had said to Julian, Yes, they have more money. But that was not humorous to Julian. He thought they were a special glamorous race and when he found they weren't it wrecked him just as much as any other thing that wrecked him.

He had been contemptuous of those who wrecked. You did not have to like it because you understood it. He could beat anything, he thought, because no thing could hurt him if he did not care.

All right. Now he would not care for death. One thing he had always dreaded was the pain. He could stand pain as well as any man, until it went on too long, and wore him out, but here he had something that had hurt frightfully and just when he had felt it breaking him, the pain had stopped.

He remembered long ago when Williamson, the bombing officer, had been hit by a stick bomb someone in a German patrol had thrown as he was coming in through the wire that night and, screaming, had begged everyone to kill him. He was a fat man, very brave, and a good officer, although addicted to fantastic shows. But that night he was caught in the wire, with a flare lighting him up and his bowels spilled out into the wire, so when they brought him in, alive, they had to cut him loose. Shoot me, Harry. For Christ sake shoot me. They had had an argument one time about our Lord never sending you anything you could not bear and someone's theory had been that meant that at a certain time the pain passed you out automatically. But he had always remembered Williamson, that night. Nothing passed out Williamson until he gave him all his morphine tablets that he had always saved to use himself and then they did not work right away.

Still this now, that he had, was very easy; and if it was no worse as it went on there was nothing to worry about. Except that he would rather be in better company.

He thought a little about the company that he would like to have.

No, he thought, when everything you do, you do too long, and do too late, you can't expect to find the people still there. The people all are gone. The party's over and you are with your hostess now.

I'm getting as bored with dying as with everything else, he thought.

"It's a bore," he said out loud.

"What is, my dear?"

"Anything you do too bloody long."

He looked at her face between him and the fire. She was leaning back in the chair and the firelight shone on her pleasantly lined face and he could see that she was sleepy. He heard the hyena make a noise just outside the range of the fire.

"I've been writing," he said. "But I get tired."

"Do you think you will be able to sleep?"

"Pretty sure. Why don't you turn in?"

"I like to sit here with you."

"Do you feel anything strange?" he asked her.

"No. Just a little sleepy."

"I do," he said.

He had just felt death come by again.

"You know the only thing I've never lost is curiosity," he said to her.

"You've never lost anything. You're the most complete man I've ever known."

"Christ," he said. "How little a woman knows. What is that? Your intuition?"

Because, just then, death had come and rested its head on the foot of the cot and he could smell its breath.

"Never believe any of that about a scythe and a skull," he told her. "It can be two bicycle policemen as easily, or be a bird. Or it can have a wide snout like a hyena."

It had moved up on him now, but it had no shape any more. It simply occupied space.

"Tell it to go away."

It did not go away but moved a little closer.

"You've got a hell of a breath," he told it. "You stinking bastard."

It moved up closer to him still and now he could not speak to it, and when it saw he could not speak it came a little closer, and now he tried to send it away without speaking, but it moved in on him so its weight was all upon his chest, and while it crouched there and he could not move, or speak, he heard the woman say, "Bwana is asleep now. Take the cot up very gently and carry it into the tent."

He could not speak to tell her to make it go away and it crouched now, heavier, so he could not breathe. And then, while they lifted the cot, suddenly it was all right and the weight went from his chest.

It was morning and had been morning for some time and he heard the plane. It showed very tiny and then made a wide circle and the boys ran out and lit the fires, using kerosene, and piled on grass so there were two big smudges at each end of the level place and the morning breeze blew them toward the camp and the plane circled twice more, low this time, and then glided down and leveled off and landed smoothly and, coming walking toward him, was old Compton in slacks, a tweed jacket and a brown felt hat.

"What's the matter, old cock?" Compton said.

"Bad leg," he told him. "Will you have some breakfast?"

"Thanks. I'll just have some tea. It's the Puss Moth, you know. I won't be able to take the Memsahib. There's only room for one. Your lorry is on the way."

Helen had taken Compton aside and was speaking to him. Compton came back more cheery than ever.

"We'll get you right in," he said. "I'll be back for the Mem. Now I'm afraid I'll have to stop at Arusha to refuel. We'd better get going."

"What about the tea?"

"I don't really care about it, you know."

The boys had picked up the cot and carried it around the green tents and down along the rock and out onto the plain and along past the smudges that were burning brightly now, the grass all consumed, and the wind fanning the fire, to the little plane. It was difficult getting him in, but once in he lay back in the leather seat, and the leg was stuck straight out to one side of the seat, where Compton sat. Compton started the motor and got in. He waved to Helen and to the boys and, as the clatter moved into the old familiar roar, they swung around with Compie watching for wart-hog holes and roared, bumping, along the stretch between the fires and with the last bump rose and he saw them all standing below, waving, and the camp beside the hill, flattening now, and the plain spreading, clumps of trees, and the bush flattening, while the game trails ran now smoothly to the dry water holes, and there was a new water that he had never known of. The zebra, small rounded backs now, and the wildebeeste, bigheaded dots seeming to climb as they moved in long fingers across the plain, now scattering as the shadow came toward them, they were tiny now, and the movement had no gallop, and the plain was as far as you could see, gray yellow now and ahead old Compie's tweed back and the brown felt hat. Then they were over the first hills and the wildebeeste were trailing up them, and then they were over mountains with sudden depths of green-rising forest and the solid bamboo slopes, and then the heavy forest again, sculptured into peaks and hollows until they crossed, and hills sloped down and then another plain, hot now, and purple brown, bumpy with heat and Compie looking back to see how he was riding. Then there were other mountains dark ahead.

And then instead of going on to Arusha they turned left, he evidently figured that they had the gas, and looking down he saw a pink sifting cloud, moving over the ground, and in the air, like the first snow in a blizzard, that comes from nowhere, and he knew the locusts were coming up from the South. Then they began to climb and they were going to the East it seemed, and then it darkened and they were in a storm, the rain so thick it seemed like flying through a waterfall, and then they were out and Compie turned his head and grinned and pointed and there, ahead, all he could see, as wide as all the world, great, high, and un-

believably white in the sun, was the square top of Kilimanjaro. And then he knew that there was where he was going.

Just then the hyena stopped whimpering in the night and started to make a strange, human, almost crying sound. The woman heard it and stirred uneasily. She did not wake. In her dream she was at the house on Long Island and it was the night before her daughter's debut. Somehow her father was there and he had been very rude. Then the noise the hyena made was so loud she woke and for a moment she did not know where she was and she was very afraid. Then she took the flashlight and shone it on the other cot that they had carried in after Harry had gone to sleep. She could see his bulk under the mosquito bar but somehow he had gotten his leg out and it hung down alongside the cot. The dressings had all come down and she could not look at it.

"Molo," she called, "Molo! Molo!"

Then she said, "Harry, Harry!" Then her voice rising, "Harry! Please, Oh Harry!"

There was no answer and she could not hear him breathing.

Outside the tent the hyena made the same strange noise that had awakened her. But she did not hear him for the beating of her heart.

John Steinbeck
1902-

WHEN so many young men were going Hemingway or involving themselves in their egos like Sherwood Anderson, John Steinbeck was making himself part of his healthful, wholesome California. The mountains around Monterey and the wide stretches of the fertile Salinas valley are his country. Here he has lived most of his life, and it is about this land and its people that he writes. He likes the bizarre Mexican-American folk scene and has pictured it in *Tortilla Flat* and *Cannery Row*. He worries about social and labor problems (*In Dubious Battle*), and romanticizes about the transient ranch worker (*Of Mice and Men*). When hard time drove the Okies into California, he immortalized them in *The Grapes of Wrath*, the finest novel about the Great Depression. But best of all, to many minds, are his stories in *The Long Valley* and *The Red Pony*, about simple, elemental people living in the hills: the pioneer grandfather in "The Leader of the People" is one of these. He received the Nobel Prize for Literature in 1962 for *The Winter of Our Discontent*.

The Leader of the People

BY JOHN STEINBECK

ON SATURDAY afternoon Billy Buck, the ranch hand, raked together the last of the old year's haystack and pitched small forkfuls over the wire fence to a few mildly interested cattle. High in the air small clouds like puffs of cannon smoke were driven eastward by the March wind. The wind could be heard whishing in the brush on the ridge crests, but no breath of it penetrated down into the ranch cup.

The little boy, Jody, emerged from the house eating a thick piece of buttered bread. He saw Billy working on the last of the haystack. Jody tramped down scuffing his shoes in a way he had been told was destructive to good shoe leather. A flock of white pigeons flew out of the black cypress tree as Jody passed, and circled the tree and landed again. A half-grown tortoiseshell cat leaped from the bunkhouse porch, galloped on stiff legs across the road, whirled and galloped back again. Jody picked up a stone to help the game along, but he was too late, for the cat was under the porch before the stone could be discharged. He threw the stone into the cypress tree and started the white pigeons on another whirling flight.

Arriving at the used-up haystack, the boy leaned against the barbed-wire fence. "Will that be all of it, do you think?" he asked.

The middle-aged ranch hand stopped his careful raking and stuck his fork into the ground. He took off his black hat and smoothed down his hair. "Nothing left of it that isn't soggy from ground moisture," he said. He replaced his hat and rubbed his dry leathery hands together.

"Ought to be plenty mice," Jody suggested.

"Lousy with them," said Billy. "Just crawling with mice."

"Well, maybe, when you get all through, I could call the dogs and hunt the mice."

"Sure, I guess you could," said Billy Buck. He lifted a forkful of the damp ground hay and threw it into the air. Instantly three mice leaped out and burrowed frantically under the hay again.

Jody sighed with satisfaction. Those plump, sleek, arrogant mice were doomed. For eight months they had lived and multiplied in the haystack. They had been immune from cats, from traps, from poison and from Jody. They had grown smug in their security, overbearing and fat. Now the time of disaster had come; they would not survive another day.

Billy looked up at the top of the hills that surrounded the ranch. "Maybe you better ask your father before you do it," he suggested.

"Well, where is he? I'll ask him now."

"He rode up to the ridge ranch after dinner. He'll be back pretty soon."

Jody slumped against the fence post. "I don't think he'd care."

As Billy went back to his work he said ominously, "You'd better ask him anyway. You know how he is."

Jody did know. His father, Carl Tiflin, insisted upon giving permission for anything that was done on the ranch, whether it was important or not. Jody sagged farther against the post until he was sitting on the ground. He looked up at the little puffs of wind-driven cloud. "Is it like to rain, Billy?"

"It might. The wind's good for it, but not strong enough."

"Well, I hope it don't rain until after I kill those damn mice." He looked over his shoulder to see whether Billy had noticed the mature profanity. Billy worked on without comment.

Jody turned back and looked at the sidehill where the road from the outside world came down. The hill was washed with lean March sunshine. Silver thistles, blue lupins and a few poppies bloomed among the sagebushes. Halfway up the hill Jody could see Doubletree Mutt, the black dog, digging in a squirrel hole. He paddled for a while and then paused to kick bursts of dirt out between his hind legs, and he dug with an earnestness which belied the knowledge he must have had that no dog had ever caught a squirrel by digging in a hole.

Suddenly, while Jody watched, the black dog stiffened, and backed out of the hole and looked up the hill toward the cleft in the ridge where the road came through. Jody looked up too. For a moment Carl Tiflin on horseback stood out against the pale sky and then he moved down the road toward the house. He carried something white in his hand.

The boy started to his feet. "He's got a letter," Jody cried. He trotted away toward the ranch house, for the letter would probably be read aloud and he wanted to be there. He reached the house before his father did, and ran in. He heard Carl dismount from his creaking saddle and slap the horse on the side to send it to the barn where Billy would unsaddle it and turn it out.

Jody ran into the kitchen. "We got a letter!" he cried.

His mother looked up from a pan of beans. "Who has?"

"Father has. I saw it in his hand."

Carl strode into the kitchen then, and Jody's mother asked, "Who's the letter from, Carl?"

He frowned quickly. "How did you know there was a letter?"

She nodded her head in the boy's direction. "Big-Britches Jody told me."

Jody was embarrassed.

His father looked down at him contemptuously. "He *is* getting to be a Big-Britches," Carl said. "He's minding everybody's business but his own. Got his big nose into everything."

Mrs. Tiflin relented a little. "Well, he hasn't enough to keep him busy. Who's the letter from?"

Carl still frowned on Jody. "I'll keep him busy if he isn't careful." He held out a sealed letter. "I guess it's from your father."

Mrs. Tiflin took a hairpin from her head and slit open the flap. Her lips pursed judiciously. Jody saw her eyes snap back and forth over the lines. "He says," she translated, "he says he's going to drive out Saturday to stay for a little while. Why, this is Saturday. The letter must have been delayed." She looked at the postmark. "This was mailed day before yesterday. It should have been here yesterday." She looked up questioningly at her husband, and then her face darkened angrily. "Now what have you got that look on you for? He doesn't come often."

Carl turned his eyes away from her anger. He could be stern with her most of the time, but when occasionally her temper arose, he could not combat it.

"What's the matter with you?" she demanded again.

In his explanation there was a tone of apology Jody himself might have used. "It's just that he talks," Carl said lamely. "Just talks."

"Well, what of it? You talk yourself."

"Sure I do. But your father only talks about one thing."

"Indians!" Jody broke in excitedly. "Indians and crossing the plains!"

Carl turned fiercely on him. "You get out, Mr. Big-Britches! Go on, now! Get out!"

Jody went miserably out the back door and closed the screen with elaborate quietness. Under the kitchen window his shamed, downcast eyes fell upon a curiously shaped stone, a stone of such fascination that he squatted down and picked it up and turned it over in his hands.

The voices came clearly to him through the open kitchen window. "Jody's damn well right," he heard his father say. "Just Indians and crossing the plains. I've heard that story about how the horses got driven off about a thousand times.

He just goes on and on, and he never changes a word in the things he tells."

When Mrs. Tiflin answered her tone was so changed that Jody, outside the window, looked up from his study of the stone. Her voice had become soft and explanatory. Jody knew how her face would have changed to match the tone. She said quietly, "Look at it this way, Carl. That was the big thing in my father's life. He led a wagon train clear across the plains to the coast, and when it was finished, his life was done. It was a big thing to do, but it didn't last long enough. Look!" she continued, "it's as though he was born to do that, and after he finished it, there wasn't anything more for him to do but think about it and talk about it. If there'd been any farther west to go, he'd have gone. He's told me so himself. But at last there was the ocean. He lives right by the ocean where he had to stop."

She had caught Carl, caught him and entangled him in her soft tone.

"I've seen him," he agreed quietly. "He goes down and stares off west over the ocean." His voice sharpened a little. "And then he goes up to the Horseshoe Club in Pacific Grove, and he tells people how the Indians drove off the horses."

She tried to catch him again. "Well, it's everything to him. You might be patient with him and pretend to listen."

Carl turned impatiently away. "Well, if it gets too bad, I can always go down to the bunkhouse and sit with Billy," he said irritably. He walked through the house and slammed the front door after him.

Jody ran to his chores. He dumped the grain to the chickens without chasing any of them. He gathered the eggs from the nests. He trotted into the house with the wood and interlaced it so carefully in the wood box that two armloads seemed to fill it to overflowing.

His mother had finished the beans by now. She stirred up the fire and brushed off the stove top with a turkey wing. Jody peered cautiously at her to see whether any rancor toward him remained. "Is he coming today?" Jody asked.

"That's what his letter said."

"Maybe I better walk up the road to meet him."

Mrs. Tiflin clanged the stove lid shut. "That would be nice," she said. "He'd probably like to be met."

"I guess I'll just do it then."

Outside, Jody whistled shrilly to the dogs. "Come on up the hill," he commanded. The two dogs waved their tails and ran ahead. Along the roadside the sage had tender new tips. Jody tore off some pieces and rubbed them on his hands until the air was filled with the sharp wild smell. With a rush the dogs leaped from the road and yapped into the brush after a rabbit. That was the last Jody saw of them, for when they failed to catch the rabbit, they went back home.

Jody plodded on up the hill toward the ridge top. When he reached the little cleft where the road came through, the afternoon wind struck him and blew up his hair and ruffled his shirt. He looked down on the little hills and ridges below and then out at the huge green Salinas Valley. He could see the white town of Salinas far out in the flat and the flash of its windows under the waning sun. Directly below him, in an oak tree, a crow congress had convened. The tree was black with crows all cawing at once.

Then Jody's eyes followed the wagon road down from the ridge where he stood, and lost it behind a hill, and picked it up again on the other side. On that distant stretch he saw a cart slowly pulled by a bay horse. It disappeared behind the hill. Jody sat down on the ground and watched the place where the cart would reappear again. The wind sang on the hilltops and the puff-ball clouds hurried eastward.

Then the cart came into sight and stopped. A man dressed in black dismounted from the seat and walked to the horse's head. Although it was so far away, Jody knew he had unhooked the checkrein, for the horse's head dropped forward. The horse moved on, and the man walked slowly up the hill beside it. Jody gave a glad cry and ran down the road toward them. The squirrels bumped along off the road, and a road runner flirted its tail and raced over the edge of the hill and sailed out like a glider.

Jody tried to leap into the middle of his shadow at every step. A stone rolled under his foot and he went down. Around a little bend he raced, and there, a short distance ahead, were his grandfather and the cart. The boy dropped from his unseemly running and approached at a dignified walk.

The horse plodded stumble-footedly up the hill and the old man walked beside it. In the lowering sun their giant shadows flickered darkly behind them. The grandfather was dressed in a black broadcloth suit and he wore kid congress gaiters and a black tie on a short, hard collar. He carried his black slouch hat in his hand. His white beard was cropped close and his white eyebrows overhung his eyes like mustaches. The blue eyes were sternly merry. About the whole face and figure there was a granite dignity, so that every motion seemed an impossible thing. Once at rest, it seemed the old man would be stone, would never move again. His steps were slow and certain. Once made, no step could ever be retraced; once headed in a direction, the path would never bend nor the pace increase nor slow.

When Jody appeared around the bend, Grandfather waved his hat slowly in welcome, and he called, "Why, Jody! Come down to meet me, have you?"

Jody sidled near and turned and matched his step to the old man's step and stiffened his body and dragged his heels a little. "Yes, sir," he said. "We got your letter only today."

"Should have been here yesterday," said Grandfather. "It certainly should. How are all the folks?"

"They're fine, sir." He hesitated and then suggested shyly, "Would you like to come on a mouse hunt tomorrow, sir?"

"Mouse hunt, Jody?" Grandfather chuckled. "Have the people of this generation come down to hunting mice? They aren't very strong, the new people, but I hardly thought mice would be game for them."

"No, sir. It's just play. The haystack's gone. I'm going to drive out the mice to the dogs. And you can watch, or even beat the hay a little."

The stern, merry eyes turned down on him. "I see. You don't eat them, then. You haven't come to that yet."

Jody explained, "The dogs eat them, sir. It wouldn't be much like hunting Indians, I guess."

"No, not much—but then later, when the troops were hunting Indians and shooting children and burning teepees, it wasn't much different from your mouse hunt."

They topped the rise and started down into the ranch cup, and they lost the sun from their shoulders. "You've grown," Grandfather said. "Nearly an inch, I should say."

"More," Jody boasted. "Where they mark me on the door, I'm up more than an inch since Thanksgiving even."

Grandfather's rich throaty voice said, "Maybe you're getting too much water and turning to pith and stalk. Wait until you head out, and then we'll see."

Jody looked quickly into the old man's face to see whether his feelings should be hurt, but there was no will to injure, no punishing nor putting-in-your-place light in the keen blue eyes. "We might kill a pig," Jody suggested.

"Oh, no! I couldn't let you do that. You're just humoring me. It isn't the time and you know it."

"You know Riley, the big boar, sir?"

"Yes. I remember Riley well."

"Well, Riley ate a hole into that same haystack, and it fell down on him and smothered him."

"Pigs do that when they can," said Grandfather.

"Riley was a nice pig, for a boar, sir. I rode him sometimes, and he didn't mind."

A door slammed at the house below them, and they saw Jody's mother standing on the porch waving her apron in welcome. And they saw Carl Tiflin walking up from the barn to be at the house for the arrival.

The sun had disappeared from the hills by now. The blue smoke from the house chimney hung in flat layers in the purpling ranch cup. The puff-ball clouds, dropped by the falling wind, hung listlessly in the sky.

Billy Buck came out of the bunkhouse and flung a wash basin of soapy water on the ground. He had been shaving in mid-week, for Billy held Grandfather in reverence, and Grandfather said that Billy was one of the few men of the new generation who had not gone soft. Although Billy was in middle age, Grandfather considered him a boy. Now Billy was hurrying toward the house too.

When Jody and Grandfather arrived, the three were waiting for them in front of the yard gate.

Carl said, "Hello, sir. We've been looking for you."

Mrs. Tiflin kissed Grandfather on the side of his beard, and stood still while his big hand patted her shoulder. Billy shook hands solemnly, grinding under his straw mustache. "I'll put up your horse," said Billy, and he led the rig away.

Grandfather watched him go, and then, turning back to the group, he said as he had said a hundred times before, "There's a good boy. I knew his father, old Mule-tail Buck. I never knew why they called him Mule-tail except he packed mules."

Mrs. Tiflin turned and led the way into the house. "How long are you going to stay, Father? Your letter didn't say."

"Well, I don't know. I thought I'd stay about two weeks. But I never stay as long as I think I'm going to."

In a short while they were sitting at the white oilcloth table eating their supper. The lamp with the tin reflector hung over the table. Outside the dining-room windows the big moths battered softly against the glass.

Grandfather cut his steak into tiny pieces and chewed slowly. "I'm hungry," he said. "Driving out here got my appetite up. It's like when

we were crossing. We all got so hungry every night we could hardly wait to let the meat get done. I could eat about five pounds of buffalo meat every night."

"It's moving around does it," said Billy. "My father was a government packer. I helped him when I was a kid. Just the two of us could about clean up a deer's ham."

"I knew your father, Billy," said Grandfather. "A fine man he was. They called him Mule-tail Buck. I don't know why except he packed mules."

"That was it," Billy agreed. "He packed mules."

Grandfather put down his knife and fork and looked around the table. "I remember one time we ran out of meat——" His voice dropped to a curious low singsong, dropped into a tonal groove the story had worn for itself. "There was no buffalo, no antelope, not even rabbits. The hunters couldn't even shoot a coyote. That was the time for the leader to be on the watch. I was the leader, and I kept my eyes open. Know why? Well, just the minute the people began to get hungry they'd start slaughtering the team oxen. Do you believe that? I've heard of parties that just ate up their draft cattle. Started from the middle and worked toward the ends. Finally they'd eat the lead pair, and then the wheelers. The leader of a party had to keep them from doing that."

In some manner a big moth got into the room and circled the hanging kerosene lamp. Billy got up and tried to clap it between his hands. Carl struck with a cupped palm and caught the moth and broke it. He walked to the window and dropped it out.

"As I was saying," Grandfather began again, but Carl interrupted him. "You'd better eat some more meat. All the rest of us are ready for our pudding."

Jody saw a flash of anger in his mother's eyes. Grandfather picked up his knife and fork. "I'm pretty hungry, all right," he said. "I'll tell you about that later."

When supper was over, when the family and Billy Buck sat in front of the fireplace in the other room, Jody anxiously watched Grandfather. He saw the signs he knew. The bearded head leaned forward; the eyes lost their sternness and looked wonderingly into the fire; the big lean fingers laced themselves on the black knees. "I wonder," he began, "I just wonder whether I ever told you how those thieving Piutes drove off thirty-five of our horses."

"I think you did," Carl interrupted. "Wasn't it just before you went up into the Tahoe country?"

Grandfather turned quickly toward his son-in-law. "That's right. I guess I must have told you that story."

"Lots of times," Carl said cruelly, and he avoided his wife's eyes. But he felt the angry eyes on him, and he said, " 'Course I'd like to hear it again."

Grandfather looked back at the fire. His fingers unlaced and laced again. Jody knew how he felt, how his insides were collapsed and empty. Hadn't Jody been called a Big-Britches that very afternoon? He arose to heroism and opened himself to the term Big-Britches again. "Tell about Indians," he said softly.

Grandfather's eyes grew stern again. "Boys always want to hear about Indians. It was a job for men, but boys want to hear about it. Well, let's see. Did I ever tell you how I wanted each wagon to carry a long iron plate?"

Everyone but Jody remained silent. Jody said, "No. You didn't."

"Well, when the Indians attacked, we always put the wagons in a circle and fought from between the wheels. I thought that if every wagon carried a long plate with rifle holes, the men could stand the plates on the outside of the wheels when the wagons were in the circle and they would be protected. It would save lives and that would make up for the extra weight of the iron. But of course the party wouldn't do it. No party had done it before and they couldn't see why they should go to the expense. They lived to regret it, too."

Jody looked at his mother, and knew from her expression that she was not listening at all. Carl picked at a callus on his thumb and Billy Buck watched a spider crawling up the wall.

Grandfather's tone dropped into its narrative groove again. Jody knew in advance exactly what words would fall. The story droned on, speeded up for the attack, grew sad over the wounds, struck a dirge at the burials on the great plains. Jody sat quietly watching Grandfather. The stern blue eyes were detached. He looked as though he were not very interested in the story himself.

When it was finished, when the pause had been politely respected as the frontier of the story, Billy Buck stood up and stretched and hitched his trousers. "I guess I'll turn in," he said. Then he faced Grandfather. "I've got an old powder horn and a cap and ball pistol down to the bunkhouse. Did I ever show them to you?"

Grandfather nodded slowly. "Yes, I think you did, Billy. Reminds me of a pistol I had when I was leading the people across." Billy stood politely until the little story was done, and then he said, "Good night," and went out of the house.

Carl Tiflin tried to turn the conversation then. "How's the country between here and Monterey? I've heard it's pretty dry."

"It is dry," said Grandfather. "There's not a drop of water in the Laguna Seca. But it's a long pull from '87. The whole country was powder then, and in '61 I believe all the coyotes starved to death. We had fifteen inches of rain this year."

"Yes, but it all came too early. We could do with some now." Carl's eye fell on Jody. "Hadn't you better be getting to bed?"

Jody stood up obediently. "Can I kill the mice in the old haystack, sir?"

"Mice? Oh! Sure, kill them all off. Billy said there isn't any good hay left."

Jody exchanged a secret and satisfying look with Grandfather. "I'll kill every one tomorrow," he promised.

Jody lay in his bed and thought of the impossible world of Indians and buffaloes, a world that had ceased to be forever. He wished he could have been living in the heroic time, but he knew he was not of heroic timber. No one living now, save possibly Billy Buck, was worthy to do the things that had been done. A race of giants had lived then, fearless men, men of a stanchness unknown in this day. Jody thought of the wide plains and of the wagons moving across like centipedes. He thought of Grandfather on a huge white horse, marshaling the people. Across his mind marched the great phantoms, and they marched off the earth and they were gone.

He came back to the ranch for a moment, then. He heard the dull rushing sound that space and silence make. He heard one of the dogs, out in the doghouse, scratching a flea and bumping his elbow against the floor with every stroke. Then the wind arose again and the black cypress groaned and Jody went to sleep.

He was up half an hour before the triangle sounded for breakfast. His mother was rattling the stove to make the flames roar when Jody went through the kitchen. "You're up early," she said. "Where are you going?"

"Out to get a good stick. We're going to kill the mice today."

"Who is 'we'?"

"Why, Grandfather and I."

"So you've got him in it. You always like to have someone in with you in case there's blame to share."

"I'll be right back," said Jody. "I just want to have a good stick ready for after breakfast."

He closed the screen door after him and went out into the cool blue morning. The birds were noisy in the dawn and the ranch cats came down from the hill like blunt snakes. They had been hunting gophers in the dark, and although the four cats were full of gopher meat, they sat in a semicircle at the back door and mewed piteously for milk. Doubletree Mutt and Smasher moved sniffing along the edge of the brush, performing the duty with rigid ceremony, but when Jody whistled, their heads jerked up and their tails waved. They plunged down to him, wriggling their skins and yawning. Jody patted their heads seriously, and moved on to the weathered scrap pile. He selected an old broom handle and a short piece of inch-square scrap wood. From his pocket he took a shoelace and tied the ends of the sticks loosely together to make a flail. He whistled his new weapon through the air and struck the ground experimentally, while the dogs leaped aside and whined with apprehension.

Jody turned and started down past the house toward the old haystack ground to look over the field of slaughter, but Billy Buck, sitting patiently on the back steps, called to him, "You better come back. It's only a couple of minutes till breakfast."

Jody changed his course and moved toward the house. He leaned his flail against the steps. "That's to drive the mice out," he said. "I'll bet they're fat. I'll bet they don't know what's going to happen to them today."

"No, nor you either," Billy remarked philosophically, "nor me, nor anyone."

Jody was staggered by this thought. He knew it was true. His imagination twitched away from the mouse hunt. Then his mother came out on the back porch and struck the triangle, and all thoughts fell in a heap.

Grandfather hadn't appeared at the table when they sat down. Billy nodded at his empty chair. "He's all right? He isn't sick?"

"He takes a long time to dress," said Mrs. Tiflin. "He combs his whiskers and rubs up his shoes and brushes his clothes."

Carl scattered sugar on his mush. "A man that's led a wagon train across the plains has got to be pretty careful how he dresses."

Mrs. Tiflin turned on him. "Don't do that, Carl! Please don't!" There was more of threat than of request in her tone. And the threat irritated Carl.

"Well, how many times do I have to listen to the story of the iron plates, and the thirty-five horses? That time's done. Why can't he forget it, now it's done?" He grew angrier while he talked, and his voice rose. "Why does he have to tell them over and over? He came across the plains. All right! Now it's finished. Nobody wants to hear about it over and over."

The door into the kitchen closed softly. The four at the table sat frozen. Carl laid his mush spoon on the table and touched his chin with his fingers.

Then the kitchen door opened and Grandfather walked in. His mouth smiled tightly and his eyes were squinted. "Good morning," he said, and he sat down and looked at his mush dish.

Carl could not leave it there. "Did —did you hear what I said?"

Grandfather jerked a little nod.

"I don't know what got into me, sir. I didn't mean it. I was just being funny."

Jody glanced in shame at his mother, and he saw that she was looking at Carl, and that she wasn't breathing. It was an awful thing that he was doing. He was tearing himself to pieces to talk like that. It was a terrible thing to him to retract a word, but to retract it in shame was infinitely worse.

Grandfather looked sidewise. "I'm trying to get right side up," he said gently. "I'm not being mad. I don't mind what you said, but it might be true, and I would mind that."

"It isn't true," said Carl. "I'm not feeling well this morning. I'm sorry I said it."

"Don't be sorry, Carl. An old man doesn't see things sometimes. Maybe you're right. The crossing is finished. Maybe it should be forgotten, now it's done."

Carl got up from the table. "I've

had enough to eat. I'm going to work. Take your time, Billy!" He walked quickly out of the dining room. Billy gulped the rest of his food and followed soon after. But Jody could not leave his chair.

"Won't you tell any more stories?" Jody asked.

"Why, sure I'll tell them, but only when—I'm sure people want to hear them."

"I like to hear them, sir."

"Oh! Of course you do, but you're a little boy. It was a job for men, but only little boys like to hear about it."

Jody got up from his place. "I'll wait outside for you, sir. I've got a good stick for those mice."

He waited by the gate until the old man came out on the porch. "Let's go down and kill the mice now," Jody called.

"I think I'll just sit in the sun, Jody. You go kill the mice."

"You can use my stick if you like."

"No, I'll just sit here awhile."

Jody turned disconsolately away, and walked down toward the old haystack. He tried to whip up his enthusiasm with thoughts of the fat juicy mice. He beat the ground with his flail. The dogs coaxed and whined about him, but he could not go. Back at the house he could see Grandfather sitting on the porch, looking small and thin and black.

Jody gave up and went to sit on the steps at the old man's feet.

"Back already? Did you kill the mice?"

"No, sir. I'll kill them some other day."

The morning flies buzzed close to the ground and the ants dashed about in front of the steps. The heavy smell of sage slipped down the hill. The porch boards grew warm in the sunshine.

Jody hardly knew when Grandfather started to talk. "I shouldn't stay here, feeling the way I do." He examined his strong old hands. "I feel as though the crossing wasn't worth doing." His eyes moved up the sidehill and stopped on a motionless hawk perched on a dead limb. "I tell those old stories, but they're not what I want to tell. I only know how I want people to feel when I tell them.

"It wasn't Indians that were important, nor adventures, nor even getting out here. It was a whole bunch of people made into one big crawling beast. And I was the head. It was westering and westering. Every man wanted something for himself, but the big beast that was all of them wanted only westering. I was the leader, but if I hadn't been there, someone else would have been the head. The thing had to have a head.

"Under the little bushes the shadows were black at white noonday. When we saw the mountains at last, we cried—all of us. But it wasn't getting here that mattered, it was movement and westering.

"We carried life out here and set it down the way those ants carry eggs. And I was the leader. The westering was as big as God, and the slow steps that made the movement piled up and piled up until the continent was crossed.

"Then we came down to the sea, and it was done." He stopped and wiped his eyes until the rims were red. "That's what I should be telling instead of stories."

When Jody spoke, Grandfather started and looked down at him. "Maybe I could lead the people someday," Jody said.

The old man smiled. "There's no place to go. There's the ocean to stop you. There's a line of old men along the shore hating the ocean because it stopped them."

"In boats I might, sir."

"No place to go, Jody. Every place is taken. But that's not the worst—no, not the worst. Westering has died out of the people. Westering isn't a hunger any more. It's all done. Your father is right. It is finished." He laced his fingers on his knee and looked at them.

Jody felt very sad. "If you'd like a glass of lemonade I could make it for you."

Grandfather was about to refuse, and then he saw Jody's face. "That would be nice," he said. "Yes, it would be nice to drink a lemonade."

Jody ran into the kitchen where his mother was wiping the last of the breakfast dishes. "Can I have a lemon to make a lemonade for Grandfather?"

His mother mimicked—"And another lemon to make a lemonade for you."

"No, ma'am. I don't want one."

"Jody! You're sick!" Then she stopped suddenly. "Take a lemon out of the cooler," she said softly. "Here, I'll reach the squeezer down to you."

John O'Hara
1905-

THE short stories of *The New Yorker,* born of Hemingway and grown to manhood in the Depression, have—in the course of fifty-two issues a year since then—worn themselves a niche quite their own. They are tight, economical, crisp stories. To a large extent they present the civilized and sophisticated judgment of the few on the helpless, the average, and the small-time majority. They spotlight foibles and note with sharp ears subtle giveaways in speech.

John O'Hara, master of this expert technique, is one of the outstanding writers who first achieved recognition in *The New Yorker.* His are stories of frustrated characters—theater ushers, grocery clerks, automobile salesmen—who are neither nice nor happy. O'Hara was born a Catholic, educated at Niagara Preparatory School, and was, in his early days, a soda clerk, a gas-meter reader, an amusement-park guard, a laborer in a steel mill, and secretary to Heywood Broun. He knows what it's all about. It is said that O'Hara wrote 25,000 words of his first novel in a furnished room in New York and then, reduced to his last nickel, sent what he had written to a publisher with a letter, and sold the book. It was *Appointment in Samarra.* Only a few years later he was living in a duplex apartment on one of New York's most expensive streets and commuting to Hollywood. . . . "Price's Always Open" appeared in *Files on Parade. Assembly,* a later collection of short stories, was published in 1961.

Price's Always Open

BY JOHN O'HARA

THE place where everybody would end up before going home was Price's. This was the second summer for Price's. Before that it had been a diner and an eyesore. The last man to run the diner had blown town owing everybody, and somehow or other that had put a curse on the place. No one, not even the creditors, wanted to open up again, and time and the weather got at the diner and for two years it had stood there, the windows all smashed by passing schoolboys, the paint gone, and the diner itself sagging in the middle like an old work horse. Then last summer Mr. Price got his bonus and he went into the all-night-restaurant business.

The first thing he did was to get permission to tear down the diner and put up his own place. It was a corner plot, and he built his place twice as wide as the diner had been. The Village Fathers were only too glad to have Mr. Price build. In other times they never would have let the place go the way the diner had. The neatness of the village was always commented upon by new summer people and bragged about by those who had been coming there for generations. But things being the way they were . . . So Mr. Price built a sort of rustic place, which, while not in keeping with the rest of the village architecture, was clean and attractive in its way. All the signboards were simulated shingles, and the lettering has been described as quaint. Mr. Price frankly admitted he got his idea from a chain of places in New York. There was one neon sign that stayed on all night, and it said, simply, PRICE'S. Nothing about what Price's was; everyone knew.

Mr. Price had one leg, having left the other somewhere in a dressing station back of Château Thierry. He was not a cook but a house painter, and he had had to employ a couple of short-order cooks from New York and Boston. But Mr. Price was always there. Not that anyone ever wondered about it, but it might have been interesting to find out just when he slept. He was at his position near the cash register all night, and he certainly was there at noon when the chauffeurs and a few summer-hotel clerks and people like that would come in for lunch. As a matter of fact, he did not need much sleep. No day passed without his leg bothering him, and seeing people took his mind off his leg. Best of all, he liked late at night.

Saturday night there was always a dance at the yacht club. That was a very late crowd. The dances were supposed to stop at one, but if the stricter older members had gone home, the young people would keep the orchestra for another hour or two, and even after that they would hang around while one of the boys played the piano. The boy who played the piano was Jackie Girard.

They were a nice bunch of kids, practically all of them, and Mr. Price had known their fathers and mothers for years, or many of them. Sometimes the wife's family had been coming to this island for years and years; then she married the husband, a stranger, and the husband and wife would start coming here and keep coming. Sometimes it was the husband who was old summer people. Most of the present younger crowd had been coming here every summer for fifteen, twenty years. One or two of them had been born here. But Jackie Girard was Mr. Price's favorite. He was born here, and unlike the others, he lived here all year round.

Jackie had a strange life with the summer people, and it probably was that that made Mr. Price feel closer to him than to the others. The others were nice and respectful, and they always said *Mister* Price, just as Jackie did. But they were summer people, and the winters were long. Not that Jackie was here in the winter any more, but at least he came home several times in the winter. Jackie was at college at Holy Cross, and naturally his holidays were spent here.

The strange life that Jackie had apparently did not seem strange to him. Jackie's father was a carpenter, the best in the village; the best out of three, it's true, but head and shoulders above the other two. Henry Girard was a French Canuck and had been in the Twenty-sixth Division with Mr. Price, but never an intimate of Mr. Price's. Jackie had three sisters; one older, two younger, Jackie's mother played the organ in the Catholic church. The older sister was married and lived in Worcester, and the younger ones were in high school. Anyway, Jackie was not a member of the yacht club, but he was almost always sure of being invited to one of the dinners before the regular Saturday-night dance. He was one of the clerks at the hotel, and that, plus an occasional five or ten from his sister in Worcester, gave him just enough money to pay for gas and his incidental expenses. He could hold his end up. The only trouble was, except for Saturday and Sunday, he did not have much end to hold up.

There were gatherings, if not parties, practically every night of the week. Every Thursday, for instance, the large group of young people would split up into smaller groups, sometimes three, four, five, and after dinner they would go to the boxing matches. Jackie was not invited to these small dinner parties. He had been invited two or three times, but his mother had told him he had better not go. For herself, she wished he could have gone, but his father would not have approved. After Jackie had regretted the few invitations he got, the summer people figured it out that all he cared about was the yacht-club dances. He was the only town boy who was invited to the yacht-club dances, and they figured that that was all he wanted. It did not take them long to decide that this was as it should be all around. They decided that Jackie would feel embarrassed at the smaller parties, but that he did not need to feel embarrassed at the club dances, because in a sense he was earning his way by playing such perfectly marvelous piano. But this was not the way Mr. Price saw it.

Almost every night but Saturday Jackie would drop in. Two nights a week he had been to the movies, which changed twice a week, but Mr. Price at first wondered what Jackie would do to kill time the other nights. Jackie would show up around eleven-thirty and sit at the counter until some of the summer crowd began to arrive. They would yell at him, "Hi, Jackie! Hi, keed! How's it, Jackie?" And Jackie would swing around on his stool, and they would yell at him to come on over and sit at a table with them. And he would sit at the table with whichever group arrived first. In the early part of the summer that did not mean any special group, because when the other groups would arrive, they would put all the tables together and form one party. Then there would be some bickering about the bill, and more than once Mr. Price saw Jackie grab the check for the whole party. It was not exactly a big check; you could not eat much more than forty cents' worth at Mr. Price's without making a pig of yourself, and the usual order was a cereal, half-milk-half-cream, and a cup of coffee; total, twenty cents. But you take fourteen ot those orders and you have a day's pay for Jackie.

As the summer passed, however, the large group did break into well-defined smaller groups; one of six, several of four. By August there would be the same foursomes every night, and of these one included the Leech girl.

The Leeches were not old people in the sense that some of them were.

The Leeches belonged to the newcomers who first summered in this place in 1930 and 1931. They had come from one of the more famous resorts. Louise Leech was about twelve when her family first began to come to this place. But now she was eighteen or nineteen. She had a Buick convertible coupé. She was a New York girl, whereas most of the other boys and girls were not New Yorkers; they all went to the same schools and colleges, but they did not come from the same home towns. Some came from as far west as Denver, as Mr. Price knew from cashing their checks. And even what few New York girls did come to this place were not New York friends of the Leeches. Mr. Leech was here only on week ends and his wife was away most of the time, visiting friends who had not had to give up Narragansett. Louise herself was away a good deal of the time.

It was easy to see, the first summer Louise was grown up, that she was discontented. She did not quite fit in with the rest of the crowd, and she not only knew it but she was content not to make the best of it. Mr. Price could hear the others, the first summer he was in business, making remarks about Louise and her thinking she was too good for this place. And they had been saying something like it in the early part of this summer, too. But after the Fourth of July, somewhere around there, they began to say better things about her. Mostly they said she really wasn't so bad when you got to know her. To which a few of the girls said, "Who wants to?" And others said, "She doesn't like us any better. We're still not good enough for her. But Sandy is." Which did explain a lot.

Sandy—Sandy Hall—was from

Chicago, but what with prep school and college and this place and vacation trips, he probably had not spent a hundred days in Chicago in the last seven years. In a bathing suit he was almost skinny, except for his shoulders; he looked cold, he was so thin. But Mr. Price had seen him in action one night when one of the Portuguese fishermen came in drunk and got profane in a different way from the way the summer people did. Sandy had got up and let the Portuguese have two fast hard punches in the face, and the fisherman went down and stayed down. Sandy looked at the man on the floor —it was hard to tell how long he looked at him—and suddenly he kicked him. The man was already out, and so there was no need to kick him, but the kick had several results. One was that Mr. Price brought a blackjack to work the next night. The other result was something Mr. Price noticed on Louise's face.

He had not had much time to take it all in, as he had had to leave the cash register to help the night counterman drag the fisherman out of the place. But he remembered the expression on the girl's face. It began to appear when the fisherman went down from the punches, and when Sandy kicked the man, it was all there. Mr. Price, standing where he did, was the only one who caught it. He thought of it later as the way a girl would look the first time she saw Babe Ruth hit a home run, provided she cared about home runs. Or the way she would look if someone gave her a bucketful of diamonds. And other ways, that would come with experiences that Mr. Price was sure Louise never had had.

Sandy had not come with Louise that night, but Mr. Price noticed she went home with him. And after that

night they were always together. They were part of a foursome of whom the other two were the dullest young people in the crowd. It took Mr. Price some time to determine why this was, but eventually he did figure it. The foursome would come into Price's and Louise and Sandy would watch the others while they ordered; then Sandy would say he and Louise wanted the same, and from then on neither Sandy nor Louise would pay any attention to the other two. Stooges.

Another thing that Mr. Price noticed was that Jackie could not keep his eyes off Louise.

Along about the latter part of August, it was so obvious that one night Mr. Price kidded Jackie about it. It was one of the nights Jackie dropped in by himself, and Mr. Price said. "Well, she isn't here yet."

"Who isn't here?"

"The Leech girl."

"Oh," said Jackie. "Why, did anybody say anything to you? Is that how you knew I liked her?"

"No. Figured it out for myself. I have eyes."

"You're a regular Walter Winchell. But don't say anything, Mr. Price."

"What the hell would I say, and who to?"

"I'll be back," said Jackie. He was gone for more than an hour, and when he returned the crowd was there. They all yelled as usual, but this time one of the girls added, "Jackie's tight." He was, rather. He had a somewhat silly grin on his face, and his nice teeth made a line from ear to ear. Several tables wanted him to join them and they were friendly about it. But he went to the table where sat Louise and Sandy and the others.

"Do you mind if I sit down?" he said.

"Do you mind?" said Sandy.

"No," said Louise.

"Thank you. Thank you," said Jackie. "Go fights?"

"Mm-hmm," said Sandy.

"Any good? Who won?"

"The nigger from New Bedford beat the townie," said Sandy. "Kicked the Jesus out of him."

"Oh, uh townie. You mean Bobbie Lawless. He's nice guy. Za friend of mine. I used to go to high school——"

"He's yellow," said Sandy.

"Certainly was," said Louise.

"Nope. Not yellow. Not Bobbie. I used to go to high school with Bobbie. Plain same football team."

"Where do you go to school now?" said Sandy.

"Holy Cross. We're gonna beat you this year."

"What is Holy Cross?" said Louise.

Sandy laughed. Jackie looked at her with tired eyes.

"No, really, what is it?"

" 'Tsa college. It's where I go to college. Dint you ever hear of Holy Cross? Give another hoya and a choo-choo rah rah——"

"O.K.," said Sandy.

"I'll sing if I wanta. I'll sing one of your songs. Oh, hit the line for Harvard, for Harvard wins today——"

"Oh, go away," said Sandy.

"Yes, for God's *sake*," said Louise.

"Oh, very well, Miss Leech. Very well." Jackie put his hands on the table to steady himself as he got to

his feet, but he stared down into her eyes and for two seconds he was sober.

"Come on, Jackie, you're stewed." Mr. Price had come around from the cash register and had taken Jackie by the right arm. At that moment Sandy lashed out with a right-hand punch, and Jackie fell down. But he had hardly reached the floor before Mr. Price snapped his blackjack from his pocket and slapped it down on the front of Sandy's head. Sandy went down and there was blood.

"Anybody else?" said Mr. Price. By this time the night counterman had swung himself over the counter, and in his hand was a baseball bat, all nicked where it had been used for tamping down ice around milk cans. None of the summer crowd made a move; then Mr. Price spoke to two of the young men. "Get your friend outa here, and get out, the whole goddam bunch of you." He stood where he was, he and the counterman, and watched the girls picking up their wraps.

"Aren't you going to do anything?" Louise screamed. "Chuck! Ted! All of you!"

"You get out or I'll throw you out," said Mr. Price. She left.

There were murmurs as well as the sounds of the cars starting. Thinking it over, Mr. Price agreed with himself that those would be the last sounds he ever expected to hear from the summer crowd.

Jerome Weidman

1913-

BORN a New Yorker, educated in New York, his youthful world bounded by the Lower East Side and the Bronx, Jerome Weidman seldom writes of anything but the city streets. Probably no other living writer does a more complete job on the mean, the double-dealing, and the cheap. If a worthy figure chances into one of his tales—and one does in "The Tuxedos" —he is at once used, pounced upon by those slicker and smarter than himself. Weidman writes with complete objectivity, but the choice of his victims shows the passion of his indignation. The humor of the Garment Center, Broadway, and Tin Pan Alley makes his stories amusing reading in spite of their bitterness. His most recent collection of short stories, published in 1961, is called *My Father Sits in the Dark*.

The Tuxedos

BY JEROME WEIDMAN

EVER SINCE the time, some ten years
ago, when I worked for Mr. Brunschweig on Canal Street, I have been
peculiarly sensitive to the half-hour
of the day that comes between five-
thirty and six o'clock in the late afternoon. Mr. Brunschweig was an excellent boss, as bosses go, except for one
lamentable defect: he was a minute-
pincher. He carried two large pocket
watches and spent a good part of each
day comparing them with each other
and with the huge Seth Thomas on
the wall. I am certain that he was a
little terrified by the inexorableness of
time and that his sensitivity to it was
a direct result of the way he earned
his living. Mr. Brunschweig rented
tuxedos.

The tuxedo-renting business, as I
knew it, was distinguished by two
cardinal rules. First, the suits had
to be made of the toughest and
heaviest materials available. And
second, it was necessary to deliver
them as close to the moment of
wearing as possible and even more
imperative to pick them up as soon
after they were taken off as the
wearer would permit. Mr. Brunschweig's timing in this respect was
so good and I was so nimble as a
delivery boy that while many of his
customers cursed him roundly for

having delayed them in getting to a
wedding, not one of them could say
with honesty that he had worn a
Brunschweig tuxedo to more than
one affair for the price of a single
renting.

My relations with Mr. Brunschweig
were amicable if somewhat exhausting, but every day, as the hands of
the clock crept around to half-past
five, a definite tension would come
into the atmosphere. My quitting
time was six o'clock. As a general
rule, Mr. Brunschweig arranged
deliveries in such fashion that the
last one carried me up to, or past,
that hour. We had an understanding
to the effect that if I took out a
delivery at any time after five-thirty
and could not get to my destination
until six o'clock or a few minutes
before, I did not have to return to
the Canal Street store that night and
was at liberty to go directly home.
However, the possibility of his only
employee departing for home five or
ten mintues ahead of quitting time
was so disturbing to Mr. Brunschweig that very often he would detain me in the store before I went
out on my final delivery, talking
about the weather or discussing the
baseball scores, just to make sure

From *The Horse That Could Whistle Dixie* by Jerome Weidman, originally published in *The New
Yorker*. By permission of Simon and Schuster, Inc. Copyright, 1938, by Jerome Weidman.

that I could not possibly complete delivery before six o'clock.

Strangely enough, I did not resent these obvious subterfuges, because I sensed that Mr. Brunschweig was a little ashamed of them. What I did resent was that unconsciously I was being forced into practices I didn't approve of to combat him.

For instance, I would instinctively stall on any delivery after five-fifteen to make certain that I would not get back to the store in time to make another delivery before quitting. Or I would rush through a four-o'clock delivery to make sure that there would be ample time for still another one before six o'clock. In either case it was very unsettling, and scarcely a day went by that I didn't have a struggle with my conscience or the clock.

There were times, of course, when my energy overcame my caution. One day, in an industrious mood, I returned from an uptown delivery at twenty minutes to six. It had been a long trip and I could have stretched it for another twenty minutes with ease, but I had temporarily forgotten Mr. Brunschweig's vice and I did not realize my mistake until I came into the store. He was boxing an unusually large order, and I could tell from his cheery greeting that this one would carry me well past six o'clock. I was about to dismiss the occurrence as simply another occasion on which I had been out-maneuvered by Mr. Brunschweig when I saw that he had stacked six boxes, one on top of the other.

"Is that *one* delivery?" I asked in amazement.

The average delivery weighed well over ten pounds and consisted of a tuxedo, a shirt, a tie, studs, and a pair of patent-leather pumps, packed neatly into a heavy card-board box. Two or three of these boxes were a load. Six of them were an incredible amount.

"Yeah," he said cheerfully. "Italian wedding. It all goes to one family. I'll give you a help to the subway."

I should have been grateful to him for this offer, I suppose, since it was an unusual move, but all I could think of was the prospect of juggling sixty pounds of tuxedos through the subway in the rush hour.

"Where's it going?" I asked.

"Brooklyn," he said. "It's just over the bridge. Won't take you long."

The boxes weighed so much I could scarcely raise them from the floor.

"Here," he said. "You take the hats. I'll take the suits till we get to the train."

I hadn't even thought about top hats. They were not very heavy, but they were the most perishable items in Mr. Brunschweig's stock and consequently were always packed with great care in individual boxes.

"We gotta hurry," Mr. Brunschweig said, handing me a slip of paper with an address on it. "It's the bride's family and I promised them early. Name is Lasquadro."

He took the lashed tuxedo boxes and I took the pile of hatboxes, tied one on top of another so that they resembled a small steamship funnel. In the street we paused for a moment while he locked the store and then we started off down Canal Street to the subway station.

The only satisfactory recollection I have of that evening is the brief memory of Mr. Brunschweig tottering along in front of me under the weight of six boxes of tuxedos and accessories. The rest was a nightmare. I remember being on the subway platform, between my two huge bundles, trying to get into train after train. I had to let seven or eight go by before I could wedge my way into one of them. Then I remember standing, perspiring and exhausted, outside the subway station in Brooklyn, looking at the two bundles and realizing that I could carry them no further. It had grown quite dark and I began to be worried, too, about being late with the delivery. Finally I worked out a plan. I dragged the tuxedos along the ground for a short distance, then went back for the hats, dragged them up to the tuxedos, and then repeated the process. It was an effective method but an extremely slow one. Though the address Mr. Brunschweig had given me was only three blocks from the Brooklyn subway station, it was almost twenty minutes later that I stopped, breathless, in front of the correct house number.

The street was deserted and dark; the house was a two-story brownstone affair and only the basement windows showed lights from behind drawn shades. As I wiped the perspiration from my face and tried to think of an excuse for being so late, I heard noises coming from the basement. Figures kept passing the windows quickly and the sounds of scuffling and angry voices reached me clearly. I was frightened and spent another precious minute trying to puzzle out a way of leaving my bundles without having to face the people inside the house.

Then, in a burst of nervous courage, I tumbled the bulky bundles down the steps that led to the basement door and knocked gently. There was no answer. The angry noises inside continued, and I knocked again. Still no answer. Then I discovered a push button on the wall beside the door, jabbed at it hastily, and a bell pealed shrilly

somewhere inside the house. At once the door was pulled open and a small young man in shirt sleeves, with a tight, dark, scowling face, shot his head out and glared at me.

"What the hella *you* want?" he demanded harshly.

"The—the tuxedos," I said awkwardly. "I brought the tuxedos."

The young man turned his head and yelled at someone in the room behind him. "He brought the tuxedos! You hear that? He brought the tuxedos!"

He laughed unpleasantly and a man's voice replied from inside the room, "Tell him he knows what he can do with them!"

The young man in front of me reached for the door and started to slam it shut. The thought that I might have to drag those two bundles back to Canal Street that night was enough to make me forget my fright. I braced my shoulder against the door and held it open.

"I have to leave these here," I said quickly. "I have to—I have to get the receipt signed."

The little dark face glared at me and the hand on the door drew back threateningly. "Aah," he started to say, and then stopped. "O.K., O.K., come on. Bring 'em in and beat it."

He dragged the bundles in and the door swung shut behind me. As I began to fumble in my pocket for the receipt book, I stole a scared look at the scene in the room. It was a large, shabbily furnished living room, with a new radio in one corner, a huge potted rubber plant in another, and embroidered mottoes on the wall. A pretty, dark-haired girl in a white wedding gown was sitting at a table in the middle of the room. Five men, all in vests and shirt sleeves and all looking as if they must be brothers of the young man who had opened the door for me, were standing over her. One of the men held the girl and was twisting her arm behind her, and she was sobbing violently. A tiny old woman, with white hair in a knot at the back of her head and wearing a black alpaca apron, hovered on the outskirts of the group around the table, jabbering shrilly in Italian. The young man who had let me in joined his brothers. Nobody paid any attention to me.

"Come on," one of the men said, leaning over the girl. "What's his address? Give us that address!"

The girl shook her head and the man who was holding her arm gave it another twist. She screamed and dropped her head forward. Another man pushed his face down close to hers.

"Come on!" he yelled. "Give it to us. We're doing this for the family, ain't we? What's his address?"

The girl shook her head again; the little old lady chattered away. One of the brothers reached over and slapped the girl's face.

"Where was he when he called up?" he said. "Come on, tell us. We ain't gonna hurt him. We'll just murder the louse, that's all. Where was he?"

She didn't answer.

"Come on, you damn fool," the man who held her arm said. "Talk! You want him to go spreading it to the whole world he walked out on you an hour before the wedding?" He shook her angrily. "Where was he when he called up? Where does he live? We'll fix him so he won't talk. What's his address?"

The girl did not answer. He started to shake her again, then he saw me standing near the door. "Get that guy out of here," he said.

The brother who had let me in came across the room in three steps and grabbed my shoulder. "Come on, kid," he said. "Beat it!"

I lifted my receipt book in front of his face. "The receipt," I said. "I must get my receipt signed. I can't leave the——" He snatched the book from me and fumbled in his vest pocket for a pencil. He couldn't find one. I held my own out to him and he scribbled his name in my receipt book.

"O.K., kid," he said sharply. "Outside!" and he shoved the receipt book and pencil at me. I took them and started toward the door. Suddenly the little old lady grabbed my arm and pulled me back.

"What the hellsa matter?" the young man asked angrily.

She gestured violently toward me and poured a stream of Italian at him.

"All right, all right," he said, and reached into his pocket, pulled out a coin, and tossed the tip to me. I caught it and turned toward the door again.

"Thanks," I said quickly. But before I could open the door the old lady was on me. She clawed at my hand until I opened it so she could see the coin. It was a quarter. She swung around to the young man and clutched his coat.

"What the hellsa matter now?" he cried. "I gave him the tip, didn't I?"

Again she started talking in Italian, pointing at the bundle of tuxedos and tapping off the boxes with her finger—one, two, three, four, five, six. She waved six fingers in his face and yelled at him. He bit his lip, dug into his pocket again, and slapped some more coins into my palm. At once the little old lady seized my hand again. Now there were two quarters, a dime, and a nickel in it. She counted them quickly, snatched up the nickel, and counted again. Sixty cents remained. Another glance at the tuxedos and another glance at the two quarters and dime in my hand. Six tuxedos. Sixty cents. She nodded sharply to herself. Now it was all right.

"Give us that address!" shouted one of the brothers. There was the sound of a slap and the girl screamed again. "Where was he when he called up?"

The little old lady pulled open the door, pushed me out roughly, and slammed it shut behind me.

Irwin Shaw
1913-

ANOTHER New Yorker born and bred, Irwin Shaw is a big fellow who, while becoming a writer, was a truck driver, a semiprofessional football player, and a private in the army (he asked to be classified 1A); he also worked in a cosmetics factory, an installment furniture house, and department stores. But through all his jobs he kept writing as his objective. He has written novels, radio scripts and screen plays. He has had several plays produced on Broadway and has published five collections of short stories. one of the best of which is *Tip on a Dead Jockey.*

Act of Faith

BY IRWIN SHAW

"PRESENT it to him in a pitiful light," Olson was saying as they picked their way through the almost frozen mud toward the orderly-room tent. "Three combat-scarred veterans, who fought their way from Omaha Beach to . . . What was the name of the town we fought our way to?"

"Königstein," Seeger said.

"Königstein." Olson lifted his right foot heavily out of a puddle and stared admiringly at the three pounds of mud clinging to his overshoe. "The backbone of the Army. The noncommissioned officer. We deserve better of our country. Mention our decorations, in passing."

"What decorations should I mention?" Seeger asked. "The Marksman's Medal?"

"Never quite made it," Olson said. "I had a cross-eyed scorer at the butts. Mention the Bronze Star, the Silver Star, the Croix de Guerre with palms, the Unit Citation, the Congressional Medal of Honor."

"I'll mention them all." Seeger grinned. "You don't think the C.O.'ll notice that we haven't won most of them, do you?"

"Gad, sir," Olson said with dignity, "do you think that one Southern military gentleman will dare doubt the word of another Southern mili-tary gentleman in the hour of victory?"

"I come from Ohio," Seeger said.

"Welch comes from Kansas," Olson said, coolly staring down a second lieutenant who was passing. The lieutenant made a nervous little jerk with his hand, as though he expected a salute, then kept it rigid, as a slight, superior smile of scorn twisted at the corner of Olson's mouth. The lieutenant dropped his eyes and splashed on through the mud. "You've heard of Kansas," Olson said. "Magnolia-scented Kansas."

"Of course," said Seeger. "I'm no fool."

"Do your duty by your men, Sergeant." Olson stopped to wipe the cold rain off his face and lectured him. "Highest-ranking noncom present took the initiative and saved his comrades, at great personal risk, above and beyond the call of you-know-what, in the best traditions of the American Army."

"I will throw myself in the breach," Seeger said.

"Welch and I can't ask more," said Olson.

They walked heavily through the mud on the streets between the rows of tents. The camp stretched drearily over the Reims plain, with the rain beating on the sagging tents. The division had been there over three weeks, waiting to be shipped home, and all the meager diversions of the neighborhood had been sampled and exhausted, and there was an air of watchful suspicion and impatience with the military life hanging over the camp now, and there was even reputed to be a staff sergeant in C Company who was laying odds they would not get back to America before July 4th.

"I'm redeployable," Olson sang. "It's so enjoyable." It was a jingle he had composed, to no recognizable melody, in the early days after the victory in Europe, when he had added up his points and found they came to only sixty-three, but he persisted in singing it. He was a short, round boy who had been flunked out of air cadets' school and transferred to the infantry but whose spirits had not been damaged in the process. He had a high, childish voice and a pretty, baby face. He was very good-natured, and had a girl waiting for him at the University of California, where he intended to finish his course at government expense when he got out of the Army, and he was just the type who is killed off early and predictably and sadly in moving pictures about the war, but he had gone through four campaigns and six major battles without a scratch.

Seeger was a large, lanky boy, with a big nose, who had been wounded at St.-Lô but had come back to his outfit in the Siegfried Line quite unchanged. He was cheerful and dependable and he knew his business. He had broken in five or six second lieutenants, who had later been killed or wounded, and the C.O. had tried to

get him commissioned in the field, but the war had ended while the paperwork was being fumbled over at headquarters.

They reached the door of the orderly tent and stopped. "Be brave, Sergeant," Olson said. "Welch and I are depending on you."

"O.K.," Seeger said, and went in.

The tent had the dank, Army-canvas smell that had been so much a part of Seeger's life in the past three years. The company clerk was reading an October, 1945, issue of the Buffalo *Courier-Express*, which had just reached him, and Captain Taney, the company C.O., was seated at a sawbuck table which he used as a desk, writing a letter to his wife, his lips pursed with effort. He was a small, fussy man, with sandy hair that was falling out. While the fighting had been going on, he had been lean and tense and his small voice had been cold and full of authority. But now he had relaxed, and a little pot belly was creeping up under his belt and he kept the top button of his trousers open when he could do it without too public loss of dignity. During the war, Seeger had thought of him as a natural soldier—tireless, fanatic about detail, aggressive, severely anxious to kill Germans. But in the last few months, Seeger had seen him relapsing gradually and pleasantly into the small-town hardware merchant he had been before the war, sedentary and a little shy, and, as he had once told Seeger, worried, here in the bleak champagne fields of France, about his daughter, who had just turned twelve and had a tendency to go after the boys and had been caught by her mother kissing a fifteen-year-old neighbor in the hammock after school.

"Hello, Seeger," he said, returning the salute with a mild, offhand gesture, "What's on your mind?"

"Am I disturbing you, sir?"

"Oh, no. Just writing a letter to my wife. You married, Seeger?" He peered at the tall boy standing before him.

"No, sir."

"It's very difficult." Taney sighed, pushing dissatisfiedly at the letter before him. "My wife complains I don't tell her I love her often enough. Been married fifteen years. You'd think she'd know by now." He smiled at Seeger. "I thought you were going to Paris," he said. "I signed the passes yesterday."

"That's what I came to see you about, sir."

"I suppose something's wrong with the passes." Taney spoke resignedly, like a man who has never quite got the hang of Army regulations and has had requisitions, furloughs, and requests for courts-martial returned for correction in a baffling flood.

"No, sir," Seeger said. "The passes're fine. They start tomorrow. Well, it's just——" He looked around at the company clerk, who was on the sports page.

"This confidential?" Taney asked.

"If you don't mind, sir."

"Johnny," Taney said to the clerk, "go stand in the rain someplace."

"Yes, sir," the clerk said, and slowly got up and walked out.

Taney looked shrewdly at Seeger and spoke in a secret whisper. "You pick up anything?" he asked.

Seeger grinned. "No, sir, haven't had my hands on a girl since Strasbourg."

"Ah, that's good." Taney leaned back, relieved, happy that he didn't have to cope with the disapproval of the Medical Corps.

"It's—well," said Seeger, embarrassed, "it's hard to say—but it's money."

Taney shook his head sadly. "I know."

"We haven't been paid for three months, sir, and——"

"Damn it!" Taney stood up and shouted furiously. "I would like to take every bloody, chair-warming old lady in the Finance Department and wring their necks."

The clerk stuck his head into the tent. "Anything wrong? You call for me, sir?"

"No!" Taney shouted. "Get out of here!"

The clerk ducked out.

Taney sat down again. "I suppose," he said, in a more normal voice, "they have their problems. Outfits being broken up, being moved all over the place. But it's rugged."

"It wouldn't be so bad," Seeger said, "but we're going to Paris tomorrow. Olson, Welch, and myself. And you need money in Paris."

"Don't I know it?" Taney wagged his head. "Do you know what I paid for a bottle of champagne on the Place Pigalle in September?" He paused significantly. "I won't tell you. You wouldn't have any respect for me the rest of your life."

Seeger laughed. "Hanging is too good for the guy who thought up the rate of exchange," he said.

"I don't care if I never see another franc as long as I live." Taney waved his letter in the air, although it had been dry for a long time.

There was silence in the tent, and Seeger swallowed a little embarrassedly. "Sir," he said, "the truth is, I've come to borrow some money for Welch, Olson, and myself. We'll pay it back out of the first pay we get, and that can't be too long from now. If you don't want to give it to us, just tell me and I'll understand and get the hell out of here. We don't like to ask, but you might just as well be dead as be in Paris broke."

Taney stopped waving his letter and put it down thoughtfully. He peered at it, wrinkling his brow, looking like an aged bookkeeper in the single, gloomy light that hung in the middle of the tent.

"Just say the word, Captain," Seeger said, "and I'll blow."

"Stay where you are, son," said Taney. He dug in his shirt pocket and took out a worn, sweat-stained wallet. He looked at it for a moment. "Alligator," he said, with automatic, absent pride. "My wife sent it to me when we were in England. Pounds don't fit in it. However . . ." He opened it and took out all the contents. There was a small pile of francs on the table in front of him when he finished. He counted them. "Four hundred francs," he said. "Eight bucks."

"Excuse me," Seeger said humbly. "I shouldn't've asked."

"Delighted," Taney said vigorously. "Absolutely delighted." He started dividing the francs into two piles. "Truth is, Seeger, most of my money goes home in allotments. And the truth is, I lost eleven hundred francs in a poker game three nights ago, and I ought to be ashamed of myself. Here." He shoved one pile toward Seeger. "Two hundred francs."

Seeger looked down at the frayed, meretricious paper, which always seemed to him like stage money anyway. "No, sir," he said. "I can't take it."

"Take it," Taney said. "That's a direct order."

Seeger slowly picked up the money, not looking at Taney. "Sometime, sir," he said, "after we get out,

you have to come over to my house, and you and my father and my brother and I'll go on a real drunk."

"I regard that," Taney said gravely, "as a solemn commitment."

They smiled at each other, and Seeger started out.

"Have a drink for me," said Taney, "at the Café de la Paix. A small drink." He was sitting down to tell his wife he loved her when Seeger went out of the tent.

Olson fell into step with Seeger and they walked silently through the mud between the tents.

"Well, *mon vieux?*" Olson said finally.

"Two hundred francs," said Seeger.

Olson groaned. "Two hundred francs! We won't be able to pinch a whore's behind on the Boulevard des Capucines for two hundred francs. That miserable, penny-loving Yankee!"

"He only had four hundred," Seeger said.

"I revise my opinion," said Olson.

They walked disconsolately and heavily back toward their tent.

Olson spoke only once before they got there. "These raincoats," he said patting his. "Most ingenious invention of the war. Highest saturation point of any modern fabric. Collect more water per square inch, and hold it, than any material known to man. All hail the quartermaster!"

Welch was waiting at the entrance of their tent. He was standing there peering excitedly and shortsightedly out at the rain through his glasses, looking angry and tough, like a big-city hack driver, individual and incorruptible even in the ten-million colored uniform. Every time Seeger came upon Welch unexpectedly, he couldn't help smiling at the belligerent stance, the harsh stare through the steel-rimmed G.I. glasses, which had nothing at all to do with the way Welch really was. "It's a family inheritance," Welch had once explained. "My whole family stands as though we were getting ready to rap a drunk with a beer glass. Even my old lady." Welch had six brothers, all devout, according to Welch, and Seeger from time to time idly pictured them standing in a row, on Sunday mornings in church, seemingly on the verge of general violence, amid the hushed Latin and the Sabbath millinery.

"How much?" Welch asked loudly.

"Don't make us laugh," Olson said, pushing past him into the tent.

"What do you think I could get from the French for my combat jacket?" Seeger said. He went into the tent and lay down on his cot.

Welch followed them in and stood between the two of them. "Boys," he said, "on a man's errand."

"I can just see us now," Olson murmured, lying on his cot with his hands clasped behind his head, "painting Montmartre red. Please bring on the naked dancing girls. Four bucks' worth."

"I am not worried," Welch announced.

"Get out of here." Olson turned over on his stomach.

"I know where we can put our hands on sixty-five bucks." Welch looked triumphantly first at Olson, then at Seeger.

Olson turned over slowly and sat up. "I'll kill you," he said, "if you're kidding."

"While you guys are wasting your time fooling around with the infantry," Welch said, "I used my head. I went into Reems and used my head."

"Rance," Olson said automatically. He had had two years of French in

college and he felt, now that the war was over, that he had to introduce his friends to some of his culture.

"I got to talking to a captain in the Air Force," Welch said eagerly. "A little, fat old paddle-footed captain that never got higher off the ground than the second floor of Com Z headquarters, and he told me that what he would admire to do more than anything else is take home a nice shiny German Luger pistol with him to show to the boys back in Pacific Grove, California."

Silence fell on the tent, and Welch and Olson looked at Seeger.

"Sixty-five bucks for a Luger, these days," Olson said, "is a very good figure."

"They've been sellin' for as low as thirty-five," said Welch hesitantly. "I'll bet," he said to Seeger, "you could sell yours now and buy another one back when you got some dough, and make a clear twenty-five on the deal."

Seeger didn't say anything. He had killed the owner of the Luger, an enormous S.S. major, in Coblenz, behind some bales of paper in a warehouse, and the major had fired at Seeger three times with it, once nicking his helmet, before Seeger hit him in the face at twenty feet. Seeger had kept the Luger, a heavy, well-balanced gun, lugging it with him, hiding it at the bottom of his bedroll, oiling it three times a week, avoiding all opportunities of selling it, although he had once been offered a hundred dollars for it and several times eighty and ninety, while the war was still on, before German weapons became a glut on the market.

"Well," said Welch, "there's no hurry. I told the captain I'd see him tonight around eight o'clock in front of the Lion d'Or Hotel. You got five hours to make up your mind. Plenty of time."

"Me," said Olson, after a pause, "I won't say anything."

Seeger looked reflectively at his feet, and the two other men avoided looking at him.

Welch dug in his pocket. "I forgot," he said. "I picked up a letter for you." He handed it to Seeger.

"Thanks," Seeger said. He opened it absently, thinking about the Luger.

"Me," said Olson, "I won't say a bloody word. I'm just going to lie here and think about that nice, fat Air Force captain."

Seeger grinned a little at him and went to the tent opening to read the letter in the light. The letter was from his father, and even from one glance at the handwriting, scrawly and hurried and spotted, so different from his father's usual steady, handsome, professorial script, he knew that something was wrong.

"Dear Norman," it read, "sometime in the future, you must forgive me for writing this letter. But I have been holding this in so long, and there is no one here I can talk to, and because of your brother's condition I must pretend to be cheerful and optimistic all the time at home, both with him and your mother, who has never been the same since Leonard was killed. You're the oldest now, and although I know we've never talked very seriously about anything before, you have been through a great deal by now, and I imagine you must have matured considerably, and you've seen so many different places and people. Norman, I need help. While the war was on and you were fighting, I kept this to myself. It wouldn't have been fair to burden you with this. But now the war is over, and I no longer

feel I can stand up under this alone. And you will have to face it sometime when you get home, if you haven't faced it already, and perhaps we can help each other by facing it together."

"I'm redeployable. It's so enjoyable," Olson was singing softly, on his cot. He fell silent after his burst of song.

Seeger blinked his eyes in the gray, wintry, rainy light, and went on reading his father's letter, on the stiff white stationery with the university letterhead in polite engraving at the top of each page.

"I've been feeling this coming on for a long time," the letter continued, "but it wasn't until last Sunday morning that something happened to make me feel it in its full force. I don't know how much you've guessed about the reason for Jacob's discharge from the Army. It's true he was pretty badly wounded in the leg at Metz, but I've asked around, and I know that men with worse wounds were returned to duty after hospitalization. Jacob got a medical discharge, but I don't think it was for the shrapnel wound in his thigh. He is suffering now from what I suppose you call combat fatigue, and he is subject to fits of depression and hallucinations. Your mother and I thought that as time went by and the war and the Army receded, he would grow better. Instead, he is growing worse. Last Sunday morning when I came down into the living room from upstairs he was crouched in his old uniform, next to the window, peering out."

"What the hell," Olson was saying. "If we don't get the sixty-five bucks we can always go to the Louvre. I understand the Mona Lisa is back."

"I asked Jacob what he was

doing," the letter went on. "He didn't turn around. 'I'm observing,' he said. 'V-1s and V-2s. Buzz bombs and rockets. They're coming in by the hundred.' I tried to reason with him and he told me to crouch and save myself from flying glass. To humor him I got down on the floor beside him and tried to tell him the war was over, that we were in Ohio, 4000 miles away from the nearest spot where bombs had fallen, that America had never been touched. He wouldn't listen. 'These're the new rocket bombs,' he said, 'for the Jews.'"

"Did you ever hear of the Panthéon?" Olson asked loudly.

"No," said Welch.

"It's free."

"I'll go," said Welch.

Seeger shook his head a little and blinked his eyes before he went back to the letter.

"After that," his father went on, "Jacob seemed to forget about the bombs from time to time, but he kept saying that the mobs were coming up the street armed with bazookas and Browning automatic rifles. He mumbled incoherently a good deal of the time and kept walking back and forth saying, 'What's the situation? Do you know what the situation is?' And once he told me he wasn't worried about himself, he was a soldier and he expected to be killed, but he was worried about Mother and myself and Leonard and you. He seemed to forget that Leonard was dead. I tried to calm him and get him back to bed before your mother came down, but he refused and wanted to set out immediately to rejoin his division. It was all terribly disjointed, and at one time he took the ribbon he got for winning the Bronze Star and threw it in the fireplace, then he got down on his

hands and knees and picked it out of the ashes and made me pin it on him again, and he kept repeating, 'This is when they are coming for the Jews.'"

"The next war I'm in," said Olson, "they don't get me under the rank of colonel."

It had stopped raining by now, and Seeger folded the unfinished letter and went outside. He walked slowly down to the end of the company street, and, facing out across the empty, soaked French fields, scarred and neglected by various armies, he stopped and opened the letter again.

"I don't know what Jacob went through in the Army," his father wrote, "that has done this to him. He never talks to me about the war and he refuses to go to a psychoanalyst, and from time to time he is his own bouncing, cheerful self, playing handball in the afternoons and going around with a large group of girls. But he has devoured all the concentration-camp reports, and I found him weeping when the newspapers reported that a hundred Jews were killed in Tripoli some time ago.

"The terrible thing is, Norman, that I find myself coming to believe that it is not neurotic for a Jew to behave like this today. Perhaps Jacob is the normal one, and I, going about my business, teaching economics in a quiet classroom, pretending to understand that the world is comprehensible and orderly, am really the mad one. I ask you once more to forgive me for writing you a letter like this, so different from any letter or any conversation I've ever had with you. But it is crowding me, too. I do not see rockets and bombs, but I see other things.

"Wherever you go these days— restaurants, hotels, clubs, trains—

you seem to hear talk about the Jews, mean, hateful, murderous talk. Whatever page you turn to in the newspapers, you seem to find an article about Jews being killed somewhere on the face of the globe. And there are large, influential newspapers and well-known columnists who each day are growing more and more outspoken and more popular. The day that Roosevelt died I heard a drunken man yelling outside a bar, 'Finally they got the Jew out of the White House.' And some of the people who heard him merely laughed, and nobody stopped him. And on V-J Day, in celebration, hoodlums in Los Angeles savagely beat a Jewish writer. It's difficult to know what to do, whom to fight, where to look for allies.

"Three months ago, for example, I stopped my Thursday-night poker game, after playing with the same men for over ten years. John Reilly happened to say that the Jews got rich out of the war, and when I demanded an apology, he refused, and when I looked around at the faces of the men who had been my friends for so long, I could see they were not with me. And when I left the house, no one said good night to me. I know the poison was spreading from Germany before the war and during it, but I had not realized it had come so close.

"And in my economics class, I find myself idiotically hedging in my lectures. I discover that I am loath to praise any liberal writer or any liberal act, and find myself somehow annoyed and frightened to see an article of criticism of existing abuses signed by a Jewish name. And I hate to see Jewish names on important committees, and hate to read of Jews fighting for the poor, the oppressed, the cheated and hungry. Somehow,

even in a country where my family has lived a hundred years, the enemy has won his subtle victory over me— he has made me disfranchise myself from honest causes by calling them foreign, Communist, using Jewish names connected with them as ammunition against them.

"Most hateful of all, I found myself looking for Jewish names in the casualty lists and secretly being glad when I saw them there, to prove that there, at least, among the dead and wounded, we belonged. Three times, thanks to you and your brothers, I found our name there, and, may God forgive me, at the expense of your blood and your brother's life, through my tears, I felt that same twitch of satisfaction.

"When I read the newspapers and see another story that Jews are still being killed in Poland, or Jews are requesting that they be given back their homes in France or that they be allowed to enter some country where they will not be murdered, I am annoyed with them. I feel that they are boring the rest of the world with their problems, that they are making demands upon the rest of the world by being killed, that they are disturbing everyone by being hungry and asking for the return of their property. If we could all fall in through the crust of the earth and vanish in one hour, with our heroes and poets and prophets and martyrs, perhaps we would be doing the memory of the Jewish race a service.

"This is how I feel today, son. I need some help. You've been to the war, you've fought and killed men, you've seen the people of other countries. Maybe you understand things that I don't understand. Maybe you see some hope somewhere. Help me. Your loving Father."

Seeger folded the letter slowly, not seeing what he was doing, because the tears were burning his eyes. He walked slowly and aimlessly across the dead, sodden grass of the empty field, away from the camp. He tried to wipe away his tears, because, with his eyes full and dark, he kept seeing his father and brother crouched in the old-fashioned living room in Ohio, and hearing his brother, dressed in the old, discarded uniform, saying, "These're the new rocket bombs. For the Jews."

He sighed, looking out over the bleak, wasted land. Now, he thought, now I have to think about it. He felt a slight, unreasonable twinge of anger at his father for presenting him with the necessity of thinking about it. The Army was good about serious problems. While you were fighting, you were too busy and frightened and weary to think about anything, and at other times you were relaxing, putting your brain on a shelf, postponing everything to that impossible time of clarity and beauty after the war. Well, now, here was the impossible, clear, beautiful time, and here was his father, demanding that he think. There are all sorts of Jews, he thought: there are the sort whose every waking moment is ridden by the knowledge of Jewishness; who see signs against the Jew in every smile on a streetcar, every whisper; who see pogroms in every newspaper article, threats in every change of the weather, scorn in every handshake, death behind each closed door. He had not been like that. He was young, he was big and healthy and easygoing, and people of all kinds had liked him all his life, in the Army and out. In America, especially, what was going on in Europe had been remote, unreal,

unrelated to him. The chanting, bearded old men burning in the Nazi furnaces, and the dark-eyed women screaming prayers in Polish and Russian and German as they were pushed naked into the gas chambers, had seemed as shadowy and almost as unrelated to him, as he trotted out onto the stadium field for a football game, as they must have been to the men named O'Dwyer and Wickersham and Poole who played in the line beside him.

These tortured people had seemed more related to him in Europe. Again and again, in the towns that had been taken back from the Germans, gaunt, gray-faced men had stopped him humbly, looking searchingly at him, and had asked, peering at his long, lined, grimy face under the anonymous helmet, "Are you a Jew?" Sometimes they asked it in English, sometimes French, sometimes Yiddish. He didn't know French or Yiddish, but he learned to recognize that question. He had never understood exactly why they asked the question, since they never demanded anything of him, rarely even could speak to him. Then, one day in Strasbourg, a little, bent old man and a small, shapeless woman had stopped him and asked, in English, if he was Jewish. "Yes," he'd said, smiling at them. The two old people had smiled widely, like children. "Look," the old man had said to his wife. "A young American soldier. A Jew. And so large and strong." He had touched Seeger's arm reverently with the tips of his fingers, then had touched the Garand Seeger was carrying. "And such a beautiful rifle."

And there, for a moment, although he was not particularly sensitive, Seeger had got an inkling of why he had been stopped and questioned by so many before. Here, to these bent, exhausted old people, ravaged of their families, familiar with flight and death for so many years, was a symbol of continuing life. A large young man in the uniform of the liberator, blood, as they thought, of their blood, but not in hiding, not quivering in fear and helplessness, but striding secure and victorious down the street, armed and capable of inflicting terrible destruction on his enemies.

Seeger had kissed the old lady on the cheek and she had wept, and the old man had scolded her for it while shaking Seeger's hand fervently and thankfully before saying good-by.

Thinking back on it, he knew that it was silly to pretend that, even before his father's letter, he had been like any other American soldier going through the war. When he had stood over the huge, dead S.S. major with the face blown in by his bullets in the warehouse in Coblenz, and taken the pistol from the dead hand, he had tasted a strange little extra flavor of triumph. How many Jews, he'd thought, has this man killed? How fitting it is that I've killed him. Neither Olson nor Welch, who were like his brothers, would have felt that in picking up the Luger, its barrel still hot from the last shots its owner had fired before dying. And he had resolved that he was going to make sure to take this gun back with him to America, and plug it and keep it on his desk at home, as a kind of vague, half-understood sign to himself that justice had once been done and he had been its instrument.

Maybe, he thought, maybe I'd better take it back with me, but not as a memento. Not plugged, but loaded. America by now was a strange country for him. He had been away a long time and he wasn't sure what was waiting for him when he got home. If the mobs were coming down the street toward his house, he was not going to die singing and praying.

When he had been taking basic training, he'd heard a scrawny, clerkish soldier from Boston talking at the other end of the PX bar, over the watered beer. "The boys at the office," the scratchy voice was saying, "gave me a party before I left. And they told me one thing. 'Charlie,' they said, 'hold onto your bayonet. We're going to be able to use it when you get back. On the Yids.' "

He hadn't said anything then, because he'd felt it was neither possible nor desirable to fight against every random overheard voice raised against the Jews from one end of the world to the other. But again and again, at odd moments, lying on a barracks cot, or stretched out trying to sleep on the floor of a ruined French farmhouse, he had heard that voice, harsh, satisfied, heavy with hate and ignorance, saying above the beery grumble of apprentice soldiers at the bar, "Hold onto your bayonet."

And the other stories. Jews collected stories of hatred and injustice and inklings of doom like a special, lunatic kind of miser. The story of the Navy officer, commander of a small vessel off the Aleutians, who in the officers' wardroom had complained that he hated the Jews because it was the Jews who had demanded that the Germans be beaten first, and the forces in the Pacific had been starved in consequence. And when one of his junior officers, who had just come aboard, had objected and told the commander that he was a Jew, the commander had risen from the table and said, "Mister, the Constitution of the United States says I have to serve in the same Navy with Jews, but it doesn't say I have to eat at the same table with them." In the fogs and the cold, swelling Arctic seas off the Aleutians, in a small boat, subject to sudden, mortal attack at any moment. . . . And the million other stories. Jews, even the most normal and best adjusted, became living treasuries of them, scraps of malice and blood-thirstiness, clever and confusing and cunningly twisted so that every act by every Jew became suspect and blameworthy and hateful. Seeger had heard the stories and had made an almost conscious effort to forget them. Now, holding his father's letter in his hand, he remembered them all.

He stared unseeingly out in front of him. Maybe, he thought, maybe it would've been better to have been killed in the war, like Leonard. Simpler. Leonard would never have to face a crowd coming for his mother and father. Leonard would not have to listen and collect these hideous, fascinating little stories that made of every Jew a stranger in any town, on any field, on the face of the earth. He had come so close to being killed so many times; it would have been so easy, so neat and final. Seeger shook his head. It was ridiculous to feel like that, and he was ashamed of himself for the weak moment. At the age of twenty-one, death was not an answer.

"Seeger!" It was Olson's voice. He and Welch had sloshed silently up behind Seeger, standing in the open field. "Seeger, *mon vieux*, what're you doing—grazing?"

Seeger turned slowly to them. "I wanted to read my letter," he said.

Olson looked closely at him. They had been together so long, through so many things, that flickers and hints of expression on each other's faces were recognized and acted upon. "Anything wrong?" Olson asked.

"No," said Seeger. "Nothing much."

"Norman," Welch said, his voice young and solemn. "Norman, we've been talking, Olson and me. We decided—you're pretty attached to that Luger, and maybe, if you— well——"

"What he's trying to say," said Olson, "is we withdraw the request. If you want to sell it, O.K. If you don't, don't do it for our sake. Honest."

Seeger looked at them standing there, disreputable and tough and familiar. "I haven't made up my mind yet," he said.

"Anything you decide," Welch said oratorically, "is perfectly all right with us. Perfectly."

The three of them walked aimlessly and silently across the field, away from camp. As they walked, their shoes making a wet, sliding sound in the damp, dead grass, Seeger thought of the time Olson had covered him in the little town outside Cherbourg, when Seeger had been caught, going down the side of a street, by four Germans with a machine gun in the second story of a house on the corner and Olson had had to stand out in the middle of the street with no cover at all for more than a minute, firing continuously, so that Seeger could get away alive. And he thought of the time outside St.-Lô when he had been wounded and had lain in a mine field for three hours and Welch and Captain Taney had come looking for him in the darkness and had found him and picked him up and run for it, all of them expecting to get blown up any second. And he thought of all the drinks they'd had together, and the long marches and the cold winter together, and all the girls they'd gone out with together, and he thought of his father and brother crouching behind the window in Ohio waiting for the rockets and the crowds armed with Browning automatic rifles.

"Say." He stopped and stood facing them. "Say, what do you guys think of the Jews?"

Welch and Olson looked at each other, and Olson glanced down at the letter in Seeger's hand.

"Jews?" Olson said finally. "What're they? Welch, you ever hear of the Jews?"

Welch looked thoughtfully at the gray sky. "No," he said. "But remember, I'm an uneducated fellow."

"Sorry, bud," Olson said, turning to Seeger. "We can't help you. Ask

us another question. Maybe we'll do better."

Seeger peered at the faces of his friends. He would have to rely upon them, later on, out of uniform, on their native streets, more than he had ever relied on them on the bullet-swept street and in the dark mine field in France. Welch and Olson stared back at him, troubled, their faces candid and tough and dependable.

"What time," Seeger asked, "did you tell that captain you'd meet him?"

"Eight o'clock," Welch said. "But we don't have to go. If you have any feeling about that gun——"

"We'll meet him," Seeger said. "We can use that sixty-five bucks."

"Listen," Olson said, "I know how much you like that gun, and I'll feel like a heel if you sell it."

"Forget it," Seeger said, starting to walk again. "What could I use it for in America?"

James Thurber
1894-1961

THURBER first became known as a creator of thin-line humorous drawings of smug, unimaginative, practical women and timid, somewhat fanciful, constantly thwarted men; of dogs that are mournful and at the same time thoughtful; of seals that manage somehow or other to get into bedrooms. But Thurber preferred to think of himself as a writer and his reputation as an essayist and short-story writer has grown steadily through the years. He was a hard worker, sometimes reversing the ordinary routine by writing through the night and sleeping by day—which is in keeping with the netherworld quality of what he produced. Such stories, one surmises, could never have been conceived in daylight or nurtured by the sun.

Thurber was born in Columbus, Ohio. His boyhood there inspired one of his most hilarious books, *My Life and Hard Times*. During World War I, having been turned down by the army because of poor eyesight, he was a code clerk in Washington and later in Paris. For seven years he worked on *The New Yorker* in its early days, doing inimitable "Talk of the Town" notes, and remained an intermittent contributor until the time of his death.

The Secret Life of Walter Mitty

BY JAMES THURBER

"WE'RE going through!" The Commander's voice was like thin ice breaking. He wore his full-dress uniform, with the heavily braided white cap pulled down rakishly over one cold gray eye. "We can't make it, sir. It's spoiling for a hurricane, if you ask me." "I'm not asking you, Lieutenant Berg," said the Commander. "Throw on the power lights! Rev her up to 8500! We're going through!" The pounding of the cylinders increased: ta-pocketa-pocketa-pocketa-*pocketa-pocketa*. The Commander stared at the ice forming on the pilot window. He walked over and twisted a row of complicated dials. "Switch on No. 8 auxiliary!" he shouted. "Switch on No. 8 auxiliary!" repeated Lieutenant Berg. "Full strength in No. 3 turret!" shouted the Commander. "Full strength in No. 3 turret!" The crew, bending to their various tasks in the huge, hurtling eight-engined Navy hydroplane, looked at each other and grinned. "The Old Man'll get us through," they said to one another. "The Old Man ain't afraid of hell!" . . .

"Not so fast! You're driving too fast!" said Mrs. Mitty. "What are you driving so fast for?"

"Hmm?" said Walter Mitty. He looked at his wife, in the seat beside him, with shocked astonishment. She seemed grossly unfamiliar, like a strange woman who had yelled at him in a crowd. "You were up to fifty-five," she said. "You know I don't like to go more than forty. You were up to fifty-five." Walter Mitty drove on toward Waterbury in silence, the roaring of the SN202 through the worst storm in twenty years of Navy flying fading in the remote, intimate airways of his mind. "You're tensed up again," said Mrs. Mitty. "It's one of your days. I wish you'd let Dr. Renshaw look you over."

Walter Mitty stopped the car in front of the building where his wife went to have her hair done. "Remember to get those overshoes while I'm having my hair done," she said. "I don't need overshoes," said Mitty. She put her mirror back into her bag. "We've been all through that," she said, getting out of the car. "You're not a young man any longer." He raced the engine a little. "Why don't you wear your gloves? Have you lost your gloves?" Walter Mitty reached in a pocket and brought out the gloves. He put them on, but after she had turned and gone into the building and he had driven on to a red light, he took them off again. "Pick it up, brother!" snapped a cop

Originally published in *The New Yorker*. Copyright, 1939, by James Thurber.

as the light changed, and Mitty hastily pulled on his gloves and lurched ahead. He drove around the streets aimlessly for a time, and then he drove past the hospital on his way to the parking lot.

. . . "It's the millionaire banker, Wellington McMillan," said the pretty nurse. "Yes?" said Walter Mitty, removing his gloves slowly. "Who has the case?" "Dr. Renshaw and Dr. Benbow, but there are two specialists here, Dr. Remington from New York and Dr. Pritchard-Mitford from London. He flew over." A door opened down a long, cool corridor and Dr. Renshaw came out. He looked distraught and haggard. "Hello, Mitty," he said. "We're having the devil's own time with McMillan, the millionaire banker and close personal friend of Roosevelt. Obstreosis of the ductal tract. Tertiary. Wish you'd take a look at him." "Glad to," said Mitty.

In the operating room there were whispered introductions: "Dr. Remington, Dr. Mitty. Dr. Pritchard-Mitford, Dr. Mitty." "I've read your book on streptothricosis," said Pritchard-Mitford, shaking hands. "A brilliant performance, sir." "Thank you," said Walter Mitty. "Didn't know you were in the States, Mitty," grumbled Remington. "Coals to Newcastle, bringing Mitford and me up here for a tertiary." "You are very kind," said Mitty. A huge, complicated machine, connected to the operating table, with many tubes and wires, began at this moment to go pocketa-pocketa-pocketa. "The new anesthetizer is giving away!" shouted an intern. "There is no one in the East who knows how to fix it!" "Quiet, man!" said Mitty, in a low, cool voice. He sprang to the machine, which was now going pocketa-pocketa-queep-pocketa-queep. He

began fingering delicately a row of glistening dials. "Give me a fountain pen!" he snapped. Someone handed him a fountain pen. He pulled a faulty piston out of the machine and inserted the pen in its place. "That will hold for ten minutes," he said. "Get on with the operation." A nurse hurried over and whispered to Renshaw, and Mitty saw the man turn pale. "Coreopsis has set in," said Renshaw nervously. "If you would take over, Mitty?" Mitty looked at him and at the craven figure of Benbow, who drank, and at the grave, uncertain faces of the two great specialists. "If you wish," he said. They slipped a white gown on him; he adjusted a mask and drew on thin gloves; nurses handed him shining . . .

"Back it up, Mac! Look out for that Buick!" Walter Mitty jammed on the brakes. "Wrong lane, Mac," said the parking-lot attendant, looking at Mitty closely. "Gee. Yeh," muttered Mitty. He began cautiously to back out of the lane marked "Exit Only." "Leave her sit there," said the attendant. "I'll put her away." Mitty got out of the car. "Hey, better leave the key." "Oh," said Mitty, handing the man the ignition key. The attendant vaulted into the car, backed it up with insolent skill, and put it where it belonged.

They're so damn cocky, thought Walter Mitty, walking along Main Street; they think they know everything. Once he had tried to take his chains off, outside New Milford, and he had got them wound around the axles. A man had had to come out in a wrecking car and unwind them, a young, grinning garageman. Since then Mrs. Mitty always made him drive to a garage to have the chains taken off. The next time, he thought, I'll wear my right arm in a sling;

they won't grin at me then. I'll have my right arm in a sling and they'll see I couldn't possibly take the chains off myself. He kicked at the slush on the sidewalk. "Overshoes," he said to himself, and he began looking for a shoe store.

When he came out into the street again, with the overshoes in a box under his arm, Walter Mitty began to wonder what the other thing was his wife had told him to get. She had told him, twice before they set out from their house for Waterbury. In a way he hated these weekly trips to town—he was always getting something wrong. Kleenex, he thought, Squibb's, razor blades? No. Tooth paste, toothbrush, bicarbonate, carborundum, initiative and referendum? He gave it up. But she would remember it. "Where's the what's-its-name?" she would ask. "Don't tell me you forgot the what's-its-name." A newsboy went by shouting something about the Waterbury trial.

. . . "Perhaps this will refresh your memory." The District Attorney suddenly thrust a heavy automatic at the quiet figure on the witness stand. "Have you ever seen this before?" Walter Mitty took the gun and examined it expertly. "This is my Webley-Vickers 50.80," he said calmly. An excited buzz ran around the courtroom. The Judge rapped for order. "You are a crack shot with any sort of firearms, I believe?" said the District Attorney, insinuatingly. "Objection!" shouted Mitty's attorney. "We have shown that the defendant could not have fired the shot. We have shown that he wore his right arm in a sling on the night of the fourteenth of July." Walter Mitty raised his hand briefly and the bickering attorneys were stilled. "With any known make of gun," he said evenly, "I could have killed Gregory Fitzhurst at three hundred feet *with my left hand*." Pandemonium broke loose in the courtroom. A woman's scream rose above the bedlam and suddenly a lovely, dark-haired girl was in Walter Mitty's arms. The District Attorney struck at her savagely. Without rising from his chair, Mitty let the man have it on the point of the chin. "You miserable cur!" . . .

"Puppy biscuit," said Walter Mitty. He stopped walking and the buildings of Waterbury rose up out of the misty courtroom and surrounded him again. A woman who was passing laughed. "He said 'Puppy biscuit,'" she said to her companion. "That man said 'Puppy biscuit' to himself." Walter Mitty hurried on. He went into an A. & P., not the first one he came to but a smaller one farther up the street. "I want some biscuit for small, young dogs," he said to the clerk. "Any special brand, sir?" The greatest pistol shot in the world thought a moment. "It says 'Puppies Bark for It' on the box," said Walter Mitty.

His wife would be through at the hairdresser's in fifteen minutes, Mitty saw in looking at his watch, unless they had trouble drying it; sometimes they had trouble drying it. She didn't like to get to the hotel first; she would want him to be there waiting for her as usual. He found a big leather chair in the lobby, facing a window, and he put the overshoes and the puppy biscuit on the floor beside it. He picked up an old copy of *Liberty* and sank down into the chair. "Can Germany Conquer the World Through the Air?" Walter Mitty looked at the pictures of bombing planes and or ruined streets.

. . . "The cannonading has got the wind up in young Raleigh, sir," said the sergeant. Captain Mitty looked up at him through tousled hair. "Get him to bed," he said wearily, "with the others. I'll fly alone." "But you can't, sir," said the sergeant anxiously. "It takes two men to handle that bomber and the Archies are pounding hell out of the air. Von Richtman's circus is between here and Saulier." "Somebody's got to get that ammunition dump," said Mitty. "I'm going over. Spot of brandy?" He poured a drink for the sergeant and one for himself. War thundered and whined around the dugout and battered at the door. There was a rending of wood and splinters flew through the room. "A bit of a near thing," said Captain Mitty carelessly. "The box barrage is closing in," said the sergeant. "We only live once, Sergeant," said Mitty, with his faint, fleeting smile. "Or do we?" He poured another brandy and tossed it off. "I never see a man could hold his brandy like you, sir," said the sergeant. "Begging your pardon, sir." Captain Mitty stood up and strapped on his huge Webley-Vickers automatic. "It's forty kilometers through hell, sir," said the sergeant. Mitty finished one last brandy. "After all," he said softly, "what isn't?" The pounding of the cannon increased; there was the rat-tat-tatting of machine guns, and from somewhere came the menacing pocketa-pocketa-pocketa of the new flame-throwers. Walter Mitty walked to the door of the dugout humming "Auprès de Ma Blonde." He turned and waved to the sergeant. "Cheerio!" he said. . . .

Something struck his shoulder. "I've been looking all over this hotel for you," said Mrs. Mitty. "Why do you have to hide in this old chair? How did you expect to find you?" "Things close in," said Walter Mitty vaguely. "What?" Mrs. Mitty said. "Did you get the what's-its-name? The puppy biscuit? What's in that box?" "Overshoes," said Mitty. "Couldn't you have put them on in the store?" "I was thinking," said Walter Mitty. "Does it ever occur to you that I am sometimes thinking?" She looked at him. "I'm going to take your temperature when I get you home," she said.

They went out through the revolving doors that made a faintly derisive whistling sound when you pushed them. It was two blocks to the parking lot. At the drugstore on the corner she said, "Wait here for me. I forgot something. I won't be a minute." She was more than a minute. Walter Mitty lighted a cigarette. It began to rain, rain with sleet in it. He stood up against the wall of the drugstore, smoking. . . . He put his shoulders back and his heels together. "To hell with the handkerchief," said Walter Mitty scornfully. He took one last drag on his cigarette and snapped it away. Then, with that faint, fleeting smile playing about his lips, he faced the firing squad; erect and motionless, proud and disdainful, Walter Mitty the Undefeated, inscrutable to the last.

Ludwig Bemelmans

1898-1962

THIS sliest of humorists was born Tirolian, but came to the United States at the age of sixteen. According to his own account of himself, his removal to this country was a matter of punishment: he had made so much trouble for his family at home, at the lyceum where they sent him to school, and in his uncle's hotel where they put him to work that he finally was given his choice between reform school and America. Happily for America, he chose the latter.

Bemelmans' life can be traced by his books: for years after his arrival in this country he worked—from busboy to waiter—in a famous New York hostelry (*Hotel Splendide*); he served in World War I (*My War with the U.S.A.*); went twice to Ecuador (*Quito Express*); had a wife and daughter (*I Love You, I Love You, I Love You*). He illustrated his own books and stories, and both drawings and tales are inimitable and unmistakable. How to tell a story the way one paints a picture, only Bemelmans knew. Though he had a serious side (*Now I Lay Me Down to Sleep*) it turned humorous on him in spite of himself. In even his airiest bubbles—and "Sacre du Printemps" is one—there is satire.

Sacre du Printemps

BY LUDWIG BEMELMANS

THE Undersecretary of the Division of Spring of the Ministry of the Four Seasons unrolled an ivy-green runner on the balcony of the Ministry of Strength-through-Joy at the precise moment that the Undersecretary of the Ministry of Discipline and Order placed thereon his microphone; then both listened to the bells strike seven in the morning and opened the door behind which stood in proper uniform, with all buttons buttoned, the Ministers of Spring, of Discipline and Order, and of Strength-through-Joy. The Minister of the Four Seasons and the Minister of Discipline and Order announced the beginning of Spring.

Dutifully, with dispatch and promptness, there appeared blossoms in their proper colors on all trees in the land, buttercups growing orderly along the brooks opened their little faces to the sun, forget-me-nots in the forests, heather in the marshes, daisies among the fields, and even edelweiss high up in the mountains.

In the windowboxes of the workingmen geraniums bloomed, tulips in the gardens of the civil servants of the classes 1, 2, 3, 4, and 5, and roses in the classes from 6 to 12. Above that, in classes 13 to 15, there was no need of Spring—

flowers were in bloom the year round in the winter gardens of generals, bishops, directors of banks and gas factories. Heartwarming and admirable was the success with which the state and particularly the Ministry of Strength-through-Joy, the Division of Spring of the Ministry of the Four Seasons, and the Ministry of Discipline had succeeded in the administration of all details, down to the orderly joy of the little girls, who marched out into the lovely greenery in proper white starched dresses and in battalion formation, starting at seven-thirty in the morning, the smallest in front, the tallest in back.

There the little girls stopped to sing the appropriate songs, simple *Lieder* written for the occasion. On this day there were sung: The *Lied* of the *Lindenbaum* for the linden trees, the song of the *Heidenröslein*, for the little wild rose. How good! How without problems was life ahead for the little blond girls! How provident was the Ministry of the Four Seasons and, for that matter, the Ministry of Youth, of Motherhood, and even of Love!

No one was forgotten. The railroads ran extra trains to take each and every citizen out into the Spring.

And even the railroad was an example of the forethought and order of the provident State. There were first-class carriages with red plush upholstery and umber curtains; there were second-class compartments with green herringbone sailcloth; third class (a) with wooden seats, soft wood tailored to conform to the curves of the body; and third class (b) with hard wooden benches, nonconforming; and sixth-class carriages, to stand up in.

Malcontents, enemies of the government, and scoffers told of a sixth-class carriage that had no floor—just a roof and sides—in which the passengers had to run along the tracks. That, of course, was not so. Besides, there were no malcontents left.

The unsleeping vigilance of the Ministry of Justice had run all nonconformists into the ground, or successfully converted them. That is, all but one man, the Outsider, the One, by name Kratzig, Emil, who walked alone in his own disorderly path.

When all the citizens were out in the Spring, Emil Kratzig sat at home with his curtains drawn and read forbidden books; and again when all were snug at home in the Winter, singing the songs of the "Oven," "Grandfather's clock, tick tock, tick tock," or "*Ich bin so gern, so gern daheim, daheim in meiner stillen Klause,*" he ran around outside in the snow and whistled.

There was a long official report under K—Kratzig, Emil. But while the Political Police shadowed him, they nevertheless left him alone. They did not disturb him. "We must save him," said the Minister of Justice. "He is the last one; we may need him as an example." Besides, Emil Kratzig was an old man, and a foreigner: his maternal great-grandfather had been a Frenchman.

So Emil Kratzig lived apart and sat alone. And on the street the policeman, Umlauf, who was stationed at the City Hall square to keep him under surveillance, filled his little notebook with the discordant reports of the goings and comings of the dissenter.

The leaves in the official notebook of Policeman Umlauf, pages 48 to 55, carry the story of the sad end of the incorrigible, insubordinate Emil Kratzig. . . .

On the sunlit morning of a green May day, when all in the city went out to look at the blossoms, take deep breaths, and sing in the new, light-flowered prints designed by the Ministry of Dress and Underwear, Kratzig, wrapped in a muffler, burdened with galoshes and heavy winter coat, fled alone to the meanest landscape he could find, a district that contained the municipal incinerators, the garbage trucks, and the street-cleaning apparatus. There he spent the day crossing and recrossing the cobblestones, with wild tirades; made free with the names of ministers, the government, the nation as a whole, and that night came home and slept with open windows. That night, of course, there was a frost, and it was this frost which took many blossoms and reached out also for the life of Emil Kratzig.

The next day Emil Kratzig was ill. A cold turned to pleurisy of the left lobar cavity, and the government doctor, who came the following day and ordered him to stay in bed, shook his head as he left the house. But Emil Kratzig got up again, in violation of the doctor's orders, and with a high fever ran to the City Hall.

"Aha," said Policeman Umlauf, and in his notebook he remarked:

"The end is near and Herr Kratzig is coming to heel."

And it looked as if at last, indeed, this misguided Kratzig had decided to mend his ways. He passed by the Bureaus of Birth, Taxation, and Marriages, and properly opened the door to the Bureau of Funerals, on the second floor. He entered the room, removed his hat, and stood quietly in the line of citizens who had business with the clerk of that department. He patiently awaited his turn with hat in hand and finally spoke his desire . . . to make arrangements for himself.

The clerk pushed forward a chair for Herr Kratzig. On the top of his desk was a large album. He opened it for Emil Kratzig's inspection.

The Chief Clerk appeared and pushed a platoon of underclerks away. With his own lips he blew dust from the funeral album (this album was used only in extraordinary cases); he washed his hands in the air with anticipation, patted Kratzig on the shoulder, cleared his throat, and opened the cover.

"Now this," said the Chief Clerk, "is the first-class funeral." He pointed to the first of the many pictures and recited, "The first-class funeral is composed of the wagon, first class," indicating with the rubber end of his pencil the four angels of Annunciation carved in the teakwood, who stood at the four corners of the wagon, at the rubber tires, at the betasseled curtains of black brocade.

"This wagon is drawn by six horses, with black cloaks and black plumes. They wear this silver harness. There is besides a bishop and two priests, sixty *Sängerknaben*, a band, the bells of all the churches ring, there is a salute of guns, incense, and, at the high Mass, twelve of these golden candelabra are used

with scented beeswax candles. But this is not for you. It is for the classes 13 to 15 of the Civil Service."

He turned the page of the second-class funeral. "Here we have the same car, rubber tires, four horses with black cloaks, black plumes, and silver harness, three priests, but no bishop, forty *Sängerknaben*, incense, six of the first-class candelabra at the high Mass, the bells of half the churches, no guns, and, in the first-class candelabra, plain unscented candles."

Again he turned a huge page. "Now we come to the third-class funeral," he continued. "There is a different wagon, but also very nice, with one mourning angel sitting on top, cretonne curtains, two horses with nickel harness, black cloaks and plumes, two priests, no *Sängerknaben*, but a male quartet, nickel candelabra, of course no guns, but the two bells of the cemetery chapel and one priest with two apprentice priests, incense, and a very nice grade of candles, not beeswax but scented. But that is not for you either."

He shifted the weight of his body to his left foot and his voice changed. "The fourth-class funeral is somewhat plainer. We have here the wagon of the third class, one horse with cloak and plume and nickel harness, one priest, one singer, two altar boys, and incense. For the Mass, organ music and two candelabra with candles.

"The fifth-class funeral," he went on, "is here." And he turned the page. "Here is a strong solid wagon, and one horse, no cloak, no plume, but it is a black horse, an apprentice priest, and one singer, one altar boy, incense, no music at the Mass and two wooden candelabra with used candles."

He paused.

"And finally we come to the sixth-class funeral," he said. "Here again you get the wagon of the fifth class, the black horse, an apprentice priest, no singer, one altar boy, two wooden candelabra with used substitute-wax candles, a little bell." And he turned the page to show a drawing. "And with this funeral goes a rented coffin—it saves you buying one."

A working drawing of this imaginative, melancholy piece of black carpentry was attached, also photographs showing its economical performance. It looked like any other frugal coffin, but had an ingenious device—two doors at the bottom opened when a lever was pulled. Once occupied and having been carried to its destination, the coffin opened at the bottom and the occupant was dropped into the grave. So

the rented coffin could be used over and over again.

"Very simple, after all," said the clerk and, turning, he left the sentence open, because Emil Kratzig was gone.

Emil Kratzig was not seen again until the middle of the next night. Policeman Umlauf, standing in the center of the market square, saw a pale man coming toward him. The man was dressed in a long, white nightshirt. On his head was a top hat. Tied to it with a piece of crepe was a black plume. In his hand he held two burning candles and he carried a shovel under his arm.

"I am Emil Kratzig," said the man. "I died last night. I am going up to the cemetery. This is a seventh-class funeral."

William Saroyan
1908-

SINCE "The Daring Young Man on the Flying Trapeze"
appeared in *Story*, in 1934, William Saroyan has written over
three hundred stories, a good third of which have been
published. "In my opinion," he writes, "I am what is known
as a natural-born writer. . . . I never use a dictionary . . . I
know nothing about formal grammar and punctuation . . .
I never talk about writing . . . I speak the same language
any other loafer speaks." Despite this protestation, Saroyan
has scarcely "loafed." At the age of eight he sold newspapers;
at thirteen he served as telegraph boy from afternoon until
midnight; at sixteen he pruned grapevines; and in 1934 and
1935 he wrote steadily in an unheated room in San Francisco,
mailing out a daily story, single-spaced and unrevised.

Saroyan, the son of an Armenian immigrant, lives sometimes in San Francisco, sometimes in Fresno, not far from
the Armenian relatives whom he dearly loves and of whom
he writes over and over again. If personality is a test of a
work of art, Saroyan's sketchy stories cannot be dismissed.
They lack what we commonly think of as technique, but they
have outstanding vitality and deep, warm sympathy. Saroyan
laughs *with* his people. It took the war to arouse his anger,
not only against the enemy, but against his superior officers
in the army, as demonstrated in *The Adventures of Wesley
Jackson.*

Seventy Thousand Assyrians

BY WILLIAM SAROYAN

I HADN'T had a haircut in forty days and forty nights, and I was beginning to look like several violinists out of work. You know the look: genius gone to pot, and ready to join the Communist Party. We barbarians from Asia Minor are hairy people: when we need a haircut, we *need* a haircut. It was so bad, I had outgrown my only hat (I am writing a very serious story, perhaps one of the most serious I shall ever write. That is why I am being flippant. Readers of Sherwood Anderson will begin to understand what I am saying after a while; they will know that my laughter is rather sad.) I was a young man in need of a haircut, so I went down to Third Street (San Francisco), to the Barber College, for a fifteen-cent haircut.

Third Street, below Howard, is a district; think of the Bowery in New York, Main Street in Los Angeles: think of old men and boys, out of work, hanging around, smoking Bull Durham, talking about the government, waiting for something to turn up, simply waiting. It was a Monday morning in August and a lot of the tramps had come to the shop to brighten up a bit. The Japanese boy who was working over the free chair had a waiting list of eleven; all the other chairs were occupied. I sat down and began to wait. Outside, as Hemingway (*The Sun Also Rises; Farewell to Arms; Death in the Afternoon; Winner Take Nothing*) would say, haircuts were four bits. I had twenty cents and a half pack of Bull Durham. I rolled a cigarette, handed the pack to one of my contemporaries who looked in need of nicotine, and inhaled the dry smoke, thinking of America, what was going on politically, economically, spiritually. My contemporary was a boy of sixteen. He looked Iowa; splendid potentially, a solid American, but down, greatly down in the mouth. Little sleep, no change of clothes for several days, a little fear, etc. I wanted very much to know his name. A writer is always wanting to get the reality of faces and figures. Iowa said, "I just got in from Salinas. No work in the lettuce fields. Going north now, to Portland; try to ship out." I wanted to tell him how it was with me: rejected story from *Scribner's*, rejected essay from *The Yale Review*, no money for decent cigarettes, worn shoes, old shirts, but I was afraid to make something of my own troubles. A writer's troubles are always boring, a bit unreal. People are apt to feel, *Well, who asked you to write in the first place?* A man must pretend not to be a writer. I said, "Good luck, north." Iowa shook his head. "I know better. Give it a try, anyway. Nothing to lose." Fine boy, hope he isn't dead, hope he hasn't frozen, mighty cold these days (December, 1933), I hope he hasn't gone down; he deserved to live. Iowa, I hope you got work in Portland; I hope you are earning money; I hope you have rented a clean room with a warm bed in it; I hope you are sleeping nights, eating regularly, walking along like a human being, being happy. Iowa, my good wishes are with you. I have said a number of prayers for you. (All the same, I think he is dead by this time. It was in him the day I saw him, the low malicious face of the beast, and at the same time all the theaters in America were showing, over and over again, an animated film cartoon in which there was a song called "Who's Afraid of the Big Bad Wolf?", and that's what it amounts to; people with money laughing at the death that is crawling slyly into boys like young Iowa, pretending that it isn't there, laughing in warm theaters. I have prayed for Iowa, and I consider myself a coward. By this time he must be dead, and I am sitting in a small room, talking about him, only talking.)

I began to watch the Japanese boy who was learning to become a barber. He was shaving an old tramp who had a horrible face, one of those faces that emerge from years and years of evasive living, years of being unsettled, of not belonging anywhere, of owning nothing, and the Japanese boy was holding his nose back (his own nose) so that he would not smell the old tramp. A trivial point in a story, a

bit of data with no place in a work of art, nevertheless, I put it down. A young writer is always afraid some significant fact may escape him. He is always wanting to put in everything he sees. I wanted to know the name of the Japanese boy. I am profoundly interested in names. I have found that those that are unknown are the most genuine. Take a big name like Andrew Mellon. I was watching the Japanese boy very closely. I wanted to understand from the way he was keeping his sense of smell away from the mouth and nostrils of the old man what he was thinking, how he was feeling. Years ago, when I was seventeen, I pruned vines in my uncle's vineyard, north of Sanger, in the San Joaquin Valley, and there were several Japanese working with me, Yoshio Enomoto, Hideo Suzuki, Katsumi Sujimoto, and one or two others. These Japanese taught me a few simple phrases, *hello, how are you, fine day, isn't it, good-by,* and so on. I said in Japanese to the barber student, "How are you?" He said in Japanese, "Very well, thank you." Then, in impeccable English, "Do you speak Japanese? Have you lived in Japan?" I said, "Unfortunately, no. I am able to speak only one or two words. I used to work with Yoshio Enomoto, Hideo Suzuki, Katsumi Sujimoto; do you know them?" He went on with his work, thinking of the names. He seemed to be whispering, "Enomoto, Suzuki, Sujimoto." He said, "Suzuki. Small man?" I said, "Yes." He said, "I know him. He lives in San Jose now. He is married now."

I want you to know that I am deeply interested in what people remember. A young writer goes out to places and talks to people. He tries to find out what they remember. I am not using great material for a short story. Nothing is going to happen in this work. I am not fabricating a fancy plot. I am not creating memorable characters. I am not using a slick style of writing. I am not building up a fine atmosphere. I have no desire to sell this story or any story to *The Saturday Evening Post* or to *Cosmopolitan* or to *Harper's*. I am not trying to compete with the great writers of short stories, men like Sinclair Lewis and Joseph Hergesheimer and Zane Grey, men who really know how to write, how to make up stories that will sell. Rich men, men who understand all the rules about plot and character and style and atmosphere and all that stuff. I have no desire for fame. I am not out to win the Pulitzer Prize or the Nobel Prize or any other prize. I am out here in the Far West, in San Francisco, in a small room on Carl Street, writing a letter to common people, telling them in simple language things they already know. I am merely making a record, so if I wander around a little, it is because I am in no hurry and because I do not know the rules. If I have any desire at all, it is to show the brotherhood of man. This is a big statement and it sounds a little precious. Generally a man is ashamed to make such a statement. He is afraid sophisticated people will laugh at him. But I don't mind. I'm asking sophisticated people to laugh. That is what sophistication is for. I do not believe in races. I do not believe in governments. I see life as one life at one time, so many millions simultaneously, all over the earth. Babies who have not yet been taught to speak any language are the only race of the earth, the race of man: all the rest is pretense, what we call civilization, hatred, fear, de-

sire for strength. . . . But a baby is a baby. And the way they cry, there you have the brotherhood of man, babies crying. We grow up and we learn the words of a language and we see the universe through the language we know, we do not see it through all languages or through no language at all, through silence, or example, and we isolate ourselves in the language we know. Over here we isolate ourselves in English, or American as Mencken calls it. All the eternal things, in our words. If I want to do anything, I want to speak a more universal language. The heart of man, the unwritten part of man, that which is eternal and common to all races.

Now I am beginning to feel guilty and incompetent. I have used all this language and I am beginning to feel that I have said nothing. This is what drives a young writer out of his head, this feeling that nothing is being said. Any ordinary journalist would have been able to put the whole business into a three-word caption. Man is man, he would have said. Something clever, with any number of implications. But I want to use language that will create a single implication. I want the meaning to be precise, and perhaps that is why the language is so imprecise. I am walking around my subject, the impression I want to make, and I am trying to see it from all angles, so that I will have a whole picture, a picture of wholeness. It is the heart of man that I am trying to imply in this work.

Let me try again: I hadn't had a haircut in a long time and I was beginning to look seedy, so I went down to the Barber College on Third Street, and I sat in a chair. I said, "Leave it full in the back. I have a narrow head and if you do not leave it full in the back, I will go out of this place looking like a horse. Take as much as you like off the top. No lotion, no water, comb it dry." Reading makes a full man, writing a precise one, as you see. This is what happened. It doesn't make much of a story, and the reason is that I have left out the barber, the young man who gave me the haircut.

He was tall, he had a dark serious face, thick lips, on the verge of smiling but melancholy, thick lashes, sad eyes, a large nose. I saw his name on the card that was pasted on the mirror, Theodore Badal. A good name, genuine, a good young man, genuine. Theodore Badal began to work on my head. A good barber never speaks until he has been spoken to, no matter how full his heart may be.

"That name," I said, "Badal. Are you an Armenian?" I am an Armenian. I have mentioned this before. People look at me and begin to wonder, so I come right and tell them. "I am an Armenian," I say. Or they read something I have written and begin to wonder, so I let them know. "I am an Armenian," I say. It is a meaningless remark, but they expect me to say it, so I do. I have no idea what it is like to be an Armenian or what it is like to be an Englishman or a Japanese or anything else. I have a faint idea what it is like to be alive. This is the only thing that interests me greatly. This and tennis. I hope someday to write a great philosophical work on tennis, something on the order of Death in the Afternoon, but I am aware that I am not yet ready to undertake such a work. I feel that the cultivation of tennis on a large scale among the peoples of the earth will do much to annihilate racial differences, prej-

udices, hatred, etc. Just as soon as I have perfected my drive and my job, I hope to begin my outline of this great work. (It may seem to some sophisticated people that I am trying to make fun of Hemingway. I am not. Death in the Afternoon is a pretty sound piece of prose. I could never object to it as prose. I cannot even object to it as philosophy. I think it is finer philosophy than that of Will Durant and Walter Pitkin. Even when Hemingway is a fool, he is at least an accurate fool. He tells you what actually takes place and he doesn't allow the speed of an occurrence to make his exposition of it hasty. This is a lot. It is some sort of advancement for literature. To relate leisurely the nature and meaning of that which is very brief in duration.)

"Are you an Armenian?" I asked.

We are a small people and whenever one of us meets another, it is an event. We are always looking around for someone to talk to in our language. Our most ambitious political party estimates that there are nearly two million of us living on the earth, but most of us don't think so. Most of us sit down and take a pencil and a piece of paper and we take one section of the world at a time and imagine how many Armenians at the most are likely to be living in that section and we put the highest number on the paper, and then we go on to another section, India, Russia, Soviet Armenia, Egypt, Italy, Germany, France, America, South America, Australia, and so on, and after we add up our most hopeful figures the total comes to something a little less than a million. Then we start to think how big our families are, how high our birth rate and how low our death rate (except in times of war when massacres increase the death rate), and we begin to imagine how rapidly we will increase if we are left alone a quarter of a century, and we feel pretty happy. We always leave out earthquakes, wars, massacres, famines, etc., and it is a mistake. I remember the Near East Relief drives in my home town. My uncle used to be our orator and he used to make a whole auditorium full of Armenians weep. He was an attorney and he was a great orator. Well, at first the trouble was war. Our people were being destroyed by the enemy. Those who hadn't been killed were homeless and they were starving, *our own flesh and blood*, my uncle said, and we all wept. And we gathered money and sent it to our people in the old country. Then after the war, when I was a bigger boy, we had another Near East Relief drive and my uncle stood on the stage of the Civic Auditorium of my home town and he said, "Thank God this time it is not the enemy, but an earthquake. God has made us suffer. We have worshiped Him through trial and tribulation, through suffering and disease and torture and horror and [my uncle began to weep, began to sob] through the madness of despair, and now He has done this thing, and still we praise Him, still we worship Him. We do not understand the ways of God." And after the drive I went to my uncle and I said, "Did you mean what you said about God?" And he said, "That was oratory. We've got to raise money. What God? It is nonsense." "And when you cried?" I asked, and my uncle said, "That was real. I could not help it. I had to cry. Why, for God's sake, why must we go through all this God damn hell? What have we done to deserve all this torture? Man won't let us alone. God won't let us alone

Have we done something? Aren't we supposed to be pious people? What is our sin? I am disgusted with God. I am sick of man. The only reason I am willing to get up and talk is that I don't dare keep my mouth shut. I can't bear the thought of more of our people dying. Jesus Christ, have we done something?"

I asked Theodore Badal if he was an Armenian.

He said, "I am an Assyrian."

Well, it was something. They, the Assyrians, came from our part of the world, they had noses like our noses, eyes like our eyes, hearts like our hearts. They had a different language. When they spoke we couldn't understand them, but they were a lot like us. It wasn't quite as pleasing as it would have been if Badal had been an Armenian, but it was something.

"I am an Armenian," I said. "I used to know some Assyrian boys in my home town, Joseph Sargis, Nito Elia, Tony Saleh. Do you know any of them?"

"Joseph Sargis, I know him," said Badal. "The others I do not know. We lived in New York until five years ago, then we came out west to Turlock. Then we moved up to San Francisco."

"Nito Elia," I said, "is a Captain in the Salvation Army." (I don't want anyone to imagine that I am making anything up, or that I am trying to be funny.) "Tony Saleh," I said, "was killed eight years ago. He was riding a horse and he was thrown and the horse began to run. Tony couldn't get himself free, he was caught by a leg, and the horse ran around and around for a half-hour and then stopped, and when they went up to Tony he was dead. He was fourteen at the time. I used to go to school with him. Tony was a very clever boy, very good at arithmetic."

We began to talk about the Assyrian language and the Armenian language, about the old world, conditions over there, and so on. I was getting a fifteen-cent haircut and I was doing my best to learn something at the same time, to acquire some new truth, some new appreciation of the wonder of life, the dignity of man. (Man has great dignity, do not imagine that he has not.)

Badal said, "I cannot read Assyrian. I was born in the old country, but I want to get over it."

He sounded tired, not physically but spiritually.

"Why?" I said. "Why do you want to get over it?"

"Well," he laughed, "simply because everything is washed up over there." I am repeating his words precisely, putting in nothing of my own. "We were a great people once," he went on. "But that was yesterday, the day before yesterday. Now we are a topic in ancient history. We had a great civilization. They're still admiring it. Now I am in America learning how to cut hair. We're washed up as a race, we're through, it's all over, why should I learn to read the language? We have no writers, we have no news—well, there is a little news: once in a while the English encourage the Arabs to massacre us, that is all. It's an old story, we know all about it. The news comes over to us through the Associated Press, anyway."

These remarks were very painful to me, an Armenian. I had always felt badly about my own people being destroyed. I had never heard an Assyrian speaking in English about such things. I felt great love for this young fellow. Don't get me

wrong. There is a tendency these days to think in terms of pansies whenever a man says that he has affection for man. I think now that I have affection for all people, even for the enemies of Armenia, whom I have so tactfully not named. Everyone knows who they are. I have nothing against any of them because I think of them as one man living one life at a time, and I know, I am positive, that one man at a time is incapable of the monstrosities performed by mobs. My objection is to mobs only.

"Well," I said, "it is much the same with us. We, too, are old. We still have our church. We still have a few writers, Aharonian, Isahakian, a few others, but it is much the same."

"Yes," said the barber, "I know. We went in for the wrong things. We went in for the simple things, peace and quiet and families. We didn't go in for machinery and conquest and militarism. We didn't go in for diplomacy and deceit and the invention of machine guns and poison gases. Well, there is no use in being disappointed. We had our day, I suppose."

"We are hopeful," I said. "There is no Armenian living who does not still dream of an independent Armenia."

"Dream?" said Badal. "Well, that is something Assyrians cannot even dream any more. Why, do you know how many of us are left on earth?"

"Two or three millions," I suggested.

"Seventy thousand," said Badal. "That is all. Seventy thousand Assyrians in the world, and the Arabs are still killing us. They killed seventy of us in a little uprising last month. There was a small paragraph in the paper. Seventy more of us destroyed. We'll be wiped out before long. My brother is married to an American girl and he has a son. There is no more hope. We are trying to forget Assyria. My father still reads a paper that comes from New York, but he is an old man. He will be dead soon."

Then his voice changed, he ceased speaking as an Assyrian and began to speak as a barber: "Have I taken enough off the top?" he asked.

The rest of the story is pointless. I said *so long* to the young Assyrian and left the shop. I walked across town, four miles, to my room on Carl Street. I thought about the whole business: Assyria and this Assyrian, Theodore Badal, learning to be a barber, the sadness of his voice, the hopelessness of his attitude. This was months ago, in August, but ever since I have been thinking about Assyria, and I have been wanting to say something about Assyria, and I have been wanting to say something about Theodore Badal, a son of an ancient race, himself youthful and alert, yet hopeless. Seventy thousand Assyrians, a mere seventy thousand of that great people, and all the others quiet in death and all the greatness crumbled and ignored, and a young man in America learning to be a barber, and a young man lamenting bitterly the course of history.

Why don't I make up plots and write beautiful love stories that can be made into motion pictures? Why don't I let these unimportant and boring matters go hang? Why don't I try to please the American reading public?

Well, I am an Armenian. Michael Arlen is an Armenian, too. He is pleasing the public. I have great admiration for him, and I think he has perfected a very fine style of writing and all that, but I don't want to write about the people he likes to write about. Those people were dead to begin with. You take Iowa and the Japanese boy and Theodore Badal, the Assyrian; well, they may go down physically, like Iowa, to death, or spiritually, like Badal, to death, but they are of the stuff that is eternal in man and it is this stuff that interests me. You don't find them in bright places, making witty remarks about sex and trivial remarks about art. You find them where I found them, and they will be there forever, the races of man, the part of man, of Assyria as much as of England, that cannot be destroyed, the part that massacre does not destroy, the part that earthquake and war and famine and madness and everything else cannot destroy.

This work is in tribute to Iowa, to Japan, to Assyria, to Armenia, to the race of man everywhere, to the dignity of that race, the brotherhood of things alive. I am not expecting Paramount Pictures to film this work. I am thinking of seventy thousand Assyrians, one at a time, alive, a great race. I am thinking of Theodore Badal, himself seventy thousand Assyrians and seventy million Assyrians, himself Assyria, and man, standing in a barber shop, in San Francisco, in 1933, and being, still, himself, the whole race.

Stephen Vincent Benét

1898-1943

STEPHEN VINCENT BENÉT came of one of America's foremost writing families. William Rose Benét, his brother, Laura Benét, his sister, Rosemary Carr, his wife, are all writers, and Elinor Wylie was his sister-in-law. In his all-too-short life, Stephen Benét himself followed no other profession but writing. Born of the generation of the disillusioned, he stood forth, almost alone among his contemporaries, with shining faith. In the postwar days of the twenties, when it was the fashion to belittle America as commonplace and dull, he was glorifying the spirit of its past as well as the achievement of its present.

This special interest in his own country may well have been heightened by the fact that though his immediate family were writers, his forebears were army folk. His father, his grandfather, and his great-grandfather were all army officers, and Stephen Benét himself was raised in an army post. Moreover, his father's library, where he did his first research, was filled with military books, which furnished him with the minute information on American history for which he was noted, and no doubt fired him with patriotism. His particular urge was to write a long narrative poem about the Civil War. To this end, in 1926, he was granted a Guggenheim Fellowship, which resulted in *John Brown's Body*, one of the great narrative poems in American literature. American folklore fascinated him quite as much as history, and his original slant on old tales, his fancy playing a new turn for an old song, made for some of his best work. "The Devil and Daniel Webster," already a short-story classic, was made into a grand opera, and "O'Halloran's Luck," quite as indigenously American as "The Devil," is filled with the same fantastic humor.

O'Halloran's Luck

BY STEPHEN VINCENT BENÉT

THEY were strong men built the Big Road, in the early days of America, and it was the Irish did it. My grandfather, Tim O'Halloran, was a young man then, and wild. He could swing a pick all day and dance all night, if there was a fiddler handy; and if there was a girl to be pleased he pleased her, for he had the tongue and the eye. Likewise, if there was a man to be stretched, he could stretch him with the one blow.

I saw him later on in years when he was thin and whiteheaded, but in his youth he was not so. A thin, whiteheaded man would have had little chance, and they driving the Road to the West. It was two-fisted men cleared the plains and bored through the mountains. They came in the thousands to do it from every county in Ireland; and now the names are not known. But it's over their graves you pass, when you ride in the Pullmans. And Tim O'Halloran was one of them, six feet high and solid as the Rock of Cashel when he stripped to the skin.

He needed to be all of that, for it was not easy labor. 'Twas a time of great booms and expansions in the railroad line, and they drove the tracks north and south, east and west, as if the devil was driving

behind. For this they must have the boys with shovel and pick, and every immigrant ship from Ireland was crowded with bold young men. They left famine and England's rule behind them—and it was the thought of many they'd pick up gold for the asking in the free States of America, though it's little gold that most of them ever saw. They found themselves up to their necks in the water of the canals, and burned black by the suns of the prairie—and that was a great surprise to them. They saw their sisters and their mothers made servants that had not been servants in Ireland, and that was a strange change too. Eh, the death and the broken hopes it takes to make a country! But those with the heart and the tongue kept the tongue and the heart.

Tim O'Halloran came from Clonmelly, and he was the fool of the family and the one who listened to tales. His brother Ignatius went for a priest and his brother James for a sailor, but they knew he could not do those things. He was strong and biddable and he had the O'Halloran tongue; but there came a time of famine, when the younger mouths cried for bread and there was little room in the nest. He was not entirely wishful to emigrate, and yet, when he thought of it, he was wishful. 'Tis often enough that way, with a younger son. Perhaps he was the more wishful because of Kitty Malone.

'Tis a quiet place, Clonmelly, and she'd been the light of it to him. But now the Malones had gone to the States of America—and it was well known that Kitty had a position there the like of which was not to be found in all Dublin Castle. They called her a hired girl, to be sure, but did not she eat from gold plates, like all the citizens of America? And when she stirred her tea, was not the spoon made of gold? Tim O'Halloran thought of this, and of the chances and adventures that a bold young man might find, and at last he went to the boat. There were many from Clonmelly on that boat, but he kept himself to himself and dreamed his own dreams.

The more disillusion it was to him, when the boat landed him in Boston and he found Kitty Malone there, scrubbing the stairs of an American house with a pail and brush by her side. But that did not matter, after the first, for her cheeks still had the rose in them and she looked at him in the same way. 'Tis true there was an Orangeman courting her—conductor he was on the horsecars, and Tim did not like that. But after Tim had seen her, he felt himself the equal of giants; and when the call came for strong men to work in the wilds of the West, he was one of the first to offer. They broke a sixpence between them before he left—it was an English sixpence, but that did not matter greatly to them. And Tim O'Halloran was going to make his fortune, and Kitty Malone

to wait for him, though her family liked the Orangeman best.

Still and all, it was cruel work in the West, as such work must be, and Tim O'Halloran was young. He liked the strength and the wildness of it— he'd drink with the thirstiest and fight with the wildest—and that he knew how to do. It was all meat and drink to him—the bare tracks pushing ahead across the bare prairie and the fussy cough of the wood-burning locomotives and the cold blind eyes of a murdered man, looking up at the prairie stars. And then there was the cholera and the malaria— and the strong man you'd worked on the grade beside, all of a sudden gripping his belly with the fear of death on his face and his shovel falling to the ground.

Next day he would not be there and they'd scratch a name from the payroll. Tim O'Halloran saw it all.

He saw it all and it changed his boyhood and hardened it. But, for all that, there were times when the black fit came upon him, as it does to the Irish, and he knew he was alone in a strange land. Well, that's a hard hour to get through, and he was young. There were times when he'd have given all the gold of the Americas for a smell of Clonmelly air or a glimpse of Clonmelly sky. Then he'd drink or dance or fight or put a black word on the foreman, just to take the aching out of his mind. It did not help him with his work and it wasted his pay; but it was stronger than he, and not even the thought of Kitty Malone could stop it. 'Tis like that, sometimes.

Well, it happened one night he was coming back from the place where they sold the potheen, and perhaps he'd had a trifle more of it than was advisable. Yet he had not drunk it for that, but to keep the queer thoughts from his mind. And yet, the more that he drank, the queerer were the thoughts in his head. For he kept thinking of the Luck of the O'Hallorans and the tales his granda had told about it in the old country—the tales about pookas and banshees and leprechauns with long white beards.

"And that's a queer thing to be thinking and myself at labor with a shovel on the open prairies of America," he said to himself. "Sure, creatures like that might live and thrive in the old country—and I'd be the last to deny it—but 'tis obvious they could not live here. The first sight of Western America would scare them into conniptions. And as for the Luck of the O'Hallorans, 'tis little good I've had of it, and me not even able to rise to foreman and marry Kitty Malone. They called me the fool of the family in Clonmelly, and I misdoubt but they were right. Tim O'Halloran, you're a worthless man, for all your strong back and arms." It was with such black, bitter thoughts as these that he went striding over the prairie. And it was just then that he heard the cry in the grass.

'Twas a strange little piping cry, and only the half of it human. But Tim O'Halloran ran to it, for in truth he was spoiling for a fight. "Now this will be a beautiful young lady," he said to himself as he ran, "and I will save her from robbers; and her father, the rich man, will ask me—but, wirra, 'tis not her I wish to marry, 'tis Kitty Malone. Well, he'll set me up in business, out of friendship and gratitude, and then I will send for Kitty——"

But by then he was out of breath, and by the time he had reached the place where the cry came from he could see that it was not so. It was only a pair of young wolf cubs, and they chasing something small and helpless and playing with it as a cat plays with a mouse. Where the wolf cub is the old wolves are not far, but Tim O'Halloran felt as bold as a lion. "Be off with you!" he cried and he threw a stick and a stone. They ran away into the night, and he could hear them howling—a lonesome sound. But he knew the camp was near, so he paid small attention to that but looked for the thing they'd been chasing.

It scuttled in the grass but he could not see it. Then he stooped down and picked something up, and when he had it in his hand he stared at it unbelieving. For it was a tiny shoe, no bigger than a child's. And more than that, it was not the kind of shoe that is made in America. Tim O'Halloran stared and stared at it—and at the silver buckle upon it—and still he could not believe.

"If I'd found this in the old country," he said to himself, half aloud, "I'd have sworn that it was a leprechaun's and looked for the pot of gold. But here, there's no chance of that——"

"I'll trouble you for the shoe," said a small voice close by his feet.

Tim O'Halloran stared round him wildly. "By the piper that played before Moses!" he said. "Am I drunk beyond comprehension? Or am I mad? For I thought that I heard a voice."

"So you did, silly man," said the voice again, but irritated, "and I'll trouble you for my shoe, for it's cold in the dewy grass."

"Honey," said Tim O'Halloran, beginning to believe his ears, "honey dear, if you'll but show yourself——"

"I'll do that and gladly," said the voice; and with that the grasses parted, and a little old man with a long white beard stepped out. He was perhaps the size of a well-grown child, as O'Halloran could see clearly by the moonlight on the prairie; moreover, he was dressed in the clothes of antiquity, and he carried cobbler's tools in the belt at his side.

"By faith and belief, but it *is* a leprechaun!" cried O'Halloran, and with that he made a grab for the apparition. For you must know, in case you've been ill brought up, that a leprechaun is a sort of cobbler fairy and each one knows the whereabouts of a pot of gold. Or it's so they say in the old country. For they say you can tell a leprechaun by his long white beard and his cobbler's tools; and once you have the possession of him, he must tell you where his gold is hid.

The little old man skipped out of reach as nimbly as a cricket. "Is this Clonmelly courtesy?" he said with a shake in his voice, and Tim O'Halloran felt ashamed.

"Sure, I didn't mean to hurt your worship at all," he said, "but if you're what you seem to be, well, then, there's the little matter of a pot of gold——"

"Pot of gold!" said the leprechaun, and his voice was hollow and full of scorn. "And would I be here to-day if I had that same? Sure, it all went to pay my sea passage, as you might expect."

"Well," said Tim O'Halloran, scratching his head, for that sounded reasonable enough, "that may be so or again it may not be so. But——"

"Oh, 'tis bitter hard," said the leprechaun, and his voice was weeping, "to come to the waste, wild prairies all alone, just for the love of Clonmelly folk—and then to be disbelieved by the first that speaks to me! If it had been an Ulsterman

now, I might have expected it. But the O'Hallorans wear the green."

"So they do," said Tim O'Halloran, "and it shall not be said of an O'Halloran that he denied succor to the friendless. I'll not touch you."

"Do you swear it?" said the leprechaun.

"I swear it," said Tim O'Halloran.

"Then I'll just creep under your coat," said the leprechaun, "for I'm near destroyed by the chills and damps of the prairie. Oh, this weary emigrating!" he said, with a sigh like a furnace. "'Tis not what it's cracked up to be."

Tim O'Halloran took off his own coat and wrapped it around him. Then he could see him closer—and it could not be denied that the leprechaun was a pathetic sight. He'd a queer little boyish face, under the long white beard, but his clothes were all torn and ragged and his cheeks looked hollow with hunger.

"Cheer up!" said Tim O'Halloran and patted him on the back. "It's a bad day that beats the Irish. But tell me first how you came here—for that still sticks in my throat."

"And would I be staying behind with half Clonmelly on the water?" said the leprechaun stoutly. "By the bones of Finn, what sort of a man do you think I am?"

"That's well said," said Tim O'Halloran. "And yet I never heard of the Good People emigrating before."

"True for you," said the leprechaun. "The climate here's not good for most of us and that's a fact. There's a boggart or so that came over with the English, but then the Puritan ministers got after them and they had to take to the woods. And I had a word or two, on my way West, with a banshee that lives by Lake Superior—a decent woman she was, but you could see she'd come down in the world. For even the bits of children wouldn't believe in her; and when she let out a screech, sure they thought it was a steamboat. I misdoubt she's died since then—she was not in good health when I left her.

"And as for the native spirits— well, you can say what you like, but they're not very comfortable people. I was captive to some of them a week and they treated me well enough, but they whooped and danced too much for a quiet man, and I did not like the long, sharp knives on them. Oh, I've had the adventures on my way here," he said, "but they're over now, praises be, for I've found a protector at last," and he snuggled closer under O'Halloran's coat.

"Well," said O'Halloran, somewhat taken aback, "I did not think this would be the way of it when I found O'Halloran's Luck that I'd dreamed of so long. For, first I save your life from the wolves; and now, it seems, I must be protecting you further. But in the tales it's always the other way round."

"And is the company and conversation of an ancient and experienced creature like myself nothing to you?" said the leprechaun fiercely. "Me that had my own castle at Clonmelly and saw O'Sheen in his pride? Then St. Patrick came—wirra, wirra!—and there was an end to it all. For some of us—the Old Folk of Ireland— he baptized, and some of us he chained with the demons of hell. But I was Lazy Brian, betwixt and between, and all I wanted was peace and a quiet life. So he changed me to what you see—me that had six tall harpers to harp me awake in the morning—and laid a doom upon me for being betwixt and between. I'm to serve Clonmelly folk and follow

them wherever they go till I serve the servants of servants in a land at the world's end. And then, perhaps, I'll be given a Christian soul and can follow my own inclinations."

"Serve the servants of servants?" said O'Halloran. "Well, that's a hard riddle to read."

"It is that," said the leprechaun "for I never once met the servant of a servant in Clonmelly, all the time I've been looking. I doubt but that was in St. Patrick's mind."

"If it's criticizing the good saint you are, I'll leave you here on the prairie," said Tim O'Halloran.

"I'm not criticizing him," said the leprechaun with a sigh, "but I could wish he'd been less hasty. Or more specific. And now, what do we do?"

"Well," said O'Halloran, and he sighed, too, "'tis a great responsibility, and one I never thought to shoulder. But since you've asked for help, you must have it. Only there's just this to be said. There's little money in my pocket."

"Sure, 'tis not for your money I've come to you," said the leprechaun joyously. "And I'll stick closer than a brother."

"I've no doubt of that," said O'Halloran with a wry laugh. "Well, clothes and food I can get for you— but if you stick with me, you must work as well. And perhaps the best way would be for you to be my young nephew, Rory, run away from home to work on the railroad."

"And how would I be your young nephew, Rory, and me with a long white beard?"

"Well," said Tim O'Halloran with a grin, "as it happens, I've got a razor in my pocket."

And with that you should have heard the leprechaun. He stamped and he swore and he plead—but it was no use at all. If he was to follow

Tim O'Halloran, he must do it on Tim O'Halloran's terms and no two ways about it. So O'Halloran shaved him at last, by the light of the moon, to the leprechaun's great horror, and when he got him back to the construction camp and fitted him out in some old duds of his own—well, it wasn't exactly a boy he looked, but it was more like a boy than anything else. Tim took him up to the foreman the next day and got him signed on for a water boy, and it was a beautiful tale he told the foreman. As well, too, that he had the O'Halloran tongue to tell it with, for when the foreman first looked at young Rory you could see him gulp like a man that's seen a ghost.

"And now what do we do?" said the leprechaun to Tim when the interview was over.

"Why, you work," said Tim with a great laugh, "and Sundays you wash your shirt."

"Thank you for nothing," said the leprechaun with an angry gleam in his eye. "It was not for that I came here from Clonmelly."

"Oh, we've all come here for great fortune," said Tim, "but it's hard to find that same. Would you rather be with the wolves?"

"Oh, no," said the leprechaun.

"Then drill, ye tarrier, drill!" said Tim O'Halloran and shouldered his shovel, while the leprechaun trailed behind.

At the end of the day the leprechaun came to him.

"I've never done mortal work before," he said, "and there's no bone in my body that's not a pain and an anguish to me."

"You'll feel better after supper," said O'Halloran. "And the night's made for sleep."

"But where will I sleep?" said the leprechaun.

"In the half of my blanket," said Tim, "for are you not young Rory, my nephew?"

It was not what he could have wished, but he saw he could do no otherwise. Once you start a tale, you must play up to the tale.

But that was only the beginning, as Tim O'Halloran soon found out. For Tim O'Halloran had tasted many things before, but not responsibility, and now responsibility was like a bit in his mouth. It was not so bad the first week, while the leprechaun was still ailing. But when, what with the food and the exercise, he began to recover his strength, 'twas a wonder Tim O'Halloran's hair did not turn gray overnight. He was not a bad creature, the leprechaun, but he had all the natural mischief of a boy of twelve and, added to that, the craft and knowledge of generations.

There was the three pipes and the pound of shag the leprechaun stole from McGinnis—and the dead frog he slipped in the foreman's tea—and the bottle of potheen he got hold of one night when Tim had to hold his head in a bucket of water to sober him up. A fortunate thing it was that St. Patrick had left him no great powers, but at that he had enough to put the jumping rheumatism on Shaun Kelly for two days—and it wasn't till Tim threatened to deny him the use of his razor entirely that he took off the spell.

That brought Rory to terms, for by now he'd come to take a queer pleasure in playing the part of a boy and he did not wish to have it altered.

Well, things went on like this for some time, and Tim O'Halloran's savings grew; for whenever the drink was running he took no part in it, for fear of mislaying his wits when it came to deal with young Rory.

And as it was with the drink, so was it with other things—till Tim O'Halloran began to be known as a steady man. And then, as it happened one morning, Tim O'Halloran woke up early. The leprechaun had finished his shaving and was sitting cross-legged, chuckling to himself.

"And what's your source of amusement so early in the day?" said Tim sleepily.

"Oh," said the leprechaun, "I'm just thinking of the rare hard work we'll have when the line's ten miles farther on."

"And why should it be harder there than it is here?" said Tim.

"Oh, nothing," said the leprechaun, "but those fools of surveyors have laid out the line where there's hidden springs of water. And when we start digging, there'll be the devil to pay."

"Do you know that for a fact?" said Tim.

"And why wouldn't I know it?" said the leprechaun. "Me that can hear the water run underground."

"Then what should we do?" said Tim.

"Shift the line half a mile to the west and you'd have a firm roadbed," said the leprechaun.

Tim O'Halloran said no more at the time. But for all that, he managed to get to the assistant engineer in charge of construction at the noon hour. He could not have done it before, but now he was known as a steady man. Nor did he tell where he got the information—he put it on having seen a similar thing in Clonmelly.

Well, the engineer listened to him and had a test made—and sure enough, they struck the hidden spring. "That's clever work, O'Halloran," said the engineer. "You've saved us time and money. And now

how would you like to be foreman of a gang?"

"I'd like it well," said Tim O'Halloran.

"Then you boss Gang Five from this day forward," said the engineer. "And I'll keep my eye on you. I like a man that uses his head."

"Can my nephew come with me," said Tim, "for, 'troth, he's my responsibility?"

"He can," said the engineer, who had children of his own.

So Tim got promoted and the leprechaun along with him. And the first day on the new work, young Rory stole the gold watch from the engineer's pocket, because he liked the tick of it, and Tim had to threaten him with fire and sword before he'd put it back.

Well, things went on like this for another while, till finally Tim woke up early on another morning and heard the leprechaun laughing.

"And what are you laughing at?" he said.

"Oh, the more I see of mortal work, the less reason there is to it," said the leprechaun. "For I've been watching the way they get the rails up to us on the line. And they do it thus and so. But if they did it so and thus, they could do it in half the time with half the work."

"Is that so indeed?" said Tim O'Halloran, and he made him explain it clearly. Then, after he'd swallowed his breakfast, he was off to his friend the engineer.

"That's a clever idea, O'Halloran," said the engineer. "We'll try it." And a week after that, Tim O'Halloran found himself with a hundred men under him and more responsibility than he'd ever had in his life. But it seemed little to him beside the responsibility of the leprechaun, and now the engineer began to lend him books to study and he studied them at nights while the leprechaun snored in its blanket.

A man could rise rapidly in those days—and it was then Tim O'Halloran got the start that was to carry him far. But he did not know he was getting it, for his heart was near broken at the time over Kitty Malone. She'd written him a letter or two when he first came West, but now there were no more of them and at last he got a word from her family telling him he should not be disturbing Kitty with letters from a laboring man. That was bitter for Tim O'Halloran, and he'd think about Kitty and the Orangeman in the watches of the night and groan. And then, one morning, he woke up after such a night and heard the leprechaun laughing.

"And what are you laughing at now?" he said sourly. "For my heart's near burst with its pain."

"I'm laughing at a man that would let a cold letter keep him from his love, and him with pay in his pocket and the contract ending the first," said the leprechaun.

Tim O'Halloran struck one hand in the palm of the other.

"By the piper, but you've the right of it, you queer little creature!" he said. " 'Tis back to Boston we go when this job's over."

It was laborer Tim O'Halloran that had come to the West, but it was Railroadman Tim O'Halloran that rode back East in the cars like a gentleman, with a free pass in his pocket and the promise of a job on the railroad that was fitting a married man. The leprechaun, I may say, gave some trouble in the cars, more particularly when he bit a fat woman that called him a dear little boy; but what with giving him peanuts all the way, Tim O'Halloran

managed to keep him fairly quieted.

When they got to Boston he fitted them both out in new clothes from top to toe. Then he gave the leprechaun some money and told him to amuse himself for an hour or so while he went to see Kitty Malone.

He walked into the Malones' flat as bold as brass, and there sure enough, in the front room, were Kitty Malone and the Orangeman. He was trying to squeeze her hand, and she refusing, and it made Tim O'Halloran's blood boil to see that. But when Kitty saw Tim O'Halloran she let out a scream.

"Oh, Tim!" she said. "Tim! And they told me you were dead in the plains of the West!"

"And a great pity that he was not," said the Orangeman, blowing out his chest with the brass buttons on it, "but a bad penny always turns up."

"Bad penny is it, you brass-buttoned son of iniquity," said Tim O'Halloran. "I have but the one question to put you. Will you stand or will you run?"

"I'll stand as we stood at Boyne Water," said the Orangeman, grinning ugly. "And whose backs did we see that day?"

"Oh, is that the tune?" said Tim O'Halloran. "Well, I'll give you a tune to match it. Who fears to speak of Ninety-Eight?"

With that he was through the Orangeman's guard and stretched him at the one blow, to the great consternation of the Malones. The old woman started to screech and Pat Malone to talk of policemen, but Tim O'Halloran silenced the both of them.

"Would you be giving your daughter to an Orangeman that works on the horsecars, when she might be marrying a future railroad presi-

dent?" he said. And with that he
pulled his savings out of his pocket
and the letter that promised the job
for a married man. That quieted the
Malones a little and, once they got
a good look at Tim O'Halloran, they
began to change their tune. So, after
they'd got the Orangeman out of the
house—and he did not go willing,
but he went as a whipped man
must—Tim O'Halloran recounted all
of his adventures.

The tale did not lose in the telling,
though he did not speak of the leprechaun, for he thought that had better be left to a later day; and at the
end Pat Malone was offering him a
cigar. "But I find I have none upon
me," said he with a wink at Tim,
"so I'll just run down to the corner."

"And I'll go with you," said Kitty's
mother, "for if Mr. O'Halloran stays
to supper—and he's welcome—
there's a bit of shopping to be done."

So the old folks left Tim O'Halloran and his Kitty alone. But just
as they were in the middle of their
planning and contriving for the
future, there came a knock on the
door.

"What's that?" said Kitty, but Tim
O'Halloran knew well enough and
his heart sank within him. He opened
the door—and sure enough, it was
the leprechaun.

"Well, Uncle Tim," said the
creature, grinning, "I'm here."

Tim O'Halloran took a look at him
as if he saw him for the first time.
He was dressed in new clothes, to be
sure, but there was soot on his face
and his collar had thumbmarks on it
already. But that wasn't what made
the difference. New clothes or old,
if you looked at him for the first
time, you could see he was an unchancy thing, and not like Christian souls

"Kitty," he said, "Kitty darling, I

had not told you. But this is my
young nephew, Rory, that lives with
me."

Well, Kitty welcomed the boy
with her prettiest manners, though
Tim O'Halloran could see her giving
him a side look now and then. All
the same, she gave him a slice of
cake, and he tore it apart with his
fingers; but in the middle of it he
pointed to Kitty Malone.

"Have you made up your mind to
marry my Uncle Tim?" he said.
"Faith, you'd better, for he's a grand
catch."

"Hold your tongue, young Rory,"
said Tim O'Halloran angrily, and
Kitty blushed red. But then she took
the next words out of his mouth.

"Let the gossoon be, Tim O'Halloran," she said bravely. "Why
shouldn't he speak his mind? Yes,
Roryeen—it's I that will be your
aunt in the days to come—and a
proud woman too."

"Well, that's good," said the leprechaun, cramming the last of the cake
in his mouth, "for I'm thinking you'll
make a good home for us, once
you're used to my ways."

"Is that to be the way of it, Tim?"
said Kitty Malone very quietly, but
Tim O'Halloran looked at her and
knew what was in her mind. And he
had the greatest impulse in the
world to deny the leprechaun and
send him about his business. And
yet, when he thought of it, he knew
that he could not do it, not even if
it meant the losing of Kitty Malone.

"I'm afraid that must be the way
of it, Kitty," he said with a groan.

"Then I honor you for it," said
Kitty, with her eyes like stars. She
went up to the leprechaun and took
his hard little hand. "Will you live
with us, young Rory?" she said.
"For we'd be glad to have you."

"Thank you kindly, Kitty Malone

—O'Halloran to be," said the leprechaun. "And you're lucky, Tim O'Halloran—lucky yourself and lucky in your wife. For if you had denied me then, your luck would have left you—and if she had denied me then, 'twould be but half luck for you both. But now the luck will stick to you the rest of your lives. And I'm wanting another piece of cake," said he.

"Well, it's a queer lad you are," said Kitty Malone, but she went for the cake. The leprechaun swung his legs and looked at Tim O'Halloran. "I wonder what keeps my hands off you," said the latter with a groan.

"Fie!" said the leprechaun, grinning, "and would you be lifting the hand to your one nephew? But tell me one thing, Tim O'Halloran, was this wife you're to take ever in domestic service?"

"And what if she was?" said Tim O'Halloran, firing up. "Who thinks the worse of her for that?"

"Not I," said the leprechaun, "for I've learned about mortal labor since I came to this country—and it's an honest thing. But tell me one thing more. Do you mean to serve this wife of yours and honor her through the days of your wedded life?"

"Such is my intention," said Tim, "though what business it is of——"

"Never mind," said the leprechaun. "Your shoelace is undone, bold man. Command me to tie it up."

"Tie up my shoe, you blackhearted, villainous little anatomy!" thundered Tim O'Halloran, and the leprechaun did so. Then he jumped to his feet and skipped about the room.

"Free! Free!" he piped. "Free at last! For I've served the servants of servants and the doom has no power on me longer. Free, Tim O'Halloran! O'Halloran's Luck is free!"

Tim O'Halloran stared at him, dumb; and even as he stared, the creature seemed to change. He was small, to be sure, and boyish—but you could see the unchancy look leave him and the Christian soul come into his eyes. That was a queer thing to be seen, and a great one too.

"Well," said Tim O'Halloran in a sober voice, "I'm glad for you, Rory. For now you'll be going back to Clonmelly, no doubt—and faith, you've earned the right."

The leprechaun shook his head.

"Clonmelly's a fine, quiet place," said he, "but this country's bolder. I misdoubt it's something in the air —you will not have noticed it, but I've grown two inches and a half since first I met you, and I feel my-self growing still. No, it's off to the mines of the West I am, to follow my natural vocation—for they say there are mines out there you could mislay all Dublin Castle in—and wouldn't I like to try! But speaking of that, Tim O'Halloran," he said, "I was not quite honest with you about the pot of gold. You'll find your share behind the door when I've gone. And now good day and long life to you!"

"But, man dear," said Tim O'Halloran, "'tis not good-by!" For it was then he realized the affection that was in him for the queer little creature.

"No, 'tis not good-by," said the leprechaun. "When you christen your first son, I'll be at his cradle, though you may not see me—and so with your sons' sons and their sons, for O'Halloran's luck's just begun. But we'll part for the present now. For now I'm a Christian soul, I've work to do in the world."

"Wait a minute," said Tim O'Halloran. "For you would not know, no doubt, and you such a new soul

And no doubt you'll be seeing the priest—but a layman can do it in an emergency and I think this is one. I dare not have you leave me—and you not even baptized."

And with that he made the sign of the cross and baptized the leprechaun. He named him Rory Patrick.

"'Tis not done with all the formalities," he said at the end, "but I'll defend the intention."

"I'm grateful to you," said the leprechaun. "And if there was a debt to be paid, you've paid it back and more."

And with that he was gone somehow, and Tim O'Halloran was alone in the room. He rubbed his eyes. But there was a little sack behind the door, where the leprechaun had left it—and Kitty was coming in with a slice of cake on a plate.

"Well, Tim," she said, "and where's that young nephew of yours?"

So he took her into his arms and told her the whole story. And how much of it she believed, I do not know. But there's one remarkable circumstance. Ever since then, there's always been one Rory O'Halloran in the family, and that one luckier than the lave. And when Tim O'Halloran got to be a railroad president, why didn't he call his private car "The Leprechaun"? For that matter, they said, when he took his business trips there'd be a small boyish-looking fellow would be with him now and again. He'd turn up from nowhere, at some odd stop or other, and he'd be let in at once, while the great of the railroad world were kept waiting in the vestibule. And after a while, there'd be singing from inside the car.

Walter D. Edmonds
1903-

WALTER DUMAUX EDMONDS has made the most of his
regional background. His country is upstate New York, where
he was born and still lives, bringing up his children on a
farm much as he was brought up. *Rome Haul* and *Drums
Along the Mohawk*, his best-known novels, deal with the
Erie Canal, and Tom Whipple, the boy in the story of that
name, came from those parts. Edmonds, though a born
storyteller, is nevertheless a hard worker. Old letters,
biographies, newspapers of another day, and almanacs are
not only his pleasure, but also his necessity. . . . "Tom
Whipple" is Edmonds' interpretation of an American legend
first recorded by Maria Child in 1840.

Tom Whipple

BY WALTER D. EDMONDS

On a late October morning in 1837, just after sunrise, a woman and a grown boy, approaching the Cortland Street wharf, asked a deck hand if that was the steamboat for Albany. When he said it was, the boy turned to the woman.

"See, Ma. You didn't miss it anyhow."

Her voice was timid. "I was only feared the Amboy boat had made us late. I'd be feared to stay all day in a big city like this one. Washington City was big enough for me." She cast an anxious glance over her shoulder. New York was waking up, and the frosty streets echoed with the clatter of drays and water carts. "Hadn't we ought to get on to the boat, Tom?"

"Might as well."

Beside her small bent figure, he looked tall. He was a big boy, anyway, with the flesh on him not yet grown up to his bones. He was carrying a small satchel and a bundle rolled up in a cotton print, and his hands hung well below the cuffs of his shabby coat, showing the wrist joints.

Choosing a corner behind the stove in the main saloon, they stowed the satchel under the seat, and the woman sat down. "This here's real nice," she said, looking up at her son. "I think it's prettier than the other boat, don't you, Tom?"

"Yes, Ma."

He was looking out of the window that faced south. He could see the bay beyond the river's mouth, the white gulls against the sky and a ship sailing past the Castle Garden.

She watched his face for a moment, thinking, perhaps, that it favored her own more than his father's.

Then he turned to her and fixed his eyes on a nail in the wall about two feet over her shawled head. "You ought to get home all right," he said.

"We ought to," she said sharply, as if she had been seeing into his mind for some time. "You don't mean——"

He nodded and said, "Yep."

She said then, angrily, "You know I'm feared of traveling alone. It ain't right of you to leave me here, Tom. This way. In this big boat." She saw that she was getting nowhere. "Ain't it enough for you to go see Washington City? Didn't we traipse all the way over to that Mount Vernon? And we rode on the cars. Ain't many boys done that much. Not even Supervisor Utley has rode on railroad cars. Besides, how'm I going to run the place?"

He was still looking over her head. His face was blank, as only a seventeen-year-old boy's can be, defensive and stubborn. She took the end of her shawl to put it to her eyes. "When Pa moved up from New Haven way out into York State, he promised I was to have a home permanent in Westernville. And then he died, and I calculated you would grow up there and take care of me. Remember how you promised Pa? What will I say to the Utleys?"

"Tell them I aim to see something of the world," Tom said. "I aim to look me around a spell. I'll come home, maybe in the spring. You'll be all right. You got your widow pension off the government, didn't you? You can hire help now."

She sniffed two or three times. "Oh, Tom," she said, "where'll you go to?"

"I don't know," he said, shuffling his feet. "Maybe Europe. Maybe I'll go to China."

"But, oh, Tom, you ain't got money. You ain't never been nowhere."

"That's it. I ain't been nowhere," he said.

Passengers were coming onto the boat, their feet crackling sharply on the deck outside. She saw that his face was set, and she looked at the freckles as if she wanted to count them over before he left her. His father had been just as stubborn; you couldn't turn him; wasn't anything more stubborn, she thought with a little twinge of pain and pride, than a Whipple man when he got dead set.

He cast a look around and saw that they were partly screened by the stove. He bent down awkwardly to kiss her.

"Good-by, Ma," he said. "See you come spring, I guess."

The warning bell began to toll as he stepped off the boat.

"Well, bub," said the man with the hedge of black chin whiskers. "What do you want?"

"You're hiring help, ain't you?" asked Tom Whipple.

The man shoved the stiff-visored cap back on his head and put his feet on the box he had been writing on. He had a square face, the skin like red leather on his cheeks. His eyes were piercing, gray, and hard.

"Yep," he said. "What can you do? Milk perty good, hey? Pitch hay? Say, maybe you can make butter too?"

"I could," said Tom. "I ain't done much, but my ma makes dandy butter. We sell ourn to Supervisor Utley."

"Yew deaow, hey?" The mate got a big laugh from the men in the three-cent-gin shop where he was signing on the crew. "Now that's real handy of yeaow."

Tom Whipple stared at him. He said, "I calculate you must come from Massachusetts State."

This time he got the laugh, and the mate's eyes narrowed. But though he let it go, anybody could see he wasn't going to let Tom Whipple out of his hands after that.

His voice was even and cold. "Ever been to sea?" he asked.

"No," said Tom.

The mate turned to the saloon-keeper for sympathy. "Jeff, did you ever see a crummier lot of ditch lice?" He wheeled round again on Tom. "This is a ship, not a farm. You'll get eleven dollars a month, and you don't milk cows. But we make a ship sail, see?"

"Yes," said Tom. "That's what I want. I want to travel."

"You'll travel all right aboard the *Flora Bascom.*" The mate smiled thinly. "Name?"

"Tom Whipple."

The mate's pen squeaked.

"All right," he said. "Next man."

"Just a minute," Tom said. "Where's the *Flora Bascom* sailing to?"

"It's none of your business," said the mate. He rose behind the box. "My name is Mr. Bullett," he said evenly. "I don't want remarks from you. I don't want questions. But when you speak, I'm 'Mister.' Understand?"

"All right," Tom said good-naturedly.

He didn't know what happened. The mate did not move from behind his box, but his fist hit Tom between the eyes. The next he knew, he was lying on the floor and Mr. Bullett was saying, "Mister!" and breathing gently on his knuckles. "Mr. Freel," he said, "take him aboard and see if you can pick some of the straws out of his ears."

A thick-shouldered man yanked Tom to his feet and shoved him toward the door. "Come along, hay-foot," he said. He smelled of tar and plug tobacco and gin and a peculiar kind of hair grease. Half a dozen of the other new hands came after them. But their sycophants' laughter stopped as they emerged into the rumbling clatter of South Street.

"The mate's a bully, ain't he?" one asked.

"Not too bad, if you look sharp and jump when he spits," replied the second mate. "Besides, he's found himself a toy." He nodded at Tom, who was giddily trying to avoid a cart horse.

Tom spent all that day trying to do what he was told, along with the other men. The idea seemed not so much to get the work done as to keep the hands busy, and there were moments when Mr. Freel scratched the bald spot on his head and looked hopefully toward Mr. Bullett.

At noon and at four the men were allowed ashore for an hour, but Tom was kept on board, for Mr. Freel had an idea he might clear out. He told Tom that somebody had to keep watch on the ship. Tom didn't know his rights, of course. Nobody told him that the one-armed old fellow smoking a clay pipe amidships was the shipkeeper, hired according to law. He was glad enough to stay on board and take the hour admiring the vessel. Mr. Freel brought him some scraps of food from the captain's table. Mr. Freel, it appeared, did not eat in the cabin, but, like other second mates, lived a kind of ghostly existence halfway between the forecastle and the cabin. And because Tom had proved handy with the ropes, he acted friendly.

One of the first things he asked was whether Tom had any money.

Tom said no, but he expected to have plenty when they docked across the ocean. Eleven dollars a month was good pay for an apprentice, he thought. Mr. Freel, whittling a plug into a horny palm, grunted.

"You'll need clothes," he said. "Sea boots and a pea jacket. You'll have to buy them from the slop chest. And you'll pay the master a hundred and fifty per cent profit on the transaction," he said.

Tom thought about it for a while before he said, "That don't seem honest."

"Maybe not," Mr. Freel said shortly. "But it's regular. He keeps good stuff in the slop, which is more than some do. You won't have such a hell of a big fortune, though, when you reach St. Petersburg."

Tom cleaned up his beans and said, "Where's that, Mr. Freel?"

"Russia. And a damned cold place, they say."

"Ain't you never been there?"

"No. And I ain't got much desire to go."

Tom lay on his back and looked up into the rigging. The sun and the wind put a kind of shine on the spars that was foreign to the hull.

"I'm glad we're going to Russia," he said. "I've had a fancy to see that place. Maybe I'll get to see the Emperor. Have you ever seen an emperor, Mr. Freel?"

"No," said Mr. Freel. "Captain Stath is emperor enough for me. Him and Mr. Bullett. What do you want to see the Emperor for, anyway?" he asked.

"Oh," said Tom, "I'd kind of like to talk to him. When you want to find out about something, Supervisor Utley says you want to ask the top man, as long as you ain't buying."

Tom Whipple had the bunk in the peak of the forecastle, where the air still smelled of the Dago Portuguese who had occupied it on the preceding voyage. When the crew laid after to be chosen into watches, he was taken by Mr. Bullett. The choosing was done under the eye of Captain Stath, a clean-shaven man with a calculating face. He was short with the first mate, and he did not speak to the second except to give orders, but he took the ship down the river in fine style. By evening the brig was a lonely box on the waves with eighteen men and a spotted cat, and America was a place on which the sun had set.

He was sick, and the cold bit as the sun went under, and Mr. Bullet, who had been driving him since the *Flora Bascom* dropped Castle Garden, ordered him aloft with a ball of marline for the boatswain.

"Stay up there till he tells you to bring it down. Maybe the wind will blow the hayseed out."

Tom took the ball in his right hand and worked himself onto the shrouds. He could hear the hiss of the water under him, and the cross ropes pushed against his chest. But he went up, and the only time he looked down he could see Mr. Bullett and Mr. Freel both looking up at him, and Captain Stath coming out of the cabin. Mr. Freel looked anxious, the captain showed nothing on his face at all, but Mr. Bullett was smiling his thin smile.

"Damn him," Tom said to himself. "I'm just as good as he is off this ship."

He didn't stop again. He felt the back wind off the sails against his face; the curve of them made dingy feather beds to lure a man to let go; but he went up.

He saw, after a while, the noncommittal face of the boatswain leaning over the yard. The boatswain's feet were like glue, and his hands were careless, and he laid a long line of tobacco spit level on the wind.

"I've seen a snail go up a bush!" he shouted. "But he got there, too, bub!"

It wasn't praise, exactly, but it made Tom feel easier. He found the yard a comfortable pressure on his belly. He let it carry his weight, gingerly, then with more confidence. Then he looked down and saw the hull slitting the water like a needle that a bug might straddle.

"It's bigger than it looks!" shouted the boatswain. "But don't look at it too long, bub! You'll see plenty of it when you're down!"

So Tom looked out while the boatswain worked. He saw the night on the Atlantic; the great heaving mass of it was leveled from that height, and he felt himself swoop over it, a little like the motion of a gull. But a gull didn't fly in the squeak and crash and booming of rigging. He had feathers to silence the wind.

Out there was Russia, he thought, and back of him was Westernville. He could imagine his mother, when she got home, telling Mrs. Utley and the supervisor what had become of him. She would say he was on a ship; maybe for Europe, maybe for China. He could imagine her crying and saying, "He didn't have any money. He didn't want any. You know how Tom is. Always going round with his pocket full of nails and things he picks up, thinking he is as good as the richest man alive." She would think of him asleep in bed, possibly. She would never imagine him up alone in the wind with the yard against his belly and his feet balanced on a spider thread. And the supervisor would clear his throat and say, "Pshaw, Mrs. Whipple," and ask where his supper was.

Thinking of supper at the Utleys' made Tom hungry. For the first time since the brig had met the Atlantic swell, he felt his stomach take a rational shape. "By holy," he said to himself, "I'm all right."

Then the marline ball was slapped against his palm, and the boatswain said, "Get down, bub. And take it easy. Any man can climb."

He went down easy, and when he hit the deck, the roll met his feet squarely. He could smell pork in the galley vent. Mr. Bullett came stamp-ing aft along the deck. His eyes had not changed, and he was still smiling thinly. But all he said was, "Take the marline back to Mr. Freel."

After a week or so, Tom was getting along well enough with the officers. But the fact that he was planning to see the Emperor was too much for Mr. Freel to keep to himself, and, once the foremast hands got wind of it, they talked about it all the way to Russia.

It didn't bother Tom a great deal, though. He didn't know, himself, how he was going to get to talk with him. He didn't even know what his name was, and nobody in the forecastle was able to tell him. They were a pretty mixed crew. Tom was the only genuine American citizen in the forecastle, except a man from New Orleans; and he wasn't hardly what Tom thought of as a Yankee. He saw they didn't mean harm; they had to have something to occupy their minds; but he thought they plain didn't understand how a man could get along. He wasn't worried, except about finding out the Emperor's name.

The bos'n told him that Russian names didn't count. You couldn't pronounce them anyway. And the carpenter said they didn't have last names in Russia at all; the names all ended in "sky," which meant "son of." The cook said, why didn't he ask the old man? So Tom said maybe he would.

But he didn't make up his mind to it till the *Flora Bascom* had worked her way across the Baltic Sea and was heading in for the gulf. At the wheel was the dim-witted Swede, but he could steer a ship like a dreaming archangel. It was Tom's turn at polishing the brasswork, and he was rubbing up the binnacle when Captain Stath came up for his morning constitutional.

All the time Tom worked he could hear the smart crack of the captain's heels on the frosty deck, measuring out his exact rectangle. It was easy to tell that the captain was feeling brisk. So Tom gave the shining brass a last flourish of the rag and caught the captain on his twenty-third quarter turn.

He touched his forelock smartly with the knuckle of the hand holding the brass polish and said, "Excuse me, Captain. Could you tell me the name of the Emperor of Russia?"

The captain wheeled like a speared sturgeon and roared, "What?" in a t'gallant bellow that brought the entire crew up standing.

Tom saw that he had put his foot in it, but he had to get out the question now, so he asked it again.

The captain's voice cut like the ice spray as he shouted for Mr. Bullett. The rest of the crew all grinned, for they had been waiting this minute; only the Swede didn't change face, but he wiggled his ears for a moment, as if he felt a shift coming in the wind. The sight of them didn't help the captain. By the time Mr. Bullett came up, he was in a state of frenzy.

"Do you know what's happened, mister?" he demanded, leveling his voice.

"No, sir," said Mr. Bullett.

"I've been interrupted on my own deck by one of the watch. Your watch, Mr. Bullett. And do you know what he wanted to know? He wanted to know the name of the Emperor of Russia, Mr. Bullett! . . . Are you going to stand there like a blasted gaping marble image, Mr. Bullett? Ain't you going to do something?"

Mr. Bullett did. He hailed Tom down amidships and had a couple of

seamen hold him over a barrel, and he put a rope's end on his bare back twenty times.

When he was through, they rolled Tom over on his back and emptied buckets of sea water over him and told him to put his shirt on and get to work. Tom felt sore, inside as well as out; the captain had taken up his walk at the exact point at which he had left off, and the only times he watched the flogging was during the short space when he was coming forward and crossing to starboard. The crew thought it was a prodigious joke, discussing it in the forecastle when the watch was off. It was the carpenter's opinion that none of the officers knew the Emperor's name.

Somehow the word of that got aft, and the rest of the voyage became pretty brisk for all of them, and Tom wasn't sorry to jump the brig as soon as she berthed in Kronstadt.

But when he reached St. Petersburg, he got to feeling better. He couldn't talk to anybody. They all looked foreign and many of them had a queer fat smell that made him think of a sheep's carcass hanging in the cool room. He was immensely excited by what he saw, and spent days walking the streets. New York, he thought, or even Washington City, wasn't in it, for strange sights. He saw all sorts of different-appearing people, and they didn't all talk one language either; even a stranger could tell that. He could tell it was a big country, and the urge to find out about it got more and more intense, and he felt surer than ever that the only way to do that was to have a talk with the man at the top, the Emperor.

He tried two or three times at the palace, and he kept watch on the gates, until he began to realize that to get next to the Emperor he would have to have letters or something of that sort.

He didn't know how to get hold of letters, and he had been there two weeks and his money was about gone. He was feeling a bit low that afternoon, standing outside a pub, when he saw a sailor ambling down the street and looking as footloose as himself.

He hadn't dared go back to the port in all this time, for fear of being picked up by Mr. Bullett. So, seeing that this sailor was a stranger, he hailed him, and they shook hands like two white men in a foreign country; fingering the few coins left in his pockets, he asked the sailor in for a drink. "It's just a pot likker," he said. "But it warms a person."

The sailor turned out to be off a British ship, and he was sympathetic. He had Tom's drink, and then he bought Tom one, and they got so friendly that Tom told him how he had been trying to get to see the Emperor, but didn't know how to go about it.

The sailor said it appeared to him like a difficult problem. "Can't your minister help you out?" he asked.

Tom said, "My minister?" and the sailor said, "Yes. The minister of the United States."

Tom said he hadn't been to see him. He hadn't thought of it; as a matter of fact, it had not even occurred to him that there could be such a job. It made him feel that the United States was a pretty fine coun try to send a minister all the way to St. Petersburg. He felt considerably better immediately; it was the next best thing to seeing a picture of Old Hickory himself on the wall. Well, said the sailor, why didn't Tom go to see him? Taking care of the interests of American citizens in Russia was what the American minister was paid to do. "And he's got to look after you same as the British minister has to look after me," he said. "That's what they collect the taxes off us for." Tom said he would go. The sailor offered to lend him the money to hire a sled with, but Tom declined. He didn't care to be beholden to a man he didn't know well, and a for eigner at that. So he said good-by and started off for the American embassy. He had a good idea of the direction because there turned out to be a Frenchman in the pub who said he knew.

Well, the minister lived in a mighty fine big house with the American flag flying over it, and when he saw it, Tom Whipple felt good. While he was looking at it, a man came walking from the other direc tion, and he was dressed in a good American coat; you could tell it a mile. He had a sealskin cap on his head, and with the flaps up, pretty near exactly like the one Supervisor Utley wore when he got into the cutter behind the bays and drove down to a Sunday dinner in Rome. But even without those garments, Tom could have told he was an American by the way he walked. He was coming right along, and you could see he meant business. So Tom stepped across the roadway, dodging a couple of droshkies with their jingling bells, and touched his hat to the American, and asked whether the American minister was to home.

The man looked Tom up and down from his worn felt hat and pea jacket to the old pants and the sea boots. He looked at Tom's freckled face and his young turkey neck and his rawboned wrists, and he gave him a smile.

"No," he said, "the minister's not home yet, but he will be in two shakes. Come in and let me see what I can do for you." He took off his hat, so Tom took his off and they went in the outer door.

"My name's Dallas," said the man. "I'm the minister."

"Whipple," said Tom. "I'm pleased to meet you."

Well, when they came to the inner door, the minister stood to one side to let Tom in first, and then a couple of Russian-dressed servants came up, and one took the minister's hat and coat and one took Tom's hat and his pea jacket. They went upstairs together to where the minister had a kind of office. There was coal burning in a tiled stove, there were books on the walls, and there was a table, something like a dresser, laid out with about every kind of bottle there was.

Mr. Dallas pointed to it and asked whether Tom would have anything to drink. But Tom declined. "There ain't nothing I'd like now except a glass of fresh buttermilk," he said. "I ain't been able to find none anywhere, Mr. Dallas. I can't figure out no Russian for it either."

Mr. Dallas smiled. He said he hadn't thought of buttermilk himself, but if there was anything that would taste good to him at that moment, buttermilk was what it would be. So he pulled a velvet rope hanging on the wall, and a servant came and went, and pretty soon he came in with two big glasses on a gold tray. Mr. Dallas took one and Tom the other; Mr. Dallas raised his and said, "Your very good health, Mr. Whipple." So Tom raised his and returned the compliment, and they took chairs and drank the buttermilk. Tom thought it wasn't near so good as what came out of his

mother's churning, but he didn't like to say so. And after being so long without it, he had to admit it tasted pleasant.

The minister talked plain to him. He asked how the U. S. A. was getting along, and Tom said that money was awful tight. He told how he and his mother had been to Washington to get her pension, and how he had seen the President go by down the avenue. He said he had gone over to Mount Vernon. And then he told about putting his mother on the Albany steamboat and how he had signed on the *Flora Bascom*. He hadn't known she was coming to Russia when he did it, but he was mighty glad when he learned, for he had heard about the Russians licking Napoleon Bonaparte, so he knew it was a great country, and he had made up his mind to see the Emperor. That, as a matter of fact, was what he had called on Mr. Dallas about. He would like to get a letter from Mr. Dallas, saying who he was and that he would like a little conversation with the Emperor.

Mr. Dallas looked at him for a moment before he said, picking his words, "You know, Whipple, the Emperor's a pretty hard man to get to see." Then he tried to explain how it was in an empire as compared to a democratic country. Tom thought it over, but he shook his head. He said he couldn't see it that way. He could see it might apply to a Russian farmer, in a manner of speaking, but he was a United States citizen. Martin Van Buren, now, he could see the Emperor, couldn't he? Mr. Dallas nodded his head; that was true. Then why couldn't Tom Whipple?

Well, they sawed away at it for a spell, and Mr. Dallas was as friendly a man as you could ask to argue with.

But Tom got the best of him at every turn, and finally he agreed to write a letter to the imperial court chamberlain for Tom. But he said there was one thing: It was the custom, when you went to call on an Emperor, to take him a present. Tom hadn't thought of that but he could see how it would be; and he stuck his hand in his pants pocket to fiddle the junk he carried, the way he always did when he was puzzled, and his fingers closed on an object he'd hardly thought of since leaving Washington City. Holding it, he thought how lucky it was he hadn't dropped it anywhere, like up on the topsail yards of the *Flora Bascom* driving off Finisterre. "All right," he said. "Tell him I got a present I'd mighty like to give the Emperor and that I figure the Emperor is going to be mighty pleased to have."

Mr. Dallas looked at Tom's face, and he wrote the message down without asking what the present was. Then he sealed the letter inside and out, prettifying it like anything, to Tom's way of thinking. He gave it to Tom, telling him to come around in the morning and he would send a man with him to be sure he got in to see the chamberlain. Then he asked Tom if he would have supper. He had to go out himself, he explained, his family was going with him, but he couldn't offer to take Tom, as it was a formal court dinner. However, if Tom didn't mind eating alone, he could have dinner here.

So Tom ate alone in the dining room, with five men to wait on him, not one of whom could talk good English; and after dinner, to save money, he found himself a stable and slept in the hay.

It meant a good deal of picking and dusting to get clear of the hay in the morning, but he turned up at the minister's house on time and was sent off with a clerk. Mr. Dallas came down to shake hands with him and said for him to come back when he was ready; he would see that Tom got a berth on a ship to go home. Tom thanked him and said he would.

He could tell that Mr. Dallas didn't expect he would get to see the Emperor at all, but he didn't hold it against him. Mr. Dallas had been as neighborly as any man could be.

The clerk was a dapper man. Tom could tell at first glance that he wasn't the quality of man Mr. Dallas was. As soon as they got round the corner, he asked Tom whether he had the minister's letter. Tom slapped his coat pocket to show he did, and the clerk said, "Well, come on, then."

It amused Tom some to see how walking alongside of him made the clerk uneasy. He kept pressing forward as if he was trying to leave Tom behind, but he couldn't walk worth a duck. It didn't bother Tom. He could imagine how the clerk would look setting out to pitch hay.

But the clerk knew where to go and whom to speak to. Inside the palace he kept whispering to Tom not to make such a hooraw with his boots; but you can't help making some noise with sea boots on a tile floor, so Tom went the quietest he could without tiptoeing, and let it go at that. He knew people were looking at him; they in their Russian costumes and he in his pea jacket made kind of a mixture, he could see. But it didn't bother him. They liked to wear that kind of clothes, and he liked his own. When they got to the chamberlain's room, the clerk gave his message to a flunky, and pretty soon this man came out and told them to go in through the inner door.

Tom had supposed that the clerk would go in with him to see the chamberlain, but the clerk was through. He said, "In there," to Tom, as if he was driving a pig to a sticker, and turned on his heel. Tom let him go. He didn't feel that the clerk would have been much help anyhow.

In the chamberlain's office there was a handsome, bearded, elderly man sitting at a desk. He got up and bowed, when Tom entered, and Tom handed him Mr. Dallas' letter, and the chamberlain said he was honored, in very unsteady English, but understandable. He read the letter, and then he looked at Tom for a spell.

He said, "You know the Emperor is a very busy man, Mr. Whipple."

"I calculate he must be, running a country this size, and without no congress either, so far as I know," said Tom.

The chamberlain bowed. "For instance, today he has five audiences in the morning; then an hour of state papers to sign and the imperial policies to consider. Then he has to go to a military review. Then he eats with the Empress. Then this afternoon he receives a delegation of Cossacks, and must inspect the Palace Guard and decorate a grand duke, and in the evening he has to appear at the opera. You see, he is busy."

"I expected he would be," Tom said. "But I don't aim to take a lot of his time."

"Well," said the chamberlain, "using my influence, I might be able to arrange an audience with him next April."

But that didn't suit Tom's book at all. "It's this way," he said: "I ain't got the money to stay here that long. In fact, if I don't see the Emperor

in the next day or two, I'll have to just take ship without seeing him at all. I'd hate to to that. You tell him, seeing he's so all-fired busy, I won't take any of his time. I'll just give him my present and wish him luck and clear out."

"Well," said the chamberlain, "I will see. But perhaps you would give me the present to present it for you."

"I wouldn't," said Tom. He wanted to be polite, though, so he added, "I got this present in America, mister, and I'd like to give it to the Emperor with my own hand."

Well, the chamberlain hadn't ever come up against a genuine Yankee, and he couldn't make him out. He looked baffled, biting the inside whiskers of his mustache as if he'd like to turn Tom over to a squad of Cossacks, maybe; but there was Mr. Dallas' letter in his hand, so he couldn't do that. And after a couple of minutes of thinking, he made up his mind.

"I'll take your letter in to the Emperor now," he said.

"That's fine," said Tom. "Just put it up to him. It's a fair proposition."

Well, in about ten minutes, back came the chamberlain, and along with him was a fine tall man. From the way he walked, Tom saw he was a man who didn't have to fiddle with this and that, but marked his first chip and axed right to the line. He was a good deal bigger than the chamberlain and he had a bold sharp eye. He wasn't dressed so fancy, but he didn't have to be dressed fancy to tell a person he was somebody. There wasn't any doubt he was the Emperor. And then Tom realized he didn't know the man's name.

He hesitated a moment, and then he decided, even though he was younger, the thing was up to him, so as not to embarrass the man. So he took three steps forward and held out his hand.

"My name's Tom Whipple," he said. "I'm from the U. S. A. I ain't been in your country long, but it seems like a fine country, and before I left I wanted to give you a present."

The Emperor looked at him a minute. His eyes went all over Tom in a glance and then rested on his face. Then he smiled and held out his own hand and they shook.

"Hello, Tom," he said. "My name's Nicholas. I'm glad to welcome you. I wish you'd come to see me sooner."

"Well," said Tom, "you're a mighty hard man to get to see, Emperor. I tried half a dozen times."

"That's the trouble with being an emperor," said Nicholas. "They run in all the people you don't want to talk to, and they keep out the people you do."

He had an easy way with him; he seemed neighborly.

He said, "Now you've got here, though, we'll have a talk. You come with me, Tom."

But the chamberlain interrupted in Russian, and from the way the Emperor talked back, it sounded like swearing. The chamberlain stepped back, and the two of them walked out on him. As soon as they were outside, Nicholas laughed and put his hand on Tom's shoulder.

"I told him to throw out everybody," he said, "and he don't like it much. But he's got to do it. That's one of the good things about being an emperor, even if there aren't many."

Well, he took Tom to another room, as big as a convention hall, to Tom's eyes, which, he said, was his own snug place where they wouldn't be disturbed, and the first thing he did was ask to see his present.

Tom was glad he had thought of it then. He pulled his hand out of his pocket, and then he opened it and he showed the Emperor an acorn resting in the palm of his hand.

The Emperor looked at it, and then he took it and said, "Thanks," in a friendly way, but Tom could see he was a mite puzzled. It made him grin.

"Shucks," he said. "I wouldn't bring you no ordinary acorn, Emperor. I picked that up in Mount Vernon. That was the place George Washington lived and died at. This nut's right off one of his own personal trees." Then he felt a little bashful, so he added, "I thought you'd appreciate it, being as it comes from the home of the greatest man of the U. S. A., greater even than Old Hickory."

"I do, Tom," said the Emperor. "I've studied the history of your country, and I admire General Washington more than about any man I know of."

"Well, you ought to," said Tom. "And over there we admire you folks too. The way you licked Napoleon Bonaparte. I calculate that took some doing too."

"I value this acorn a lot, Tom," said the Emperor, "and I'll tell you what I plan to do. We'll have a good talk till the day warms up some, and then we'll go out and plant this acorn. I'll have them thaw out a piece in my own palace garden, and you and I'll plant this acorn there together. An American and a Russian."

"That sounds just proper to me," Tom agreed.

"And then we'll have lunch with my wife and family," said the Emperor, just as Supervisor Utley might have said it. "But now you sit down."

Well, the Emperor put Tom right through the business. He wanted to know all about America. He was most interested in the railroads and the schools and the steamboats, and Tom was proud that he had been through grammar school and had ridden on the railroad cars. He was able to tell the Emperor a lot he didn't know.

Then they talked about tight money, and the Emperor told him about a famine he had had, and it seemed in Russia you didn't have a money panic at all, you had a famine —which was simpler, in a way, but Tom thought it amounted to much the same thing for the people who were hard up to start with.

They kept at it till noon, and Tom gave the Emperor some of Supervisor Utley's ideas about banking, which interested the Emperor a whole lot. Then they went out and planted the acorn. There was a squad of Cossacks standing round, but they kept out of the way.

The Emperor wondered whether the acorn would grow, and Tom didn't see why not. It was a sound nut from a sound tree, he said.

So then they took a turn round the palace grounds, and a couple of big, spotted, silk-haired dogs, kind of like greyhounds, joined up with the Cossacks. They looked at some horses, which, Tom could see, were dandies, and he asked where the Emperor kept his cows. He was mighty keen to see a Russian milch cow, he said, but the Emperor told him he would have to go out of the city, and he said he would send him out tomorrow. He couldn't go himself, because an Emperor might kick over the thills once in a while, but

he had to keep on the road, too, by and large, to get along, just like an ordinary man.

Well, they had their food in another apartment of the palace, and the Empress turned out to be obliging. She talked English better than the Emperor did, and she wanted to know all about housekeeping in the U. S. A. Tom told her all he knew, which wasn't so much, since his mother took care of that end of their lives. But he told her how they made butter and maple sugar, and mincemeat, and corn bread, and she called a servant and had it all written down, just as he said it. Then she said she guessed she was right in thinking that there weren't any servants in America. And Tom had to laugh at her, and said she must have been reading Mrs. Trollope's book. He hadn't read Mrs. Trollope's book himself, but he had heard Supervisor Utley talk about it enough to know the kind of nonsense that was in it.

The Empress admitted she had, so Tom told her that while poor folks did their own work—and weren't ashamed to, either—rich people in U. S. A. were just like other folks, and had servants, and plenty of them. But the Empress said you didn't call them servants, but help, and Tom said that was so, but it always seemed to him like a good idea. The Emperor semed pleased by the conversation, and he made one of his daughters go out for some crocheting or some kind of fancywork she had been doing, and Tom admired it. The Emperor's girls were fine girls, modest and well mannered, but shy of him. When he praised the fancywork, the girl that had made it colored all up and made him a curtsy, and then asked him if he would take it back to his mother as a present from her.

That made Tom blush, but he said he would. He hadn't felt so much at home since he left Westernville, and he made up his mind he would have to show the crocheting to Mr. Dallas.

Well, they talked all through the afternoon, and the Emperor called in some Russian dancers to show Tom how they danced in Russia, and he tried to show them a square dance, but only the girl who had given him the fancywork and the Emperor himself seemed to catch on. The rest weren't handy at it at all. But he put that down to their being bashful and foreign, and it didn't bother him.

Then the Emperor said he would have to get back to work, but he asked Tom where he was staying, so he could send round a sleigh for him in the morning to go see the cows. Tom told him he was getting hard up, so he was sleeping in barns, but would meet the sleigh at the palace door. The Emperor wanted him to stay at the palace, but Tom wouldn't. He said he could take care of himself, and wouldn't put anybody out, so the Emperor shook hands with him and said to see him after he had looked at the cows.

Tom looked at them next day. He went out in a sleigh with three horses, and a fine fur robe over him, and a squad of Cossacks ahead and another behind.

He saw the Emperor the next day and told him he had a nice barn, and that he had milked a couple and thought they were a fair-to-middling good breed, and there was one of the springers he downright fancied. The Emperor said he was glad of Tom's opinion; he had never been able to judge a cow himself.

Then he asked Tom whether there was anything else he wanted to see, and though Tom didn't like to ask so much, he finally admitted he would like to look at Moscow, where Napoleon was licked. So the Emperor sent him to Moscow, and this time Tom traveled with all the luxuries and stayed in the palaces and the best hotels, and the officer who went with him took him to the theater and gave him a champagne supper every night.

Tom found it hard to keep going, not being used to so much high life, and he had to admire the Russians for the way they could keep it up. But he enjoyed it, too, and he had to tell the Emperor he was sorry to think of leaving for home. "But I got to get back and get to work," he said. "Ma's expecting me." And he pointed out that even an ordinary man had to work, like an Emperor.

The Emperor said he was sorry to see him go. But if Tom had to get back he would have to go down into Europe to Germany, for the gulf was frozen over and no ships leaving. To Tom that seemed like putting the Emperor to a lot of trouble, but he told Tom to think nothing of it. If a man had to get to work, he had to. So they shook hands, and Tom said good-by to the Empress and her girls, and he called on Mr. Dallas, who was surprised and interested to hear his story. Then the Emperor's Cossacks took Tom out of Russia.

When he got to Westernville in the spring, though, he was mighty glad to be home. He had kept thinking of maple sirup and buckwheat cakes all the way across the Atlantic; and sure enough, his mother had them for him when he sat down to supper.

After supper they went up to the Utleys', and there he told them all about the trip. The women could hardly credit the wonders Tom had seen, till he pulled out the fancy-work the Emperor's girl had sent to Mrs. Whipple. Then he showed them a big watch and chain with a ruby stone hanging to it that the Emperor had given him in return

for the acorn. It struck its own hours and half-hours, and was made of gold.

But even then it seemed like a fairy story to Mrs. Whipple—the great people treating her Tom like a prince—and she remarked on it so often that Supervisor Utley was obliged to say, "Pshaw, Mrs. Whipple. Any American lad, like Tom here, can get along anywhere on earth."

Conrad Aiken
1889-

SINCE his undergraduate days, Conrad Aiken has known exactly where he wanted to go. At Harvard he cut classes for ten days in order to turn a French story into an English poem. In World War I he refused to serve, claiming that as a poet he was in an "essential industry"—and was excused on that ground. He has been determinedly independent and has always stood clear of literary or propaganda groups. The Harvard of his day, however, contained a group that definitely did not stand clear: Heywood Broun, Walter Lippmann, T. S. Eliot, Robert Edmond Jones, Van Wyck Brooks, John Reed. It was the period of Freud, and Aiken, like so many undergraduates of those years, was steeped in psychoanalysis, if not in politics and sociology. His concern with the subconscious gives subtle depths to his character studies, as in "Silent Snow, Secret Snow." Aiken has remained preeminently the poet, and his rather rare stories are written in a poet's beautiful prose.

Silent Snow, Secret Snow

BY CONRAD AIKEN

I

Just why it should have happened, or why it should have happened just when it did, he could not, of course, possibly have said; nor perhaps could it even have occurred to him to ask. The thing was above all a secret, something to be preciously concealed from Mother and Father; and to that very fact it owed an enormous part of its deliciousness. It was like a peculiarly beautiful trinket to be carried unmentioned in one's trouser pocket—a rare stamp, an old coin, a few tiny gold links found trodden out of shape on the path in the park, a pebble of carnelian, a sea shell distinguishable from all others by an unusual spot or stripe—and, as if it were anyone of these, he carried around with him everywhere a warm and persistent and increasingly beautiful sense of possession. Nor was it only a sense of possession —it was also a sense of protection. It was as if, in some delightful way, his secret gave him a fortress, a wall behind which he could retreat into heavenly seclusion. This was almost the first thing he had noticed about it—apart from the oddness of the thing itself—and it was this that now again, for the fiftieth time, occurred to him, as he sat in the little schoolroom. It was the half-hour for geography. Miss Buell was revolving with one finger, slowly, a huge terrestrial globe which had been placed on her desk. The green and yellow continents passed and repassed, questions were asked and answered, and now the little girl in front of him, Deirdre, who had a funny little constellation of freckles on the back of her neck, exactly like the Big Dipper, was standing up and telling Miss Buell that the equator was the line that ran round the middle.

Miss Buell's face, which was old and grayish and kindly, with gray stiff curls beside the cheeks, and eyes that swam very brightly, like little minnows, behind thick glasses, wrinkled itself into a complication of amusements.

"Ah! I see. The earth is wearing a belt, or a sash. Or someone drew a line round it!"

"Oh, no—not that—I mean——"

In the general laughter, he did not share, or only a very little. He was thinking about the Arctic and Antarctic regions, which of course, on the globe, were white. Miss Buell was now telling them about the tropics, the jungles, the steamy heat of equatorial swamps, where the birds and butterflies, and even the snakes, were like living jewels. As he listened to these things, he was already, with a pleasant sense of half effort, putting his secret between himself and the words. Was it really an effort at all? For effort implied something voluntary, and perhaps even something one did not especially want; whereas this was distinctly pleasant, and came almost of its own accord. All he needed to do was to think of that morning, the first one, and then of all the others—

But it was all so absurdly simple! It had amounted to so little. It was nothing, just an idea—and just why it should have become so wonderful, so permanent, was a mystery— a very pleasant one, to be sure, but also, in an amusing way, foolish. However, without ceasing to listen to Miss Buell, who had now moved up to the north temperate zones, he deliberately invited his memory of the first morning. It was only a moment or two after he had waked up—or perhaps the moment itself. But was there, to be exact, an exact moment? Was one awake all at once? or was it gradual? Anyway, it was after he had stretched a lazy hand up towards the head rail, and yawned, and then relaxed again among his warm covers, all the more grateful on a December morning, that the thing had happened. Suddenly, for no reason, he had thought of the postman, he remembered the postman. Perhaps there was nothing so odd in that. After all, he heard the postman almost every morning in his life—his heavy boots could be heard clumping round the corner at the top of the little cobbled hill street, and then, progressively nearer, progressively louder, the double knock at each door, the cross-

ings and recrossings of the street, till finally the clumsy steps came stumbling across to the very door, and the tremendous knock came which shook the house itself.

(Miss Buell was saying, "Vast wheat-growing areas in North America and Siberia."

Deirdre had for the moment placed her left hand across the back of her neck.)

But on this particular morning, the first morning, as he lay there with his eyes closed, he had for some reason *waited* for the postman. He wanted to hear him come round the corner. And that was precisely the joke—he never did. He never came. He never had come—*round the corner*—again. For when at last the steps *were* heard, they had already, he was quite sure, come a little down the hill, to the first house; and even so, the steps were curiously different —they were softer, they had a new secrecy about them, they were muffled and indistinct; and while the rhythm of them was the same, it now said a new thing—it said peace, it said remoteness, it said cold, it said sleep. And he had understood the situation at once—nothing could have seemed simpler—there had been snow in the night, such as all winter he had been longing for; and it was this which had rendered the postman's first footsteps inaudible, and the later ones faint. Of course! How lovely! And even now it must be snowing—it was going to be a snowy day—the long white ragged lines were drifting and sifting across the street, across the faces of the old houses, whispering and hushing, making little triangles of white in the corners between cobblestones, seething a little when the wind blew them over the ground to a drifted corner; and so it would be all day, getting deeper and deeper and silenter and silenter.

(Miss Buell was saying, "Land of perpetual snow.")

All this time, of course (while he lay in bed), he had kept his eyes closed, listening to the nearer progress of the postman, the muffled footsteps thumping and slipping on the snow-sheathed cobbles; and all the other sounds—the double knocks, a frosty far-off voice or two, a bell ringing thinly and softly as if under a sheet of ice—had the same slightly abstracted quality, as if removed by one degree from actuality—as if everything in the world had been insulated by snow. But when at last, pleased, he opened his eyes, and turned them towards the window, to see for himself this long-desired and now so clearly imagined miracle —what he saw instead was brilliant sunlight on a roof; and when, astonished, he jumped out of bed and stared down into the street, expecting to see the cobbles obliterated by the snow, he saw nothing but the bare bright cobbles themselves.

Queer, the effect this extraordinary surprise had had upon him— all the following morning he had kept with him a sense as of snow falling about him, a secret screen of new snow between himself and the world. If he had not dreamed such a thing—and how could he have dreamed it while awake?—how else could one explain it? In any case, the delusion had been so vivid as to affect his entire behavior. He could not now remember whether it was on the first or the second morning— or was it even the third?—that his mother had drawn attention to some oddness in his manner.

"But, my darling—" she had said at the breakfast table—"what has come over you? You don't seem to be listening. . . ."

And how often that very thing had happened since!

(Miss Buell was now asking if anyone knew the difference between the North Pole and the Magnetic Pole. Deirdre was holding up her flickering brown hand, and he could see the four white dimples that marked the knuckles.)

Perhaps it hadn't been either the second or third morning—or even the fourth or fifth. How could he be sure? How could he be sure just when the delicious *progress* had become clear? Just when it had really *begun*? The intervals weren't very precise. . . . All he now knew was that at some point or other— perhaps the second day, perhaps the sixth—he had noticed that the presence of the snow was a little more insistent, the sound of it clearer; and, conversely, the sound of the postman's footsteps more indistinct. Not only could he not hear the steps come round the corner, he could not even hear them at the first house. It was below the first house that he heard them; and then, a few days later, it was below the second house that he heard them; and a few days later again, below the third. Gradually, gradually, the snow was becoming heavier, the sound of its seething louder, the cobblestones more and more muffled. When he found, each morning, on going to the window, after the ritual of listening, that the roofs and cobbles were as bare as ever, it made no difference. This was, after all, only what he had expected. It was even what pleased him, what rewarded him: the thing was his own, belonged to no one else. No one else knew about it, not even his mother and father. There, outside, were the bare cobbles; and here, inside, was the snow. Snow growing heavier each day, muffling the world, hiding the ugly, and deadening increasingly—above all—the steps of the postman.

"But, my darling—" she had said at the luncheon table—"what has come over you? You don't seem to listen when people speak to you. That's the third time I've asked you to pass your plate. . . ."

How was one to explain this to Mother? or to Father? There was, of course, nothing to be done about it: nothing. All one could do was to laugh embarrassedly, pretend to be a little ashamed, apologize, and take a sudden and somewhat disingenuous interest in what was being done or said. The cat had stayed out all night. He had a curious swelling on his left cheek—perhaps somebody had kicked him, or a stone had struck him. Mrs. Kempton was or was not coming to tea. The house was going to be house cleaned, or "turned out," on Wednesday instead of Friday. A new lamp was provided for his evening work—perhaps it was eyestrain which accounted for this new and so peculiar vagueness of his—Mother was looking at him with amusement as she said this, but with something else as well. A new lamp? A new lamp. Yes Mother, No Mother, Yes Mother. School is going very well. The geometry is very easy. The history is very dull. The geography is very interesting—particularly when it takes one to the North Pole. Why the North Pole? Oh, well, it would be fun to be an explorer. Another Peary or Scott or Shackleton. And then abruptly he found his interest in the talk at an end, started at the pudding on his plate, listened, waited, and began once more—ah how heavenly, too, the first beginnings—to hear or feel—for could he

actually hear it?—the silent snow, the secret snow.

(Miss Buell was telling them about the search for the Northwest Passage, about Hendrik Hudson, the *Half Moon.*)

This had been, indeed, the only distressing feature of the new experience: the fact that it so increasingly had brought him into a kind of mute misunderstanding, or even conflict, with his father and mother. It was as if he were trying to lead a double life. On the one hand he had to be Paul Hasleman, and keep up the appearance of being that person—dress, wash, and answer intelligently when spoken to; on the other, he had to explore this new world which had been opened to him. Nor could there be the slightest doubt—not the slightest—that the new world was the profounder and more wonderful of the two. It was irresistible. It was miraculous. Its beauty was simply beyond anything—beyond speech as beyond thought—utterly incommunicable. But how then, between the two worlds, of which he was thus constantly aware, was he to keep a balance? One must get up, one must go to breakfast, one must talk with Mother, go to school, do one's lessons—and, in all this, try not to appear too much of a fool. But if all the while one was also trying to extract the full deliciousness of another and quite separate existence, one which could not easily (if at all) be spoken of—how was one to manage? How was one to explain? Would it be safe to explain? Would it be absurd? Would it merely mean that he would get into some obscure kind of trouble?

These thoughts came and went, came and went, as softly and secretly as the snow; they were not precisely a disturbance, perhaps they were even a pleasure; he liked to have them; their presence was something almost palpable, something he could stroke with his hand, without closing his eyes, and without ceasing to see Miss Buell and the schoolroom and the globe and the freckles on Deirdre's neck; nevertheless he did in a sense cease to see, or to see the obvious external world, and substituted for this vision the vision of snow, the sound of snow, and the slow, almost soundless, approach of the postman. Yesterday, it had been only at the sixth house that the postman had become audible; the snow was much deeper now, it was falling more swiftly and heavily, the sound of its seething was more distinct, more soothing, more persistent. And this morning, it had been—as nearly as he could figure—just above the seventh house—perhaps only a step or two above: at most, he had heard two or three footsteps before the knock had sounded. . . . And with each such narrowing of the sphere, each nearer approach of the limit at which the postman was first audible, it was odd how sharply was increased the amount of illusion which had to be carried into the ordinary business of daily life. Each day, it was harder to get out of bed, to go to the window, to look out at the—as always—perfectly empty and snowless street. Each day it was more difficult to go through the perfunctory motions of greeting Mother and Father at breakfast, to reply to their questions, to put his books together and go to school. And at school, how extraordinarily hard to conduct with success simultaneously the public life and the life that was secret. There were times when he longed—positively ached—to tell everyone about it— to burst out with it—only to be checked almost at once by a far-off

feeling as of some faint absurdity which was inherent in it—but *was* it absurd?—and more importantly by a sense of mysterious power in his very secrecy. Yes: it must be kept secret. That, more and more, became clear. At whatever cost to himself, whatever pain to others——

(Miss Buell looked straight at him, smiling, and said, "Perhaps we'll ask Paul. I'm sure Paul will come out of his daydream long enough to be able to tell us. Won't you, Paul." He rose slowly from his chair, resting one hand on the brightly varnished desk, and deliberately stared through the snow towards the blackboard. It was an effort, but it was amusing to make it. "Yes," he said slowly, "it was what we now call the Hudson River. This he thought to be the Northwest Passage. He was disappointed." He sat down again, and as he did so Deirdre half turned in her chair and gave him a shy smile, of approval and admiration.)

At whatever pain to others.

This part of it was very puzzling, very puzzling. Mother was very nice, and so was Father. Yes, that was all true enough. He wanted to be nice to them, to tell them everything— and yet, was it really wrong of him to want to have a secret place of his own?

At bedtime, the night before, Mother had said, "If this goes on, my lad, we'll have to see a doctor, we will! We can't have our boy——" But what was it she had said? "Live in another world"? "Live so far away"? The word "far" had been in it, he was sure, and then Mother had taken up a magazine again and laughed a little, but with an expression which wasn't mirthful. He had felt sorry for her. . . .

The bell rang for dismissal. The

sound came to him through long curved parallels of falling snow. He saw Deirdre rise, and had himself risen almost as soon—but not quite as soon—as she.

II

On the walk homeward, which was timeless, it pleased him to see through the accompaniment, or counterpoint, of snow, the items of mere externality on his way. There were many kinds of bricks in the sidewalks, and laid in many kinds of pattern. The garden walls too were various, some of wooden palings, some of plaster, some of stone. Twigs of bushes leaned over the walls; the little hard green winter buds of lilac, on gray stems, sheathed and fat; other branches very thin and fine and black and desiccated. Dirty sparrows huddled in the bushes, as dull in color as dead fruit left in leafless trees. A single starling creaked on a weather vane. In the gutter, beside a drain, was a scrap of torn and dirty newspaper, caught in a little delta of filth: the word ECZEMA appeared in large capitals, and below it was a letter from Mrs. Amelia D. Cravath, 2100 Pine Street, Fort Worth, Texas, to the effect that after being a sufferer for years she had been cured by Caley's Ointment. In the little delta, beside the fan-shaped and deeply runneled continent of brown mud, were lost twigs, descended from their parent trees, dead matches, a rusty horse-chestnut burr, a small concentration of sparkling gravel on the lip of the sewer, a fragment of eggshell, a streak of yellow sawdust which had been wet and was now dry and congealed, a brown pebble, and a broken feather. Further on was a cement sidewalk, ruled into geo-metrical parallelograms, with a brass inlay at one end commemorating the contractors who had laid it, and, halfway across, an irregular and random series of dog tracks, immortalized in synthetic stone. He knew these well, and always stepped on them; to cover the little hollows with his own foot had always been a queer pleasure; today he did it once more, but perfunctorily and detachedly, all the while thinking of something else. That was a dog, a long time ago, who had made a mistake and walked on the cement while it was still wet. He had probably wagged his tail, but that hadn't been recorded. Now, Paul Hasleman, aged twelve, on his way home from school, crossed the same river, which in the meantime had frozen into rock. Homeward through the snow, the snow falling in bright sunshine. Homeward?

Then came the gateway with the two posts surmounted by egg-shaped stones which had been cunningly balanced on their ends, as if by Columbus, and mortared in the very act of balance: a source of perpetual wonder. On the brick wall just beyond, the letter H had been stenciled, presumably for some purpose. H? H.

The green hydrant, with a little green-painted chain attached to the brass screw cap.

The elm tree, with the great gray wound in the bark, kidney-shaped, into which he always put his hand—to feel the cold but living wood. The injury, he had been sure, was due to the knawings of a tethered horse. But now it deserved only a passing palm, a merely tolerant eye. There were more important things. Miracles. Beyond the thoughts of trees, mere elms. Beyond the thoughts of sidewalks, mere stone, mere brick, mere cement. Beyond the thoughts even of his own shoes, which trod these sidewalks obediently, bearing a burden—far above—of elaborate mystery. He watched them. They were not very well polished; he had neglected them, for a very good reason: they were one of the many parts of the increasing difficulty of the daily return to daily life, the morning struggle. To get up, having at last opened one's eyes, to go to the window, and discover no snow, to wash, to dress, to descend the curving stairs to breakfast——

At whatever pain to others, nevertheless, one must persevere in severance, since the incommunicability of the experience demanded it. It was desirable of course to be kind to Mother and Father, especially as they seemed to be worried, but it was also desirable to be resolute. If they should decide—as appeared likely—to consult the doctor, Doctor Howells, and have Paul inspected, his heart listened to through a kind of dictaphone, his lungs, his stomach —well, that was all right. He would go through with it. He would give them answer for question, too—perhaps such answers as they hadn't expected? No. That would never do. For the secret world must, at all costs, be preserved.

The birdhouse in the apple tree was empty—it was the wrong time of year for wrens. The little round black door had lost its pleasure. The wrens were enjoying other houses, other nests, remoter trees. But this too was a notion which he only vaguely and grazingly entertained— as if, for the moment, he merely touched an edge of it; there was something further on, which was already assuming a sharper importance; something which already teased at the corners of his eyes,

teasing also at the corner of his mind. It was funny to think that he so wanted this, so awaited it—and yet found himself enjoying this momentary dalliance with the birdhouse, as if for a quite deliberate postponement and enhancement of the approaching pleasure. He was aware of his delay, of his smiling and detached and now almost uncomprehending gaze at the little birdhouse; he knew what he was going to look at next: it was his own little cobbled hill street, his own house, the little river at the bottom of the hill, the grocer's shop with the cardboard man in the window— and now, thinking of all this, he turned his head, still smiling, and looking quickly right and left through the snow-laden sunlight.

And the mist of snow, as he had foreseen, was still on it—a ghost of snow falling in the bright sunlight, softly and steadily floating and turning and pausing, soundlessly meeting the snow that covered, as with a transparent mirage, the bare bright cobbles. He loved it—he stood still and loved it. Its beauty was paralyzing—beyond all words, all experience, all dream. No fairy story he had ever read could be compared with it—none had ever given him this extraordinary combination of ethereal loveliness with a something else, unnamable, which was just faintly and deliciously terrifying. What was this thing? As he thought of it, he looked upward toward his own bedroom window, which was open—and it was as if he looked straight into the room and saw himself lying half awake in his bed. There he was—at this very instant he was still perhaps actually there— more truly there than standing here at the edge of the cobbled hill street, with one hand lifted to shade his eyes against the snow-sun. Had he indeed ever left his room, in all this time? since that very first morning? Was the whole progress still being enacted there, was it still the same morning, and himself not yet wholly awake? And even now, had the postman not yet come round the corner? . . .

This idea amused him, and automatically, as he thought of it, he turned his head and looked toward the top of the hill. There was, of course, nothing there—nothing and no one. The street was empty and quiet. And all the more because of its emptiness it occurred to him to count the houses—a thing which, oddly enough, he hadn't before thought of doing. Of course, he had known there weren't many—many, that is, on his own side of the street, which were the ones that figured in the postman's progress—but nevertheless it came to him as something of a shock to find that there were precisely *six*, above his own house— his own house was the seventh.

Six!

Astonished, he looked at his own house—looked at the door, on which was the number thirteen—and then realized that the whole thing was exactly and logically and absurdly what he ought to have known. Just the same, the realization gave him abruptly, and even a little frighteningly, a sense of hurry. He was being hurried—he was being rushed. For —he knit his brows—he couldn't be mistaken—it was just above the *seventh* house, his *own* house, that the postman had first been audible this very morning. But in that case— in that case—did it mean that tomorrow he would hear nothing? The knock he had heard must have been the knock of their own door. Did it mean—and this was an idea which

gave him a really extraordinary feeling of surprise—that he would never hear the postman again?—that tomorrow morning the postman would already have passed the house, in a snow by then so deep as to render his footsteps completely inaudible? That he would have made his approach down the snow-filled street so soundlessly, so secretly, that he, Paul Hasleman, there lying in bed, would not have waked in time, or, waking, would have heard nothing?

But how could that be? Unless even the knocker should be muffled in the snow—frozen tight, perhaps? . . . But in that case——

A vague feeling of disappointment came over him; a vague sadness, as if he felt himself deprived of something which he had long looked forward to, something much prized. After all this, all this beautiful progress, the slow delicious advance of the postman through the silent and secret snow, the knock creeping closer each day, and the footsteps nearer, the audible compass of the world thus daily narrowed, narrowed, narrowed, as the snow soothingly and beautifully encroached and deepened, after all this, was he to be defrauded of the one thing he had so wanted—to be able to count, as it were, the last two or three solemn footsteps, as they finally approached his own door? Was it all going to happen, at the end, so suddenly? or indeed, had it already happened? with no slow and subtle gradations of menace, in which he could luxuriate?

He gazed upward again, toward his own window which flashed in the sun: and this time almost with a feeling that it would be better if he *were* still in bed, in that room; for in that case this must still be the first morning, and there would be six more mornings to come—or, for that matter, seven or eight or nine—how could he be sure?—or even more.

III

After supper, the inquisition began. He stood before the doctor, under the lamp, and submitted silently to the usual thumpings and tappings.

"Now will you please say 'Ah?' "

"Ah!"

"Now again please, if you don't mind."

"Ah."

"Say it slowly, and hold it if you can——"

"Ah-h-h-h-h-h—"

"Good."

How silly all this was. As if it had anything to do with his throat! Or his heart or lungs!

Relaxing his mouth, of which the corners, after all this absurd stretching, felt uncomfortable, he avoided the doctor's eyes, and stared towards the fireplace, past his mother's feet (in gray slippers) which projected from the green chair, and his father's feet (in brown slippers) which stood neatly side by side on the hearth rug.

"Hm. There is certainly nothing wrong there . . ."

He felt the doctor's eyes fixed upon him, and, as if merely to be polite, returned the look, but with a feeling of justifiable evasiveness.

"Now, young man, tell me—do you feel all right?"

"Yes, sir, quite all right."

"No headaches? no dizziness?"

"No, I don't think so."

"Let me see. Let's get a book, if you don't mind—yes, thank you, that will do splendidly—and now, Paul, if you'll just read it, holding it as you would normally hold it——"

He took the book and read:

"And another praise have I to tell for this the city our mother, the gift of a great god, a glory of the land most high; the might of horses, the might of young horses, the might of the sea. . . . For thou, son of Cronus, our lord Poseidon, hast throned herein this pride, since in these roads first thou didst show forth the curb that cures the rage of steeds. And the shapely oar, apt to men's hands, hath a wondrous speed on the brine, following the hundred-footed Nereids. . . . O land that art praised above all lands, now is it for thee to make those bright praises seen in deeds."

He stopped, tentatively, and lowered the heavy book.

"No—as I thought—there is certainly no superficial sign of eye-strain."

Silence thronged the room, and he was aware of the focused scrutiny of the three people who confronted him. . . .

"He could have his eyes examined—but I believe it is something else."

"What could it be?" This was his father's voice.

"It's only this curious absent-minded——" This was his mother's voice.

In the presence of the doctor, they both seemed irritatingly apologetic.

"I believe it is something else. Now, Paul—I would like very much to ask you a question or two. You will answer them, won't you—you know I'm an old, old friend of yours, eh? That's right! . . . ."

His back was thumped twice by the doctor's fat fist—then the doctor was grinning at him with false amiability, while with one finger-nail he was scratching the top button of his waistcoat. Beyond the doctor's shoulder was the fire, the fingers of flame making light prestidigitation against the sooty fireback, the soft sound of their random flutter the only sound.

"I would like to know—is there anything that worries you?"

The doctor was again smiling, his eyelids low against the little black pupils, in each of which was a tiny white bead of light. Why answer him? why answer him at all. "At whatever pain to others"—but it was all a nuisance, this necessity for resistance, this necessity for attention: it was if one had been stood up on a brilliantly lighted stage, under a great round blaze of spotlight; as if one were merely a trained seal, or a performing dog, or a fish, dipped out of an aquarium and held up by the tail. It would serve them right if he were merely to bark or growl. And meanwhile, to miss these last few precious hours, these hours of which every minute was more beautiful than the last, more menacing——? He still looked, as if from a great distance, at the beads of light in the doctor's eyes, at the fixed false smile, and then, beyond, once more at his mother's slippers, the soft flutter of the fire. Even here, even amongst these hostile presences, and in this arranged light, he could see the snow, he could hear it—it was in the corners of the room, where the shadow was deepest, under the sofa, behind the half-opened door which led to the dining room. It was gentler here, softer, its seethe the quietest of whispers, as if, in deference to a drawing room, it had quite deliberately put on its "manners"; it kept itself out of sight, obliterated itself, but distinctly with an air of saying, "Ah, but just wait! Wait till we are alone together!

Then I will begin to tell you something new! Something white! something cold! something sleepy! something of cease, and peace, and the long bright curve of space! Tell them to go away. Banish them. Refuse to speak. Leave them, go upstairs to your room, turn out the light and get into bed—I will go with you, I will be waiting for you, I will tell you a better story than Little Kay of the Skates, or The Snow Ghost—I will surround your bed, I will close the windows, pile a deep drift against the door, so that none will ever again be able to enter. Speak to them? . . ." It seemed as if the little hissing voice came from a slow white spiral of falling flakes in the corner by the front window—but he could not be sure. He felt himself smiling, then, and said to the doctor, but without looking at him, looking beyond him still——

"Oh, no, I think not——"

"But are you sure, my boy?"

His father's voice came softly and coldly then—the familiar voice of silken warning. . . .

"You needn't answer at once, Paul —remember we're trying to help you —think it over and be quite sure, won't you?"

He felt himself smiling again, at the notion of being quite sure. What a joke! As if he weren't so sure that reassurance was no longer necessary, and all this cross-examination a ridiculous farce, a grotesque parody! What could they know about it? These gross intelligences, these humdrum minds so bound to the usual, the ordinary? Impossible to tell them about it! Why, even now, even now, with the proof so abundant, so formidable, so imminent, so appallingly present here in this very room, could they believe it?—could even his mother believe it? No—it was only too plain that if anything were said about it, the merest hint given, they would be incredulous—they would laugh— they would say, "Absurd!"—think things about him which weren't true. . . .

"Why no, I'm not worried—why should I be?"

He looked then straight at the doctor's low-lidded eyes, looked from one of them to the other, from one bead of light to the other, and gave a little laugh.

The doctor seemed to be disconcerted by this. He drew back in his chair, resting a fat white hand on either knee. The smile faded slowly from his face.

"Well, Paul!" he said, and paused gravely, "I'm afraid you don't take this quite seriously enough. I think you perhaps don't quite realize— don't quite realize——" He took a deep quick breath, and turned, as if helpless, at a loss for words, to the others. But Mother and Father were both silent—no help was forthcoming.

"You must surely know, be aware, that you have not been quite yourself, of late? don't you know that? . . ."

It was amusing to watch the doctor's renewed attempt at a smile, a queer disorganized look, as of confidential embarrassment.

"I feel all right, sir," he said, and again gave the little laugh.

"And we're trying to help you." The doctor's tone sharpened.

"Yes, sir, I know. But why? I'm all right. I'm just *thinking*, that's all."

His mother made a quick movement forward, resting a hand on the back of the doctor's chair.

"Thinking?" she said. "But my dear, about what?"

This was a direct challenge—and would have to be directly met. But before he met it, he looked again into the corner by the door, as if for reassurance. He smiled again at what he saw, at what he heard. The little spiral was still there, still softly whirling, like the ghost of a white kitten chasing the ghost of a white tail, and making as it did so the faintest of whispers. It was all right! If only he could remain firm, everything was going to be all right.

"Oh, about anything, about nothing—*you* know the way you do!"

"You mean—daydreaming?"

"Oh, no—thinking!"

"But thinking about *what*?"

"Anything."

He laughed a third time—but this time, happening to glance upward towards his mother's face, he was appalled at the effect his laughter seemed to have upon her. Her mouth had opened in an expression of horror. . . . This was too bad! Unfortunate! He had known it would cause pain, of course—but he hadn't expected it to be quite so bad as this. Perhaps—perhaps if he just gave them a tiny gleaming hint——?

"About the snow," he said.

"What on earth!" This was his father's voice. The brown slippers came a step nearer on the hearthrug.

"But, my dear, what do you mean!" This was his mother's voice.

The doctor merely stared.

"Just *snow*, that's all. I like to think about it."

"Tell us about it, my boy."

"But that's all it is. There's nothing to tell. *You* know what snow is?"

This he said almost angrily, for he felt that they were trying to corner him. He turned sideways so as no longer to face the doctor, and the better to see the inch of blackness between the window sill and the lowered curtains—the cold inch of beckoning and delicious night. At once he felt better, more assured.

"Mother—can I go to bed, now, please? I've got a headache."

"But I thought you said——"

"It's just come. It's all these questions——! Can I, Mother?"

"You can go as soon as the doctor has finished."

"Don't you think this thing ought to be gone into thoroughly, and *now*?" This was Father's voice. The brown slippers again came a step nearer, the voice was the well-known "punishment" voice, resonant and cruel.

"Oh, what's the use, Norman——"

Quite suddenly, everyone was silent. And without precisely facing them, nevertheless he was aware that all three of them were watching him with an extraordinary intensity —staring hard at him—as if he had done something monstrous, or was himself some kind of monster. He could hear the soft irregular flutter of the flames; the cluck-click-cluck-click of the clock; far and faint, two sudden spurts of laughter from the kitchen, as quickly cut off as begun; a murmur of water in the pipes; and then, the silence seemed to deepen, to spread out, to become world-long and world-wide, to become timeless and shapeless, and to center inevitably and rightly, with a slow and sleepy but enormous concentration of all power, on the beginning of a new sound. What this new sound was going to be, he knew perfectly well. It might begin with a hiss, but it would end with a roar—there was no time to lose—he must escape. It mustn't happen here——

Without another word, he turned and ran up the stairs.

IV

Not a moment too soon. The darkness was coming in long white waves. A prolonged sibilance filled the night —a great seamless seethe of wild influence went abruptly across it— a cold low humming shook the windows. He shut the door and flung off his clothes in the dark. The bare black floor was like a little raft tossed in waves of snow, almost overwhelmed, washed under whitely, up again, smothered in curled billows of feather. The snow was laughing: it spoke from all sides at once: it pressed closer to him as he ran and jumped exulting into his bed.

"Listen to us!" it said. "Listen! We have come to tell you the story we told you about. You remember? Lie down. Shut your eyes, now—you will no longer see much—in this white darkness who could see, or want to see? We will take the place of everything. . . . Listen——"

A beautiful varying dance of snow began at the front of the room, came forward and then retreated, flattened out toward the floor, then rose fountainlike to the ceiling, swayed, recruited itself from a new stream of flakes which poured laughing in through the humming window, advanced again, lifted long white arms. It said peace, it said remoteness, it said cold—it said——

But then a gash of horrible light fell brutally across the room from the opening door—the snow drew back hissing—something alien had come into the room—something hostile. This thing rushed at him, clutched at him, shook him—and he was not merely horrified, he was filled with such a loathing as he had never known. What was this? this cruel disturbance? this act of anger and hate? It was as if he had to reach up a hand toward another world for any understanding of it—an effort of which he was only barely capable. But of that other world he still remembered just enough to know the exorcising words. They tore themselves from his other life suddenly——

"Mother! Mother! Go away! I hate you!"

And with that effort, everything was solved, everything became all right: the seamless hiss advanced once more, the long white wavering lines rose and fell like enormous whispering sea waves, the whisper becoming louder, the laughter more numerous.

"Listen!" it said. "We'll tell you the last, the most beautiful and secret story—shut your eyes—it is a very small story—a story that gets smaller and smaller—it comes inward instead of opening like a flower—it is a flower becoming a seed—a little cold seed—do you hear? we are leaning closer to you——"

The hiss was now becoming a roar—the whole world was a vast moving screen of snow—but even now it said peace, it said remoteness, it said cold, it said sleep.

Dorothy Canfield

1879-1958

ALTHOUGH Dorothy Canfield Fisher was born in Kansas and educated in Ohio, where her father was a college president, she was a Vermonter. She lived in Vermont, on the farm of her Canfield forebears, took an active interest in all phases of Vermont life, and wrote an inspired book which might be called a biography of that state: *Vermont Tradition*. Her work, however, is not "regional," because Vermont, as she presents it, is not limited to local talk and customs. Her country people, with their independent ideas, might as easily be Norwegians (to whom she often compares them) or Scots or French peasants. She lived many years in France, and besides French, which she spoke fluently, she knew Danish, German, Spanish, and Italian. It is this knowledge and understanding of the peoples of many nations that add another dimension to her plain Vermont characters and to her thoughtful stories, so simple on the surface, of the why and how of their lives. "Sex Education" is a particularly striking example of the wide application of a single moment's experience. Dorothy Canfield's novels, *The Deepening Stream, Her Son's Wife, Bonfire,* and *Seasoned Timber,* as well as the earlier ones, *The Bent Twig* and *Understood Betsy,* are widely translated and known nearly as well throughout Europe as in the United States.

Sex Education

BY DOROTHY CANFIELD

It was three times—but at intervals of many years—that I heard my Aunt Minnie tell about an experience of her girlhood that had made a never-to-be-forgotten impression on her. The first time she was in her thirties, still young. But she had then been married for ten years, so that to my group of friends, all in the early teens, she seemed quite of another generation.

The day she told us the story, we had been idling on one end of her porch as we made casual plans for a picnic supper in the woods. Darning stockings at the other end, she paid no attention to us until one of the girls said, "Let's take blankets and sleep out there. It'd be fun."

"No," Aunt Minnie broke in sharply, "you mustn't do that."

"Oh, for goodness' sakes, why not!" said one of the younger girls, rebelliously, "the boys are always doing it. Why can't we, just once?"

Aunt Minnie laid down her sewing. "Come here, girls," she said, "I want you should hear something that happened to me when I was your age."

Her voice had a special quality which, perhaps, young people of today would not recognize. But we did.

We knew from experience that it was the dark voice grownups used when they were going to say something about sex.

Yet at first what she had to say was like any dull family anecdote; she had been ill when she was fifteen; and afterwards she was run down, thin, with no appetite. Her folks thought a change of air would do her good, and sent her from Vermont out to Ohio—or was it Illinois? I don't remember. Anyway, one of those places where the corn grows high. Her mother's Cousin Ella lived there, keeping house for her son-in-law.

The son-in-law was the minister of the village church. His wife had died some years before, leaving him a young widower with two little girls and a baby boy. He had been a normally personable man then, but the next summer, on the Fourth of July when he was trying to set off some fireworks to amuse his children, an imperfectly manufactured rocket had burst in his face. The explosion had left one side of his face badly scarred. Aunt Minnie made us see it, as she still saw it, in horrid detail: the stiffened, scarlet scar tissue distorting one cheek, the lower lip turned so far out at one corner that the moist red mucous-

From *The Yale Review*. By permission of the author and publishers. Copyright, 1945, by Yale University Press.

membrane lining always showed, one lower eyelid hanging loose, and watering.

After the accident, his face had been a long time healing. It was then that his wife's elderly mother had gone to keep house and take care of the children. When he was well enough to be about again, he found his position as pastor of the little church waiting for him. The farmers and village people in his congregation, moved by his misfortune, by his faithful service and by his unblemished character, said they would rather have Mr. Fairchild, even with his scarred face, than any other minister. He was a good preacher, Aunt Minnie told us, "and the way he prayed was kind of exciting. I'd never known a preacher, not to live in the same house with him, before. And when he was in the pulpit, with everybody looking up at him, I felt the way his children did, kind of proud to think we had just eaten breakfast at the same table. I liked to call him 'Cousin Malcolm' before folks. One side of his face was all right, anyhow. You could see from that that he *had* been a good-looking man. In fact, probably one of those ministers that all the women——" Aunt Minnie paused, drew her lips together, and looked at us uncertainly.

Then she went back to the story as it happened—as it happened that first time I heard her tell it. "I thought he was a saint. Everybody out there did. That was all *they* knew. Of course, it made a person sick to look at that awful scar—the drooling corner of his mouth was the worst. He tried to keep that side of his face turned away from folks. But you always knew it was there. That was what kept him from marrying again, so Cousin Ella said. I

heard her say lots of times that he knew no woman would touch any man who looked the way he did, not with a ten-foot pole.

"Well, the change of air did do me good. I got my appetite back, and ate a lot and played outdoors a lot with my cousins. They were younger than I (I had my sixteenth birthday there) but I still liked to play games. I got taller and laid on some weight. Cousin Ella used to say I grew as fast as the corn did. Their house stood at the edge of the village. Beyond it was one of those big cornfields they have out West. At the time when I first got there, the stalks were only up to a person's knee. You could see over their tops. But it grew like lightning, and before long, it was the way thick woods are here, way over your head, the stalks growing so close together it was dark under them.

"Cousin Ella told us youngsters that it was lots worse for getting lost in than woods, because there weren't any landmarks in it. One spot in a cornfield looked just like any other. 'You children keep out of it,' she used to tell us almost every day, *'especially you girls.* It's no place for a decent girl. You could easy get so far from the house nobody could hear you if you hollered. There are plenty of men in this town that wouldn't like anything better than ——' she never said what.

"In spite of what she said, my little cousins and I had figured out that if we went across one corner of the field, it would be a short cut to the village, and sometimes, without letting on to Cousin Ella, we'd go that way. After the corn got really tall, the farmer stopped cultivating, and we soon beat down a path in the loose dirt. The minute you were inside the field it was dark.

You felt as if you were miles from anywhere. It sort of scared you. But in no time the path turned and brought you out on the far end of Main Street. Your breath was coming fast, maybe, but that was what made you like to do it.

"One day I missed the turn. Maybe I didn't keep my mind on it. Maybe it had rained and blurred the tramped-down look of the path. I don't know what. All of a sudden, I knew I was lost. And the minute I knew that, I began to run, just as hard as I could run. I couldn't help it, any more than you can help snatching your hand off a hot stove. I didn't know what I was scared of, I didn't even know I *was* running, till my heart was pounding so hard I had to stop.

"The minute I stood still, I could hear Cousin Ella saying, 'There are plenty of men in this town that wouldn't like anything better than ——' I didn't know, not really, what she meant. But I knew she meant something horrible. I opened my mouth to scream. But I put both hands over my mouth to keep the scream in. If I made any noise, one of those men would hear me. I thought I heard one just behind me, and whirled around. And then I thought another one had tiptoed up behind me, the other way, and I spun around so fast I almost fell over. I stuffed my hands hard up against my mouth. And then—I couldn't help it—I ran again—but my legs were shaking so I soon had to stop. There I stood, scared to move for fear of rustling the corn and letting the men know where I was. My hair had come down, all over my face. I kept pushing it back and looking around, quick, to make sure one of the men hadn't

found out where I was. Then I thought I saw a man coming towards me, and I ran away from him —and fell down, and burst some of the buttons off my dress, and was sick to my stomach—and thought I heard a man close to me and got up and staggered around, knocking into the corn because I couldn't even see where I was going.

"And then, off to one side, I saw Cousin Malcolm. Not a man. The minister. He was standing still, one hand up to his face, thinking. He hadn't heard me.

"I was so *terrible* glad to see him, instead of one of those men, I ran as fast as I could and just flung myself on him, to make myself feel how safe I was."

Aunt Minnie had become strangely agitated. Her hands were shaking, her face was crimson. She frightened us. We could not look away from her. As we waited for her to go on, I felt little spasms twitch at the muscles inside my body. "And what do you think that *saint*, that holy minister of the Gospel, did to an innocent child who clung to him for safety? The most terrible look came into his eyes—you girls are too young to know what he looked like. But once you're married, you'll find out. He grabbed hold of me—that dreadful face of his was *right on mine*—and began clawing the clothes off my back."

She stopped for a moment, panting. We were too frightened to speak. She went on, "He had torn my dress right down to the waist before I—then I *did* scream—all I could —and pulled away from him so hard I almost fell down, and ran and all of a sudden I came out of the corn, right in the back yard of the Fairchild house. The children were staring at the corn, and Cousin Ella ran out of the kitchen door. They had heard me screaming. Cousin Ella shrieked out, 'What is it? What happened? Did a man scare you?' And I said, 'Yes, yes, yes, a man— I ran———!' And then I fainted away. I must have. The next thing I knew I was on the sofa in the living room and Cousin Ella was slapping my face with a wet towel."

She had to wet her lips with her tongue before she could go on. Her face was gray now. "There! that's the kind of thing girls' folks ought to tell them about—so they'll know what men are like."

She finished her story as if she were dismissing us. We wanted to go away, but we were too horrified to stir. Finally one of the youngest girls asked in a low trembling voice, "Aunt Minnie, did you tell on him?"

"No, I was ashamed to," she said briefly. "They sent me home the next day anyhow. Nobody ever said a word to me about it. And I never did either. Till now."

By what gets printed in some of the modern child-psychology books, you would think that girls to whom such a story had been told would never develop normally. Yet, as far as I can remember what happened to the girls in that group, we all grew up about like anybody. Most of us married, some happily, some not so well. We kept house. We learned —more or less—how to live with our husbands, we had children and struggled to bring them up right— we went forward into life, just as if we had never been warned not to.

Perhaps, young as we were that day, we had already had enough experience of life so that we were not quite blank paper for Aunt Minnie's frightening story. Whether we thought of it then or not, we couldn't have failed to see that at this very time, Aunt Minnie had been married for ten years or more, comfortably and well married, too. Against what she tried by that story to brand into our minds stood the cheerful home life in that house, the good-natured, kind, hard-working husband, and the children—the three rough-and-tumble, nice little boys, so adored by their parents, and the sweet girl baby who died, of whom they could never speak without tears. It was such actual contact with adult life that probably kept generation after generation of girls from being scared by tales like Aunt Minnie's into a neurotic horror of living.

Of course, since Aunt Minnie was so much older than we, her boys grew up to be adolescents and young men, while our children were still little enough so that our worries over them were nothing more serious than whooping cough and trying to get them to make their own beds. Two of our aunt's three boys followed, without losing their footing, the narrow path which leads across adolescence into normal adult life. But the middle one, Jake, repeatedly fell off into the morass. "Girl trouble," as the succinct family phrase put it. He was one of those boys who have "charm," whatever we mean by that, and was always being snatched at by girls who would be "all wrong" for him to marry. And once, at nineteen, he ran away from home, whether with one of these girls or not we never heard, for through all her ups and downs with this son, Aunt Minnie tried fiercely to protect him from scandal that might cloud his later life.

Her husband had to stay on his job to earn the family living. She was the one who went to find Jake. When it was gossiped around that Jake was in "bad company" his mother drew some money from the family savings-bank account, and silent, white-cheeked, took the train to the city where rumor said he had gone.

Some weeks later he came back with her. With no girl. She had cleared him of that entanglement. As of others, which followed, later. Her troubles seemed over when, at a "suitable" age, he fell in love with a "suitable" girl, married her and took her to live in our shire town, sixteen miles away, where he had a good position. Jake was always bright enough.

Sometimes, idly, people speculated as to what Aunt Minnie had seen that time she went after her runaway son, wondering where her search for him had taken her—very queer places for Aunt Minnie to be in, we imagined. And how could such an ignorant, homekeeping woman ever have known what to say to an errant willful boy to set him straight?

Well, of course, we reflected, watching her later struggles with Jake's erratic ways, she certainly could not have remained ignorant, after seeing over and over what she probably had; after talking with Jake about the things which, a good many times, must have come up with desperate openness between them.

She kept her own counsel. We never knew anything definite about the facts of those experiences of hers. But one day she told a group of us—all then married women—something which gave us a notion about what she had learned from them.

We were hastily making a layette for a not-especially welcome baby in a poor family. In those days, our town had no such thing as a district-nursing service. Aunt Minnie, a vigorous woman of fifty-five, had come in to help. As we sewed, we talked, of course; and because our daughters were near or in their teens, we were comparing notes about the bewildering responsibility of bringing up girls.

After a while, Aunt Minnie remarked, "Well, I hope you teach your girls some *sense*. From what I read, I know you're great on telling them 'the facts,' facts we never heard of when we were girls. Like as not, some facts I don't know, now. But knowing the facts isn't going to do them any more good than *not* knowing the facts ever did, unless they have some sense taught them, too."

"What do you mean, Aunt Minnie?" one of us asked her uncertainly.

She reflected, threading a needle. "Well, I don't know but what the best way to tell you what I mean is to tell you about something that happened to me, forty years ago. I've never said anything about it before. But I've thought about it a good deal. Maybe——"

She had hardly begun when I recognized the story—her visit to her Cousin Ella's Midwestern home, the widower with his scarred face and saintly reputation and, very vividly, her getting lost in the great cornfield. I knew every word she was going to say—to the very end, I thought.

But no, I did not. Not at all.

She broke off, suddenly, to exclaim with impatience, "Wasn't I the big ninny? But not so big a ninny as that old cousin of mine. I could wring her neck for getting me in such a state. Only she didn't know any better, herself. That was the way they brought young people up in those days, scaring them out of their wits about the awfulness of getting lost, but not telling them a thing about how *not* to get lost. Or how to act, if they did.

"If I had had the sense I was born with, I'd have known that running my legs off in a zigzag was the worst thing I could do. I couldn't have been more than a few feet from the path when I noticed I wasn't on it. My tracks in the loose plow dirt must have been perfectly plain. If I'd h' stood still, and collected my wits, I could have looked down to see which way my footsteps went and just walked back over them to the path and gone on about my business.

"Now I ask you, if I'd been told how to do that, wouldn't it have been a lot better protection for me —if protection was what my aunt thought she wanted to give me-— than to scare me so at the idea of being lost that I turned deef-dumb-and-blind when I thought I was?

"And anyhow that patch of corn wasn't as big as she let on. And she knew it wasn't. It was no more than a big field in a farming country. I was a well-grown girl of sixteen, as tall as I am now. If I couldn't have found the path, I could have just walked along one line of cornstalks—*straight*—and I'd have come out somewhere in ten minutes. Fifteen at the most. Maybe not just where I wanted to go. But all right, safe, where decent folks were living."

She paused, as if she had finished. But at the inquiring blankness in our faces, she went on, "Well, now, why isn't teaching girls—and boys, too, for the Lord's sake don't forget they need it as much as the girls—

about this man-and-woman business, something like that? If you give them the idea—no matter whether it's *as* you tell them the facts, or as you *don't* tell them the facts, that it is such a terribly scary thing that if they take a step into it, something's likely to happen to them so awful that you're ashamed to tell them what—well, they'll lose their heads and run around like crazy things, first time they take one step away from the path.

"For they'll be trying out the paths, all right. You can't keep them from it. And a good thing too. How else are they going to find out what it's like? Boys' and girls' going together is a path across one corner of growing up. And when they go together, they're likely to get off the path some. Seems to me, it's up to their folks to bring them up so when they do, they don't start screaming and running in circles, but stand still, right where they are, and get their breath and figure out how to get back.

"And anyhow, you don't tell 'em the truth about sex" (I was astonished to hear her use the actual word, taboo to women of her generation) "if they get the idea from you that it's all there is to living. It's not. If you don't get to where you want to go in it, well, there's a lot of landscape all around it a person can have a good time in.

"D'you know, I believe one thing that gives girls and boys the wrong idea is the way folks *look!* My old cousin's face, I can see her now, it was as red as a rooster's comb when she was telling me about men in that cornfield. I believe now she kind of *liked* to talk about it."

(Oh, Aunt Minnie—and yours! I thought.)

Someone asked, "But how *did* you get out, Aunt Minnie?"

She shook her head, laid down her sewing. "More foolishness. That minister my mother's cousin was keeping house for—her son-in-law— I caught sight of him, down along one of the aisles of cornstalks, looking down at the ground, thinking, the way he often did. And I was so glad to see him I rushed right up to him, and flung my arms around his neck and hugged him. He hadn't heard me coming. He gave a great start, put one arm around me and turned his face full towards me— I suppose for just a second he had forgotten how awful one side of it was. His expression, his eyes—well, you're all married women, you know how he looked, the way any able-bodied man thirty-six or -seven, who'd been married and begotten children, would look—for a minute anyhow, if a full-blooded girl of sixteen, who ought to have known better, flung herself at him without any warning, her hair tumbling down, her dress half unbuttoned, and hugged him with all her might.

"I was what they called innocent in those days. That is, I knew just as little about what men are like as my folks could manage I should. But I was old enough to know all right what that look meant. And it gave me a start. But of course the real thing of it was that dreadful scar of his, so close to my face— that wet corner of his mouth, his eye drawn down with the red inside of the lower eyelid showing——

"It turned me so sick, I pulled away with all my might, so fast that I ripped one sleeve nearly loose, and let out a screech like a wildcat. And ran. Did I run? And in a minute, I was through the corn and

had come out in the back yard of the house. I hadn't been more than a few feet from it, probably, any of the time. And then I fainted away. Girls were always fainting away; it was the way our corset strings were pulled tight, I suppose, and then— oh, a lot of fuss.

"But anyhow," she finished, picking up her work and going on, setting neat, firm stitches with steady hands, "there's one thing, I never told anybody it was Cousin Malcolm I had met in the cornfield. I told my old cousin that 'a man had scared me.' And nobody said anything more about it to me, not ever. That was the way they did in those days. They thought if they didn't let on about something, maybe it wouldn't have happened. I was sent back to Vermont right away and Cousin Malcolm went on being minister of the church. I've always been," said Aunt Minnie moderately, "kind of proud that I didn't go and ruin a man's life for just one second's slip-up. If you could have called it that. For it *would* have ruined him. You know how hard as stone people are about other folks' let-downs. If I'd have told, not one person in that town would have had any charity. Not one would have tried to understand. One slip, *once*, and they'd have pushed him down in the mud. If I had told, I'd have felt pretty bad about it, later—when I came to have more sense. But I declare, I can't see how I came to have the decency, dumb as I was then, to know that it wouldn't be fair."

It was not long after this talk that Aunt Minnie's elderly husband died, mourned by her, by all of us. She lived alone then. It was peaceful October weather for her, in which she kept a firm roundness of face and figure, as quiet-living country-women often do, on into her late sixties.

But then Jake, the boy who had had girl trouble, had wife trouble. We heard he had taken to running after a young girl, or was it that she was running after him? It was something serious. For his nice wife left him and came back with the children to live with her mother in our town. Poor Aunt Minnie used to go to see her for long talks which made them both cry. And she went to keep house for Jake, for months at a time.

She grew old, during those years. When finally she (or something) managed to get the marriage mended so that Jake's wife relented and went back to live with him, there was no trace left of her pleasant brisk freshness. She was stooped and slow-footed and shrunken. We, her kinspeople, although we would have given out lives for any one of our own children, wondered whether Jake was worth what it had cost his mother to—well, steady him, or reform him. Or perhaps just understand him. Whatever it took.

She came of a long-lived family and was able to go on keeping house for herself well into her eighties. Of course we and the other neighbors stepped in often to make sure she was all right. Mostly, during those brief calls, the talked turned on nothing more vital than her geraniums. But one midwinter afternoon, sitting with her in front of her cozy stove, I chanced to speak in rather hasty blame of someone who had, I thought, acted badly. To my surprise this brought from her the story about the cornfield which she had evidently quite forgotten telling me, twice before.

This time she told it almost dreamily, swaying to and fro in her rocking chair, her eyes fixed on the long slope of snow outside her window. When she came to the encounter with the minister she said, looking away from the distance and back into my eyes, "I know now that I had been, all along, kind of *interested* in him, the way any girl as old as I was would be, in any youngish man living in the same house with her. And a minister, too. They have to have the gift of gab so much more than most men, women get to thinking they are more alive than men who can't talk so well. I *thought* the reason I threw my arms around him was because I had been so scared. And I certainly had been scared, by my old cousin's horrible talk about the cornfield being full of men waiting to grab girls. But that wasn't all the reason I flung myself at Malcolm Fairchild and hugged him. I know that now. Why in the world shouldn't I have been taught *some* notion of it then? 'Twould do girls good to know that they are just like everybody else—human nature *and* sex, all mixed up together. I didn't have to hug him. I wouldn't have, if he'd been dirty or fat and old, or chewed tobacco."

I stirred in my chair, ready to say, "But it's not so simple as all that to tell girls——" and she hastily answered my unspoken protest. "I know, I know, most of it can't be put into words. There just aren't any words to say something that's so both-ways-at-once all the time as this man-and-woman business. But look here, you know as well as I do that there are lots more ways than in words to teach young folks what you want 'em to know."

The old woman stopped her swaying rocker to peer far back into the past with honest eyes. "What was in my mind back there in the cornfield —partly anyhow—was what had been there all the time I was living in the same house with Cousin Malcolm—that he had long straight legs, and broad shoulders, and lots of curly brown hair, and was nice and flat in front, and that one side of his face was good-looking. But most of all, that he and I were really alone, for the first time, without anybody to see us.

"I suppose, if it hadn't been for that dreadful scar, he'd have drawn me up, tight, and—most any man would—kissed me. I know how I must have looked, all red and hot and my hair down and my dress torn open. And, used as he was to big cornfields, he probably never dreamed that the reason I looked that way was because I was scared to be by myself in one. He may have thought—you know what he may have thought."

"Well—if his face had been like anybody's—when he looked at me the way he did, the way a man does look at a woman he wants to have, it would have scared me—some. But I'd have cried, maybe. And prob-

ably he'd have kissed me again. You know how such things go. I might have come out of the cornfield halfway engaged to marry him. Why not? I was old enough, as people thought then. That would have been nature. That was probably what he thought of, in that first instant.

"But what did I do? I had one look at his poor, horrible face, and started back as though I'd stepped on a snake. And screamed and ran."

"What do you suppose *he* felt, left there in the corn? He must have been sure that I would tell everybody he had attacked me. He probably thought that when he came out and went back to the village he'd already be in disgrace and put out of the pulpit.

"But the worst must have been to find out, so rough, so plain from the way I acted—as if somebody had hit him with an ax—the way he would look to any woman he might try to get close to. That must have been——" she drew a long breath, "well, pretty hard on him."

After a silence, she murmured pityingly, "Poor man!"

Eudora Welty
1909-

UNLIKE many contemporary Southern writers, Eudora Welty is not ridden by anger. She takes her home town of Jackson, Mississippi, philosophically, and when writing of it, does so without bitterness, though darkness and weirdness may not be far away. She describes herself as "underfoot locally," which seems to mean that she is open to invitations, has no special job (writing in a small town is not a "job"), and, as it works out, is content with the small ways of uneventful living. Not that she hasn't tried other careers, however—at one time it was music, another time advertising. But writing, which she regards as an avocation, has always been her true love. When *A Curtain of Green,* a volume of subtle, expert stories, was published in 1941, it took the critics entirely off guard: who was Eudora Welty? *The Wide Net,* also a superb collection of short stories, followed, and in 1946 her first novel, *Delta Wedding*.

Petrified Man

BY EUDORA WELTY

"Reach in my purse and git me a cigarette without no powder in it if you kin, Mrs. Fletcher, honey," said Leota to her ten-o'clock shampoo-and-set customer. "I don't like no perfumed cigarettes."

Mrs. Fletcher gladly reached over to the lavender shelf under the lavender-framed mirror, shook a hair net loose from the clasp of the patent-leather bag, and slapped her hand down quickly on a powder puff which burst out when the purse was opened.

"Why, look at the peanuts, Leota!" said Mrs. Fletcher in her marveling voice.

"Honey, them goobers has been in my purse a week if they's been in it a day. Mrs. Pike bought them peanuts."

"Who's Mrs. Pike?" asked Mrs. Fletcher, settling back. Hidden in this den of curling fluid and henna packs, separated by a lavender swing door from the other customers, who were being gratified in other booths, she could give her curiosity its freedom. She looked expectantly at the black part in Leota's yellow curls as she bent to light the cigarette.

"Mrs. Pike is this lady from New Orleans," said Leota, puffing, and pressing into Mrs. Fletcher's scalp with strong red-nailed fingers. "A friend, not a customer. You see, like maybe I told you last time, me and Fred and Sal and Joe all had us a fuss, so Sal and Joe up and moved out, so we didn't do a thing but rent out their room. So we rented it to Mrs. Pike. And Mr. Pike." She flicked an ash into the basket of dirty towels. "Mrs. Pike is a very decided blonde. She bought me the peanuts."

"She must be cute," said Mrs. Fletcher.

"Honey, 'cute' ain't the word for what she is. I'm tellin' you, Mrs. Pike is attractive. She has her a good time. She's got a sharp eye out, Mrs. Pike has."

She dashed the comb through the air, and paused dramatically as a cloud of Mrs. Fletcher's hennaed hair floated out of the lavender teeth like a small storm cloud.

"Hair fallin'."

"Aw, Leota."

"Uh-huh, commencin' to fall out," said Leota, combing again, and letting fall another cloud.

"Is it any dandruff in it?" Mrs. Fletcher was frowning, her hair-line eyebrows diving down toward her nose, and her wrinkled, beady-lashed eyelids batting with concentration.

From *A Curtain of Green* by Eudora Welty. By permission of the publishers, Harcourt, Brace and Company, Inc. Copyright, 1941, by Eudora Welty.

"Nope." She combed again. "Just fallin' out."

"Bet it was that last perm'nent you gave me that did it," Mrs. Fletcher said cruelly. "Remember you cooked me fourteen minutes."

"You had fourteen minutes comin' to you," said Leota with finality.

"Bound to be somethin'," persisted Mrs. Fletcher. "Dandruff, dandruff. I couldn't of caught a thing like that from Mr. Fletcher, could I?"

"Well," Leota answered at last, "you know what I heard in here yestiddy, one of Thelma's ladies was settin' over yonder in Thelma's booth gittin' a machineless, and I don't mean to insist or insinuate or anything, Mrs. Fletcher, but Thelma's lady just happ'med to throw out—I forgotten what she was talkin' about at the time—that you was p-r-e-g., and lots of times that'll make your hair do awful funny, fall out and God knows what all. It just ain't our fault is the way I look at it."

There was a pause. The women stared at each other in the mirror.

"Who was it?" demanded Mrs. Fletcher.

"Honey, I really couldn't say," said Leota. "Not that you look it."

"Where's Thelma? I'll get it out of her," said Mrs. Fletcher.

"Now, honey I wouldn't go and git mad over a little thing like that," Leota said, combing hastily, as though to hold Mrs. Fletcher down by the hair. "I'm sure it was somebody didn't mean no harm in the world. How far gone are you?"

"Just wait," said Mrs. Fletcher, and shrieked for Thelma, who came in and took a drag from Leota's cigarette.

"Thelma, honey, throw your mind back to yestiddy if you kin," said Leota, drenching Mrs. Fletcher's hair with a thick fluid and catching the overflow in a cold wet towel at her neck.

"Well, I got my lady half wound for a spiral," said Thelma doubtfully.

"This won't take but a minute," said Leota. "Who is it you got in there, old Horse Face? Just cast your mind back and try to remember who your lady was yestiddy who happ'm to mention that my customer was pregnant, that's all. She's dead to know."

Thelma drooped her blood-red lips and looked over Mrs. Fletcher's head into the mirror. "Why, honey, I ain't got the faintest," she breathed. "I really don't recollect the faintest. But I'm sure she meant no harm. I declare, I forgot my hair finally got combed and thought it was a stranger behind me."

"Was it that Mrs. Hutchinson?" Mrs. Fletcher was tensely polite.

"Mrs. Hutchinson? Oh, Mrs. Hutchinson." Thelma batted her eyes. "Naw, precious, she come on Thursday and didn't ev'm mention your name. I doubt if she ev'm knows you're on the way."

"Thelma!" cried Leota stanchly.

"All I know is, whoever it is'll be sorry someday. Why, I just barely knew it myself!" cried Mrs. Fletcher. "Just let her wait!"

"Why? What're you gonna do to her?"

It was a child's voice, and the women looked down. A little boy was making tents with aluminum wave pinchers on the floor under the sink.

"Billy Boy, hon, mustn't bother nice ladies," Leota smiled. She slapped him brightly and behind her back waved Thelma out of the booth. "Ain't Billy Boy a sight? Only three years old and already just nuts about the beauty-parlor business."

"I never saw him here before," said Mrs. Fletcher, still unmollified. "He ain't been here before, that's how come," said Leota. "He belongs to Mrs. Pike. She got her a job but it was Fay's Millinery. He oughtn't to try on those ladies' hats, they come down over his eyes like I don't know what. They just git to look ridiculous, that's what, an' of course he's gonna put 'em on: hats. They tole Mrs. Pike they didn't appreciate him hangin' around there. Here, he couldn't hurt a thing."

"Well! I don't like children that much," said Mrs. Fletcher.

"Well!" said Leota moodily.

"Well! I'm almost tempted not to have this one," said Mrs. Fletcher. "That Mrs. Hutchinson! Just looks straight through you when she sees you on the street and then spits at you behind your back."

"Mr. Fletcher would beat you on the head if you didn't have it now," said Leota reasonably. "After going this far."

Mrs. Fletcher sat up straight. "Mr. Fletcher can't do a thing with me."

"He can't!" Leota winked at herself in the mirror.

"No siree, he can't. If he so much as raises his voice against me, he knows good and well I'll have one of my sick headaches, and then I'm just not fit to live with. And if I really look that pregnant already——"

"Well, now, honey, I just want you to know—I habm't told any of my ladies and I ain't goin' to tell 'em —even that you're losin' your hair. You just get you one of those Stork-a-Lure dresses and stop worryin'. What people don't know don't hurt nobody, as Mrs. Pike says."

"Did you tell Mrs. Pike?" asked Mrs. Fletcher sulkily.

"Well, Mrs. Fletcher, look, you ain't ever goin' to lay eyes on Mrs. Pike or her lay eyes on you, so what diffunce does it make in the long run?"

"I knew it!" Mrs. Fletcher deliberately nodded her head so as to destroy a ringlet Leota was working on behind her ear. "Mrs. Pike!"

Leota sighed. "I reckon I might as well tell you. It wasn't any more Thelma's lady tole me you was pregnant than a bat."

"Not Mrs. Hutchinson?"

"Naw, Lord! It was Mrs. Pike."

"Mrs. Pike!" Mrs. Fletcher could only sputter and let curling fluid roll into the ear. "How could Mrs. Pike possibly know I was pregnant or otherwise, when she doesn't even know me? The nerve of some people!"

"Well, here's how it was. Remember Sunday?"

"Yes," said Mrs. Fletcher.

"Sunday, Mrs. Pike an' me was all by ourself. Mr. Pike and Fred had gone over to Eagle Lake, sayin' they was goin' to catch 'em some fish, but they didn't, a course. So we was settin' in Mrs. Pike's car, is a 1939 Dodge——"

"1939, eh," said Mrs. Fletcher.

"—An' we was gettin' us a Jax beer apiece—that's the beer that Mrs. Pike says is made right in N.O., so she won't drink no other kind. So I seen you drive up to the drugstore an' run in for just a secont, leavin' I reckon Mr. Fletcher in the car, an' come runnin' out with looked like a perscription. So I says to Mrs. Pike, just to be makin' talk, 'Right yonder's Mrs. Fletcher, and I reckon that's Mr. Fletcher—she's one of my regular customers,' I says."

"I had on a figured print," said Mrs. Fletcher tentatively.

"You sure did," agreed Leota. "So Mrs. Pike, she give you a good look —she's very observant, a good judge of character, cute as a minute, you know—and she says, 'I bet you another Jax that lady's three months on the way.'"

"What gall!" said Mrs. Fletcher. "Mrs. Pike!"

"Mrs. Pike ain't goin' to bite you," said Leota. "Mrs. Pike is a lovely girl, you'd be crazy about her, Mrs. Fletcher. But she can't sit still a minute. We went to the travelin' freak show yestiddy after work. I got through early—nine o'clock. In the vacant store next door? What, you ain't been?"

"No, I despise freaks," declared Mrs. Fletcher.

"Aw. Well, honey, talkin' about bein' pregnant an' all, you ought to see those twins in a bottle, you really owe it to yourself."

"What twins?" asked Mrs. Fletcher out of the side of her mouth.

"Well, honey, they got these two twins in a bottle, see? Born joined plumb together—dead a course." Leota dropped her voice into a soft lyrical hum. "They was about this long—pardon—must of been full time, all right, wouldn't you say?—an' they had these two heads an' two faces an' four arms an' four legs, all kind of joined *here*. See, this face looked this-a-way, and the other face looked that-a-way, over their shoulder, see. Kinda pathetic."

"Glah!" said Mrs. Fletcher disapprovingly.

"Well, ugly? Honey, I mean to tell you—their parents was first cousins and all like that. Billy Boy, git me a fresh towel from off Teeny's stack—this 'n's wringin' wet—an' quit ticklin' my ankles with that curler. I declare! He don't miss nothin'."

"Me and Mr. Fletcher aren't one speck of kin, or he could never of had me," said Mrs. Fletcher placidly.

"Of course not!" protested Leota.

"Neither is me an' Fred, not that we know of. Well, honey, what Mrs. Pike liked was the pygmies. They've got these pygmies down there, too, an' Mrs. Pike was just wild about 'em. You know, the tee-niest men in the universe? Well honey, they can rest back on their little bohunkus an' roll around an' you can't hardly tell if they're sittin' or standin'. That'll give you some idea. They're about forty-two years old. Just suppose it was your husband!"

"Well, Mr. Fletcher is five foot nine and one half," said Mrs. Fletcher quickly.

"Fred's five foot ten," said Leota, "but I tell him he's still a shrimp, account of I'm so tall." She made a deep wave over Mrs. Fletcher's other temple with the comb. "Well, these pygmies are a kind of a dark brown, Mrs. Fletcher. Not bad-lookin' for what they are, you know."

"I wouldn't care for them," said Mrs. Fletcher. "What does that Mrs. Pike see in them?"

"Aw, I don't know," said Leota. "She's just cute, that's all. But they got this man, this petrified man, that ever'-thing ever since he was nine years old, when it goes through his digestion, see, somehow Mrs. Pike says it goes to his joints and has been turning to stone."

"How awful!" said Mrs. Fletcher.

"He's forty-two too. That looks like a bad age."

"Who said so, that Mrs. Pike? I bet she's forty-two," said Mrs. Fletcher.

"Naw," said Leota, "Mrs. Pike's thirty-three, born in January, an Aquarian. He could move his head—like this. A course his head and mind ain't a joint, so to speak, and I guess his stomach ain't either—not anyways. But see—his food, he eats it, and goes down, see, and then he digests it"—Leota rose on her toes for an instant—"and it goes out to his joints and before you can say 'Jack Robinson,' it's stone—pure stone. He's turning to stone. How'd you like to be married to a guy like that? All he can do, he can move his head just a quarter of an inch. A course he *looks* just *terrible.*"

"I should think he would," said Mrs. Fletcher frostily. "Mr. Fletcher takes bending exercises every night of the world. I make him."

"All Fred does is lay around the house like a rug. I wouldn't be surprised if he woke up someday and couldn't move. The petrified man just sat there moving his quarter of an inch though," said Leota reminiscently.

"Did Mrs. Pike like the petrified man?" asked Mrs. Fletcher.

"Not as much as she did the others," said Leota deprecatingly. "And then she likes a man to be a good dresser, and all that."

"Is Mr. Pike a good dresser?" asked Mrs. Fletcher skeptically.

"Oh, well, yeah," said Leota, "but he's twelve-fourteen years older 'n her. She ast Lady Evangeline about him."

"Who's Lady Evangeline?" asked Mrs. Fletcher.

"Well, it's this mind reader they got in the freak show," said Leota. "Was real good. Lady Evangeline is her name, and if I had another dollar I wouldn't do a thing but have my other palm read. She had what Mrs. Pike said was the 'sixth mind' but she had the worst manicure I ever saw on a living person."

"What did she tell Mrs. Pike?" asked Mrs. Fletcher.

"She told her Mr. Pike was as true to her as he could be and, besides, would come into some money."

"Humph!" said Mrs. Fletcher. "What does he do?"

"I can't tell," said Leota, "because he don't work. Lady Evangeline didn't tell me near enough about my nature or anything. And I would like to go back and find out some more about this boy. Used to go with this boy got married to this girl. Oh, shoot, that was about three and a half years ago, when you was still goin' to the Robert E. Lee Beauty Shop in Jackson. He married her for her money. Another fortune-teller tole me that at the time. So I'm not in love with him any more, anyway, besides being married to Fred, but Mrs. Pike thought, just for the hell of it, see, to ask Lady Evangeline was he happy."

"Does Mrs. Pike know everything about you already?" asked Mrs. Fletcher unbelievingly. "Mercy!"

"Oh yeah, I tole her ever'thing about ever'thing, from now on back to I don't know when—to when I first started goin' out," said Leota. "So I ast Lady Evangeline for one of my questions, was he happily married, and she says, just like she was glad I ask her, 'Honey,' she says, 'naw, he isn't. You write down this day, March 8, 1941,' she says, 'and mock it down three years from today him and her won't be occupyin' the same bed.' There it is, up on the wall with them other dates—see, Mrs. Fletcher? And she says, 'Child, you ought to be glad you didn't git him, because he's so mercenary.' So I'm glad I married Fred. He sure ain't mercenary, money don't mean a thing to him. But I sure would like to go back and have my other palm read."

"Did Mrs. Pike believe in what the fortuneteller said?" asked Mrs. Fletcher in a superior tone of voice.

"Lord, yes, she's from New Orleans. Ever'body in New Orleans be-lieves ever'thing spooky. One of 'em in New Orleans before it was raided says to Mrs. Pike one summer she was goin' to go from state to state and meet some gray-headed men, and, sure enough, she says she went on a beautician convention up to Chicago. . . ."

"Oh!" said Mrs. Fletcher. "Oh, is Mrs. Pike a beautician too?"

"Sure she is," protested Leota. "She's a beautician. I'm goin' to git her in here if I can. Before she mar-ried. But it don't leave you. She says sure enough, there was three men who was a very large part of making her trip what it was, and they all three had gray in their hair and they went in six states. Got Christmas cards from 'em. Billy Boy, go see if Thelma's got any dry cotton. Look how Mrs. Fletcher's a-drippin'."

"Where did Mrs. Pike meet Mr. Pike?" asked Mrs. Fletcher primly.

"On another train," said Leota.

"I met Mr. Fletcher, or rather he met me, in a rental library," said Mrs. Fletcher with dignity, as she watched the net come down over her head.

"Honey, me an' Fred, we met in a rumble seat eight months ago and we was practically on what you might call the way to the altar inside of a half an hour," said Leota in a gut-tural voice, and bit a bobby pin open. "Course it don't last. Mrs. Pike says nothin' like that ever lasts."

"Mr. Fletcher and myself are as much in love as the day we married," said Mrs. Fletcher belligerently as Leota stuffed cotton into her ears.

"Mrs. Pike says it don't last," re-peated Leota in a louder voice. "Now go git under the dryer. You can turn yourself on can't you? I'll be back to comb you out. Durin' lunch I promised to give Mrs. Pike a facial.

You know—free. Her bein' in the business, so to speak."

"I bet she needs one," said Mrs. Fletcher, letting the swing door fly back against Leota. "Oh, pardon me."

A week later, on time for her ap-pointment, Mrs. Fletcher sank heavily into Leota's chair after first removing a drugstore rental book, called Life Is Like That, from the seat. She stared in a discouraged way into the mirror.

"You can tell it when I'm sitting down, all right," she said.

Leota seemed preoccupied and stood shaking out a lavender cloth. She began to pin it around Mrs. Fletcher's neck in silence.

"I said you sure can tell it when I'm sitting straight on and coming at you this way," Mrs. Fletcher said.

"Why, honey, naw you can't," said Leota gloomily. "Why, I'd never know. If somebody was to come up to me on the street and say, 'Mrs. Fletcher is pregnant!' I'd say, 'Heck, she don't look it to me.'"

"If a certain party hadn't found it out and spread it around, it wouldn't be too late even now," said Mrs. Fletcher frostily, but Leota was almost choking her with the cloth, pinning it so tight, and she couldn't speak clearly. She paddled her hands in the air until Leota wearily loosened her.

"Listen, honey, you're just a virgin compared to Mrs. Montjoy," Leota was going on, still absent-minded. She bent Mrs. Fletcher back in the chair and, sighing, tossed liquid from a teacup onto her head and dug both hands into her scalp. "You know Mrs. Montjoy—her husband's that pre-mature-gray-headed fella?"

"She's in the Trojan Garden Club is all I know," said Mrs. Fletcher.

"Well, honey," said Leota, but in a weary voice, "she come in here not the week before and not the day before she had her baby—she come in here the very selfsame day, I mean to tell you. Child, we was all plumb scared to death. There she was! Come for her shampoo an' set. Why, Mrs. Fletcher, in a hour an' twenty minutes she was layin' up there in the Babtist Hospital with a seb'm-pound son. It was that close a shave. I declare, if I hadn't been so tired I would of drank up a bottle of gin that night."

"What gall," said Mrs. Fletcher. "I never knew her at all well."

"See, her husband was waitin' outside in the car, and her bags was all packed an' in the back seat, an' she was all ready, 'cept she wanted her shampoo an' set. An' havin' one pain right after another. Her husband kep' comin' in here, scared-like, but couldn't do nothin' with her a course. She yelled bloody murder, too, but she always yelled her head off when I give her a perm'nent."

"She must of been crazy," said Mrs. Fletcher. "How did she look?"

"Shoot!" said Leota.

"Well, I can guess," said Mrs. Fletcher. "Awful."

"Just wanted to look pretty while she was havin' her baby is all," said Leota airily. "Course, we was glad to give the lady what she was after—that's our motto—but I bet a hour later she wasn't payin' no mind to them little end curls. I bet she wasn't thinkin' about she ought to have on a net. It wouldn't of done her no good if she had."

"No, I don't suppose it would," said Mrs. Fletcher.

"Yeah man! She was a-yellin'. Just like when I give her her perm'nent."

"Her husband ought to could make her behave. Don't it seem that

way to you?" asked Mrs. Fletcher. "He ought to put his foot down."

"Ha," said Leota. "A lot he could do. Maybe some women is soft."

"Oh, you mistake me, I don't mean for her to get soft—far from it! Women have to stand up for themselves, or there's just no telling. But now you take me—I ask Mr. Fletcher's advice now and then, and he appreciates it, especially on something important, like is it time for a permanent—not that I've told him about the baby. He says, 'Why, dear, go ahead!' Just ask their *advice*."

"Huh! If I ever ast Fred's advice we'd be floatin' down the Yazoo River on a houseboat or somethin' by this time," said Leota. "I'm sick of Fred. I tole him to go over to Vicksburg."

"Is he going?" demanded Mrs. Fletcher.

"Sure. See, the fortuneteller—I went back and had my other palm read, since we've got to rent the room again—said my lover was goin' to work in Vicksburg, so I don't know who she could mean, unless she meant Fred. And Fred ain't workin' here—that much is so."

"Is he going to work in Vicksburg?" asked Mrs. Fletcher. "And ____?"

"Sure, Lady Evangeline said so. Said the future is going to be brighter than the present. He don't want to go, but I ain't gonna put up with nothin' like that. Lays around the house an' bulls—did bull—with that good-for-nothin' Mr. Pike. He says if he goes who'll cook, but I says I never get to eat anyway—not meals. Billy Boy, take Mrs. Grover that *Screen Secrets* and leg it."

Mrs. Fletcher heard stamping feet go out the door.

"Is that that Mrs. Pike's little boy

here again?" she asked, sitting up gingerly.

"Yeah, that's still him." Leota stuck out her tongue.

Mrs. Fletcher could hardly believe her eyes. "Well! How's Mrs. Pike, your attractive new friend with the sharp eyes who spreads it around town that perfect strangers are pregnant?" she asked in a sweetened tone.

"Oh, Mizziz Pike." Leota combed Mrs. Fletcher's hair with heavy strokes.

"You act like you're tired," said Mrs. Fletcher.

"Tired? Feel like it's four o'clock in the afternoon already," said Leota. "I ain't told you the awful luck we had, me and Fred? It's the worst thing you ever heard of. Maybe *you* think Mrs. Pike's got sharp eyes. Shoot, there's a limit! Well, you know, we rented out our room to this Mr. and Mrs. Pike from New Orleans when Sal an' Joe Fentress got mad at us 'cause they drank up some homebrew we had in the closet —Sal an' Joe did. So, a week ago Sat'day Mr. and Mrs. Pike moved in. Well, I kinda fixed up the room, you know—put a sofa pillow on the couch and picked some ragged robins and put in a vase, but they never did say they appreciated it. Anyway, then I put some old magazines on the table."

"I think that was lovely," said Mrs. Fletcher.

"Wait. So, come night 'fore last, Fred and this Mr. Pike, who Fred just took up with, was back from they said they was fishin', bein' as neither one of 'em has got a job to his name, and we was all settin' around in their room. So Mrs. Pike was settin' there, readin' a old *Startling G-Man Tales* that was mine, mind you, I'd bought it myself, and all of a sudden she jumps!—into the air—you'd 'a' thought she'd set on a spider—an' says, 'Canfield'—ain't that silly, that's Mr. Pike—'Canfield, my God A'mighty,' she says, 'honey,' she says, 'we're rich, and you won't have to work.' Not that he turned one hand anyway. Well, me and Fred rushes over to her, and Mr. Pike, too, and there she sets, pointin' her finger at a photo in my copy of *Startling G-Man*. 'See that man?' yells Mrs. Pike. 'Remember him, Canfield?' 'Never forget a face,' says Mr. Pike. 'It's Mr. Petrie, that we stayed with him in the apartment next to ours in Toulouse Street in N.O. for six weeks. Mr. Petrie.' 'Well,' says Mrs. Pike, like she can't hold out one secont longer, 'Mr. Petrie is wanted for five hundred dollars cash, for rapin' four women in California, and I know where he is.' "

"Mercy!" said Mrs. Fletcher. "Where was he?"

At some time Leota had washed her hair and now she yanked her up by the back locks and sat her up.

"Know where he was?"

"I certainly don't," Mrs. Fletcher said. Her scalp hurt all over.

Leota flung a towel around the top of her customer's head. "Nowhere else but in that freak show! I saw him just as plain as Mrs. Pike. *He* was the petrified man!"

"Who would ever have thought that!" cried Mrs. Fletcher sympathetically.

"So Mr. Pike says, 'Well, whatta you know about that,' an' he looks real hard at the photo and whistles. And she starts dancin' and singin' about their good luck. She meant our bad luck! I made a point of telling that fortuneteller the next time I saw her. I said, 'Listen, that magazine was layin' around the house for a month, and there was five hundred dollars in it for somebody. An' there was the freak show runnin' night an' day, not two steps away from my own beauty parlor, with Mr. Petrie just settin' there waitin'. An' it had to be Mr. and Mrs. Pike, almost perfect strangers.'"

"What gall," said Mrs. Fletcher. She was only sitting there, wrapped in a turban, but she did not mind.

"Fortunetellers don't care. And Mrs. Pike, she goes around actin' like she thinks she was Mrs. God," said Leota. "So they're goin' to leave tomorrow, Mr. and Mrs. Pike. And in the meantime I got to keep that mean, bad little ole kid here, gettin' under my feet ever' minute of the day an' talkin' back too."

"Have they gotten the five hundred dollars' reward already?" asked Mrs. Fletcher.

"Well," said Leota, "at first Mr. Pike didn't want to do anything about it. Can you feature that? Said he kinda liked that ole bird and said he was real nice to 'em, lent 'em money or somethin'. But Mrs. Pike simply tole him he could just go to hell, and I can see her point. She says, 'You ain't worked a lick in six months, and here I made five hundred dollars in two seconts, and what thanks do I get for it? You go to hell, Canfield,' she says. So," Leota went on in a despondent voice, "they called up the cops and they caught the ole bird, all right, right there in the freak show where I saw him with my own eyes, thinkin' he was petrified. He's the one. Did it under his real name—Mr. Petrie. Four women in California, all in the month of August. So Mrs. Pike gits five hundred dollars. And my magazine, and right next door to my beauty parlor. I cried all night, but Fred said it wasn't a bit of use and to go to

sleep, because the whole thing was just sort of coincidence—you know: can't do nothin' about it. He says it put him clean out of the notion of goin' to Vicksburg for a few days till we rent out the room agin—no tellin' who we'll git this time."

"But can you imagine anybody knowing this old man, that's raped four women?" persisted Mrs. Fletcher, and she shuddered audibly. "Did Mrs. Pike *speak* to him when she met him in the freak show?"

Leota had begun to comb Mrs. Fletcher's hair. "I says to her, I says, 'I didn't notice you fallin' on his neck when he was the petrified man —don't tell me you didn't recognize your fine friend?' And she says, 'I didn't recognize him with that white powder all over his face. He just looked familiar,' Mrs. Pike says, 'and lots of people look familiar.' But she says that ole petrified man did put her in mind of somebody. She wondered who it was! Kep' her awake, which man she'd ever knew it reminded her of. So when she seen the photo, it all come to her. Like a flash. Mr. Petrie. The way he'd turn his head and look at her when she took him in his breakfast."

"Took him in his breakfast!" shrieked Mrs. Fletcher. "Listen— don't tell me. I'd 'a' felt something."

"Four women. I guess those women didn't have the faintest notion at the time they'd be worth a hundred an' twenty-five bucks apiece someday to Mrs. Pike. We ast her how old the fella was then, an' she says he musta had one foot in the grave, at least. Can you beat it?"

"Not really petrified at all, of course," said Mrs. Fletcher meditatively. She drew herself up. "I'd 'a' felt something," she said proudly.

"Shoot! I did feel somethin'," said Leota. "I tole Fred when I got home

I felt so funny. I said, 'Fred, that ole petrified man sure did leave me with a funny feelin'.' He says, 'Funny-haha or funny-peculiar?' and I says, 'Funny-peculiar.'" She pointed her comb into the air emphatically.

"I'll bet you did," said Mrs. Fletcher.

They both heard a crackling noise.

Leota screamed, "Billy Boy! What you doin' in my purse?"

"Aw, I'm just eatin' these ole stale peanuts up," said Billy Boy.

"You come here to me!" screamed Leota, recklessly flinging down the comb, which scattered a whole ash tray full of bobby pins and knocked down a row of Coca-Cola bottles. "This is the last straw!"

"I caught him! I caught him!" giggled Mrs. Fletcher. "I'll hold him on my lap. You bad, bad boy, you!

I guess I better learn how to spank little old bad boys," she said.

Leota's eleven-o'clock customer pushed open the swing door upon Leota paddling him heartily with the brush, while he gave angry but be-littling screams which penetrated be-yond the booth and filled the whole curious beauty parlor. From every-where ladies began to gather round to watch the paddling. Billy Boy kicked both Leota and Mrs. Fletcher as hard as he could, Mrs. Fletcher with her new fixed smile.

"There, my little man!" gasped Leota. "You won't be able to set down for a week if I knew what I was doin'."

Billy Boy stomped through the group of wild-haired ladies and went out the door, but flung back the words, "If you're so smart, why ain't you rich?"

William Faulkner
1897-1962

WILLIAM FAULKNER made common cause with Thomas Wolfe and Erskine Caldwell in uprooting the "genteel" tradition of the South. But this aim, possibly unconscious, and the fact that they were all born in the South, are their only similarities. In Faulkner, degeneracy and morbidity lurk behind pillared porticos. Not only are his characters decadent; more often than not, their story is told from the point of view of a narrator still more degenerate. Their lives are grotesque, their neighbors mysterious, their victims helpless. Born in Mississippi of a line of governors and statesmen, Faulkner belonged to the impoverished-Southern-gentleman class about which he wrote: in fact, his family and his town make up the basis of many of his novels and stories.

At the outbreak of World War I, Faulkner joined the Canadian air force, had two planes shot down under him in France, and was wounded. Once back in Mississippi, with the new and mature vision of the returning soldier, he saw the South as a wasteland and himself bound up with it. His education had included very little actual schooling; his jobs were haphazard and insignificant. It was not until he began to write seriously, in New Orleans, under the influence of Sherwood Anderson, that the found himself. Then, like Balzac, he set himself the goal of compressing a world into the pages of fiction. This strange world of mansions and shanties, miscegenation and fruitless snobbery, he wove into an intricate pattern in which familiar figures unexpectedly turned up and as unexpectedly disappeared, the confusion deepening the suspense. His short stories, also dark with violence, are more straightforward than his novels.

The Hound

BY WILLIAM FAULKNER

To COTTON the shot was the loudest thing he had ever heard in his life. It was too loud to be heard all at once. It continued to build up about the thicket, the dim, faint road, long after the hammerlike blow of the ten-gauge shotgun had shocked into his shoulder and long after the smoke of the black powder with which it was charged had dissolved, and after the maddened horse had whirled twice and then turned galloping, diminishing, the empty stirrups clashing against the empty saddle.

It made too much noise. It was outrageous, unbelievable—a gun which he had owned for twenty years. It stunned him with amazed outrage, seeming to press him down into the thicket, so that when he could make the second shot, it was too late and the hound too was gone.

Then he wanted to run. He had expected that. He had coached himself the night before. "Right after it you'll want to run," he told himself. "But you can't run. You got to finish it. You got to clean it up. It will be hard, but you got to do it. You got to set there in the bushes and shut your eyes and count slow until you can make to finish it."

He did that. He laid the gun down and sat where he had lain behind the log. His eyes were closed. He counted slowly, until he had stopped shaking and until the sound of the gun and the echo of the galloping horse had died out of his ears. He had chosen his place well. It was a quiet road, little used, marked not once in three months save by that departed horse; a short cut between the house where the owner of the horse lived and Varner's store; a quiet, fading, grass-grown trace along the edge of the river bottom, empty save for the two of them, the one squatting in the bushes, the other lying on his face in the road.

Cotton was a bachelor. He lived in a chinked log cabin floored with clay on the edge of the bottom, four miles away. It was dusk when he reached home. In the well house at the back he drew water and washed his shoes. They were not muddier than usual, and he did not wear them save in severe weather, but he washed them carefully. Then he cleaned the shotgun and washed it too, barrel and stock; why, he could not have said, since he had never heard of fingerprints, and immediately afterward he picked up the gun again and carried it into the house and put it away.

He kept firewood, a handful of charred pine knots, in the chimney corner. He built a fire on the clay hearth and cooked his supper and ate and went to bed. He slept on a quilt pallet on the floor; he went to bed by barring the door and removing his overalls and lying down. It was dark after the fire burned out; he lay in the darkness. He thought about nothing at all save that he did not expect to sleep. He felt no triumph, vindication, nothing. He just lay there thinking about nothing at all, even when he began to hear the dog. Usually at night he would hear dogs, single dogs ranging alone in the bottom, or coon- or cat-hunting packs. Having nothing else to do, his life, his heredity, and his heritage centered within a five-mile radius of Varner's store. He knew almost any dog he would hear by its voice, as he knew almost any man he would hear by his voice. He knew the dog's voice. It and the galloping horse with the flapping stirrups and the owner of the horse had been inseparable: where he saw one of them the other two would not be far away—a lean, rangy brute that charged savagely at anyone who approached its master's house, with something of the master's certitude and overbearance; and today was not the first time he had tried to kill it, though only now did he know why he had not gone through with it. "I never knowed my own luck," he said to himself, lying on the pallet. "I never knowed. If I had went ahead and killed it, killed the dog . . ."

He was still not triumphant. It was too soon yet to be proud, vindicated. It was too soon. It had to do with death. He did not believe that a man could pick up and move that irrevocable distance at a moment's notice. He had completely forgotten about the body. So he lay with his gaunt, underfed body empty with waiting, thinking of nothing at all, listening to the dog. The cries came at measured intervals, timbrous, sourceless, with the sad, peaceful, abject quality of a single hound in the darkness, when suddenly he found himself sitting bolt upright on the pallet.

"Nigger talk," he said. He had heard (he had never known a Negro himself, because of the antipathy, the economic jealousy, between his kind and Negroes) how Negroes claimed that a dog would howl at the recent grave of its master. "Hit's nigger talk," he said all the time he was putting on his overalls and his recently cleaned shoes. He opened the door. From the dark river bottom below the hill on which the cabin sat the howling of the dog came, bell-like and mournful. From a nail just inside the door he took down a coiled plowline and descended the slope.

Against the dark wall of the jungle fireflies winked and drifted; from beyond the black wall came the booming and grunting of frogs. When he entered the timber he could not see his own hand. The footing was treacherous with slime and creepers and bramble. They possessed the perversity of inanimate things, seeming to spring out of the darkness and clutch him with spiky tentacles. From the musing impenetrability ahead the voice of the hound came steadily. He followed the sound, muddy again; the air was chill, yet he was sweating. He was quite near the sound. The hound ceased. He plunged forward, his teeth drying under his dry lip, his hands clawed and blind, toward the ceased sound, the faint phosphorescent glare of the dog's eyes. The eyes vanished.

He stopped panting, stooped, the plowline in his hand, looking for the eye. He cursed the dog, his voice a dry whisper. He could hear silence but nothing else.

He crawled on hands and knees, telling where he was by the shape of the trees on the sky. After a time, the brambles raking and slashing at his face, he found a shallow ditch. It was rank with rotted leaves; he waded ankle-deep in the pitch-darkness, in something not earth and not water, his elbow crooked before his face. He stumbled upon something; an object with a slack feel. When he touched it, something gave a choked, infantlike cry, and he started back, hearing the creature scuttle away. "Just a possum," he said. "Hit was just a possum."

He wiped his hands on his flanks in order to pick up the shoulders. His flanks were foul with slime. He wiped his hands on his shirt, across his breast, then he picked up the shoulders. He walked backward, dragging it. From time to time he would stop and wipe his hands on his shirt. He stopped beside a tree, a rotting cypress shell, topless, about ten feet tall. He had put the coiled plowline into his bosom. He knotted it about the body and climbed the stump. The top was open, rotted out. He was not a large man, not as large as the body, yet he hauled it up to him hand over hand, bumping and scraping it along the stump, until it lay across the lip like a half-filled meal sack. The knot in the rope had slipped tight. At last he took out his knife and cut the rope and tumbled the body into the hollow stump.

It didn't fall far. He shoved at it, feeling around it with his hands for the obstruction; he tied the rope about the stub of a limb and held the end of it in his hands and stood on the body and began to jump up and down upon it, whereupon it fled suddenly beneath him and left him dangling on the rope.

He tried to climb the rope, rasping off with his knuckles the rotton fiber, a faint, damp powder of decay like snuff in his nostrils. He heard the stub about which the rope was tied crack and felt it begin to give. He leaped upward from nothing, scrabbling at the rotten wood, and got one hand over the edge. The wood crumbled beneath his fingers; he climbed perpetually without an inch of gain, his mouth cracked upon his teeth, his eyes glaring at the sky.

The wood stopped crumbling. He dangled by his hands, breathing. He drew himself up and straddled the edge. He sat there for a while. Then he climbed down and leaned against the hollow trunk.

When he reached his cabin he was tired, spent. He had never been so tired. He stopped at the door. Fire-flies still blew along the dark band of timber, and owls hooted and the frogs still boomed and grunted. "I ain't never been so tired," he said, leaning against the house, the wall which he had built log by log. "Like ever'thing had got outen hand. Climbing that stump, and the noise that shot made. Like I had got to be somebody else without knowing it, in a place where noise was louder, climbing harder to climb, without knowing it." He went to bed. He took off the muddy shoes, the over-alls, and lay down; it was late then. He could tell by a summer star that came into the square window at two o'clock and after.

Then, as if it had waited for him to get settled and comfortable, the hound began to howl again. Lying in the dark, he heard the first cry come up from the river bottom, mournful, timbrous, profound.

Five men in overalls squatted against the wall of Varner's store. Cotton made the sixth. He sat on the top step, his back against a gnawed post which supported the wooden awning of the veranda. The seventh man sat in the single splint chair; a fat, slow man in denim trousers and a collarless white shirt, smoking a cob pipe. He was past middle age. He was sheriff of the county. The man about whom they were talking was named Houston.

"He hadn't no reason to run off," one said. "To disappear. To send his horse back home with a empty saddle. He hadn't no reason. Owning his own land, his house. Making a good crop ever year. He was as well fixed as ere a man in the county. A bachelor too. He hadn't no reason to disappear. You can mark it. He never run. I don't know what; but Houston never run."

"I don't know," a second said. "You can't tell what a man has got in his mind. Houston might a had reason that we don't know, for making it look like something had happened to him. For clearing outen the country and leaving it to look like something had happened to him. It's been done before. Folks before him has had reason to light out for Texas with a changed name."

Cotton sat a little below their eyes, his face lowered beneath his worn, stained, shabby hat. He was whittling at a stick, a piece of pine board.

"But a fellow can't disappear without leaving no trace," a third said. "Can he, Sheriff?"

"Well, I don't know," the Sheriff said. He removed the cob pipe and spat neatly across the porch into the dust. "You can't tell what a man will do when he's pinched. Except it will be something you never thought of. Never counted on. But if you can find just what pinched him you can pretty well tell what he done."

"Houston was smart enough to do ere a thing he taken a notion to," the second said. "If he'd wanted to disappear, I reckon we'd a known about what we know now."

"And what's that?" the third said.

"Nothing," the second said.

"That's a fact," the first said. "Houston was a secret man."

"He wasn't the only secret man around here," a fourth said. To Cotton it sounded sudden, since the fourth man had said no word before. He sat against the post, his hat slanted forward so that his face was invisible, believing that he could feel their eyes. He watched the sliver peel slow and smooth from the stick ahead of his worn knife blade. "I got to say something," he told himself.

"He warn't no smarter than nobody else," he said. Then he wished he had not spoken. He could see their feet beneath his hat brim. He trimmed the stick, watching the knife, the steady sliver. "It's got to trim off smooth," he told himself. "It don't dast to break." He was talking; he could hear his voice: "Swelling around like he was the biggest man in the county. Setting that ere dog on folks' stock." He believed that he could feel their eyes, watching their feet, watching the sliver trim smooth and thin and unhurried beneath the knife blade. Suddenly he thought about the gun, the loud crash, the jarring shock. "Maybe I'll have to kill them all," he said to himself—a mild man in worn overalls, with a gaunt face and lackluster eyes like a sick man, whittling a stick with a thin hand, thinking

about killing them. "Not them; just
the words, the talk." But the talk
was familiar, the intonation, the
gestures; but so was Houston. He
had known Houston all his life: that
prosperous and overbearing man.
"With a dog," Cotton said, watching
the knife return and bite into another
sliver. "A dog that et better than me.
I work, and eat worse than his dog.
If I had been his dog, I would not
have. . . . We're better off without
him," he blurted. He could feel their
eyes, sober, intent.

"He always did rile Ernest," the
first said.

"He taken advantage of me," Cotton said, watching the infallible
knife. "He taken advantage of ever
man he could."

"He was a overbearing man," the
Sheriff said.

Cotton believed that they were
still watching him, hidden behind
their detached voices.

"Smart, though," the third said.

"He wasn't smart enough to win
that suit against Ernest over that
hog."

"That's so. How much did Ernest
get outen that lawing? He ain't never
told, has he?"

Cotton believed that they knew
how much he had got from the suit.
The hog had come into his lot one
October. He penned it up; he tried
by inquiry to find the owner. But
none claimed it until he had win-
tered it on his corn. In the spring
Houston claimed the hog. They went
to court. Houston was awarded the
hog, though he was assessed a sum
for the wintering of it, and one
dollar as pound fee for a stray. "I
reckon that's Ernest's business," the
Sheriff said after a time.

Again Cotton heard himself talking, blurting. "It was a dollar," he
said, watching his knuckles whiten

about the knife handle. "One dollar." He was trying to make his
mouth stop talking. "After all I taken
offen him. . . ."

"Juries does queer things," the
Sheriff said, "in little matters. But
in big matters they're mostly right."

Cotton whittled, steady and
deliberate. "At first you'll want to
run," he told himself. "But you got
to finish it. You got to count a hundred, if it needs, and finish it."

"I heard that dog again last night,"
the third said.

"You did?" the Sheriff said.

"It ain't been home since the day
the horse come in with the saddle
empty," the first said.

"It's out hunting, I reckon," the
Sheriff said. "It'll come in when it
gets hungry."

Cotton trimmed at the stick. He
did not move.

"Niggers claim a hound'll howl till
a dead body's found," the second
said.

"I've heard that," the Sheriff said.
After a time a car came up and the
Sheriff got into it. The car was driven
by a deputy. "We'll be late for supper," the Sheriff said. The car
mounted the hill; the sound died
away. It was getting toward sundown.

"He ain't much bothered," the
third said.

"Why should he be?" the first said.
"After all, a man can leave his house
and go on a trip without telling
everybody."

"Looks like he'd a unsaddled that
mare, though," the second said. "And
there's something the matter with
that dog. It ain't been home since.
And it ain't treed. I been hearing it
ever night. It ain't treed. It's howling.
It ain't been home since Tuesday.
And that was the day Houston rid

away from the store here on that mare."

Cotton was the last one to leave the store. It was after dark when he reached home. He ate some cold bread and loaded the shotgun and sat beside the open door until the hound began to howl. Then he descended the hill and entered the bottom.

The dog's voice guided him; after a while it ceased, and he saw its eyes. They were now motionless; in the red glare of the explosion he saw the beast entire in sharp relief. He saw it in the act of leaping into the ensuing welter of darkness; he heard the thud of its body. But he couldn't find it. He looked carefully, quartering back and forth, stopping to listen. But he had seen the shot strike it and hurl it backward, and he turned aside for about a hundred yards in the pitch-darkness and came to a slough. He flung the shotgun into it, hearing the sluggish splash, watching the vague water break and recover, until the last ripple died. He went home and to bed.

He didn't go to sleep though, although he knew he would not hear the dog. "It's dead," he told himself, lying on his quilt pallet in the dark. "I saw the bullets knock it down. I could count the shot. The dog is dead." But still he did not sleep. He did not need sleep; he did not feel tired or stale in the mornings, though he knew it was not the dog. He knew he would not hear the dog again, and that sleep had nothing to do with the dog. So he took to spending the nights sitting up in a chair in the door, watching the fireflies and listening to the frogs and the owls.

He entered Varner's store. It was in midafternoon; the porch was empty, save for the clerk, whose name was Snopes. "Been looking for you for two-three days," Snopes said. "Come inside."

Cotton entered. The store smelled of cheese and leather and new earth. Snopes went behind the counter and reached from under the counter a shotgun. It was caked with mud. "This is yourn, ain't it?" Snopes said. "Vernon Tull said it was. A nigger squirl hunter found it in a slough."

Cotton came to the counter and looked at the gun. He did not touch it; he just looked at it. "It ain't mine," he said.

"Ain't nobody around here got one of them old Hadley ten-gauges except you," Snopes said. "Tull says it's yourn."

"It ain't none of mine," Cotton said. "I got one like it. But mine's to home."

Snopes lifted the gun. He breeched it. "It had one empty and one load in it," he said. "Who you reckon it belongs to?"

"I don't know," Cotton said. "Mine's to home." He had come to purchase food. He bought it: crackers, cheese, a tin of sardines. It was not dark when he reached home, yet he opened the sardines and ate his supper. When he lay down he did not even remove his overalls. It was as though he waited for something, stayed dressed to move and go at once. He was still waiting for whatever it was when the window turned gray and then yellow and then blue; when, framed by the square window, he saw against the fresh morning a single soaring speck. By sunrise there were three of them, and then seven.

All that day he watched them gather, wheeling and wheeling, drawing their concentric black circles, watching the lower ones wheel down and down and disappear below the trees. He thought it was the dog. "They'll be through by noon," he said. "It wasn't a big dog."

When noon came they had not gone away; there were still more of them, while still lower ones dropped down and disappeared below the trees. He watched them until dark came, until they went away, flapping singly and sluggishly up from beyond the trees. "I got to eat," he said. "With the work I got to do tonight." He went to the hearth and knelt and took up a pine knot, and he was kneeling, nursing a match into flame, when he heard the hound again; the cry deep, timbrous, unmistakable, and sad. He cooked his supper and ate.

With his ax in his hand he descended through his meager corn patch. The cries of the hound could have guided him, but he did not need it. He had not reached the bottom before he believed that his nose was guiding him. The dog still howled. He paid it no attention, until the beast sensed him and ceased, as it had done before; again he saw its eyes. He paid no attention to them. He went to the hollow cypress trunk and swung his ax into it, the ax sinking helve-deep into the rotten wood. While he was tugging at it something flowed silent and savage out of the darkness behind him and struck him a slashing blow. The ax had just come free; he fell with the ax in his hand, feeling the hot reek of the dog's breath on his face and hearing the click of its teeth as he struck it down with his free hand. It leaped again; he saw its eyes now. He was on his knees, the ax raised in both hands now. He swung it, hitting nothing, feeling nothing; he saw the dog's eyes, crouched. He rushed at the eyes; they vanished. He waited a moment, but heard nothing. He returned to the tree.

At the first stroke of the ax the dog sprang at him again. He was expecting it, so he whirled and struck with the ax at the two eyes and felt the ax strike something and whirl from his hands. He heard the dog whimper, he could hear it crawling away. On his hands and knees he hunted for the ax until he found it.

He began to chop at the base of the stump, stopping between blows to listen. But he heard nothing, saw nothing. Overhead the stars were swinging slowly past; he saw the one that looked into his window at two o'clock. He began to chop steadily at the base of the stump.

The wood was rotten; the ax sank helve-deep at each stroke, as into sand or mud; suddenly Cotton knew that it was not imagination he smelled. He dropped the ax and began to tear at the rotten wood with his hands. The hound was beside him, whimpering; he did not know it was there, not even when it thrust its head into the opening, crowding against him, howling.

"Git away," he said, still without being conscious that it was the dog. He dragged at the body, feeling it slough upon its own bones, as though it were too large for itself; he turned his face away, his teeth glared, his breath furious and outraged and restrained. He could feel the dog surge against his legs, its head in the orifice, howling.

When the body came free, Cotton went over backward. He lay on his back on the wet ground, looking up at a faint patch of starry sky. "I ain't never been so tired," he said. The dog was howling, with an abject steadiness. "Shut up," Cotton said. "Hush. Hush." The dog didn't hush. "It'll be daylight soon," Cotton said to himself, "I got to get up."

He got up and kicked at the dog. It moved away but when he stooped and took hold of the legs and began to back away, the dog was there again, moaning to itself. When he would stop to rest, the dog would howl again; again he kicked at it. Then it began to be dawn, the trees coming spectral and vast out of the miasmic darkness. He could see the dog plainly. It was gaunt, thin, with a long bloody gash across its face. "I'll have to get shut of you," he said. Watching the dog, he stooped and found a stick. It was rotten, foul with slime. He clutched it. When the hound lifted its muzzle to howl, he struck. The dog whirled; there was a long fresh scar running from shoulder to flank. It leaped at him, without a sound; he struck again. The stick took it fair between the eyes. He picked up the ankles and tried to run.

It was almost light. When he broke through the undergrowth upon the riverbank the channel was invisible, a long bank of what looked like cotton batting, though he could hear the water beneath it somewhere. There was a freshness here; the edges of the mist licked into curling tongues. He stooped and lifted the body and hurled it into the bank of mist. At the instant of vanishing he saw it—a sluggish sprawl of three limbs instead of four, and he knew why it had been so hard to free from the stump. "I'll have to make another trip," he said; then he heard a pattering rush behind him. He didn't have time to turn when the hound struck him and knocked him down. It didn't pause. Lying on his back, he saw it in mid-air, like a bird, vanish into the mist with a single short, choking cry.

He got to his feet and ran. He stumbled and caught himself and ran again. It was full light. He could see the stump and the black hole which he had chopped in it; behind him he could hear the swift, soft feet of the dog. As it sprang at him he stumbled and fell and saw it soar over him, its eyes like two cigar coals; it whirled and leaped at him again before he could rise. He struck at its face with his bare hands and began to run. Together they reached the tree. It leaped at him again, slashing his arms as he ducked into the tree, seeking that member of the body which he did not know was missing until after he had released it into the mist, feeling the dog surging about his legs. Then the dog was gone. Then a voice said:

"We got him. You can come out, Ernest."

The county seat was fourteen miles away. They drove to it in a battered Ford. On the back seat Cotton and the Sheriff sat, their inside wrists locked together by handcuffs. They had to drive for two miles before they reached the highroad. It was hot, ten o'clock in the morning. "You want to swap sides out of the sun?" the Sheriff said.

"I'm all right," Cotton said.

At two o'clock they had a puncture. Cotton and the Sheriff sat under a tree while the driver and the second deputy went across a field and returned with a glass jar of buttermilk and some cold food. They ate, repaired the tire, and went on.

When they were within three or four miles of town, they began to pass wagons and cars going home from market day in town, the wagon teams plodding homeward in their own inescapable dust. The Sheriff greeted them with a single gesture of his fat arm. "Home for supper, anyway," he said. "What's the matter,

Ernest? Feeling sick? Here, Joe; pull up a minute."

"I'll hold my head out," Cotton said. "Never mind." The car went on. Cotton thrust his head out the V strut of the top stanchion. The Sheriff shifted his arm, giving him play. "Go on," Cotton said, "I'll be all right." The car went on. Cotton slipped a little farther down in the seat. By moving his head a little he could wedge his throat into the apex of the iron V, the uprights gripping his jaws beneath the ears. He shifted again until his head was tight in the vise, then he swung his legs over the door, trying to bring the weight of his body sharply down against his imprisoned neck. He could hear his vertebrae; he felt a kind of rage at his own toughness; he was struggling then against the jerk on the manacle, the hands on him.

Then he was lying on his back beside the road, with water on his face and in his mouth, though he could not swallow. He couldn't speak, trying to curse, cursing in no voice. Then he was in the car again, on the smooth street where children played in the big, shady yards in small bright garments, and men and women went home toward supper, to plates of food and cups of coffee in the long twilight of summer.

They had a doctor for him in his cell. When the doctor had gone he could smell supper cooking somewhere—ham and hot bread and coffee. He was lying on a cot; the last ray of copper sunlight slid through a narrow window, stippling the bars upon the wall above his head. His cell was near the common room, where the minor prisoners lived, the ones who were in jail for minor offenses or for three meals a day; the stairway from below came up into that room. It was occupied for the

time by a group of Negroes from the chain gang that worked the streets, in jail for vagrancy or for selling a little whisky or shooting craps for ten or fifteen cents. One of the Negroes was at the window above the street, yelling down to someone. The others talked among themselves, their voices rich and murmurous, mellow and singsong. Cotton rose and went to the door of his cell and held to the bars, looking at the Negroes. "Hit," he said. His voice made no sound. He put his hand to his throat; he produced a dry croaking sound, at which the Negroes ceased talking and looked at him, their eyeballs rolling. "It was all right," Cotton said, "until it started coming to pieces on me. I could a handled that dog." He held his throat, his voice harsh, dry, and croaking. "But it started coming to pieces on me . . ."

"Who him?" one of the Negroes said. They whispered among themselves, watching him, their eyeballs white in the dusk.

"It would a been all right," Cotton said, "but it started coming to pieces . . ."

"Hush up, white man," one of the Negroes said. "Don't you be telling us no truck like that."

"Hit would a been all right," Cotton said, his voice harsh, whispering. Then it failed him again altogether. He held to the bars with one hand, holding his throat with the other, while the Negroes watched him, huddled, their eyeballs white and sober. Then with one accord they turned and rushed across the room, toward the staircase; he heard slow steps and then he smelled food, and he clung to the bars, trying to see the stairs. "Are they going to feed them niggers before they feed a white man?" he said, smelling the coffee and the ham.

Thomas Wolfe

1900-1938

THOMAS CLAYTON WOLFE tried to put his contemporary world, complete and unexpurgated, into his novels. What he succeeded in writing was a series of novels about himself that included all the experiences of his short, passionate, hard-working lifetime. Scarcely a thought was untold, scarcely an emotion left untouched. Every person he had known, every place he had seen, became part of his written page.

Wolfe's South was Asheville, North Carolina, the scene of his first book, *Look Homeward, Angel*, a novel of 350,000 words, written when he was twenty-seven. After a year in London, where he went on the Guggenheim Fellowship *Look Homeward, Angel* had won him, he returned to America with the material for another novel—a package of manuscript two feet high, containing some 3000 sheets of typewritten paper. Merely to arrange the sheets in order took him six weeks. For two years he worked all day and into the night over this material, under the supervision of an understanding editor. As the editor cut, Wolfe added, and when the publisher finally called a halt, the novel was already twelve times average size. The next year he wrote another novel, combined it with the first, and, what with more cutting, sometimes as much as 50,000 words at a sitting, finally brought forth the magnificent *Of Time and the River*.

Wolfe was a tremendous man—six feet seven, weighing two hundred and fifty pounds, with tremendous energy and great talent. "I had created a labor so large," he wrote, ". . . that the energy of a dozen lifetimes would not suffice for its accomplishment." Actually, when he died there was enough material left for ten more novels.

While Wolfe was writing *Of Time and the River*, he was living in the Syrian colony of south Brooklyn, in a basement flat. This is the scene of "No Door," taken from the volume *From Death to Morning*, which Wolfe believed was as good writing as he had ever done.

No Door

BY THOMAS WOLFE

IT IS wonderful with what warm enthusiasm well-kept people who have never been alone in all their life can congratulate you on the joys of solitude. I know whereof I speak. I have been alone a great deal in my life—more than anyone I know—and I also knew, for one short period, a few of these well-kept people. And their passionate longing for the life of loneliness is astonishing. In the evening they are driven out to their fine house in the country where their wives and children eagerly await them; or to their magnificent apartments in the city where their lovely wife or charming mistress is waiting for them with a tender smile, a perfumed, anointed, and seductive body, and the embrace of love. And all of this is as a handful of cold dust and ashes, and a little dross.

Sometimes one of them invites you out to dinner: your host is a pleasant gentleman of forty-six, a little bald, healthily plump, well-nourished-looking, and yet with nothing gross and sensual about him. Indeed he is a most aesthetic-looking millionaire, his features, although large and generous, are full of sensitive intelligence, his manners are gentle, quietly subdued, his smile a little sad, touched faintly with a whimsy of ironic humor, as of one who has passed through all the anguish, hope, and tortured fury youth can know, and now knows what to expect from life and whose "eyelids are a little weary," patiently resigned, and not too bitter about it.

Yet life has not dealt overharshly with our host: the evidence of his interest in unmonied, precious things is quietly, expensively, all around him. He lives in a penthouse apartment near the East River: the place is furnished with all the discrimination of a quiet but distinguished taste, he has several of Jacob Epstein's heads and figures, including one of himself which the sculptor made "two years ago when I was over there," and he also has a choice collection of rare books and first editions, and after admiring these treasures appreciatively, you all step out upon the roof for a moment to admire the view you get there of the river.

Evening is coming fast, and the tall frosted glasses in your hands make a thin but pleasant tinkling, and the great city is blazing there in your vision in its terrific frontal sweep and curtain of star-flung towers, now sown with the diamond pollen of a million lights, and the sun has set behind them, and the red light of fading day is painted upon the river—and you see the boats, the tugs, the barges passing, and the winglike swoop of bridges with exultant joy—and night has come, and there are ships there— there are ships—and a wild intolerable longing in you that you cannot utter.

When you go back into the room again, you feel very far away from Brooklyn, where you live, and everything you felt about the city as a child, before you ever saw or knew it, now seems not only possible, but about to happen.

The great vision of the city is burning in your heart in all its enchanted colors just as it did when you were twelve years old and thought about it. You think that same glorious happiness of fortune, fame, and triumph will be yours at any minute, that you are about to take your place among great men and lovely women in a life more fortunate and happy than any you have every known—that it is all here, somehow, waiting for you and only an inch away if you will touch it, only a word away if you will speak it, only a wall, a door, a stride from you if you only knew the place where you may enter.

And somehow the old wild wordless hope awakes again that you will find it—the door that you can enter —that this man is going to tell you. The very air you breathe now is filled with the thrilling menace of some impossible good fortune. Again you want to ask him what the magic secret is that has given his life such power, authority, and ease, and made all the brutal struggle, pain, and ugliness of life, the fury, hunger, and the wandering, seem so far away, and you think he is going to tell

you—to give this magic secret to you—but he tells you nothing.

Then, for a moment the old unsearchable mystery of time and the city returns to overwhelm your spirit with the horrible sensations of defeat and drowning. You see this man, his mistress, and all the other city people you have known, in shapes of deathless brightness, and yet their life and time are stranger to you than a dream, and you think that you are doomed to walk among them always as a phantom who can never grasp their life or make their time your own. It seems to you now that you are living in a world of creatures who have learned to live without weariness or agony of the soul, in a life which you can never touch, approach or apprehend; a strange city race who have never lived in a dimension of time that is like your own, and that can be measured in minutes, hours, days, and years, but in dimensions of fathomless and immemorable sensation; who can be remembered only at some moment in their lives nine thousand enthusiasms back, twenty thousand nights of drunkenness ago, eight hundred parties, four million cruelties, nine thousand treacheries or fidelities, two hundred love affairs gone by— and whose lives therefore take on a fabulous and horrible age of sensation, that has never known youth or remembered innocence and that induces in you the sensation of drowning in a sea of horror, a sea of blind, dateless, and immemorable time. There is no door.

But now your host, with his faintly bitter and ironic smile, has poured himself out another good stiff drink of honest rye into a tall thin glass that has some ice in it, and smacked his lips around it with an air of rumination, and, after two or three reflective swallows, begins to get a trifle sorrowful about the life harsh destiny has picked out for him.

While his mistress sits prettily upon the fat edge of an upholstered chair, stroking her cool and delicate fingers gently over his knit brows, and while his good man Ponsonby or Kato is quietly "laying out his things" for dinner, he stares gloomily ahead, and with a bitter smile congratulates you on the blessed luck that has permitted you to live alone in the Armenian section of South Brooklyn.

Well, you say, living alone in South Brooklyn has its drawbacks. The place you live in is shaped just like a Pullman car, except that it is not so long and has only one window at each end. There are bars over the front window that your landlady has put there to keep the thugs in that sweet neighborhood from breaking in; in winter the place is cold and dark, and sweats with clammy water, in summer you do all the sweating yourself, but you do plenty of it, quite enough for anyone; the place gets hot as hell.

Moreover—and here you really begin to warm up to your work—when you get up in the morning the sweet aroma of the old Gowanus Canal gets into your nostrils, into your mouth, into your lungs, into everything you do, or think, or say! It is, you say, one huge gigantic Stink, a symphonic Smell, a vast organ note of stupefying odor, cunningly contrived, compacted, and composted of eighty-seven separate several putrefactions; and with a rich and mounting enthusiasm, you name them all for him. There is in it, you say, the smell of melted glue and of burned rubber. It has in it the fragrance of deceased, decaying cats, the odor of rotten cabbage, prehistoric eggs, and old tomatoes; the smell of burning rags and putrefying offal, mixed with the fragrance of a boneyard horse, now dead, the hide of a skunk, and the noisome stenches of a stagnant sewer; it has as well the——

But at this moment your host throws his head back and, with a look of rapture on his face, draws in upon the air the long full respiration of ecstatic satisfaction, as if, in this great panoply of smells, he really had found the breath of life itself, and then cries:

"Wonderful! Wonderful! Oh, simply *swell! Marvelous!*" he cries and then throws back his head again, with a shout of exultant laughter.

"Oh, John!" his lady says at this point with a troubled look upon her lovely face, "I don't think you'd like a place like that at *all*. It sounds simply *dreadful!* I don't like to hear of it," she says, with a pretty little shudder of distaste. "I think it's simply terrible that they let people live in places like that!"

"Oh!" he says, "it's wonderful! The power, the richness, and the beauty of it all!" he cries.

Well, you agree, it's wonderful enough. And it's got power and richness—sure enough! As to the beauty —that's a different matter. You are not so sure of that—but even as you say this you remember many things. You remember a powerful big horse, slow-footed, shaggy in the hoof, with big dappled spots of iron gray upon it that stood one brutal day in August by the curb. Its driver had unhitched it from the wagon and it stood there with its great patient head bent down in an infinite and quiet sorrow, and a little boy with black eyes and a dark face was standing by it holding some sugar in his hand, and its driver, a man who had the tough seamed face of the city, stepped in on the horse with a bucket full of water which he threw against the horse's side. For a second, the great flanks shuddered gratefully and began to smoke, the man stepped back on to the curb and began to look the animal over with a keen deliberate glance, and the boy stood there, rubbing his hand quietly into the horse's muzzle, and talking softly to it all the time.

Then you remember how a tree that leaned over into the narrow little alley where you lived had come to life that year, and how you watched it day by day as it came into its moment's glory of young magic green. And you remember a raw, rusty street along the water front, with its naked and brutal life, its agglomeration of shacks, tenements, and slums and huge grimy piers, its unspeakable ugliness and beauty, and you remember how you came along this street one day at sunset, and saw all of the colors of the sun and harbor, flashing, blazing, shifting in swarming motes, in an iridescent web of light and color for an instant on the blazing side of a proud white ship.

And you start to tell your host what it was like and how the evening looked and felt—of the thrilling smell and savor of the huge deserted pier, of the fading light upon old rusty brick of shambling houses, and of the blazing beauty of that swarming web of light and color on the ship's great prow, but when you start to tell about it, you cannot, nor ever recapture the feeling of mystery, exultancy, and wild sorrow that you felt then.

Yes, there has been beauty enough —enough to burst the heart, madden the brain, and tear the sinews of your life asunder—but what is there to say? You remember all these things, and then ten thousand others, but when you start to tell the man about them, you cannot.

Instead you just tell him about the place you live in: of how dark and hot it is in summer, how clammy cold in winter, and of how hard it is to get anything good to eat. You tell him about your landlady, who is a hardbitten ex-reporter. You tell him what a good and liberal-hearted woman she is; how rough and ready, full of life and energy, how she likes drinking and the fellowship of drinking men, and knows all the rough and seamy side of life which a newspaper reporter gets to know.

You tell how she has been with murderers before their execution, got the story from them or their mothers, climbed over sides of ships to get a story, forced herself in at funerals, followed burials to the graveyard, trampled upon every painful, decent, sorrowful emotion of mankind—all to get that story; and still remains a decent woman, an immensely good, generous, and lusty-living person, and yet an old maid, and a puritan, somehow, to the roots of her soul.

You tell how she went mad several years before, and spent two years in an asylum; you tell how moments of this madness still come back to her, and of how you went home one night several months before, to find her stretched out on your bed, only to rise and greet you as the great lover of her dreams—Dr. Eustace Mc-Namee, a name, a person, and a love she had invented for herself. Then you tell of her fantastic family, her three sisters and her father, all touched with the same madness, but without her energy, power, and high ability; and of how she has kept the whole crowd going since her eighteenth year.

You tell about the old man who is an inventor who does not invent; of how he invented a corkscrew with the cork attached that would not cork; an unlockable lock; an unbreakable looking glass that wouldn't look. And you tell how the year before, he inherited $120,000—the first money he had ever had—and promptly took it down to Wall Street, where he was as promptly shorn of it, meanwhile sending his wife and daughters to Europe in the nuptial suite of a palatial liner and cabling them when they wanted to come back: "Push on to Rome, my children! Push on, push on! Your father's making millions!"

Yes, all this, and a hundred other things about this incredible, mad, fantastic, and yet highhearted family which I had found in a dingy alleyway in Brooklyn I could tell my host. And I could tell him a thousand other things about the people all about me—of the Armenians, Spaniards, Irishmen in the alley who came home on weekdays and turned on the radio, until the whole place was yelling with a hundred dissonances, and who came home on Saturday to get drunk and beat their wives—the whole intimate course and progress of their lives published nakedly from a hundred open windows with laugh, shout, scream, and curse.

I could tell him how they fought, got drunk, and murdered; how they robbed, held up, and blackjacked, how they whored and stole and killed—all of which was part of the orderly and decent course of life for them—and yet, how they could howl with outraged modesty, complain to the police, and send a delegation to us when the young nephew of my landlady lay for an hour upon our patch of back-yard grass clad only in his bathing trunks.

"Yuh gotta nekkid man out deh!" they said, in tones of hushed accusatory horror.

Yes, we—good sir, who are so fond of irony—we, old Whittaker, the inventor, and Mad Maude, his oldest daughter, who would grumble at a broken saucer, and then stuff lavish breakfasts down your throat, who would patiently water twenty little feet of back-yard earth from April until August, and until the grass grew beautifully, and then would turn twenty skinny, swarthy, and half-naked urchins loose into it to stamp it into muddy ruin in twenty minutes while she played the hose upon their grimy little bodies; we, this old man, his daughters, and his grandson, three bank clerks, a cartoonist, two young fellows who worked for Hearst, and myself; we, good sir, who sometimes brought a girl into our rooms, got drunk, wept, confessed sinful and unworthy lives, read Shakespeare, Milton, Whitman, Donne, the Bible—and the sporting columns—we, young, foolish, old, mad, and bewildered as we were, but who had never murdered, robbed, or knocked the teeth out of a woman; we, who were fairly decent, kind, and liberal-hearted people as the world goes, were the pariahs of Balcony Square—called so because there was neither square nor balconies, but just a little narrow alleyway.

Yes, we were suspect, enemies to order and the public morals, shameless partakers in an open and indecent infamy, and our neighbors looked at us with all the shuddering reprehension of their mistrustful eyes as they beat their wives like loving husbands, cut one another's throats with civic pride, and went about their honest toil of murder, robbery, and assault like the self-respecting citizens they were.

Meanwhile a man was murdered, with his head bashed in, upon the step of a house three doors below me; and a drunken woman got out of an automobile one night at two o'clock, screaming indictments of her escort to the whole neighborhood. "Yuh gotta pay me, ya big bum!" she yelled. "Yuh gotta pay me now! Give me my t'ree dollehs, or I'll go home an' make my husband beat it out of yuh!"

"Staht actin' like a lady!" said the man in lower tones. "I won't pay yuh till yuh staht actin' like a lady! Yuh gotta staht actin' like a lady!" he insisted, with a touching devotion to the rules of gallantry.

And this had continued until he had started the engine of his car and driven off at furious speed, leaving her to wander up and down the alleyway for hours, screaming and sobbing, cursing foully and calling down the vengeance of her husband on this suitor who had thus misused her—an indictment that had continued unmolested until three young ambitious thugs had seized the opportunity to go out and rob her; they passed my window running, in the middle of the night, one fearful and withdrawing, saying, "Jeez! I'm sick! I don't feel good! Wait a minute! Youse guys go on an' do it by yourself! I want a cup of coffee!"— And the others snarling savagely:

"Come on! Come on, yuh yellah bastad! If yuh don't come on, I'll moiduh yuh!" And they had gone, their quick feet scampering nimbly in the dark, while the woman's drunken and demented howls came faintly from the other end, and then had ceased.

Your host has been enchanted by that savage chronicle. He smites himself upon the brow with rapture, crying "Oh, grand! *Grand!* What a lucky fellow you are! If I were in your place I'd be the happiest man alive!"

You take a look about you and say nothing.

"To be free! To go about and see these things!" he cries. "To live among real people! To see life as it is, in the raw—the *real* stuff, not like this!" he says with a weary look at all the suave furnishings of illusion that surround him. "And above all else to be *alone!*"

You ask him if he has ever been alone, if he knows what loneliness is like. You try to tell him, but he knows about this too. He smiles faintly, ironically, and dismisses it and you, with a wise man's weary tolerance of youth: "I know! I know!" he sighs. "But all of us are lonely, and after all, my boy, the real loneliness for most of us is *here*"—and he taps himself a trifle to the left of the third shirt stud, in the presumptive region of his heart. "But you! Free, young, and footloose, with the whole world to explore—you have a fine life! What more, in God's name, could a man desire?"

Well, what is there to say? For a moment, the blood is pounding at your temples, a hot retort springs sharp and bitter to your lips, and you feel that you could tell him many things. You could tell him, and not be very nice or dainty with it, that there's a hell of a lot more that a man desires: good food and wonderful companions, comfort, ease, security, a lovely woman like the one who sits beside him now, and an end to loneliness—but what is there to say?

For you are what you are, you know what you know, and there are no words for loneliness, black, bitter, aching loneliness, that knows the roots of silence in the night.

So what is there to say? There has been life enough, and power, grandeur, joy enough, and there has also been beauty enough, and God knows there has been squalor and filth and misery and madness and despair enough; murder and cruelty and hate enough, and loneliness enough to fill your bowels with the substance of gray horror, and to crust your lips with its hard and acrid taste of desolation.

And oh, there has been time enough, even in Brooklyn there is time enough, strange time, dark secret time enough, dark, million-visaged time enough, forever flowing by you like a river, even in cellar depths in Brooklyn there is time enough, but when you try to tell the man about it you cannot, for what is there to say?

For suddenly you remember how the tragic light of evening falls even on the huge and rusty jungle of the earth that is known as Brooklyn and on the faces of all the men with dead eyes and with flesh of tallow gray, and of how even in Brooklyn they lean upon the sills of evening in that sad hushed light. And you remember how you lay one evening on your couch in your cool cellar depth in Brooklyn, and listened to the sounds of evening and to the dying birdsong in your trees; and you remember how two windows were thrown up, and you heard two voices—a woman's and a man's—begin to speak in that soft tragic light. And the memory of their words came back to you, like the haunting refrain of some old song— as it was heard and lost in Brooklyn.

"Yuh musta been away," said one, in that sad light.

"Yeah, I been away. I just got back," the other said.

"Yeah? Dat's just what I was t'inkin'," said the other. "I'd been t'inkin' dat yuh musta been away."

"Yeah, I been away on my vacation. I just got back."

"Oh, yeah? Dat's what I t'ought meself. I was t'inkin' just duh oddeh day dat I hadn't seen yuh f'r some time, 'I guess she's gone away,' I says."

And then for seconds there was silence—save for the dying birdsong, voices in the street, faint sounds and shouts and broken calls, and something hushed in evening, far, immense, and murmurous in the air.

"Well, wat's t' noos sinct I been gone?" the voice went out in quietness in soft tragic light. "Has anyt'ing happened sinct I was away?"

"Nah! Nuttin's happened," the other made reply. "About duh same as usual—*you* know?" it said with difficult constraint, inviting intuitions for the spare painfulness of barren tongues.

"Yeah, I know," the other answered with a tranquil resignation—and there was silence then in Brooklyn.

"I guess Fatheh Grogan died sinct you was gone," a voice began.

"Oh, yeah?" the other voice replied with tranquil interest.

"Yeah."

And for a waiting moment there was silence.

"Say, dat's too bad, isn't it?" the quiet voice then said with comfortless regret.

"Yeah. He died on Sattiday. When he went home on Friday night, he was O.K."

"Oh, yeah?"

"Yeah."

And for a moment they were balanced in strong silence.

"Gee, dat was tough, wasn't it?"

"Yeah. Dey didn't find him till duh next day at ten o'clock. When dey went to look for him he was lyin' stretched out on duh bat'room floeh."

"Oh, yeah?"

"Yeah. Dey found him lyin' deh," ıt said.

And for a moment more the voices hung in balanced silence.

"Gee, dat's too bad. . . . I guess I was away when all dat happened."

"Yeah. Yuh musta been away."

"Yeah, dat was it, I guess. I musta been away. Oddehwise I woulda hoid. I was away."

"Well, so long, kid. . . . I'll be seein' yuh."

"Well, so long!"

A window closed, and there was silence; evening and far sounds and broken cries in Brooklyn, Brooklyn, in the formless, rusty, and un-numbered wilderness of life.

And now the red light fades swiftly from the old red brick of rusty houses, and there are voices in the air, and somewhere music, and we are lying there, blind atoms in our cellar depths, gray voiceless atoms in the man-swarm desolation of the earth, and our fame is lost, our names forgotten, our powers are wasting from us like mined earth, while we lie here at evening and the river flows . . . and dark time is feeding like a vulture on our en-trails, and we know that we are lost, and cannot stir . . . and there are ships there! there are ships! . . . and Christ! we are all dying in the darkness! . . . and yuh musta been away . . . yuh musta been away. . . .

And that is a moment of dark time, that is one of strange million-visaged time's dark faces.

Erskine Caldwell

1903-

ERSKINE CALDWELL, the son of an itinerant Presbyterian minister, was born in a spot in Georgia that had no name. Throughout his boyhood the family wandered from church to church, covering the South in a year, and living on an income that averaged $300 annually. Young Caldwell went to primary school in Virginia, grammar school in Tennessee, high school in Georgia, and was admitted to the University of Virginia on a scholarship. There, while attending classes by day, he worked at night in a poolroom. His later jobs covered the field: professional football player, real-estate salesman for Alabama lots deep under water, bodyguard for a Chinese, stagehand in a burlesque theater. The people he writes about, however, are the Georgia folk he knew and the Maine folk among whom he lived, farmed, and brought up a family. Lynching, rape, murder, and violence abound in his stories, but he approaches these horrors with such gusto that as many of his tales come out comic as brutal. "Saturday Afternoon" is probably America's classic lynching story.

Saturday Afternoon

BY ERSKINE CALDWELL

TOM DENNY shoved the hunk of meat out of his way and stretched out on the meat block. He wanted to lie on his back and rest. The meat block was the only comfortable place in the butcher shop where a man could stretch out and Tom just had to rest every once in a while. He could prop his foot on the edge of the block, swing the other leg across his knee and be fairly comfortable with a hunk of rump steak under his head. The meat was nice and cool just after it came from the icehouse. Tom did that. He wanted to rest himself a while and he had to be comfortable on the meat block. He kicked off his shoes so he could wiggle his toes.

Tom's butchershop did not have a very pleasant smell. Strangers who went in to buy Tom's meat for the first time were always asking him what it was that had died between the walls. The smell got worse and worse year after year.

Tom bit off a chew of tobacco and made himself comfortable on the meat block.

There was a swarm of flies buzzing around the place: those lazy, stinging, fat and greasy flies that lived in Tom's butchershop. A screen door at the front kept out some of them that tried to get inside, but if they were used to coming in and filling up on the fresh blood on the meat block they knew how to fly around to the back door where there had never been a screen.

Everybody ate Tom's meat, and liked it. There was no other butchershop in town. You walked in and said, "Hello, Tom. How's everything today?" "Everything's slick as a whistle with me, but my old woman's got the chills and fever again." Then after Tom had finished telling how it felt to have chills and fever, you said, "I want a pound of pork chops, Tom." And Tom said, "By gosh, I'll git it for you right away." While you stood around waiting for the chops Tom turned the hunk of beef over two or three times businesslike and hacked off a pound of pork for you. If you wanted veal it was all the same to Tom. He slammed the hunk of beef around several times making a great to-do, and got the veal for you. He pleased everybody. Ask Tom for any kind of meat you could name, and Tom had it right there on the meat block waiting to be cut off and weighed.

Tom brushed the flies off his face and took a little snooze. It was midday. The country people had not yet got to town. It was laying-by season and everybody was working right up to twelve-o'clock sun time, which was half an hour slower than railroad time. There was hardly anybody in town at this time of day, even though it was Saturday. All the town people who had wanted some of Tom's meat for Saturday dinner had already got what they needed, and it was too early in the day to buy Sunday meat. The best time of day to get meat from Tom if it was to be kept over until Sunday was about ten o'clock Saturday night. Then you could take it home and be fairly certain that it would not turn bad before noon the next day—if the weather was not too hot.

The flies buzzed and lit on Tom's mouth and nose and Tom knocked them away with his hand and tried to sleep on the meat block with the cool hunk of rump steak under his head. The tobacco juice kept trying to trickle down his throat and Tom had to keep spitting it out. There was a cigar box half full of sawdust in the corner behind the showcase where livers and brains were kept for display, but he could not quite spit that far from the position he was in. The tobacco juice splattered on the floor midway between the meat block and the cigar box. What little of it dripped on the piece of rump steak did not really matter: most people cleaned their meat before they cooked and ate it, and it would all wash off.

But the danged flies! They kept on buzzing and stinging as mean as ever, and there is nothing any meaner than a lazy, well-fed, butchershop fly in the summertime, anyway. Tom knocked them off his face and spat them off his mouth the best he could without having to move too much. After a while he let them alone.

Tom was enjoying a good little snooze when Jim Baxter came running through the back door from the barbershop on the corner. Jim was Tom's partner and he came in sometimes on busy days to help out. He was a great big man, almost twice as large as Tom. He always wore a big wide-brimmed black hat and a blue shirt with the sleeves rolled up above his elbows. He had a large egg-shaped belly over which his breeches were always slipping down. When he walked he tugged at his breeches all the time, pulling them up over the top of his belly. But they were always working down until it looked as if they were ready to drop to the ground any minute and trip him. Jim would not wear suspenders. A belt was more sporty-looking.

Tom was snoozing away when Jim ran in the back door and grabbed him by the shoulders. A big handful of flies had gone to sleep on Tom's mouth. Jim shooed them off.

"Hey, Tom, Tom!" Jim shouted breathlessly. "Wake up, Tom! Wake up quick!"

Tom jumped to the floor and pulled on his shoes. He had become so accustomed to people coming in and waking him up to buy a quarter's worth of steak or a quarter's worth of ham that he had mistaken Jim for a customer. He rubbed the back of his hands over his mouth to take away the fly stings.

"What the hell!" he sputtered, looking up and seeing Jim standing there beside him. "What you want?"

"Come on, Tom! Git your gun! We're going after a nigger down the creek a ways."

"God Almighty, Jim!" Tom shouted, now fully awake. He clutched Jim's arm and begged: "You going to git a nigger, sure enough?"

"You're damn right, Tom. You know that gingerbread nigger what used to work on the railroad a long time back? Him's the nigger we're going to git. And we're going to git him good and proper, the yellow-face coon. He said something to Fred Jackson's oldest gal down the road yonder about an hour ago. Fred told us all about it over at the barbershop. Come on, Tom. We got to hurry. I expect we'll jerk him up pretty soon now."

Tom tied on his shoes and ran across the street behind Jim. Tom had his shotgun under his arm, and Jim had pulled the cleaver out of the meat block. They'd get the God-damn nigger all right—God damn his yellow hide to hell!

Tom climbed into an automobile with some other men. Jim jumped on the running board of another car just as it was leaving. There were thirty or forty cars headed for the creek bottom already and more getting ready to start.

They had a place already picked out at the creek. There was a clearing in the woods by the road and there was just enough room to do the job like it should be done. Plenty of dry brushwood near by and a good-sized sweetgum tree in the middle of the clearing. The automobiles stopped and the men jumped out in a hurry. Some others had gone for Will Maxie. Will was the gingerbread Negro. They would probably find him at home laying-by his cotton. Will could grow good cotton. He cut out all the grass first, and then he banked his rows with earth. Everybody else laid-by his cotton without going to the trouble of taking out the grass. But Will was a pretty smart Negro. And he

could raise a lot of corn too, to the acre. He always cut out the grass before he laid-by his corn. But nobody liked Will. He made too much money by taking out the grass before laying-by his cotton and corn. He made more money than Tom and Jim made in the butchershop selling people meat.

Doc Cromer had sent his boy down from the drugstore with half a dozen cases of Coca-Cola and a piece of ice in a washtub. The tub had some muddy water put in it from the creek, then the chunk of ice, and then three cases of Coca-Cola. When they were gone the boy would put the other three cases in the tub and give the dopes a chance to cool. Everybody likes to drink a lot of dopes when they are nice and cold.

Tom went out in the woods to take a drink of corn with Jim and Hubert Wells. Hubert always carried a jug of corn with him wherever he happened to be going. He made the whisky himself at his own still and got a fairly good living by selling it around the courthouse and the barbershop. Hubert made the best corn in the county.

Will Maxie was coming up the big road in a hurry. A couple of dozen men were behind him poking him with sticks. Will was getting old. He had a wife and three grown daughters, all married and settled. Will was a pretty good Negro too, minding his own business, stepping out of the road when he met a white man, and otherwise behaving himself. But nobody liked Will. He made too much money by taking the grass out of his cotton before it was laid-by.

Will came running up the road and the men steered him into the clearing. It was all fixed. There was a big pile of brushwood and a trace-chain for his neck and one for his feet. That would hold him. There were two or three cans of gasoline, too.

Doc Cromer's boy was doing a good business with his Coca-Colas. Only five or six bottles of the first three cases were left in the washtub. He was getting ready to put the other cases in now and give the dopes a chance to get nice and cool. Everybody likes to have a dope every once in a while.

The Cromer boy would probably sell out and have to go back to town and bring back several more cases. And yet there was not such a big crowd today, either. It was the hot weather that made people have to drink a lot of dopes to stay cool. There were only a hundred and fifty or seventy-five there today. There had not been enough time for the word to get passed around. Tom would have missed it if Jim had not run in and told him about it while he was taking a nap on the meat-block.

Will Maxie did not drink Coca-Cola. Will never spent his money on anything like that. That was what was wrong with him. He was too damn good for a Negro. He did not drink corn whiskey, nor make it; he did not carry a knife, nor a razor; he bared his head when he met a white man, and he lived with his own wife. But they had him now! God damn his gingerbread hide to hell! They had him where he could not take any more grass out of his cotton before laying it by. They had him tied to a sweetgum tree in the clearing at the creek with a trace-chain around his neck and another around his knees. Yes, sir, they had Will Maxie now, the yellow-face coon! He would not

take any more grass out of his cotton before laying it by!

Tom was feeling good. Hubert gave him another drink in the woods. Hubert was all right. He made good corn whiskey. Tom liked him for that. And Hubert always took his wife a big piece of meat Saturday night to use over Sunday. Nice meat, too. Tom cut off the meat and Hubert took it home and made a present of it to his wife.

Will Maxie was going up in smoke. When he was just about gone they gave him the lead. Tom stood back and took good aim and fired away at Will with his shotgun as fast as he could breech it and put in a new load. About forty or more of the other men had shotguns too. They filled him so full of lead that his body sagged from his neck where the trace-chain held him up.

The Cromer boy had sold completely out. All of his ice and dopes were gone. Doc Cromer would feel pretty good when his boy brought back all that money. Six whole cases he sold, at a dime a bottle. If he had brought along another case or two he could have sold them easily enough. Everybody likes Coca-Cola. There is nothing better to drink on a hot day, if the dopes are nice and cool.

After a while the men got ready to draw the body up in the tree and tie it to a limb so it could hang there, but Tom and Jim could not wait and they went back to town the first chance they got to ride. They were in a big hurry. They had been gone several hours and it was almost four o'clock. A lot of people came downtown early Saturday afternoon to get their Sunday meat before it was picked over by the country people. Tom and Jim had to hurry back and open up the meat-market and get to work slicing steaks and chopping soup bones with the cleaver on the meatblock. Tom was the butcher. He did all the work with the meat. He went out and killed a cow and quartered her. Then he hauled the meat to the butcher-shop and hung it on the hooks in the icehouse. When somebody wanted to buy some meat, he took one of the quarters from the hook and threw it on the meatblock and cut what you asked for. You told Tom what you wanted and he gave it to you, no matter what you asked for. Then you stepped over to the counter and paid Jim the money for it. Jim was the cashier. He did all the talking, too. Tom had to do the cutting and weighing. Jim's egg-shaped belly was too big for him to work around the meatblock. It got in his way when he tried to slice you a piece of tenderloin steak, so Tom did that and Jim took the money and put it into the cashbox under the counter.

Tom and Jim got back to town just in time. There was a big crowd standing around on the street getting ready to do their weekly trading, and they had to have some meat. You went in the butcher-shop and said, "Hello, Tom. I want two pounds and a half of pork chops." Tom said, "Hello, I'll get it for you right away." While you were waiting for Tom to cut the meat off the hunk of rump steak you asked him how was everything.

"Everything's slick as a whistle," he said, "except my old woman's got the chills and fever pretty bad again."

Tom weighed the pork chops and wrapped them up for you and then you stepped over to Jim and paid him the money. Jim was the cashier. His egg-shaped belly was too big for him to work around the meatblock. Tom did that part, and Jim took the money and put it into the cashbox under the counter.

Richard Wright

1908-1960

In *Black Boy,* the autobiography of his youthful years, Richard
Wright uncovers a world of poverty and hunger, ugliness and
intolerance, which most Americans prefer not to face: "I found
that to tell the truth is the hardest thing on earth. . . . If you
try it, you will find that even if you succeed in discounting
the attitudes of others to you and your life, you must wrestle
with yourself most of all, for there will surge up in you a
strong desire to alter facts, to dress up your feelings. You'll
find that there are many things that you don't want to admit
about yourself or others." Richard Wright wrestled with himself and brought out a book comparable to no other in American literature except perhaps Theodore Dreiser's *Dawn.* But
for all the bitterness of that youth, he had an unflinching determination to see things straight. He was kindly and open
and friendly, his writer's point of view objective, not personal.

With no opportunities whatsoever, actually with the world
opposing him at every turn, this young black boy became
literate, a reader of good books, and finally a writer. As an
artist, not a propagandist, Richard Wright became one of the
top half-dozen writers in America. In 1938 he won the $500
prize offered by *Story* for the best story written by a worker
on the Writers' Project. A volume of short stories, *Uncle
Tom's Children,* appeared the same year. The next year he was
awarded a Guggenheim Fellowship, which brought forth the
best seller *Native Son.*

Almos' a Man

BY RICHARD WRIGHT

DAVE struck out across the fields, looking homeward through paling light. Whut's the usa talkin wid em niggers in the field? Anyhow, his mother was putting suppper on the table. Them niggers can't understan nothing. One of these days he was going to get a gun and practice shooting, then they can't talk to him as though he were a little boy. He slowed, looking at the ground. Shucks, Ah ain scareda them even ef they are biggern me! Aw, Ah know whut Ahma do.... Ahm going by ol Joe's sto n git that Sears Roebuck catlog n look at them guns. Mabbe Ma will lemme buy one when she gits mah pay from ol man Hawkins. Ahma beg her t gimme some money. Ahm ol ernough to hava gun. Ahm seventeen. Almost a man. He strode, felling his long, loosejoint limbs. Shucks, a man oughta have little gun aftah be done worked hard all day....

He came in sight of Joe's store. A yellow lantern glowed on the front porch. He mounted steps and went through the screen door, hearing it bang behind him. There was a strong smell of coal oil and mackerel fish. He felt very confident until he saw fat Joe walk in through the rear door, then his courage began to ooze.

"Howdy, Dave! Whutcha want?"

"How yuh, Mistah Joe? Aw, Ah don wanna buy nothing. Ah jus wanted t see of yuhd lemme look at tha ol catlog erwhile."

"Sure! You wanna see it here?"

"Nawsuh. Ah wants t take it home wid me. Ahll bring it back termorrow when Ah come in from the fiels."

"You planning on buyin something?"

"Yessuh."

"Your ma letting you have your own money now?"

"Shucks. Mistah Joe, Ahm gitting t be a man like anybody else!"

Joe laughed and wiped his greasy white face with a red bandanna.

"Whut you plannin on buyin?"

Dave looked at the floor, scratched his head, scratched his thigh, and smiled. Then he looked up shyly.

"Ahll tell yuh, Mistah Joe, ef yuh promise yuh won't tell."

"I promise."

"Waal, Ahma buy a gun."

"A gun? Whut you want with a gun?"

"Ah wanna keep it."

"You ain't nothing but a boy. You don't need a gun."

"Aw, lemme have the catlog, Mistah Joe. Ahll bring it back."

Joe walked through the rear door.

By permission of Paul R. Reynolds & Son, 599 Fifth Avenue, New York 17. Copyright, 1940, by Richard Wright.

Dave was elated. He looked around at barrels of sugar and flour. He heard Joe coming back. He craned his neck to see if he were bringing the book. Yeah, he's got it! Gawddog, he's got it!

"Here, but be sure you bring it back. It's the only one I got."

"Sho, Mistah Joe."

"Say, if you wanna buy a gun, why don't you buy one from me? I gotta gun to sell."

"Will it shoot?"

"Sure it'll shoot."

"Whut kind is it?"

"Oh, it's kinda old . . . A left-hand Wheeler. A pistol. A big one."

"Is it got bullets in it?"

"It's loaded."

"Kin Ah see it?"

"Where's your money?"

"Whut yuh wan fer it?"

"I'll let you have it for two dollars."

"Just two dollahs? Shucks, Ah could buy tha when Ah git mah pay."

"I will have it here when you want it."

"Awright, suh. Ah be in fer it."

He went through the door, hearing it slam again behind him. Ahma git some money from Ma n buy me a gun! Only two dollahs! He tucked the thick catalogue under his arm and hurried.

"Where yuh been, boy?" His mother held a steaming dish of black-eyed peas.

"Aw, Ma, Ah jus stoped down the road t talk wid th boys."

"Yuh know bettah than t keep suppah waitin."

He sat down, resting the catalogue on the edge of the table.

"Yuh git up from there an git to the well n wash yosef! Ah ain feedin no hogs in mah house!"

She grabbed his shoulder and pushed him. He stumbled out of the room, then came back to get the catalogue.

"Whut this?"

"Aw, Ma, it's jusa catalog."

"Who yuh git it from?"

"From Joe, down at the sto."

"Waal, thas good. We kin use it around the house."

"Naw, Ma." He grabbed for it. "Gimme mah catlog, Ma."

She held onto it and glared at him.

"Quit hollerin at me! Whut's wrong wid yuh? Yuh crazy?"

"But Ma, please. It ain mine! It's Joe's! He tol me t bring it back t im termorrow."

She gave up the book. He stumbled down the back steps, hugging the thick book under his arm. When he had splashed water on his face and hands, he groped back to the kitchen and fumbled in a corner for the towel. He bumped into a chair; it clattered to the floor. The catalogue sprawled at his feet. When he had dried his eyes he snatched up the book and held it again under his arm. His mother stood watching him.

"Now, ef yuh gona acka fool over that ol book, Ahll take it n burn it up."

"Naw, Ma, please."

"Waal, set down n be still!"

He sat down and drew the oil lamp close. He thumbed page after page, unaware of the food his mother set on the table. His father came in. Then his small brother.

"Whutcha got there, Dave?" his father asked.

"Jusa catlog," he answered, not looking up.

"Ywah, here they is!" His eyes glowed at blue and black revolvers. He glanced up, feeling sudden guilt. His father was watching him. He eased the book under the table and rested it on his knees. After the blessing was asked, he ate. He scooped up peas and swallowed fat meat without chewing. Buttermilk helped to wash it down. He did not want to mention money before his father. He would do much better by cornering his mother when she was alone. He looked at his father uneasily out of the edge of his eye.

"Boy, how come yuh don quit foolin wid tha book n eata yo suppah?"

"Yessuh."

"How you n ol man Hawkins gittin erlong?"

"Suh?"

"Can't yuh hear? Why don yuh lissen? Ah ast you how wuz yuh n ol man Hawkins gitting erlong?"

"Oh, swell, Pa. Ah plows mo lan than anybody over there."

"Waal, yuh oughta keep you min on whut yuh doin."

"Yessuh."

He poured his plate full of molasses and sopped at it slowly with a chunk of cornbread. When all but his mother had left the kitchen, he still sat and looked again at the guns in the catalogue. Lawd, ef Ah only had tha pretty one! He could almost feel the slickness of the weapon with his fingers. If he had a gun like that he would polish it and keep it shining so it would never rust. N Ahd keep it loaded, by Gawd!

"Ma?"

"Hunh?"

"Ol man Hawkins give yuh mah money yit?"

"Yeah, but ain no usa yuh thinkin bout thowin nona it erway. Ahm keepin tha money sos yuh kin have cloes t go to school this winter."

He rose and went to her side with the open catalogue in his palms. She was washing dishes, her head bent low over a pan. Shyly he raised the open book. When he spoke his voice was husky, faint.

"Ma, Gawd knows Ah wans one of these."

"One of whut?" she asked, not raising her eyes.

"One of these," he said again, not daring even to point. She glanced up at the page, then at him with wide eyes.

"Nigger, is yuh gone plum crazy?"

"Aw, Ma——"

"Git out here! Don yuh talk t me bout no gun! Yuh a fool!"

"Ma, Ah kin buy one fer two dollahs."

"Not ef Ah knows it yuh ain!"

"But yuh promised me one——"

"Ah don care whut Ah promised! Yuh ain nothing but a boy yit!"

"Ma, ef yuh lemme buy one Ahll never ast yuh fer nothing no mo."

"Ah tol yuh t git outta here! Yuh ain gonna toucha penny of tha money fer no gun! Thas how come Ah has Mistah Hawkins t pay yo wages t me, cause Ah knows yuh ain got no sense."

"But Ma, we needa gun. Pa ain got no gun. We needa gun in the house. Yuh kin never tell whut might happen."

"Now don yuh try to maka fool outta me, boy! Ef we did have gun yuh wouldn't have it!"

He laid the catalogue down and slipped his arm around her waist.

"Aw, Ma. Ah done worked hard alla summer n ain ast yuh fer nothin, is Ah, now?"

"Thas whut yuh spose t do!"

"But Ma, Ah wans a gun. Yuh kin lemma have two dollahs outa mah money. Please, Ma. I kin give it to Pa . . . Please, Ma! Ah loves yuh, Ma."

When she spoke her voice came soft and low.

"What you wan wida gun, Dave?

Yuh don need no gun. Yuhll git in trouble. N ef you Pa just thought Ah let yuh have money t buy a gun he'd hava fit."

"Ahll hide it, Ma. It ain but two dollahs."

"Lawd, chil, whuts wrong wid yuh?"

"Ain nothin wrong, Ma. Alhm almos a man now. Ah wans a gun."

"Who gonna sell yuh a gun?"

"Ol Joe at the sto."

"N it don cos but two dollahs?"

"Thas all, Ma. Just two dollahs. Please, Ma."

She was stacking the plates away; her hands moved slowly, reflectively. Dave kept an anxious silence. Finally, she turned to him.

"Ahll let yuh git tha gun ef yuh promise me one thing."

"Whuts tha, Ma?"

"Yuh bring it straight back t me, yuh hear? It be fer Pa."

"Yesum! Lemme go now, Ma."

She stooped, turned slightly to one side, raised the hem of her dress, rolled down the top of her stocking, and came up with a slender wad of bills.

"Here," she said. "Lawd knows yuh don need no gun. But yer Pa does. Yuh bring it right back t me, yuh hear? Ahma put it up. Now ef yuh don, Ahma have yuh Pa lick yuh so hard yuh won ferget it."

"Yessum."

He took the money, ran down the steps, and across the yard.

"Dave! Yuuuuuh Daaaaave!"

He heard, but he was not going to stop now. "Naw, Lawd!"

The first movement he made the following morning was to reach under his pillow for tha gun. In the gray light of dawn he held it loosely, feeling a sense of power. Could killa man wida gun like this. Kill anybody, black or white. And if he were holding his gun in his hand nobody could run over him; they would have to respect him. It was a big gun, with a long barrel and a heavy handle. He raised and lowered it in his hand, marveling at its weight.

He had not come straight home with it as his mother had asked; instead he had stayed out in the fields, holding the weapon in his hand, aiming it now and then at some imaginary foe. But he had not fired it; he had been afraid that his father might hear. Also he was not sure he knew how to fire it.

To avoid surrendering the pistol he had not come into the house until he knew that all were asleep. When his mother had tiptoed to his bedside late that night and demanded the gun, he had first played possum; then he had told her that the gun was hidden outdoors, that he would bring it to her in the morning. Now he lay turning it slowly in his hands. He broke it, took out the cartridges, felt them, and then put them back.

He slid out of bed, got a long strip of old flannel from a trunk, wrapped the gun in it, and tied it to his naked thigh while it was still loaded. He did not go in to breakfast. Even though it was not yet daylight, he started for Jim Hawkins' plantation. Just as the sun was rising he reached the barns where the mules and plows were kept.

"Hey! That you, Dave?"

He turned. Jim Hawkins stood eying him suspiciously.

"What're yuh doing here so early?"

"Ah didn't know Ah wuz gittin up so early, Mistah Hawkins. Ah wuz fixin t hitch up ol Jenny n take her t the fiels."

"Good. Since you're here so early,

how about plowing that stretch down by the woods?"

"Suits me, Mistah Hawkins."

"O. K. Go to it!"

He hitched Jenny to a plow and started across the fields. Hot dog! This was just what he wanted. If he could get down by the woods, he could shoot his gun and nobody would hear. He walked behind the plow, hearing the traces creaking, feeling the gun tied tight to his thigh.

When he reached the woods, he plowed two whole rows before he decided to take out the gun. Finally, he stopped, looked in all directions, then untied the gun and held it in his hand. He turned to the mule and smiled.

"Know whut this is, Jenny? Naw, yuh wouldn't know! Yuhs jusa ol mule! Anyhow, this is a gun, n it kin shoot, by Gawd!"

He held the gun at arm's length. Whut t hell, Ahma shoot this thing! He looked at Jenny again.

"Lissen here, Jenny! When Ah pull this ol trigger Ah don wan yuh t run n acka fool now."

Jenny stood with head down, her short ears pricked straight. Dave walked off about twenty feet, held the gun far out from him, at arm's length, and turned his head. Hell, he told himself, Ah ain afraid. The gun felt loose in his fingers; he waved it wildly for a moment. Then he shut his eyes and tightened his forefinger. Bloom! A report half deafened him and he thought his right hand was torn from his arm. He heard Jenny whinnying and galloping over the field, and he found himself on his knees, squeezing his fingers hard between his legs. His hand was numb; he jammed it into his mouth, trying to warm it, trying to stop the pain. The gun lay at his feet. He did not quite know what had happened. He stood up and stared at the gun as though it were a live thing. He gritted his teeth and kicked the gun. Yuh almos broke mah arm! He turned to look for Jenny; she was far over the fields, tossing her head and kicking wildly.

"Hol on there, ol mule!"

When he caught up with her she stood trembling, walling her big white eyes at him. The plow was far away; the traces had broken. Then Dave stopped short, looking, not believing. Jenny was bleeding. Her left side was red and wet with blood. He went closer. Lawd have mercy! Wondah did Ah shoot this mule? He grabbed for Jenny's mane. She flinched, snorted, whirled, tossing her head.

"Hol on now! Hol on."

Then he saw the hole in Jenny's side, right between the ribs. It was round, wet, red. A crimson stream streaked down the front leg, flowing fast. Good Gawd! Ah wuznt shootin at tha mule. . . . He felt panic. He knew he had to stop that blood, or Jenny would bleed to death. He had never seen so much blood in all his life. He ran the mule for half a mile, trying to catch her. Finally she stopped, breathing hard, stumpy tail half arched. He caught her mane and led her back to where the plow and gun lay. Then he stopped and grabbed handfuls of damp black earth and tried to plug the bullet hole. Jenny shuddered, whinnied, and broke from him.

"Hol on! Hol on now!"

He tried to plug it again, but blood came anyhow. His fingers were hot and sticky. He rubbed dirt hard into his palms, trying to dry them. Then again he attempted to plug the bullet hole, but Jenny shied away, kicking her heels high. He stood helpless. He had to do something. He ran at Jenny; she dodged him. He watched a red stream of blood flow down Jenny's leg and form a bright pool at her feet.

"Jenny . . . Jenny . . ." he called weakly.

His lips trembled. She's bleeding t death! He looked in the direction of home, wanting to go back, wanting to get help. But he saw the pistol lying in the damp black clay. He had a queer feeling that if he only did something, this would not be; Jenny would not be there bleeding to death.

When he went to her this time, she did not move. She stood with sleepy, dreamy eyes; and when he touched her she gave a low-pitched whinny and knelt to the ground, her front knees slopping in blood.

"Jenny . . . Jenny . . ." he whispered.

For a long time she held her neck erect; then her head sank, slowly. Her ribs swelled with a mighty heave and she went over.

Dave's stomach felt empty, very empty. He picked up the gun and held it gingerly between his thumb and forefinger. He buried it at the foot of a tree. He took a stick and tried to cover the pool of blood with dirt—but what was the use? There was Jenny lying with her mouth open and her eyes walled and glassy. He could not tell Jim Hawkins he had shot his mule. But he had to tell something. Yeah, Ahll tell em Jenny started gittin wil n fell on the joint of the plow. . . . But that would hardly happen to a mule. He walked across the field slowly, head down.

It was sunset. Two of Jim Hawkins' men were over near the edge of the woods digging a hole in which to bury Jenny. Dave was surrounded by a knot of people; all of them were looking down at the dead mule.

"I don't see how in the world it happened," said Jim Hawkins for the tenth time.

The crowd parted and Dave's mother, father, and small brother pushed into the center.

"Where Dave?" his mother called.

"There he is," said Jim Hawkins. His mother grabbed him.

"Whut happened, Dave? Whut yuh done?"

"Nothing."

"C'mon, boy, talk," his father said.

Dave took a deep breath and told the story he knew nobody believed.

"Waal," he drawled. "Ah brung ol Jenny down here sos Ah could do mah plowin. Ah plowed bout two rows, just like yuh see." He stopped and pointed at the long rows of upturned earth. "Then something musta been wrong wid ol Jenny. She wouldn't ack right a-tall. She started snortin n kickin her heels. Ah tried to hol her, but she pulled erway, rearin n goin on. Then when the point of the plow was stickin up in the air, she swung erroun n twisted herself back on it. . . . She stuck hersef n started t bleed. N fo Ah could do anything, she wuz dead."

"Did you ever hear of anything like that in all your life?" asked Jim Hawkins.

There were white and black standing in the crowd. They murmured. Dave's mother came close to him and looked hard into his face. "Tell the truth, Dave," she said.

"Looks like a bullet hole ter me," said one man.

"Dave, whut yuh do wid tha gun?" his mother asked.

The crowd surged in, looking at him. He jammed his hands into his pockets, shook his head slowly from left to right, and backed away. His eyes were wide and painful.

"Did he hava gun?" asked Jim Hawkins.

"By Gawd, Ah tol yuh tha wuz a gun wound," said a man, slapping his thigh.

His father caught his shoulders and shook him till his teeth rattled.

"Tell whut happened, yuh rascal! Tell whut . . ."

Dave looked at Jenny's stiff legs and began to cry.

"Whut yuh do wid tha gun?" his mother asked.

"Whut wuz he doin wida gun?" his father asked.

"Come on and tell the truth," said Hawkins. "Ain't nobody going to hurt you . . ."

His mother crowded close to him.

"Did yuh shoot tha mule, Dave?"

Dave cried, seeing blurred white and black faces.

"Ahh ddinnt gggo tt sshoooot hher. . . . Ah ssswear ffo Gawd Ahh ddint. . . . Ah wuz a-trying t sssee ef the ol gggun would sshoot——"

"Where yuh git the gun from?" his father asked.

"Ah got it from Joe, at the sto."

"Where yuh git the money?"

"Ma give it t me."

"He kept worryin me, Bob. . . . Ah had t. . . . Ah tol im t bring the gun right back t me. . . . It was fer yuh, the gun."

"But how yuh happen to shoot that mule?" asked Jim Hawkins.

"Ah wuznt shootin at the mule, Mistah Hawkins. The gun jumped when Ah pulled the trigger . . . N fo Ah knowed anything Jenny was there a-bleedin."

Somebody in the crowd laughed. Jim Hawkins walked close to Dave and looked into his face.

"Well, looks like you have bought you a mule, Dave."

"Ah swear fo Gawd, Ah didn't go t kill the mule, Mistah Hawkins!"

"But you killed her!"

All the crowd was laughing now. They stood on tiptoe and poked heads over one another's shoulders.

"Well, boy, looks like yuh done bought a dead mule! Hahaha!"

"Ain tha ershame."

"Hohohohoho."

Dave stood, head down, twisting his feet in the dirt.

"Well, you needn't worry about it, Bob," said Jim Hawkins to Dave's father. "Just let the boy keep on working and pay me two dollars a month."

"Whut yuh wan fer yo mule, Mistah Hawkins?"

Jim Hawkins screwed up his eyes.

"Fifty dollars."

"Whut yuh do wid tha gun?" Dave's father demanded.

Dave said nothing.

"Yuh wan me t take a tree lim n beat yuh till yuh talk!"

"Nawsuh!"

"Whut yuh do wid it?"

"Ah thowed it erway."

"Where?"

"Ah . . . Ah thowed it in the creek."

"Waal, c mon home. N firs thing in the mawnin git to tha creek n fin tha gun."

"Yessuh."

"Whut yuh pay fer it?"

"Two dollahs."

"Take tha gun n git you money back n carry it t Mistah Hawkins, yuh hear? N don fergit Ahma lam you black bottom good fer this! Now march yosef on home, suh!"

Dave turned and walked slowly. He heard people laughing. Dave glared, his eyes welling with tears. Hot anger bubbled in him. Then he swallowed and stumbled on.

That night Dave did not sleep. He was glad that he had gotten out of killing the mule so easily, but he was hurt. Something hot seemed to turn over inside him each time he remembered how they had laughed. He tossed on his bed, feeling his hard pillow. N Pa says he's gonna beat me. . . . He remembered other beatings, and his back quivered. Naw, naw, Ah sho don wan im t beat me tha way no mo. . . . Dam em all! Nobody ever gave him anything. All he did was work. They treat me like a mule. . . . N then they beat me. . . . He gritted his teeth. N Ma had t tell on me.

Well, if he had to, he would take old man Hawkins that two dollars. But that meant selling the gun. And he wanted to keep that gun. Fifty dollahs fer a dead mule.

He turned over, thinking how he had fired the gun. He had an itch to fire it again. Ef other men kin shoota gun, by Gawd, Ah kin! He was still listening. Mebbe they all sleepin now. . . . The house was still. He heard the soft breathing of his brother. Yes, now! He would go down and get that gun and see if he could fire it! He eased out of bed and slipped into overalls.

The moon was bright. He ran almost all the way to the edge of the woods. He stumbled over the ground, looking for the spot where he had buried the gun. Yeah, here it is. Like a hungry dog scratching for a bone he pawed it up. He puffed his black cheeks and blew dirt from the trigger and barrel. He broke it and found four cartridges unshot. He looked around; the fields were filled with silence and moonlight. He clutched the gun stiff and hard in his fingers. But as soon as he wanted to pull the trigger, he shut his eyes and turned his head. Naw, Ah can't shoot wid mah eyes closed n mah head turned. With effort he held his eyes open; then he squeezed. Blooooom! He was stiff, not breathing. The gun was still in his hands. Dammit, he'd done it! He fired again. Blooooom! He smiled. Blooooom! Blooooom! Click, click. There! It was empty. If anybody could shoot a gun, he could. He put the gun into his hip pocket and started across the fields.

When he reached the top of a ridge he stood straight and proud in the moonlight, looking at Jim Hawkins' big white house, feeling the gun sagging in his pocket. Lawd, ef Ah had jus one mo bullet Ahd taka shot at tha house. Ahd like t scare ol man Hawkins jussa little. . . . Jussa enough t let im know Dave Sanders is a man.

To his left the road curved, running to the tracks of the Illinois Central. He jerked his head, listening. From far off came a faint hoooof-hoooof; hoooof - hoooof; hoooof - hoooof . . . That's number eight. He took a swift look at Jim Hawkins' white house; he thought of Pa, of Ma, of his little brother, and the boys. He thought of the dead mule and heard hoooof-hoooof; hoooof-hoooof; hoooof-hoooof . . . He stood rigid. Two dollahs a mont. Les see now . . . Tha means itll take bout two years. Shucks! Ahll be dam!

He started down the road, toward the tracks. Yeah, here she comes! He stood beside the track and held himself stiffly. Here she comes, erroun the ben. . . . C mon, yuh slowpoke! C mon! He had his hand on his gun; something quivered in his stomach. Then the train thundered past, the gray and brown boxcars rumbling and clinking. He gripped the gun tightly; then he jerked his hand out of his pocket.

Ah betcha Bill wouldn't do it! Ah betcha. . . . The cars slid past, steel grinding upon steel. Ahm riding yuh ternight so hep me Gawd! He was hot all over. He hesitated just a moment; then he grabbed, pulled atop of a car, and lay flat. He felt his pocket; the gun was still there. Ahead the long rails were glinting in moonlight, stretching away, away to somewhere, somewhere where he could be a man. . . .

Katherine Anne Porter
1894-

WHEN Katherine Anne Porter puts the old South into a story, she does so with finesse and delicacy. No fiery outpouring hers, no scenes of violence. Daniel Boone was her ancestor, Indian Creek, Texas, her birthplace, but here all relation to pioneer life ceases. She is a scholar, has lived in many countries, has translated books from other languages. In her own writing she is an extremely slow worker and has published relatively little. Nevertheless she has made herself a solid reputation with her short stories and her recent—and only—novel, *Ship of Fools*. "The Old Order" comes from *The Leaning Tower*.

The Old Order

BY KATHERINE ANNE PORTER

IN THEIR later years, the Grandmother and old Nannie used to sit together for some hours every day over their sewing. They shared a passion for cutting scraps of the family finery, hoarded for fifty years, into strips and triangles, and fitting them together again in a carefully disordered patchwork, outlining each bit of velvet or satin or taffeta with a running briar stitch in clear lemon-colored silk floss. They had contrived enough bed and couch covers, tablespreads, dressing-table scarfs, to have furnished forth several households. Each piece as it was finished was lined with yellow silk, folded, and laid away in a chest, never again to see the light of day. The Grandmother was the great-granddaughter of Kentucky's most famous pioneer: he had, while he was surveying Kentucky, hewed out rather competently a rolling pin for his wife. This rolling pin was the Grandmother's irreplaceable treasure. She covered it with an extraordinarily complicated bit of patchwork, added golden tassels to the handles, and hung it in a conspicuous place in her room. She was the daughter of a notably heroic captain in the War of 1812. She had his razors in a shagreen case and a particularly severe-looking daguerreotype taken in his old age, with his chin in a tall stock and his black satin waistcoat smoothed over a still-handsome military chest. So she fitted a patchwork case over the shagreen and made a sort of envelope of cut velvet and violet satin, held together with briar stitching, to contain the portrait. The rest of her handiwork she put away, to the relief of her grandchildren, who had arrived at the awkward age when Grandmother's quaint old-fashioned ways caused them acute discomfort.

In the summer the women sat under the mingled trees of the side garden, which commanded a view of the east wing, the front and back porches, a good part of the front garden and a corner of the small fig grove. Their choice of this location was a part of their domestic strategy. Very little escaped them: a glance now and then would serve to keep them fairly well informed as to what was going on in the whole place. It is true they had not seen Miranda the day she pulled up the whole mint bed to give to a pleasant strange young woman who stopped and asked her for a sprig of fresh mint. They had never found out who stole the giant pomegranates growing too near the fence: they had not been in time to stop Paul from setting himself on fire while experimenting with a miniature blowtorch, but they had been on the scene to extinguish him with rugs, to pour oil on him, and lecture him. They never saw Maria climbing trees, a mania she had to indulge or pine away, for she chose tall ones on the opposite side of the house. But such casualties were so minor a part of the perpetual round of events that they did not feel defeated nor that their strategy was a failure. Summer, in many ways so desirable a season, had its drawbacks. The children were everywhere at once and the Negroes loved lying under the hackberry grove back of the barns playing seven-up, and eating watermelons. The summer house was in a small town a few miles from the farm, a compromise between the rigorously ordered house in the city and the sprawling old farmhouse which Grandmother had built with such pride and pains. It had, she often said, none of the advantages of either country, or city, and all the discomforts of both. But the children loved it.

During the winters in the city, they sat in Grandmother's room, a large squarish place with a small coal grate. All the sounds of life in the household seemed to converge there, echo, retreat, and return. Grandmother and Aunt Nannie knew the whole complicated code of sounds, could interpret and comment on them by an exchange of glances, a lifted eyebrow, or a tiny pause in their talk.

They talked about the past, really —always about the past. Even the future seemed like something gone and done with when they spoke of it. It did not seem an extension of their past, but a repetition of it. They would agree that nothing remained of life as they had known it, the world was changing swiftly, but by the mysterious logic of hope they insisted that each change was probably the last; or if not, a series of changes might bring them, blessedly, back full circle to the old ways they had known. Who knows why they loved their past? It had been bitter for them both, they had questioned the burdensome rule they lived by every day of their lives, but without rebellion and without expecting an answer. This unbroken thread of inquiry in their minds contained no doubt as to the utter rightness and justice of the basic laws of human existence, founded as they were on God's plan; but they wondered perpetually, with only a hint now and then to each other of the uneasiness of their hearts, how so much suffering and confusion could have been built up and maintained on such a foundation. The Grandmother's role was authority, she knew that; it was her duty to portion out activities, to urge or restrain where necessary, to teach morals, manners, and religion, to punish and reward her own household according to a fixed code. Her own doubts and hesitations she concealed, also, she reminded herself, as a matter of duty. Old Nannie had no ideas at all as to her place in the world. It had been assigned to her before birth, and for her daily rule she had all her life obeyed the authority nearest to her.

So they talked about God, about heaven, about planting a new hedge of rosebushes, about the new ways of preserving fruit and vegetables, about eternity and their mutual hope that they might pass it happily together, and often a scrap of silk under their hands would start them on long trains of family reminiscences. They were always amused to notice again how the working of their memories differed in such important ways. Nannie could recall names to perfection; she could always say what the weather had been like on all important occasions, what certain ladies had worn, how handsome certain gentlemen had been, what there had been to eat and drink. Grandmother had masses of dates in her mind, and no memories attached to them: her memories of events seemed detached and floating beyond time. For example, the 26th of August, 1871, had been some sort of red-letter day for her. She had said to herself then that never would she forget that date; and indeed, she remembered it well, but she no longer had the faintest notion what had happened to stamp it on her memory. Nannie was no help in the matter; she had nothing to do with dates. She did not know the year of her birth, and would never have had a birthday to celebrate if Grandmother had not, when she was still Miss Sophia Jane, aged ten, opened a calendar at random, closed her eyes, and marked a date unseen with a pen. So it turned out that Nannie's birthday thereafter fell on June 11, and the year, Miss Sophia Jane decided, should be 1827, her own birth year, making Nannie just three months younger than her mistress. Sophia Jane then made an entry of Nannie's birth date in the family Bible, inserting it just below her own. "Nannie Gay," she wrote, in stiff careful letters, "(black)," and though there was some uproar when this was discovered, the ink was long since sunk deeply into the paper, and besides no one was really upset enough to have it scratched

out. There it remained, one of their pleasantest points of reference.

They talked about religion, and the slack way the world was going nowadays, the decay of behavior, and about the younger children, whom these topics always brought at once to mind. On these subjects they were firm, critical, and unbewildered. They had received educations which furnished them an assured habit of mind about all the important appearances of life, and especially about the rearing of young. They relied with perfect acquiescence on the dogma that children were conceived in sin and brought forth in iniquity. Childhood was a long state of instruction and probation for adult life, which was in turn a long, severe, undeviating devotion to duty, the largest part of which consisted in bringing up children. The young were difficult, disobedient, and tireless in wrongdoing, apt to turn unkind and undutiful when they grew up, in spite of all one had done for them, or had tried to do: for small painful doubts rose in them now and again when they looked at their completed works. Nannie couldn't abide her newfangled grandchildren. "Wuthless, shiftless lot, jes plain scum, Miss Sophia Jane; I cain't undahstand it aftah all the raisin' dey had."

The Grandmother defended them, and dispraised her own second generation—heartily, too, for she sincerely found grave faults in them—which Nannie defended in turn. "When they are little, they trample on your feet, and when they grow up they trample on your heart." This was about all there was to say about children in any generation, but the fascination of the theme was endless. They said it thoroughly over and over with thousands of small variations, with always an example among their own friends or family connections to prove it. They had enough material of their own. Grandmother had borne eleven children, Nannie thirteen. They boasted of it. Grandmother would say, "I am the mother of eleven children," in a faintly amazed tone, as if she hardly expected to be believed, or could even quite believe it herself. But she could still point to nine of them. Nannie had lost ten of hers. They were all buried in Kentucky. Nannie never doubted or expected anyone else to doubt she had children. Her boasting was of another order. "Thirteen of 'em," she would say, in an appalled voice, "yas, my Lawd and my Redeemah, thirteen!"

The friendship between the two old women had begun in early childhood, and was based on what seemed even to them almost mythical events. Miss Sophia Jane, a prissy, spoiled five-year-old, with tight black ringlets which were curled every day on a stick, with her stiffly pleated lawn pantalettes and tight bodice, had run to meet her returning father, who had been away buying horses and Negroes. Sitting on his arm, clasping him around the neck, she had watched the wagons filing past on the way to the barns and quarters. On the floor of the first wagon sat two blacks, male and female, holding between them a scrawny, half-naked black child, with a round nubbly head and fixed bright monkey eyes. The baby Negro had a potbelly and her arms were like sticks from wrist to shoulder. She clung with narrow, withered, black-leather fingers to her parents, a hand on each.

"I want the little monkey," said Sophia Jane to her father, nuzzling his cheek and pointing. "I want that one to play with."

Behind each wagon came two horses in lead, but in the second wagon there was a small shaggy pony with a thatch of mane over his eyes, a long tail like a brush, a round, hard barrel of a body. He was standing in straw to the knees, braced firmly in a padded stall with a Negro holding his bridle. "Do you see that?" asked her father. "That's for you. High time you learned to ride."

Sophia Jane almost leaped from his arm for joy. She hardly recognized her pony or her monkey the next day, the one clipped and sleek, the other clean in new blue cotton. For a while she could not decide which she loved more, Nannie or Fiddler. But Fiddler did not wear well. She outgrew him in a year, saw him pass without regret to a small brother, though she refused to allow him to be called Fiddler any longer. The name she reserved for a long series of saddle horses. She had named the first in honor of Fiddler Gay, an old Negro who made the music for dances and parties. There was only one Nannie and she outwore Sophia Jane. During all their lives together it was not so much a question of affection between them as a simple matter of being unable to imagine getting on without each other.

Nannie remembered well being on a shallow platform out in front of a great building in a large busy place, the first town she had ever seen. Her father and mother were with her, and there was a thick crowd around them. There were several other small groups of Negroes huddled together with white men bustling them about now and then. She had never seen any of these faces before, and she never saw but one of them again. She remembered it must have been summer, because she was not shivering with cold in her cotton shift. For one thing, her bottom was still burning from a spanking someone (it might have been her mother) had given her just before they got on the platform, to remind her to keep still. Her mother and father were field hands, and had never lived in white folks' houses. A tall gentleman with a long narrow face and very high curved nose, wearing a great-collared blue coat and immensely long light-colored trousers (Nannie could close her eyes and see him again, clearly, as he looked that day) stepped up near them suddenly, while a great hubbub rose. The red-faced man standing on a stump beside them shouted and droned, waving his arms and pointing at Nannie's father and mother. Now and then the tall gentleman raised a finger, without looking at the black people on the platform. Suddenly the shouting died down, the tall gentleman walked over and said to Nannie's father and mother, "Well, Eph! Well, Steeny! Mister Jimmerson comin' to get you in a minute." He poked Nannie in the stomach with a thickly gloved forefinger. "Regular crowbait," he said to the auctioneer. "I should have had lagniappe with this one."

"A pretty worthless article right now, sir, I agree with you," said the auctioneer, "but it'll grow out of it. As for the team, you won't find a better, I swear."

"I've had an eye on 'em for years," said the tall gentleman, and walked away, motioning as he went to a fat man sitting on a wagon tongue, spitting quantities of tobacco juice. The fat man rose and came over to Nannie and her parents.

Nannie had been sold for twenty dollars: a gift, you might say, hardly sold at all. She learned that a really choice slave sometimes cost more than a thousand dollars. She lived to hear slaves brag about how much they had cost. She had not known how little she fetched on the block until her own mother taunted her with it. This was after Nannie had gone to live for good at the big house, and her mother and father were still in the fields. They lived and worked and died there. A good worming had cured Nannie's potbelly, she thrived on plentiful food and a species of kindness not so indulgent, maybe, as that given to the puppies; still it more than fulfilled her notions of good fortune.

The old women often talked about how strangely things come out in this life. The first owner of Nannie and her parents had gone, Sophia Jane's father said, hog-wild about Texas. It was a new Land of Promise, in 1832. He had sold out his farm and four slaves in Kentucky to raise the money to take a great twenty-mile stretch of land in southwest Texas. He had taken his wife and two young children and set out, and there had been no more news of him for many years. When Grandmother arrived in Texas forty years later, she found him a prosperous ranchman and district judge. Much later, her youngest son met his granddaughter, fell in love with her, and married her—all in three months.

The judge, by then eighty-five years old, was uproarious and festive at the wedding. He reeked of corn liquor, swore by God every other breath, and was raring to talk about the good old times in Kentucky. The Grandmother showed Nannie to him. "Would you recognize her?" "For God Almighty's sake!" bawled the judge, "is that the strip of crowbait

I sold to your father for twenty dollars? Twenty dollars seemed like a fortune to me in those days!"

While they were jolting home down the steep rocky road on the long journey from San Marcos to Austin, Nannie finally spoke out about her grievance. "Look lak a jedge might had better raisin'," she said, gloomily, "look lak he didn't keer how much he hurt a body's feelin's."

The Grandmother, muffled down in the back seat in the corner of the old carryall, in her worn sealskin pelisse, showing coffee brown at the edges, her eyes closed, her hands wrung together, had been occupied once more in reconciling herself to losing a son, and, as ever, to a girl and a family of which she could not altogether approve. It was not that there was anything seriously damaging to be said against any of them; only—well, she wondered at her sons' tastes. What had each of them in turn found in the wife he had chosen? The Grandmother had always had in mind the kind of wife each of her sons needed; she had tried to bring about better marriages for them than they had made for themselves. They had merely resented her interferences in what they considered strictly their personal affairs. She did not realize that she had spoiled and pampered her youngest son until he was in all probability unfit to be any kind of a husband, much less a good one. And there was something about her new daughter-in-law, a tall, handsome, firm-looking young woman, with a direct way of speaking, walking, talking, that seemed to promise that the spoiled Baby's days of clover were ended. The Grandmother was annoyed deeply at seeing how self-possessed the bride had been, how

she had had her way about the wedding arrangements down to the last detail, how she glanced now and then at her new husband with calm, humorous, level eyes, as if she had already got him sized up. She had even suggested at the wedding dinner that her idea of a honeymoon would be to follow the chuck wagon on the round-up, and help in the cattle-branding on her father's ranch. Of course she may have been joking. But she was altogether too Western, too modern, something like the "new" woman who was beginning to run wild, asking for the vote, leaving her home and going out in the world to earn her own living . . .

The Grandmother's narrow body shuddered to the bone at the thought of women so unsexing themselves; she emerged with a start from the dark reverie of foreboding thoughts which left a bitter taste in her throat. "Never mind, Nannie. The judge just wasn't thinking. He's very fond of his good cheer."

Nannie had slept in a bed and had been playmate and workfellow with her mistress; they fought on almost equal terms, Sophia Jane defending Nannie fiercely against any discipline but her own. When they were both seventeen years old, Miss Sophia Jane was married off in a very gay wedding. The house was jammed to the roof and everybody present was at least fourth cousin to everybody else. There were forty carriages and more than two hundred horses to look after for two days. When the last wheel disappeared down the lane (a number of the guests lingered on for two weeks), the larders and bins were half empty and the place looked as if a troop of cavalry had been over it. A few days later Nannie was married off to a boy she had known ever since she came to the family, and they were given as a wedding present to Miss Sophia Jane.

Miss Sophia Jane and Nannie had then started their grim and terrible race of procreation, a child every sixteen months or so, with Nannie nursing both, and Sophia Jane, in dreadful discomfort, suppressing her milk with bandages and spirits of wine. When they each had produced their fourth child, Nannie almost died of puerperal fever. Sophia Jane nursed both children. She named the black baby Charlie, and her own child Stephen, and she fed them justly turn about, not favoring the white over the black, as Nannie felt obliged to do. Her husband was shocked, tried to forbid her; her mother came to see her and reasoned with her. They found her very difficult and quite stubborn. She had already begun to develop her implicit character, which was altogether just, humane, proud, and simple. She had many small vanities and weaknesses on the surface: a love of luxury and a tendency to resent criticism. This tendency was based on her feeling of superiority in judgment and sensibility to almost everyone around her. It made her very hard to manage. She had a quiet way of holding her ground which convinced her antagonist that she would really die, not just threaten to, rather than give way. She had learned now that she was badly cheated in giving her children to another woman to feed; she resolved never again to be cheated in just that way. She sat nursing her child and her foster child, with a sensual warm pleasure she had not dreamed of, translating her natural physical relief into something holy, God-sent, amends from heaven for what she had suffered in childbed. Yes, and for what she missed in the marriage

bed, for there also something had failed. She said to Nannie quite calmly, "From now on, you will nurse your children and I will nurse mine," and it was so. Charlie remained her special favorite among the Negro children. "I understand now," she said to her older sister Keziah, "why the black mammies love their foster children. I love mine." So Charlie was brought up in the house as playmate for her son Stephen, and exempted from hard work all his life.

Sophia Jane had been wooed at arm's length by a mysteriously attractive young man whom she remembered well as rather a snubby little boy with curls like her own, but shorter, a frilled white blouse and kilts of the Macdonald tartan. He was her second cousin and resembled her so closely they had been mistaken for brother and sister. Their grandparents had been first cousins, and sometimes Sophia Jane saw in him, years after they were married, all the faults she had most abhorred in her elder brother: lack of aim, failure to act at crises, a philosophic detachment from practical affairs, a tendency to set projects on foot and then leave them to perish or to be finished by someone else; and a profound conviction that everyone around him should be happy to wait upon him hand and foot. She had fought these fatal tendencies in her brother, within the bounds of wifely prudence she fought them in her husband, she was long after to fight them again in two of her sons and in several of her grandchildren. She gained no victory in any case, the selfish, careless, unloving creatures lived and ended as they had begun. But the Grandmother developed a character truly portentous under the discipline of trying to change the characters of others. Her husband shared with her the family sharpness of eye. He disliked and feared her deadly will-fullness, her certainty that her ways were not only right but beyond criticism, that her feelings were important, even in the lightest matter, and must not be tampered with or treated casually. He had disappeared at the critical moment when they were growing up, had gone to college and then for travel; she forgot him for a long time, and when she saw him again forgot him as he had been once for all. She was gay and sweet and decorous, full of vanity and incredibly exalted daydreams which threatened now and again to cast her over the edge of some mysterious forbidden frenzy. She dreamed recurrently that she had lost her virginity (her virtue, she called it), her sole claim to regard, consideration, even to existence, and after frightful moral suffering which masked altogether her physical experience she would wake in a cold sweat, disordered and terrified. She had heard that her cousin Stephen was a little "wild," but that was to be expected. He was leading, no doubt, a dashing life full of manly indulgences, the sweet dark life of the knowledge of evil which caused her hair to crinkle on her scalp when she thought of it. Ah, the delicious, the free, the wonderful, the mysterious and terrible life of men! She thought about it a great deal. "Little day-dreamer," her mother or father would say to her, surprising her in a brown study, eyes moist, lips smiling vaguely over her embroidery or her book, or with hands fallen on her lap, her face turned away to a blank wall. She memorized and saved for these moments scraps of high-minded poetry, which she instantly quoted at

them when they offered her a penny for her thoughts; or she broke into a melancholy little song of some kind, a song she knew they liked. She would run to the piano and tinkle the tune out with one hand, saying, "I love this part best," leaving no doubt in their minds as to what her own had been occupied with. She lived her whole youth so, without once giving herself away; not until she was in middle age, her husband dead, her property dispersed, and she found herself with a houseful of children, making a new life for them in another place, with all the responsibilities of a man but with none of the privileges, did she finally emerge into something like an honest life: and yet, she was passionately honest. She had never been anything else.

Sitting under the trees with Nannie, both of them old and their long battle with life almost finished, she said, fingering a scrap of satin, "It was not fair that Sister Keziah should have had this ivory brocade for her wedding dress, and I had only dotted swiss . . ."

"Times was harder when you got married, Missy," said Nannie. "Dat was de yeah all de crops failed."

"And they failed ever afterward, it seems to me," said Grandmother.

"Seems to me like," said Nannie, "dotted swiss was all the style when you got married."

"I never cared for it," said Grandmother.

Nannie, born in slavery, was pleased to think she would not die in it. She was wounded not so much by her state of being as by the word describing it. Emancipation was a sweet word to her. It had not changed her way of living in a single particular, but she was proud of having been able to say to her mistress, "I aim to stay wid you as long as you'll have me." Still, Emancipation had seemed to set right a wrong that stuck in her heart like a thorn. She could not understand why God, Whom she loved, had seen fit to be so hard on a whole race because they had got a certain kind of skin. She talked it over with Miss Sophia Jane. Many times. Miss Sophia Jane was always brisk and opinionated about it: "Nonsense! I tell you, God does not know whether a skin is black or white. He sees only souls. Don't be getting notions, Nannie—of course you're going to heaven."

Nannie showed the rudiments of logic in a mind altogether untutored. She wondered, simply and without resentment, whether God, who had been so cruel to black people on earth, might not continue His severity in the next world. Miss Sophia Jane took pleasure in reassuring her; as if she, who had been responsible for Nannie, body and soul in this life, might also be her sponsor before the judgment seat.

Miss Sophia Jane had taken upon herself all the responsibilities of her tangled world, half white, half black, mingling steadily and the confusion growing ever deeper. There were so many young men about the place, always, younger brothers-in-law, first cousins, second cousins, nephews. They came visiting and they stayed, and there was no accounting for them nor any way of controlling their quietly headstrong habits. She learned early to keep silent and give no sign of uneasiness, but whenever a child was born in the Negro quarters, pink, wormlike, she held her breath for three days, she told her eldest granddaughter, years later, to see whether the newly born would turn black after the proper interval

. . . It was a strain that told on her, and ended by giving her a deeply grounded contempt for men. She could not help it, she despised men. She despised them and was ruled by them. Her husband threw away her dowry and her property in wild investments in strange territories: Louisiana, Texas; and without protest she watched him play away her substance like a gambler. She felt that she could have managed her affairs profitably. But her natural activities lay elsewhere, it was the business of a man to make all decisions and dispose of all financial matters. Yet when she got the reins in her hands, her sons could persuade her to this and that enterprise or investment; against her will and judgment she accepted their advice, and among them they managed to break up once more the stronghold she had built for the future of her family. They got from her their own start in life, came back for fresh help when they needed it, and were divided against each other. She saw it as her natural duty to provide for her household, after her husband had fought stubbornly through the War, along with every other man of military age in the connection; had been wounded, had lingered helpless, and had died of his wound long after the great fervor and excitement had faded in hopeless defeat, when to be a man wounded and ruined in the War was merely to have proved oneself, perhaps, more heroic than wise. Left so, she drew her family together and set out for Louisiana, where her husband, with her money, had bought a sugar refinery. There was going to be a fortune in sugar, he said; not in raising the raw material, but in manufacturing it. He had schemes in his head for operating cotton gins, flour mills, refineries. Had he lived . . . but he did not live, and Sophia Jane had hardly repaired the house she bought and got the orchard planted when she saw that, in her hands, the sugar refinery was going to be a failure.

She sold out at a loss, and went on to Texas, where her husband had bought cheaply, some years before, a large tract of fertile black land in an almost unsettled part of the country. She had with her nine children, the youngest about two, the eldest about seventeen years old; Nannie and her three sons, Uncle Jimbilly, and two other Negroes, all in good health, full of hope and greatly desiring to live. Her husband's ghost persisted in her, she was bitterly outraged by his death almost as if he had willfully deserted her. She mourned for him at first with dry eyes, angrily. Twenty years later, seeing after a long absence the eldest son of her favorite daughter, who had died early, she recognized the very features and look of the husband of her youth, and she wept.

During the terrible second year in Texas, two of her younger sons, Harry and Robert, suddenly ran away. They chose good weather for it, in mid-May, and they were almost seven miles from home when a neighboring farmer saw them, wondered and asked questions, and ended by persuading them into his gig, and so brought them back.

Miss Sophia Jane went through the dreary ritual of discipline she thought appropriate to the occasion. She whipped them with her riding whip. Then she made them kneel down with her while she prayed for them, asking God to help them mend their ways and not be undutiful to their mother; her duty performed, she broke down and wept with her

arms around them. They had endured their punishment stoically, because it would have been disgraceful to cry when a woman hit them, and besides, she did not hit very hard; they had knelt with her in a shamefaced gloom, because religious feeling was a female mystery which embarrassed them, but when they saw her tears they burst into loud bellows of repentance. They were only nine and eleven years old. She said in a voice of mourning, so despairing it frightened them: "Why did you run away from me? What do you think I brought you here for?" as if they were grown men who could realize how terrible the situation was. All the answer they could make, as they wept too, was that they had wanted to go back to Louisiana to eat sugar cane. They had been thinking about sugar cane all winter . . . Their mother was stunned. She had built a house large enough to shelter them all, of hand-sawed lumber dragged by oxcart for forty miles, she had got the fields fenced in and the crops planted, she had, she believed, fed and clothed her children; and now she realized they were hungry. These two had worked like men; she felt their growing bones through their thin flesh, and remembered how mercilessly she had driven them, as she had driven herself, as she had driven the Negroes and the horses, because there was no choice in the matter. They must labor beyond their strength or perish. Sitting there with her arms around them, she felt her heart break in her breast. She had thought it was a silly phrase. It happened to her. It was not that she was incapable of feeling afterward, for in a way she was more emotional, more quick, but griefs never again lasted with her so long as they had before. This day was the beginning of her spoiling her children and being afraid of them. She said to them after a long dazed silence, when they began to grow restless under her arms: "We'll grow fine ribbon cane here. The soil is perfect for it. We'll have all the sugar we want. But we must be patient."

By the time her children began to marry, she was able to give them each a good strip of land and a little money, she was able to help them buy more land in places they preferred by selling her own, tract by tract, and she saw them all begin well, though not all of them ended so. They went about their own affairs, scattering out and seeming to lose all that sense of family unity so precious to the Grandmother. They bore with her infrequent visits and her advice and her tremendous rightness, and they were impatient of her tenderness. When Harry's wife died—she had never approved of Harry's wife, who was delicate and hopelessly inadequate at housekeeping, and who could not even bear children successfully, since she died when her third was born—the Grandmother took the children and began life again, with almost the

same zest, and with more indulgence. She had just got them brought up to the point where she felt she could begin to work the faults out of them —faults inherited, she admitted fairly, from both sides of the house— when she died. It happened quite suddenly one afternoon in early October, after a day spent in helping the Mexican gardener of her third daughter-in-law to put the garden to rights. She was on a visit in far-western Texas and enjoying it. The daughter-in-law was exasperated but apparently so docile, the Grandmother, who looked upon her as a child, did not notice her little moods at all. The son had long ago learned not to oppose his mother. She wore him down with patient, just, and reasonable argument. She was careful never to venture to command him in anything. He consoled his wife by saying that everything Mother was doing could be changed back after she was gone. As this change included moving a fifty-foot adobe wall, the wife was not much consoled. The Grandmother came into the house quite flushed and exhilarated, saying how well she felt in the bracing mountain air—and dropped dead over the doorsill.

ABOUT THE EDITOR

BERNARDINE KIELTY has had considerable experience in the short-story world. As one of the first editors of *Story* magazine she participated in the discovery of many a fledgling writer since become famous, and as a fiction editor of the *Ladies' Home Journal* she dealt with the stories of authors already arrived. As a reader for the Book-of-the-Month Club she reviews fiction and biography and covers the field of anthologies. She originated the book column "Under Cover" in the *Journal* and has written several historical biographies for young readers.